KALINDA

Also by Evan Green

ALICE TO NOWHERE
ADAM'S EMPIRE

KALINDA

Evan Green

Macdonald

A Macdonald Book

First published in Great Britain in 1991 by
Macdonald & Co (Publishers) Ltd
London & Sydney

Typeset by Leaper & Gard Limited, Great Britain
Printed and bound in Great Britain by
BPCC Hazell Books
Aylesbury, Bucks, England
Member of BPCC Ltd.

British Library Cataloguing in Publication Data
Green, Evan
  Kalinda: (Adam's empire II).
  I. Title
  823.[F]

ISBN 0 356 17630 4
ISBN 0 356 18158 8 (PB – Export only)

Macdonald & Co (Publishers) Ltd
Orbit House
1 New Fetter Lane
London EC4A 1AR

A member of Maxwell Macmillan Pergamon Publishing Corporation

For my children,
Gavin, Linda, Randall and Alison,
with love

And with grateful thanks to my agent,
Selwa Anthony, for her faith and
boundless support.

BOOK

O·N·E

The Reunion

O·N·E

September, 1939

Harry Quinlan brushed a fly from his face and squinted towards the horizon. There was still no sign of the train. He walked between the rails, counting each sleeper until he lost count and, confused, turned and paced his way back to the small siding. Fifty-six sleepers. Same as his age. That must mean something. He brushed his beard and a disturbed swarm of insects buzzed his face. Fifty-six paces, fifty-six years. He stepped them out again. One, two, three. That was how old he was when his mother died. Never knew his father. Eight, nine, ten. He'd been working at ten, distilling eucalyptus with that stingy bastard Cullen. Fifteen. What happened at fifteen? He couldn't remember but it had been important. Taking off his hat, he wiped perspiration from a forehead of speckled pink skin, felt the lump that was growing on the side of his head just above the ear, and again searched for the train. It was already six hours late.

Where was he? Fifteen. He resumed pacing. Seventeen. He remembered the party for the end of the century. First time he'd got really drunk. Couldn't remember where it was. Maybe Ceduna. He searched the sky for inspiration but a spiral of crows high above him caught his attention and drifted away, taking the answer with them. He ran back to the deserted siding and, puffing from the sudden exertion, opened his canvas bag and took out a shotgun. He fired at the birds. They were too far away. He picked up a stone and threw it at them and stayed there at least a minute, panting and glowering at the departing birds until the raw sky hurt his eyes and he had to turn away.

Shotgun in hand, Quinlan walked back down the line, counting once more. Twenty-seven. That's when he met Elsie. The next three steps were agony. Thirty. Just thirty when she'd run off, chasing that shearer with the bald head and red beard. Quinlan stopped. He couldn't walk any farther. What was the point? She'd gone. And where the hell was the train?

The railway lines and sleepers laddered their way to infinity, the tapering rails shining and rocking in the midday heat haze. If Elsie was on the train, he'd kill her. Put the gun under her jaw and blow her head off. Imagining she was standing with him, he mimed the action and pulled the other trigger and felt the closeness of the blast scorch his face. See how you like that, he thought, and grinned with malice. Maybe she would still be with the shearer. No worries. He had two barrels. He closed his eyes and saw the red beard disappear and come out through the top of the shearer's bald head.

He hurried back to the siding to reload.

There was no platform, merely a three-sided shed with a roof angled towards a water tank. The train, which would be travelling north towards William Creek, Oodnadatta, Finke, and Alice Springs, would stop only on demand.

On either side of the line stretched a plain covered in clumps of dry grass that were as gaunt and menacing as the frayed ends of unravelled wire. Quinlan selected a clear patch of gravel near the shed. There he squatted and cleaned the gun and loaded new cartridges. Then he took a shirt from the bag and used it to wipe and polish the weapon until the barrels shone a lethal grey. The shirt was the only other garment he possessed. He put it in the bag and then, as though recalling a forgotten plan, hid the shotgun beneath the shirt and closed the bag.

He walked to the water tank and, with difficulty, forced the tap open. A thin ring of water drizzled on the ground. He removed his hat, cupped his hands and drank. The taste was vile. Birds must have got in the tank, become trapped and drowned in the water. He spat out the last mouthful and ran a moist tongue around the inside of his lips, soothing the driest places.

The Depression was in its final phase but it had bypassed Harry Quinlan. Long before the stockmarket crash of 1929, he had been depressed, an alcoholic and a drifter. He had come back from the Great War with his nerves wrecked and had not had a steady job since 1919. His wife had run off even before then, recognizing the first signs of the madness that now consumed him.

For the last few years, Quinlan had roamed the more remote parts of the Australian outback, hunting animals, living in the most squalid aboriginal camps, sometimes doing a few days' work to earn money for cartridges and grog. Occasionally, and especially after drinking some vile liquor, he would imagine that Elsie was returning. When those moments came, he would head for the nearest settlement. Usually, it meant a fight and a beating and a few days in gaol. But he was ready this time.

4

Cradling the canvas bag, he sat in the middle of the tracks and waited for the train.

The train had left the terminus at Port Pirie one and a half days earlier. Now, it had passed the last of the salt channels that led to the shores of Lake Eyre South and was travelling north-west, crossing a plain whose edges shuffled and rose in a gaseous heat dance.

The train was known locally as The Ghan. The name was a nostalgic tribute to the Afghan traders who used to drive their camels over this route before the line was laid. If the title was an abbreviation, the train itself was stretched – an absurdly long and unbalanced contraption that carried all the things that needed to be hauled from the settled south to Alice Springs, in the near-empty centre of the continent. At the front was the steam-engine and its coal-bearing tender. Then followed more than a quarter of a mile of flat goods-waggons. In turn, these were followed by two tankers, three wooden carriages, and a boxed guard's van.

It was a serpent crawling through the desert, a primeval monster that emitted smoke and steam at its head and had a long, thin body dragging a bulbous tail.

Josef Hoffman sat in the rear of the third carriage. He was in a corner, with his head resting against the wooden window frame. The carriage swayed and the wheels rattled and chattered and the wind that rushed through the row of open windows was thin and scorched and laced with the biting aroma of smoke. Left and right, the carriage rocked, jolting regularly on the uneven track. Click-etty-clack went the wheels over a joint in the rails. Left, right. Clicketty-clack. It was a raucous, rhythmical accompaniment to a journey of stupefying boredom.

A milepost flashed past.

'Five hundred and ten,' Josef announced.

The young woman beside him stirred. The side of her face that had been pressed against the leather seat glistened with perspiration. 'Five hundred and ten what?' She had not been able to sleep and her voice was slurred.

'Miles from Adelaide.'

'It feels more like a thousand and ten. Are we almost there?'

'About another hour, I think.'

'We're late.'

'The train's always late.'

She sat up, shook her head, and used her fingers to comb her hair. She put her chin on his shoulder and gazed out the window. 'The country's getting worse. It looks awful.'

5

'Everyone says that the first time.'

'Everyone's right.'

Josef gave her a veteran's smile. 'You get used to it.'

'Is it better where your friend lives?'

'Much nicer.' He patted her knee. She had long legs. 'The sand's more colourful.'

She frowned and moved her leg out of range. 'You mean he lives on a beach?' He turned away, but she was quick at reading faces and pouted. 'You said sand.'

'I know. Not beach sand, though.' He looked at her with eyes that were suddenly loving and understanding. 'Kalinda has sand-hills. Red dunes.'

'Oh,' she said, not comprehending but presuming he was apologizing. She allowed the knee to sway back within reach of his waiting hand. 'I knew you were pulling my leg.'

'It's such a lovely leg.' It *was* a lovely leg and he began moving his fingers on an upward journey of exploration.

She gripped his wrist. 'You'll have to stop mocking me.'

'I know what I'd like to do to you.' His trapped fingers teased the inside of her leg.

'You're a monster,' she whispered, her face close to his cheek.

'Don't you ever forget it,' he said, trying to sound gruff, but the tip of her tongue had entered his ear and he twitched, unable to control himself.

'Some monster,' she laughed softly. 'But I like it.'

He turned away, feeling a wave of contentment wash through him. She leaned on his shoulder. For some minutes they travelled like that. With the long journey almost at an end, he began searching for familiar sights but the landscape that rolled past was a treadmill of even desolation.

Without lifting her head, she said, 'Will this Adam Ross be waiting for us?'

'Adam will be there.'

Josef had written weeks ago, telling his friend he wanted to come to Kalinda and to bring with him the woman he intended to marry. Adam had even written back. It was a short reply, but good for a man who had not been to school and was still learning to read and write: 'Good on you, Joe. Will meet you and the unfortunate victim at William Creek railway station.' Adam had misspelt 'unfortunate' and 'victim' but Josef knew what he meant. Adam would certainly be there, probably in the old red Alfa-Romeo.

'Do you think he'll like me?' she asked.

'*I* like you. That's what matters.' He spoke with sufficient determination to convince them both.

6

'That's different. I mean, do you think he'll approve?'

She was smart, Sarah Mandelton. Not necessarily intelligent, but smart. Josef had never said he was taking her all this way just to have a friend bestow approval on his choice of a wife but it was true, and he was honest enough to realize it. His parents didn't like Sarah, and thus he found her all the more attractive. At twenty-five, Josef was thoroughly tired of having his parents, with their old-fashioned German ideas of what was proper and what was not, telling him how to live his life. So he had told them he would marry Sarah and to hell with them. They had had a few arguments lately about his ideas on how to run the winery and how to sell the wine and this was the best, most spectacular way he knew to show them he was a grown man who knew his own mind and would no longer tolerate being treated like a boy. However, he was impetuous and when he cooled he knew it and was inclined to go through stomach-wrenching sessions of self-doubt, so another vote on the wisdom of getting married seemed a good idea. Adam Ross might have lived in the middle of nowhere but he was Josef's closest friend and the person whose opinion he most respected. There were plenty of men who would slap his back and give him a wink of envy and not say what they really felt, but Adam was different. He would quietly watch Sarah and let her talk, and after a week or so say 'She seems a nice girl, Joe' or 'Do you think you're rushing things a bit, Joe? Do you think it might be an idea to wait on for a while ...' To his surprise, and not knowing why, Josef found himself wishing Adam would urge him to reconsider.

Of course, it had all happened pretty rapidly. He'd only known Sarah for four months. He'd met her at a dance at Tanunda and discovered that she was interested in grapes and wine-making, or so she said. Within a week, he had been showing her over the vineyards. She seemed to have an accountant's eye for things, being interested in yields and gallonages and, to Josef's delight, even more fascinated by his plans for future marketing of the family wines. They were adventurous schemes; he was sure the prospects for wine in Australia were good and that the Hoffmans would make a lot of money.

Apart from her surprising interest in the business, Sarah had shown herself to be a remarkably vigorous and talented fornicator. He had never met a girl – or was it a woman? She was already twenty – who could be so proper in company and yet rollick with such an absolute, almost dedicated abandon in their private moments. She was also disarmingly frank.

'I love sex,' she had told him during their first coupling. She said it in a way that made him assume she meant only with him, and he

7

felt flattered and, somehow, older and stronger. He had never heard a grown woman use that expression before. In any case, he couldn't argue with the proposition because it entirely matched his own philosophy. So they did a lot of the thing they both loved and here he was, taking her all the way to a sheep station on the western shores of Lake Eyre to have his best friend, whom he hadn't seen for three years, tell him he was a lucky man or a fool. And Josef knew he was sufficiently corroded by doubt to accept the verdict.

There were only two other men in the carriage. One had been on the train since Port Pirie. He was dressed inappropriately in a three-piece blue serge suit and spent much of his time nursing a briefcase. The other man had boarded the carriage later, at Beltana in the Flinders Ranges. He had introduced himself as the Reverend Victor Rawlinson, a patrolling padre for the Australian Inland Mission. He was on his way to Oodnadatta. He did not look like a minister. He wore bush clothes and sported a grey beard peppered with faded remnants of a once distinctive colouring. He was bald and scratched his scalp a lot.

The rocking and the clattering eased. The train slowed.

'Is this William Creek?' Sarah asked hopefully, above the grind of brakes.

Josef looked out of the window. The line was straight and smoke from the engine obscured his view but there were no fettlers' cottages in sight. 'It's too soon,' he said and checked his watch. 'We must be stopping for someone at one of the small sidings.'

Carrying the canvas bag in his left hand, Harry Quinlan climbed into the third passenger carriage. He walked past the man in the three-piece suit, who clutched his briefcase defensively but did not look up. Quinlan moved down the corridor, to where the padre was sitting.

Rawlinson smiled a greeting. 'You look as though you've had a long, hot wait out in the sun, friend.'

Quinlan did not answer. He stared down at the padre for several seconds and his scabbed and blotched forehead crinkled into a map of complex intersections.

'Something wrong?' the padre asked.

Quinlan shook his head. 'Just thirsty,' he mumbled and turned away.

'There's water up there,' the padre said, indicating a water-flask and glasses in the stand above a window near him. He noticed Josef smiling and returned the smile. 'Wouldn't be too good out there today in the sun,' he called out.

Quinlan had taken down the flask and was drinking directly from

8

it. 'What was that?' he snapped, wiping his lips and breathing with satisfaction.

'Just talking to my young friend,' Rawlinson said. And then he added gently, 'You know, you're supposed to use one of the glasses. Health. Germs. All that sort of thing.' His expression suggested health and germs were of no great concern to him but might bother other people.

Quinlan ignored him. He drank again, in such haste that water trickled from either side of his mouth.

'Must be close to the hundred mark,' Josef said, anxious to end the awkward silence.

With the flask still raised, Quinlan swung towards the voice and, for the first time, noticed Sarah Mandelton. He lowered the flask and looked from Sarah to the padre and back again.

'Elsie?' His face twisted in uncertainty. He put the water container on the seat beside his bag. He lifted both his hands, until they were level with his shoulders.

By now, Josef was sitting upright. He no longer felt like smiling for Quinlan had begun flexing his fingers. It was a weird, menacing gesture which carried the threat of some impending and sudden action. Josef had seen a cowboy movie in which a gunfighter did that before he drew his six-shooter. This was ridiculous, he thought, but he felt frightened. The man was staring, fingers moving. Sharing the sense of menace, Sarah pressed against Josef.

'Elsie!' Quinlan shouted.

'Not Elsie,' Josef said, trying to sound bright and relaxed but noting to his dismay that his voice cracked. 'She's my girl-friend. My fiancée.' And then, when the man continued to stare and to flex his fingers: 'Sarah. The lady's name is Sarah, not Elsie.'

Very slowly, Quinlan turned to face the padre, who was gazing at the floor, hoping the man might sit down if he took no notice of him.

'Red beard,' Quinlan growled.

Rawlinson looked up.

'You had a red beard?'

'And red hair. Once.' The padre rubbed his bald scalp.

'Jesus Christ. Still shearing?'

'I beg your pardon?'

'Still shearing, I said.'

'I'm not a shearer, friend. I'm a minister of religion.' Quinlan's eyes had rolled upwards, searching for a vision from twenty-six years ago. The padre kept talking, forcing good humour into his voice. 'I'm Victor Rawlinson, patrolling padre with the Presbyterian Church. I'm from the Smith of Dunesk Mission at Beltana.

9

On my way to Oodnadatta. There's a couple there I have to marry, and some children I have to baptize. All in the same family.' It was the favourite joke of his profession and he smiled at the retelling but Quinlan was insulated from the present.

'Phillips,' he said suddenly, snatching a name from the past. He swept the flask from the seat. It hit a seat frame on the other side of the corridor and exploded in a shower of glass and water. Bright slivers covered the floor, shivering to the carriage's vibrations.

Rawlinson stood, rubbing his hands in apprehension. He was wondering if he should alert the guard to put this man off at the next stop.

'You're Phillips, aren't you?'

The padre shook his head as though genuinely sorry to disappoint the man. 'No, I'm Rawlinson. The Reverend Victor Rawlinson.'

'You bastard, Phillips. I've been looking for you.' He reached out and grabbed the padre by the shirt.

Josef rose and walked towards them. He moved awkwardly because his legs were stiff from the long journey. 'Now look, mate,' he said, one arm extended as though he wanted to shake the man's hand, 'take your hands off the Reverend and sit down.' Josef was tall and he squared his shoulders to increase the impression of advancing bulk. He rolled forward like a sailor just off his ship.

Quinlan seemed not to see him.

For a normally gentle male, few things are more disconcerting than having a rare display of aggression ignored. Josef stopped, wondering what to do. Quinlan was not looking at him but was staring at a point on the opposite wall of the carriage. Pictures of South Australian scenery were ranged above the window line, and there was another water flask.

'What's up? Do you want a drink of water?' Josef said, attempting to sound reasonable. Releasing the padre, Quinlan turned slowly.

'That's better,' Josef said, taking care to keep his shoulders square-on to the man and rocking on his soles, to exaggerate his height advantage. Now was the time to let this man know he would take no nonsense.

Quinlan hit him.

The blow was so unexpected that Josef made no effort to protect himself. Quinlan was a powerful man and his fist hit just below Josef's left ribs, bending him like a banana and sending him sliding across the back of a seat. He hit the wall and fell to the floor, where he lay coughing and retching.

The padre jumped up. Quinlan pushed him back on to the seat, then opened his canvas bag and extracted the shotgun. 'Any more of your mates?' he said, letting the twin barrels write their own message of threat in the air between the two men.

'I never saw that young fellow before last night,' Rawlinson protested, swaying backwards to avoid the moving barrels. Josef was squirming and groaning on the floor.

Quinlan twisted suddenly so that he could see the man in the suit, who was sitting at the front of the carriage with his briefcase protecting his chest.

'Who are you then?' he roared and the man, too frightened to speak, shook his head.

Quinlan blinked many times, as though trying to absorb information from a long and complex conversation, and then said abruptly: 'Cut out all that crap. Just don't move. I only want Phillips and Elsie.'

He spun towards the back of the carriage where Sarah was sitting. 'Come here. Come and join your boy-friend before I blow his bloody bald head off.' He seized Rawlinson by the shirt again.

Sarah had wriggled into the corner vacated by Josef. 'I don't know that man. He's not my boy-friend.'

'Elsie!' Quinlan growled the word, as threatening as a savage dog giving its final, low warning.

'I'm not Elsie,' she whimpered.

'You come back here to me or I'll turn his brains into tomato soup.'

'What have you done to Joe?' she said, her voice so soft it blended with the rumble and rattle of the wheels.

His eyebrows arched in triumph. 'So it's Joe, is it? I never knew his first name. Joe Phillips.' He swung the gun towards the padre. 'Well, how would you like your darling Joe with nothing above the beard, eh.'

'He's not Joe.' Her voice quivered but it was louder, with the first suggestion of anger.

'You just come here, Elsie.'

'I'm *not* Elsie. That man's *not* Joe.'

He lifted the shotgun and fired into the roof. Wood and paint chips cascaded around them. 'Come here,' he shouted, before the echoes had settled.

She stood, hands clasped in front of her chin, her anger dissipated in a rush of fear, her legs trembling so severely that her body sagged and rolled like a puppet on loosened strings. 'I want to see you two together.' He pulled the padre closer to him. 'Just you and Elsie, Joe. See what a fine couple you make.'

'Dear friend, my name's not Joe,' the padre said. He spoke with

11

difficulty because Quinlan had such a firm grip on the man's collar that he was partly choking him. 'I'm Victor Rawlinson.'

'And I'm Haile Selassie.' Quinlan lifted the padre, exerting so much pressure that the man's eyes bulged, and then pushed him savagely. Rawlinson tripped and slid along the corridor.

Both hands back on the gun now, Quinlan focused all his attention on Sarah. 'You have five seconds to get here,' he said, and then tilted his head at an acute angle. 'Jesus Christ, woman, is that asking too much? Five bloody seconds after all these years?' He beckoned her with one finger and she started to move. 'I was in the war. Did you know that?'

Sarah had shuffled into the corridor. The train swayed violently and she steadied herself on the back of the seat.

'I was in France. Did you know that, Elsie?'

She shook her head.

'In the trenches. All my mates were killed.'

She moved a few steps, grasping seat backs as she went.

'Darkie Thompson had his legs blown off. You remember Darkie?'

'No.' She shook her head without looking at the man. She was near the place where Josef had fallen. He was trying to rise, but a rush of vomit filled his throat and he slumped back, legs splayed beneath a seat.

'They shelled us for two weeks once. Never stopped. All the officers were killed.'

She was close now, and stopped.

'Why'd you leave me?'

She stared at the floor, not daring to look at either Quinlan or Josef. The carriage swayed. The wheels drummed on a rough joint. Rawlinson was getting to his feet.

'I was a good husband.' Quinlan wiped his lips, as though uttering such words had hurt him. At times he would examine her through eyes that were unnaturally wide. Now he narrowed them to slits. 'You been dyeing your hair?'

'No.'

'Your hair's changed.'

She didn't look up. 'My hair's always been this colour.'

'Don't lie to me, woman,' he shouted, his eyes wide again. 'I've had enough of your lies.'

'I'm not Elsie. I'm not your woman.'

He roared, a wild, animal sound that came from deep in his chest, and he lifted the gun. The padre, thinking he was about to shoot, lunged forward. He grabbed Quinlan's shoulder. Off balance, Quinlan turned. His finger squeezed the trigger.

12

The shot made a deep, ugly sound that bounced around the carriage. The padre spun backwards and rammed a seat. His face froze in a comical expression of disbelief. Almost mechanically, his right hand sought the left elbow. Blood oozed between the fingers.

'You mongrel, Phillips,' Quinlan said rapidly. 'I didn't mean to do that. I wasn't ready. What the hell's going on here?' He turned to Sarah. 'What are you two up to?'

'We're not up to anything,' she sobbed. 'He's a minister, don't you understand, you raving lunatic. He's not my boy-friend. He's a man of God.' But she could have been addressing one of the pictures lining the carriage walls. Quinlan began to smile.

'He doesn't look so good, don't you reckon?' he said, studying the injured man and letting his head tilt from side to side. He gave her time to consider. 'You don't like him more than me, do you, love?' He removed his hat, revealing a mat of oily grey hair. A crease from perpetually wearing the hat ringed his hair, leaving a mark as distinct as a headband.

'Come back, eh?' he said reasonably. 'He's gone. Forget him.'

There was a shuffling sound from the floor and Josef peered from above the seats. Quinlan pointed the gun at him.

'Just go and look after your mate,' he said. 'Me and Elsie are talking.'

T·W·O

From a distance, the great flock of cockatoos could have been a ribbon of mirrors, linked in some miraculous way and flashing and sparkling with each synchronized change of direction. But then the mass of birds drew closer, wheeling, soaring, darting, and the mirrors became wings and the faint chatter that had seeped through the distance became a raucous din. The stream of white broke into fluttering mobs. Over the town the birds circled, separating into even smaller groups and then, in a bedlam of flapping and screeching, settled on the railings of the stockyards.

The town of William Creek was tiny. Apart from the stockyards, it had a collection of railway cottages, the station, a side line with a string of empty stockwagons, a water tank, a store and a hotel. As with all small and remote bush towns, the hotel was the community centre. It was where people met, talked, drank, ate and waited for the train.

The hotel was a small, squat building, rather like a bigger structure that had partially melted in the heat. The roof was low-pitched and made of corrugated iron. It had once been painted but the paint had either faded or blistered so that the effect was of blotched decay. Some peppercorns grew at the back and they cast shadows over a cluster of small and uneven outhouses.

The main building was made of stone. A verandah covered its front. The verandah wall was enclosed along the bottom with iron sheets to keep out the dust from the frequent wind storms, and across the top with fly wire to keep out the perpetual onslaught of insects.

A young woman was on the verandah, holding a child in her arms. She stopped at a water bag suspended from a ceiling hook, and filled an enamel drinking mug. She offered it to the child.

'Here, Cassie,' she said soothingly, supporting the mug while the girl drank. 'Your Uncle Joe will be here any minute. He's coming on the big choo-choo train.'

Cassie Ross, three years of age, had been waiting for the train since dawn, and excitement had given way to restlessness and boredom.

'He is not,' she said, holding out the mug for more water. 'Uncle Joe got frightened by the wabbits and went home.'

'No,' the woman said and smiled. Cassie had spent the last hour in the bar being entertained by a few of the old timers who gathered there each morning. Rabbits were in plague proportions in the district and old Ted had told Cassie the train would be frightened by the rabbits and would turn around and go back to Adelaide.

She refilled the mug. 'Uncle Joe has seen plenty of rabbits. He won't be frightened and he won't let the train get frightened. Uncle Joe is very brave and ... Use both hands. Don't splash yourself.' As the child drank, she gazed through the wire screen for any sign of the train.

Nellie Arlton was a woman of extraordinary beauty. A half-caste with an aboriginal mother and Finnish father, she had lustrous dark skin, a fine Nordic nose, lips that were just a touch too full but hinted at sensuality, high cheekbones and large brown eyes. Her hair was curly. Her body was slender. She was thirty-two and supremely content to be living at Kalinda homestead, north of William Creek, as the mistress of Adam Ross.

She glanced to the right and saw the cockatoos. 'Let's go and see the birds,' she suggested and, putting Adam's daughter on the floor, took the child's hand and led her from the building.

She moved cautiously because she knew the parrots would be easily frightened. A hundred or more had glided from the railings to the ground and were pecking for seeds. Others, the younger and bolder birds, had lined up on a taut strand of wire and, like circus performers, were turning somersaults and revolving around the wire in a blur of outstretched white wings and raised yellow crests.

Halfway to the stockyards, Nellie paused and checked the railway once more. Rising above the shimmer of the distant haze was a smudge of smoke. 'Here comes Uncle Joe,' she said excitedly and, lifting Cassie, turned and hurried back towards the hotel.

The cockatoos on the ground rose in alarm, as uniform as floating seaweed rising on a high wave, and settled again.

Adam Ross was in a corner of the public bar, holding a partly consumed glass of lemonade and trying to appear interested in what the man sitting next to him was saying. The man was a stockman. He hadn't worked for a few months and intended catching the train up to Alice Springs. He wore a hat which had the appearance of never having left his head. It was soiled by grease and dirt and the wide brim had rotted in several places. The

15

stockman was convinced there was going to be another war. Adam had found that interesting when the man had first told him, but that had been two hours ago.

'I was reading a paper the other day,' the stockman said, as though being required to offer proof for his theory. He waited a long time before continuing. Adam said nothing. He was tired. He had driven from Kalinda yesterday and he and Nellie and Cassie had camped near the creek. He had been up since four.

'There's this joker called Adolf Hitler who's causing a lot of trouble,' the stockman said.

Old Ted joined in. He was sitting at the other end of the room, under a poster advertising a race meeting that had been held the previous autumn. 'Should have wiped them all out last time,' he said, in a voice that whined unevenly, as though produced by someone turning a handle. 'Greatest mistake the Allies ever made was not marching through Berlin in 1918. Half the bloody Huns don't even think they were beaten.'

Adam checked his watch.

'He's a Nazi,' the stockman said, and sipped his rum.

'Who is?' Ted called. He was annoyed that his pronouncement had been ignored but Ted had been in the bar most mornings for the past year and no one took much notice of him. It was rumoured that he had once had a good job in the city. No one knew what as.

'This Hitler I was telling you about.'

'What's a NAR-ZEE?' It was not a question but the retort a man gives when he knows he will not get an answer. Ted waited, glass poised in expectation of triumph.

It was a moment spoiled, for Nellie appeared in the doorway. 'The train's coming,' she announced and the room creaked as each man moved on his seat, uncoiling himself from the stresses of the long wait.

'Good on you, Nellie,' one man said, as though she had personally delivered the missing train.

The bar emptied. Even the publican walked outside, for the arrival of a train was an event of significance to everyone in town. There might be no passengers to meet, no one to bid farewell, no parcel to collect, no freight to despatch, but the train represented the only regular link William Creek had with the rest of the world. It was the outside, touching them briefly.

The sudden emergence of so many people sent the great flock of cockatoos into the air, to wheel above the town and then curl in a long, rippling banner towards the trees that lined the creek.

To the south-east, the train was becoming visible, its black serpent's head distinct and puffing smoke, its tail writhing in the

16

vapours that boiled on the horizon.

Some of the dozen people who gathered to await the train's arrival stayed in the middle of the dusty street. Adam and Nellie took the few extra steps to the station. There they stood linked by the outstretched arms of his daughter.

Sarah was the first out of the carriage. She was pushed, and fell on her knees. Harry Quinlan followed. He descended the steps with the shotgun in both hands. When he reached the ground, he stood behind Sarah and stared defiantly at the people gazing at him. There was a murmur, but no one spoke.

Josef appeared at the doorway. His face was bleached.

'This man shot the Reverend,' he said, as though delivering a prepared speech. 'We need a doctor.'

Quinlan bent forward and grabbed Sarah's shoulder. She rose, brushing small stones from her palms and her knees.

Adam pushed Cassie behind him. 'Take her away,' he said softly to Nellie. 'Just get behind me and then move away. Do it slowly.' Nellie obeyed. Josef had resumed talking.

'The gentleman says this is his wife and she's going with him and no one is to try and stop him.'

Quinlan, one hand still on Sarah's shoulder, nodded at the completion of the words. 'Me and Elsie are going off together,' he said, still nodding. 'I won't hurt no one. Just keep away from us.'

Adam moved a step forward. Behind him, he could hear the shuffling of feet and frightened whispers.

'G'day, Joe,' he said.

Josef gulped. 'Hello, Adam. I didn't see you there.'

'You all right?'

Josef nodded. Quinlan was staring at Adam. Josef took the chance to put one finger near his temple and spin it in the air.

So the man's mad, Adam thought, and nodded acknowledgement of the signal.

'It's Sarah, Adam,' Josef said.

'Elsie,' Quinlan snapped.

'Hello, Elsie,' Adam said and moved a few steps closer. He glanced back. Some people had retreated towards the hotel. Nellie and Cassie were in the middle of the street. Nellie had lifted the girl into her arms and was still walking slowly away from the railway, but not taking her eyes off Adam.

At the far end of the train, the guard got down from his van. He was a grey-haired man who moved slowly, and limped.

'Can I give you a hand, Elsie?' Adam said and took another step.

'You just keep clear,' Quinlan said.

17

'But the lady had a fall.'

'I can look after her.'

Adam scratched his cheek. 'I know you, don't I?'

Quinlan narrowed his eyes.

'You were looking for work. You came through about six months ago.'

Quinlan retreated behind the woman. She was staring at Adam, her eyes glazed with fear.

'Harry!' Adam said and the man nodded automatically. 'I couldn't give you work but I gave you tucker.'

The man blinked, groping for recollection. He had the shotgun in one hand. The barrels were pointing at Adam.

'How've you been, Harry? Get any work?'

He shook his head.

'Don't you remember me?'

'No.'

'Ross. Adam Ross.' He stepped forward.

'Just keep back.'

Adam nodded. 'Where are you heading for, Harry?'

'None of your business.'

Adam risked another look behind him. Nellie had reached the hotel verandah. 'Mind if I talk to my friend?' he asked.

'You can do that later. After me and Elsie have gone.'

Adam nodded agreement but spoke to Josef nonetheless. 'Who was hurt?' he asked.

'The Reverend.'

'I said to shut up,' Quinlan said.

'I will, Harry, I will.' But still he talked to Josef. 'Alive?'

Josef nodded.

'Need a doctor?'

Quinlan waved the gun. 'Can't you understand what I bloody well tell you?'

'Of course. It's just that I haven't seen my mate for three years.'

Quinlan blinked in confusion.

Josef waited a few moments and then nodded. 'He's bleeding a lot.' He touched his arm. 'Shot in the elbow.'

Adam was looking at the twin barrels of the gun. 'Once or twice?'

'I said not to talk,' Quinlan shouted and so tightened his grip on Sarah's shoulder that she cried out in pain.

Josef held up one finger.

'Only one shot,' Adam said softly and stroked his chin.

'He fired twice,' Josef said, suddenly realizing what information Adam wanted. 'Once into the ceiling.'

18

'Jesus Christ,' Quinlan snapped.

'And reloaded?'

'No.'

Quinlan spun towards Josef. 'I told you what you was supposed to say ...' he began, but Adam had sprung towards him. Adam wrenched Sarah clear, saw Quinlan lift the gun, and kicked hard at the man's arm. His boot struck the wrist. The shotgun flew in the air.

Sarah had fallen. Adam stepped around her. Quinlan ran to the gun.

'The gun's empty,' Adam said as Quinlan bent to retrieve the weapon.

The man was snarling. Teeth bared, animal noises in his throat, he snapped open the breech, saw the empty barrels and hurled the gun away. Arms outstretched like a bear about to crush an intruder, he advanced on Adam.

'It's all right, Harry,' Adam said and retreated, hoping to draw the man away from the woman. 'No one's going to hurt you.'

'I'll break your bloody neck.'

'I gave you a feed when you were hungry.'

Quinlan stopped. His brow creased in worry. 'I don't remember that.' His arms were still raised but his head sagged.

'Six months ago.' Adam stopped. Quinlan was well past the woman. Josef had run down the steps to help her. The old guard had retreated to his van and reappeared with a fire-axe.

From behind him, Adam heard Nellie's voice. 'Mr Peterson has a rifle.'

Peterson, the publican, called out, 'Just move to one side. I can drop him from here.'

Adam held up a hand. 'No need. No one's going to get hurt.'

Slowly Quinlan raised his head. 'Where's Phillips?' he asked.

The guard had joined Josef, who passed Sarah into his care and took the axe.

'Who's Phillips?' Adam asked.

'Bloody hell, you're all liars, every one of you.'

Josef was moving towards them.

'Tell me about Phillips,' Adam said.

'You know, you lying bastard.'

'Wally Phillips?' Adam thought of a fencing contractor he had met.

'Joe Phillips,' Quinlan roared and threw himself at Adam.

Adam gripped the man's hands. He staggered back under the thrust of the charge but kept his balance. The men stood forehead to forehead, arms out wide, fingers locked in a test of brute strength.

19

Josef was close, the axe raised above his shoulder.

'No,' Adam shouted and Josef stopped.

The man was powerful, supercharged by an eruption of hatred. 'He took Elsie,' he roared, and tried to bite the side of Adam's face. There was an appalling stench on his breath and Adam's memory flashed back to another struggle, with another man. He had killed that man ...

For a moment he faltered and Quinlan began to force his arms back.

Locked together, legs splayed wide, backs arched, they matched strength. For a full twenty seconds they wrestled, grunting, wheezing for breath, boots scratching an accompaniment on the coarse gravel. Then Adam felt the other's power start to wane as the madness eased. Quinlan took a step back, then tottered and fell to one knee. His fingers cracked and he gasped with pain. Adam forced him further down, until Quinlan suddenly opened his hands in a gesture of surrender. He slumped to the ground. 'What have I done?' he croaked.

Adam stood over him, aching and breathing heavily.

'He ran off with Elsie.' Quinlan looked up, a dog eyeing its master and expecting a beating.

Adam put a hand on the man's shoulder.

Peterson had walked up, rifle at the ready. 'What's wrong with him? Is he a lunatic or something?'

'Just had some hard times,' Adam suggested. 'Been on his own too long.'

'I didn't want her to go,' Quinlan said. He was exhausted and sat with his hands in his lap.

'I've got a set of handcuffs,' the publican said, and withdrew them from his pocket. 'Very handy for the wild ones.'

Quinlan, used to the routine, held out his arms. 'I must have been drinking, officer,' he mumbled and waited for the handcuffs to click around his wrists.

Adam moved to Josef, who was still holding the axe.

'Going to chop some firewood?'

Josef dropped the axe and grinned. 'Glad you could get here,' he said and the two men embraced.

They drove to Kalinda that afternoon. Cassie, frightened by the happenings in town, was still in shock and clung to Nellie throughout the journey. She found her Uncle Joe a terrifying stranger. She had seen him near the man attacking her father; and since Josef had been wielding an axe, she presumed he meant to use it on her father. And now he was sitting here in the car, talking a lot and laughing. She was confused, and shivered whenever he made a loud noise, which he did many times. Cassie had her face pressed against Nellie's shoulder. Only occasionally did she allow an eye to wander towards the couple in the back seat, the tall and raucous uncle she could not remember, and the strange, silent woman who sat beside him.

Adam had been anxious to return to Kalinda. They waited until a contrite and manacled Quinlan had been placed in the guard's van for the journey to the police station at Oodnadatta and left only after a fettler's wife had tended to the wounded padre. The woman was a commanding figure: so fat you would doubt she could survive in such heat and yet she moved swiftly and decisively, bullying men into carrying the injured padre from the train and growling at the pale and bleeding man as though the shotgun blast was self-inflicted. But she worked expertly and with a tender touch, using the gruff approach as a verbal anaesthetic to stun the patient into silence. She had once been a nurse, and had seen some appalling injuries inflicted on men who worked along that lonely stretch of railway line.

No one had taken much notice of the man in the three-piece suit. Only after the padre had been carried from the carriage did he get out and cross the road to the hotel. There he took a room, intending to rest and make some enquiries.

T·H·R·E·E

Behind the homestead was a hill. It was worn and low and crazed like broken pavement, and when the wind blew it sighed a lament of decay and great age. It was a relic of a time before animals trod the earth, when cataclysmic upheavals rumpled the land and tilted it in layered slabs. This had been a patch of harder rock which defied the inexorable grind of nature by an extra millennia or two and now stood, jutting and forlorn, as a reminder of an unimaginable time. It was surrounded by the debris of a billion years, reduced to gravelly plains and rows of wispy, shifting dunes.

Just before sunset, Josef took Sarah to the hill. Holding hands, they climbed to the top. It was an awkward ascent because the way up was over layers of broken rock and across ridges which bared rows of flinty teeth in a perpetual snarl. The climb was all the more difficult because Sarah was wearing raised heels. Josef did not mind. It gave him the chance to put his arm around her and demonstrate his strength and sure-footedness. She had been acting strangely since the train, scarcely speaking to him and avoiding his eyes as though, somehow, he had offended her. Josef was in a mood to reassert himself.

'Kalinda means "beautiful view",' he said when they reached the top, and then added 'I think,' which he immediately regretted because it made him appear uncertain and that was not the image he wished to project. He kept his arm around her. 'It's an aboriginal word.'

She gazed at the wide plains and the rows of sand ridges.

'This is beautiful?'

'Yes.' And then, feeling qualification was necessary, he added, 'This part of the country, that is.'

She turned in a slow circle, studying everything but saying nothing.

'It gets to you,' he added. 'It just takes time to appreciate it, to understand it.'

She raised her eyebrows, as though to say 'If you say so', and he felt better. They sat on a large flat rock.

'Where's Lake Eyre?'

He pointed to the east.

'You can't see it,' she said, straining to see beyond the dunes.

Rimming the horizon was a dark line, thin as a fine thread of cotton. 'That could be it,' he said, but her eyes were not as good as his and no matter how much he pointed and held her hand to make sure she was facing in the correct direction, she could not see it.

'Anyhow, it's there,' he added and felt stupid. 'Biggest lake in Australia.'

'Oh,' she breathed.

'Sixteenth biggest lake in the world.' He'd read that somewhere. Probably in one of his father's magazines.

'Then why can't we see it?'

There was a suggestion of a smile and he thought she must be joking.

'Well, we can't see Lake Superior either and that's even bigger,' he said and grinned. But there was no acknowledgement of either his wit or learning.

'What are you talking about?' she said, after a long pause.

'The lake,' he said tentatively. 'Just because it's big doesn't mean you can see it.'

She gave him a short, uncomprehending glance.

'I mean, it depends how close you are, not how big it is,' he said, trying to sound reasonable.

'Are you saying I'm stupid?'

'No, of course not.'

'Well, what was all that about Lake Superior or whatever it was?'

'I thought you were joking.'

'And?'

'And ...' He groped for the correct answer. 'And I said Lake Superior. It's in America.'

'I went to school.'

It's time to follow another course, he thought and, not knowing what to do, kept quiet. He tossed a stone and watched it bounce down the broken rocks.

'You're always mocking me,' she said.

'I'm not.'

'You are.'

A bird was circling high above them. He strained his eyes to see what it was. An eagle. He could distinguish the broad tail, the lazy warp of a wing-tip to set it spiralling slowly in another direction. It soared as free and as weightless as a scrap of charred paper rising above a fire. He would like to be a bird. If humans were born again

23

as animals, he would choose to be an eagle: big, majestic, afraid of nothing, and able to glide effortlessly above the world.

Her stare, demanding something, brought him back to earth. 'I'm sorry,' he said.

'That's better. But you don't mean it.'

He leaned towards her and kissed her cheek. 'I do.'

She stood, temporarily appeased. 'Does Adam own all this?'

'As far as the eye can see.'

'All the way to the lake?'

He nodded. He had a feeling she was adding up the acres.

'The first time we came here was terrible,' he said, anxious to swing her interest back to him.

'Why?' It took her a long time to answer. She sounded bored.

He should have remained silent. The four of them had vowed never to talk about that time but there was something about her manner that goaded him on.

'We were almost killed,' he said and, keen as a child who has told an outrageous lie to attract attention, awaited her reaction. But this was no lie.

She brushed something from the side of her nose and examined her fingertip.

'We were,' he said.

Very slowly, she turned to him and she had the look of a woman who expects anything but the truth.

'We were nearly shot.' You shouldn't be telling her this, a small voice whispered, but he was extraordinarily tired and he had had a damaging day and he was beyond caution. Besides, it had all happened a long time ago.

Now she was interested. 'Shot? Who? You and Adam?'

He was about to tell her everything. The other names. Mailey. The voice was warning him and it acted like a gate being swung shut in front of bolting horses. He knew he should close it as quickly and as firmly as he could. But the compulsion was too strong and some words, some of the frenzied horses, got out.

'There was this terrible man. He tried to smash my head in with a shovel.'

Her mouth was agape but she believed him; he could see it in her eyes. She was deep in some imagined horror.

'Adam jumped on his back.' There was a long silence.

'You said the man was going to shoot you.' The horror had gone and the doubt was back in her voice.

'I shouldn't be telling you this,' he said and looked away. 'You won't tell anyone?'

'Well, I don't know anything except that someone was supposed

24

to be shooting you and Adam jumped on his back.'

The eagle had drifted to the east.

'Was he a lunatic like that man on the train?'

'No.'

She followed his eyes to the eagle, then waited for him to continue. 'And what happened then? Did he run away when Adam jumped on his back?'

He had said far too much, and it had done him no good because she was treating the whole thing as a joke. A foolish joke, and he was the fool.

'Did the nasty man run away?'

Avoiding her eyes, he stood up. His belly still hurt from the pounding and he winced with pain. He breathed deeply.

'He was killed,' he said softly.

The last slice of the sun slipped from sight and the sky turned a fiery bronze. Josef took another deep breath.

'*Adam* killed him?' she said, emphasizing the name. 'He shot this man?'

'No.' He held up his hands.

'He killed him with his bare hands?' Josef blinked many times but did not answer. 'Who was this man that he killed?'

'It doesn't matter.'

'What do you mean, it doesn't matter? You're the one who insisted on telling me this story.'

'I shouldn't have.'

'You're not just making this up?'

'Do I make up stories?'

'Sometimes I think you do, yes. You keep telling me how rich you're going to be but I haven't seen any sign of real money yet,' she said, twisting each word to hurt on entry. She took Josef's arm and made him face her. 'How could Adam kill someone with his bare hands? Did he punch him or strangle him or something?'

Josef shook his head miserably.

'I don't think I understand you, Josef Hoffman. You let that man make a fool of you in the train today and now you insist on telling me some cock-and-bull story about you and Adam coming here and killing a man.'

He could feel the heat rise around his neck. 'What do you mean, let the man make a fool of me?'

'Well, you went up like Flash Gordon and you went down like Mickey Mouse.'

'That's very unfair.'

'One hit and you fell down. And you were sick everywhere.'

'I wasn't expecting it.' His voice rose higher than he would have

25

liked. He coughed. 'I was trying to calm him down.'

'He didn't do it to Adam.'

By now his whole face was flushed. 'Of course he didn't. Adam saw he had a gun, and I told him what the man had done.' He breathed deeply, trying not to feel envious of his friend. 'In any case, Adam's bloody strong.'

'Strong? Is that how Adam killed this man you were telling me about? Just by being strong?'

He was really angry now. What the hell was she trying to say? She had released her grip on his arm. Now he took hers. 'You mustn't mention this to anyone.'

She looked puzzled. 'Why?'

'Because no one else knows.'

'You didn't tell anyone?'

'No.'

'My God.'

'You must promise.'

'That I won't tell anyone?' she shrugged. 'Why would I?'

'Good. You mustn't mention it to Adam either.'

She arched an eyebrow. 'Surely he knows.'

'Of course,' he said, warding off the sarcasm. 'It's just that I promised never to tell anyone.'

Her eyes blazed with an intensity that intrigued Josef. It was as though she had scored some secret triumph. She blinked and the expression was gone. 'Don't worry,' she said soothingly. 'I won't tell a soul. Not even Adam Ross.'

She looked about her with an interest so fresh it was as if she had just reached the site. Josef, pleased at the silence, joined her in a survey of the stark panorama.

'Is he rich?' she enquired, the words spoken casually in the way some people ask the question that most concerns them.

Josef laughed. 'Adam?'

Her eyes had regained that strange intensity. She waited, piercing him with the look.

'Haven't you seen the house?' They were both facing the distant homestead. The building was dappled by shadows which softened the roughness of its construction but did nothing to disguise its diminutive size. Adam had built it himself.

'But you were saying he's only been here a couple of years,' she said as though she were carrying on a defensive argument, 'and I've heard that people on the land put all their money into the property in the first years, not the house. He must have stashed a lot away.'

'My God, you remind me of someone,' Josef said grimly and when she enquired, he laughed. 'Just someone.'

26

'Like me?' Her look suggested she could be hurt or praised; it was up to him.

'Not at all like you.' He kissed her forehead. 'Come on. Let's get back while we can still see where we're walking.'

She took his hand. 'He drives a very fancy car,' she said, leading the way and choosing each step with great care.

'It's a very old car.'

'It's smart. Continental?'

'Italian.'

'He must have paid a fortune for it.'

He stopped and laughed again. Joined by his grip she turned, wrenched off balance.

'We found it.' He enjoyed her look of consternation.

There was so much more he could have said and probably should have because he had given her a wrong impression but what the hell, let her be curious. The more she talked, the more she reminded him of Heather. Why had he never noticed that before? The same innuendos, the same sly questions, the same fascination for hidden wealth.

'You mean you just took it?' she said.

His face was a merry-go-round of whirling expressions. 'Not exactly,' he said eventually. And when that did not satisfy her he added: 'It's a very complicated story. And you probably wouldn't believe it.' She certainly wouldn't. If he told her the whole story of the Alfa – that the owner had been shot and buried in a creek bed in the outback of Western Australia, that they had used the car to save their own lives, that the only way they could drive it was by stuffing the tyres with grass – she'd be certain he was inventing a colourful tale to impress her. So he said no more, but gently prodded her into resuming the descent.

'You're not making all this up, are you?' she said and he felt unnerved, as though she could read his mind. She often did that; said something that made him feel as though she had slipped inside his brain and was examining the contents. 'I mean, you're not just saying all this to take my mind off the fact that you were beaten up by a smaller man.'

'He wasn't a small man.'

She sniffed disagreement.

'How about the padre? Was he made to look a fool too?'

'That was different. He was trying to help me.'

'Well, what do you think I was trying to do?'

'I have no idea. You just walked up to this man and said something ridiculous about having a drink of water and he hit you in the belly.'

27

Josef stopped and leaned against a large rock. 'You're a very cruel person,' he said slowly.

'Oh, don't be so serious,' she chided. 'The world's full of cowards. You just happen to be one of millions.'

'How *dare* you say that.'

She waited a long time, enjoying the sight of him stewing in the juice of his anger. Then she touched him lightly on the stomach. 'Josef, I'm only joking.' And, when he didn't answer: 'I am, truly. You were getting so serious with all that talk. And you've been teasing me – all the time. That's all you've done all day. Teased me and made me seem stupid.' He tried to protest, but she placed her fingers over his mouth. 'So I was just getting my own back. I was only joking.'

'You've got a funny sense of humour.'

Her hand had slipped down to his stomach. 'How's the bruise? Very sore?' She felt for the place and he guided her fingers to the spot beneath his ribs.

'Not bad,' he said, holding her hand so she didn't press too hard.

'It was a terrible thing he did, hitting you like that when you weren't expecting it.'

'I just didn't expect it,' he echoed and felt foolish. He had felt foolish all day and he suddenly realized why. It was the comparison with Adam, even if only implied. Adam did everything well. Josef tripped over things.

Her hand was moving. The fingers played with his belt. 'Not hurt anywhere else, I hope?' she said.

'No damage.' He grinned. This was more like the Sarah he knew.

'You might need an expert to examine you,' she said wickedly.

'Probably do.' He had difficulty swallowing.

'Tonight,' she promised and strummed a chord across the front of his trousers. 'I think I should check for any sign of swelling.'

If Josef's vision had not been so misted by spray from the waves of desire, he might have noticed a pattern to all this. Sarah would often show a hard edge to her nature and goad him to the point of anger. But then, cautioned by a finely honed instinct for not going too far, she would stop, suggest he had misunderstood, and then scramble all his thoughts by short-circuiting him through the loins.

'It might be a bit hard,' he said.

'It better be.' She patted him. 'I'm expecting big things.'

Involuntarily, he pulled away. He could never grow used to her touching him like that. 'I mean tonight,' he said. 'I'm not sure where we'll be sleeping.'

'Don't tell me he's coy about who sleeps with who out here?'

'What do you mean?'

'Really, Josef, sometimes you're so naïve I wonder whether you were born like other boys or were delivered in a parcel, all nicely wrapped so you didn't see anything improper on the way. What I mean is, who fucks who around this place?'

He was shocked but felt compelled to smile, to prove there were few men more wordly than he. 'You mean Adam and Nellie?'

'Who else? Do they sleep together?'

He picked up a stone and threw it as far as he could. 'There *is* only one bedroom.'

'She could always sleep in the shed. Or he could.'

He lifted his shoulders.

'I've never known a white man who sleeps with a black woman,' she said. 'I've heard about it, of course, but never actually met one. He doesn't look the type.'

'They've known each other for a long time.'

A sudden thought occurred to her. 'They're not married?'

'No.'

'They just pretend.'

'It's none of our business, Sarah.'

Her face suggested it *was* their business and that they'd have answers before too long. 'The baby. That's his?'

He nodded.

'She doesn't look like him. She's so dark and he's so fair.'

'She's a lovely little thing, isn't she?'

'The mother's dead?'

'Yes. It happened when I was here last. She, ah, drowned in the lake.'

'You told me. She was a white woman?'

'He smiled. 'Very.'

'What's that mean?'

'She was very fair. Blonde hair, blue eyes, all that.' They had reached the bottom of the hill and were walking towards the homestead.

'Beautiful?'

He could sense a comparison looming. 'In a way.'

'What way?'

He lifted his eyebrows, as though it were difficult for him to remember what Heather had looked like, but he remembered her with absolute clarity. 'Tall,' he said, continuing the pretence. 'She was tall.' He lifted a hand to indicate the height.

'Taller than me,' she said flatly.

He adjusted the level. 'No. About your height. She had lovely hair.' He presumed that was safe.

'Good face?'

29

'Yes. But a bit severe.'

'How?'

'She didn't smile a lot.'

'I can understand that, living out here. Nice eyes?'

He hesitated. There was a time when Heather could look at Josef and he would dissolve into a jelly of helplessness. 'A bit cold.'

I wonder where Sarah keeps all these facts? Josef thought. She was always pumping him to extract details about people, or about the family business.

'Good figure?' she asked.

'So-so.' They walked a few more steps and he knew he was required to add to the description. 'A bit skinny.' In fact, she was luscious. God, it was a shame what had happened to her.

'And she drowned?' Another silence. 'I thought the lake was dry.'

He took careful aim and kicked a stone. 'Heavy rain fell. Everything flooded.' He couldn't tell her that Heather had drowned in mud beneath the lake's salty crust. That was too ghastly.

She made the intended assumption. 'How unlucky for her. I mean for Adam too. To drown in a storm out here when it's usually so dry.'

Already there were stars in the sky.

'Has he ever thought of remarrying?'

'I haven't seen him since then. But he's with Nellie. He should have married her in the first place.'

She gave him a long, pitying look. 'He wouldn't marry a woman like her,' she said. 'Never.'

Nellie had fed Cassie and put her on the floor, where Adam played with her. They sat facing each other, each with legs apart, and rolled a cotton reel from one to the other. Adam pushed the reel to her. She grabbed it with sure hands and shoved it back hard towards him. She laughed a lot.

The house had only two rooms: the bedroom that Nellie and Adam shared and the other room that served as kitchen, dining-room and living-room. Nellie checked the lamb sizzling in the oven. A kettle on the top hotplate began to boil and she moved it to one side, away from the most intense heat.

'I'll need more wood soon.'

Without answering, Adam scooped up Cassie on one arm and left the building. He was back in minutes, his daughter slung under one arm and several chopped pieces of firewood under the other.

'Which would you like?' he asked cheerfully.

Nellie rested both hands on her hips and surveyed the choices.

30

'Well, I'm not sure,' she said and Cassie kicked her legs in protest. 'They're both good-looking lumps of wood.'

'It's me, Nellie!' Cassie shouted, almost laughing but just sufficiently concerned to lift her face so there could be no mistake.

'Did you hear a piece of wood call out?' she said.

'Not me.' Adam lifted both arms. 'Hurry up. My arms are getting tired.'

'It's me, Daddy!' She kicked even more vigorously.

'Goodness me,' Nellie said, reaching forward and touching the child's flushed cheek. 'This one looks just like Cassandra Ross.'

'It *is* Cassanda Woss.'

Then, as always, there was the mock surprise and the rejoicing at being reunited. It was a favourite game, but it only lasted a few seconds and the child was back on the floor, seeking the cotton reel. She found it near the door to the bedroom and began pushing it across the floor. She made the noises of a steam-train as she followed the reel around the room, crawling, puffing, whistling.

Adam put a piece of wood on the fire and stacked the rest. 'They're coming,' he said. 'I could just make them out, walking back from the hill.'

Nellie, bending at the oven, ladled boiling fat over the meat. Her face danced with fiery reflections. 'What do you think of Sarah?'

Adam shrugged.

'Me, too.'

'I didn't say anything,' he protested.

'I know what you mean.' She straightened and wiped perspiration from her forehead. 'I'm not sure, either, but I don't think I like her.'

'It's too early to say.'

'Maybe.' She checked once more that the table was set. It was a new table, delivered by Saleem Benn only a month before. It was the first thing they had bought for the house. Josef and Sarah were their first guests.

'But you've got a feeling?' Adam respected Nellie's instinctive reaction to strangers. She was rarely wrong, but he also knew she could be illogical and stubborn and was not immune from an attack of female jealousy.

'Just a little feeling at the moment,' she said. 'I hope I'm wrong, for Joe's sake.'

'We'll wait and see.'

Nellie smiled. Adam was a rare mixture: he was a man who could do almost anything, from building his own house to subduing a crazed man with a gun, and if things had to be done quickly he could act faster and more positively than anyone she knew, but

31

when it came to making judgements about people, he would wait. And wait. He gave everyone a second chance. He hated being unfair, or hurting people.

'I'll put Cassie to bed,' she said, and took the girl into the other room. There, Nellie bathed Cassie's face and hands once more in the basin in the corner of the tiny room, and lifted her into bed. She heard Josef and Sarah return to the house. Josef began talking about the likelihood of a war in Europe, just as he had in the car. She wished people wouldn't talk about war. There were enough men around who'd been gassed or injured in the Great War, and who spent all their time coughing and spluttering and talking about it, without Josef bringing stories about a new war, one that would cripple a whole fresh crop of young men. And Adam was only twenty-nine.

She checked her hair in the mirror and, standing sideways, patted her stomach. No, no one could tell yet.

F·O·U·R

Saleem Goolamadail was in his early twenties. He had glossy black hair and unnaturally large eyes but since babyhood no one had ever been tempted to describe him as good looking.

The eyes and the sleek, brushed-back hair were good enough features but it was the rest of his face that let him down. His nose was a prominent hook, his cheeks were cadaverous hollows and his teeth projected. To see him staring at you from a corner of the store at William Creek – and he normally sat in the shadows, where he could observe newcomers while their eyes adjusted to the light – was to feel you were being watched by a rat.

The man in the three-piece suit entered the store and peered into the deepest shadows. He stood near the entrance, waiting for someone to come forward but having the uncomfortable feeling he was being observed. A wave of smells greeted him. The sickly aroma of chaff and grains and sweet molasses mixed with the raw dryness of jute and the rich tang of newly cured leather. He blew his nose. In the faint light, he could distinguish sacks and crates and barrels against the walls and smaller items hanging in rows from the rafters. There were saddles and hats, raincoats and buckets, pick-axes, pipes and pots, but there was no sign of a human being.

The man felt his way along a row of sacks. 'Anyone there?' he called.

He heard the rustle of moving limbs from the far corner, peered into that dark area and saw Goolamadail's rat face staring at him. He retreated a step and bumped a rack of shovel handles.

'Can I help you?' Goolamadail said in a flat voice, and moved into the light.

The man was busily restacking the shovel handles. He cleared his throat. 'I was looking for a Mr Saleem Benn.'

'He's my uncle.'

'May I see him please?' He found he was grasping a handle. He thrust it into the rack, and they all fell again.

'Leave it to me,' Goolamadail snapped, brushing past the man and bending to pick up the handles. 'My uncle is not here.'

'They told me he might be.'

'He will be.' Goolamadail examined the man with an insolent expression that dared him to upset the rack once more. 'To-morrow.'

'Oh.' The man had locked his hands in front of his waist. 'I was hoping to engage him. Actually, I had written.'

Goolamadail raised one eyebrow in an extravagant gesture that could have implied curiosity or contempt. Given the choice, most people in William Creek would have assumed he meant contempt. In a town of few people where everyone had strong feelings about everyone else, he was easily the most disliked person. Certainly not because he was an Afghan, because Afghans generally were admired and his uncle was an honourable man who was much respected throughout the district; and not because he ran the only general store for several hundred miles and charged what he liked when his uncle was not around to temper the young man's avarice. He was disliked because he possessed the one flaw which prevented anyone of any shape or colour being accepted in a bush town. He behaved as though he were superior to other people.

He was known in town as the Boa Constrictor. Goolamadail rather liked that. He presumed the name was in recognition of his toughness as a negotiator and the way he could squeeze a desperate person to his price. In fact, Boa was an acronym for that 'bastard of an Afghan'. Some wag had added Constrictor.

'Your uncle is a transport contractor?'

Goolamadail gave him the look of an old man peering over his spectacles.

The man cleared his throat. 'Well, I need to travel to a homestead.' He coughed more firmly. 'To see someone.'

'You want my uncle to take you?'

'I did write. I'm told there is no one else.'

'That is true. You are fortunate. He is not always here.'

'Oh.' Unable to help himself, the man felt for a shovel handle. His fingers stroked the smooth wood.

'Where do you wish to go?'

'Kalinda homestead.'

Both eyebrows rose. Slowly tilting his head, the Afghan used his nose as a gunsight. 'Why?' he fired, having paused until the whites of the man's eyes were prominent.

'It is my business.' And then he became flustered. 'I don't mean it is not your business. I mean it is the business that brought me here.'

'It is forty-seven miles,' Goolamadail said, to prove he was no longer concerned with the reasons for the visit. 'A very long walk.' There was a hint of a smile. 'You wish to see Mr Ross?'

'Yes.' Neither man spoke. It was a silence which compelled an explanation or, at least, an introduction.

'I am a lawyer.' The man had thought of saying solicitor but lawyer sounded more impressive. 'Jeremy Pollard, of Pollard and Pollard.'

Goolamadail sucked in his cheeks and the rat's eyes shone wickedly. 'You have money for Mr Ross?'

'No.' A discreet cough. 'It's a private matter.'

'Of course.' Goolamadail brushed dust from a bin.

'You know him well?'

'Very well. I know everyone.' The young Afghan was moving towards the back of the store. Pollard followed, hands clasped in front of him.

'Your uncle is out of town?'

'He will be here tomorrow.'

'And he can take me?'

'He has a truck.'

'Someone at the hotel said he had camels.'

'He has.' The eyes flashed a sideways glance. 'You would prefer to ride a camel?'

Pollard smiled nervously. 'No.'

'It's all right. He has a very good truck. It is only new.'

They had reached the end wall. In a corner was a table with jars and cups. Goolamadail indicated a spirit stove. 'I was about to make a cup of tea. Would you care to join me?'

'Thank you.' Pollard looked around the store. 'The store is yours?'

'My uncle's.'

'Oh. He is an important man?'

Goolamadail's head tilted to one side, acknowledging such a perceptive remark. 'I am the manager.' The teeth flashed. 'One day, who knows?' He lit the stove. 'You are comfortable at the hotel?'

'It is primitive.'

'This is a primitive town.' The flames hissed. He checked the water level in the kettle.

'I thought the people at the hotel were joking with me.'

Goolamadail sat in a chair in the corner. He waved towards a second chair with a broken armrest. Pollard sat down. 'I mean about the camels,' he added.

'They are not nice people.'

Pollard's expression was noncommittal, the practised deflection

35

of a legal man. 'They were not very helpful,' he said grudgingly.

'You needed help?' Goolamadail was sitting like a judge, arms evenly spread, legs wide, head up so that his incredible nose was poised to detect a droplet of fact in a flood of fiction. Pollard felt uncomfortable.

'Er, just some details about Mr Ross. Really simple, basic things. They were most reluctant to help.'

'They are not nice people,' Goolamadail repeated and checked the water. 'What did you want to know?'

'Elementary things.' Pollard seemed distressed at having found such obstinacy. 'He has a daughter?'

'Of course. Very little.' His hand indicated how tall. 'Her mother died.'

'So I understand.' Goolamadail looked interested, as though he'd like to hear more of what Pollard understood, but the solicitor was intent on the floor. 'Who looks after the girl?'

The Afghan smiled as though vital pieces of a puzzle had just clicked into place. So it was not money that had brought this city man to William Creek but something to do with Adam Ross and his daughter. And maybe the woman who was living with Adam Ross, the half-caste bastard Nellie Arlton? The woman who had worked for him, resisted his advances and then humiliated him by going to live with Ross at Kalinda. He risked a sly glance at Pollard. Was he here because of her? Was something happening at last?

His smile had thinned. 'I don't know who looks after the girl.'

Pollard looked as though he were thinking of something else. 'I'd heard there was a black woman.'

The Afghan's eyes half closed.

'You haven't heard?'

'I do not gossip.'

'Of course not.' Pollard coughed, to clear such improbable thoughts from his mind.

The kettle whistled and Goolamadail turned down the flame. 'You mean the half-caste prostitute?' he said softly.

'Prostitute?' Pollard had difficulty uttering the word.

'She is quite notorious.' He smiled apologetically. 'You must appreciate that in a small community everyone knows everything about everyone else. Even distasteful things are common knowledge.' His voice, which had sunk almost to a whisper, suddenly rose and became bright. 'Now, I have no milk but I can offer you sugar.' He raised one eyebrow expectantly, and smiled his warmest smile.

Adam and Josef had gone riding to the Number Two Bore, where Jimmy Kettle was camped. The women were together in the house.

36

Nellie was not looking forward to being alone with Sarah all day, for her initial feelings were being confirmed. She did not like Josef's girl-friend. Not that Sarah had said a lot; in fact, it was her long silences that unsettled Nellie. She preferred someone to say what she thought, not sit quietly and listen and give the impression she was judging you, which is what Sarah did. There was a calculating look about her that suggested she was adding up points and coming to a score.

Nellie began by suggesting Sarah might like to hold Cassie for a while. Sarah agreed, with the mildest display of enthusiasm, but Cassie ended the prospect by refusing to budge from Nellie's arms. She burrowed her face into Nellie's shoulder.

'She's shy,' Nellie said.

'Of course. She wouldn't be used to people.' The words were bland enough but somehow the remark suggested criticism, as though the child mixed with some other species.

What the hell do you mean by that, Nellie thought, but said, 'Oh she's normally very good with people. She loves Jimmy.'

'This is the one-armed aboriginal?'

'Adam's friend. And Josef's.'

'Quite ... He sounds ...' She groped for an appropriate expression. '... different.'

'He's weird.' Nellie smiled, pleased at the look on the other woman's face. Sarah hadn't expected that and seemed shocked, but the look only lasted a brief moment before she brought herself under control.

'I'll tell him you said that,' Sarah said and matched smiles. The smile was supposed to suggest a joke but Nellie presumed she *would* tell Jimmy. Sarah, she was certain, was the sort of woman who would hurt one person to score off another.

'Oh, he knows,' Nellie laughed. 'We're always trading insults.'

Sarah seemed intent on watching Cassie, who was nervously pulling at a strand of Nellie's hair. 'You must be old friends,' she said.

'Me and Jimmy?' Nellie spent some time as though adding up the years. What was this woman up to, and when would she get around to the subject she wanted to discuss, which was Adam? She'd noticed the way Sarah looked at him, studied him, judged him. 'Oh,' she said eventually, 'we've known each other a long time.'

'Before you met Adam?'

'Just before.'

'Really? How long ago was that?'

'Too long.' She put Cassie on the floor. The girl ran out the door. 'Don't go too far,' she called after her.

'Will she be safe?' Sarah did not sound concerned.

'She's very responsible.'

Sarah gazed about her. 'Adam built this?'

'Yes.'

'For you?'

'For him.'

Sarah's eyes swept over the ceiling, the wall, the door, Nellie, the stove. 'Clever man.'

Nellie said nothing.

'I'd like a cup of tea.' It was perilously close to a demand and Nellie felt the hairs on her neck tingle with incipient anger.

'I was just about to offer you one,' she said and was surprised that her voice sounded so friendly.

'I have that knack. I'm always saying what people are thinking. Josef says it's quite unnerving.'

'Really?'

'Yes. He thinks about something and I say it before he can.'

'Poor Joe.'

Sarah looked puzzled. 'Why poor?'

'Well, he likes to say things for himself.' She moved the kettle over the hotplate on the stove and checked the water level. 'Have you met his parents?'

'Many times.'

'Well, you know what I mean.'

Sarah seemed not to know, but she said nothing. She was losing control of the conversation. And now, to make things worse, Nellie went to the door and spent some time checking that the child was safe.

'In sight?' Sarah said breezily, when Nellie re-entered the room.

'Yes. Happily playing with a brown snake.'

'You're joking!'

'Yes.'

Sarah's legs twitched in agitation, as though the snake were about to be brought into the house. 'You *are* joking?'

'Yes.'

The legs relaxed. 'You have the strangest sense of humour.'

'It helps me smile.' Her smile was so sincere Sarah found herself responding. 'No matter how I feel.'

'She's not really playing with a snake?'

'She's quite capable of it, but no.' It was merely a snake skin that Cassie was using as a toy, whirling it around her head like a stock whip but Nellie felt disinclined to offer any further explanation.

'What was her mother like?'

The abruptness of the question surprised Nellie.

38

'You knew her?' Sarah added.

'Yes. Not well.'

'Was she as nice as Josef said.'

'It depends on what Josef said.'

The women sparred with smiles.

'Beautiful?' Sarah suggested.

'I don't think Adam has a photograph or else I could show you.'

'She was very fair.' Sarah's fingers sketched an outline. 'Blonde. Blue eyes.'

Not black, you mean, you nasty bitch, Nellie thought.

'She died,' Sarah continued as though breaking the news. 'Josef told me. It must have been very sad.'

The kettle was boiling. Sarah made no effort to move but sat, back to the stove, waiting for the tea to be made. 'Do you think he'll marry again?' she asked.

'Adam?'

'I mean a man should be married. It's natural, don't you think? Especially a man living out here on his own.'

Nellie brought the kettle to the table. 'He's not exactly on his own,' she said slowly.

'I know.' Sarah smiled sweetly. 'But living with his baby daughter makes it even worse, don't you think? I mean, it's hardly *being* with someone is it?'

'What is it, then?' Nellie said evenly. Her eyes managed a rapt expression, as though the answer were important to her although she feared she might have overplayed the expression. She was torn between either laughing or pouring hot water down Sarah's back, and she felt her face must be twitching between possibilities. Sarah seemed not to notice, and accepted the offered cup. Oh Josef, Nellie thought, you never were very clever where women were concerned, but where did you find this one?

'It's just ... different,' Sarah said profoundly. 'A wealthy grazier, living on his own, trying to raise a baby daughter ... it's not good, is it?'

I don't know how *you'd* know whether it's good or not, Nellie thought, but the last two years I've spent with Adam and Cassie have been the best of my life.

'Were you the housekeeper before ...?' Sarah let the question slide into silence.

Nellie held her forehead between thumb and forefinger. 'No, it doesn't work,' she said.

Sarah looked up in surprise. 'What doesn't?'

'I was trying to think if I could be as smart as you and know what the other person was trying to say. But I can't. I can't pick up any suggestion of any thought coming from you.'

Sarah wiped her lips, chasing an elusive tealeaf. 'What a strange thing to say.'

Nellie smiled.

'It was almost offensive. I think I could be offended by what you said and the tone you used.' She avoided Nellie's eyes. 'All I was asking was if you were the housekeeper before Heather died.'

'Meaning am I the housekeeper now?'

Sarah was involved in sipping tea.

'You may not have noticed, but Adam and I live together.'

Sarah extended the sip.

'You were here last night. I'm sure you know that we slept together, in that room.' She pointed to the doorway. 'There are only two rooms.'

'There's no need to become vulgar. I was merely enquiring if Adam ever thought of marrying again. It seemed to me to be a perfectly normal question.'

'I think you were being ... what was your word? Offensive.'

'Not at all.' Sarah tilted her head, a fresh thought having knocked it off-centre. 'You don't intend to marry him yourself?'

'I don't think that's any of your business.'

'My God, you do.'

Defiantly, Nellie glared at her.

'How quaint,' Sarah said quickly. 'Impossible but quaint.'

'What is impossible?'

'You marrying Adam Ross.'

'Why?' The word took a long time to leave her mouth.

'My dear, you must have noticed. You're black and he's white.'

Nellie touched her nose in thought. 'How perceptive of you. I'd never realized.'

'White men do not marry black women.'

'Really?' Nellie was now talking to the wall. 'White men seem to like black women.'

'That's not the same thing.'

'Adam and I ...' She was about to say 'are in love' but that was such a personal thing, such a pure thing that she didn't want to taint the thought by exposing it to this woman. Instead, she said, 'We don't think that matters.'

'Everyone else would.'

'I'm not concerned with what anyone else thinks.'

Sarah shook her head vigorously. 'He won't marry you. Never in a thousand years.'

Nellie breathed deeply. 'Why are you doing all this, saying all these things?'

'I believe in speaking honestly, in saying what I think.'

'So do I.'

'Good, we understand each other.'

Sarah had finished her tea. She rattled her cup. 'I'd like some more tea.'

'You're lucky. There's some left in the pot.' And when she didn't move, 'It's on the stove.'

'If you worked for me, I'd soon drum some manners into you,' Sarah snapped.

Nellie circled her. 'Have you been sleeping with Joe?'

'How *dare* you ask such a thing!'

'I'll bet you have. It's the only thing I can see about you that might attract him.'

'You bloody black bitch.'

'Ooh, the walls are cracking, aren't they.'

Sarah frowned. 'What do you mean?'

'The real Sarah is showing through.' She touched her forehead in an exaggerated gesture. 'I knew Joe was silly about women, but I didn't think he could be this silly.'

Sarah looked as though she might choke, but eventually managed to swallow and said loudly, 'I'm going outside.' She advanced to the doorway and screamed. Cassie was on the verandah, playing with the snake skin. 'She does have a snake,' she said, her voice thin.

Nellie joined her. 'Cassie,' she said softly, 'I've told you so many times not to pull the snakes out of their skins.'

Sarah ran from the house. Frightened by the noise and sudden movement, the child hurried to Nellie and wrapped her arms around her legs. 'Remind me to tell your father something tonight,' Nellie said, watching the other woman. 'We'll tell him Uncle Joe should have a nice big bath. And we should fill it with Lysol.'

Sarah had stopped running. She turned but, seeing Nellie looking at her, swung her hips and walked away.

Nellie felt sick. Adam would be angry when he found the women had argued, and he'd blame her. He knew she had a temper and he wouldn't believe the other woman had said all those things. She covered her stomach protectively. Sarah was probably right, she thought, and felt even more miserable. Adam would never marry her.

Adam and Josef had dismounted and were resting in the shade cast by a solitary tree. Having not ridden for some years, Josef was sore and already a little stiff. He sat at the base of the tree. Adam leaned against the trunk. Their horses grazed nearby – a listless, fruitless exercise, for the ground was hard and without grass and the few weeds that showed were withered and as bleached as straw.

41

Prompted by instinct, rather than hope, the horses covered the ground in a languid way, their heads moving slowly, nostrils twitching, lips curled in an expectation soured by constant frustration.

'It's funny,' Josef said and Adam waited, knowing there was no need to answer. One of the horses tried to sample a leaf on a stunted shrub but the plant was covered in ants and the animal moved away sharply, snorting loudly and lifting its head in distress. Deep in his own thoughts, Josef seemed not to have noticed. 'I thought of living in the outback once but I don't think I could now.'

'Got too used to the city?'

'Not the city. The Barossa Valley's hardly Adelaide.' He rubbed the inside of his calf where his horse's flank had chafed his skin. 'No, it's just that things are so dry. So hard. Nothing grows without a struggle.'

'You get used to it.'

Josef uttered a soft laugh. 'That's what I was telling Sarah.'

Adam changed his position slightly, to avoid a projecting piece of bark. 'And?'

'Oh, I said the sort of things you say and she said the sort of things that I'm thinking now.'

Adam moved again. 'So you're going to stay down south?'

Josef nodded. 'I think so. The business is going well. And there's so much green grass. We've even got to mow the stuff.'

'There you are, that's one advantage we have. Up here, we don't have to cut the grass.'

Josef rubbed the other calf. 'I'd rather have it and have to cut it than not have it and not cut it.'

The horse had attempted to nibble the bush once more and again, it retreated, snuffing and shaking its head. 'Just look at that,' Josef said. 'The poor beggar hasn't got a thing to eat.'

They both watched the horse, and said nothing for a long time. Eventually Adam spoke. 'With water we could grow anything.'

Awkwardly, Josef got to his feet. 'Everyone out here always says that. But you haven't got any water. It never bloody well rains.'

'It rained last time you were here,' Adam said.

'And I nearly drowned in a flood.' He almost added 'And your wife died' but stopped in time. 'Anyhow, that was three years ago. Had any rain since?'

Adam grinned.

'See? It's either everything at once or nothing for years. Feast or famine. You can't live in a place like this.'

'*I* can.'

Josef studied his friend.

42

'Yes, you can, but not many could.'

'That's all right.' Adam brushed an ant from his elbow.

'No, it's not all right,' Josef said earnestly. 'I worry about you. Life's so much easier down south.'

'I don't like the city.'

'I'm not talking about the city. There's a lot of good country down south, with water, grass, trees.'

'I couldn't afford a property down there. Besides, this is the country I know.'

'It'll beat you, Adam.'

Adam looked surprised.

'I don't mean you're not good enough to run a property up here or anything like that. You're the best I know. It's just that no one can win on land as poor as this.'

'I'm getting by.' Adam still smiled. He remembered how intense Josef could be.

'One day it won't rain for four years. Or five years.' He flung the additional period at his friend like a curse.

'Well, don't wish it on me.'

Josef stretched a leg. 'I wouldn't do that. God forbid. It's just that it could happen and no matter how good you are, you couldn't go on if there was a really long drought. Everything would die. You'd lose the lot.'

Adam shrugged. 'Could happen I suppose. But I've made a lot of improvements. I've got the two bores down so there's good underground water and I'm thinking of sinking a third, up north and nearer the lake. There's good feed up there.'

Josef nodded, accepting the information but not agreeing. 'It's too hard, Adam. For the same amount of work, you could do so much better down south.'

'The properties aren't as big,' Adam said simply, withdrawing to his last line of defence.

'You're not a Sidney Kidman. You haven't got a hundred properties to shuffle your cattle around, so that if there's a drought in one place, you can move your stock elsewhere.'

Adam kicked a stone to one side. 'So what do I do?'

'Move south.'

'Can't afford to.'

'Make your money here, then come south.'

Adam smiled. 'I'll think about it. But this is the sort of country I was raised in. I love it.'

'You're up against nature, Adam, and nature will beat you.'

Adam rolled the stone back to where it had been. 'Life's easy for a prosperous wine grower?'

43

Now Josef laughed. '*Touché.*'

Adam was puzzled. 'What's that mean?'

'It's a fencing term.'

'I've never heard a fencer use it.'

'Wrong sort of fencer. It's a word used in sword fighting when someone scores a point.'

'I scored a point?'

'You did. We have birds that eat the fruit and insects that eat the leaves and bacteria that attacks what's left.' He looked worried. 'And we have too much rain and too little sun or too much sun and too little rain.'

'And that affects the plonk you produce?'

Josef's face was transformed into a mask of great suffering. 'Don't call it that, please. Anything but plonk.'

'I don't think I've heard it called anything else.'

'I know,' Josef agreed sadly. 'But one day it will change, and Australians will learn about wine and develop a taste for wine and become real connoisseurs.'

'That's the aim?'

'That's it. The grand Josef Hoffman plan.'

'How does your father feel?'

Josef grunted. 'He's not as optimistic, but you know my father. He's a really good, maybe even a great wine-maker but he's no marketer. And he's getting a bit despondent. You know, when you get trodden on often enough, the heel marks start to show.'

Flies had discovered them. Adam brushed away a flight that had settled on his face. 'I like your father.'

'I know,' Josef said grudgingly.

'How do you get on with him these days?'

'Same as always. I'm his son which in his eyes means I'm always a boy. He just can't understand that I'm a grown man with a mind of my own, and able to think about things and do things for myself.'

'I'll tell you what,' Adam said, his hand now steadily clearing the flies from his face, 'seeing you've got trouble with birds and insects and ...'

'Bacteria.' Josef filled the pause.

'Whatever that is, and with people who don't appreciate what a fine drop of plonk you make ...' His grin broadened as Josef winced. '... and seeing your father –'

'– is a pain in the arse.'

'Right. Considering all those things, I reckon you should give away something as troublesome as trying to grow grapes and move up here where all you've got to worry about is the rain.'

'You bastard,' Josef said amiably.

Adam got the horses. 'So you're going to stay down south, get married and make wine?' he said offering Josef his reins.

'Something like that.' He stretched his back. 'I've got a feeling I'm going to regret all this riding tomorrow.'

'You never were one to do things gradually.'

Josef mounted, groaning with the effort. 'I think that's what I like most about wine-making. You don't have to ride a horse.'

Adam swung to the saddle. There was a faint squeak of leather. 'When's the big day?' he asked.

'The wedding?' Josef realized he had been dreading the question. He bent to fit his right boot in the stirrup. 'In a few months I suppose,' he said, still leaning down and out of sight. 'We haven't really discussed it.' He lifted his head sufficiently to see Adam across the saddle. 'What do you think of her?'

Adam was sitting quietly, hands crossed on his mare's neck.

'She seems ... nice.'

'Good looking isn't she?'

Adam nodded. He stretched, as though the gesture had exhausted him. 'The important thing,' he said deliberately, 'is what you think of her.'

Josef sat up and adjusted his hat. 'Well, I'm going to marry her,' he said and smiled a little too artificially, to indicate it had been a foolish question. 'Now, how about you?'

Adam waved his hand across his face to disperse the flies. 'I don't think I'll marry Sarah.'

'Silly goat. I mean you and Nellie.'

Adam shrugged.

'You must have discussed it.'

'Not really.'

'Thought about it?'

There was a long silence.

'Has it been hard?' Josef asked. Adam had begun to move off and Josef prodded his horse into action. 'There must have been some talk. I know what these things are like.'

'No one's said anything to me.' Adam slowed to allow Joseph's gelding to catch up. 'But a few people have told me what other people are saying.'

'All shock and horror and how disgusting?'

'Something like that.' There was another long silence. Adam turned the mare to cross a sand-hill. Josef followed. 'Plus of course, people saying that I haven't even buried my first wife.'

'Oh my God.' The gelding stumbled in the soft sand. Josef

steadied himself and then drove the horse to catch up. 'People can't accept the idea of a white man living with a black woman.'

'Nellie's half white,' Adam said rapidly and immediately regretted the remark. He didn't care what colour she was and deplored hearing the defensive clichés about blacks that some whites kept uttering. The more self-professed sympathetic whites spouted phrases to underline their own good intentions, the more he doubted them. 'I mean,' he began, but realized he didn't know what he meant.

'Sure,' Josef interrupted, 'but a touch of black is black to most people, and they just can't seem to accept the idea of a white man living with a black woman. Even a half-caste,' he added, as a sop to Adam's last remark. Josef was quiet for a moment and then said, 'Gee, that's a terrible expression.'

Adam, still miserable from his own foolishness, looked across sharply.

'Half-caste. It doesn't sound human, but only half of something. Like an imperfect piece of machinery.'

Adam reached the top of the ridge. He stood in the stirrups and repositioned himself in the saddle. 'Did I ever tell you you talk too much?'

'Many times. I'm just an impulsive talker. I say what comes into my head.'

'I wouldn't let Nellie hear you call her an imperfect piece of machinery.'

'Has she still got the same temper?'

They grinned at each other. 'She keeps it pretty well bottled up,' Adam said.

Josef let his horse take up position beside Adam's. The dune sloped down to a gravelly plain. The sand was beautiful, a rich terracotta in colour and layered by the wind into a series of parallel terraces so that the slope seemed to be covered by an army of shadowy red snakes, all slithering in unison.

'You are happy?' Josef asked. He would never have asked Adam such a simple question a few years ago, but their relationship then had been different. Adam had always seemed so much older, and the master. Now Josef felt more equal; he'd matured a lot in the last three years.

Adam, who had been admiring the view, nodded.

'That's good. To hell with what people say.'

'That's exactly what Nellie says.' Adam let the mare start down the dune. It slid with each step, its hooves pulverizing the finely sculpted terraces and leaving a trail of soft craters.

'People are bastards,' Josef said.

The mare floundered to the bottom of the dune and then delicately picked its way through a barrier of spinifex to reach the gravel plain.

'Only some,' Adam said. 'Not everyone's been gossiping. There are a few on our side.'

'Anyone I know?' Josef said with a show of joviality. He felt it was about time to change the subject.

'Saleem Benn. He's been a good friend.'

'Of course. He's a terrific bloke. How is the old feller?'

'Good. We see him every now and then. His business hasn't been doing too well down Marree way and he's spending more of his time up here. He drives a truck now.'

Josef stopped his horse. 'Whatever happened to the camels?'

'He's still got a few. He almost got put out of business by carriers using trucks so he reckoned it was time to make the change himself.'

'I can't imagine him in a truck. It's like Noah being in a motorboat and not the ark.'

'He's the world's worst driver,' Adam continued. 'He makes a gear change like he was whipping a camel.'

'This I've got to see.'

'You probably will. He's due to bring some supplies up.'

'When?'

'Tomorrow. Next week. Next month. Whenever he gets here.'

Josef smiled with affection for the man who had once saved their lives. He was looking forward to seeing the old Afghan. Saleem had always treated Josef as a boy, the junior to Adam and Jimmy Kettle. Josef wanted to tell him how well the business was going in the Barossa Valley, and to show him Sarah. And to make sure Saleem realized he had changed in the last few years and was now a man, independent of Adam and successful in his own right. He stood in the saddle and rubbed the seat of his pants. 'How much further?'

'You never could find your way to the bore,' Adam said, shaking his head ruefully. He pointed towards a dune on their right. 'Just over that sand-hill. Jimmy will be pleased to see you. He's got a surprise for you.'

'What is it?'

'Just wait.'

'Is it a big one or a little one?'

'It depends.'

'Oh come on, Adam.'

But Adam would not be provoked into saying more. 'Just wait another ten minutes and you'll find out for yourself,' he said.

47

Josef, whose horse had fallen behind again, dug his heels into its flanks and urged it to go faster. Adam's mare was only walking, but the gelding refused to increase its pace.

'You've given me a real dog,' Josef complained.

'It's the quietest one I have. Just wait till you turn it round and point it towards home. You'll have to hang on.'

Josef pressed one hand against the small of his back. 'I can hardly wait.'

'You've grown soft,' Adam observed.

'Yes,' Josef admitted, still holding his back. 'And I like it. This is not a natural way for a man to live, punishing himself every day. And don't tell me you get used to it.'

'You can get used to anything.'

'Well from now on, I just want to get used to what I like.'

'And you know what that is?'

'What sort of question is that?'

'A serious one.' Adam let the mare stop at a patch of low bushes to nibble at the leaves. He turned in the saddle and waited for Josef to draw level. 'Not many people know what they want. They can tell other people what they should do, but they don't know what's best for them. At least, that's what I reckon. So what do you want to do?'

Josef lifted one shoulder in a manner which suggested he didn't really care. 'Grow grapes. Become a famous wine-maker. Make a lot of money.'

'Get married?'

Josef let his breath out slowly. 'I suppose so.'

Adam's eyes were penetrating. 'You should think about it carefully.'

Josef concentrated on the meagre bushes, which both horses were now attacking. 'You're not exactly the best one to be offering advice on getting married.' He looked up briefly, saw no sign of hurt, and went on. 'I mean after Heather. That was a disaster.'

'You're often wiser after you make a mistake,' Adam said softly

Jose. nodded. 'I didn't mean to say that. Not the way it sounded anyhow.'

'That's all right.'

'No. I'm sorry. For a moment you reminded me of my father.' His smile confirmed the apology. 'You know how he's always giving me advice. I just snap back automatically now. We've had some terrible arguments in the last year or so.'

'You always did.'

'They're worse these days.'

Adam reined in his horse. 'That's a shame,' he said. 'You're both such nice people.'

Josef did not want to look up. His hat bobbed an acknowledgement of the compliment. 'Some people just argue. It happens automatically, like paper burns if you hold a match to it.'

'Someone has to strike the match.'

'He's the match striker,' Josef said. 'He just can't help himself.'

They rode towards the last dune, their horses side by side.

'My father says there's not going to be a war,' Josef said, his voice suddenly loud and cheerful, relishing the chance to pass on news that emphasized the poor state of his father's mind.

'You think there is?' Adam sounded surprised.

'Pounds to peanuts.'

'There's been talk of it around William Creek.'

'There's also talk of it in other more influential parts of the world,' Josef said with heavy sarcasm. 'Chamberlain says there won't be a war which is why I think there will be.'

'Who's Chamberlain?'

'The British Prime Minister. Weak as piss. My father believes him. The reason is, you see, my father looks like Neville Chamberlain – same moustache, same grey hair, same thin face and sad eyes – so when he saw him on the newsreel saying there would be peace in our own time, the old man thought it was himself speaking. Silly old goat. Of course there'll be war.'

'Why?'

'Because the world wants it.'

Adam twisted in the saddle. 'You're joking.'

'No. There's been a depression, and a good war would fix that. Get all the industries back on full steam, and make lots of money for everyone.'

Adam looked shocked.

'It's true, Adam. I know you're not a man of the world so you wouldn't understand, but there are a lot of people who would want a war. The Germans for instance.'

'Why on earth would the Germans want another war?'

'To get their own back. Revenge. Restoring national pride. All those things.'

'Sounds crazy.'

'The world's full of crazy people.' Feeling secure in a subject on which he knew Adam had little knowledge, Josef raced on. 'There are American industrialists who would welcome a big war so they could sell ships and trucks and guns and God knows what, and there are a million Frenchmen just waiting to have another crack at the Huns; and the English of course are mad enough to go to war

49

on a matter of principle, even if half the slobs who'd end up doing the fighting wouldn't understand what the principle was ...' He paused. He was breathing heavily. He pushed his hat away from his forehead. 'I'd like to go to war.'

Adam made the mistake of smiling.

'I would,' Josef repeated, frowning. 'I'd like to go and fight the bloody Germans.'

'But you are a German.'

'Not me. My father is, but I'd love to go over there and shoot a few of them.'

F · I · V · E

The bore was a pipe in the ground, sunk to a depth of more than a thousand feet to tap an underground reservoir of hot water. The hole had been drilled in a valley bounded by tall and almost parallel ridges of sand. The valley was narrow but long, and its floor was flat and strewn with small stones. Red was the predominant colour; dark red clay was the surface and a lighter, faded shade where low islands of sand protruded and linked together, chain-like, to divide the clay into broad pools. From a height, the scene could have been mistaken for some coral reef, all rocks and sandy islets and curving lagoons which, miraculously, had changed from the translucent blue-green of the tropics to the opaque red of the outback.

The illusion was destroyed by the additions which Adam and Jimmy Kettle had made to the site. The bore pipe was an ugly jumble of metal tubes and valves. It was rusted, and near its open end had become encrusted with barnacles of lime and grown a beard of dark green weed. A gush of water, rising from its dark and pressurized basin deep beneath the earth's crust, emerged from the pipe in a hissing, steaming, stinking jet. The water splashed into a wide pool. Steam curled from the surface. The edge of the pool carried a sour mix of froth and flaking crust. Bore-drain grass, the rush-like, spiky growth that alone can tolerate the chemical brew and great heat, was thriving. It encircled the pool, adding a dark green outer ring to the colourful bands at the water-line.

There was a windmill. A light breeze turned its blades and the pump clanked, sucking water from the pool and transferring it to a tank. There, the water cooled and ran into a long trough where sheep could drink. A pipe carried more water to a stockyard. Two camels were tethered within the yard.

Further back and close to the edge of one sand-dune was a hut made of timber and corrugated iron. A small rainwater tank stood on a frame beside the hut.

Josef stopped his horse. 'My God, you've built a house. Is that the surprise?'

'No,' Adam said, shaking his head, enjoying the secret.

'Where's Jimmy?' Josef looked around him, smiling in anticipation of seeing his friend.

'Knowing Jimmy, he's been watching us for the last half hour.' Adam twisted in the saddle, and joined in the search for the aborigine. Jimmy could move more quickly and blend into the scenery more completely than any other person he knew. Jimmy would not have left the bore. He knew Josef was due today. He was probably observing them, enjoying their inability to see him and content to bide his time and let Josef grow more and more agitated.

Adam's eyes roved the side of one dune, trying to distinguish which of the shadowy lumps were clusters of spinifex or salt bush and which might be a man, bent over, unmoving but unable to stop grinning at the joke he was playing on his visitors. Jimmy knew these hills well. He spent little time at the homestead these days but stayed with the sheep at either the Number One or the Number Two bore. A slight movement drew Adam's eye to the far end of the dune but it was a sheep moving. There were several there, scattered across the slope and difficult to distinguish from the salt bush that peppered the sand. Adam looked hard, but he could see no other living creature.

Josef urged his horse forward. 'Maybe he's in the hut,' he said hopefully. Near the small building, he dismounted and, holding his sore back with one hand, led the gelding towards the door. The hut had an old and worn look about it. The iron was second-hand, and came from a shed that had once stood on an outstation at Anna Creek. That shed had collapsed from the combined effects of wind storms which had blasted its sides and gnawing termites which had rotted the timber supports. Saleem Benn had transported the iron to Kalinda, knowing Adam and Jimmy could use it. He also brought in the timber, great hand-cut posts that he had found on an abandoned station in the northern Flinders Ranges. United in a lonelier location than either had previously known, the iron and timber had already shared a few sand storms at the Number Two bore. It was a stout little structure, and the weathered walls and the high ridge of sand and pebbles that crept up its base gave it a look of suffering and permanence.

Josef paused near the door. He wasn't sure what to do with the horse.

A voice challenged from the distance. 'Not going to take the nag inside, are you?'

Josef turned, a grin of delight on his face. He saw no sign of Jimmy Kettle. 'Where is he?' he asked Adam, after a few moments spent scanning the hills.

52

Adam was still mounted. 'Search me,' he said, shrugging. The voice seemed to have come from behind them but this was a confusing place, given to echoes.

'Where are you Jimmy?' Josef shouted in exasperation.

'Right in front of you,' Jimmy replied. Josef was looking towards the dune they had descended.

'That's it,' Jimmy called. 'You're looking right at me. How are you going, mate? All right?'

Still there was no movement. 'I can't see the bugger,' Josef whispered, his eyes nearly shut as he squinted into the bright light.

'You won't until he wants you to,' Adam said, not bothering to look.

'Please, Adam,' Josef said, still speaking softly so his voice would not carry. 'Your eyes are better than mine.'

Only when Adam turned did Jimmy move. It seemed that a bush on the far slope rose. It was almost beside the track they had ridden down. The shape stretched into a man, dressed in ragged pants, a coat, and carrying a rifle. These days Jimmy almost always carried his Winchester.

Even at this distance, they could see his teeth exposed in a broad smile. 'I thought you pair of eagle-eyed bushmen was going to ride over the top of me,' he called, and hurried down the side of the hill.

There was something strange. Adam noticed it first. Jimmy was carrying the rifle under the left sleeve of his coat. Jimmy had only one arm, and it was the left one that was missing. The arm was bent, holding the gun correctly. The hand was buried in the coat pocket.

Jimmy sauntered the last few paces to avoid any suggestion of eagerness. 'Well, how the hell are you, kid?' he enquired. The Winchester was still under his arm.

'Good,' Josef said and felt so happy he thought he might cry. 'I'm good. How are you?'

Jimmy pulled a face that covered the distorted expressions of a rubber mask being stretched into place. 'Not bad,' he said when his face had settled, and nodded agreement with his own assessment.

Suddenly, Josef noticed the arm. 'Jesus Christ!'

Jimmy was delighted, but there was no hint now of a smile. 'What do you think of it?' he asked, glancing down at the sleeve. 'Took me eighteen months to grow.'

'What?' Josef let go the reins and the horse immediately ambled towards a patch of salt bush.

'I grew it just for you,' Jimmy said. 'Been eating emu eggs. Didn't know they made arms grow, but there you are. You're always learning something.'

53

Using his right hand, and watching Josef's face all the time, Jimmy unbuttoned the coat and slipped the sleeve from his right arm. The left stayed securely in the pocket. Withdrawing the rifle, he removed the coat. The left arm, firm as ever, stayed bent, with the hand in the pocket. 'Emu eggs,' Jimmy repeated.

'You lying bastard,' Josef said and embraced him. 'What did you make it of?'

The embrace finished, Jimmy delivered a playful punch to Josef's ribs. 'Stuffed grass. Wire. Like it?'

'Terrific,' Josef laughed but it was more from the joy of seeing his friend than from the joke.

'Took me a day to get it right. I had to make two. The first one wouldn't hold the gun.'

'You silly bugger,' Josef said in a voice that wavered with affection.

'I'd have done it quicker, but I was a bit short-handed.' He laughed and scored with another soft punch to the body. He stood back and studied Josef. 'You're getting fat. Too much of the good life.'

'You can't have too much.'

Adam dismounted. 'I don't think he'll be able to walk tomorrow.'

'I haven't ridden since I was here last.' Josef gripped Jimmy's shoulders again. 'Jesus it's good to see you.'

'Me too.'

Josef smiled at Adam. 'So this is the surprise you promised me.'

'No.' Adam let the mare wander off to join the gelding.

'You didn't know about it?'

Jimmy answered for him. 'This was just my own little surprise for both of you. Hey!' He turned to Adam. 'You really didn't spot me when you rode down the hill? Your mare almost trod on me.'

Adam shook his head. 'We were too busy looking for you.'

They all grinned. Then Josef scratched his chin and said to Adam, 'Well if you didn't know about the new arm, how did you know Jimmy had a surprise for me?'

Again Jimmy answered. 'Because I have. Want to see it?' He said the words slowly, without any suggestion of concern which, Josef recalled, meant just the opposite. Jimmy was bursting with a desire to show him something.

'Sure.' Josef attempted to display an equal lack of interest. 'If you want to.'

'Why not?' Jimmy said. Rifle in hand and coat over his shoulder with the wired arm still branching from the pocket, he advanced towards the hut. He whistled shrilly. 'OK,' he yelled.

54

The door opened. It swung inwards, creaking a bird song on hinges that were not perfectly aligned. Josef heard a giggle. He was determined to show no surprise, to score a point in the game that Jimmy had so far dominated, but he had not expected this. Someone was inside. His mind raced through the possibilities but all he could think of was Saleem Benn, and that was ludicrous. The Afghan wasn't on the property, wouldn't hide in a hut and certainly wouldn't giggle. He folded his arms, reinforcing himself against emitting a sudden gasp or an uncontrolled laugh.

A woman stepped through the opening. She was a shadow at first, and all Josef could be sure of was that she was tall and slim and young; he could tell the latter from the way she moved, with a fluid, animal-like grace.

She emerged slowly, with a delicate swaying motion. Then she was in the sun. She was black but her skin had a curious grey sheen that suggested a statue carved from a pure, dark marble. She had long hair, and she was shy. He looked at her closely. She could be no more than eighteen. She smiled and Josef found himself gaping at her. He kept staring, entranced by the simple beauty of this girl. She had thin legs and she was bare-footed – but he had not yet progressed that far, being unable to break the link with her eyes.

She broke it. She turned to Jimmy and the smile became mischievous.

Hands still across his chest, Josef coughed. 'Well,' he said, trying to sound as unimpressed as was polite, 'what have we got here?'

Jeremy Pollard was growing restless. He had been in William Creek for two days now and the transport contractor who was to drive him to his destination had still not arrived. Pollard was used to accounting for every minute of his time, and he was feeling guilty as he always did when he wasted time. He should have been doing work for the firm instead of being incarcerated in some primitive hotel, waiting for an Arab to turn up whenever the wretched heathen felt like it. Time is money, his father always said, and his father would be extraordinarily angry, even by his colourful standards, if he knew his son was spending his time in a hotel bar rather than accomplishing his mission.

Jeremy Pollard wore his guilt like itchy underwear. He sat in a corner of the bar of the William Creek hotel, fidgeting and scratching and worrying about the time he was wasting on what was essentially a simple matter, although one compounded by the fact that the client, whom he'd never met, was a friend of a close friend of his father. Cecil Pollard was given to the occasional grand gesture and, with a modest 'friend in need is a friend indeed', had promised to despatch his only begotten son (he said it in his most biblical voice) to the wilds of the South Australian hinterland.

'You look like you could do with a drink,' a man said. Pollard had been gazing at a section of the wall to which was pinned a number of old calendars. They all had paintings of beaches or snow-capped mountains and, despite the fly specks and curled edges, served as a kind of visual refuge in the really hot months when the temperature inside was a hundred and five and the air beyond the verandah had been burnt to such a searing thinness that it scorched the nostrils and gave sinners a reasonable foretaste of the hereafter. People could gaze at those calendar pictures and believe there was another world, and resolve to try and survive another summer, and have another drink. Pollard was facing the wall but saw nothing other than the scowling visage of his father.

He blinked and looked up. 'I beg your pardon.'

'You look like you could do with a drink,' the man repeated. 'You look agitated.' He said the word with the clumsy deliberation of one who had been practising it for some time. He tried to give a friendly smile but there was a desperation lurking in his eyes. He licked his lips. He was the one who needed the drink.

'No,' Pollard said weakly, shaking his head. 'I'm all right thank you.'

'Mind if I join you?' The man sat down. Cadger Ferguson had a reputation from Hawker to Finke as a man who never bought a drink but had never been seen to walk sober from a bar. 'What are you drinking?' he asked, his tongue unable to leave his lips for a longer time than it took to ask the question.

Pollard shook his head, wishing the man away.

'Nothing? I'll have a rum thanks.' He turned to the publican. 'A rum please, Harry.'

Harry Peterson poured the drink slowly, eyeing Pollard all the time, inviting him to cancel the order. Pollard said nothing.

'Thank you sir, that's very kind of you,' Ferguson said and lifted the glass with a hand that shook slightly.

'On your account Mr Pollard?' Peterson asked, giving the solicitor a final chance to withdraw.

Pollard did his best to make his shoulders meet in front of his body. He was wondering how he would account for this expense. 'Yes,' he said. 'Of course. Certainly.'

Ferguson's tongue had retreated, to savour the rum. He beamed. 'Up here on business, I hear,' he said.

'Yes.'

'I hear you're a city lawyer.'

Pollard wanted to excuse himself but he didn't know the appropriate words to use with a man like this. Decent words, that would

56

allow him to walk away with dignity. Other men in the bar were looking at them. He hesitated and was lost. He thought of his father.

The man was sipping his drink, coaxing it from the glass, eager for its warming flow yet desperate to conserve every drop.

'Adelaide?'

Pollard turned his head, defeated. Where was that vile truck driver? 'Yes,' he said and found his eyes looking into those of an old stockman wearing a filthy hat. The man was sitting at the bar and smiling, as though Pollard had done something foolish.

'Nice down there.'

Pollard removed a hair from his coat.

'You're going to see Adam Ross.'

'Who told you that?' Pollard said frowning.

'Gooly.' Ferguson had decided to make the rum last. This man wasn't likely to buy him another drink without a lot of work. He licked his lips. The lawyer looked puzzled. 'The storekeeper,' Ferguson added.

'The man is a talker,' Pollard said in his sternest courtroom voice.

'Oh, he's all right.' The other lifted the glass and held it just beneath his nose, testing and demonstrating his restraint. 'What do you want to see Ross for?' he asked, his eyes intent on the delicious colour of the spirit.

Pollard clasped his hands. His face was grim. He hated being pressed like this, particularly by such a vulgar character, but Ferguson misread the expression.

'Hope it's something bad,' he said cheerfully and drank again. It was a prodding remark, designed to dislodge a clue. Cadger liked to know other people's secrets, and if the business that had brought this pallid man in the suit to William Creek was bad for Adam Ross, so much the better. Ross had never bought him a drink. Most men bought him at least one rum.

'He's a nasty one, that,' he added when he saw a flicker of response in the solicitor's eyes. This man, Ferguson deduced with a cunning that had eased him into drunkenness on most days of his adult life, wanted to hear that Adam Ross was not good. Why, he had no idea. He didn't really care. If he could please the man, he could keep him talking and get him to pay for a few more drinks. 'Any man that lives with a nigger ...' he said and grinned slyly as he saw he had scored a bullseye.

'You know him? And this woman?'

'Oh yes.' He finished the drink in one gulp. They faced each other. Ferguson held the glass expectantly. The lawyer wanted

57

more words. 'It's a real scandal,' Ferguson offered and saw that he was certainly on the right track. This man would love scandals, so he bolted ahead. 'He owns a lot of land. Just bought another five hundred sheep. You know, a real squatter, country gentleman, that sort – or that's what he'd like you to think. Never touches a drop. But, do you know something?'

Pollard's anxiety to learn was well restrained, but clear.

'He lives with blacks.'

'Aborigines?'

'The place is full of them. You know something else?'

Pollard did not shake his head for fear that this man might mistake the movement for lack of interest. If he got genuine information from this conversation it could help the client in her case and, also, allow him legitimately to charge any drinks to expenses.

'There isn't another white person on the place.'

'Really.'

'He has two women.'

'Two?'

'Both niggers. One older, about his age. She's been there a while, but now they reckon he's taken another one. Younger. Good-looking sort. Part Abo, part Indian or something. He's got a bloody harem going.' He laughed.

'You said scandal?' the solicitor reminded him.

'Well, that's right,' he said and caught the eye of the old stockman. The man winked at him. 'I mean it's one thing to like a bit of smoked log but you don't have to live in the bloody fireplace, if you follow me.'

Pollard did not, and studied his fingernails rather than stare stupidly at the man.

'It'd be different if there was just him.'

Pollard risked a quick look. Ferguson waved the empty glass to make sure it was noticed.

'Decent folk are ...' He paused to think of the strongest expression he knew. '... horrified.'

'Horrified?'

Cadger Ferguson wondered if he'd used the wrong word. 'Yes,' he said, trying to bluster his way through. 'There's a kid, you know,' and he saw the man did know and realized he had said precisely the right thing. He could afford to slow down now. 'By the way,' he said, leaning back, 'what are you having to drink this time?'

In the afternoon, Nellie went for a walk. Normally she would have stayed in the house with Cassie in the hope that the child might

58

sleep. She always put her to bed after lunch but Cassie had grown so vigorous and alert in recent weeks that the habit had become an exercise in futility, ending with the pair of them playing games on the floor. Even so she tried, reasoning that a three-year-old required sleep during the day. But Nellie needed to get away from Sarah and she was not prepared to leave Cassie in the house with the other woman.

Sarah had not spoken since their clash. When she returned to the homestead, she sat in one corner, in the only comfortable chair in the room, and resumed reading a book she had brought with her on the train. Her silence bristled with malevolence. She crossed and uncrossed her legs constantly, using her long limbs alternatively as defences to repel Nellie's glances or as the branches of a catapult to hurl silent insults upon her enemy. Wherever Nellie moved around the room, Sarah shuffled accordingly, always keeping those long legs between them.

It was a tiring game and so Nellie left the house. She carried the girl – delighted at the prospect of doing something outside rather than being imprisoned in the cot – all the way to a tree that laid an emaciated shadow on the bare earth. There she sat down, and put Cassie near her feet, expecting the child to pick up a stick or a stone and start to play. Instead, Cassie examined her intently, staring with an expression that seemed to demand an explanation for so unusual an action as to desert the house at this time of the day.

Nellie laughed. Cassie's expression hovered in doubt, then dissolved into a smile of contentment.

'You don't like it when I'm not happy, do you?' Nellie said, ruffling the girl's hair. Cassie smiled more broadly, not understanding but happy to be the cause of sudden good humour. 'And you're wondering why I've brought you out here, instead of putting you behind bars in that cot of yours.'

Again, she ruffled the child's hair. This time the movement produced a serious look.

'I just can't stand that bitch inside,' Nellie explained. The child stared at her, big eyes unblinking. 'Couldn't bear the thought of leaving you on your own with her. Rather leave you alone with a room full of spiders.' She breathed in the warm air and tried to calm herself. Cassie's eyes had not left her.

'Want a game?' Nellie said cheerfully. She threw a small stick towards the girl. Normally, Cassie liked trying to catch things but she let the stick spin past her.

'What would you like to do then?'

Cassie shuffled closer, and lay across Nellie's outstretched legs.

'Don't tell me you want to sleep?'

59

The eyes stared up at her. The lids blinked with the first hint of weariness.

Nellie put a hand on Cassie's shoulder. 'There's no doubt about you, darling,' she said and squeezed the child. 'I put you to bed in the house in a good clean, soft cot and you yell your lungs out and won't go to sleep, but when I bring you out here in the heat and the dust you want to have a nap. OK.' She patted the girl's bottom to emphasize the decision she had reached. 'From now on, I'll put you out here with all the flies, and I'll sleep in the cot.'

Cassie seemed to understand some of that and produced a tired smile. Contentedly, she closed her eyes.

I wish you were mine, Nellie thought. Mine and Adam's. It was a wish she expressed every day, and each day it was meant more fervently. Nellie had hated Heather the mother, but truly loved Cassie the daughter. Unkind people – and there were plenty of them around, she thought – would say the love was a kind of gratitude, for without the child there would be no need for Adam to keep a woman at the homestead. Cassie, therefore, was the reason that so upstanding a man as the boss of Kalinda homestead did the unthinkable and lived with a coloured woman, and the reason that a person like Nellie Arlton had a good home and a good man, instead of drifting around the outback, the plaything of wandering drunks, as others of her kind were inclined and even expected to do.

No one had ever said that to her face, but she had little doubt people thought it. There had been so much gossip. It had been transmitted by friends on occasional visits and dispensed casually, like dust brushed from a jacket.

Well, it wasn't true. She loved Cassie because she genuinely loved her, not because she was the tool that gave her a man in bed and a roof over her head.

The child could so easily pass for her own. That was a strange thing. Cassie looked more like Nellie, with her fine features and big brown eyes and dark hair, than she resembled the blonde and regal Heather. She could so easily be accepted as their daughter, the logical mix of a good-looking half-caste and a fair and handsome white man. And then, as always happened, the biting hurt returned and Nellie reminded herself that no one would ever make that mistake. Not in this district, where everyone knew of Adam's wife and her terrible death. That was the awful thing: they knew of Heather and still talked about her with a kind of reverence because of the way she had died. Few of them had ever met her. But she had died in the lake and was still there somewhere, deep beneath the salt, so people conjured images of a saint who sacrificed herself to save her baby, and when they spoke of her, it was always of a good woman who had loved her husband and been taken from him in the most cruel fashion.

Adam would never say anything but one of these days Nellie would tell the truth. She would walk past the pub at William Creek and scream out 'Heather Ross was a monster. She was cruel and selfish, and she was a schemer and she was mad, and she tried to destroy her husband and she didn't love her baby!'

She grinned ruefully. They'd never believe that. Heather Ross was a lovely woman. Why, in time they'd build a memorial to her. Beautiful white women with blonde hair and blue eyes were meant to be heroines, particularly if they died young, and were almost guaranteed immortality if they died mysteriously, let alone disappeared under a salt lake.

Dark haired, dark skinned, brown-eyed half-castes were never likely to contaminate an heroic mould. They were not the stuff of legends, but the inspiration of smutty jokes.

The bitch. If only she'd gone away, as she should have, instead of blundering on to the lake and killing herself and damn-near killing the baby too. But she *had* killed herself and now she was haunting them. Some nights, Nellie dreamed Heather was laughing at her, and when that happened she awoke sweating and shivering and had to get up and light the lantern and walk through the house to make sure it was deserted.

Cassie was now almost asleep.

She loves me as she would her real mother, Nellie assured herself and tightened the grip on Cassie's shoulder so much that the girl squirmed.

'Hush,' she soothed, relaxing her hold. 'Go to sleep.' She brushed a fly hovering near the fluttering eyelids.

For the first time, she thought of going away. All of them. Just pack up, sell the sheep, the camels, the horses, sell the property (if anyone wanted it) and drive off. It would be so good for all of them. Good for Adam. He had been working too hard. He would end up a worn and wrinkled man at forty. She'd seen it before on other men who'd tried to tame the outback. A long drought and all the stock would die and that would be it. The railway line from the south was dotted with ghost towns that stood like neglected cemeteries, commemorating countless battles between men and nature. They were sad places, all rubble and lonely smokeless chimneys and wagon wheels with weeds sprouting through the spokes; places that were built on lofty hope but were memorials to man's habit of failing. She didn't want Adam to fail.

It would be good for Cassie too, even though Adam mightn't see

61

that. Warming to the argument, her lips were mouthing the words to give them more emphasis but making no sound, because a noise might have woken Cassie, and it would certainly have sounded foolish. But – and she nodded in agreement with the thought she was about to express – Cassie could grow up in a place where there were other children to play with. Where she could go to school and learn to read and write, and maybe even teach her father. She smiled at that. That would be good to see.

And it would be good for her. In another place no one would know about Heather, and she and Adam could pretend they were married, even if Adam didn't want to get married, and she could pretend Cassie was her daughter. Cassie didn't remember her mother. She would grow up thinking Adam and Nellie were her parents. Damn it, it would be so good, so right, so simple. Damn it, because she knew Adam would never agree. He wouldn't leave this land. It was his. He was bound to it by an instinctive love.

The sun was now playing on her back and gently she moved Cassie until they were once more in the shadow of the tree. She sighed. She would speak to Adam. She had vowed never to complain about anything at Kalinda because she knew how much this place meant to him and because she had never been so content, but this would not be a complaint but a reasonable suggestion. It would be in all their interests to move, although she wasn't sure what Adam would do to make money. He had said he would never work for anyone again but he just might have to, at least for a year or two.

How would he react? You had to be careful when you made demands on men. Her mother had tried to get money from her father and he had punched her. She thought of her mother, unconsciously stroking Cassie just as her mother had comforted her in the early years.

Her mother often used to speak of her father. He was an officer on a ship, or so she said. Her mother liked to boast, and Nellie had heard her tell other people that the man was a ship's captain, but to Nellie she'd always said that he was only an officer. He could have been a humble seaman. What did it matter? There was no greater honour in being taken behind the bond stores at Port Pirie and being screwed by a man wearing braid than by one without. Nellie had long since given up wondering about the truth. Something had happened, obviously, and she was living proof of its potency. All she was certain of was that the man was from a ship and that he was Finnish. She was proud of that. Someone had told her Finns were fair and that had made her feel superior, just as the story about him being a sea captain had made her mother feel less violated. In later years, someone else had told her Finns tended to be dark and were not Nordic blonds, but as she had never seen one, she had no way of checking. She preferred the initial concept: the idea of having a truly fair-haired father was appealing.

A year after the incident, her father's ship had returned to Port Pirie and her mother, with the persistence and naïvety which were her strongest characteristics, had waited for him on the wharf holding Nellie in her arms. She had suggested marriage. The crew, lined up within hearing range, tittered with laughter. Being quick to recognize an impossible situation, she had then demanded money. The father had pushed her away. She had tried to give him the infant, but he had pushed her away again. Once more she tried. That was when he hit her. The crew could no longer restrain themselves and roared with glee to see the man and the black woman so humiliated. More than the blow, her mother said, it was the laughter that hurt.

Her mother had died years ago. Nellie didn't want to lose her man and spend her years in loneliness, polishing and enlarging memories as a substitute for happiness.

S·I·X

Saleem Benn arrived at William Creek that evening. He was asleep when he reached the town, a slumbering passenger in his own truck which was driven by his brother's sixth son, Yunis. The old Afghan had no sons but eight nephews, and all worked for him. Yunis was nineteen, and the youngest. His sole duty was to load and drive the truck. Some of his brothers worked in Saleem's stores. The oldest and cleverest worked with the camels, the rationale being that creatures which had inhabited the earth since the beginning of time required the attention of only the most mature and wisest of men.

The truck was a Reo. It was red, the colour common to most trucks of the era, and had been purchased ten months earlier at Hawker. The Reo was not new but little used. It had been bought at a bargain price from the widow of a road-making contractor who had grown clumsy in his use of explosive.

Saleem Benn had learned to drive the truck but had little understanding of it. Anything that did not require feeding or would not respond to soothing words or a sharp command was unnatural. As such, he told others, it did not deserve his fullest attention. To emphasize his contempt for a device that he could not master (and that was threatening, as a species, to put his camels out of business) he assigned most of the driving to the least competent and most juvenile of his nephews. It was a subtle insult, wasted on an inanimate beast like the red Reo.

While surrendering the wheel, Saleem Benn did not relinquish control and imposed strict limits on the way the truck was to be driven. Believing that the higher the gear engaged, the more the vehicle was inclined to have its head and race out of control, he forbade Yunis to select any gear other than reverse, first or second. As a result, the one hundred and forty miles from Marree to William Creek had taken eleven and a half hours and all the time, the engine had shrieked at nearly maximum revolutions as the Reo ground its way over the ruts and potholes. Saleem rather liked the sound of the motor's pained bellowing. He was becoming deaf and welcomed the reassurance of a constant, vigorous noise and besides, he had paid good money for this truck and the desperately striving engine suggested he was getting his money's worth. Weren't some of his best camels the ones that belched the loudest and complained the most? He slept for most of the journey, lulled by the comforting roar of the motor, while young Yunis clung to the vibrating steering-wheel and pondered the delights that lay beyond second gear.

In town, Saleem Benn descended from the cabin to be confronted by Jeremy Pollard. The solicitor had discarded his coat but still wore a waistcoat and tie. He was hot and glistened with sweat, to which a fine coating of dust adhered. He used a handkerchief to mop his brow, a frequent action which turned the dust into mud and ground it into the wrinkles across his forehead, so that he presented a finely striped face to the startled Afghan.

'You must be Mr Benn,' he said and frowned.

Slowly, Saleem raised his nose. He performed the feat in a way that suggested great control over a considerable object. 'And you?'

The solicitor shuffled his feet. This was not the sort of man he had expected. 'Jeremy Pollard. My office wrote to you.' He coughed, and produced a business card.

Saleem took it delicately, with his thumb and third finger. He turned it over, his expression suggesting there might be a poisonous insect on the other side.

'Your office wrote to me?'

'Yes.'

'No.' He returned the card.

Pollard was not sure what to do with the card, so held it with both hands and twisted it. 'What do you mean, no?'

'Your office did not write to me.'

The card was now bent and useless. Pollard put it in a waistcoat pocket. 'You didn't get a letter?'

'*My* office did.' Saleem stressed the first word. 'From a Mr Pollard. That was you?'

'Yes.' The brow wrinkled and the mud lines deepened. 'I wrote to you. Some weeks ago.'

'Ah!' The nose was still high. 'So it was you who wrote to my office, not your office who wrote to me.'

Pollard shook his head, then wiped his brow. He felt he was involved in some form of verbal chess and had started the game badly.

Point made, Saleem continued. 'My brother told me there was a letter. He conducts business affairs for me.'

Pollard felt he should start again. 'I need transport from here to a nearby property.'

65

'Yes, yes.' The old man turned to remove a small bag from the floor of the truck cabin. 'That was quite clear in the letter. My brother told me.' He glanced towards Pollard. 'My brother handles all correspondence. He runs the office.' It was the tone one uses with a person who has difficulty grasping simple facts.

'Of course.' Pollard swallowed noisily.

'Good. I am pleased we have now established the facts.' He smiled indulgently.

'I have to go to Kalinda.'

'Yes. Mr Ross's property.'

'I have been here for several days.'

Saleem's head nodded sympathetically. 'There are not enough trains.' And when Pollard did not respond, he added, 'With one train a week, many people have to wait, often in unpleasant surroundings.'

'I was expecting you sooner.' There was a hint of accusation.

Saleem's eyes narrowed. 'You are fortunate I am here today.'

'Indeed?' Pollard had taken a deep breath.

'It is a long journey from Marree. I have many things to deliver to many clients.' He patted the side of the truck, which was heavily laden with drums, crates and cartons.

'But I wrote specifying the date I would be here.'

'But you did not enquire when I would be here.' He smiled benignly.

'I've waited two days.'

'There are those who wait two weeks.'

'That is very unsatisfactory,' Pollard said and it was clear he was referring to his inconvenience, not that of others.

The Afghan shrugged. 'You presumed I would be here. You presumed I would be able to drive you to Kalinda. Happily you were correct. I think you will come to realize you have been most fortunate. I am not without other demands on my time.'

'In Adelaide, I can telephone for a taxi cab and have it outside my office in half an hour.'

Saleem shook his head. 'Truly, you must be a man of great influence.'

Pollard frowned and searched for fragments of sarcasm. He detected none. The old man in the strange robes seemed suitably deferential. 'But of course that is Adelaide,' Pollard added, feeling the need to offer a concession.

Saleem lifted both eyebrows and let his head bob in acknowledgement of such remarkable perception.

Pollard felt uncomfortable. 'When can we leave?' he asked.

'Possibly tomorrow.'

'Possibly?' The question was a squeak.

'I have goods to deliver, things Mr Ross has ordered.'

'And there will be a delay?'

'That depends on you.'

Pollard looked around him, as though seeking support. He dabbed his forehead. 'I don't understand.'

'It depends on your requirements.'

'I want to get to Kalinda.'

'You have nothing to take? No machinery, no furniture, no large items to be loaded on my vehicle?'

'Of course not.'

'Your letter was most unclear. I anticipated some time spent in loading ... whatever it was you brought with you.'

'Mr Benn, there is just me.'

'How extraordinary.' Saleem stroked his nose. 'You will be staying there?'

'No. I will be returning.'

'You mean I am being engaged in the manner of an Adelaide taxi cab? A truck just to carry one person?' Again the eyebrows were raised and Pollard had the uncomfortable feeling he was being assessed unfavourably. 'This humble man,' Saleem continued, 'who once led caravans of fifty noble camels laden with the necessities of life for pioneers who had settled the most remote regions ... this humble but proud man is now reduced to delivering ... one person?'

Pollard scowled. 'Is this the prelude to a demand for more money, a larger fee?'

The eyebrows descended to crowd the eyes and Pollard, alarmed by the sudden change in expression, stepped back.

'If the fee suggested in your letter to my office had not been sufficient, I would not have travelled here today,' Saleem growled. He breathed deeply, the incoming air hissing through clenched teeth. The eyebrows rose to a normal level. 'It was not a threat, sir, or, as you suggested, a prelude to something dishonourable. It was a lament.'

'I'm sorry.' Pollard cleared his throat. 'When can we leave?'

'At seven, if that is not too early an hour.'

'The earlier the better. I've wasted so much time.'

'To handle something badly is to waste it,' the old man said, nodding as though that had been Pollard's meaning. 'It is a sin we all commit at some time. By the way, I presume you are a friend of Mr Ross?'

The solicitor was still interpreting the remark. 'Ah, no, I'm not,' he said, fumbling to rejoin the conversation. 'I've never met him.'

Adam Ross, my friend, what have you done to bring such a man to your house? Saleem wondered. For a moment, he contemplated refusing the job but then thought better of it. He would deliver Mr Pollard to Adam Ross and if the man's mission was as unpleasant as his manner, he could always deposit him on a sand-hill on the way back to town, at a point beyond walking distance.

'Do you know him well, Mr Benn?' Pollard smiled.

'We have met,' he said, 'but he owns much land and I am but a simple camel driver forced by poor circumstances to become a taxi cab driver.' He began to walk towards the store.

'Mr Benn,' Pollard protested, anxious to ask more questions. But the old man was off, waving one hand feebly as he walked away.

Yunis appeared around the front of the truck.

The solicitor gave the courtroom smile he used on juveniles required to furnish vital information. 'Hello,' he said. 'Had a long, hard drive?'

Yunis stayed close to the radiator.

'Do you know Mr Ross?'

Yunis let a finger trace a path around the rim of one headlight.

'Adam Ross,' Pollard prompted. 'Do you know him?'

Yunis gave a shy smile. 'No English,' he said.

'No English. Oh my God.' Pollard examined the backs of his hands and found them so comforting he addressed them in a low, confiding voice. 'I spend two days wasting valuable time and then my driver arrives and he's an old imbecile of an Arab with a companion who turns out to be a grinning idiot who can't even speak the King's English.'

He looked up. Had he been faster, he might have seen the flash of anger in Yunis's eyes but the youth was quick, as well as cunning, and his face now carried a suitably vacant expression.

'So I'm to be blessed with your company too,' Pollard said, hiding his hands in his pockets. He stared at the silent youth who continued to run a finger around the headlight. 'Obviously, an exception to the rule that empty vessels make the most sound,' he grunted, and enjoyed the novel experience of being able to speak his mind. 'I'll guarantee you were parted with your money at an early age,' he said, smiling pleasantly and nodding when Yunis returned the smile.

He checked his watch. He would be out of this town in thirteen hours, and, hopefully, on the train south in a few more days. The business with Ross was distasteful but he should be able to complete it quickly and to the satisfaction of his client. When first apprised of the case, he had felt a certain sympathy for Ross but that had disappeared in the last few days. The man was obviously an immoral monster which, perhaps, was not so surprising when he considered that the people who lived in this God-forsaken part of the world all seemed to be crude and uncouth. The client was absolutely correct. This was a totally unsuitable, even alien, environment for the child and the sooner she was removed and taken back to civilization, the better.

Cassie was asleep. The adults were seated around the new table but there was little conversation. Josef attempted to brighten the evening by recounting the story of how Jimmy Kettle had hidden from them and then produced his surprise.

'I have never got such a shock,' Josef said and laughed, and Nellie and Adam smiled with him. 'The last thing I would have guessed was that Jimmy had found himself a ... a companion.'

Adam nodded. 'He had to go down south a few months ago. He met his lady at Beltana. He just brought her back with him.'

'Like some people bring home a stray dog,' Nellie said.

'How appropriate,' Sarah said and wiped her lips daintily.

'They get on very well,' Adam said. 'Jimmy's a different man since he met Stella.'

'Stella means star,' Sarah said and when the others looked at her, felt compelled to explain. 'I know because I had an Aunt Stella and she told me.'

There was a silence. Josef felt he should say something.

'I haven't met your aunt, have I?'

'No you haven't. She died five years ago.'

'Oh. I'm sorry.'

'Josef, don't keep making an ass of yourself.' Sarah displayed a humourless smile. 'You weren't responsible for her death so there's no need to apologize.'

'I just meant I was sorry for reminding you of her death. You know, stirring up the past and all that.'

'You do talk a lot of nonsense.' She sought agreement from the others, but Nellie was offering Adam more potatoes and he was absorbed in the task of refilling his plate. 'I was not particularly hurt when she died, only when I found she'd left me nothing in her will. She was a stingy old thing and I didn't like her.' The silence that followed seeped into every corner of the room. 'Well,' she added, 'I believe in speaking the truth, don't you? If you have something worth saying, say it.'

'*If,*' Nellie whispered, so softly only Adam heard.

'But as I was about to say, Stella is such a strange name for a woman like that,' Sarah continued. 'A star is white.'

'And bright. I think the name suits her,' Nellie said, as though she had missed the insult.

'She seems a lovely lady,' Josef added.

'You are being generous.'

'No,' Josef disagreed. 'You'd call her lovely.'

'But not a lady.'

Adam coughed. 'Anyhow,' he said, 'you'll have a chance to judge for yourself. Jimmy and Stella are coming in tomorrow.'

She smiled sweetly. 'Your one-armed friend and his little stray dog. I'm looking forward to it.'

Josef decided it was time to defuse the conversation by adding erudition.

'I always thought Jimmy was a misogynist,' he said and studied Adam's face keenly, awaiting his reaction.

Adam ate some potato. 'Well, I didn't,' he said eventually. 'Never.'

'You lying bastard,' Josef said, grinning. 'You don't even know what it means.'

'Which is why I never thought it.'

'It means woman hater.'

Only Sarah was not smiling. 'You're not just an ass at times, Josef, but you're a pompous ass.'

'It's a game Adam and I play,' he protested.

'You sound as though you're boasting.'

'He is,' Adam said, hoping to persuade her to join in the fun. 'What was that word again?'

'Misogynist.'

'Sounds like a sickness.'

'It means hating all women.'

Nellie said, 'I could understand some men hating some women.'

'Or some women hating other women,' Sarah rejoined, and smiled at Nellie.

'What's it called when women hate men?' Adam said. It had been a strained evening and he was anxious to alter it or end it.

'When a woman hates a man it's just unnatural,' Josef said solemnly and Nellie and Adam laughed.

Wanting to sustain the joviality, Josef said, 'A man who hates the idea of getting married is a misogamist.' Suddenly realizing the implications of his remark, he immediately regretted having uttered the words but it was too late. Nellie glanced down. Sarah arched an eyebrow in a way he knew was ominous.

Adam looked pleased. 'You said that before,' he exclaimed, triumphant in the belief that his educated friend had snared himself in his own wordy trap.

'No, no,' Josef said, too committed to withdraw. 'That was a misogynist. This is a misogamist.'

70

Adam was sure he was being teased. 'You're saying the same word.'

'One has an "n" and the other has an "m".'

'But they mean the same thing.'

'No they don't. The one with the "n" hates women. The one with the "m" hates marriage.'

'That's not the same?'

'No. It's very different.'

Sarah yawned, a feat performed with theatrical intensity. 'Josef, you're a ponderous bore.'

'Well that's better than being a pompous ass,' he said, and turned to Nellie who grinned.

'Not when you're both a pompous ass and a ponderous bore,' Sarah said and touched her lips to stifle more yawns.

'I've never heard so many big words in one night,' Adam said.

'He's trying to impress everyone,' Sarah said, and turned on Josef. 'And Adam's got a point. What is the difference? They mean the same thing.'

Josef galloped into the trap. 'They're very different,' he said. 'Someone who hates marriage mightn't hate women. Just the opposite. He might like women so much he hates the idea of getting married.'

'Buying a book when he could belong to a library?'

'Well, maybe,' he said, shrugging. There was no suggestion of mirth in her eyes.

'Like you,' she continued. 'You must be a ... misogamist.' She pronounced the word precisely.

'Not me.'

She ignored him. 'And Jimmy Kettle. Is he married to this Stella, the black star that he brought home like a stray on a leash?'

'Sarah.' Josef turned the name into a plea for silence.

'Obviously not,' she continued. 'So Mr Kettle is a misogamist. Or is he just a dirty old man?'

'Please,' Josef said.

'They're not married,' Adam said and he was not smiling.

'Nor are you,' she said. 'Although in your case, I can understand why.'

Nellie stood, holding her hands in front of her in a way that suggested one side of her body was fighting the other. Knowing how fiery her temper could be, Adam prepared to rise, to forestall any violence, but Nellie surprised him.

'I was thinking of making a cup of tea,' she purred. 'Would anyone else like one?'

* * *

71

They were in bed. Nellie was lying with her arms folded tightly across her chest. She was shaking.

'I was proud of you,' Adam said.

'I could have killed her.'

'She's not worth it.'

'I still could have. How on earth could Josef have got himself involved with a bitch like that?'

It was a question that required no answer but he thought of several suitable responses, and they were all to do with Josef's inability to resist a woman who showed interest in him. He said nothing.

'Were you really proud of me?' Still in shock from the scene in the kitchen, her mind trailed the conversation by several sentences.

He touched her shoulder. 'I was. I thought you were going to hit her.' He paused and heard her grunt in a way which suggested she thought it was still a good idea. 'You would have, a few years ago.'

'I've changed.'

Cassie stirred in her cot and they were silent until the noises ceased.

'We had a terrible argument,' Nellie whispered.

'Who?'

'Me and Sarah.' She unfolded her arms. 'While you were away at the bore.'

It confirmed what he suspected. The atmosphere in the house had been poisonous when he and Josef returned but neither woman had said anything and Josef had been too busy talking to notice. 'I was waiting for you to tell me what happened.'

'She said a lot of things. She said I must have been Heather's maid. She said you'd never marry me.'

'She said that?'

'Yes.' Nellie clasped her hands and stared at the ceiling where a pattern as fine as a spider web moved across the surface. The light was faint and blue as the night and came from the open window where a lace drape stirred in the breeze. 'I thought you'd be angry.'

'Why?'

'Because we'd argued. I know you think I've got a bad temper and I thought you'd blame me. But it wasn't my fault, believe me.'

'I do.'

'I didn't start the argument. She said terrible things.'

'I said I believe you.'

'She has a horrible mind.'

'I've seen that for myself.'

'And you're not angry?'

'I'm just sorry for Joe. And for you. You've had to put up with her all day.'

72

'Do you think Joe'll marry her?'

'No.'

'Why?'

'He's got too much sense.'

She hesitated. 'I'm not sure.' The light was brushing the ceiling with ghostly strokes. 'Joe's so particular with his words but so careless with his women.'

Adam laughed.

'It's true.' She put a hand across his mouth. 'You'll wake the baby.' She let her hand slide to his chest. 'I don't think he's a migosamist or whatever the word is.'

He put his hand across hers.

'He likes women too much,' she said. 'That's his trouble. He's a pushover for a scheming woman and that Sarah is as scheming a woman as I've ever seen.'

Adam lifted her hand and kissed it.

'Are you a migosamist?' she asked.

'Which one is that?'

'The one who hates to get married.'

She felt his grip tighten. 'No,' he said.

'Have you ever thought about getting married?' she asked, inflecting enough of a lilt into the words to suggest it was not entirely a serious question.

'I did some years ago,' he said with mock seriousness and she hit him. It was a playful slap on the arm.

'You know what I mean.'

'Do I have to spell everything I say out for you, word by word?'

'Yes.' Again, she tried to hit him. He caught her hand and pulled her to him. She was wearing no nightgown and her breasts touched his face. He sought and kissed a nipple.

'You're just a dirty old man,' she said but did not move.

'And getting older every day.'

'We all are.'

'It'll be too late, soon.'

'For what?'

'Getting married.'

He let her go. She lay on him. 'I'm not going to get off until you give me an answer,' she said.

'I like it like this,' he said, speaking with difficulty for her breasts were across his face.

She rolled clear. 'I'd like to marry you.'

He said nothing.

'Is it such an awful thought? I mean, is the idea of living with me for the rest of your life a bad one?'

73

His hand felt for her waist. His fingers lifted a fold of flesh. 'I'd like someone who wasn't so skinny.' He converted the grip into a tickle and she wiggled clear of him.

'I want you to be serious.'

He rolled on his back and crossed his arms across his chest.

'You look like a corpse.'

'That's as serious as I can get.'

She raised herself on one elbow so that her body was all sweeping curves and arched shadows. His head turned towards her. Even in the dark, she knew he was smiling.

'You do love me, don't you?' she asked.

'Yes.'

'I love you.'

'I know.'

Cassie uttered a single cry and Nellie sat up, prepared to move to the child's side. 'She must be dreaming,' she said softly when there were no more sounds. 'I love her too.'

'I know.'

'I love her like she was my own.'

'You're wonderful with her.'

'Would you like to have ...' Nellie began and then paused, uncertain how to express herself. She reached out and stroked Adam's head, pushing the hair from his forehead. 'Have you ever thought of having another baby? I mean, the two of us?'

Adam rolled his head to one side, so she could scratch the nape of his neck.

'I hadn't thought of it,' he said.

'I think it would be nice.'

'There are so many other things we should do first.'

'Like what.'

'I want to build a better and bigger house.'

'That can wait.'

'Put in another bore.'

'You're a bore.'

'And get married.'

'You mean that?'

'One day.'

She hit him on the chest and, grinning, he made no attempt to defend himself.

'I don't like your order of doing things,' she said. 'Build a house, drill another bore and then get married.'

The grin widened. 'There's no hurry.'

Oh yes there is, she thought, but lay back on her pillow and felt warm and good. She remained like that for a long time, thinking and listening to his steady breathing.

It was probably Heather. That and all the talk about him living with a coloured woman. That was why he didn't want to get married right away. He hadn't loved Heather, not at the end anyhow, and so it wasn't that he was pining for her or anything like that. Despite his lack of education, or maybe because of it, Adam was a very proper sort of man who was aware of what was right and what was wrong and was greatly influenced by what people might say or think. And there had been a lot of talk about Heather and people who'd never met her now reckoned the sun's rays shone out her earholes. Bitch. She was to blame for so much. Anyhow, Adam was trapped by this false image and probably wanted to wait as long as possible, so people stopped pitying him for the loss of such a fine young woman and got around to saying it was time he took himself another wife. That's what he was thinking. He wanted to protect her as much as himself. He wouldn't want people saying he'd been rushed into marriage by this black tart and that he wasn't thinking clearly because he was still in love with his first wife. The white one.

She rearranged her pillow.

'Can't sleep?' Adam asked quietly.

'I thought you were asleep.'

'No. I've been thinking. About Joe. About us.'

'And what were you thinking?' Her teeth played nervously with her lower lip.

'I can't see Sarah staying here much longer. And if she storms off and Joe doesn't want to go, that'll be the end of things between them.'

'Good riddance.'

'Probably.' There was a long silence.

'He only brought her here to get your blessing,' she said. 'He's still a boy, Joe. He wants people to approve the things he does. It's all to do with his father.'

'Maybe.'

'There's no maybe. If you say yes, he'll marry her. If you say no, he'll give her the arse.'

'Nellie!'

'Well, he will.'

'You know what I mean. I don't like to hear a lady talk like that, 'specially you.'

She giggled. She liked being called a lady. 'Well, if you say no, he *will* tell her that the affair has ended.'

'That's much better.'

'And she'll give *him* the arse.'

75

He clucked disapproval. She tickled his stomach. 'You said you were thinking about us.'

'Uh-huh.'

I have to drag things out of this man, she thought, and tickled him again. 'What about us?'

'About what sort of house I should build. I've got a few ideas.'

The tickle became a scratch. 'I don't want a new house.'

'One day.'

The faint light had gone from the ceiling and she stared into blackness. 'Adam, have you ever thought of moving?'

He propped himself on an elbow. 'Have you been talking to Joe?'

'No. Why?'

'He spent half the day telling me I should sell up and move south.'

'And what did you say?'

'Nothing.'

'That doesn't surprise me. You're the original brick wall when it comes to talking.' She touched his cheek gently. 'What do you think?'

He sighed. 'I'd never thought of leaving here. I wouldn't want to.' And then, after a pause: 'Don't you like it here?'

'I love being here, but that's because I'm with you. You and Cassie. I'd love it anywhere, if we were together.'

'Joe was saying it would be a lot easier down south.'

'I suppose it would be.' She knew she mustn't push.

'I don't think I could afford a property down there.'

She left her hand on his cheek. He covered it with his. His hand was rough and calloused but surprisingly gentle. 'It would be so good for Cassie,' she said softly. He breathed deeply. 'She'd have friends. She could go to school. She could become a real lady.'

'She's happy here.'

'But she doesn't know anyone else.' She moved her hand to grip his chin and turned his face towards hers. 'It would be good for us too, Adam. We're never going to be accepted here. If we went away –'

'Nellie, where would we go to?'

'Somewhere. If we went away, people would think we were married and they'd think Cassie was our daughter. It would be so much easier.'

She had tightened her grip and he had difficulty speaking. Gently, he took her hand away.

'But I love it here, Nellie. I love this place so much.'

* * *

76

Adam and Nellie slept on a bed without a mattress. They had covered the base with newspaper and horseblankets and an old rug. They slept tolerably well, with Nellie clutching Adam's arms and pulling them around her body.

Their mattress was out in the main shed, on the bed Adam had made for Sarah. It was placed in one corner of the building which was three-sided and open at the front. He and Nellie had spent two days making and decorating a temporary bedroom. Two of the walls, being part of the shed's structure, has been whitewashed with lime. A framed picture from the house had been hung on the wall. A calendar was on the other. Adam had made a simple wardrobe and they had carried a large mirror on a stand from their own bedroom. There was a table with a waterjug and glasses and an enamelled washbasin. There were two chairs and two towels. The front of the room was sealed by a tarpaulin. The side was a curtain, which could be pulled back to make a doorway. In the central part of the shed were the normal occupants – the stacks of animal feed, the tools and farm implements, drums of petrol, oil and lighting kerosene, and the red Alfa-Romeo. At the far end was Josef. His 'room' was much more modest in size and was separated from the car by a curtain made of chaff bags. It had only a small table, filled by a washbasin, and the crude bed used by Josef on his last stay.

Nellie had laughed at Adam for insisting they provide separate quarters for their visitors. 'Josef will wait until he sees our light go out,' she had said, 'then count to ten and sneak up to the double bed.'

On this night, Josef stayed on his own bed. He had been there an hour, awake and listening to the noises of the night, the rustle of a horse, the faint scurry of a mouse in the hay, the thud of a bird's wings beating the cool air as it flew low, past the shed. He heard the rattle of metal touching metal.

'Shit!' It was Sarah, from somewhere in the middle of the shed.

Josef still found it difficult to accept a woman swearing. He knew it was modern, like smoking and he tried to appear unaffected whenever Sarah did it in company, but privately he winced. His mother never swore and men rarely used bad language in her presence. He wasn't sure what there was about his mother that commanded such respect, but he admired the quality.

'Can you come and bloody well help me?' Sarah called, in an urgent whisper.

He got out of bed and groped for the lantern.

'I don't want a light,' Sarah said, and Josef felt uneasy. She couldn't have seen what he was doing, yet she seemed to know.

'Have you hurt yourself?' he asked.

77

'No, and don't speak so loudly.'

He felt his way past the car, and found her holding a long-handled rake. 'I don't know where this goes,' she said, handing it to him. Not being able to see clearly, he fumbled the exchange and dropped the rake.

'For God's sake, try to be quiet.'

'I couldn't see the thing.'

'Well, pick it up and put it where it goes.'

'Where does it go?' Josef knelt and felt for the handle.

'How would I know?'

'I thought you might have a clue, seeing you ran into it.' He straightened, holding the rake in both hands.

She stood there fidgeting and waiting for him to say something. Eventually the silence became too threatening. 'I was coming to see you,' she said.

'Why?'

She shuffled her feet. 'Aren't you going to put that bloody rake away?'

'You're swearing a lot tonight.'

'I feel like swearing.'

He felt stronger for not moving. Normally, he did what she suggested; sometimes slowly, often indirectly, but he always followed her bidding.

'You look ridiculous,' she said and he was tempted to move but resisted.

'Why were you coming to see me?'

'Why not, for heaven's sake?' She turned her head. Her fine profile was a black cut-out on a field of deep blue. She lifted her chin. 'I was lonely.'

He had never heard her make such an admission. He put the rake against a post that was still rounded in the shape of the original tree trunk.

'And I wanted to be with you.' She reached for his hand.

'You're freezing.'

She pulled him close.

'Is that why you wanted to be with me?' he said.

'No.'

He started to move towards his area. 'My bed's bigger,' she said, and led him the other way, across the shed and through the open curtain.

'Quick, get under the blankets,' she urged and he held her until both had stopped shivering.

'It's so quiet,' she said.

'It's great, isn't it?'

'It's creepy. I like to go to sleep with the radio on. I like to hear trams rattling by.'

'We're a long way from the nearest tram.'

'I don't know how people can live in such primitive conditions. I mean, honestly, this is basic.'

'I like it.'

'You're used to it. And I'm used to trams.' She squeezed him. 'Oh, you're so cold. I really love the sound of trams. They make me feel safe. We used to live near the tram line when I was a kid and I used to lie in bed at night and hear the trams go by. It's very comforting.'

'There aren't any trams at Tanunda.' It was a reminder of their commitment.

'There are in Adelaide.'

'The family business is in the Barossa Valley. My family. The one you're going to join?' He said it as a question and was surprised at his audacity. He was challenging her to say she wasn't going to marry him, not if it meant living away from a tram line. This was a new Josef, provocative, firm, daring. He enjoyed the role and realized his strength came from a growing realization that he didn't really care about her. But before he could think it through, she was kissing him and saying: 'Your father grows the grapes and makes the wine. You're the salesman. You could sell more in Adelaide than in a tiny town like Tanunda.' She squeezed him to prepare him for the climax. 'You should have an office in the city, and we should live there.'

So we're still getting married, he thought, and the new, stronger Josef didn't think to question the decision.

'I don't know if we could afford that,' he said.

'I don't know if you could afford not to. Not if you want to grow, and make money. You'll never make a fortune in a hick town like Tanunda.'

'I like Tanunda.'

'But you won't make money there. The real money's in Adelaide.' She lifted her nightdress. 'Here, let me make you warm.'

'I am warm,' he said but it was a mild protest and she pressed herself to him and he found himself shaking.

'Isn't it a shame it's so cold,' she said, rubbing her body against his.

'But I'm warm.'

'I mean outside. I feel like making love.'

He panted into her ear. 'I've always thought the colder the night the better.'

'I feel adventurous. I'd like to try something different. Something

79

that would take both of us out of the blankets.' He grabbed her buttocks. 'But we can't,' she said, thrusting against him. 'We'd freeze.'

'Not me,' he said. 'I'm hot.'

'You're an animal.'

'Takes one to know one.'

'Talking of animals,' she said, putting her hand inside his pyjama jacket and lightly scratching his back, 'isn't that black woman just the most offensive person you've ever met?'

'Nellie?' His fingers, which had just negotiated her most rounded regions to make their first, tingling contact with pubic hair, stopped immediately.

'I don't know how someone as nice as your friend Adam could have got mixed up with her.' She reached back and touched one hand. 'Don't stop. That's nice.'

Josef was trapped between passion and reason. 'Nellie?' he repeated and knew he sounded foolish. Worse, he sounded as though he didn't believe Sarah, who was guiding his fingers into even more exciting territory.

'What she's trying to do to that poor man is just amazing.'

Josef dared not speak. She took the silence to express doubt.

'Surely you don't like her?' Her voice and body could have belonged to separate persons. The voice was soft but controlled, that of a woman having a pleasant conversation, but the body was moving and suggesting the spasms that might soon engulf them.

'Were you lovers?' Sarah asked, holding his hand tightly in place.

'Who? Me and Nellie?'

'Don't stop.' She licked his ear, and then whispered into it. 'Didn't you take her to bed, just once or twice, when you knew her all those years ago?'

Josef tried to pull away. 'What are you saying?'

'There's nothing to be ashamed of.'

'I've never done this with Nellie.'

'Never even thought of it?'

He was silent. She held his hand firmly, neither letting him move nor withdraw. 'Well, I was a bit keen on her, I suppose, but that was when I was about fourteen.'

'That's old enough.'

'I was only thinking about her, not sleeping with her.'

She squeezed his hand.

'I wouldn't have known how,' he added, attempting a laugh, to show the matter was of no concern.

'Who would you rather be doing this to?' He kissed her neck. She turned to face him. 'If it's me, prove it.'

Josef lay back, heart pumping and staring with unfocusing eyes at the faint light seeping through the edges of the curtain. She nestled in his arm.

'You've never done that with Nellie?' she asked and kissed his armpit. She ran her tongue around the crater of hair. He pulled away.

'What's wrong?'

'I'm ticklish.'

She settled her head against his chest. 'You haven't answered me.'

'Of course not.'

'I believe you.' She raised her face, to be kissed. 'Do you think she'd be good?'

He kissed, and then said, 'Sarah, I don't want to keep on talking about this.'

'Not feeling guilty?'

She wriggled into a more comfortable position. 'I wonder if Adam does?'

'Sarah, don't.'

'I'm just interested.'

'We've been through all this.'

'I'll bet he does.'

Josef was silent.

'Poor man.'

Under her weight, his arm was becoming numb and he moved it. She found a new position, and then added, 'Having to sleep with a dirty little slut like that. The poor man.'

'Please.'

'I mean, I can understand it. There's no one else and he must get desperate out here, but imagine having to take someone like that, just because there was nothing else available.'

'I don't think you should call Nellie a dirty slut.'

She might not have heard him. 'I'm told men use sheep when there are no women around.'

He pushed her clear. 'My arm's gone to sleep,' he said, and wondered why he felt compelled to excuse his action.

'Who was the man Adam killed?' That was another thing she did: ask a question that had no place in the previous conversation.

Josef's eyes focused on the opening in the curtain. Nellie had put up a rod for the curtain to slide on. One of the curtain rings had come off and the corner of the curtain hung in a fold, so that the opening looked a bit like a map of Africa. He sighed. 'Just a man.'

'Yes, but who?'

'No one you'd know.'

81

'I'm beginning to think you made up the story.'

It wasn't really like Africa. The hump wasn't big enough. He sighed again, more noisily this time as though breathing had become painful. 'I did.'

'Really?'

'It was all a lie. I was just trying to impress you.'

'I don't believe you.'

'I can't win, can I? No matter what I say, you don't believe me.' She stroked his stomach.

He recoiled.

'Ticklish?'

'Very.'

'You weren't before. Not down there.'

'I am now.'

'Who was it, Joe?'

'No one. There was no one.' Why did I ever tell you, he thought. We're not going to get married and yet I've told you a secret Adam and Jimmy and I swore we'd reveal to no one. He stopped, struck by another thought. I'm not going to marry her. I've decided, but the decision just slipped out. He felt relieved, and like laughing.

'What is it?' she asked, prodding him.

'Nothing.'

'You were breathing funny.'

'I thought of something funny.'

'How strange.' She rapped his chest. 'Don't be a meany. Tell me who it was, or at least what happened.'

'I made it up.'

'You did not.'

'No one's ever lived up here. There was no one for Adam to shoot.'

'You said strangle. Or was it break his neck?'

'I forget. You see, tell a lie and you get caught out.'

She pulled a blanket across her. 'You're taunting me, Josef Hoffman, and I hate you for it.'

Good, Josef thought. Keep hating me because it'll make it easier when I tell you I don't want to marry you. He wouldn't tell her now. He needed to wait for a better time. And he wanted to see what Adam had to say.

'You'd better go back to your own bed,' she said. 'We don't want someone wandering in here at dawn and finding you like that.'

He got up feeling angry. He had intended going back to his own bed. He didn't want her ordering him around.

'And don't make any noise,' she said.

'I'll try not to walk into the rake,' he said and went through the curtain, ruining the map of Africa.

82

S·E·V·E·N

In the days when he was a boxer in Cedric Carter's circus, Jimmy Kettle liked to boast that he'd had more women than breakfasts. It wasn't an extravagant claim although, as in so many of the things he said, there was joke buried in such a way that only the teller fully appreciated it. The joke was that Jimmy rarely ate breakfast. He did, however, have a lot of women. In all the time he spent as the star of the boxing troupe, disarming the crowds with his gleaming smile and lithe grace and destroying foolhardy challengers with his sniping right and vicious left, Jimmy rarely spent a night alone in bed. The circus travelled throughout South Australia and Western Victoria and even visited a few remote towns in the far west of New South Wales, and in all the places where the tents were pitched there was always one girl waiting for Jimmy to return, and several anxious to make his acquaintance.

He loved the life. Pummelling men to the ground and surrendering to women in bed seemed an ideal way to spend his nights. There was no question of becoming enmeshed in a romantic entanglement. One night, maybe two, break a nose, break a heart, and he'd be off to the next town.

It was a game and, for a while, he tried to break records. In one eight-month season, while the circus played one hundred and seventy-five towns from Streaky Bay to White Cliffs, Jimmy tried to take at least two women to bed each night. His record was seven in one night, but that was when he began faking orgasms, being more intent on demonstrating his incredible virility and irresistible attraction to women than on gaining gratification from any encounter. He was a numbers man, and made everyone aware of the score.

'Had four last night,' he would say and if a man doubted him there were two possibilities: a swift punch on the nose or an invitation to see for himself. He would station the doubter in the tent opposite his and from that tantalizing viewpoint, the man could see the women come and go. That's what Jimmy would promise, then add, laughing: 'Well, you mightn't see them come but you'll sure as hell hear them.'

Once, there'd been a queue. Three girls lined up outside his tent, giggling and complaining but waiting. Jimmy liked that. He'd seen men lined up, but never women. He often boasted about it, and those who didn't believe him got bloodied without getting five bob for bleeding in public, as most of Jimmy Kettle's victims did.

He told Stella everything about those early days and because he was absolutely honest he was, naturally, not believed. She presumed the stories about the women were a joke because Jimmy was a joker and the more serious the subject, the more he was inclined to say outrageous things. Even the account of boxing matches were suspect. She knew Jimmy only as a one-armed man. She recognized the athletic way he moved, was impressed by the rapidity of his reflexes and was aware that he was only in his early thirties, but he was a man with one arm and she could not imagine him with two. Therefore, she could not picture him as a boxer. But she liked to hear him talk about those days, because it made him happy and he told funny stories.

In recalling those days, Jimmy did not talk about two things. One was his last fight. It had been in Port Augusta against a young fellow called Adam Ross, who had hammered his belly until he had no wind left. He hadn't been himself that night because there was a man in the crowd who intended to kill him after the fight. Instead of killing him, the man had slaughtered half his family.

The other thing he never talked about was Nellie. She'd been one of his girls, but then he did something he'd never done with anyone else. He began to care for her. But she left him and now she was with Adam. There was plenty of irony in the situation at Kalinda, where he was working with the man who had ended his boxing career and was now his friend and who was living with a woman he had once almost loved and later truly hated. It was ironic all right; if it didn't matter, he could have told the story and changed a few things and put a twist into the ending and had people in stitches of laughter, but it did matter and so he never spoke about it.

Jimmy and Stella met in a strange way. He had gone to Peterborough to check on some rams Adam was proposing to buy. He also wanted to see his mother at Beltana so on his way south he stopped at his old home town, intending to catch the next train. That train had been derailed just out of town. No one was hurt. Nor was anyone surprised. Trains were often derailed, particularly after rain and there had been some local flooding after a storm. One advantage of a railway service that suffers frequent derailments is

84

that the people along the line know what to do, through practice. The people of Beltana took the passengers to their homes while the line was being repaired. Stella was allocated to Jimmy's mother. Stella was possibly the least important person on the train. Mrs. Kettle's house was possibly the least desirable in Beltana. Mrs Kettle was equally unimpressive, having slipped into steady drunkenness in recent years. The result was that Jimmy had to look after the guest. So well did he accomplish the task that when the line was repaired he travelled to Peterborough with Stella and returned to Kalinda with the rams and the girl.

Stella's features were not perfect, but they combined in an attractive way and she had dazzled Jimmy from their first meeting. Her mother had been part-Indian and part-Portuguese. Her father had been part-aboriginal. The other part had been a confusion of Spanish and English blood. There was even talk of Tahitian ancestry. That seemed altogether too exotic, until people saw Stella.

The mother had died ten years before. The father had been a stockman who became head man on a station in the northern Flinders Ranges. Stella had worked in the homestead. The father was a strong rider who met a stronger horse which put him into the side of a tree and broke his thigh. The fracture severed an artery and he bled to death. They didn't know what to do with Stella at the station so they sent her south, to a cousin from whom she had never heard and with whom she had no desire to live. She had been thinking of leaving the train at some station in the north and chancing her luck, when luck derailed the train.

She had become devoted to Jimmy. She had also become pregnant.

They travelled to the homestead with one camel. They rode some of the way, and walked the rest because Jimmy preferred to walk and because Stella was feeling sick. Jimmy smiled. He presumed she was suffering from travel sickness. Like so many who are not afflicted, he found the idea of being made ill by rolling and jolting both inexplicable and amusing, especially if the cause was a camel. So he smiled tolerantly and led the animal and, when she felt better, even let her take the lead so that he could hold her hand, letting go only when the homestead came in sight and he thought they might be seen.

It was mid-morning. Adam was working in the stockyard. Josef had joined him, wanting to talk about Sarah but not knowing how to start. They saw Jimmy and Stella in the distance.

'Blast,' Josef said which surprised Adam, because he knew Josef and Jimmy were such good friends.

'What's wrong?'

'I wanted to talk to you about something. In private.'

Adam wiped his hands on his trousers. 'He'll be another five minutes getting here. You can say anything in five minutes.'

Josef mumbled agreement but continued to look miserable. 'He's got Stella with him,' he said as though that made it even more difficult for him to speak in the allotted time.

'Is it about Sarah?'

'How did you know?' And then, without waiting for an answer, he said, 'We had a fight last night.'

Adam concentrated on trying to remove a splinter from his finger. 'Apparently Nellie and her had a fight or an argument or something during the day.'

'Oh? She didn't tell me.'

'They don't like each other.'

'No.' Josef had not taken his eyes from the approaching couple. 'She sure doesn't like Nellie.'

'Nellie doesn't like her.' Adam grinned ruefully. They could have been talking about a pair of cats.

'What do you think?' Josef looked around, to make sure no one was within hearing range. 'I mean about Sarah.'

'Well,' Adam said, still trying to pincer the end of the splinter and sparing Josef only the briefest of glances, 'you must have doubts.'

'What do you mean?'

'About getting married to her. That is what you're talking about, isn't it?'

Josef shrugged. 'Sure.'

'Do you want to marry her?'

'I was asking you what you thought, that's all.'

'I think what you think.'

'And what's that?'

'That she might be a bit of fun but she'd be very difficult to live with.'

Josef felt an urge to smile. He tried hard to look worried because he felt he should seem concerned, even disappointed instead of relieved that his friend felt the way he did. Adam extricated the splinter and looked up.

'You want some advice?'

'Why not?' He tried to retain the worried expression.

'Well, I think she's nice looking and she talks nicely.'

Josef nodded, and waited. This was the part to ensure he wouldn't be embarrassed by what was to come.

'And I can understand any bloke liking her.'

'She is good looking.' He nodded agreement, as though her appearance was something he had never seriously considered.

'But she's cruel. She's got a real mean streak in her. And I think she's very selfish.'

Josef studied the dust. He smoothed a patch with his toe, but said nothing.

'In other words, if it's my opinion you're after ...' Adam paused long enough for Josef to plane a square foot of dust, or to offer an objection. He concentrated on smoothing the dust. 'Joe, I'd say no.'

'No?' Josef looked up. Jimmy was nearer and gave a lazy wave.

Adam returned the greeting. He moved to the fence and leaned against the rail. 'I think it would be a mistake.'

Josef nodded. 'I came to that decision last night.'

Adam nodded several times. 'I think you're doing the right thing.'

'I'll tell her today.' Josef breathed deeply. The air tasted sweet.

'It's good to have you back up here, Joe.'

He smiled sadly. 'I was hoping Sarah would like it here.'

'She doesn't?'

'I think she was expecting something different. You know how it is, no one can imagine what this country's like until you see it for yourself, and then it can be a bit of a shock.' He turned his heel and cut a groove through the smoothed patch. 'I think she was expecting a couple of thousand acres of the Adelaide Hills.'

Adam scratched an ear. 'Do you think maybe that's why she's been acting like she has?'

Josef took a long time to answer. 'No,' he said. 'I think I've always known that she was ... well, she could be a problem.'

'It's not my decision really,' Adam said quickly. 'You've got to make up your own mind.'

'I know.'

'What do your parents think of her?'

'Mother doesn't say much but looks worried. Father hates her.'

'And that makes you like her?'

Josef grinned. 'Well, not exactly but I always reckon if my old man doesn't like someone then that person must have a lot of good points.'

Jimmy was within shouting range, and shouted. Josef raised a fist in acknowledgement. 'That's a good-looking girl Jimmy's got,' he observed, and his expression was sad.

'Nice too. She's fair dinkum.'

'Good for Jimmy?'

'Very.'

'That must be a good feeling.' He searched for a stone to kick.

Jimmy had a definite image of the girl Josef had brought to Kalinda. She would be like Josef, with a good sense of humour and yet a little slow, so you could pull her leg and have fun before she woke up to the fact that you were joking. She'd be well educated, use big words but be a person who fumbled with shoelaces and had no idea how to do basic things, like dig for water or make a damper. In other words, Jimmy expected a female Josef. He assumed she'd be good looking and have big breasts but he also knew if she had really big breasts she needn't be so good looking, because he knew Josef's tastes very well, and understood his priorities.

Jimmy was looking forward to the meeting. He was determined to have some fun and was sure the new girl would join in. He recalled the way Josef had greeted Stella. 'What have we got here?' He'd nearly died laughing. Joe, trying so hard not to look surprised had put on the face of a parson who'd just swallowed half a lemon. His words said one thing but his face gave him away. Stella had stunned him; it had taken him ten minutes just to get his breathing back to normal.

The camel tethered, Josef led Stella and Jimmy to the house. Sarah was at the door. She had been there for some time, not watching anyone or waiting for Josef but merely making a point of ignoring Nellie, who was cooking.

Before Josef could begin his introduction, Jimmy stopped and scratched his head and walked to one side, the better to inspect Sarah. 'What have we got here?' he said, doing a fair imitation of Josef's voice.

Sarah examined him slowly, beginning at the feet and assessing one distasteful feature after the other until she reached the eyes. 'Who is this creature?'

'I'm the beast from the bore.'

She twitched an eyebrow.

'The Number Two bore which probably makes me the Number Two beast.' Jimmy flashed a huge smile. 'After Joe.'

Sarah turned to Josef. 'I assume this is your friend with the strange name?'

'Jimmy Kettle,' Jimmy said, before Josef could answer. He waited for her to drop the façade of sourness and return his smile. 'And this is Stella.' He inclined his head towards Stella, who was with Adam. Stella had read Sarah's mood immediately and accurately and was not smiling. She was standing stiffly to attention and rolling her eyes nervously, a schoolgirl confronting the headmistress and awaiting a reprimand.

Again Sarah drew her eyes up Jimmy's body and her expression became even more distasteful. 'I do not appreciate being inspected like a side of beef,' she said, glaring at Josef, and walked inside.

Jimmy looked at Josef. The smile had been replaced by a stunned blankness.

'That was Sarah,' Josef said weakly.

'Please to meet you,' Jimmy said and offered his hand to the empty doorway. Suddenly he began slapping his neck.

'What's up?' Josef said.

'I thought I might have had a tiger snake around the neck. Makes people act strange.'

Cassie burst through the doorway and hurled herself at Jimmy. They had a noisy reunion. Jimmy passed her to Stella, who held the child in one arm.

'Did I say something wrong, mate?' Jimmy asked, his eyes wide with innocence.

Josef, anxiously looking into the room, felt his stomach knotting with worry. She still had that effect on him: he knew what he had decided, or almost had, but one sharp look could start him trembling. Jesus Christ, she was as bad as his father.

'I was only joking,' Jimmy said.

'I know.'

'Do you want me to say something to her? I'll go in and say I'm sorry if you like.'

'No, it's all right.'

'I'm sorry, mate. I hope I haven't caused you any trouble.'

'Nothing I can't handle,' Josef said with an extravagant show of confidence.

Sarah reappeared. She folded her arms. 'And what can you handle, Josef Hoffman?'

There was silence.

Adam started to walk away. 'Come and give me a hand to put the camel in the yard, Jimmy.'

'Dogs slinking into the night,' Sarah said, and they stopped. 'And what was it you were saying, Josef?'

He straightened. 'I was saying I could handle the situation.'

'Oh really?'

'Jimmy was joking.'

'I have decided to leave here.'

'You see, when I met Jimmy and Stella, I said "what have we got here?" as a kind of joke, and Jimmy was saying the same thing back to me. We always joke with each other.'

'Did you hear what I said?'

'And *I* said Jimmy didn't mean to offend. He was just joking.'

'I have absolutely no interest in whether he was joking or not. I have no interest in him whatever. I said, I have decided to leave. Can't you understand plain English?'

Jimmy stepped forward, managing a smile. 'Look, I'm sorry, Sarah.'

'If I were you I'd be sorry too,' she said, looking down to avoid the eyes of the others. 'Josef, when can we leave here?'

'There's no need to go just because I done the wrong thing,' Jimmy said.

'It's got nothing to do with you.'

'We've only just arrived,' Josef complained.

'And now we're going.'

'We were going to stay two weeks.'

'Two days is quite enough.'

'I think I better go back to the bore,' Jimmy said.

'I keep telling you,' she snapped, her chin buried in her chest, 'it has nothing to do with you. I'd decided I'd had enough of this miserable place yesterday.'

'Sarah, you're being ridiculous,' Josef said.

'That is the pot calling the kettle black.' And then she stopped and looked around her, with a mirthless smile. 'Oh, I've made a joke, haven't I?'

Adam was furthest from her. 'There's a train going south the day after tomorrow. I'll drive you to the station. That's if that's what you really want.'

'I do. Thank you. Could we go earlier? This afternoon possibly?'

Josef was twitching under the combined attacks of embarrassment and indecision. 'Adam said the train doesn't go for two days.'

'We could stay at the hotel. I saw a hotel in town.'

'What do you mean "we"?'

'Exactly that.' Her voice was firm but the face betrayed surprise. 'We. You and me.'

'I came up here for a couple of weeks.'

'And you're going to stay?'

'Yes.' He felt cleansed. The hands which had been trembling were suddenly steady. 'You can go back if you want to. I'm staying.'

She looked at the ring of people. Behind her was Nellie, still within the shadows of the building, arms folded, teeth just visible in a smile. Sarah stepped forward, to be further away from her.

'I see.'

'You are welcome to stay longer,' Adam said. He felt sorry for her. He was reminded of an animal ringed by hounds.

'No, thank you.' She made the words hard, almost insulting. And then, to Josef: 'You know what this means?'

He hesitated and Jimmy spoke. 'It means you've got to spend a couple of nights in the pub and that's no good. I usually camp in the creek.'

'He's only joking,' Josef said, withering Jimmy with a look which was intended to jolt him out of the conversation, but Jimmy had now made up his mind about Josef's girl-friend and was relaxed and ready for some entertainment. He ignored the glance.

'I could take you to town on the camel if you like.'

'It's a joke, Sarah. Jimmy, please stop.'

'This is the end of our marriage,' Sarah said. 'I hope you realize that.'

'I do.'

'Isn't that what you say when you are married?' Jimmy said, grinning at Stella who lifted Cassie to hide her face.

'I will sue you for breach of promise.'

'What's that, Joe?' Jimmy said cheerfully.

'Keep out of this, Jimmy.'

'It means,' she said, her eyes fierce, 'I will take him to court and get what is coming to me. In other words, everything.'

That annoyed Josef. 'Bullshit!'

'Good on you, Joe,' Jimmy said. 'It's about time we had some plain language.'

'Everything you've got,' she said, ignoring the others and jabbing a finger at Josef.

'Get your old man to give her a bottle of plonk,' Jimmy said. 'She looks like the sort of sheila who'd be stopped by one bottle.'

'Will you shut up?' she screamed.

'Just joking.' He raised his one hand in a token of surrender.

'I'm going to pack,' she said, and now directed the finger at Adam. 'You promised to take me to the station. You will do that?'

'Straight after lunch.'

'I am not hungry.'

'I am.'

'We all are,' Jimmy said brightly. 'I could eat a horse, but Adam won't let me. I tell you what I'll do.' She tried not to appear interested. 'When Adam goes to town, I'll nick a horse and put it on the barbecue tonight. Why don't you sneak back and have some?' He smiled at her.

She sniffed and strode past the group towards her room in the shed.

'Thanks, mate,' Josef said when she was gone. 'You were a big help.'

'You wanted her to stay?'

Josef was staring after her. 'No.'

'Well, what's the problem?'

'You made me look like a gig.'

Jimmy pulled a long face. 'Gee, that's hard.'

'I was trying to have a serious talk to her.'

'I thought it got pretty serious.'

'Yes, but I wanted to lead up to things.'

'Sheilas don't like a bloke who beats around the bush. You got to get in there and whack them right in the arse. Right, Stella?'

'You talk a lot,' she said softly.

He nodded. 'That's true.'

Josef was blinking rapidly. 'I didn't think she'd go off like this.'

'You don't want her around, do you?'

'There were things I wanted to say.'

'Like what? Don't forget to write?'

'No, you goat. Just things. I wanted to tell her in a gentle way, so she understood.'

'I think she's got the message.' Jimmy turned to Adam. 'You really going to drive her to town?'

'I think it's best.'

'Maybe I should take her,' Josef said, sounding as though he wanted to be talked out of the idea.

'That's a good idea,' Jimmy said and Josef was dismayed. 'Then you could give her the long speech you've been preparing and she could reach in the back of the car and grab the jack handle and beat your brains out.' Suddenly, Jimmy looked serious. 'She's a wild one, Joe. Just piss her off and let her go.'

Nellie moved out of the doorway. 'Maybe none of you will have to worry,' she said. 'Here comes the local taxi.'

In the distance was the dust trail stirred by Saleem Benn's red Reo.

E·I·G·H·T

Only after Saleem Benn had climbed from the truck and greeted his friends did Jeremy Pollard descend. He waited for the Afghan to announce that he had a passenger who had business with Mr Adam Ross, and then made as impressive an entry as was possible, which wasn't as dramatic as he would have liked, because he was stiff from the journey and had to be helped down.

'That was a ghastly experience,' he said when both feet were on the ground. 'I don't think I have ever undergone such a punishing journey.'

The others stood back, waiting politely for the man to introduce himself. He brushed dust from his shoulder. He examined the house and its surroundings. He was having trouble with his eyesight but the cost of spectacles, in both cash and loss of dignity, had persuaded him to resist the need. As a result, he squinted about him with his nose wrinkled and teeth bared in support of the effort required to focus on anything.

'Do people really live out here?' he asked. Back in Adelaide, the woman who did his typing would have thought that a good question, and kept a conversation going for five minutes.

'I don't know,' said Jimmy pivoting to examine the total scene. 'We haven't seen none. How about you? Run into any on the way out?'

Pollard was confused. He also felt uncomfortable talking to an aborigine. He had never spoken to a black man. 'No,' he said.

'Well, that settles it. The answer must be no.'

'What answer?' Pollard had found dust on the other shoulder and began to brush it vigorously.

'Yours.'

'I don't understand.'

'Well, you asked the question.'

Adam stepped forward. 'I'm Adam Ross. Saleem Benn said you came here to see me.'

Pollard frowned. 'Haven't I seen you before?'

Jimmy waved his hand. 'You ask the strangest questions. I tell you what, you try to answer it first and then we'll have a go.'

Adam put a restraining hand on Jimmy's shoulder. 'I don't think I've seen you before,' he said.

Pollard stabbed the air with a well-manicured finger. 'At the railway station.'

Adam waited.

'You were the man who wrestled that maniac to the ground.' He slapped his forehead. 'Oh good heavens.'

'What's wrong?'

'I could have given it to you then. I had no idea it was you.'

Adam shook his head. 'I have no idea what you're talking about.'

'Me neither,' said Jimmy, feeling it was safe to speak again. Saleem Benn was smiling broadly. This was an unusual sight and it encouraged him. 'How about you, Josef?' Josef shook his head. 'Stella, Nellie? No? That's it mister. Five to one. None of us know what you're talking about. If you don't know either, that's six-nil and we'll have to start again.'

'You might start by telling me who you are,' Adam said. He was beginning to feel worried. Saleem Benn had stopped smiling and was transmitting signals of caution.

Pollard produced his business card. Adam glanced at it and passed it to Josef. Fortunately for Adam, Pollard made a formal introduction. 'And, Mr Ross,' he continued, 'what I was alluding to a moment ago was that I had not expected to find you at the railway station. Had I known you were there, I could have done my business immediately and saved myself this journey and the long and I must say, extremely uncomfortable stay at the hotel.'

'No,' Saleem corrected. 'You might have avoided the journey but not the delay. There has been no train to the south.'

Pollard waved him away. 'He keeps correcting me,' he said, chatting as though among friends discussing an unwelcome intruder, 'and over the most obscure points.'

'I thought you were a man of the law,' Saleem Benn said and examined his fingernails. Pollard felt uneasy. His father had that mannerism and used it when he had scored in a discussion.

Adam introduced the others, even Sarah who had wandered back from the shed and was standing to one side.

'And that little girl is who?' Pollard said, smiling at Cassie, who had transferred from Stella to Nellie.

'My daughter Cassie.'

'Ah. Short for Cassandra.'

Adam noticed Nellie's grip tighten. 'How did you know that?' he asked.

94

'Actually, it is Cassandra Ross who has brought me here.' From his briefcase, he took a folded document and handed it to Adam. 'Thank you.'

Adam turned the paper in his hand. 'What is it?'

'Put simply, Mr Ross, that piece of paper requires you to be in court in Adelaide in a month's time to respond to a claim that you should surrender the child into the care of a more responsible person.'

Nellie pulled Cassie so close the child wheezed in distress. 'What are you saying?'

The solicitor studied her intently. 'I've forgotten your name,' he said.

'Nellie Ross,' she said and immediately regretted the lie.

'Ross?' He took his time with the question.

She lifted her chin and stared into his face. 'Nellie Arlton.'

'Ah yes.' He was thinking of the stories the young storekeeper had told him about this woman. He had never met a prostitute before; not knowingly and certainly never professionally. She looked like a normal woman, although dark and rather attractive in an unrefined way.

Nellie shifted her feet nervously. The way he examined her reminded her of those days in Port Pirie, and how certain customers, the ones with big money, would take their time before making a choice and assess you and humiliate you without saying a word.

'What I am saying, Miss Arlton, is that another person has made a claim to the court that Mr Ross is not the appropriate person to be entrusted with Cassandra.'

'Adam, what's he saying?'

Adam was holding the order in both hands as though it were a delicate but deadly thing. 'I'm not sure. Someone wants Cassie?'

'Well,' Pollard said, 'that's possibly an oversimplification but yes. Someone does.'

Josef joined in. 'Who?'

'It's on the order.'

Josef grabbed the paper and opened it.

'Bloody hell,' he said. 'It's Heather's mother.'

They were inside the house. All sat around the table except Sarah. She was leaning against the doorway, arms folded and listening, but staring out, not to look at the view, which was bleak, but to emphasize that she had no interest in the proceedings.

'What it means,' the solicitor said, 'is that doubt has been placed on the future well-being of the child if the child continues to live

95

here.' He paused, to make sure they were following him. 'It's not merely a question of who would be a better person to raise the child, the father or the grandmother, but of the environment in which the child would live and the ultimate effect on the child's well-being and the child's future.'

'Don't keep calling Cassie "the child",' Nellie said. 'You make her sound like something you buy in the shop.'

Pollard sniffed. 'Mr Ross, there's one thing I'd like you to do. Do you see the order?'

It was in front of Adam. He nodded.

'The third paragraph is particularly relevant and I want to be sure you understand. Would you please read it out for me?'

Adam pushed it from him. 'Why?'

Josef, seated across the table, took the form. 'What's so important about it?' he asked gruffly and ran his finger down to the third paragraph.

Pollard had not taken his eyes from Adam. 'You couldn't read it, could you?'

'Because I took it from him,' Josef said.

Pollard waved the remark aside. 'You can't read, Mr Ross, can you?'

Nellie took Adam's hand. 'Not easily,' he said.

'Not at all?'

'I can read some things.'

'You never went to school?'

'No.'

'That is as I understood it.' He clasped his hands and stared mournfully at them.

'He's been teaching himself,' Josef said.

Again, Pollard ignored the remark. 'It really is remarkable that in this day and age a man cannot read or write.'

'It has been a question of opportunity, not intellect,' Saleem Benn said. He was at the end of the table but with his chair so far away that he had to lean forward to put one hand on the edge. 'That is, Mr Pollard, if you are suggesting a lack of intelligence.'

Pollard wiped his forehead.

'Can you speak Pushtu?'

'I beg your pardon?'

'Mr Adam Ross is fluent in Pushtu. I myself taught him.'

'It is your language?'

'Indeed.'

'Well that is commendable, but hardly practical. Unless you're suggesting, of course, that the child should stay here to learn how to speak ... what is it?'

96

Saleem Benn sat back in the chair, and ignored the question. To answer would have been to trivialize the language and diminish the argument. 'Mr Adam Ross is learning to read and to write in your language and has made the most praiseworthy progress. I am in no doubt that the child will be taught to read and write.'

Nellie and Adam chorused agreement.

'I'm sure the court would be impressed by your confidence, Mr Benn,' Pollard said, 'but for the time being I shall have to confirm that the father is illiterate.'

'Why should it be a factor?' Josef asked and Adam was pleased he spoke because he had not understood Pollard's last remark.

'Because there is no schooling out here and the ability of the parent to educate is crucial.'

Nellie had Cassie on her knee. 'What the hell does Mrs Maguire want her for, anyhow?'

'It's natural. She's the grandmother. She is concerned about the future of her granddaughter.'

Jimmy used his finger to rap a drum beat on the table. 'The old lady was here, and she nicked off,' he said. 'Tried to walk away.'

'I beg your pardon.'

'It's true,' Adam said. 'She came here with Heather and the baby. That was a couple of years ago.'

'And she left?'

'She was frightened of her own daughter,' Jimmy said. 'I found her out in the scrub. She was nearly dead.'

'She was running away,' Nellie added.

'I tried to bring her back,' Jimmy said. 'She wouldn't come back here.'

'I can't say that I blame her,' Pollard said and a brittle laugh came from the doorway. Josef waved a finger at Sarah. She raised two to him. 'And that has nothing to do with this application,' the solicitor continued. 'The court will be concerned not with the past, but with the future. With what the grandmother can provide and what the father can provide. Which brings me to another point.'

They waited. Sarah changed position. Still leaning against the door post, she now faced the group at the table.

'It concerns you, Miss Arlton. You have assumed the role of mother?'

Nellie put Cassie on her other knee. Cassie played with a blouse button and Nellie hissed a warning to stop. 'What do you mean?' she said, gripping the girl's hand.

'Do you feed her, dress her, bathe her, punish her? Do all the things a mother does?'

97

'I don't know about punishing her,' Nellie said, looking to Adam for support.

'She's a good girl,' he said.

'Yes she is. We hardly ever have to smack her.'

'You cook all the meals, sweep the house, do those things?' Pollard asked.

Nellie nodded, a frown growing on her face.

'And how much does Mr Ross pay you for all this?'

'What do you mean?'

'You have the role of nurse, housekeeper, acting mother,' he said nodding with each category. 'Presumably, you are paid to perform all these duties.' He paused, awaiting her answer and there was silence. 'The duties would seem to be onerous. People are normally paid to perform work. Unless, of course there are special conditions. Say, a special relationship?'

Adam stood up and leaned on the table. 'I think we should stop right now,' he said.

Josef also rose. 'I was thinking the same thing. If you're just a messenger boy delivering a document, well, you've done it and you can go.'

'I assure you sir –' Pollard said taking such a breath that he puffed up.

'You look like a frill-neck lizard when you do that,' Jimmy said.

'There's no need to be offensive.' The solicitor drew back.

'I like frill-neck lizards,' Jimmy said and smiled with a beatific innocence.

'Do you know what I think?' Josef said. 'I think you're asking questions so you can go into court and win the case for your client. You do represent Mrs Maguire, don't you?'

'I thought he was from the court,' Nellie said. 'Like a policeman or something.'

'No,' Josef said, pulling the business card from his pocket. 'He's Mr Pollard from Pollard and Pollard.'

'I'm Mr Kettle from Kettle and Kettle,' Jimmy said. 'Like a cup of tea?' Stella laughed, and then there was silence.

'I do represent Mrs Maguire,' Pollard said eventually. 'I never suggested anything else.'

'Tell me something,' Adam said. 'What made Mrs Maguire do this?'

Pollard touched his forehead. 'A grandmother's love for and concern for her dead daughter's only child.'

'Bullshit,' Jimmy said softly and Pollard grimaced.

'You came here with a lot of information,' Adam said. 'You knew all about me. You know about Nellie.'

Pollard became interested in his hands once more.

Josef nodded. 'I get it. You've been asking questions all around William Creek. You're a slimy toad, Pollard.'

Pollard bent his head, to ward off the offensive words. 'Sticks and stones,' he began, but Jimmy was talking to Josef: 'I prefer lizard to toad, Joe.' And Josef was still talking, 'You've probably been listening to all the gossip from all the no-hopers in town so you can take a man's daughter from him and –'

'Calm down, Joe,' Adam said. 'It's more than that.'

'What do you mean, more?' Josef was red faced.

'Something brought him here in the first place.'

Josef turned to Pollard who seemed fascinated by a ring on one finger. He gripped it and turned it.

'We haven't heard a word from Mrs Maguire in years. And now this city law man turns up with a piece of paper from the court that says they want to take my daughter away from me. Just read what the paper says, Joe.'

Without looking up, Pollard said, 'It is merely an order for you to appear in court on the first Wednesday in October, 1939.' He lifted his hands. 'Simple as that.'

'Like hell,' Josef said, scanning the pages of the order. 'It says you can't read or write, Adam, and makes you sound like some sort of drongo. Jesus Christ, it's full of accusations.'

'What's wrong now?' Adam said anxiously.

'It says you're living with an aboriginal woman of ill repute.'

'What's that mean?'

Jimmy rocked back in his chair. 'It means Nellie's repute's got sick.'

'It means I'm a wicked woman,' Nellie said and pressed Adam's hand tightly.

'It says the father is not a fit person to care for the child,' Josef added, turning to the final sheet.

'Call her Cassie,' Nellie said.

'Well, that's what it says. And the statement is signed by Emily May Maguire of Strathfield.'

'That's a Sydney suburb,' Pollard interjected. He now sat forward, elbows on the table, a hand over each ear.

Adam nodded, absorbing the information. 'You can see what's happened.' He looked around.

'No,' Jimmy said brightly. 'I got lost about the time our mate here did his impersonation of a frill-neck.'

Saleem Benn moved in his chair and the noise of the squeaking timbers focused everyone's attention on him. 'Someone sent information,' he said solemnly. 'Long before Mr Pollard came here.'

'Right,' Adam said. 'Someone in William Creek.'

'Or in the district,' Josef said, nodding as he grasped the implica-

99

tion. 'Someone who wanted to do you harm.'

'They did what?' Nellie asked, still gripping the hand of Cassie who was striving to reach the button.

Adam faced Pollard. 'Someone up here got in touch with Mrs Maguire, and stirred her up. That's right, isn't it?'

Pollard pursed his lips as though whistling, but made no sound.

'I can't believe it,' Nellie said.

'Well, here's the proof,' Josef said, indicating the solicitor. 'Mr Pollard of Pollard and bloody Pollard.'

'We had no part in this case until recently,' Pollard said. 'Mrs Maguire's solicitors are in Sydney. We have merely been retained.'

'If this thing goes to court –' Adam began.

'Oh I assure you, it will. You have to appear. I have served the order on you.'

'And if he doesn't?' Nellie said.

'He will be arrested.'

'All right,' Adam resumed, leaning forward. 'When this thing goes to court, what's likely to happen?'

'You mean what will the court decide? I can't presume to think for the court, of course, but I'd say, on the basis of what I know about the case and what I've seen here today that you will lose.'

'And what'd happen to Cassie?' Nellie said, scarcely breathing.

'Oh, she will go to her grandmother in Sydney.'

'For ever?'

'It will be a permanent order, yes.'

Sarah Mandelton went back to William Creek that afternoon, travelling in the truck with Saleem Benn and Jeremy Pollard. Before leaving, she had three conversations. The first was with Adam.

'I'm sorry for you,' she said. 'About your daughter, I mean, and what that solicitor was saying.'

He accepted her sympathy with a slight tilt of the head.

'I have to say, however, I think it would be the best thing. For Cassie, I mean.' She was not meeting his gaze but seemed to be more concerned about the truck. They were standing near it. Adam had just finished helping Saleem Benn unload the Reo.

'Why do you have to say that?'

'Because I'm honest. I have to say what I feel.'

'And you feel he's right?'

'This is the wrong place for a child, Mr Ross.' She had never called him that.

'A lot of kids are raised in this sort of country. I was.'

'You want Cassie to grow up like you?'

100

He knew there were two sides to such a remark, and he groped for the pleasant one. 'I'd like her to be more like a girl,' he said slowly and grinned, not because he thought he'd been amusing but to cover the clumsy way he'd replied.

She looked at the ground and shook her head in despair. 'It's such a waste.'

He shook his head too, not knowing what she meant.

'About you,' she said, risking a brief engagement with his eyes. 'You're being wasted here. This is terrible country. And you're living with a black woman who doesn't wear shoes half the time ...'

Adam hadn't thought of that – Nellie did go barefoot around the house.

Now Sarah looked at him directly and shook her head in frustration. 'If only you lived in civilization.'

He let his eyes bore into hers until she turned away. His father had taught him to do that with animals, as a way of exerting dominance. 'What would happen?'

She was staring at the truck, and folded her arms tightly across her chest. 'If you could read I'd draw you a diagram,' she said acidly.

Adam waited a long time before speaking. 'I'm sorry you're going home.'

The eyes flashed. 'Really?'

'We'd hoped you'd stay longer.'

'We?'

'Nellie and me.'

'Hm.' The head tossed like a cranky horse. 'You should get rid of her. She's trouble.'

Adam scratched an ear. 'Is that so?'

'Yes it is. You should do two things. You should kick her out and you should leave this place. You know what's going to happen if you stay on, sleeping with a gin and living in a shanty in the middle of the desert.' It wasn't a question and she didn't pause for him to comment. 'You'll end up a real dead-beat, a man who's done nothing with his life, and she'll get fat and lose her teeth, and they'll have taken your daughter away and you'll have nothing, absolutely nothing, whereas if you just woke up to yourself ...'

He was feeling uncomfortable and folded his arms to match her stance.

'Well, don't you see?' she said, and then, seeing no understanding, turned her back,. 'No, you're just as stupid as Josef. Stronger but just as stupid.' Quickly, she spun around again. 'Haven't you got anything to say?'

'I was just wondering.'

101

'What?'

'How you and Joe ever got together.'

She laughed. 'I must have been mad to think I ever saw anything in him.'

'I've been feeling sorry for Joe.'

'Well you might.'

'And for you.'

'Me? Why me?' Her chin was up; an eyebrow arched, ready for the firing of a devastating glance.

'Because you're more mixed-up than a tin full of odd-sized nuts and bolts.'

She looked about her, as though she were a buyer given five seconds to assess the value of the property. 'Mixed up,' she said at the end of the inspection, but still did not look at him. 'Well, Mr Ross, I hope you stay here, and I hope that black gin of yours leaves you, and I hope they take your daughter away, and I hope you're very happy.'

Adam walked away.

Her second conversation was with Pollard. 'I'm afraid it will be uncomfortable,' she said when they were together near the truck cabin.

'It will be awful,' he said. 'The track is rough and that man is a terrible driver.'

'At least we might as well be friends,' she said and he looked at her in surprise. 'I mean, we're going to be together all the way to Adelaide.'

He tugged at his collar.

'Will they really take the child from him?'

'Possibly.'

'You said it was likely.' When he said nothing, she added, 'You mustn't treat me like a hostile witness. I'm not family and I'm certainly not a friend.'

He frowned. 'I thought ...'

'I hope they *do* take the child away.'

The frown was erased by the elevated wrinkles of surprise.

'Because I've seen what goes on here,' she added in a hushed voice.

He coughed. 'This is probably not the place to talk.'

'We'll have plenty of time,' she said. 'By the way, did I hear someone say you own your own business?'

'Pollard and Pollard? It was started by my father and his brother.'

'And you're the second generation.'

'I am the only son.'

'Of your father?'

'On either side.' He smiled apologetically.

She nodded and the smile had become sweet. 'Is it a big business?'

The third conversation was with Josef. 'I'm sorry it's ended like this,' he said.

'I'm not.' She was about to board the truck.

'Will you be all right?'

'What do you think?'

'Are you going home?'

'I might spend some time in the city.'

'Near the trams,' he said and forced a smile. She did not respond, but busied herself, placing a shoe on the footrest.

'Will I see you again?' he asked and immediately regretted the question. That was the weak Josef talking and the weak Josef, he thought, had gone, despatched to the past.

'I think not,' she said, pulling herself into the seat.

He nodded, accepting the rebuffs. 'Well,' he said, head still going up and down, 'it's been good, Sarah.'

'For you,' she said and slammed the door.

Pollard, crammed in the space between Saleem Benn and the woman, had a brief glimpse of Josef's anguished face. 'Do you want another minute?' he asked, in a gallant attempt at compassion.

'No,' she snapped, the sharp answer more for Josef's ears than for his. 'Let's go. It's a long way.'

With the truck gone, they sat in the house and stared through the spaces separating them. Eventually, Nellie opened a tin of biscuits that Saleem had brought with the supplies.

'What we should do,' Nellie said and waited for all the heads to turn towards her, 'is just nick off. We should just pack up what we can carry and take Cassie and go somewhere.'

'Run away?' Adam said.

'Yes.'

He looked at her intently.

'Where?' she said interpreting the stare. 'Who cares? Somewhere where they don't know us. We can change our names, pretend we're married ... we could even *get* married and say we'd been married for three years and that Cassie was our daughter.'

'You couldn't do that,' Josef interrupted.

Nellie had been about to broadcast her favourite fantasy and she was angry at the unexpected challenge. 'Do what?' she snapped.

'Get married. Not if you changed your names.'

'Why?'

'Because you'd have no identity.' He saw her frown intensify. 'No birth certificate or driver's licence. Things like that.'

'Well, we could just pretend. No one ever looks at your marriage certificate. People just say they're married and everyone believes them.'

Adam held a biscuit in front of him. 'I don't like the idea of just running away. It's like saying you'd done something wrong.' He took a bite. 'And we haven't done anything wrong. Cassie's my daughter.'

'The courts are weird,' Nellie said. She was still angry at Josef. It would be so easy for her and Adam to act like a married couple and pass off Cassie as their daughter. 'Anyhow, you ran away once before, and that worked out well.'

Adam thought: that was different, and a long time ago. He glanced at Stella. She was keeping out of the conversation. Eyes down, she hadn't reacted to Nellie's statement. Jimmy wouldn't have told her about Mailey, so Nellie's words meant nothing to her.

'I don't want to run away like a thief. For heaven's sake, it would mean leaving everything. The property, the sheep, everything.'

'And I don't want to lose Cassie.'

He put the biscuit on the table and used the hand to support his head. 'Maybe Mrs Maguire won't go ahead with this business.'

'She will. There's already a date for a court hearing.'

'Next month,' Josef said gloomily. 'Doesn't give you much time to do anything. You wouldn't even have time to sell the place.'

'I don't want to sell Kalinda.'

'No, but if you had to.'

'I don't have to. I don't want to. This is all I've got.'

'Except Cassie,' Nellie said. 'And me.'

There was a long silence.

'I have to go to Adelaide to this court?' Adam asked, chin still resting on his hand.

'Yes,' Josef said. 'You heard what Pollard said.'

'If it comes to Cassie or Kalinda, there's no choice,' Nellie said. 'Or is there? Does this place mean more to you than that little girl?'

'Don't be silly.'

'Well, it's hard to tell, by the way you're acting.'

'I'm not acting.' He sat up straight. 'I just don't think it's right to have to walk off a property and go into hiding just so's a man can hold on to his own kid.'

'It mightn't be right but it's sensible,' Nellie said.

'I just never expected this,' Adam said.

'No,' Josef said, feeling a word of support was needed. It was inadequate but he couldn't think of anything else to say.

'Maybe I could write to Mrs Maguire,' Adam said, looking towards Josef who, he knew, would be needed to put the necessary touch of eloquence to the letter. 'You know, I could tell her how happy and well Cassie is and make her realize things are good here.'

'She doesn't want a letter,' Nellie said. 'She wants her grand-daughter. She's probably senile and lonely and hasn't got a cat so she wants a kid.'

'She wasn't a bad old thing,' Adam said.

'I wish you wouldn't defend people who try to do rotten things to you.'

'I'm trying to be fair.'

'Well, be fair to Cassie. If you don't want her, good, go to court, let the old lady throw shit in your face.'

'Don't talk like that.'

Nellie stood and pounded the top of the table. 'But you're not taking Cassie. If you don't want her, I'll take her. I'll disappear with her and they'll never see her again and I'll raise her to be a good girl and I'll tell her her father died when she was young and I won't tell her he was a spineless bastard who thought more of his land, his rotten, sandy, rocky piece of nothing, than he did of his own daughter.'

'Jesus,' Josef said, and rocked back on his chair.

'She hasn't changed, mate, has she?' Jimmy said.

'You can shut up for a start,' Nellie said.

Jimmy grinned broadly. He took another biscuit.

'I am not going to hand over Cassie,' Adam said.

Nellie sat down and slumped as though exhausted.

'No matter what happens or what I have to do, I am not going to give her to someone else.'

'She's yours,' Nellie prompted.

'Of course she's mine,' Adam said, his voice raised. 'And don't you ever say I think more of a piece of land than I do of my girl.'

'Well, I thought –'

'And you were wrong. For heaven's sake, Nellie, you rush in and say crazy things without thinking.'

'I don't want them taking her away.'

'Neither do I.' He slammed the table.

Jimmy's smile stretched to new greatness. 'I've never seen the old feller go on like this,' he said admiringly.

'Well, I'm angry at what that solicitor's trying to do and I'm angry at what Nellie was saying. Nellie,' he said, reaching out and

105

touching her wrist, 'she's almost like your own daughter.'

Nellie nodded. 'She is.'

'You love her too.'

'Like my own.'

'Well we've got to find a way to keep her. If we have to leave this place, change our names, do any of those things we will. I just didn't want to have to do that.' He felt Nellie stiffen. 'But I will if there's no other way.'

Nellie and Stella were cooking. 'It's awful what's happened, isn't it?' Stella said.

'It was such a shock.'

'What will you do?'

'I don't know. Adam takes a while to decide things sometimes but he usually makes the right decision.'

'Will you go away?'

'I'd like to.'

'I might have to go into town later,' Stella said, smiling nervously.

'What do you mean? This week?'

'No. In six or seven months.'

'Oh Stella!'

They stood facing each other, each wide-eyed, each biting her lip. Nellie giggled. 'Are you happy?'

'I think so. I've never had a baby before.'

'Me neither.'

Stella had started to smile. 'You don't mean –'

'About the same time. Maybe sooner.'

'Ooh-ah.'

'That's what I thought.' Both giggled.

'Does Adam know?'

Nellie shook her head vigorously.

'Are you going to tell him?'

'I guess I'll have to sometime. How about Jimmy?'

'Not yet. But he won't mind. It's different with us, isn't it?'

Nellie sat down. 'I suppose so.'

'Jimmy and me are just people who drift along, living on the edge of things. No one takes much notice of us. But it's different with you and Adam. He's a big land owner, he's already got a daughter, he'll be rich one day –'

'And I'm just a stone around his neck.'

'Oh, I didn't mean that.'

'I know that, Stella, but it's true. That's why I haven't told him. I know he loves me, I know he'd want the baby, but there'll be so

106

much talk. So much trouble for him. And now this business with the court and Cassie.'

'It'll go against you? I mean you and him, having a baby and all?'

'I don't know. Probably. They already reckon he's lowered himself by living with a coloured woman. What did they call me? A woman of ill repute.' And then she got angry again. 'I wonder who told them that?'

N·I·N·E

Sarah spent the next morning in her room at the William Creek hotel. With some pleasure she told the publican that Adam Ross's former mother-in-law was now claiming custody of his daughter. She knew the story would sweep through the town.

Harry Peterson seemed sad. 'I wouldn't have expected that of her,' he said. 'She seemed a nice old lady. She stayed here on her way home a couple of years ago. She was very distressed, I seem to recall.'

'She seems to have recovered,' Sarah observed.

'She wrote to me, you know.'

'I didn't know.'

'Yes, some months later. Nice letter. Just to say thank you and to apologize for not being herself. She never paid for the room, you know.'

'Truly?'

'Didn't matter.'

'I'll remember that.'

He laughed and eyed her apprehensively.

'I will pay for my room, Mr Peterson,' she said, reaching out as if to give his hand a reaassuring pat.

'I had no doubt about that, ma'am.'

If I left without paying, you wouldn't sleep for a month, she thought, but smiled and said, 'You wrote back to her?'

He scratched his cheek. 'I think so. Hard to remember what I wrote now.'

'Just that your granddaughter is well and in good hands,' she prompted.

He looked at her strangely, but smiled and went to serve a man in the bar.

In the afternoon Sarah walked to the store and discovered Goolamadail in the shadows.

'You gave me a fright,' she said.

'A thousand pardons,' he murmured.

'One would be sufficient.'

'Then one pardon, offered most humbly.'

'And accepted. What a strange shop.'

'It is all we can offer. Is there something you were seeking?' He had not moved and she could not see him clearly.

'Not really. To be honest, I'm just filling in time.'

'You are waiting for the train?'

'How did you guess?' Her voice was heavy with irony.

'I am remarkably perceptive.' He moved from the shadows and gave his rat smile.

'Really?' She fingered a saddle that was displayed on a wooden rig. 'And what else do you perceive?'

He shrugged. 'I perceive that you are returning home earlier than expected.'

'How very clever of you. How do you know that?'

'You are the friend of Mr Josef Hoffman.' He pressed his palms together, pleased to have demonstrated his knowledge of who was linked with whom in his territory.

She was impressed. 'You know him?'

'I know everyone.'

'How remarkable.'

He bowed, missing the sarcasm in his rush to agree with the assessment. 'Mr Josef Hoffman was here before. He stayed with my uncle in Marree many years ago, when I was but a boy.'

'You knew Josef then?'

'Indeed.'

'How long ago was that?'

'Ten, twelve years. He came with his friends. Mr Adam Ross and Mr Jimmy Kettle. Mr Ross had been badly burned. I remember the time well.'

She moved to another saddle and toyed with a strap. 'Who was the man who died?'

'Died?'

'Yes. Back in those years.' She twisted the leather, unable to disguise her interest in his answer. He remained silent. She frowned. 'When they were here, the first time,' she added.

'I do not understand.'

She sighed, as though retelling a familiar story and being forced to prod the memory of a dull child. 'There was a man who died. He was killed.'

He rubbed the whiskers on his throat with the back of his fingers.

'You don't know about that?'

He shook his head slowly.

'I thought you knew everything.'

He lifted his hands. 'Everyone. Not everything.'

'Of course. But you didn't know the man who was killed?'

He lowered his head to his chest and he seemed to deflate, like a balloon having some of its air removed.

She displayed her most tolerant smile. 'The one Mr Ross slew with his bare hands, like some modern Theseus.'

He shook his head. 'I know nothing of that.'

'It's just a myth then,' she said with exaggerated cynicism. 'Not of ancient Greece but of good old William Creek.'

His face became a patchwork of puzzle lines, and she felt compelled to explain. 'Something like a fairy story. Do you understand?'

'A fairy story? Oh yes.'

'Good. How much is this saddle?'

The change of topic unsettled him. 'You wish to go riding?' he asked.

'I am just asking the price.'

'Thirty-five pounds.'

'That seems a lot.'

'It depends.'

'On what?'

'Whether you need a saddle.'

'Quite. Good day.' She walked to the front of the store. 'So there was no one?'

'I beg your pardon?' He followed and straightened the twist in the saddle strap.

'No one killed?'

He raised one hand and smiled apologetically. 'Not that I am aware of.'

'People do talk, don't they? I mean, they say things that aren't true.'

'Indeed.'

'Well, I must be going.'

'Your train is coming?'

She smiled without suggesting an appreciation of his humour. 'Eventually.'

'A most appropriate word.'

'Thank you. Goodbye.'

He bent forward in the slightest of bows. When she was gone he retreated to his corner and tried to remember the time when his uncle had brought the three young men to the house in Marree, and to recall the things they had spoken about.

Over the next five days, those at Kalinda did a great deal of talking.

110

Because the problem had such potentially devastating consequences and because the result was to be determined by strangers
in the alien territory of a court room, many of the conversations
turned in circles, fuelled by fear and steered off course by despair.
All agreed the action was unfair. All believed Adam should keep
Cassie. All were frightened.

Nellie continued to urge Adam to leave. She had an old map of
Australia and began selecting towns to which they could travel.
One night she began packing his bag and for ten frantic minutes she
put clothes in the bag while Adam took them out. It ended with her
throwing clothes at him, and him laughing and her crying. On
another night, the idea came to her that he wouldn't leave because
he didn't want her to go with him. 'I'm all right while I stay here
where no one can see me,' she shouted at him, 'but you're ashamed
to take me anywhere.'

'The only shame,' he said, 'is when you lose your temper because
then you talk a lot of nonsense.'

'You're the one who talks nonsense because you're the one who
won't leave. You're too stupid and stubborn to do what any
sensible person could see was the only thing to do.'

'I don't see why I should walk away from this place like a
criminal when I haven't done anything wrong.'

'The thing you'll do wrong is let that stupid old woman take
Cassie away from us.'

'From me.'

'That's right. Don't consider me.'

'I am thinking of you but you're not the one who has to go to
court.'

'I wish I could. I'd tell the judge a thing or two.'

Jimmy joined in the conversation. 'I'd like to be there,' he said,
talking to Josef as though Nellie and Adam were actors on a stage
and the rest were in the audience. 'It'd be worth a week's wages to
see Nellie spit at the judge and then hear him put her away for a
few months for whatever they call it.'

'Contempt of court,' Josef suggested.

'That's it. Handy thing that. You smile the wrong way and the
beak puts you in the slammer.'

'You'd know,' Nellie sniped.

'Sure would.' He grinned and was content that the argument had
been defused.

It was Josef who suggested he should go south on the next train
and see a solicitor he knew in Tanunda. He could then telegram
that man's advice to William Creek.

'The law's a mystery to all of us,' he said and Adam concurred.

111

'If we just blunder along and do what we think's right, we'll lose the case. We'd be sitting ducks for some legal eagle.'

Jimmy scratched his head. 'Is this thing going to be held in a court-house or a birdcage?'

Josef, earnestly addressing Adam, hesitated. 'In a court-house of course. What are you talking about?'

'Just shut up, Jimmy,' Nellie said.

'Ducks, eagles. I felt like a galah.' Jimmy rolled his eyes and sought encouragement from Stella. She looked down but she could not hide the smile.

'You need to have a solicitor to counter this Pollard bloke,' Josef continued. 'So let me do that. That's the first thing. When we hear what he's got to say, we can decide what to do.'

'Like go away,' Nellie said stubbornly.

Josef inclined his head, in the manner of a lawyer acknowledging a last resort. 'If necessary,' he said grudgingly.

Adam tapped the table and Nellie kept quiet, sensing he was about to deliver judgement.

'I'm not going to lose Cassie,' he said and tapped the table again. 'That's the first thing.'

'The important thing,' Josef said, again in his lawyer voice and nodding sagely.

'And I will walk away from Kalinda if I have to.' He turned to Nellie. 'We will. You, me and Cassie. We're going to stick together, right?'

She nodded, her face still flushed.

'But I can't just move out of here with nothing. Things are tough enough without trying to make a fresh start without a zac to your name.'

'I don't mind,' Nellie said quietly.

'I do. And there's a way around it.' They all looked at him. 'I could sell it to someone before we went to Adelaide for the court case.'

Nellie was disappointed. 'We've been through all that. We don't have time. You're not going to get a buyer in a couple of weeks. And if you sell out for next to nothing, and then you win the court case, you've lost everything for nothing.'

Adam was shaking his head. 'Not a real sale.'

'What do you mean?' Josef asked.

'I'll sell it to you.'

'Me?' He fluttered his hands. 'I haven't got that sort of money.'

'You don't need any. You get your lawyer friend in Tanunda to draw up a contract, I sign it over to you for a few quid and if Nellie and I have to go into hiding with Cassie, then you sell it, properly

112

and for a reasonable sum of money, and send the cash on to us.'

Josef scratched an ear. Nellie smiled. 'You'd do that?' she said.

Adam waved a hand. 'At least we wouldn't lose everything.'

She was beaming. 'And we could go anywhere, change our names –'

'Get married,' Jimmy said.

'Will you shut up?'

'I was just trying to help.'

'Well, don't bother.'

'It's what you want, isn't it?' They were sitting but Jimmy faced Nellie with his right shoulder towards her and his body jiggling, a boxer ready to deflect his opponent's first blow.

'But,' Adam said loudly, and Jimmy let his shoulder drop, 'the first thing is that Josef should see this lawyer in Tanunda.'

'I don't know what he can do,' Josef said, his face creased in thought. 'Or what he might say. He might say you haven't got a hope in hell.'

'We'll wait and see,' Adam said.

Nellie frowned at Josef. 'But you were so confident a moment ago.'

'I just said we should get our own lawyer. I didn't say he was going to win the case for us.'

'He might.'

'Of course he might. I just said we wouldn't win without him.'

'Is this bloke that good?' Adam asked.

'I don't mean him,' Josef said feeling more worried as he realised how much their hopes depended on him. 'I just meant a lawyer. A solicitor to tell us what to do, what our chances are. We need someone who understands the law.'

They regarded him in silence.

'That's all I meant,' he said.

Nellie leaned back, and studied the ceiling. 'It isn't fair,' she said, repeating a sentiment she had expressed many times in the past five days.

'Neither is the world,' Jimmy said.

'It's good to hear you say something sensible at last,' she said, not bothering to look at him. She faced Josef. 'When do you reckon you'll know something?'

Josef thought of the solicitor. He was an old man, who handled his father's affairs. The man was notoriously slow. 'I'll see him immediately I get home,' he said, injecting enthusiasm into his words so he himself might feel encouraged. 'I'll tell him how important it is.' My God, he recalled with dismay, this man had once delayed sending an urgent letter for eight months. Even his

113

father reckoned he was slow. They joked about him in town. His name was Richard Mawbis but the locals called him Rigor Mortis. What would he do if Mawbis didn't give him a quick answer, and good, practical advice?

'And?' Adam prompted.

'And I'll telegram you. You'll have to go into town to get the message.'

'Every day if necessary.'

Nellie sighed. 'I'd just as soon go now. I can't stand the thought of waiting around.'

'Wait till you hear from me,' Josef advised, and smiled confidently.

'We couldn't just walk out right now,' Adam said. 'There are things to do.'

Jimmy shrugged. 'You can go when you like. Me and Stella can handle things here.'

Nellie covered her mouth. 'I hadn't thought about that.' She gazed at Stella with large, sad eyes. 'If we leave, what will you and Jimmy do?'

Stella turned to Jimmy. There was no question of her making the decision. 'That's easy,' he said. 'We'd come with you. You might as well have three kids as one.'

Nellie stared accusingly at Stella. Surely she hadn't told Jimmy? 'What do you mean?' she said.

'Cassie, Stella and me,' he said, brow wrinkled in a wedge that was matched by his lop-sided smile. He leaned towards her. 'What did you think I meant?'

Stella and Nellie were together. 'You haven't told him?' Nellie said and the question bordered on an accusation.

'Of course not.'

'I think Jimmy knows.'

'No. He always likes to have you think he knows what's going on but it's all a game. He's just out to make you feel uncomfortable.'

Nellie shook her head, still doubting.

'You two say some funny things to each other,' Stella observed.

'We always fight.'

'You used to be his girl?'

'Sort of. It was a long time ago.'

'Was it serious?' They were standing at the stove. Stella rubbed her palms against her hips, wishing the past would be wiped as easily.

'No. Not really.' She smiled at Stella. 'Jimmy had lots of girlfriends. None of them were serious. Certainly not me.' Nellie liked

114

Stella and hesitated before speaking again. 'Does it worry you?'

'No.' Her hands rubbed vigorously on the seams of her dress. 'It's just that I've never had boy-friends. Having a lot seems ... I don't know, strange.'

'He was a good boxer.'

'So he told me.'

'He was. People loved him.'

'Truly? He tells me the most amazing stories ... I don't know whether to believe him.'

'If they're amazing enough, they're probably true.'

Both laughed.

Now Stella clasped her hands. 'I think at heart he really likes you. I tell him he shouldn't keep chipping at you. He's always saying things that make you angry.'

'I get angry easy.' They smiled.

'You should tell Adam.'

'What?' Nellie said softly. She put more wood on the fire.

'About the baby. It would change so many things. You can't go racing around the country with you pregnant, and if he knew you were going to have a baby he'd marry you. He's that sort of man.'

Nellie rattled the ashes. 'I don't want him marrying me because he's sorry for me.'

'He wouldn't feel sorry for you. He'd be happy. I'm sure. Oh Nellie, look at me.'

Nellie straightened.

'You've got to tell him. It would change things so much.'

'He couldn't marry me before the court case,' Nellie said.

'Well that doesn't matter. You've got time afterwards.'

'No, it does matter. I've been thinking these last few days. If Adam loses Cassie it won't be because he lives up in the bush or because the kid won't get properly educated or any of those things. He'll lose her because he's living with a black gin.'

Stella walked to the table, turned and sat on it.

'But you're a good woman, and you look after Cassie so well. You really love her and she adores you.'

'Which won't mean a thing to the judge,' Nellie said. 'I'm black. A nigger. A boong. Not the right sort of person to help bring up a nice little white kid.'

'Which is why you want to leave?'

'Yes. As soon as they hear he's living with me, they'll give Cassie to the grandmother.'

Stella advanced and took Nellie's hands.

'Tell Adam.'

She shook her head.

'You should. It'd make all the difference. Tell him about the baby. Tell him what you just told me about the judge. Tell him everything.'

'He'll think I'm trying to make him marry me. You know the old trick: get pregnant to get the man.'

'He won't think that.'

'I just want him to come away with me because he wants to marry me, not because he has to.'

Stella lifted Nellie's chin until they were looking directly at each other. 'I think you're being very silly.'

'It's not for the first time. Anyhow,' she said, brightening her expression, 'when are you going to tell Jimmy?'

Stella turned away. 'Later.'

'Why not now?'

'I don't think he's ready for it.'

'You're frightened of what he'll say?'

Now it was Nellie's turn to lift the other woman's face. 'Do you think he'd leave you?'

Stella avoided Nellie's eyes. 'He likes it too much here. But he might make me go.'

'Oh why?' Nellie saw the first suggestion of tears. 'He loves you. He's mad about you. I can tell.'

'But he's had so many girls. He wouldn't want a woman with a fat tummy who was sick every morning.'

'Why don't you give him the chance? Tell him and see what he does.'

'He's not like Adam.'

Nellie agreed. 'If I was with Jimmy I'd just tell him and if he complained I'd hit him.' She picked up a saucepan. 'Here. Tell him and dong him if he makes a fuss.'

Stella put the saucepan back on the stove. 'I'll tell him after you tell Adam,' she said. 'If he knew Adam was going to be a father, he might be able to handle the news.'

Nellie folded her arms. 'So neither of us are going to tell our man?'

Stella looked at the ceiling and then at Nellie. She shook her head vigorously, and laughed. 'We're a great pair, aren't we?' They hugged, and then made tea and Stella went outside and called the men.

Two days before Josef was due to leave they had a visitor. He came in a Model A Ford and they could see his smile through the yellowed insect stains on the windscreen even before he stopped at the homestead. The arrival of an unexpected motor vehicle was an

116

almost unheard-of event and Adam and Josef walked from the house to meet the visitor.

'It *is* you,' the man called out and climbed from the car. His was an awkward exit because the door was reluctant to open and his foot missed the running-board. The man stood there, rubbing a scraped shin. 'I heard it was you. They told me in town but I didn't believe it.' He was wearing a clergyman's collar. Even with his face coated by dust they could see he was young.

Not yet recognizing the man, Adam rubbed his chin. Josef looked to him for some guidance and rubbed his chin, too.

'Roger?' Adam said eventually and the clergymen's grin became a laugh that somehow managed to permit the word 'yes' to emerge. He moved towards them, arm outstretched.

'From Carnarvon?' Josef said, astonishment lifting his voice an octave.

'Right!' He gripped Adam's hand. 'Been hitching rides in any more aeroplanes?'

'Jesus Christ,' Josef said, grabbing the hand when it was free, 'where the hell did you come from?'

'Well, that's a strange mixture, but I think I know what you mean.' He laughed and stood back and examined the house but could not stop smiling, nor control his head which continued to shake in disbelief. 'You two. This is amazing. Oh, and I came from Adelaide.' With his free hand he dabbed his eyes with a crumpled handkerchief.

Adam and Josef had met the Reverend Roger Montgomery four years earlier, when they had travelled to the west in a futile bid to buy land. They took him inside, and introduced him to Nellie.

'This is the Reverend Montgomery,' Adam said. He too was now smiling broadly and shaking his head.

'Roger,' the clergyman corrected pleasantly.

'He's a Methodist minister,' Josef said.

'Presbyterian.'

'Well, almost the same thing.' Josef shrugged. His parents were Lutheran. Other Protestant faiths confused him.

Roger Montgomery nodded tolerantly and happily. 'We met in Western Australia. I used to be the minister at Carnarvon. Have you ever been there ...?' He hesitated, having forgotten her name.

'Nellie,' she said. She was standing in a pose of languid grace, her hands lightly clasped in front of her, one knee bent inward to touch the other in a stance that drew her body and legs into a series of flowing lines. It was the pose affected by a fashion model after years of training; she held it naturally, feeling relaxed in the mood of happiness that filled the air. 'No, I haven't.' She turned to Adam.

117

'That was when you tried to buy Cobargo?'

He nodded. 'I know that story,' she said. 'Adam's told me many times. You were the priest?' She looked at Adam, her question filled with doubt.

Roger wiped his face and examined the grime on his handkerchief. 'No. That was Father Ryan. I was the other one in the story. The young novice parson that Father Ryan used to bully.'

'He was a good bloke,' Adam said, fondly recalling the old priest.

'He still is, I'm pleased to say. He's continuing to terrorize the north-west.'

'Still trying to convert people?' Josef asked.

'It's a never-ending quest. Unhappily for those on my side of the net, he's scoring a few more points than we'd like. However, I suppose in the end, we're all playing the same game, if you know what I mean?'

Adam did not but smiled understanding. 'And what are you doing here?' He led the way inside.

'Well,' Roger said, accepting a seat at the table, 'I was transferred about a year ago. I'm now with the Australian Inland Mission and when Victor Rawlinson was wounded –' He looked at each man, his eyes seeking recognition of the name. 'You know, the padre who was shot on the train?' They nodded in unison. 'You should,' he continued, 'I'm told you were actively involved in the whole affair. That's when I heard your names, at William Creek, when they were telling me the whole story –' Again, he gave a broad smile and paused to muster his thoughts. 'Anyhow, he can't work for some time and they needed a replacement, and I was there and I suspect they didn't know what else to do with me, and so they gave me that decrepit heap of well-used metal that they loosely call a motor car, and here I am.'

There was a silence, broken by the snap of burning wood. The sound jolted Nellie into uttering the question that always marked the end of the initial, excited, phase of a meeting.

'Would you like a cup of tea?' she asked.

It was only when they had begun to drink their tea that Roger Montogomery suddenly sat back and said, 'You won't have heard the news.' He wiped his lips. 'No, of course not. You're so remote here. You don't get the newspapers do you?'

'They don't, Roger,' Josef said, his face bright with amused curiosity. 'I brought them the last glad tidings from the world and since then, nothing but silence.' He waved his hands. 'What's happened? Has Don Bradman scored five hundred not out or has Sydney Harbour dried up?'

118

'Neither, but the news is of that magnitude.' Roger managed a weak smile. 'England has declared war on Germany, and so have we. Australia is at war.'

The Reverend Roger Montgomery stayed that night. With Jimmy and Stella back at the bore and Sarah gone, there was a surfeit of accommodation by the normally meagre standards of Kalinda. He was given the bed in the area formerly assigned to Sarah. He argued that there was no need for them to go to such trouble. He carried his own tent and sleeping bag, and he produced both in enacting the polite ritual that preceded his inevitable acceptance of the offer. They talked until midnight. He slept well and woke late, to discover that Adam and Josef had gone to inspect the place where Adam was contemplating drilling a new bore. They would return later in the morning.

Nellie confided that the real reason they had ridden away was to talk more about the war. Josef was determined to enlist in the army on his return to Tanunda. Adam was trying to persuade him to wait. After all, Roger had said few people had expected the war to last long, so Adam couldn't see the sense in rushing off to someone else's fight when it would end before Josef got there to turn the tide.

Nellie liked the young parson. There was an engaging innocence and openness about the man that made her want to mother him, and the lack of any apparent pretence or conceit that invited confidence.

'May I talk to you?' she asked, when he had finished breakfast.

'I've been talking non-stop since I got up,' he said, which was true. He had been telling her about his experiences in Carnarvon. He dabbed his lips. 'It's only fair you should have a turn.'

She smiled shyly. 'It's hard to know how to start.'

Cassie walked to the table. Surprisingly, she had liked the stranger almost immediately and now Roger lifted her on to his knee. 'It sounds very serious,' he said, as he pushed a strand of hair from Cassie's face.'

'It is.' Nellie sat opposite him. She put both elbows on the table and locked hands, moving them constantly against each other like two wrestlers seeking to gain a winning hold. 'It's about Adam and me.'

Cassie reached up and grabbed his collar. He made no attempt to move her hand.

'As you know, we're living together.'

'Well, I ...' He moved Cassie to a more comfortable part of his leg.

119

'We're not married.' She hesitated, to gauge his reaction but he seemed engrossed in the girl. 'What you might call, living in sin.'

His head was bent but he looked up, so that his eyes were at an acute angle. It was an expression Nellie had noticed on dogs that lie outside hotels waiting for their masters, and watch strangers pass without daring to move their heads. There was a sadness in the eyes but instead of seeing the wrong person, as the dog would, this man was hearing the wrong message.

He groped for excuses. 'You've known him a long time. You're very fond of each other.'

'We love each other.'

'Well, that's good, Nellie.' He moved one hand as if drawing aside a curtain that had been between them. 'It's not uncommon, I'm told, for people in this part of the world to live together until someone like me turns up to tie the knot, as it were.'

Her right hand had gained control and was bending back the fingers on the other hand.

He leaned forward. 'Would you like me to marry you two?'

She used her forehead to separate the hands. 'Well, yes I would.'

'It would have to be next time. Unless you've already attended to all the formalities?'

She shook her head. 'It's not that.'

'Not about getting married?'

'No. Well, yes and no. I'd like to get married. We'd both like to get married,' she added hastily in case he suspected reluctance on Adam's part and hysteria on hers. 'But there's something else. Something that's only cropped up in the last few days.'

She told him about Jeremy Pollard's visit, and the claim by Mrs Maguire. As he listened, he put both arms around Cassie and rocked her on his knee. His face grew sombre and the embrace tightened, until Cassie became restless, and was put on the floor. She scampered to Nellie's side of the table.

'I know the war has made personal issues seem unimportant,' he said, when Cassie was settled on Nellie's lap. 'But for you two to have to hand Cassie to some other person would be grossly unjust.'

Nellie felt warmth spread within her when he said 'you two'. This man considered Cassie their child, just as she did, and he was the first outsider to have expressed such a feeling. 'That's what I think,' she said, resting her chin on top of Cassie's head. The girl squirmed away and slid to the floor.

'She's full of beans,' Roger said.

'She's very healthy.' Nellie beamed with pride.

'She's extremely fond of you.'

'Yes. We're close.'

120

He watched Cassie pursue a small lizard that scurried along the base of the wall. 'And what are you going to do?' he asked as the youngster chased it out of the door.

Nellie told him of the various schemes they had discussed.

He shook his head. 'You can't run away and hide, Nellie. That is unthinkable.'

'Why not? It's not as unthinkable as having someone take her away.'

'But you would be like criminals.'

She faced him defiantly. 'It's not a crime to take your own child.'

'No, of course not, but she is not your child, not in the eyes of the law anyhow.' He paused to make sure she understood that point.

'Then who cares about the law?'

'That is a very silly thing to say, with all due respect.'

She was beginning to wonder what this young unmarried parson would know about love and children? He had resumed talking, only it was beginning to sound like a lecture.

'You mightn't like the law but you have to respect it. Do you understand what I am saying?'

Now he's saying I'm stupid, she thought. He probably thinks I'm like Adam and didn't go to school. 'Of course,' she mumbled.

'If you defy a court order and don't go to the hearing, or if you just leave and take Cassie with you, you will be breaking the law. And the law will pursue you. You don't want that, do you?'

Her hands resumed their struggle. 'Why don't they just leave us alone?'

He smiled. 'Yes, why don't they?' He nodded agreement while his face struggled with the unpleasant reality. 'But unfortunately they won't. If you abscond, they'll pursue you. Forever. You'll have no peace.'

The fingers hooked in a test of strength. 'So we have to go to court?'

'Adam does. Yes. He must.'

'And what will happen then?'

He let his right hand stir the air. He used his hands a lot, which was unusual for the son of dour Scottish parents, but he couldn't find the appropriate words, which was not.

'We could lose Cassie?' she asked.

'Yes.' He knew what to say now. 'I think you have to face the fact that losing the girl might not be fair or even right but it is a very real possibility. That is, on the strength of what you said that Adelaide solicitor told you.' Another silence. 'It could happen,' he added, compelled to speak because the silences were too full of

121

pain.' I don't know what you should do, but you must go to court. If you don't, you'd lose everything and the first thing you'd lose would be Cassie.'

'But it's only over one little girl. Surely they wouldn't be so worried about a three-year-old who's with her father anyway.'

'It wouldn't be that. It would be that you and Adam have flouted the law. They wouldn't stand for that. The law can stand anything except having its nose pulled.'

Cassie was crawling after some other object. It was too small for Nellie to see but its movement fascinated the girl. 'What have you got there?' Nellie called out, her question edged with irritation.

'A thing,' Cassie said. She was following a brightly coloured insect of a kind she hadn't seen before, and her eyes stayed on the floor.

'Well, go outside and see if you can see your father and Uncle Joe coming home.'

'You said they'd be a long time.' She put one finger on the insect but withdrew her hand suddenly when it contracted its legs.

'Well, it is a long time. Just go outside and see if they're coming.'

Summoning her courage, Cassie gripped the insect and went to the door. 'They're not there.'

'You can't see them from there. Go around the back. Throw that thing away and don't go too far from the house.'

'Can I keep it and not throw it?'

'All right, but don't let it bite you. And don't hurt it.'

Roger Montgomery had spent the time rubbing an itchy eye. 'She talks well,' he said when Cassie had gone.

'Yes. I'd be a good teacher.'

'I'm sure.' He finished rubbing the eye and tested it by giving Nellie another mournful look. 'You know the trouble, don't you?'

The hands, now more gently entwined, covered her mouth. Her eyes, seeming larger than ever, gazed sadly at Roger.

'It's something you must have thought about, must have realized,' he went on, turning away under the intensity of her stare. 'The thing that will count against Adam at the hearing is the fact that he is living with you.'

'Because I'm black,' she said rapidly.

'No. At least, that shouldn't be a factor. Not in a court of law anyhow, where all people are supposed to be equal.'

'Be nice if it was true.'

'Well, it should be.' He rubbed the eye again.

'White people can't stand the idea of a white man living with a black woman.'

'*Some* white people,' he said. 'I don't suppose the fact that

122

you're coloured is a help, seeing that Cassie is white.' He put his hands towards her, offering support. 'I don't want to sound brutal but that could be a factor. You do understand?'

'I understand everything you say,' she snapped.

He withdrew his hand. 'Good. But there are two other aspects to this that worry me. The first is that the court will note that he's living with a woman but that the two of you aren't married.'

She lifted an eyebrow. 'So we should marry?'

He looked even sadder. 'There's no time. Not before the hearing anyhow.'

'We could tell the court we were getting married.' Her face brightened with hope.

'But the worst thing,' he said, ploughing doggedly along the same line, 'is what you told me the solicitor said about your, ah, reputation.'

'A woman of ill repute?' Nellie said weakly.

He let his head drop. 'Yes. Why did they say that?'

'To get Cassie.'

'But why ill repute?' He breathed noisily, labouring to produce the next question. 'Is there something ... was there something ...' He looked at her helplessly.

'You mean is it true?'

'Well, is there some reason for them to have made such a statement? In other words, is it just spiteful gossip or is there some basis in fact?'

She stood and walked to the door. 'When Adam and I first met, all those years ago, I was living in Port Pirie and there was a man who wanted to hurt me. That's why we all ran away. We went to Coober Pedy. We met Josef that way.'

She had been facing the bright day, arms folded and seeing nothing. She turned, her head low and her eyes sweeping the floor. 'But it was a long time ago. Ten years. We were just kids.'

'I don't follow all that,' Roger said, trying to make contact with her eyes. 'Who was the man who was trying to hurt you?'

'Just a slimy little man who ran a brothel in town. You know what a brothel is? Well, I worked for him. I was leaving and he wanted me back.'

There were insects buzzing near the doorway. She heard them clearly and even had time to wonder what they were, in the time it took him to speak again.

'You were a prostitute?'

'Yes.' She felt reckless, and almost added, 'And a good one.'

He moved his head as though searching for air. 'Does Adam know?'

123

'Of course.'

'And how long were you in that place.'

'I was a prostitute for a few years.'

'Oh Nellie, how could you?'

'Easy. I needed money. I didn't want to starve. Ever gone hungry, Roger? Ever been so desperate you'd do anything to eat?'

He was still gasping for breath. 'But how could you do that? Something so ...'

'Dirty?' she suggested.

'Vile.' He shook his head. 'I'm sorry. I shouldn't have said that. It was just such a surprise. I didn't expect something quite like that from someone –'

'Someone living with a man like Adam.'

He raised his palms. 'You realize this is a disaster, Nellie?'

'But it all happened more than ten years ago,' she said, her voice growing sharper.

'I'm afraid that doesn't matter. You were a prostitute and somehow the other party, the grandmother, has found out about it and intends to use that information as a means of prising the child from Adam.'

Nellie shrugged. 'I could deny it. It would be my word against hers.'

'They'd bring forward witnesses. The man who was trying to hurt you, for instance.'

'He's dead.'

'Then someone else. The local police. Someone. And if you perjured yourself ... Do you know what that means?'

'No. It doesn't sound good.' She attempted a smile.

'It means told a lie. If you did that, Adam's case would be destroyed.'

'Isn't it destroyed anyhow? Once they're told I was a prostitute and I'm the woman who's now looking after Cassie ... well, that'd be it, wouldn't it?'

His face was drained of colour. 'Yes,' he said, his voice almost a whisper. 'I'd say it would be certain they'd give the child to the grandmother.'

She crossed the room to its only window and stared out. 'So the best thing would be for me to disappear.'

'What do you mean?'

'Go away. Nick off. Can't you understand plain English?'

'Of course, of course,' He frowned. 'But you mean leave Adam?'

She turned. 'If I was gone, would he have a chance? Would they let a man living on his own keep his own daughter, even if he lived in a place like this?'

124

'How can I say? I don't have much to do with the courts.'

'Don't start running around corners on me now, Roger. I want the truth.'

His eyes registered a protest.

'OK, so a man like you can only tell the truth. Isn't it the truth that the court wouldn't, shouldn't take a daughter away from her father if he was doing his best to raise her, and he loved her and she loved him?'

He scratched his chin.

'Isn't it? Let's be honest, Roger; if there was no wicked woman, a sinful, black, unmarried woman living with Adam, he'd have a hell of a good chance of keeping his daughter? Surely they wouldn't take her away?'

'Really, Nellie ...'

'Please Roger. Stop trying not to hurt me. That doesn't worry me. Look, all this isn't about whether I'm going to get hurt or not. It's about whether Cassie can stay with her father. I love that girl almost as much as I love Adam and if I had to leave and not see her again I'd never get over it, but I'd rather do that than have Cassie taken away and raised by some old woman in Sydney because if that happened Adam would die and then I'd die too, so for God's sake be honest with me. If I left, Adam could keep Cassie. That's right, isn't it'

He coughed. 'I think so.'

'So do I.' She pursed her lips, pondering a new thought. 'And what about me? How would they explain me?'

His hands shaped the boundaries of the argument. 'You would have been the housekeeper who, unfortunately, had moved on to some other job. Adam could say he was employing someone else, to satisfy any question about looking after the things a woman does so well. You know what I mean.'

'I know what you mean.' She turned back to the window. 'So even if I married Adam it wouldn't help things?'

'It wouldn't erase your past,' he said softly.

'No. Of course not. Roger, answer me one other question.' She braced her hands against the sill. 'What if Adam told the court that he wanted to get married and that I was having a baby.'

'Good heavens, Nellie,' he said, his words dragging with fresh concern.

She laughed. 'Oh don't worry. I'm only joking. It was just that I was wondering what the judge might say. You know, he might think that things would be better out here for little Cassie if she had a brother or a sister to play with.'

'If you were having a baby it would be an absolute disaster,' he

125

said and looked at her keenly.

'I'm not,' she said and briefly let him see the reassuring smile she had forced on her face. 'Just a crazy idea.'

'Thank heavens for that.' He returned her smile. 'For the judge to be told that the father was living with a former prostitute and that he and she were going to have an illegitimate child would mean the case would be settled in two minutes.'

'And he'd lose Cassie.'

'Certainly. So don't even think of making up such a story.'

'So there's only one thing to do.'

He walked to her side. 'You can't just go away, surely? Adam wouldn't want that. And you love them both so much.'

'Oh,' she answered brightly, 'it would only be for a while. Just until the case was over. Then I could come back again, couldn't I?'

He managed to nod and seem doubtful at the same time. 'You'd have to be careful,' he said. 'There would be all sorts of questions raised at the hearing and Adam might be required to give certain assurances.'

'Meaning?'

'Just that you should be careful when, and how, you returned.'

'You mean not come back too soon?'

'Something like that.'

'I'll just stay away until the right time.'

He was still frowning. 'There'll be a lot of pain.'

'But he will keep Cassie?'

He nodded.

'Well then, it's simple isn't it?'

126

T · E · N

A strong wind had begun to blow. It came from the west, where most of the bad winds started, and it swept the claypans and dunes as it gusted towards the vastness of Lake Eyre. Spring had started but it was a winter wind, cold and dry and with a breath that bore the stench of desert refuse. Sand and dust and fragments of leaves and shredded grass were carried in its mad, swirling clouds. It was a low wind, scraping the surface and staining the air reddish brown and howling as it came. It bore down on the two riders.

Adam and Josef stopped and turned the rumps of their horses towards the first gust. 'Great weather you have here,' Josef shouted and began tying a handkerchief across his nose and mouth.

'Outback snow,' Adam replied and tucked his face into the upturned collar of his shirt.

'You've got to move to some other place,' Josef said, still tying the handkerchief in place. 'This country wasn't meant for human beings to live in.'

'You used to like it once.'

'That was when I was young and silly and I didn't know any better.'

Adam edged the mare closer to Josef's horse. 'If you go off to Europe and some German puts a bullet in your tail, you'll wish you'd never left here.'

Josef acknowledged the wisdom of the remark with an exaggerated nod of the head. He held his hat in place. 'I really do like this country,' he said. 'It's just that I couldn't live here any more and I think it's just such a hell of a waste for you to spend all your life up here.'

'Instead of?'

'Well, instead of coming south and living where people live.'

'People live here.'

Josef, head hunched in his shoulders, risked a look to one side. 'Not bloody many.'

'Enough for me. I don't like crowds.'

'But you don't have to be fanatical about it. You could at least live in a place where you're likely to see one stranger a day instead of one every six months or so.'

'You never give up, Joe,' Adam said, laughing into his collar.

'It's my greatest virtue. I'm persistent.'

Adam looked back, shielding his eyes against the wind. 'I think we might as well keep on riding. This isn't going to get any better for a while and we'll be sand-blasted down to the bones if we just stay here.'

An uprooted bush cart-wheeled past them. 'Time to go,' Josef yelled, 'before they start throwing the gum trees at us.'

They rode off, horses moving briskly to escape the stinging onslaught and each rider holding his hat and bending his head towards the wind.

'You really are going to enlist?' Adam asked. He had taken the windward side and while it meant he bore the worst of the blow, he could also look towards Josef without having his face peppered by sand.

Josef, keeping close to gain what shelter Adam provided, did not turn his head. 'Too right. Soon as I get home.'

'Are you still going to see the solicitor?'

Josef lifted the hat brim momentarily. 'Of course. That'll be the very first thing I'll do.'

'And then you'll join up?'

'That'll be the very second thing I'll do.'

'And then you'll go home?'

'The third thing.'

They laughed and the wind swept the noise away so that neither heard the other. They rode to the end of the sand ridge and turned along its sheltered side. It was quieter there.

'I know you won't forget, Joe.'

Josef, still holding the brim tightly, lifted his hand to clear his view of his friend. 'Forget what?'

'About seeing the solicitor.'

'Of course not. I promise I will see old Mawbis the minute I reach town.'

'And he'll get straight on to it?'

Josef shifted uncomfortably in the saddle. 'If he doesn't I'll twist his arm. Don't worry. The family's used him for a long time.'

Adam had been worrying about something. 'Joe,' he began, finally expressing his doubts, 'what if it takes this solicitor of yours a little time to get things under way, you know, to do what he has to do to make sure we don't lose Cassie, and in the meantime you've joined the army, and gone off to fight the Germans. What do we do then?'

Josef rode on with his head tilted forward, not speaking.

'It could happen,' Adam said. 'You could join up and be sent off somewhere the next day and while I don't want Australia to lose the war, I don't want to lose Cassie either.'

'I don't think they'd want me that quickly,' Josef said.

'You never know.'

'No. I suppose not. I hadn't thought about that, but I'll tell you what. I won't join up until Mawbis gets on the job and tells us what to do. How's that?'

Adam considered. 'That's good,' he said.

Josef's horse had taken the lead. He pulled on the reins and turned the animal to block Adam's path. He bent forward. 'Why don't you come with me and join up too?'

'I'd thought about it.'

'True?' Josef was delighted.

'I thought a lot about it last night, after Nellie went to sleep. I reckoned that if you and me were in the war, it'd be over in a few weeks.'

'Yeah but who'd win?'

'That's what I was trying to work out.' He grinned. 'Couldn't get to sleep for hours, but I reckon we'd make a good combination.'

'It'd be great.' Josef moved his horse closer. 'You know you don't really have to volunteer. You're a primary producer and I can't see them wanting blokes like you in the army when you could be growing things.'

'They don't have to know what I do for a living.'

'That's true. But you don't have to go. I do, and that's the difference. I'm only involved in a small grape-growing business and making wine is about as vital to the war effort as blowing up balloons, but you're in the sheep business and that means wool and hide and meat and you could stay here forever and no one would ever point a finger at you. But me, I've got to go.'

'I'd like to.' Adam sounded disappointed, as though there were no chance of his achieving an ambition. 'I've heard so many blokes talking about the Great War that it'd be interesting to see what they were talking about. And you and me'd see a bit of the world, wouldn't we?'

'We sure would. Come with me, Adam. Let's both go south on the train and join up.'

Adam shook his head. 'Can't. Not until this business with Cassie is cleared up. And by then you'd already be in the army and off somewhere, and I wouldn't see you again until the war was over.'

'In a couple of weeks' time,' Josef said, echoing the opinion Roger had expressed.

129

'Maybe.' Adam hunched in the saddle. 'No, I'm stuck here for a while I think.'

Josef leaned even closer. 'If you did enlist, Mrs Maguire wouldn't be able to take Cassie away.'

Adam straightened.

'When this court case came up, you could be in the army and on your way to the war. She'd never find you.'

Adam thought about that for a long time. The mare grew impatient and moved towards a clump of bushes. He pulled her back. 'I don't know,' he said. 'What would I do with Cassie?'

'Leave her with Nellie.'

'And what if they found me?'

'They wouldn't. Nellie or Jimmy wouldn't tell and by the time the police had worked out where you'd got to, you and me would be walking down the main street of Berlin.' He saw Adam's uncomprehending look, and added, 'That's the capital city of Germany.'

'I still don't know. I'd rather face this thing and clear it up before I got on to something else. I ran away from the police once before and I've never felt good about it.'

'After Mailey?' Josef could only see his eyes, revealed between the lowered brim of the hat and the turned-up collar. 'Well, that was different. This time it's not just a case of pissing off until the heat dies down. This time it's a court case and if it goes against you, you could lose Cassie.'

'I've been thinking some more about that, too, and I don't see how they can take her away. I'm her dad and I love her and look after her and she's happy here, so why should they give her to someone else?' He moved the mare past Josef's mount and resumed the journey home.

'Just think about enlisting,' Josef called out. 'Just give it some thought.' He lowered his hat to shield his face, and followed.

Nellie found Roger Montgomery pumping up a rear tyre on his Ford. 'There's a dust storm to the north,' she said, indicating the thin stain on the horizon. 'I hope the men aren't in it.'

'More washing?' he said and smiled.

'I wanted to ask you to do me a favour,' she said and he stopped pumping and looked serious. He was young for a parson but he seemed younger than his years and he had found he had to adopt a stern look if people were to take him seriously. 'Actually, two favours,' she continued, facing him with an equally stern expression. 'I don't want you to tell Adam what we were talking about earlier.'

130

'That was our own private conversation.'

'Good. So you'll tell no one?'

'It was between you and me and the Lord.'

'That's good. Thank you.' She felt she should do something to demonstrate that they had made an agreement so she shook his hand. He blushed. 'And the second thing is I'd like a lift with you when you go.'

The blush became an embarrassed flush. 'Well, I was planning to leave this afternoon.'

'That's OK.'

'But where are you going?'

'Where are you going?'

'Well I'm heading for Oodnadatta. You want to go to William Creek I presume, and Adam's going there tomorrow to take Josef to the train ... Nellie, I'm confused. Are you going shopping? Do you want me to drop you into town so Adam can pick you up tomorrow?'

'I just want to go away. If you're heading for Oodnadatta, that's fine.'

'What are you doing?'

'I'm doing what we both agreed was the best thing for me to do.'

'But surely you'll want to discuss it with Adam and then the two of you can work out what would be best.'

'No.' She shook her head. 'I've been thinking about it. There are things you don't understand, Roger, which is why I've got to do it this way.'

'He will be terribly hurt, if you just rush off like this.'

'It's best, believe me. Will you give me a lift?'

He wiped his lips. 'What if I don't?'

'Then I'll walk.'

He chewed a knuckle. 'This is terrible.'

'It is best. And you promised not to tell Adam so don't go running to him and have him try to stop me.'

He coughed and straightened. 'Look me in the eye please, Nellie,' he said and, surprised, she did as he asked. 'Answer me one question: you were talking hypothetically this morning – do you know what that means?'

'No, but go on.'

'Well it doesn't matter. You were talking about a baby. Nellie, are you pregnant?'

She dropped her eyes.

'Look at me.'

She lifted her head and breathed deeply. 'Yes.'

Roger sighed and put his arm on her shoulder.

'You won't tell Adam?' she asked, her voice thin with anxiety.

'He doesn't know?'

She shook her head. 'You mustn't tell him. Promise me you won't.'

'You should tell him.' He tried to look her in the eye but she had lowered her face.

'Not yet,' she said.

'But he should be told. This is his child too.'

'I'll let him know when the time's right. I don't want you telling him.'

'No. I understand.' He fidgeted nervously.

'You promise?'

'Very well,' he whispered.

'And you'll take me with you?'

'Have you seen a doctor?'

'No.'

'There's a hospital at Oodnadatta. I'll take you there.'

'You'll tell no one? About the baby, I mean.'

'No. Not if you don't want me to.'

'I don't want anyone to know.' She gripped his hand. 'Roger, I just want Adam to keep his daughter.'

'And what about your child? Yours and Adam's?'

She shook her head sadly. 'I don't know what else to do. If anyone finds out I'm having a baby, the court will hear about it and then Adam will have Cassie taken away from him, and if I stay here with him he'll lose her anyhow, even if I wasn't having a kid, so there's nothing else for it. I just have to go.'

Roger stepped away from her and put both hands on his hips. He gazed at the sky, his face ravaged by worry. 'Nellie, this is all so dreadful. This is going to cause you all so much pain and suffering.'

'It's best for everyone,' she said softly.

'You will come back?'

'Someday.'

'But before you have the baby?'

Her head was bent forward and one hand covered her face. 'When the time's right. That's when I'll come back.'

Being a person in whom enthusiasm easily overwhelmed prudence, Josef continued to talk about enlisting during the journey back to the homestead. Adam rode as though not listening. The wind eased and gusting swirls of dust chased the storm. When the noise had gone, Josef urged his horse to move alongside the mare.

'Do you want me to talk to Nellie?' he said, his voice louder than it need have been.

Adam had removed his hat and was hitting it against his knee to shake out the dust. 'About what?' he asked, looking across in surprise.

'About joining up.'

'You?'

Adam's smile made Josef blink. His friend was laughing at him, just as his father did with that surprised expression of his whenever Josef came up with a good idea. 'Why not?' he said, his voice even louder. 'I get along with her pretty well, you know, and I reckon she'd listen to me.'

Adam put his hat back on and adjusted the brim. He liked it bent down at the front. 'Look Joe, I haven't made up my mind what to do about the army but when I do, *I'll* tell Nellie.'

'I just thought it might be easier if I did some of the groundwork for you.'

Again Adam smiled. He could imagine the damage Josef could do tilling unreceptive soil. 'Let me talk to her first, Joe.'

'But you never say anything.'

'Better than saying too much.'

Josef wondered if that were a barb to prick his ego but decided it was not. It was merely a piece of Adam's homespun philosophy: when in doubt, shut up. The man could be frustrating but he was rarely hurtful. 'So you don't want me to?'

'No.' Adam tapped the crown of the hat, nailing it in place. 'If you don't mind.'

'I just want to help.'

'You just want to get me in the army.'

Josef grinned. 'Well, you wouldn't want to miss out, would you?'

Only when they were nearing the last sand-hill before the homestead did Josef speak again.

'What do you think Nellie would do if you went off to the war?'

Adam's eyes fired a warning shot to halt the conversation.

'I'm only saying "if",' Josef said, raising a hand in defence. 'I'm not saying you should join up or anything like that. I was merely asking a hypothetical question.'

'I followed all that until the last bit.'

'I was merely asking a "what if" question. You know, supposing this happened?'

'And what's the word again?'

'Hypothetical.'

Adam nodded, filing it away. 'I think the war would soon be over if you wrote this Adolf Hitler a long letter using all your big words, because it would take him so long to work out what you were talking about that he wouldn't have time to fight.'

'Very funny. You just don't appreciate an educated man.'

'Oh I appreciate you. I just don't understand you.'

'I get the feeling you're trying to dodge the question.'

'What question?'

'You're either very smart or very dumb and I can't work out which.' He took off his hat and pretended to throw it at Adam. 'About Nellie, knucklehead! What would she do?'

Adam thought for a few seconds. 'She'd stay and look after Cassie, I suppose.'

'You two should get married.'

Adam looked at him keenly. 'Is that what you've been getting around to?'

'What do you mean?'

'I know you too well, Mr Hoffman. You start a conversation and talk about something but you always get to the point sooner or later, when you've worn the other person down.'

'And you never give a direct answer. Why don't you and Nellie get married?'

'Maybe we will.'

Josef's horse shied away from something on the ground and he took some time to control it and bring it back alongside the mare.

'This animal's as frisky as hell,' he complained, tugging the reins.

'It knows who's in charge, and it's not the rider,' Adam said, his face set in sober judgement of the horse.

'Well let's not talk about horses. You said maybe you'd get married.'

Adam nodded.

'Have you discussed this with Nellie?'

'Not a lot.'

'Knowing you, you probably haven't said a word. You probably expect the poor woman to read your mind.'

Adam pulled at the brim of his hat.

'Does she want to get married?'

Adam shrugged.

'What's that mean?'

'It means who knows, but I reckon so.'

'She really loves you. Anyone can see that. She dotes on you.'

Adam narrowed his eyes.

'It means she adores you,' Josef interpreted. 'She'd do anything for you. You love her?'

Again Adam shrugged.

'Who knows, but you reckon so. Jesus, Adam, having a serious conversation with you is about as useful as talking to a gum tree.' He stood in the stirrups and adjusted his pants which were chafing

134

his thighs. 'If you and Nellie get married it would solve a lot of your problems.'

'Do you reckon?'

'Absolutely. The locals would stop talking and the judge would be impressed if he knew you had a wife who was looking after the kid.'

'Think so?'

'Sure. So why don't you marry the woman?'

Adam rubbed his nose. 'We're too busy looking after a guest who's causing us a lot of trouble.'

'What's he do?'

'Talks too much.'

'You will ask her, though?'

Adam nodded. 'I intend to.'

'When?'

'Soon. Maybe when we're alone.'

'After I'm gone?'

'Probably on the way back in the car.'

Josef smiled broadly. 'Tomorrow. Great. Why not do it on the way to the station?'

'I'll do it on my own and without some smart alec in the back cracking jokes and using big words.'

'Let me be the first to extend my heartiest and most sincere felicitations,' Josef said, and leaning towards the other man, held out his hand.

'I don't know what you said, but thanks.' Adam shook his hand.

They rode around the end of the sand-hill. The blades of the windmill near the house were in sight.

Nellie was standing at the door. Roger's car was nearby. All his gear was packed.

'Roger has to go,' Nellie said. 'He's been waiting. You're late.'

'It took longer than we thought,' Adam said, perplexed by her aggressive tone. 'We got caught in the wind storm.'

'Can I talk to you?' Nellie said, barring the door to prevent him entering. 'But away from here.' She walked from the house. Mystified, Adam followed.

'What's happened?' he asked.

'Nothing. There's just something I have to ask.' Beyond the car and out of sight of the others she turned, arms tightly folded across her chest. 'I've been doing a lot of thinking while you were gone.'

Adam stopped two paces from her. He too folded his arms, unconsciously mimicking her defensive stance but he cocked his head to one side, curious about what she had to say and sensing it would not be pleasant. He had seen her this way before. It usually meant she was angry. It always meant she was about to deliver a pronouncement and had little intention of giving equal time to any reply.

'Why so serious?' he said, brow crinkled in worry.

She ignored the question. 'Are you going to stay around for the court case?'

'Nellie, we've talked about this.'

Her eyes were closed and her head nodded rapidly, as though she were fending off each word. 'Just answer me, please.'

'We decided what to do. Joe's going to talk to his solicitor.'

'*You* decided. And I don't trust solicitors. Or police, or anyone to do with the law. Neither should you, after the things that have happened to you.'

He transferred weight from one leg to the other. 'What are you trying to say?'

'That if you wait around for those court people to decide who owns Cassie, you'll lose her. And you'll deserve to.'

'What brought this on?'

'Don't talk to me as though I'm sick or something.' She turned her head to one side but kept her eyes closed. 'I asked you if you were going to sit around like a dummy and wait for them to take Cassie away from you.'

He moved towards her. She looked quickly at him and stepped back. 'I suppose what you're trying to say is no, you're not moving anywhere,' she said, holding one hand aloft to indicate he should come no closer.

'We decided to wait and see what the solicitor said,' he repeated, his voice weary. He was growing tired of people repeatedly bringing up the same subjects. If it wasn't Nellie talking about running away with Cassie, it was Josef urging him to buy a property down south or join the army.

'You always wait,' she said.

'No, I don't, but I think we should this time.' Again he stepped closer and again she moved back. 'Nellie, why have you changed your mind?'

'I never changed my mind,' she snapped, looking directly at him. 'I've always known what was the best thing to do. Always. And that was to go, and to get out of here before they come and take Cassie away. That's what I've always said and that's what we should do. I've been thinking about it and I know it's right.'

He shook his head sadly.

'Anyhow,' she continued, 'I need an answer. A yes or no. Are we going to go and take Cassie – and keep Cassie – or are you going to hang around.'

136

'Oh Jesus, Nellie.'

'Don't start crying.'

He was offended. 'I'm not crying. I'm just –'

'Well don't go on with all your bullshit. Just give me a yes or no, for Christsakes.'

'Nellie, what's going on?'

'Yes or no.' She pounded the air with both fists.

'No. I'm not going. Not now – you know that.'

'Good. See you later then.' She began to walk back to the house.

'What are you talking about?'

'I'm talking about not living with a man who won't do the right thing to keep his own kid.'

He hadn't moved but she was still walking. 'It's not the right thing,' he shouted after her.

'You're just a spineless no-hoper,' she called, half turning her head, but not stopping. She entered the house.

Roger Montgomery had been at the shed, talking to Josef. He walked to Adam.

'She asked me to drive her to town,' he said quietly. He thought of saying 'to Oodnadatta' but he was worried by the pledge he had given Nellie and thought the fewer details he gave, the less trouble his involvement might cause.

'Why?' Adam asked limply. He was still staring at the open doorway.

'She seems very distressed.'

Adam turned back to Roger. 'Did you hear what she said?'

The minister blushed. 'Some of it, yes. She spoke very loudly.'

'I don't know why she's doing this.'

Roger pressed his hands together in the symbol of prayer and brought the tips of his fingers to his lips. 'I think she's doing it for you.'

Nellie emerged from the house. She carried a suitcase. She stopped near Adam. 'I was packed ready to go. I'd thought you'd say no, so I was prepared. Cassie's still asleep. Say goodbye to her for me will you?' She walked past Adam. 'Ready, Reverend?'

'You're just walking out, like this?' Adam said.

'Why not? I can see I'm only wasting my time by hanging around.' She turned on Roger. 'You said you were in a hurry. 'Let's go.' She climbed into the Ford's front passenger seat.

'Where are you going?'

She looked straight ahead, not answering Adam. Josef had walked from the shed.

'What's up?' he asked.

'Nellie's going.'

'Where?'

'To town.'

'Why?'

'Because I won't walk off the property right now.'

Josef turned to Nellie. 'You mean she's leaving?' He took a step towards the car. 'Oh Nellie, don't be silly. We were going to wait to hear what the solicitor advised, remember?'

'You can keep your mouth shut, Josef Hoffman,' she said, staring through the windscreen and ignoring Josef.

He turned to Adam. 'What brought this on?'

Adam raised his hands helplessly.

Josef moved closer to the car. 'Jesus, Nellie, it's one thing to lose your temper but it's another thing to run out like this.'

She concentrated on the view through the screen. 'I have not lost my temper and for once in your life you should keep your nose out of other people's business.'

Josef swung first to Adam and then back to Nellie. 'How long are you going for? And where are you going to?'

'Roger!' Nellie shouted. Both hands were on her lap. The fingers had resumed fighting.

Roger found Adam's hand and shook it. Adam was not looking at him. 'I'll make sure that she's all right,' the parson said.

Adam suddenly realized Roger was saying goodbye. 'I'll follow you into town,' he said, trying to get his brain working so that he could plan what he should do. 'She's likely to change her mind in another hour and then I'll bring her back.'

Nellie heard him. 'If you follow me and try to make me come back, I'll kill myself.' Although the car door was closed, she opened it and slammed it shut with great force. 'Can't you understand? I want to be on my own.'

Roger had kept his grip on Adam's hand. 'Just leave her be,' he advised. 'She's very upset. I'll make sure she's in safe hands.'

'But how will I know where she is or when she wants to come back?'

'Who said I'm coming back?' Nellie shouted.

'I'll be in touch,' Roger said softly. 'And I'm sorry. Believe me, I think she's doing this for you.' He got in and drove away, the car chased by an angry cloud of dust.

'What the hell was that all about?' Josef said, scratching his head. In the house, Cassie began to cry. The sound stimulated Adam into action.

'It doesn't make sense,' he shouted, and threw his hat on the ground. He gripped Josef's wrists, so strongly that his friend

138

flinched. 'See what's wrong with Cassie, will you?' Without waiting for an answer, he sprinted for the stockyard where the mare was now standing. He flung open the gate with such gusto that the mare reversed into a corner, feet dithering nervously. He had already removed the saddle and bridle but leaped on her bare back and, hands clutching the mane, urged her into a gallop.

Leaning forward so that he was close to the animal's neck he raced from the yard and sped off in pursuit of the distant cloud of dust.

Half a mile from the house, the track turned right to pass round a low sand-hill. There was a dip in the middle of the ridge. Adam turned the mare towards the dip and dug his heels into her flanks, spurring her on to meet the track on the other side before the car passed.

The horse floundered in the sand and, at the top, stumbled and almost threw the rider. Flung forward, Adam locked his arms around her neck and, his body and legs draped along the animal's body, hung on for the wild ride down the other side.

The car was approaching. Roger Montgomery stopped as the mare, with Adam jolting along her back, slid down to the road. The horse stopped suddenly. Adam fell on to the track. Roger leaned out, his face anxious, but Adam was on his feet. He ran limping to the car.

'Are you OK?' Roger called out.

Adam ignored him. He stopped in front of the car. 'You can't just go like this. We've got to talk.'

She turned away. 'We've done our talking.'

'Nellie, what you're doing doesn't make sense.'

'Not to you. It does to me. Roger,' she said, turning to the driver, 'can't we get moving?'

The young parson did not know what to say. He gripped the wheel tightly. 'He's in the way,' he said meekly.

'Well run him over,' she screamed.

'I can't do that.' He lifted one hand in protest and let it flutter helplessly back to the rim of the wheel.

She made a sound that could have been a sob or a growl and picked up the crank-handle, which Roger had left on the floor. She pushed open the door and holding the handle high, advanced on Adam. Tears streamed down her face.

'Can't you see I want to go away.' She swung at him and he stepped back. 'Now will you get out of the way?'

'Roger said you were doing this for me,' Adam said. 'Just explain that. I don't understand.'

'You don't understand nothing,' she shouted and swung again,

139

so hard she lost her grip on the long metal handle. It flew high over Adam and landed near the horse, which shyed away.

'Just leave me alone,' she sobbed. 'This is hard enough without you making it harder.'

'Please come back.'

'No. I wrote you a letter. Read it.' She got in the car. 'Go Roger. Now, or I'll find something else and next time I'll hit him.'

'Can I have the crank-handle please?' Roger asked. 'I can't start the car without it.' Adam retrieved the handle and passed it to him. 'Are you all right? You didn't hurt yourself when you fell?'

Eyes fixed on Nellie, Adam shook his head.

'I'll be in touch,' the parson said. 'Don't worry. I'll look after her.' He drove away, pulling off the track to pass the horse.

Adam watched them go. He brushed his trousers and then led the mare back to the homestead.

Inside the house, Adam found a note. It was printed in pencil.

> I am not coming back. You made your choice very clear. You love this rotten piece of land more than you love Cassie or me. Don't come after me. I won't be around.
>
> Nellie

That night, Adam made several decisions. He would go south with Josef and enlist. He would take Cassie to Tanunda and leave her in the care of Mrs Hoffman until the war was over. Jimmy and Stella could run the property in his absence.

He slept badly that night. Many times he thought he heard the sound of Roger's car returning but it was always the wind or a bird or his imagination. There was one good thing about the situation. With him in the army and Josef's mother looking after Cassie, there was no chance of the court finding and taking his daughter from him.

Just before dawn, while tossing in a bed that was suddenly too large for him, he had a thought. What if he was killed? People died in wars. And if he was shot or blown up or gassed, any of the things he'd heard old soldiers from the Great War talk about, then he'd never see Cassie again. He couldn't recall ever thinking of dying before, not even when he was down the old shaft the time Jimmy lost his arm. He felt like crying; not for himself but for his daughter. She'd have no father and no mother. And Nellie wouldn't be there to look after her, as he'd always imagined she would be.

140

BOOK
T·W·O

Greece

O · N · E

February, 1943: near Sparta, Greece

The man sitting on a stool in a corner of the room was forty-two years of age but looked a good deal older. A boyhood fall from a tree had broken his spine with the result that his neck and head protruded, tortoise-like, from the curved shell of his shoulders. His hair was grey and unruly, as though it had been ruffled many times in the last hour. It had.

The lieutenant pacing the area in front of the stool took off his cap and used it to hit the top of the man's head. He spoke German. 'Ask him again.'

Near the far wall, a civilian sat on a chair, reversing it so that he could fold his arms across the back and rest his chin on his forearms. He was bored. 'What were you doing there?' he repeated in Greek.

'I've told you.' The man on the stool was watching the German officer who had stopped his pacing and was now warming himself near a small stove. The officer clasped both hands behind his back. His legs were wide apart and he was rocking backwards and forwards on his boots. They were beautiful boots. The man wondered how much they would bring if he could somehow get hold of them and sell them at the Wednesday market; provided, of course, the Germans were not there. 'I had been hunting for rabbits.'

'You were coming down the mountain,' the civilian said without bothering to translate. 'You had no rabbits. You had no snares, no traps, no rifle.'

'You and your German friends would let me carry a rifle?' The eyes, which supported bags as deep and wrinkled as old leather purses, spared the man a second of derision.

'How do you catch rabbits?'

'With traps.'

'Which you leave in the hills.'

'That's right.' The man rotated his tortoise head to look at the blank wall.

'What's he saying?' the officer asked, checking his watch.

The civilian replied in German. 'The same. Always the same story of rabbits.' He sat upright, stretching his back which was beginning to ache.

'And you think he might know where these men are?'

'He could have been seeing them.'

'You believe the stories?'

'My information is from a good source, normally very reliable.'

'How many soldiers are there?'

The civilian gripped the back of the chair. 'Who knows? My informant merely says he has heard these stories.'

'Of soldiers?'

'Yes.'

'But not how many?'

'No.'

The officer was a tall man with a long nose and short temper, which flared in bursts. He was becoming tired of this stubborn Greek with the hunched back. He strode to the man and ruffled his hair, ending, as always, with a hard, hurting push on the back of the skull.

'And how are the soldiers, eh?' He stepped back, holding his cap as a weapon, poised to strike.

The civilian waited until he was certain the officer had finished speaking, before translating.

The man repositioned himself on the stool. He put his hands on his knees to stop them shaking. 'What soldiers?'

The officer moved towards him but stopped, taking satisfaction from the way the man cringed.

He put on his cap and turned to the interpreter, presenting the victim of his inquisition with a close view of the back of his highly polished boots. Again he rocked from toes to heels.

'You know this man?'

'Yes,' the civilian answered. 'Not well, but I know him. He has an orchard.'

'Does he eat rabbit?'

'I don't know lieutenant.'

'Is he stupid?'

'Yes.' The man answered instantly. He wanted to go home and his village was three kilometres away.

The German went back to the stove. 'How stupid? Stupid enough to go hunting rabbits without carrying anything to catch rabbits with?' He cocked an eyebrow. 'Or stupid enough to try

144

carrying messages to British soldiers?'

'I don't know if they are British soldiers, lieutenant. My informant merely said soldiers, meaning enemy soldiers.'

'Our enemy?' The lieutenant's lips compressed to a fine line. 'Or your enemy?'

The man smiled. 'We have a common enemy.'

The German scratched an ear. 'I'll tell you what we will do. Tell him to go home. Tell him we believe him. Tell him the next time he gets a brace of rabbits, the first one comes to me. Tell him.' He waited for the message to be delivered. The man on the stool looked up and nodded.

'Good,' the lieutenant said. 'You have someone who could watch this man without arousing his suspicion?'

The civilian puffed his cheeks and let his eyes roll, as if moved by the pressure from below. 'It could be arranged, I suppose.'

'Good. Arrange it. Next time this stupid fruit grower goes hunting for rabbits, I want to find out where he goes.'

'He may *be* hunting rabbits.'

'Good. Then I will eat rabbit. But, my dear friend,' he said, wagging a finger at the man on the chair, 'if he is not after rabbit, we may find something far more interesting in the burrow he visits, eh?'

Despite his bent back, Dimitri Raftopoulos walked at a surprisingly rapid pace. For the last four months, he had been into the mountains at least three times a week and his legs, always the most efficient part of him, had grown even more powerful from the succession of punishing climbs. He stopped at the edge of the village and turned to make sure no one was following; it had become a habit. He saw a curtain flutter in the window of the last house but that was only the widow Mouskouri and she always watched people entering and leaving the village. He bowed. Even though she was hidden from sight, he knew she would be returning his greeting because custom demanded it and she could not control the reflexes of seventy years. When she thought about the way she had been tricked, she would be angry. Dimitri felt pleased. The German and that imported traitor of his had made him angry and he wanted to spread the emotion. With a final exaggerated wave – a wave that could have been a polite gesture and therefore would offend no one but the widow Mouskouri – he resumed walking.

The orchard was half a kilometre from the village. Light snow sprinkled the hills and from a distance his fruit trees could have been blackened sticks rising from the powdery ashes of a fire. How he longed for spring, when the hills would be green and the only

145

white would be from sunlight sparkling on the bleached and ancient rock outcrops. And how he longed for the Germans to go away.

The house was made of stone. It had been built by his grandfather's grandfather and, while small, it was a good house that should last for a few more generations. Water trickled from the roof, where the last of the previous night's snow was melting.

His wife was out the back, splitting firewood. Her face was anxious. 'There was trouble? You are late.'

He nodded once, enough to start a ripple across the folds of loose skin. 'There was a patrol. They stopped me on the hill.'

She readied the axe for the next blow.

'I told them I had been hunting rabbits.'

The axe struck and the split wood fell neatly on either side of the block. 'That was not a clever thing to say.'

'I was not feeling clever. I was tired and I was worried. The sick man is worse.'

She put another piece of wood on the block. 'You will have to get the American woman. They say she is good.'

'I will have to be careful, that is what I'll have to do.'

She struck twice before splitting the wood. One piece flew towards Dimitri. He picked it up and tossed it on the pile of firewood.

'They are suspicious?' she said, resting on the axe handle.

'The patrol was looking for something. The Germans are not so keen on exercise that they go for long walks when snow has been falling.' As he spoke, he shuffled around the chopping block, retrieving small pieces of wood that would be handy for kindling. 'Someone must have heard something and talked to the Germans.'

She made a clucking sound, agreeing with him and admonishing the traitor in one economical expression.

'So it is becoming dangerous to go into the mountains,' he said, head nodding and eyes searching for any more errant chips.

'How bad is the young man?'

'He needs attention. It is beyond me.'

'He will die?'

He shrugged, a curious move in which his shoulders seemed likely to engulf the protruding neck. 'They need some things within the next day. We will have to get the American woman and her medicines.'

She was still leaning on the axe, watching him intently.

'I think they will be observing me,' he said. 'The Germans will watch to see if I go anywhere.'

His wife put down the axe and wiped her hands on her ample hips. 'Do you want me to go to the woman?'

'Yes. Tell her it is urgent. She should come here at night and be prepared to leave before dawn. And you must take care. There are many soldiers in the area now.'

'Looking for these men?'

He shrugged. 'Is Alex inside?' He began to walk to the door.

'Yes.' And then she grew alarmed. 'Dimitri, he is too young.'

'He knows the way,' he said and went in the house.

It was more than four kilometres to the house where the American woman was staying. Dimitri's wife walked. She took their twelve-year-old daughter and a jar of preserved apricots. The girl went with her to make the scene a normal one; the apricots were in case they were questioned. They were visiting a friend in another town and the fruit was a gift.

There were many German soldiers in town, but none showed any interest in the poorly dressed woman clutching a jar of apricots, or the girl who held the woman's free hand.

The address Dimitri had given her was that of a friend who would then direct them to the house they sought. It was a big town, many times larger than the village. Not being familiar with the streets, she had to ask directions and took so long to find the friend's house that she was beginning to worry about the prospect of returning in the dark. If they were stopped after sunset, there would be awkward questions.

Dimitri's friend was a furniture maker. He answered the door to his workshop, holding a chisel as a robber wields a knife. He was in a foul mood.

'The wood is not good. You cannot get good wood these days.'

The woman clucked agreement. 'I have to see the American woman.'

The man raised the chisel and waggled it. 'Never call her that. Did Dimitri not warn you?'

She shook her head.

'She lives with her grandmother. No one knows she was born out of Greece. At least no one who will talk.' He stepped outside the building, being conscious that the conversation was arousing the curiosity of his apprentice. He pointed down the road as though giving directions. 'Call her Nina,' he whispered. 'Never mention that she is American or it could be very bad for her.'

He told her where Nina lived. 'It is behind me,' he said, still facing down the road and occasionally pointing. 'First go the other way and walk around the block. Do you understand?'

'But that is further and we have already walked a long way.'

'But it is safer. Better to walk around the block than walk into prison. And have me there in the next cell. Now off you go. I have much work to do.' The last words were spoken loudly and were for the benefit of the apprentice who had moved near the door.

'Thank you,' the woman said, seeing the lad. 'Up here and turn right.'

The address was above a bakery. Feeling foolish, because she was bearing a gift she did not intend to give, the woman climbed the steps, pushing her daughter ahead of her. She stopped, suddenly filled with doubt. What if Nina did not speak Greek? She was not sure what language Americans spoke but she knew it was not Greek. She had met a man who had been to America and he said no one had understood him.

Sensing her mother's doubt, the girl stopped, only to be prodded to the first floor. There were two doors. Dimitri's friend had said it was the door on the right. She knocked.

A young man opened the door. He was tall and slender and, she decided immediately, far too good looking for a man. She disliked 'pretty men'. They were all right as statues but poor value as workers or husbands. Better someone like Dimitri who was strong and ugly enough to be beyond the interest of another woman. This person appeared to be dressed for a journey. There was a cap and loose fitting jacket and the trousers were tucked into boots.

What should she say? She had not expected this. 'I was looking for someone else,' she said and tried to peer in the room. An arm barred the way. Such delicate hands. Could he be a homosexual? She had heard of such men but, as far as she knew, she had never seen one. People said Mrs Papadopolous' son who had gone to live in Athens slept with men but he was particularly ugly, with a nose even larger than his father's, so she found the rumour unlikely.

'Who was it you wanted to see?'

The woman licked her lips. 'A woman,' she said, shifting the jar to her other hand. 'I have something for her.'

'She is your friend?' There was something peculiar about the voice: husky, as though with a cold, and with a strange way of saying some words. Perhaps a visitor from the north, she thought, and said, 'Yes. Well, no, not exactly. She's a friend of my husband.'

'And who is your husband?'

'Dimitri Raftopoulos.'

'I don't know him.'

'Why should you?' she said, frowning.

A smile, revealing flawless teeth. They were too good to be natural, she decided. He must have money to afford teeth like that.

'How did you find this place?'

148

Had Dimitri's friend said the door to the right or the left? She looked at the other door.

'No one lives there.' Such a quiet voice. 'Who told you to come here?'

She pulled her daughter close to her. 'My husband.'

'Who is a stranger to me.'

'If you say so.' The girl gazed inquiringly at the man but her mother turned her head. She did not want her daughter looking at such types.

'Are you looking for Nina?'

Was it safe to mention her name? The furniture maker had said to avoid saying 'American woman,' not Nina. She nodded.

'Why didn't you say so? What's your name?'

'Eleni Raftopoulos.'

'I'm Nina.' The cap was removed and hair spilled around her ears.

Eleni Raftopoulos' eyes widened. 'I thought you were a man.'

'I find the dress convenient.' She signalled them to enter. 'Please come in and tell me why you've brought me those delicious apricots.'

She clutched them tightly. 'They were in case we were stopped by the soldiers. I was going to say I was bringing them to a friend.'

'Where do you live?'

'At Methera. It's about an hour and a half from here.'

'I know it. You walked?'

She nodded and eagerly accepted an invitation to sit.

'And you have to walk back and you need the jar in case you are stopped by the Germans on the way home?'

'Yes.' She smiled but retained her grip on the apricots.

'What a shame. They look delicious. How did you find me?'

'A friend of Dimitri's.'

'Were the soldiers interested in you?'

'No.'

'Anyone else?'

'No.'

Nina sat on a couch beneath a fading photograph of a man with a large moustache. 'My grandmother is out; we can talk freely. What do you want?'

'There is a sick man. My husband thinks he has pneumonia.'

'Why does he not see a doctor?'

'He cannot.'

'Is he in your village?'

'No.'

'I am not a doctor.'

'But you treat sick people.'

'Only when there is no one else.'

'There is no one else.'

Nina stretched a hand across her mouth and chin. The women looked at each other, eyes not wavering. There was a resemblance, Eleni Raftopoulos noted, between Nina and the man in the old photograph. The eyes and the forehead were the same.

'Mrs Raftopoulos, my father is a doctor and a very good one but that does not mean I know anything about medicine.'

'You helped young Stavros when he broke his leg.'

'People talk too much.'

The older woman looked around the room. There was more furniture than she had ever seen. She wished Dimitri had become a baker.

'My husband thinks the man might die.'

Nina sighed. 'I've never treated pneumonia.'

The other woman was silent.

'And he's not in Methera?'

She shook her head.

'And not in this town, of course?'

'No.' She was still shocked from having found a woman dressed as a man but relieved that her earlier fears were unfounded. 'I can trust you?'

'You came here for my help.'

'He's in the mountains.' Nina was leaning forward calming her, luring her into trust. 'He is a soldier. An Australian.'

'Oh my God. I didn't realize there were any left.' She stood. 'I thought they'd all been caught.'

The woman shook her head vigorously. 'There are two of them. They have been there all winter.'

'And one has pneumonia?'

'Dimitri thinks so.'

'Where are they?'

'We can show you but I cannot tell you. My husband says it is urgent.'

Nina faced the portrait and scratched her head. 'I can't go today or tomorrow. I could come the next day.'

'As soon as you can, please. My husband says they are good men.'

'How will I get there? On foot?'

'Yes. It is very rough where they are.'

'And we leave from your place?'

'It is being watched, or so we believe. My husband was questioned by the Germans today.'

150

Nina faced her. 'So what do we do?'

'You will go to a neighbour's house and wait there the night. Before dawn, my husband will come to the house and show you the way into the mountains. It is very cold so take your warmest clothes.'

'And how will I find your neighbour's house?'

The woman patted her daughter's head. 'The day after tomorrow, my daughter will return to the bakery. She will take you there.'

She stood and pressed the jar into Nina's hands.

'You'll need them,' Nina said. 'What if you're stopped and questioned?'

'I'll say I was delivering fruit to a friend.'

The woman and her daughter left. Nina went to the window and watched them enter the street below. There were mountains in the distance and their peaks were brilliant with the flash of sunlight on snow. For a few moments, she imagined she was back in Vermont. And then she thought: 'I am never going to get back to Vermont because this war is never going to end and people will continue to expect me to perform miracles and one of these days the Germans will catch me and put me up against a wall, like they did those three men a week ago; and all I want to do is go home and become a journalist and maybe marry Mark James if he isn't married already, and do nothing more adventurous in the mountains than go skiing.'

The sunlight left the peaks and the mountains became grey and forbidding. She thought of the Australian soldier with pneumonia, and wondered if he would survive another three days.

Alex Raftopoulos was nine. He shared a bed with his sister and younger brother. His father told the other two to get up and sit by the fire for a few minutes. They obeyed immediately; being allowed out of bed was unheard-of. Dimitri sat on the end of the mattress.

'You know the way?'

The boy nodded. He was thickset and had a shock of black hair which, every two weeks, his mother cut in a straight fringe.

'Remember, you must do as I showed you and walk through the stream. No matter how cold, you must stay in the water.'

'And when I get out, I will leave no footmarks.'

'Good.' Dimitri's forehead remained knotted with worry.

'You know the place?'

'Yes, Papa. It is a big rock.'

'And you will leave no marks anywhere?'

'No, Papa.'

151

'No broken sticks, no footmarks in the mud?'

'None, Papa.'

'There are many soldiers about. If you see any, hide. Do not move. If you become frightened come home.'

'I am not frightened.'

'I know, but don't be ashamed if you are. We are all frightened at some time. Now,' he said, standing, 'everything is packed. You know what to say?'

'Yes.'

'Good. I will wake you at four.' He walked towards the fireplace. 'What are you two still doing out of bed?'

The children laughed, knowing he was joking. Like a sheepdog mustering a flock, he drove them back to bed and tucked them in. He kissed his daughter and the little boy. Alex was too old to be kissed but that night, Dimitri kissed him too.

Alex was ready to leave at four-fifteen. His father helped him put on the haversack and then wrapped his own scarf around the boy's neck. 'It is warm and it is dark,' Dimitri said. 'If you see any soldiers, lie low and pull the scarf up over your face. The dark colour will hide your pale face.'

'But then I won't be able to see.'

'Not over your eyes,' he snapped. 'Only over your nose and mouth.' He pulled the scarf roughly into place to demonstrate. Dimitri had been lecturing the boy for the full quarter hour, and his concern at sending his first-born son on a dangerous mission was erupting in flashes of irritation. He should be going himself, but someone might come to the house to check on his whereabouts or he might be wanted for more questioning, or a soldier might recognize his misshapen and distinctive outline from a distance and then there would be terrible trouble for everyone. Alex passed through the forest as the breeze rustles leaves. He was good, better, at blending into the background than his father, and he was clever. More important, he could be trusted. But he was young and he was Dimitri's favoured son and the worry and the guilt brought on an uncommon bout of irascibility.

The boy's mother fussed in the background. She had a small bag of food for him. She tugged at the loose end of Dimitri's shirt. 'Do you think this is wise?' she murmured, and the boy turned concerned eyes on her. He was longing to go, to prove his ability and independence, and he was suddenly fearful that his mother might persuade his father to cancel the mission. The man was dominant outside the house, but within the walls of the old stone building, the mother often got her way.

'We have no choice,' Dimitri growled and the boy nodded agreement. 'They need food and they should be told the American woman is coming or else the strong one might kill her in one of his traps.'

'Do you know the way in?' the woman asked, suddenly confronted by a fresh worry.

'Of course he does,' Dimitri said quickly. He ruffled the boy's hair and pulled the scarf from his nose. 'Don't wear it like that in the house. Save it for when you go outside.'

'Yes, Papa.' The boy smiled, content at the father's victory.

It was cold outside. There was no hint of dawn, no faint glow to trace the horizon or frame a building against the sky. A blackness clogged the air, as thick as drapes mourning the passing of light. There was a mist, too. Alex felt it against his bare cheeks and nose and he lifted his father's scarf to shut out the biting cold. He put on a cap, and pulled it down over his eyebrows.

It would take him at least three hours to get to the cave. He would move across the fields in the darkness and reach the forest before the sun rose. There he would wait for the first light and then follow the stream into the mountains. He knew the way. He had made the journey several times with his father, although that had been before the extra soldiers came into the area.

Once he heard a noise, like metal striking metal. He stopped and tugged the cap lower until it almost met the scarf. The sound had been faint but could have carried a long way, maybe from the farmhouse of Kostas Stefanis. A kettle being rattled? He stood still and counted to ten, finding the intense darkness so disorienting that he almost lost his balance. There was no further noise, no faint light in a window, no torch flashing, no voice shouting a challenge.

A dog barked, but it was a lonely, distant sound.

He resumed walking. He made slow progress, feeling his way through the bushes that lined the goat track through the depression in the north-eastern corner of the field and stopping once when he heard the rustle of moving animals. He was frightened at first but then remembered that this was where the herd of goats always assembled at dawn, to catch the first rays of warm sunlight away from the hindrance of trees and shadows. He thought of imitating their bleat. He made good goat noises but the sound would carry and if he disturbed the goats, the farmer might come and then there'd be trouble. Besides, there was no point; he wouldn't be able to see the goats and he only bleated for the pleasure of making them cock their heads, all in unison, and stare at him with their strange post-box eyes.

153

On the boundary of the field was an old stone wall that Nicholas Kaleides' grandfather had built on top of the ruins of an older wall. The stones were set and cold. He groped for a low, safe place to climb. A loose stone rattled to the ground. There was a murmur of movement from the goats and he stayed astride the wall, fingers, knees, feet aching from the cold, awaiting the challenge.

He could hear the goats moving, their hides rubbing and hooves sloshing in the wet grass. They settled again and he slid down from the wall and tackled the rougher, rising ground that led to the forest.

It took him another half an hour to reach the first tree. Several times he became lost, not knowing from where he had come or in what direction he should head, but by climbing all the time, he finally reached the tree line and sat down. He ate from the food his mother had given him.

He wanted to sleep but it was too cold for sleep so he took the blanket from his pack and spread it over his shoulders. Hunched and tent-like, he awaited the dawn.

When the first wash of light greyed the eastern sky, Alex rose, repacked the blanket, and used a small branch to brush any footmarks from the ground. He moved deeper into the forest. He could hear noises now, strange, disembodied sounds that drifted up from the distant village: a rooster crowing, a truck engine being whirled into life, one dog barking and another taking up the challenge.

The land between the village and the forest was emerging from the night. Trees; the roofs of buildings; a curl of smoke; squares of snow on the grass; wisps of mist clinging to the low places; the depression that had been so difficult to cross; the goats huddled together; the old stone wall glinting with frost. All grew brighter, more distinct, more real as the sky brightened and a rosy glow spread across the sharp outline of the most distant hills. The sun should be up in another fifteen minutes. He rubbed his legs to warm the muscles and set off towards the stream.

There was a path into the mountains but his father always avoided that. Other people used it and so would the Germans.

He moved quietly, pausing every few minutes to listen for sounds. The birds were chorusing their dawn songs and once he heard a small animal running across a bed of dead leaves, but the noises were normal and friendly and he kept moving. He began to descend towards the gully where he would enter and follow the stream. It meant crossing a path, a track that climbed to a saddle between two peaks where there was a long grassy meadow and where some of the farmers took their cattle in spring. He was within fifty paces of the path when he heard the noise. It was someone

154

talking, and saying words he didn't understand. Then he heard boots scuffing stony ground.

Alex was in an open place, a small clearing covered with rocks and edged by low bushes. He thought of darting for the shelter of the nearest big bush but it was too far, and his father had said it was better to stay low and remain still rather than move towards shelter because people saw moving objects clearly, so he sank to the ground, lowering his body as gently and quietly as he could. He lay face down. A sharp rock pressed against his chin and it hurt, but he didn't move.

Four German soldiers appeared, moving down the path. *Down* the path. They must have been camped up in the mountains, maybe on the meadow at the place where the small waterfall tumbled into the valley. They had rifles slung casually over their shoulders. The man at the back was talking. The others were smiling.

They walked past the place where he lay, as silent as the stones around him. One of the soldiers laughed and another spoke sharply and they were all silent. Their boots crunched on the rocky path. The sounds faded.

Only when they were gone and the few sounds reaching him were the twittering of birds and the faint gurgling of water from the stream did Alex move. He breathed heavily and rolled on his side and felt frightened. Had they seen him, they would have chased him and caught him and beaten him. He was not frightened of being shot but he was frightened of being beaten. His best friend had told him that a man his father knew had been taken into the hall and beaten with sticks and then had his fingernails torn out. Alex could not stand the thought of having his nails pulled out.

With his hands under his armpits he stood up and, hearing nothing, ran across the track and down into the bushes on the other side. Safely in their cover, he sat down again, breathing heavily as though he'd run a long distance. He had seen German soldiers before and even waved to one who had smiled at him but that was in the village where there were many people. Out here, he was on his own and the soldiers were the hunters and he was the hunted and they were the enemy. Quite suddenly, he knew what enemy meant. It meant a man would kill another person no matter how nice that person was and no matter whether he waved to you in town or not, because that person was your enemy and when you were on different sides in war, you killed the other side. He was on the other side to the Germans so they would kill him. But first they would tear out his fingernails because that was what they did to the people they caught. Why, he had no idea but he had known boys who caught frogs and cut their legs off and put salt on the wounds to

155

make them squirm even more, so it seemed to be the rule that if you caught something or someone you were entitled to hurt it before you killed it.

He began to shake. It was not fear but the growing realization of how lucky he had been not to be seen by the Germans. Every time he had climbed the mountain with his father there had been no soldiers. It had been a great, adventurous game. Even when he had thought of going on his own, he had presumed he would see no Germans up here. If he did, he would do what he had done when he was only little and playing games with his father in these woods. He would hide behind dense bushes or climb high in the branches of a tree, watching the stupid soldiers who could not possibly see him.

But he had been caught on a stony plain with nothing to hide behind and he had not thought it would be like that.

He would take off the pack and hide it in the bushes and go home. He could run faster, hide better, without the pack.

Alex had begun to slip off one shoulder strap when he heard a noise. It was faint but he listened, not moving. Another noise. A sharp rasping sound. A boot striking stones. Gently parting the branches of the bush covering him, he peered towards the path. Two more German soldiers were walking down the hill. They were not talking. The leading man had his rifle in his hands and was looking around him, as though searching for something.

They were level with Alex when the second soldier stopped and pointed. At first, the boy thought he was pointing at him but the man held out his hand again, and he was aiming to one side of the hiding place. The soldiers said something to each other, speaking in low voices, and the first man left the track and walked down the slope. The other stayed where he was, unslinging his rifle and looking about him.

The leading soldier detoured around the clump of bushes in which Alex was hiding and walked to the edge of the steep slope that led to the stream. Alex watched him, moving only his eyes.

The man found an animal track that led down the bank. He called to the other soldier and, without waiting for his companion to join him, slid down the track and out of sight.

The other man walked by, still looking around him. He reached the top of the embankment and said something, and laughed. He turned his back on the stream, slipped the rifle's sling over his shoulder, and lit a cigarette.

Alex was in an uncomfortable position but dared not move. He could see the soldier clearly, a figure mottled by leaves but distinct and close. Could he see Alex, if he looked this way? And what was

156

the other man doing? Had he found the tracks made by his father on the last journey?

There was the sound of a man breaking wind. The soldier at the top of the bank said something and laughed. The reply was a longer and riper blast of escaping gas. The soldier near Alex laughed again and walked away from the stream. He stopped near the bushes and turned his back towards the boy. He called out, and the man down by the stream replied in a strained voice.

Alex had never thought of a soldier taking off his trousers, let alone defecating when he was on patrol. The idea was ludicrous. What sort of monsters were these, who did things boys did?

After a few minutes, the first soldier reappeared, adjusting his belt. The other soldier threw down his cigarette. The two men climbed to the path and resumed the journey.

Alex stayed in the bushes for some time. So they had not seen him, which meant they were not looking for him, and they were certainly not skilled hunters. And they farted.

They were humans, and inferior ones at that. He felt his confidence flooding back. He could outwit stupid soldiers who farted besides creeks and stood with their backs to him while they smoked cigarettes. What a story he would have to tell his father! But what was the polite word for 'shit'? That was a problem.

He was greatly tempted to walk down the track and to examine the soldier's droppings. He had little doubt that they would be normal but his curiosity was great. Greater still, however, was the realization that any other soldier who scrambled down the same track might see a smaller set of footprints and grow suspicious, so he kept to his original plan and headed for the old tree that had been struck by lightning. The trunk had split, so that one half sloped down and across the water.

He followed the bank to the tree, walked down the jagged face of the trunk with the precision of a tight rope artist and, when he was above the far bank, lowered himself into the water.

The stream was shallow, with a rocky bed over which the running water curled and hissed. It was widest at the point where the fallen tree formed a bridge but for most of its passage through the valley it narrowed to little more than a trench. Here the banks were a mass of tall grass and bushes that entwined and dripped dew and shadows.

Alex's boots were high and laced to the top. He had smeared the leather with grease to make them waterproof but water trickled in at the calves, and soon his ankles and feet ached with cold and then went numb. He moved slowly, searching for a footing and taking care to minimize the noise he made. Occasionally, the bushes above

157

the stream parted and he could see a clear, cold sky but mostly he waded through a tunnel of mottled and muted shades.

He came to the boulder where he had to leave the water to begin the climb. He slithered up the great slab of rock and took off his boots and drained them of water. He listened for sounds but all he could hear, apart from the rush of the stream, was the distant thud of the waterfall. He squeezed his socks as dry as he could and let the water run across the marks he had made climbing from the stream. Satisfied that he had left no discernible trail, he put on his boots and began the ascent from the valley.

His father had put a dead bush across the start of the trail up to the cave. He lifted the bush, used it to sweep away any hint of a footprint, and put it back in place, taking care to set it naturally among the living bushes.

The climb was mainly over rocks. It was neither steep nor precarious, for the way Dimitri Raftopoulos had found up the mountain weaved between boulders and sharp outcrops in a steady zigzag. There was one long section where no trees or bushes grew but that side of the mountain was still in shadow and the rocks were large. Alex paused many times, to wipe away a footprint or to crouch behind a rock, to scan the valley and the far side of the mountain. There was snow on the uppermost ridge and the bright light drew sharp outlines around the trees and boulders that covered the slope.

The waterfall was still out of sight but he could see fine spray drifting in the rays of early sunlight. The sounds of water bouncing off the unseen cliff face and striking the hidden pool reached him in a series of shrill echoes.

Near the top, a row of trees stood against the raw whiteness of an escarpment that guarded the mountain like the ramparts of a ruined fortress. Alex crawled to the trees, just as his father had shown him. Only when he was behind the trunk of the first tree did he stand.

It was a quick walk along the ledge behind the trees. A natural path, flat and thickly carpeted with pine needles, ran to a great mound of fallen rocks which rose from a corner of the cliff face. Alex took care to follow a precise path. There was another way, an easier and more obvious path over the rubble but he knew the dangers of going that way, and followed the more difficult but safer route.

Beyond the fallen rocks, the cliff face turned sharply to the right. Here was a breathtaking view. The two peaks, the one to his right and the other far across the deep valley, were clearly in sight, each flashing mirrors from its cap of snow. The high grassy plain, where he thought the German soldiers might be camped, stretched between the mountains. A forest was on one side of the plain, its trees wet and green at this time of the day. Near the forest, the waterfall spilled down a series of steps until it splashed into the pool where the stream began its course through the valley.

Alex got down on his knees and crawled along a widening ledge to a place where the escarpment tucked into a narrow fold. A thick fuzz of vegetation guarded its entrance. Snow sprinkled the tops of low bushes, as delicate as icing sugar on small cakes. He went to one bush, shook the snow clear, lifted its lower branches and crawled through, to reach a small clearing. There he sat on his haunches, took off his pack, and whistled softly. He waited for an answering signal.

He felt a hand touch his shoulder and quivered with fright.

'Hello Alex,' a voice said in English.

The boy turned, still shaking but smiling with relief when he saw the big bearded man behind him.

'Hello Adam,' he said.

T·W·O

Dimitri Raftopoulos had found this place eight years before, while hunting. A small spring provided water. There were caves in the cliffs and the ground was riddled with holes and covered by a dense mat of low bush. The gap was only narrow but it ran deep under towering walls and folded behind the face of the escarpment in a way that made the opening difficult to distinguish from a distance. The sides were sheer and met at a point where the floor rose steeply, so that the effect was like looking at the inside of a great ship's bow. The walls and floor joined in a jumble of rocks. Some of the rocks were huge; great chipped boulders that were poised on the slope like battered bowling balls at the top of a chute.

Alex recalled with pride that only his father, of all the men in the valley, knew this place. It was here that he had led the Australian soldiers. There had been four then. Two had been shot when the group had tried to reach the coast and ran into a squad of Germans. The strong one, Adam, had carried his wounded companion back to the cave.

Adam led the way through the maze of bushes. He followed a specific trail to avoid the traps. There were many deep holes. Some had been covered by flimsy lids of sticks and grass, to hide deadly pits that would snare an intruder blundering through the tangled growth.

They talked but, as always, it was a strange conversation. The boy spoke no English other than 'hello', 'goodbye', 'yes', and 'no'. And he knew the names of the men: Adam, who was the powerful one with the big smile and the shock of fair hair that was so out of place in a land of dark men, and the sick one, Josef, who had been shot in the leg but had got better, only to go down with the coughing sickness.

Adam Ross had acquired some Greek during the eighteen months he had been in the country, and so they conversed in Greek, with the boy pouring out words and Adam stumbling to comprehend, each relying on signs and smiles to understand the other.

Near the end of the gap, they climbed a great slab of fallen rock. At the top was a ledge crested by bushes. Adam parted the bushes, waved Alex through, and followed him into the cave. The bushes closed behind them.

The cave had three chambers. The first was small but domed and high enough for a tall man to stand. Just inside the opening was a stack of rocks, sufficient to fill the opening. The second chamber was as vast as a cathedral. It was reached through an opening shaped like a human ear. Inside, the walls curved upwards into a region of perpetual darkness but down low, the chamber glistened with reflected light. Its sides were smooth and concave and streaked with tints of grey, giving the effect of being within some gigantic baroque pearl. The third chamber, reached by climbing a ledge that ran around part of the far wall, was high but no wider than a telephone box and partly filled with fallen stone. When it rained, water trickled over the debris, pulsing liquid echoes through the whole cave system. The roof of the third chamber tapered into a shaft that ran off at an angle, like a broken staircase, until it reached the surface of the mountain on a ridge behind the escarpment. The opening was shaded by rocks and large enough for a man to squeeze through. On several occasions, Adam had climbed to the top but that was before snow covered the area and partly sealed the exit.

Josef Hoffman was in the main cavern. He was near a wall, lying on a blanket spread over a thick layer of cut grass that had been put on the sandy floor. It was the driest and warmest part of the cave, well out of the breeze that sometimes swept through the entrance and into the third, flue-like chamber.

'Look who came today,' Adam said.

Josef raised himself on an elbow. 'G'day, Alex.'

The boy smiled shyly. He had never known Josef to be well and was a little fearful of him, as some children are of perpetual invalids.

'Where's your old man?'

'Your father,' Adam translated.

'He could not come,' the boy said, shaking his head vigorously. He gave the pack to Adam, who began removing items. 'The Germans stopped him yesterday and took him to the hall. They asked him questions. He was there for hours. They are watching him now. That is why he could not come.'

Josef lay back on the blanket, one arm under his head. 'What did he say?'

'Something about the Germans,' Adam said and Alex stared at him intently, willing the translation to be accurate. 'I think they must have nabbed old Dimitri.'

161

'Jesus Christ. Is he all right?' Josef struggled to rise again. He looked at the boy. 'Dimitri OK?'

The boy nodded, understanding the universal expression.

'Where is he?' Adam asked. 'At home?'

'Yes.'

'He's OK, he's at home,' he said to Josef and then in Greek: 'Not sick?' He didn't know the word for hurt. 'Father not sick?'

The boy smiled. 'Father OK,' he said and tapped his chest. 'I had to come, because they are watching my father.'

'Watching?' Adam repeated, not understanding.

The boy pointed to his eyes. 'The Germans watching ... my father.'

Josef was staring into the black vault above them. 'What's he saying?' he said wearily.

'I think the Germans are keeping an eye on Dimitri.' In Greek he said 'Germans' and pointed to his eyes and said 'father?'

The boy nodded.

'Yes. They're watching his dad. That's why he came on his own.'

'Good kid,' Josef raised a hand, as though giving benediction.

'They've sent up another blanket,' Adam said and put the new cover on his friend.

'You take it,' Josef said, trying to push it clear. 'You haven't got one.' He began to cough. Alex frowned and took a step back. His grandfather had coughed like that before he died.

'You have it today,' Adam said, pulling the blanket back in place. 'I'll take it off you tonight when it gets cold.'

'You would too, you bastard.' Josef pulled the blanket up to his chin. 'Thanks. Still snowing?'

'No. It's a nice day.'

'A doctor is coming,' Alex said.

'Doctor?' Adam said eagerly.

'Yes. A woman. My mother spoke to her yesterday. She will be here the day after tomorrow.' When he realized that was too complex, he said: 'Doctor. Woman doctor,' and waited for Adam to nod. 'Two days.' He held up two fingers.

'There'll be a doctor here in two days,' Adam said.

'Why, what's wrong with you?' Josef attempted a smile.

'Not me, mate. She's for you.'

'She?'

'The boy says it's a woman doctor.'

Josef coughed and the boy rummaged in the bag and took out a partly-used bottle of cough medicine that his mother had borrowed from a cousin.

When the spasm had finished, Josef drank some of the medicine

162

and said, 'Ask him if she's got big tits.'

'You sound as though you're getting better.'

'Go on, ask him.'

'You ask him.'

'Hey Alex,' Josef said, his eyes searching for the boy who had moved to fetch a lantern. He intended refilling it with the oil he had brought. 'This doctor, has she got . . .?' and his hands outlined large breasts on his own chest. The effort seemed to exhaust him.

Alex looked from Josef to Adam, seeking an explanation.

'The doctor,' Adam said. 'Is she good?' He could not think of more appropriate words.

Josef drew another simpler outline and the boy grinned.

'My mother says she is like a man.'

Adam translated.

Josef sighed. 'I bet she's like an ugly man, too.' He closed his eyes.

It was the afternoon of the next day. Two German soldiers arrived at the house of Dimitri Raftopoulos and escorted him to the hall.

He was taken to the room where he had been questioned but this time he was made to stand against a wall. The interpreter sat in a corner. He was reading papers in a folder. He did not speak. After thirty-seven minutes – Dimitri counted them on the clock on the wall opposite him – the tall lieutenant entered the room. He was wearing an overcoat and gloves. The civilian stood but the German indicated that he should sit again.

'Well,' the officer began with a suggestion of cheerfulness, 'have you two had a pleasant conversation?'

'We have not spoken,' the man said, well aware of the danger of having private conversations with another Greek in such a place.

'Not even a few pleasant words?'

'None.'

'How extraordinary.' He removed a glove. 'I thought you Greeks were compulsive talkers.'

The man said nothing.

'Ask him what he has done with my rabbits.'

'I beg your pardon?' The interpreter twisted the folder.

'My rabbits. Ask him where they are.'

The man stood, turned the chair and sat facing its back. 'Where are his rabbits?' he asked speaking Greek.

Dimitri had been wondering why he had been brought back. Had Alex been seen on his journey to or from the cave? That was his greatest fear. But the rabbits . . .

'Well?' the other Greek persisted. 'He wants his rabbits.'

The lieutenant had removed the second glove. He slapped them together. 'What did you say?' he demanded, and the civilian felt a prick of concern. Did the German understand the question?

'I said you wanted your rabbits.'

'I did not say "I want my rabbits.". I said "Where are my rabbits?". It is a very different thing.'

'Of course, lieutenant.' He asked the question.

'I have not caught any rabbits,' Dimitri said, both arms raised.

'He has not caught any rabbits, lieutenant.'

'Of course not,' the German said, walking close to Dimitri and using a glove to brush the man's cheek.

Dimitri blinked.

'I have not been out of the house.'

'He has not been out of the house, lieutenant.'

'I know that. And therefore he has not been hunting rabbits even though, only a few days ago, he was so passionately fond of rabbit that he climbed into the mountains, wanting to hunt and catch the animal with his bare hands. And since then, he has stayed home, not even leaving the house.' He brushed Dimitri's face once more. 'I find that very curious.'

'Do you want me to translate, lieutenant?'

The German waved a glove. 'Ask him why he has stayed at home.'

'I have been sick,' Dimitri answered and tapped his sunken chest.

'He has been sick.'

'Please offer him my sympathy. And ask if that is why his wife went to another person's house and asked for cough medicine.'

Dimitri thought it best to cough while the others were talking. When he heard the question, he coughed again, to give himself time to think. The devils. Their accursed spies were watching everyone, asking questions. When the war ended and the Germans left, he would throttle a few traitors and bury them in the hidden caves. Already, he had a list.

'I did not know she had borrowed it,' he said.

The German walked to the stove. 'She is a good woman, this wife of yours?'

Dimitri nodded when the question was put to him.

'She does a lot of things for you.'

He shrugged.

'She seems to leave the house quite a lot.'

Again he shrugged. 'Women have things to do. They like to talk.'

The lieutenant advanced and let a glove tickle Dimitri's nose. 'Why has your son not been to school?'

164

His face went white. The foul bastards. They have been checking on Alex. He swallowed awkwardly. 'I did not know,' he said, conscious of the long delay. 'The young rascal. Are you sure?'

The interpreter smiled. 'He asked if you were sure.'

'Oh we are sure. Did he not know?'

Dimitri shook his head. One advantage his broken back gave him was that he did not have to look at people, or have them peer directly into his eyes. 'He has never done this before,' he said, keeping his head well down. 'He has been a good boy. Smart, and he works hard.'

'He does things for you?'

Compose yourself, Dimitri thought, as the interpreter listened before posing the question. He knows nothing. He is trying to unsettle you. 'Yes,' he said, nodding. 'He does many jobs around the orchard. He came home at the usual time. I had no reason to suspect he had not been to school.' He felt safe with that addition because Alex, as planned, had come back from the cave at the same time as all the children were returning from school.

The officer lit a cigarette. 'What day are we talking about?' he said and blew smoke at the ceiling.

The dog of an interpreter would not have made a good card player, Dimitri decided, because he smiled as he asked the question and played his trump.

'Any day,' Dimitri snapped. 'He always leaves on time and comes home on time.'

'He does not carry messages for you ... as your wife does?'

'All wives carry tales,' he answered and enjoyed the frown on the German's face. The man might blame that turd on the chair for a clumsy piece of translation.

The German walked to the door. 'I have to go. We have people up in the mountains and there are things I must do. But I would still like to eat rabbit. Tell this man to catch me a rabbit tomorrow and have it here for my supper.' He paused to put on his gloves. 'Tell him to make sure his son is a good boy and goes to school. He should beat the boy if necessary. A little of the strap is a good thing.'

He left.

The man translated but as he talked, Dimitri was thinking about the American woman. Nina would already be on her way to the village and somehow, either he or Alex would have to show her the way to the cave.

Dimitri's daughter led Nina to the house of old Stavros. They arrived just after sunset, when the faded sky gave enough light to

165

outline the simple stone house where the widower lived, but not enough to reveal faces. Stavros was deaf. Dimitri had thought it safer to use someone who would not be tempted to ask questions.

Nina wore dark clothes: a thick woollen cap which could be rolled down to cover her ears, a heavy jacket, trousers of the sort fishermen wear and high boots. Stavros thought she was a man. That surprised him at first, but only briefly. He had expected a woman because that was what he thought Raftopoulos had said but he was always misunderstanding what people were trying to tell him. He gave the visitor a bowl of soup and some bread, and went to bed.

Nina had brought a sack which she put on the table. Then she took off her boots and lay on a couch in the corner. Stavros had indicated that she should sleep there. She pulled a single, thick blanket around her and then undid it to go and blow out the room's only lantern. Back on the couch, she fashioned a tight cocoon from the blanket. And thought.

Four years. This was supposed to be a pleasant visit to the land of her forefathers or whatever you called your maternal ancestors; a visit to meet her grandparents and develop her Greek and see the town where her mother was born. It had been her father's idea which was typical of a man who had never been to Europe but wanted his daughter to do all the things that had been denied him. 'Greece is the cradle of civilization. Get yourself some culture,' he had said, making that commodity appear to be a purchasable item. He always talked like that. He had made so much money he could buy anything. She had agreed, planning to spend the minimum time in Greece before heading for Paris and sampling as many of its degenerate pleasures as she could experience.

Two things had happened. She had fallen in love with Greece, and Europe had fallen apart.

Four years.

She would never get home. It was the dream. Six months ago she became convinced she would die young. God, she was getting to be more Greek every day, believing a stupid dream like that, but she had seen herself in the mountains with soldiers chasing her and she had tried to cross a river and a soldier had shot her. It had been so real. Since that dream, she had known she would die in this war. There was no point in feeling frightened. It was just fate and fate had decreed that twenty-three was long enough for her to live. What did it matter? There were millions dying and she was no better or worse than any of the others; there was no special reason for her to survive; no God-given gift she had to bestow on a waiting world that merited her being spared while masses were being

166

slaughtered. No, she would die and it would be a shame because she was curious about what was going to happen to the world in ten, twenty, or thirty years' time but it wasn't important. Her father would miss her terribly and say nothing and her mother would miss her and put a picture above the fireplace, the one of the three of them after her graduation, and she would never let her father forget it was his idea that they should send their only child to Greece.

It was cold, and the man was coming before dawn. She rolled on her side. Would tomorrow be the day? The German soldiers in pursuit, and the river to cross? And all for what? To give help she wasn't qualified to give to a man she had never met and who was probably beyond help. That was the trouble with this war. Everything was so pointless.

She had seen the bodies of the two Australian soldiers who had been shot last November. One had bright red hair. His head had been hanging over the back of the truck. Why? Why had some red-haired boy come to Greece in the first place as part of an army that was too small and had no chance from the outset? Why send red-headed boys from Australia to fight Germans in Greece?

She scarcely slept. She thought of many things during the cold night. She never considered not going up the mountain to help the sick man.

Dimitri entered the house a few minutes before four. He was carrying a lantern in one hand and had rabbit snares over the other arm. A cape covered his head and back, and shielded the lantern so that its light shone only to the front. Snow had been falling and the cape sparkled with white flakes. Nina, woken by the intrusion, had the sudden impression of a walking, speckled mushroom.

He gazed at her intently and bobbed his head up and down, spilling snow on the floor. Nina had the uncomfortable feeling he was assessing her, to decide whether she was up to the task ahead of them. She wriggled out of the blanket.

He put the lantern on the table and held the snares aloft.

'There is a German officer in the village who would like me to catch him a rabbit,' he said. 'So I must look as though I am trying to get him his dinner.'

'Why does he expect you to catch him a rabbit?' The woollen cap was off and she ran her fingers through her hair.

He removed the cape, spreading it across the stone floor. He sat at the table, hunched forward and head turned to one side so he could see her more clearly. His wife had said Nina looked like a man. In fact, he thought, she was a remarkably good-looking woman, if taller than was usual although it was difficult to tell how tall while she was seated. She was certainly slender and graceful in the way she moved her arms and hands.

He rubbed his chilled fingers together. 'The last time I returned from visiting my friends in the mountains, I had the bad luck to be seen by a patrol. I am not hard to distinguish.' He smiled. 'No one else in the village walks like me. So they questioned me and asked me where I had been and I said "hunting rabbits".'

'Your wife told me you had been taken in for questioning.' She put on the woollen cap, tucking her hair well out of sight.

He watched with undisguised curiosity. Now she did look like a man, but a child who had become an adult without losing his innocence. She returned his stare.

'Well,' he said, looking away, 'the lieutenant suggested I should bring him the next rabbit I caught.'

She pulled on a boot. 'There are many soldiers around?'

'They are everywhere.'

'Did they give you a hard time?'

He shrugged.

'Did they believe you? I mean about hunting rabbits.'

He toyed with the knob on the lantern, lowering the flame a little. 'They are watching me and my family.'

'So they didn't believe you.'

'They believe no one.'

Nina, still fitting the first boot, paused. 'Will they be watching you today?'

'They will not see me.' He gave her the faintest of smiles. 'We will be in the forest before the sun rises.'

'And then?'

'I may come down separately. Carrying a rabbit, of course.' His wrinkles set into an expression of cunning. 'The German thinks he is being very clever but he is, in fact, being very kind.'

She inclined her head, but concentrated on getting the boot over her thick sock.

'You see, he thinks he has stopped me from going where I want to go but, in fact, he has given me the perfect alibi for being in the hills.' The cunning became triumph. 'If I am stopped, I will merely say I am following the lieutenant's wishes. I have a perfect excuse.'

'And me?'

He fiddled with the lantern but said nothing.

'I gather I should not be seen?' First boot in place, she began on the second.

'You must be a ghost. You can move quietly?'

'You won't know I'm there.'

He smiled without looking at her. 'It is dangerous,' he said softly.

168

'What isn't these days?' She removed the boot to adjust the sock and started again. 'This sick man, the one we are going to see ... how is he?'

'My son saw him yesterday. He is alive. He is talking. He even tries to make jokes but that is the way of these people. But he must get better soon because he must leave. The Germans are searching the mountains. If he stays, he will be caught.'

'So I am to make him better?'

'If you can.'

'How long do they have?'

'Who knows. Maybe a few days.'

'Tell me,' she said, her lips tight with exertion, 'in these mountains we're going into ... is there a river?'

He picked up the cape and shook it, to dislodge the last of the snow. 'Yes.'

'And do we have to cross it?'

Slowly, he put the cape back over his shoulders. 'You are worried about your boots?'

'No.'

He gave a sly, sideways smile. 'That is good because they will get very wet. We have to walk some distance through the water.'

'Oh. Through the river?'

He nodded. 'Why do you ask?'

'No reason. I was merely wondering.' Quickly she moved to the table and picked up her pack. 'Well, I'm ready.'

T·H·R·E·E

At dawn, Adam went to the ledge where the pine trees grew. Lying on the soft needles between the second and third trees, where he had most cover, he searched for any signs of movement. Smoke was rising near the waterfall at the place where the soldiers were camped. Each morning, he had seen squads moving out to cover the other mountain and go down into the valley. He wondered when they would start on this, the shadowed side.

Thick cloud covered the far peak. From its slate-grey base trailed long swirls of falling snow. He had never seen snow before coming to Greece. On the way over on the ship, Josef had told him how warm it was going to be, and had gone on as though they were heading off on some sort of holiday escapade. Anywhere would have to be good after Egypt, Josef had said. Adam had liked Egypt. The land reminded him of home, only with people.

It would be the hottest time of the year at Kalinda. Jimmy would be worried about feed for the sheep and would probably be moving them from one watering place to another in search of grass and bluebush. How many lambs had the ewes had last spring? How many for the last three years? He tried making calculations, to help pass the time, but it was all speculation. The drought might have continued and there mightn't be an animal left alive. They could have perished or Jimmy might have sold them at rock-bottom prices. Or there could have been three good seasons and the ewes might have been dropping fat, healthy lambs by the hundreds. He might have become a rich man or remained a poor one. He had been away so long, and so much could have happened.

A sound drifted up to him. It was someone shouting an order. Very carefully, he scanned the far mountainside for any sign of movement. Then he inspected the lower slopes of the mountain, with their flanks of rocky soil and sparse peppering of bush. They reminded him of the worn hills in the Flinders Ranges. He hadn't been through that country for ten years, not since the time when he and Jimmy and Joe had gone there to keep away from people.

He thought about Mailey. It was a crazy world. For five years, he had avoided towns, and his mates had gone with him, because he had killed a man – violently but unintentionally and certainly in self-defence – and to have stayed around would have meant going to gaol or being hanged. And here he was, hiding on a mountain in Greece, because the same Government that would have hanged him was now wanting him to kill men. The more he killed, the better they would like it. Kill enough and they might give you a medal.

How long would he stay in hiding this time? Another five years? Already, he and Joe had been running from the Germans, fighting the occasional skirmish, killing them and seeing his mates killed, for more than a year. Now there were just the two of them.

He looked again for any sign of movement. The tracks where he had seen patrols in past days were empty; just faint, static scratches on the bleak slopes. He squirmed forward for a better view of the line of timber which followed the stream from the waterfall to the broad valley. Again, he could see no one, but he sensed that the sound had come from somewhere near the water, and he grew anxious, because that was the way Dimitri or Alex, whoever came, would bring the doctor.

The sun rose a little higher and snow stopped spilling from the cloud astride the far mountain top.

Adam closed his eyes and breathed in the cool, delicious air. He thought of Cassie. He always thought of her in the morning; she used to crawl into bed with him in the mornings. He was having terrible trouble remembering what she looked like. When he saw a Greek girl of about three, he would fantasize that she was Cassie and now, whenever he tried to conjure up an image of his daughter, he saw the face of a Greek child. Not that he really knew what she looked like. Not now. Cassie was nearly seven. My God, she'd been going to school for two years. Mrs Hoffman would be sending her off in the morning and meeting her in the afternoon when school was over and doing all the things mothers and fathers did. She had written to Josef a few times, saying what a good girl Cassie was, but the last letter had reached them in Cairo, two years ago.

He thought of Nellie and closed his eyes tightly. If only she was still at Kalinda ... but that was a regular lament, and a selfish one. She'd gone in a fit of temper. God knows why, but she was stubborn and had a temper that popped like a mortar and did just as much damage.

He often thought of Nellie at night, when he was less able to control his thoughts. It still hurt.

A bird soared overhead. How he longed to be at Kalinda,

171

watching the eagles circle high above the plains.

He looked down. Far below, ten men, German soldiers with helmets shining in the sun, were near the trees that lined the stream and they were advancing, line abreast, as though stalking prey.

Dimitri, up to his knees in the water and bent low beneath the overhanging bushes, turned and held up his hand. Obediently, she stopped. He signalled her to move closer.

When she was beside him, bending low to hear his words, he said, 'They are coming, this way. If they keep coming, they will certainly see us.' He felt her shake, and seized her wrist. 'Listen. This is what you must do.' He moved forward a step and risked a glance between two thick bushes. 'They are still a few minutes away. You must stay here, where the cover is thickest, and not move.'

'And you?' she whispered.

'I'm going to hunt rabbits.' He attempted a smile but his expression was too intense. He took her wrist again and she was surprised at the power in the grip. Because he was so misshapen, she had expected him to be weaker than other men.

'I am going back,' he said in a way that would accept no argument. His grip became even stronger and she winced with pain. 'I shall let them catch me. I shall tell them I am trying to catch a rabbit for their beloved leader. There will be a great discussion. All the soldiers will become involved.'

'And what do I do?' she asked and her voice trembled.

'You wait here until they go away.'

'And then you'll come back?'

He shook his head. 'You will go on alone.'

'But I don't know the way.'

He glanced towards the approaching soldiers. 'About two hundred metres further on there is a large rock. On the right-hand side. It is the biggest rock you will see. Get out of the water there.'

She blinked rapidly, then nodded.

'Above you on the mountain you will see a line of pine trees. They are very distinct. Climb to there.'

'And?'

'Wait there out of sight. The cave is close.'

'Should I call out when I get there?'

He was anxious to move and began jiggling with agitation. 'Do not move. There are traps. Wait. I will come, or send Alex.'

He left, leaving her crouching in the deepest shadows.

* * *

She saw him reach the first bend in the stream. He looked back, and then waded out of sight. A few moments later and to her astonishment, she heard him whistling a tune. He must have left the water because the sound came from somewhere to her left.

From the other side of the stream, several men shouted at once. Near her, a man began running but almost immediately slipped and fell. He swore in German, got up and crashed through bushes so close to her that she felt the air move as he passed, running parallel to the creek.

Dimitri was calling out. Despite her fear she couldn't help smiling because he was complaining that all the noise had frightened a rabbit, but he was shouting in Greek and the others were shouting in German.

Only twenty metres from her, a soldier blundered across the creek. She could hear others splashing through the water but they were out of sight.

Dimitri was making a lot of noise.

Other men were shouting but, gradually, only two voices could be heard: Dimitri's coarse growl, as he maintained his pretence of rage and a higher-pitched voice attempting to assert dominance.

The voices faded. They are taking him away, she thought, and began to shiver as a variety of thoughts bombarded her. The Germans are going away, so I am safe. They have Dimitri, so he is in danger. And I am left on my own.

For ten minutes, Nina stayed crouched beneath the overhanging bushes. Her back ached and her feet and ankles were numbed by the cold but she remained motionless, listening for the sounds of other soldiers. The Germans were cunning; they could have other men, following much later, looking for a second person.

It was possible that she and Dimitri had been seen much earlier, and that the Germans had been searching for two people. If so, they would surely look for her. That would make the dream come true. Crossing a river. Shot trying to run away. But then birds began to twitter and the only sound she could hear was the musical rush of the water and the cold became so intense she thought she might not be able to walk so, very slowly, she moved on. Her boots cut twin wakes in the running water. The noise she made seemed appalling, and every few steps she stopped, to listen for the sounds of pursuit. Once she heard a splash but it was only a lump of snow falling from the branch of a tree.

She reached the boulder and paused, uncertain as to whether this was the place where she was supposed to leave the water. Dimitri had said she should climb out on the biggest rock she could see, but there could be other, bigger rocks further on. He had said two hundred metres. She was not good at judging metres, even after four years in Europe but in any case she had no idea how far she had come. The boulder sloped upwards with its top projecting beyond the sheltering branches of a tree. She climbed into the sunlight. Above her was the mountain and high up on its side was a line of pine trees. Behind the trees rose a sheer cliff face. On top of the cliff lay snow, dripping at its lower edges like icing running from a cake. Dimitri had said she was to go to a line of trees. These were distinctive; tall and arranged in what seemed to be a straight line and growing from a rocky ledge.

She lay on the rock for a while, letting the sun warm her and flexing her toes to bring feeling back to her feet.

The climb was slow and difficult. She had no idea which way she should head and, finding no path, climbed straight up. Much of the way was over open ground. The soil was light and crusted with rocks and she knew her dark clothes, so perfect for the night, were now making her as obvious as a seal on ice. Scrawny bushes clung to the mountainside so she climbed from one scrap of vegetation to the next, pausing beside each one and blending into its shadow.

Several times she dislodged stones. When that happened, she pressed herself to the slope and waited for the rattle of the falling stone to trigger a challenge. Once she slipped and slid back several body lengths, skinning the palm of her hand as she clutched desperately for grip.

There was no challenge, no distant voice, no sign of another person.

Nearer the trees were several larger rocks. She rested in the shade cast by one, regaining her breath and wrapping a handkerchief around the bleeding hand. The climb had made her hot and she longed for a drink.

She stayed there fifteen minutes, feeling more secure beside the bulk of rock. She had no water and wondered how long she would have to wait at the trees for Dimitri or his son. Without them she could not find the cave. And he had said not to go on. There were traps. Traps? Man traps, rabbit traps? She took off the woollen cap, shook her hair, scratched her scalp and put the cap back on again, pulling it low over her eyes. There was nothing so distinctive through a pair of binoculars as a human face. Belatedly, she decided she should camouflage herself. Scooping up some damp earth, she rubbed it across her cheeks and chin and dabbed the tip of her nose. If her mother could see her now, she would faint with horror. Her mother, a simple Greek girl from a simple Greek town,

174

happened to possess a glorious singing voice and had gone to America seeking fame and fortune. She had found neither until marriage to a wealthy American surgeon gave her access to a fortune beyond anything she could have imagined. She hardly ever sang these days. These days, Nina thought; I mean until the beginning of 1939, when I last saw her.

What sort of traps?

She'd seen a bear trap once. That was a hideous device with metal jaws that could snap through an ankle.

Maybe she should wait here. Dimitri would have to come up this hill to reach the trees. Or would he? There might be another way and he would never find her. In any case, if a squad of Germans came up the hill and looked straight at the rock, they would see her. There was no cover; just shade and the reassuring mass behind her. No, she should continue to the trees. There might even be water. There had to be some moisture up there for so many trees to be growing. Even melted snow would be good.

She crawled around the rock and began the last part of the climb. It was steeper now but there were more rocks. Some were huge; great, flat-topped boulders that jutted from the stony soil. One gave her a vantage point from which she could spy on the valley below. There was still no sign of another person.

As the day warmed, she began to relax and plan the things she should do during her wait for Dimitri or the boy. She would clean her hand and put a proper dressing on it. She would search for water, taking care not to stray into any place where a trap could be hidden, and she would sleep. She had had only a few hours of restless sleep at the Stavros house, and she was tired from all the walking.

The last part of the climb was the most difficult. She clawed her way up, reaching the ledge at a point near the middle of the line of trees. Safely over the edge, she crawled to the nearest tree and sat against its trunk.

The view was magnificent. She could see the stream and the forest, and in the distance, the village blurred by smoke wisping from a dozen chimneys.

She took off the pack and searched for the things she needed to tend her scraped palm.

A rough hand covered her mouth. There was no question of screaming or struggling. The hand pulled her head sharply back. An arm wrapped itself around her body and jerked her to her feet, so roughly that the wind was forced from her lungs. She was carried behind the trees to the cliff face and flung to the ground. She got to her knees and looked up. A tall man, bearded and with hair so fair

175

it was almost white, stood over her.

'Who are you?' he said, in halting Greek.

She shook her head. The gesture was not meant to signify defiance. She had no breath and words were impossible.

He grabbed the collar of her jacket and pulled her to her feet. He pushed her against the rock.

'Why?' he said. That was all.

Why what? she thought but she still couldn't speak.

'Here,' he said, stabbing the air. 'Why here?' The hand stayed high, poised to strike.

She lifted a hand to guard her face. She shook her head. 'No,' she managed to gasp in Greek, as air once more flowed through her lungs. 'Please don't hit me. You've hurt me already. Don't hit me.'

His look told her he had not understood. 'My God,' she said, speaking to herself, 'I had to come to Greece to find a genuine Tarzan.'

He looked at her in astonishment. 'You speak English?'

She leaned forward, hands on her knees, breathing painfully. 'Who the hell are you, mister?'

He walked a few paces along the face of the cliff and returned with a long piece of wood with a sharpened end.

'Is that a spear?' she gasped.

He put it against her chest.

'Just tell me your name, mate.'

'I don't believe this.' Her voice was raspy and each bundle of words was separated by a wheeze of pain. 'I thought I was going to be shot ... by a German soldier crossing a river ... but here I am ... with some blond wildman ... about to run me through with a ...' She ran out of breath.

'With a sharp stick.' He finished the sentence for her and pressed the point against her jacket. 'Who are you and what are you doing here? And how come you speak English?'

'Who I am ... and what I'm doing here ... is none of your business.' She paused to get more air in her lungs. 'And I speak English ... because I do.'

He pulled the spear back a few inches.

'Are you a digger, mate?'

Her ribs were sore and she folded her arms across her chest. 'A what?'

'An Aussie. Australian.'

'Oh my God,' she said, letting her arms drop. 'Are you one of the Australians?'

He stepped back but kept the spear in place.

'And who are you?'

176

She removed the cap and ruffled her hair. 'The name's Nina.'

'A sheila!'

Puzzled, she tilted her head.

'A woman.'

'So I've been told.' She wiped her forehead and examined the mud on her fingers. 'And you're one of the Australians?'

He nodded.

She pushed her hair back. 'Do all Australians introduce themselves like that?'

He grinned and lowered the spear, slowly. 'Sorry. You're the doctor?'

'Not exactly. But I've been sent to help.' She smiled ruefully.'Let me guess. You're the one that's not sick?'

Another officer entered the room. Dimitri, legs and boots still wet, had expected the lieutenant and had rehearsed his protest. He had not expected a different man, and nervously fidgeted with his cap. The soldier near him stood to attention.

'Tell him to stand up straight,' the officer said. He was wearing a darker uniform than the others, and Dimitri felt even more apprehensive. He had heard of these special soldiers.

The interpreter did not bother to pass on the instruction. 'He cannot. He broke his spine many years ago and that is the way he stands.'

The officer sniffed and rubbed his palms briskly.

'I was trying to catch a rabbit for the lieutenant,' Dimitri said.

'Tell him to be quiet. He is only to speak in answer to my questions.' The officer paced to a vacant wall and stared up at its bare boards while the message was delivered. Then he turned to the soldier. 'What was he carrying when you intercepted him?'

'These, sir.' The soldier produced the snares.

'What else?'

'Nothing, sir.'

'No food?'

'No, sir.'

'No water, no drinks?'

'Nothing, sir.'

'No paper? No messages?'

'No, sir.'

'You searched him thoroughly?'

'Yes, sir.'

'He was alone?'

'Yes, sir.'

'You're sure?'

177

'Yes, sir.'

'You searched the area?'

The soldier, who had been staring resolutely ahead of him, allowed his tongue to moisten his lower lip. 'Yes, sir.'

The officer turned but looked at the interpreter, not Dimitri. 'I want to hear no more of this nonsense about trying to catch rabbits.' He paused to allow the interpreter to speak. 'Tell him his friend the lieutenant is no longer here and that I am not his friend, and that we know he has been carrying messages to British soldiers.'

The interpreter looked surprised. 'We do?'

'Just tell him,' the officer snapped.

'That is not true,' Dimitri answered. He stepped forward, but the soldier pushed him back. 'The lieutenant asked me to bring him a rabbit. Ask him.' He wagged his head at the other Greek.

'It's true,' the interpreter said.

'Will you stop joining in the conversation or would you rather I made you the subject of this interrogation?'

The man was silent.

'Ask him where the soldiers are.'

'I do not know of any British soldiers,' Dimitri answered.

'Why was he soaking wet?'

Dimitri waited. 'I fell in the water. I am not steady on my feet.' He held up a wavering hand, to indicate his poor balance. 'I stumble a great deal.'

The officer sniffed loudly. 'Why was he out before dawn?'

'Because that is when the rabbits are out.'

'Who was he with?'

'I was on my own.'

'How many soldiers are there?'

'I don't know anything about soldiers.'

The officer walked from the wall and stood in front of Dimitri. 'Would you like a cigarette?' He spoke in English and watched for a flicker of response.

Dimitri kept his head down. He knew a few words of English. This man was as cunning as a fox. 'I don't understand,' he answered in Greek, looking to the other man for assistance. The interpreter shrugged.

'How long have they been there?' the officer asked, again speaking English. When there was no response he repeated the question in German.

'Who?'

'The British soldiers you are in communication with.'

Dimitri shook his head.

178

'Does he know the penalty for helping these people?'

'I am not helping anyone.'

The interpreter held up his hand. 'Excuse me, sir, but when the lieutenant last questioned this man, he said he had been sick and couldn't leave his house. He doesn't look sick now.'

The officer looked from one Greek to the other, sniffing after each inspection. 'What was wrong with him?'

'He had a cold, sir. He was coughing.'

'And now he goes swimming at dawn.'

'Yes, sir.'

He walked to the heater, stood there briefly and returned. 'Tell him if we find British soldiers in the mountains in the next twenty-four hours, he and his family will be shot.' He waited. 'And tell him he has until tomorrow to tell me where they are.' Another pause for the translation. 'If he does that, his family will be spared.' He smiled. 'A bargain, an exchange. His family for the enemy soldiers.'

Dimitri shook his head sadly. 'I know nothing. I was just hunting rabbits.'

'Then he has nothing to fear.' The officer walked to the interpreter and tapped the back of his chair. 'Tell him he is to stay here. Tell him I will question him again tomorrow and if I do not get satisfactory answers, I will adopt more drastic measures.' He turned to the soldier, and spoke while the interpreter translated.

'I do not believe there was only one person out there. I think you found the decoy, not the quarry. Go back to the place where you found this man and search the area. There may be a place where he hides food or messages. There must be other tracks. You will find them. Do not return until you have found something.'

While Nina attended to Josef, Adam went back to his look-out on the ledge. To his dismay, he saw troops in two places. One lot was on the far mountain, but instead of following the usual track, the men had turned down what appeared to be a stony slope and were heading towards the base of the waterfall. He had never seen soldiers there. The other men were coming from the direction of the village. They had just walked from the first forest.

He stayed there a long time. The first group disappeared from sight in the dense growth near the waterfall. Occasionally, he heard voices: thin, disembodied, sounds that were fragments of a shout or a laugh, playing trills on the steady boom of the falling water. Once, there were many laughs. He hadn't thought of German soldiers laughing, but they were probably the same as Australians or anyone else. They bled when they were cut, died when they were shot, and laughed when someone did something funny or foolish. He wished

179

he could have seen whatever it was that caused so much laughter. Maybe the sergeant had fallen into the water. He thought of a few sergeants he would like to have seen backside up in a river. And he was envious of those men down there by the water. He felt caged, with only the ledge and the space near the cave as relatively safe territory. He longed to move away and be out in the open.

They might have to move very soon, he thought, looking towards the other soldiers. They were making for the little river. He didn't like that. Maybe Dimitri had talked.

Adam rolled the spear in his hand. Normal blokes or not, he would kill the Germans if they came up here because that was what war was all about. He didn't understand what caused wars, but he knew the simple rules. A lance-corporal who'd been the first to die on that awful day when the paratroopers had landed behind them, had put it succinctly. 'Kill the bastards before they kill you.'

So, since he had carried the wounded Josef back to the cave before the first snows of winter, he had dug or made many traps to maim or kill anyone who ventured up here. There was a pit at the entrance to the ledge. He had widened it from a natural fissure. The opening was narrow and covered with a mat of pine needles. The pit was deep enough to hold two men standing one on the other, but at the bottom he had placed a sharp and lethal rock. At the end of the ledge was the massive fall of rock and here he had created an obvious path which crossed a slab so precariously balanced that a man's weight would cause it to tip and pitch the intruder over the ledge. There were more pits in the area immediately before the cave. Only one safe path led to their shelter and he could protect that path with a cascade of stones from the pile at the end of the gap.

Not that he had any illusions about the result of a fight in which one side was armed with spears and stones and the other with rifles and grenades. With any luck, he and Josef would be away long before anyone reached their secluded eyrie. The work, however, had given him something to do and filled in the months of tedium.

The second group of soldiers reached the stream and spread along the bank closer to him. They were searching for something. Worried, he returned to the cave.

Nina was at the entrance.

'How's Joe?' he said.

'Sleeping.'

'Going to be all right?'

'I hope so.'

'I didn't know what to do for him.'

'You were looking after him fairly well, I'd say.'

180

He nodded and brushed his hair back. He put the spear on the ground.

Puzzled by the spear, she said, 'You've got a rifle inside.'

'This is quieter. And you don't need bullets.'

'Which you don't have?'

He held up four fingers.

'Just four?'

He nodded and glanced back down the gap. He's as nervous as a wild animal, she thought.

'You were gone a long time. I thought you weren't coming back.'

'Just seeing what's going on.' He sat beside her.

'And what is?'

'Lots of Jerries down there. It seems they're looking for something. Any idea what it might be?'

She shook her head. 'Where are they?'

'Near the little river. Where they caught Dimitri.' He had watched the whole episode and followed her climb to the ledge. 'Did you leave anything or drop anything?'

'No, I've got everything in my pack. Even Dimitri's lantern.'

He nodded but his teeth played with his lower lip.

'What are you thinking?' she asked when the silence had stretched beyond endurance.

'That they're looking for tracks.'

'Mine?'

'Perhaps. They might have guessed there were two of you. Or Dimitri might have talked.'

'You don't think he'd tell them?'

'No I don't. But they can do terrible things to make people talk.'

She rested her chin on her bent knees. 'So what should we do?'

'Nothing much.' He stroked his beard. He hadn't shaved for fifteen months, or had his hair cut except for the occasional rough trim with a sharp knife. 'I thought I might go back to the trees and keep an eye on things.'

'In case they come up the mountain?'

He nodded.

'Do you think they'll find my tracks?'

He lowered his head. Hair fell across his eyes. 'Do you think you left any?'

She couldn't see the upper half of his face. 'Well, I don't know.'

'You came up there like a wombat.'

She wrapped her arms around her knees. 'What's a wombat?'

'An animal. It's about the size of a pig and it's covered in hair and when it goes somewhere, it heads straight for the target and anything that gets in its way, it just knocks over.'

'Oh.' She gripped her knees more firmly. 'And I came up like that?'

'Straight up.'

'It was a very difficult climb.'

'I've never seen anyone come up that way before.'

She cleared her throat. 'So you think they'll find my trail.'

He pushed the hair from his face. 'It depends how good they are in the bush. If they're city boys, we should be all right.'

'And if they're not? If there's a hunter in the group?'

'We might have to move.'

'I don't think we can move your friend.'

'Then we'll have to get ready for them.'

Their eyes met and for several seconds neither spoke. He was a man, she thought, who was used to long silences. She found such types unsettling. If there was a gap in a conversation, she felt compelled to fill it.

'How long have you been here?'

'We came here first last autumn. We'd had a bit of a skirmish with the Jerries and were trying to get away and had the good luck to run into Dimitri.'

'Run into?'

'I think he came looking for us. There was quite a big dust-up.' He gestured with his thumb. 'Over there, on the other side of the other mountain. Dimitri heard the shooting and came looking for us. He's got a lot of guts, that bloke.'

'I only met him this morning.'

'He's a good bloke. Anyhow, he brought us here. We tried to leave just before winter but ran into trouble.'

She nodded. 'I heard about that. The man with the red hair?'

'Bluey Baker.' He looked at her with curiosity.

'I was in town when they, ah, brought him and the other man in.'

Adam was silent for a while. He pushed his hair back. 'I've got to get a hair cut,' he muttered.

'I'll do it for you.'

'Yeah?'

'If we have time.'

'We'll make time.'

She smiled, and there was another silence. 'How long are you going to stay here?'

'Only as long as it takes Joe to get better. I don't think we've got much time. The Germans are getting closer every day.'

'Where will you go?'

'To the coast. Dimitri has a friend with a fishing boat. He reckons he could take us to Egypt.'

182

'That's a long way in a little boat.'

'Better than staying here. A man feels like a mouse in a hole.'

They were facing a sheer cliff face. She bent forward, looking to the right and then left along the narrow gap.

'Is there another way out of here?'

With his thumb, he motioned towards the cave. 'Up the top. It's a fair climb. You go through the last cave.' Their eyes met again. 'We should get you out of here, shouldn't we?'

'I don't know the way back to town.'

He nodded, his brow knotted in thought. 'Dimitri said he'd come back for you?'

'Yes. Or he'd send his son.'

'They wouldn't make it at the moment, not with all those men down there.'

'They'd walk into a trap?'

He raised his eyebrows. 'If the soldiers stay down there.'

'When does Dimitri normally come up here?'

'Every few days. Always first thing in the morning.'

'So he won't come before tomorrow?'

Adam shook his head. 'If he comes even then. Let's hope he waits a while.'

'And in the meantime?'

'I'm going to see what they're doing. Want to come?'

'Can I? If I promise not to walk like a ... what's that animal's name?'

'Wombat.'

He picked up the spear. Crouching, to stay below the level of the bushes, he led her towards the ledge.

They lay on the fir needles, so close their shoulders touched. They could see the second group of soldiers climbing the mountain. Still near the stream, the men moved slowly, methodically, with heads down and rifles slung over their shoulders. As they watched, the soldiers all turned to the right.

'They're looking for tracks,' Adam said.

'Was that the way I came?'

'No. You were further over that way.' He pointed to the right laying his arm across hers. 'About a quarter of a mile.'

'What we need is a good snowstorm.'

'I've had enough snow for a while,' he said.

'I mean to cover my tracks.'

He looked at the sky. 'Could be lucky. There are plenty of big clouds.'

'Let's pray.'

'You pray.'
'Why me?'
'I don't know how.'
'Don't you have churches in Australia?'
'Plenty of them. I just wasn't taken to any.'
'Didn't your mother and father take you? Going to church is about the earliest thing I can remember.'
'Didn't have a mother.'

She wriggled to a more comfortable position. 'What do you Australians have instead of mothers?'

He ignored the question. He was watching the Germans who, having turned, had begun to climb again. Their movements were synchronized, obviously in obedience to shouted commands. If they maintained the present search pattern, they would reach the steepest part of the climb in another hour and be within stone throwing distance.

'Never had a mother, never went to church, never went to school,' he said quietly.

'Australia sounds a most unusual country.'

He didn't reply.

'Your mother's dead?' she asked.

'Yeah. Died when I was young.'

She didn't say she was sorry. She deplored people offering sympathy when they found out that someone they didn't know had died a long time ago. It sounded so ... American. We Americans gush a lot, she had decided soon after coming to Europe, and she had resolved never to gush. 'And you truly didn't go to school?'

He shook his head. 'I was never taught to read or write.'

'You'd be at home in the town where I'm staying,' she said. 'They're such simple folk they think I'm a doctor just because my father's a doctor.'

'And people there can't read or write?'

'Many of them. Maybe half the town.'

'Oh.' He felt pleased. He had always thought he was a rarity in modern society. 'Where do you come from?'

'America.'

He turned on his side. 'I've never met an American.'

She shook his hand. 'You have now. You're the first Australian I've met, so we're all square. By the way, what's your name?'

'Adam Ross.'

'Melina O'Sullivan.'

'I thought you said you were Nina?'

'I'm called Nina. Greek mother, American father.'

He peeped over the edge. 'They're climbing up again. There's

184

another lot over there.' He nodded to the right.

She wriggled forward. 'Where?'

'Near the waterfall. I can't see them now but they were there this morning. They must be checking the trees, along the river.'

'It's not really a river. It's not big enough.'

'It'd be a river where I came from.'

'Where's that?' She retreated from the edge.

'South Australia. In the outback.'

'What's that?'

'The bush. The donger. The back of beyond.'

'I'm none the wiser.'

'It's a long way from anywhere.'

'And you don't have many rivers?'

'It's desert country. A lot of sand and salt lakes. The nearest town's maybe five hundred miles away.' He scratched his forehead. 'You'll have to come and see us some day. If you've got a year or two to spare, I'll walk across the country with you.'

'How big is it?'

'Don't know exactly. From east to west though, it must be a good three thousand mile or so.'

'And you'll take me across?'

'If you've got the time, and I'm not doing anything else, and we get out of here.' A cold wind reached them. He looked up. 'You must have been praying. There's snow falling on the other mountain, and it's moving across this way. It's heavy too.'

Below them, the soldiers had begun to retreat towards the stream.

F·O·U·R

Heavy snow fell. They went back to the cave, ducking under the bushes and having snow trickle down their necks. It was warm inside the main chamber. They sat on the sandy floor near the ear-shaped entrance.

Josef still slept. He was covered by the new blanket. Leaning against the wall was a stack of spears. On the floor beside them were several bent pieces of wood. She picked up one.

'It's a boomerang,' Adam said, answering the question posed without words. 'Or it's supposed to be.'

'What's a boomerang?'

'It's something the aborigines use. A kind of weapon.'

'You brought it with you?'

'Made it here. It's a bit rough.'

She held it in the middle. 'What's it supposed to do?'

He took it from her and demonstrated the correct grip. 'It's a throwing stick. Supposed to come back to you.' With his free hand, he described a circle and twisted his forefinger to simulate the boomerang turning in flight.

'You used that against the Germans?'

He laughed. 'It's for ducks and things like that.'

'Why kill birds?'

'Because it beats starving.' He pretended to throw the stick. 'You toss it into the middle of a flock of ducks and it hits one and knocks it out of the sky. And if you miss, it comes back to you and you can have another go.'

'And who uses these in Australia?'

'The aborigines. Black fellas. I grew up with them.'

'Wild people?'

'They're only wild if you tread on their toes.' He grinned.

'And you were raised with them?'

'More or less. My dad and I used to roam around the country. That's why I never went to school.'

'But you learned how to throw a boomerang?'

'And a spear. It's good for hunting. Very quiet.' He put the boomerang back in place. 'My best mate's an aborigine. He works with me on the property.'

'What's that? A property?'

'The place I own. The land. I run sheep.'

An eyebrow rose. 'You have a ranch?'

He lifted a shoulder to match her raised eyebrow. 'I don't know what you call it. We call it a property. You know, a sheep station.'

'Ranch,' she said emphatically. 'How big?'

He ran his fingers through his beard. 'Bit over thirteen hundred square miles.'

'Square miles!'

He smiled. He had found even his mates in the infantry had been impressed.

'Are you sure you're not from Texas?'

'No.' He looked puzzled. 'I met a bloke from there once, though.'

'You said you hadn't met any Americans.'

'It's near the Queensland border.' His face crinkled in earnest lines. 'Not far from Goondiwindi. Never been there myself but this bloke reckoned it was a good town.'

She coughed. 'I think we must be talking about different Texases. Tell me about your best friend, the aborigine.'

Adam described Jimmy Kettle. He told Nina about the boxing troupe, about their days in Coober Pedy, about the accident that cost Jimmy his arm and about Kalinda. He left out Mailey and Heather.

'And your friend here, Joe. Did you meet in the army?'

'No,' he laughed. 'He's my other best friend.' Without saying any more, he got up, walked to the cave entrance and went out. He returned a few minutes later, brushing snow from his hair and shoulders.

'Still snowing,' he said. 'In fact, it's getting heavier. No sign of the soldiers.'

'So we're safe?'

'Tracks are all nicely covered.'

'That's good. No one can get up the mountain. I guess it also means no one can get down; specifically me. I'll tell you what. If I'm going to stay here a while' – she waited for him to nod acquiescence – 'then I might as well be useful. I'll cut your hair while you tell me about your other best friend.'

'Good,' he said and moved so that he sat with his back to her.

She waited. 'What would you like me to use?' she said eventually. 'A spear or a boomerang?'

187

He turned his head. 'I've got a knife.'

'No scissors?'

'Bit short of scissors. Haven't got a comb either.'

'Or a razor.'

'There used to be a barber shop next door,' he said, 'but he took one look at me and closed up.'

'Very funny.' She went to her pack and took out the first-aid fit. She extracted a tiny pair of scissors. 'Just as well I'm a woman and carry everything. Sit still. This may take some time.' She sat behind him, legs crossed, scissors in her right hand. 'How do you want it cut?'

'No blood and I'd like to be able to see. Otherwise, it's up to you.'

She cut his hair and he told her about Josef.

Eleni Raftopoulos put the children to bed early that night. She had been crying for most of the day, which had been embarrassing because six people had called at the house to tell her they had seen the Germans take Dimitri to the hall. The last woman had come only half an hour before sunset to say Dimitri was still in the hall and the Germans were not going to feed him until he told them where the British soldiers were hiding in the mountains. How the woman would know such things Eleni had no idea, but the news made her cry anew.

Alex could not sleep. She sat on his bed.

'I know what your father said but you are not to leave this house.'

'He said I was to bring the woman back if he couldn't,' Alex said.

'That was before the Germans caught him.'

'She will starve.'

'And they will shoot you. And stop arguing with me.'

The boy was silent for a few moments, but only a few. 'I'm not arguing, Mama. But Papa said the Germans might catch him and if they did I was to go and bring the woman doctor back.'

'It has all changed. Your father thought the Germans would not hold him for long but they have. And it is snowing and you would freeze out there.'

'The woman will freeze.'

'She will not. She looks like a man and is probably very strong.'

'Papa said if the Germans came, he would tell her to wait at the ledge with the row of trees. She will die there, out in the snow and with no food.'

'The Australian will find her.'

He ignored that remark. 'And if she goes looking for the cave,

188

she will either get caught in the rock trap or fall into a pit and die.'

Eleni grasped Alex by both shoulders. 'Better she die than you.' The boy was quiet. 'I've lost my husband. I'm not going to lose my son.'

He wriggled free. 'Papa will come back. He says the Germans are fools.'

'He's a fool if he thinks that.' She stood and shook a finger at him. 'You are not to leave this house. If your father does come back, he can go to the mountain or send someone else. You are not walking through that door, do you understand?'

He glared at her. 'What about the woman doctor?'

'She's a doctor. She can look after herself. Now you be quiet and go to sleep.'

Eleni went to the fire. Alex lay in bed, with the blanket pulled to his chin.

His father had been so clear, so insistent. If the Germans came, then his plan was to draw them away from the woman and she was to go on her own to the ledge where the trees grew. And Alex was to go there and take her to the cave to treat the sick Australian and then bring her back. His mother was a nervous old woman. He'd heard his father call her that many times. Even stupid woman. They kissed a lot when they thought he wasn't watching but they argued a lot too, and his father called his mother many names, and he was right. She was a stupid, nervous old woman. He, Alex Raftopoulos, wasn't frightened of German soldiers. They took off their trousers and farted and stood next to you without seeing you.

He would go to the mountain in the morning and not tell his mother. He would find the woman doctor and save her, and she would save the sick soldier. His father would be proud of him.

Adam made a small fire near the opening that led to the third cavern. He made a broth from some of the potatoes that Alex had brought. Nina fed Josef.

'I thought you were supposed to look like a man,' Josef said, glancing up while sipping the broth.

'Well, I'm sorry.' She held the spoon clear of his mouth. 'Don't talk or I won't feed you.'

'I thought you were going to be ugly, too.'

'Were you wrong or disappointed?'

He closed his eyes. 'I'm too crook to work that out. But I'm pleased.'

'I please you?'

'Yes.'

'Good. Now drink your soup.'

189

When he had finished, he said, 'How about a kiss?' His voice was weak so that what was intended to sound like a raunchy advance emerged on a breath that just made the journey past the lips.

She turned to Adam, who was leaning against the wall near the fire. 'Is he always like this?'

'He's worse when he's feeling good.'

'Thank heavens he's sick.' She poured some liquid from a bottle and made Josef drink.

'What's that?' he whispered.

'Cough medicine. Better than any kiss. And it'll make you sleep.'

'Are you doping me?' he sighed.

'Yes.' She recorked the bottle. 'If you want me to kiss you, you'd better be strong.'

'Jesus Christ.' He closed his eyes and smiled.

'That'll give you something to dream about.'

She rearranged his bed clothes. Her jacket was on top of the blanket. Eyes still closed, Josef nodded thanks. She walked to the fire.

'He needs rest and warmth,' she said, and accepted the cup of broth that Adam passed her. 'In a week or so he should be strong again.'

'We may have to move before then.' Adam offered her a chunk of bread.

'Thanks.' She bit into the bread. 'Let's hope not,' she said, chewing vigorously. 'He's not up to walking in the snow.' She paused to swallow. 'How strong is he normally?'

'Like a horse.'

'He's funny. That bit about kissing ...' She smiled but her eyes just missed making contact with his.

You should have seen him in Cairo, Adam thought. I had to drag him out of every brothel between the Sphinx and the sea. 'Yes, he's always joking,' he said.

'This is good.' She drank more broth. 'How am I going to get back?'

'How long can you stay? I mean, are people going to look for you, or ask questions if you're not there?'

'I'm only staying with my grandmother. She's all right. I was just wondering how I was going to get down the mountain again. I suppose the same way?'

'Could you find your way?'

'I could try.'

Adam put a small stick on the fire. There was little smoke and what there was drifted into the third cavern. Even so, he only lit a fire at night, when there was little risk of someone seeing smoke emerging from the exit at the top of the escarpment. 'We'll see what happens tomorrow. If Dimitri or the kid don't turn up, I'll take you down.'

'Would that be safe?'

'Depends on the Germans. You might have to stay here for a day or two.'

She raised a hand. 'I'm not in any hurry to get back. No job to go to. No husband waiting for his dinner. I might stay for the whole skiing season.'

His hand swept around the chamber. 'The house is yours.'

'How are we off for food?'

'We've got some and I can always catch ducks.'

'In winter?'

'Well, something. If it moves, I can catch it. We've eaten some strange animals.'

'Like what?'

'I don't know what they're called but they've got fur on and you need a couple to make a meal.'

She grimaced. 'I hope you're not talking about rats.'

'Not rats. I know them.'

'You've got rats in Australia?'

'Little rats.' He lifted his hand to the same level as his head. 'And big rats.'

'You have rats that high?'

'We call them kangaroos.'

She pointed an accusing finger at him. 'I've heard of them. They're the things that hop.'

'Right.' He sipped more soup. His eyes smiled above the rim of the cup.

'I've got a silly question,' she said.

He nodded, as though he'd been answering silly questions all his life.

'Where do we sleep?'

'Wherever you like.'

She looked around, probing the shadows.

'Where do you sleep?'

'On the ground.'

'That's what I was afraid you'd say. What's it like?'

'Better than standing up.'

Rubbing her back in anticipation of an uncomfortable night, she inspected the cave. The floor was a mixture of rocky ridges and flat slabs of boulder, but between the outcrops were patches of sand. Only the area around the fire was brightly lit. She walked as far as she could see, until the streaks of shadow merged into constant

191

darkness. But if the floor was a black and forbidding place, the walls sparkled. The surface was so clean-cut it could have been polished, and the concave recesses danced with fiery reflections.

'It's beautiful. It reminds me of *Tom Sawyer*. You know the part where Tom goes in the cave and he's chased by Indian Joe?' She was looking at the walls, not him. 'I loved that as a kid. It was kind of spooky but I like reading those sort of things.'

She turned. He was in front of the fire, a shadow surmounted by a golden fringe. He said nothing and she remembered. 'It's a book,' she said and shrugged. 'Just a kid's book.'

'I've taught myself to read.' He spoke softly.

There's a lot of dignity about this man, she thought, and I've embarrassed him by my silly prattling. And I'm not going to say 'that's good' or 'how clever of you' because that would be patronizing, and this man is far too good to be treated that way.

So she turned her back, to study the walls again. 'I want to be a writer.'

'To write books?'

'No. Well, maybe one day. I want to be a journalist. You know, write articles for newspapers or magazines. Preferably magazines. Maybe take pictures too. Then I could roam the world, writing stories for *Life* and *National Geographic* and the *Saturday Evening Post* and taking the photographs that illustrate them.' She faced him again. He had moved and firelight brushed his profile into a glowing outline. He was a good-looking man. Not a Tyrone Power or an Errol Flynn but handsome in a rugged way. A little gaunt but that was to be expected. A month eating her mother's food in Vermont would soon fatten him.

What am I thinking about? I'm not taking him home, like some stray cat I found on the street. 'And what have you brought home this time, Melina?' 'It's an unusual breed, mother. It's called an Australian.' 'How quaint.' 'Yes. And very large.' 'Will it eat a lot?'

She smiled. Her imagination was always racing down strange roads.

'What are you laughing at?' he said.

'I didn't think you could see me over here.' She couldn't see his face, because he had turned again and there was just the bright outline of his hair, but she knew he was looking at her with that intense expression he sometimes had. 'I was thinking about me taking photographs for *Life*,' she lied. 'I can't even use a camera properly. My photographs are awful. All blurred scenery and chopped-off heads.'

'But one day you'll be good.' There was no hint of mockery or doubt. He believed.

'Yes.'

192

He offered more soup and she walked to him, to have her cup refilled.

'I can do most things when I set my mind to it,' she said.

'I bet you can. More bread?'

'We have enough?'

'So much I'm thinking of opening a bakery.' He passed her a piece. 'What's the name of that book, the one about the cave?'

'*Tom Sawyer.*'

'I'll read it.'

'Good.' She could see his face now. Each was looking directly into the other's eyes. 'You'll become a great reader.'

'And you'll be a great picture taker.'

They tapped cups.

They began by sleeping apart, one on either side of the fire. It was a small fire that soon reduced itself to glowing coals, and spread little heat. There was only one blanket, which Adam had wrapped around Nina. He lay on a canvas groundsheet. As the fire diminished, she moved closer to it until she could have reached out and put her hand in the glowing embers.

'We don't have a lot of wood,' he apologized. 'We can't have too big a fire anyhow. It would light up the cave and someone just might see the glow, or smell the smoke.'

'That's all right.' She was shivering.

'Are you still wet?'

'My legs are. They never really got dry after wading through the water.'

The sleeping Josef burst into a bout of coughing. He had coughed many times since nightfall.

Adam got up. He climbed to the ledge that led to the third cave and returned with several long sticks and a length of twine. He tied the sticks at one end and set them up as a tripod.

'What are you doing?' she asked, sitting and spreading her hands in front of the fire.

'Just a minute.' He climbed the ledge once more. When he returned, he was carrying a log.

'What's that?'

'It's known as a piece of wood.' He put in on the fire.

'I thought we didn't have any?'

'I was going to use this for something else.' He knelt and began blowing on the embers to stir flames into life.

'What was it doing up there, in the other cave?' She watched him with interest and moved even closer, in anticipation of new warmth.

'That's our special hiding place. There are all sorts of things up

193

there. The idea is that if we ever had a sudden visit from someone, we could nick up there out of sight and we wouldn't have our things scattered all over the place.' He grinned. 'It's our store-room.'

A fresh crop of flames sprouted around the log.

She groaned with delight but then added: 'What about the light?'

'I need your help.'

Hands still extended, she pressed her chin to her knees. 'What can I do?'

'Take your trousers off.'

Her arms coiled around her legs. 'I beg your pardon?'

'Take 'em off and put them on this.' He indicated the stick tripod. 'That'll block the light. It'll also dry your pants.'

She pressed her face to her knees. 'I don't have anything else. I didn't bring a change of clothing.'

'Well you can't stay like that. You'll freeze with wet duds on and end up like Joe.'

'I'll freeze without them.'

'No you won't.' He brought his groundsheet to her side of the fire and spread it on the sand so that one end almost reached the ring of ashes. 'Now, if you get in the blanket and then wrap yourself in the groundsheet, and keep your feet towards the fire, you'll be as warm as toast.'

She eyed the canvas, and then Adam. She tugged at the cuff of her pants. 'But I have to take these off?'

'Unless you want to end up with pneumonia.'

A large flame licked the side of the log. She stared into it. 'I've never heard of this approach,' she said, more to herself than to him. He had walked away.

'Do you want me to turn my back?' he asked.

'Couldn't I dry them on?'

'No. Your legs'd be cold all night. Besides, we need something to block the light, remember?'

'Something for a curtain?'

'That's right.' He had his back to her. He folded his arms, a figure of finite patience. There was a long silence. 'I'll count to twenty.'

After ten seconds, she said: 'They're stuck. My legs are wet and the material's shrunk.'

'Want a hand?'

'No.' She giggled. 'This is ridiculous. I've known you less than a day, it's snowing outside and I'm freezing, and here I am getting my pants off.'

'Tell me when you're in the blanket.'

She extricated a foot from the last leg and draped the pants over

194

the tripod. Her legs were clammy. She rubbed them vigorously.

'What are you doing?' he called softly.

'Trying to dry my legs and get the circulation going.'

'I'll help if you want.'

'No thanks.'

'I have seen girls' legs before.'

'I'm sure you have. Probably rubbed a few too.'

He said nothing. Why do his silences make me feel so bad? she thought. I make with smart words and he says nothing and I feel as though I've uttered the most banal remark imaginable. Which I probably have. 'Nearly ready.'

'It's getting cold over here.'

She had opened the blanket and was standing up, preparing to wrap herself. 'Almost there.'

'OK.' His stockinged toe pawed the sand. 'I was married once,' he said.

'I can't imagine someone like you being married.'

'Well, I was.'

'What was she like?'

'Awful.'

Nina laughed. Blanket tight around her, she tried to sit down on the canvas but sprawled clumsily across it. She laughed again. 'You can turn now,' she said as she scrambled to a more dignified position.

He came back, arms still folded and body shaking from the cold.

'You poor thing. Get close to the fire,' she said. Adam squatted opposite her. 'What happened? Were you divorced?'

'She died.'

She almost said 'I'm sorry,' but stopped herself. So she said nothing and felt bad for asking the question about divorce. She'd forgotten. Divorce was an American custom. 'I'm not married,' she said.

'No,' he said.

No. How do you follow a remark like that? 'I've got a boy-friend though,' she said and immediately thought it a bad follow on. Banal, again. Even trite, or was that the same thing? I'll make a great journalist, she thought; all I have to do is learn the language ... which will be awkward, after all these years in Greece. 'He's not really a boy-friend. I haven't seen him for four years.'

'What's he like?'

'He's a drip.' They both smiled. 'But he can ski. He's studying to be a dentist. Or he was.'

'Four years is a long time.'

'Yes. My parents sent me to Europe. For experience. My mother

195

was born here. My father's a doctor. A very good one. Filthy rich.' Each sentence was followed by a pause. Adam nodded solemnly with every statement she made. 'I was supposed to go back years ago. I got caught up in the war.'

'So did I,' he said.

She stared into the fire. 'I'm going to study journalism when I get back . . . if I get back. What will you do when you get back to Australia?'

'Get warm.' He rubbed his hands.

'What else?'

'Don't know.'

'Raise sheep?'

'Probably.'

The fire had dulled her but suddenly she rocked back on her haunches and looked at him with concern. 'You're going to freeze to death.'

His face bore an expression of mild surprise. 'Not if I can help it.'

'But I've got the blanket and I've got your groundsheet.'

'That's all right.'

'It's not all right. It's unfair.'

He shook his head, warding off her words. 'I'll sit near the fire.'

'And when it goes out?'

'I'll jump in.'

She lay back on the canvas and stared up. There was nothing there; just walls tapering into shadows and a blackness that could have reached beyond the stars.

'We should share,' she said in a quiet but determined voice.

'I'm all right.'

But she was not listening. Her eyes were unfocused, her thought an argument which needed to be outlined. 'What the hell does it matter if a man and a woman sleep together, I mean beside each other, when it's so cold that one of them could die? 'Specially when there's only one blanket.'

He stared through the fire. 'What are you suggesting?'

She sat up. 'One question?'

'Another silly one?'

'An important one. Do you snore?'

He shrugged.

'What's that mean?'

'I don't know.'

'In other words, no one's ever complained. OK. Hop in.' She unpeeled the blanket and shuffled to one side. She pulled down the tail of her shirt so that it reached to her thighs.

'How are your legs?' he asked.

'If you mean are they warmer, the answer's yes, thank you.'

196

'That's what I meant.'

'You could at least say they're nice. An American man would.'

'They're nice.'

'Good. Now hop in.'

He wore all his clothes except his boots. 'I'd offer you my pants only –'

'I'm perfectly all right thank you.' She waited for him to take his place on the blanket. 'How are we going to lie? There isn't much room.'

'How about side by side?'

'I was thinking of back to back,' she said.

'Fine by me. Keep the kidneys warm.'

'Very practical.'

'I'm a practical bloke.' He lay with his back towards her. 'What happens when we want to roll over?'

She had been trying to pull the groundsheet over the blanket. 'Oh. I hadn't thought of that.'

He rolled on his back. 'Why don't we just go to sleep and see what happens.'

She grunted agreement. She was silent for a few seconds. 'Do you get up early?'

'In a bed like this, we'll both be glad to get up early. Besides, I want to be out before dawn to see what's going on in the valley.'

There was a long silence. Her leg pressed against his as she scratched one foot with the other.

Josef coughed. Adam felt her stiffen, to relax only when the bout of long, hacking coughs ended.

'That's a bad cough,' he whispered, when all was quiet.

'That's why we have to keep him warm.'

An ember popped in the fire.

'Thanks for coming up here.'

'My pleasure,' she mumbled.

He lay there for a long time, not daring to roll on his side and aware of the growing warmth from her body. She was tall. The top of her head came up to his ear. Taller than Nellie. He thought of Nellie. He usually did at this time of the night.

Nina's breathing became slower and deeper. He was still awake when she rolled on her side and, quite naturally, put one arm across his chest.

F·I·V·E

Alex meant to get up at four o'clock but he had no alarm and slept until ten to five. It was still intensely dark. Taking care not to wake his sister and younger brother, he dressed and groped his way to the far side of the room, where he got some bread from the tin near the stove. The woman doctor would be hungry. He found his hat and took the oilskin that hung near the door. He went outside.

Snow was still falling. That was good, he tried to convince himself. Certainly it would be cold and miserable out in the open but the fresh snow would cover his tracks and the Germans would probably stay indoors on such an unpleasant morning. He could be back in time for lunch. And possibly a beating. Never mind. He was doing what his father had told him to do and his father might be back in the house to greet him and then there would be nothing but rejoicing.

He started to cross the field but the snow was too deep and he sank to his knees. He doubled back to the road. There was snow there too, but he was able to make a path by following the stony ridge on the crown.

He left the road at the forest.

It was not the normal place, but he had to guess because it was still so dark. The bank was steep and he struggled to climb to the trees. He slipped several times, and made many tell-tale holes in the snow. They were too deep for the fresh snow to fill before dawn, so he spent some time trying to hide his tracks. The task was difficult because he couldn't see what he was doing but he could feel some of the depressions and trenches his lunges and slides had cut on his progress up the bank. Lying on the oilskin, he used his hands as shovels to fill them in. When he was reasonably sure no one would notice the trail, and when his hands were numb from cold, he got up and moved into the woods.

A vague grey light, as subtle as the first watery stroke on a land-scape painting, touched the sky. He hurried through the forest. He found his way surely, not being worried about leaving footmarks.

He emerged from the trees, knowing the sun must have risen but welcoming the grey murk that covered the mountain. Snow fell in a shuffling, powdery mist and he could see no more than twenty paces in front of him. That was good, he reasoned. Any Germans would have to be close to see him. The falling snow would also blanket any noise he made so he would be well protected this morning. But there were dangers. Just as approaching soldiers wouldn't be able to see him, nor could he see them, and their words and noises would be muffled too. He would have to be as stealthy as a fox, or he could blunder into trouble.

He came to the path and paused to listen for any noise. There was just the soft hiss of falling snow. He crossed the path, found the split tree with the leaning trunk and entered the stream. The cold was awful. Now his feet ached too. His hands were still numb, despite continuous rubbing, and his ears throbbed and his face was taut with the cold and his nose ran and his eyes watered so much he had to wipe them with the back of his hand.

The big rock was powdered with snow and difficult to ascend. It was slippery and his fingers wouldn't work properly and once he slid and almost went back into the stream. He only got to the top by grabbing the branch of an overhanging tree and hauling himself up. The act dislodged a line of snow which sprung from the rebounding branch and showered the area. Once at the top of the rock, he didn't stop to pour water from his boots or wring out his socks. He began the climb immediately. He was too cold not to keep moving.

He reached a small tree whose branches drooped under the burden of snow. Beneath it was a clear patch. There, he spread his oilskin and took out some bread. He looked back towards the stream. His trail led to the tree, as sharp and ugly as ink stains on white paper. He bit off some bread, put the rest away for the woman doctor, and tried to estimate how long it would take for the falling flakes to fill the holes.

Only then did he glance down to the left. Just visible was a ghostly figure in a grey uniform. The man was putting on a helmet. A rifle slanted from one shoulder. He was standing still at first but then began trudging through the snow, moving parallel to the stream. He was looking ahead, not up towards Alex. Another man spoke. The voice was soft but clear, and enquiring. Without stopping, the soldier answered. He blew in his cupped hands.

Alex crawled behind the narrow trunk. He searched the mist behind the man. There was something there, a faint outline of light grey in the floating haze of flakes. A tent. He felt a sudden need to urinate.

The Germans were camped there.

The man was walking towards the boulder where Alex had left the stream. He must have heard the bough snapping back into place. He will get there, Alex thought, and see the footmarks and follow them straight up to the tree.

The soldier neared the rock. He saw the tracks and unslung his rifle. The voice in the tent called out again. The soldier answered. Just one word. But he was looking towards the stream, as though the tracks ran down the mountain, not up.

Grabbing the oilskin, Alex began scrambling up the hill, keeping the tree between himself and the soldier. He was not concerned about leaving marks in the snow. He wanted to get away as quickly as he could. Let them search the stream. If they stayed there long enough, the trail would be covered, for the snowfall was getting heavier.

The cave was a place of mysteries, with no boundaries, no form, no colour. The void was total, a blackness without dimension. When the first light penetrated, it came as a stain. It seeped through the low opening and gradually spread until it touched walls and rocks and ripples of sand, creating shapes and shadows and chilling the large chamber with the first hint of reality.

Adam was awake. He was stiff and cold because Nina had turned and taken the blanket with her, and he was under the gap where the two ends no longer met. He rose and put on his boots. He had left them on a rock beside the ashes of the fire, to soak in the lingering warmth. He ruffled his hair. Nina was still asleep. He put his part of the blanket and groundsheet over her and walked towards the first cave, stretching his back as he went.

Josef coughed and raised a hand in greeting. Adam bent to adjust Nina's coat, so it covered his friend's chest.

'How are you feeling?' he whispered.

'As though I've got a ton weight on me.' Josef's voice was a croak.

'I forgot to take my blanket back.'

'Bastard. Trying to crush me to death.'

'Had a good night?' Adam rubbed his hands vigorously.

'Don't know. I was asleep.' The grey shadow that was Josef's head moved slightly as he looked towards the opening. 'Going out?'

'Just thought I'd see what's happening.'

'If you're going down to the shop, would you bring us back a paper?'

Adam bent to touch Josef's brow. 'I can never tell whether you're delirious or whether you're normal.'

'There's no difference.'

'You're still hot but you must be feeling better.'

'If I say I am, will you take this bloody weight off me?'

'It's Nina's coat.'

Josef reached from under the blankets and felt the heavy coat. 'How is the doc?'

'Asleep.'

'If she's cold, tell her I know where there's a warm bed.'

'You're better.' Adam got a spear from the wall.

'I'm never that crook.' He breathed unevenly, the air rasping in his throat.

'Stop talking.'

Josef took some time to answer. 'You're the one that started the conversation.'

Spear in one hand, Adam leant over him. 'Want a drink or something?'

'When you come back will do. I wouldn't mind a piss.'

'You'll have to do that yourself.'

'With a sheila around?'

'She's asleep.'

'Which wall will I use?'

'No wall. Don't get up. Just do it over the side of your bed. There's plenty of sand.'

There was a pause while Josef marshalled his breath. 'You must have been raised in a stinking house.'

'I wasn't raised in a house. Now just shut up. I'm going out.'

'Don't forget the paper,' Josef wheezed, as Adam left the cave.

The narrow gap was coated in snow. Where there had been bushes, there were now folds in a blanket of virgin white. Adam hissed dismay. To reach the ledge would mean cutting a clear and easily seen path. And getting wet. For a moment, he thought of returning to the comfort of the cave and being there when Nina woke, but to do that would have been careless and the only careless soldiers he had lived with in Greece were now either dead or prisoners of the Germans. Every day of their stay up here on the mountain, he had gone out before dawn to check for movement in the valley or the mountainsides. It was a rule for survival.

So he went. He pulled up the collar of his army shirt and tucked his khaki jumper in his pants and crawled under the bushes. Dislodged snow thudded on him and he was soaked by the time he reached the ledge. Sitting against the cliff face, he rubbed his arms and legs to restore circulation. He'd often spent a chilly winter's morning in the outback and had made ice crackle under his boots as he walked the hollows between sand-dunes, but that was nothing

201

like this. Oh, what he'd give now to be back at Kalinda with the air hot and dry and the temperature up around the one hundred and twenty mark. He thought about that and tried to feel warm but his fingers ached and his nose ached and his back ached and he was hungry, and try as he might to feel warm, he felt cold.

He got his hands working. God they were freezing! Leaving the spear against the cliff, he moved past the trees to the brink. The snow was only ankle-deep here. He used his feet to clear a space where he could lie on his belly and scan the scene beyond the ledge. He always looked from here and had even dug a U-shaped opening, like a crenel in a fortress wall, so he could peek at others without having his head project above the natural rim of the ledge. The top layer of pine needles was damp but he scooped up a lower and drier layer, to make himself a tolerably comfortable mattress. He put a little snow in his mouth and rubbed his wet hands across his lips. He wriggled into position.

Layers of cloud striped the mountains. Snow was not falling on him but there was a flurry on the far hillside and more falls further down the valley, all of which was choked with fog. The trees and the stream were hidden. Higher up and to the right the plateau where the Germans had set up camp was obscured by cloud. Nor could he see the waterfall but he could hear it tinkling and splashing down the broken rock face. The noise was not as loud today, the dense cloud and mist and curtains of falling snow deadening all sound. He had a sensation of being remote and cut off from the world, of being in a place that was floating and silent and not quite real.

For the first time, he realized it must be later than he had thought. The sun was well up, although the clouds so blocked the light that the air had the vague promise of pre-dawn. He had no watch. He tried to guess the time but the European winter confused him. He was used to the sharp certainty of an Australian sunrise, not the lingering doubt of a northern dawn where the sun hinted at its presence half way between breakfast and lunch. He shouldn't have thought of food. He was hungry.

He normally spent at least an hour at his observation post, looking, listening, checking the known paths and, if he saw people moving, trying to work out where they were going and what they were likely to be doing. There was nothing to see today. He checked the clouds again. If more snow fell, there was little chance of anyone venturing out. It could be a quiet day. He could talk to Nina. Josef could lie peacefully and get better.

Dimitri would not come. Even if he had been released by the Germans, he would not venture into the mountains on such a day.

With so much fresh snow about, he would leave a trail that even the dumbest boy from Berlin could follow.

He heard a noise. It could have been the rattle of a loose stone. It came from somewhere below him and to his left. Adam crawled forward, projecting his forehead and eyes beyond the opening. He peeped down. Mist wreathed the mountainside and the boulders below the ledge were bubbles in a swirling soup. There were other noises. Stones were dislodged, snow was being stamped underfoot. Someone was down there, climbing rapidly and recklessly.

He felt his stomach knot as other sounds reached him. There was more than one person down there. They must be soldiers scrambling up the hill. And he had left a sharply defined track through the gap to the cave. Dimitri had talked; a squad of soldiers had been sent up to catch them.

The spear was against the cliff. The rifle was back in the cave, where Josef was sick and the girl asleep. Jesus, who'd have thought the Jerries would come up on a day like this? And yet he should have known. They hadn't overrun Europe by doing conventional things.

His mind raced through the choices open to him, but there weren't many. He might be able to show himself and not get shot and yet lead them on such a chase that they'd fall into his traps. He thought of moving to the far end of the ledge where the first deep pit had been dug. Let them start by trying to cross that. The snow disguised it perfectly. Christ, they would have guns and he had one miserable stick with a sharp end.

He slithered back a little, until his eyes were just clear of the rim. The first figure loomed into sight. He had a cover over him and he was climbing frantically. But there was something odd. He knew the path, because he turned at precisely the correct places and was scurrying up like a rabbit. A German wouldn't know the way. And the figure was small.

The person stopped, looked back quickly and then glanced up. It was Alex.

A second figure came out of the mist. No mistaking this one. He was a soldier, rifle in one hand, other arm out to steady himself on the steep climb.

Horrified but fascinated, Adam watched the pursuit. The German couldn't see the boy, who was above him and out of sight behind boulders, but he could certainly hear him, and was being guided by the noise of the boy's clattering progress. The soldier cleared the mist. He stopped, chest heaving from exertion, and transferred the rifle to his other hand. He looked around and behind him, as though expecting support but then, seeing no one, hitched up his belt and resumed the climb.

Alex, what are you doing? Adam thought. You're bringing them straight up to us. Go back. Go sideways. Go somewhere but go away. And then he caught sight of the boy's face. The kid was terrified and was running for his life, towards the only person who might be able to help him.

Adam slid back from the edge, got to his hands and knees, and scuttled across to retrieve his spear. Still crouching low he hurried to the far end of the line of trees. The trail Alex was following joined the ledge near this point. The boy would come up, keep wide to avoid the first pit, and then duck behind the trees. It was the path he always used, the only safe way on to the ledge.

The first pine was a young tree but the second was old and broad. Adam stood behind its trunk, the spear held against his chest. He heard Alex reach the top and scramble on to the ledge. In his haste he dislodged some stones and they tumbled down the slope. The boy slithered past, ducking low to avoid a branch and not seeing Adam. He raced on, slipping several times but not looking back.

Adam heard the soldier reach the edge. There was a clatter as he put his rifle on stones, a long gasp of effort as he hauled his legs up, the scrape of boots and the noisy, painful breathing of someone who had almost reached the limit of his endurance. Then the man began to run, resuming the chase. Adam bent his knees, ready to spring.

There was a crashing sound. Adam jumped clear of the tree, spear extended. The soldier had hit the trap at full charge. Instead of falling through, he had fallen across the opening. One leg had penetrated the cover. The rest of him was sprawled across the side. Adam ran to him. The man looked up. His eyes were wide with surprise and his mouth was open in pain. He was older than Adam and he hadn't shaved and a grey stubble lined his chin, and for an agony of time, a full half-second, Adam looked into the face of the man who would kill him or be killed by him. The soldier raised the rifle.

Adam thrust down hard with the spear. The point, which he had lovingly hardened in the coals of a fire, penetrated the man's skin between neck and collar. There was a dull bursting sound, like a pick being driven into a sack of wheat. The man twitched so violently the spear was torn from Adam's grasp. The open mouth distorted even more but the only sound to emerge was a soft gutter gurgle. The rifle fell on the snow. The soldier slumped on his back. The shaft of the spear vibrated, counting the last heartbeats.

At the far end of the row of trees, where the jumble of rocks formed a corner in the cliff face, the boy had stopped and looked back.

'Adam?'

Adam held a finger to his lips, but Alex was beyond obedience. He rushed back, tears flooding his eyes and making a low, crying sound as he ran. He wrapped his arms around Adam's hips.

Adam patted his head but pressed the boy's face into his body, to muffle the noise of his sobbing as much as to comfort him.

'Quiet,' he said, but in English. Urgently he looked around him. 'You've got to be quiet.'

The boy pulled back and stared at the dead man, and then up at his friend. He wiped his cheeks. His eyes were blank with horror.

'Shh.' Again Adam put a finger to his lips. 'It's OK. Everything's OK.' Then in Greek: 'No talk ... stop.'

The boy sniffed and nodded. He glanced again at the dead soldier and the long projecting spear and stepped back. By now, Adam had gone to the edge. There was no sign of another soldier. He signalled Alex to come to him.

'More?' he whispered and pointed down.

'Yes.' Alex nodded. He wiped his nose. 'They were camped down there by the stream. I saw a tent. There were other men talking. This one was down at the –'

Adam waved a hand, stopping the flood of words he hadn't understood. He held up one finger, then two, then three. 'Man?' he asked.

Alex shrugged. 'I don't know. There was a tent.'

'Tent?'

The boy drew the shape of a tent around him, then mimed a person sleeping. 'Near the water,' he added.

This Adam understood. 'One man, two man, three man?' he prompted, remembering his numbers.

'I could not see. There was fog.'

From somewhere far below came a shout. It was a plaintive sound, faint and as lost as a misplaced echo. Alex gripped Adam's arm. They waited. Another shout followed, but it was even weaker and seemed to come from farther down the valley.

'They're searching for him,' Adam said and the boy, comforted by the distance of the sounds, nodded seriously.

'Stay,' Adam commanded and pointed at the spot where Alex crouched. 'You look. Understand?' The boy nodded.

Adam crawled back to the soldier. The spear had gone through the base of the man's neck and diagonally into the chest. To extract it, he had to put a foot on each shoulder and tug hard on the shaft. It came out, ripping flesh and smeared with gore. He saw Alex staring at him, and jabbed his finger in a silent command to look the other way. Dutifully, the boy turned.

Adam wiped the spear in the snow, pulled the cover off the trap, removed the man's ammunition belt, and tipped the body down the hole. He scooped up the bloodstained snow and threw it after the body. The flimsy cover having being pierced, he rethatched the broken section and put it back in place. He spread snow across the trap, gathered the rifle and rejoined the boy.

'Man?' he asked.

The boy shook his head.

Low, slate-grey clouds were scudding across the mountain. Snow started to fall. The boy grinned. 'It will cover any tracks,' he said and then repeated the words slowly until Adam understood. 'We are lucky,' he said and Adam nodded.

The boy produced some bread. 'Where is the woman doctor?'

'In the cave.'

'OK?'

'She's OK.'

Another shout filtered through the fog but the sound was so faint the boy had a sudden surge of confidence. 'The stupid pigs are going the wrong way.' He smiled at Adam. 'Pigs' was a word he had heard his father use to describe the invading soldiers and, at this moment, he felt adult enough to mimic the expression. 'Only that one man saw me. The others won't know where he has got to, and with this snow they'll never track him.'

The mist below the line of trees had thickened. Even the boulders had faded and the fall of snow, which had begun as fine, waffling flakes, had become a thick deluge.

'Time to go,' Adam said, gripping the boy's shoulder and then standing.

Alex joined him. He nodded towards the pit. 'That man, the German, he is dead?'

'Yes.'

He kept nodding. His lips were so compressed his cheeks bulged. 'He was going to pull out my fingernails.'

Adam looked at him quizzically. 'What?'

'Fingernails.' The boy touched his and then pulled at them.

'I don't understand.'

The boy repeated the performance.

'Not that man,' Adam said.

'Oh yes. The Germans pull out your nails.' Again there was a demonstration.

'Not all Germans do that,' Adam said. 'There are some nice ones.' Including, he thought, the man I just killed. He was probably

206

a good bloke with a wife and kids back in Germany. Oh God, what have I done? Kill the bastards before they kill you. We're all brutal, as rotten as each other.

The boy was staring up at him, eyes still unnaturally wide.

'Here.' Adam handed him the rifle. 'Can you carry this?'

Alex beamed. He gripped the gun and stood, holding it stiffly in front of him while Adam used the spear to level the snow where they had been crouching and where the German soldier who hadn't shaved that morning had died.

S·I·X

The cave was darker than normal because the entrance was now partly blocked. Adam, Nina and Alex rolled several of the larger rocks that were piled inside the first chamber into the opening. They had no way of knowing how it looked from the outside, but reckoned that the fresh covering of snow, the thick bushes, and the new plug of rocks would make the opening extraordinarily difficult to detect.

'What if my father comes?' Alex asked.

'We'll pull the rocks away,' Adam said, and the boy smiled at him.

The floors had been cleared. Everything, except the rifles, a couple of spears and the crude boomerangs, had been carried up to the third cavern. A few sticks glowed on the fire but it was at the far end of the chamber and out of sight from the entrance. It could be extinguished and the embers scattered in a few seconds.

Josef was sitting with them, a blanket over his shoulders. Nina wore her coat. Her arms were tightly folded. 'So what do we do?' she said.

'Get out of here.' Adam had removed his wet jumper and shirt and had a blanket over his shoulders. His clothes were on a tripod near the fire.

'The mountain will be crawling with soldiers,' she said, shaking her head sadly.

'We'll go up to the top.'

'How?'

'Through the last cave. There's a way out that takes you to the top of the mountain.'

Alex looked concerned. 'My father said I was to bring the doctor back to the village.'

'I don't think we'll be going back to the village for a while,' Nina said in English.

'Not down the way you came, anyhow,' Adam said.

'So?' She eyed Adam.

'We climb out the top. Go over the mountain. Then you and Alex go home. Me and Joe go south to the coast.'

'And?'

'Find Dimitri's friend and take a boat to Egypt.'

She frowned. 'So we all go out together, get down off this mountain, and then Alex and I circle back to the village and you and Joe head for the coast?'

'Yes.'

'I don't like it very much.'

'Neither do I but I can't think of anything better. The Germans will be swarming up this mountain as soon as the snow clears.'

'Joe's not well enough to travel.'

'They'll catch us, all of us, if we don't get out of here quick smart.'

'We could stay,' Josef interjected, his brow creased in thought. 'With the front sealed like that, they won't find the cave. We've got water. We don't need much food. We can just sit it out until they go away.'

Alex had been watching the others but not understanding the English. He tugged Nina's jacket. 'I have to take you back to the village.'

'We have to go out through the cave,' she explained. 'And then climb down the other side of the mountain.'

'What are Adam and Joe going to do?'

'Find your father's friend, the one with the fishing boat.'

'They will not find him on their own. It is very difficult. They need a guide.'

'Who?'

'My father.' He paused, troubled by a new thought. 'Or me.'

'You know the way?'

'Oh yes. I have been there. It is a nice place.'

She explained to Adam. 'It is too dangerous,' he said. 'We couldn't take the boy.'

'So what will you do?'

He wrapped the blanket more tightly around his body. 'Leave first thing in the morning. Be up at the top by sun-up.' He paused. 'I'd rather be going now, this very instant, but I don't think Joe could make it.'

'I'm OK,' Josef said brightly.

'You are not,' Nina said. 'You go out now in the snow storm and we'd be carrying you within minutes.'

'Well that's all right,' Josef said. 'Although it depends who carries me.' He lifted his eyebrows at her, and attempted his most winning smile.

209

'I had a dog who used to look at me like that.'

'Jesus, thanks.'

'Just be quiet,' Adam said, having enjoyed the exchange. 'Save your strength for tomorrow.'

'Tomorrow will be all right?' she asked hopefully. 'I mean as far as the Germans are concerned. They won't be up the top?'

'Who knows?' He wiped his face. 'We don't have much choice, do we?'

She coughed. 'Have you thought of surrendering?' She avoided his eyes. 'You know, just give yourself up and become prisoners of war.'

He stared at the floor of the cave. 'You remember that fellow you saw in town? The bloke with red hair and a dozen bullet holes in his belly?'

She nodded, her lips tight.

'He was surrendering.'

The officer in the sinister uniform entered the room and shook snow from his cap. He strode to the stove. The interpreter and two soldiers followed. Dimitri was sitting on the floor, his back against the wall. He scrambled to his feet.

'Do you know what's happened?' the officer snapped. He did not wait for the interpreter to finish. 'One of our men is missing. He was up in the mountains. He went to investigate a noise by the river.' The interpreter was being flustered. 'Oh for heaven's sake, hurry up.'

He walked to the other end of the room and rapped on the door. A soldier appeared, escorting Eleni Raftopoulos. The officer motioned the two of them to a corner.

Eyes wide in alarm, Dimitri began squeezing his hands together.

'This is your wife?' The officer didn't require a translation. 'Good. I'll come to her later. I was telling you about a missing soldier. He heard a noise, went to a spot on the bank of the river, and disappeared.'

'Possibly he fell in the water,' Dimitri suggested, eyes still on his wife.

'Quiet!' the officer roared when the other Greek translated Dimitri's remark. 'If you think this is funny, I guarantee you won't be smiling for long. He did not fall in the water. He vanished, taken by someone.' He waited until there was silence. 'You know the river? It was near the place where you were allegedly hunting for rabbits. You *do* remember?'

Dimitri nodded.

'I asked you yesterday to tell me where the British soldiers were.

210

You recall that?'

Again he nodded.

'You will now tell me. Where are they?'

'I do not know.'

'I have no time for your games.' He withdrew his pistol from its leather holster and marched to the corner. He put the pistol to the forehead of Dimitri's wife. 'You will now tell me.'

'How can I tell you something I don't know?' His wife's eyes were boring into his. There was no fear in that proud face. The eyes oozed defiance.

'I do not believe in fairies. I do believe in enemy soldiers who have become nothing more than mountain bandits. And I believe those bandits have taken one of our men. Now, will you tell me where those bandits are hiding?'

The question was translated. Eleni shook her head while the officer was looking at Dimitri.

'You have till five.' He began to count.

Dimitri wrung his hands. 'Your excellency, how can I give you information I don't have –'

'Three.'

'Please, let my wife go home.'

'You will tell me? Four.'

'I don't know!' Dimitri's answer was a high-pitched wail.

The officer pulled the trigger. One of the soldiers ducked as red froth sprayed across him. Eleni's dumpy body slid down one wall.

'I have your children outside,' the officer said.

The interpreter blinked. He said nothing.

'Have you lost your tongue?'

The man translated. Dimitri began to move to his wife but was pulled back.

'Bring in the girl.'

Dimitri's daughter was led in. She saw her mother and began screaming.

The officer held the pistol high above his shoulder. 'You will talk now.' He aimed the barrel at the girl. 'We have your son outside. I have enough bullets. Just tell me.'

Dimitri fell to his knees. The girl tried to run to him but was restrained.

'Just tell me.'

'There is only one,' Dimitri sobbed.

'Go on.'

'He is sick.'

'I do not believe you.'

'It is true.' His head touched the floor.

211

'He is British?'

'I do not know. He speaks a strange tongue.'

'Where is he?'

'In a very difficult place. It is hard to find.' A terrible anger had begun to well within the Greek. He would kill this man and as many others as he could. He didn't care about himself. They could kill him but he would kill some of them first. He thought of charging the monster with the Luger and choking him but they would shoot the girl and him and nothing would be gained.

'Tell us.'

He shook his head. 'You would not understand. You would not find it.'

'Is this man armed?'

'He is sick. I think he is dying. I found him by chance, while hunting.'

'For rabbits, of course.'

His head nodded, brushing the floor.

The officer clicked his boot heels. 'Very well. You will take us there. Now.'

Dimitri looked up. Already a plan was forming. 'We are going now?' Better to appear reluctant. 'My wife –'

'I assure you, she will not be going anywhere. You!' He pointed to the interpreter. 'Come with us.'

The man's hand dived on to his chest. 'Me?'

'Of course. We need to know what this fool is saying.'

'But it is snowing.'

'Wear a coat.'

'I have a bad leg.'

'You will have two bad legs if you don't hurry.' He turned to one of the soldiers. 'Six men. Immediately.'

The nine men went in a truck. They stopped at the forest and Dimitri led them to the stream. He walked beside it until they reached a place where three tents were pitched. The storm had passed but the field was deep in snow.

'This is where you were hunting rabbits,' the officer said. Dimitri pointed to a field further down the stream.

'Down there,' he said.

The man ignored him. 'And this is where the soldier disappeared. The others found some footmarks leading down from the mountain.' He waited for the translation. The civilian was puffing badly.

'Obviously,' the officer continued, 'your sick British soldier was not too sick to come down to the water.'

A private at the tents led them to the large rock. 'We found the tracks here,' he said. 'Unfortunately, heavy snow fell and filled in all the footprints.'

The officer dismissed him with a nod. He faced the mountain. 'He came down from there. Is that where he is hiding?'

Dimitri, hands clasped in subservience, nodded.

'Where?'

Dimitri closed his eyes. Please forgive me Adam, but there is nothing else I can do. 'You see the tall trees?'

All looked up. The mist had lifted and the trees were sharp outlines against the white escarpment.

'He is there?'

'Yes. He lives in a hole.'

'A hole?'

'Beneath the ground. It is just behind the trees. Very hard to find.'

'Show us.'

'The climb will be difficult. There is so much snow.'

'Do not make it more difficult than it truly is. You understand me?' The officer raised a gloved finger.

'Yes.'

Dimitri began the climb. He followed his normal path. There was no point in going any other way. The officer assigned two soldiers to follow immediately in his steps. He came next, with the other soldiers labouring after him. The interpreter, wearing ordinary shoes, floundered at the rear.

They stopped many times. When he could, Dimitri glanced at the ledge, and the place where he knew Adam had his observation point. He could see no sign of the big Australian.

Towards the end of the climb, he moved at a faster pace and the two men with him struggled to keep up. He reached the ledge and was about to haul himself up when one of the soldiers grabbed his wrist, holding him while his partner crawled over the edge. The man stood, rifle at the ready and inspected the ledge. He waved the others on.

Dimitri went next, then the second soldier. The officer had dropped back and was still negotiating the last of the boulders.

Hunched forward, Dimitri moved towards the trees. The closer soldier grabbed his arm. The Greek shook it free, taking care to appear annoyed at the restraint rather than anxious to get away. He skirted the edge, walking on the outer rocks.

'Come back,' the soldier barked, but the order was in German and Dimitri felt safe, as long as he did not hurry. He counted his steps, moved slowly in from the brink, and faced the soldiers. The

213

leading man strode angrily towards him. One boot crashed through the cover shielding the narrow pit. The soldier's other foot was still on firm ground and, for a moment, it seemed he might balance there but he fell forward, landing heavily on his chest on the far side. The rifle, knocked from his grasp, cart-wheeled over the snow.

The second soldier ran to help his friend. Dimitri picked up the rifle and shot him. The soldier sagged to his knees, his mouth open in an expression of comic disbelief. The momentum of his run carried him, sliding on his knees, into the pit.

The first man was slipping back. Arms outstretched, hands grasping at snow, he looked up to Dimitri with a forlorn plea for help on his face. The Greek put his boot on the helmet and pushed. The man disappeared.

Others were shouting. Dimitri saw the tip of a rifle appear above a stone bordering the ledge and he turned and ran. He was strong at walking but poor at running and before he was halfway along the row of pines a shot rang out and something tugged at his side and sent him spinning into the trunk of a tree. He lost his grip on the rifle and bent to pick it up. A bullet snarled above him. He felt dizzy and a sudden sickness was in his throat. He tried to lift the rifle. Instead, he fell on his face. The cold snow cleared his brain and he looked up to see a soldier charging. Dimitri was a good hunter and he preferred shooting from the prone position. The soldier had ducked behind a tree but now reappeared, sprinting towards him. The Greek took aim and fired and the impact of a direct hit in the chest turned the man into a rag doll with arms and legs twisting at improbable angles.

The officer was partly behind a tree. Dimitri fired again but the man had moved. Dimitri got up. There was a fearful pain in his side and he couldn't run. He headed for the boulders, ambling like an ape with one hand touching the ground, helping to balance and propel him.

He slipped through the gap between the two largest rocks, turned and, resting against one gigantic slab of stone, waited for the Germans to come.

They heard the shots in the cave. Adam pulled at one of the rocks blocking the entrance.

'What are you doing?' Nina said, her voice strained but hushed. She tried to push the rock back and looked at Adam as though he had gone mad.

He shoved her away. She landed on Josef. 'They can only be shooting at one thing,' he said harshly, wrenching the rock clear.

'That's got to be Dimitri out there.'

Josef helped her to her knees. 'The old bloke must have tried to get up here and they followed him,' he said.

'And I'm going out.' Adam rolled another rock away from the opening.

'You can't go out,' she said.

'I'm not going to stay here and have him killed. Don't you understand? It's got to be him. No one else knows the way.' He was breathing heavily from the effort of moving the rocks.

Another shot boomed. The shrill whine of a ricochet threaded its way through the echoes.

Adam stared at her, his face torn by dread.

'What will you do?' Her voice was soft, apologetic.

'Whatever I can. Joe!' He gave him the Lee Enfield. 'We've only got four rounds.'

Josef nodded. 'What do you want me to do?'

'Stay at the entrance. Do what you have to.' Adam took the German rifle and thrust a boomerang in his belt. He gripped his friend by the arm. 'If I don't get back, take Nina and Alex out through the top.'

Josef grunted acknowledgement. Adam was gone.

Adam found Dimitri at the end of the great pile of boulders. The Greek had retreated along the safe path and was guarding the exit. He was on his knees. He held the rifle by the barrel, grasping it as a baseball player holds a bat. The back of his jacket was torn and a dark stain spread across his hips.

Adam touched the Greek's shoulder and the man almost dropped the rifle. His face was a deathly white, but when the shock had passed, he managed to smile.

'Eh Adam, where've you been?' he said in Greek.

'Are you OK?' Adam said in English.

Dimitri tilted his head in a way that meant everything was fine. Adam pointed to his back and the Greek dismissed the wound with a wave of the hand.

'They killed Eleni,' he said, and Adam understood.

There was the sound of a boot slipping on rock. Dimitri tightened his grip on the barrel. He smiled and the effort seemed to hurt him. 'There were eight,' he said, and showed eight fingers. He pointed beyond the rocks. Adam nodded.

'I have got four.' He displayed four fingers, and touched the rifle.

Adam held up four fingers and pointed in the direction of the trees.

215

'Yes. There are four left, including the scum who murdered my wife.'

'Why are you holding the gun like that?' Adam asked, tapping a finger on the German weapon.

'No more bullets.' He shrugged. 'Empty.'

There was another scraping sound, and a grunt of pain. One of the soldiers was trying to climb the rocks.

Adam gave him his gun. He waved towards the gap in the escarpment. 'Quickly. Go back. Let them come through.'

Dimitri passed the other gun to him.

Adam shook his head. He tossed the rifle to the ground between the boulders and the bushes. Dimitri looked at him in astonishment and then, slowly, began to grin.

'That's right,' Adam said, still in English, because the adrenalin was pumping so hard he could remember no Greek. 'They'll think you've got no gun. Go right to the end. Wait there. Surprise them ...' And he added softly: '... those that get through.'

Dimitri was off, dragging himself painfully into the bushes. He left a distinctive trail.

There was a space between two tilted boulders, with a third slab forming a natural roof. Adam slipped into place and took the boomerang from his belt. A man is mad, he thought. I'm in the middle of Greece with nothing but a home-made boomerang and there are four Germans out there with guns. Jimmy would be cackling his head off. If only he were here. He moved like the wind and hit like lightning. He'd relish a situation like this ... even with one arm....

A pair of boots landed on the rock above him. One leg appeared, then another, and a soldier dropped to the ground. Adam, crouched in the opening, had the boomerang ready but the man ran forward to the rifle. He picked it up and emitted a shout of triumph. Another man joined him. They saw the drag marks made by Dimitri and ran into the bushes.

He heard the footsteps of another man. This one had come a different way, following the path Dimitri had defended. Adam risked a look. He saw the back of a tall man wearing an officer's cap and overcoat. He carried a pistol in his hand.

The officer stood there, unwilling to enter the bushes. He was joined by a civilian whose long coat and dark trousers were stained with mud. The officer said something and the other man laughed. The news seemed to make him much more relaxed. He turned, smiling broadly, and saw Adam. He grabbed the officer's arm.

Adam stepped into the open and lifted the boomerang.

The German swung around, saw Adam had no gun, and spent a

216

moment examining him from his head to his boots. Two expressions crossed his face, the first curiosity, the second distaste. Very slowly, he raised his pistol.

Adam threw the boomerang. The distance was short. The angled piece of wood was heavy and tapered at the tips, and it spun with a whirring sound. It struck the German in the neck. His cap fell off. Then he collapsed without uttering a sound.

The other man stepped back, his feet stuttering, and then ran in a wide circle. He bolted for the broad, outer path back through the boulders. Adam chased him but stopped short of the area where he had undermined the rocks. The man, running clumsily, trod on the flat slab, which turned and pitched him over the edge. It was at least one hundred feet to the first landing.

'I don't know who you were,' Adam said, 'but I don't think you were a friend.'

That was six. The two soldiers were still at large, somewhere in the bushes.

The pain had gone, but so had his energy, and Dimitri was struggling to reach the place where the cave was, let alone go further along the gap and draw the soldiers away. He could hear his pursuers crashing after him. They must be supremely confident, he thought. Young and inexperienced hounds, anxious to make the kill. Well, this old fox would be waiting. He rolled on his belly and put the rifle in place.

The regular sound of the two men pushing their way through the bushes was suddenly broken by a snapping noise and a hideous scream. One of the bearded man's terrible traps, Dimitri said to himself, and nodded contentedly. Just wait there, my young hound, and I will come back and put you out of your misery.

The other soldier stopped and called out but the only answer was another scream of pain.

Dimitri waited. He glanced towards the cave and saw Josef, sitting beneath the bushes and nursing the heavy Lee Enfield rifle. Josef waved, a mere movement of the hand, and then did an astonishing thing. He called out, but in German.

'It's all right,' he shouted. 'I have them.'

There was no answer. 'Where the devil are you,' Josef called out, his voice agitated and shrill. 'I need you. Come at once.'

Dimitri heard the soldier start pushing through the bushes. It was so easy. The man emerged from the thickest of the growth just near him, stared stupidly at him, and was shot by him.

There are two more, Dimitri thought, and they are the main ones. He heard another noise, but this was a different sound; slight

217

and made by someone who knew what he was doing. Adam's face appeared from beneath a bush.

'There are two more,' the Greek called out urgently and held two fingers aloft.

Adam shook his head. He raised two fingers, and knocked them over.

'The officer?' Dimitri said, struggling to one elbow.

Adam nodded. He brandished the boomerang.

'The officer? Dead?'

Adam shook his head. He put his cheek on one hand, mimicking sleep, and said, 'Very sore head. He's back there.' He indicated with his thumb. He crawled from the bushes and went to the Greek. 'How are you, old friend?'

Dimitri waved him away. 'OK,' he said.

Adam climbed to the cave. He grinned at Josef. 'Who was that screaming out in German?'

'I just tried to sound like an officer.' Josef looked concerned. 'But the bloke came out and Dimitri shot him. There was no need for that.'

'They killed his wife.'

'Oh God.' He coughed and clutched his chest. 'What happened?'

'I don't know. There wasn't much time for talk.'

Nina crawled through the opening. The boy followed. Adam explained what had happened. 'You'd better go to Dimitri,' he said to Nina. 'He must have been shot. He's covered in blood.'

'Where is Papa?' Alex asked, and they turned. Dimitri had gone.

The trail was simple to follow. Crushed snow and smears of blood led back through the bushes. Adam moved cautiously. Dimitri had said four people remained, but there could have been more. He stopped several times to listen. The euphoria of victory had gone, replaced by the fear – no, the certain knowledge – that others would come and there would be more of them and that there was no way they could win next time.

The soldier who had fallen in one of the pits was silent. There'd been no sound for some time, Adam realized. Keeping below the bushes, he followed Dimitri's trail to the trap. The soldier was at the bottom. He was dead, his head a bloody mess. There were two rifles in the pit. The stock of one was covered in gore. The trail led back to the boulders and the place where Adam had felled the officer. Dimitri was there, lying on his side near the other man. He was panting heavily. He held a rock in one hand.

Adam walked closer, but then stepped back, shocked by what he saw. The German's face was crushed.

218

Dimitri raised his great, baggy eyes. 'He was looking at me when I killed him.' He tried to spit but the frothy liquid refused to leave his lips. He wiped his face and smiled wickedly. 'He did not enjoy it.'

'Let me get you back to Nina.'

'He killed Eleni. That man.' He pointed to the faceless figure beside him and lay back again. 'Bastard. May he already be in hell.'

'Come, friend. We must hurry.'

Painfully, Dimitri rolled on his bent back. 'We have done a good day's work, you and I, eh?' He held up a hand and Adam grasped it. He pulled the Australian close. 'Take the coat. It is good. You will need it.'

Adam did not understand.

'The coat, the coat.' His hand fluttered up and down, pretending to undo buttons. Adam undid the coat, pulled it free and laid it across Dimitri. He shook it off. 'No, no. It is for you. You will need it. You will have to go.'

'Go?'

'Yes, go. To the coast. Immediately. First, get him out of the way.'

Adam dragged the German to the pit and tipped the body on top of the dead soldier. Then he returned and hauled Dimitri back to the clearing. Once out of the bushes, he picked him up and carried him to the cave.

Dimitri saw Alex for the first time. His eyes opened in wild surprise. 'What are you doing here?'

The boy saw the great stain across his father's coat and trousers and began to weep. 'I came for the woman doctor, Papa, as you told me.'

The Greek grasped his son's hand and the grip was so powerful he hurt.

'Your mother is dead. You will have to look after the family now.' The boy's cry became higher pitched. Dimitri squeezed even harder. 'Don't cry.'

'But you are hurting my hand.'

He pulled his son to him and kissed his cheek. 'You're a good boy, Alex. I'm very proud of you.' He held him, saying nothing. Then he pushed the boy away. 'I want you to be a lawyer. I want you to be a good man. A good rich man. That is better than a good poor man.'

'Yes, Papa.'

'Stop crying. I'm not hurting your hand now.'

'I can't help it, Papa.'

Nina joined them. 'While you two are talking, let me have a look

219

at your back.' With difficulty, Dimitri moved. She lifted his torn coat, and sucked in her breath. Adam bent over her. 'Can you get me my first-aid box please,' she said in a thin voice.

'Before you go home to look after the others,' Dimitri told his son, 'there is something you must do.'

Alex nodded and waited for his father to gain sufficient strength to speak again.

'You must take Adam and Joe to Ari's place. You know the way?'

'Yes, Papa.'

'Take them there. Make sure they are safe.'

The boy blew his nose and nodded.

Nina had been delicately peeling away the shirt. 'I will go with him,' she said. Dimitri raised a hand and she gripped it. 'And I will take Alex home again.'

'Promise?'

'A promise.'

He twisted to look at her. 'They said you were a good woman.' Still holding her hand, he sank to the floor. Slowly, he breathed out, and the air left his body with the sigh of a distant wind. His eyes stared at the domed roof of the small cavern.

'Jesus Christ,' Josef muttered, after a long silence.

Nina pulled the boy against her and cried with him.

Adam stood up. Roughly he wiped an eye. 'I'll be outside for a few minutes,' he said, not looking at anyone. 'I have to make sure there's no one around and I've got some clearing up to do.'

'Please take care,' Nina said.

'I'll be back soon. There are things I must do.'

220

S·E·V·E·N

Working quickly, Adam smoothed the snow around the boulders and along the path through the bushes. He retrieved another rifle and ammunition and took the coat from a tall soldier shot by Dimitri. There were two dead soldiers near the trees. He left the bodies there. Better for the Germans to think there had been a fight only among the pines and that the survivors had gone back down the mountain. Then he returned to the cave, brushing over his own footmarks as he retreated.

Inside the cave, they blocked the entrance with rocks once more. Then they carried Dimitri's body into the big cavern and, using the light from a lantern, laid it gently near one wall and covered it with the dry grass that had formed Josef's bed. They scattered the ashes of the fire.

Josef, now wearing the officer's overcoat, was gathering the boomerangs and spears.

'We won't be able to take all those,' Adam said. He frowned, not wanting to discard what had taken him so long to make.

'Take one of your sharp sticks and one piece of bent wood.' Josef handed him a spear and a boomerang. He stacked the others near the ashes of the fire place. 'That'll give them something to scratch their heads about. Whoever comes in here will think they've made a discovery of great anthropological significance.'

Nina laughed, more loudly than she need have, but it was a relief to find something funny after the events of the last few hours.

'Boomerangs and pre-Bronze Age spears found in remote Greek cave.' Josef, encouraged by the laughter, was reading the headlines. He coughed. 'We could be rewriting history.'

'We'll *be* history if we don't get out of here,' Adam said, and led the way into the third cavern.

The climb out of the cave was awkward but not dangerous. They paused many times, so each could gain the benefit of the lantern light to negotiate a more difficult part of the ascent. The tunnel was formed along a fault in the rock and rose in a series of steps, ledges and small caverns. Sometimes, the roof was sufficiently high to stand. Mostly, they had to crawl on hands and knees. In one place, where they could feel cold air from the opening on the plateau above, the tunnel spiralled through a series of small openings which required them to slither on their bellies and drag their gear behind them, so tight was the squeeze.

Adam led the climb. Alex followed, carrying the lantern. Nina was next, her rucksack in her hands, and then Josef, who found the going exhausting and was glad for every opportunity to rest.

After forty-five minutes, they reached the top. The exit was blocked by snow but they wormed their way through and emerged among rocks at the top of the escarpment. The sun was already low. A cool wind was blowing.

'Now what?' Josef said, desperately short of breath but trying to sound bright. 'Having gone to all that trouble to get up' – he paused to get air – 'I suppose we now have to go down.'

The boy pointed to the south, where hills rolled to the horizon. 'That way.'

'You know the route?' Nina said.

'It is that way,' he said with absolute confidence.

'He knows where we are?' Adam asked her. She put the question to Alex.

'Sure. Our village is over there.' He pointed. 'And we have to go that way, beyond the hills.' Again he indicated the south. 'I was up here once, before the Germans came. My father was hunting. He brought me. I was only small but I remember.'

'When you were only small ... Must have been years ago,' Josef said kindly, and the boy looked at him with serious eyes.

The area they had reached was raw and exposed. Boulders projected from the snow. There were no trees.

'If we get moving, we could be down in the woods before sunset,' Adam said. 'We could do with some shelter.'

'I'm ready,' Josef said, answering the unspoken question. He extended a hand. 'Let me take one of those.'

Adam was carrying both rifles, one over each shoulder, plus a spear. 'I'm OK. We'll only keep these until we're down off the mountain. Then we'll get rid of them. Right?'

Josef remained seated on a rock which he had carefully cleared of snow. 'Right.'

Nina moved beside Adam. 'Let me take this,' she said, reaching for the spear.

'I'm OK thanks.' He kept his head down.

'I could do with something to lean on. Besides, if anything happens and you need to use one of those guns, you could probably do with two free hands.'

He passed her the spear. his hands were shaking.

She looked at him with concern. 'You're cold?'

'Who isn't?' He tried to smile but his teeth were clenched and his breath came in sharp little waves.

'Are you feeling sick? Have you got what Joe's got?'

'Nothing like that.' He was still gripping the spear shaft. Her hand was above his, and she let her fingers droop and touch his.

'What is it?'

Again, the attempt at a smile. 'I think it's called shock or something. Maybe fright, although I thought you were supposed to be scared before things happened, not after.' He shook the shaft. 'I stuck this through a bloke today.'

She returned his grave stare.

'He was about to shoot me. He was lifting his gun. If I'd waited maybe half a second –'

'You had to do what you did.'

'He was looking straight at me. Right into my eyes.'

'We wouldn't be here, alive. . . .' Gingerly, she took the spear. 'I'll carry this.'

'Then there were the others . . . and Dimitri.'

She nodded. 'It's been a horrible day.'

'We killed nine men, Dimitri and me.' He stared blankly at the snow. 'I was counting on the way up. Nine.'

Alex had gone to help Josef. The boy was looking at them, agitation on his face. 'We must go,' the boy called.

She smiled. 'Our little leader.'

Adam took a deep breath, and wiped the tip of his nose. 'The kid's right. There'll be Germans swarming all over these hills within an hour or two.'

'Are you OK? All right to move?'

'Right as rain.' He adjusted the weight of the rifles on his shoulders. 'It was just that everything's been happening so fast and climbing up from the cave was the first chance I've had to think.'

'I know.' She held the spear like a staff, with the tip facing the sky.

'A bloke shouldn't think.'

'I'm glad you do.'

'No.' He scratched at his lips, cleansing them after having uttered such words. 'Thinking's dangerous. You end up feeling sorry for the other bloke, and then he shoots you.'

They left and began the long descent down the southern side of the mountain. Alex led the way.

Apprehensively, the German soldier hauled himself on to the

ledge. Again, he called out to the missing officer but there was still no answer. Eight men had come up, plus that Greek farmer they had found the previous day, and there was no sign of any of them. Rifle at the hip, he examined the scene. There was a line of pine trees, a narrow and rough-looking strip of land covered in snow, and the sheer wall rising to the top of the mountain. No one else was standing on the ledge, but he could see something projecting from the base of one of the trees. It could have been a branch, or a root.

He signalled to the other men and they joined him on the ledge.

'Wait here,' he said, patting the air with one hand, and then walked forward, travelling cautiously.

They had heard faint shots echoing off the mountain and what sounded like a man screaming, and then absolute silence. That had been almost an hour and a half ago.

'Go and see what the devil's going on,' the sergeant had said, and they followed the tracks all the way up.

Neither he nor the other soldiers had seen anything on the long climb to the ledge and now there was nothing here, except that strange object farther down the row of trees.

He took care to avoid a deep cleft in the rocky surface. He did not look down. Rifle extended, slightly crouched, he moved along the ledge, his attention focused on the object projecting beyond the trunk of the tree. It was a man's leg. He stopped. There were two legs, neatly arranged. A few more steps. He could see clearly now. Boots, German uniform. And a little further, slumped around the base of another tree and covered with a sprinkling of snow was the body of another man, but minus the coat.

One of his companions called out. The man was standing above the hole in the ground and waving for him to come back. He seemed greatly agitated.

The sun was setting when Alex led the three adults down a track that grooved its way through an outcropping of boulders. Ahead was his immediate goal, a grove of trees. They were the first trees the party had seen since leaving the escarpment and while not big and only sparsely dotted down the slope, they offered some shelter.

Josef was near exhaustion. Adam had dropped back to help him but when they paused, before tackling a short but steep descent from the region of boulders, it was Josef who seemed concerned for his friend.

'You all right now, mate?' he wheezed, holding his ribs. 'You seemed a bit shaky back there.'

'Just thinking about things.' Adam slipped the rifles from his shoulders. 'You know, Dimitri getting it, and all the things that happened up there. It got to me for a while, that was all.'

Josef nodded. 'How many were there?'

'Nine. First the bloke I speared. Then another eight.'

'Jesus Christ. All dead?'

'Every one of them. Even a civilian. Got no idea who he was but he was very pally with the Jerries. He went over the cliff.'

Josef breathed heavily, sucking in air through his teeth. 'When do you reckon the Huns will get to the cave?'

'Now.'

'Not in the cave, surely?'

'No, probably not and finding the opening might be a bit tricky for them, but they'd certainly be up on the mountain by now. Alex said there was a camp down by the little river. You can bet that someone's gone up to see what the hell happened to the eight men.'

'And they'd have found a yard full of bodies. Christ, what will they think?'

'That the English Army was hiding up there.'

Josef's face creased with a new thought. 'They will reckon there were a lot of us, won't they? Which means –'

Adam lifted the rifles back on his shoulders. 'Which means they'll call in hundreds of troops.'

'And they'll be everywhere.' The words rattled in his throat.

'So we should keep going. The further we get, the better.'

'Be dark soon.' It was a simple statement but it contained a plea for rest.

'How long do you reckon you can keep going?'

'Long as you like.'

'No, Joe, seriously.'

'When I faint, I'll fall on you. That'll be my secret signal' – he stopped to suck in several deep breaths – 'just a code between you and me ... so no one else knows.'

'You're a nut.'

Josef tried to smile but the deep, laboured breathing ruined the effect. 'A sane man'd be no use to you out here.' A few gasps, and a twisted smile. 'Not in a crazy war like this.'

They reached the trees, but it was an unsettling place, for the trunks and branches were gnarled and set in the twisted postures of people recoiling from horror. It was a place to breed nightmares and the tortured shadows stretched the illusion. They hurried through.

A copse of taller, more densely packed timber lay beyond. By the time they reached those trees, the last trace of daylight was draining from the sky.

Nina, hair tucked in her cap and sack on her shoulders, had been walking with Alex. She turned and waited for Adam and Josef to reach her.

'What do you think?' The spear was angled across her shoulder. 'Stay or go?'

'We should cover as much ground as we can,' Adam said. Josef had been leaning on him, one arm around a shoulder so that Adam now carried both rifles on one side. 'But maybe this is a good place to stay.'

'I'm all right,' Josef protested but in a voice so soft Nina scarcely heard him.

'Let's sit down anyhow.' Adam slipped the rifles from his shoulder and put them on the ground. Josef sagged against a tree and eased his body to the ground.

'Don't get wet or cold,' Nina said.

'The one thing I couldn't do,' he gasped, 'is get up.' She moved to him and put her hand on his forehead. He closed his eyes and smiled. 'Did I ever tell you you remind me of my mother?'

'Not until now. Is that a compliment?'

He sighed. 'I'll tell you when I feel stronger.'

'His mother's nice,' Adam said. He sat near Josef. 'She's looking after my daughter.'

Nina turned to him in surprise. 'You've got a daughter?'

'Cassandra.'

'She'd be at home in this country with a name like that. A blondie like you?'

'Dark like you.'

'How old?'

Adam had to think. 'Seven.'

'When's her birthday?'

He scratched his head. 'I can't remember. That's terrible, isn't it?'

'Hasn't seen her for more than three years,' Josef said quickly. 'Easy thing to forget in a war.'

'And she's staying with your mother?' Her hand was still on his forehead.

'Yeah. Gives the old girl something to fuss over. She loves fussing.'

'I bet she's nice, your mother.'

'I bet she's not.'

'You're awful.'

He nodded. 'You're probably right there.'

226

Alex had watched the conversation, bewildered by the sudden animation. Even in the growing darkness, Nina could see the intensity of his expression. 'I'm prattling away,' she said to Adam, 'and I'd almost forgotten that poor boy and the terrible thing that happened to him today.'

'He's a good kid.'

'He's a terrific kid. A real little man.'

Josef let his head loll against the tree trunk. 'He'd kill you if he heard you call him that. He reckons he's a real big man. Don't you, Alex?'

Realizing they had been talking about him, the boy let his mouth reveal a willingness to smile. It all depended on what they were saying about him. The prospect he dreaded was a decision to send him home before he could take the two men to the coast.

'There are villages nearby,' he said to Nina. He always spoke to her now, and it would be good to show them he had been thinking about the task of getting them to the coast and, therefore, was of practical value to them.

'How close?' she asked. The men looked on, curious.

'I do not know exactly. I do know there are villages. They are where the hills are not so big.'

'And we have to go through them? We cannot go around them?'

He shrugged. He had always been driven when he accompanied his father to Ari's house, and the road went through the villages. He did not know if it were possible to pass the villages without being seen. She translated for the others.

As soon as she finished, he said, 'We shall certainly be seen as we get near the coast. The country is very open. Many people live there. We shall have to be very careful. We should try to make ourselves look like the people who live there. We don't want people asking questions.'

The men nodded when his words were put into English. They pondered his remarks and he was pleased that something he had said had been perceived as being wise. His family had never responded that way. Much had happened today; many changes had taken place. Never again would he be considered a little boy whose words were just prattle.

'We may need a little fire,' he said.

Adam understood the word fire. 'No.' He shook his head.

'Not for cooking,' the boy responded, shaking his head even more vigorously. 'To change Adam.'

'Change?' Nina asked, before translating.

Alex continued while she spoke. 'Yes. When we walk through

227

the villages, people will look at Adam. He is so fair. He does not look like a Greek.' He waited for her to explain. Adam stroked his beard. 'We need the ashes to stain his hair. To make him dark. To make him seem like an old Greek man.'

'What's this "old Greek man"?' Adam asked.

'The ashes will make your beard and hair black and grey,' the boy said, rubbing his fingers over an imaginary set of whiskers. 'Now if you walked with a stoop or with a stick, you would be even less noticeable.'

'I haven't got a walking-stick,' Adam growled at Nina.

'Yes you have.' She produced the spear. 'Just cut a bit off it.'

Wearily, Josef looked up. 'Are we staying here the night?'

Adam went scouting. He returned in an hour, groping his way through the trees and guided by occasional bird calls whistled by Alex. The woods, he reported, were only narrow. On the southern side of the trees was a clearing on which he had found the ruins of a stone building. It offered shelter, with walls to screen them from the wind and even a partial roof to protect them from any snow or rain. A small fire could be lit in a place where the flames would be hidden from the outside.

They moved slowly through the trees. It was now extremely dark and the person in front was just visible to the one following. No snow had fallen since they climbed from the cave, but the ground here was wet from the constant dripping of leaves and thick with the detritus of ages. Every step seemed a squelching, crackling betrayal of their presence.

Aloof from such temporal fears, a gentle wind soughed through the topmost branches. The moon rose, frosty, fat and slatted by cloud.

In the faint light, they were able to move more rapidly. From the edge of the woods, the ruins could be distinguished as a collection of broken lines and jumbled shadows. The building, or what remained of it, was near the far side of the clearing. Beyond it loomed the curved outlines of more trees.

'It's an old farmhouse,' Nina said with the conviction a woman uses when determining the answer to a question that had puzzled only her.

'Not occupied?' Josef whispered. He was still among the trees, leaning against a projecting limb.

'No. No one lives there.' Adam hitched the rifles in place.

'I was wondering if you'd found an old temple,' Nina said.

Josef unhooked himself from the limb and joined the others.

'Give you a race,' he gasped. 'Last one there's lousy.'

'You're on,' she said.

'Hang on, you two,' Adam said, catching Josef and putting a hand on his shoulder. 'You stay here and keep quiet and I'll go on.'

'And make tea?' Josef said.

'And make sure there's no one there.'

Josef pulled the collar of his overcoat up to his chin. 'You said it was deserted.'

'It was. But that was more than an hour ago. And you never know.'

Josef emitted a sound that resembled the run down of an electric motor in a vacuum cleaner. It was, Adam knew, a whine of protest.

'We've stayed alive for the last year or so by not taking risks,' Adam said and passed him the Lee-Enfield. 'Here, take this. And wait in the trees.'

'Anything else I can do?'

'Yes,' Adam said, studying the ruins intently. There was no sign of movement but he didn't want to lead the group blithely into a trap. Someone could have gone to the ruins in the last sixty minutes: a patrol searching for them or just a couple of soldiers looking for a place to spend the night. He had to make sure the building was still empty. 'You can get some firewood and bring it over when I give the signal.'

'Which will be?'

'A bird whistle.' Very softly, he produced a sample.

Alex cocked his head to one side. He answered the whistle.

'Just like being in a cage full of canaries,' Josef said.

'Very good,' the boy said and nodded gravely.

'So I'll whistle when I get there and find things good.'

'Find things *are* good,' Josef corrected, wheezing as he spoke. 'Or better still, that everything is satisfactory.'

'He swallowed a dictionary when he was a kid.' Adam leaned close to Nina. 'Just try and keep him quiet while I'm gone.'

'Be careful.' She touched his wrist.

Adam counted the steps to the ruins. One hundred and sixty-three. He carried the German rifle (it was lighter and they had more ammunition for it) and when he reached the farmhouse he knelt, just as he had on the first visit, with the weapon at the ready and his senses alert. He examined the building's broken outline, and listened. Only the wind murmured.

He stood and walked around the ruins, feeling uneasy but not knowing why. There was a well. He hadn't noticed that before. He passed the leaning remains of a timber shed. The main building had been constructed of stones and timber and was two storeys high. The front had collapsed, giving the structure the profile of a staircase.

Adam entered the ruins at a place where a wall had crumbled. He stopped and listened and, there being no sounds, felt his way towards the back where he knew a corner room was still relatively intact.

He entered the room. It was so dark that he prodded with his rifle, as a blind man uses his cane, to explore the area. There was no furniture, but the walls were solid except for one glassless window, and the roof seemed sound.

He was about to leave the room, aiming for the rectangle of faint light that was the doorway, when he heard a noise. It was a rumbling, grating sound and it took Adam only a few seconds to identify it. A truck was approaching. He went to the front of the building and, using the remains of a wall as a shield, looked out. A light flittered through the trees.

There must be a road. Stupid. He hadn't thought of that. He gripped the rifle more tightly. The truck was approaching from the left and someone on board was shining a powerful light at an angle through the trees. Another light, he now noticed, played on the other side of the road.

The truck reached the clearing and a dazzling beam shone towards the old farmhouse. Adam dropped behind the wall. He heard voices, the peremptory issuing of an order, and the crunch of boots.

The light stayed on the ruins, cutting it into slices of bright stone and stark shadow.

There was a shout, and the clump, clump, clump of several men jogging towards his hiding place.

The others? He had a despairing thought that Josef might have grown restless and started to move across the clearing but there was no shout of alarm, no sudden firing, no burst of acceleration from the truck. And then, with a shiver of fear, he realized that he'd better move himself because the sound of boots advancing towards the farmhouse was growing louder. Bent double and keeping to the dark places, Adam hurried towards the corner room. Before he could get there, the truck moved a few feet and the light shone fully on the room's open doorway. He ducked behind a short wall. It was low, little more than waist high and weeds grew along its base. With light bouncing off walls, he crawled to the corner, where a few rotting planks stood at an angle. He pulled up some weeds, shifted the planks, slipped behind them, and then covered himself with the weeds. It was an appalling disguise. He put the rifle on the ground, its barrel towards the opening in the wall, and covered it with another hastily plucked weed.

He sat there, feeling absurdly vulnerable. His stomach knotted in fear, but he kept his right hand on the trigger.

Bootleather crunched on rubble. Two men were talking. There was at least one torch, for he could see a bright spot running across the stonework on the upper floor. One man with an exceptionally deep voice was talking constantly. He drew closer to Adam, the voice growing more distinct, his boots rattling loose stones.

The man seemed to be beside him. Adam held his breath and looked up. The soldier was on the other side of the wall, and leaning on it. He had the torch. Adam could see his forearm and the extended torch, which he was using as a pointer to indicate the places that should be searched. He jiggled the beam towards the corner room.

A soldier stepped into sight. He came around the end of the low wall and walked past Adam towards the open doorway. The view was neatly divided by the sloping planks but Adam could see that he was young, maybe no more than eighteen.

The soldier leaning above Adam said something in a soft, conspiratorial voice and the other soldier half turned and smiled nervously. He went into the room.

The one above him sniffed and spat.

The young soldier reappeared in the doorway. He lifted a hand to shield his eyes from the truck's spotlight and turned towards his companion. Adam prepared to lift the rifle. He would shoot the man above him, then the one in the doorway. God knows how many there were in the truck. He waited for the shout that would come when the youth saw him.

The soldier with the torch flashed the light in his companion's eyes. The young man uttered a curse and staggered forward, blinded. The soldier above Adam laughed. He spat again, and moved away from the wall. Still complaining and covering his eyes, the younger soldier walked out of sight.

They left. Adam waited for the truck to move before he pushed the boards away and crawled out of the corner.

Crouching low, he moved to the front of the ruins. The truck was passing the woods, playing both its spotlamps on the trees. The lights flashed a code of dashes on bright trunks and then the truck swung to the left, and followed the road on a winding ascent of a hill.

Adam waited until the lights had faded and the sound of the last

231

grinding gear change had drifted off with the breeze. He whistled. It was not a good bird call but to his great relief, there was a faint but immediate answer.

E·I·G·H·T

They ate salted fish and the bread Alex had brought. The well was dry but they found water in some recesses in the stone. A small fire burned in the corner of the room. Adam stood in the doorway, watching the road.

'You're sure it's safe staying here?' Nina asked him.

'No.' He didn't turn. 'But we need the shelter.'

'You don't think they'll come back?'

'Who knows?' He shrugged. 'But they're not likely to search the same place again. Anyhow, if we see lights, we move out. We're not going to risk being bottled up in here.'

'That means watching all night?'

'Indeed it does.' He yawned in anticipation of a long night. 'We'll take it in turns.'

Alex joined them. 'If I'd had a gun, I'd have blasted them.' Nina smiled indulgently but didn't bother translating. 'We were all lying behind trees,' he went on, excited by the triumph of evasion, 'and they didn't see us and I could have shot every one of them. I could see them clearly.'

'Alex is saying he could have shot all the Germans,' she said.

Adam nodded and smiled at the boy, not because of what he had said but because Alex was smiling up at him. The boy's face, shining with reflected firelight, was the colour of old bronze.

'The fire's getting a bit big, mate,' Adam said to Josef, who had put another stick on the flames. Josef was lying beside the fire and, without getting up, pulled the stick away.

'I am a very good shot,' the boy went on, not knowing what had been said between the men, but assuming it related to him.

'I'm going to get rid of the guns,' Adam said.

She looked surprised. 'After what's happened?'

'By tomorrow, we'll be walking near towns and the guns would be a dead give-away. I'll tip them down the well in the morning – provided the Jerries don't come back tonight.'

'I can carry a gun,' Alex offered, but when she told him what

Adam had said, he looked stunned. 'How will we kill the Germans?'

His face was innocent; he might have been asking about the next meal.

'We will not be killing Germans,' she said. 'Your job is to get Adam and Josef on to a boat and safely away. If we start shooting Germans, they will start shooting back.'

'I'm not frightened of the Germans. They are fools.'

'Only fools believe that,' she said, and smiled in a way that made the boy feel he was exempted from the criticism. 'Why don't you go and sit by the fire and get warm. Keep Joe company.' She leaned closer to whisper. 'And make sure he doesn't put too much wood on the fire.'

He looked doubtful.

'It's very important that we have enough heat to keep Joe warm, because he is so sick,' she continued, smiling across at Adam who was not following the conversation, 'but also very important that we don't make too much light.' She put one hand on the boy's shoulder while she spoke to Adam. 'I've asked him to go to the fire and make sure Joe doesn't put too much wood on. But I think he thinks I'm trying to get rid of him, and I don't think he likes taking orders from a woman.'

Adam squatted beside the boy. 'The important thing,' he said and waited for Nina to translate, 'is to make sure there's no light thrown on that wall.' He pointed to the stone wall facing the open doorway, and waited again. 'If that wall was lit, someone outside would see it, and come in and have a look.'

The boy nodded.

'So I want you to be in charge of the fire.' He paused again. The boy nodded gravely. 'We need a little fire, to help keep Josef warm. But no light on that wall.'

Alex left. 'He adores you,' she said.

'Don't know about that.' He was fascinated by what the boy was now doing. Alex was carrying a large piece of cut stone to the side of the fire.

'And you're quite a psychologist.'

'I am?'

'Very clever.'

He smiled. 'Do you want to get some sleep?'

'No. Not yet. I'm still a bit on edge after all that excitement.' She folded her arms. She did that a lot but rarely kept the arms in place for long. She was always moving her hands and arms, usually as an accompaniment to conversation.

Alex had gone to get another stone.

'It's just that if we're going to keep a look-out,' Adam said moving

234

away from the doorway to get a clearer view of the sky, 'you and me aren't going to get much sleep.'

She followed him out, trying to pick a path through the rubble. The moon glowed behind a veil of cloud.

'Meaning,' he continued, 'there's just the two of us. Joe's not up to it and it's a bit rough expecting a nine-year-old to keep watch.'

'So it's you and me,' she said, standing so close their shoulders touched. She was wearing her boots, the blue pants, the jacket and the woollen cap. She folded her arms again.

He began to laugh quietly.

'What's wrong?'

'Nothing. It's just that you look like a bloke.'

She swayed away from him.

'I don't mean you look like a man,' he said hurriedly, no longer laughing. 'You look like a woman.'

'Thank you.'

'But with all that gear on, you could be a bloke. Particularly when you stand like that.' He mimicked her stance. 'All you need is a pipe and you could be a young bloke standing around the town square.'

'It's my disguise,' she said. 'I've found it was much better to be mistaken for a young man.'

Adam turned his head towards the doorway. 'Look at that.'

'At what? I can't see anything.'

'That's it,' he said. 'The light's gone. Stay here a minute.' He walked back to the room and when he rejoined her, he was smiling. 'The kid's bright. Know what he's done?'

She had thrust her hands in the pockets of the jacket, and was standing with one knee inclined towards the other. Now she looks like a woman, he thought, and a good-looking one – even with all that winter gear on. As if aware of his assessment, she removed the cap and shook her hair.

'No, what?'

'He's built a wall. The little bloke's carried a lot of stones to one side of the fire and made a barrier that blocks off the light.'

'Smart boy. Poor Dimitri said he wanted Alex to be a lawyer.'

'He'd make a good bricklayer.'

She dug her hands deeper into the pockets. 'He's the sort of boy who could probably do anything, given the chance.'

'That's the thing, isn't it? Being given the chance.' He looked up at the sky and turned a circle examining all the heavens. 'Could be a fine day tomorrow.'

'Thank heavens it's not snowing.'

He walked through the ruins towards the front door. When he

235

showed no sign of returning, she joined him.

'What are you thinking?'

'That we'll have to change our clothes.' He used his fingers to brush his shorter hair in place. 'Me and Joe, that is. We can't go walking through towns wearing what's left of our uniforms.'

'We'll have to find a shop,' she said and even in the faint light he saw her wry smile.

'I'm a bit strapped for cash.' He lifted one foot on to the remains of a wall, and leaned forward on the raised knee. 'We might have to raid someone's clothes line.'

'We could always ask.' Her eyebrows were raised and her hands came out of the pockets, to open like flowers greeting the sun. 'It's quite possible,' she said, hands continuing to rise in a gentle, flowing motion. 'The Greeks are such good people that they'd probably want to help you.'

'Give you the shirt off their back?'

She folded her arms and nodded. 'They would.'

'Who's going to ask?'

'I will.' Her eyes flashed mischievously. 'I'll get an old man's clothes for you, to go with the grey hair we'll give you in the morning.'

'Reckon that'll work?'

'I think it's a good idea.'

He was silent for a few moments. 'I don't suppose we can go waltzing up to this friend of Dimitri's looking like a pair of diggers and ask for two tickets to Egypt.'

He was looking up at the sky again and she matched his pose. 'What's a digger?'

'An Aussie soldier.'

'Why digger?'

'Don't know. They've always been called diggers. You'll have to ask Joe. He knows everything.'

She put her hands back in the pockets. 'He's a real brain, is he?'

He grinned. 'Not really. He does some pretty stupid things at times, specially with women. But he's smart. You know, good with words and things like that.'

'Stupid with women?'

'Unable to resist.'

Her eyebrows shot up.

'He almost got married before the war and in Cairo he was always falling in love.'

'In Cairo? With Egyptian women?'

'Didn't matter where they came from. There was a French woman, a British army officer's wife, and God knows what country

236

the others came from. If Joe hadn't been so busy, I reckon we could have concentrated on the war and driven the Germans out of North Africa a couple of years ago.'

She laughed. 'He's such a funny man, even when he's sick. So he's a real Lothario.'

Never heard him called that before, Adam thought. Scoundrel was the word the British army officer had used.

'What will he do after the war?'

'Probably go back to the family business and worry about who he should marry.'

'Maybe he's the sort of man who'll never marry.'

'Maybe.' Adam hunched his shoulders. A mist was drifting over the field and it was cold. 'I think he's the sort of bloke who'll keep trying to find someone.'

'Not like you?' She looked at him but he had turned the other way in his constant scanning of the night. She heard a slight rush of breath. It could have been a laugh.

'You told me what Joe did but I've forgotten.'

'His family grows grapes. They make wine.'

'In South Australia.'

'Right.' He was now looking towards the woods and seemed to discover her face close to his. 'What are you going to do?'

'When?'

'After the war.'

She locked fingers behind her head and stretched. 'Will it ever end?'

'It better,' he said. 'Got a lot of sheep to shear.'

'You should write to Hitler and tell him.'

'Can't write.' He smiled in case she was embarrassed. He could not see her eyes at this angle. The face was a shadow topped by the most delicate halo where her hair caught the moonlight. 'At least not good enough to write to him. Anyhow, what's the answer?'

'What'll I do?' She sang a few words of the song, then stretched again and buried her hands under her armpits.

'You sing good, but didn't you say you wanted to write?'

She smiled at the compliment and nodded at the remark. 'I did. For one of the big magazines.'

There was doubt in her voice and he gripped her shoulders and turned her, until the faintest of light reflected from her face. 'You sound as though you don't expect it to happen.'

She pouted. 'Who knows?'

'I reckon you'd be a good writer.'

'I want to be great. But I don't think I'll have the time.'

He still had her by the shoulders. He said nothing, but the gentle

237

grip and the long silence demanded that she explain.

'I've got this premonition,' she said. 'You know, a feeling. You'll probably think I'm silly.'

'Won't know unless you tell me.'

She looked at him and now he could see her eyes. 'I don't think I'm going to live very long.'

He took his hand off one shoulder. That was the way old Tiger Miller, the man who raised him after his father died, had broken the news that he was dying. 'Are you sick or something?' Adam said, the first hint of concern crinkling his forehead.

She let her head lean to one side until it touched the hand on her shoulder. 'Goodness me, no. I'm as strong as a horse.'

'What is it then?'

'I had a dream.'

He smiled, a soft expression of relief.

'I knew you'd laugh at me,' she said, lifting her head.

'Not laughing. I'm just glad you've not got something wrong with you.' He put his free hand under her chin. 'What was the dream about?'

'I dreamed I was crossing water and I was shot by a German soldier.'

He nodded, as though he had had similar dreams.

'It was very realistic.'

'Dreams can be.' He turned away for a moment, to check on the road. 'I used to dream the one dream over and over again.'

'I've dreamed this several times. It's not always exactly the same' – she gave a nervous laugh – 'but that soldier always gets me.'

'I used to dream about my mother.'

'Who died when you were young?'

'That's right. I was always chasing her and I could never catch her.'

'Do you still dream about her?'

'No. Haven't for years.'

'Maybe we grow out of dreams.' She pressed her head against his hand. 'This one is horrible.'

'It's only a dream.'

'I know.' She lifted her head and looked up, as if the night sky was of great interest. 'I've had a few close calls already.'

He gripped both her arms. 'If we get to this place where there's a fishing boat, what are you going to do?'

'If we get there,' she said, speaking the words firmly, 'I'm going to see you two safely aboard and then I'm going to take Alex back home, just as I promised his father.'

'You could come with us. You and Alex.' She turned away and

238

he shook her gently, to bring her eyes back to his. 'His parents are dead. It will be dangerous going back.'

She tossed her head. 'No. I promised. I've got a grandmother who will worry. Alex has a brother and sister to look after. Besides, I get seasick.' She attempted a smile.

He let her go and sat on the low wall. She sat beside him but faced the other way. 'Would you like to get some rest? I can take first watch.'

'No. If that truck comes back, it's likely to be in the early part of the night. They might just have gone up into the mountains for a couple of hours and then head back down to their base, wherever that is. Why don't you sleep for a while?'

'I'm not sleepy.'

'Not frightened of dreaming?'

'No. If the dream comes, it comes.' She breathed deeply. 'I know we all think we're invulnerable, but it's the height of madness or vanity or both for anyone involved in war to believe that he or she is going to survive, don't you think?'

'I hadn't thought about it,' he said after a long hesitation.

'Haven't you ever thought you were going to die?'

'Often.' He was silent for a while. She was learning to interpret his signals and knew he had not finished. 'Usually, though, after things happen. That's when I think I should have been killed. Like this morning.'

She was rocking backwards and forwards, arms tightly clasped across her chest.

'That German was going to shoot me. I could see it in his eyes. He didn't hate me, or anything like that. It was just that he saw me there with the spear and he knew he had to shoot me.'

She stopped, leaning so far forward her body almost touched her knees.

'I was just quicker than him. I didn't want to kill him. I'd never seen the bloke before.' He gave a cynical grunt. 'Heaven knows how many blokes I've killed in this war. You just lie behind your rifle and fire away. You might hit a dozen or miss a dozen.' He stood up but then sat down again immediately. 'But this poor bloke was right there. I could see his eyes. He wasn't frightened. He was just surprised. Didn't know what to do for a second. I could have put my hand out to help him up or run the spear through him.'

'He was going to shoot you,' she said.

He drew in a long, noisy breath. 'I even thought "Why should he die and not me?" Do you know that? I had time to think that. And if I'd kept on thinking that, he'd have put a bullet through my head.'

'Thank God he didn't.'

'Yeah. I suppose so.' He breathed deeply again. 'When we were in training, we had a sergeant-major who said, any private who stops to think for himself in wartime is dead. Which is why so many of the good ones die and the morons live.'

'And why we have wars,' she said. 'They're fought by people doing their duty and not thinking.'

'Do you know what this war's all about?'

'No.' She shook her head sadly.

'I don't think about it that much. What I can't work out is what good's going to come from all this. I can't even tell you why it started, what it's going to achieve or who's going to get what if they win. I've heard some people say this is a war of good against bad, but that's a load of crap, if you'll excuse the language, because Joe's a German and so are his parents, of course, and they're terrific people who'd do anything for you, and I've met a few Italians who were really nice fellers, so why are we fighting each other? The only thing I'm sure of is I'd rather we won than they won but the way things are going, I'm not too sure.'

There was a long pause. Then she got up without speaking, and went to the room where the others were sheltering. She returned with a blanket. Again, she sat beside him but this time she faced the same direction. She spread the blanket across their shoulders.

'I thought you were going to get some rest?' he said in a voice of mock complaint.

'I am. I'm going to rest here.'

'Hang on then.' He went to the room and returned with his canvas groundsheet. He spread it on the ground outside the crumbling wall, at a place where a pile of broken masonry formed a natural shelter. He sat with his back resting against the wall. 'Going to join me?'

Once more, she spread the blanket across their shoulders. 'What time does the movie start?' she said and leaned against him.

Just before midnight, the truck returned.

It was travelling with masked headlamps and its reappearance caught Adam by surprise. Having seen it with spotlights fanning the countryside, he had expected it to come back the same way, flashing its presence from a great distance. But he heard it before he saw it and the sound snapped him from a state of reverie, in which he'd been thinking about Nellie and Kalinda and sleep and Nina and Dimitri. The growl of the gears and the popping of the vehicle's exhaust as it came down the hill were noises from a dream and he thought at first he had drifted into sleep.

Then he saw the twin slits of light, already down from the hill and approaching the woods. With a start, he realized the truck would be level with them within thirty seconds.

Nina was asleep. She had dozed off an hour earlier. At first she had leaned against his shoulder but since then she had slumped across his lap. He patted her head. She awoke instantly.

'Company,' he said, and scrambled to all fours. 'Go and wake the others.'

She began to stand, at the same time tugging her cap over her ears. Roughly, he pulled her down.

'What is it?'

'The truck. It's come back.'

She got to her hands and knees and turned to look. He slapped her rump, as he would to make a horse move. 'Go. It'll be here in a second. And make sure the fire's out.'

She left, still on all fours. He put the blanket with the groundsheet and rolled them together. He crawled behind the wall. The German rifle was there, propped against the stone. He lowered it, heard anxious voices behind him and then the swishing sound of someone scattering the embers of the fire.

The moon shone through a gap in the clouds. Hell, Adam muttered to himself, of all the times for the moon to come out. He squirmed flat behind the wall, then risked a quick look.

The truck had reached the edge of the forest. Moonlight glinted from the cabin roof and seeing its great bulk towering above the hooded lights, he had the impression of viewing some monstrous insect, emerging from the woods for its nightly prowl.

A spotlight clicked on. The beam shone through the trees, sagged momentarily to ground level, and then slashed across the clearing. Adam ducked his head below the wall. The light reached the ruins, went past and then returned immediately. There was a cry of triumph.

The truck's engine roared. It jolted forward, grinding along in low gear. The light stayed on the farmhouse, the beam bouncing with each bump on the road. There were more voices. The truck stopped.

Adam searched the shadows for a way to the room where the others were hiding but the beam shone straight to the doorway. He was cut off.

Thoughts tumbled through his mind. The others should get out through the back window and head for the trees. Was the fire out? Why had the Germans stopped? If they came to the ruins, he'd have to shoot. He wasn't going to surrender meekly. How many of them were there?

241

A truck door slammed. He could hear voices, raised and threatening as though an argument were in progress. Then the light dipped. It was still shining, but no longer on the building. He crawled to the end of the low wall and peeped around.

The light had been lowered to shine on two men, who were standing near the truck. They had their backs to Adam, but their heads were turned, trying to avoid the glare. They wore cloth caps and were in civilian clothes.

A soldier wearing the insignia of a sergeant walked into the circle of light and shouted, waving one arm vigorously at the two men. One shook his head. The other slumped to his knees. The sergeant clicked his fingers and two other soldiers walked into the light. Adam recognized them. They were the men who had searched the ruins earlier in the night. The older soldier put a hand under the armpit of the man on his knees and lifted him to his feet. The man seemed to have trouble standing and the soldier steadied him. The younger soldier pushed the other man, who turned. They walked towards the farmhouse.

The light was switched off.

Adam slithered away from the entrance, He thought of trying to reach the room but the soldiers were close and they might hear him or the light could be turned on again, so he crawled backwards along the wall to the corner, dragging the rolled groundsheet, and waited.

The soldiers stopped short of the building. Torch light flashed across the stones. Again the sergeant called out in his distinctive, high-pitched voice. Adam knelt, rifle at the ready.

The sergeant strode into the ruins, torch in hand. He made one cursory sweep of the building and then used the torch to summon the others. The first civilian appeared, followed by the young soldier. Then the older soldier came into view, still supporting the other man, who seemed to be injured. He kept one hand pressed against his shoulder.

That was all. Two civilians and three soldiers. There must be a driver, and maybe other soldiers back at the truck.

Adam was close, and exposed, but the Germans were concentrating on their prisoners. The man with the torch used it to examine the building. He found a wall that was more than head high and ordered the two civilians placed against it. Only then did Adam realize what was going to happen. This was a firing squad.

Adam stood. No one heard him move. Choosing each step with care, he walked to the group and put the barrel of the rifle against the neck of the sergeant who was still giving orders. The man stopped talking, gave a strange, strangled cough and started to turn.

Adam jabbed the rifle into the side of his skull and the man pitched forward, throwing the torch against the wall.

The other soldiers swung around in alarm. The light was faint but there was no mistaking the figure facing them with a rifle, and Adam had stepped forward and was so close he could not have missed either man. The older soldier licked his lips and lowered his gun. His companion followed his example.

Adam prodded the older man, who was closer, and he let the rifle fall to the ground. The younger soldier did the same. Both raised their hands.

The injured civilian, his back to the wall, slid slowly to the ground. The other man picked up the torch.

'Who are you?' he said in Greek, shining the torch on Adam.

Adam waved the light away. 'Australian,' he said and the other man smiled.

The sergeant was trying to get up. Adam used his boot to push him down again. He stood with his foot on the man's ear. 'Are you there Joe?' he called softly.

'Right here,' Josef said and appeared from behind a side wall. He was carrying the Lee-Enfield.

'Tell Nina and Alex to stay out of sight.' Adam kept his boot on the sergeant's head and his rifle on the other two soldiers. 'It'd be better if they weren't seen.'

Josef bent out of sight momentarily and then reappeared. 'Message understood,' he said.

'Can you come over here for a moment?'

'Be delighted.' He muffled a cough.

'Just take care. I think there are still some blokes in the truck.'

'You did that rather well,' Josef said when he had joined Adam. 'What's going on here? Any idea?'

'I think they were about to shoot these two.' He inclined his head towards the civilians. He beckoned for the torch. The man gave it to him, staring first at Adam and then at Josef.

'Two Australians,' Adam said in Greek and the man nodded and smiled at Josef.

'Greek?'

'I suppose so,' Adam said. 'Let's get this lot inside.'

They moved the soldiers into the room where they forced them to lie with their heads against the wall.

'How's your German?'

Josef scratched his chin. 'Well, unless it's gone off in the last few hours, it should be OK.'

'Good. Ask them how many more there are out in the truck.'

As Josef asked the question, Adam shone the torch on the

sergeant's face. The man was lying with his head to one side and his one visible eyebrow arched in surprise.

'You are German?' he asked, his voice muffled by the dirt floor.

'Of course.'

The man tried to move but Adam lowered the rifle until steel touched the man's ear.

'You are a traitor?' the sergeant asked. There was only curiosity, not hostility in the question. The man was confused and needed a solid basis of fact before he turned loose his emotions.

'No,' Josef said in a jovial tone. 'There's been a revolution. Adolf Hitler went mad and was put in the zoo and I'm the new Führer, so you'd better do as I say or you'll end up with him in the monkey cage.'

The man uttered a profanity and glared balefully at his inquisitor.

'What's he saying?' Adam asked.

'Nothing much yet. He's a bit surprised to find someone who speaks German.' And, to the sergeant: 'How many in the truck?'

He did not answer. The other two soldiers kept their faces to the ground.

'How many?'

'Find out.'

'If you don't talk, my friend will shoot you.'

The man sneered. 'He would not dare pull the trigger. At the sound of a shot, my men would come running.'

Josef coughed, and paused to regain the breath to speak. The civilian, who had helped move his friend to the corner furthest from the doorway, made a clucking noise of concern. Josef tapped his chest and tried to smile and then, with a deep wheezing breath, turned back to the German. 'What a load of bullshit,' he said and coughed again. 'You were about to shoot those two Greeks. If there aren't any shots, your men will wonder why.'

Adam interrupted. 'Any luck?'

'Still doesn't want to talk. There are other men out there, though. He told me that.'

'Get him to call them in.'

Josef cleared his throat. 'I think that could be dodgy. He's a bit of a death and glory boy, this fella. Why don't I just call them over?'

'Reckon you could talk like this geezer?'

'Dead easy.'

The sergeant swore again, in a louder voice.

'What's he saying?'

'It's too rude for young ears.'

244

Adam touched the man's nose with the toe of his boot. The sergeant turned his face to the floor, silencing himself instantly.

'Tell him if he makes another sound, I'll kick him in the nose.'

Josef translated. The man grunted and cross his ankles. Josef scratched an ear. 'I hope you don't mind but I changed the message a bit. I said you'd kick him in the balls.'

'Just as long as he's quiet. We don't want to have a gun battle.' Adam took out the man's handkerchief, knelt on his lower back and began gagging him. 'So what we have to do is get them to come in here and persuade them to join their mates.'

'Right.' Josef nodded agreement and watched as Adam moved to the second man.

'I'll go outside,' Adam said. The second soldier kicked as the knot was tightened and Adam pushed his face in the dirt. 'Give me about twenty seconds to get in place.' He got up and knelt on the third man, who was breathing heavily but lay still while his handkerchief was removed. There was money in his pocket. Adam passed it to Josef. 'Then you signal with the torch and call out and get them to come here.'

'What about Nina and the kid?'

'Where are they, I wonder?' Adam said, standing again.

'Out here.' The whispered voice came from the window.

Adam stepped to the opening. He lifted the torch, shading its beam with one hand. He could just distinguish Nina and, beyond her, the bright eyes of the boy.

'Are you OK?' she whispered.

'Fine. You?'

She nodded. He reached through the wide window opening and pulled the woollen cap down over her eyes.

'Keep yourself covered. You'll get cold.'

'You too.' She lifted the cap above eye level.

'Just stay out of sight. We've got a couple more to take care of. Why don't you get behind the well?'

She nodded and was gone.

'I'm set,' Josef said.

'You know what to do?'

'Errol Flynn couldn't do better.'

Adam went to the doorway. On knees and elbows, and with the rifle cradled in his arms, he crawled for the low wall.

Josef waited more than a minute. He's forgotten, Adam thought and grew agitated. The soldiers in the truck would be growing suspicious. But then Josef came to the doorway and flashed the torch. He shouted in German. 'Come here. Immediately.' He stepped out of sight.

The spotlight was switched on, searing the mist and bathing the ruins in brilliant light.

'Straight away!' Josef shouted, in a voice that was meant to be thunderous, but had a croaking edge to it. He remained concealed.

'Is everything all right?'

Josef appeared in the doorway and Adam knew why his friend had taken so long to act. He was dressed in the sergeant's uniform. He had his hand raised, covering his face from cap to chin. 'Turn that thing off,' he roared. 'And get over here. Now!' He withdrew into the room.

The light went off.

Adam raised his head above the wall. A torch was bobbing towards the farmhouse. He lowered himself again and listened. He could hear the sloshing of boots on damp grass and the rasping of men breathing under the strain of running in battle dress.

A soldier with a torch entered the ruins. Another man was at his heels. Both stopped.

'Where are you, sergeant?' one called out.

'Here. Through the door.' Josef couldn't control himself. He began to cough.

The man with the torch hurried forward. The other followed for a few paces, then stopped.

There was no question of waiting. Adam had to move, before the man turned and saw him. He darted forward. The soldier heard him and twisted sufficiently to get the butt of Adam's rifle on the cheek. A roar of pain gushed from his mouth. He fell, but knocked Adam's rifle to the ground.

The first soldier had already spun around. The beam of his torch wavered from the fallen man to Adam, who jumped to one side, then charged. Even as he ran, he knew the distance was too great. The soldier dropped the torch and raised his rifle. Adam dived and landed on the patch of ground illuminated by the fallen torch. Desperately, he rolled to one side, hurting as he crossed sharp stones. He expected a shot, but there was a thud and a gasp and the German pitched forward, to land near him.

Adam got to his feet and picked up the torch.

Josef stood near the doorway, the Lee-Enfield held butt-first in his hands. 'Well, that's my bit for the war effort,' he said and sat down.

Adam put the rifle down and dragged both men into the room. Then he returned to help Josef. 'That took all the energy I had,' Josef said in a weak voice.

The civilian, a rock in each hand, was standing guard over the first three soldiers. The one whose uniform Josef had taken was

246

sitting up. Josef flashed the torch on him. Despite the gag and the cold, he seemed to be smiling.

'What the hell's he got to laugh about?' Josef gasped and leaned against the window sill. A moment later he retreated across the room. Slowly, he raised his hands. The barrel of a rifle appeared through the opening.

'Bastard,' Josef said, shooting a despairing glance at Adam. 'There's one more ... and he went round the back.'

The sergeant pulled the handkerchief from his mouth. 'You were a little hasty,' he said and scrambled to his feet. 'There were three, you see.'

The man with the rocks menaced him.

'Shoot this man,' the German ordered.

Instead of a shot, there was a clanking sound, like a wooden drumstick striking metal. The rifle at the window disappeared.

'Adam.' It was Nina, pleading for help.

Adam scrambled through the window. He landed on a man, who was on his hands and trying to rise. The impact flattened the soldier. Adam sprawled beyond him and when he got to his knees, he could see the other man clearly outlined against the lighted window. The soldier was holding the back of his neck and trying to stand. Adam rose with him and punched him hard in the belly. The man hit the wall and let his head sag through the window. Adam lifted his legs and tipped him into the room. He caught a glimpse of the civilian standing over the undressed sergeant, who was holding his head and had blood trickling down his fingers, and of Josef, white faced and grasping the Lee-Enfield.

'Look after this bloke, will you?' Adam said and then sought Nina.

'I'm here,' she said but he could not see her.

'Are you all right?'

'I've got a sore hand.'

'What happened?'

She advanced into the light. 'I hit him with the wombat.'

Adam began to laugh.

'What's wrong?'

'You mean boomerang.'

247

N·I·N·E

The wounded Greek had been shot in the shoulder. Nina talked to the men while she dressed the wound. Alex sat next to her, listening avidly, watching the flow of blood being stanched, admiring the way the man bore his pain. Occasionally, he joined in the conversation. When Nina had finished, she moved to where Adam and Josef were sitting.

'They come from a village in the hills. They are members of what you would call the Greek underground, the resistance.' The two Australians nodded greetings. The Greeks solemnly responded. 'They were up in the mountains,' she continued, 'and got caught in all the sudden activity. I told them what happened, and what we're trying to do.'

'They know where Ari lives,' Alex said.

'At least, they know the town where he lives,' she corrected, after the translation. 'It is about an hour away ... by car.'

'Or truck,' Adam said softly.

'Jesus Christ,' Josef said, shaking his head in disbelief, 'this isn't like driving to catch the ferry to Kangaroo Island.'

Adam raised his hand. 'Hang on a minute. I've been thinking. The longer we take to get to the coast, the more dangerous it gets. Right?'

Josef had his head in both hands.

'So the quicker, the better. If we could drive, we'd be there by the morning.' He aimed a thumb at the five soldiers, who were trussed and blindfolded with strips torn from the blanket. 'Before the search starts for these characters.'

'To say nothing of their flaming truck. What are we going to do? Park it at the fishing wharf?'

Adam shook his head. He turned to Nina. 'Can the one who's not hurt drive?'

She asked him.

'Yes.'

'Would he be prepared to take us somewhere near the town ...'

He looked at Josef. 'Not to the wharf but near the town. Then he could drop us off in some safe place and drive to wherever he likes. He could either keep the truck or abandon it, but leave it nowhere near the coast and nowhere near here.'

'What about these blokes?' Josef asked while Nina was speaking to the Greeks. 'What are we going to do with five Krauts?'

'Leave them here. I suppose they'll be found in a day or so.'

Josef shook his head, liking nothing of the plan.

'Or put them in the back of the truck and let the Greeks look after them,' Adam went on.

'You know what *they'll* do to them.'

Adam had no time to answer because Nina turned, hands clasped, eager to release the stored information she had to impart. 'Yes, he would be prepared to drive us to the coast. In fact, he would be honoured. Yes, he knows a place where he can leave us. It is the house of a friend. They can even give us clothes. No, he does not want to keep the truck.' The Greek said something and she smiled. 'He says his ambition is to own a truck but he thinks this one might be an embarrassment. But he can hide it in the hills where no German would ever find it and after the war he might come back and get it and use it to deliver vegetables to the market.'

The Greek made sure she had finished and then smiled broadly, revealing large, tobacco-stained teeth.

'We leave straight away?' Adam asked. 'There may be other people coming along the road and I don't want them finding a parked truck.'

She checked. 'Yes. Immediately.'

'What about his friend? That's a nasty wound.'

The friend raised a hand in a deprecatory gesture.

'You have saved their lives,' she said. 'I think he is quite prepared to spend a few more hours out of bed.'

'And the Germans? Should we leave them, or take them with us?'

She passed on the question and both men looked at Adam in astonishment. The injured man smiled and drew his hand across his throat.

Adam shook his head. 'No killing.'

'They were going to kill us,' the first man said.

'We're not going to kill them.'

The two Greeks talked. Nina listened, nodding at each point they made.

'They will take the Germans in the truck, tied up and blind-folded. They will drop them in the mountains, a long way from anywhere, and dressed only in their underwear.' The Greeks smiled at the end of the translation.

'I don't trust them,' Josef said. 'They'll cut their throats the moment we're off-loaded.'

Adam picked up the rifle. 'We've got to trust them. And it's their war in their country.' He turned from Josef and beckoned to Alex. He pointed to the ashes of the fire and to his hair. 'I think it's about time you made me a grey-headed old man.'

The mist thickened which, the Greek said, was a good omen. It meant nature, as well as right, was on their side and was offering protection for the start of a perilous undertaking. He now wore the uniform of one of the soldiers. The sleeves and trousers were too long but a few tucks had rectified the problem.

'If anyone takes the time to check my trouser length, I will have the time to slit his throat,' he said cheerfully, producing a bayonet taken from one of the soldiers. He drove. Josef sat in the cabin beside him. He still wore the sergeant's uniform.

They passed only one vehicle, another truck with similarly masked headlamps. It emerged from the mist, a great dark and damp shape pursuing two feeble lights, and was swallowed by the night.

The town where the driver's friend lived was thirty-five kilometres away but because of the poor visibility and the wretched road, the journey took an hour and a half. The driver parked in an alley and went to the back of his friend's house. He returned a few minutes later, smiling broadly.

'Nick almost died from shock,' he told Nina, who had been travelling in the back with the wounded Greek, Adam, Alex and the prisoners. 'For one thing, he is never very good around three in the morning. And for another, I'd forgotten I was wearing this uniform.' He tilted his head back and opened his mouth as though issuing a mighty guffaw, but made not a sound.

Nina waited until the man's humour was restrained.

'He can assist us?'

'Certainly.' He helped them from the truck. 'Please hurry. I want to be well into the mountains before dawn.'

'Your friend in the back will be all right?' she asked.

The wounded Greek waved feebly. He was cradling the Lee-Enfield. Adam gave the German rifle to the driver. 'Add this to your collection,' he said.

The man shook his head. 'No, you will need it,' he said, but gripped the rifle with joy while continuing with the pantomime of protesting against the presentation of a gift he coveted. Still shaking his head, he held the weapon at arm's length.

Adam gave him a handful of ammunition. 'We cannot take the gun,' he said. 'You would be doing us a great favour.'

Nina translated and the man beamed. They shook hands and the Greek put the rifle on the front seat.

A man came from the house. He was introduced as Nick.

'Inside,' he said, counting heads. 'Quickly.'

They raised their hands in farewell and the truck drove away.

Nick was nervous. Even after he had moved them off the street he went back to make sure no one had been watching. He returned to the kitchen where the others waited. His wife had risen and was standing near the stove.

'You are hungry?' he asked, in a manner which suggested an affirmative answer would cause him great distress.

Nina, hands under her armpits, shook her head vigorously.

'Good. You would like to sleep?'

She nodded.

'Good. The longer you sleep the better. I will get a message to your friend this afternoon.' He pointed to the boy. 'He is your father's friend?'

'Yes.' Alex had not slept in the truck and his face sagged from weariness.

'Sleep first. When you wake, you can tell me where he lives and you and I will go and see him.' He signalled to his wife. 'Put him to bed out the back.'

Head bobbing, she led the boy away.

'Which of you is the sick one?'

Nina touched Josef's shoulder.

'Come with me.' He took Josef's arm.

'Where am I off to?' Josef asked in a voice that suggested little concern about the destination, provided there was a bed at the end of the journey.

'Somewhere quiet, I think,' Nina said.

'Get some rest,' Adam said. 'You'll need your strength for a long boat trip.'

'Oh Jesus, I hadn't thought about that,' Josef said, as the Greek led him out of the room. 'I get seasick.'

The Greek hissed him into silence.

When they were alone, Nina moved to the stove, where Nick's wife had rekindled the fire. She spread her hands to catch the radiated warmth. 'It's been a long day.'

'And a lucky one.' And then Adam remembered Dimitri. 'Mostly.'

251

'You make your own luck, I believe,' she said, marching up and down on the flagging to warm her feet, 'and I think you're a great creator of good fortune.'

'There were a dozen times today we could have been dead. Even should have been.'

'We're not, though.'

He rubbed his hands. 'Wouldn't be this cold if we were.' He shivered. 'I've never known such a cold place.'

'Why don't you come nearer the fire?' All she revealed was a segment of shadowed face. The cap was pulled low, the jacket collar was raised. As he approached, she admired his darkened hair. 'Bend over a bit,' she suggested. 'Let me see what you look like as an old man.'

Adam had shortened the spear and he used it as a walking-stick. He bent forward, one hand on the stick, the other across his lower back.

'Very good,' she said, turning to warm her back. 'I don't know whether you really look like an old man but you certainly look different. Not like a fair-headed Aussie digger. Digger? Is that the right word?'

'Yes.' He blew into one clenched fist. 'What about this Nick bloke? Do you think we can trust him?'

'Yes.' Her head, buttressed by hunched shoulders, nodded slowly but definitely. 'He's probably in the underground, like our friends in the truck.'

'They took a hell of a risk driving us here.' He considered for a few moments. 'Brave blokes.'

'There are a lot of brave people in this country.'

'The world's probably full of brave people,' Adam said. He moved closer to the stove. 'It just helps when the ones you meet are on your side.'

The Greek returned carrying a candle. He signalled them to follow. He went into another room and led them down steps to a cellar. It was a small room, with one wall cut from rock. A bundle of old clothes lay in a corner. There was a powerful smell of stale sweat and urine. Nick put the candle on the table beside a stretcher. 'It is cold,' he said to Nina, 'And there is only one bed. It is all we have and I am sorry, but you look like two strong men and one night sharing the same bed won't hurt you.'

'No.' She nodded and looked at Adam who, not understanding, smiled at the Greek. 'This will be fine.'

The man grunted to himself and climbed the steps. He said, 'I am blocking the entrance so no one can come down by accident, if you understand me.'

252

'That's all right.'

'It is much safer in these times. Please be quiet. Once the sun rises, there will be people around. I will come back for you around midday. Sleep well.' He opened the door. 'Oh, if you want to have a piss, do it against the wall. The others always did. Otherwise, use the bucket in the corner. If you get thirsty, there's water in the bottle near the bed. I'll bring some food when you wake up. Sleep well.'

He closed the door. They heard the scrape of a heavy piece of furniture being dragged into place.

'Where are we sleeping?' Adam said, peering around the cellar.

She sat on the stretcher and removed the cap. 'I don't know. Is there another bed?'

'Can't see one.' He rubbed his nose. 'What was Nick saying?'

'Not to make too much noise and he'll see us again about midday. This afternoon, he's going to go with Alex to see Dimitri's friend. You know, the one with the boat.'

'We could be gone in a day or so.'

'Yes.' She undid her jacket. 'God, I feel as though I've been wearing these clothes for a month.'

'A bath would be good.' He paced around the cellar. 'So would another bed. I'm about dead on my feet.'

'There's only one,' she said, jacket undone and hands clasped between her knees.

Miserably, Adam looked at the brick floor. 'Could be another cold night.' Since leaving the ruins of the farmhouse, he had been wearing the officer's overcoat. He spread it on the floor.

'What do you think you're doing?'

'Making a warm spot for me to collapse on to.'

'And what's wrong with the bed?'

He straightened and faced her. His hair, beard and eyebrows were streaked with ash and the more sharply defined eyebrows gave his eyes a new intensity.

She felt embarrassed. It was like confronting a stranger. 'There's no point in freezing on the floor,' she said, looking away from him. 'There are several good, warm if somewhat rough blankets here and, after all, you have slept with me before.' She glanced at him. 'Unless of course you don't want to.'

'I don't want to freeze.'

She folded the jacket and put it on top of the slim pillow. She was wearing a high-necked navy jumper. The candle-light played on the soft swellings in the wool.

'I'd like you to sleep with me.'

He rubbed his beard and gazed, seemingly forlorn, at the new

253

stains on his fingers. 'Look, I'm going to be going away in a day or two.'

'Precisely.'

He picked up the coat, and moved a step closer. 'And what's that mean?'

'Tomorrow might be the last time we ever see each other. For all we know, it might be the last day we ever spend on this earth.' She reached out. He took her hand. 'You don't believe me?'

'Oh I think the odds are lousy. They have been for the last year and a half.'

She pulled him closer and wrapped her arms around his waist. 'You must have been through a pretty terrible time. You were in the cave for a few months?'

'And in the mountains to the north for a year before that.'

'What happened? I mean, how did you start this game of hide and seek?'

'We were caught in a trap when the Germans parachuted behind us. So we had one army in front of us and another army behind us.'

She held on, the side of her face pressed against him.

'Things got confused. Some of us fought our way through.' He paused. 'We met up with a few other blokes in the mountains. At one stage, there were twenty-five of us.'

He put his hand on her head and began stroking her hair. 'You've got nice hair.'

'I haven't had anyone say that for a long time.' She moved her head, relishing the soft strokes through the scalp. 'But go on. What happened?'

'Oh, we had the odd skirmish. Met up with some of the local guerrillas. Blew up a bridge or two. Shot the tyres out of the occasional army truck. Lost the occasional man.'

She dipped her head to meet his soothing fingers. 'And?'

'In the end, there was just me and Joe.'

'All the others were killed?'

'Don't know what happened to some of them. We just got separated.'

She dropped her arms to his thighs.

'Do you know the last time a man made love to me?'

'I didn't know anyone ever had.'

'I'm no virgin, Mr Aussie digger, but it's been a long time.' She paused for a deep, reflective breath. 'Do you know why I came to Europe?'

'To see your grandmother?'

'Ha.' She folded her arms and leant back, touching the wall beside the bed. 'That's what my parents thought. My plan was to

254

spend the minimum time in Greece and the maximum time in Paris and to discover if it was true what they said about Frenchmen.'

'What do they say?'

'That they're the world's greatest lovers.'

With surprising speed, she pulled off her jumper and the warm checkered shirt beneath it. They came off in one movement. She wore no underclothes or brassiere. She had large breasts, which wobbled from the sudden movement and whose shape and size had been compressed into anonymity.

'You'll get cold.'

She stood and wriggled out of her trousers. 'Not if you get into bed with me.' She climbed under the blankets, and shivered. 'The wool's rough. It tickles.' Only the top half of her face was exposed. Her eyes seemed unnaturally large.

Adam's thumb was hooked through his belt and his feet were widely spaced. It was the stance of a cautious, even suspicious man but his face was in conflict with his body, and warming to the frank invitation in those eyes. 'Are you sure you haven't been drinking?' he said and one shoulder sagged as though his defences had been breached and resistance was flowing from him.

She smiled wickedly and poked one hand above the blanket. 'So help me God.'

He sat on the edge of the bed. 'You're a real surprise.'

'And you're real slow.'

He blew out the candle.

The wonder of rediscovery charged his body. He'd forgotten. After all the dreams he'd had about Nellie, all the wild longings interspersed with the bitter confusions, he had truly forgotten what a woman felt like, and forgotten how powerful was the urge that coursed within him. He was burning and bursting, as out of control as a river that has meandered across a vast plain and suddenly narrows to plunge through a series of cataracts where each fall is an accelerating frenzy of roaring and swirling and surging power.

'Slower, please,' she groaned and gripped the back of his hand. 'Oh, your hands are so hard.'

He lifted his fingers, afraid of hurting her.

'Don't stop.' She pressed down. 'I love them. They're so strong. You're so strong. I can feel every muscle in your body. Oh Jesus.' She fought to free herself from his grip.

He released her.

'Don't let go. Oh Adam, don't stop.' He held her again, hard, and she groaned a deep throated, savage noise that she stifled only by filling her mouth with his. Back curved, legs curled around him, she gave herself completely, drawing him deeper and deeper within her.

He burst in a shower of sweet pain and then was frightened, for her intensity remained. He was spent. She was a wild creature, groaning, scratching, sucking, hurting.

When it ended, she softened and lay limp with her head on his shoulder. She began to cry.

'What's wrong?' he whispered, still surprised by the frenzy he had aroused.

'I'm going to miss you.' He wiped her cheek and her finger followed his, clearing the missed tears.

They lay together, awake and warming each other. Adam thought about the last few days. Like a film being rewound and stopped and started, his mind flickered through scenes. Their first grappling encounter on the ledge. The night in the cave. Sitting with her, beside the ruined wall at the old farmhouse. So much had happened in so few days. He felt a surge of warmth for this remarkable woman. How many days had it been? Three or four? He'd lost track of time but all that seemed real in his life were the events that had happened since Nina had first blundered into his arms. His arms! He laughed to himself. He'd almost broken her neck.

She felt his body shaking. 'What's wrong?'

'I was thinking of the time we met.'

'I much prefer the way you treated me tonight,' she said and held him tightly. They were silent for a long time. When she next spoke, Adam was almost asleep.

'Do you know my trouble?' The voice was a little high pitched, the throat constricted in anticipation of allowing a secret to escape.

He yawned. 'You talk too much?'

'Don't be silly.' She prodded his ribs. 'No, I'm frightened.'

She had to prod him again to make him speak. 'Well, who isn't?' It wasn't the answer she wanted.

'What I can't figure out,' she said, wriggling into a position that allowed her to fit more comfortably against him, 'is why I still do things when I'm so scared.'

'You don't look scared.'

'Well, I am. And yet I do things, like go up into the mountains to tend some sick Australian, when it would be much more sensible to stay in my room above my grandparents' bakery and just wait for the war to go by. I mean, why do I do such things?'

'Because you want to?' Adam felt compelled to guess. She was asking questions to which he had no answers and he suddenly realized he knew almost nothing about this woman except that she

256

was American and brave and lived somewhere above a shop with her Greek grandmother. And that she acted as if she loved him. He certainly cared for her, maybe even felt the first stirrings of love, but he neither knew nor truly understood her. She was a woman and in the months after Nellie had left, he had concluded that he didn't understand women and never would. Such a decision had, somehow, made Nellie's departure more tolerable. If being illogical was a logical thing for a woman to do then it made the incomprehensible action a natural thing for her to have done. All his mates in the army reckoned women regularly did things that were beyond reason.

She took a long time to answer. 'No,' she said, stretching the word to breaking point, 'I certainly didn't want to go up into the mountains to help some Australian I'd never met.'

'You went because you had to,' he said.

He felt her head nodding against his chest. 'Yes. You're right. I had to. I didn't want to, but there was something in me that made me do it. And yet I was scared stiff. Can you understand it, because I can't?'

'If you don't stop asking questions, I'll have to do something to shut you up.'

'Be serious. It was a serious question.'

'Well,' he said slowly, 'I've been scared stiff since we landed in this country.'

'I can't believe that.' She tightened her grip on him.

'Look, I've been frightened since the day I turned around and saw the sky behind us full of parachutes.'

'Why did they send you to Greece?'

'No idea.'

'But why such a small army?'

'Maybe because we don't have a big one.'

'Then why send it, and lose all those men?'

He sighed. 'Do you remember what I said?'

'About what?' She snuggled closer.

'About asking questions.'

She reached down. 'Oh,' she said, her voice a mixture of surprise and admiration. 'I see you were serious.'

257

T·E·N

In the morning, Nick went to the town square where the old men gathered. The sun shone, weak and cold but clear in a sky of unblemished blue. The square was a severe place, with white stone buildings and grey stone walls and leafless trees that cut the flagstones with razor-sharp shadows. The old men sat in the warmest places. They wore cloth caps and thick, hairy coats and hunched over their walking-sticks, pecking at gossip with the sombre intensity of vultures dissecting a carcass.

Nick sat on a low wall beside an old friend with white side-whiskers. Three trucks rumbled past. Each was laden with rows of soldiers. The old man spat, taking a long time to summon the necessary moisture to make the gesture sufficiently contemptuous.

Many trucks had gone through town, he told Nick. There was talk of a battle up in the mountains. He had heard many Germans had been killed. He hoped so. He tried to spit again but achieved little more than dampening his chin. He wiped his face and cursed old age and suggested today would not be a good day to be out on the road. Nick nodded gravely. He stayed a little longer, heard other gossip, and went home.

He woke Alex. Together, they followed the longer route to the fishing village where Ari Rentzis, the friend of Dimitri Raftopoulos lived. The route avoided the road and followed a track over a rocky spur that ran from the hills. It was a track favoured by fishermen who used it to hike to a promontory west of the village. After half an hour of walking in silence, Nick and the boy topped a rise and saw the sea. They were on a ridge above a wide bay. Beneath them were rocky headlands and pocket-shaped beaches of white sand. To the left was the promontory. At its edge, the disturbed waters of a reef sparkled in the sunlight.

A strong breeze cuffed the sea.

The main track went left along the ridge. The man and the boy turned right and followed a narrow path to a beach. After another half an hour of walking on sand and skirting rocks, they came to a place where several fishing boats were beached. There was a jetty in the distance with two larger boats moored to its pylons. Near the jetty were several small houses.

As they walked past the beached boats, an aircraft flew towards them. It was a single-engined, high-winged aeroplane, flying low and following the curving coastline. It was travelling slowly, its engine bleating a flat, raucous sound.

'Wave,' Nick commanded. Dutifully, Alex waved. Nick lifted a hand to shield his eyes, even though he was not looking into the sun. Why show the enemy your face? he reasoned and caught a glimpse of the pilot staring intently at him. A gloved hand returned the boy's greeting.

'He smiled at me,' Alex said. 'I could see his face.'

'He was looking for your friends.' Nick walked on, towards the jetty. 'It will not be easy, this business.'

'But that was only a little plane,' the boy said. He had seen the Stukas and the big bombers.

'He could bring the big planes. Or the soldiers.' He hurried on, shaking his head and muttering to himself.

At the jetty, Nick turned to the boy. 'Is this the place?'

'Yes, I think so but we came from the other direction.'

'And you're not sure which house?'

Alex breathed deeply. He was always being tested. He pointed to one of the houses. 'I think it is that one.'

The man nodded but patted the boy's shoulder. 'Wait.' He walked along the jetty to one of the fishing boats, where a man was mending a net. He asked some questions and returned, the beginnings of a smile on his face.'

'You have a good memory for a pup,' he said and ruffled the boy's hair. 'Come.'

It was the middle of the afternoon. Nick had returned to his house. He was in the cellar with Nina and Adam and he had just discovered that one of his guests was a woman. His face had purpled with embarrassment.

'It is all right,' she said, as Adam looked on curiously, not knowing the cause for the Greek's sudden agitation. 'This is war and, as you say, it is too dangerous for us to go out.'

'Even to leave this room,' Nick said glumly.

'We understand.'

'But you have to remain here. You cannot leave until tomorrow night.'

'That's all right.'

259

He glanced at Adam, then at her. 'Do you wish to speak in English, to explain?'

'No. It's all right. He understands.'

His expression sharpened. 'You are not Greek?'

She shook her head. He nodded, that revelation having explained her acceptance of an impossible situation.

'What's happening?' Adam asked.

She sought Nick's permission to translate. 'This friend of Dimitri's, Ari ... the one who has taken other soldiers away ... can't leave before tomorrow night. Maybe even later. It depends on the weather.'

Nick grunted, as though approving that batch of information.

'We have to stay in the cellar. He is sorry, because it is so cold and smelly, but he says it is too dangerous to move around. There are Germans everywhere. They even have aircraft patrolling the coast.'

Adam considered. 'The longer we stay, the more dangerous it will become.'

She agreed. 'But he says Ari cannot take you before tomorrow night at the very earliest.'

'How's Joe?'

'He is fine. They have him hidden in the loft in a building out the back. He says it is drier than here, and better for his health.'

'Many Germans?' Adam said in Greek and Nick smiled. He had not heard Adam speak in his language.

'Very many,' he said. 'What did you do to cause so much of a fuss?' Nina began to translate but he held up a hand. 'Don't tell me. It is better that I do not know.'

He left the cellar but returned a few minutes later with a small coarse mattress. 'It's from a child's bed,' he said, eyeing Nina. 'But one of you can rest on it and it will at least keep your body warm.'

Adam lay on the mattress on the floor. The candle was low, its flame spluttering and colouring the cellar walls with a wavering golden light.

'Are you awake?'

'Yes.' She sat up.

'This is strange,' he said, staring up at a shadow flickering across the ceiling. His hands were behind his head. 'A man spends the last year and a half living on his wits ... you know, as nervous as a rabbit in a paddock full of dingoes –'

'What are dingoes?'

'Wild dogs. They love eating rabbits.' He got up to change the

260

candle. 'And anyhow, now there's nothing to do but wait and I don't know how.'

'To wait?'

'To relax. I've got so used to getting up before dawn, crawling out to see if anyone's around, jumping at any noise, not lighting fires, that I can't do this.'

'Do you want to talk?'

'No. I wonder what time it is?'

'I've no idea. It's so dark in here. And I want to use the bathroom. Desperately.'

Adam lit one of the new candles and put it in the holder. 'You might have to wait until you get to your grandmother's place to have a bath.'

'I am not talking about having a bath.' She patted both hands on her knees in a nervous drum roll. 'I am talking about using that revolting bucket.'

Adam had flopped on to her mattress and was lying with his face to the wall. 'It seems many have been here before us,' she said, her voice trailing away. 'If you know what I mean ...'

'Our friend Nick must have been running a regular ferry service.' His eyes were closed. She sat beside him.

'These people take a lot of risks, don't they?' she said.

'And suffer for it. The Germans shoot a few of them every now and then.'

'They're special people, the Greeks. I'm glad I came to this country.'

'I used to think Greeks were people who ran cafés. Didn't even know there was a country called Greece.'

'Seriously?'

'Dead serious. In Australia every country town you go to has a Greek café.'

His hair was in disarray and she used her fingers to comb it. 'And these cafés, they serve Greek food?'

'Not the food they have over here. Back home we get mainly steak and eggs and potato chips. If it wasn't for the Greeks, a man'd go hungry.' He tried to dismiss a sudden longing for steak and eggs and chips.

Her hand touched his cheek. 'Let's talk about other things. Who are your special people?'

'You mean my friends?' He took her hand and rolled on his back.

'Your girl-friends. I'm curious.'

'Don't have any.'

261

'You had a wife.'

'She wasn't a friend.'

'She must have been once.'

He gripped her hand. 'I don't want to talk about her.'

'Was she that bad?'

The look of reproof was softened by a smile, but he did not answer.

'She died?'

'Yes.'

'How long ago?'

'A few years. Come on. No more.'

She pulled his nose. 'I hate people who keep secrets.'

'I hate people who can't keep them.'

'I can keep secrets.'

'Good. That makes you pretty unusual.' He closed his eyes.

'Are you sleepy?'

'No. Just resting.'

'Tell me about your girl-friends.'

He opened one eye. 'I thought we'd gone through all that?'

'No. We just talked about your wife. Or rather, we didn't talk. You must have had girls. Tell me about them.'

'You ask too many questions.'

'It's the sign of a healthy and curious mind.'

'All right. It's my turn.'

'Good.' She settled in place, ready for an onslaught. 'What do you want to know?'

He had to think. 'How old are you?'

'You should never ask a lady that question.' And then, before he could speak: 'Twenty-three.'

He laughed. 'Well, that was hard. I really had to twist your arm to make you tell me.'

She ran a finger down his chest. 'I just like to put up a bit of a fight before surrendering. How old are you?'

Adam stroked his beard. 'What year is this?'

'Nineteen forty-three as you probably know very well.'

'I'll be thirty-three.'

'You're only ten years older than me.'

'You sound surprised.'

'Well, I thought you might be older.'

'It's this grey beard. It fools all the girls.'

'Tell me about them.'

He smiled. 'You never let up, do you?'

'No. Tell me.'

'Well,' he said, with a sigh of resignation, 'just before I joined up

262

I was living with a black woman.'

'This is a true story? No jokes?' She reversed her grip on his hand.

'True. It doesn't shock you? I mean, me living with a black woman?'

'Why should it? If I loved a black man, I'd live with him.'

'Good on you. That's how I felt.'

'You loved her?'

He hesitated. 'Yes. I think so.'

'What do you mean "think so"?'

'Yes. I loved her.'

'That's better. Never be ashamed to admit you love someone. I told you I loved you last night, remember?'

His eyes were closed. The beard tilted in the slightest of acknowledgements. 'How about today?'

'I'm not saying,' she said and smiled when he opened an eye. 'A girl has to have a few secrets. But tell me more about this black woman that you loved. Was she nice? Were you friends?'

'Yes. Her name was Nellie.'

'Was? She's not dead too?'

'No. At least I hope not. I haven't heard from her since the war started.'

'What happened?'

'She left me.'

'Why?'

'Would you believe I don't know? There was an argument, although I'm not sure what started that.'

She paused and with her other hand touched his shoulder. 'People often fight over things that aren't important, and then the fight becomes the important thing, and they forget what started it.'

'It wasn't like that. It was almost as though she was looking for some reason to go away.'

'Was she unhappy?'

'Not that I knew of.' He told Nina about Cassie, and the visit by the lawyer with the demand from Mrs Maguire.

'Was Nellie beautiful?' she asked.

His eyes were open now and he had been gazing at the brightest spot on the ceiling. 'Yes. I think you could say she was beautiful. Her father came from Finland.'

'So she wasn't black? I mean, not completely.'

'Half-caste.'

'Some people like that are the very best looking of all. Was she?'

He thought for a few moments. His images of Nellie were becoming fewer. Those that remained were still clear, like prized

263

photographs, but they were recollections from certain times in set poses. He said, 'She was good looking, yes.'

'Nice figure?'

He laughed. 'You ask more questions than anyone I know.'

'Well, did she have a nice figure?'

'You're not going to ask if it was better than yours?'

'Of course not.'

'Good.'

'Good what? Good that I'm not going to ask, or good figure?'

'Both.'

She squirmed with frustration. 'You don't give much away, do you?'

He smiled, eyes closed, content.

'Did you two have any children?'

He looked at her in surprise. 'We weren't married.'

'My dear Australian digger, the process of having a baby is not dependent on the partners being married.'

'I beg your pardon?' He propped himself on an elbow.

'What I'm saying is that you and Nellie could have had a baby without being married.'

'Well, we didn't.'

She leaned forward to get water from the table. 'Do you want a drink?'

'No thanks.'

She sipped from the bottle. 'And you haven't heard from Nellie since the war?'

'Not a word.'

'You've tried to get in touch?'

'Joe and me've written a few letters; you know, got in touch with a few people.'

'And nothing?'

'Nothing. She just disappeared.'

'You say she loved your daughter.'

He nodded.

'Do you still love her?'

'Hang on.' He sat up and swung his legs over the edge of the bed. 'It's about time I got a question in.'

'Answer mine first.'

'Why?'

'Because I'm interested.'

He stood and walked to the opposite wall. 'I feel just like I'm in a cage.' He tapped the rock. 'The cave was bad enough but at least there was a front entrance and a back entrance and you could always get out.' He turned and faced her and he was a tall shadow, rounded by an edge of flickering light.

'You were badly hurt, weren't you?' she said, sitting with her hands clasped.

The light playing on his face wavered. He said nothing.

'You loved her so much and you didn't want her to go. It must have been awful for you. And you really don't know why she left?'

'I know what she said.'

'But it didn't make sense?'

'No. Not to me.' He moved towards her, hands in his pockets. 'How long did Nick say we'd have to wait?'

'Until tomorrow night. Maybe longer.' She crossed her legs on the bed. 'Maybe Nellie tried to write to you. There could be a dozen letters waiting for you.'

'Maybe.' He breathed deeply, folded his arms, unfolded them almost immediately and walked back to the wall. 'If the Germans catch us down here, we'll be sitting ducks. No guns. No way out, nothing.'

'I think Nick's a good man.'

'Hope so. We're in his hands. I was thinking,' he said leaning with his back to the wall, 'if the Jerries nab Nick, we'd never get out of here. We couldn't open the door at the top of the stairs.'

'What a horrible thought.'

He walked to the bed and sat beside her. 'It's funny to think Joe and I could be out of Greece in a day or so.' He gripped her knee so tightly she flinched. 'Are you sure you won't come with us?'

'I promised Dimitri.'

'I know, but Alex could come too.'

'Frankly, I think it would be safer for Alex to go home than to get on that boat and try to sail to Egypt.' She took his hand and pulled it to her mouth. She kissed his fingers. 'Do you know how far it is across the Mediterranean?'

'I should. We came here by boat.'

'But that was a big boat. The thing you'll be going on is tiny.'

'We can't stay.'

She turned his hand and kissed the palm. 'And *we* can't go.'

German soldiers came late that afternoon. They had been searching all the houses. One man stood at the front and another at the rear while others went through Nick's house. Alex was sitting at the kitchen table, eating some bread. They ignored him. They searched both floors of the house and walked past the old and heavy wardrobe that hid the entrance to the cellar. Then they went to the backyard building which Nick used as a store-room. It was cluttered with tools and junk and the things that Nick, an incredible hoarder,

265

kept in case of need. One soldier even squeezed his way between rows of boxes filled with pieces of timber, old doorhandles, rusting locks and an accumulation of used nails to climb a ladder that led to a shallow loft.

Had he pulled away one box, he would have been able to crawl into a larger space where he would have discovered some most interesting items: a stool, a small table, a half-eaten loaf of bread and a partly consumed sausage, a metal bucket, and a mattress on which lay a wide-eyed and fearful Josef. But the soldier saw only a row of boxes that stretched from the loft's floor to its ceiling and he retreated down the steps.

The next morning, Nick went to the town square and sat with the old men. There was talk of a German truck having been stolen, and of a gun battle somewhere up in the hills. A number of soldiers had been found dead. As a result, even more troops had been brought into the area. However, they were all going towards the hills. Things were quiet today in the town and down on the coast. There had been no more searching of houses. Several army trucks had gone through the town last night but there had been none since daylight. The men puffed their pipes and agreed the hills would be an unhealthy place to visit in the next few days.

'We go tonight,' Nick said, standing on the bottom step. He carried a freshly lit candle. 'It is quieter on the coast, but that may not last. By tomorrow, if the Germans find no one in the hills, they will be back. They work that way.' He advanced to the cellar floor. 'And the wind has eased, so it will be good on the water.'

While Nina translated for Adam, Nick went to the small table and put down some bread and a pot of boiled potatoes.

'We will go in two groups,' he said. 'I will bring you clothes this afternoon.' He indicated Adam. 'For him. You are all right.'

Nina nodded and explained.

'I will go first with the sick one.'

'How is Joe?' Nina asked.

'He does not like being alone.' A faint smile lightened his face. 'But he is getting better. He is strong enough to walk. A few minutes after we leave, the boy will take you two. Your friend must pretend he is an old man. That is a good idea.'

'How far is it to the coast?' Adam asked when the translation was done.

'About an hour. It is a quiet track. There is a climb, then a descent to the beach. You will pretend to be fishermen. I have lines for you to carry.'

266

He nodded mechanically as Nina spoke to Adam. 'Eat well and get some rest,' he said. 'And pray that we are lucky and the soldiers stay in the hills.'

Twenty-eight kilometres to the north-east, a German patrol was searching a valley in a region where gnarled and unkempt olive trees grew on the flanks of the hills. At the entrance to the valley, a keen-eyed soldier had seen the imprint of a tyre on a patch of soft ground. The patrol had gone deep into the hills, following the course of a wide but dry watercourse. At first, they found no more wheel tracks but at a place where the valley forked into two arms, one of which was narrow and filled with a dense growth of low timber, they found a strip of sand serrated by the bold tread of a truck tyre. It pointed towards the trees. They followed a bed of stones into the narrow valley and just within the outer line of trees, they found a great quantity of cut branches and bushes, stacked like a fence. They removed the barrier. A German army truck was revealed.

The soldiers then searched the copse. At its far end, the ground was softer and at one place, soil on the bank appeared to have been cut away to fill in a large hollow. One soldier probed with the tip of his bayonet and touched metal. He dug it up and produced a German helmet. The others joined him and, at a shallow depth, uncovered the body of a man dressed in underwear.

They dug for another hour. They found the bodies of five men. All had been shot in the back of the head.

It was almost dark when the colonel in charge of the operation got the message. He had commandeered the dining-room of the small hotel in the town nearest the mountains and was sitting at a corner table. He tapped his knee nervously.

'You're sure they are the men?'

The captain facing him jerked his head forward sharply, like a parrot pecking at food. 'There is no doubt sir. The men have been identified.'

'And it was their truck?'

'Yes sir.'

He gazed out of the window at the hills where his men had been killed. The hills, so bright and harsh during the day, were glowing a soft bronze in a last flush of colour before being swamped by the night. 'What does this suggest to you Eberhardt?'

The captain was surprised. The colonel rarely called him by his first name. 'That we are dealing with many men. Maybe even some men who have been dropped behind our lines.'

'Not partisans?'

'I don't know sir.'

'No.' The colonel still tapped his knee. 'Neither do I. It does suggest however that whoever is responsible for this sudden outbreak is moving this way. First, the dead men in those pits up in the mountains. Second, dead men in a grave down in the hills. It's almost, Eberhardt, as though the persons responsible are heading towards the coast.'

'Yes sir. That's possible.'

'In which case, they may not be partisans but soldiers. Men trying to leave the country.'

Again, the captain's head jerked forward. 'I suppose that is possible.'

'But you doubt it?'

The captain tilted his head to one side. 'These last men seem to have been executed. That is the way of guerrillas, not regular soldiers.'

The colonel looked out of the window. 'Before the war, I came to Greece on holidays. Have you been here before, Eberhardt?'

'No, sir.'

'It is a most beautiful country. And the people were delightful. Friendly. They would give you everything. And now, they shoot us in the back of the head just because we are Germans. What do you think of that?'

'It is war, sir.'

The colonel nodded. The hills were beginning to flush a deep red. 'I had once thought of coming to live in Greece. Possibly on one of the islands. But I could never do that now. Even after the war is over and things have settled down, there would always be the risk that some Greek with a long memory – and they have long memories, the Greeks – would one day come up behind me and fire a pistol into the back of my head. So ...' He turned from the window. 'So we should do what we have to do and forget about our dreams. You'll keep your patrols searching the hills?'

'Yes sir. We are combing the area where the bodies were found. I have also ordered some squads up into the mountains, but it is very rough country.'

'Good, but I suspect the birds have well and truly flown. May I suggest you take some of your men and keep an eye on the coast.'

'Sir?'

'I have a feeling that the people responsible will try to leave the country. Let us make sure they do not.'

'I will have extra men patrolling the coast first thing in the morning, sir.'

'Do it tonight, Eberhardt, do it tonight. And take charge personally. I have a feeling ...' He smiled, his attention focused on some point far beyond the captain. 'You know how I am with intuition and my instincts tell me these men are heading away from the mountains, not back into them. So I want you' – and his eyes snapped back into focus and burned into the other man so acutely that the captain shifted uncomfortably from one leg to the other – 'I want you to make sure they do not get away. We will have no more of our men being trussed like fowl and shot in the head, eh?' He sighed and stared out the window. 'It will be a glorious night. Cold, but fine.'

Captain Eberhardt Klammer clicked his heels, gave a salute sufficiently casual to match the atmosphere in the room, and left. Outside the dining-room he paused, frowning. He had intended to spend the evening with his mistress, not waste his time following another of the colonel's hunches. Never mind, he thought, brightening as an idea firmed in his mind. He could do both.

As the sun was setting, Alex led Nina and Adam down the path that led to the beach. Adam followed the others. He was dressed in worn clothes and used the cut-down spear as a walking-stick. His hair had been given a fresh coating of fine ash and he affected an old man's stoop. He felt slightly ridiculous and extremely vulnerable; a soldier in fancy dress parading unarmed through enemy territory.

Josef and Nick were already on the beach. Playing the role of fishermen, the Greek stopped several times to examine the water and even went through the charade of casting a line at a place where a spit of sand projected into the sea. Just beyond a rocky headland and within ten minutes' walk of the Korgos jetty, Nick stopped again. While Josef sat on a rock, Nick cast his line once more into the water, and waited for the others to join him.

Nina went ahead.

'Caught anything?' Her tone was so genuine that Nick looked behind him, thinking there must be some other person within hearing distance.

He nodded, contented that she should maintain the pretence. One never knew who was watching. He looked out to sea, not at her, and said: 'Have the boy stay here with Josef. You and the one with the beard walk another twenty metres and pretend to fish.'

'And if we catch something?' she said, making a great effort to be jocular. Her arms were tightly folded across her chest, containing and disguising her nervousness.

He allowed her a flicker of admiration. 'Then it will be a miracle.

You have no bait to put on the hook.' He sniffed loudly. 'The important thing is that you must appear to be fishing ... not anxious, or in a hurry to go anywhere.' He paused to make sure she understood and then went on to explain his plan. The fishing boat of Ari Rentzis was moored at the end of the jetty. Ari intended to leave at ten, when the tide was on the ebb and before the moon rose. Nick would walk to the jetty and meet Ari. If there were no Germans in the village and if Ari intended to proceed with the plan, Nick would flash twice with his torch. The Australians, however, were not to leave the beach until Nick sent another signal. Three long flashes would mean they should walk along the jetty and get into the boat.

'If there is no signal?' she asked.

'If you do not get two flashes within fifteen minutes, leave the beach. Go back the way you came. Wait up on the hill.' He began pulling in his line. 'You understand all that?'

'Yes.'

'You have any questions?'

Her hands were still tightly folded. 'Does your torch work?'

He turned. She was trying to smile and he nodded, understanding. 'It is good to have a sense of humour at such a time.' He was still nodding. 'My torch works and if it does not, I will strike a match. You will get your signal.' He pulled in the last of the line. There was weed on the hook. 'Now you have bait,' he said and handed her the line. 'Tell me, how good will the two men be if there is an emergency? You have seen them –'

'Josef has been sick. I don't really know.'

The man nodded gravely. 'He is getting better.'

'The other is excellent. Very quick. Very decisive.'

'So my friend said. That is good. May there be no need for any decisive action, eh?'

He left.

E·L·E·V·E·N

Eberhardt Klammer was enjoying his stay in Greece. The life of a conqueror was a pleasant one with plenty of wine, women and song, even if the wines were resinous locals, the women costly imports and the songs were played on twangy instruments and inspired dancing that resembled a drunken frenzy. Even the occasional skirmish with the partisans had its advantages because it meant there was sufficient action to keep him here. If there was no fighting, he could be transferred elsewhere, to a place where there was real warfare; even, God forbid, the Russian front.

The captain's mistress was part Egyptian, part Greek. He had met her in Athens. She spoke German, having lived in Germany where her father had worked as a chauffeur before the war. She was a good-looking woman with a nose that projected sufficiently to disqualify her from any claim to beauty. However, she was shapely and she moved with a fluid grace that made observing her in motion extraordinarily exciting for a man with a hunger for females, as the captain had been on his first visit to the Greek capital. She had no liking for Greeks which meant, automatically, that she was attracted to Germans because the Greeks disliked them. And she had a gnawing desire for money and the things a man with influence could acquire. She had been Klammer's mistress for four months. Six weeks ago, he had moved her into a small hotel near the coast.

At eight-thirty, having already given the necessary orders to bring some men back from the hills, he had his driver take him to the hotel where the mistress was staying. There, they dined. He ate goose and was amused by his own mischievous choice.

'I am on a wild goose chase,' he said, anxious to share his wit. 'The colonel is forever being inspired to act according to his instincts, rather than reason, and I have to obey, being a mere captain.' He waited for the expression that confirmed he was anything but a mere captain, or a mere anything for that matter. She was well skilled in the art of prospering through flattery. 'It is quite obvious that whoever murdered these men went back up into the hills. We have seen movements. There are tracks.' He sipped some wine and grimaced. 'We need all our men up in the mountains. However, he is the colonel ...'

She smiled and slowly spun the glass in her hand. 'You said we would be together tonight.'

'Ah!' He raised his eyebrows in triumph. 'I have ordered men back. They are being assigned to various locations along the coast. I will inspect several of these places, to make sure everything is being done properly.'

, She sipped her wine. She liked it, but took care to frown and waited for him to reveal the latest example of cleverness.

'That inspection should take only the briefest amount of time. Then I shall move to my temporary headquarters, the place where I will wait for any reports of activity.' He moved his glass to touch hers. 'Do you remember the inn where we once spent a night? It was in a little village on the beach, where there was a long jetty and fishing boats. It was very romantic.'

'Korgos?'

His head bobbed forward, as though acknowledging an order from the colonel. 'Precisely. I will take a room at the inn. We might even have time for a stroll. It is a beautiful night.'

She reached forward and patted his hand. 'You are more cunning than a fox.'

'Of course,' he said and refilled his glass.

It was quiet on the beach. Only the lap of the waves and the faint sighing of the breeze ruffled the silence. Josef sat among the rocks, an unnoticed extension of the shadows. Alex stood on the beach with a line trailing uselessly into the sea. Twenty paces away were Nina and Adam. He sat, she stood. They took it in turns to hold the fishing line.

'I think I just got a bite,' she whispered.

'That's a dozen times you thought there was a fish on the line.' He spoke as softly as she, conscious of the way sound carried at night.

'Well, it feels like it. There's something tugging on the hook.' She pulled on the line. 'I think it's gone. What do you think it was?'

'Your imagination.'

'You're a beast.' She sat beside him and transferred the line to her left hand. 'In any case, what do you know about fishing?'

'Nothing.'

'There you are. I don't know why I bother to ask you questions.'

'I do.'

'Why?'

'Because I'm the only bloke around who wouldn't tell you to shut up.'

'Do you think I talk too much?'

'I don't know. You certainly don't stop to get your breath often.'

'It's just so spooky out here in the open. It's so dark. I feel better when I talk.' She hugged her knees. 'You've never gone fishing?'

'Not in the sea.' He looked towards the jetty but there was still no signal. The first one had been on schedule, but that had been hours earlier. 'Caught a lot of fish in the Cooper once.'

'What's the Cooper?'

'A river. Its real name is Cooper's Creek.'

'A creek's a river?'

'We have funny things in Australia. You'll have to come there one day and see for yourself.'

'Would you like me to?'

'Yes.' He lay on his back with his hands under his head. 'They were callop.'

'What were?'

'The fish I caught in the Cooper. Used a wire net and a piece of rotten old meat. Had 'em for breakfast. Joe, Jimmy and me.'

'Were they good? The fish, I mean.'

'Great.'

There was silence, broken by the sound of a door slamming in the distance.

'What was it like to be thirty?' she asked.

'You ask the strangest questions.'

'No I don't. It's a serious thought. Thirty seems so far away and it's like a barrier. You know, something you go through and it changes you. You're never the same again after you turn thirty, so what's it like?'

'Never thought about it.'

'Didn't you feel bad, as though you'd lost something?'

'We lost a few sheep in the drought.'

She used her fist as a gavel to pound his knee. 'I'm being serious and you're trying to make a joke of it.'

'I'm not. I'm just frightened that if we get into serious talk you'll tell me you don't expect to live until you're thirty or something like that.'

'Well, I don't.'

'You see?'

'Oh please, don't go through all that again. I just happen to feel that way and nothing is going to make me change.'

He sat up and reached for her hand. 'Look, I want you to

promise me something. I want you to give me your word that you're going to try and see this war out. That you're going to try and live.'

'All I want to do is see you and Joe safely on the boat.'

'And then get Alex back home?'

'Yes,' she said. 'I want to do that, of course.'

'And then get back to your grandmother's?'

'If I can.'

'You can.' He squeezed her hand. He searched again for the signal. There were faint lights in the village, subtle glowings in curtained windows, but no torch flashed from the jetty. 'How are you going to get back?' he asked. 'You and the boy. It's a long way and there are Germans everywhere.'

'I'll go back to Nick's and wait for things to quieten down. Then we'll walk home.'

'Simple as that.'

'Why not? The Germans shouldn't be too interested in a young woman and a nine-year-old boy.'

'You dress like a man.'

'I'll dress like a woman. I *am* capable of looking like a woman, you know.'

'Oh, I know that.'

She dug her fingers into the muscle of his thigh. 'The first thing I'm going to do when I get back,' she said, 'is find a map of the world and see exactly where Australia is. If I'm going to go there one day, I should know where it is.'

He laughed softly. 'I'll be waiting.'

'Really?'

'Well, I'll be there.'

'It's not the same thing.' She reached out and touched his face. 'I wish I could see you.'

'I can see you.'

'I mean clearly. You're just a smudge. I'd like to be able to see your eyes. So I could look at you and say goodbye.' She pulled him close and kissed his forehead. 'Let's say goodbye now. It's going to be a shambles when you get on the boat.'

He found her lips and kissed her. 'I wish you were coming.'

'So do I in a way but I can't.'

'I know. I'll just worry about you.'

'Don't worry. Don't feel sad. Don't even think of me.' He began to protest but she covered his lips. 'Just be glad we had these few days together.'

'Yeah.' She could feel his head nodding. 'I am.'

'Go back and find your Nellie.'

From the jetty, a light flashed three times.

Nick stood beside Ari Rentzis. 'The wind is good,' the fisherman said. 'I can hoist the sail and drift out with the tide and be well clear before I need to start the engine.' All the supplies were packed. His assistant stood near the bow of the boat, gazing nervously back to the village.

'Good fishing,' Nick said. It was not a joke. Ari meant to fish on the way back.

'Yes.' He nodded his thanks. 'Where are your friends?'

'Ten minutes along the beach. They will be here soon.'

'I will be on board. We leave immediately they get here.'

Nick turned to walk down the jetty. He had taken only a few steps when he heard the sound of a motor cycle approaching the village. He stopped.

'Who is it?' Ari called, his voice strained with worry.

'I don't know. Stay on board. Be ready to go.'

There was another sound now. A car engine. A motor cycle and a car meant Germans. They had come at the worst possible time. The Australians were exposed on the beach, Ari was on a boat rigged to sail, he was standing on the jetty. He ran and when the beach was near, jumped on to the sand. He crouched low, sheltering beside the wooden structure.

The flat beat of the motor-cycle engine grew louder. There was a squeal of brakes, then voices. A car door slammed. They were at the hotel, out of sight near the little square but no more than two hundred metres away. Were they going to search the village, or was it no more than another visit by some officer here for a dirty night with his Athenian whore?

Where were the two Australians?

He thought of flashing the torch but that would only confuse them and possibly send them back. If they were quick, and if the Germans stayed at the hotel, Ari could have them on board and away in minutes.

He waited, listening for noises, trying to count so that the fear simmering within him could be controlled by reason. He had taken ten minutes to walk to the jetty. There had been some light then. Now it was dark and they would take longer. How long since he had flashed the signal? Seven minutes? Eight? He counted another two minutes.

From the square came the wheezing, pumping sound of the motor cycle engine being kicked into life. It had a distinctive beat and Nick, who was good with motors, could picture the machine. It was a side-valve motor, probably a Zundapp, and there would be a

275

side-car. That meant a rider and another man, probably sitting with a rifle across his lap.

He could see its light. It was coming towards the jetty. He crawled under the decking and now reversed his wishes. He wanted the Australians to be far away, beyond the range of the feeble lamp on the motor cycle.

It was a side-car outfit. Nick saw it approach but then lost sight of it as the rider turned in towards the jetty. He heard the rough thump of the engine at idle, heard two men talk, and saw a torch-beam flash quickly across the sand. They were most interested in the fishing boat at the end of the jetty. Ari and his deckhand would be out of sight. He prayed the two Germans didn't leave the bike to search the boat.

The engine beat increased, there was the crunch of a gear being selected, and the motor cycle swung in a semi-circle. It accelerated away.

Nick crawled from beneath the jetty to watch the motor cycle. It left the village. So, he thought, there is just the car and it is at the hotel. And he prayed: may there be an Athenian whore of such prodigious skill that the officer with her cannot wait to remove his pants.

He heard the crunch of boots on sand. His eyes, well used to the dark by now, distinguished four shapes. Shielding the torch with one hand, he flashed the light on his feet.

They moved quickly to him.

Adam led. 'Germans?' he asked.

'Yes. Quick. We have no time to talk.'

'You must hurry,' Nina said. She stood back, her hand on Alex's shoulder.

The men climbed on the jetty.

'Goodbye Alex, Nina,' Josef said. He was stiff with cold.

'Get well,' she said. Alex raised a hand.

'Thanks for everything.'

'Hurry.' She turned her face towards Adam. 'I'll see you in Australia sometime.' He bent down but she stepped back. 'No more farewells,' she said. Nick spoke urgently. 'He says he thinks there are more Germans in town,' she explained. 'You're to go straight on to the boat.'

'I don't even know your proper name,' Adam said. 'You told me back in the cave, but I've forgotten.'

'Just remember me as Nina.'

'I thought I might write to you in America one day.'

'No,' she said, shaking her head. 'I'll come to Australia. I've got to see me a wombat.'

276

'Please!' Nick was dancing in agitation.

Adam and Josef followed him along the jetty. Josef, weak from the long walk, leaned on his friend.

They were halfway to the fishing boat when a bright light played on their backs.

'Halt. Do not move.' The voice was German. The light flicked away, scanning the boat, then came back to them. 'Who are you? What are you doing?'

Adam turned, to be dazzled by a light being held by someone standing on the road that ran parallel with the beach. 'Get in the boat,' he said quietly to Josef and then raised a hand to shield his eyes. He still carried the walking-stick. Once more he bent forward in the exaggerated posture of an old man.

'What are you people doing out there?'

Josef stopped. 'He wants to know what we're going.'

'Tell him,' Adam whispered.

'What are we doing?'

'Going fishing.'

'Sir, we are going fishing,' Josef called out and bent his body in automatic imitation of Adam's pose. 'My friend and I go fishing every week. We have....' He paused, wondering how daring he should be. '... we have gone fishing like this every week for the past twenty years.'

The light advanced, bobbing with each step the man took. 'You speak German?'

'My mother was German,' he said.

Adam was trying to see the figure behind the torch. There could be two people; it was difficult to see. He had also lost sight of Nina and the boy. They might have retreated along the beach or hidden themselves beneath the jetty.

'Are there any more people on the boat?' The German was on the jetty now. He shone the torch on each of the three men.

'Just us,' Josef said. He pointed at Nick. 'This man owns the boat. He and my father have been friends for many years.'

The German, feet stamping against the cold, let the powerful torch beam roam across the boat. He turned and spoke softly to someone behind him. The light reflected from the boards between them. Adam saw a woman. The man turned and shone the beam in Josef's face.

'You will not leave until your boat has been cleared.'

Josef shielded his eyes from the glare. He was feeling foolish stooped so low, but it was too late to straighten. Let the man think he had inherited a spinal defect from his aged father.

'What do you mean cleared?'

277

'Searched.' Captain Eberhardt Klammer advanced on the three men. He had a Luger in one hand, a long torch in the other and he allowed the light to tilt upwards sufficiently to reveal that they were faced by an armed and senior officer. 'Other men will be here in a few minutes. They will search your vessel.'

'But why, sir?'

'You ask far too many questions.'

'We don't want to miss the tide.'

'You don't want to be insolent, either.' Klammer had drawn level with Adam who was keeping his head low. The German shone the torch on him. 'And how about your father? Does he speak German too?'

'He is deaf.' Josef shuffled his feet, suddenly aware of the fact that despite the change of clothes, he was still wearing his army boots.

Adam had not understood any of the conversation but was in no doubt the captain meant to have their boat searched. The men on the motor cycle would return soon. They had to leave now.

'Look at me,' Klammer said, tapping Adam on the shoulder with the torch.

It was done in a series of rapid movements. Adam straightened and swung the stick up, striking Klammer on the hand that held the Luger. The pistol spun into the night. Before the captain could complete his cry of pain, Adam's boot had caught him in the groin and as the man pivoted forward, a fist hammered his jaw. He fell on his side, bent as though praying. He did not move.

Nick whistled in admiration. Josef picked up the torch. 'That was well done,' he said but his hands shook so much the light danced unevenly. The beam rested on a woman standing near the entrance to the jetty. She began to run but Alex, who had been hiding under the boards, emerged and tripped her so that she sprawled on the sand. Nina, following the boy out of their hiding place, jumped on her and held a knee across the back of the woman's neck.

Adam ran down the jetty and pulled the woman to her feet. She began to scream. Roughly, he hooked an arm across her face, silencing her. He dragged her, kicking and scratching, back to the fallen captain.

'What are we going to do with these two?' he said, turning the hold into a headlock, to stop the woman struggling. Nina had followed him. 'Ask Nick,' Adam snapped.

Nick had seen the Luger on the edge of the jetty and retrieved it. He spoke before Nina had finished the question.

'They must go on the boat. Throw them overboard, give them to the British in North Africa, do what you like, but take them. If they

278

stay here, everyone in the village will be shot.'

'There will be questions –' she said.

'There are always questions. For God's sake, tell them to go.'

Ari and his man had reappeared on the deck. They were hoisting a sail.

'Can you look after this one?' Adam said to Josef and, when his friend nodded, Adam thrust the woman at him. Josef wrapped his hands across her mouth.

'One word out of you,' he said in German, 'and I will stick an oar down your throat.' He had seen an oar on the fishing boat and was pleased at the way her eyes widened in fright. He shone the torch on Adam, who was lifting the unconscious German.

Nina ran forward and kissed Adam. 'I meant what I said the other night,' she said, standing back.

Adam hoisted the man on to one shoulder. 'You said a lot of things.'

'Think of the most important thing.' She turned and ran after Nick who was hurrying from the jetty. Alex was already on the beach.

'Nina!' Adam called but she didn't stop or look back. He stood there, the German draped across his shoulder like a bent roll of carpet, until Nick tugged at his coat.

'They have cast off,' he shouted and there was no mistaking the urgency in his voice.

Adam jumped for the boat and was grasped by Ari's steadying hand. He dropped Klammer on the deck. The Greek grabbed the captain's boots and dragged him towards the stern. With a snap of canvas, the breeze filled the sail. Leaning slightly, the boat swung towards the sea with its rigging creaking and water hissing along the hull.

'The bitch is strong,' Adam heard Josef say, the words punctuated by grunts of exertion, but he was searching the shore for a sign of Nina. From somewhere on the beach came a brief stab of light. Nick signalling farewell? There was a second flash. Was it a warning?

The answer came within seconds. He saw another, constant light moving from the village and heard the dull beat of an engine. The motor cycle had returned.

It followed the road along which Klammer and his mistress had been walking. A bright spotlight shone from the side-car, raking the beach on one side of the jetty and then following the wooden structure, pier by pier, out to sea. Finally, it settled on the boat.

The woman jolted Josef with her elbow and broke his grip. She screamed. Josef tried to restrain her but she pushed him and he

279

stumbled over coiled rope and fell. Bright in the light, the woman shouted in German. Adam leapt at her. The motor cycle accelerated to the wharf.

The woman was in a frenzy and more powerful than Adam expected. He grabbed her across the mouth and she bit him. He punched her in the kidneys and her legs went limp and she stopped screaming.

He didn't hear the rifle shot. He felt a kick in his back, like a violent blow on sunburnt skin, and let the woman fall and then, with the world suddenly tipping upside down, fell on top of her.

Two more shots rang out but they were lighter, sharper sounds.

Nick stood with the Luger in his hand. The lamp on the motor cycle still shone out to sea, even though the rider sprawled dead across the handlebars and the man with the rifle had pitched forward over the nose of the side-car.

He switched off the spotlight. Nina, gasping with shock, joined him.

'They have killed the one with the beard,' he said. 'God, what a disaster this has become.' Ignoring her, he stuffed the body of the rider into the side-car so the two soldiers were wedged together. He straddled the saddle. 'Can you and the boy find your way back to his village?'

She had not moved. Shivering with the horror of the last minute, Nina stared helplessly into the void where the boat had sailed. She shook her head.

'Not your home?' she mumbled, somehow recalling that that had been the plan.

'No. It will be far too dangerous. Get as far away from here as you can. I have things to do at once.' He put the machine into first gear and bore his grisly load down the jetty and on to the road. Its lights off, the motor cycle disappeared. The steady bubbling of its exhaust blended into the soft lament carried on the wind.

Alex leaned against her. 'They shot Adam?'

'Yes.'

The night had closed on the boat and Adam and her life. And she thought: so it was you, my darling, who was to be shot by the German soldier. Across the water, as in the dream.

The boy, who had not cried since his father died, began to weep.

'Come,' she said, letting her own tears run unhindered down her cheeks, 'I promised to take you home and we have a long way to go.'

* * *

It was morning. The sun shone and the sea sparkled as though the night had not been a time of terrible happenings. Ari had bound Klammer and his mistress and silenced the woman with a gag that bit cruelly into her cheeks. Josef sat on the deck. Adam lay across him, eyes closed, not moving, scarcely breathing. His head was cradled in Josef's arms. They had tried to bandage the terrible hole in his back, but Adam's clothing and Josef's trousers and the deck were stained with blood.

Ari had lowered the sail before dawn. The steady pump, pump, pump of the engine sent shivers through the deck.

Two hours after sunrise, they were challenged by a small warship. It was grey and had white numbers painted on its bow and came straight towards them.

'Jesus, mate,' Josef said out loud. He had been talking to the unconscious Adam for hours. 'We go through a year and a half of hell to keep out of the bastards' hands in the mountains and they catch us on the water.'

The ship had slowed and turned. Josef, eyes glazed, was not looking.

'Who are you?' Identify yourself.' The voice was a distortion of metallic echoes.

Josef heard Ari call out in Greek, and only then realized the challenge had been in English. He looked up at a line of white uniforms.

'Who are you?' he shouted.

'Royal Navy. Who the hell are you?'

'Jesus Christ,' Josef said softly and had trouble breathing. His eyes and nose were running. He wiped his face and put Adam's head comfortably on the deck and stood. 'Australian,' he shouted. 'AIF.' And then the words began to tumble out. 'My friend's been shot. He's very badly hurt. I think he's . . .' He couldn't say 'dying'.

'Just a minute, matey. We've got a doctor and we'll have you on board in a minute.'

Josef wiped his eyes. Suddenly, the day looked good.

BOOK

T·H·R·E·E

Nellie

O·N·E

May, 1943: William Creek, South Australia

Saleem Goolamadail was wishing his uncle would either get better or die. The old man had been sick for more than a week and because he had become ill while travelling through William Creek he was staying at Goolamadail's house and lying in Goolamadail's bed. The fact that Saleem Benn owned the house and all its furniture and paid him his wage made the young storekeeper even more bitter, for without these obligations, he would have told the sick old fool to take his truck and camp down by the dry creek bed and spread his germs over the galahs. Goolamadail hated sickness almost as much as he hated having to do things for other people.

Grumbling loudly to ensure his uncle would be aware of the inconvenience he was causing, he carried in a bowl of canned soup that he had heated on the spirit stove at the back of his store.

The spoon fell to the floor. He picked it up and put it back in the bowl.

'I'm sorry I could not come this morning,' he began, but the old Afghan was asleep. Goolamadail put the bowl on the table beside the bed. If the soup became cold, that would not be his fault. His uncle was old enough to know when it was lunch time and to stay awake in the middle of the day, rather than sleep like a child.

He sat on the rickety stool at the foot of the bed. It might be better if Saleem Benn lived, he reasoned. If he died now, he would probably leave all his property to his brother and that would make life more difficult because Goolamadail's father had no particular love for his son. Indeed, Saleem Benn treated Goolamadail rather well and was the one who had entrusted him with the William Creek store. His father would never have done that. So, if only Saleem Benn outlived his younger brother, there was a reasonable chance that Saleem would leave all his property to Goolamadail. Saleem was rich. Goolamadail would be rich.

He closed his eyes and prayed that Saleem Benn would survive this illness and prayed that his own father would die soon, to relieve him of the worry about the inheritance. That was not an unreasonable request; his father had been sick and was not enjoying life.

Goolamadail, who had been the darling of his mother and had been persuaded by her that he was a gift from Allah, felt on reasonably intimate terms with his creator. Therefore, his prayer was delivered as a petulant request from one who was on a plane that justified special consideration.

Saleem Benn groaned and opened one eye.

'How are you, uncle? I have brought you soup.'

The old man's tongue explored his lips, dabbing at the skin like a lizard searching for flies. With a sigh of irritation, Goolamadail fed him a spoonful of soup.

'I have news for you, uncle.' He filled the spoon again but held it clear of the eager mouth until the single, opened eye focused on him. 'It is about your friend Adam Ross. The man who used to live with the black woman.'

He gave him the soup.

'He is not missing in action any more. He has been found, but he has been wounded. Do you understand me?'

Saleem Benn's lips curled to receive more food.

'I am talking about Adam Ross.'

'Adam Ross?' The voice was weak.

'Yes. The message came today. He has been wounded. Shot.' He smiled and Saleem Benn nodded so that his great nose gently sliced the air.

'Adam Ross?'

'Yes. I do not know how badly he has been hurt.'

'Adam Ross?'

'Yes. He is being sent back to Australia.' He dispensed more soup.

Saleem Benn lifted his right hand. The fingers, always long and thin but now skeletal from the fever and lack of nourishment, stroked the air.

'Where is your hand?' he croaked.

Goolamadail put down the soup and held his uncle's hand. The old Afghan smiled.

'I feared I would never see you again.' He pulled the hand to his chest.

Was this the moment? Was his uncle about to bestow upon him his property? He knelt beside the bed.

Saleem Benn breathed painfully but continued to smile. 'You were so strong. So brave.'

What was he talking about? Only his mother had ever flattered

286

him. Men had called him clever and cunning, even devious, but never strong and brave. They said men confessed their true feelings on their death-bed. He clasped his uncle's hand with both his. Did the old fool truly love and admire him?

'That devil. He would have killed us all.'

'Devil?' Goolamadail frowned.

'I can still feel the burning of that accursed rope around my throat. No matter how I struggled I could not free myself.' He tried to rise on one elbow.

'Uncle!' He released Saleem Benn's hand and attempted to feed him more soup but the old man brushed the spoon away.

'That dog, Mailey. May ants be eating him in hell.' He slumped to the pillow.

'Mailey?'

'Oh Adam Ross, I thought you were dead. Now there is joy in my heart.'

Goolamadail was silent. He put the bowl on the table and sat on the stool.

'They tell me you were wounded.'

'Yes,' Goolamadail hissed.

'I thought he would kill you.'

'Who?'

The bushy brows formed wings that soared above puzzled eyes. 'The policeman. The devil Mailey. He was like a bull. You remember?'

Goolamadail locked fingers. 'Of course.'

Saleem Benn lay still. Goolamadail thought he had gone back to sleep and was about to rise when his uncle spoke again.

'No one has ever guessed.'

Goolamadail leaned forward, a bird of prey waiting to drop on its victim. There was a long pause, sawn into intervals by the old man's harsh breathing.

'We were very clever, eh?'

Goolamadail waited.

'I thought we would all die.'

'Yes.'

'He meant to kill us, that son of Satan.'

'Yes.'

'Where is your hand?' The voice was a whine of distress.

Hurriedly, Goolamadail knelt beside the bed and proffered his right hand.

'People said you had died in the war.'

'I am here.'

Saleem Benn tried to rise and Goolamadail hid his face in the sheet. He felt the old man settle back on the pillow.

'When I heard his neck break ...' The old man shook his head. 'We have never talked about it. You have told no one?'

'No.'

There was a loud sigh. 'Neither have I. We must not.'

'Never.'

'Good. Good.' Abruptly, he sat up, his eyes staring at the wall. 'They've got away.' He squeezed his nephew's hand with a strength that almost made the young man cry out. 'Quickly, you fool. After them.'

Goolamadail sought an answer on the wall, then in the glazed eyes. The old man was shouting now.

'Yes, yes. She is worth a hundred pounds. Five to you if you stop her.' He wrenched his hand free and thumped the bed. 'The load, the load. It is slipping. Did your father not teach you to tie a simple strap so it would stay in place? I swear when we return –'

Saleem Benn wiped his brow with the back of his hand and slumped forward. 'I cannot do that.'

The pause was too long for Goolamadail. 'What?' he asked.

'No, most reverend one. You must not ask me to do that. Tell my friend. I beseech you.' Distress contorted the wrinkled face.

'To do what?' Goolamadail prompted.

'There is but one God. We each believe that.' He sat erect once more and raised a finger. 'We call our two Gods by different names but that is a result of the accident of birth. Had I been born a Presbyterian, I would believe in your God and had you been born a Moslem, you would believe in my God. The true one.' The face crinkled into a smile and the old man extended his arm and shook an imaginary hand. When the shaking was finished, he let the hand dangle, supporting that arm with the other. 'It is not possible. Oh, it is possible but it is not right. Even a promise to that woman does not make it right. Most reverend one, she is but a woman.'

Saleem Benn turned his head at an angle, the better to hear a counter argument. He lowered his eyes.

'But it is the child of Adam Ross.' Again he listened, and then shook his head. 'I feel like a man who has been tricked. And all because of what you call honour and I call foolishness.' He raised a hand. 'All right. I gave you my word and I am a man who keeps his word. Unto death.'

He fell back on the pillow. After a while, Goolamadail stood. The old man's eyes flickered towards him.

'Who are you?' he growled.

In the weeks after Saleem Benn recovered and left William Creek,

288

Goolamadail thought about that day of delirium and of the strange things that were said. The first part of his uncle's ramblings interested him most. The rest did not make sense. But the early part ... *You are strong ... someone was going to kill me ... a rope around my neck ... the devil ... the policeman ... Mailey ... we were all going to die ... I heard his neck break ... our secret.* Goolamadail wrote them all down and wondered if the words were just nonsense or had some meaning, some substance that could be of value to himself.

It was a few weeks before he recalled the conversation he had had with the pugnacious young woman who had come to William Creek with Josef Hoffman. That had been four years earlier. She had been a tart, and so he had taken no notice of what she had said. But she had said someone had been killed and ... what was it? ... Adam Ross had slain some man with his bare hands.

Bare hands ... I heard his neck break.

Was it possible that Ross and his uncle and, presumably, someone else had been in the area a long time ago and that Ross had killed a man?

The prospect excited Goolamadail. Possessing such information could give him great power over those involved. His uncle, whom he despised, Ross whom he hated and whoever else was there at the time. Blackmail was not the word he thought of; leverage was better. With such information, he could apply great pressure to gain whatever he wanted. Some of Ross' land perhaps. His uncle's business. Who knew the limits?

He was not liked around town, but people talked to him and in the next few days, he asked many questions. They were sly, subtle conversations and no one, he was sure, would guess his motive. One of the men who frequented the bar seemed most likely to have the information he sought. He managed to persuade the man to come to the store and it cost him a bottle of rum, because Cadger Ferguson was notorious for not talking unless being well primed with alcohol.

At first Goolamadail feared he had wasted his money.

'Maybe you mean that bloke who broke down in a car out near the lake,' Cadger said and took another swig from the bottle. 'That would have been, oh, thirteen or fourteen years ago.'

'No.' Eyes narrowed, Goolamadail was watching the liquor disappear. He should have tried offering methylated spirit. It was so much cheaper and he had sold quite a bit of it to drifters. The more desperate they were, the more inflated the price he charged, and they didn't seem to mind its taste.

'No?' Cadger eyed the Afghan over the rim of the bottle. 'He's the only bloke I can think of. Died of thirst.'

Goolamadail's prominent nostrils narrowed and tightened as though he begrudged sharing air with this man. 'The person my friend mentioned died violently.'

'No, mate.' Cadger drank again and lifted a fist to muffle the burp that followed. 'The copper died of thirst.'

'Copper?'

'Yeah.'

'He was a policeman?'

Goolamadail's eyes widened and Cadger knew there was a chance of a second bottle.

'He was a big bastard, or had been. I saw his body, or what was left of it, when they brought it in. Come to think of it, it was your uncle that found him.'

'My uncle?'

'Yeah. Old Saleem Benn. I was working on the railway when he brought him in. He had him in a bag on the back of one of his camels.'

Each began to smile, a fox confronting a fox. Cadger took a long drink but his eyes never left the Afghan's.

'Do you know his name?' Goolamadail asked.

Cadger wiped his lips without removing the smile. 'I think I could remember.' There was a long pause. 'I was wondering if you had another bottle of rum?'

'I have high quality metho.'

The other man looked amused. 'No,' he said shaking his head. 'To make the memory work proper, I need rum. You're not a drinker so you wouldn't understand.'

Goolamadail got another bottle. He offered it.

'Let's see now,' Cadger said, eyes raised to seek inspiration from the shadowy ceiling of the store. One hand reached out to grip the bottle's neck but Goolamadail retained his hold.

'The name,' he said.

'Mailey,' Cadger said. 'Jesus, mate, don't shake like that or you'll drop it.'

A few days later, Goolamadail thought about the other things his uncle had said. Some of it, obviously, was worthless, a meaningless jumble of words inspired by the fever. But the part about Ross and his child ... Why was his uncle talking about the Ross girl? Or was he talking about someone else, another child? And the person he called 'most reverend'. Was that a derogatory phrase or was he serious? He'd talked about a Presbyterian. The only Presbyterian Goolamadail knew was the Australian Inland Mission padre who

290

made an occasional visit, the man called Montgomery.

What had his uncle said? He had been tricked, but he had given his word. He had given his word, about the child of Adam Ross, to Montgomery?

Surely there was a way here to cause damage to Adam Ross. Years before, he had tried with a futile letter to Ross's mother-in-law, Mrs Maguire. He had told her terrible things were happening at Kalinda, but the whole scheme had been spoiled when the child was whisked away and Ross joined the army.

He had since heard the grandmother had died. Never mind. There would be other opportunities to hurt Adam Ross and, inadvertently, his uncle might have shown him the way.

Goolamadail spent weeks grappling with the pieces of the puzzle. The policeman Mailey. The name his uncle had mentioned. The same name Cadger Ferguson had given him. Mailey died of thirst yet his uncle – who found the body – had talked of a broken neck. So had Josef Hoffman's woman. And Adam Ross had killed someone, with his bare hands. Mailey?

And the child, whose father was Ross, and the reverend Presbyterian, and the promise that Saleem Benn had been tricked into giving. One puzzle, or two?

Instinctively, Goolamadail knew he possessed information that could be of great value to him, but the facts were cloudy and incomplete. There were too many missing pieces for the puzzle to make sense. At first, he was anxious for quick answers and went through the items he had written down until his head ached from confusion and frustration.

Then he grew calmer. Ross would be back soon. They said he was being invalided home. There was time for him to gather more information about the two prime elements: Mailey and the child. He would listen, ask questions when he thought it was appropriate, and wait. For years, if necessary. The longer he had to wait for his revenge, the more exquisite it would be.

T · W · O

November 1943: William Creek

The drought was still bad, the road exceptionally rough and the
heat intense, and when the Reverend Roger Montgomery reached
the store he spilled rather than stepped from the car seat, and
staggered into the shade. He took off his hat and wiped his forehead. He saw nothing but deep, cool shadows for his eyes were still
accustomed to the glare of the road from Oodnadatta.

Goolamadail had been thinking of the padre. His voice came
from the darkest corner.

'You have the look of a chicken that has escaped the pot.'

Roger laughed. It was a thin sound, produced through a throat of
painful dryness. 'Hello, Gooly. I can't see you, as usual, but I
suppose it's you.'

'Indeed it is. You would like a lemonade?'

'I would give almost anything for a drink.'

There was a metallic click and the sharp hiss of escaping gas.
Goolamadail materialized from the darkness. He offered an opened
bottle of lemonade.

'And how is my most reverend friend?'

Roger drank and laughed, spluttering drink down his chin.
'That's what your uncle calls me.'

'Really?' Goolamadail lowered his eyes. Inwardly, he soared.
Another piece had slipped into place.

The padre wiped his mouth. 'And how is my dear friend Saleem
Benn? Better?'

'I believe so. I have not seen him for some time. I get no news
from Marree.'

'He was very sick.'

Goolamadail agreed, and then assembled the items that Roger
needed for his journey south. He was returning to the mission at

Beltana, after a three-month drive through the north-western portion of his territory.

'Have you heard any more news about my good friend Mr Adam Ross?' the Afghan enquired, while packing sugar and tea into a cardboard carton.

'No, Gooly. I've been out of touch for a while. They were talking of sending him home but the last I heard was he'd made such a good recovery that there was a chance he'd stay over there.'

'Oh,' he said, concentrating on the packing. 'Mr Ross is a redoubtable character.'

Roger smiled.

'I have said something amusing?'

'No. I was merely thinking that you sound more like your uncle every day.'

'Ah!' He fashioned an oily smile. 'I am very close to my uncle. His favourite nephew, as the saying goes.'

'Then you are fortunate.'

'Indeed.' He bowed. Now was the time to try. 'We are very close. I am his confidant.'

'That is good.'

'Yes. I nursed him and fed him when he was sick.'

Roger almost said 'that was very Christian of you' but remembered in time.

'We talked a great deal. But back to Mr Adam Ross. Tell me,' Goolamadail went on and Roger nodded, to indicate his readiness to comply, 'has the child been told?' He paused to ensure the next dart would hit the target. 'The little one my uncle was talking about.'

Roger stared at him in astonishment.

'The child of Mr Adam Ross. Does the poor little creature know that misfortune has befallen its father?'

'How –?' Roger said. 'Who –?'

Goolamadail's eyes closed, so that no one could peek in to share his triumph. So it was certain. There was another child. Now, he would have to be cautious. Better to miss more facts than alarm this man who could go running to his uncle, for if he did there could be trouble of the most unpleasant kind.

'Saleem Benn told you?'

The eyebrows said 'of course' but Goolamadail was clever enough to remain silent.

'I don't know what to say.' Roger shook his head in distress.

'My question is so difficult?' the Afghan asked, his face beaming innocence.

293

'Well, it's just ... I mean.' Roger turned and faced the opening of the store and the parked Ford, scorching in the sun.

He would say no more. Time to make him feel foolish. 'Has she been told?' Goolamadail asked.

'She?' The padre turned and the desperate concern that cemented his face began to crumble into a smile. 'Oh, you mean the girl?'

'Yes.' He returned the smile. 'I have never met her. What is her name?'

'Cassie. Cassandra's her proper name I think.' His body softened with relief. 'I suppose she's been told. She's in Adelaide I believe. I haven't seen her since she was just a tot.'

'I have never had the pleasure of seeing Mr Adam Ross's child.'

'She's a lovely girl.'

'I'm sure.' And there is another child and it's a boy. Which means, Goolamadail thought, that the mother has to be the black bitch Nellie Arlton.

December 1943: Marree

The washing hanging from the clothes-line was so dry it crackled at the touch. Nellie gathered it and was walking to the house, counting the steps because the heat in the open yard was so fierce, when she saw the Ford approaching. She threw the washing on an old and decrepit couch that sprawled across the back verandah, and waited, hand shielding her eyes. Roger Montgomery stopped the car near the peppercorn tree and wrote something in a notebook. He was always writing things in that book, she thought, as she walked to the wire fence at a place where there was shade from the tree.

Roger got out of the car. Pencil clenched between his teeth, he waved. Then he removed the pencil, smiled, walked into the shade to greet her, and looked sombre, an expression suitable for the news he had heard in the town. Nellie had lost her job at the hotel. There was no question of incompetence or dissatisfaction. Roger had checked with the publican. Business was poor. The man had no money to spend on the wages of a barmaid and assistant cook.

'What will you do?' he asked.

'Dunno,' she said, her arms crossed and leaning on a fence post.

'How's the boy?'

'Good.' She smiled and he thought what a marvellous looking woman she was. 'Well, no, he's not that good because he's sick. Got a cold.'

He offered sympathy and they talked about the paradox of catching a cold in a town as hot as Marree.

A man leading two camels walked past. He raised his hat and both acknowledged the greeting. Hawks circled above them, wing tips flexing as they caressed the rising currents of hot air. The birds were up every day, drifting across the three parts of town in their search for scraps. Marree was divided neatly. The white part was on the western side of the railway line. The Afghan part was on the other side of the line and the aboriginal part lay further to the east on the fringe of a gibber plain. The hawks began their search over the area inhabited by the whites, where the pickings were fewer but likely to be richer, as the whites threw out things the others would not, and then gradually moved across towards the rubbish heaps surrounding the aboriginal camps. Nellie was in the middle section of town, sharing a house with Ramala, an Afghan woman whose dead husband had been a friend of Saleem Benn.

'So you have a sick child and no money coming in,' Roger said, gazing up at the birds.

'I've saved some money.'

'But you'll need a job.' She nodded and he took off his hat and wiped his forehead and scalp. 'Goodness me, it's hot. How's Ramala?'

'She's thinking of getting married again.' Nellie's expression was as glum as her voice.

'So she'll need the room?'

She nodded. 'She's been very nice.'

'But now you need a job and a new place to live.'

'Any offers?'

'There is a possibility.' He had to wear glasses now and he took them off to polish the lenses. They were constantly being coated with fine dust. The more he rubbed, the more rapidly they seemed to become dusted again. 'Have you ever heard of Innamincka?'

'Sort of. It's up the Birdsville Track?' She glanced across to the set of tracks that meandered out of town to the north-east. The tracks stood out clearly, twin ribbons of dusty white curving across the purple grey expanse of the gibber plain.

'No. It's up the Strzelecki,' he corrected. 'It's on the Cooper, near the Queensland border.' He explained what he had in mind. The Australian Inland Mission operated a small bush hospital at Innamincka. There was no town there, just a hospital which served a vast but sparsely populated area. The nearest homesteads were Nappa Merrie, just over the border in Queensland, and the huge

295

cattle station of Innamincka, north of Cooper's Creek. The hospital needed a nurse.

He put his glasses on and tested them by focusing on her face. 'What do you think?'

She stared back, equally intense. 'About what?'

'Going to Innamincka.'

She smiled, dazzling him with a broadside of sparkling teeth. 'Come off it. I'm not a nurse.'

She would be trained on the job. The matron was a great woman. The need was desperate. And he felt sure Nellie would make a good nurse. He blinked. His eyes were fading behind a fine coating of dust that formed in swirling patterns on his glasses.

'I'd be cleaning bedpans?'

'Yes.' He nodded enthusiastically. 'And other things. You might have to do some of the cooking.'

'And you get paid?'

'Three pounds ten shillings a week. Plus board and all meals.'

She let her head hang. 'I don't think so.'

'It'd be a great place for the boy. Quiet. Healthy. The people on the various cattle stations seem a good lot.'

'I was thinking of going up to William Creek.'

'For good?'

'No. Not yet, anyhow.' She lifted her arms on the post. 'I just thought I might go up for a few days and see how Jimmy and Stella were getting on. And I haven't seen their kid since Stella and I were in hospital at Oodnadatta together.'

'It's a year since I was out at Kalinda. They seemed fine then.'

'And the girl?'

'Full of beans.'

'I'd like to see them.' She turned and folded her arms. She leaned against the post. 'Adam might have written to them. He could be back soon.'

He removed his glasses and put them in their case. It was simpler than cleaning them constantly. 'What will you do when he comes back?' He squinted at her.

'Depends. He might bring someone home with him.'

'I don't think so. He'll be hoping to find you waiting for him.'

'Do you reckon?'

'I think so, Nellie. And it will be so much easier for you now, since poor old Mrs Maguire, God rest her soul, passed away. He'll be able to keep Cassie. There'll be no more worries about someone trying to take her away from him and you can all be together. All four of you.'

Again, she overwhelmed him with her smile. She had a large mouth and the teeth were magnificent. 'What do you reckon he'll say when he sees Daniel?'

Roger searched for the birds but it was a futile quest for, without his glasses, the sky was a blur of glaring vapours. 'I think he'll be very surprised.'

'Pleased?'

'When he gets over the shock.' He wiped his forehead. 'You *will* go back to him?' It was a plea rather than a question.

'It depends. That's why I'd like to go up to William Creek for a few days and see Jimmy and Stella. They might have heard from Adam.' Her toe traced a delicate pattern in the yard's dust. 'You know, he might have said something in a letter.'

His head bobbed agreement, then sagged in doubt. 'Would you take Daniel?'

'No. He's got a cold,' she said, burying her hands beneath her folded arms. 'Besides, it's better that others don't see him for a while. Not up there, anyhow.'

He brightened. 'And what about Innamincka? It's a job, there is accommodation provided, and they do need help.'

Her toe swept the dust to one side. 'Would you mind if I went to William Creek first? Then I might know what's best for me to do.'

'Of course.' He breathed deeply and took advantage of his temporarily slimmer waist to tuck the loose ends of the shirt into his trousers. 'I'm due to drive up to Innamincka in three weeks' time. I'd like to know by then.'

The train was late and reached William Creek just before midnight. Nellie was the only passenger to alight. A lantern hung on the platform. Another light glowed softly from the verandah of the hotel. There was no sign of Jimmy Kettle, to whom she had written, and no sign of any other person. The few passengers on the train slept. The locomotive hissed steam. Insects slapped against lantern glass.

All day the air had been thin and scorched and drained of taste. Now it was alive with aromas, a tangy mix of smoke and dust and withered vegetation and the left-over smells of evening meals and doused cooking fires.

The train guard walked past, swinging his own lantern.

'There's no one here,' Nellie complained, gripping her small suitcase in both hands. 'Isn't there a station master?'

'There's a war on.' He pulled on a silver chain and a watch emerged from his vest pocket, spinning like a small fish on a line.

'We'll be here an hour.'

'I'm getting off here.'

'We'll still be here an hour.' He pocketed the watch. 'Someone meeting you?'

'Yes.' She looked around hopefully.

'Is it that gentleman over there?' He nodded towards the street, where a man stood. The guard touched his cap and walked towards the engine.

The man on the road did not move. It was not Jimmy. This person had two arms and was tall and thin. Nellie waited several minutes and then walked to the tiny waiting room and sat near the hanging lantern. She heard steps. The man walked into the light.

It was Goolamadail.

'I thought it was you.' He frowned.

'You always were clever.'

'What are you doing here?' he said, untouched by her irony. He had been lusting for a woman all night and had come to look at the train, in case there were pretty women travelling north.

'Visiting,' she said, not bothering to look at him.

'I thought you had gone.'

'See. Even you can make a mistake.'

'Why did you come back?'

'I told you.'

'Why did you go away?'

'To visit friends. I have friends here and I have friends somewhere else and that's what I do, I go from here to there. Now I'm here. Next time I'll go there.'

One arm lifted, he leaned against the corner post of the waiting room. It was a pose he liked. He had practised it in front of the mirror and thought it gave him a lithe, romantic look, like Rudolph Valentino, whose picture in a similar stance he had found in an old book.

'Who is coming to meet you?'

'Santa Claus. It's nearly Christmas.'

'I think you're making jokes.'

Now she turned her eyes on him. 'Have you hurt your back?'

'Why?' He smiled his Valentino smile.

'Because of the way you're standing. You look like a lizard trying to climb a broken drainpipe.'

He straightened and frowned. 'Someone is coming to meet you?'

'Yes.'

'They are very late.'

'So was the train.'

'That's what I mean. They should have been here.' He moved to the opposite side of the entrance way. She changed position on the seat, to face another wall.

'Would you care for a cup of tea?'

She regarded him with astonishment. 'Have you got some condemned stock or something?'

His face drooped in dismay. 'I don't know why you say such things. Is it only because you joke?'

'It's only because I know you so well.'

'It is a genuine offer. You must be very tired and very thirsty. It was one hundred and eight degrees today.'

She was tired, she was thirsty and she was worried. She had sent a follow-up telegram to Jimmy and Stella a week ago and someone would have got the message out to them. Jimmy might be inclined to let her wait but Stella would insist they be at the station to meet her.

'Well?' He made his best attempt at smiling brightly. It was not difficult because he felt great joy. Here, delivered to him was the one person who could answer the questions that had plagued him for months. And once he'd gained the information he needed, he would make passionate love to her, after she had oiled his body and teased him almost to the point of madness. And when it was all over and she lay on the bed stunned by the perfection of his body, he would thrash her.

'What if they arrive?' she said.

'We will see them. The store is just across the way. Surely you remember.'

'Only too well.'

'It is settled then. A cup of tea to show you I have no hard feelings.' He led the way from the station.

'You have no hard anything,' she said softly and not hearing her clearly, he turned and smiled when she smiled. He went to the store, produced a torch and moved to the corner area at the back. There he lit a lamp and chatted while he made tea. Business had been bad, he said, because of the drought and the fact that food was rationed and other items were not available and all the young men were away at war.

'Not you, Gooly?' she said and he tapped the side of his head to indicate great cunning. There was a problem with his eyes, he said, and winked.

I'll bet there is, she thought. The only trouble with his eyes was strain from looking after himself.

The poor business did not really matter, he continued. This was his uncle's enterprise and his uncle paid him a weekly wage no matter how much he sold. The quieter the business, the better. He smiled. She half smiled, and having drunk some of the tea and slaked her thirst, regretted having come in here. The man was loathsome slime, so unlike the Afghans among whom she had been living in Marree.

'And how is my uncle?' he said and she sensed a trap. He would not know where she had been or that she had had any contact with Saleem Benn. The old man had sworn to tell no one. He would certainly not tell Goolamadail who would have told all William Creek.

'Saleem Benn? How would I know? I was about to ask you.'

He had settled into the corner and sat with one leg raised on the chair. He had the look of someone who knows your most personal secrets, and she felt uncomfortable.

'Oh,' he said, scratching the raised knee. 'I have not seen him for many weeks but after my last conversation with my esteemed uncle, I formed the impression that you and he were, shall we say, very close.'

She put the cup on top of a crate. 'What are you talking about?'

'The baby.' Bullseye. No doubt. Unable to resist, he squeezed his knee in triumph. Her reaction was perfect: shock, a face that paled, an open mouth, disbelief then, possibly, admiration for his guile.

'What baby?' she said but her voice was weak, and only strengthened as she continued to talk. 'Really, Gooly, you talk a lot of rubbish. Your uncle hasn't got a baby.'

His eyes narrowed, his own way of showing admiration. She was quick but it was a pathetic attempt to turn the conversation.

'Please,' he said, looking down so that it seemed that he was inspecting his crotch, 'don't play silly word games. My uncle confides in me.'

'Bully for him.'

'How is the boy?'

She was silent but her eyes grew even wider.

'I'm only making a polite enquiry,' he said.

'Like hell. Did Saleem Benn tell you I had a son?' She tried to make the question appear ridiculous.

'He tells me everything.'

'Bullshit,' she said and he winced at the word. 'If he told you the time, he'd check his watch to make sure you hadn't nicked the minute hand.'

He sighed. 'You are still extremely coarse. You need to be taught a lesson.'

'Not by you.' She gripped the cup.

'You have a son,' he said and extended his hand as a magician does the instant before performing his greatest trick. 'The father is Adam Ross. You are not married. Your son is a bastard.'

'You're the bastard around here.'

His neck sagged, dumping the chin on the chest. 'And all I wanted was to be polite. I knew about your child. My uncle told me. Why shouldn't he? It does not matter to me whether you have one boy or two dozen. I was attempting to make what you would call pleasant conversation. Small talk. But you insist on being insulting.'

She leaned back. 'What do you want?'

He matched her pose. For several seconds they faced each other, each attempting to suggest amused tolerance.

He spoke. 'I could suggest a bargain of sorts.'

'Like what?'

'I have been thinking about what happened last time you were here.'

Nellie smiled with pleasure. He had tried to maul her and she had belted him with a pickaxe handle.

'I realize now,' he added, 'that what you did was an expression of feeling.'

'It certainly was.'

'Ah! You see.'

'I was expressing a feeling of hatred.'

'You say that because you are too proud to confess your deepest emotions.' He raised a hand to stifle any protest. 'But I understand how you truly feel.'

'I'm so pleased,' she purred.

'Good.' He stood and she stood, not wanting to give him the high ground.

'You said a bargain?' Nellie retreated two steps and realized that he had placed her in a trap. To get out, she had to pass him. She looked around for possible weapons. There was a broom against the wall, within reach. He remained where he was, a contented smirk seeping across his face. Spreading his hands, he prepared to define the limits of the bargain he was proposing. But first, there was another question.

'Who was coming to meet you?'

'Jimmy Kettle.'

The smirk became contemptuous. He moved a hand as though brushing away a fly. 'He might be here today, tomorrow, next week. With such a person there is never reliability.'

She wished Jimmy were here. Even with one arm he could frighten this man into bowing obsequiousness. 'He used to be a boxer,' she said.

One eyebrow arched. 'And you used to be a whore, rented by the night.'

She still had the cup and she held it now like a stone, ready for throwing. 'Who told you that?'

His hand brushed aside such an unimportant question. 'Everyone knows.'

'I'm going back to the station.' She lifted the cup.

He reached behind him and produced a breadknife. He smiled. 'First, there is a bargain to discuss.'

She backed against the wall.

'When this Jimmy Kettle comes, tell him to go away. Tell him you are staying here.'

'You're nuts.'

He ignored her. 'You will remain here with me. I will make you very happy. You will make me very happy.'

Slowly, she reached for the broom and pulled it towards her. A broom against a knife wasn't much but she could get in one blow that would hurt. If he came one step closer, she would hit him. The thought of his touch sickened her.

'I need a woman. It is very lonely here. And you need a man. A man like me.' He spoke as though the logic were irrefutable.

She held the broom in front of her. 'I need a man like you like I need a dose of rat poison.'

His nostrils flared and she recognized the sign. It wasn't anger. He began twisting the knife so the blade flashed in the lantern light. She'd known men like him when she was young and working down at Port Pirie. They were the cruel ones, who got out of control.

'You said there was a bargain,' she prompted, hoping to calm him, because he looked as though he was about to lunge at her with the knife.

He put the flat of the blade to his nose, breathed deeply and closed his eyes. 'It is very simple,' he said rapidly, eyes still shut. 'You do as I say or I reveal what I know about your bastard child. It will ruin Mr High and Mighty Adam Ross and you two will never be able to live here again.'

'What are you talking about?'

The eyes opened and studied her from either side of the blade. 'His reputation already is a poor one. Living with a notorious black trollop like you so soon after his wife died ... people do not like dealing with men of low morals.' She laughed defiantly and he

302

slashed at her, so that she pressed back against the wall. 'Do not laugh at me! It is true. If I tell all I know, he will never be able to return to his property because no bank would lend him money, no store would give him credit, no company would buy his wool. I know everything, you see.'

'Like what?' She was shaking now, frightened by the knife and the blaze in his eyes and not understanding all that he was saying but sensing there was a certain logic to it.

'I know about Mailey the policeman and what your Mr Adam Ross did.' There was a long silence, broken by the faint hiss of steam from the locomotive at the station.

'My uncle,' he said, answering the question in her eyes.

'He wouldn't tell you.' The words were soft and despairing, a lament for a broken trust.

'I know everything.' His voice was equally gentle but the eyes gloated.

'And you think I'll stay with you?'

'For a while.'

'How long?'

'Until I have no further need of you.' He put the knife down and folded his arms, content that she had seen the power of his reasoning.

She shook her head, trying to separate fantasy from reality. 'You haven't been bitten by a mad dog recently? I mean, do you know what you're saying?'

'It is perfectly clear.' He beamed with satisfaction. 'You do as I say or I'll ruin Adam Ross and I'll ruin you as well. It is all very simple.'

She tried to hit him with the broom. He saw the blow coming and moved so that the handle, aimed for the groin, struck him on the hip. It hurt and he spun to one side but he laughed and caught the second blow and pulled her towards him. He snatched at her blouse, hooked his fingers in the collar and jerked her off balance. The blouse ripped and she fell.

He reached for the knife. On her knees, she put her hands around both his ankles and pulled. He tipped backwards, cannoned off a pile of crates, and fell on her. She struggled and elbowed his face. He grabbed the torn blouse and pulled it off her.

She crawled clear and tried to stand. He caught an ankle. She kicked him with her free foot but fell and he, bleeding from the nose and snarling, grabbed her leg again. She kicked free and heard him grunt with pain. Rising, she stumbled into a corner of the darkened store.

He got the torch and ran past her. At the front, he turned. She hid behind a stack of sacks.

'It will be good,' he said, wiping his face and glancing at the blood on his hand. 'I will have much pleasure from you and then I will kill you. There's no use hiding. I will find you.'

The beam roamed the store. It flitted past a row of handles. She stood and grabbed one and felt the weight of a shovel in her hands.

'There you are,' he said, and advanced. He had the knife in one hand, the torch in the other. He examined her with the beam, probing her section by section. 'You have a very good body. The mind of a whore but the body of an angel.' He noticed the shovel. 'What have you got there?'

She held the heavy implement like an extended lance.

'That's worth seven and sixpence,' he said. 'If you damage it, I'll add it to your bill.'

'My bill?'

'Oh yes. There are many things we have to settle.'

He moved closer and she jabbed at him with the shovel blade. It was so heavy the move was clumsy. He avoided the jab with ease.

'You are being ridiculous.' He flicked at the shovel with the knife. In a clatter of metal, the knife fell but he seized the shovel and pulled it from her grasp.

'Now we shall see,' he said and flashed the torch in her eyes.

She retreated. Reaching back to feel her way, her hand touched a row of chains. She remembered them from her days in the store. Gooly hadn't changed a thing. Her fingers closed on one heavy chain and lifted the final link off its hook. She lashed out at the torch. There was a squeal of pain and the light clattered to the floor. She pulled the chain back and struck again but the Afghan had slithered to one side and the metal links thudded to the floor.

A hand clutched her wrist and pulled and she fell and he was on top of her, dripping blood and mumbling words she didn't understand. He held one wrist. With his free hand, he began to choke her. She kicked but he was astride her and she could not breathe.

Her right hand groped for something and upset a row of cast-iron pots. She grabbed one by the rim and swung it upwards. The blow hit his arm. He let go her throat and clawed for her arm but she was swinging again. She took better aim this time. There was the fearful clang of metal striking bone and he released her left wrist and rocked back off her body. By the light of the fallen torch, she could see him on his knees with both hands pressed to his face. She still had the pot. Once more she struck and she hit as hard as she could, a two-handed blow to the top of the head.

'You animal,' she screamed and stood up. Gripping the heavy pot, she thought of hitting him again for a fury had burst within her. But she shook so much she dropped the pot and he was on the floor, curled and helpless as a rag doll, and all her anger evaporated to be replaced, instantly, by a cold fear.

I've killed him, she thought. She retrieved the torch and flashed the light across Goolamadail's body. He was breathing. That was the first thing she saw. In fact, he was whimpering, holding his hands to his face and making bubbling noises. She touched his ribs with her shoe and the whimpering rose one level. She picked up the chain and, at the sound of the links rattling, he rolled on to his chest with his head buried in his arms.

'My nose is broken,' he moaned.

'Good. It was ugly anyhow.'

'I can't get up.'

'If you do I'll break your nose again.' She rattled the chain and his body shivered. 'You're such a turd, Gooly,' she said and threw the chain on his back.

She walked to the corner area and washed her face and hands. Then she went to the shelf where women's clothes were kept and selected a blouse. She put it on. She flashed the torch towards the man. He was sitting up. His face was red with blood.

'What are you doing?' he said, his voice muffled by swollen lips.

'Getting a new blouse.'

'You have to pay for that. I'll put the police on to you.'

'Gooly, you're not only the ugliest man on earth, you must be the most stupid.'

He was standing now. He had picked up the knife.

'Put that back,' he mumbled through a hand that covered his lips and nose. He waved the knife at her.

'You tell the police and I'll tell them you tried to rape me, although I don't think you'd know how to do it, seeing you spend all your time playing with yourself.'

'How dare you speak to a man like that.'

'Easy, when it's a man like you. Or do you spend your time fondling your uncle's camels? I've heard that's what you do.'

'I will kill you,' he said and stumbled towards her. She backed away, retreating through racks of clothing and past great piles of

305

cans and sacks until she was back among the chains and shovels and pots.

He kept covering his nose and saying 'I will kill you.'

Her foot touched the pot she had used to knock him down. She picked it up. 'You come one step closer,' she said, aiming the torch at his eyes, 'and your nose will be so flat you'll have to blow your earholes whenever you get a cold.'

'First I will cut your throat. Then I will slice you into little pieces.' He advanced another step, blinking in the bright light.

She swung the pot over her head in a tight arc. It hit him on the forehead. He fell to his knees, with his body as vertical as a post being driven into the ground. Then he fell forward and did not move.

'Oh Jesus,' she said and dropped the pot.

The train whistle blew.

She got her bag, which was in the place where they had had tea. On the side-table was a tin with money. She would have to get on the train but it was going north. She would need more money to pay for the extra ticket and get back to Marree. There was more than twenty pounds in the tin. She took ten. Without it she couldn't get home. She would pay it back to Saleem Benn.

Goolamadail was unconscious and there was fresh blood on the floor but he was breathing. She stepped over his body, and hurried out of the store.

The train had begun to move. She climbed back into the carriage and stood at the doorway, facing the blackness that lay beyond the small town. There was still no sign of Jimmy Kettle. Where the hell was he? Tears were forming in her eyes and she shook her head in despair. If only Jimmy had been waiting at the station as she'd asked, there'd have been no trouble. But now the police would be after her and she could never come back to William Creek.

The Alfa-Romeo reached the town just as the hotel opened next morning. Jimmy Kettle was angry. He had never been a good driver and controlling such a car with one arm was not easy. Because gear changes were awkward, he tended to leave the car in third or fourth, and let that ratio do all the work but on one long sandy creek crossing that he had attempted in top gear, the wheels had dug in and stalled the motor. His efforts to drive out had merely spun the tyres deeper into the sand. He and Stella had spent thirty-two hours stuck there, digging, pushing, arguing, sleeping and occasionally laughing at the absurdity of the situation. Stella's abiding worry was that Nellie would be waiting for them and would be worried by the long delay. She was also wondering if Nellie had brought the boy, but she said nothing about that to Jimmy because he was unaware of the child's existence.

The people at the hotel told them the train had been late and had left some time after midnight. As far as they knew, no one had got off. The only thing they wanted to talk about was the attack on the storekeeper. He had been assaulted by someone overnight and the store had been robbed.

Harry Peterson told Jimmy the story. 'Gooly reckons someone came up behind him and hit him on the head with an iron bar, and then gave him a real hammering. He's got a broken nose and a big cut on the forehead and there's a chance he could have concussion. You can't tell with Gooly. He always looks a bit dopey. We reckon it could have been some cove who got off the train, hit Gooly and robbed the store and then got back on the train again.'

'What's Gooly say?'

'Nothing yet. He can't talk much.' The publican grinned. 'The blokes in the bar say they hope the police find whoever it is so they can all chip in to buy him a medal. Gooly's not the most liked man in town.'

Jimmy reported the conversation to Stella, who had stayed in the car with their daughter.

'So Nellie didn't come,' he said and gripped the wheel in anger. 'After all the trouble we had in getting here.'

'Something must be wrong.'

'No. You don't know her like I do. She says she's going to do one thing and does another.'

In a foul temper, Jimmy turned the car and drove back to Kalinda. On this occasion, he stopped before the long sandy crossing, and put the car into first gear.

Nellie returned to Marree a week before the Reverend Roger Montgomery was due to leave for Innamincka. Roger was back at Beltana. She went to the post office and telephoned him. She wanted the job at the hospital but there were two conditions: the first was that he must not ask her what had happened at William Creek, and from that he assumed she had learned that Adam no longer wanted to see her. Maybe he had even found some other woman overseas, as Nellie had feared. He made a note to pray for her that evening, and then asked about the other condition.

She wanted to change her name. She regarded this move as the start of a new life for herself and her son, and so a new name was needed. She had thought of Khan. It was a good Afghan name and

Daniel was being raised as an Afghan boy. Danny Khan sounded good.

'So you're to be Nellie Khan?' he said, trying to sound jovial because it was a clergyman's lot to bring cheer to those whose lives were going through a process of disintegration.

'Well,' she said slowly, 'I'd thought of a different first name too. You know, if you're going to start afresh, you might as well go the whole hog.' She didn't give her real reason: any police search for the woman who had beaten and robbed the storekeeper at William Creek could be interested in a coloured woman called Nellie. 'Maybe Betty, Ellen, Ellie ... something like that?'

'You choose. It's your name.'

By the time she and Roger Montgomery were driving up the Strzelecki Track towards Innamincka, Nellie had decided she preferred Ellen. It was on that long drive that Roger also told her the news from William Creek. Gooly had been attacked and robbed.

'Really?'

'You didn't hear about it while you were up there?'

'No.'

'He was beaten rather badly. They think it must have been someone passing through town.'

'You say there was a robbery. What was stolen?'

'Clothes. A lot of cash.'

'A lot?'

'About seven hundred pounds. Everything that was in the safe.'

'Seven hundred!' She choked trying to say the words.

'Yes. It's a lot of cash. Poor Gooly.'

'Poor Saleem Benn. It's his money.'

'Yes,' he said but looked at her with curiosity as they drove on.

So Gooly was robbing his own uncle, she thought. She could tell Saleem Benn. But then Gooly would talk about the boy and do all the things he said he would do with the banks and that would ruin Adam, and he knew about Mailey and that would put Adam in gaol ... No, better to keep quiet and disappear.

'What's at Innamincka?' she asked.

'Not very much. The creek's just near the hospital. It's pretty.'

'Good. I like pretty creeks. Any water?'

'In places. I should warn you that Innamincka is a little like the end of the earth.'

'Sounds great,' Nellie said. 'Just what I need.'

'They certainly need you up there.'

'Well, that's something.' Daniel had been sleeping on her lap. He

308

woke and to entertain him, she pointed out a mob of kangaroos that were flowing in effortless bounds along the side of a distant hill.

BOOK
F·O·U·R
Nina

O·N·E

April, 1953: San Francisco

Melina O'Sullivan got off the cable-car and walked to the Stanford Court Hotel. At thirty-three, she was a good-looking woman. Tall and with the dark features of her Greek mother, she had curly hair from her Irish-American father and legs long enough to have won her a place in the Radio City Rockettes. Not that she was a dancer. Melina O'Sullivan was a writer and a good one, as she liked to advise anyone sufficiently foolish to challenge her. In recent days, a few people had doubted her judgement, if not her writing ability, because she had just resigned her position with the *Chronicle* to join the ranks of freelance writers, which, as one friend put it, was like an actress giving up a part in *South Pacific* in the hope that something better might come along.

Carl Zimmerman was waiting in the foyer. They kissed. She presented her cheek and he offered compressed lips and an onslaught of after-shave, then led her to the coffee lounge.

'This is all rather grand isn't it, Carl?' She placed her bag beside the seat, crossed her legs and examined him with wry amusement.

He offered her a cigarette. 'Well, it is a special occasion. Not every day someone like you walks out on me. Here.' He spun a large envelope across the table. 'One ticket on the *Mariposa*. San Francisco–Sydney and return. The last word's the important one.'

'You *are* a darling.' She drew heavily on the cigarette, put it on the ashtray and opened the envelope.

'Not the best cabin on the ship, but a good one,' he said as she examined the ticket. 'You sail in four days.'

She put the ticket back into the envelope and crammed it into her bag.

'Don't lose it,' he said and then, recognizing the expression on her face, raised both hands in surrender. 'Don't say it. I know what you're thinking. You're thinking "Thank you for that advice, Carl. I don't know how I would have managed without it." Right?'

She didn't laugh but the smile was genuine. 'It was good of you to collect the ticket for me.'

He'd been a theatre critic and had learned to give flawless imitations of those he had destroyed. The hand clasping his cigarette struck a lily-like pose. 'It is the essence of all good tragedy,' he said, wagging the cigarette, 'that those who are to suffer most become the agents of their own destruction.'

'Which means?'

'That I, who don't want you to go and will die when you do, went and got your ticket.'

She laughed. 'I'm going to miss you.'

'If you don't come back in six months, I'll have them inscribe that on my tombstone. "She's going to miss me." It's got a certain ring to it, don't you think?'

A waiter interrupted. They ordered coffee.

'Heard from Mark?' he asked, sitting well back in his seat and directing a jet of smoke at the ceiling.

'No. Last I heard of him he was in Boston. Opening a new practice.'

'Serves him right. May he gaze into many a foul mouth.' He drew on the cigarette. 'Miss him?'

'Of course not.'

'How long's it been? Two years?'

'The divorce went through two and a half years ago.'

'Best thing you ever did. Not so sure about this present move, though.'

'Carl, you know why.' Seeing the coffee approaching, she stubbed out the cigarette. They were silent until the waiter had gone.

'It's what you want to do, I know. And the *Geographic*'s good.'

'They're paying good money.'

'And lots of free Kodachrome?'

'We can have a slide night when I come back.'

'Now there's a prospect.' He sipped his coffee. 'Why Australia? The last frontier? Is that the challenge?'

'Partly. They have a number of unusual things down there. Did you know they have the world's longest coral reef?'

'No.' His eyes, just showing above the cup, displayed no interest. 'To tell you the truth, my love, I'm not even sure where the place is, except that it takes you six months to go there by ship and come back again.'

She laughed.

'You find me amusing?'

She reached across the table to touch his wrist. Not his hand, he

314

noted, but the wrist. 'You remind me of me,' she said and his eyebrows shot up. 'A long time ago, I had a similar conversation. You see, there was an Australian man I met and I had to confess I had no idea where he'd come from.'

'Oh.' He seemed to find the coffee particularly interesting. 'And would he be the reason you're going there?'

'No, Carl. He's dead. He was killed in the war. We met in Greece.'

He nodded. 'Were you good friends?'

'If I didn't know you better I'd say you were jealous.'

He smiled brightly. 'If you knew me better, you'd *know* I was jealous.'

'I only knew him for three or four days. He was trying to escape from the country and I got involved with the escape attempt.'

'He got away? Or ...'

'There were two of them. The man I'm talking about was shot on the boat, just as they were pulling away.'

'Sorry.' He offered another cigarette. 'So you're going to write about the world's longest ... what was it?'

'Coral reef. Not just that. I'm looking at a few things. There's an enormous rock in the centre of the country and I'm going there. I believe we have to ride out by camel.'

'My God. I can imagine you on many things but not on a camel.'

'And there's a salt lake that makes the one in Utah look like a puddle. The local aborigines believe demons live there.'

'I'm terribly impressed. Isn't Australia the place that has those things that hop? What are they called – kangaroos?'

'It is.' She uncrossed her legs. 'I hope to see some kangaroos but the animal I want to see is the wombat.'

He produced his Olivier look: a hint of a smile, a studied cynicism, a trace of interest. 'The name sounds like something Disney might have dreamed up. Why a wombat?'

'Personal reasons, Carl.'

'Ah.' He blew smoke at the ceiling. 'This young man must have made quite an impression on you, Nina.'

'It was a long time ago, Carl. A long time ago.'

June, 1953: Far Western Queensland

Josef Hoffman was becoming more nervous as the flight progressed. Once again, he put his hand on the throttle without changing its setting, as he had done at least once a minute for the last ninety minutes, and tapped a beat that matched the drone of

315

the engine. He scanned the instruments. Fuel was on the wrong side of half. Then the compass. Two forty degrees, plus or minus a wobble or two, as it had been since he had taken off from the strip at Quilpie. As a youth, he had ridden over country like this and been overwhelmed by the sensation of being surrounded by miles of nothing. From the air it was even more impressive. Hundreds and hundreds of miles of nothing. Two thousand feet beneath the Piper the ground resembled a vast sheet of faded red blotting-paper soiled by an occasional stain or blotch. The stains were shadows: the line of a dry creek bed or the rough edge to some low and decaying whelk of a hill. The blotches were trees: hardy, patient species that would go for years without rain and had fine, grey leaves and gnarled trunks that looked more like rough metal castings than living, growing, suffering timber.

Josef had flown for five years but this was the first aircraft he had owned. He had bought it from a man in Toowoomba. Getting there had meant a long train journey but he'd had business to do in Sydney and Brisbane so there had been no real hardship in travelling the extra distance to Toowoomba. Another two hours after nearly three days in the train was a joy because he knew that acquiring the Piper meant he wouldn't have to undertake any more long rail journeys. Aircraft were the way of the future for Australia, he was convinced and, as one of the leaders in the burgeoning wine industry, he felt it appropriate that he should set an example by being the first to have his own plane. Within ten years, he would have his salesmen travelling the country by air, selling his wines. Marketing was the key to success in business and selling wine was like selling anything. Quality wasn't enough. You had to know your market, have good distributors and keep in touch with them, and be able to respond quickly to any opportunity or challenge. The only way to do that, Josef reasoned, was to have a few really good people who knew the product and the market, and be able to move them around the country in hours, not days.

Whoops. He was dreaming again. The compass had swung to one forty seven. He brought the nose back on course. There was a fuzz of darker colour on the horizon. That could be the Cooper. Once he got there he'd be right. He'd follow the river all the way to the refuelling point.

The early stages of the flight had been simple. He had wanted to go to Charleville to see a friend about a business deal. He had flown north-west then west, and only occasionally referred to the map. He had followed the railway line, the 'iron compass' of bush pilots, and as the weather had been fine and he only flew in daylight, there had been no problems. He'd even come low and waved to a train driver near Roma and had sung for much of the way from the sheer joy of uncomplicated, exhilarating flight.

The terrain west of Charleville was even drier and flatter but the flight to Quilpie gave him a chance to practise his navigation, with the comforting knowledge that he would encounter another railway line about halfway along his course. From Quilpie to the Cooper, however, was real cross-country flying, and the country was appalling. There were a few tracks to intersect and some channels that an enthusiastic cartographer had labelled as rivers but otherwise, he might have been tackling the crossing of a fossilized ocean. There were no small towns to overfly, no distinctive peaks to use as reference points, and no twin lines of steel running straight to the horizon. He was alone. The comforting world of people and houses and roads and patches of green and high hills and low valleys had disappeared, spun into the past by the monotonous whirl of the propeller. In its place was a buffed and eroded panorama of reddish-brown nothingness. It frightened him, not in the spiritual way that great space and endless plains had affected him when walking on such land, for that was no more than a realization of the insignificance of man. This was a sharper fear, the prelude to panic, and the air in the cabin where he alone sat was charged with it. The fear fed from the fact that he had done a stupid thing. On his first outback flight, he had chosen as a landing and refuelling point a settlement that was probably the smallest in the country. If he, an imperfect navigator even on the ground, miscalculated and flew off course by a few degrees he would not see the tiny cluster of buildings and fly over land like this until he ran out of fuel.

The blur of colour that he had seen on the horizon rolled towards him and gradually became distinct. At first it was a long serpent of green and grey, a winding strip of darker tones that came from the north and then, off to his left, swung to the west and wriggled to the horizon. The serpent's skin was a band of trees and shrubs and grass and the central spine was a curling line of thicker vegetation that marked the main channel of a river. He flew closer, and began humming to himself. There was no water in the river but he knew what it was and even more important, where he was. This was Cooper's Creek, one of the great inland rivers of Australia, and he was on course. All he had to do now was follow the Cooper to Innamincka.

There was water in the Cooper at Innamincka. Josef flew low along the river, leaving a trail of shrieking birds. White cockatoos and gaudy parrakeets rose from the giant eucalypts, fluttering in the wake of the Piper like leaves ruffled by a gust of wind. A squadron of pelicans that had been feeding on the placid surface of one waterhole ascended in layers of flashing white and, necks tucked into their great bodies, soared north towards the safety of the gibber desert. The aircraft banked to the left, to pass over a monumental pile of empty bottles and then buzz the large stone building that was the Australian Inland Mission hospital.

The airstrip was on a gibber plain. Only the larger stones had been removed. Josef gained altitude, still singing from the joy of hitting his target so accurately, and then turned to land.

It was a rough landing, but the only person watching was an aborigine who had driven to the strip in a battered truck.

'You want petrol?' he asked, as Josef walked towards him.

'Yes,' Josef said and smiled pleasantly. There was a row of drums at the end of the strip. 'Any chance of me getting something to eat first? A sandwich maybe?'

The aborigine, an old man with a broad face and a hat that was several sizes too big for him, stroked his chin.

'You'll have to go to the hospital,' he said gravely.

'Is the food as bad as that?'

The man did not smile.

Josef looked around him. 'Could I get a lift with you?'

'Hop in.' The man adjusted his hat. 'Where're you from?'

'Adelaide.' Josef settled in the seat beside the driver. 'I've flown from Toowoomba.' He realized he might as well have said Timbuctu and quickly added: 'Quilpie. I left there a couple of hours ago.'

'Ah,' said the driver, recognizing the name even though he had never been out of the Channel Country. He drove Josef to the hospital, parked and pointed to the entrance. 'Ask for Ellen.'

Josef entered the building and found a room where a woman was kneeling in front of a filing cabinet and trying to pull open a reluctant drawer. Her back was to him.

'Excuse me,' he said and then tapped on the open door. 'I was looking for Ellen.'

'You've found her,' the woman said and tugged despairingly at the drawer. 'And if you can open this thing, she'll be your friend for life.' She turned, wiping her nose as she got to her feet and, for the first time for nearly fourteen years, Josef and Nellie stood face to face.

They were seated at a wooden table. Each had a cup of tea. Josef had eaten a sandwich made of freshly baked bread and tinned beef. Beside them was a window which overlooked a huge pile of empty bottles. As high as the hospital building but covering an area many

318

times greater, the glassy dump had been ravaged by an occasional flood but still represented an impressive memorial to the drinking prowess of those who had lived in the district or had become thirsty while passing through. There used to be a hotel at Innaminkca, Nellie had explained, and while it was worth the cost of having crates of full bottles hauled by camel train up the Strzelecki Track, no one was prepared to pay for the empties to be taken back down south. The dump, therefore, represented more than half a century of draining beer, whisky, gin, rum, brandy, wine and even the occasional lemonade from its container and chucking the empty on the heap. Thousands of bottles had been washed downstream by the Cooper floods. Tens of thousands remained. Square-sided, rounded or warped, filled with silt, roughened by sand or dulled by decades of sunshine, they glinted in the clear, harsh light.

'You look great,' Josef said, still dazed from encountering Nellie in such a remote and unlikely place, and she said the same thing about him. Privately, each noted the changes. Meeting an old friend can be like revisiting the family home after an absence of many years. There is the shock of discovering that memory was flawed, and the sadness of perceiving the damage wrought by time.

Josef was taller and thinner than Nellie remembered. He was balding a little at the temples and there was grey in the hair around his ears. Lines which had once shown only during moments of hearty laughter were now set in his face but it was, she noted with satisfaction, the face of a person who seemed content with life. He was thirty-eight. One third of his life had passed since they had last met.

Josef talked about the wine business and why he had purchased the aircraft, and his plans for the future. He was in Innamincka because he'd had to go to Charleville and he'd gone there because a friend who used to haul bulk wine in the Barossa Valley had gone to Queensland to open his own transport business. Josef had thought of diversifying into carrying bulk wine and as Jimmy Flynn was the best operator he knew, he'd flown to Charleville to see him.

'And to fly your new plane,' Nellie added.

He grinned, and she remembered Josef at fifteen. 'It's great to see you so happy,' she said. 'Not married or anything like that?'

'No. I'm neither married nor anything like that. No time. Too busy.' He tapped the table to emphasize his joy at seeing her. 'This is unbelievable. You look so good. You just haven't changed.'

She smiled, accepting the lie with grace. Nellie had not been well for two years. She'd lost weight, her face was drawn, and every morning she seemed to discover a new grey hair.

'I won't see forty-five again.'

319

'You're joking.' He had never thought of her as being so much older than he was; except, of course, when they were at Coober Pedy and he'd been just a boy and she had been a willowy and fiery-tempered young woman. He scratched his head. 'Where have the years gone, Nellie?'

'The usual place.' She smiled wistfully. 'Behind us.'

He drank some tea and emptied the cup. 'The old fellow who picked me up at the strip called you Ellen.'

She gazed at him. He'd forgotten how large and beautiful her eyes were. 'A lot of things have changed.'

'You mean it wasn't a mistake?'

'No. I'm called Ellen these days.' She poured some tea.

'It's a nice name,' he said. 'More suited to a mature woman.'

'That's what I thought. Tell me,' she added casually, 'do you ever see anything of Adam these days?'

He lifted the cup. The water was steaming and he blew gently across its surface. 'I haven't been up there for five years. I get letters every now and then. Cassie writes, usually.'

Nellie let her chin drop on to the arch formed by her clasped hands. 'Dear little Cassie. I've really missed her.'

'She's not so little, I wouldn't think. She's seventeen.'

She looked at him and the expression was so full of regret that Josef had to turn away.

'I never really understood what happened,' he said after a long pause. 'I was there when you left but I didn't really know why and Adam never truly understood.'

'There were a lot of reasons.'

'I know you must have been angry with Adam and I know how frustrating he can be ...'

'It wasn't that.' She was staring out the window, as though mesmerised by the flashes of colour winking from the monstrous pile of glass.

'What was it then?' He hesitated. 'Nellie, I know he was so unhappy.'

'I did it for him. Let's leave it at that.'

'He hasn't married.'

She shrugged, but continued to gaze out the window. 'I've been up here for ten years now. It's been good. The best thing I've ever done. I've been doing something useful.' She swung to face him. 'If I'd stayed, Adam would have lost Cassie, lost the property, lost everything.'

'Maybe not.'

'You don't know the fully story, Joe. Even Adam doesn't know.' She sighed. 'I was trouble. It was better that I left.'

320

He drank but kept the teacup poised at his lips. 'He looked for you, you know.'

She said nothing.

'Adam spent the first year after he got back from the war travelling around, trying to find you. He searched Port Augusta, Port Pirie, all those places. He went across to Whyalla and Port Lincoln. Even Adelaide. He was there a month. Can you imagine Adam in a city?'

Her eyes flickered.

'He even hired a detective agency. They took six months and most of his cash and told him you'd disappeared. Vanished. I don't think anyone ever thought of Innamincka.'

She turned towards him. 'It's better that he didn't find me,' she whispered.

'He's never forgotten you, never stopped hoping.'

She lowered her eyes.

Josef cleared his throat. 'Did you ever try to get in touch with him?'

'I started to go back to Kalinda once. During the war.'

'What happened?'

'Never made it. Trouble seems to follow me like a bad smell and there was trouble and I had to turn around and go away.'

Josef frowned. 'What sort of trouble?'

She shook her head. 'It doesn't matter. How are Jimmy and Stella?'

His brow wrinkled, pushing up one topic to make room for the next. 'They're well, or so Cassie said in their last letter. They've got a few kids. Three girls, I think.'

Nellie laughed softly. 'I can't imagine Jimmy as a father.'

They smiled at each other.

'It'd be good to see them all again,' she said, in a voice people reserve for hopeless causes.

'Why not?' Josef stirred from the feeling of despair that had engulfed them both. He sat upright and put the cup on the table. 'It'd be so good. Adam would love to see you again. He doesn't know whether you're alive or dead. He certainly cares.'

Her expression softened. 'I'd like to see Cassie again. Seventeen. I can't imagine her grown up.'

'She was twelve when I last saw her.'

'Beautiful?'

'Gawky. She was tall for her age and tough as a bag of nails.'

Nellie shook her head slowly. 'I have to go to Adelaide.'

'When? Why?'

'In a month. To see a doctor. I haven't been well. The flying

321

doctor wants some tests carried out.'

'And then?' He sat back and patted the table with both hands.

'After that? I suppose I come back here. It's where I work.'

'Why not take the train to William Creek?'

'Never. That's one town I'm never ever going back to.' She had been gazing out the window again but turned and, seeing his puzzled expression, said, 'Now don't spoil it all by asking me why, because then I'd tell you to mind your own business and then we'd start arguing and that would spoil a lovely day.'

He pursed his lips. 'Fair enough. But would you go to Kalinda if you didn't have to go to William Creek?'

She stood up, examining him quizzically. 'That's like saying you can go to heaven without ever going to church first.' She picked up the teapot. 'I'm making more tea. Want some?' He nodded and gave her the little-boy smile she remembered. 'By the way, Joe, are you able to stay the night? We've got a few spare beds. Everyone's healthy around here at the moment.'

'No I can't. I've got to be in Leigh Creek this afternoon.'

She went to the sink to fill a kettle.

'There is a way,' he said.

'Of doing what?'

'Getting to Kalinda without going through William Creek.'

'There's a new road?'

'No. There's me and my aeroplane.' His fingers rapped a triumphant beat on the table top. 'When you're through with the doctor in Adelaide, I'll put you in my Piper and fly you up.'

'No, I couldn't,' she said, but her eyes held a plea for contradiction.

Josef knew Nellie's looks. 'Why not?'

'I've never flown before.'

'There's got to be a first time.'

'Well then, it'd be too expensive.'

'I won't charge you a penny.'

'I didn't mean that. I meant expensive for you.'

'I want to go up there anyhow. It's been five years since I've seen them and now I've got the plane. And there's a seat in it that would fit you perfectly.'

'Do you have the time? You sound very busy.'

'I was going to take some time off. A week in the north would be good.'

'Would it only take a week?'

'A day up, a day back, and five days there.'

'Planes are marvellous things, aren't they?' she said and he agreed. Nellie lowered her head. 'I'd be frightened Joe. It's been so long.'

'I'll be with you ...' He started to call her Nellie but then hesitated. 'What do I call you now? Ellen?'

'No. I'd like you to call me Nellie.'

They talked about the war and the time both Adam and Josef spent recuperating after Greece. 'He was pretty sick,' Josef said, watching her closely. 'When the bullet hit him it spread and took out a lot of his lung.'

'He's all right now?'

'Last time I saw him he was as fit as a scrub bull. Nellie, you never got married?'

'No.'

'Why not?'

She laughed. 'Have a look around you. There aren't a lot of eligible men.'

She had work to do and he had to leave. Back at the strip, Josef taxied the plane to the drums. He was helping the aborigine refuel when a Chevrolet drove across the gibbers and parked behind the Piper. A woman in matron's uniform got out.

'Are you Mrs Khan's friend?' she said, smiling. She was a middle-aged woman with skin sunburned to the texture of fine leather.

'Ellen's friend?' the woman prompted when Josef did not answer. He said yes and introduced himself. She shook his hand and raised one arm to shield her face from the sun. Even then, the eyes squinted and the skin folded like a soft bag being squeezed. 'Pleased to meet you. I'm sorry I was busy when you were over there. Moira Buttenshaw. I'm the matron. Ellen tells me you live in Adelaide.'

'Near there,' he said. 'At Tanunda, actually.'

'Nice place.'

'You've been there?'

'I was born in Gawler.' Small talk over, Matron Buttenshaw went straight to the reason for her visit. 'We're worried about Ellen.'

'Oh?' Josef let the other man pump fuel.

'She's been an absolute treasure. Practically runs the place. But she's been so sick for such a long time. She has to go to Adelaide to see a specialist.'

'She told me she was going south. I didn't realize it was anything serious.'

'It is. I'm worred about her being on her own while she's down there. Can she stay with you, or with some of your friends?'

'Well, yes.' He was confused. 'Of course. I'll arrange something.'

'Good. I'd appreciate it. Give me your address. I'll write and let you know when she's coming down.'

Josef fumbled for a pencil and paper.

'What do you think of our little town?' she asked.

'It's very little.'

'That's one of the kindest things that's ever been said about it.' He wrote out his address and passed it to her. She studied it with the profound squint of a person who needs reading glasses. 'My arms are getting too short,' she said and laughed heartily. 'There won't even be a hospital here soon.'

'Why?'

'There's talk of closing it. First the pub, then the hospital. The town's dying.'

'Have you been here long?'

'Twenty-six years.'

He had trouble putting the pencil back in his shirt pocket. 'What will you do if they close it?' he asked, head down, intent on the task.

'When they close it, I will go to Adelaide and live on the beach somewhere. I have a sister at Glenelg.'

'And ... Ellen?'

'That's another worry. If she gets over this –' and her eyes narrowed to slits – 'she'll need a place to live and another job. Pity the boy isn't older. Well!' She held out her hand and he shook it spontaneously. 'Mustn't keep you. Been nice meeting you, Mr Hoffman. I'll write. You *will* look after her when she comes down?'

'Yes.'

'Good. Have a nice trip.'

She got in the Chevrolet and accelerated away. Josef watched her depart, his mind whirling with confused thoughts, until the aborigine tapped his shoulder to advise him the aircraft was ready to leave.

That night, Nellie wrote a letter:

Dear Daniel,

I have not been feeling too good for a while and the last time the doctor was here he said I should go down to Adelaide to see another doctor. It's nothing serious but you know how doctors worry! I'll be going down the track with the mailman to Lynd-hurst in about four weeks' time. I'll get the train from there. I don't suppose there'll be a chance to see you unless there's a job

324

Saleem Benn is doing down that way. Anyhow, I will be away for a few weeks so there is no point writing for a while. I hope school is going well and your uncle isn't working you too hard. I will try to write to you from Adelaide. That will be a thrill. I don't think you have had a letter from the city before. Be a good boy.

Love
Mother.

She addressed the letter to Daniel Khan, care of Saleem Benn, Marree, South Australia.

T · W · O

July, 1953: Kalinda

Adam Ross was in a reflective mood. The new homestead had been completed only the week before and now that the last of the tradesmen were out of his hair he was more able to relax and enjoy the house. With the diesel generator throbbing in the shed and the verandah lights turned on, he shut the flyscreen door, walked down the steps and turned to examine the building.

Four bedrooms. He must have been nuts to agree to such an extravagance although Cassie insisted she was right. After putting up with the old home and its single bedroom for seventeen years – he'd built it about the time Cassie was born – it made sense to have too many rather than too few bedrooms in the new place. But four! Who the hell was going to fill them all? One for his daughter, and one for him meant that there were two left over and even if they did have a steady stream of guests, say two or three a year, it was hard to see both the spare rooms being used.

'You need a good woman, Dad,' Cassie would say, 'and then you'd soon fill them up.'

'I've got a good woman,' he would say and aim a slap at her bottom. He rarely connected because she was quick and smart on her feet.

Adam walked further from the building to get a better view. It was a huge house and the construction of it had been a nightmare. When he had made the first house, he had done everything with his own hands except make the stove, and the work had taken him a few months. He had experts do this job for him and it had taken them eighteen months from digging the foundations to putting the last brush stroke of paint on a wall. There had been shortages of materials, the wrong items had been sent and tradesmen hadn't turned up when they promised. He didn't know what the world was coming to.

In his day, people did what they promised to do and delivered on time. And didn't send screws when you'd ordered nails, or freight ten gallons of grey paint when you asked for twenty of white.

Still, it was finished and it looked good. There was a large cellar under the house where he could store all his supplies and the things that needed to be kept cool. There was a big kitchen with the biggest wood-burning stove he'd ever seen, and one of those modern kerosene-burning refrigerators, and tables and chairs that he'd bought rather than made himself. There was a dining-room, and a lounge-room with dark varnished walls and thick curtains so you could shut out all the sunlight and sit in the dark on a hot day and try to persuade yourself that it was cool. There was a room that Cassie called his study where he could sit and do any bookwork that needed to be done or talk to any stranger he didn't want to invite into the lounge-room, and there was the radio-room where the new but cumbersome two-way radio had been fitted. Cassie had also put her sewing machine in there because it was a long room with a lot of space. A laundry had been built – *inside* the house, of all places – and there was a store-room for his boots and wet weather gear and rifles.

It was the only house he'd ever heard of that had two bathrooms. He and Cassie had a long argument over that because he couldn't see the sense in having two rooms where you could wash yourself, let alone go to the expense of having to buy two bathtubs when they were often so short of water there wasn't sufficient to fill one washbasin. But Cassie had won that argument. She usually did.

And there was a verandah that surrounded the house. It was completely sealed from insects by wire screens. A lavatory was out the back. Adam had expected Cassie to suggest two of those but all she had insisted on was that the little building be hidden behind a wooden lattice. She had already planted a vine, so that the structure would be covered by a creeper, both to camouflage a potential eyesore and to make it habitable, if that was the word, in summer.

The old house was a couple of hundred yards away. It had been extended by the addition of another two bedrooms and a living-room. Jimmy, Stella and the three girls lived there.

Mrs Wilson, who had been the cook, housekeeper and one-time tutor to help Cassie with her school work, lived in a three-roomed cottage that Adam and Jimmy had built a couple of years ago. A grey-haired woman in her sixties, she had been at Kalinda since 1947. For the first years, Adam had put her in his house. He had slept in the shed.

Adam looked around him. He had three houses, a variety of sheds and his own generator supplying electricity. A great deal had changed since he had first come to Lot B, Lake Eyre West at the end of 1935.

The greatest change was that he now had money. The Korean war had brought astronomical increases in the demand, and the price paid, for wool. He was a rich man. At least on paper, he was probably worth a million pounds. He had taken a lease on an adjoining block and now controlled more than two thousand square miles of country. He had thirty-five thousand head of merino sheep growing the fine fleeces that brought the highest prices. He also ran a couple of hundred head of beef cattle.

He had borrowed from the bank and was on such good terms they sent him a card each Christmas; he had an A1 credit rating with the stock agents; a new Holden was parked in the shed (alongside the old Alfa-Romeo which was now stored under a sheet); and, if most of his assets were in property and stock, he was still well enough placed financially to be amused by losing an argument with his daughter on the subject of one bathroom or two.

The years immediately after the war had been tough. The drought had continued, wool prices had been low and the effects of his wartime injuries had persisted. He coughed a lot in dust. Dingoes, made daring by hunger, had moved in to attack his flocks and each night had meant constant patrols to protect the sheep and, at lambing time, to save the new-born animals from predators.

The sheep had been split into two main groups. Jimmy and Stella, when she was not heavily pregnant, would look after one lot. Adam and Cassie cared for the other.

At nine years of age, Cassie had been a deadly shot with a rifle. She had her own light .22 Remington and was capable of dropping a dingo on the run, or a rabbit at a hundred yards. The limiting factor was the performance of the rifle, not her skill. She spent the years after the war awake at night and sleeping in the day until Mrs Wilson complained that the child would not only grow up to be as nocturnal as a possum but would excel at rifle shooting, trapping, and baiting and be a dunce at reading, writing and arithmetic.

Food had been scarce in the hard years too. The flock of merinos had diminished during the war because of the drought, and Adam had returned to find he owned about four hundred sheep. He borrowed a thousand pounds and bought another thousand sheep and a few items for the house. There had been no question of ever eating lamb or mutton, unless an animal was injured and had to be destroyed. As had been the case in the first months on the property, the staple diet at Kalinda became galah and rabbit. Cassie shot her share of game and now, at seventeen, could handle any gun and drop anything that moved within sight. She was also a fine horsewoman, being strong and fluent in the saddle rather than graceful. She could bully a camel into submission if not silence, could shear sheep, and knew how to crack a stock-whip.

She was nearly as tall as her father and, having spent most of her energy in growing up, was only now beginning to fill out. She was good looking without being beautiful, wrinkled her forehead a lot and liked to arm-wrestle with her father or anyone foolish enough to accept her challenge. She had little interest in young men, having met very few, but had become a voracious reader. Mrs Wilson, whose late husband had been a school teacher, brought with her a small library of books and kept ordering more. Cassie had read them all. She could recite pieces of Keats and Shelley and most of the poems of Banjo Patterson. Her favourite was 'The Man from Snowy River'. The images excited her, although she had trouble picturing the slope down which The Man rode, because she had never seen such a mountain.

Mail and supplies were now delivered by a contractor, Giuseppe Portelli. He worked for Saleem Benn whose operations had expanded and become Northern Outback Stores and Transport Limited.

The locals abbreviated the title to 'Nostril', an acronym they found particularly suitable in view of the Afghan's most prominent physical feature.

Portelli was a thick-set and jovial Italian who was typical of a new breed of outback settler; the migrant who, having escaped from the structured and constrained demands of European society, found the challenge of a big and near-empty continent irresistible. At a time when most native-born Australians were being drawn to the cities, the more adventurous of the European migrants were spreading into the remote areas where greater opportunities were a counter-balance to the isolation and ferocious climate. Portelli had migrated just after the war. Equipped with a funny accent and a love of being left alone to get on with his work, he had adapted almost instantaneously to life in the bush. He liked the hot weather and he liked being able to stop on some lonely track and look around and see no one else. Out here, you survived or perished, succeeded or failed, according to your own efforts. He liked that. Giuseppe Portelli and Adam Ross had become good friends.

Portelli was based at Marree but spent most of his time delivering mail and goods in the triangle of country bounded by William Creek, Oodnadatta and Coober Pedy. He travelled to Kalinda more often than economic prudence suggested, partly because Adam was his friend and partly because Portelli was finding Cassie increasingly attractive.

It was a cold but sunny morning when Portelli arrived un-expectedly with mail and a drum of power kerosene, hardly a suffi-cient load to justify the long journey from the railway.

'No worries,' he said, when Adam had delivered his usual polite remonstration. 'It's no problem. Just a-tought you might need somating for the new 'ouse. Then I bring it next a-time and 'ave it for you has you like it.' He was adventurous with the English language and took care to sound every consonant and even throw in the occasional 'h' if he thought there was doubt. His face was classically Italian with the mischievous eyes of a street wise Neapolitan. He managed to sustain a stubble that consistently suggested three days' growth of beard. He was twenty-five.

''Ow is Cassandra?'

'Fine thanks, mate. She's in the house. Why don't you go inside and ask her yourself?' This was the standard conversation.

'Oh no, it don't matta. I'm in a 'urry.'

'I think she's about to make a cup of tea.'

'Yeah?'

'She'd like to say hello.'

'Well, just-a for uno momento.' He would hesitate. 'You come, Adam?'

'I'll be in in a minute or two. You go ahead.'

Adam would delay his entry to the house, knowing that both Cassie and Portelli enjoyed these brief encounters. She liked him, thought his shyness amusing and teased him unmercifully about his accent.

'Anda 'ow are you today Peppino me boy?'

'Fine.'

'Foine? That'sa good.'

He grinned.

'One of these days Cassandra –' and he delivered her name with a flourish of the tongue – 'I will teach-a you to speak Italian.'

Hands on hips, trying to confront him with her masculinity and only managing to look provocatively feminine, she said, 'Whata for?'

The grin almost split his face. 'If you donna know my language, 'ow you gonna talk-a my folks?'

'Your folks?' The hands moved from the hips to the waist, the elbows jutting at a more challenging angle. 'What I wanna meet you folks for, eh?' Cassie might not have met many young men but she had a wild animal's instant and instinctive recognition of the initial moves in the mating game. As yet, she had little idea of the final sequences in this entertaining ritual but the first stages were a lot of fun.

Their eyes met in a cheeky challenge and she knew she controlled this man as effectively as a Border Collie musters a young and awkward sheep.

'You wanna biscuit?' she said.

'You gotta biscuit?'

She was a good mimic and imitated his exaggerated hand movements, flinging a hand in the air as if tossing a plate. 'What you think I offer you-a biscuits for if I no got 'em, eh?'

He began to laugh. 'You sure you never been-a to Italy?'

'Not this week.'

'I 'ave han aunty in Lipari just-a like you.'

'Beautiful, eh?' She wrinkled her nose.

He shook his head. 'She make a lot of-a noise.'

The banter ceased when Adam entered. Cassie regarded the game as private, her first mild intimacy with a man, and she did not want to give such a revealing performance in front of her father. For his part Portelli regarded Adam as an older man and deserving of respect, as was the custom in the old country. There was, additionally, the consideration that Adam was the father of this bewitching young creature, and fathers of such women required special treatment. He was also aware that she made a fool of him. Now, a man in love, or preparing himself for that state, can tolerate a degree of ridicule if it means the woman gives him her total attention and if she does it with humour and laughs a great deal, as Cassie did. He cannot accept ridicule if it is done to impress others. Portelli, a simple man fashioned in a complex mould of honour, knew the boundaries of such conversations. Cassie's instincts guided her as unerringly. Both were serious the moment Adam rattled the wire screen door.

'You'd like a cup of tea, Dad?' she asked and Portelli smiled from behind his biscuit.

'What's in the mail?' Adam asked. Cassie always opened the mail.

While she went through the bills, newspapers, magazines, and letters – opening them in that order because she liked saving the best for last – Adam sat on the table and talked to Portelli.

Adam was now forty-three. The extra years suited him. He was still trim from constant work and exercise, and as strong as he had ever been but the main changes had been to his face. Even as a youngster he had the look of a man but, inevitably, the impression had been flawed by the innocence of youth and the uncertainty and gullibility that were the companions of inexperience. The war had changed him. It had inscribed a few new lines on the face and set the mouth in a firmer pattern. In later years, success and the money

331

that came with it had allowed the face to relax, so that lines of contentment hovered around the eyes and the lips. It was a good face. Interesting, worn but strong, and good humoured. The eyes were honest but could unsettle people by not leaving them. He was a six-footer but so broad, and inclined to wear such ill-fitting shirts, that his height was deceptive. His hair had not greyed and was still thick.

He had not worn a beard since a Royal Navy barber shaved him on a destroyer speeding along the North African coast.

Cassie emitted a squeal of delight. 'Uncle Joe's coming to visit us.'

'Josef?' Adam got off the table. Portelli, eyes curious, looked from Cassie to Adam. 'He's a friend of mine,' Adam said, then sipped his tea. 'Haven't seen him for years.'

'They were in the war together,' Cassie said, then turned to her father. 'Guess what?'

'He's married.'

'No. Better than that. He's got an aeroplane.'

'I hope he can handle it better than he handles women,' Adam said and Portelli, realizing the remark had been for his benefit, smiled.

'He's going to fly here.'

Adam had put in an air strip when he first installed a pedal radio for the Flying Doctor network. In such flat country, the work required to construct a strip had been minimal: clearing a few stones, levelling a couple of ant hills and erecting a metal pole with a wind-sock. 'When's he coming?'

'In a few weeks. He doesn't say exactly when.'

'He's your huncle?' Portelli asked.

'Not exactly. He's just a friend.'

'An old bloke?'

'Actually,' Cassie said, sensing the young man was sniffing out a potential rival, 'Joe's quite young. Much younger than Dad.'

'But they were in-a war together.'

'Joe lied about his age,' she said and winked at Adam. 'Oh, I just can't wait. It's been so long since we saw him.'

'Must be five years,' Adam said.

'I wonder what he'll look like.'

'Five years older, probably.'

'I wonder if he'll take me flying.'

'Over my dead body.'

'You wouldn't.' She studied her father and saw that he would. 'Surely you'd want to go up?'

'I've got on this long without flying, I reckon I can last a little

332

longer. Anyhow, I tried it once. Didn't like it.'

'When?' she challenged.

'Years ago. In Western Australia.'

'You never told me.'

'Never asked. Joe and I got a lift in a plane. There were no seats, it was freezing cold and we had to share the space with the body of a dead man wrapped up in a canvas sheet.'

'Yeah?' Portelli said, forehead creased in interest.

'Don't you believe him, Peppino. Dad's always making up stories about the things he did when he was young.'

'It's true,' Adam complained.

'We know,' she said in a gently derisive voice. 'Who wants more tea or another biscuit? By the way ...'

Adam looked up.

'Uncle Joe said he might bring a surprise with him.'

'Like what?'

'Really, Dad, if I knew, it wouldn't be a surprise, would it?'

Adam drank more tea. 'And when's he coming?'

'In a few weeks.'

'I bet it's a woman.'

The next morning, Mrs Wilson wrote down a telegram that had been relayed over the radio. Adam was still in the house.

'Got a reply-paid telegram,' she called out.

'What's that?'

'I don't know, Mr Ross. I presume it's someone wanting an answer and paying for it.'

He walked into the radio room. Cassie joined them and read the telegram.

'*National Geographic*?' she queried. 'What's that?'

'An American magazine, and a very good one,' Mrs Wilson said. 'It's very educational. They have lovely pictures.'

'What do they want?' Adam asked, growing exasperated with the lack of information.

Cassie pulled a face. ' "This is to advise," ' she read, ' "that *National Geographic* is preparing a major article on Australia stop." ' She looked at Adam. Whenever she read 'stop' on a telegram, he was supposed to say 'go'.

'Go.'

She grinned. They had been doing it since the first pedal radio was cranked into life. ' "I wish to research ..." ' She turned to Mrs Wilson for an explanation.

'You know that word, Cassie. It means to study, to delve into.'

'Oh. "I wish to research Lake Eyre, get information, take photographs, stop."' She paused but Adam waved his hand for her to continue. '"Would greatly value your co-operation and would much appreciate possibility of staying at Kalinda from fifteenth this month for some days to accumulate material for story."'

'It was a long telegram,' Mrs Wilson said, flexing her writing hand.

'He uses a lot of words,' Cassie said, re-reading the telegram. 'Must have a lot of money.'

'Who's it from?' Adam said wearily.

'Oh.' Cassie scanned the paper. 'Someone called M. O'Sullivan. It was sent from the South Australian Hotel, Adelaide.'

'When's the fifteenth?'

'In two days,' Mrs Wilson said.

'Wonder how the hell he's getting out here?' Adam said. 'There's no train.'

'If it's the *National Geographic*, they would probably hire a car. They're a very wealthy organization. Very prestigious.' In Mrs Wilson's eyes, money and prestige were linked by unbreakable bonds.

Cassie held the paper delicately between thumb and forefinger. 'They want a reply. What do we say?'

Adam shrugged. 'OK.'

'Just that?'

'Well, that's OK with me. So just send back a reply saying OK.'

Cassie glowered at Mrs Wilson. 'Here we have a big American magazine – as big as *Women's Weekly*?'

'Goodness me, child, much bigger,' Mrs Wilson said and laughed at such naïvety.

'– bigger even than *Women's Weekly*,' Cassie continued, 'and they send the world's longest telegram full of big words, and want a reply and even pay for it and all my father can think of to say is OK.'

'It says all I need to say.'

'You should say "delighted to have you", or something like that,' Cassie said. 'Or, "be most pleased to accommodate you at Kalinda. Kindly stay as long as you like.".'

Mrs Wilson beamed. 'That's very good.'

Adam said: 'I like OK, but send what you like. It's their money.'

Cassie spun in a circle. 'I wonder what Mr O'Sullivan is like? Maybe he's young and good looking.'

Mrs Wilson clucked in admonition but smiled.

'It's all those poems she reads in bed, Mrs Wilson,' Adam said. 'We should never have let her go to bed at nights. I liked her better when she was out shooting dingoes.'

Cassie aimed a punch at him. Jimmy had shown her how, but she delivered it slowly and Adam, matching her playful pace, swayed out of the way.

'Got to go,' he said. 'Things to do.'

Cassie struck an oratorical pose. '"There was movement at the station for the word had passed around ..."'

He stopped at the door. 'You'd just better give Mrs Wilson a hand to clean up. If we're going to have visitors, you make sure all those extra bedrooms you wanted are ready.'

She charged him, hoping to ruffle his hair because he hated that, but he was already out the door.

T·H·R·E·E

The pilot of the twin-engined Dragon Rapide could not find the airstrip, so he landed the biplane on the track running to the big homestead. Cassie, already waiting on the steps, walked out to greet him. The pilot slid back a side-window.

'Where's your airfield?' he shouted.

She pointed. 'Over there.'

'OK. I'll take her over. This is Kalinda?'

'Yes.' She walked closer.

'Don't get near the propellers.' Cassie stopped and took a step back. The pilot turned to speak to a person beside him. 'I'll just drop someone off while I'm here.'

She nodded and strained to see who it was.

'Be a good idea to paint your name on the roof,' he yelled. 'Stop people like me getting lost.'

'I'll get Dad to do it,' she called back. A pair of legs descended from the other side of the fuselage.

The pilot waved. The level of engine noise rose and the aircraft waddled off, trailing a dust storm. Cassie turned and covered her face.

'Noisy thing, isn't it?' It was a woman's voice but with a curious accent.

Cassie wiped the grit from her eyes. A tall woman dressed in slacks walked towards her. She carried a bag on one shoulder and a briefcase in the other hand.

'Hi.' The woman put the briefcase on the ground.

'Hello.'

The woman looked around her. 'So this is Kalinda.'

Cassie hooked a thumb in the direction of the Dragon Rapide 'Was that Mr O'Sullivan?'

'No. That was Mr Lunney. I'm O'Sullivan.' She advanced, offering her hand. 'Melina O'Sullivan. Who are you?'

Nervously, Cassie wiped the palm of her right hand on her hip. 'Ah, Cassandra Ross.' They shook hands.

'Pleased to meet you, Miss Ross. Your family runs this property? I know I shouldn't call it ranch. Property is correct, right?'

'We call it property. Or station.' The women smiled at each other, one shy, the other waiting for an answer to the rest of her question. 'My father owns it,' Cassie said after a pause.

'Is he around? I sent a telegram.'

'Yes, I know. I sent you the reply.'

'Oh. Thank you. It was very short.'

'We didn't want to waste your money. Dad'll be back soon. He's out but he'll have heard the plane. Is it yours?'

Nina laughed. 'No. We've only hired it for a few more days.'

'My uncle has an aeroplane.'

'Does he?' Nina was studying the homestead. 'What a lovely big house.'

'It's new. We've only been in it for a week or so.'

'How wonderful. Do you know why I've come here?'

'Yes. To write something for an American magazine.'

'And there's no problem?'

'No. Dad said OK.' She smiled, feeling more relaxed. She liked this woman. 'In fact, we're delighted to have you. You're welcome to stay as long as you like.' Cassie wished Mrs Wilson could have heard her say that. She would have been pleased. The smile broadened. 'Dad'll be surprised. He was expecting a man.'

'I hope he won't be too disappointed.'

Cassie picked up Nina's briefcase. 'Come inside. Mrs Wilson will be making you a cup of tea.'

'I'd love a coffee,' Nina said. 'Although I've found coffee about as hard to find in your country as gold nuggets.'

'We have coffee.'

Nine rubbed her hands. 'I know I'm going to love it here.'

Mrs Wilson rarely made coffee and prepared Nina's drink with the zeal of someone determined to convert the recipient to tea.

'I don't know how you can drink that stuff,' she said cheerily and Nina, after the first sip, understood her confusion. Mrs Wilson returned to the kitchen and put away the jar of coffee and chicory mixture that had been opened for some other visitor four years before.

'I've never tried coffee,' Cassie said, watching Nina's efforts with intense interest.

'Don't,' Nina said and smiled. 'At least not this lot. When I get back to America, I'll send you some real coffee.'

Cassie was concerned. 'Isn't it any good?'

'It's fine.' She shook her head, either in denial or disgust; Cassie couldn't tell which. 'It's just that I'm a coffee freak, an addict and we addicts are very particular about our coffee.' She pulled a packet of cigarettes from her bag. 'Do you mind if I smoke?'

Cassie had read that women smoked but had never seen one actually light a cigarette. 'No.'

Nina inhaled deeply and Cassie watched in fascination.

'Oh, I'm sorry,' Nina said, moving uncomfortably 'I should have asked. Do you smoke?'

'No. No thanks.'

Nina tried another sip of coffee. 'My God, that's awful,' she said and laughed.

Cassie leaned forward, not sure whether to join in the laughter or appear concerned. She chose the latter course. 'Can I get you something else?'

Nina ran her fingers through her hair. 'No, it's all right, really. It's just that I've been on the job in this country for a few weeks now and I am truly dying for a good cup of coffee. I would kill for it.'

Cassie blinked.

'I'm just using a figure of speech. Cassandra?'

'Yes.'

'Lovely name.' She stopped, a faint memory jogged. Puzzled, she tilted her head.

'What is it?'

'I almost thought of something,' Nina said. 'You know how it is when you almost think of something but then it goes away before you can catch it?'

Cassie nodded.

'Well, when you said your name it almost brought something back but now I can't think what it was. Must be all the riding in airplanes.'

'Or bad coffee.'

'Could be.'

'Where's the man who flies the plane?'

'Oh, he'll fuss around that thing for another half an hour yet, tying it down, putting it to bed for the night.'

'My father's been in an aeroplane.'

'Has he?'

'It was a long time ago. He says there were no seats and there was a dead man wrapped in canvas.'

Nina put her coffee on the table. 'It must have been a memorable flight.'

They heard the sound of a horse.

'That's Dad.'

338

'Good. I'm looking forward to asking him questions. We don't have that much time. We were delayed up on the Great Barrier Reef and lost three days. Have you ever been there?'

'No.'

'You must go. It is absolutely, unbelievably beautiful. How long have you lived here, Cassandra?'

'All my life.'

'Ever been to Queensland?'

'No.'

The wire door clanged. Boots scraped on the verandah mat. Nina smiled at Cassandra, rose, and turned to meet the owner of Kalinda.

The light outside was bright, and when Adam stepped into the room he was a silhouette etched by the noonday glare. He took off his hat and hung it on a stand. The door closed.

'Dad, this is the Mr O'Sullivan we were expecting,' Cassie said. She, too, had risen and stood deferentially with her hands behind her back.

'As you can see, I was a surprise,' Nina said, still not seeing Adam clearly. He had been brushing the knees of his pants, and straightened.

'It's Miss O'Sullivan, is it?' he began. 'It's so dark in here, I can hardly see a thing after –'

They faced each other, hands outstretched but not touching.

'Oh my God!' She sat down.

'Nina?'

She put a hand to her lips and then looked up, her face white. 'But you're dead.'

He swallowed awkwardly and sat on the seat facing her.

Mouth agape, Cassie had been following the exchange like an enthralled spectator at a tennis match. 'You two know each other?'

'Cassie!' Nina said. 'That's it. He spoke about you.' She slapped her forehead. 'I don't believe this. It's not happening.'

'We met in Greece,' Adam said. 'Nina came to help Joe when he was sick. She helped us escape.'

Nina flopped back in the seat. 'You were shot. I saw it.'

'But I wasn't killed.'

'We were certain.' She folded her arms tightly across her chest. 'We were so certain you'd been killed.'

'You got back all right?'

'Yes.' She reached for a handkerchief. 'Obviously.'

'And Alex? The boy?'

She managed to wipe her eyes and nod at the same time.

339

'And the man who took us there. What was his name?'

'Nick? I don't know. The Germans came later and did some terrible things in the village.'

Cassie's hands fluttered in front of her. 'I think I should leave you two alone. So you can both have a good cry.'

'This is my daughter Cassie,' Adam said, staring at Nina.

'I know. We've been talking. You told me all about her. I never thought I'd meet her.' Temples grasped between thumb and forefinger, she slowly shook her head.

'Well,' Adam said, and took a deep breath. 'You never know, do you?'

'Would you like a cup of tea?' Cassie asked.

'Don't ask for coffee,' Nina said and tried to laugh but began to cry.

They talked for hours. Cassie sat, knees under her chin, listening and saying nothing. Nina told her story first. She and Alex had walked clear of the fishing village just in time. As they climbed the track into the hills they had heard shots fired in the village and by the time they reached the town where Nick lived, the road was busy with trucks and motorcycles racing towards the coast. By avoiding the main roads they managed to reach Alex's home in four days. An aunt had moved in to look after the children. Nina had then walked back to the bakery.

'Just like that?' Adam asked.

'Well, by then all the heat was down on the coast. You see, Nick shot the man who shot you, and the other man on the motor-bike. There were rumours of terrible reprisals.'

Adam was silent for a long time.

'Anyhow,' she said when she felt it appropriate to resume. 'I spent the next two years with my grandmother, living above the bakery.'

'And going out at night, curing pneumonia and mending broken bones?'

'Occasionally.' They smiled at each other, and Cassie wondered.

After the war, Nina had gone to Britain and then home to America. She had taken her course in journalism, worked on a Boston newspaper, married the boy she'd known before the war, divorced him after two years, and gone to work in California.

'I had a good job on a San Francisco paper but then the old stirrings got too strong. You remember? To write for magazines and take my own photographs?'

He nodded, eyes closed and remembering the cellar at Nick's and the smells and the flickering candle and the passionate young

340

woman who'd frightened him with the intensity of her love making.

'I got a few offers, would you believe, but there was this fascinating assignment with the *Geographic* and the chance for me to see what a wombat was really like –'

He laughed.

'And here I am.'

He shook his head. 'I didn't think you'd see the war out. What you were doing was so dangerous, and you seemed to have a death wish.'

'That dream? When I saw you get shot, I said to myself, "That's it. That's what the dream was all about." And do you know, I never had that dream again.' She leaned forward. 'What happened to you? How come you're still alive?'

'Bit of good luck. This boat picked us up.'

'What boat?'

'A British destroyer. Apparently we ran into it the next morning. It was on its way to Tobruk, in Libya. There was a good doctor on board and he took the bullet out. It had gone through a lung and hit a few other things on the way. I ended up in hospital in Cairo. Took about six months to get back on my feet. They sent me to New Guinea.'

'And?'

'Walked through a lot of mud.'

They enjoyed a short silence.

'How about Joe?'

'They put him in hospital too. The pneumonia got worse for a while but one day they found him chasing a nurse so they shipped him home and somehow he ended up training younger blokes in the art of warfare.'

'He's all right? You still hear from him?'

'He's coming here in a few weeks.'

'Oh, I'd love to see him ...' Her voice trailed into regret.

'You have to go?'

'Must. I only have the plane for four days and there's so much to do.'

'Where to from here?' He studied his clasped hands.

'Adelaide. Then up to Sydney and back to the States.' She stood up. 'Tell me, do you folks ever eat around here?'

Mrs Wilson, who had been in the doorway, listening but not speaking, said, 'I fed the man who flew that thing that almost ran into the house. There's plenty left. Would you like more coffee with your lunch?'

'I might try tea,' Nina said.

* * *

341

Nina went to work that afternoon, using her Leica to take photographs of the homestead and portraits of the residents. Jimmy who had been out at the bore, returned just before sunset. He drove the Land Rover that Adam had purchased the previous year and Nina, anxious to make best use of the perfect light, put him straight back in the four-wheel-drive and drove with him to the nearest sand-hills for a series of portraits in the red dunes.

She sat next to Jimmy at dinner that night. They were eating beef. The days of galah and rabbit were far behind them. Mrs Wilson had cut Jimmy's meat into small slices.

'I like you Americans,' Jimmy announced, delicately spearing a piece of beef with his fork.

'Oh? What do you like about us?'

'Most things.' He drove the meat into his mouth and parked it inside one cheek. 'But you do three things that are funny.'

'What are they?' She braced herself, having already been exposed to Jimmy's humour.

'Well, you do things as though there'll be no time tomorrow for nothin', and you take pictures as though films were free.'

She eyed him with suspicion. 'How many Americans have you met?'

'In person? Only you.' He smiled to suggest the barb had been meant kindly.

'We don't have much time for this job,' she said, feeling compelled to offer some defence, 'and the film *is* free, courtesy of *National Geographic.*'

'When you've known Jimmy for twenty or so years,' Adam interjected, 'you'll realize he may only have one hand but he's very good at pulling people's legs.'

'I'll remember that,' she said and confronted Jimmy. His eyes sparkled with an hypnotic intensity. He was enjoying himself and the fun had not ended. 'You said three things,' she challenged. 'You've only listed two. What's the other?'

'You got a strange way of talking.' He dropped his voice from its normal zone of production, somewhere behind the nose, to deep in his throat and emitted the words with enough twang to fire an arrow. He had seen many cowboy films in his young days and the memories were strong. 'Say, pardner, that's a good lookin' hoss you got there.' With his one hand, he tipped back the brim of an imaginary hat. 'Better lookin' than you.'

She pushed back her imaginary hat. 'Smile when you say that.' Her drawl matched his.

'To tell you the truth mister, I don't feel like smilin'.' Without standing, he managed to imitate the roll of a cowboy advancing on bowed legs.

'Why's that?'

'Because I put my six-gun on the wrong side.' He made a light-ning draw from an empty holster. He roared with laughter and almost lost the meat in his mouth.

'Jimmy spends too much time on his own,' Cassie said.

'Not as much as someone I know,' Jimmy said and looked point-edly from Adam to Nina. She blushed.

They went to bed at ten. At ten-thirty, Adam heard a discreet knock on his door and saw the knob turn. He had been thinking about Nina and wondering how they could see each other in private, but had dismissed as outrageous any thought of walking to her bedroom and tapping on the door. And now, here she was ...

Cassie's head came into view. 'Good, you're still awake. Can I come in?'

Adam shuffled into an upright position. 'What do you want?'

'To talk.' She tiptoed to the bed. 'Move over.'

'Hang on. What's all this about?' It was years since Cassie had come to his bed. The protest had no effect. She lifted the sheet and used her hip to push him to one side.

'Now,' she said, squirming into a comfortable position alongside him, 'tell me about Nina.'

'You heard all about her today. Why don't you go back to bed and let your dad get some sleep?'

'You weren't asleep. You were thinking about her.'

He began to remonstrate but she elbowed him. 'Oh Dad, come on, tell me. I'm sure it's very romantic.'

'What is?'

'The story of how you and Nina met in Greece. Mrs Wilson has told me all about Greece. Byron went there. She read me his poems. She said it was the most romantic country on earth.'

'Mrs Wilson hasn't been to Greece.'

'Did you fall in love?'

He tried to push her out of bed but she dug her arm into his side and, for a few moments, their elbows engaged in a duel.

'I won't leave till you tell me,' she said, laughing but with a stubborn edge and he recognized the signal. She would stay there all night until she heard what she thought was the truth.

'Greece was cold,' he said. 'It was so cold your Uncle Joe got pneumonia. There was snow everywhere.'

She gave him a tolerant but disbelieving look. 'Greece is idyllic,' she said, using a word she had only recently discovered. 'It is so warm all the gods wear practically nothing and the men have tight curls and the women are very tall and beautiful and have straight

343

noses.' She lay a finger along her nose. 'They don't always have arms.'

He took her hand. 'Who don't?'

'The most beautiful women. Some of them, anyhow. I've seen pictures.'

'When I was in Greece, I didn't see any beautiful women without arms.'

'But you were in a cave, weren't you?'

'I did spend some of my time out in the open.' He patted her hands. 'What's this about gods, and not wearing clothes?'

'Greece is where the gods came from. You know, Zeus and Poseidon and Aphrodite and all those people.'

'I met a Dimitri and a Nick and a boy called Alex.'

She used his hand to thump his own thigh. 'Don't be ridiculous. And don't try to get away from answering the question.' When he said nothing, she squeezed his fingers. 'I saw the way you two looked at each other today. You both had that sick cow look that Peppino gets.'

'We were surprised to see each other.'

'I mean after you got over the surprise.'

'What did you see? I mean, apart from a pair of sick cows?'

She studied her father as though about to measure him for a suit. 'I saw a man who's been very lonely.'

'Who?' His tone was indignant.

She pinched the flesh below his ribs. 'I wasn't looking at the pilot and there weren't any other men.' He kicked because she had started to tickle him. 'I saw this man who met a beautiful young woman during the war and fell in love with her and thought he'd lost her and then found her.'

'Aren't you getting me mixed up with the prince who turned into a frog or something?'

'I know exactly what I saw.'

'You've been reading too much poetry.'

'You can never read too much.' She snuggled closer. 'Do you know what else I saw? I saw a woman who had met this handsome soldier during the war and thought he had been killed but then, when she went to a strange land, she found that he was alive after all.'

She put her hand against his shoulder and purred with satisfaction. 'I think it's just so romantic.'

'There's a better word for it but you're too young to hear it.'

She twined her arms around his chest. 'Dad, do you think I'll ever get married?'

Surprised, he pulled away. She sat upright. 'I suppose so,' he said. 'Why do you ask such a thing?'

'I've been wondering. I was thinking when I saw you and Nina today that you'd probably get married again and then I thought, if you got married, what's going to happen to me?'

'All because I met an old friend?'

'Oh,' she said, pinching him again, 'she's more than an old friend. She's your lost love.'

'Cassie.' He held her hand to stop the attacks. 'Me and Nina only knew each other for a few days.

'Some of the world's greatest romances have been between couples who never even spoke. Just a glance was enough.'

'I'm going to talk to Mrs Wilson tomorrow.'

'And do what?'

'Get her to stop letting you read poems and put you on to some good reading, like *Stock and Station Journal* or *Cattleman's Monthly*.'

She pulled her hand free and tickled him again. 'And stop changing the subject.'

'About what?'

'Me. Whether I'll ever get married.'

'I said yes, I suppose so. That's what women do. Get married.'

'Who'd want me?'

He shrugged. 'I think Peppino's pretty keen.'

'He wants to take-a me to Italy to meet-a his folks.'

'Don't poke fun at him.'

'I'm not. I just wouldn't marry him.'

'Why not?'

'I don't want to. There's no other reason.' She gazed up at the ceiling. 'Do you think I'm beautiful?'

'In an ugly sort of way.'

She threatened him with her raised hand. 'Do you want me to deliver Jimmy Kettle's demon right jab?'

He raised his hands in surrender. 'Anything but that.' Her fist remained, poised to strike. 'No, seriously, I think you're so beautiful that if I wasn't your father I'd want to marry you.'

'You're just saying that to be nice.' She kissed him on the cheek. 'You've always said my mother was beautiful. Am I starting to look like her?'

'You're dark. She was fair. But you are going to be devastatingly beautiful. Now, why don't you go back to your own bed. If I'd known you didn't mind sharing a bed I could have saved a lot of money on this house.'

She ignored the remark. 'The trouble is, there aren't any men.'

'Where?' He knew she wouldn't move until she was talked out.

345

'Around here. There's no one.' She held up her fingers and counted off the single men. 'Peppino is nice but he never shaves. There's that dreadful Gooly at the store but he's got that ugly broken nose and anyhow, he's about a hundred and one.'

'I think he's a little younger than that.'

She sat bolt upright. 'You wouldn't want me to marry him?'

'Look Cassie,' he said, pulling her hand down and demolishing the line of unnamed suitors, 'I don't want you to marry anyone. Not for a while anyway. You've got plenty of time. There are a lot of sheep to shear before you have to think about racing off to get married.'

'What a romantic way to put it.' She swayed away, rocking to the edge of the bed, to focus on him more accurately. 'Tell me, Dad, do you love me? I mean really, so you'd give your life for me, that sort of thing?'

He knew better than to smile but he almost succumbed to the temptation. 'What do you think?'

Again, she gave him the tailor's examination. 'I think so. Yes.'

'You're right.'

'Good.' She leaned over and kissed his cheek. 'Do you know how I knew that?'

'No. Tell me.'

'By the look in your eyes.'

'Go on.'

'It's true. I saw the same look today when you were talking to Nina.' She swung her legs off the bed and stood up. 'I just wanted to let you know that I know how you feel and I understand.'

'That's very kind of you.'

'And I'm very happy for you and if you want to go ahead and marry her, that's all right with me.'

'Cassie, you're about seven thousand steps ahead of me.'

'As always.' She blew him a kiss and walked to the door, swinging her hips in an exaggerated way because one slipper was partly off her foot. She bent to refit it. 'Who was that woman I remember? When we were first here.'

'Woman?'

'Yes. The one that used to nurse me.'

'Nellie.'

'She wasn't my mother?'

'No.'

'She was black?'

'A bit like Stella.'

'As pretty as Stella?'

He nodded.

'Did you love Nellie?'

'Do I love Mrs Wilson?'

'Don't be silly.'

'Can't you see it in my eyes?'

She pulled a face. 'After my mother died, why didn't you ever marry? When I was little, I can remember how sad you used to be.'

'I think you were mixing up being sad with being tired.'

'No.' The slipper was in place. She reached the door. 'Why didn't you marry someone?'

He knew she was a big girl but, until that moment he hadn't realized she was grown up. 'I don't know,' he said and made no effort to disguise the sadness in his voice.

'Don't let this one go, will you?' She closed the door.

F·O·U·R

An hour after sun-up next day, they flew to the lake. Cassie sat beside the pilot. Adam was in the next row. Nina sat at the back of the cabin with her camera equipment in the seat opposite her. She said she needed room to move from one side of the cabin to the other. Soon after take-off, she moved to the seat beside Adam.

'I'll go back when we get to Lake Eyre,' she shouted to be heard above the din of the twin motors.

Adam had never flown above the property or the lake, and was enthralled by the view. They swung east, over a row of sand-hills that embroidered the plain in rows of parallel stitching.

'What are you thinking?' she said, leaning towards him to see out of his window.

'Better than a map.' He rubbed his chin. 'A man ought to have one of these. Be very handy.'

'You could land anywhere. Your ranch, sorry, your property is like one big airfield with a few rows of sand every now and then just to make things interesting.' She looked around the cabin, which buzzed and resonated like the inside of a drum. 'You wouldn't buy one of these, though.'

Adam joined her in the examination. 'Bit big for me.'

'And old. The pilot and I keep having arguments. He tells me what a great plane it is and I tell him it must have been left over from the ark. Two wings! It's positively ancient.'

'The Flying Doctor has a plane like this. He says it's good. It can take people on stretchers and use very rough strips. Some of the new planes are a bit like new cars, he reckons. They're built for the city, not the bush.'

'Does he fly into Kalinda often?'

'Hardly see him. He came over to pick up Jimmy's eldest girl when she broke her collarbone. Otherwise he just drops in for an occasional cup of tea if he's on his way somewhere.'

'Sounds cosy.'

'It's good. Transformed this country having a doctor, believe me.'

'And when you want him, you just call him on the radio?'

'Yeah. There's the lake.' Visible through the whirling disc of the starboard propeller was the first sign of Lake Eyre, a smudge of white and grey where the shoreline of a bay bruised the horizon. They were flying at five hundred feet and gradually, eerily, the lake revealed itself. Flat, swirling in monotones and awesome in size, it marked the place where form and colour, no matter how drab, gave way to a great nothingness. It was as if the edge of the world had broken away.

They flew closer and the lake spread wider. More bays came into view. The main body of the lake stretched north and south, its boundaries lost in haze. There were some small islands and sashes of mud and great areas of smooth salt where millions of crystals formed mirrors to bounce blinding sunlight at the intruding aircraft.

Nina grabbed Adam by the shoulder. 'It's like flying over a gigantic painting,' she said excitedly. 'The only thing is all the colour is back there. The lake is like the edge of the canvas, where the artist cleaned his brush.' Her other hand pointed to the places where stains of colour or darker tones of grey showed on the salt.

'You're a poet,' he said.

'I'm a writer.' She squeezed his shoulder, then, remembering her mission, went to the back of the cabin and got her camera bag. For the next twenty minutes, she took photographs. They could still not see the opposite shore. When the pilot indicated they should return, he banked to the right with the intention of flying back along the southern coastline. At first, they flew deep into a bay. Ahead they could see land and, south of that, another expanse of salt.

'Must be Lake Eyre South,' Adam said. 'It all looks so different from up here.'

Nina photographed him. 'I want a picture of the man who owns Lake Eyre getting his first view from the air.'

He laughed. 'I don't own Lake Eyre.'

'Well you own the land that runs up to the lake.' She began unloading the Leica, to put in her fifth roll of film for the flight.

'I own part of the land around the lake,' he said. 'A small part.'

She nodded agreement. 'Not small but a part. I've read the figures. The lake covers four thousand eight hundred square miles. It's one hundred and eighty miles from south to north – that's Lake Eyre North, if that's what you call the main lake?'

He shrugged. He was fascinated by the way she could change film without looking at the camera.

'And it's the lowest part of the continent. Thirty-two feet below sea level?'

'Don't ask me,' he said. 'I just live here.'

349

'Well, if you want to learn all about it, read next February's edition of *National Geographic.*'

'I'll go down to the shop and get one.'

'Better still, I'll mail a copy to you.'

'Always the way, isn't it,' he said, when she had finished reloading. 'If you want to find out about the place where you live, you got to ask a stranger.'

'Who are you calling a stranger?' She smiled and he smiled and she took his photograph.

They followed the shore to a long promontory, crossed that, and then flew over a deep bay shaped like a jackboot.

'Anything more you want, Nina?' the pilot shouted.

'No thanks, Geoff. I'll get some ground shots this evening.' She turned to Adam. 'Would you mind driving me out to the lake? I want some sunset shots.'

'Be glad to.'

She lowered her head and covered her eyes.

'What's wrong?'

She looked up, her eyes bright. 'I just can't believe you're still alive.' She shook her head. 'I've thought of you a lot, but as someone from the past. I couldn't sleep last night.'

Nina reached for his hand. He took it but only after checking to see if Cassie was looking. His daughter seemed intent on the view through the front screen. Having crossed the mouth of the bay, the Dragon Rapide flew over a low headland. A mob of kangaroos took fright. Adam pointed them out to Nina. He counted about forty animals before the lower wing obscured his view. The plane swung a little to the right and began crossing a much wider bay.

Halfway across, the plane lurched, then steadied. Cassie swung around, one arm across the back of her seat. She was smiling and when she saw Adam holding Nina's hand, she winked at him.

'How'd you like that?' she asked gleefully.

'Like what?' he asked, still holding hands but as embarrassed as a schoolboy caught with his first cigarette.

'That!' she repeated, her face animated with joy. 'The flight. I've been flying the plane for the last ten minutes.'

With his free hand, Adam covered his eyes.

'She's good, isn't she?' the pilot called out, sparing Adam a brief glance. 'You'll have to buy her her own plane one day.'

Cassie raised her eyebrows. Adam recognized the expression. It was the prelude to a campaign.

'A plane would be perfect out here,' the pilot continued and Adam wished he would concentrate on his flying. 'They'll be as common as cars in a few years.'

Cassie nodded with each word and kept her eyes on her father.

Adam aimed a finger at her nose. 'Just let me pay for all those extra bedrooms before you start pestering me for something else.'

'Who's in a hurry?' she said and winked again. She slipped back into the seat. 'Can I have another go?'

The pilot raised both hands. 'Be my guest.'

'I like flying, don't you Dad?' Cassie called and there was mischief in her voice.

Nina laughed. 'That's a very special young lady you have for a daughter.'

'And one who knows how to get what she wants,' Adam said softly. He felt especially contented with life, and as they flew towards Kalinda, he recalled the nights when there were no galahs to go into the pot.

In Adelaide, Josef Hoffman had been waiting at the hospital for several hours. He was thinking of getting some lunch when a nurse came and asked him to follow her. She led him to an office where a grey-haired surgeon sat behind a desk. He was sipping tea and offered Josef some. Josef declined and sat down.

'Well, Mr Hoffman, the operation was a success, I think.' He paused before uttering the last words. 'Mrs Khan will be a bit woozy for a day or so but you should be able to see her tomorrow.'

'You got it all, do you think?' Josef fidgeted with the buttons of his coat.

'You can't be sure with cancer.' The man drank some tea. He looked exhausted, and Josef wondered how many operations he had done that day and what was his score. How many saved, how many lost, how many uncertain? 'At least she wasn't riddled with it. Some we just sew back up, but there's good reason for hope in her case.'

'It was such a surprise.' Josef was still numb. Nellie had only been diagnosed as having cancer two days before. She had gone straight into hospital.

'It usually is. Of course, if we'd got her earlier ...'

'She lives up in the bush.'

'Six months earlier, and I'd be feeling reasonably confident.'

'The matron told me she'd been sick for a while.'

The surgeon drank more tea. 'People tend to tough it out,' he said and wiped his lips. He had long, delicate fingers that were so pink it seemed a layer of skin had been removed. 'And that's a shame. People perceive it as a virtue when a sick person doesn't complain but it makes it harder for us. And harder for them, of course. Does she have to go back to Innamincka?'

'I guess so.' Josef slouched over his knees. 'I was going to fly her up north to see some friends. I've got my own plane, you see, and I was wondering if she'd be well enough to travel.'

'Better the plane than the long train journey, I would think. When are you planning to leave?'

'In a couple of weeks.'

The surgeon made a bridge with his fingers. 'I don't see why not. As long as she doesn't carry heavy bags or do something strenuous.'

'She won't.' Josef sat up and shook his head.

'Friends you say? That could be good. Cheer her up.' He put his hands on the table. The talk was over.

Josef stood. 'I can see her tomorrow?'

'Tomorrow night.'

They shook hands. The man's fingers were cold.

'Mr Hoffman, it was a good operation, a successful operation, but there are no guarantees.'

'I understand,' Josef said, but didn't.

Outside, Josef breathed deeply. He hated the smell of hospitals.

The sunset was a particularly beautiful one. Adam had taken the Land Rover and driven Nina to the western shore of Lake Eyre. They had gone to the site where a wide, sandy creek broke into many channels and ran into the lake through a series of mud flats and soured, swampy basins. Several low headlands, divided by the varying mouths of the watercourse, jutted into a bay. It was a colourful place. The headlands, like everything else in that region, bore the pain of ages on their worn faces, which were striped with the geological deposits of the aeons. Layers of pink, yellow, grubby grey, and stark white were exposed, along with thin fillings of shale and ancient muds, and bubbling rows of small boulders. All had been revealed by the abrasive tongues of floods; rare moments when water had filled the lake and swirled around these sentinels and made a fine cut to brighten the colours.

'So the lake has had water,' she mused, when the sun had gone but the last of its light lingered. It was a time when the lake seemed soft, and the bed could be seen, clear and smooth, running all the way to the first hint of night.

'It is a lake,' he said. 'Lakes do have water.'

She held his hand. It was the first time they had touched since the flight that morning. 'I must sound like a ... what's the appropriate Australian expression?'

'Drongo?'

'That'll do. I know lakes have water but this looks as though it

352

should always be like this. Dry. Mystic. Sort of sinister in the daytime and spooky at night.' She turned to him. 'I love it.'

'I've never seen water fill Lake Eyre,' he said, determined to be practical. 'We had a scientist bloke up here a couple of years ago and he said the lake's often flooded.'

'Really?'

'Maybe a couple of times every hundred years.'

She stood beside him, facing the salt, which was turning a soft purple colour. 'You wouldn't want to buy tickets for the big happening.'

'He reckoned,' Adam persevered, 'that the salt gets a little thicker every time it floods. The water comes down in the rivers, either from Western Queensland,' he pointed to the north east, 'or from the Northern Territory up on the other side.'

'This is all very educational.'

'Good. And the water had salt in it, you see, just naturally. So when the flood goes and the water evaporates, the salt's left.'

'And makes the bed of the lake thicker.'

'That's right.'

'When are you going to kiss me?' She gripped his hand so he couldn't pull loose. He didn't try but she felt him stiffen. 'Just a welcome kiss. One that says "I'm glad you're here".'

'I thought you wanted to write a story?' Tenderly he kissed her on the forehead. 'I'm still trying to convince myself it really is you.'

'It really is. Same girl who shared your cave, kept your bed warm in the cellar and put you on the boat.' She paused. 'And saw you get shot.'

He kissed her lips and the kiss became so hard that she pulled back.

'Is that to say you're pleased to see me?'

'Yes. Among other things.'

'What other things?' She had placed her hand on his chest and gently stroked him.

'It says I remember what happened in Greece. It says that I feel as though this is a dream, that I'm living in some kind of miracle.'

'That's a lot for one kiss.'

He kissed her again, a gentle kiss that allowed their lips to explore each other. She put her arms around his neck.

'I remember you as such a strong man; the strongest, bravest man I'd ever known.'

'I remember you in the cellar.'

She pushed her face into his shoulder. 'I've never made love to anyone else like that.'

'I've never made love to anyone since then.'

353

She lifted her head. 'My God. That was 1943.'

'I know.' He locked his arms behind her waist, and drew her tightly to him.

She lifted both hands and gently touched his biceps. 'I think you're still the strongest man I've ever known. I can't break loose.'

'You're not trying.'

'I don't want to.'

They stayed together until the remaining light drained into a fine, golden line that rimmed the western dunes. Over the lake, the first stars appeared.

'I can't believe these skies,' she said.

'What can't you believe?'

'They're so clear. Normally the sky's like a roof. You know, with a limit to it? But here, it goes on forever and there are so many stars.'

'It's our nice clean air.'

She breathed deeply. 'It smells so good.'

'Gets a bit dusty in the summer.'

'I'd like to see this country in the summer.'

'That's easy. Just stay.'

She drew away from him, but held his hands 'You'd really like me to?'

He nodded.

'Say it.' She was at arm's length and shook his hands, to help dislodge the words.

'Yes. I'd like you to.'

'Why?'

He pulled her closer with the ease of someone who knows he is much stronger but uses his power to demonstrate a gentle affection. 'I'd forgotten how you were always asking questions.'

'That's me. The enquiring journalist. Just shows you I haven't changed.'

'Oh yes you have.'

'In what way?'

She put her head against his shoulder.

'You're older,' he began and when she tried to draw away he pulled her back. 'And better looking.'

She relaxed. 'That's better. And it *has* been ten years.'

'You're more interesting.'

Softly, she stroked the back of his neck. 'Calling a woman interesting is sometimes a polite way of saying she's a bit of a dog. I hope this is going to be better.'

'I mean you look as though you've got a few brains.'

354

The stroking became firmer. 'Whereas, before –'

He began to laugh. 'I've got big feet, haven't I?'

'Which you put in your mouth?'

'Constantly.'

'Maybe you should just stay the strong silent type.'

'I was trying to say nice things. I think you look lovely.'

'Well, that's better, even if it is an exaggeration. I may be many things but I'm not lovely. It's just this marvellous light.'

Adam tilted his head down. 'But I can hardly see you.'

'That's what I mean. By the way, never compliment a woman on her brains. That *is* saying she's a dog. You can say she's got a pretty face or a lovely figure but never, ever say she's got a good mind. It puts out the fire as effectively as a bucket of water.'

He stroked her hair. 'I'm not doing very well, am I?'

'The start wasn't very good. I'm just hoping for a big ending.'

'To tell you the truth, I feel that I should be saying something, something clever, but I don't know what to say.'

'Try something simple. Tell me you've missed me.'

'But I didn't.' He felt her head lift, and used his hand to put it back against his shoulder. 'I don't mean I didn't think of you. I did. Often. 'Specially on the boat and in hospital in Egypt. I thought about you all the time then. But when I came back to Australia, I thought: well, that's it. She's over there and I'm here and if she's still alive, which I doubted because of the way things were going in Greece, she'll go back to America maybe or stay in Greece or do God only knows what and I'll never see her again. That's what I thought. And do you know something else?'

Her head shook against his chest.

'I didn't even know your name. I knew Nina, but not your real name – you told me once, while we were in the cave I think, but I forgot. I could hardly have gone off to America after the war and said "I'm here to find Nina".'

'Would you have?' she asked. 'If you thought I was alive?'

He hesitated. 'I would have when I was in Egypt. That was close. I don't mean only in distance. I mean close in time, and Greece still seemed real then. It's hard to explain, but the further you get from a place, the less real it seems. The same with the people you met there. By the time I'd sailed back to this part of the world and gone to New Guinea and then come back here, Greece seemed like . . . well, a bit like a dream, you know, as though it hadn't really happened.'

'So you wouldn't have come to America?'

She felt his head rise and fall several times before he spoke. 'I would have if I'd known you were OK, and I'd known your name and knew where you lived. And if I was sure you weren't married.'

355

'Not married? Was that important?'

'Yeah.'

She pressed hard against him. 'I thought about you,' she said. 'And I used to dream about you a lot. Weird things. Fantasies, nightmares, those sorts of dreams. But I never thought we'd ever meet again. I was convinced you were dead. You were my lost love. It was all very sad, and very romantic.' She sighed. 'It was also a long time ago.'

'And you've been married?'

'And divorced. You don't do that sort of thing over here, do you?'

'Never tried it myself.'

'Don't. He was a dentist. Or rather, is. He's still alive and drilling in Boston.'

'Why'd you get divorced?'

'I went to work. He went to bed ... with other women. It didn't matter really. I knew it was a mistake after the first month.'

More stars were shining.

'And here we are,' he said.

'I love your daughter.'

He nodded. 'She's a bit of a character.'

'She adores you.'

'She makes my life hell.'

'Go on. You love the way she fusses around you and teases you. You two are good friends.'

'Mates.'

'I like that word.'

'She came into my bedroom last night,' he said. Nina cocked her head. 'She wanted me to come clean about the big romance in Greece.'

'You'd talked to her about us.'

'No. She'd just looked at the two of us yesterday and started jumping to conclusions.'

'A perceptive young miss.'

'She's got a very active imagination.'

The first puffs of a cool breeze touched them. Nina shivered. They set off towards the Land Rover, which was parked on solid ground well clear of the lake's edge. Nina walked with her arms across her chest. Adam had his arm around her waist.

'You've raised Cassie yourself?' she asked as they walked.

'Mrs Wilson helped with her schooling. It was pretty tough before she came along. Stella was great. She's really good at reading and writing and she helped with the lessons. I wasn't too good at that, remember?'

356

'You never went to school.'

'That's me.'

'How about now?' Nina posed the question frankly, as though men who couldn't read or write were her regular companions.

'I'm pretty good,' Adam said, pride lifting his voice. 'Mrs Wilson has been a real gem. She's very well educated and she'd give me lessons when we'd put Cassie to bed at night. I can read anything now and I'm pretty good at writing. I read books, magazines, whatever papers I can get hold of.'

'Not the *National Geographic*?'

'I'm starting with the February issue. Do you know one thing I'm good at?'

'What?' She patted the hand that held her waist.

'Arithmetic. Mrs Wilson says I should have been an engineer or something like that.'

They were silent while he led her across a marshy area.

'She's the only woman in your life?' Nina asked when they were on firm sand.

'Mrs Wilson?' He laughed. 'Yes.'

'You've never found anyone else? Or gone looking for someone?'

'No.'

'It must be a lonely life. I mean, I don't think I've ever been to a place where there are so few people and so much space. The years since the war must have been awfully difficult for you.'

He dismissed the problems with a shrug. 'There's been a lot of work. That keeps me busy.'

'What happened to the woman you were telling me about? The one who went away?'

'Never heard from her.'

'You didn't know why she'd gone.'

'Still don't.'

'Do you think about her?'

He was silent and she counted six paces before he spoke. 'Yes.' Another silence. Nina had learned to keep quiet. (Her first editor had taught her: 'Ask your question, then shut up. People can't stand a verbal vacuum. They feel compelled to fill 'em with words.' She smiled. That man had never met Adam Ross.) It was a long silence. Their feet crunched on plates of dried salt. 'I used to think about her a lot,' he said eventually, as though there had been no pause. ''Specially when I came back here and brought Cassie from the city.'

Another silence. Nina had to speak. 'And you never found her or ever heard where she went to?'

'Not a sign, not a word.' He sighed. It was a sound not meant for others to hear. 'I searched for her. Almost went mad, the first couple of years.'

'Was there another man?'

He grunted, the beginning of a laugh that couldn't be sustained. 'Not too many men up here.'

'Was it the loneliness? This place is very isolated.'

'Don't think so. She was used to this sort of country.' He supported her as they crossed a ridge covered with tussocky grass. The light was feeble but sufficient for him to find the path. 'I got the feeling that she left for a good reason.'

'Well, obviously. Good for her, anyhow.'

'No, I don't mean that. I mean good, like noble. Nellie was a bit like that. Inclined to do something and not tell you why.'

'Do you think she ... I mean, is she still alive? Do you know?'

'No. She might be dead.' He shook his head. 'It's been a long time.' More silence. 'When she left, she was given a lift by a parson. I've asked him a few times if he knows where she is. I think he might, but he's not saying.'

'So she could still be around?'

'Who knows? Probably married with kids and living happily somewhere.' They were near the vehicle. 'It was a long time ago. I stopped worrying about her or why she had left, years ago.'

'Still –' Nina began, not believing him.

'Nina,' he said, 'she left here fourteen years ago. Before the war. End of story.' They reached the Land Rover. Following the custom of bush people, he had left both doors open. She climbed in and he closed her door. 'The important question,' he said, having trouble with the catch, 'is how long you're staying.'

'We're due back in Adelaide in a couple of days.'

'Do you have to go back then?' she slammed the door again and the vehicle shook but the catch held.

'The charter ends on Friday.'

'Send the pilot back with the plane. You stay.'

'And how do I get back?'

'On the train. That's an experience. Worth a story in itself.' He slid into place behind the steering-wheel.

'I have to write my story.'

'Do it here, at the homestead. It's nice and quiet.'

'I need access to information.' She reached across and touched his wrist. 'I have to write about the Great Barrier Reef and Ayers Rock as well. I must go to Adelaide. Believe me.'

They followed their own tyre marks, first across a stretch of sand and then up a rise where the ground was patterned like the skin of a burnt rice pudding.

358

'When are you going back to America?'

'The *Mariposa* sails from Sydney in three and a half weeks.'

'So you'd have to leave Adelaide in three weeks' time.' She agreed. 'And how long would it take you to write your story?

She sensed the trap and raised a finger. 'Maybe a week, but it could take me another week to collate all the information.'

'But you'd have at least a week to spare. A week you could spend up here.'

She ran her fingers through her hair and left the hands locked behind her head. 'And then I'd miss the plane ride and have to take the train, and that's a long way on my own.'

He changed gear to tackle a dry channel filled with soft sand. 'Who said you'd be on your own?'

Josef had visited her the night before. Now the surgeon made a call. His ulcer was aching and he was not in the mood for small talk.

'The operation went well, Mrs Khan,' he told Nellie. 'How are you feeling?'

'She's fine,' the nurse answered for her, a little too quickly for Nellie's liking. 'Aren't you, Mrs Khan?'

Nellie smiled. 'Still feeling a little dopey.'

'Of course,' he said, and checked her chart.

'Am I going to be all right?'

He attempted a bright smile but his ulcer intervened and the expression became distorted by pain. 'We'll just have to wait and see,' he said. When the answer seemed to displease the nurse, he added, 'Don't worry, we'll soon have you out of here and on your way home,' and moved on to the next bed.

Later that day, Nellie asked the nurse for a pen and paper.

'Are you well enough to write?'

'Yes. There's a letter I must send.'

'Very well, pet, but better make it a short letter, eh?'

Nellie wrote to Saleem Benn. First she addressed an envelope, then began the letter.

'Dear Saleem Benn,
You've been so good to me and I'm very grateful. I wanted you to know that. I can never repay you for what you done for me and what you're doing for Danny.'

She read what she had written and crossed out Danny and substituted Daniel.

'There are two things I want to say. The first is that if I die,

359

Adam should be told that Daniel is his boy. I know Adam would want to look after him. I don't mean give him cash but make sure he got a good start in life. Maybe Daniel could get a job with him. I like the idea of the two of them working together.

She was tired and rested for a few minutes. The nurse came to check. Nellie smiled and waved the pen.

'Only a few more lines,' the nurse said and went away.

The other thing (Nellie continued) is about Gooly. I should have told you a long time ago. Remember when he said he was robbed of seven hundred pounds? Well, he took that himself. I know because I was there. He's got a filthy mind and he tried to attack me and I hit him and broke his nose. I took a tenner because I never had the cash for the train. I was going to pay you back but then he took the money.

The nurse returned. 'You look exhausted. Is it finished?'

'I haven't signed it,' Nellie said.

The woman waited for Nellie to sign, then took the letter. 'I'll post it, pet. Just get some rest.'

Nellie couldn't sleep for a while. There was something else she meant to add. Only later did she remember. She was going to warn Saleem Benn that his nephew knew about Mailey, but by then it was too late. The letter had gone.

F·I·V·E

Cassie spent most of the day with the pilot. When she was not talking to him, she sat on her own in the cabin of the aircraft, studying the display of inactive instruments and gently dabbing the rudder pedals. When Adam asked what she was doing, she explained that she was studying the fundamentals of flying. He was amused, rather than concerned by her long solo efforts in the stationary biplane but her talks to the pilot had him behaving, for the first time in his life, like an anxious father.

The only young man who visited the homestead, Peppino Portelli, was a bit of fun. He was also essentially a decent person and, just as impressive a qualification, he was a local, living no more than two hundred miles away which, by the standards of the outback, made him a neighbour.

The pilot was different. Geoff Lunney was in his late thirties, had been in the air force, and lived in Adelaide. In the eyes of Adam, the worried and protective parent, those three facts were interchangeable with the three deadliest vices. Lunney was too old, too experienced and lived too far away to be displaying interest in an attractive but naïve seventeen-year-old.

Therefore, when he persuaded Nina to stay an extra week, he suggested that the aircraft leave a day ahead of schedule, to save on the charter fee. When Lunney explained that the fee depended on hours in the air, not time spent on the ground, Adam proposed that the extra day could be gainfully spent doing additional charter work.

There wasn't that much work around, Lunney said and anyhow he didn't own the plane so it didn't worry him.

In that case, Adam proposed, he could spend the saved day with his wife or girl-friend, a subtlety that was lost on Cassie but was quickly absorbed by Lunney who was not only a skilled pilot but good at reading between the lines of a message.

He left after lunch.

'My father used to behave like you,' Nina said, when he and Adam were alone.

'I like the sound of your dad,' Adam said. He was trying a cup of coffee. Mrs Wilson had said Nina prepared it.

'He was hopeless. As soon as any young man appeared, he started behaving like a frog with palsy.'

'And I remind you of him?'

'The way you behaved with Geoff, yes.' She was needling him and enjoying it. There was a vulnerable side to Adam after all.

'I didn't like the way Mr Lunney was looking at my daughter.'

'Mr Lunney was looking at Cassie like any young man would. With interest. And she was enjoying it.'

Adam had raised the cup and was using it as a pointer. 'He is not a young man. He was in the war. The air force at that.'

'What was wrong with the air force?

'I knew blokes in the army who'd chase anything with skirts but the fellers in the air force were worse.'

She sat back in her chair. 'I think you're delightful like this, acting this new role.'

'What role?'

'The old-fashioned father.' She grinned. 'You'd be hopeless in the city, with boys living next door.'

'Well, thank God we don't live there.' He drank some coffee, mainly to stem the need for any further words on the subject. As the coffee went down his face lifted in anguish. 'God, how can you drink this stuff?'

'Who's drinking it?' She sipped her tea. 'What you have in your kitchen masquerading as the world's greatest drink is not only old and stale but as much like genuine coffee as ...' She clicked the fingers of her other hand, attempting to summon the appropriate words.

'As what?' He pushed the coffee away and waited, taunting her.

She started to giggle. 'Anything. Your boots.'

He crossed his feet. 'What's wrong with them?'

'Apart from the fact that they seem to be very well used, nothing. It's just that I wouldn't want to drink them. I'll tell you what, when we get to Adelaide, I'll buy you two things: new boots and proper coffee.'

'I don't want coffee. I'm happy with tea.'

'If you want me to come back you'll need to have good coffee.'

Adam whistled softly and the frivolity in the conversation escaped with this breath. He played with the cup, spinning it slowly on the saucer. 'You would come back?'

'It depends on my work.' She avoided his eyes.

'I'd like you to come back,' he said after a long pause.

'It's such a long way.'

Mrs Wilson entered the room. 'Anyone for more tea or coffee?' She noticed Adam's almost full cup. 'Would you rather have tea?' She took his cup and smiled at Nina and left the room.

'You do have to go back?' Adam said.

'To America?' Her surprise was unnaturally vigorous. 'I live there. I work there.' He was sitting back, saying nothing. 'And I have to get this story back, and all the photos. They have to be developed.'

'We have a new invention in this part of the world. Could be very handy.'

'What's that?'

'It's called the mail.'

She clasped her hands and hid behind them. 'What are you suggesting?'

'That maybe you shouldn't go back home.'

She stood up. 'I have to make some notes.'

He nodded gravely. 'I got work to do too. I'll see you later.' They went through different doors. As she was leaving, he said: 'Think about it, won't you?'

That afternoon, Nina spent several hours with Cassie. They walked out to the rocky hill behind the homestead and climbed to the top. There, they sat together and admired the view. Cassie pointed out the features of the property. Most were out of sight, either because of their great distance from the homestead buildings or because they were hidden by the dunes that trimmed the horizon. She talked of artesian bores and mound springs, knew the region where the cattle were grazing – it was forty miles away – and described the places where the two main mobs of sheep were located. She discussed price trends for wool and the potential market for beef. When Nina said what most newcomers said – that there seemed to be almost no grass for the animals to eat – Cassie explained the importance of top feed and listed the bushes the animals could eat. Standing up and pointing, she indicated the sections of the vast property where the best top feed grew. Standing atop the highest peak in the district she resembled, Nina thought, some ancient goddess dispensing favours to the mortal creatures below her heavenly perch. At some length, Cassie described how the bores worked and the difference between the deep bores which gushed their scalding-hot water at high pressure and filled the surrounding air with sulphurous fumes, and the shallow springs which bubbled on the surface. The bores allowed them to work the land, for there was not enough water above the surface to keep animals or people alive. There was, however, a huge amount of water underground, in the great artesian basins that spread beneath

363

much of inland Australia. Just south of Muloorina, a homestead to the east of Lake Eyre South, was the most prolific bore in Australia. It poured out nearly two million gallons of water a day through a pipe that reached half a mile into the ground.

'But the water from these bores is so hot,' Nina said. 'You could make tea from it.'

'We dig long drains and let the water cool off as it runs away. The animals drink it downstream.'

'It smells terrible.'

'Maybe to us. The stock seem to love it. In fact, they prefer bore water to rain water.'

'Europeans drink a lot of mineral water,' Nina said and Cassie, whose thoughts had been firmly within the boundaries of Kalina, was perplexed and stared at the other woman.

Suddenly, Nina realized she had sounded dangerously like a species she detested: the boring sophisticate returned from her pilgrimage to the Continent. 'What I was thinking of,' she said smoothing her forehead to eradicate even a hint of pretension, 'was that humans drinking mineral water and cattle drinking bore water that's full of minerals are not all that different. It's a matter of taste and habit I suppose.'

But Cassie's interest was not in mineral water, but in the Europeans who drank it. 'What are Europeans like?' she asked, her eyes bright with curiosity.

Nonplussed, Nina laughed. 'They're all different.'

'How?'

'Well, they speak different languages, have different customs, even look different.' She could see Cassie wanted more. 'A German person often looks very different to a Frenchman, while an Italian is different again. Darker, particularly if they come from the south.'

'Peppino Portelli is Italian. He's our mail contractor. He talks funny.'

They walked towards the homestead. 'Have you ever thought of going to Europe?' Nina asked.

'Mrs Wilson has books on Europe. Switzerland looks nice. Are the mountains really that big?'

'I guess so. I've never been to Switzerland.'

'But you've been to Europe.'

'I saw a lot of Greece, or rather, one part of Greece. I didn't see a lot of Europe.' Nina kicked at a stone. 'You should go. A girl like you would get so much benefit out of spending a year or so over there.'

Now it was Cassie's turn to laugh. 'I couldn't leave here for a year. There's too much to do.'

'Surely your dad could spare you?'

'He says I'm his right-hand man. Jimmy says that too, but he's only joking.' She waited for Nina to show understanding but the other woman shook her head. 'You've seen Jimmy,' Cassie continued and touched her right arm in explanation.

'Oh,' Nina said, raising her head in understanding. 'Your friend Jimmy's got a sense of humour, hasn't he?'

'Jimmy's nuts.'

'But nicely nuts.'

'You never know when he's serious. But he's really nice. My dad saved his life.'

'How?'

'Jimmy got stuck down a well once, a long time ago, and rocks fell on him. That's how he lost his arm.'

'And your father rescued him?'

'He went down and got Jimmy out, even though there were still rocks falling on top of them.'

'Did your father tell you exactly what happened?'

'He never talks about it. Jimmy and Uncle Joe told me about it.'

'Your father doesn't talk much, does he?'

'Jimmy says he has better conversations with a sand-hill.'

They laughed and walked on. Near the house, Nina said: 'Cassie, if you really wanted to travel to Europe, would your father let you go?'

'Probably. We've never talked about it.'

'He's told me you do a lot of work around the place but he could manage without you for a while, surely?'

'I'm not sure that I want to go.'

Nina stopped. 'For goodness sake's, why?'

'Dad says Australia's the best country on earth, and other people have told me that too.'

'Well, that might be so, but you still ought to have a look at some other countries for yourself.'

'What's the point of going somewhere if it's better where you live? That's just wasting time and good money.' Cassie walked on, head bowed in thought. 'Anyhow we've got the shearing in a month or two.'

'I don't mean right away,' Nina laughed. 'Travelling isn't or shouldn't be a matter of only going to the best countries. It's a matter of seeing the most interesting places and some of them can be pretty terrible. I can tell you some stories ...' Nina's eyes flared with innuendo and Cassie, longing to hear the tales but knowing intuitively that now was not the time, kept her head down but anticipated some interesting evenings when Nina might be persuaded to unlock her chest of wicked stories.

Near the house, they stopped. 'What's the best country you've been to?' Cassie asked.

'Oh, that'a difficult question to answer. Best for what? Food, clothing, scenery, men?' Both laughed.

'If you had your choice, where would you live?'

'Now that is hard.' Nina pondered. 'The States I suppose.'

'The States?'

'The United States. America. Where I live. But I guess that's natural. Most people would prefer to live in the country where they were born.'

'I suppose so. Could you ever live in Australia?'

Nina was about to answer when she realized she was stepping into a gently-laid trap. This long conversation, which she thought she had engineered, had been steered towards this point. She glanced at Cassie who had her head down, trying not to display too much interest.

'Well, I don't know,' she said, as if the thought had never occurred to her. 'It would depend on so many things. Like whether you were living among friends.'

'That's what you'd miss in America, I suppose. I mean, if you lived somewhere else, you'd miss all your friends.'

'Yes. I guess when it came down to it, friends are the key to living in any place.'

Cassie stood by the steps, letting her head nod as though absorbing all the points Nina had made on the walk from the hill. 'Well,' she said, giving her head a final shake, 'I have to go over to the shed. There are a few things I've got to do.'

'Thank you for the lovely talk,' Nina said. 'I've learned a lot.'

'I'm pleased you're staying.' They smiled at each other.

Cassie came to Adam's bedroom again that night, and climbed under the blankets.

'It's cold,' she said.

'It'd be warmer if you stayed in your own bed.'

'I like her.' She pulled the blankets up to her chin. Adam was sitting up.

'Who?'

'Oh Dad, you can be the world's biggest drip. Nina of course.'

'Well, I wasn't sure.'

She elbowed his hip. 'Did you think I was talking about Mrs Wilson? She lives here forever and then one night I come up to you and say I like her? Is that what you think?' She elbowed him again.

He grinned. 'What brought this on?'

'I had a long talk to Nina today. She was interviewing me for her story. She took some photographs. Do you think they'll use them in her magazine?'

'Maybe. Depends on how good a magazine it is.'

She tugged the blankets, pulling them higher. 'I won't ask what you mean by that.'

He hunched his knees and she struggled to keep the blankets over her. 'What did you two talk about?'

'The property. The underground water. Things like that.'

'And she was interested?'

'Very.' She rolled on her side and faced Adam. 'She said something interesting.'

'What was that?'

'She said I should see the world.'

'Why?'

'She said travel was an essential part of every modern young woman's education.'

'Whatever happened to reading and writing?'

Cassie propped herself on one elbow. 'You sound so old-fashioned at times. Reading and writing is just the beginning of education.'

'And you want to move on? To see the world?'

'Well, I don't know. I rather like it here. I'm not so sure how I'd like other countries.'

'Only one way to find out, I suppose.'

'You'd let me go?'

'Maybe. Not yet. You're too young.'

'I'm always too young.'

'I was thirty before I went overseas.'

'You were in the army. Do you want me to wait for another war and join up?'

'I want you to go back into your bed so I can get some sleep.' He tried to push her out of bed, but she fought back.

'I've got an idea,' she said, when they paused in the struggle. 'I know you can't really do without me here –'

'Who says?'

'So I won't go until you have an extra hand, who can help with all the difficult jobs.'

'That's big of you. Who've you got in mind?'

She leaned across and kissed his forehead. 'Nina.' Quickly, she slid out of range and stood up. 'When you marry her, you can send me around the world, as a wedding present.'

'You cheeky young pup,' Adam said swinging a pillow at her. He

367

missed. 'Anyhow, wedding presents are given to the people who are getting married.'

'You can be different.' She slipped out of the room.

Adam stayed awake, thinking. He tried to analyze his feelings about Nina, consider the implications of her staying, even assess the positive and negative points of marrying, but his thoughts were constantly short-circuiting. He began by wondering if she'd want to marry and exchange a career in writing for a life on one of the most isolated properties in a big, empty and strange country. He wondered what being a writer involved, but while he was trying to unravel that puzzle, he remembered the night they had been in the ruined farmhouse in Greece and she'd hit the German soldier on the head with the crude boomerang. He chuckled. What had she called it? A wombat. He must make another boomerang and put it on the wall, as a trophy. A trophy to what? The miracle of Greece. Finding Nina, losing her, finding her again. It was a fluke that he and Josef had got out alive. He remembered nothing about the fishing boat and only a little about the voyage on the British destroyer. He recalled waking in the sick bay and seeing the German officer, head bandaged and arms bound, sitting in the corner, glaring at him with a hateful intensity. Poor bloke, it was his bad luck that he'd chosen that night to go for a walk with his girl-friend along the beach. The German had ended up in a prisoner-of-war camp. Adam didn't know what had happened to the woman. Josef reckoned the men on the fishing boat cut her throat and threw her overboard, but no one knew. She was not on the destroyer. The war had been rough on civilians. The Germans would have done something terrible to Nina if they had caught her. Probably treated her as a spy. She was lucky. Plucky too. He remembered the way she had climbed up the mountain on her own just to treat some sick soldier she'd never met. Very gutsy.

That first night in the cave, when she'd gone to sleep in front of the little fire and, subconsciusly, put her arm around him. That was good. It had been so completely dark in that cave at night that he'd lost all sense of reality. It was like being in some immense, limitless space where the silence and the darkness were so total that they pressed in on you and destroyed all your balance and sense of perspective. It had been like that at Coober Pedy, in the underground home. That was a long time ago. A candle burning yellow and smoking oily fumes, a basin of precious water, and Nellie, naked and provocative and daring him to bathe her.

He rolled over on his side.

Nellie wouldn't go away. The burning door at Coober Pedy gaol, and Nellie and Josef – he was only a boy then – using Mailey's car to break them out. Jimmy wouldn't go through the flames. Josef screaming out. Nellie trying to drive the car when she couldn't drive, and setting fire to it. He rubbed his knees. They were still scarred.

Nellie at Port Augusta, years later, when he and Josef were coming back from the west. He could see her now in the café, and the look when she recognized them. She was beautiful.

He almost fell asleep but then woke again and it was Nellie he was thinking about. All those wasted, lonely years. Why? He tossed in the bed. Where was she now? Dead? Could have been dead for years. Or living with some other man, somewhere ... That thought hurt, as it had most nights since he'd come back to Kalinda. But whatever she'd done, wherever she was, she was out of his life.

He pressed his eyes tightly shut. Think about Nina. Nellie was gone. For heaven's sake, she'd run out on him before the war during one of her fits of anger about something or other. She was too unpredictable, too tempestuous, to have lived with in a loving, stable relationship. He turned on his side. No she wasn't. She was warm and lovely and she'd have raised Cassie as though she were her own mother. They could have had such good times. Even the bad times would have been good, more bearable, if he could have shared them with her.

Stop that. Forget about her. She was out of his life as surely as his dead mother, whom he couldn't remember and his dead father, who died on that terrible day ... Forget that too. Forget everything. Think about the future. Think about Nina.

Nina was not beautiful but she was an attractive woman with a fire in her eyes which was both exhilarating and intimidating. Exhilarating because life would never be dull with her around; not with those eyes that showed an interest in so many things and sparkled with the promise of joyous moments. Intimidating because the eyes were so clever that Adam felt not so much threatened but inferior, as many men do in the presence of superior women. Even so, she was magnificent and any suggestion of being a tomboy, which was so evident in Greece (but mainly, he reasoned, due to her clothes) was now gone. She was an essentially feminine woman, and he felt more uncomfortable because of that.

There was a lot of determination and intelligence in Nina; more than he remembered in Greece. She had matured and improved with the years, just like Josef reckoned his wines did. Josef would be coming up in a few weeks. What was the surprise? Bound to be a woman. Josef was always falling in love.

Love. Was that what he felt for Nina? It couldn't be, not after

369

knowing her only a few days in Greece and then, ten years later, for another couple of days at Kalinda. It had to be something else. Maybe the beginnings, the first wild stirrings that were so exciting but were not to be trusted. And he was no boy, no youngster caught up in a vortex of new and irresistible emotions. He had been in love before. He even had a seventeen-year-old kid. And yet . . .

That night in the cellar, when that Greek had locked them in to keep them safe from the enemy and Nina had unleashed a power of love-making that had brought him close to fear. She had been wonderful, but fierce and out of control, as though consumed by demons. He'd never known that in a woman before.

Nellie had been gentler, even in the early days when she had been such a wild woman in so many other ways. What a temper. He saw Nellie in the headlights of the car Mailey had used to chase them.

He rolled on to his other side.

She had gone. Forget her, but don't forget the mistakes. He shouldn't have let her go. There was some reason she didn't divulge. He should have kept her here, even by force if that was the only way to make her stay, and make her tell him what was on her mind. It wasn't just the things she said. She wouldn't have gone away and stayed away all this time if there weren't other, deeper reasons. He should have forced her to tell him what they were. What? The question had tormented him for years.

Well, Nellie had gone. He loved her and he would have married her and maybe they would have had children of their own. How many? Jimmy had three girls. Maybe Nellie and he would have had three sons. Three sons and Cassie. Would have been a nice family. The boys would have been handy around the property, too.

Stop it, stop it. Think of Nina. Sort things out. Cassie liked her. That's important because it would be a nightmare marrying a woman that your daughter disliked but Cassie genuinely liked Nina. He could tell, just from watching the way they got on together. A freelance writer. That meant she could do stories for anyone. Therefore, she wouldn't have to go to an office, like people who had ordinary jobs. Was it possible she could live at Kalinda and keep on writing? Would she have to travel a lot? That might be possible, although she would soon get sick of that long train journey.

Should they get a plane? It seemed a bit fanciful. People having their own aircraft was like the stuff you read in some of the magazines he got now. He liked *Popular Mechanics*, only the magazine made him feel guilty because there were so many projects he'd like to do and he never had enough time to do any of them. He had not seen *National Geographic* and wondered if it looked like *Popular Mechanics.*

He tried to sleep. He had to get up early.

If Nellie had only told him why she was leaving, given him the true reasons, he might have been able to stop her and they wouldn't have had those wasted fourteen years.

If he let Nina go without telling her how he felt ... How *did* he feel? Confused. He needed time. He would go with her to Adelaide, spend more time with her, ask her lots of questions, get to know her better.

I'd like to be with her now, he thought, and even contemplated getting up and going to her room. Just to talk and maybe hold hands. To lie with her, without saying a word. He had been so lonely for so many years.

He thought of the cellar in Greece, and fell asleep.

Once more, Adam took Nina out to Lake Eyre. This time they left at dawn and spent the morning walking on the salt, travelling so far from the shore that the coastline thinned to a fine ribbon that fluttered on the layers of heat haze. The salt seemed as hard as concrete. Adam had brought an auger and drilled a hole. He struck mud at five inches. He explained that there was a layer of dried salt over a sea of mud, a gypsum slush that extended to a depth of at least fifteen feet. Then there was another layer of salt and then coal – huge deposits that were not mined because of the economic impracticability of working such a site.

'The blacks would never come to the lake,' he said, 'because they believed there was a monster of some sort that ate people. There was a monster all right, but it was called mud.'

'Tell me more?' she asked but he refused, just saying that no one should wander on to the lake without testing the surface.

'There are parts where the salt's so thin it starts to rock if you step on it. If that happens, get the hell off.'

'And this mud. Is it like quicksand?'

'Worse,' he said and changed the subject, talking about the Adelaide scientist who had visited the lake and taught him so much about it. 'You should see him when you go to Adelaide,' he said and then told her he had decided to travel south with her.

'I was hoping you would.' She held his hand. He seemed shy and she laughed. 'I don't think anyone's going to see you out here.' She kissed him.

'What was that for?'

'That was to say thank you for coming to Adelaide with me.' She kissed him again. 'How long can you stay?'

371

'A week or so. There are a few things I should do. I haven't been south for a long time.'

'What about Cassie?'

'She can run the place. She thinks she runs it now, anyhow.'

She bent to examine the encrusted remains of an insect that had been blown from the land and perished on the desolate surface. It was a beautiful object, more a crystalline piece of jewellery than a once-living creature, with each delicate limb and outstretched feeler evenly coated in a translucent skin of salt.

Adam coughed and she looked up. 'There's something I wanted to ask you,' he said and she straightened, curious, for his voice was now soft and serious.

'How important is this writing to you?'

She still held the insect and, absent-mindedly turned it so that refracted light coated its fine limbs in pinks and violets. 'My writing? You mean the article I'm doing?'

'Well no. I mean your writing. Your career.'

'Very important. It's something I've wanted to do for a long time.'

Hands in pockets, he seemed to be focusing on some object on the distant and wavering shore. Eyes crinkled against the glare, he said, 'What will you be doing next? What's the story? Where will you be going?'

'I don't know.'

'How do you get work in a job like yours?'

'Through contacts. I know some people in important positions.' She joined him in gazing into the distance. 'I've let a few of the magazines in the States know who I am and that I'm available. And I think of stories and tell the appropriate person on the right magazine. Or newspaper. I write for newspapers too.'

'Do you have to live in America to do a job like that?'

She laughed softly. 'It helps. In my game, out of sight is very definitely out of mind.'

'Have you ever thought of writing for Australian magazines?'

'No. But it's not a bad idea. British magazines and papers too. The more the merrier. As long as they pay enough, I'll write for them.'

He was silent. The land rimming the lake was splitting and dividing and rejoining, all depending on the whim of the intervening layers of shuffling hot air.

'It *is* very important to me, Adam. For years, I've wanted to do this.'

He nodded. He would understand that. 'I was just wondering whether you had to live in America to do that.' He glanced at her.

'Apparently you do.'

'Well,' she said, angling her head in a way that allowed some discussion. 'It'd be easier.'

'But not essential?'

'There are a lot of freelance writers living out of America, I guess. And I suppose one or two of them make good money.'

He brightened but still seemed to be concentrating on the horizon. Nina moved in front of him. Deliberately, she rapped on his chest. 'Excuse me, but I have a message for whoever's living inside.' He looked down. She presented him with a wide, innocent face. 'I would like to know what's going on in the mind of this man who's asking me such a lot of personal questions.' Adam looked away, smiling foolishly, but touching his chin, she guided him back to her. 'I would like to know why he's so interested. Please ask him. I'll wait for the answer, thanks.'

'You're mad,' he said, touching the hand against his chin.

'I'm just curious. They impressed me as being very serious questions and I was wondering why you asked them.'

'Because,' he said and then was quiet for so long she thought he had finished. She squeezed his hand. 'Because I don't want you to rush off back to America.'

'I'm not exactly rushing off.'

'I don't want you to go at all.'

'I see,' she said and let her head settle against his chest. 'Have I ever told you I feel very safe whenever you're around?'

'Not for a long time.'

'Well, I do.'

'I feel good when you're with me.'

'Me too.'

'Nina, why are you going back?'

'Because I ... Oh God, Adam, I don't know.'

'If you go to America, we're not going to see each other again. I know that. I've got a feeling. And Nina, I couldn't stand that.' He put a hand on each shoulder. 'I can't believe how lucky we were to meet again. And if I let you go again ... I should have made you get in that boat in Greece, and come with us to Egypt. Then we could have been together for the last ten years, instead of you going back to America and marrying the wrong bloke and me being stuck out here on my own.'

'What are you saying, Adam?'

'That I want you to stay.'

'In Australia?'

'Here. With me.'

She kissed him. 'I should go back.'

373

'Why?'

'I don't know.' She shook her head in despair. 'I can't think clearly. I just know something is telling me I should return to America.'

'You could write your story here.'

'Yes. I'm sure I could. It's just that I'd always thought of working in the States. I'd never thought of anything else. Oh Adam, there are so many things to consider. This has all been such a surprise. These last few days ...'

He held her at arms length. 'Why don't we talk about this again when we're in Adelaide? Away from here, and back in a city, where you'll probably feel much more at home.'

'I'd like that.'

Holding hands they walked towards the shore. After a while, she said, 'Were you saying what I think you were saying back there?'

'I don't know,' he said. 'You might have to knock and ask the bloke inside again.'

'I'll be going south on the train with Nina,' Adam told Cassie. 'There are a few things I have to do in Adelaide, so I'll be able to keep her company on the way down.'

'Yes, Dad.' Her look stripped him of all pretence. He had intended listing the people he meant to see, then business he had to do, but she smiled at him, the knowing adult not being deceived by the bumbling words of the child.

He wiped his lips. She was still smiling. 'Will you be all right?' he said.

'I'll be good.'

'I'll be fine, thank you,' Mrs Wilson corrected. She was at the kitchen table, having placed herself discreetly to be beyond the range of whispers but close enough to supervise the grammar. It was particularly important at this time, she felt, for Mr Ross to be aware that his daughter would not lack supervision during his absence. She waited for Cassie to repeat her words, but missed the face the girl pulled for her father.

Adam ran through the list of work that had to be done on the property. It was a quiet time, and the jobs were things that Jimmy and Cassie could handle easily.

'Let me know if there's something you want me to pick up for you in Adelaide,' he said.

'I'll write you a list tonight.'

'*One* thing.'

She tugged at the pocket of his shirt. 'How often do you go to Adelaide?'

'Maybe two things.'

'I'll tell you what. You stay here and I'll go and keep Nina company. Then I could do the shopping when we got there. She'd probably prefer a woman anyway. Someone to hold her hand.'

'Very funny. What sort of things do you want?'

'Clothes.'

'We just built a house, remember?'

'I can't wear a house.'

'And I don't own a bank.'

She wrinkled her nose, dismissing the last remark. 'Get Nina to help you. I'm sure she's got good taste.'

Adam turned to the housekeeper. 'What can I do, Mrs Wilson?'

'Take the list, Mr Ross, and try not to lose it.'

'I've got a feeling I'm losing this battle,' Adam said.

'You haven't won a battle, Mr Ross, since she was fourteen.'

Cassie tugged the pocket, signalling she needed his attention.

'What about Uncle Joe? Will you be back before he gets here?'

'He's not due for three weeks. I'll be back in two. If you behave yourself, you might even be able to put on your new dress for him.'

'I need more than a new dress,' she said, smiling sweetly.

S·I·X

The truck pulled up outside the William Creek store. Stiff from age and the punishment of the long drive from Marree, Saleem Benn descended from the passenger's seat. As instructed, his nephew Yunis stayed on board. The young man switched off the motor, which popped and banged for some seconds before shuddering to a halt, and then drank some water from the flask he kept behind the seat. He settled down for a long wait. Saleem Benn had said he wanted to see Goolamadail in private, and the meeting could take some time.

There was no one in the store. Saleem Benn went to the warehouse at the back. It was an older building and he noticed with concern that the door with the loose hinges was sagging as it had on his last visit, which meant it could not be closed properly.

Goolamadail was inside. He came forward to greet his uncle, brushing dust from his clothes and looking like a man who had had his sleep disturbed.

'I was doing some cleaning,' he said, his mouth curling beneath the bent nose.

'You are well?' the old man enquired, while sweeping his eyes around the warehouse.

'Most well, thank you. And you, uncle?'

Saleem Benn allowed his head to wobble from side to side, as pliant as a tethered balloon in a crosswind. The mannerism could be an accompaniment to any emotion. On this day, Goolamadail was in no doubt his uncle was displeased but, as yet, there was no talk of the reason for his unhappiness. Following the required formalities of polite conversation, they discussed other things: the road journey from Marree, the state of health of the other members of the family, rumours of government plans to rebuild the railway line. Wondering what had displeased his uncle but daring not broach the subject, Goolamadail suggested they drink tea. They went to the store, and sat in the corner recess.

'I notice with sorrow,' Saleem Benn said, speaking slowly to emphasize his feelings, 'that the door to the warehouse is still not repaired.'

Goolamadail raised his eyebrows, preparing to deliver his excuse when the old man had finished. He was relieved. This was a simple matter, requiring only a few glib, lying words.

'The angle of the door,' Saleem Benn said, demonstrating with his hands, 'bears little relationship to the angle of the building.' Respectfully, Goolamadail nodded. 'It is therefore impossible to close. Dust can get in. So can any person. The dust will cover the goods inside. An intruder could steal them.'

'Yes, uncle.' The younger man thought it safe to speak.

'I mentioned this to you last time. The door, if anything has become worse.'

'By an amazing coincidence, I was in the warehouse searching for the correct hinges when you arrived.'

'It is many weeks since I was here last. Have you been searching for the correct hinges all that time?'

'There have been other things to do, uncle. I know there is little need to remind you but I am here on my own, and I have been very busy.'

'You mean you have begun to sell a few items?'

The sarcasm lifted Goolamadail's eyebrows into a roof that was remote from the battered pillar of his nose. 'There is so much to do, even when there are no customers in the store.' His hands rose, fingers groping for understanding. 'There is the ordering, the cleaning, the constant bookwork.'

'Ah yes, the bookwork,' Saleem Benn's eyes roamed the store. What he saw appeared to distress him for his face became sadder. Goolamadail shifted uncomfortably on his seat.

'You were not expecting me?'

'No. Otherwise ...' He shrugged and attempted a smile.

'Otherwise you might have fixed the door.' Saleem Benn aimed his formidable nose at his nephew. 'But it was not the door I wished to discuss.'

As the smile became real, the eyebrows settled nearer the nose. 'Please have some more tea,' he purred, presuming the issue was settled.

The older man raised a hand in refusal. 'Tell me, was this the area where you were attacked? When you suffered your injury?' He tapped his nose.

Goolamadail frowned. 'Uncle, that was many years ago.'

'You don't remember?'

'Of course I remember.' He frowned, not liking the trend in the conversation. 'Yes. It was here. The man came from behind. I did

377

not see him at first. It was dark. I was working late, doing book-work.' He could not resist adding the last words.

'But you saw him eventually?'

Goolamadail shrugged helplessly.

'You must have seen him. For him to strike you such a deforming blow to the nose, he must have been standing in front of you.' He waited for the other man to pout agreement. 'What did he look like? You have never given me a truly comprehensive description and it was a very large sum of money he stole. How much was it again?'

'Seven hundred pounds,' Goolamadail whispered, as though mourning the loss of a dear relative. He thought it the best voice to use: his uncle loved money.

'And the man?'

'Well, he was large.'

'As tall as you?'

Goolamadail hesitated. 'No, larger.'

'I think not. I would say your size. And his hair. Light or dark?'

'Dark.'

'As dark as yours?

'It's hard to say.'

'On the contrary, it is very easy to say. I can tell you his hair was precisely the same colour.'

Goolamadail blinked rapidly. 'What are you saying?'

'I am saying, you miserable wretch, that I know who took the money.'

Seeking to do something with his hands, Goolamadail reached for his cup but it rattled so noisily that he let go.

'I know you were not attacked by a man, this so-called stranger who was supposed to have come off the train and assaulted you and then robbed the safe. It was you who did the attacking. You tried to assault a woman, may God understand and forgive you. She in fact overwhelmed you, you miserable weakling, and inflicted the injury which has transformed your face into a sight which sends dogs whimpering in distress.' He stood and shook his fist at his nephew. 'You were too ashamed by that incident to confess the truth. That is lamentable but, perhaps, understandable. No man could happily accept being beaten and disfigured by a woman. But you, vile and ungrateful creature, you worm from a decaying womb, you seized the opportunity to steal from me.' Saleem Benn beat his chest so hard he began to cough.

The halt in the Afghan's tirade gave Goolamadail opportunity to gather his thoughts, which had been scattered in the initial onslaught. He had been stealing from his uncle for years. The seven hundred pounds had been the start but since then, by careful manipulation of the books, and occasional private deals with some of the local residents, he had organized for himself a steady, illicit, and tax-free income. The total sum now exceeded five thousand pounds. It was not just the amount but the ease of cheating his uncle that had made the gathering of this money such a sweet exercise. Adding to the sum and plotting new ways to steal from the trusting old fool had become a passion, just as gambling is for some men. It had even ousted his desire for revenge against Nellie Arlton as the prime interest in his life. He still wanted to hurt her and that black-lover Adam Ross, but he was too shrewd, and too greedy for money, to let desire hamper profit. Even now he was working on a deal with a grazier west of Anna Creek – a man who had no idea of the dishonest nature of the arrangement – and within two weeks expected to make at least four hundred and sixty pounds for himself. He was moving into an area of activity in which he could make much greater sums of money using his uncle's business as a cover, but keeping the profits for himself. He had even found a truck driver who was prepared to steal cattle from various properties and sell them down south. The locals had so little idea of how many cattle they had, or where they had strayed, that taking a few from each of them, in a properly organized operation, should be a safe and profitable enterprise.

Holding his chest, Saleem Benn studied his nephew through rheumy eyes.

'I have had your cousin Mohammed examine your record of accounts for the last few years,' the old man said, his voice wavering, his hand spread across his chest. 'It would seem there are a number of irregularities –'

'Really?' Goolamadail managed to look uninterested. 'And tell me, uncle, how is Mohammed?'

Saleem Benn, who had been attempting to regain the momentum of his accusations, almost choked. 'I am not discussing the health of your cousin!'

'I'm not sure what you *are* discussing, esteemed uncle.'

The old man leaned back, hand still holding his chest, and regarded his nephew with eyes that seemed to be leeched of all emotion. It was a look that Goolamadail used to dread, but now, realizing his uncle knew something of his doings and anticipating exposure, he felt a curious composure. The moment was one he had been expecting. He knew what to do.

'It is not merely the findings of your cousin, about whose health you are so concerned, that has brought me here,' Saleem Benn continued in words that slid, viper-like, between the two men. 'I have other information.'

379

'About what?' Goolamadail said, trying to sound bored and succeeding, but attempting to avoid his uncle's eyes and failing.

'Were you not listening? About the seven hundred pounds you stole. I know precisely what happened.'

The only other person who knew what had happened was the black bitch. 'You mentioned a woman?'

'Yes. Would that it had been a man, that he might have crushed your skull, but it was a woman.' Saleem Benn seemed to have trouble breathing and he paused, head down.

Goolamadail shook his head. 'Truly, the years have not dealt kindly with you, uncle.' He waited for the old man's eyes to rise and meet his once more. 'Some men are spared the indignity of senility. Unhappily, you have lived too long.'

With difficulty Saleem Benn rose. He raised his hand. 'Were I younger, I would do to you what the woman could not.'

'For what? Taking what is rightfully mine?'

'You admit stealing the money?'

'Ha!' Goolamadail moved out of reach. 'It is is not theft to take money that I raise, through my own efforts, in the God-forsaken town where I work, with no assistance.'

'Work! You spend your days sleeping and dreaming of fornication.'

'With no assistance,' Goolamadail continued, ignoring the old man's remarks as he walked around him in a semi-circle, 'and what do you expect? That I meekly hand over the fruits of my labour to an old man whose brain has turned to camel dung?'

Saleem Benn sat down heavily. 'You are dismissed,' he said in a weak voice. 'Were it not for the disgrace that would be brought to the family, I would put the police on to you.' He used the back of his long hand to brush the other man away and out of his life.

'I am not dismissed.' The younger man faced him, his arms folded.

Again Saleem Benn brushed him away. It was a weary gesture but performed with a haughty grandeur.

'I am not dismissed. In fact, we will be discussing a new financial arrangement which will see me become a partner in your enterprises,' Goolamadail said.

'This is the raving of a madman,' the old man said, addressing a sack of potatoes.

'Furthermore, there will be no police called, unless it is by me.'

Now he had Saleem Benn's attention.

'I know the name of the person who attacked me,' he said, 'and even though the assault took place some years ago, I could still press charges and see your favourite whore go to prison.' With pleasure, he noted the flash of fire in his uncle's eyes. Maybe she was his woman now. It could only be Nellie Arlton who had told the story of their fight and who knew that no thief had entered the store that night. 'But that is of minor concern to me. I would bring the police to arrest *you*.'

The old man's lip curled, revealing a keyboard of large yellow teeth. 'You have truly taken leave of your senses.'

'The police would also arrest your intimate friend Mr Adam Ross.' Goolamadail moved to a stand where a saddle was displayed and stroked the leather. 'Do you understand what I am talking about? It is to do with an incident that occurred many years ago.' He glanced sideways at his uncle. 'It is to do with a policeman. A policeman who died in the area and was erroneously reported as having perished of thirst. I understand you found the body.' He left the saddle and walked towards the store entrance, touching the goods on display as he went. Near the opening he turned. 'I'm sure you remember the incident. The man's name was Mailey.'

There was silence. He brushed dust from the tops of a row of canned fruit. 'So you see, you will not be dismissing me, as you so foolishly suggested.' Saleem Benn had sagged forward. His face was in shadow. 'You will, instead, make me your partner in the store. That will do to start with.'

Saleem Benn's breath rasped noisily, a bellows fanning a dying fire.

'Who told you about Mailey?'

'You did.'

Saleem Benn raised his head.

'When you were sick and I, your loving and dutiful nephew, put you to bed and fed and cared for you. Remember?' He thumped the yellow tape binding a car tyre. 'You were feverish. Delirious. You imagined that I was your friend, Mr Adam Ross, and you talked accordingly. You talked at great length.'

The hollows beneath the old man's cheekbones appeared to have deepened. 'That was years ago.'

'I have a very good memory for such things.'

'Why have you said nothing until now?'

'There was no need.' He smiled. 'So now let me outline for you the new business arrangement that you and I will have.'

Josef found Nellie on the verandah of his parents' house. It was a sunny day and she was sitting in the old rocking-chair that Mr Hoffman lugged around the building, seeking the warmest and quietest locations for the family's guest. Nellie had little say in this. Josef's father, having retired from the business, had made the care

381

of the patient his prime activity. She stood as Josef approached.

'What are you doing standing up?'

'Using my muscles. I'm so fit now I could race you around the vineyard. It's all this moving about the house, following your father and his chair.'

'He's a bit much, isn't he?'

'Yes.' She giggled. 'But he's sweet.'

Nellie had been out of hospital for almost a week. Josef had brought her to his parents' home to recuperate but as he had been busy at the winery, the responsibility of entertaining her had been assumed by Hans Hoffman. The entertainment had consisted mainly of long monologues by the old wine-maker. Nellie enjoyed them. She was a good listener and relished the attention the Hoffmans gave her.

Josef was shuffling on the spot, his feet unable to disguise his anxiety to say something. Nellie recognized the sign. 'What's brought you home at this time of the day?' she asked.

'Do you think you'd be fit to travel a little earlier than we planned?'

'Sure,' she said. 'When?'

'In a couple of days.'

She sat in the rocking-chair, her confidence deflated. 'But we were going to fly up in a couple of weeks.'

'I know.' Josef had developed the mannerism of bobbing his head up and down when he was talking on one subject but in a hurry to get on to another topic. He was bobbing now. 'But something's cropped up. I have to be in Adelaide in about three weeks' time. Big business.' He cleared his throat. 'But if we leave earlier, I can still fly up for a week or so. If you're up to the journey, that is?'

She rocked back and splayed her hands. 'As long as I don't have to get out and push.'

'In the long history of Josef Hoffman Airlines, no passenger has ever had to get out and push.'

'How may passengers have you carried?'

Josef spent some time counting on his fingers. 'You're the first.'

She let the chair tilt forward. 'You're certain this is a good idea?'

'Positive. It's the most comfortable as well as the quickest way to cover this country. And I'm a terrific pilot, even if I do say so myself.'

'I don't mean that.' The chair rocked and a loose floorboard squeaked. 'Does Adam know we're coming?'

'He knows I'm flying up sometime soon. I said I'd have a surprise.' His eyebrows wobbled and they exchanged knowing smiles. 'But I'll send another telegram and tell him I'll be arriving earlier.'

'You think it will be all right?'

'Guarantee it.'

She held out a hand and he took it. 'Joe, I'm scared.'

'I told you I'm a good pilot.'

'I'm not frightened of the plane. I'm scared of seeing everyone again.' She let go his hand and gripped the armrests. She smiled nervously. 'And look at me. I look terrible. I'm all yellow in the eyes and my body's so thin. I'm like a starved alley cat.'

'You look terrific to me.'

'That's a lie, but a nice one.' She gave him a motherly smile, and let the chair rock a few times. 'You know what I'm really worried about, don't you?'

'Seeing Adam again?'

She nodded. 'The thought of seeing him, just standing in front of him again, really terrifies me.'

'Last time I saw him he didn't look too terrifying. Still only had one head.'

'You know what I mean. After what happened, I'm not sure what he'll do when we come face to face.'

'It'll be just like you've never been away.'

'I wish I could believe that.' She let the chair rock back as far as it would go. 'I'm looking forward to seeing Cassie again. She'll be a real little lady now.'

'She was a tomboy when I last saw her.'

The board creaked several times.

'I've never told you what happened or why I left, have I, Joe?'

'No.' His head was still but his fingers played elusive games with each other.

'One day.' She shot him a guilty look which was immediately overwhelmed by a smile. 'Maybe when we get to Kalinda I'll tell you the whole story.'

'OK with me.' He checked his watch. 'I have to go. You're sure you don't mind flying up earlier like this?'

She shook her head. 'The sooner the better. Get it over with.'

'You make it sound like going to the dentist, instead of going home.'

She reflected. 'I guess that's what it is. Going home.'

Two things happened to persuade Adam to change his mind about travelling south with Nina in the train.

The first was a radio report that heavy rain had fallen around Pedirka, north of Oodnadatta, and washed away the railway line. A bridge had to be rebuilt. The train could be a week late.

The second was another radio report about a motor sporting

383

event that deeply interested him. This was the Redex Around Australia Reliability Trial. One hundred and eighty seven cars had left Sydney on a six thousand, five hundred mile event that had begun as a test of motor-car reliability but had quickly developed into a madcap race over the best and worst of outback roads. It had generated huge public interest. Cars had travelled up the Queensland Coast as far north as Townsville, raced west to the mining town of Mount Isa, entered the Northern Territory and gone all the way to Darwin on the coast. They were now driving south on the Stuart Highway to Alice Springs. They were due to pass through Coober Pedy, to the west of William Creek, in a few days' time. There was a major refuelling point at the opal mining settlement.

Adam now proposed that Nina and he drive to Adelaide in the Holden. They would follow the track to Coober Pedy to see the Redex Trial cars pass through. Then, if Nina wished, they could visit some of the opal mines there and maybe look at the underground house where Adam lived when he was digging for opal in 1929. They would then drive south, skirting the new Woomera rocket range before reaching the sealed road at Port Augusta. From there, it was only a whisker over two hundred miles to Adelaide.

'How far altogether?' Nina asked.

Adam had the look of someone who fears he will miss out on a treat by revealing too much. 'Not far.' She waited. 'Well, about five or six hundred miles,' he added.

She shook her head, laughing silently. 'I keep forgetting that out here a hundred miles is next door.'

'If it's too far ...' Adam let his voice trail to within reach of disappointment.

'If you don't mind driving so far, I don't mind going.'

'Could be a good story,' he suggested.

'As long as it's a good experience.'

Cassie had been listening. 'It'll be an experience all right. I want to know what those Redex cars are like because I'm going in the next trial. I'd love to drive around Australia.'

'You don't have a licence,' Adam said.

'I'm still a good driver.'

'I'll observe things for you Cassie,' Nina said. 'I'll watch everything – the cars, the drivers, what they wear and what they eat – and I'll give you a report.'

'Oh, good.' Cassie fluttered her eyes at Adam. 'Does that mean Nina's coming back?'

Nina blushed. 'It means,' Adam said, 'that there are such things as letters. Nina can write you a letter.'

'After all, I am a writer,' Nina said, still blushing.

Three hours after Adam left to drive Nina to Coober Pedy, a telegram from Josef was transmitted through the Flying Doctor two-way radio. It said that Josef would now be arriving in two days' time.

S·E·V·E·N

Possum Kipling had been trying to overtake the car in front of him since the road had taken a long and lazy turn to the east around the boundaries of Mount Clarence station. The problem was that Kipling could not see the car he was chasing. The sun was shining and the South Australian driver, hat tilted at an angle, had good eyesight yet he was driving blind, deep in the dust trail of the car he had been pursuing for almost twenty minutes. The dust was appalling. It billowed from the tail of the speeding car in choking masses and fired a barrage of small stones at Kipling's Holden. It was a lethal mix: dust to obscure a boulder or pothole, and stones to shatter a windscreen or punch a hole through the radiator.

The road turned slightly. Kipling, not seeing the bend, ran wide and, during the few seconds it took him to regain the road, his car bucked and reared across the gibber plain that edged the so-called Stuart Highway. Stones rapped the floor of the Holden, giving the driver and his crew the sensation of riding inside a machine-gun. But being out wide had given him a brief glimpse of the other car. It was big and it was white. It could be the Humber of Tom Sulman, one of Kipling's great rivals. The veteran Sydney driver was, with Kipling, one of the few competitors in the Redex Trial to have lost no points at all on all of that marathon journey. Sulman had left the Alice Springs control ahead of the South Australian. The realization that it could be the Humber spurred Kipling on. The section to Coober Pedy was one of the most difficult and the fastest in the event and if he could pass Sulman, he might gain valuable points at the control. And he would also get to the refuelling point ahead of the big British car, which had a huge tank and would take longer to fill, and could delay him at the start of the long section to Adelaide.

The road surface became softer and more dust, even thicker and whiter and more choking, spiralled towards Kipling. He decided to take a risk and pass.

He eased to the left, daring not pull to the right for fear of hitting an oncoming vehicle – even though they had not seen a northbound car or truck for more than three hours. He felt the rumble of rocks, which indicated they were crossing from the graded surface of the highway to the gibber plain, but saw nothing. This was the most perilous part of the operation. As with boats travelling at speed, a car racing through dust leaves a distinctive wake. The thickest, most violently disturbed stream is at the outer edge and it was through this vortex that Kipling now passed. He saw nothing, but heard above the roar of the Holden engine the deep clang of rocks hammering metal and the sharper, more spiteful crack of stones striking glass.

Two things happened. He cleared the wake and saw the car clearly. It was Sulman's big white Humber. And he saw, directly in the Holden's path and unavoidable, a collection of larger rocks.

Kipling swerved. He saw the look of alarm on the face of Sulman's navigator who turned and realized a car was attempting to overtake, and he felt a wheel hit one rock. The effect was instantaneous. A tyre exploded. There was a great clanging and bouncing and the steering wheel dragged to one side.

With a curse, Possum Kipling slowed and drove back on to the road. He stopped to change the wheel. The snarling cloud of dust raced into the distance.

He noticed another Holden, a private car, parked well off the road. While Kipling opened the boot to get the tools and a spare wheel, the driver of the other car started the motor and drove towards him. Kipling noticed a man and a woman in the car and then got on with the job of changing the wheel.

Adam Ross got out of the car. 'G'day,' he said and, Kipling, straining to loosen a wheel nut, grunted. 'Want a hand?'

'No thanks, mate. We'll be all right.' Kipling noted with gratification that the stranger did not wander too close or indulge in small talk. The bane of a trial driver's life was the stranger who talked too much or got in the way. The woman had got out of the car, he saw, and was taking photographs.

He and his navigator were trying to juggle the new wheel on to the studs when the jack began to collapse. The wheel, not in place, began to fall. The men shouted in dismay as the car swayed towards them.

Adam ran forward and grabbed the front kangaroo bar. Knees bent, back straight, he took the strain.

'Can you get it on in five seconds?' he grunted.

'Bloody hell,' the navigator muttered, eyes wide in astonishment at the sight of a man holding the car off the ground. Kipling slipped the wheel onto the hub, then dexterously spun a nut along the thread of one stud.

'Fixed,' he said. 'You can let go.'

Adam straightened. Noisily, he sucked air through clenched teeth.

'What do you train on?' Kipling said. 'Razor blades?'

Adam grinned and massaged his fingers. 'Glad to help.'

'Live around here?'

'Not far.'

'Possum Kipling, Port Wakefield.' He extended his hand.

'Adam Ross, Kalinda.'

'Glad you came to have a look.'

'Glad to be able to help.'

The navigator had begun to pack the deflated tyre and tools in the car's boot. 'Hey Possum,' he called out. 'Get her going. Here comes Antill.'

A dark car was racing towards them. As they watched the sound of its roaring motor and the constant patter of stones rapping its undersides grew in volume.

Waving farewell, Kipling sprinted around the car and jumped behind the wheel. He started the motor and was moving before the navigator had closed his door. The other car was now only two hundred yards away, a roaring, quivering metallic monster that was pursued by a corkscrewing frenzy of dust.

Instinctively, Adam stepped back. He had never seen a car travel so quickly.

It was a Plymouth, a big, square-sided car covered with lavish signwiting. The driver flashed the lights and blew the horn in a futile signal to Kipling that he wished to pass, but Kipling's car, accelerating so hard that the tail wagged in a series of power sides, was already disappearing behind its own dusty screen. The Plymouth's great side-valve six emitted a deep snarl, a bass to the smaller Holden's ringing tenor, and as the car thundered past, Adam caught a glimpse of three men. The driver wore a beret. The man beside him was leaning forward, peering anxiously into the dust trail. The man in the back turned his head and waved.

Adam waved back, then retreated, coughing in the dust, to the place where Nina was standing. She had fitted the long lens to the Leica.

'I got some great shots,' she said. 'I didn't expect anything like this.'

'You see,' Adam said, still rubbing his hands and gazing at the two racing tunnels of dust, 'this country's full of surprises.' He turned to face her. 'Just stay here instead of going back to America and you'd get stories no other writer would get.'

She blew the dust from the lens. 'Are you saying I should remain in this part of the world for professional reasons?'

'I'm saying you should stay here and marry me.'

She let the camera dangle from its strap. 'Did I hear you say what I thought I heard you say?'

'I said I want you to marry me.'

'Goodness me.' She lifted the Leica and searched for more dust. 'I thought we were going to talk in Adelaide.'

'We are. I'm just letting you know what I think.'

She snapped a photograph of him, stepped back and examined him critically. 'Is this the new, straight-talking, say-what's-on-your-mind Adam Ross?'

'Same old me.'

'I didn't think I'd ever hear you say you wanted to marry me.' She smiled. 'I thought you might mean it, and talk around it but I never thought you'd come right out and say it.'

'There's nothing like lifting a motor car for cleansing the head.'

She took his hand. 'I think you're the finest, sweetest man I've ever known.' She laughed. 'And probably the strongest. Were you really holding that car?'

'It was still in the jack. I just stopped it from falling.' He squeezed her hand. 'What's the matter?'

'No rushing. I told you we'd talk in Adelaide.'

'Any hints? I mightn't be able to wait till Adelaide.'

'Let's just say I'm tempted.' She kissed him.

Another balloon of dust was growing on the horizon. 'Here comes another car.'

'This is exciting,' she said, and checked the camera's settings. 'Why don't we watch this car pass and then go back to Coober Pedy and see them being refuelled? I promised to take notes for Cassie.'

'I do love you,' he said.

She took another photograph of him. 'That's for the album,' she said. 'Adam at the moment he first told me he loved me.'

'When do I get to take a picture?'

'Oh, Adam,' she said moving to him. 'You don't need a camera. You just love me; that's good enough.' They were embracing when the car raced past. It was a grey Peugeot but they didn't notice.

They spent the rest of the day at Coober Pedy. At first they watched more of the Redex cars refuelling from the hand-pumps outside the store and then, while stragglers still arrived to end their long journey from the centre of Australia, Adam showed Nina some of the town. It was a unique settlement. Most people lived under the ground. There were two inhabited surface buildings, the

389

store and, just down the road, the settlement's only hotel. As always, there was a water shortage and the hotel, despite having a bathroom for guests, had no water for bathing. They had spent the night there.

Adam took Nina to the hill where the Hoffmans and he used to live. Someone else was living in the house he had dug. The miner was out at the diggings so Adam did not go into the house but stood at the entrance and described how old Horrie Smith had helped him dig the two-roomed residence back in the days when Coober Pedy was still a relatively new opal mining centre.

They were standing there, with Adam lost in the past, when a man hobbled by, walking slowly and using a stick. Adam recognized him.

'Mr Paradine?'

The man turned and peered at Adam through glasses that had lenses as thick as the bottoms of beer bottles.

'Yes,' he said and edged closer. Adam introduced himself and then Nina and the man smiled broadly. 'Never thought I'd see you again,' he said and shuffled awkwardly to retain his balance.

Adam explained that Dexter Paradine had been one of the leaders of the mining community back in the late twenties. He had the finest singing voice Adam had ever heard. The old man beamed at that.

'What are you doing these days?' Paradine asked, still glowing from the compliment.

'Got a place over near William Creek.'

'Doing well, I hope.'

'Not bad.'

Paradine nodded contentedly. 'I'm still here,' he said and Adam angled his head as though the news was a revelation. 'Not singing much these days. The old town's not the same.'

'No. Lot more people. 'Specially today.'

Paradine adjusted his glasses. 'Never seen so many people in a hurry in my life.' He tapped his bent leg. 'I can't hurry much myself these days.'

'What happened?'

'Fell down my own mine. They say that's the first sign.' He waved the stick at Adam. 'What happened with that dreadful man Mailey? Did he ever catch up with you?'

Adam laughed nervously. 'No. That was a long time ago.'

'It certainly was. Dreadful man. Simply appalling. Must go.' He used the stick to wave farewell. 'Nice to have seen you again. You'll be back?'

'Maybe.'

'Good.' He lifted a hand as though tipping the brim of his hat in a farewell to a lady, and hobbled away.

'What was that about a dreadful man?' Nina asked, when Paradine had gone.

'Coober Pedy used to be full of characters,' Adam said, taking her hand and leading her away from the hill. 'One day when you've got plenty of time I'll tell you all about it.'

'I've got plenty of time.'

'No you haven't. There's too much to see and not a lot of time.'

She let him tow her back towards the car. 'Why not? What do we have to do?'

'I thought I might take you out to where the diggings are. Go down a mine.'

'And then?'

'And then I thought we might drive south a bit and camp by the road. We can probably find a bore and have a bath, rather than spend another night in the pub with no water. I'll cook tea for you.'

'Not coffee?'

'I mean the tea you eat. Dinner. What would you like?'

'What's on the menu?'

'I'll surprise you.' He paused to let her draw level. 'How about goanna?'

'What's goanna?'

'Big lizard.'

'You wouldn't dare.'

'The way I feel today, you never know.'

By the time they reached the car, Nina had forgotten about the conversation with Dexter Paradine.

Adam had been searching for a windmill. Two hours before sunset, he saw one to the far right of the road. Its blades, stationary in the windless afternoon, towered above an even line of scrub. The highway had been rough, with long troughs of talcum-fine bulldust interspersed with outcroppings of rock or, even worse, interminable stretches of saw-tooth corrugations that set the car buzzing and dithering from one side of the road to the other. They had been passed by several of the Redex cars, tail-enders who struggled to keep up with the fliers out front. Each had passed with a shriek of tortured metal. Differentials howled, shock absorbers rattled, exhaust pipes dragged on the road, engines groaned and grated but, without exception, the crews waved cheerily as they passed.

Wheeltracks ran from the road to the windmill. They were smoother than the highway. The tracks crossed a narrow claypan and then curled through a grove of dead trees. Little bigger than bushes, they had been scorched by a wildfire and lay in naked clumps, as coiled and intertwined as abandoned rolls of wire. The timber would be good for a fire, Adam noted, and followed the wheeltracks to a wooden stockyard. On the other side was the windmill and beneath it was a large metal tank.

Adam parked the car near the tank. He cleared a space beside the car and spread his groundsheet on the red soil. Then he collected dry wood for a fire. And then he proposed a bath.

'I'd kill for a bath,' Nina said, pushing dusty hair off her forehead. 'But where?'

Adam had begun unbuttoning his shirt. 'In there,' he said, indicating the water tank. 'There must be a good ten thousand gallons in there.'

'Good water?'

Adam went to a wooden frame that stood on one side of the tank. He climbed to the top and put his hand in the water. 'Crystal clear. A bit cool. Looks good. No dead birds.'

'Dead birds?'

'Sometimes the galahs get in and can't get out.' He dropped back to the ground. 'The only rule is you mustn't dive. The shock could break the wall of the tank.'

'Well, that's all very well,' she said, giving him the look a calf reserves for its first sighting of the slaughterman, 'but I haven't exactly brought my swimming wear with me.'

'Nina,' he said, struggling with a button, 'this is the Australian bush. If you want to go native, you should dress like one.'

'Are you suggesting that I swim naked?' She folded her arms and spread her legs out wide.

'Unless you want to get your clothes wet.' He took off his shirt.

'They could do with a wash.'

Adam was undoing his belt.

'Just a minute,' she said, and climbed up the side of the tank. At the top of the wooden frame, she took off her shoes, her watch and a ring she wore on her right hand.

She sat and dangled her legs in the water. 'Oh it's lovely. Are you decent?' Without waiting for an answer, she looked. He was wearing underpants. 'Oh, I thought you were doing it *au naturel*?'

'How natural do you want me to be?' He waited at the bottom of the timber structure.

'Well, if you're going to do these things, I always believe you should do them wholeheartedly.' She smiled condescendingly. 'Or not at all.'

'Look who's talking. The lady who's going to wash her clothes.'

'I am.' She took off her blouse and threw it in the water. Then she undid her brassière and tossed that after the blouse. She stood, and smiled, and let her skirt fall. She kicked it into the tank, took off her pants and, when they were around one ankle delicately lobbed them into the middle of the water. She sat down again.

'Well?' she said.

'Well what?'

'Well, how do I look after ten years?'

Adam breathed deeply. 'Better than I remember.'

'And what do you remember?'

'That you were pretty good.'

'I think you called me sensational.'

'Well, now you're more than sensational.'

She giggled.

'What's up?'

'Those underpants aren't doing a lot to hide you.' He kicked them off.

'Like me to do some washing for you?' she asked.

He threw his shirt, socks, and underpants into the tank, then climbed on to the stand. He sat beside her.

'I think I could get to like this country of yours,' she said, and lowered herself into the water.

The flames crackled and lifted long tongues to lick the night. There was no breeze. The windmill was stark and static, its face a full moon of dull golden blades.

Normally, Adam made small fires, burning no more wood than was needed to heat a can of water, cook his food or warm his body. He had learnt that from those natural masters of conservation, the aborigines. But on this night, he was wilfully lavish, throwing on sticks and branches and boughs and even the trunk of a dead tree he had dragged to the site.

They sat together, dulled by the warmth and seduced by the feeling the fire engendered: that they were at the centre of things and whatever existed beyond their island of light was of no consequence.

At first, they talked. They squatted on sleeping bags, staring into the fire and drifting with the stories. Nina recalled the years, beginning with her recent days in San Francisco and telling Adam of the work she did and the friends she had, and then going back to the time she was married and lived in the east. She talked frankly. Adam sat silently, chewing the end of a stick and listening, and recalling the lively, slightly morbid young woman he had known.

'When did you decide you weren't going to die?' he asked and she looked at him with curiosity, not understanding the question at first. Then she smiled.

393

'Oh. I remember. That dream? I was so sure I wouldn't see out the war, wasn't I?'

'I was frightened you'd talk yourself into it.'

She laughed. 'I was going through my realist phase. I had been through the usual juvenile business of considering myself immortal – you know, like all young people do – but then suddenly there was so much death and destruction around me that I was jolted out of that and into the opposite school of thought. I was convinced I'd never live to become what I am: a hoary old woman of –' she paused, leaned towards Adam and stroked his arm – 'somewhere in her thirties.'

'What phase are you in now?'

'The phase of excitement. I've just realized that I'm living in a big and interesting world that I know very little about, and I want to learn as much about that as I can.'

Adam removed the stick, examined it, and began chewing the other end. His eyes had a wistful look. 'Did you ever get to Paris?'

'Never.'

'So you never found out?'

For several seconds she gazed deep into the fire. 'About French men?' she ventured and, when he nodded, burst into laughter. 'You remember too much.'

'It's all coming back.'

'You said you'd forgotten.'

'No I didn't. I said I hadn't thought about the days in Greece a lot because everything seemed to have happened in another time, like the things you think of in a dream. But I've never forgotten.'

She wriggled into position beside him, delicately took the twig from his mouth, and offered her lips. He kissed her, softly and lovingly.

'I still can't believe all this,' she said.

'You keep saying that.'

'I keep meaning it.' She settled into his lap. 'I have to tell you something.'

'Now, you're not going to say "you'll think I'm silly but" ...'

She put a hand over his lips. 'Stop reminding me of my foolish youth.'

'Your realist phase.'

'Ssh. What I'm trying to say is important. I've slept around a little. In fact, more than a little.'

'Which means?'

She let a finger stray to his nose. 'I'd forgotten I was dealing with a primitive. It means I've had sex with quite a few men. So –'

'So?'

'Well, what do you have to say?'

'Nothing. I'm listening.'

'I'd also forgotten how infuriating you could be. I'm trying to make a confession. I have made love to other men since we were together in Greece. But I have to say, and I know this is going to sound silly and a bit like an excuse but I think in some of those cases, I was really trying to find you again. Can you understand that?'

He thought for a long time. She remembered his silences.

'Yes.'

'Just yes?'

'Yes. I can understand that. I've been lonely. I dream. I miss things.'

'Things?'

'People.'

'Me?'

'Yes, but in a strange sort of way, as though I could never see you again, which made the feeling easier to bear. You can put up with something, a longing, when you know there's absolutely no chance of it ever happening again.' He paused. 'That's how I felt about you.'

'And now? How do you feel about me?'

'As though a dream has come true.' He kissed her fingers. 'I don't mean a dream like a wish. I mean I feel as though the impossible has become ... possible.'

'The dream has become reality?'

'Yes. That's how I feel.'

'I'd like you to make love to me.'

He tapped her lightly on the nose. 'I don't think you'd be strong enough to stop me. Not the way I feel.'

'Good. I remember you as being strong. I don't mean crude or brutal. Gentle, but very determined and powerful.'

'That was good?'

'That was wonderful.' She put her hands behind his face, pulling him towards her and kissed him. Then she squirmed clear. She sat up. 'But first, I'd like to eat.'

'You like to torture a man.'

'I like to eat. If I don't eat I grow weak, and if I'm weak I can't make love to you. Not properly.'

He gripped her hand.

'What would you like me to prepare for you? More important, what have we got?'

He stood. 'This is my country and that means I cook.'

'Always?' She smiled mischievously.

'At least for tonight. You sit where you are. I'm cooking.'

He dragged some coals from the fire and made what he called a cooking corner at one side of the blaze. She expected him to prepare a simple meal: possibly fried eggs and bacon, with toast grilled over the coals, and the inevitable tea. Instead, Adam produced potatoes, tomatoes, onions and carrots and some canned beef (there was no fresh meat in Coober Pedy) and made a stew. While that was simmering, he cooked a damper. This bushman's staple was, he explained, best cooked in a cast-iron camp oven, although he had seen men produce good ones using the blade of a shovel as the cooking utensil. He had neither but displayed a baking dish he carried in the car's boot. He made the damper from flour and water, with salt for taste and raisins and sultanas to give the sweet interest required of a dish served as a dessert.

'Where did you learn to cook?' Nina asked when they were eating the damper. 'In Greece?'

'In the bush.'

'When?'

'When I was hungry.' He finished one slice and licked the crumbs from his fingers. 'After my father died, I was raised by an old character called Tiger Miller. He used to drink.'

'And was too drunk to cook for you?'

'He got too drunk to do anything.'

'So you learned to cook rather than go hungry.'

'And to prevent old Tiger starving. He was usually too full to fend for himself.'

'And who taught you?'

'No one.' He laughed. 'You soon learn.'

She cut him another slice, and buttered it. She passed it to him but he took her wrist and still on his knees, shuffled closer and placed one hand on the top button of her blouse.

'Oh, where did you learn this?' she said and dropped the damper.

'There was this strange girl who used to dress like a man.' He began undoing the buttons.

'A man? How strange. What did she look like?'

'Let me show you.' He removed the blouse, folding it neatly and putting it on the ground beside her sleeping bag. 'From memory she looked exactly like this.'

She looked down at her body, bronzed by the firelight, then up at Adam. 'A perfect copy?'

'Perfect.'

She started to undo her brassière.

'I'll do it.'

'You're doing everything tonight.'

He moved behind her and fumbled with the hooks.

'You're better at cooking.'

'I just need practice.'

'And where do you think you're going to get that?'

'It all depends on you,' he said and as the brassière fell, he kissed her ear and slowly slipped his arms around her, to cup her breasts.

'Do you think I need support?'

'I think you need me.'

She turned her face. 'You're starting to convince me.'

He moved in front of her, kissing one breast, then the other. She undid his shirt. 'I don't know why we bothered getting dressed.'

'It makes it more exciting.'

Both stood. Each removed the other's remaining clothes.

'You have so many scars.' Slowly she walked around him, touching each place. She put her hand across the large scar on his back. 'That's the only one I know the story of. Greece, 1943.'

'I'll take you on a tour someday.' He ran his fingers slowly and tenderly over her body. 'I can't find a thing.'

'I hope you mean scar. There are things that should interest you.'

'There are things that fascinate me.'

She sank to the ground and reached up for his hands. 'If you want me to stay, you'll have to start convincing me it will all be worthwhile.'

They began impatiently, in a physical, almost ferocious way. Once more Adam unlocked passions that poured from her in wild, uncontrolled, exhilarating bursts but then it became a sweet, loving experience and as the fire grew smaller, they lay holding each other, just as they had in a dark cellar in Greece.

Nellie enjoyed the flight. The day was clear but cool and the air so smooth that the Piper droned to the north undisturbed by any rough or rising currents. The noise of the engine and the rush of air prevented easy conversation so Nellie entertained herself by looking at familiar places from a novel angle.

They landed once to refuel. That was at the coal-mining town of Leigh Creek. Nellie found the landing exciting, whooping like a child on a roller coaster as the plane descended, drifting to one side and yawing as Josef pushed on the rudder pedals. Beyond Marree they followed the railway line to William Creek.

'It's so small,' Nellie chortled, amused at the insignificance of a settlement that had always seemed so important when viewed from ground level. While she found familiar features – the hotel, the fettlers' cottages, Gooly's store, the stockyards and the rail siding –

397

Josef searched for the track to Kalinda. To his great delight, he saw it almost immediately. No more than twin parallel ruts, they had been worn by seventeen years of sparse traffic into stark, white ribbons that cut across the rusted landscape and were as distinct and as easy to follow as the railway.

He circled the town once, drawing a speckled patch of upturned faces on to the road in front of the hotel, and then followed the track. The compass hovered around forty-two degrees but he knew the way. Across the flat plains. Around the ends of a pair of sand-hills, looking like fat grubs from this altitude. Across a sandy creek. More plains. Then towards the Douglas. The sandy creek was wide and its surface striated, raked in even patterns by the last rush of water, two or maybe three years ago. The regularity was broken only by islands that were slivers of sand, formed around trees whose trunks were buttressed by rotting debris. He had almost drowned in that creek. Now, there was not a sign of water. He was tempted to say something to Nellie, to remind her about that awful day, but when he turned she was looking down and smiling sadly. She remembered. The creek passed below them, tranquil and apparently lifeless until a flock of cockatoos burst from some trees and scattered in whirling confusion.

'It's beautiful,' Nellie said and, without hearing her words, Josef nodded agreement. He could not live in the outback any more but it did have a certain beauty. There was a sinister majesty about the desolation, the monotony, the endlessness of this country. It was beautiful but forbidding, a place not for humans. The outback was where nature revealed how all the world would be one day, when the mountains wore down and the valleys filled, the lakes dried into salt pans and the rivers silted up. It was a place to inspire a feeling of dread or of reverential awe, but it was not a place where any but a special few could live. Distances were too great, the isolation too profound, the threats to survival too real. He felt an intruder. He had grown too used to the comfort of neighbours and the convenience of towns.

By contrast, Adam understood the outback. He loved it with the feeling a kangaroo has for the plains or an eagle has for the rocky crags of a desert range. He could never live anywhere else. Josef realized that now. To put Adam in a town would be to fence in the kangaroo or cage the eagle.

He was looking forward to seeing his friend. 'Won't be long,' he shouted.

Nellie smiled, her lips compressed. She seemed smaller, even frail, having sunk into the seat the way old women do. 'I'm nervous,' she called back.

Josef reached out and grasped her hand. 'They'll be so happy to see you.'

'We should have told them.'

'And have everyone in the district know? This new two-way radio system's great but there's no such thing as a personal, confidential message.' He leaned close to make sure she could hear. 'Besides, it'll be better to surprise them.'

'What if they're not there?'

'I told them I was coming. And where do they ever go to?' He gripped her hand. 'Relax.'

Cassie and Jimmy were at the airstrip. The landing was not as Josef would have liked it because he bounced the aircraft three times and finally settled one wheel at a time. Still, if the landing was imperfect, so was the strip and, wheels rumbling on the stones and angry streams of dust billowing out behind, he taxied the Piper to the waiting Land Rover.

Cassie was at the wheel. She stayed there, to make sure Josef recognized that she could now drive a car. Jimmy, however, was out of the vehicle quickly and ran to the pilot's side of the fuselage.

'Who's at the wheel?' he shouted as the propeller fluttered its last strokes. 'A flamin' roo? They were three of the best hops I ever seen.'

Josef stuck his head out. 'If you made a decent strip, I'd make a decent landing.'

'Never known you to do anything decent in your life.' Jimmy's smile was so broad that his facial muscles were beginning to ache. 'Anyhow, how the hell are you?'

'Not bad, you old bastard. How are you?' They clasped hands.

For the first time Jimmy was aware of a passenger. He stepped back and trimmed the smile to more modest dimensions. 'Who'd you bring up? Must have more guts than I got to fly with you.'

Josef, leaning across to help Nellie open her door, had disappeared from Jimmy's view.

'Where you gone?' he called out, and then heard Nellie's feet hit the ground. Keeping well clear of the propeller, even though it was now motionless, he walked around the front of the aircraft.

'Jesus Christ,' he said, and the smile vanished.

'Hello Jimmy,' Nellie said. She came forward and shook his hand. 'Been a long time.'

Josef had followed Nellie and, before Jimmy could speak, he advanced with arms outstretched. He embraced the other man and pulled him off balance. 'What's this?' he said. 'Only a one-man welcoming committee? Where are the others? I hope they're

399

getting lunch ready because I could eat a horse.'

'You're lucky,' Jimmy said, getting his balance back, 'We're having horse for tea tonight.'

Disentangling himself, Josef stepped back and put a paternal arm around Nellie's shoulder. 'And what do you think of my surprise?'

Jimmy looked from one to the other. 'A real good one.' He smiled slowly at Nellie. 'I sure wasn't expecting you.' The horn of the Land Rover, out of sight behind the aircraft, tooted several times. 'That's Cassie. She won't leave the car until her Uncle Joe sees her behind the wheel.'

'She can drive a car?' Josef took his arm from Nellie and began to walk around the Piper.

'She can fly a plane,' Jimmy said, reckoning that a few minutes at the controls of the Dragon Rapide established Cassie as someone who could fly.

Hand on a propeller blade, Josef negotiated the front of the aircraft and, seeing Cassie, stopped. He gasped. 'You're Cassie?'

She got out of the vehicle. One hand still resting on the door, she beamed at him. 'I drove here. I've been driving for years, practically since you were last here.'

He shook his head. 'I wouldn't have believed it.'

'That I can drive?'

'That you're so big. You've grown up.'

'People do that.' And she ran to him and threw her arms around his neck. Josef was still shocked. He could remember cuddling Cassie and kissing her goodnight and even helping to bathe her, and he knew she was now seventeen, but he had expected a girl. Instead, he was being embraced by a young woman who had thrown herself recklessly into his arms. To his horror, he felt the first stirring of desire. Gently, he pushed her away.

'Let me look at you,' he said. In her excitement, she had risen on to her toes. 'My God, you're so tall.' Laughing, she lowered herself. 'You're still tall,' he said, holding her by the shoulders to keep her at bay for, like a puppy, she was straining to get closer.

'Five foot nine,' she said and then saw Nellie.

'This is the surprise I promised,' Josef said and walked back the few paces to where Nellie was standing. 'Do you two remember each other?'

Cassie, who had not witnessed the greetings on the far side of the aircraft, looked to Josef for guidance.

'The last time your Uncle Josef came here, that I remember,' Nellie said, a shy smile on her face, 'you thought he might be frightened away by the rabbits.'

'I did?' She had the baffled, disbelieving look of a person who is told she had talked in her sleep.

'Only you called them "wabbits".' Nellie stood with her hands clasped together. Nervously, she scratched the back of one ankle with the instep of her other foot, a pose that stressed her aboriginality.

At last, Josef responded to Cassie's plea. 'Cassie, this is Nellie.'

'Nellie?' Her brow furrowed as she chased memories. 'You used to look after me?'

'Yes.'

It seemed Cassie would run forward, but she hesitated. Then she began to extend a hand but withdrew it, recalling what Mrs Wilson had said about greeting people. 'How do you do?' she said and smiled.

Nellie nodded. 'I'm good, thanks.' Jimmy who had been examining the interior of the aircraft through the open door, joined the group and stood beside Nellie.

'Where you been?' he asked.

'Different places.'

'I been there too. Funny I didn't run into you.' He winked at Cassie. 'And what are you doin' up this way?' It was the pleasant enquiry one would make of a stranger passing through.

'Nellie's been sick,' Josef interjected. 'We ran into each other a couple of months ago. I invited her up for the ride. To convalesce, to get better.'

'Oh,' Cassie said, looking concerned. Jimmy was still grinning. 'Are you all right now?'

'I'm as right as rain.'

Ignoring Mrs Wilson's dictum, Cassie moved forward and shook Nellie's hand. 'I'm so pleased you came back.' Still holding the other woman's hand, she said, 'Did I really say "wabbit"?'

Nellie had been standing stiffly. Now she relaxed. 'You did. You used to call yourself Cassandra Woss.' She was about to add 'you used to have trouble with your r's' but Jimmy was beside her and she knew what he could make out of a remark like that so she said nothing but returned Cassie's deepening smile.

'I'm trying to remember,' Cassie said. 'When were you here?'

'You were just over three when I left.'

'Oh,' Cassie nodded as though much had been explained. 'Dad's got Mrs Wilson as housekeeper now. She's been with us for years. She used to be so strict with me. You know with my English. If I said something wrong, like "you done" instead of "you did", she'd jump on me. Were you strict with me?'

Nellie managed to smile and looked distressed at the same time. 'You were only a baby.'

'Anyhow,' Josef said as though it were time to move, 'where's Adam?'

'Not here,' Jimmy said and looked anxiously towards Cassie. She missed the signal.

'He's in Adelaide,' she said and sighed in exasperation. 'He'd only been gone for a couple of hours when your telegram came.'

Josef breathed out, and his strength seemed to ebb with the breath. 'Will he be long?'

'He was going to get back in time to be here when you got here.' She giggled. 'If you know what I mean.'

'Where's he staying?'

She looked at Jimmy with a knowing expression but failed to intercept his glare of caution. 'We don't know,' she said, her eyes bright and wide, 'but it's all very romantic.'

'Romantic?' Josef said.

She turned towards him and touched his arm. 'Guess who's been here.'

He shook his head wearily. 'Give me a clue. Man, woman or beast?'

She pulled his arm. 'Don't be silly. It's a woman of course, and it's someone you know.' Without waiting for his answer she turned to Nellie, 'Oh, it's been so funny, Dad pretending he wasn't interested and all that but I think this is the big love of his life, and she thought he was dead.'

Nellie said nothing but her face seemed to grow longer.

'What on earth are you talking about?' Josef said.

'Yeah, don't go over the top,' Jimmy said.

'Oh Jimmy,' she said amiably, 'you were hardly here. You didn't see what went on.' She concentrated on Josef, as though the subject was of no interest to the others. 'Think of someone he met, you both met, during the war. In Greece.'

'A woman?'

'I said it was a woman.'

Josef risked a quick glance at Nellie, who suddenly seemed unsteady on her feet. 'Not Nina?'

'Yes.' She clutched his arm. 'She just turned up. She's working for an American magazine and didn't know Dad was here. They almost died when they saw each other.'

'Who's Nina?' Nellie said in a quiet voice.

'An American woman. She and Dad met in Greece. I think they had a passionate love affair.'

'Oh, cut it out,' Josef said lamely.

'No, it's true. I think they're going to get married. Oh, Uncle Joe, she's lovely and it's so exciting. You've got to tell me all about what happened in Greece.'

Josef swallowed awkwardly. 'And Adam's gone to Adelaide?'

'They've both gone to Adelaide.'

Nellie swayed. Jimmy caught her arm. 'Jesus, what's wrong?' he said.

Josef held her other arm. 'She's been very sick. She's only been out of hospital for a few days.' And as they helped Nellie to the Land Rover, he knew what a terrible mistake he had made in bringing Nellie back to Kalinda.

E·I·G·H·T

Nellie was in bed. Stella was in the room with her, having brought the three girls to be presented to her old friend. Jimmy had gone to check the sheep at the Number One bore. In the living-room, Cassie and Josef were talking. They had eaten lunch and Josef had explained about Nellie's operation.

'What does she do these days?' Cassie asked.

'She's a nurse in a hospital.' That was not accurate, he thought, but it would do. He did not say where. The girl presumed he meant Adelaide and he let it go at that.

'I don't really remember her. There are a few vague things that come back at times ...' She shook her head. 'She seems nice.'

'She is.' He scratched his nose, temporarily lost in the recollection of Nellie in the early days, when he was just a boy and she was the most gorgeous woman he had ever seen. 'For a couple of years, she was the one who raised you. You know, washed you, dressed you, fed you while your dad was out working.'

Her eyebrows arched in surprise. 'I hadn't realized. Dad talks about her every now and then, whenever he's telling me one of his stories about the old days.' She grinned. 'Ones that involve you and Jimmy usually. I always thought she was fat and dumpy like Mrs. Wilson.'

'Mrs Wilson would love to hear you call her that.'

'She's outside.' She leaned forward. 'Tell me about Nina.'

Josef moistened his lips. There was something he had to say and he had little idea of how to begin. Inevitably, he began badly. 'We shouldn't talk about Nina in front of Nellie,' he said and found something in his shoes that needed to be examined.

'But she's not here.'

'I know,' he said, knotting his eyebrows. 'But when she is around, it probably would be a good idea not to talk about Nina.'

'Why?'

He was still concentrating on his shoes and was slow to answer.

'Uncle Joe, are you saying she's keen on Dad?'

He looked up and shrugged. 'Well, she might have been once.'

Cassie leaned back, her face doubtful. 'You're not pulling my leg?'

'No. I think she was.' He straightened and leaned back, matching her casual pose with his legs crossed and one arm draped over the back of the chair. 'Well, maybe. Who knows? It just might be a sensitive subject. A good one to avoid. You know?'

She was studying his face intently.

'Well,' he continued, 'it was a long time ago and Nellie was one of those people we kept running into. She was at Coober Pedy and then we didn't see her for a long time. Then we met her again at Port Augusta when your dad and I were driving back from Western Australia.' She nodded. She knew about the adventure in the west. 'And then she was working at William Creek about the time your dad started this place.'

'She was our housekeeper here,' she said, feeling the need to prompt.

He turned his head and nodded and his mouth moved, but he said nothing.

'And you ran into her in Adelaide.'

'Well not in the city, actually. She was working in a hospital at this place where I landed my plane ...'

'Where was that?'

He waved to the east. 'Oh, a long way from here. Anyhow, she said she was going to see this doctor in Adelaide and I got the idea of bringing her up here for a bit of a holiday. So she could see her old friends. It's funny,' he raced on, not wanting to give her the chance to ask a question, 'but we always seem to run into each other. She's a nice person. I think she's had a pretty hard life.' He glanced towards the bedroom. The girls were noisy and they could hear occasional juvenile laughter. 'I probably shouldn't have brought her up. The flight was a long one. Possibly too much for her.' He had run out of words.

'Did Dad like her?' Her eyes bored into his.

He smiled and scratched at a mark on the side of his shoe. 'I know that I used to like her. She was a very good-looking woman. Still is, of course.' The eyes remained on him. Even as a little girl, she had had a way of staring intently into the eyes of another person. Just like her father. 'But your dad? Oh, I don't think so. Mind you, it was a long time ago and we were only kids.'

'Why shouldn't I talk about Nina then?'

'Well,' he said, raising his shoulders to an extravagant height, 'she hasn't been well.'

Cassie started to laugh.

'What's wrong?'

'It's you.' she said. 'You're funny. You've taken pity on Dad living on his own and brought an old girl-friend up here. Uncle Joe, you're nothing but an old match maker.'

'No. It's not that.'

'Well what is it?' she taunted.

He spread his hands. 'She's not well and we'd hoped to see Adam and she's disappointed, and if you talk about him chasing off to Adelaide after an American woman ...'

Her eyes narrowed and a smile hovered at the corners of her mouth. 'I still think you're pulling my leg but I can't work out what it's all about. Anyhow,' she continued, when he seemed to grow more uncomfortable 'we won't talk about Nina in front of anyone else. So let's talk about her now.'

For the next ten minutes, a relieved Josef told her what he could recall of the few days he and Adam had spent with Nina in Greece.

'Were they lovers?' she asked, with the breathless innocence of a child talking about fairytale characters.

He laughed uneasily. 'We were fighting the Germans. It was pretty desperate stuff. I don't think there was too much time for people to be falling in love. It was also very cold and I was sick and she was looking after me, not your father, so there wasn't too much time for anything else.'

'No kissing?'

'No kissing, Cassie.'

'Rats. I was hoping they'd had this passionate love affair.'

His face crinkled into a smile. 'What have you been reading in the last five years?'

'Lots of things. Mrs Wilson gets all the latest books. I've read a great deal of poetry. Do you think they'll get married?'

'Cassie, they hardly know each other.'

'He needs a wife.'

'So do I,' he said trying not to smile, 'but these things take time. Other people can't organize such private happenings.'

She leaned forward, resting her elbows on her knees. 'Do you think I'll ever get married?'

Much happier with the trend of the conversation, he leaned back and locked his fingers behind his head. 'I think it's very likely.'

'Why?'

'You're a pretty girl.'

'Is that the most important thing?'

He laughed.

She beat her fists on her knees. 'You're a man of the world. You'd know. Tell me.'

'Well, I don't know if any of that's true but being pretty is a good start. It makes men look at you and once they're taking notice, you can start impressing them with all your other attributes.'

'What are attributes?'

'Your good features.'

'What are mine?'

He lowered his hands. 'I don't know you well enough yet.'

She jabbed a finger at him. 'You've known me all my life.'

'But only as a baby or a little girl. You're a young woman now.'

'And that's different?' She puffed with pleasure.

'Very different.'

'Do you know the main problem here?' she said after a lengthy pause. 'There are no men.'

'That is a problem,' he conceded.

'Nina says I should travel.'

'She's probably right.'

'Could you take me somewhere?'

He stiffened. 'Where?' His mind raced to the thought of escorting Cassie through the streets of London or Paris.

'Over Lake Eyre. We flew over the southern part of the lake in the big plane that brought Nina here. The pilot let me fly it for a while.'

'Really?'

'He said I was very good. But now I'd like to see up north. We live on the lake but I've never been up there.'

'I've got to be a bit careful of my fuel.'

'That's all right. It wouldn't be far in a plane.'

He used the expression he normally displayed when tasting a rival wine. 'We'll think about it,' he said grudgingly.

'Dad's going to buy a plane.'

'When did Adam decide this?'

'He hasn't yet but he will.' She smiled cheerily, with the supreme confidence of one who knows she can manipulate her father.

'He could do with one. I'm a great believer in the future of aircraft.'

'We'll work on him together.' They shook hands. Her skin was roughened from hard work but her touch was light and cool.

'You don't know where he's staying in Adelaide?' he said, anxious to take his mind away from thoughts of how her skin felt.

'No. But he said he was going to telephone you when he got there.'

'So he will ring my parents and they'll tell him I'm up here. Which means,' he said, nodding each item on its way, 'that he'll then turn around and catch the next train up.'

'He went by car.'

'He's game,' he said his face stretched in admiration of the feat Adam had attempted. 'So he can turn around and drive home again.'

'You won't go away?' she asked anxiously. 'You'll stay?'

'We'll wait till we hear from your father.'

'And maybe while we're waiting, you could take me for a fly?'

'Maybe.' He smiled. She really had become a most attractive young woman.

Nellie was asleep. Stella sat beside the bed, holding her friend's hand and recalling the last time they had been together. That was in hospital at Oodnadatta, when she had had Marie and Nellie had given birth to Daniel. She had sent the girls out of the room as soon as Nellie had become drowsy. Marie had gone to help Mrs. Wilson. The younger ones, Yvonne, ten, and Elizabeth, eight, had returned to the old homestead to do their homework for the School of the Air.

A blowfly was caught between the window blind and the glass. It tapped the pane repeatedly, buzzing nosily until Stella went to the window and deftly crushed it, cornering it behind the blind and then applying sufficient pressure to silence it permanently without squeezing its juices on to the glass. It was the technique of an experienced fly killer, which most bush women were. When she returned to the bed, Nellie was awake.

With the girls gone, they talked about Daniel. He was now in his fifteenth year and living at Marree. He was being cared for by Saleem Benn. He was tall for his age, strong, not interested in school work and brown enough, both through natural colouring and a perpetual suntan, to be accepted without question as one of the Afghan community. He now spoke Pushtu fluently as well as English and showed no inclination to pray either as a Moslem or a Christian.

He was allegedly in his final year at school – and it was so he could go to a proper school and round off his education that Nellie had sent him to stay with Saleem Benn – but it seemed, Nellie confessed, that the boy was more interested in working with camels and trucks than with books. More and more, she heard reports of his accompanying Saleem Benn or one of his men on a delivery run to some homestead out near Lake Frome or up the Birdsville Track. During school holidays, he had even gone with the Birdsville mail contractor, Fred Crawford, all the way to the tiny Queensland settlement. The Cooper had been up, and Daniel had helped Crawford and his assistant, a bearded Russian whom locals knew

408

only as Ivan, to ferry supplies across the flooded river. The Cooper flowed every few years and Crawford kept a barge-like ferry at a crossing near Lake Killamperpunna. It had taken the two men and the boy several days to unload the original truck, haul the goods bit-by-bit across the broad flood, and then reload everything on to a second truck parked on the other side of the river. The load consisted of forty-four gallon drums of fuel, crates of beer for the Birdsville Hotel, motor tyres, rolls of wire, sacks of flour, tea and sugar, cartons of supplies, cans of food, newspapers and mail. It was exhausting work. Daniel had loved it.

'He's a real bushie,' Nellie laughed.

'He sounds like his father's son,' Stella said and Nellie smiled wistfully.

'He's like Adam in so many ways.'

'When will you be seeing Daniel again?' Stella forced brightness into the words.

'On the way back. I have to go back to Innamincka, so I'll stop off at Marree and see him.' She realized then, at the moment of discussing her return, that she had been hoping to stay at Kalinda; if not forever, at least long enough to see Adam again and make sure they could be friends. And she had desperately wanted to see Cassie, and spend time with her. God knows what she should do now, after what Cassie had said. She breathed out and produced a groan.

'What's up?' Stella leaned forward anxiously. 'Are you in pain?'

'Just tired.' She smiled. 'They must have taken more out of me than I thought.'

Each was silent for a while.

'Who's this woman Cassie was talking about?' Nellie said, staring at the wall.

'She's an American. A writer of some sort. She takes pictures too. She had a bag with a real expensive camera and bits and pieces. I never seen anyone take so many pictures of the same thing.'

'Like what?' Nellie managed to sound interested.

'Anything. People. Bushes. Sand. Camels. The houses. She took Jimmy's photo about fifty times.'

'Must have a lot of money.'

'Mrs Wilson says Americans are rich.'

Nellie closed her eyes and imagined Adam with a rich woman. The woman she could see was older than Adam and had big earrings and a pearl necklace and rings on every finger. The woman was heavily made up and, even then, not good looking.

'What's she like?'

Stella let her eyes roam the room, as though seeking some comparison. 'She's nice,' she said with some reluctance.

'Real nice?'

Stella let her eyes settle on Nellie. She pursed her lips.

'What's that mean? Come on Stella, I'm a big girl. I can stand a bit of truth every now and then.'

The other woman looked down. 'Yes. Real nice.'

'That's good. How old is she?'

'Thirty. Maybe a bit more.' She saw Nellie gulp. 'Probably more.'

'Younger than Adam then?'

'Yes.' The word came out with great reluctance.

'That's good. A man needs a younger woman.'

Stella looked towards the window. Another blowfly was buzzing against the glass.

'Nice looking?'

She nodded, her attention still on the window. 'Funny voice though.'

'How?'

'Hard to say. Jimmy does a real good imitation.'

'What do you think? Is Adam really going to marry her?'

Stella laughed, a soft, genuine sound. 'Cassie's got the best imagination of any person I know. I didn't see anything happen that would make you think that Adam and the American woman were going to get married.' She found a loose thread on her sleeve and twisted it into a ball. 'He just drove her down to Adelaide because he had to go there himself.'

Nellie nodded and closed her eyes. Stella thought she had fallen asleep again but Nellie moved her hand to brush something from her forehead.

'Are you going to tell Adam about Daniel?'

Nellie opened one eye.

'He's such a good man. I'm sure he'd want to know, so he could help and that sort of thing.' Carefully Stella entwined her fingers and placed the locked fingers on her lap. 'He doesn't know he has a son. I think he'd be very proud, particularly if Daniel's such a good boy.'

Nellie held out a hand and Stella took it. 'I wrote to Saleem Benn. He's been terrific.' There was a long pause.

'What did you write about?'

'I said that if I died –' She felt Stella's hand jerk and she gripped it more tightly. 'I said if I died, he was to tell Adam. Just so he could keep an eye on him, make sure he didn't get in with the wrong crowd or anything like that. Give him a job, maybe.'

410

'What's all this talk about dying?' Stella said in her soothing mother's voice.

Nellie opened both eyes. 'I've been pretty sick. The doctor said it could come back.'

Stella leaned closer. 'Why don't you wait here for Adam to come back and tell him?'

'There are reasons.'

'It doesn't make sense to me.'

'I don't know that I've ever made sense,' Nellie said, wrinkling her forehead. 'But I'm not going to tell him. Not now. Specially now that he might have found himself a nice rich American lady.'

'Oh, that's just Cassie talking.'

But Nellie smiled and closed her eyes.

A customer entered the store and Goolamadail in most untypical fashion, hurried to serve her. The wife of one of the fettlers, she bought canned food, cereal and soft drinks. She was on her way home in five minutes, whereas a visit to the store normally entailed a ten-minute wait before the Afghan appeared and then slow service accompanied by much gossip. On this day, Goolamadail escorted her to the front of the shop, gave her a slight push to make sure she kept going and then returned to the darkened rear of the building where his visitor was waiting.

Ginger Thompson was a short, slightly-built man with not a trace of red colouring in his hair. 'Ginger' was a preferred simplification of his given name Jingellic, which was the town in southern New South Wales where he had been born. His father had followed a family tradition by being a cattle thief and to escape local opprobrium as well as the police, had left the rich mountain country along the Murray River to work in South Australia just after the First World War. Ginger Thompson had spent the last twenty years trapping rabbits and shooting dingoes in the arid country around the Flinders Ranges. The five years before that had been spent in gaol, for armed robbery. He now owned a truck and was Goolamadail's partner in his new cattle-stealing venture.

'I can get in pretty easy, I think,' Thompson said, stretching himself out in the corner chair. 'There's a bit of a track in from the road near Anna Creek turn-off. That way I can come in from the southern side of the Neales, just near Umbum Creek. He's got about a hundred head of cattle up there. Saw 'em myself the other day.'

'And you can get them out safely, without being seen?'

'There's an old yard along the creek, off his property. I'll fix it up and move a few truckloads down there.'

411

'Not too many.'

'Leave it to me. I've got a buyer close enough for me to move 'em out right, one load at a time.'

'Good.' Goolamadail gabled his fingers. 'And you'll leave no trail?'

'Not that he'll find.'

Goolamadail nodded contentedly. 'He's away, anyhow. Mr Adam Ross will lose some of his best cattle and will be quite unaware of it. Now, would you care for something to drink?'

'Got some Scotch?'

Goolamadail's damaged nose flattened a little more in an expression of distaste. 'I was thinking of tea.'

'Come on, Gooly,' Thompson said, crossing one leg over the other. 'This is big business. We're gonna make a lot of money, you and me.'

The Afghan opened a cupboard and extracted a bottle of whisky.

'We'll have a toast,' the other man said. 'To all those mug cockies who won't have a clue they're being robbed and are gonna make us rich.'

Goolamadail poured tea for himself. 'To us,' he said, clinking his cup against the other man's glass. He disliked this man and resolved to dispense with him if ever he could find another equally gifted partner.

It was late afternoon and a golden light seeped through the branches of the trees. A dozen young men, wearing laterally striped football jumpers and shorts but barefooted, ran past, breaths rasping, faces glistening. Adam and Nina, holding hands, paused to let them pass. They were walking in one of the broad parks that surrounded the one square mile of buildings that formed the city of Adelaide.

'How could I still write and take photographs?' Nina said in the tone of a person content to be defeated.

'There's one room in the new house that would be perfect for writing.'

'And taking photographs?'

'You take them while you get your stories, I supose.'

'It would mean having to travel every now and then.'

He shrugged.

'I wouldn't be much of a housekeeper.'

'I've already got a housekeeper.'

'What would you do when I was away?' She swung his arm in an exaggerated movement that caused them both to sway as they walked.

412

'Either miss you or go with you.'

'You'd travel with me?'

'If I could.' He locked her swinging hand in mid-air and she stumbled, off balance. 'If you wanted me to.'

'That would be really good.' She walked a few steps with her head down. 'Really good. I'd like that. You'd be able to come with me?'

'Sometimes. Depending on where and how long and when.'

'And all those things.' She laughed.

'Couldn't leave at shearing time.'

'You could do with more help, possibly.'

'Been thinking of getting someone else.'

'You really think you could put up with an American city slicker? You, the classic Aussie bushman.'

'Why not? Could you put up with me?'

She leaned her head on his shoulder. 'I don't think I could live without you.'

'It's pretty lonely up there.'

'Don't try and talk me out of it.'

'I'm not, believe me.' He let his ear rest on the crown of her head and together they walked with heads touching. 'I've thought about this. I want to marry you – but I want you to be happy.'

'As long as I don't have to give away my career entirely. If I could just write occasional stories. Good ones.' She considered. 'Very good ones. In fact, exceptional ones.'

'There's a lot in this country to write about.'

'I could be a specialist. "By our Special Correspondent in Australia."'

'Why don't you use your name? "By Melina Ross."'

'Melina O'Sullivan. I'd like to keep using that name professionally.' She laughed. 'That way, if I do a really terrible article, no one in this country will know who I am.'

'You couldn't write a terrible article.'

She moved her head from his shoulder and kissed his ear. 'Do you think we should wait?'

'No.'

'Maybe a year? To let Cassie get used to the idea, to make sure you really want to go ahead with this.'

'Cassie was smelling a romance within five minutes of you getting off the plane.'

'Would I be her stepmother?' She looked worried. Nina had been raised on fairy-stories and the term had nasty connotations.

'You'd be her friend.'

'I like her.'

413

'I'm sure she likes you. You'd be good for her too. She needs company.'

'Not just a wife but a companion.' She pulled a face.

He stopped and faced her. Another group of runners was approaching. 'Look, I've thought this out. I've got no doubts. We met ten years ago. We liked each other –'

'We certainly did.' Gently, she pinched his nose.

'And we got separated. Split up by the war.' He held her by both shoulders. 'We're not going to lose any more time. I love you, Nina.'

'And I love you.'

They kissed. The runners thudded by. 'Get into it, mate,' one of them panted. The others departed in a volley of whistles.

'So what are we going to do?' she asked brushing her hair back with one hand.

'Get married as soon as we can.'

'How about my return ticket on the *Mariposa*?'

'We either cash it in or we frame it and put it on the wall and you can write underneath it: "This is how much I love my husband."'

'I don't seem to be able to think of any more arguments.'

'Good.' He resumed walking, holding her hand and swinging it once more. 'I've got to make a telephone call and I'll need your help because I'm not too good with the phone.'

'Delighted to help. Who are we calling?'

'Josef. I'm going to need a best man.'

The telephone booth was in the foyer of the hotel. Adam put the telephone down and walked out, his face creased with worry.

Nina reached out to touch his hand. 'What's wrong?'

'Josef's not there. He's gone to Kalinda.'

'But you said he wasn't going for a couple of weeks.'

'That's what he said in his telegram.' He led her into the coffee lounge where they sat at a table decorated with an elegant white vase holding a single paper rose. Adam summarized the conversation. He had spoken to Mrs Hoffman. Josef had sent a telegram and then left two days ago. He intended staying a week. There had been a change in his business arrangements, Mrs Hoffman thought, which had made him leave several weeks earlier than he had originally intended.

'So we're down here and he's up there,' Nina said. 'What do we do now?'

'Send him a telegram. Get him to hop into his flying machine and come back to Adelaide.' He eyed Nina. 'Unless we drive back up to Kalinda. I know a good parson.'

414

Smiling, she shook her head. 'I have to be here for a while. Get the colour transparencies developed, write my story, mail everything off. There are people I must write to and telephone. I have to stay here, just for a few weeks.'

'All right. Help me write the telegram.'

'What do you want to say?'

'You're the writer.'

'Don't ever say that to a writer. Come on, tell me.'

'Something like "What are you doing up there when I need a best man down here."'

'Great. Send it. Plus the hotel's address so he can reply.'

She wrote out the telegram for him. They lodged it, for transmission the next day.

Adam's conversation with Mrs Hoffman had been brief because Josef's mother had grown deaf and any exchange of words was difficult. He had promised to ring that night and speak to Mr Hoffman. And it was Josef's father who told Adam about Nellie.

'My God,' Nina said when Adam relayed the news. 'That's the one you told me about in Greece?'

He nodded, his face still pale from the news. 'Joe's taken her to Kalinda.'

'Why would he do that? And without telling you?' He didn't answer, and she thought for a while. 'To bring you two together again. Would that be it?'

'Who knows with someone like Joe? He tends to rush off and do things.' He led her up the stairs, towards their suites. They were staying in separate rooms. 'She's been sick, apparently. She had a big operation and came to stay with the Hoffmans while she got better.'

'Where has she been all these years?'

'I'm not sure. Mr Hoffman said Josef had run into her somewhere in the bush. He found out she was sick and had to come south to see a doctor.'

'Why didn't he tell you?'

They paused while she searched her bag for the key to her room. 'I don't know,' he said. 'All I can think of is that Joe wanted to surprise me. Or surprise us, rather. I mustn't forget Cassie. Nellie would have wanted to see Cassie. She used to be very fond of her.'

They entered the room and sat on the bed.

'So what do we do now?'

He shook his head. 'Why would Joe do something as stupid as this?'

'I don't know him very well. And I've never met Nellie. There

415

could be all sorts of reasons.' She took his hand. 'You should go back.'

He looked alarmed. 'We're going to get married.'

'You should still go back and see what's happening. And meet Nellie again. She how she is and clear up anything that has to be cleared up.' She felt his hand clench and touched it soothingly. 'It's important. If there are any ghosts they should be laid to rest.'

'Nina, she walked off in 1939. That was before the war. The whole world's changed since then. Cassie was a baby. Now she's a woman. I'm a different man.' He hunched over the end of the bed. 'There are no ghosts.'

'At least you can find out why she left. I'm curious. I'd like to know the answer to that myself.' When she felt him moving in an agitated manner, she added: 'I know you love me. You know I love you. I think you're the finest man I've ever known. Very sexy too.' She nipped his thigh with her fingers. 'But I could use some time to do all this work I have to do. And we can't get married instantly. I presume this is not Reno. We do have to have permits or licences or something.'

He lifted his shoulders. 'I don't know.'

'I'll find out. I can do my writing, get the pictures processed, and attend to all the paperwork relevant to the marriage of Adam Ross and Melina O'Sullivan.' She leaned against him. 'You can go home, see Josef, see Nellie, find out what the hell's going on and then come back. That's if you don't mind all that driving.'

'I'll go back the short way, up along the Flinders Ranges and through Marree.'

'It's still a lot of driving.'

'Only two days. I'll pretend I'm in the Redex Trial.'

'Don't you dare. You take it easy. I want you back here safe and sound. I've got plans for you.' She kissed his cheek.

Adam left the next morning. He sent another telegram. He tried to cancel the first one but it had already been sent.

N·I·N·E

Mrs Wilson was working the radio when the telegram was read out, in slow precise terms, by the operator at the Flying Doctor base. She wrote the message on a piece of paper. As the telegram was addressed to Josef, she put the paper on top of the cabinet in his bedroom. Josef was out with Jimmy. She said nothing to Cassie, who had been working in the stockyard during the radio session.

'Any interesting news?' Cassie enquired when she returned to the house. Everyone listened to the telegrams.

'The father of Margaret Stevens is very sick. He's in hospital in Port Augusta.'

'I don't like her.'

'It doesn't make her father being sick any better news.'

'Suppose not. Anything else?'

'Stuart Creek are ordering more cattle. Janice Taylor is going south in a few weeks' time and wants to stay with her husband's sister. They had two points of rain at Mount Sarah.'

'How boring. Nothing for us?'

'A telegram for Mr Hoffman.'

Cassie reacted as though she had touched a live wire. 'Who from?'

'Your father.'

'What's he say?'

'It's for Mr Hoffman.'

'Where'd you put it? In his room?' And before Mrs Wilson could answer or stop her, Cassie had bolted for Josef's bedroom. She emerged waving the paper and shouting in triumph.

'I told you, I told you. They're going to get married.'

'Calm down. He doesn't say that at all. He just makes reference to Mr Hoffman being the best man. That could mean anything.'

'Oh Mrs Wilson,' Cassie said, putting the message on the table where Josef would see it immediately he entered the house, 'You can be such a drip. But a nice one.' She bounced away. 'Of course they're going to get married. I knew it. No one believed me, but I knew it.'

She ran from the house and went to the old homestead. Nellie was now staying there, to be close to Stella. Cassie skipped into the kitchen, smiled at Nellie who was sitting at the table near the stove, and went straight to Stella.

'Guess what?' She gave the woman no time for even one attempt. 'Dad and Nina are getting married. Dad sent a telegram to Uncle Joe. He wants him to be best man. He said "what are you doing up there when I need a best man down here"', or something like that.'

Stella wiped her hands as though rolling down rubber gloves. 'When did the telegram arrive?' she said in a weak voice.

'Just now.' At that moment, Cassie recalled Josef's plea not to speak about such matters in front of Nellie. Her feet performed a nervous tap dance. 'It came over the radio.' Her voice trailed away. She folded her arms, in the way she had noticed Nina did. 'He's staying at some hotel in North Terrace, Adelaide. What's that like?'

Stella shook her head in a gesture so forlorn she seemed unlikely to produce any words. 'I don't know,' she said eventually, 'I never been to Adelaide.'

'It's pretty,' Nellie said. 'There are parks all around it.'

Cassie sat on a chair beside her. 'Did you really play with me when I was young?'

'I certainly did.' Nellie felt an overwhelming desire to hug the girl but instead smiled down at the table. 'Do you know what your favourite game was?'

'I can't remember.'

'Pushing a cotton reel around the floor.'

'A cotton reel?' Cassie looked up at Stella for confirmation that such a thing was possible.

'We weren't ... your father wasn't too well off in those days. I don't think it would have mattered. He could have bought you the world's most expensive toy and you'd still have pushed that cotton reel around the place. You were always getting under our feet.'

They talked for another half an hour until Cassie, remembering some unfinished chores with the horses, ran off.

'Well, that's it,' Nellie said, staring at the empty doorway.

'Wait till he gets here, tell him about Daniel,' Stella said.

'No. A man about to marry a rich American woman doesn't want a half-caste son for a wedding present.'

'Nellie, that's an awful thing to say.'

'Didn't you know? I say awful things.' She sighed. 'No, I'll just leave when Joe leaves. If he takes me to Leigh Creek, I can then get up to Lyndhurst and get a lift with the mailman back to Inna-mincka. That's where I belong.'

'I know you're doing the wrong thing.'

'That's me. I say awful things and do wrong things. Not much variety but it makes for an interesting life.' She smiled. 'What's left of it.' She was still staring at the door. 'She's a lovely girl, isn't she? I always used to think I could pass her off as my own daughter. What do you think?'

Stella touched the side of one eye as though dabbing away a speck of dirt. 'I reckon she would have loved you as her mother.'

'Yes,' Nellie said softly and turned away.

A few miles past the Farina rail crossing, Adam stopped his car, got the tools from the boot, and slid under the back axle to tighten a rear shock absorber. While he was there, he checked the nuts holding the U-bolts on the rear springs and made sure no oil was leaking from the differential. Everywhere were signs of stone damage, for the road north of Hawker had been coated in coarse, deep gravel. There had also been a long stretch of road with scores of deep, sharp dips – what locals called jump-ups because of the way cars reared on the exit. Adam believed it was the hammering of the jump-ups that had shaken loose the shock absorber.

The sun was low enough to be throwing long shadows across the gibber plain as he drove over the final rise in the road before Marree. The town stretched across the horizon, the big rail sheds on the western side of the line dominating the skyline. He drove past the crossing that would have taken him into the white part of town where the pub, the post office, a shop and the police station were clustered near the railway station. He went straight on, towards Saleem Benn's store in the Afghan part of town, near the start of the Birdsville Track.

Yunis, who was gradually being entrusted with duties other than driving, was in the store. He smiled pleasantly when he saw Adam and went outside to help him refuel the Holden. Saleem Benn was in town and while Adam checked the car's oil and water levels, Yunis went to fetch his uncle.

The old Afghan emerged from the store, his face warm with good feelings. He insisted Adam eat with him and sleep on the back verandah of his house. He had two small boys, children of his older nephews, move a pile of tyres and an old ice chest to make room for the stretcher that was assembled in the space allocated to Adam.

A larger boy put the pieces of the bed together and then carried Adam's bag from the car. He was good looking and a little fairer than the others.

'He is a good lad,' Saleem Benn confided, speaking softly even

419

though the boy was beyond hearing range. 'Industrious and very smart although, regrettably, his interests do not extend to study. He is one of those who will begin his learning only when he is old enough to realize the need.'

Adam smiled sympathetically.

'In truth, he reminds me of you.'

'One of your nephews?' Adam enquired.

'Remarkably, no. He is the son of a friend.' He called to the boy, who responded immediately. 'Daniel, this is my good friend, Mr Ross.'

The boy was shy. He performed a greeting which was between a nod and a bow. 'Hello, Mr Ross.'

'How are you, Daniel?' Adam offered his hand. The grip he received was surprisingly strong.

'Very well thank you, Mr Ross.' The boy saw the slight movement of Saleem Benn's head and excused himself.

'What a polite lad,' Adam said, knowing this would please his friend, who so valued good manners.

'Indeed.' Saleem Benn's eyes glowed. 'I have taken some care with this one.'

'Your friend is lucky to have such a son.'

Slowly the Afghan spread his hands. 'The more fortunate we are, the less we value our good fortune. My friend is scarcely aware of the treasure he has created.'

'It's often the way,' Adam said, nodding.

They dined and discussed Adam's long drive from Adelaide. Adam said he was contemplating marriage. This did not surprise the Afghan. A man should have a woman, he said and enquired, most casually, whether it was someone he knew. When Adam said no, he offered his felicitations and talked about something else. After the meal, they walked out on the street. For some minutes, Adam's host seemed to be enjoying the brilliant sky.

'A most unusual and grave matter has arisen,' Saleem Benn said, angling his eyes towards Adam but leaving his face aimed at the heavens.

'If I can be of help ...' Adam remembered the long conversations they used to have. The preamble was always lengthy but eloquent. Nothing was rushed.

'Your thoughts would be valued.' He examined the stars once more. 'I find great comfort in studying that part of God's universe we are permitted to see. The days can be a misery and the nights a delight and yet it is the same heaven above us. Do you not find that curious?'

'I never thought about it.'

'Ah! Consider that when we have most illumination we see nothing of the infinite.' He paused. 'One bright light, a minor star we call the sun, blinds us to what lies beyond. It is only when that necessary but distracting light disappears that we catch a glimpse of what surrounds us. It is so in life too, is it not?'

'Very often. As always you speak great truth.' He spoke the last words in Pushtu, which greatly amused the old man.

'Your memory is excellent but your accent has deteriorated.' He raised and extended his hand, a signal for Adam to grasp it. 'Truly, Adam Ross, I enjoy your company as much as that of any man I know.'

'I am honoured.'

'That was better,' he said; Adam had again used Saleem Benn's language. 'Truly, a month with me and I would have you speaking with the fluency of a merchant in the bazaars of Jalalabad.'

'I trust I am honoured,' Adam said in English and the old man nodded his head vigorously. Again, he looked up.

'Just as a bright light blinds us to the truths of the universe, so have I been blinded as to the truth of what was happening around me.' He sighed, making a whimpering sound. 'By one of my own family.'

Adam was silent. He stood beside his friend, examining the same expanse of sky.

'You know my nephew Goolamadail?'

'Of course.'

'Do you like him? Be honest.'

Adam hesitated. 'No.'

Saleem Benn stroked his fine grey beard. 'I do not like being in one place. I do not like serving in a store, or keeping books, or weighing flour and adding this and taking away that. I prefer to be under the stars. Once with my beloved camels, now with that wretched motor truck, may God preserve it from mishap. I prefer to trade, to see my customers in their fine homesteads or humble tents. Where they live and work. I do not want them to come to me, to see me in the confines of a shop. That is for women.' He scratched his nose. 'Do you understand me?'

'Yes.'

'As a result, I have been foolish enough to trust others to run parts of my operation, the parts which I find onerous. Some in those positions of trust have been excellent. They are honest men. Even women.' He paused for a long time. 'So you do not like Goolamadail?'

'I don't know him well,' Adam said, not understanding the trend of the conversation.

421

'What do you not like? Be frank.'

Adam cleared his throat. 'He strikes me as being shifty.'

'Not to be trusted?'

Adam shrugged.

'Why did you not say something to me, your old friend?' The question was asked kindly.

'It was my opinion. Just a feeling. I don't know him well.'

The Afghan grunted. 'Neither do I apparently.' He faced Adam. 'He has been robbing me. The first time I am aware of, was about ten years ago. On that occasion, he took a very large sum of money and claimed he had been beaten and robbed.'

Adam had heard of the incident.

'Since then he has been steadily defrauding me. Cooking the books is the term, I think.'

'That is terrible. Your own nephew.'

Saleem Benn waved the problem aside with a sweep of his hand. 'Distressing yes, but no great problem. The world is full of dishonest men, even relatives. I know how to deal with them.'

There was a long pause. From the other side of the railway came the sound of a sudden burst of recorded music. Someone had opened the door of the Great Northern's lounge bar.

'The problem is even greater?' Adam said eventually.

There was another whimpering sigh. 'He is making threats.'

'What kind of threats?'

Saleem Benn lowered his head and several times pulled on the tip of his nose. He sniffed. 'I was ill some time ago.'

'I remember – you are well now?'

'Completely. Thank you. Perfectly well but as you may recall, I was taken ill in the region of William Creek and was compelled to seek the care of my nephew Goolamadail.'

'I wish I'd been there to care for you.'

The old man raised both hands, as in prayer. 'Then my troubles would never have occurred.' He lowered his arms and clasped hands behind his back. He began walking. 'I had a fever. Apparently I talked. That viper of a nephew listened, and made notes.'

Adam walked with him in silence.

'As a result of what I said, and I am most ashamed of my lapse, Goolamadail now appears to know about the abominable Sergeant Mailey.' He stopped and Adam, shocked, stood beside him.

'How much?'

'That I do not know. But possibly enough. And because of that knowledge, he is now threatening me. And, I should add, you too.'

'Threatening?'

'He wants me to give him the store. He says I am not to tell the police of his transgressions.' His hands, graceful as butterfly wings, fluttered at his sides. 'Unless I do as he demands, he threatens to expose me, you and all involved with the death of that Satan, Mailey.'

'What have you told him?'

'Nothing. He has, however, a supreme confidence which I find especially irritating. He is certain he will get all he demands. And these demands, of course, are but the first. My friend,' he said touching Adam on the shoulder, 'you are the one with most to lose through my unfortunate but unintended lapse. With me it does not matter. With you, a man of substance and, of course, the man who saved our lives by fighting and destroying the monster, it does matter. Which is why it is so propitious that you should call in tonight.' Saleem Benn turned and walked back towards his house. 'He knows many things. Other matters too, which are of no concern now. My words must have flowed like a stream in flood.' He laughed, a bitter sound. 'God protect us from our own weakness, eh?'

'Truly.' When Adam was with Saleem Benn, he found himself talking like the old man. 'Yes,' he added. 'Very true.'

They stopped outside the house.

'You want me to say what I think you should do?'

'Indeed. Your advice is always valued because of its great wisdom.'

'Kick him out.'

Saleem Benn looked surprised. 'Throw him out of the store?'

'Out of South Australia if you can. But certainly don't do what he asks. Just kick him out. Tell him to go to the police. And tell him that if he does, you'll have him in gaol for thieving from you.' Adam looked sharply at the old man. 'You can prove he stole from you?'

'Yes. We have the books. I could even summon a witness.'

'We'll play his game. Give him the choice of getting out or going to gaol. He strikes me as being a bit spineless. I'll bet he'd run.'

Saleem Benn slapped his knee. 'You would take the risk?'

'Sure.'

'Then I will throw him out.' He swung his arms with gusto. 'Into the dust. I would have him grovelling. And while he was there, I would help him cover the first yard of his journey by assisting him with my foot.' He launched a swinging kick into the night but then grew serious. 'Unhappily I will not be there for some time.'

'I'll be there tomorrow.'

The Afghan narrowed his eyes. 'You would pass on my

423

message? You would do this for me?'

'With pleasure.' Adam raised a finger. 'But if I throw him out, who will run the store for you?'

'Close it. It is only losing money with that worthless individual in charge. I will send someone up later. You would really do that for me?'

'It is my problem too.'

Saleem Benn grasped both Adam's hands. 'Truly, I would give a month of my life to see you confront this worm. Do not be gentle. Try to have his bowels palpitating before you actually throw him out on to the dust. Oh,' he said, pumping both hands up and down, 'I feel so much better. These last few days have been excruciatingly miserable.'

'If you say so,' Adam laughed.

The old man cocked his head. 'As well as correcting your Pushtu, I see I have also still to reveal to you some of the gems within your own language.'

'One day, my friend.'

Saleem Benn nodded contentedly. 'May we each be spared for that day.'

Flying into the early morning sun, the Piper had reached the eastern shores of Lake Eyre. Josef showed Cassie how to execute a left turn and slowly, straining to be smooth, she swung the nose to the north.

'Keep it up,' he called out. 'Aim it at the horizon. Your right wing's gone too far down. Bring it up again.'

Tongue out of the side of her mouth she coaxed the aircraft into level flight.'

'I didn't think it would be so hard keeping it straight,' she said.

'I thought you'd done this before.'

'I've never made a turn before.'

'You did it very well.'

'It was fun.' Glowing with joy, she concentrated on keeping the nose aimed at the horizon, the rudder steady, the wings level, and the throttle in the position Josef had shown her. There was little time for her to admire the view.

The coastline was a quilted maze of sandy mounds and ridges, grey-white salt pans and mud-streaked inlets. From a height, the effect was like fat splashed from a dish. They droned to the north. She checked the altimeter. Fifteen hundred feet.

A great channel of mud and sand, fringed by salt bush and low trees, came writhing across the eastern landscape. Josef checked his map. 'Cooper Creek,' he announced.

The coastline broke into a tangle of inlets and smaller lakes that sparkled in the sun. Josef pointed towards the left. The top of the lake was coming into view off to the north-west. Cassie applied minute pressure to the controls.

Josef laughed. 'Come on, give it a bit a muscle.' He took over and aimed the aircraft at a long, dark stain that spread down the bed of the lake in the distance.

She squealed with disappointment. 'I thought I was flying it.'

'You were trying to be so delicate we'd have been in the Northern Territory before we'd have turned.'

'Well I don't want to hurt it.'

'You won't hurt it.' He thrust the nose down, let the aircraft gather speed, then pulled it hard back. He levelled of at thirteen hundred feet.

'That was fun. Can I try?'

'Certainly not.' He raised his hands. 'But she's all yours. Just try and keep it straight.'

They flew towards the distinctive muddy stripe that projected into the lake. Josef consulted the map.

'That's the Warbuton Groove. It's where the Warburton spills on to the salt.' He checked the map again. 'The Warburton River runs from Goyders Lagoon, up on the Birdsville Track, and the Mulligan and the Diamantina run into Goyders Lagoon.' He put the map down and examined the groove. 'So whatever water gets down here to leave that filthy stain probably starts as rain, way up in Queensland.'

She peered out the side. 'I've heared of those rivers,' she said, smiling quickly at him and then checking to ensure the plane's altitude was correct. 'It's wonderful to see them.'

'That's flying for you.'

'Will you help me talk Dad into getting a plane? He should have one.'

He smiled. 'Who should?'

'We should.'

'You're a natural flyer. You'd get your licence really quickly.'

'I haven't even got my car licence.'

'But you can drive.'

'I know. I can drive anything on the property but I haven't got a licence because there's no one up here to give it to me.'

'I'll get one for you.'

'How will you do that?'

'You've just got to apply for one in this state. There's no test. I'll apply for you.'

'Would you?'

'Promise.' He looked down. They were over land. 'Where are we going? Alice Springs?'

'Well, where do we go?'

'Just keep turning left. Follow the edge of the lake.' Josef settled back. It was sunny and he felt drowsy. They came to the northern part of the delta where the Neales entered Lake Eyre. A broad arm of salt swept in from the west. Gently, proud of her skill in changing direction with such delicacy, Cassie followed the line of the river.

Josef, eyes open but seeing nothing, was thinking of the news about Adam. He was trying to imagine what Nina looked like. She'd be in her early thirties. He wondered if she still wore men's clothing. Funny but that was his most vivid recollection of her. He couldn't remember her face clearly, but he could have drawn with great accuracy what she wore: the cap, the jacket, the baggy pants, the long boots. And God, poor Nellie. He'd been hoping for so much. The big reunion. So maybe they wouldn't have got married but at least they could have become friends again; maybe more, who knows. All those lost years. He yawned and glanced at the compass. Almost west.

'Jesus Christ, where are we going?' He sat up in the seat.

Cassie was perplexed. 'Well I was following the edge of the salt but it seems to have got narrow.'

'It's got narrow all right. It's a river.' He looked at the map, checked his watch. 'Must be the Neales. No worries. Just turn south.'

She hesitated confused by the compass.

'Turn south. To the left, ninety degrees.'

'Where will that takes us?'

'Turn first, then ask questions.'

She banked the aircraft to the left and concentrated on keeping the nose on the horizon.

'Very good,' he said when she had completed the turn. He glanced out the window. 'Wonder where we are?'

'Well, if that was the Neales, we're probably over the northern part of our property. We run all the way up to the river.' She glanced to the left and right. 'It all looks so different from up in the air.'

They flew over a set of wheeltracks that stood out as clearly as fresh scratches on skin. Cassie was busy maintaining level flight and trying to comprehend the markings on the compass. Josef was intrigued by the tyre marks. 'Have you got a road up here?'

'No.' She kept her eyes on the horizon, wanting to be the first to see the homestead.

'Well, someone's been driving up here.' Eyes wrinkled against the glare, he followed the line of the tracks back towards the north west. The twin line ended in a puff of dust. 'Hang on a minute,' he said, taking over the controls. 'There's a car or a truck up there.'

'But it's our land,' she said, swivelling to the right. 'No one's up here today.'

'Well, there's someone there. Let's have a look.'

They chased the dust trail. It was being made by a large truck, travelling slowly over the virgin ground. As they drew closer, the truck crossed a small salt pan and the dust ceased. The vehicle had high, fenced sides. It was laden with cattle. The truck slowed to negotiate some sand at the end of the salt pan. The man behind the wheel looked up as the aircraft passed.

'Friend of yours?' Josef asked and began to turn the Piper.

'Don't think so. Never seen the truck before. What are you doing?'

Josef had put the plane into a dive. 'Going down to have a closer look. I think we might have caught ourselves a cattle duffer.'

'You mean he's nicking our cattle?'

'I don't think he's taking them away to clean their teeth. Hang on,' he said, levelling out at a hundred feet above the ground. 'Have a good look and see if you recognize the bloke as we go past.'

Throttling back almost to stalling speed, Josef flew towards the truck. There was only one man on board. He ducked low as they roared past.

'Didn't see his face,' Cassie called out as Josef applied more power and climbed to turn again.

'OK. We'll have another look.'

'This is fun.'

'Could be expensive fun. They're your stock he's stealing.'

'Wish we had a bomb. We could drop it on him.'

'And make a lot of hamburgers. Anyhow, this is a Piper, not a Flying Fortress. Here we go again. Now have a good look this time.'

He flew lower, and to the left of the vehicle so Cassie could get a clear view. The truck stopped. The driver got out and reached in the cabin for something.

With the aircraft yawing because of the low speed, they flew past the truck. Josef concentrated on keeping the plane flying at such a perilous altitude while Cassie peered intently at the man. He had lifted a rifle to his shoulder. Each heard the zing of a bullet striking the aircraft.

'He's shooting at us,' she exclaimed, her voice high in disbelief.

'Get your head down.' He pushed her down in the seat, applied more throttle and climbed away.

'No one hurt?'

'What a rotten type,' she said, and he laughed, excited by the action.

'People who steal other people's stock usually are. You're sure you're OK?'

'Good as gold. Did he hit the plane?'

'Somewhere.' He looked around the cabin. 'No broken perspex.' He bent to examine the undersides of the wings. 'No holes that I can see.'

'I didn't see his face that time either,' she said in a voice that suggested she was prepared for another attempt.

'We're not going back. I don't like men shooting at my nice new aeroplane.'

'So what do we do?'

'Go back to Kalinda and get on the radio. Call the police and alert the homesteads up this way.'

'Why don't we see where he's going?' She pointed ahead of them. 'He's following wheeltracks. He must have made them on the way in. Let's see where they go and if someone's waiting for him.'

He glanced at her with his mouth ready to smile. 'Have I ever told you you sound like your father?'

They followed the wheeltracks for another three minutes. The lines ran faint but straight across a flat and grassless plain and then dipped through a sandy creek bed. On the other side of the creek, the ground was rougher and sprinkled with low bush. Only then did Josef examine the instruments. 'Oh Jesus,' he said, and she turned to him in alarm. 'Look at the fuel.' He tapped the gauge. The needle was descending.

'We're losing gas,' he said frantically and began searching for a place to land.

'It's almost empty.'

'Indeed it is,' he said and banked towards the right. 'He must have hit the tank or a fuel line. We'll have to land.'

'Why not go back to that big plain?'

'Because he's driving along on that plain in a truck full of your cattle and he's got a gun and he likes shooting at us.' The engine stuttered. He pointed to the right. 'Over there.'

A long patch of hard ground, bare but for a few islands of spinifex, ran towards a wide expanse of salt. In the middle distance was a cluster of trees. Fishtailing on the rudder, Josef angled the Piper on a line that would avoid the spinifex clusters. As he drew closer, he saw the ground was rougher than he thought but it was

428

too late to change his mind. With a spluttering cough, the engine stopped and the comforting bellow of the motor gave way to the eerie whistle of rushing wind.

'Got your belt done up?'

'Yes.' She had her hands out.

'Cover your face. Know any prayers?'

'Yes.'

'Say one.'

Her lips began to move.

'Don't forget to include me,' he said and she laughed, just as the wheels touched the ground.

It was a perfect landing. The aircraft did not bounce or kick sideways. It just rolled along the ground, making a great rumbling noise from the tyres, but missing all the spinifex and larger rocks.

'That was good, Uncle Joe,' she said and smiled innocently at him.

'Good! It was bloody miraculous.' He leaned over and kissed her and she drew back, startled. The plane rolled near the group of trees before he braked. 'You must be my good luck charm,' he said. 'I can't land like that on a good airstrip with a full tank of fuel.'

She was smiling now, sharing her relief. 'So what do we do now?'

'You keep asking me that.' He scratched his head. 'We get out, hope our cattle-duffing friend doesn't come looking for us, and wait.'

'It's too far to walk,' she said, examining the country they would have to traverse to reach the homestead. 'Maybe seventy or eighty miles. I'm not sure. I've never been up here.'

She got out of the plane and he followed.

The belly of the fuselage was covered in petrol. He found a bullet hole just astern of the engine and searched for the damage. 'Lucky shot,' he said, wiping his hands. 'The bullet cut a fuel line.'

'Can you fix it?'

'I can't fix it and I haven't got any petrol to put in it. So we're here for a while, at least until someone comes looking for us.'

'How about your radio, Uncle Joe?'

'Doesn't work too well on the ground.' He grinned and rubbed his hands. 'But not to worry. There's food and water on board. We can have a little picnic. And seeing we're survivors of what's possibly the first and certainly the finest forced landing near the shores of Lake Eyre, you'd better stop calling me uncle because it makes me feel a hundred and ten.'

'What do I call you?'

'Josef. When you know me better you can call me Joe.'

They heard the truck pass in the distance but could not see it. Josef carried some of the gear from the aircraft and put it under a tree. Cassie collected wood for a signal fire. They settled down to await rescue.

T·E·N

Peppino Portelli arrived at Kalinda with a load of supplies, to be greeted by the news that no one was home. Mrs Wilson met him. She was there, of course, as were Stella and her children and Nellie, but the people the young Italian liked to see – Jimmy, Adam and, above all, Cassie –were all out.

'Mr Ross is in Adelaide,' Mrs Wilson said, enjoying the responsibility of passing on so much bad news. She regarded Portelli as a potential suitor of the eligible Cassandra Ross and he was not, she felt sure, of a sufficiently high calibre. Not until he had made some money, anyhow. 'Jimmy is out working at the Number Two and won't be back till this evening and Miss Cassie is in an aeroplane'.

'Sheeza what?' Portelli asked.

'In an aeroplane. Flying. A very good and old friend of the family arrived with his own personal aeroplane and he and Cassie have gone for a flight.' She was amused by the expression on Portelli's face. His jaw had dropped to a distance which invited dislocation.

'Where?'

'In the air.' She spun a forefinger above her head. 'Would you please take those supplies down to the shed and unload them? I'd give you a hand but I'm busy cooking.'

'Oh?' The jaw rose and the eyes showed interest.

'Cakes. They should be ready for morning tea. Possibly you'd care to join us? That's if you can spare time from your busy schedule.'

'Sure,' he said breezily. 'I gotta mainly drums a fuel.'

'You know where they go.'

'Yes sir, lady.' He jumped back in the truck. 'Ah, when the plane gonna come back?'

'When it does,' she said and went to bake her cakes.

Mrs Wilson was busy in the kitchen when the radio session was scheduled so she asked Stella to operate the set. The second telegram from Adam came through. She told Mrs Wilson.

'Did he say when he'd be here?'

'The telegram was lodged in Adelaide yesterday morning. He could be here today or tomorrow.'

'It's amazing,' Mrs Wilson said, resuming her whisking of the contents of a bowl with a vigour approaching ferocity, 'how many times a telegram telling you there'll be more people at the table arrives after you start cooking.'

'We hardly ever have visitors, but.'

'It still happens.'

Still tackling the logic of Mrs Wilson's complaint, Stella went in search of Nellie. She found her talking to Portelli at the shed.

'Got more news,' she said, drawing Nellie away from the truck. When they were on their own, she held Nellie by both arms. 'He's coming back.'

'Who?' At first Nellie turned towards the Italian but Stella pulled back.

'Adam. He'll be here today or tomorrow. We just got a telegram.'

Nellie's teeth played with her lower lip. 'Is he bringing her with him?'

'Didn't say. It was a message for Josef. It just told him to stay where he was because Adam was on his way up. Nellie, he probably wants to see you.'

'Don't be a drip, Stella. He doesn't know I'm here. He's probably bringing his wife up.'

'He's not married.'

'He could be by now.' Stepping back, she called out to Portelli. 'When are you going in to William Creek?'

He was rolling a drum into place in the shed. 'This morning. Soon as I finish.'

'Got room for a passenger?'

He pointed at her and smiled. 'You?'

'Me.'

'You catching tonight's-a train?'

'Yes.'

He noted Stella's sudden frown, and looked at her in case there was an objection. She shrugged. 'Sure,' he said. 'It's a bit rough.'

'That's all right.'

'She's had an operation,' Stella said. 'She shouldn't be shaken up.'

'I will drive-a very carefully.'

'I'll go and pack,' Nellie said.

'Nellie!'

'It's settled,' she said and walked back to the old homestead, the

432

building she and Adam once had shared.

Portelli, out of the shed once more, gazed up at the sky.

'Wonder where Cassie is?' he said.

'She's with a rich man from down south,' Stella said, and then winked. 'But it's all right. He's much older than you.'

Adam reached William Creek at midday. He had stopped to repair a puncture on the way and his hands were covered in grease and rubber dust. He drove straight to the store. Two women were in the shop. Goolamadail served them with a practised and languid insolence. As a result, Adam had to wait nearly fifteen minutes before the store was clear.

Goolamadail had watched him but not spoken while the women were present. He delivered a vestigial bow. 'Mr Adam Ross. I had heard you were in Adelaide.'

'I am in William Creek.'

The directness confused Goolamadail. He blinked.

'Doing good business?'

The man tilted his head and compressed his mouth to a degree which indicated modest success.

'A little for your uncle and a lot for you, eh?'

Goolamadail straightened. 'What do you mean?'

'I spoke to Saleem Benn yesterday. He told me you have been robbing him. He has proof. I told him he should go to the police.'

The Afghan was standing beneath a row of buckets that hung from the ceiling. A large and roughly hewn pole supported the roof. He put both hands on it, to steady himself. 'What do you mean?'

'That I think your uncle should go to the police and have you put in gaol for ten years or so.'

The man breathed deeply, struggling to regain composure. 'Is that all my uncle said?'

'He told me you were making threats. What they call blackmail.'

Goolamadail's teeth showed in a derisive smile. 'And you suggest the old fool calls the police. Do you know what I would tell the police?'

'Yes, and they wouldn't believe you. But they would believe your uncle. He has proof. There's no doubt. You're a thief and you'd go to gaol.'

Goolamadail put his face against the pole. 'I know about Mailey!'

'Mailey who?'

He blinked. 'You cannot bluff me, Mr Adam Ross. I will tell the police all about Mailey.'

433

'Good. Go ahead. When you've finished, we'll tell them all about you. Like to take a bet on who ends up in prison? They'll laugh at your story and put the handcuffs on you as soon as they hear about all the money you've stolen.'

'You have a bastard child.' He spat the words at Adam, who hit him. It was a wild, impulsive blow and it struck Goolamadail on the chest. He gasped with surprise and pain. Adam stood back.

'Don't you ever call my daughter that word.' He held his fists high.

'Your daughter?' He was about to speak further but Adam advanced. Goolamadail retreated. On the way he passed a scythe. He picked it up, flashing the wicked blade at Adam. 'Now we will see who is so strong,' he said and slashed in a crude semi-circle. The tip of the blade pierced a sack and stuck there. Grain spilled to the floor.

Adam took the scythe from him and put it against the wall.

Goolamadail, still retreating, passed a stand of rifles. He grabbed one but in the same instant Adam took it from him.

'Your uncle is a man of extraordinary generosity,' Adam said, catching Goolamadail by the shirt and lifting him from the ground. 'He said if I threw you out of the shop, he would not go to the police. Isn't that good of him?' He pressed Goolamadail against the wall at the back of the store. 'Me, I'd hang you from a hook on the ceiling, but your uncle is a much kinder man than me. So I'm only going to throw you out.' He banged the man against the wall. 'You happy with that?'

Goolamadail's eyes rose like twin full moons.

'Good. You have five minutes to pack what you need. If you say one word, about my daughter or anything else, I will knock your teeth out. If you say two words, I'll put them back in – but not in your mouth. Understand?' Adam shook him.

Teeth chattering, Goolamadail tried to nod.

Holding him by the collar, Adam guided the man to his room at the back of the store.

'I cannot pack in five minutes,' he said.

'I told you, one word.' Adam displayed his clenched fist. 'Believe me, I'd love to flatten you.'

'Where will I go?'

'To hell eventually. Just for the time being, make it as far away from here as you can.'

While Adam spoke, Goolamadail opened a drawer and wrapped a shirt around the leather pouch that contained the money he had accumulated. He put the shirt in a large canvas bag.

'What you are doing is illegal,' he said, putting other clothes in the bag.

'If you don't shut up, I'll carry you across to the pub,' Adam said, his voice rising, 'tell everyone there what you've been up to, and then carry you out to the shithouse and drop you into the pit.'

'You are a vulgar man.'

'I'm an angry man and you're a thief who's been robbing his uncle.' He took the bag. 'That'll do. Come on. You're catching tonight's train.'

'I will not go.'

'I'll wait and put you on the train myself. Unconscious if I have to.' He lifted the man and draped him over his shoulder.

'What are you doing?'

'I promised Saleem Benn I'd throw you out.' He carried the man, kicking and struggling, to the front of the store. There, he threw the bag on the dirt and then dumped Goolamadail at his feet. As he tried to rise, Adam planted a boot on the man's buttocks and pushed. Goolamadail sprawled in the dust.

'I promised Saleem Benn I'd do that,' he said, and realized he had an audience. Peppino Portelli had pulled up in his truck.

'What are you doing here?' Adam said, putting one foot on Goolamadail's back.

Astonished, Portelli looked from the man on the ground to the man standing on him. 'Justa drop someone at the pub,' he said. 'Whatsa hell goin' on?'

Adam scratched his chin. 'Where are you going now?'

'Down-a south.'

'Got room for this?'

'Whatsa hup?'

'Our friend Gooly has been robbing his uncle. Saleem Benn asked me to kick him out. I was going to put him on the train, but if you're going south ...'

'Robbin' the old-a man, hey?' Portelli got out of the truck and he too put a foot on Goolamadail's back. 'Wanna take 'im to the police?'

'No, just take him away. Anywhere.'

'Coward Springs OK?'

'Sounds perfect. Just watch him, Peppino. He's tricky.'

The Italian bent down and pulled Goolamadail to his feet. He held his fist up. 'You try-a somethin' tricky anna I do this.' He hit the Afghan hard on the forehead. The man's knees sagged. 'That'sa only a demo, understand?'

'Not too rough.' Adam had calmed down.

'Oh.' Portelli hit him again, but a little softer. The Afghan staggered back and tripped over his bag. Portelli picked him up and held him by one arm. 'Was that-a better?'

435

Adam shook his head and bit back a smile. 'Much better.'

'Good. I like-a the old man Saleem. If I a-tink about what he done, this bloke, I might-a hit 'im again, what you reckon?'

'Try and leave something to get off the truck at Coward Springs, won't you, Peppino?'

'Donna worry, Mr Ross.' He steered Goolamadail to the truck. 'When are you off?'

'Now. I'm a runnin' late. Hey, I was out your place. That Cassie. You know whatsa she doin?'

Adam shook his head.

'Flyin' in-a sky. Stella reckons a rich bloke's-a got a plane.'

'He's my friend Josef Hoffman and he's not rich man, Peppino.'

'Not-a rich, hey?' Portelli smiled. 'That'sa good. See ya.'

Adam watched him drive away. Then he walked to the hotel, to let people know the store would not be manned for a few days. He knew what would happen. People would take what they needed, make a list and pay whoever came to replace Goolamadail.

Goolamadail sat beside the driver, his hand to his sore forehead, his mind trying to absorb all that had happened in the last quarter of an hour. He would make this oaf beside him pay, and devise a truly exquisite method of revenge to hurt the devil Ross. Where was he being taken? Coward Springs, down the line towards Marree. That was fortunate. Coward Springs was where Ginger Thompson lived. Good. He would spend some time with him and devise ways to expand their cattle stealing enterprise, at the particular expense of Mr Adam Ross.

The train was due about eleven-thirty which, uncharacteristically, was only three hours behind schedule. Rather than wait at the station or anywhere else where she could be seen and recognized, Nellie booked one of the tiny rooms at the hotel. The publican had only been in town for two years, so she was a stranger to him. She planned catching the train to Marree, to spend a few days with Daniel and Saleem Benn and then go on to Lyndhurst, the railway settlement where the Strzelecki Track began. Then she would travel with the mail contractor on his rough and lonely drive to the Cooper. But first, she had to buy a train ticket.

She opened the door, walked along the dark corridor towards the hotel's side entrance and was about to step outside when she noticed a man on the verandah. He had his back to her and was leaning against a verandah post. Even after all these years, she recognized Adam immediately.

She had come to William Creek to avoid meeting Adam but now

that he was here and on his own, the desire to talk to him, to touch his hand, to explain everything, flooded through her. She was about to call out and step through the door when she realized he was not alone. There was another man, just out of sight.

'Yes, glad I ran into you,' the other man said in a slow voice that was cracked with age. 'And you haven't lost any cattle?'

'Not that I know of,' Adam said.

'Have a bit of a check. There seems to be something going on.'

'I will, Bert.'

'Anna Creek lost some about two weeks ago. They reckon about thirty head.'

'Yeah? Didn't stray?'

'Possible. They're tighter than most, though. Know what they've got and what's missing.'

'Good operation.'

'Bloody good.'

The other man walked into view. His legs were bent and he wore a large hat stained with grease spots. He had a stiff back and as he walked his arms moved like paddles. 'I'd keep an eye out if I was you,' he said and moved away from the building. Adam walked with him, slowing to the man's pace.

Nellie wanted to reach out and call Adam back, but she hesitated, intimidated by the presence of the other man. The two men walked out of sight, around the front of the building.

I'm being a fool, Nellie told herself. I should see him, say hello, and talk for a few minutes. I haven't got to tell him everything. Just make sure he knows I had good reasons for doing what I did, and that it wasn't his fault, and that I was thinking of him. Even if he's going to marry this American woman, I want us to be friends.

She heard the sound of a car engine starting.

I want him to understand, she thought, and not go through life thinking I'm just some sort of crazy bitch who gets angry and does hurtful things. I'm not like that although I do more stupid things than most people. But I don't try to hurt people and I didn't want to hurt him or Cassie.

Maybe we could talk and I could even go back with him to Kalinda and spend a few days there just talking and being there with him and Cassie. I'd like to see more of Cassie, seeing she was like my own kid once.

Breathing deeply with new-found resolution, Nellie walked to the front of the hotel. A cream Holden, its windscreen splattered with the remains of insects, drove past her. She saw Adam clearly. He had his head down, checking something on the seat. She called out and waved but he drove on, not hearing or seeing her.

Behind her on the hotel verandah, a man stood teetering on the brink of drunkenness. 'Like a drink, love?' he called out, brandishing a bottle as enticement.

Nellie wiped her face. 'No thanks.' She walked towards the railway station, to buy her ticket.

Josef spent much of the afternoon trying to fix the broken fuel line. There was a hacksaw blade in his tool kit and he cut away the damaged ends of the pipe. With a length of thin rubber hose and some wire to lock it in place, he began to fix the line. He had no petrol, but he felt it important to try and do something. Cassie watched him all the time, handing him pliers and taking away the blade when he no longer needed it. She said nothing that was not constructive but all the time he was aware of the feeling that if Adam had been here, he would have fixed it quickly.

The line repaired, he searched the cabin for items they would need if their stay stretched into days. He had no illusions about the likelihood of an early rescue. Someone would come looking for them eventually but Josef had a gnawing worry that it might take a while for a proper search to be organized. Adam was in Adelaide so Jimmy was in charge at Kalinda. Jimmy was no organizer. He was a do-it-yourself man and his reaction to hearing that the aircraft was missing would be to jump on one of the camels and go and look for himself. He was a magnificent tracker, but aircraft left no footprints.

The women, either Mrs Wilson or Stella Kettle, would get on the radio and alert the nearest homesteads but there were precious few in this part of the world and the nearest ones, like Muloorina and Anna Creek, were a couple of hundred miles away. The Flying Doctor might come looking. The trouble was, Josef realized, no one knew where they were. He had said they were going for a flight over the lake. The lake was bigger than many countries (he'd once gone through the index of his father's big atlas and found one hundred and thirty eight nations or states that were smaller than Lake Eyre) and the plane was not even on the lake. They were somewhere on the north-west side near the Neales River, on a desolate stretch of land. The only person who had seen them had shot them down, so there was no chance of that man telling anyone.

He emerged from the cabin with a carton of matches, a mirror which could be useful for signalling, a can-opener, a pocket knife, a one-gallon can of water and a small box containing food supplies. He had packed the box before his first flight in the Piper, when he had travelled from Toowoomba through Innamincka to Adelaide, but he had never opened it. He could not remember what was inside.

438

Cassie opened the box and found two bars of Cadbury's dark chocolate, a Hoadley's Violet Crumble bar, a packet of Lifesavers, a can of baked beans, a tin of sliced peaches in syrup, and a packet of Sao biscuits.

They sat in the shade beneath the wing. 'You were going to have a party?' she said, holding up one of the chocolate blocks.

'They were for nibbling. I wasn't exactly expecting to be in a situation like this.'

'How about this then?' She displayed the baked beans.

'In case I spent a night somewhere where there was no pub.'

He began to divide the food according to the days of the week. 'This will be for Tuesday,' he said, indicating half of a chocolate block. He pointed to the other half. 'This is for Wednesday. We'll have a splurge on Thursday and have half the can of baked beans and eat the rest on Friday. We can have a Sao every day for breakfast and a Lifesaver for supper.'

'How about the peaches?' Her eyes sparkled with the joy of joining in a game.

'They'll be our weekend treat.'

'And the other chocolate and the Violet Crumble bar?'

'They're for next week.' He was not smiling.

'Are you serious, Uncle Joe? Do you think we could be here that long?'

'I hope not, but it could be. And don't call me Uncle Joe.'

'I might start the fire.' She had already collected a large supply of dead wood. 'By the way, I took a rubber mat from the plane. I'll keep it beside the fire and throw it on if we need to make smoke. Do you mind?'

'No. That's a good idea.'

'Do you know, Josef,' she said standing and putting her hands on her hips, 'I think you and me are going to have a good time.'

'Don't let Mrs Wilson hear you talk like that.'

'What's wrong with having a good time?'

'Nothing. But you said you and me. It should be you and I.'

She sighed. 'You're as bad as Mrs Wilson.'

'I wish I could cook like her.' He surveyed their meagre rations. 'Do you really think we could be here for a week?'

'No,' he said, mustering as much confidence as he could. 'But it could be a few days before anyone gets here.'

She nodded, accepting that. 'I'll light the fire. At least there's plenty of wood.' She walked away. Watching her, Josef thought how uncommonly attractive she was from the rear.

Marie Kettle was well clear of the houses, waiting for Adam's car.

She had run down the road when she saw the dust of the approaching Holden. Adam stopped for her and the fourteen year-old climbed on to the front seat.

'Cassie's not back,' she announced breathlessly.

'Back from where?' Some of the station dogs had run to greet the car. They barked furiously and Adam shouted at them to get out of the way. 'Back from where?' he repeated, not being particularly curious.

'She and Mr Hoffman went up in the plane and they haven't come back.'

'They've missed lunch, have they?' he said, smiling at the girl.

'They missed breakfast too.'

Adam stopped the car. A sickening feeling stirred in his stomach. He could see Mrs Wilson and Stella waiting for him at the homestead steps. 'Did they go before breakfast?'

'Yes.'

'And they haven't come back?'

'No.'

He bent closer to the girl and his expression was so intense that she felt frightened, as though she were about to be accused of something.

'Were there just Mr Hoffman and Cassie in the plane?'

She nodded.

'Where did they go?'

She remained silent.

'Marie, where?'

'I don't know.'

He patted her shoulder and jumped from the car.

'When did they leave?' he called out to the women as he ran to the house.

'About seven,' Mrs Wilson said. 'I was expecting them back for breakfast. I cooked something special.'

Adam knew she was about to run through the menu so he held up a hand. 'What sort of plane has Joe got?'

Stella answered. 'A little one. It has a wing on top.'

'So they certainly wouldn't still be flying.' He checked his watch. It was after three. 'Do you know where they went?'

The women looked at each other and both spoke at the same time. To the lake, they chorused. Stella yielded seniority.

'Cassie wanted to see the lake,' Mrs Wilson said, wiping her hands constantly on her apron. 'She flew over it the other day as you know, and she said she wanted to see the rest of it.'

Adam stroked his chin. 'We went around the southern part. Which means they've probably gone up north.' He looked up at the women. 'Who else knows the plane's missing?'

Mrs Wilson lifted the apron and screwed it between her hands. 'Just us.' Nervously she glanced at Stella.

'We didn't want to start a scare,' Stella said. 'We didn't know ...'

Adam ran up the stairs. They moved back to make way for him. 'Are there just the two of them in the plane?'

Their heads bobbed in unison.

Adam looked along the verandah. 'Where's Nellie then?'

Neither spoke.

'She's here,' he said, irritated by their hesitancy. 'Mr Hoffman told me she flew up with Joe.'

Stella stood on one leg, hooking the other behind her knee. 'She's gone.'

'What do you mean gone? You said only Joe and Cassie were in the plane.' Nellie would have done something. She'd have been on the radio and started a search hours ago.

'Gone back.'

Mrs Wilson moved forward. 'She went back to William Creek. Mr Portelli gave her a lift.'

'Peppino? I saw him in town. He was on his own.'

Again the women found support in their mutual surprise.

'But she went with him,' Stella said. 'I saw them leave.'

Wait a minute, Adam thought. Peppino had said something about dropping someone at the pub. He had been so concerned about getting rid of Goolamadail that he hadn't thought any more about it.

'Doesn't matter for the moment,' he said, holding his hands in the air. 'She's not here so let's worry about the missing plane. Now, here's what we do. Mrs Wilson, get on the radio now. Call up Elliot Price at Muloorina, then see if you can raise Anna Creek or anyone else nearby, and tell them what's happened. Ask Elliot if he could send someone out to check the southern part of the lake. You never know. And get on to the Flying Doctor. Tell him we think we've got an aircraft down.'

She nodded. 'And what do I say?'

'Tell them who's on the plane, tell them it's a little one ...' He paused. 'How many engines?'

The women looked at each other. 'It's got one propeller,' Stella said.

'Tell them that it's got one engine, that they took off at seven and that we think they might have gone to the north of the lake.'

'But you want Mr Price at Muloorina to check the southern part,' Mrs Wilson added.

'That's right. Where's Jimmy?'

Stella answered. 'At the Number Two bore. He took the Land Rover .'

'OK. I'll drive over there and see him. We'll have a look around until dark, then we'll come back here. Stella, could you fetch a few things for me?'

Anxiously, she nodded.

'The first aid kit,' he said and each woman put a hand to her face. 'A little food and a four-gallon drum of water.'

'You think they'll be hungry and thirsty?' Mrs Wilson asked, her professional interest in feeding people being aroused.

Adam gave a wry smile. Mrs Wilson would attend a funeral and be more concerned about feeding the living than farewelling the dead. 'It's in case I get stuck,' he said. The women went inside.

Alone, he shivered. There was some bad country up north. At least the lake was big and flat and much of it would make a perfect landing field. As long as Josef didn't try to land near the edges, because the thin crust near the shore was deadly. That's if Josef was able to make a landing. The alternative was too horrifying to contemplate. He had seen a plane crash during the war. It had been a terrible sight.

He turned from the house. Dear God, don't allow that to have happened to Cassie and Josef. Not those two. Let them be safe, and let me find them. Marie was near the car and staring at him, surprised to see him looking up at the sky and moving his lips. Feeling foolish, he smiled at her and got back in the car.

In a conventional car, the drive to the bore was extremely difficult. Several times, Adam had to engage low gear and charge through areas of soft sand. He arrived at the windmill going so fast that when he braked, the back end of the car spun wide and he stopped in a storm of dust and pebbles. The two camels in the yard reared like rocking horses and gurgled foul sounds. Jimmy was not there. However, he soon arrived, driving the Land Rover down the valley between the dunes, having heard the sound of the Holden racing towards the site. He knew it was an emergency. Adam never brought the car here.

'I thought you were in Adelaide,' he began but Adam silenced him and told him what had happened. The most likely occurrence, Adam said (and hoped that he was correct) was that Josef had suffered some minor mechanical problem and had made a landing on the salt. Neither knew what the lake was like up north because neither had been that far but, Adam recalled, the scientist who had come to the area a couple of years ago had said the lowest part of the lake was down south. That meant the thickest salt would be there too.

'Therefore,' Adam continued, 'if he's had to land up north, he could have broken through the crust.'

Jimmy completed the thought. 'And tipped the thing arse over head.' Each was silent for a moment. They were probably a hundred miles from the northern shore of the lake. 'So what do we do?' Jimmy said.

'Check the lake as far as we can while there's light. We take the camels. We can't drive on to the salt because the crust is too thin at the edges.'

They saddled the camels, put their supplies, first aid kit and two rifles in the panniers, and rode together to the east. The journey took half an hour. They reached the lake near the point where Adam had taken Nina. The camels reared and curled their long necks and both men had to dismount and lead the animals on to the crust. The salt swayed under their weight. In places it cracked into large plates and they walked as though stepping from one moored barge to another. But as they progressed from the shore, the salt became firmer and the camels quietened. They remounted and, travelling side by side, trotted from the bay towards the main body of Lake Eyre.

A squadron of pelicans flew overhead, *en route* to their nesting grounds.

The two men halted, so far from the shore that no land was visible. They were surrounded by a static ocean of white.

'Be dark in an hour,' Jimmy said. 'Don't want to get stuck out here.'

Adam was still looking around them, anxiously seeking some break in the awful symmetry of salt. He took one rifle. 'You ride south, I ride north. Go for twenty minutes. Then we come back.'

'And if we see something?'

'Fire one shot.'

Jimmy turned his camel. 'See you back here in forty minutes.'

'No longer,' Adam warned.

'Don't worry. For an old blackfeller like me, every minute out here is a minute too long. Come on.' He goaded his camel into a run.

The lake's surface was patterned like a mammoth net. Fine ridges criss-crossed the salt. Formed from lines of pure, sparkling crystals, they were as low and meandering as the furrows left by tunnelling worms. Within this network of ridges, the surface was littered with foreign objects that had been blown on to the lake and consumed by the salt: insects, a dead bird, an uprooted bush, twigs, leaves. All had been overwhelmed by the rising moisture and the growing crystals and were forming salt islands. Some islands, which had grown over the years from a foundation of one dead grasshopper, were big, as much as twenty yards across, and because their edges rose precipitously they caught any wind-blown dust. They were rimmed in brown and, from a distance, resembled gigantic upturned fried eggs.

Adam, stretching the camel to its fastest pace, passed a pair of white lizards which broke their perfect camouflage to scurry away from the galloping intruder.

After a few minutes he slowed. The pace was too fast and he was concentrating on staying in the saddle, not searching the lake. At a cruising jog he continued, conscious now of the wheezing of the beast and aware that no matter how far he travelled, the view seemed never to change. This was a terrifying, empty place, ringed by mirages.

Eventually he stopped and checked his watch. Seventeen minutes. The sun was low now. With cooler air, visibility was improving but the view was the same: an endless expanse of salt, pimpled by flat salt islands and criss-crossed by delicate salt ridges. There was no sign of land, no sign of an aeroplane, no sign of humans. He searched for smoke or for any suggestion of movement. He listened for a sound. There was nothing. He shouted and the noise disappeared.

It was time to go back. Rather than return along his own tracks, Adam rode the camel half a mile to the east and then turned south, riding at a gentler pace and concentrating on the view to the west. The surface was now a pastel pink and he could see an immense distance, but all he saw was salt.

He was, perhaps, one tenth of the way across the lake. To search the whole area would take weeks, for there was the mass of the lake to check, plus gulfs and bays and estuaries.

He first saw Jimmy's camel when they were still several miles away. As if by signal, each man turned towards the west, so that their paths would intercept near the coast. Now that the light was fading, each was anxious to reach land as soon as possible. The lake was no place to be lost in the dark.

Only then, when he had abandoned hope of sighting the plane that day, did Adam think of Nellie. Why had she returned and gone away without seeing him? It was a question that puzzled him all the way to the shore where, ten minutes after sunset, he and Jimmy were reunited.

E·L·E·V·E·N

Mrs Wilson was waiting at the homestead when the two vehicles drove in, the headlamps of one spearing the dust trail of the other. She had been on the radio, as Adam had requested. The Flying Doctor would send an aircraft in the morning to fly over the lake. It would take off at first light and land at Kalinda around nine, to report on what the pilot had seen. The people at Muloorina would start a search in the morning. Two parties would go out, one to scour the shores of Madigan Gulf, the other to check the area around Jackboot Bay.

'That's good of Elliot,' Adam mused. 'They'll be out at least two days.'

'I also asked the Flying Doctor to get in touch with Mr and Mrs Hoffman,' Mrs Wilson said. 'I'd hate them to hear on the radio that Josef was missing.'

'I'd forgotten,' Adam said. 'That was very thoughtful of you.' He looked up. 'I must send a telegram to Nina, too.'

She wiped her hands on her apron. 'I'll send one for you in the morning. You'll be busy.'

Adam planned spending the night in the workshop finishing a special vehicle that could take him around the perimeter of the lake. He had begun to construct the device months ago, but had never found time to finish it. No ordinary vehicle would do the journey. The Land Rover, despite its advantage of four-wheel-drive, was too heavy and its narrow tyres sawed through salt, sand or any soft surface and left the machine bogged to the chassis.

Adam's creation was crude but had the advantages of simplicity and light weight. He had already welded together a metal ladder-frame and bolted to that an old wooden door, which acted as a floor and splash guard. The engine was a twin cylinder air-cooled motor from a BSA motor cycle. It drove the back wheels through the motor cycle gearbox and a chain. There was a single seat, a steering wheel and a fuel tank. As yet, the vehicle had no brakes but they had never been a priority because Adam reckoned there weren't too many things to hit in the country where he intended to drive.

This was a vehicle to romp over sand-hills, coast across the salt and even float through the swamps that ringed the lake. It was so light he could lift it out of a bog and roll it, like a wheelbarrow, to firmer terrain.

The wheels had yet to be fitted. Adam had bought four old aircraft tyres that were fat and almost treadless, which made them perfect for sand. The wheels were much wider than on any car but he had to weld plates to them and drill those plates to fit the hubs he had made. With low pressure in the ultra-wide tyres, he and the 'flying ladder' as Jimmy called it, should be able to accomplish a journey that would defeat any other wheeled vehicle.

If the Flying Doctor found nothing, he would set off immediately to the north, and would keep going in a clockwise direction and drive around the lake until he reached the far side of Madigan Gulf. Jimmy would take the camels and head south, searching the hundred miles of coastline that led to Jackboot Bay. That way, between the people of Muloorina and themselves, they would cover all the coastline.

Before going to the workshop, Adam took Stella to one side. 'Why did Nellie come back?'

Her eyes swept the room, longing to find some diversion. There being none, she said, 'She wanted to see Cassie.'

'Did Cassie remember her?'

'Not really.' She smiled sadly.

Adam went to the kitchen to get some water. 'How is she?' he called out.

'She's been sick.'

'So I heard. Is she better?'

'She's still very weak.' She waited for him to finish drinking. 'She had to rest a lot.'

'And she's going back on tonight's train?' She said nothing and he came back into the room. 'That's a rough trip for anyone.'

'I know.' She nodded, her face mournful in anticipation of the miseries Nellie would have to endure.

He faced her. 'Why, Stella? Why did she come back? And where's she been?'

She shook her head.

'You mean she just came, and went away again. After all these years?' Again silence. He took a deep breath. 'And you don't know why she left?'

She didn't face him.

He went to the door. 'Maybe we'll talk about it later. There's too much to think about at the moment.' He walked to the workshop. A cool breeze was blowing. Later on, it would be freezing out on the lake, he thought, and hurried to start work on the vehicle. He wanted to have it completed, running and tested by the time the Flying Doctor arrived.

A gust of wind blew through the place where Cassie and Josef were camped, tearing a sheaf of sparks from the fire and scattering shooting stars into the night. Cassie had built a big fire, both as a bright signal to any potential rescuer and as a boost to her own confidence. She felt better with flames driving back the boundaries of darkness, and the bigger the flames, the better she felt. While Josef had spent the last hours before sunset going over the aircraft to check for any other damage, she had dragged timber to the campsite. Fortunately, they had landed near a slight rise littered with the withered branches of dead scrub and she had already gathered sufficient wood to keep the blaze going for several days. They would have a small, smoky fire in the daytime, and a big, crackling, cheerful fire at night.

The wind drove smoke towards her and she moved away, shivering. 'I didn't bring a jumper,' she said.

'I didn't bring a toothbrush.' Josef was wearing a short-sleeved shirt and he wrapped his arms across his shoulders.

She smiled and shivered again and said, 'Neither did I. We had a shearer here last year who was such a good-looking man but when he opened his mouth he had a breath that would drop a bullock at a hundred yards.'

'Really?' Josef wondered about his own breath.

'What are we having for dinner tonight?'

'Half a chocolate bar.'

'You don't think we should be daring and start with baked beans, do you Uncle Joe?' She saw his reproachful look and immediately corrected herself. 'Josef. What do you say?'

'I say chocolate. If you behave yourself, we'll have a biscuit for supper.'

'One between us?'

'One each.'

'Tonight's a special occasion, is that it?'

'Right.'

'What is it?' Her face was eager, anticipating a witty reply.

He groped for an adequate response. 'This is the first night we've been out together,' he said and she regarded him seriously.

'You mean like boy-friend and girl-friend?'

'Absolutely.' He beamed his most avuncular smile.

447

'I've never had a boy-friend.'

'Well, let me be your first.'

'What do boy-friends do?'

He coughed. 'The first thing a good boy-friend should do is feed his young lady.'

'Am I your young lady or your girl-friend?' she asked as he took one of the chocolate blocks from the box and broke it in half. It did not part evenly.

'Girl-friend,' he said. 'It sounds more exciting. Now, we have a problem.' He displayed the two parts of the chocolate. 'One is bigger than the other so we have a dilemma. Do we eat the larger one or the smaller one?'

'Are you asking me?'

'Lady's choice.'

'Well, seeing I'm your first girl-friend . . .'

'Cassandra,' he said sombrely, 'I may be your first boy-friend but I have to advise that you are not my first girl-friend.'

'Let's have the big piece, seeing it's tonight. And while we eat, you can tell me about your other girl-friends.'

Twenty-five miles away, another campfire was burning. This was much smaller, only large enough to roast meat and boil a billy of water. In the darkness beyond the fire, a windmill turned slowly, its many blades flashing faint reflections of spluttering flames. Cattle were penned in a makeshift stockyard built among some trees. Two trucks – one big, one smaller – were parked nearby. Two men sat at the fire, talking to the accompaniment of the clanking windmill and the restless lowing of the cattle.

The younger man drank from an enamel mug. 'Reckon it's safe to go back tomorrow?'

'Flamin' oath,' Ginger Thompson said. 'I got a dozen head ready to be picked up and I'm not leavin' those for the dingoes.'

'But what about that plane?'

'They won't be back.' He stared in the fire. 'I'll give 'em another belly full of lead if they do.'

'Where were they from?'

'Wouldn't 'ave a clue.'

'What if they tell someone?'

'Course they'll tell someone. But who?' He laughed. 'Ross is in Adelaide and no one could get up here by tomorrow morning from any other property. In any case, I'm making another track.'

'Jeeze, I don't like it.'

'You don't have to like it. Just do like I tell you.'

448

The other man cleared his nose. 'Why don't we just nick off? We got enough now.'

Thompson grinned. 'They're for Gooly and me. This lot tomorrow's for you and me.'

By eleven, Josef had run through an edited and entertaining account of his affairs with various women. While not of the fairy-tale quality, they were still reasonably pure, the story of an innocent's quest for the perfect woman.

'You've been very unlucky, Josef.' Cassie, being certain of her wood supply, had started a second fire and they sat between them, warming each side. 'You say I met Sarah Mandelton. I don't remember her.'

'You were tiny.'

'She sounds nice.'

'She was.' Josef was enjoying the pretence. Not only were the events of his various courtships suitably modified but the participants had been pruned of most vices.

'Why did she leave you, then?'

'I decided I didn't love her.' He paused for dramatic effect, and to shuffle a little closer to one fire. His back was cold. 'She behaved rather strangely. I think it was the effect the outback had on her. It unsettled her in some way.'

'Why should it do that?'

'Some people find the distances alarming. You know, if you're used to crowds it's hard to cope with the space and the emptiness up here. Anyhow, it rattled her, and shook away the veneer, and that beautiful, elegant, sophisticated exterior just crumbled and fell and, for the first time, I saw her as she truly was.'

She glanced at him admiringly. 'You use nice words.'

He played with a small, smooth stone. 'I like nice words. You can't express your thoughts adequately if you don't know the words that convey exactly how you feel.'

'I suppose not.' She shivered. 'I'm sleepy but I'm too cold to go to sleep.'

They had tried sitting in the aircraft's cabin but it was freezingly cold away from the fire. Josef had found an empty box in the back of the plane, and had spread the cardboard on the ground.

'I've got to lie down,' she said. 'Otherwise I'll fall over and miss this warm cardboard mattress you found.'

He moved out of the way.

'No, you lie down too,' she said. 'You get on your side and I'll lie in front of you and I can cuddle into you and then we'll both feel warmer.'

'Cassie! I can't do that.'

'Why not? There's room.' She smiled, recalling earlier years. 'Dad and I used to do it when we were out trapping dingoes at night and it got cold.'

'But how old were you then?'

'I don't know.' She searched the fire for inspiration. 'Eight or nine.'

'And now you're seventeen.'

'So what? I'm just as cold. Come on.' She got into place, lying on her side with her knees bent up. 'Now you get behind me and do the same thing.'

He did not move.

'Josef,' she chided. Then, smiling, 'Uncle Joe! I'll freeze and then who'll get wood to keep you warm. Come on.' She reached for his hand and pulled him down.

He lay behind her, legs straight.

'Bend your knees,' she said, hooking one foot around one of his legs and pulling it into her. 'That's better.' She searched for his arm. 'Here, put it around me like this.' She pulled his hands around her waist and held her arms tightly over his. 'Isn't that good?'

'Jesus,' he muttered, and she wormed her body closer into his.

Adam completed the 'flying ladder' by three-thirty in the morning, slept until five and had it tested by six. He took it for a run over the nearest dune. It went well. He had built a long extension to the BSA gearbox and while the lever rattled a lot, the gear changes worked. He took the machine back to the workshop and packed on board extra fuel and oil, water, food, the first aid kit, tools, a shovel, axe, rope and his rifle. He had breakfast and prepared to wait for the Flying Doctor.

At eight, the homestead received a radio message to say the Flying Doctor would not be landing. The aircraft had been diverted to a station on the Birdsville Track, where a stockman had broken his leg. However the pilot had already flown up the lake, keeping close to the eastern perimeter, and had begun to cross to the western shore when he received the distress call. He had seen no sign of the missing Piper.

Within minutes, Adam was driving north in his strange machine.

He had wrapped his mixed load in a canvas sheet and tied it to the wooden floor but, after half a mile, it began to shake loose so he stopped and resecured the ropes. There was room for two people to sit on the platform, although their comfort would be minimal and he wondered if he should have brought cushions. There was also space, he noted sombrely, for two people to lie or be placed along the structure, one either side of his driving seat.

The vehicle had no springs but the tyres were so pliant – he had set them at five pounds per square inch – that the flexing rubber absorbed most of the bumps.

He drove to a place where he could see the lake's glistening salt clearly and where he estimated he was within half a mile of the shore. Then he turned to the north, and followed that line as consistently as he could. Occasionally he stopped to climb a low hill and check the view. Sometimes he veered to the right, when a spit of land projected into the lake and he felt he was driving too far from the salt. At other times he had to loop to the left to avoid a bay or the marshy overflow of some scoured water-course.

He crossed sand-hills with ease, charging up the sides and soaring from the sharpest ridges. The fat, soft tyres floated on the loose surface. To the delicate patterns of lizard tracks, the star-like imprints of fossicking birds and the gentle terraces formed by the wind, he added his own urgent and incongruous set of marks: the broad and parallel lines left by a man growing more concerned by the minute. Each dune, each crumbling crest, revealed the same outlook: more ridges, scoured salt pans, the vastness of the lake and not a sign of another being.

He came to a wide expanse of sand and salt. This was where the southern branch of the Neales ran towards the lake. He knew, from previous journeys by camel, that a large triangular island lay beyond the river. If he drove across the island for another twenty miles, he would come to the northern and larger branch of the delta. To keep within sight of the lake, he had to cross the river but the river crossing was wide and the mud and salt looked perilously soft.

He tried at a place where the crust seemed firm. The front wheels immediately broke the salt into thin plates that showed glutinous black mud on their exposed undersides. The vehicle stopped, its front tyres already coated with mud. As no reverse gear was fitted, Adam got out and dragged the device back to firm ground.

He turned to the right and drove to the point where the river entered the lake. He climbed a low and eroded headland and spent several minutes squinting into the glare, to search the lake for any sign of the plane. Finding nothing, he drove back along the river bank, seeking a safe place to cross.

The river remained wide, with a base as treacherous as quicksand. Several times he stopped to explore on foot but always the inviting salt layer cracked and his boot would sink to the ankle.

Chafing at having to make such a detour, he crossed a sandy creek and then drove along the edge of a wide plain that stretched south from the river bank. The ground began to change. There was less sand. The surface was rock hard and covered in patches of white, as though cement had spilled across the plain. Keeping as close to the river as practicable, Adam came to a small dip filled with powdery dust. He stopped, astonished, for the dust was neatly cut by a set of wheeltracks.

He got out. No vehicles ever came up here. He walked around the hollow, studying the tracks. They were the imprints of big, bar-tread tyres, and they were fresh. No wind had burred the sharp edges moulded in the dust, so they might have been made during the night or earlier that morning. He bent to examine the tracks. They had been made by a truck, and a large one. Whose? He stood up, scratching his head.

Someone might have seen the plane going down, and driven up here, searching for it. Which way had the truck been travelling? He presumed it had come from the west and had been heading towards the lake but when he examined the tracks again, the distinctive tyre pattern indicated the truck had been heading away from the lake. Maybe the driver had found the plane, picked up Cassie and Josef and was taking them west to the railway line or one of the other homesteads south of Oodnadatta. That was more like it. Heart pounding, he jumped into his vehicle and set off to follow the tracks.

Despite the hard ground and the cold wind, Cassie and Josef had eventually fallen asleep around two in the morning. As a result, the fires burned down. Well before dawn, the couple awoke chilled and stiff, and spent the last part of their night carrying wood to rekindle the flames.

They made one large fire only and stamped around it to get some warmth in their limbs. When the sun rose, they greeted its welcome arrival by eating a biscuit and drinking a little water.

With the air warming, they let the fire settle but added bark and leaves and sprinkled them with engine oil from the aircraft. A thin column of black smoke rose in the air.

Josef looked on with satisfaction. 'I reckon it would have taken all yesterday for people to realize we were in trouble and to get organized. They'll be out today. What are the odds we see someone this morning?'

Cassie smiled cheerfully.

For the next half hour, they busied themselves by gathering more wood until they had built a high pile of dry timber at the side of the fire.

At one stage, they thought they heard the distant drone of an aircraft but the sound faded and though they searched the sky for

452

many minutes afterwards, there was no sign of a search plane. They discussed the sound and agreed that it could have been an aircraft over the lake or the wind ruffling a distant grove of trees. They preferred the latter explanation. It was easier to accept.

About two hours later, they heard another noise. At first it seemed to flirt with their imaginations, a will o' the wisp of sound that buzzed and retreated and floated on the edge of certainty. Then it went away, but within a minute the noise returned, loud and clear. It was a motor, working hard.

'Someone's coming,' Cassie said. She had the sharper hearing but Josef nodded and they smiled at each other, the tension of the last twenty-four hours seeping away with the prospect of rescue.

Josef handed her the remaining part of the chocolate block. 'Go you halves.' Eagerly she took it and they were eating chocolate when the vehicle came into sight. They stopped chewing. It was the truck they had seen the previous day.

The big vehicle was at the far end of the strip on which Josef had made his forced landing. It stopped, then turned and came towards them.

Josef spat out his chocolate. 'He fired at us yesterday. God knows what he'll do today.'

'He might give us a lift,' he said but her face contradicted the words.

Josef shook his head savagely. 'Let's get out of here.'

She looked around them at the sparse cover. 'Where to?'

He was breathing quickly but thinking too slowly. 'Well, you go. Hide in the trees. Lie behind the pile of wood. Do something. Get out of the way.'

'What about you?'

'Go.' He slapped her bottom.

Bent double, she ran for the shelter of the stack of dry timber and knelt behind it. She took one long piece of wood and held it like a club.

Again, the truck was laden with cattle. It rolled up to the crippled Piper, stopped while the driver examined the plane, and then turned in a slow circle that brought the truck between the aircraft and the fire.

With the truck engine still running, Ginger Thompson got out and brought a rifle with him.

'What 'ave we got 'ere?' A cigarette bobbed with each word.

'G'day,' Josef said, trying to be bright. 'Glad someone came along.'

'Yeah? What ya doin'?'

'Just waiting for our service crew.' Josef hadn't planned saying

453

that but he was pleased with the words, and the reaction from the other man.

Thompson looked around him, scanning the sky and the wide plain with great concern. Eventually he moved the cigarette to the other side of his mouth. 'This your plane?'

'Yes.'

'On your own?'

'No, I've got the plane.' He attempted a laugh. 'Actually, I'm out of fuel. Haven't got any aviation gasoline, I don't suppose?'

'Not on me.' The man put the rifle under his arm. 'What ya doin' out here anyhow?'

'Aerial survey work,' Josef said.

'Survey?'

'My company's looking for minerals.'

'What sort?'

Josef blew his nose, to give himself time to think. 'Beryllium,' he said and the man's expression did not flicker. 'Lithium, rutile, obsidian.' He winced as he said the last one; his mother had an ornament made of obsidian on the mantlepiece at home, but it was the only word he could think of. 'Those sorts of things,' he added as though the man were familiar with mineral exploration. 'There's a lot of interest in this area.'

'Yeah?' Thompson took the cigarette from his lips and blew smoke. 'What's the trouble with your plane?'

'No gas.'

'You told me. But why?'

Josef coughed. 'Actually a funny thing happened. I was flying on a set course yesterday, you know one of those low runs where you have to go backwards and forwards over the same piece of ground to get the readings, and there was this big yellow truck on the ground.'

'Yeah?' Thompson's truck was red. He looked back to make sure.

'The fellow must have been mad. He took a shot at me.'

'The driver?'

'Yes. Hit a fuel line. I was lucky to land.'

'What did the bloke look like?'

'I wasn't even taking much notice of the truck, let alone the driver. I was concentrating on the instruments. You know, the ones that show what minerals are in the ground.'

'That so?'

'Yes. I don't know what he was up to.'

'No.' Thompson took the rifle in one hand. 'Let's look at this plane of yours.'

454

'Sure.' Josef looked up. 'The others should arrive any minute. They said they'd be here by ten. Any idea of the time?'

'No.' He waved the rifle for Josef to lead him to the Piper. 'I want to see all these instruments of yours.'

'Be glad to show you.' They walked around the truck.

Behind the pile of wood, Cassie sat up. She saw the man leave and strained to hear what they were saying. 'Carryin' any money?' she heard the other man ask Josef.

'Don't have any need. No shops up here.' There was a laugh, but only from Josef.

'Don't give me that bullshit.'

Cassie heard the click of a rifle bolt. She stood up and ran to the truck. The voices were clearer now.

'You know who put the bullet into you yesterday so don't give me all this crap.'

'Was that you?' Josef said, as though he'd been pleasantly surprised.

Hidden from the men by the back wheels, Cassie leaned against the wooden side of the truck. It pulsed with vibrations from the idling motor. The cattle were restless and the rails creaked as the animals, frightened by her sudden appearance, shuffled away from her. They were a wild lot, the cattle up here. Jimmy had brought them up and her dad said Jimmy could bring them back again. The truck swayed as one particularly nervous beast cannoned into the side. The wood made an alarming noise, as though it were about to split and, in confusion, she heard another sound above all the others; a strange noise like a motor bike in the distance.

She still had the piece of wood in her hand. She could slip around the back of the truck and hit the man on the head – provided he didn't see her or shoot Josef first.

'Ya got bloody money,' the man was saying and then he shouted an oath and there was the sound of a scuffle.

Cassie ran to the back of the truck. Josef was fighting the man. He had grabbed the rifle and they were wrestling, each gripping the gun. She thought of running to them and clubbing the man but as she watched they fell and rolled in the dust.

The motor-bike noise was growing louder. She looked down the strip and saw a strange sight. A platform with four wheels and a man sitting in the middle was driving towards them.

Thompson got up first. The rifle was still on the ground. He saw Cassie, picked up the gun and prepared to fire. She jumped for the back of the truck. The cattle surged away from her. A bullet ricochetted off a metal hinge on the tail gate.

Cassie wanted to help Josef, she wanted to stay alive, she didn't

455

want to lose Kalinda's stock to a cattle duffer and, in an instant, she thought of a way to assist each cause.

She pulled the bolt that held the gate in place. The rear swung down. It formed a ramp to the ground and the cattle, wild and wide-eyed, backed away from the sudden opening. Working her way along the rails, she leaned over the top yelling and beating on the hide of the nearest animal. One steer bolted for the opening and stumbled down the ramp. She shouted and whacked another animal. As one, they raced to get out.

She dropped to the ground, shouting and waving her arms to force the cattle to the other side of the truck.

Thompson was confused. He had now seen the man approaching on the spindly vehicle, Josef had regained his feet and was shaping up for a fist fight, and six steers being driven by a girl were charging him. He ran for the front of the truck.

A steer knocked Josef and sent him spinning to his knees. Cassie ran to him. She heard the truck engine roar and pulled Josef to one side as Thompson drove away, tail ramp dragging on the ground. And then her father arrived, jumping from the crude car she now recognized as the machine he had been working on for months, and running towards them while the car rolled on.

'Are you all right?' he shouted and she flung herself into his arms.

'Joe?'

Josef waved an arm. 'I'm OK. Just did a spot of bullfighting,' he wheezed.

Cassie was jumping up and down in excitement. 'He's getting away.'

'What the hell's happening?'

'We're OK,' she said, breathing heavily from the exertion of the last few minutes. 'But that man was stealing our cattle and he's getting away.'

'He shot us down,' Josef gasped.

'Daddy,' she pleaded, watching the truck roar further away.

Adam ran after the machine, which had rolled to a stop beyond the fire. 'Come on!' She sprinted after him. Laboriously, Josef got to his feet.

Adam turned the machine. Cassie jumped on the front, clutching the rope holding the canvas bundle in place. He drove back to the plane.

'Are you all right, Joe?'

'Sure.' Still bent over, Josef waved.

'Be back in a minute.' Adam opened the throttle and raced in pursuit of the truck.

456

'This is great!' Cassie shouted, her hair streaming in the rushing air. 'When did you finish it?'

'Last night. Get the rifle. It's in the bundle.'

She extricated the gun.

'Reckon you could hit his tyres if I got close?'

She turned with a huge grin on her face.

'Get me close enough and I'll take the wax out of his ears.' She held her hair with one hand. 'How did you find us?'

'The tyre marks from that truck. I followed them. I thought he might have given you a lift.'

'He tried to shoot me,' she shouted, and then checked the rifle, for they were catching the truck and were now in its dust trail.

'Hang on,' Adam called. Blinded by dust, he pulled to one side. They ran over a bush, and had a few frantic moments disentangling themselves from pieces of broken branch. He slowed momentarily but then accelerated, now clear of the trail of dust and able to see where he was driving.

In his run to the north, Adam had never engaged a gear higher than second because he had been intent on searching the countryside and needed no more than a modest pace. Now, for the first time, he changed into fourth gear and gave the engine full throttle. Cassie screamed with delight.

Bouncing, weaving slightly and occasionally leaving the ground when they were launched from a ramp of raised earth, Adam and Cassie overhauled the fleeing Thompson. They drew level and Adam slowed to the pace of the truck.

'Now,' he shouted, 'go for his tyres, not the wax in his ears.'

She was close enough to see Thompson's face staring at them, his expression a mixture of fear and astonishment. She lifted the rifle and he ducked out of sight.

They hit a bump.

'It's too rough,' she shouted.

'Like me to have a go?' Adam said and that was all the provocation she needed. She was as good a shot as he was. Both knew that.

She raised the rifle, letting her knees and body absorb the bumps and holding the sights on the front wheel. She fired.

The wall of the tyre burst and the wheel went into a violent wobble. The truck swung to one side, slewing so violently Adam had to turn to avoid it. The big vehicle ran into a sandy depression, tipped on two wheels and seemed about to roll on its side but then, in an explosion of dust and rattling wood, fell back on all its wheels.

Adam rolled to a stop, got off and walked to the truck. A shaken Thompson climbed from the cabin.

'My daughter tells me you tried to shoot her,' Adam said.

457

Thompson looked at the expression on the man facing him, saw the girl advancing with the gun, and raised his hands.

Cassie walked up to Adam. She had a strange expression on her face and Adam thought she was fearful of what he might do.

'Don't worry,' he said, fixing his eyes on Thompson. 'I won't hit him. We'll just pass him over to the police.'

She put the butt of the rifle on the ground, gripped the weapon by the barrel, and swung it hard across the man's shins. Thompson fell back, howling in pain.

'That's for stealing our cattle and shooting Josef's plane.'

Adam took some rope and tied Thompson's wrists and ankles. They put him across the front of the platform. Cassie sat with her feet on his back.

Adam was about to start up. 'What's this "Josef" business? I though you called him Uncle Joe?'

'Not any more. He says I'm too big for that.'

'Does he now?' He started the motor and engaged first gear. 'There's food in the bag and water if you need it.'

She searched for the food.

'Must have been cold last night.' he said.

'It wasn't bad. Me and Josef slept together.'

Adam missed the gear change. 'I think Joe and I better have a talk when we get back,' he said and she looked at him with an innocent curiosity.

458

T·W·E·L·V·E

The journey back to the homestead was slow. Adam left some of the gear with the aircraft but even with the lesser burden, the 'flying ladder' was heavily laden and short of space. Cassie, who had helped Adam in the early stages of the vehicle's construction, wanted to drive. When Adam pointed out that this was an inappropriate time to start playing with a new toy, she became miffed and prepared to sit between Josef's spread knees. Adam was even less happy with this arrangement and suggested she stand over the back axle 'to give the wheels better traction' as he put it. She liked that idea and so they travelled with Josef on one side of the platform, the trussed and bruised Thompson on the other and Cassie at the back. She had one foot on each side of the chassis and was bent forward, body over the engine and arms resting on the back of the single seat. In that angled stance, like some modern but inelegant charioteer, she travelled happily. Hair flying in the wind and face close to her father's, she used the time to tell Adam all that had happened since he had last seen her.

She asked about Nina. He confirmed that they were going to be married and she hugged him so eagerly that he almost spun on the top of a dune. Adam drove on feeling good. His daughter and friend were safe and Cassie genuinely was pleased at the prospect of him remarrying.

He thought a lot about Nina; even while Cassie was shouting in his ear, telling some story about the flight or what she and Josef had eaten, he thought of the woman waiting for him in Adelaide, and longed to be with her again. His mind raced in strange directions. He would put two seats on the 'flying ladder' and take Nina driving in the sand hills. Zooming over the hills was exhilarating. They could travel to parts of the property that couldn't be reached by other means, even camel. They might drive around the perimeter of the lake. No one had ever done that. What a story that would give her.

Would she be happy? It was a long way from the hills of San

Francisco to the plains of Kalinda. She might become bored, or even hate the place, as Heather had. And what if she went away for long periods, to write stories while he had to stay and supervise a muster or the shearing? That could happen. She might be happy at first but then find the isolation too great to bear, and long for city life. She might try to persuade him to move, to have a town house, and leave a manager up here.

If only they had a telephone: he could ring her and talk to her and be reassured by having her at the other end of the line. Talking by telegram was impossible; too cold, too clipped, too slow and too public, with every other station listening in.

If they had a telephone, what would they talk about? She wouldn't have heard about the missing plane yet, so she would say ... what? He had to think back to their last conversation. Of course. How is Nellie, and what did she say?

Cassie had stopped chatting and was wiping her lips, which were drying in the wind. Adam passed her a handkerchief.

'Put this over your nose and mouth.' And when she did: 'You saw Nellie and spoke to her?'

'Sure.' The voice was muffled. 'She's nice. I'd like to talk to her more about the old days.'

'She's gone.'

Hands gripping the seat, Cassie leaned so close that her hair whipped his face. 'She was there when we left. What happened?'

'Don't know. She was gone when I arrived.'

She let her head touch his shoulder.

'Are you getting tired?' he asked.

'No, this is great.' She nuzzled his ear. 'Was Nellie our house-keeper?'

They were crossing a small salt pan and the surface cracked under the wheels. He hesitated to answer and pretended to be concentrating on his driving. Patiently, she awaited his answer.

'Well, in a way,' he said.

'I always imagined her to be grey haired and fat. She's got some grey hair now but she's not fat. She's a bit skinny.'

'She's been sick.'

'In fact,' Cassie pressed on, 'I think she must have been a beautiful woman when she was young.' She pulled Adam's ear. 'Were you in love with her?'

He laughed but any sound was engulfed by the flat beat of the engine.

'Were you, Dad?'

'You've been reading too many books. I told you that the other day.'

'I'll bet you were,' she said and nuzzled his ear through the hand-kerchief.

The policeman drove from Oodnadatta and collected Ginger Thompson that evening.

'He says he was working on his own,' the policeman told Adam after his first session with the cattle thief. 'There's been a bit of stealing going on and some people were thinking it was organized. You know, a gang.'

'I don't think we've lost any,' Adam said. 'At least not till now.'

'I'll have a chat to him tonight,' the policeman said and winked, and went to talk to Josef about the shooting incident.

After dinner Adam took Josef out on the verandah. 'Tell me about Nellie,' Adam said. So they talked, Josef covering everything from his arrival at Innamincka to their flight to the homestead.

'She's been really sick,' Josef said. 'Cancer. One of those women's problems, you know?' Adam knew no more than Josef but waited for his friend to resume. 'I spoke to the surgeon in Adelaide. He said it might come back. At least, that's what he

Adam was silent for a long time. 'She knows?'

'I think so.' He sniffed and affected a smile. 'She looks good. A bit tired and thin but she's still a good-looking woman.'

Adam settled into a cane chair. 'Why did she come here?'

'I suppose in a way it was my idea.' Adam looked up sharply. 'I thought you'd like to see her again. I didn't know about Nina of course.'

'Might have been an idea to get in touch with me first.'

'I thought it'd be a pleasant surprise. And I was worried about her.' His face set in defensive lines. 'She's been a good friend. We shared some experiences with her and you used to live with her, for Christ's sake.' He looked around to make sure no one was listening. 'And I didn't want her going back to that bush hospital and doing nothing but sitting out in the sun on her own. Have you ever been to Innamincka?'

'With Saleem Benn, years ago.'

'Well, you know what it's like. It's about one stage away from being buried. She'd die of loneliness. Anyhow,' he said slumping into a chair near Adam, 'I thought she'd like to see her old friends. She certainly wanted to see Cassie.'

Adam spent a long time thinking. 'Did she ever tell you why she left here all those years ago?'

He shook his head. 'She said she might tell me – tell us I suppose she meant – when she got here.'

461

'But she didn't say?'

'No.' He scratched his forehead. 'I think she might have got married.'

Adam let his head tilt back. There was no moon and the sky was ablaze with stars of miraculous clarity.

'I think she might have had a kid,' Josef added. 'The matron at Innamincka said something funny, about it being a shame the boy wasn't old enough to look after her. Something like that.'

'What boy?'

'I don't know. The matron didn't say any more and Nellie didn't say anything of course.'

'You didn't ask her?'

'She wouldn't talk about her private life. She said she might say something when she got here. Could be anyone's boy I suppose.' He put his feet on the verandah rail. 'Mightn't mean anything.'

'No.' Adam walked to the edge of the verandah. 'I hope she is married. I don't like the idea of her being on her own.' He searched for the constellation of Orion, the one his father used to describe to him. He found the hunter's feet and the sword of stars that was the bushman's guide to the celestial south.

Josef cleared his throat. 'How do you feel about her?'

'You mean now?'

'Right now. I mean, how would you have reacted if you'd been sitting here and Nellie had walked in off the plane?'

Adam considered the question. 'I'd have been pleased to see her.'

'That's all?'

'Joe, she walked out, for whatever reason, in 1939. I've lived a third of my life since then. So has she. She's probably married and got kids. It's all history.'

'But you were going to marry her once. You told me.'

'That was then. This is now.'

'No feeling left?'

''Course I've got feelings. And I feel sorry for her, 'specially if she's been sick, but too much has happened for me to say I still love her, if that's what you're driving at.' Josef's face was a mask of innocence. 'And I'd have liked to have seen her, to find out what she's been doing, how she is, all that.'

'And why she left?'

'If she wanted to tell me. It doesn't matter now.'

'But if she'd stayed back in '39, you'd have married her.'

'She didn't and I didn't. The world full of ifs, Joe.'

Josef nodded sagely. 'And now it's you and Nina. I still can't get over that.' They had discussed Nina at dinner. 'I'd love to see her again.'

'You will. I suppose you'll be our best man.'

'Delighted.' Josef paused for a moment. 'You're sure about this?'

'About you being best man?'

'Nina, you goat. You've only known her a few days.'

Adam smiled. 'This reminds me of conversations we used to have, only it was me asking you those sort of questions.' Josef was still waiting. 'Yes, I'm sure,' Adam said.

'Good. You need a woman.'

'What man doesn't? And look at you. Almost forty and still a bachelor. Which reminds me ...'

Josef shifted uncomfortably, predicting the question to come. 'What's all this about Cassie calling you Josef?'

He produced his most innocent smile. 'I feel like Methuselah when a girl that big calls me uncle.' Adam was nodding but seemed unconvinced. 'Besides, we were just talking and I said "call me Josef, not Uncle Joe" to cheer her up, for something to say. It was pretty lonely out there, and I was frightened the kid might be scared. You know what it's like.'

'She said you slept with her.'

Josef was prepared for a question about how they passed the night but the words still hit so hard he felt winded. A chain of excuses rattled through his brain. In the end, he said, 'Well, I did.'

Adam breathed deeply.

'We just huddled up.' Josef almost used Cassie's word 'cuddled' and trembled at the near-miss. 'It was freezing.' He paused. Adam was not looking at him. 'We didn't have any warm clothing. We lit two big fires and sat between them.'

'Sat?'

'Well, she got tired and lay down and said "you lie behind me and keep me warm" and I did. I kept the wind off her back.' He scratched his head again, but more vigorously. 'Jesus Adam, you didn't think I slept with Cassie, you know, as in sleep with a woman? My God.'

Adam shook his head. 'She doesn't know much about men.'

Josef laughed, feeling the crisis had passed. 'She certainly doesn't. She says some funny things at times.'

'Like what?' A hint of suspicion had returned.

'Oh, just things that would have a different meaning if they came from someone else. Like when she suggested I lie down with her. She said "I want you to sleep with me" or something like that.'

There was a long silence.

'She's a nice kid.' Josef felt compelled to say something. 'I like her a lot. Lovely looking.' Immediately he wished he had remained quiet, but he had difficulty coping with Adam's silences.

463

'Joe,' Adam said, his voice low, 'she's seventeen. You're more than twenty years older than she is.'

Josef took his feet from the railing. 'You don't think something happened out there, do you? What do you think I am, some kind of monster?'

'I've seen you in action, remember? I was the one who had to fish you out of all those brothels in Egypt.'

'That was the war. And those women weren't the daughters of my best friend.' He sat up straight. 'Or the man I thought was my best friend.'

Adam studied the stars again. 'If you kept her warm, thank you.'

'Is that an apology?'

'Do you need one?'

'No, but I don't have to make one either.' He put his feet back on the railing. 'I did nothing wrong.'

'Good.' Adam turned. 'Sorry. It's been a tough few days.'

Josef dismissed the problem with a wave of his hand. But later that night he found himself thinking about Cassie, and wondering about the twenty-two year gap between their ages. She was developing into an extraordinarily interesting young woman.

Adam was in bed. There was a light knock on the door and Cassie entered.

'I thought you'd have been asleep an hour ago,' he said.

'Nope.'

'What's this "nope" business? Mrs Wilson would have your hide if she heard you talking like that.'

'No,' she said, rounding the vowel extravagantly. 'But I'm still too excited to sleep. Move over.'

'You getting a taste for sleeping with old men?'

'I'm not getting in.' She sat on a corner of the bed. 'I'm too old for that now.'

'Thank God for that. I might get some sleep.' She pulled his toe.

'Gosh, it was cold last night,' she said. 'I thought I would freeze to death. I made two good fires, though.'

'You made them?'

'You know me. Best fire maker west of Lake Eyre.'

'Is that so?'

'The fires were terrific. I'll never forget last night.' She felt him stiffen but did not understand why. 'Or yesterday or today.' She jabbed his ribs. 'Hey, how about that shot. One bullet, one truck tyre.'

'Pretty sensational.'

'I thought so too. Tell me about Nellie.'

'Nellie?'

She tickled his ribs. 'You know, the woman you used to love.'

'Here we go again. A few weeks ago it was Nina and our passionate love affair in Greece.'

'Come on, tell me about Nellie.' Without waiting, she went on. 'She told me all sorts of interesting things. I couldn't remember her which was awful. She said that my favourite toy was a cotton reel? Was that true?'

'I think it was.'

'What a drip I must have been.'

'You were a lovely drip.'

She bounced into a more comfortable position. 'Was I? What was Nellie like then? Did you two kiss goodnight?' Suddenly she straightened. 'Where did she sleep? We only had the little house then.'

'What do you mean?' he said and a hollow feeling began to spread within him.

'Well, where did she sleep? There wasn't much space. Did you make her sleep in the shed?' She turned and leaned towards him. 'Were you two married?'

He put his hand on her shoulder and pushed her back. 'Why are you so interested in all this?'

'Because she came here. And I've been thinking about her.'

'You liked her?'

'Yes. I wish she'd stayed. Do you know why she left?'

'No. Stella said something about her having to catch the train but Joe knows nothing about that. He was going to fly her back in a few days.'

'Maybe something came up.'

'Maybe.' Adam paused, content that he had defused the conversation. He touched Cassie's arm. 'I'm glad you're back safely.'

'Were you worried?'

'Of course I was.'

'Good.' She moved closer.

'You wriggle a lot. You're pulling the blankets off me. And how about going to your own room?'

'OK.' She grabbed the blankets and piled them around his face. 'Where did she sleep, Dad?' The blankets had covered his eyes. She pulled them clear. Her eyes were bright with humour and curiosity. 'You didn't make her sleep in the shed, did you? That would have been awful.'

'No.' He stared back, and thought of lying, but couldn't. 'She slept in the house.'

'Not in the kitchen?'

465

'No.'

Her lips rounded. 'In the bedroom?'

'We were not married,' he said, 'but I intended to marry her.'

'Nellie?' She lay across his legs, propping herself on one elbow. 'So you did love her?'

'Yes.'

She smiled triumphantly. 'I knew.'

'Can't fool you, can I? Not the best little fire maker west of Lake Eyre.'

Cassie's smile dissolved into a perplexed frown. 'Why didn't you marry, then?'

'She decided to go away.'

'Why?'

'I guess she didn't like it here.'

She moved closer and gently rested a finger on his nose. 'Did she break your heart?'

'Into a thousand pieces.'

She flattened the tip of his nose. 'I'm serious.'

'Well, I didn't like it but there wasn't anything I could do about it.'

She rolled across the end of the bed and gazed at the ceiling. 'You've been unlucky in love, haven't you? I mean, my mother died and then Nellie ...' Her head turned sharply. 'This *was* after my mother died?'

He smiled. He was glad she knew. 'Yes.'

She played with her fingers, shuffling all the facts into place. 'I won't say anything to Nina.'

'She already knows.'

She sat up, dragging the blankets off Adam. 'You told her?'

'Of course.'

'Were you going to tell me?'

'I just did.'

'But I had to ask. Would you have told me without being asked?'

'Only when you were a big girl,' he said and she hit him with a pillow. He pulled it off her and chased her to the door. She turned and kissed him on the forehead.

'Don't worry, Dad, I love you.'

'I know. I love you too.' He couldn't recall ever saying that before.

'Thanks for coming to get us.'

'It was a pleasure.'

'Can I drive the flying ladder tomorrow?'

'If you let me get some sleep.' She waved mischievously and closed the door.

* * *

A week later, two groups of visitors arrived on the same day. The first came by aircraft. With the pilot, who was *en route* to Oodnadatta, was an aero-mechanic hired by Josef to fix his Piper. Cassie was an eager volunteer for the job of driving the mechanic and Josef out to the stranded aircraft. The man was to check the damage, and make any further repairs. Then Josef and he were to fly the Piper back to the Kalinda airstrip. Cassie would drive back on her own, a prospect that made Adam nervous but filled her with joy.

The second lot of visitors came by truck. Saleem Benn arrived with Yunis driving and the boy Daniel riding on the back. While the others unloaded some supplies, the old man took Adam to one side. The supplies, he explained, were a gift in recognition of the services Adam had rendered in ridding the William Creek store of Saleem Goolamadail. There were a few staples like flour and tea, plus delicacies such as tinned fish, jams, jelly crystals and dried fruits. He dismissed Adam's polite protests with a flourish of his hands.

'They are nothing, the merest tinkle of coins spilling from the chest of riches I will save by having had the viper thrown from the nest.' It was an unusually colourful statement even by the exotic standards of Saleem Benn. The old man was happy and Adam smiled and accepted the gifts.

'You have someone to run the store?' Adam asked.

'Yunis.' The Afghan twisted his mouth as though he had gum stuck between his teeth. 'He is not my brightest nephew but he is honest. I will see how he manages. He might need help for some time, so I may be up this way quite often.'

'That is our good fortune.'

Saleem Benn nodded, allowing a sufficient interval to acknowledge the compliment. 'You said you were contemplating marriage?'

'Yes'

'To an American woman.'

'Yes.'

'What are American women like? Forgive such a frank question but I am curious.'

Saleem Benn had dropped his head to one side, as though the inclination would assist Adam's reply. Adam matched the angle. 'Well, I don't know what American women are like. This American woman ...' he paused and then said in Pushtu 'is very good.'

The old man's eyes had a wicked glint. 'You deserve a good woman. I trust she will be exceptional.'

'I'll give you a report.'

This delighted Saleem Benn and he grasped both Adam's shoulders. 'Such talk! We prattle like a pair of eighteen-year-olds, each contemplating his first sip of the elixir of love. Whereas ...' He wagged a finger. 'Each of us has drunk our fill and knows not the torment of curiosity but the desire to quench our thirst once more. Is that not true?'

'If you say so.'

'Oh I do. Unhappily, I may have to wait longer than you.'

'You're considering remarriage?' Adam teased.

'Not in this life.' He laughed heartily, then took Adam by one shoulder and walked with him even further from the others. 'I have a favour to ask.'

'Certainly.'

'Please, do not agree until you hear what it is.'

'I'm sure you wouldn't ask unless you thought I could help.'

He looked back. Yunis and Daniel, having unloaded the supplies, were sitting side by side on the tray of the truck. 'It concerns the boy, Daniel. You remember him?'

'Of course.'

'He has finished school. There is no purpose in sending him any more. He is a practical lad, who chafes at being confined within a classroom. But he is clever.'

'I remember what you said about him.'

'It is now time for him to start working. But it must be work that would keep him out of doors. To attempt to turn this boy into a storekeeper would be as cruel as clipping the wings of an eagle. And it must be work with a future and I fear, my friend, that the type of operation I am running does not have prospects for someone I treasure as my own son. So, while he needs to work, and to learn the things that will be important to him in his adult life, I cannot in all conscience give him the opportunity.'

Adam waited but Saleem Benn had finished. 'What would you like me to do?'

'To have him work for you.'

Adam had need of extra help. But a boy ... 'He's still so young,' Adam said.

'You yourself were working at that age.'

'I couldn't pay him much.'

'He seeks nothing but the privilege of working for you and learning from you. His keep and possibly a pittance to give him a feeling of some independence, is all that is suggested.'

'I would have to give him a reasonable wage. And where would he sleep?'

The old man turned in a gesture of theatrical intensity. 'He is one

468

of the old kind. The stars are his roof.'

Adam smiled tolerantly. The concept of a station hand sleeping in the open was as archaic as camel caravans. Both, he reflected, came from the era in which he had met his friend. He had often slept under the stars; Saleem Benn had hauled goods by camel.

'In any case,' the Afghan continued, 'you have sheds of great size and the boy is skilled with his hands. He could build a hut for himself.'

'I might have to show him how,' Adam said. 'That's a bit much for a youngster to tackle.'

The Afghan was delighted with the response. 'If you were to show him, it would be a structure of great presence, I am sure, and the lad would have learned an invaluable lesson. Please, my friend.' He raised both hands. 'Only if it is possible, of course, but if it were possible I would be in your eternal debt.'

'It's a bit awkward right away,' Adam said, knowing that he would be returning to Adelaide and wanting to be on hand when any new worker started. 'Maybe in three months' time or so?'

Saleem Benn extended his hand. 'I wished merely to have your assurance that you would employ such a talented lad at some time in the future. I feel you will not regret it.'

Adam was puzzled. 'This boy Daniel – he means as much to you as that?'

'Although the son of a friend, he has become as dear to me as my own offspring.'

Adam shook his hand. 'Then I shall treat him as I would your son.'

'I could ask nothing more.' The Afghan nodded contentedly. The woman, Nellie, for whom he had developed so much affection, would now have one small pleasure added to her life, however short that might be. And it was proper that Adam Ross should see his son grow into a man.

It had been a long drive for Mick Mason, the young man who had been Ginger Thompson's helper. Having dispensed with the first lot of cattle stolen from the northern plains of Kalinda, he joined the main Marree to Oodnadatta track near Edwards Creek railway station and travelled through Anna Creek, William Creek and Coward Springs to Marree and then followed the line south past the majestic folds of the Flinders Ranges to the township of Hawker. He turned his truck into a street near the main shops and stopped at the house whose address he carried on a slip of paper.

Saleem Goolamadail answered the doorbell. He had been at

469

Hawker for a week, having stayed with Ginger Thompson at Coward Springs only long enough to plot the next moves in their cattle stealing scheme. Hawker, being the largest town in the area and strategically placed, was a more suitable headquarters for the operations he planned; he had moved down and rented a small house owned by a friend of Thompson.

Mason handed him an envelope stuffed with notes of various denominations. 'This is what we got,' he said, as Goolamadail began to count the pounds. 'I think Ginger got caught.'

Goolamadail dropped a five-pound note. 'Who caught him?' he asked. A train whistled at Hawker station, carrying the shrill tone in the Afghan's voice a couple of octaves up the scale.

'The cops, I think.' Mason was flustered. 'I dunno what happened.'

Goolamadail sat down. 'Tell me.'

On the second day of stealing cattle, Thompson had seen an aeroplane and fired at it, Mason said.

'He shot at the plane?' Goolamadail said and thumped his forehead. 'The man is an idiot.'

Mason shrugged and continued. Thompson had decided to go back for another haul – Mason did not reveal who was to profit from this additional excursion – and not had returned. Mason waited all day at their camp and then went looking for his companion in the evening. He found the truck, empty and abandoned and with a flat tyre, in a sandy depression.

'He may have merely wandered away and died,' Goolamadail said, his face poised to break into an expression of relief.

The other man shook his head. 'I heard up north that they'd caught someone for cattle duffing. The copper at Oodnadatta 'ad 'im.'

'Did they say who?'

'No, but it sounded like Ginger. They said this bloke Ross caught 'im red 'anded.'

'Adam Ross?'

Mason nodded. 'I thought 'e was supposed to be in Adelaide?'

'He came back.'

'The bloke in the plane musta told 'im, and Ross came out and nabbed Ginger.'

Goolamadail's mind raced. He began by thanking God for not having stayed in Coward Springs, where the police would most certainly go to ask questions but changed the thanks to a reflection on his own cleverness for having the wit to distance himself from the base of a vulnerable and idiotic operator.

'He will talk?' he asked. 'Is he likely to implicate us?'

470

'Ginger wouldn't tell a copper nothin',' Mason said, compressing his lips in certainty.

'And was the truck still there?' Goolamadail asked. He was adding up costs. The truck had been stolen but it was a valuable asset.

Mason smiled at the crassness of such a question. How could he move the cattle without the big truck? No, he had changed the wheel and driven back to the camp. The small truck had been hidden among some trees.

'You left it there?' The Afghan was still offended by the supercilious expression on the young man's face and his words were intended to cut.

'Can't drive two trucks at once,' Mason said, smiling. 'Don't worry. There are no plates on it. No one can trace it, that's if they ever find it out there.'

'You will not leave it there.'

'No?'

'We need it. Next time you are up north, you will take a companion and drive out and recover the vehicle. It is worth a lot of money.'

'It's a heap of crap, if you ask me.'

Goolamadail aimed the imperfect barrels of his flattened nose at Mason. 'If you continue to work for me, which I assume you wish to do' – he waited for the other to nod, if somewhat insolently – 'then you will learn that I will rarely ask your opinion on any subject. I will, however, tell you what to do, and you will carry out my instructions. And my instructions are that you will return and get the truck. It is essential to our operations.'

'I can pinch another one.' Mason examined his soiled fingernails.

'Certainly, when I tell you. First, you will go back and get the truck. The longer you leave it, the more likely someone is to find it. It will be associated with the incident and someone will recall seeing you driving in such a vehicle, and then you too will be arrested. You can understand such basic logic?'

Mason blinked. 'I only just got down here.'

'Rest a day. Then return.'

Mason picked at a splinter in his hand. 'What are we gonna do now? I mean about pinchin' more stock.'

'Nothing. At least not for a while. I have some plans for other areas. I need time to complete my studies. Tell me, how long is Ginger likely to be in prison?'

The young man shrugged. 'Maybe a few years. Who knows?'

Goolamadail resumed counting the money. 'There are some things I have in mind that might require his particular experience. I

471

think it is important we let him know that if he keeps silent, there will be a job for him in the future. But he must not talk.'

'How are we going to do that?'

'I will handle that matter.' He looked up. 'I have in mind a project that will bring disgrace to Mr Adam Ross. It is complex and it will require someone like Ginger. If we have to wait a few years, so be it. I am a patient man.'

'What are we gonna do till then?'

The eyebrows rose in broad arches. 'Oh, many things. There seems to be a lucrative market in motor vehicles and motor parts. We might dabble in that.'

'Dabble? You mean knock 'em off?'

'Make money, my simple friend, make money.' He put the notes back in the envelope. 'Cash first, then sweet revenge.'

Adam left Kalinda with Josef in the repaired Piper. He intended rejoining Nina in Adelaide, but no sooner were they airborne than Adam asked if they could detour via Innamincka. He had been thinking: he wanted to see Nellie, to try to resolve once and for all the mystery of her disappearance so many years ago.

'It's something I have to do,' he said, and nodding sombre understanding, Josef swung the plane to the east.

The flew over the lake and then across the soured and sandy desert that spread beyond. They passed over the Birdsville Track, seeing it as a white scar on a plain of mottled pink, and then followed the meandering path of Cooper's Creek to Innamincka.

They landed on the stony strip that Josef had used a few months before, but this time there was no one to meet the aircraft. They walked to the hospital.

Only the matron was there. The hospital was being shut down. No, Ellen Khan had not come back. The matron had received a telegram from her, saying merely that she had decided to stay down south. Where? Maybe Adelaide? The matron spread her hands in a helpless gesture.

Was Ellen Khan married? Adam asked. The matron became more guarded. Ellen had been married, she offered, but the husband had died in an accident, or so Ellen said. She had rarely talked about her private life.

'Any children?'

The question made the matron's lips pucker into a defensive ridge. Ellen didn't talk about the boy to anyone. A long time ago, the Reverend Roger Montgomery had hinted at some trouble to do with custody and the courts. She studied this man who had come with the pilot who had known Ellen. So unsmiling, so intense. He

472

could be the one who'd cause all the strife, so she shook her head and said, 'I've never seen any children,' which was true.

Josef scratched his chin. 'When I was here before, you said something about a boy ...'

'A boy?' The matron spent some time removing a speck of dust from her eye.

'Yes. You said "if only the boy could help", or something like that.'

She smiled, her eye and mind clear. 'That must have been the lad who gave her a hand around the hospital. His family moved on. Went walkabout.'

'I see.'

Adam said, 'We wanted to see her. We're old friends.' He thought of asking the matron to let him know if 'Ellen' got in touch and left an address where she could be contacted, but the woman was dissecting him with chilling glances. What's the use? he thought. Obviously, Nellie was determined to keep away from him. He didn't understand, but if that was the way she wanted it, that was the way it would be.

He and Josef thanked the matron and walked in silence back to the plane. They took off for Leigh Creek.

Over Mount Hopeless, where the last of the Flinders Ranges crumbled into the sand-hills and salt pans of the Strzelecki Desert, Josef turned to him. 'That's it then? The end of Nellie? I mean as far as you're concerned?'

Adam had been staring down at the appalling landscape. Its bleak emptiness matched his mood. 'I just felt I should make one more effort to locate her and talk to her. Sorry to have taken you so far off course.'

'No problem. I wish we had seen her.'

'Me too.' The rough peaks around Arkaroola were coming into sight. He sighed. 'I wanted to discover the answers to all those questions, Joe. The things that have puzzled me for years.' He glanced anxiously at his friend. 'It wasn't that I'd changed my mind about Nina or anything like that. I just wanted to know.'

'Sure.'

They were over Arkaroola before Adam spoke again. 'Why on earth would a woman stay away all those years, hide herself in a place like Innamincka and then come back to Kalinda and shoot off again without waiting to talk to me?'

Josef shook his head sadly. 'Don't ask me. I gave up trying to understand women a long time ago.' He slapped Adam's knee. 'Are you sure you're not having second thoughts about Nina?'

'Of course not.' He was concentrating on the mountains below

473

them. The peaks rose like the stumps of decayed teeth. The plane bucked in a sudden updraught and the men smiled in mutual re-assurance. 'It's just that I had to go there,' Adam continued when the Piper had settled. 'I had to try and make contact. One last time, as it were.'

Josef mumbled sympathy. After a while, he said, 'Are you going to keep on looking?'

'No. She doesn't want that, pretty obviously. She wants to be left alone. I'll go along with that.'

'I was so sure she wanted to see you,' Josef said, recalling the flight to Kalinda. The plane shuddered again. The movement seemed to rattle the foundations of his certainty because he said, 'At least, I thought so. Who knows, eh? I'll bet there's another man. It'd be logical, wouldn't it? It's been a long time.'

Adam grunted. 'It's such a strange feeling.'

'What is?'

'The feeling that a part of my life has just ended. The Nellie episode. Closed. That's it. No more.'

'Like closing the final page of a good book,' Josef said, determined to sound cheerful.

Adam laughed cynically. 'It was a long book. And it was a real mystery. Just like reading something and then finding the last pages have been torn out.'

Josef checked the instruments. 'One book closes and another opens.'

'Don't you mean door?'

'Doors, books. Same thing. You shut one, you open another.' He looked down. 'Remember when we rode through this country?'

'That was a long time ago,' Adam said. 'That was another world, filled with other people.'

In Adelaide, Adam stayed with Nina until she completed her assignment for *National Geographic.* Then, they travelled by train to William Creek.

They were married in the first week of November, 1953. The ceremony was performed in the homestead by the Reverend Roger Montgomery. A shy guest was the boy, Daniel, who began work at Kalinda that week.

474

BOOK

F · I · V · E

The Newcomers

O · N · E

Before coming to Kalinda, Daniel Khan had a strange conversation with Saleem Benn, the man he knew as his uncle. 'From now on, you will not be known as Khan, nor should you ever mention that name,' the old man told the boy. 'Your name henceforth is Khalid, Daniel Khalid.'

The boy regarded him with astonishment. 'Khalid?'

'It is the surname of your dead father.'

Daniel was too surprised to speak. He had never heard mention of any family name other than Khan.

Saleem Benn shifted uncomfortably. 'Khan is the name of your mother's family. She reverted to it when separated from your father. She did it to protect you. There was a legal problem.'

Saleem Benn saw the boy frown and added quickly, 'The courts in this country can sometimes take children away from their parents. Do you understand?'

'No.'

'Never mind. One day it may all be clear. The thing you must remember, however, is that you are now Daniel Khalid.'

The boy nodded and tried to sweep his doubts behind him, because that would please his uncle. 'Daniel Khalid. It sounds good.'

'Indeed it does. It has a noble ring to it.'

'And there are too many Khans,' the boy said without enthusiasm but repeating a saying among the Afghans of Marree. He smiled bravely.

'In truth, the town is full of Khans.' The old man returned his smile and patted him on the head. 'To call yourself Khan from now on would be dangerous for your mother. It would put her in a very difficult situation and you wouldn't want to do that, eh?'

'No, Uncle.' A pause. 'Did my mother do something wrong?'

Saleem Benn raised both hands in a fluttering ascent. 'In heaven's name, no. How can I explain it?' He stroked his long nose, trying to think of some way to extricate himself from the mire of deceit into which he was blundering. Adam knew Nellie called herself Ellen Khan. It would take one question of a lad named Daniel Khan to expose her secret. He bent down, so that his face was level with the boy's. 'Do you know how aboriginal children are sometimes given into the custody of white parents?'

Daniel did not know but nodded, not wishing to disappoint the old man.

'Good.' Saleem Benn beamed. 'It is like that.' He straightened. The matter was closed. Let the boy think he might have been taken from his mother and given to someone else. 'You must remember then, you are now Daniel Khalid. It is a fine name. In any case, it is only proper that you now call yourself by your father's name.'

'If it was once dangerous to call myself Khalid, why is it not dangerous now, Uncle?'

Saleem Benn sighed. It was his fault. He had raised the boy to have an inquiring mind. 'Matters, legal matters, change with the years.' He coughed, clearing his throat for the next deceptive passage. 'It is because you are now working. In the eyes of the law, you are now a man.'

'Oh.' Clearly the boy did not understand. How could he?

'Legal matters are as entangled as a nest of snakes,' the old man said, smoothing Daniel's hair. 'But you must trust me. You must give me your word.'

'Of course Uncle. Should I tell Mr Ross?'

'No. He especially must not be told.'

'Why him especially?'

'Because he will be your employer. He will have to write your name on forms. These will be sent to government officials in Adelaide. Such forms could come to the notice of the courts ...'

'It is to protect my mother?'

'Yes. And it is your correct name.'

The boy nodded. 'Very well. I am Daniel Khalid.'

'And you must forget that you were ever Daniel Khan.'

'Yes.'

Later that day, Saleem Benn had prayed that he would be forgiven for lying so shamelessly to one so innocent and trusting.

Daniel soon settled into life at Kalinda. Adam Ross treated him well. The station owner was a patient man who took time to show him how to do jobs and who seemed pleasantly surprised to discover that the boy already knew a great deal; all those journeys with the Afghan caravans had taught him much about the bush. And hardened him. He was as tough and uncomplaining as a man.

Daniel liked being treated as an adult. At Marree, he had been

478

one of a group of teenage Afghans and half-castes. Most were older than he, which made him a lesser member of an inferior pack – inferior when judged by the standards of the white people who lived on the other side of the railway line.

He didn't like being one of a mob. He liked to do things on his own or, at least, be with only a small number of people. And there weren't many people at Kalinda: Adam Ross, Jimmy, the women and Jimmy's pretty daughters.

The women were very different to any females he had known at Marree. Mrs Ross used to hide away in her special room when she was writing stories. He wondered what sort of stories they were. He knew people who read books and he'd even read a couple himself, but he'd never met anyone who wrote books.

Mrs Ross – call me Nina, she said, but he hadn't dared so far – seemed nice, but he was a bit frightened of her. He had never met a woman who had a room where no one else was allowed to go and who didn't spend all her day cooking or washing clothes or chopping wood or doing other menial work. Sometimes she walked around in a bit of a daze and looked as though she were talking to herself. He would smile but she wouldn't see him.

'She's creating,' Cassie had explained.

Cassie was nice, too, but a real bully. From the first day, she'd made it clear that she knew as much about running the place as the boss did and that she didn't think much of younger boys.

He got on well with Jimmy's girls, but they were only girls and inclined to stick together and giggle. Marie was as much of a bully as Cassie. Young Lizzie was the friendliest and the prettiest, but she was only a kid and she followed him everywhere, which got on his nerves.

Stella mothered him. In fact, she paid him so much attention that he became embarrassed. It was as though she knew him or was a long-lost aunt or something. He kept away from her.

Most of his time at the big house was spent with Mrs Wilson. She liked people who enjoyed her food and he loved eating. And there was one particular factor that set them apart from the others. She worked for the Rosses and so did he, whereas everyone else was either family or behaved like family. He and Mrs Wilson were the employees.

Some nights, they would sit in the kitchen after dinner. She would wash up and he'd wipe or she'd be cooking something and they'd talk. He enjoyed those nights.

'Going to be all right, is he?' Jimmy asked Adam one day. Daniel was busily sawing timber. The three of them were sealing off one

479

end of the shed where the old car was kept, to make living quarters for young Daniel.

'Yes. I think he'll be good.'

'Industrious little bugger.'

'He's not so little.' Already, Daniel had the broad shoulders of a man.

'Do you know who he reminds me of?' Jimmy asked and went on without waiting for an answer. 'You.'

'Oh fair go, Jimmy.' Adam was hammering and didn't bother looking up.

'No, it's true. A bloke needs a chisel to chip words out of him, just like you. He's got your shoulders and he even stands like you.'

Adam laughed. 'Do you mean on two legs?'

'No, he leans against posts like he was part of the original tree. Haven't you ever noticed?'

Adam straightened and examined Daniel. 'No,' he said and resumed hammering.

'You didn't get stuck into any of those Afghan sheilas when you were down in Marree a few years back, did you?'

Playfully, Adam took a swipe at him with the hammer. 'No I did not.'

'Anyhow, he's a nice young bloke.'

'Yes, he'll be handy around here.'

'What do you know about his family?'

'Not much.'

'His father's a friend of a cousin of one of Saleem Benn's nephews, or something like that, isn't he?'

'Something like that.'

'Haven't you asked him?'

'No.'

'Why?'

Adam put down the hammer. 'By crikey you ask a lot of questions, Jimmy. Have I ever bothered you with a bunch of silly questions about who your mother or father were?'

'No. Would you like me to tell you?'

'No.'

'I'll say this for you Adam. You've got all the curiosity of a sleeping goanna.'

'I don't like to pry into other people's affairs, that's all. All I know is that Saleem Benn thinks highly of him. He's virtually raised him as one of his own.'

'So Daniel's old man must have been a good friend.'

'Yeah. That's what Saleem told me.'

'Did he say whether Danny's old man is alive or dead?'

'I don't remember.'

Jimmy turned in a circle, like a dog settling for the night. 'Having a conversation with you is about as productive as having a chat with a gum tree, except you don't give any shade. In fact, you don't give anything away.'

'Why don't you talk to Daniel, if you're so interested in him?'

'I will, I will.'

'But wait until he's finished.'

'Jesus, you're a hard taskmaster.' Jimmy flashed his magnificent smile and wandered over to where Daniel was working.

He lifted a leg, to steady the piece of timber that Daniel was cutting.

'Thanks,' Daniel said and kept on sawing.

'Don't you ever get tired?'

The boy stopped, leaving the saw wedged in the wood. He straightened his back, rubbed his hands together and nodded.

Jimmy laughed.

'What's up?'

'I was just thinking. You remind me of someone.'

'Who?' Daniel's chest was heaving from exertion.

'Doesn't matter. Have a blow. Take it easy for a while.' Jimmy sat on a block of wood. 'How are you liking it here?'

'Good, Jimmy.'

'It's not bad is it?'

'No.'

Again Jimmy laughed.

'What's so funny?'

'You don't say much.'

Daniel shrugged.

'You've got to talk a bit more, son,' Jimmy said. 'Communicate. Otherwise, you'll end up like Adam over there.'

Daniel seemed puzzled. 'What's wrong with Adam?'

'Nothing. He just doesn't talk much.'

'No.'

Jimmy shook his head. 'Having a conversation with you two would be like playing ping pong with no ball.'

Daniel lifted the tail of his shirt to wipe his face. Clever, Jimmy thought. The kid not only wipes his face but he covers it so that he hasn't got to answer a smart-arse like me.

Jimmy picked up a stick and began tracing patterns in the dust. 'How's your dad?'

Daniel stared at Jimmy. 'He's dead.'

'Oh, I'm sorry kid. I didn't know.'

'You knew him?' The question chimed with hope; Daniel had

481

never met anyone who had known his father.

'Ah, no. I don't think so. What was his name?'

Daniel hesitated, suddenly remembering Saleem Benn's words of caution. No, it was all right to talk about his father's real name. Only Kahn had to be avoided. 'Henry Khalid.'

Jimmy stroked his chin. 'No. No donger there.'

'Pardon?'

'Doesn't ring a bell.' His eyes flashed. 'What was he into? Camels?'

'Horses. He was a stockman.' And that, he realized, was really all he knew about his father. Henry Khalid, or Khan, as he used to think, was a good horseman; got a job that had taken him away from home; killed in some accident in the north-east of the state. It wasn't much in the way of a life story but that was all he knew. It would be good to meet someone, some day, who had known his father and could tell him more.

Jimmy used a boot to scrub out the marks he had made on the dust. 'Is Saleem Benn your uncle?'

'Yes. I mean no.' Jimmy looked up. 'I mean he's not my real uncle.'

'You just call him that?'

Daniel nodded and got back to sawing the wood.

'Your dad must have been a good mate of his.'

'Yes. So Mum says.'

Jimmy began scratching a circle around his left boot. 'Your mum still alive?'

'Yes.'

'She live in Marree?'

'No. Not now.' Careful, Daniel told himself. He might start asking her name. What am I supposed to call her: Ellen Khalid? Saleem Benn hadn't said. Not Khan. That was all he said.

'But she used to?'

'Of course. I went to school there.'

'Lot of Afghans in Marree, aren't there? More than us poor abos.'

Daniel grinned because Jimmy was smiling. Then a thought struck him. He and Jimmy were both from people who were required to live in certain places. In Marree, it was on the eastern side of the railway line. Only the whites lived on the other side, the better side. He hadn't thought of that before, and he hadn't thought of Jimmy as being like him. They were different. A pair of outsiders.

'Got any brothers and sisters?'

'No.'

'Most of the Afghans I know seem to have dozens of them.'

'Not me.'

'So what's your mother do?'

'Nothing much. She used to work for the Flying Doctor.'

'What was she? A pilot?' They exchanged sly glances. Yes, I am joking, Jimmy's eyes said.

'She worked in the hospital,' Daniel said.

'Where? Broken Hill?'

He was about to say Innamincka but Jimmy would never have heard of it and he was tired of schoolboy jokes about 'mincka' and 'stinker' so he nodded.

'So you don't see much of her?'

'No,' he said and cut the final stroke. He picked up one end of the sawn piece of wood and tested its weight.

Jimmy stood and lifted the other end. Together they carried it towards Adam.

'Did you used to be a boxer?' Daniel said, with what sounded like awe in his voice.

'Matter of fact, yes.'

'Would you mind telling me about it sometime?'

'When I've got time,' Jimmy said and began whistling.

'So what did you find out?' Adam said when they were servicing the car later that day.

'His dad was a great horseman. You must have heard of Henry Khalid.'

Adam thought for a while. 'Don't think so.'

'He was killed in an accident over near the New South Wales border. Horse fell on him.'

'Poor bloke.'

'Yeah. He was a good mate of old Saleem's.'

'Well, I knew that. Didn't know he'd been killed on a horse.'

'Happened some time ago, apparently,' Jimmy said, wondering how far he should go with the tale. 'He was after some missing cattle and his horse got spooked by a snake.'

'Really?'

'His mother's a nurse with the Flying Doctor over at Broken Hill.'

'I didn't know that.'

'How could you? You don't learn nothing if you don't ask nothing.'

'So now you know.'

'Yeah. He's a nice kid. Were you telling him I used to be a fighter?'

'Not me.'

'No you wouldn't, you miserable old coot.' Jimmy grinned. 'Must have been Cassie. He wants me to tell him some of my stories about the boxing troupe.'

'That'll be hard. A modest bloke like you, who doesn't like talking about himself, having to yarn about the old days.'

'Yeah, it'll be tough,' Jimmy said and wondered which story he should start with.

T·W·O

It was summer and every day was hot. The mercury in the thermometer hanging from a hook on a wall of the lounge, one of the coolest parts of the homestead, never sank below 95 degrees. The air inside the house was warm and still, for all doors and windows were closed to keep out the pervasive dust. To step out from the shaded verandah on a bright, windless day was to open the door of an oven. It was usually 120 or more out there, a dry, baking, suffocating heat that sucked out moisture and sapped energy and scorched the nostrils of anyone foolish enough to draw in a deep breath.

There were frequent dust storms. The little ones came in swirling, stinging, snarling gusts. The big ones advanced stealthily, gigantic curtains that billowed hundreds of feet above the land in graceful folds of filmy brown. Only when they were close enough for the howling to be heard could you observe the reality. Then, the curtain resolved itself into the outer wave of a monstrous aerial whirlpool that carried grit, grass, shredded leaves and uprooted bushes in its tumbling spirals.

It was not a good time for a city woman to be introduced to life in the outback. There were three big dust storms in the first month Nina spent at Kalinda as Mrs Adam Ross. During the hottest hours, she locked herself in her writing room. She had a desk, a special typing chair, a filing cabinet, her typewriter and an electric fan. She would take in a basin of water and a cloth, dab her face and arms and sit in the draught of air letting the evaporating moisture cool her skin.

Although she had no commissions for articles or contracts with any newspaper or magazine, Nina began writing almost immediately she returned to Kalinda. There were three reasons for such an early burst of activity. She didn't want to allow her career to lose its momentum; she felt lost and useless around the homestead; and she couldn't stand the heat outside. In the locked room, she was shielded from the realities of outback life and, with the fan going, her working zone was tolerable, if claustrophobic.

She found Mrs Wilson intimidating. The housekeeper did her best to make the new Mrs Ross feel like the boss's wife, but that involved such an awesome display of industry and an impervious-ness to heat that Nina soon retired from the kitchen. In trying to impress, Mrs Wilson set a standard no newcomer could match. She cooked monumental amounts of food, rose at four-thirty to prepare breakfast and was constantly cleaning, tidying and polishing.

The kitchen had a refrigerator which worked on kerosene. This meant it had to be refilled regularly, a task which Mrs Wilson insisted on performing herself so that the operation of a contraption regarded as miraculous by the others remained shrouded in mystery. The stove burned wood. It cooked things beautifully but reduced Mrs Wilson to a sweating, glowing stoker who was forever bending and opening an iron door and wiping her brow.

There was running water, an innovation they'd had for years but which continued to delight Adam. Half a dozen times in the first week, he told Nina stories of the days when he and Cassie used to carry water from the tank outside. Even with the miracle of running water, there was a secret switch somewhere which had to be turned on regularly to pump water from a big tank to a smaller, higher one. No one showed Nina where the switch was. Again, flicking the switch was something Mrs Wilson did. Like stoking the fire and filling the refrigerator's tank, pumping the water was a duty she regarded as her own. She had done those things for years; she would do them for ever.

The one thing Nina did was to make the coffee. She had brought some good coffee beans from Adelaide and arranged for a regular supply which Peppino Portelli delivered and, being Italian, appreci-ated.

This was why, finding that writing was the one thing she could do well and no one else seemed to do at all – except the indefatigable Mrs Wilson who wrote occasional letters to a cousin down south – Nina devoted much of her time to it.

Her articles for the *National Geographic* had not yet been published. Before leaving Adelaide, she had sent letters to a few newspapers in America and received polite acknowledgments which made her realize that, by moving to Kalinda, she had entered a professional backwater of profound isolation. Most interesting,the editors had replied. Let's know next time you're in the States.

So she began a novel. She had been thinking about writing fiction for some time and started a story about the adventures of an American in the Australian outback. She made the main character a man, to avoid the inevitable charges of autobiography. She spent

486

a week writing the first chapter, completed it on a day when a dust storm shook the windows and darkened the house, and tore it up.

She decided to concentrate on feature articles. Where to start? She had already written about the Great Barrier Reef and the big rock south-west of Alice Springs. She was so far from anywhere; that was the problem. She pinned a map to the wall and studied it. Cape York? The Kimberleys? Tasmania? What could be found at those places? But they were so far away. Roads were bad in this country and towns so widespread that any journey was going to involve huge distances and great amounts of travelling time.

Maybe she should concentrate on a character, a personality who would fascinate readers in New York, Chicago or Los Angeles. Someone from this part of the world. Maybe the driver of the Ghan, the train that ran up to Alice springs? That charming old Afghan, Saleem Benn? The publican at the funny little hotel at William Creek?

She spent a day, sitting in her tiny room and splashing water on her forehead and wrists before she realized that the ideal subject was the man she slept with.

Adam Ross: a man of the desert, living and prospering where few could survive. Resourceful, self-educated, a genuine war hero now fighting the cruel heat and isolation of the Australian outback. The Americans would love it.

She told Adam and he laughed. Why would the Americans be interested in him? She told him and he said nothing but looked at her in a strange way which told her he was still laughing. Even so, he promised to co-operate. What did she want?

She wanted to see him at work. To take photographs of him on horseback or, better still, riding a camel. To have him talk to her about underground water, which was the sole reason people and stock could survive in such country, and picture him working at a bore, with a windmill clanking in the background and steam rising from the gush of hot water. To have him rounding up his sheep ('please call it mustering,' he suggested, wincing at the Americanism) and posing on top of a dune, surveying this vast empire in the Never Never.

'The Never Never?'

'Yes,' she said, looking pleased with herself. 'You see? I'm coming to grips with the language.'

'Never Never,' he muttered. But Adam did take Nina out with him on the next few days. They were calm days, with no wind. She carried the household thermometer with her and recorded 124 degrees in the shade of a stunted palm that Adam had planted near a mound spring. He posed for her by filling his hat with water and pouring it over his face. 'Man in the desert,' she said, snapping several shots and then changing the lens filter to darken the sky. 'The owner of one of the world's largest sheep ranches – correction, sheep stations – refreshing himself at one of the rare mound springs which are a feature of this part of the world.' She looked up. 'How do you like the sound of that?'

When she put the camera down, he tipped water over her. Then they took their clothes off and went for a swim.

The morning with the sheep was awful. The sheep were smelly and raised dust and Nina thought she would faint in the heat. He drove her back to the homestead, primed her with iced tea and insisted she lie down until dinner. She did, but felt more inadequate than ever.

The time in the dunes was good. She wanted to film Adam in the soft light preceding sunset. He agreed, not understanding a photographer's requirement of light but knowing it would be cooler then. The dunes would be impossible in the middle of the day. The sand would be too hot to touch, the glare painful to the eyes and the reflected heat would have them gasping for air.

At six in the evening, they went out to the most extravagantly contoured and colourful of the sand-hills within range of the homestead. It was a thirty-minute drive.

They trudged up and down the dunes, taking care not to leave cratered footprints on the sections Nina intended to photograph. She took a whole role of film, twenty-four shots, of Adam: standing with hands on hips, with one hand in his pocket, looking left, looking right, hat on, hat off, perched on a finely sculptured rim of wisping sand, sitting down near a bush. Then she shot off a roll of film of the dunes themselves. Hunched, kneeling or lying down, she pursued shapes and shadows with a boundless determination.

'Magnificent,' she enthused and Adam shook his head.

'Never seen anyone take so many pictures of sand,' he said. 'Matter of fact, I've never known anyone to take a picture of sand.'

'You're hopeless,' she said, smiling benignly as she fitted another roll of film into the camera. 'You live in beauty and don't recognize it.'

'I'll bring you out here at noon one day. If the wind's blowing, you won't see a thing after five minutes.'

'Beauty is in the eye of the beholder,' she said stubbornly, glancing around her at the soft, superb colours and forms.

'You, my beauty, will have an eye full of sand.'

She sat beside him and they waited there, holding hands and talking until the sun had gone and the first stars were twinkling in a sky of unblemished purity.

488

When they returned, Mrs Wilson was annoyed because the dinner was spoiled. When the housekeeper wasn't looking, Adam winked at Nina. And Nina felt better. He was intimidated by Mrs Wilson, too.

Adam was reluctant to be photographed on a camel. 'It'll make me look like a real old-timer,' he complained and suggested that she photograph him beside the Holden or even the old Alfa-Romeo.

'I don't want you looking like a modern man,' she said, wrinkling her nose. 'If I send pictures of you with a car, the Americans will think you're one of them. Even on a horse, you could be mistaken for a Texan cowboy. But on a camel, you could only be an Aussie from the outback.'

'Or an Arab,' he said. 'Or a prize dill.'

'I want you on a camel.'

'Only if you ride one, too.'

She agreed. Half a mile from the homestead, her camel took fright when it almost trod on a snake. Nina was thrown to the ground and broke her ankle.

The Flying Doctor came that afternoon.

'It's a nasty break,' the doctor told Adam. 'I think we might have to send her down to Adelaide.'

'She'll be there some time?'

'Probably. Do you want someone to go with her?'

Cassie volunteered.

It was the fifth day in a row that Roger Montgomery had been to the Adelaide office of the Australian Inland Mission. The answer was the same: there was no news about his next posting. Today, however, he heard a rumour that he might be assigned a ministry at Port Lincoln. Miss McKillop, who was first with most of the rumours, told him in confidence and said, as she had every day, that he would just have to wait a little longer. The Lord moved in slow and mysterious ways, she reminded him and then smiled as though she believed the Lord had little to do with the procrastinations of the Presbyterian Church.

Roger returned to his room to find a letter waiting for him. It was from Saleem Benn. He admired the calligraphy for some time before reading the old Afghan's words. Saleem Benn, he mused, must have used a quill. The down lines were thick, the up lines delicate, the flourishes as elaborate as the swoopings of swallows in flight.

The first paragraph enquired about his health. Roger smiled. Saleem Benn wrote like he talked: a ritual of good manners had to

489

be performed before he moved on to the matter that concerned him.

I have presented the boy Daniel with a new surname. He now calls himself Daniel Khalid. This is to avoid any link with his mother, who Adam Ross now knows has been using the name Ellen Khan. Please remember this if ever you are in the area or in communication with Adam Ross. The boy, of course, was confused, but I spun a story which seemed to satisfy him. And this brings me to the main purpose of the letter.

I am deeply concerned about the maintenance of the cruel deception we are all practising with regard to the boy's true origins. Adam Ross has accepted him without question as Daniel Khalid, the son of an old friend of mine, and the boy seems to have settled in most harmoniously, may God be praised.

Whose God? Roger thought, recalling some of the theological debates they'd had in Marree. He'd enjoyed those jousts, even if a neutral judge would probably have scored in favour of the Muslim.

I am a man who detests lies, and yet I have been compelled to spin a web of deception. I have lied to Daniel and I have lied to Adam Ross and my nights are filled with torment. Most reverend Roger, I am an old man and I have not been in good health lately and I am growing more and more uncomfortable at the prospect of undertaking the Ultimate Journey and facing the Supreme Being, as you would call him, with so much deceit gnawing at my conscience. And verily, having thought about it a great deal lately, I cannot see what good purpose the maintenance of this deception will do.

It is a situation bristling with the utmost irony that father and son are living together without either being aware of his true relationship to the other. It would transform the boy, in terms of dignity and pride, to know that his father is so fine a man as the owner of Kalinda, and not some phantom created in my own feeble and tainted imagination. And, my dear reverence, Adam Ross should know. Every man should be aware of his first born son and Daniel is a fine boy, who would bring joy to his father's heart.

Therefore, I am writing with a request. I believe you know the whereabouts of Daniel's mother. Please see Nellie and beg her to release us from the promise we all made so long ago. Explain to her what benefits would accrue to her own son. Tell her I believe there would be no risk to the recent marriage of Adam Ross, if that is a concern. I think his new wife, while from a strange land,

490

is a worldly person, well able to accept such a situation.

I beg you to see her and try.

With salutations and the most fervent wishes that this letter finds you in good health,

Your servant, Saleem Benn.

Nellie was staying with a widow at Glenelg. The house was old and small but close enough to the beach for the air in the front room to be spicy with images of sailing boats and freshly beached seaweed. The widow was a former nurse who had been a friend of the Innamincka matron. Nellie's stay was only temporary, good for the few weeks it might take her to find permanent accommodation.

Nellie told Roger she had a job at a local café. She worked there three days a week. Her health was good, she said, but she seemed gaunt and sat all the time they talked.

Roger told her of the letter.

'No.'

Roger polished his glasses vigorously and avoided her eyes. 'Saleem Benn is an honourable man. Persevering with a lie is causing him deep distress. He says he feels tormented.'

'I'm sorry.'

He handed her the letter. She turned it in her hands like a person examining a rare object. 'He's a good writer, isn't he?'

'Yes.' He smiled, hoping to persuade her by his own bene-volence. 'Please read it for yourself.'

She read slowly, then gave the letter back to Roger. 'He didn't say how Daniel was. Is he all right?'

'I'm sure he is. Saleem Benn said he was fitting into life at Kalinda in a harmonious way. That means he's well and he's happy.'

He waited expectantly. She shook her head.

'You don't know the whole story, Roger, but Adam would be in more trouble if people found out about Daniel than if they didn't.'

'There's no question of Adam losing Cassie now,' he said, shaking his head earnestly.

'I know. It's not that.'

He waited.

'No, Roger,' she said firmly. 'People mustn't know. You have to keep your promise.'

There was a long silence. 'Times have changed since you had the baby, Nellie.' He cleared his throat. 'Folk are a lot more broad-minded about unmarried mothers these days. They wouldn't think badly of you, or talk behind your back, if that's the problem.'

She laughed softly. 'It's not me I'm worried about, Roger. It never has been.'

491

T·H·R·E·E

Nina spent only one night in hospital. She had a touch of concussion as well as the broken ankle, and was released on the understanding that she report back to the doctor in one week. So she booked into an Adelaide hotel which had a spacious, air-conditioned suite and, dosed with pain killers, lay on the bed and relished the cool breeze that blew from the vents in the wall. She missed Adam, but had no desire to hurry back to Kalinda; not while the bottom of her leg was encased in a jacket of plaster and her head ached and the temperature near Lake Eyre stayed above the century mark. The accident, she decided, had given her a providential, if temporary release from the horrors of her first outback summer.

The suite had two bedrooms, a lounge and, wonder of wonders, a bathroom with a marble floor, a large bath, shower recess, toilet and a wide, brilliantly lit make-up mirror. It was the hotel's dearest suite, but Nina had grown used to living on an expense account and had little taste for an inferior standard of accommodation.

Cassie had never seen such a suite. She was fascinated by the bathroom and spent hours there, lolling in the tub or posturing in front of the mirror.

After three days, Nina's headaches eased and she became restless. Anxious to do some writing, she had Cassie go down to the office to see if she could borrow a typewriter. Cassie had become friendly with the receptionist, who came from Peterborough. As Adam had occasionally bought sheep at the Peterborough sales, the two girls felt like neighbours and got on well. So well, that when Cassie returned to the room she was carrying a nearly new Remington.

With her leg supported on pillows, the typewriter on a small table beside the bed and a stream of cool air playing on her face, Nina began to write the article about Adam.

Cassie knew Nina preferred privacy when she was being creative, so whenever Nina wrote, Cassie left the room. For the first couple of days, she walked through the city. She was used to the dark, jumbled confusion of the store at William Creek, which had every-thing from saddles and shirts to shovels and seeds. But Adelaide had stores which dazzled and stores which specialized: bright shops with big windows and sparkling lights and mirrors on the walls and shops which sold nothing but shoes or clothes or food, or displayed racks of cosmetics, chocolates and books. She gazed in windows and gaped at tall buildings. She marvelled at the traffic, the crowds, the statues and the green grass in the parks.

Near the hotel was a War Disposals store and on the second day Cassie returned with a stout pair of desert boots.

'For your father?' Nina asked hopefully as the girl began to demonstrate her purchase by pulling on one boot.

Cassie was puzzled by the humorous glint in Nina's eye. 'Of course not. They're for me. The first shoes I've ever bought in the city. They'll be terrific back home.'

'Just don't wear them down here.'

'Why?' Cassie admired the deep rubber soles and the prominent stitching.

'You might be snapped up by a talent scout for a football team.' Nina's mouth shrivelled, prune-like in distaste.

'Don't you like them?'

'Well, they're not very feminine.'

Cassie shrugged, her pride sliding, her doubt growing. 'These'll be terrific around the property.'

'I'm sure they will.'

Doggedly, Cassie laced up the boot. 'Do you want me to get you a pair of these for when we go back to Kalinda? They'd be good for your ankle. You know, give it support.'

'I'm sure they would, but no thank you.'

'They had other things. Jerry cans, axes, compasses, camping gear, clothing.'

'Really?'

'They had a trenching tool that Dad might like.'

'What's a trenching tool?'

'A sort of folding spade. He could carry it in the car for when he gets bogged in sand.'

'I don't think I've ever met a man who owns more spades than your father. I doubt that he'd need another one.' She reached out to grasp Cassie's hand. 'As soon as I can move out of here without too much bother, you and I are going shopping.'

'What for?'

'Lovely things. Quality things. Feminine things.'

Cassie nodded eagerly, then frowned, determined to make a

point. 'But it's a good shop where I got the boots. I've never seen a place like it.'

'I'm sure you haven't,' Nina said and smiled gently.

On her third day of exploration, Cassie took a tram to the beach. She got off at Glenelg. Roaming the sand, she watched people swimming and playing in the shallow waves. Some women were wearing skimpy two-piece bathing costumes which looked just like underwear and that shocked her. She had never seen women display themselves so immodestly in public. Other women, however, wore one-piece suits. She approved of them so she went to a shop, bought herself a navy costume and a yellow towel with sea horses printed on it, and went to the pavilion where the women got changed. Then she had her first swim in the sea.

She was not good in the water, having had so little practice. Her father had taught her how to swim in one of the mound springs, but the water there was smooth and the distance from one side of the spring to the other wasn't great. She could swim to the other bank and take only four breaths.

The sea intimidated her. There were waves, and other people shouting and splashing, and the water surged and swept her feet from under her, and there was no land on the other side; just more water than she had ever seen and an occasional ship steaming in the distance.

So she sat in the shallows and let the small waves break against her back. A little girl, maybe four, joined her. The girl had a bucket and spade and began building a sand-castle at the water's edge. Cassie helped her. The girl's mother, who was sitting on the beach and wearing a costume that bulged like the corrugated sides of a water tank, watched them. She was suspicious at first, looking at Cassie as a cow would eye her if she played with its calf, but after a while the woman relaxed and Cassie and the little girl had a good time. They kept on building simple sand-castles and the waves kept on washing them away.

When the girl and her mother left, Cassie waded out beyond the rippling breakers until she was standing waist-deep in water. She swam a few strokes, but the sea was rising and falling and she kept on swallowing salty water. Two youths, maybe her age or a little older, ran into the sea and dived on either side of her. They splashed each other and her, because she was in the middle, and swam with a great deal of kicking and extravagant strokes, but they didn't talk to her. That surprised her because it seemed obvious that they were trying to attract her attention.

She caught the tram to Glenelg again the next day. Around

noon, a cool wind sprang up so she dressed and went for a walk in the town. It began to rain. To get out of the weather, she entered a café and ordered a cup of tea and a toasted sandwich.

Nellie was about to walk out from the kitchen when she recognized Cassie. She swayed backwards and sat down.

'Not feeling well, love?' the woman who ran the cafe asked. She took the tray from Nellie's hands. 'You stay there a minute. Who's this for?'

Nellie pointed to a couple in the far corner of the cafe.

'You just take it easy. Things are quiet so you just sit down until you're feeling better.' The woman liked Nellie and always took over when she had one of her turns. Then, with the flourish of an actress making a grand entrance, the woman swept out through the swinging doors.

Nellie stood up, but was so shaky she had to grasp the back of the chair. Maybe she was mistaken. She'd only glimpsed the girl for a few seconds and she'd been thinking a lot about Adam and Cassie and the people at Kalinda. It might be someone who simply looked like her. Nellie peeped over the door. It *was* Cassie. She was sitting side-on, but there was no mistake. On her own? A glance around the café. Yes. No one else. Surely she wasn't visiting Adelaide by herself? Adam must have brought her down which meant he would be nearby.

For one soaring moment, she thought of walking out, very nonchalantly, and sitting beside the girl she had raised. 'Hi,' she would say, straight-faced, and enjoy Cassie's expression of consternation. And then they would hug and kiss.

She sighed. Who was she fooling? She would probably burst into tears. And Cassie, who had the curiosity of ten cats, would want to know where she lived and what she was doing down here and why she had dashed away from Kalinda without waiting to see Adam.

And they wouldn't kiss. She loved Cassie like her own daughter, but Cassie didn't remember her.

Nellie slumped, all strength draining down her body. She couldn't go out. Cassie would tell Adam, who would come looking for her, find her, coax the whole story from her and then the truth would be out. Adam Ross, just married to a rich American lady, had a half-caste bastard son. And the son was working for him as the hired hand. What a joke!

Adam would be disgraced, his new wife would probably walk out on him, and Goolamadail, who could store a grudge longer than anyone she knew, would ensure that no one ever did business with Adam again. Gooly would do more than tell people the truth about Daniel. He would invent the most shocking stories about

Adam and tell them in such a way that people would believe them. She knew Gooly. Once he started something, he would go to astonishing lengths to harm someone he hated, and he hated Nellie and Adam.

Nellie normally finished at two. That was when Cassie left the café. It was still raining. Nellie followed Cassie, keeping well back and shielding her face behind an angled umbrella. She wasn't sure why she followed her. Maybe in case Cassie led her to Adam. Not that she would talk to him, but if he were somewhere close, she might see him. Even if he were with the other woman, she wanted to see Adam again.

Cassie boarded a city tram. Nellie watched it leave, then went home.

Nellie saw Cassie again the next day. Nellie wasn't working and it was a hot day so she had gone down to the beach to sit on a wooden bench beneath a shady tree. It was a favourite spot. Cassie arrived at about ten o'clock. She went to the women's changing pavilion and emerged in her navy one-piece. Nellie sucked in her breath. Cassie had become a woman and a shapely one at that. She began to cry, little tears that bothered her eyes and made her blink rapidly and feel immensely sad. Where had the years gone? The little girl who used to play with cotton reels had somehow become a woman. And such a woman. She saw the men turn and look, just like they used to look at her in the years when Nellie was proud of her body and men would fight each other to determine who'd spend the night with her.

She watched Cassie swim and saw some young men splash and shout at her. Cassie swam away.

After her swim, Cassie dressed and caught a city tram. This time, Nellie caught the tram, too. Like most newcomers to the city, Cassie sat in the front of the tram to get a better view. Nellie sat at the back. She wasn't sure why she was following the girl. Presumably to discover where Cassie was staying and to see if she met anyone. Probably so that she could hang around the front of the hotel, out of sight, and catch a glimpse of Adam.

And then what? I'm not going to speak to him, she reminded herself, but now, sitting in the back of a tram and rocking from side to side, she wasn't so sure. If she saw Adam, she might go up to him and blurt out everything. She didn't know. But she was feeling weak, a prisoner of undiagnosed instincts. All she knew was that she wanted to follow Cassie.

'I'm nuts,' she moaned and was staring out the window, lost in dreamy thoughts, when Cassie got off. The tram was moving again before Nellie could reach the door.

* * *

It was two days before Cassie returned to the beach. On the day in between, which was the day Nina had her appointment with the doctor, Cassie stayed in Adelaide and met Alexander McWhinney. She thought it was the strangest name. McWhinney reminded her of a horse, she said, and laughed when he seemed offended. He bought her a chocolate milk shake. He was the first man ever to buy her a drink.

They met in one of the parks edging the city. He was Scottish, twenty-three years old and travelling the world with only a haversack to hold his few possessions. When she first saw him, McWhinney was sitting on a bench with the pack on his back but with his shoes off. He was vigorously massaging his feet. Ever curious, she sat beside him and asked what he was doing.

His boots were worn, he explained, and the frayed lining was rubbing his toes. He had tramped through Iran, India and Nepal, had hitched a ride across the Nullarbor and was planning to go north to Alice Springs and Darwin. He needed new boots but didn't have much money. She told him about the War Disposals store and took him there. The milk bar was next door.

'I just met an interesting young man,' Cassie said when she returned to the suite.

Nina was wrestling with a difficult paragraph. 'Really?' She didn't look up but scowled at the sheet of paper that refused to fill with the rows of words she needed.

'He's walking around the world.'

Nina nodded without looking at Cassie and then, in a sudden gush of energy, thumped out a batch of text. With the plug removed, the sentences flowed. The typewriter clattered, fingers moving so rapidly that sometimes the keys jammed. Cassie watched in amusement as Nina's lips kept pace with the keys, mouthing the desired phrases before they appeared on the paper.

Finally, Nina grunted, either in triumph or exhaustion, and turned to Cassie.

'I'm sorry. What did you say?'

'I met a man who's walking around the world.'

'That's what I thought you said.' Nina frowned, then scratched her forehead. Suddenly, she was filled with guilt. She had been so obsessed with her own injury, her comfort and the writing of the story, that she had been ignoring Cassie. After the remorse came alarm. Her step-daughter had been roaming the streets of a strange city. 'A man. How old is he?'

'Twenty-three.'

497

'How do you know?'

'I asked him. He's got a beard. Guess what his name is?'

'I couldn't possibly.'

'McWhinney.' Cassie laughed. 'I told him he reminded me of a horse.'

Nina arched an eyebrow. 'And what did he say about you?'

'He reckoned I had a funny accent.'

'You two must have had a great conversation.'

Cassie nodded. 'You should have heard the way he spoke. I could hardly understand him.'

'Why? Where does he come from?'

'Scotland. He talks like this.' She rolled some r's. 'And instead of saying yes, he says "aye". He's funny.'

'Where did you meet this Scotsman of yours?'

'In the park. He was rubbing his toes.'

'His toes?'

'His boots were nearly worn out. I showed him where to get new ones. I took him into the shop and he bought some. He reckons they're great.'

'Desert boots?'

'Yes.'

Nina laughed, feeling relieved. A meeting that ended in a War Disposals store sounded innocuous.

'He bought me a drink.'

Nina stopped laughing. 'He did what?'

'Bought me a drink. At the milk bar not far from here.'

'He bought you a milk shake?'

'Yes. It was good.'

Nina nodded, trying to remember the last time she had drunk a milk shake. Or the first time a boy bought her one. She took a deep breath, determined to expunge all feeling of concern and guilt. Cassie and the young Scot had gone into a shop to buy a pair of desert boots and had had a milk shake together. She could think of nothing more innocent, or ridiculous. 'How did you meet him?'

'I told you. He was rubbing his toes.'

'I mean, did you speak to him or did he speak to you?'

Cassie tilted her head, like a dog puzzled by its owner's actions. 'We spoke to each other.'

'Who spoke first?'

'I don't remember.' She thought. 'Me, I think.'

'You went up to him and spoke?'

'I asked him why he had his shoes off.'

Nina rubbed the back of her neck in the universal gesture of someone who disapproves of an action but is reluctant to criticize.

'Why, what's wrong?'

'Cassie, it's not wise to go up to strange men in a park and ask them why they've got their shoes off, or why they're rubbing their toes.'

'He wasn't a strange man.'

Nina had to pinch her nose to stop herself laughing. 'I don't mean he wasn't normal. I mean you didn't know him.'

Cassie raised her hands. Where she came from, everyone spoke to strangers. She didn't know what she should say; Nina seemed to be switching from being concerned to being amused about something. So she said, 'I don't know why. I just wanted to talk to him. I wanted to talk to someone.'

'You've been lonely?'

She shrugged. 'Well, I've missed having someone to yarn with.'

Nina extended her hand, inviting Cassie to sit beside her on the bed. 'I've been neglecting you,' she said.

'No.'

'Yes. We'll spend more time together.'

'But you want to write.'

'I've almost finished.'

'Does that mean we can go home soon?'

Nina spent a great deal of time examining her fingers. The innocent Cassie's action in befriending a nomadic Scotsman in the park had shocked her. She had allowed Adam's daughter to go off wandering unescorted around the city, and cities were potentially dangerous places. Even a city as compact and proper as Adelaide would contain the sort of men who preyed on young girls, and she had let her walk around on her own because she wanted time to finish a story.

And she was frightened of going back, to the heat and challenge of Kalinda.

'Don't you want to be home with Dad?' Cassie asked.

'Of course I do. I miss him terribly.'

'What did the doctor say?'

'He's happy with my head.' She touched her forehead and laughed. 'You know what I mean. He said the concussion's all cleared up.'

'And the ankle?'

'I just have to keep it in plaster for a couple of weeks.'

'So we can go home?'

Nina raised her shoulders, more in surrender than enthusiasm. 'I don't suppose your father would have any reason to travel to Adelaide? No urgent business that would keep him down here for a month or two?' She smiled hopefully.

Cassie returned the smile but in a way that made Nina feel exposed. That was the disarming thing about this girl: so naïve one moment, then able to peel away all the layers of your sophisticated pretences the next.

'You'd have to leg rope him to get him to leave now. He hates cities.'

They were in the lounge, separated by a table. Nina extended her hand towards Cassie but stopped just short of contact. She tapped the table top with her fingers in a nervous, confessional gesture. 'I want to be with your father. Believe me.'

'I wish you'd call him Adam.'

'I beg your pardon?'

'Don't call him "your father". It puts a wall between us.'

'Oh.' Nina withdrew her hand. 'All right, I'll call him Adam.'

'Good. So will I. Everyone else calls him Adam. I feel so young calling him Dad. Even Daniel calls him Adam and he's even younger than me.'

'You will not call your father Adam.' Nina spoke forcefully. She was losing control of this conversation. Cassie was a nice girl, but if she established dominance at this stage of their relationship she would gain a position from which she would never retreat. Cassie had already bullied young Daniel in the instinctive way that one animal will quickly dominate another, and Nina had no intention of being the inferior member in a partnership with her step-daughter. 'You will call your father – sorry, Adam – Dad. It sounds much closer and loving than his first name. That's for friends and acquaintances. You're more special than that. You're his daughter.'

Cassie said nothing but looked at Nina in the manner of one who is adding up points.

'I think it's very precocious, don't you?' Nina said, feeling she must say something to interrupt the calculation. 'Do you really like daughters calling their fathers by their first names?'

Cassie's eyes rolled from side to side, counting off the limited number of girls she knew. 'I don't think I know any. I have read about it, though, in one of Mrs Wilson's novels.'

Nina shook her head disapprovingly. 'It's not nice. I knew a girl back home in America who called her father Hank and it sounded awful.'

'Hank!' Cassie covered her mouth to suppress a laugh. 'What sort of name is that?'

'A variation of Henry. Common enough in America. I guess you'd say Harry.'

'America must be a funny place.'

'It's very different to Australia. You must go there one day. You and me.'

'And Dad.'

'If he can leave the property.'

Cassie let her head sag. 'Is it just the heat you don't like at Kalinda?'

Nina swayed back in her chair. 'Why do you say that?'

'I've been watching you. You seem to prefer it down here.'

Nina wiped her lips. 'I do find it hot at Kalinda.'

Cassie grinned. 'It's awful, isn't it?'

'I thought you liked the heat?'

'You can get used to it, but I don't know anyone who likes it.'

'I got the feeling I was the only one up there who couldn't take the high temperatures.'

'No one likes it. The summer's terrible.'

'But you go outside and work and ride your horse and do things like that. I take one step outside the door and feel as though I'm on fire. I can't breathe. I feel useless, ashamed. Everyone else seems to be able to cope except me.'

Cassie nodded all through this confession. 'It's really only bad for a couple of months. Then it's good. Dad always says you can tell newcomers by the way they rush around in the heat. They dash out and try to hurry through some job and then they collapse.'

'Like I do?'

'Everyone does it at first. Dad says we should all behave like sheep.'

'Sheep?'

'He says no one should walk faster than sheep. They're never in a hurry. They wear woolly coats and they cover big distances, but they never get exhausted because they always take their time.'

Nina was about to speak but laughed.

'What's up?'

'I was going to ask how long it took you to get used to the summer, but then I remembered: you've always been there.'

Cassie wiggled her chair closer to Nina's. 'So you like Kalinda but not the heat?'

'I don't know Kalinda very well yet, but I'm sure I'll grow to like it. I haven't had a chance to see too much of it, and there's so much.'

'I'll take you around when it gets cooler.'

'Please. I'd like that.'

Cassie leaned on the table, pressing her face into her arms. 'Can I ask you something? A very personal question?'

'Go ahead.'

'What happened in Greece?'

'Do you mean when your father and I met?'

501

A finger tapped the table in admonition. 'Call him Adam. It sounds so stuffy the other way.' She turned her face and she was grinning. 'And yes, that's what I mean.'

'How much time do you have?'

'All night. I feel like talking.'

They talked for hours. When she went to bed that night, Nina felt good.

The next day was hot. It was one of the days Nellie didn't work, so she went down to the beach and sat on the bench under the tree. She wore a floppy hat, not for protection from the sun but to cover her face in case Cassie arrived. I'm becoming stupid about all this, she told herself. I'm sneaking around like some spy in the movies, hiding under a big hat, sitting in the shade where people won't see me, travelling in the back of a tram so that I can hide behind other passengers, and all because I'm hoping to see a young woman who could have been raised as my daughter. But I won't speak to her. Seeing her these past days has wrenched at my heart and I long to see her father, who is the only man I've truly loved, but I'm not going to say a word. I'll just keep waiting, to watch her in secret, until, one day, she won't turn up and that will mean she's gone back to Kalinda. And when that happens, I'll know I may never see her again.

She laughed bitterly and a man walking past turned to stare.

I'm a fool. I should either keep away or go up to Cassie and say something.

She thought of going back to her room in the little house one street from the beach, but then Cassie arrived. As always, she was on her own. Cassie changed and went down to the sand where she spread out her towel and sunbaked for a while.

Three young men hovered near her, bees drawn to the flower. Nellie studied them closely. They were the same young men who had been swimming near Cassie the other day. She didn't like the look of them. They reminded her of a hunting pack, moving innocently, doing normal things, but relentlessly closing on their prey. They were throwing a ball, occasionally hurling it too far which forced one to run back, until, eventually and unremarkably, they surrounded her.

One spoke to Cassie. She got up and walked to the water. The three followed.

Cassie came out of the water and walked down the beach. They followed. All four walked out of sight.

The road ran parallel to the beach. Nellie got up and followed the footpath past some buildings until she could see Cassie and the men once more. Cassie was fifty yards ahead of them. Forty yards. Thirty. They were closing on her and as they drew nearer they fanned out, hunters spreading the net to prevent the quarry escaping.

Nellie quickened her pace but could not keep up. Cassie, looking back at the men, started to run. The others ran. Nellie could hear them calling out. Then Cassie did something that made Nellie shudder with fear. She stopped and turned to face her pursuers.

'Run,' Nellie screamed, but Cassie could not hear her.

The first man stopped with his hands on his hips. Head leaning forward he said something and Cassie took one step backwards. He moved closer and reached out to push her shoulder. She pushed him. He swung a punch which she ducked with the ease of a boxer. Cassie hit him with a left hook.

That was pure Jimmy Kettle, Nellie thought, her mouth open in astonishment. Then she grew angry. That bastard Jimmy had been teaching her little girl how to fight. She would have raised Cassie as a lady but Jimmy had to teach her how to box like some circus ruffian.

The man had staggered back and was shaking his head. His companions encircled Cassie. They held their fists high.

A car was coming. Nellie ran into the middle of the road and waved the driver to a stop.

'There's a girl being attacked on the beach,' she shouted as she moved to the driver's door. The man was middle-aged and dressed for bowls.

He got out of the car and squinted towards the beach. The man had difficulty seeing that far. 'What do you want me to do, lady?'

'Stop them.'

'But there are a lot of them.'

'Three. And only one of her.'

'I've got a back problem.'

One of the men charged Cassie from the front and another from the rear. She fell, kicking and punching.

The bowler hadn't moved.

'Oh for God's sake,' Nellie screamed and, leaving the car, ran across the footpath and on to the sand. She charged the three men, shouting for them to stop. Behind her, she heard a car horn being blown. At least the bowler was doing something.

She wished she had one of his bowls to throw at the men, but she had nothing. 'Get away from her,' she shouted when she was about fifty yards from them. One of the young men turned.

He pulled a companion clear and pointed towards Nellie. They turned and ran down the beach. Cassie had the other one in a headlock. The man was struggling to free himself.

Another horn was blowing and Nellie could hear men calling out. A dog was barking excitedly.

The third man broke free and Cassie, lying on her back on the sand, kicked him hard in the belly. Doubled over, he staggered after the others.

A man wearing only shorts and with a dog on a leash galloped past Nellie, showering her with sand. She stopped.

'Are you all right?' the man called out and Cassie got to her feet, wiping sand from her face. She nodded.

'You were doing all right,' the man said cheerily, and let his dog go. It set off in pursuit of the three men.

'I could have handled one,' Cassie said and the man laughed because he knew she meant it.

Nellie turned and walked back towards the road. She started to cry.

I'm useless, she told herself. I couldn't have stopped those men. There was a time, but not now.

She reached the footpath and turned towards her house. She didn't look back. She knew she would not see Cassie again.

Nina and Cassie caught the next train north. Adam was horrified when he heard the story of the beach attack. It reinforced his opinion of cities: they were not a place where civilized people should live.

Two weeks after their return, Alexander McWhinney arrived at Kalinda, having hitched a ride with Peppino Portelli. Adam regarded him with such suspicion that the young Scot stayed only three days, after which Jimmy drove him back to William Creek.

There followed a period of abnormally cool weather, during which Cassie drove Nina around the property, showing her the bores and sand-hills and mound springs.

'I can see how this place gets under your skin,' Nina told Adam one night.

'You really like it?'

'I'm starting to. It grows on you. There is so much space, so much emptiness. Even the trees are different, sort of stunted and tortured, and there are so many strange colours. It looks so old, so ancient. I feel as though I've strayed on to a part of the world where humans aren't supposed to be. Do you ever feel that?'

He raised his eyebrows. It meant, she assumed, that he hadn't thought about it.

'I was intimidated by Kalinda at first. It was just so big and so different to anything I'd ever known before. And here I was, a city girl from the USA, about to spend the rest of my days here.'

'You came at a bad time. It was pretty hot.'

'I thought I'd melt.'

He wagged a finger. 'Take your pace from the sheep.'

She laughed. 'Cassie told me that story. Haven't you noticed? These days, I'm strolling like the slowest, fattest merino on the property.'

'I thought it was the walking-stick.'

She shook her head. 'It's the new me.'

In the months that followed, the weather grew cooler and Nina, with her ankle mended, saw more of Kalinda and began to blend into station life. She learned about sheep and cattle, read books on animal husbandry, studied the subject of underground water, and even learned how to refill the refrigerator with kerosene.

Often, she would drive off on her own, either to take photographs or just to sit and look. The dunes were favourite territory. The colours were vivid and changeable, flashing fiery tones to match a red dawn or turning a sombre blue in the cool of a moonlit night. The patterns on the sand were equally fascinating, for the dunes were always wrinkling and folding in parallel terraces shaped by the passing of a vagrant breeze.

In particular, she loved the lake. Sometimes in the evening, she and Adam would drive out to one of the bays and watch the sun set over the eroded and weirdly coloured headlands.

She learned to ride and even joined Adam at mustering time. She was not a great deal of help, she thought, but he liked to have her near and she loved being with her man.

Daniel was marvellous. So quiet and yet so strong. He was just like Adam in many ways and fitted in perfectly with the way life was at Kalinda.

Her main worry was Cassie. She was not meeting any men of her own age. There was always the amusing Peppino, but his visits were becoming less frequent because his work was taking him to other places. In any case, it was important that a girl of Cassie's age meet as many young men as possible.

Nina was frightened that her step-daughter would marry the first grazier she met and spend the rest of her life living on a property just like Kalinda. That was fine in its way, but someone as bright and capable as Cassie deserved to be given the chance to do something else. She should see more of the world and meet more of its people before she locked herself into perpetuating the only sort of existence she had known.

Cassie ought to be exposed to other people with other thoughts

505

and other values. She might still marry a grazier, but that was all right as long as she made a choice based on a knowledge of what else was available – in both men and lifestyles. She needed to meet a man of the world. Someone truly international and exciting.

BOOK

S · I · X

The Lake

O · N · E

May, 1960: Monaco

Michel Klemansky read about Lake Eyre in an article in *Life* magazine. The story was written by Melina O'Sullivan, a writer who, friends said, had had a number of good stories on Australian subjects published in the last couple of years. What intrigued Klemansky, however, was one photograph. It was spread over two pages and showed a vast expanse of flat, virginal salt. Across the top of the picture stretched a thin, blue-grey fuzziness that marked the place where the lake bed met the sky. That vague, distant line was without blemish; so pure that the curvature of the earth bent its way across the top of the pages. And the promise of that blurred line was that even more of that perfect salt surface lay beyond the horizon.

It was precisely the location for which Klemansky had been looking.

The first girl came out of the bathroom. She was naked except for a long and lavish necklace of diamonds and rubies. They were so large as to be obvious fakes, and hung between breasts that were small enough to be genuine. She walked to the bed, strutting for his benefit but pouting because he was still looking at the magazine. She took it from his hands. 'I thought you might be looking at girls,' she said in heavily accented English. She put the magazine on the floor and stroked his belly.

'Girls are the present, that's the future,' he said. She sat beside him. 'Where's Monique?'

The other girl appeared on cue. She had put flowers in her hair and reeked of perfume. She was taller than the first, and plumper. She sat on the other side of the bed.

'Why are you so interested in that magazine, when we are here?' the first girl said, her face creased by a worried expression that hovered, begging to be erased by a flattering remark. 'Are we so boring?'

'It's just that I'm very interested in salt,' he said and grinned at the consternation his remark caused. The girls attempted to translate for each other. One went through the motions of pouring salt from an imaginary shaker, and he nodded. They giggled.

'Kinky?' One ventured. He grabbed her wrist.

'You will not be able to race tomorrow,' she said, offering a warning but smiling at the futility of it. Was he not paying exceptional money?

'I'll drive better than ever. Come here.'

Klemansky was a Grand Prix racing driver. He was an American. His father, French by birth but Russian by ancestry, had moved to the USA before the war and amassed a fortune importing and selling furs.

Now thirty-one, Klemansky had been racing internationally for six years. Motor racing has a saying that 'the way to make a small fortune from the sport is to start with a big one'. The American was proof that the axiom was fallible. He had started with a big fortune and still had one, but the depth of his financial reserves was due to the American woman's dream of owning a mink coat, rather than any great success on the track. He ran his own team which he called Mustela Racing, an oblique reference to the Mustela Vison which gave its coveted skin to help sustain his passion for motor racing at the highest and most expensive level.

He was not a great racing driver, as Ascari, Fangio or Moss were great, but, having wealth, he was able to drive great cars. He had driven Ferrari sports cars at Le Mans and in the Targa Florio, and crashed a Maserati at Daytona, an accident which left a few intriguing scars on his chin and cheek. He had thought of growing a beard, but found the scars attracted women, who liked to run cool fingers along the jagged lines.

For the past two seasons, he had concentrated on Grand Prix racing. He had begun with a Maserati but it was outclassed and so, for 1960, he had switched to a Cooper-Climax, one of the most successful of the new breed of British rear-engined designs. His car was one of last year's factory machines, built for the final rounds of the Formula One series. Bought from Cooper with spare engines, gearboxes and a truckload of wheels and other components, it was identical to the dark green model used by Jack Brabham to win the world championship.

He had painted the car red, white and blue. White, the colour assigned to America in international racing, was the dominant feature of the design but the red and blue flashes were prominent. With such a colour scheme, he felt he could show allegiance to

America, affection for France and respect for Britain. Thus, in one package, he could honour the countries where he, his father and the car had all been produced.

Never one wanting or forced to do things in a small way, the American had hired some of the best men in Formula One to form the Mustela Racing team. Head of the equipe was Paolo Rotondo who had been with Ferrari. Rotondo was an engineer with special expertise in chassis design and in aerodynamics, the latter an area of racing that was still regarded as a black art – primarily because motor racing people had been more concerned with raw power than with the subtleties of saving energy through slippery shapes. Rotondo, it was rumoured, was working on a new project: perhaps Klemansky's own Grand Prix car, to challenge marques like Ferrari, Lotus, Cooper and BRM.

The Monaco Grand Prix is the most traditional and least typical of all the events that count towards the Formula One World Championship. The race is held not on a special circuit, but through the streets of the tiny principality's capital, Monte Carlo. The start is near the harbour. The road is narrow and climbs to a square near the casino, then plunges through a series of bends, all lined with wheel-breaking kerbs, and kinks through a long tunnel. Back in the sunlight, the road sweeps along the harbour to a hairpin bend, which takes cars back to the start. The track is too narrow and too dangerous but tolerated because Monaco is the way motor racing used to be. The Monaco Grand Prix is also a side-show in which the main attractions are not the drivers but the spectators. It is the one race of the season attended by the ultra rich, who come to be ogled by the envious. Some stay in Monte Carlo's grandest hotels. Others bring their yachts and anchor them in the harbour, knowing that their boats, their women and their suntans will be admired and compared by the less fortunate masses.

Klemansky stayed in a villa in the mountains beyond the Principality. On the morning of the Grand Prix, he drove down in his gull-wing Mercedes. He joined the Grande Corniche at a time when traffic was relatively quiet although a Cisitalia and an MG, locked in mortal combat, soon caught his silver coupé. The Cisitalia had Italian registration, the MG French. Each driver, his imagination catapulting him into a close pitched battle for national honour, weaved across the road in frustration, unable to pass the big German sports car. For several kilometres Kelmansky led them down the road, blocking their progress and stifling their illusions. And then, when the road tightened even more, he blasted away from them, sliding the bends and leaving his pursuers slack-jawed

511

and contemplating careers in banking. He liked doing that. He might not be able to match Moss, Hill or Brabham but he could teach ordinary drivers a lesson.

He wondered how long he might continue racing. It was not a question of money, but pride. Being a Grand Prix driver was fine for a season or two, but being an unsuccessful one was becoming an embarrassment. There was a definite pecking order in the Formula One Circus, and he was firmly established in the lower level. Not a star but a lesser light. He was not used to that. He thought about Rotondo, in America working on the new project. That could give him the prestige he desired. He must send him the magazine and ask him to check out that lake.

Twenty-four cars had been entered for the race but only sixteen were allowed to start, because of the narrowness of the track. Practice had been frantic with drivers striving not merely for a good starting position – and the fastest practice lap gained the number one position on the grid – but for a start in the Grand Prix. The eight who did not make it included Scarlatti's strange Cooper-Castellotti, which was a Cooper chassis with a four-cylinder Ferrari engine, two of the three Cooper-Maseratis and both Lance Reventlow's American-made Scarabs. Reventlow was the son of Woolworth heiress Barbara Hutton, and even richer than Klemansky.

At least Klemansky made the grid. He qualified twelfth which put him in the middle of the third-last row, but he had a bad feeling about the race. The car had not been good in three days of practice. Since the last race, the team had made changes to extract more power from the engine in an effort to match the latest works cars, but power was now erratic down low and Monaco was a place where you needed your horsepower to be unleashed progressively, not in one mammoth punch at the high end of the rev scale. Nervously, he adjusted his gloves. Damn it, Rotondo should have been here to supervise things.

He made a good start. The man on his left stalled and Klemansky caught a glimpse in his mirrors of weaving cars and a set of wheels rearing high in the air. That's someone out, he thought and flicked his eyes back to the tachometer. Into second gear. On his right were the pits where anxious bodies bent towards the chaos at the rear of the field.

He was close to the car in front, the nose of his Cooper chasing the other car's exposed gearbox and spinning drive shafts. Ahead and through a haze of exhaust gases, he could see other cars, weaving, darting for openings, racing up the hill as though all were

512

pulled by a common string. Oil mist smeared his goggles. The Cooper that had been on his right had made up two places. Damn it, the man was getting away from him. Last in the queue, he roared up and away from the harbour, changing gear, losing revolutions with that wretched engine until it burst back into full song and, as always, in the opening moments of a race, frightening himself with the rush of speed and the closeness of the other cars.

Up to the Casino, across to the right and his stomach was somewhere up in his chest as the Cooper lifted for the crest. Then down, and he straightened the wheels for the run towards the difficult right-hander. He'd never got this bend right in practice.

He was losing ground to the car in front. The leaders had disappeared. How the hell did these guys go so fast?

Braking, changing gear, correcting slides; this was a diabolical circuit with well over a thousand gear changes to be made during the race. He'd covered the palm of his right hand with adhesive plaster but he knew that the glove and the plaster wouldn't be enough and he'd have a raw hand from moving that short lever by the time the chequered flag came out.

Into the tunnel, sweeping to the right with a flicker of lights on the left and the marshals watching him but not waving their flags, which meant there was no trouble in front and no one trying to overtake him.

Klemansky began to settle down. He came out of the tunnel and had time to admire the yachts.

He could see cars ahead of him again, the leading ones already as small as insects. By the second lap, they were out of sight: Moss, Brabham and von Trips in the new rear-engined Ferrari. Klemansky's race settled into a personal duel with the driver immediately in front of him. The car was a BRM. Its driver, Klemansky deduced, was having gear selection problems. He would catch the BRM on the parts of the circuit which demanded a series of slick gear changes but lose it on the run around the harbour and on the long climb up the hill.

On lap eighteen it began to rain, and he needed all his concentration to hold the car on line, to stay away from the kerbs, to avoid the slippery spots where oil had been spilled. By lap twenty-five he was right on the BRM's tail. The other car was laying a fine trail of smoke which mixed with the spray to make a lethal fog.

Into the tunnel they raced and he moved the Cooper to one side so he could see more clearly. The marshals were leaning forward and one man was frantically waving a blue flag. It was the signal that one car was about to pass another. Klemansky assumed it was for the benefit of the BRM driver. Only when they were about to

513

leave the tunnel did he glance in the vibrating mirror to the right of the steering wheel and see the two cars immediately behind him. First there was the fright, then the realization: at last, here was his chance to overtake the BRM.

They came out of the tunnel and he was engulfed in spray. He kept left, blinded by water from the tyres of the car in front, and a Cooper and a Lotus thundered past. The two leaders were lapping him. He pulled out, to be sucked along in their slipstream and get the extra pace he needed to pass the BRM.

There was a sharp clout on a back wheel and his car went sideways. Something struck his helmet. He spun, seeing a merry-go-round of white boats and tubular grandstands. The sky turned upside down and with a sickening thud, he hit something. And then everything slowed down and water began filling his helmet.

The American regained consciousness that night. Not two but three cars had been overtaking him. The third car had hit his back wheel and spun him into the fence. From there, the Cooper had somersaulted high in the air and gone into the harbour. A crewman on one of the luxury yachts dived in and released him from the car. He had concussion and his ankle was badly broken.

In the next few weeks, Klemansky made several important decisions. He would retire from Grand Prix racing. He didn't enjoy being lapped at one quarter distance of a race, and in front of a harbour full of pretty girls at that. Nor did he want to hurt himself again. More important, the injury had shocked him into a bit of honest thinking. He wasn't good enough to be a Grand Prix driver.

So he decided to concentrate on the other project because that gave him a chance to be the best in the world. When he could move on crutches, he flew back to America and conferred with Dr Paolo Rotondo. He showed Rotondo the *Life* magazine and they agreed. Next year, Michel Klemansky would make an attempt on the world's land speed record.

Rotondo was designing a car to run with a jet engine. The target speed was five hundred miles an hour. The salt lakes at Utah, where previous records had been set, had been affected by rain and currently were not long enough. They would go instead to Lake Eyre, in South Australia.

May, 1960: Hawker, South Australia

Ginger Thompson had been out of gaol for two months. The charge of cattle stealing had resulted in a two-year sentence but the judge had been even more impressd with Thompson's inclination to use his rifle. Firing at and bringing down an aircraft, and firing at Cassie when she was on the back of the truck had been viewed with such displeasure that Thompson was given a ten-year term in prison. He had been released after six. Thompson had behaved himself, being encouraged by information from Saleem Goolamadail that big money was to be made, provided he got out soon.

He went to Goolamadail's house at Hawker.

The house was still the simple residence that the Afghan had rented in 1953. Now he owned it, but was too cunning to spend any money on its appearance. In nearly seven years, Goolamadail had made a considerable fortune and had gone to pains to ensure few people knew of his growing wealth.

Dealing in stolen cars, trucks and automotive parts had been a profitable enterprise. His cattle- and sheep-stealing business had also flourished. In each zone of illegal activity, he had followed the same principles: regularly move the areas in which his teams operated, and get rid of the spoil through the same trusted outlets. The system worked well. None of his men had been arrested, he was regarded as a respectable if inconspicuous resident of Hawker, and he was rich.

He was not content to continue like this, however, and planned a few spectacular coups over the next twelve months. Then he would move out of town, take his money to Queensland and live the life of a rich man with all the trappings he coveted: a big house, a large American car with high fins at the back, and many women.

'Watcha got in mind?' Thompson asked, his voice high-pitched and whining.

'Your language has grown even more appalling,' Goolamadail said, shaking his head sadly.

'Cut the crap, Gooly. For a couple of years now I've been wondering what the big deal was. No bull. Just tell me.'

The Afghan sighed. 'I have a buyer who can take an extremely large shipment of stock. Both cattle and sheep. This is not small time but a very large business deal. Do you understand?'

'I been in gaol, not the moon. I still speak English. Go on.'

'It will require much organization. I have already done a large part of the necessary work. I need you to help me in the final stages.'

Thompson nodded and poured himself a drink. They were seated in a back room of Goolamadail's house.

'What we are going to do, Ginger, will be on such a large scale that there will be an immediate investigation. Police everywhere.'

'Don't need that.'

Goolamadail was smiling in anticipation of the objection. 'That is all part of the plan, don't worry. Someone else will be the suspect.'

515

He paused to straighten the seam of one trouser leg and avoided Thompson's eyes, being sure the man was staring intently at him. 'And that suspect will be the centre of a great scandal and, hopefully, go to prison.'

'Yeah?' Thompson didn't seem greatly interested in this part of the scheme.

Goolamadail leaned forward. 'Who would you like to see hurt?'

'Watcha mean?' He hated being asked questions when he didn't understand the question, let alone know the answer.

'Who was the man who sent you to prison? Who was the man who threw me out of William Creek?'

'Ross?'

'Mr Adam Ross.' Goolamadail beamed in anticipation of revenge. 'We will steal everyone else's stock other than his. A small proportion of animals will be found in a secret place on his property. This area will appear to have been used for many years for the purpose of hiding stolen stock. It will all be done in such a way that, even if he doesn't go to prison, Mr Adam Ross will never be trusted again. His reputation will be ruined.'

'You got it all worked out Gooly?'

'All.' Goolamadail let the fingers of one hand rest gently on the other.

'Jeeze, you're a devious bastard.'

He smiled serenely. 'Thank you.'

May, 1960: Marree

One of the diesel motors that powered the station generators at Kalinda had broken down and Daniel was taking it to Leigh Creek, the open-cut coal mining centre which had grown into the largest settlement in the north. Leigh Creek had the only automotive workshop in the region that could handle the job of repairing the big diesel unit. Daniel had the motor in the back of a truck that Adam had recently acquired. The truck was not new – it was an ex-Army four-wheel-drive unit that he had bought from Fred Crawford, the Marree-Birdsville mail contractor – but it was good on rough tracks and it was strong and it was big enough to carry the heavy engine. On the way down, Daniel stopped at Marree to see his mother.

Nellie was staying in a house near Saleem Benn's depot. She had not seen Daniel for three years.

When they met, she caught her breath. How could Adam not suspect that this tall young man was his son? Certainly he was

516

darker, with deeply tanned skin and glossy brown hair but the build and the walk and the way he stood, always looking like a spring about to uncoil, were pure Adam Ross.

'They closed the hospital?' he said, after she had kissed him and they had exchanged the conventional greetings.

She nodded sadly. 'There's nothing at Innamincka now, except an empty hospital, the ruins of the pub and a great pile of bottles. Even the bottles are mostly gone. We had a flood.'

'I heard.'

He's as talkative as Adam, she thought. She examined him as mothers do when a son returns after an absence. The boy had gone, leaving no trace except in his smile. That was still the same. The hair had some golden patches but that was probably the sun, not a legacy of Adam's fair locks. His arms were heavily muscled and covered in curly hair, his neck was thick and bull-like in its suggestion of strength – just like Adam's – and he hadn't shaved for a couple of days. She had never seen him with whiskers. He was twenty, legally a youth but undoubtedly a man.

'You're so big,' she said and smiled.

'It's all the work.'

'And food. Mr Ross looking after you?'

The boyish smile stretched the whiskers. 'Adam's terrific.'

'Adam? Shouldn't you call him Mr Ross?'

'No one else does. Except Mrs Wilson.'

'She's the cook?'

'Yeah. She's nice. She's been giving me books to read.'

'What kind?'

'Everything.' He rubbed his chin. 'Forgot to shave.'

'I noticed.'

He smiled at her without speaking, enjoying being with her, just as Adam had done. When he was ready, he said, 'Sometimes I read cowboy books. I like them. Sometimes I read a big book. *Treasure Island, Kidnapped.* Ever read those?'

She shook her head, basking in his pride.

'I even read poetry. Books that Cassie has read. I don't always follow them but I like some of them. She reads a real lot.'

His eyes sparkled at the mention of Adam's daughter and she tilted her head. 'Do you see much of Cassie?'

'Fair bit.' He looked at her with surprise. 'You know her?'

'I know of her,' she said, slowing down to make sure she didn't say too much. 'You've talked of her and mentioned her in your letters.'

He nodded, his thoughts having turned inwards. 'She's good.' The eyes were still bright.

517

'You're not keen on her?' she said anxiously.

'Oh, cut it out.' He grinned.

'She's older than you.'

'So what?'

'Danny, she's the boss's daughter.' Nellie licked her lips in dread. She had never thought of Cassie and Danny as possible lovers.

'Well, what's that got to do with it?' The voice was amused, not challenging, but he was firm, wanting an answer.

She looked away. 'It'd be awkward. I mean if you liked her and she never liked you, it could be difficult. Your job there could be unpleasant. You might have to leave.'

He laughed. 'There's no risk of her liking me.'

He said it so positively she relaxed and smiled at him. 'She got a boy-friend or something?'

'No boy-friends. She's strictly a man-hater. She gives me a hard time.'

'Like what?'

'Oh, treats me like a little brother, you know.'

Nellie skewered him with a glance. 'You don't mind?'

'I'll keep working away.'

'At what?' she asked, alarmed.

'Work. There's plenty of that to keep me busy.'

'But there are other girls there.' She thought of Stella's daughters.

'Yeah. Jimmy's got three girls.'

'What are they like?' She could not disguise the hopeful edge to the question.

'Marie's not bad.'

'How old is she?' Nellie asked, knowing the answer.

'About my age.'

'That's nice.'

He touched her shoulder making her feel frail. 'Mum, I have to be in Leigh Creek this arvo. Is there anything to eat?'

They had lunch. She had been in Marree since the previous December, as always able to depend on the generosity of Saleem Benn. In recent weeks, Nellie had not been well and she feared the old complaint was returning.

'I have to go to Adelaide in a week or two,' she said.

'Oh?' He looked up, concerned, patient, waiting for her to say more, and she shifted uneasily in her chair because that was the way Adam would have responded.

'To see a doctor.'

'Something wrong?'

'I had a problem some years ago. I had to go down for an operation. Remember?'

518

His eyes had not left her, boring in, trying to tap the truth.

'It's nothing serious.' She busied herself clearing the plates. 'But I just have to go and see him again. Have a check up. I'm supposed to do it every now and then.'

He nodded, not quite convinced. 'Do you think I should come back here? To live, I mean. I could get a job, I'm sure.'

'Whatever for?'

'To look after you.'

She laughed. 'I'm only going to Adelaide and then I'm coming back. I'm not exactly helpless.'

'What will you do?'

'Your uncle has said I can work in the store.' With Daniel, she always referred to Saleem Benn as 'uncle'. 'He's enlarging it and putting in a counter where people can buy food and take it away. We're starting to get tourists coming through to drive up the Birdsville Track and the new railway has brought more business into town.' The line had been changed to Standard Gauge three years earlier and the old steam driven Ghan had gone, to be replaced by modern diesel locomotives. The trains were even running on time. She smiled brightly. 'You stay where you are. You just keep learning what you can and one day you'll have your own property.'

'If you ever want me to come back here, let me know.' He reached for a biscuit.

'I don't know if I could afford to feed you.'

'No, I'm serious.'

'I'll remember.' She watched him devour the biscuit. 'They are feeding you up there at Kalinda?' He nodded. 'And you are happy?'

'I could stay there forever.'

I thought that once, too, she reflected, and took the last of the dishes to the kitchen. 'And how's Mr Ross?' she called out.

'Good.'

'And Mrs Ross?'

'Good.'

'What's she like?'

'Good.'

She came back into the room. 'You're full of information.'

'What do you mean?' He was now standing and making signs that he was about to leave.

'Well, I wasn't asking if she was good or bad.'

He thought. 'She takes a lot of photographs. She just had a big story printed in an American magazine. It came in the mail the other day.'

'She must be a clever woman.'

519

His eyebrows played with various possibilities. 'Must be,' he said and smiled at the frustrated expression on his mother's face. 'The kid's good, too,' he added.

'Oh yes, I'd forgotten,' she said but she hadn't. She just found it difficult to talk about Adam's other son.

T · W · O

April, 1961

Patrick Adam Ross was five years and eleven months old and he was wondering what all the excitement was about. Strange things had been happening at Kalinda for many months, certainly since Christmas which he remembered well because he'd been given his own horse for Christmas.

There were all those strange men who came to talk to his father and then went out to the lake and worked there for weeks and weeks. They built a road on to the lake, dumping earth on the soft edges and using big trucks that tipped their loads in a great cloud of dust. He'd liked watching that and had become a special favourite of the man they called Oscar. Oscar carried him around and put him in the truck and even let him pull the lever. And then they had gone out on the lake, so far that he couldn't see the land, and used trucks pulling pieces of wood to make the salt even smoother, until there was a wide mark across the lake like a white road, where they had scraped the rough little bits off the top of the salt.

It *was* salt, because he'd tasted it.

When he'd asked Oscar what he was doing, he was told they'd been making a track for the car, and now everyone was getting excited, even Mrs Wilson who got excited about nothing, because they said the car was coming. He wondered what sort of car could generate such excitement. At Kalinda, they had his father's old Holden and the funny red car that was always kept under the sheet so dust wouldn't get on it, and the new Mercedes-Benz and the two new Land Rovers and the old truck that Danny drove. There was the funny little car that he played with that his Daddy called the 'flying ladder' and the newer and bigger model that was much faster and had two seats. And there were all the cars and trucks that Oscar's friends and Peppino had brought with them.

Then, of course, there was the helicopter his father had made with help from Danny. Everyone laughed at that because it was made from waterpipe and had a Beetle engine – he couldn't understand that but that's what everyone said – but even though people made jokes about the helicopter, it flew and it had been used to check the water troughs and bores all over the property until they had bought the Cessna, which his father and Cassie flew and Danny was learning to fly. So with all the things they already had on Kalinda, he didn't know why they needed a new car, and why they had to make a special road for it on the lake.

'It's a very special kind of car,' Nina told him. 'It has an engine that was made for a jet plane, and the man who owns it wants it to be the fastest car in the world.'

'Doesn't Daddy own it?'

'No. It's owned by an American called Mr Klemansky.'

'Why's he coming here?'

'Because he needs a very long, flat, smooth road and Lake Eyre is the longest, flattest, smoothest place in the world.'

'Do you know him?'

'Mr Klemansky? No, although he's a famous racing driver.'

'But you're an American.'

She laughed and tousled his hair. He was fair-headed like Adam, but with her slender features.

'There are a lot of Americans. Millions of us. We don't all know each other.'

'Are you going to write a story about him?'

'Probably.'

'What are you going to say?'

'It depends on what he does.'

'What are you writing now?' He had seen his mother working in the room where she went when he wasn't supposed to talk to her.

'It's a secret.'

Patrick had large eyes and they widened at the mention of the word. He loved secrets that were shared but hated those that were kept from him. 'What kind of secret?'

'If I told you, it wouldn't be a secret.'

He pondered that and thought it sounded suspiciously like the unpleasant kind of secret.

'I'll tell you what,' she said, reading the disappointment on his face. 'It's only a secret at the moment because I'm not quite sure what sort of story I should write. As soon as I decide, I'll tell you.' He brightened. 'But then you must promise me that you won't tell anyone.'

'I promise.'

She laughed. 'You're a bit early. Wait till I'm ready.' Nina, now approaching forty-one, had established a fine reputation as a free-lance contributor to a number of the world's most important magazines and newspapers. Not needing the money, she could be selective and only wrote about subjects that really interested her. The *Life* article about Lake Eyre had been one of her best, and simple to write because it was about two subjects she loved: the lake and the man who lived nearby, her husband. With the success of that feature, she had decided that her next subject should be Jimmy Kettle. She had talked to Jimmy for hours, with him never suspecting that he was providing the information for her next journalistic triumph. He had chatted about the old days in the boxing troupe, about digging for opals at Coober Pedy, about losing his arm and the early years at Kalinda. It was a fascinating story.

That was her secret. She intended writing the story of a remarkable man who had once been a flamboyant and champion boxer but who now seemed content to hide himself away in the outback. He was, despite his almost shy way, a very funny man, and he was Adam's most loyal friend. She would write the story, tell no one here, have it published, and present it to Jimmy as a gift, because this man, she felt, deserved some public recognition. Besides, it was a hell of a good story.

Peppino Portelli no longer worked for Saleem Benn. For the last six years, he had run his own transport business and had developed into one of the largest operators in the north of the state. Portelli had begun with one truck, an old unit he had purchased from his former employer, but now owned a fleet which ranged in size from simple one-tonners to a couple of big semi-trailers. He specialized in servicing companies drilling for oil and natural gas, and hauled supplies and equipment to rigs in the north-east of South Australia, to the southern part of the Northern Territory and to Western Queensland. The search for oil was booming, and so was Portelli's business.

Saleem Benn had helped the young Italian by giving him a year's free use of the truck before he had to start paying for it. Since then, the Afghan had lent him money and now was a partner with a twenty-five per cent interest in Portelli Transport Proprietary Limited.

Not anticipating the intense activity of the oil exploration era, the old man had decided to get out of the trucking side of his business and concentrate on stores. Hence he had been keen to sell the old truck to Portelli, although at the time he thought the young man was a fool, blinded by enthusiasm and optimism. Saleem

523

Benn's trucking operation had been badly hurt by the improved freight service being offered by the railways with their new diesels. Additionally, the homesteaders who had been his main customers were buying their own large vehicles to carry supplies. some were even getting aircraft and he had witnessed the extraordinary spectacle of a grazier flying his wife to Leigh Creek so she could shop in the large air-conditioned supermarket which had been opened in the mining town.

The world was changing, too rapidly for the Afghan to keep pace, but he had been astute enough to recognize that Portelli was not merely keen but clever. The young man had an analytical brain and when he heard people were searching for oil in South Australia, he quickly learnt all he could about oil exploration, and specifically about the needs of the exploring companies. As a result, he had persuaded Saleem Benn to inject the necessary capital for them to purchase or have constructed special vehicles to suit the new clients. Initially, they had acquired refrigerated vans, which were used to carry food supplies to drilling sites or to teams of geologists at survey camps. The concept of refrigerated transport, miraculous though it may have been, the Afghan could comprehend. After all, that was merely an extension of what he had been doing all his life and a truck hauling milk and frozen foods was no more than a modern and logical successor to the camel caravans laden with flour and sugar that had established the business.

What he found hard to understand was that Portelli Transport made much of its money from mud. Peppino Portelli had discovered that oil drillers needed huge quantities of a special substance called drilling mud to lubricate the bits and pipes that bored deep into the ground. He had become an importer of the lubricant and hauled it to the sites in vast quantities.

Portelli had built a reputation for being able to handle difficult and unusual assignments. He would go anywhere and he was reliable. As a result, his company was the obvious choice for the job of transporting Michel Klemansky's jet car to Lake Eyre.

The car and its accompanying equipment had been shipped from America to Port Adelaide and then put on to three of Portelli's trucks for the journey to Kalinda. Portelli himself drove the semi-trailer that carried the jet car. It was not only the most valuable cargo his company had carried, it was by far the most publicized and he felt the burden imposed by these twin factors was too great for any employee to bear. He also had a natural flair for publicity, and reasoned that if the newspaper photographers and television cameramen failed to show the company name on the side of his truck, the journalists covering the story would want to know the name of the truck driver. Better for business that they write about Giuseppe Portelli than Bluey Wilkins, who was his senior driver and the man he normally entrusted with the most important jobs.

There had been so much publicity about the car that the journey north was unnaturally slow. Every town had its crowd, every intersection its knot of people to see the procession pass. Portelli needed a police escort all the way to Quorn, more than two hundred miles from Adelaide, to guide the trucks and the accompanying cars carrying Klemansky and members of his crew along the prescribed route. The police were also busy ensuring that no over-enthusiastic motorist, passing and waving and peering, wandered off course and ended up beneath the wheels of one of Portelli's giant vehicles.

Klemansky's record breaker had been developed and constructed in America but the testing had been done in secret. As a result, few people knew what it looked like. For the road journey north, the car travelled without cover, its primarily white body glinting in the bright sunlight.

The first surprise was that it was so big. Those expecting either something of racing-car proportions or a recognizable variation on the theme of the ordinary motor car were astonished by its size and shape. It was thirty-two feet long and so functional in its appearance as to be brutal. The heart of the machine and the vital component that determined its shape was the jet engine. Taken from a Sabre fighter, the engine needed to suck in copious amounts of air to help burn its fuel. Then it had to blast a super-heated stream of gas out the back. The car's body, therefore, required a hole in the front, a hole in the back and sufficient room in between to accommodate the long jet engine. The driver was tucked into a space near the front intake with his head protected by a perspex bubble canopy. The four wheels were sheathed within large streamlined arches. The rear of the body carried a high fin, to stabilize the car at speed.

The machine had the look of a monstrous fish. The wheel arches and tail could have been fins and the cockpit canopy an eye. The intake was a mouth and, to add to the effect, the painter had lined the opening with great teeth. He had done it as a joke but his inspiration had helped determine the name of the large vehicle: the Great White Shark.

The official world land speed record was held by the Englishman John Cobb at 394.196 miles per hour. He had set his time on the salt lakes at Bonneville, Utah, in 1947. Cobb was one of a line of drivers who, for a quarter of a century, made record breaking at its ultimate level a British preserve. His car, the Railton Special, was a thunderingly powerful streamliner that was the successor to such machines as Eyston's Thunderbolt, Sir Malcolm Campbell's Bluebird and Henry Segrave's Golden Arrow.

Record breaking is as infectious as it is risky and after setting the new standard on land, Cobb turned to the water. He was going for the world water speed record at Loch Ness in Scotland when his boat, Crusader, hit a ripple. That was sufficient to start the nose pattering. Its even and delicate touch with the lake's surface broken, Crusader reared and plunged and took its brave driver the way of many who fail in record attempts.

At Utah in 1947, Cobb had been forced to follow the stringent rules that applied to land speed record attempts. He had to cover a precisely measured mile and do it twice. The runs had to be in opposite directions, and the second attempt had to be made within one hour of the first. The Railton Special had been powered by two Napier Lion aero engines. They developed two thousand, eight hundred horsepower and, as the rules required, drove the wheels.

The Great White Shark was different. The wheels were not driven. Propulsion came from the violent expansion of burning fuel, whose exhaust gases then rushed through an outlet at the tail of the car. The Great White Shark was a jet engine, on four tyres.

'It was Dr Rotondo's idea,' Klemansky said, waving a generous hand in the direction of the Italian engineer. They were in the lounge at Kalinda. Adam and Nina faced Klemanksy. Cassie sat beside him. Little Patrick was outside, still looking at the car on the back of Portelli's semi-trailer. 'A pure jet car is not strictly legal but we're fighting that. In any case, we're convinced it's the way to go.'

The others waited, certain they would be told why.

'You can remember what happened last year to Donald Campbell?' Klemansky scanned the group. Nina nodded, the others shook their heads. Klemansky changed the grip on his walking-stick. He had used a cane since the Monaco accident. It was not a question of needing support to move properly: the ankle was serviceable, if not perfectly mended. The stick was carried as a cosmetic accessory because the American had discovered a cane and a slight limp made him more attractive to women. It also short-circuited difficult conversations. With him leaning on the stick no one pursued the awkward subject of why he had retired from Grand Prix racing.

Klemansky turned to Cassie. 'Campbell is the son of Sir Malcolm Campbell who was a perpetual record breaker back in the twenties and thirties.' He waited for her smile to guarantee he had won her total attention. 'A very great man.' She nodded, not agreeing but

526

absorbing his assessment. 'The son, Donald Campbell, holds the water speed record. Two hundred and sixty miles per hour. Now that is some achievement, believe me, but it seems the son wants to emulate the father and get the land speed record too.'

He rested both hands on the cane. 'Last year Campbell took his car, which he calls Bluebird, to Utah and went for Cobb's record. Now, the salt at Bonneville is short, maybe only eleven miles long, and to get up to four hundred you've got to put a lot of power on early. That means there's the risk of wheelspin. You all follow me?'

Nina took Adam's hand. This man was starting to make her feel uneasy, as though she were hearing the opening lines of a long sales pitch, but Adam and Cassie were absorbed in his words.

'Campbell had a huge accident. The car turned upside down, tore its wheels off, nearly killed Campbell. And all because it got wheelspin.' He took one hand off the stick and used it to chop the air. 'Big wheels spinning at those speeds can act like gyroscopes. They do strange things like invert cars, and believe me, this business is risky enough without having to judge how much power you should be feeding to your rubber, especially when you're sitting over a few thousand horsepower and the slightest mistake – the slightest mistake –' He pointed at Cassie, to make sure she appreciated the fine margins he was describing. Eyes wide, she nodded. 'Get it wrong and you can feed in a hundred horsepower you don't need.

'So, Paolo here' – he reached across and grabbed the engineer's shoulder – 'came up with the concept of a pure jet. More power. No wheelspin. Campbell's going to try again I believe, but he's following an antiquated, not to say deadly formula. Once you get up around the four hundred miles an hour mark, it's almost impossible to transmit the power needed on to the track through a tyre.'

'But with a jet?' Cassie said, anxious to ask the correct questions.

'With a jet it is still dangerous,' Rotondo said. He had hardly spoken. Now his voice was flat, as though expressing an opinion he had forwarded many times in losing an argument.

'With a jet there's no wheelspin,' Klemansky said, ignoring Rotondo and concentrating on Cassie. 'The wheels are purely the means of rolling across the smooth surface. No frantic spinning, no savage abrasion of the tread, no great heat build-up.'

'They still get hot,' Rotondo corrected. His English was immaculate. 'Very hot.'

The American smiled. 'But not as hot. And with a jet engine, you can go faster, much faster, than with an old-fashioned piston engine.'

Adam had been anxious to ask a question that bothered him.

'But you say the run won't be legal, that the authorities, whoever they are, won't recognize whatever speed you do as a record.'

Klemansky leaned back. 'They'll have to change their rules. If we come out and do five hundred –'

'Four hundred would do,' Rotondo said, smiling.

'We'll say five hundred, because that's what we're aiming for. When we do five hundred, those men who run motor sport and sit in a beautiful office in Paris will have to recognize our achievement. After all, it will look ridiculous saying John Cobb has the record at three hundred and ninety-four if Michel Klemansky had gone a hundred and six miles an hour faster and cracked the magic five hundred. Now won't it?'

Cassie agreed with enthusiasm. She pinned her hands between her knees. 'Is it hard to drive?'

'I'll let you know,' he said, meeting her look of curiosity with an expression that posed its own, more subtle question.

'You mean you haven't driven it?' Adam said and Klemansky turned to him.

'In a few trials. Nothing much yet.'

'When are you going to test it?'

'When I get on to your lake. The trouble is, sir, when you design for five hundred there's not much point in testing at that speed. If you're going to go that fast, you might as well go for the record. As a matter of fact, there aren't too many places on this earth where they welcome you driving at two hundred, let alone five hundred.' He enjoyed a solitary laugh, and put both hands back on the cane. He looked across to Cassie. 'You'd like to drive the Great White Shark?'

She laughed. 'Why did you call it that?'

'Don't you think it's a good name?'

'It's funny.'

'Why?'

'Sharks eat things.'

'This will eat records.' His eyebrows levelled. 'You really want to drive the Shark?'

'You'd let me?'

'Don't badger the man,' Adam said, standing. 'There's no question of you driving a thing like that. It's too big, too powerful and too expensive.'

'And dangerous,' Nina added quietly, and Klemansky smiled, pleased at the addition.

Adam excused himself. 'I've got a sheep station to run. Nice to have you here, Mr Klemansky.'

'Nice to be here, sir. I wasn't sure what we were going to find at

528

Lake Eyre.' He smiled at Cassie. 'Now I know we'll have a great time.'

'Good,' Adam said, and looked uneasily at Cassie.

'Take my word,' Klemansky said as Adam went out, 'we'll break the world record for you.'

Adam waved his thanks and went to see Daniel and Jimmy about the new water tank they were putting in.

'What's he like?' Jimmy asked. As usual, Daniel listened and kept on working. He didn't talk a lot.

'Very good with words,' Adam said.

'That's the biggest car I ever seen,' Jimmy said.

'Wouldn't carry too many bales of wool.'

Daniel grinned at that.

'Tell me,' Jimmy said, hand on the shovel that he held in readiness for Daniel's use, 'what do you reckon this Yank's most interested in? The record or Cassie?'

'What exactly do you mean?' Adam said and Daniel, a suggestion of alarm on his face, stopped working to hear the answer.

Jimmy's smile was so heavy his head fell forward. 'You know exactly what I mean. I saw the way this codger looked at her when he got here. One minute to sum up the place, the rest of the time for the women. He gave everyone the once-over. Even Mrs Wilson.'

'I noticed.'

'What was he like in the house?'

'Like I said. Talked a lot.'

'Eyes on Cassie?'

Adam shrugged. He began chewing his top lip.

'Well, I don't suppose it matters,' Jimmy said. 'She's a good-looking sheila and this bloke probably thought there'd be nothing out here but kangaroos. I'd still watch him though.'

'I will.'

'Mind you, if he plays up and you want to thump him, you'll never catch him.'

Daniel laughed. Jimmy passed him the shovel. 'By the way,' Jimmy continued, 'I thought I might take a run up to the top boundary in the next day or so.'

'Yeah?' Adam looked up, roused from his thoughts about Cassie. She was nearly twenty-five and if he wasn't worrying about the lack of men for her to meet then he was worrying about the calibre of the men she did meet. And she had never met a worldly character like Klemansky. 'What for?' he asked.

'Just to have a look. I got a funny feeling we might be short a few head.'

Adam nodded sagely. He had a great respect for Jimmy's funny feelings.

'Stella was in town the other day and she heard that a few of the places around here have been losing the odd steer. Anna Creek are missing a stud bull.'

'I'll go with you, if you like,' Daniel said but Adam was shaking his head before the offer was completed.

'No, Danny, I want you to stay around the house for the next day or so.'

'What he means,' Jimmy said, 'is that he's going to be busy doing a few things and he wants you to keep an eye on Cassie and make sure that Yank doesn't give her a hard time, or any sort of time.'

'What are you, a mind reader or something?' Adam said, grinning with embarrassment.

'I've known you long enough to know exactly what's going on in that empty space of yours you call a mind.'

'What do you want me to do?' Daniel asked, looking from Jimmy to Adam and trying not to smile.

'There are a few things I want you to do around the homestead.'

'But most of all he wants you to keep an eye on Cassie,' Jimmy said.

'I'm just not sure I trust these new people.'

Daniel, his heart pumping in anticipation of spending the next few days near the boss's daughter, nodded earnestly.

'What I don't want, Danny, is them putting her in one of their fast cars. She could hurt herself.'

Jimmy made a great show of inspecting Daniel, who was now twenty-one, taller than Adam and probably just as strong. 'Reckon the kid could look after her?' he teased. He was well aware of Daniel's interest in Cassie and her total lack of response.

'I just want Danny to be around to keep an eye on things.'

'I'll be pleased to, Adam,' Daniel said, and looked pleased.

Ginger Thompson drove Saleem Goolamadail to the yards he had constructed inside the north-western boundary of Adam Ross's property. The structure was crude but strong and had room for a couple of hundred head of cattle. It was built near a mound spring that rose within a grouping of low hills. It was hidden from all sides except the north, and no one ever came from the north.

Cattle had found the spring. Thompson had followed the cattle and then built the yards near the water. He had run a pipe to a trough within the enclosure.

'I guarantee Ross don't know about the spring,' Thompson said, leading Goolamadail to the gate. 'With a couple of thousand square miles to his name, he won't 've been everywhere.'

Goolamadail looked around. The ground had been well trampled.

'I been bringing 'is cattle in 'ere for months,' Thompson said. 'Then I let 'em out again. The place looks like it's been used for years.'

'You have his brand?'

Thompson took a branding iron that had been leaning against the fence. 'It's an exact copy.'

'And the others?'

'All the ones you asked for.'

'And you will brand these tomorrow?'

'Do the lot.' He cast an eye over the cattle standing sullenly in one corner of the yard. 'You sure about the bull? We could get a lot for that.'

'The bull must be included.'

'Gooly, it's got to be worth a couple of thousand.'

'Good.'

'That'd be nice money in our pockets.'

Goolamadail touched the top rail with the caution of one who expects splinters. 'But it will cover our trail and hopefully put our friend in prison.' He took his hand away and brushed the palms. 'Because the animal is so valuable, the owners will identify it positively, and be very angry at the man they think has stolen it. Be sure to brand it very well, so there is no sign of the other mark.'

'I'll do it as though I worked for Ross.'

'That is precisely the way to do it.' He patted the air with his hands. 'As though you were genuinely stealing the animal to add to Kalinda's herd. It must be done in such a way that no one is in doubt that Mr Adam Ross stole this bull and, by inference, had stolen all the other animals. That will make it much simpler for us.'

'And put him in gaol?'

'Hopefully.'

'You must hate this bloke.'

'Surely you do too? He put you in prison for many years.'

Thompson smacked the top rail. 'Don't think I'd go to all this trouble.'

'Think of it this way. By diverting blame, we achieve two objectives. It is a very good plan.'

'Suppose so. And we go for the big haul on schedule?'

'In three days' time.'

'And then that's it. We take the money and run.'

'We disappear.' Goolamadail smiled contentedly.

'Seems a shame. We got such a good operation.'

531

'Don't get greedy, my friend.' His finger described a series of cautionary arcs in front of the other man's face. 'The operation we are about to undertake is so big we could not possibly continue after its successful conclusion. I can assure you the people who lose stock will be livid. Ready, in fact, to hang someone.'

'This Ross bloke?'

'With luck.'

The train from the south reached Marree late at night. Nellie got off to find Saleem Benn waiting for her. The son of one of his nephews was with him. The boy was sleepy and rubbed his eyes but carried Nellie's bag and walked ahead of the others.

'It's so late. You shouldn't have come,' she told the Afghan, but leaned on his arm. They walked slowly, he feigning feebleness to keep his pace to a level she could manage.

When he spoke, his voice was thin with anxiety. 'What did your friend the doctor say? How is the news?'

'What I expected.'

'He will operate again?'

'He said there's no point.' They walked in silence. The boy reached the house. He turned and Saleem Benn signalled him to take the bag inside. 'The doctor said I might have another six months,' Nellie continued. 'He was very nice. We sat down and we had a cup of tea and some biscuits and he asked me if I wanted to stay down there or come home. I said I wanted to come back here. I hope you don't mind.'

He stopped and gripped her hand. 'I have been praying constantly since you went to Adelaide. Unhappily, it seems my prayers have not been answered.'

'Well,' she said softly, 'it can't be helped.'

He scratched the tip of his nose. 'Six months?'

'At the most. That's what he said anyway, if you can believe what doctors say.' She smiled.

'Life may be good or life may be bad, but life is never easy to understand. Why I have been spared all these years defies logic.'

'You're a good man.'

He patted her hand. 'That is kind of you but the remark shows how little you know of me.' He too attempted a smile. 'You know that I would willingly take your place if, by so doing, you could be spared, but that is merely the impossible wish of a foolish old man who has grown to love you as a daughter and who has been ...' He stopped and scratched his nose again. 'I have been told I talk too much.'

'I like to hear you talk.'

His head bobbed from side to side. 'What will I do when you are not here to flatter me?'

She blinked and smiled brightly. 'I haven't cried once. Don't you start me now.'

Before going to bed, Nellie wrote a long letter to Daniel. In the morning she gave it to Saleem Benn.

'It's for Daniel,' she said. 'I want you to give it to him ... well, you know when.'

T·H·R·E·E

Klemansky established two bases. One was on the lake. Eventually, the car, most of its equipment and a few key personnel would stay there. The other, the larger base, was near the homestead. Klemansky and Dr Rotondo slept in long and luxuriously equipped caravans. The rest of the team stayed in the shearers' quarters.

The American had offered Adam one thousand pounds a week to accommodate and feed the crew. When Adam hesitated, thinking the offer absurdly high, Klemansky immediately raised the figure to twelve hundred and fifty pounds and they had shaken hands on the deal. Feeling guilty, Adam tried to rationalize his acceptance by reminding himself of two things. Firstly, he had no idea how long the team would stay. All Klemansky said was they would remain until they broke the record. It could take two weeks or two months. Adam knew a long stay would interfere with the normal operations of the station, and if the record attempt continued until shearing time, he would be faced with the expense of providing additional accommodation for the record breakers. There was no question of asking the shearers to stay elsewhere; he had little desire to cause a walk-out by asking short-tempered and irreplaceable shearers to stay anywhere but in their designated quarters. Secondly, he could do with the money. He was thinking of buying more cattle to improve the quality of his herd, and had even begun negotiations to purchase a stud bull with an impressive pedigree. The extra thousands from Klemansky should provide the funds for that investment.

Adam had brought in builders to construct the shearers' quarters two years previously. By the standards enjoyed or endured (it depended on one's perspective) by those who had worked at Kalinda in the past, these were buildings with almost lavish facilities. There were four main structures in the complex. Two of them, long buildings in the style of motels, contained twenty rooms. Each room had two beds, electric light, a concrete floor, fly screens for the doors and windows and a fan in the ceiling. Between these buildings was a large toilet block with hot water, showers and a laundry, and the row of lavatories linked to that recently arrived outback miracle, a septic tank system to dispose of waste.

The fourth building housed a kitchen and dining-room. Adam had engaged the cook who normally came to Kalinda at shearing time. He was a first-class chef, who had once worked in a city restaurant. Stella and her elder daughters helped the cook, acted as waitresses and cleaned the units.

Klemansky had a team of twenty-one. There were six men who worked on the track and had been at Lake Eyre since April, four refuellers who would now also help with track preparation until the runs began, a tyre specialist and two fitters, two mechanics who had worked on Klemansky's racing cars for a number of years, a chassis specialist, the body builder who had constructed the car to Rotondo's design, and a panel beater, a painter and Oscar Gronwald, once pit chief for Mustela Racing and now superintendent of this operation.

Others would arrive when summoned: the timekeepers who would record the runs, and officials of the Confederation of Australian Motor Sport, who would supervise the attempt.

In the morning, Adam flew out to the lake. He went in the home-made helicopter. This was a flying machine that had evolved in a curious way. Cassie who was a voracious reader, had seen an article about a miniature helicopter. It was designed to carry one person, had no engine and was intended to be towed behind a speedboat. The machine illustrated had floats and apparently rose in the air when the speedboat reached a sufficiently high speed to turn the single rotating blade fast enough to generate lift. It was called a Fli-Ski. Cassie, wishing she had a helicopter, a speedboat and a lake with water in it, showed the article to her father.

The Fli-Ski was a fun machine, virtually a set of flying water skis, but Adam saw a serious purpose for such a device. Built for land use – with wheels or skids rather than floats – it could be towed behind a car and rise high above the scrub that grew over parts of the property. In this way, he would be able to spot stock hidden in the scrub. The machine, he argued, would be handy at mustering time.

Cassie saw through the argument. Her father regarded the Fli-Ski as a toy, and would have fun with it, but would never admit to such thoughts. So she agreed with him, presuming he might write to the American manufacturer and order one.

Adam, however, meant to built it himself.

With the article was a scale plan of the helicopter. From that, Adam built his own Fli-Ski. He used unconventional materials like waterpipe and galvanized iron and took the wheels from an old welding trolley. He spent seventy-eight pounds on materials he needed, and made the aircraft larger than on the plan because he thought the original looked too small to work properly.

He had only seen one helicopter before attempting to build his own. That one had been chartered by a geological survey team on its way to the Simpson Desert, north of Lake Eyre. It had developed a mechanical problem and put down at Kalinda. The helicopter was there only six hours but Adam had spent all that time examining it and talking to the pilot. He felt he understood the basic principles.

Having completed his own, larger version of the Fli-Ski, Adam spent the next six months trying to make it fly. The main problem was the lack of wind. To get into the air, the helicopter needed either a strong breeze or a faster car than Adam possessed.

When a wind began blowing one night, Adam leaped out of bed, woke Daniel and Cassie, and had them drive one of the Land Rovers across the paddocks with the helicopter in tow. It flew well. The problem was the paddocks were fenced and the fences had gates. When Cassie stopped to let Daniel open a gate, Adam fluttered back to earth.

Feeling he had proved the aerodynamic soundness of the design, Adam then thought about powering the aircraft. He worked out a way to drive the main rotors and turn the smaller rear propeller, which was needed to overcome any tendency for the body to spin in the opposite direction to the big blades. All he needed was an engine.

The motor was delivered by a young man driving around Australia and working his way from town to town. He came to Kalinda in an old Volkswagen. Two hundred yards from the homestead, the car's front suspension collapsed. The battery was flat, both headlights had been broken by impacts with kangaroos, and the tyres were so worn that the driver had mended seven punctures in the last three days. He was short of money and temper and gave the car to Adam in exchange for ten pounds and a lift back to William Creek.

The Volkswagen engine was in reasonable condition but Adam and Daniel pulled it apart and gave it new rings and bearings, fitted new spark plugs and points, converted its oil storage to a dry sump lubrication system and then mounted the motor in the helicopter.

It flew sluggishly and seemed reluctant to rise more than a hundred feet from the ground but, in country where few things projected above the flat surface, that was no great disadvantage.

If Adam loved his machine, Nina was appalled by it. The sight of

536

her husband chasing a flock of cockatoos in something he had made out of bits and pieces filled her with dread. Nor was she impressed by the flat, uneven beat of the VW motor. She liked her aircraft to be big, powerful-sounding and with bodies that had walls and windows.

However, Adam wanted to use the helicopter. It was not only fun to fly but it would get into places where a conventional plane could not land, so he and Nina reached a compromise. He agreed to fly no higher than twenty feet above the ground. It meant dodging an occasional tree but she let him soar over the dunes, her rationale being that if he fell on the sand he was less likely to hurt himself, and so many of his flights took him across the dunes, because following the contours of the ridges was more exciting.

When he flew to Lake Eyre, Adam did so for more practical reasons.

The Cessna would have been quicker and possibly safer but Adam had no intention of landing his precious aircraft on salt. He knew what the lake's corrosive surface could do to metal. A couple of landings, in which a fine film of salt was sprayed into the wheel bearings, across the landing gear and up into the engine and fuselage, could cause thousands of pounds worth of damage.

In the past months, he had been to the lake many times and had come to respect its destructive potential. He had also learned some surprising facts. One fact was that even on the hottest days, there were times when the salt became moist. He could scrape away part of the surface, and watch a pool of water form. Adam deduced that the lake had a weird, subterranean tide, which rose and fell beneath the crust. When the tide was high, the water level hovered near the surface, and when this occurred, the corrosive powers of the salt were at their worst.

When Klemansky's track crew first arrived, they drove their vehicles on to the lake in a quest to discover a twenty-mile stretch of salt to use as the record strip. Oscar Gronwald drove his hired car further than the others. He revelled in the smooth conditions, but listened with great interest to the sound his tyres made, for that was a guide to the smoothness and firmness of the surface. Sometimes the noise would be a rumble as he sped across thousands of thimble-sized pinacles of salt. At other times the tyres would hiss, as though running through shallow water.

By the end of the first day, the car seemed to have grown a white skin over all its lower surfaces. After a week, the skin had expanded to great lumps which filled the wheel arches and hung like stalactites beneath the doors. The exhaust pipe swelled into a monstrous tube which grew and grew in layers of baked enamel whiteness.

After two weeks, the car was discarding great crags of salt, as an iceberg at sea jettisons floes. One morning on the third week, Gronwald got in the car and put his foot through the floor.

An examination showed the steel was eaten through in several places. The paint that had originally protected the bottom of the bodyshell had been chipped away by stones, probably on the long drive from the south. The car had then been driven on the lake. Damp salt had stuck to the bare metal and the relentless onslaught of corrosion had begun.

Gronwald, who knew his way around Klemansky, had immediately telegramed the American in Adelaide to report that the floor had fallen out of one of the hired cars. He did not report the cause, and he knew precisely what his boss would do. Klemansky telephoned the general manager of the car rental company to complain that the team had been given a dangerous vehicle. He demanded a replacement, which was railed to William Creek immediately, and with profuse apologies.

Gronwald did not take the new car on to the salt. From then on, only trucks and the aluminium bodied Land Rovers went on to the lake, and they were first cleaned and had their chassis painted with a heavy rubberized undercoat.

Adam flew low across the lake, heading straight for the camp which he could just distinguish as a dark spot on the horizon. He did not follow the wheeltracks. Made by the trucks that hauled gear out of the base, they curled off to the right, to avoid the shoal of mud which lay close to the shore and was covered by a deadly trap of thin salt. There were other shoals and raised salt islands to avoid and the wheeltracks meandered around them. Adam had spent weeks with Gronwald, surveying a safe route out to the site where the car, its fuel and wheels were to be kept. The camp was twenty-three miles from the shore but the supply track skirted thirty-nine miles of hazards to reach it.

The car was to be housed at one end of the strip Gronwald had selected as being suitable for the record attempt. Dr Rotondo had asked for twenty miles of good salt, and Gronwald had surveyed a huge area of the basins, checking the depth of salt (six inches or more was the preferred thickness) and trying to find one absolutely straight line that avoided salt islands or thin patches. He had found nineteen point seven miles of perfect salt, which everyone agreed was sufficient. Several weeks had been spent in smoothing the strip. The salt could not be graded in a conventional sense because scraping the surface with a heavy blade weakened the crust and brought moisture to the top, which softened the crystals. The

538

levelling had been done by dragging pieces of flat timber behind a Land Rover. It was a tedious business, requiring the patience of a gem polisher. It also required a good eye, as the lines had to be straight.

Once the strip had been smoothed to a width of a hundred and fifty yards and polished so fastidiously that it resembled a satin ribbon laid across the lake, the task of measuring was begun. Markers were erected at every mile, and identified by their distance from the base. At the halfway mark were the critical posts: a red marker for the start of the timed section, a blue marker to indicate the end of the flying kilometre and a yellow marker for the mile.

Gronwald was waiting for Adam. He stood well clear of the slowing rotor and, when the pilot stepped out of the machine, walked with him to the large red, white and blue marquee where equipment was stored.

'How's the flying flea?'

'Getting faster every day. We'll be able to go for the record ourselves, I reckon.'

'That must be the slowest, smallest, craziest contraption I ever did see.'

Adam acknowledged the compliment. He got on well with Gronwald. The man was a Swede who had once been a mechanic with the Saab rally team, before switching to racing and joining Klemansky. He was an indefatigable worker who, despite his Scandinavian origins, seemed to perform best in hot weather. He liked the lake. Even in winter it was warm and the white surface reminded him of snow.

'You said I could help you,' Adam said.

Gronwald nodded and outlined his need. He had a special blue dye which would be used to mark the salt. It was to be the guide line that Klemansky would follow on the record runs.

'It sounds crazy I know, but at five hundred miles an hour, Michel could easily move off course and if he gets off line, then it's a big disaster.'

Adam agreed.

'The car has a small cockpit. The driver only sees this much.' Gronwald used his hands to outline a small window. 'So we must paint him a line. I have the dye. We have one of our trucks set up to paint. Do you know what the problem is?'

Adam waited. Gronwald had reached a drum of blue dye and tried to budge it.

'The problem is,' he said, when the drum proved too heavy to shift, 'is to travel in a straight line. We must be absolutely straight. Neither to the left or right. No bends. No wiggles. But, Adam, how do we go in a straight line?'

539

Adam grinned. Gronwald made a point like some farmers plant crops; he spent most of his time preparing the ground. 'You tell me, Oscar. I bet you've worked it out.'

'There is nothing on the ground for us to follow. Nothing to aim at.'

'That's right.'

'So we need you and your incredible piece of flying scrap metal to help us.'

'Which is why you asked me to bring it.'

'Yes.' Gronwald walked out of the tent and past the truck with the painting apparatus fixed to its rear. He faced the strip. 'We want you to fly down the track about five miles. We think we could still see you at five miles. We cannot see anything on the ground at that distance because of the heat haze. You understand?'

'Yes, Oscar.' Adam peered along the strip, which tapered into steamy vagueness. 'So you want me to hover above the track, where you can see me.'

'Precisely. Stay exactly in the centre of the strip if you can.'

'And what will you do?'

'I will drive this truck very fast, aiming straight at you, and dropping a spot of paint every fifty yards. When I reach you, you will fly down another five miles, and so on, until we do all twenty miles. Then, if the dots seem to form a straight line, we will go slowly along the row of dots and paint a nice blue line for Michel to follow.'

Adam laughed. 'This doesn't seem a very scientific way to be doing it.'

Gronwald lifted his hands helplessly. 'I don't know any other way to do it.'

'I thought you'd have all the latest and best equipment.'

'No one makes equipment to build roads on salt or to paint straight blue lines on salt. We are pioneers of a lonely craft.'

So Adam spent the morning helping Oscar Gronwald mark the track. After acting as an aerial target, he landed and travelled in the back of the truck while the blue line was applied. One man drove. Adam and Gronwald tended the painting equipment, which consisted of the drum of dye, a long pipe shaped to project behind the truck and almost touch the track, a valve to regulate the flow of liquid and a shower rose on the end of the pipe.

'How dangerous is this business, Oscar?' Adam asked as the truck rumbled down the centre of the strip.

'Record breaking?' Gronwald had been leaning over the back, concentrating on the flow of dye. He straightened and rubbed a flake of sunburnt skin from his lips. 'If they built a club for people

540

who had broken the land speed record, it would be a very quiet place. There'd be a lot of plaques on the wall, but no one on the leather chairs.'

'Meaning?'

'It's dangerous. Parry Thomas killed himself going for the record on the Pendine Sands. A chain broke and cut him in two. John Cobb holds the record but he's dead. Killed himself on the water. Donald Campbell almost died last year. Cracked his skull and had an ear torn off. When his mechanic got to the wreck of the Blue-bird, the gas turbine was still going and sucked the poor man into the opening in the front of the car. Luckily there was a split intake and one of the man's legs went up one opening and the second leg went up the other. Almost took his balls off.' He checked the paint line. 'It's a dangerous business all right.'

'Well, why is he doing it?'

'Michel?' Gronwald checked ahead, then bent over the back of the truck again. 'He used to drive Formula One and that isn't much better. I guess he's doing it because he wants to, or has to.'

'Has to?'

Gronwald took a deep breath. 'Some men feel compelled to do dangerous things. Don't ask me why. With Michel, it's not the money.'

'He's rich?'

'Got more than you and me will ever see.'

'Funny bloke?'

'A bit strange. Not bad though.'

Adam scratched his jaw. 'I'm a bit worried by the attention he's paying my daughter.'

'Yes?' Gronwald made a minute adjustment to the rate of flow of the dye.

'I wouldn't worry if Cassie wanted to walk through a paddock full of snakes because I know she could handle that. But she's not used to men. Not men like Klemansky, anyhow.'

Gronwald laughed. 'There aren't any other men like him.'

'She'd be lucky to see a dozen men in a year.'

The Swede nodded in sympathy. 'She seems a nice young lady.'

'She is. And I don't want to see her get hurt.'

'Well, if she can handle snakes, she can probably handle Michel.' He looked deep into Adam's eyes. 'All the same I'd keep her away from him if you can. Michel's good with men, good with cars but not so good with women. They're a bit of a sport. Do you know what I mean?'

'I do. Only too well.'

'Well maybe you should have a word with her. When it comes to

541

good-looking young ladies, Michel sometimes can't help himself.'

'He'd better learn how,' Adam said. Subconsciously, he had been rubbing one fist in the palm of his other hand.

The truck rolled slowly along the strip. It had laid another quarter of a mile of blue line before Gronwald spoke again. 'Maybe I should have a word with Michel, just to make sure he understands the situation.'

'Maybe,' Adam said.

Gronwald nudged Adam with an elbow. 'I don't want this fancy car of ours being driven by a man who can't see because he's got two black eyes, now do I?'

'I'm not being stupid about this, Oscar. It's just that I've seen the way he looks at her.'

'I'll talk to him. He listens to me. All we want is for him to break records, not hearts, eh?'

The Great White Shark was about to leave on its journey to the lake. Again Giuseppe Portelli was to drive the truck. He spent an hour adjusting the pressure of the tyres, so the heavy vehicle would cope with sand and not break through the salt. Cassie watched. Occasionally, she was joined by Klemansky, who would spend several minutes with her and then return to his caravan, which was part bedroom, part business office. He said he had many letters to write.

Portelli approached Cassie, who was staring up at the jet car.

'He's a busy man,' he said.

'Heeza very busy manna,' she said, stretching each word to the limit.

'Have I ever told you that you talk like a wop?' He dodged the jab she aimed at his shoulder. Portelli's English had improved as dramatically as his fortune. He retained the Italian habit of enunciating all consonants but his sentences were framed correctly and he chose and uttered his words with precision. In fact, it was this precision, rather than any accent, which made it obvious that he had not been born in Australia.

Apart from a casual greeting on his arrival, Cassie had not spoken to Portelli. 'How was the trip, Peppino?' she asked in a normal voice. The old joke about his accent was only good for one sentence these days. 'Michel tells me there were a lot of people on the road.'

'I've never seen such crowds. There must have been a thousand people at the turn-off south of Port Augusta, and we had to stop at the turn into the main street of Quorn. There were so many people there, I couldn't swing the semi around the corner.'

542

'Is business good?'

'Very good.' He gestured with one hand to catch her eye. 'How long have you been calling him Michel?'

She grinned proudly. 'Since yesterday. He asked me to.'

'He calls me Portelli.' His face was a mask of exaggerated sadness.

'Poor Peppino. What do you call him?'

'Sir.' Both laughed. 'Hey,' he said, accelerating from sadness to enthusiasm, 'you should have come down to Adelaide and travelled up in the truck. We'd have had a lot of fun, waving to everyone.'

'You think I'd like to spend a few days in your semi-trailer?'

He did his best to touch an ear with a shoulder. 'You could have pretended you were the Queen.'

'You think the Queen would ride in a truck?'

He tapped her arm. 'The Queen used to drive a truck.'

She laughed derisively.

'Want to bet?'

'You wanna bet, uh?' She supported the words with flapping hands.

He ignored the reminder of past years. 'The Queen drove a truck during the war. She was only a princess then, and she was in the army.'

'Are you serious?'

'You know me. I never joke.'

'Not much. I'll tell you what, Peppino. Next time you've got a jet car to bring up from Adelaide, let me know and I might do the trip with you.'

'You're full of promises.' He took a deep breath and adjusted his belt. 'Why don't you come down with me when I take the car back?'

'When's that?'

'I don't know. When he breaks the record, I suppose. The crowds will be twice as thick then.'

'He might fly back.'

Portelli was surprised. 'How do you know?'

'He told me just a few minutes ago. He asked me if I'd like to fly him down in the Cessna.'

'He asked you?'

'Why not?' Her back stiffened.

'I thought he'd go back the way he came up.'

'He said it was such a long trip he got bored.'

'And he asked you to fly him back?'

'Yes. He knows I fly.'

543

'And what did you say?'

Before she could answer, Klemansky emerged from his caravan. 'Are we ready to roll, Portelli?' he called out.

'He does call you Portelli,' she whispered and he blushed.

'Ready, Mr Klemansky,' he said and turned back to her. 'You see? I've stopped calling him sir.' He walked to the cabin of his truck.

Klemansky joined Cassie. He shouted to Portelli, 'You go on and get the car to the lake. I'll be there later.'

Portelli waved, and started the truck engine.

'He's a good man,' Klemansky said, firmly nailing the truck driver into his social niche. They watched the truck leave, the big vehicle following a litter of Land Rovers. Daniel had been on the other side of the truck. He stayed in position, facing them.

Klemansky saw the tall station hand and turned his back. He took Cassie by the arm. 'Now, about tonight,' he said, as though the topic had been interrupted by the departure of the jet car.

'Tonight?' She turned, the movement made awkward because he had his arm locked through hers.

'Yes. What are you and I going to be doing tonight?'

'Well, I don't know.'

He walked with her. Hesitantly, and maintaining his distance, Daniel followed.

'Is there a dance we could go to?' Klemansky continued. 'Some show in the nearest theatre? A concert perhaps?'

She sought out his smile. 'There's never anything on around here.'

'Not even a movie?'

'Dad gets pictures sent up sometimes. Usually when the shearers are here.'

'And what do you see?'

She attempted a nonchalant shrug, but her arm was still held by his. He twirled the cane with his free hand and gave her his most winning smile.

'Different things,' she answered. 'We had *Singin' in the Rain* and *Thirty Seconds Over Tokyo.*'

'Oh,' he said, stick rapping the ground. 'All the latest films.'

'I suppose so.'

'Let me make a suggestion.' He had led her towards his caravan. 'But first a question. Do you like French cooking?'

She was nonplussed.

He raised his cane. 'What a ridiculous question for me to ask. Of course you do. Well, it just so happens that I am one of the world's great cooks.' He paused for her reaction.

544

'You?'

'Me. My speciality is French cuisine. I like nothing more than to prepare a meal for intimate friends.' He leaned towards her. 'The fewer the better. I believe that if you try to give a dinner party for too many, the effect is lost, don't you?'

'Well, I don't know,' she said, hoping the answer sounded doubtful rather than confused.

He squeezed her arm. 'It's true, believe me. So what I'm proposing is this. Tonight, there'll be a dinner party in my caravan. The group will be very exclusive. I'll cook. Veal. You like veal?'

Struggling to stay in the conversation, she smiled. 'Yes.'

'Good. Very few things are still fresh after the long run up from Adelaide so this might be the last dinner party without canned food for a while. We'll have to make sure it's memorable.' He stopped at the doorway to his caravan. 'I have some letters to write, some more work to do. Shall we say seven-thirty?'

He released her arm and put one foot on the step of the caravan. She had not been inside. It looked huge.

'Here?' She said.

'Should I send the car?' He smiled.

'It's only a couple of hundred yards. I can walk.'

'On my steps at seven-thirty then.'

She wanted to ask what she should wear but that would make her seem too much like a country bumpkin. She would ask Mrs Wilson. Instead, she said, 'Michel, who'll be at this party?'

'You and me. Don't forget, seven-thirty.' He entered the caravan and closed the door.

At first she was excited and then worried. Just the two of them? And why hadn't he invited her father? No one asked her to do anything or go anywhere without asking him or inviting him. She began walking back to the homestead. Daniel was watching her.

'What *is* up with you today?' she asked.

He twined one ankle around the other. 'Nothing.'

'You've been watching me like a calf that's lost its mother.'

'No I haven't.'

'Haven't you got anything to do?' She was close to him now and she stopped.

'I'm just waiting for Adam to get back from the lake,'

'Would you do something for me then?'

'Sure. What?'

'Go away. I don't like people staring at me.'

F·O·U·R

Jimmy drove as far north as the new bore but found only fifty head of cattle in the area. There should have been at least two hundred. He knew the animals would not wander away from the bore unless they had found another water supply. That was an interesting possibility. Supposing they had strayed and discovered a natural spring or water hole? With more water on the property, they could run a few more hundred head of cattle. Not sheep. There would be dingoes in the area and this was too far from the homestead to offer the vulnerable stock any protection.

When he was sure that no more cattle were to be found near the bore, Jimmy went to the trough beside the windmill and washed – this was good water with a lower soda content than most bores in the district – and did some thinking. At the current market price for beef cattle, the missing stock represented a potential loss of around eight thousand pounds. That was a sobering thought. That amount of money would keep everyone on the station in food for a couple of years. He looked at the bleak landscape surrounding him. The animals could not have roamed off the property; no rain had fallen for months and, without water, they would perish before they crossed Kalinda's unfenced boundary. Or they could have been removed; either driven away by stockmen on horses, or trucked out, just like that thieving character Thompson had been trying to do seven or eight years ago.

Jimmy got back into the two-seater buggy and drove in a wide circle around the bore. He saw no wheel marks or signs of a mob having been driven off.

Searching for tracks, he continued on to the southern branch of the Neales River and, keeping well clear of its salt and mud flats, travelled west to Sunny Creek. He crossed that dry watercourse at a place where the banks had broken into mounds of soft white sand. On the other side of the creek he found some cattle tracks. They headed a little north of due west, but petered out on a gibber plain that stretched beyond the limits of his phenomenal eyesight.

The plain was an amazing sight. So flat, so evenly pebbled and so colourful, it looked like a manufactured article, perhaps a metal plate, once painted but now blistered and rusting. Each stone was the size of an orange. The hues were reds and purples, and the gibbers jostled each other for space. They were iron-hard, but the insidious and abrasive caress of a million years of dust storms had polished the stones to a uniform gloss, size and smoothness.

It was vile country for tracking, so Jimmy set his course to the west, and let the buggy rumble over the stones. He travelled slowly, constantly scanning the horizon.

On previous journeys north, Jimmy had followed the boundary along the upper branch of the Neales, and he had ridden a camel as far west as it was possible to go on the property, but he had never been to this segment of the land. That did not strike him as being unusual. There were many parts of the property he had not seen. Kalinda now sprawled across an area of more than two thousand five hundred square miles and not to see pockets of twenty or fifty square miles merely meant missing a small part of the total. Up here was miserably dry country anyhow, useful only if there was surface water to keep stock alive.

The gibber plain ended and the jarring patter of the stones was replaced by the soft rush of sand beneath the tyres. There were low trees ahead. They formed a grey strip that seemed to hover in haze above the rim of the earth, but they were something to aim at, and he headed that way.

He was within half a mile of the trees when the buggy crossed some tracks. He stopped and walked back. They were hoof marks. Cattle. He scouted the area and found the imprint of a large tyre. All tracks headed to the north-west. He peered into the distance. Off to his right was something; a blur that played games with his eyes. It would appear, skip capriciously into the sky, disappear, emerge as a flat, dark stain, and then dissolve.

Jimmy turned towards the object. In this area of mirages, distances were impossible to judge, sizes deceptive and shapes elusive. But as he drove closer, he decided his target was too wide for a car or truck, too dense for a thin line of trees. It must be a hill.

He was experienced enough to know that a low, narrow hill could be distorted by heat haze to appear like a mountain range and, in such country, he was expecting the object to solidify into a low mound. Instead, and to his surprise, he found he was travelling towards a series of hills. They were low but substantial and covered by outcrops of coarse, broken rocks.

He drove to the base of the first hill. A few stunted trees grew within a ring of fallen rock. Grass rimmed the hill. Jimmy felt a tremor of excitement. There must be water here.

He searched for hoof marks but the ground was rock – not broken into small stones as on the gibber plain but covered in great slabs that lay tilted and superimposed on each other like scales on a fish. Finding no tracks, he turned the buggy towards a patch of softer ground where he might again see signs left by the cattle. Having discovered trees and grass and rocky slopes that were covered in vegetation, he felt reasonably sure that he would find a spring or some other permanent water within the folds of the hills. And that would explain the puzzle of the missing cattle; they had picked up the scent of water and walked to this place.

He began to romanticize. The herd would be somewhere within the hills, their hides sleek and bodies bulging with feed, standing within a lush valley whose grasses were fed by the constant flow of water from a spring. And that would transform Kalinda and perhaps open up an extra few hundred square miles of land for grazing. Adam might even have to build an out-station up here.

He was still dreaming as he drove around the side of the hill and found more low hills running towards the north. He and Stella could move out to this low range. If there was water here and plenty of grass, it would be a good site for a homestead. He could manage the northern part of Kalinda. This would be fine country for cattle. Adam would keep the sheep down near the main bores, and all the cattle could be up here, watering at the new bore and at the spring he would find in these hills.

The house would be built on the side of a hill. Jimmy loved hills. He had grown up at Beltana, on the western side of the Flinders Ranges, and it was those hills, with their colours and craggy ridges and mysterious valleys that he missed most since coming to Kalinda. Each day of his boyhood at Beltana, it seemed, had been fashioned by the ranges. He learned to track there, played there, hid there, speared his first kangaroo there, took his first girl there.

These hills were low, a mere spattering of bubbles on a flawless plain, but Jimmy felt excited as he followed the line of the last curving hill. He had the sensation of being an explorer on the verge of a significant discovery. The hill ended in a jumble of rocks and squat trees. There were more hills on the other side and he realized he had been circling a compound that was in the shape of a horseshoe.

He crossed a patch of soft ground and it was pockmarked with hoof prints. He drove around the point formed by the rocks and trees. The ground here seemed particularly arid and infertile, and a sudden rush of pessimism overwhelmed him, sapping him of strength. It was as though the romantic dreams of the last ten minutes had been swept away by a preview of reality. Jimmy often had these sensations of imminent happenings and he was now limp with the certainty of impending disappointment. He would find little of value. Maybe a trickle of water from some miserable rock hole, no grassy fields, a few scrawny cattle, nowhere to build a house with a view across the hills.

The way in was narrower than he expected, for once past the trees a row of rocky ridges blocked his path. The ridges tapered down to a pavement of crazed stone and for an instant, he had an image of fossilized lizards basking in the sun. The entrance to the ring of hills lay at their tails.

With the buggy wheels bumping over the last rough tip of outcropping rock, he turned into the valley. What he saw made him stop.

The area was half a mile long and almost as wide. The flanks of the hills sloped gently and were well covered with bushes and low trees. There was grass on the floor of the valley. A few guttered depressions marked the course of small creeks that flowed after rain. But what seized his attention was the scene to his right. A large stockyard had been built and it was crammed with cattle. Other cattle milled near the yard. They were being herded by a man on horseback. He swung a whip whose cracking echoes whistled through the hills. Three trucks were parked near the enclosure.

At first Jimmy was confused. It was such a normal scene – but there should be no one out here. A thin column of smoke rose from a fire behind the fence. Part of the ground within the yard was damp. So there was water, he reasoned, and the fire probably meant branding was in progress. With the realization of what he was seeing came anger. They were cattle duffers. Now he had no illusions about what had happened to the missing cattle, nor what was going on here. And he was also angry, in an intense but illogical way, that other people had found such a beautiful place and cheated him of its discovery.

He drove straight towards the man on horseback. His concentration focused on the rider, he passed a collection of large boulders, each as tall as a two-storeyed building. Jimmy did not glance back into the deep shade cast by the boulders. Had he done so, he would have seen a tent and two men holding a map, and talking.

Jimmy stopped the buggy, took his rifle and walked to the man on horseback. The man had not turned.

Jimmy fired one shot in the air and the rider almost fell as the horse shied to one side.

'G'day,' Jimmy said when he knew he had the man's attention. 'Like to get off that horse?'

549

The man dismounted. 'Who the hell are you?'

'I'm the bloke with the gun that's pointing at the spot where your breakfast has got to. Who are you?'

The man did not answer. He took off his hat and wiped his forehead.

'I asked you a question,' Jimmy said, advancing a few paces. 'Who are you and what are you doing with our cattle?'

'They're not your cattle.' The man put on his hat and raised a defiant chin.

'Oh yes they are.' Jimmy lifted the rifle barrel so that it pointed between the man's eyes.

'No boong owns cattle out here.'

Jimmy licked his lips. The insult didn't worry him. He'd flattened many a cocky white man in his early days.

'Specially a one-armed abo. What are you doing with only one arm?'

Jimmy let the barrel drop a fraction. 'I'd have brought the other one but I was in a hurry.'

'You're a real comedian aren't you?'

'And you haven't told me what you're doing here.'

The man was grinning. Alarmed, Jimmy began to turn but it was too late. Something struck him on the head and his eyeballs seemed to burst and, much later, like an echo from a far-off place, he heard the sound of his body hitting the ground.

Some of Nina's best stories had been the most difficult ones to write. They required weeks of research and were followed by lonely hours spent staring at the keys of the typewriter while she tried to construct the sentences that were perfect enough to express her thoughts. She hated doing those stories, although the results were especially satisfying, like producing a beautiful baby after a long and difficult pregnancy.

The article about Jimmy Kettle, however, had been easy to write. And it was good. Jimmy was such a colourful character, and his stories of the early days in the boxing troupe were so bizarre and often hilarious, that it had been simple to string it together. One day was all that it had taken her to write the fifteen hundred words requested by the *Sunday Mail* for its feature section. She had used a lot of direct quotations, which made it a boisterous, rollicking yarn and added her own observations which, she thought (and smiled wickedly at her conceit) gave it a touch of class.

Jimmy, of course, had no idea that the hours spent talking had, in fact, been interview sessions. His surprise would be all the greater, and funnier to observe when he saw his photograph and the article in the Sunday paper. It would be good for him, she thought, and no more than he deserved. A man with as interesting a background as her husband's loyal friend shouldn't hide himself among the sand-hills. He deserved publicity.

A twin-engine plane landed at the strip that afternoon. It brought the timekeepers and the equipment they needed for the record attempt. The pilot was returning to Adelaide immediately. Nina spoke to him and he agreed to take back the big envelope with the article and photographs. He would see that it was delivered to the newspaper office the next morning.

Someone was hitting the inside of a steel boiler with a hammer and Jimmy was inside the boiler and every time the hammer struck, his body shook and his head hurt. The noise was awful. So was the pain. His head throbbed and the pain came from the base of the skull. Maybe the head had shifted on the neck. He thought of moving but nothing would work. He tried to open his eyes but that was agony. His ears worked. He could hear.

He was on the back of a moving truck. He could distinguish the sounds of the motor, and the noise of the wooden floor shaking, and the back wheels bumping and hammering on rough ground. Men were speaking. He couldn't understand what they were saying because of all the roaring and hammering but they were talking. There were two. One man spoke most of the time. Something in the man's voice, muffled though it was by the other noises, scratched at the door to his memory.

The truck stopped and the noises died. The toe of a boot explored his ribs.

'You musta killed him.' The man standing above him shouted, calling to a distant companion.

'Nah,' another voice answered. It was fainter. Jimmy heard a door slam and when the man spoke again, his voice was louder. 'He's got a head like a brick. He's not dead.'

'A bullet through him wouldn't be a bad idea.'

'No.' This was a third man, the one whose voice Jimmy had heard before. 'Let him die of thirst. If they find him with a hole in his head, we will have a very different sort of investigation.'

'He saw me, but.'

'But not us. And he will not survive. He is now at least twenty miles from water.'

'Want me to break his leg?'

'You are a sadist,' the familiar voice said and chuckled. 'But we leave him. It is better for us this way.'

The boots touched him again. 'He feels like he's ready for the maggots.'

551

Again, the chuckle. 'Throw him over the back.' Jimmy strained, trying to make his brain work. Who was it? 'Come on. We haven't got all day. There is much to do and this has been a diversion we could ill afford.'

Rough hands grabbed Jimmy's wrist and his ankles. He was dragged across splintery boards and thrown from the back. The fall seemed to take an abnormal amount of time. He tried to put out his arm and bend his knees but his mind and his hearing were in one place and his body was somewhere else. No matter how he tried, he could not connect the pieces and so he fell like a sack and landed on his back in sand.

The fall helped, for now everything connected. He tried to open an eye and succeeded. The back of the cattle truck loomed above him. Two men were jumping down. Neither looked at him, but walked out of his line of vision towards the front. The third man must already be behind the wheel, because the beat of the motor had risen.

With great difficulty Jimmy rolled on one side. He was in a region of sand ridges. What had they said? Twenty miles from water. He wasn't thinking clearly but he knew he couldn't stay where he was and survive. He was close to the truck. There was a frame beneath its tail, a big metal cradle to carry a spare wheel. He shuffled nearer and grabbed the rearmost bar.

The truck started to move.

Rolled on to his back, Jimmy was dragged along. He was on sand but as soon as the truck reached gibbers or salt, his back would be cut to pieces. A large rock would divide him at the shoulder blades. The strain on his arm was severe. He was about to let go when the truck slowed, then stopped. A door opened.

Jimmy released his grip on the bar and waited, expecting discovery. But the man who got out went to the front. Jimmy heard the scrape of metal, the slosh of water. The man was drinking from the water bag.

'Hurry up,' a voice shouted. That voice again.

Jimmy crawled under the vehicle and climbed into the spare wheel carrier. He put his legs on top of the axle tube, one each side of the differential, and grabbed the top of the frame with his hand.

He was frightened now. Surely one of them would look back and see he was gone, and then they would use the gun. But the truck rolled forward, drove around the end of a sand-hill, and turned slowly to the left.

He was aching in many places, and great clouds of exhaust smoke and sand swirled around him, but Jimmy hung on.

* * *

His arm was numb from fatigue when the truck slowed to wind its way through the rocky ridges that guarded the entrance to the horseshoe valley. He had to get off now. For all of the journey, he had been thinking of this moment and practising what to do. When the dust threatened to choke him or the oil fumes surrounded him with poisonous mist, he had kept himself alert by rehearsing the moves, for he would have to act quickly and precisely. Otherwise, he could get caught under the back axle and be run over, or stay trapped on the metal cage and be discovered when the three men got out.

Straining to lift himself, he pulled back his legs, bending into a foetal crouch. He was entirely within the spare wheel cradle. Now he had to spin around, so that his legs were to the rear of the truck. The vehicle hit a bump, and a metal brace cut into his spine. The pain numbed his back and he lost valuable seconds before he could move again.

He was facing the correct way now, but the truck was speeding up. Jimmy thrust out his legs, felt his heels drag on the ground and worked his way along the frame until only his head and shoulders were within the structure. He pushed clear.

He hit the ground, rolled into a ball, and turned several untidy somersaults. The truck drove on, following the track to the stock-yard.

Jimmy tried to stand, but his muscles would not work properly. Nearby was a small clump of bushes. He crawled to them, arriving within their shelter as the truck stopped on the far side of the large boulders. The driver got out. He was a young man. Jimmy had not seen him before. The other two men were hidden by the vehicle. The first one walked into sight and Jimmy recognized the man he had seen on the horse. The third man stayed out of sight for some time but, eventually, he appeared near the tail of the truck. At first, he was partly obscured by one of the other men but Jimmy, crouched within the bushes, could see he was taller than the others and had black hair. Then he moved away and Jimmy saw him clearly. Saleem Goolamadail.

At the homestead, the plane had taken off to return to Adelaide and Nina, watching it disappear in the south-eastern sky, had a feeling of exceptional contentment. The story could appear this Sunday. It was a good weekend-paper feature. It might even be syndicated to newspapers in other states. She wasn't concerned about the money but felt that the wider the exposure, the more Jimmy would be honoured. Knowing the way the Press worked, she anticipated other newspapers and magazines, even radio and television, wanting to interview Jimmy Kettle. Lake Eyre would soon be in the national focus because of Michel Klemansky's attempt on the land speed record. All the press would be searching for off-beat colour stories and the Jimmy Kettle story was, to use an Australian expression, a real beauty.

Nina began to walk back to the house. Cassie joined her. 'You seemed pleased with yourself.'

Nina put her arm through Cassie's. 'I was just thinking of something.'

'It must have been good.'

'It was.' She saw concern on Cassie's face and tightened her expression. 'Is something bothering you?'

'Well, not really.' Cassie frowned. 'It's about tonight. Michel's asked me to have dinner with him.'

'Michel?' Nina's face became elongated in surprise. 'Where?'

'Well, that's the problem. In his caravan. He's going to cook.'

'And who's going to be there?'

'No one. Just me.' Cassie managed to appear excited and then miserable while uttering only four words.

'And what's the worry? The fact that it's in a caravan, or that he's going to cook a meal?'

Cassie laughed. 'It's not that. He says he's one of the world's great cooks.'

'I don't think modesty is a burden Michel Klemansky has to bear. Mind you,' she said, applying pressure to Cassie's arm, 'he probably is a great cook. You should have an interesting evening.'

Cassie stopped. 'You think I should go?' It was the question of a little girl being allowed to do a normally forbidden thing.

'Of course. I think you could handle anything he's likely to dish out.'

'He said we were having veal.'

Nina dropped her face to disguise her smile. 'I was thinking of other things.' She took Cassie's other hand. 'My dear, you're a grown woman, very attractive, able to fly, drive a car, ride a camel, break a horse, crack a whip, shoot a gun and do God knows what else. But how much do you know about men?'

Cassie wasn't sure whether she should smile, but decided the proper response was to be serious because Nina's eyes burned with a deep concern. 'How do you mean?' she said.

'I mean men. The other sex.' Nina let go Cassie's hand and folded her arms, as she often did when something serious had to be said. 'We've never really talked about this but maybe we should. Now, forgive me for asking but what do you know about sex?'

Cassie grinned. 'You mean about babies? Stella's had three and

554

we've talked a lot. You had Patrick. And Nina, this is a property and we breed horses, cattle and sheep. I know what goes on.'

'Have you ever slept with a man, like that strange Scotsman you met in Adelaide?'

'Of course not.' Cassie blinked and looked down.

'There's nothing to be ashamed of. Women sleep with men these days. Unmarried women, like you. It's perfectly normal.'

'I've slept with Dad.'

Nina laughed, making no sound but rocking her folded arms. 'A long time ago when you were a little girl?'

Cassie nodded.

'I was thinking of something different. Of sleeping with a man who was not your father, when you were grown up, and the two of you made love. Do you understand what I'm talking about?'

'Nina, I'm not fifteen.'

'I know that and I don't want to seem crass or insensitive, but you do live – we live – in a most unusual environment. We don't meet many people. You are not a sophisticated person –' She saw a look of alarm on Cassie's face and extended a hand. 'Don't misunderstand me. That's a compliment. You are a very straightforward, lovable, loving person without all the devious twists of most sophisticates. The trouble is, when you meet one – and Michel is a very sophisticated, charming and experienced man – a person such as yourself can be at a loss to know how to deal with him. You don't know what to believe and what not to believe. You can be so impressed by all the charm and the worldly manners that you can fail to see what the real person is like. Cassie, a person like Michel is very good at disguising his motives, at hiding his real self, so it can be very hard to know what he really is up to.'

'Are you saying I shouldn't go, now?'

'No.' She laughed and again touched the young woman's hand. 'But I am saying you should go with your eyes open and understand what he really wants.'

'And you know what it is he wants?'

'I think so.'

Cassie was silent for a moment. Klemansky's caravan was in sight and she looked from it to her step-mother. 'And what does he want?'

'He wants to take you to bed.'

Cassie put her hand to her mouth.

Nina folded her arms and let her head slowly fall to one side. 'That would be his ultimate objective. There's nothing terribly sinister about it. It's normal. Woman needs man, and man must have his mate or whatever it is the song says. It is a very common

555

thing for a red-blooded male, or even one who thinks he's blue-blooded like our friend Michel, to be so attracted to a woman that he develops an overwhelming desire to take her to bed. To make love.'

'I don't want to go to bed with him,' she protested.

'Good. But just be aware that that is almost certainly his ultimate objective. For a man like him, anyhow. Some men I would trust. Not him. He's the type who doesn't make love because he's in love or passionately fond of a person. He'd take a woman to bed to score points. Do you understand? He's out to prove he's irresistible.'

Cassie cupped her chin. 'You make him sound horrible.'

'Not horrible. Just typical. Of all the attractive men in the world, a good fifty per cent are like that. The trouble for we women is to find a man who comes from the other half of the male population.'

'So what should I do?'

'By all means go. You'll probably have a great time. And he probably is a good cook. Just be cautious.'

'Should I take the shotgun?' Cassie smiled impishly.

'Not a shotgun. For some men, that has other implications.'

'Like what?'

'Oh, Cassie. I can see you and I should have a long, long talk.'

'I had a talk with Mrs Wilson once.'

'I think you and I would cover much more ground.'

Adam was late in returning from the lake. Daniel stood by as he landed the helicopter.

'The engine was misfiring a bit on the way back,' Adam said as they walked from the shed where he housed the machine. 'I think we might take the heads off and check the valves.'

Daniel agreed. He liked working on motors. 'I was wondering what time you were expecting Jimmy back?' he asked.

'Not back yet?'

'No. He took the buggy. He's been gone seven or eight hours already.'

Adam examined the sky. There was still an hour of daylight left. 'He could be all day,' he said. 'There's a lot of country up there.'

'What if he doesn't get back tonight?'

'We'll worry about that when it happens. How did you get on today?'

'All right.'

'Keep an eye on Cassie?'

'Yeah.'

'She get into any trouble?'

556

'Not her. Only me.'

'What do you mean?' Adam took out his handkerchief and wiped the back of his neck.'

'Well, she caught me watching her and didn't like it.'

He examined the grime on the handkerchief. 'Well, I'm sorry about that, Danny. I didn't mean to cause you trouble.'

'That's all right.'

'What's Klemansky been up to?'

'Nothing much. He's spent most of the day in the caravan. The blokes who are going to clock the run arrived in a plane.'

'Oh good.'

'And he sent the car out to the lake.'

'I know. That's why I'm late. I gave them a hand getting it off.' He looked keenly at Daniel. 'What did Cassie say to you?'

'She told me to go away.'

'You're lucky. She's often said worse things to me.' Adam waved and walked to the house. Daniel remained near the shed, watching the track to the north. He was worried about Jimmy.

F·I·V·E

Jimmy felt wretched. His head and back ached and his ankles were sore from being chafed by the truck's axle. He could move his arm only with difficulty. Across the back of his skull was a swelling surmounted by a jagged cut which was hardening into a scab. Blood matted his hair. He was desperately thirsty. Still hiding in the bushes, he waited and watched.

Just before sunset, the two men with Goolamadail finished branding the cattle and joined the Afghan in his camp among the boulders. They were out of sight there, but the aroma of cooking meat drifted across to Jimmy and he could hear murmured fragments of their conversation. One wall of the tallest boulder glowed with the quivering reflections of a fire. At the base of that boulder was a low but dense patch of scrub. That fringe of vegetation was where Jimmy intended to spend the night. He could hide there and be close enough to hear what the men were saying. He might even find water.

Jimmy planned to stay out of sight until the men left. He was in no condition to confront them. He would listen to their conversations, learn what he could, and when they were gone, get in the buggy, drive back to the homestead and have Adam radio the police.

He could not see the buggy. He presumed it was parked somewhere behind the boulders.

He waited for sunset before moving. Walking was difficult and he was so dizzy he had to pause several times to regain his balance. The men's voices grew louder. One man, not Goolamadail, talked most of the time. He laughed a lot. It was a bitter, hard sound. They would be cruel stories he was telling, Jimmy thought, and he felt a hatred for those men. Fervently, he wished to be fit enough to strut around the rocks and take on all three. Normally, he could whip them, even with one arm. In his imagination, he saw himself confronting them. He was muscular, dynamic – and twenty years younger than he really was. He moved among them with dazzling speed, jabbing his fist out, hammering their heads, ducking their crude swings. And when they sprawled flat on the ground, bleating for mercy, he pushed each man's face in the dirt.

He stumbled on a stone and nearly fell. He was near the low bushes but had to pause, one hand on the ground, while his head stopped spinning. Had he felt stronger, he might have laughed. Fight three men? He couldn't stand up.

The man laughed again. The sound seemed so close, so intimidating that it startled Jimmy and he stumbled towards the bushes, anxious to be hidden before someone walked behind the boulders and discovered him. When he reached the first bush, he let himself fall and crawled beneath its low branches. To his shame, he realized that he was frightened.

Jimmy Kettle, the star performer in the boxing troupe with Cedric Carter's Circus hadn't been afraid of anything or anyone.

Gasping for breath, he lay under the bush and thought about those days. He'd had his last professional fight in 1929, and it was now 1961. How could so many years have gone by? How many years? He forced his battered head to think. Thirty-two. Was it really thirty-two years since he'd stood on the boards in front of the boxing tent, with his hair slicked back and his hands taped ready for the night's destruction, and wore his silk dressing-gown and genuine leather lace-up boxing boots, and been booed by the men and adored by the women? The men were always noisy and as restless as roosters when there was a fox around. The women were silent but had hungry eyes.

Thirty-two years since he'd met Adam? He might never see Adam again. Jimmy hadn't thought about dying, not as though it were about to happen, but now he thought about it. If the men found him, they would shoot him. No question. They wouldn't bother driving out into the sand-hills again and dumping him over the back. If they spotted him, it would be a bullet through the head. And what if they'd done something to the buggy? He hadn't considered that, but it was logical. All they had to do was drain the tank and he wouldn't be able to drive it one inch. And then how would he get back? It was a hell of a long walk back to the homestead. Maybe eighty, ninety miles and dry country all the way. The condition he was in, he'd be battling to cover half a mile.

Jimmy had fallen face down, and, being too sore to roll on his back or side, he stayed that way. He cleared the earth near his face, so he could rest comfortably.

After a while, he felt a little better. He had moved to these bushes, he reminded himself, to be closer to the three men and overhear what they were saying. It was time for him to do some listening.

559

The man with the hard laugh had stopped talking. Goolamadail was now speaking, and the others must be listening intently, Jimmy decided, because they rarely interrupted to ask a question. For some time now, he had heard nothing but the drone of the Afghan's voice.

'We will take only those ones,' Goolamadail was saying, 'and leave the others to be found here in a few days' time. You, Ginger, will make sure that Milson is told his cattle have been seen here.'

'Got it.' Thompson held a long stick which he used to poke at the fire.

'As Milson will lose more cattle than anyone else, he will be most interested in the rumour that reaches him, I am sure.'

'He's a good mate of Ross's.' Thompson jabbed at a log.

'Nevertheless, he will come here to see for himself. He might think it possible his cattle have merely strayed this far. Once he sees the elaborate set-up and the branding irons ...' Goolamdail paused, pleased with the subtlety of his plot. 'There is nothing so guaranteed to destroy a friendship as the suspicion that your good friend and neighbour has been stealing your cattle. And that is just what Mr Milson will think about Mr Ross.'

The third man, who had been squatting on his haunches in front of the fire, refilled his cup from a bottle of rum. 'I still think it's a shame to leave all these cattle.'

Goolamadail eyed him with distaste. 'We are taking so many in the other operation, these will be as nothing.'

'Nothin'?' The man drank from the mug. 'I wouldn't mind 'avin' what these'll bring at market.'

'You do not understand. A diversion is necessary.'

'Yeah?' The man's face was set in doubt. 'What I can't understand is why we spent all this time branding cattle we're gonna leave 'ere.'

Goolamadail looked across the flames towards Ginger Thompson, who offered him no support. Ginger didn't like the idea of leaving so many cattle either.

'We take the trucks loaded only with the animals we have selected,' the Afghan said, his voice surly because of the need to repeat himself.

'And leave the steers that we went to all the trouble of branding twice?' the third man growled.

'You have been branding the animals twice for a very good reason.' There was anger in Goolamadail's voice. He waited, to let the heat dissipate. When he spoke again, his voice was lower. 'Once with the brand of other stations, and then over the top with the

Kalinda brand, so that Mr Milson and all the others will believe their good friend has been trying to rob them.'

'Seems a waste of time to me.' The man drank more rum.

Goolamadail stood and stretched his arms. 'Your lack of comprehension saddens me, but does not surprise me. You explain it to him, Ginger. And both of you, be ready to load up at first light.' He walked towards one of the trucks.

The third man scratched his head. 'What did 'e say Ginger?'

Thompson smiled. 'He said you're too much of a dill to know what's goin' on.'

'I'm gonna thump him one day.'

'Wait till he makes us rich. Then I'll give you a hand.'

'You like what he's doin'?' He refilled the cup. 'I've been 'ere three days brandin' and double brandin' and we're just gonna waltz off and leave most of 'em. Doesn't make sense.'

'Yes it does.'

'How? That's what I don't understand.'

'It makes sense because while we're movin' all those cattle down south, the blokes we been robbin' will be up 'ere, screamin' for the blood of this Ross character.'

The other man stared in the fire seeking an explanation in the crackling flame. 'Then why not leave just a few? We could take the rest. Some of them gotta be worth a hundred quid a head.'

'Because you need to leave a lot, with all different brands on 'em, to make it look like Ross has been stealing from everyone. Gooly wants this Ross to look like a big-time cattle duffer.'

'Yeah?' He gazed across the rim of his cup.

'I'd go easy on that stuff if I was you. We got a couple of big days comin' up. You'll need your wits about you.'

'You just worry about yourself, Ginger. I'll be all right.' He wiped his lips and looked away from the flames. 'You reckon Gooly knows what he's doin'?'

Thompson prodded the fire with his long stick. 'Gooly might be a bastard, but I reckon he's a clever bastard.'

'Maybe too clever.'

'Maybe.'

'Probably get his arse burnt.' He drank rum and then sucked in air through clenched teeth. 'Hope he does. Serve the oily bugger right.'

Thompson stood up. 'Better not hope that, mate. If he gets singed, we burn too.' He threw the stick on the fire. 'Wonder how the abo's gettin' on?'

The other man remained squatted in front of the fire. 'Should a put a bullet through 'is skull while we 'ad a chance.'

561

'Don't worry, mate. That bugger was half-dead when we left him.'

'Still better to've made sure.'

'Tell you what.' Ginger stretched his back. 'You can go out before breakfast and see 'ow 'es gettin' on.'

'Why don't you?' He drained the cup.

'Because I got too much else to do.'

'Well, so've I, for Chrissake.'

'Quit belly-achin' then.' Thompson stretched again. 'Jesus mate, the nigger's no worry. He'll just die out there and if anyone ever finds 'im they'll think 'e just run out of water.'

'I don't like it, Ginger.'

'That's nothin' new. You never like nothin' anyhow.' He gave a brittle laugh as a signal that the conversation was terminated, and walked to his tent. The other man stayed by the fire until the bottle was empty. Then he too rose and, stiff with cold, went to the tent.

With the Great White Shark safely unloaded and parked in its tent on the lake, Oscar Gronwald drove back to Kalinda with Klemansky. They reached the homestead well after dark, and went straight to Klemansky's caravan.

'I'm running late,' the American said as he got out of the Land Rover. He glanced at his watch for confirmation and muttered an oath. 'She'll be here in a minute. Got to fly. See you in the morning, Oscar.'

Gronwald leaned across the cabin, one arm outstretched to prevent the door being closed. 'What's on?'

Kleamsaky grinned at him. 'I'm having one of my cooking nights.'

'Michel, take care.'

The Swede often offered advice on mechanical matters but rarely intruded into Klemansky's personal affairs.

The grin vanished. 'You know something I don't know?'

'Who are you having dinner with, Michel?'

'Any of your business?'

'If it's the young lady who's the old man's daughter, yes, it could be.'

'What the hell are you saying, Oscar?'

'I had a talk with Adam out on the lake today. He's a trifle worried that you're showing more interest in the young lady than's healthy.'

'Is he now?'

Gronwald recognized the tone. Klemansky's voice had dropped. It was a signal that Klemansky was about to slam a door, punch a

562

face, or tip a table on its end. The first two were possibilities, but he pressed on. 'We need these people, Michel. Without Adam Ross, there's no access to the lake and without the lake, there's no record.'

Klemansky leaned forward, to see Gronwald more clearly. 'What did he goddam well say?'

'That she's a young and unworldly woman and he doesn't want to see her get hurt.'

'And what did you say, Oscar?'

Gronwald shrugged, pleased that the heat had gone from the American's voice.

'I just said you were a good guy.'

'Gee, thanks, Oscar.' His voice was heavy with irony. 'But you ought to know that the women I like are the young and unworldly ones. When they're as good looking and as interesting as this one, it's a bonus.'

'Michel, I think this one's a nice lady.'

'Well, thank you for the recommendation. But I want you to remember two things, Oscar.' His finger jabbed the vacant seat. 'You don't talk to other men about what I do in my own time. That is none of your goddam business. And you do not tell me who I can and cannot fuck!'

He slammed the door. Gronwald slid across the seat.

'Michel, this could cost us the project.'

'Oscar, if you want to keep your job you stick to handling cars and leave me to handle women. All right?' He rapped the side of the vehicle, and went into his caravan.

Cassie was about to leave the homestead. She was at the door when Adam came out on the verandah.

'I believe you're having dinner with Mr Klemansky?'

'Yes. Michel asked me before he went out to the lake. He's going to cook me a French meal.'

Adam was uneasy, like someone wanting to say something but unable to find the words. He glanced through the wire screen in the direction of the light that shone from Klemansky's caravan.

'I'm going to meet him at seven-thirty,' she said, hand on the door.

'He's probably running late. He only got back a little while ago.'

'He said seven-thirty.' She faced him, daring him to say more.

'I had a talk out on the lake to Oscar. He knows Klemansky pretty well.'

'And?'

Adam's eyes flitted from Cassie to the light in the caravan. 'Well, he says he's a bit of a ladies' man.'

563

'That's OK. I spoke to Nina.'

'Oh. And what did she say?'

'To be careful.'

Adam nodded. 'That's good advice.'

'We reckon he wants to get me in bed with him.'

'Bed?' It took him a long time to utter the word.

'Yes,' she said casually. 'Nina said most men want that.'

'That's what you were talking about?'

'Sure.'

'And you're still going?'

'Of course.' She nudged him. 'You know me. Anything for a free feed.' He was horrified and she laughed. 'Oh Dad, I'll be all right. It should be interesting.'

'You'll be careful?'

'Of course.'

'Do you want me to come and collect you? Say at nine o'clock?'

'You do and I will die of shame.'

He scratched his forehead, sheltering behind his hand. 'You won't be late, will you?'

'I won't be late but I won't be early and I won't be in any trouble.' She blew a kiss and left. By the bottom step, her confident smile had vanished. Nervously, she headed for the caravan.

The caravan had a shower recess and every day, Klemansky had one of his men fill the tank with bore water. In addition he kept a bucket of precious rain water for washing his hair. He was showering when Cassie knocked on the door. His hair was dark and curly and he had just rinsed away the last of the shampoo. He put his head out of the shower doorway and called for her to come in.

She saw his wet curls. 'Oh I'm sorry. I'll come back later.'

'Nonsense. I'll only be a moment.' He began drying his hair. 'Take a seat. There are drinks on the shelf or in the refrigerator. What would you like?'

Hesitantly, she entered the caravan.

'There's sherry, wine, gin, whisky, beer. Just help yourself.'

She selected a beer. The caravan rocked as he dried himself.

'Don't look now. I've got to come out.'

She faced the wall. 'Why don't I come back later?'

'Because I'll only be two minutes.' She heard the pad of his feet and the sound surprised her. It took her several moments to work out what was different and then she knew: he was not limping.

'Can I start to get dinner ready? Maybe put the potatoes on or something?'

'No.' There was a rattle of curtain rings. 'And if you're still

564

facing the other way, like a good little girl, there's no need. I'm now decent and out of sight.'

She relaxed but still took care to face the wall. 'Did you get the car off all right?'

'Absolutely no problems. It's installed in its canvas workshop out there and we can start our runs in a day or so.'

'Tomorrow?'

'Possibly. Just a low speed trial perhaps to make sure everything works.'

'I'd love to see that.'

'Come with me in the morning.'

'You'd take me?'

'Sure.' He drew the curtain and appeared, dressed entirely in white. He often wore white, both because of the colour link with the car and because it suited him. He was one of those persons who appeared perpetually suntanned and the stark outfit made a dramatic and flattering contrast.

He wore white shoes, too, but no socks. Cassie was surprised. The only men she had seen sockless were the poor drifters. Rich men, she assumed, always wore socks.

'Something wrong?' He followed her eyeline.

She blushed, but went ahead. 'You're not wearing socks. Did you forget?'

'No. I rarely wear socks when I'm dressing casually. I find them a bore.' He lifted his cuffs. One ankle was badly scarred. She noticed the scars, as she was supposed to.

'Oh that?' he said, although she had asked no question. 'Does it offend you?'

'No. Of course not.' She sipped her beer. 'What happened?'

'I was racing at Monte Carlo. I was doing very badly.'

She smiled, not believing him.

He poured himself a gin and tonic. 'There was a crash. Another driver and I tangled. He was coming third and was rather anxious to catch the leading pair. Have you ever been to Monaco?'

She executed a minute shake of the head.

'There is a harbour. For the Grand Prix, it is full of yachts. Beautiful boats, big boats, luxurious boats, all crowded with gorgeous girls in their bikinis and, sometimes, not in their bikinis.' He waved his glass, dismissing the vision. 'Well, this rash character's car hit mine and launched me into the air. Over the safety fence, and into the harbour.'

'Oh my goodness. Into the water?'

His spare hand executed a neat dive. 'Luckily, I did not land on any of the beautiful yachts or the beautiful women. My car somer-

565

saulted into the water. I was knocked unconscious, and did this.'
He raised the ankle and waited for her to ask the question all
women now asked, which was how did he get out of the car.

But Cassie did not speak. Obviously, he had got out of the car
without drowning and she sensed he was in the middle of a story
which she had no desire to interrupt.

Klemansky sipped his gin and tonic. 'Fortunately, my car sunk
near one of the largest cruisers in the harbour. On board was a
Moroccan princess who happened to be an accomplished skin-
diver. She had been sunbathing but without hesitation dived overboard and managed to undo my seat belts and pull me to the
surface.'

'A princess?'

'I am told she was very beautiful. A dark woman, with lustrous
skin.' A bearded young Spanish deckhand had dragged him from
the wreck but Klemansky preferred the imaginary Moroccan
princess.

'You were very lucky.'

'No, very unlucky. I did not see my rescuer, the woman who
saved my life, and I am told she was the most beautiful woman in
all of Monaco.'

'Not even after, when you were in hospital?'

'I was unconscious for some days.' He paused, to make sure she
understood the implications of that statement. 'I believe she came
to see me several times. With her face covered, of course, which is
the way she normally appeared in public. But she had to return to
the palace, and so I never saw her. Which is why I say I was
unlucky.' He stood and limped to the gas stove. 'But I think it is
time for the chef to take over from the raconteur.' He spent some
time assembling the ingredients and implements he needed. 'And
you've never been to Monte Carlo?'

'No.'

'Overseas?'

'No. We've been going to go a few times but something's always
cropped up.'

'Like what?'

'Well, two years ago we could have gone around the world or
bought the Cessna, so we bought the plane.' She laughed. 'It cost
more, anyhow.'

'You should go.'

'Nina's talking about going next year. She wants to see her
parents in America. Her mother hasn't been well.'

'That's very laudable.' He brandished the frying-pan. 'But you
should go on your own, not with your parents. Part of every young

566

woman's education should be a visit to Europe, for at least a year. You would enjoy it, you would develop, you would learn so much, and you would have so much fun.'

Cassie was feeling confused. Sometimes Klemansky spoke like an American using the expressions and with the accent Nina used. At other times he sounded European, almost like a refined and sophisticated version of Peppino. Tonight he sounded European.

'I intend spending quite a bit of time in Monaco next year,' he said lighting the gas. 'You should be there. I could show you around.'

Klemansky was a good cook and a charming host. He took away Cassie's beer and gave her champagne and while he prepared the meal and while they ate, he talked about the most fascinating places he had visited.

Afterwards, he escorted her back to the homestead, stick in one hand, torch in the other. Throughout the evening, he had not touched her. Near the house, he said, 'Cassie, my love, do you have a typewriter?'

'We have two. Nina has one and there's another in the office.'

'And, by some miracle of good fortune, do you type?'

'Yes.' She turned towards him, anxious to please. 'What would you like me to do for you?'

'Well, back home I have a secretary who attends to all my correspondence. There are a few things that need to be done....'

'I type Dad's letters and accounts.

'Could you type a few things for me?'

'Michel, I'd be pleased to.'

They reached the steps to the verandah. 'Actually Cassie, I have need of someone who could travel with me and take care of my personal matters. Letters, phone calls, handling money, making travel arrangements. It would be an excellent way of seeing the world. Good money, too.'

She put one hand to her chest. 'You mean me?'

'We'll discuss it tomorrow. I will let you know first thing in the morning if we are contemplating a run on the lake. Thank you for being such delightful company.' He kissed her hand.

He walked back to the caravan, aware that she was still on the steps, watching him. Screw you Oscar and screw you Adam Ross, he thought. I'll have this girl but I'll do it my own way and in my own time.

Adam was in the kitchen making a cup of tea. 'Have a nice night?'

'Yes.'

567

'Klemansky behave himself?'

'Oh Dad, you sound like someone out of the nineteenth century.' She looked at him suspiciously. 'You haven't been waiting up for me?'

'No. I've just come back from Stella's. Jimmy's not home and she's a bit worried.'

'He went up north?'

'Yes. Checking the cattle.'

'That could take him days.'

'I know but he told Stella he'd be back this afternoon.'

She took a second cup and saucer from the cupboard and put it beside his. He poured tea into both cups.

'About nine, I took the Land Rover and drove all the way to the bore,' Adam said.

'And no sign?'

'Nothing. Not a lot of cattle either.'

'You think Jimmy might have gone looking for them?'

'Possible. Anyhow, if he's not back in the morning I'll go up and have a good look around, just in case he's broken down. Want to come?'

She concentrated on the cup. 'I might go out to the lake tomorrow. They're talking of giving the Shark its first run tomorrow.'

He nodded into his cup. 'And what happened tonight?'

They leaned against the kitchen sink while she told him of Klemansky's racing accident and the Moroccan princess and of all the countries he had talked about. She did not tell him of the American's suggestion that she work for him.

Later that night, when only the restless push of cattle in the compound disturbed the night, Jimmy crawled from his shelter and moved slowly to the other side of the boulders. His legs were sore and wobbly and his back responded to every step by firing darts into the base of his skull. His arm was numb and as he moved, he flexed his fingers in a vain attempt to restore feeling.

The campfire had died to a feeble glow of coals. No light shone from the tent where the men slept. Jimmy could hear the rustle of a person snoring. For a while, he was tempted to enter the tent, seize a rifle and either arrest the men on the spot – he'd heard ordinary people could do that – or put a bullet through each of them. He favoured the latter course but it was merely a dream. In his present condition, he couldn't hold a rifle, let alone use one. Realistically, all he could attempt in the next few days was to survive.

He found a can with water and drank a large amount, pausing

568

several times to breathe deeply and enjoy the satisfying rush of cool air over moist lips. With his thirst slaked, the pangs of hunger became sharper. Careful now, a voice warned him. These men mightn't bother to check the level of water in a can but they would certainly know how much food was in the camp.

From the stockyard, a steer bellowed. Others joined in the melancholy chorus. Alarmed, Jimmy retreated to the darkest fold in the wall of the nearest boulder. He expected a torch to flash, or a head to project from the tent flap but no one stirred. Eventually, when the cattle had quietened, he moved back near the fire. Some plates and jars were scattered across the top of a small, flat rock. He opened a jar and dipped his finger in jam. He tasted it. Marmalade. He screwed up his mouth in disapproval; marmalade, he thought, was an invention by the whites to poison the blacks. He tried the next jar and found honey. He ate some and was tempted to empty the jar but prudence prevailed. These men would like their honey, he reasoned, and if in the morning, the supply was gone or dramatically reduced, there would be arguments and accusations and, after the denials, there would be suspicion and that could lead to a search of the area. So instead of having more honey, Jimmy groped for other items.

He discovered a can of biscuits. Because it was almost empty, he took only one. At the bottom of the small rock, his searching fingers found a cardboard box with the remains of a loaf of stale bread and a knife. He cut himself a thick slice. He drank some more water and returned to his hiding place on the far side of the boulders.

There, he ate the bread and thought about the conversation he had overheard earlier in the night. Later, he wondered how he would get back to the homestead. His eyes were abnormally good in the dark, but in all the time he had spent near the fire, he had not been able to see any sign of the buggy.

S·I·X

Soon after dawn, Goolamadail and the others erected a makeshift fence that blocked the narrow entrance to the valley.

Leaving one panel of the fence unfinished so that the trucks could pass through, the three men returned to the stockyard, where they put Thompson's horse and all the equipment on the back of the smallest vehicle. Selected cattle were then loaded on the larger trucks. The rest of the animals were turned loose. There was no shortage of water and ample grass within the hills to sustain them for several weeks.

The men drove away, the three trucks stopping briefly while Thompson tightened the final strands in the fence that now sealed the valley. Next, the convoy swung south-east, the drivers deliberately leaving a trail that pointed towards the Kalinda homestead. However, on reaching the gibber plain, where no tyre marks could be seen, the trucks swung westward and followed a course that would intercept the main Oodnadatta Track.

Jimmy watched them leave. He stayed within his hiding place in the bushes for some time because he had seen the three men leave much earlier in the morning, only to return and load the cattle. When he was sure they had gone, he crawled from his shelter. Still dizzy and aching in several places, he walked to the campsite, searching for food. He found none. The men had made no effort to hide the site – in fact, the suggestion was that the camping area had been used many times and would be used again – but no food or cooking implements had been left. The only things he found were an axe and a couple of branding irons bearing the Kalinda design.

Of the buggy, there was no sign. Jimmy searched around the boulders and examined the area behind the stockyard and around the hills. Eventually, he decided Goolamadail and his companions had either carried the buggy with them or more likely, had taken it somewhere else the previous day and hidden it.

So that was it. He either had to walk or await rescue – except no one at Kalinda knew of this place.

Most of the cattle had left the yard, but two heifers were inside, drinking at the trough. Jimmy entered the yard and pushed the gate shut. The heifers bolted for a corner. There they stood, wild-eyed and with hooves pattering in the dust in nervous anticipation of his next move. Jimmy went to the trough, drank some water and began to remove his clothes. This took him several minutes, because his arm was still numb and his fingers had difficulty undoing buttons.

Clothes off, he immersed himself in the trough. The water was tepid. A brilliant mossy weed grew on the tin walls of the trough but he lay clear of the sides, delighting in the sensation of being submerged in water that was tolerably clean. He washed caked blood from the back of his head and shoulders. He sat up, using the long trough as a tub, and ran his fingers along the cut at the base of his skull. It was still swollen. He wondered what the wound looked like. He longed for a mirror. Being injured and not being able to see the injury was frustrating. A glimpse of the cut and the long ridged swelling might explain why his head ached and why he still felt so bad.

He spent some minutes cleaning caked blood from his hair and then scrubbed his face and feet, and felt the sore spots on his legs, and massaged the muscles nearest them. He lay back in the trough.

The two heifers, constantly backing into each other in the corner of the yard, eyed him with suspicion.

He regarded them with aroused interest. If he had to stay here and wait for someone to discover this place, the heifers might be his only source of food. He grinned ruefully. Trying to slaughter and skin a wild young beast using only an axe and a branding iron could be a slow and messy business. Just catching one would be interesting.

He lifted himself from the trough and bent to retrieve his clothes. He threw his shirt and underpants in the water, and checked the contents of his trouser pockets. All he carried was a penknife, a half-empty box of matches and a handkerchief. Putting them to one side, he threw the trousers in the trough. He kneeled to scrub his clothes.

A sudden giddiness welled within him and, although he tried to grab the side of the trough for support, he fell to the ground. The ache in his head flamed into a searing pain.

He lay in the dust, face down, holding his head and unable to move.

The first thing Adam did in the morning was to see Stella, to confirm that Jimmy had not returned overnight. The second thing

571

he did was see Daniel, to tell him he would be leaving in half an hour to search for Jimmy. He wanted the young man to fill the tank of one Land Rover and put some things in the back: another ten gallons of fuel, a tow rope, shovel, water and some food that Stella was preparing.

Daniel took the opportunity to raise a subject that had been on his mind for some days.

'I was wondering if I could have a few days off to go and see my mother?' Daniel saw uncertainty building on Adam's face, and added, 'I know things are pretty busy at the moment, but she's sick.'

Adam's expression softened. 'I'm sorry to hear that, Danny. Where's your mother living these days?'

'At Marree. She moved there last year. I haven't seen her for a long time.'

Adam scratched his forehead, a sure sign he had a problem he wished he could solve. 'When do you want to go?'

'Soon as you can spare me. It'll only take a couple of days.'

'Well, you know what's got to be done. Why don't you go as soon as you're clear.'

Daniel's hat brim tipped in a nod of thanks.

'How bad is she?' Adam asked, suddenly aware that he should have asked the question earlier. 'Nothing too serious I hope.'

'I don't know. I just got a message the other day that she wasn't too good.'

'Well, you drive down to Marree as soon as you think you can get away.'

'That's good Adam, thanks.' Daniel went to get the Land Rover. He wished he could bring his mother up to Kalinda one day. He would like to show her where he worked, and let her meet Adam.

The third thing Adam did was eat a hasty breakfast. Cassie was about to dash off, to see if the Klemansky camp intended to test the car. Patrick had been feeding his horse and had just been brought inside to eat. He was fond of his horse and did not appreciate the interruption. It was Mrs Wilson's day off and already Nina looked weary.

'Cassie had a good night,' she said, bending to pick up a spoon that Patrick had dropped.

'So I believe.' Adam was thinking about Jimmy and Danny's sick mother and a few jobs he had to do around the place. He made straight for the teapot.

'This Mr Klemansky is either a much nicer man than I imagined, or more devious.'

'Why do you say that?'

572

'From the way he behaved.'

Adam had been engrossed in pouring tea. He looked up. 'Cassie said he behaved himself.'

'That's what I mean. He reminds me of a snake with a brilliant skin. Marvellous to look at but deadly all the same.'

'I understand you told Cassie she should go and have dinner with this snake.'

'So I did and I've got no doubt she could handle any nonsense but apparently he was the perfect gentleman, and I don't think that's what he is.'

'So?'

'We were either wrong, or he's up to something.'

He mumbled in his tea.

'How's Stella?'

'Worried but all right.'

'How long do you think you'll be out?'

'Back by lunch-time. I hope. Could be later. Depends on where he's got to.'

'Back for dinner?'

'Definitely.'

She was frying eggs and bacon in a pan, and asked him to put on the toast. 'There was something I wanted to talk to you about. It concerns Patrick.'

The boy looked up, ready to deny any accusation.

'I've been thinking we should make a decision about his schooling.'

The word 'school' had been involved in too many recent conversations for Patrick's liking. 'I don't want to go to school.'

'Everyone has to go to school,' Nina said.

'I don't.'

'Do you want to grow up to be a dummy?' Adam said from the toaster.

'You didn't go to school.' Jimmy had given Patrick a vivid account of his father's lack of formal education.

'You eat your breakfast.'

'But I want to be like you.'

Smiling, Nina joined Adam at the bench. 'I think he's got the makings of a lawyer, don't you?' she said softly.

'Or a con man.'

'I was thinking about boarding-school again yesterday,' she said and pulled a face at Patrick, who was undecided whether to eavesdrop or eat his breakfast. 'It was while I was talking to Cassie. It made me realize how much she's missed by being stuck up here all the time.'

573

'It's better than living in the city.'

'I know.' She touched his shoulder. 'And I didn't mean stuck in a derogatory sense, but the fact that she has never been anywhere else is a real handicap for her. It had made her very unworldly.'

'I think she's pretty good.'

'Oh Adam, she's wonderful, but she's no match for a svelte piece of goods like Klemansky, simply because she hasn't been around. She's not experienced enough to handle such people.'

'What's this got to do with Patrick?'

'I don't want him to grow up under such a handicap. I want him to be educated at the best schools, meet interesting people, get to know the world.' She looked back. Patrick had a mouthful of food and was watching her intently.

'What are you talking about?' he said, dripping some corn flakes on to the table cloth.

'Nothing,' Adam said.

'Cassie,' Nina said.

'What's Cassie done wrong?'

'Cassie has done nothing wrong. She's a good girl.'

'She's not a girl. She's as big as you are. Bigger.'

Nina turned back to Adam. 'I think boarding-school would be very good.'

A loud hammering came from the workshop as Adam left the house. He heard the hiss of the welding torch. A galaxy of sparks shot out of the big doors. Klemansky's men were making something. He had told them to use whatever equipment they needed but he still found it strange to find other men working around the homestead talking in odd accents and building devices that seemed so alien to this simple outback setting.

He was beginning to feel overwhelmed by problems. Stella was convinced that Jimmy had suffered an appalling accident and he had spent twenty minutes trying to assure her that Jimmy was not lying under the upturned buggy on some remote sand-hill. She had a fear of dingoes, and had dreamed that Jimmy was caught under the buggy with wild dogs circling him and occasionally darting in to rip at his unmoving feet.

Now there was the worry of Daniel and his sick mother. He had never been greatly concerned about the young man's parents. He had always regarded Daniel as belonging to Saleem Benn, because of the old man's special regard for him. Daniel had never spoken of his father. He occasionally mentioned his mother, who seemed to move around from town to town. Maybe she had taken up with another man. He knew a few of the Afghans from Marree, but didn't think he'd met Mrs Khalid. He liked Daniel. He would be a good man to manage the place one day.

And then there was Cassie and Klemansky. Nina was right. For all her strengths, Cassie was a naïve bush girl and she had absolutely no experience of dealing with a character like Klemansky. In her eyes, he probably resembled a hero out of one of her romantic novels, suddenly transformed into flesh. Klemansky was clever enough to have realized this. He would find the experience amusing.

And now Patrick, and the question of his being sent to boarding-school. Adam had not spent as much time with his son as he would have liked. He certainly didn't know him as well as he had Cassie, and that was odd because when his daughter was young, he'd had no money and only Jimmy to help him on the property and he had never worked so hard or so constantly in his life. The difference was that then, he had taken Cassie with him all the time. She had watched him build fences, fetched wood for his fires, helped him track dingoes and potted galahs for their dinner. She had been with him because there was nowhere else for her to be. He reflected; that had been after Nellie had gone and after the war. Cassie had been older than Patrick was now, but there was no question of his son spending all night plodding the sand-hills at his side, tracking down a marauding dingo. He had done that with Cassie. He would never do it with Patrick. Nina would be horrified, and there was no need.

He did not relish the thought of his son being sent off to some distant school. That was like losing him. Children should be with parents, to be loved and taught and enjoyed. Even so, he suspected that Nina was correct. If Patrick stayed here, he would have an inferior education and be as limited in his outlook or his ability to deal with other people as Cassie was. The world was changing and there was going to be no space, in the arena thronged by successful people, for simple bushmen like himself.

He got into the Land Rover and drove away from the home-stead, pleased to have one easily grasped problem to deal with. Jimmy had not come home. He understood that. He had listed all the likely reasons for the delay and was looking forward to the challenge of tracking down his friend.

It was a beautiful morning, still cool and with the sunlight sparkling on the sculptured flanks of the dunes. He began to whistle.

Dr Paolo Rotondo had done more than design the Great White Shark. He had also drawn up specifications for the track and the weather.

It was he who dictated the measurements of the record strip. Twenty miles long, (or the nineteen-point-seven clear miles that Oscar Gronwald had eventually found and graded) was to allow the jet car to be accelerated and then slowed gradually. He estimated the car would need nine miles to get up to its maximum speed. This distance would minimize the risk of it careering out of control from too sudden a blast of power. The driver would then cover the measured mile and be faced with the problem of stopping. At five hundred miles an hour, Rotondo theorized, the car would need eight or nine miles to slow in safety. That distance would allow Klemansky to brake in a way that diminished his speed progressively. A shorter distance would require heavier braking and that would apply such pressure on the surface that a wheel could cut through a soft patch of salt and send the car cart-wheeling to destruction.

The track had a minimum width of one hundred and fifty yards. There were two reasons. One was to give the driver space if, for some reason, the car drifted away from the central guide line. Without backing off, he could keep the car running parallel to the blue line and still go for the record. Rotondo had no idea how stable the Shark would be under full throttle and needed that width to cover any tendency for his design to waver under power.

The fact that he had little more than theory to guide him worried the Italian but he consoled himself with the reminder that he was a pioneer in unknown territory. No one had ever driven at these speeds. No one before him had attempted to design a land-traversing vehicle that would travel at such a velocity. Aircraft went faster, but the aerodynamic problems generated by flying were vastly different to those of a device that hugged the ground. An aircraft was designed to stay away from the ground. His machine had to stay on it. Conventional wind tunnels were a guide, but little more. There was, for example, no facility that could simulate the effect of wheels spinning at such high speeds. He had to guess.

Which brought him to the second reason: survival. If the car become unstable, if the nose began to lift because he had got his sums wrong, if a tyre brust or – and this was the horror that had haunted him since the first day he stood on the lake and sensed its vastness – if a sudden gust of wind came racing from some uninhabited shore and turned the car by a few degrees, Klemansky might not have room to bring it back under control.

He would have liked to have had a mile on either side of the blue line but both Klemansky and Gronwald had argued against that. Klemansky's argument had been a combination of bravado and ridicule. He was prepared, he said, to run on the raw salt; just give him a narrow strip and he would keep the car on line. What did

Paolo want? All the lake levelled? And what was wrong with the car? Wouldn't it run the way the wheels were pointed? Whenever Klemansky sensed the designer was worried about something, he would retreat to the role of driver, acting the part of a simpleton who possessed nothing but skill and daring. He knew such a stance made the Italian uncomfortable because it thrust even more responsibility on his shoulders.

Gronwald had ended the discussion with a simple statement. Nowhere on the lake could he find a strip twenty miles long by two miles wide. There were too many small islands, shoals, and patches of thin crust. But he had sympathized with Rotondo. Understanding and sharing the man's concern, he graded the track to one hundred and fifty yards, which, in practical terms, was as wide a swathe of solid, flat salt as he could cut anywhere on the lake.

Having compromised on the track, Rotondo was insistent about the weather. They could only run the car at speed on calm days. Gusting from the side, a wind could blow the car off course. Rotondo did his sums. Any wind above two knots was dangerous.

Because the morning was still, and therefore met Rotondo's specification, Klemansky decided to give the Shark its first test run.

Gronwald and the mechanics drove from the homestead base before dawn. The American left two hours later. He took Cassie. Rotondo sat in the back of the vehicle, gazing through a window and thinking of side winds, soft patches of salt and unexpected deficiencies in his design.

For Cassie's benefit, Klemansky ran through their schedule for the morning. The car would make several low-speed runs to make sure all systems worked. Then the refuelling crew would rehearse filling the tank at the far end of the strip. Because the rules of record breaking required two runs in opposite directions and because the second run had to be completed within one hour of the first, the speed and efficiency of the refuellers was vital. They had to be in the right place, know what flap on the car's body to open, pour in the precise amount of jet fuel, close off everything properly and not get run over or start a fire. He went through every facet of the refuelling operation. Cassie was impressed.

'How slow is slow?' she asked.

'You mean today?'

'Yes. You said you'd make a couple of slow runs.'

He took his hand from the wheel and measured a minute quantity of air. 'No more than two hundred.'

'Miles an hour?' Her face, he noted, carried the right mixture of surprise and admiration.

577

'If nothing falls off, we might turn the wick up a little and do a couple of threes.'

Cassie was silent. Threes, she presumed, meant three hundred but to ask would seem crass, so she nodded knowingly.

In the back, Rotondo made a soft growling sound.

'The eminent doctor wants to make a few tests to see if he's got the aerodynamics right.' Klemansky smiled into the rear vision mirror. 'You know, make sure the nose is at the front and the tail fin's at the back. Complex stuff like that.'

The track to the lake had been cut into two well-worn ruts. Near the base of one dune, however, the sand had spilled across the track and Klemansky followed a rough detour. When he was back in the ruts, he turned to Cassie.

'Have you thought about what I said last night?'

'About typing some letters for you?'

'About working for me.'

Rotondo shifted his position on the back seat and made a great deal of noise.

'Were you serious?' she said. 'You don't know if I could do the work.'

'I'm sure you could. It's not very difficult.'

Then why do you need someone to do it? she thought briefly, but then dismissed the response as uncharitable. After all, this man was offering to take her around the world. Nina had said she should travel. Here was her chance, and with a rich and exciting character like Michel Klemansky.

'Maybe I should type a few letters for you first.'

'I'm sure you can spell.' He reached out and touched her hand, which was resting on the facia to brace herself against bumps. 'But typing is only a small part of the job. I need someone who can handle the little worries that drive me mad. Look after the details. Organize me. Do you think you could do that?'

She blushed. 'I don't know.'

'I'm sure you could. What do you think Paolo?'

'I was not listening.' Rotondo's voice, strained and high, suggested he had been, did not approve of the conversation but had no desire to become involved.

'Paolo thinks only about technical matters. The man's a genius but an insufferable bore when it comes to other things.' He glanced up at the mirror and winked. 'What's up, my friend? Worried about the way the Shark will behave?'

Rotondo shrugged. 'It is an important day. We have to learn many things.'

'You're a worrier. The car will be perfect. We might even go for the record today.'

'That is nonsense and you know it.'

'The CAMS stewards are due tomorrow. We can go for the record any time after they arrive.'

'We need many trial runs.'

'Not too many. I don't mind dying at speed but I don't want to die of boredom.'

Rotondo closed his eyes. 'You should not say such things, even in jest.'

'I'm deadly serious. We're not going to waste time out on the lake.'

'There are things that must be done, tests that must be carried out before we can try for the record.'

Klemansky turned to Cassie. He smiled conspiratorially. 'Paolo's the sort who'd like a couple of test runs at six hundred before we see if we can do five hundred officially.'

Rotondo leaned forward, grasping the back of Cassie's seat.

'This is not some little barrow he is going to push down the street. This is a jet-powered device, unlike any other car that has ever been constructed or driven.'

'A car is a car.' Klemansky winked at Cassie. 'Some just go faster than others.'

'You say that to torment me. You do not believe it.'

'We'll have the record within a week.' The American lifted his right hand, prepared to shake on a wager.

'We need much more time. This is a dangerous business.'

'The only things that are worthwhile in life involve some element of danger. Ask Miss Ross. I'm sure she agrees.'

The vehicle lurched across a bump. 'I'm not sure,' Cassie said when she had resettled herself in the seat.

'Well, take this job I'm offering you. There's a risk in that, isn't there? It means leaving all this, your home, and going out into the world. The world's a dangerous place.'

Cassie laughed.

'It is,' Klemansky said, his face serious. 'It's full of thieves, cut-throats, murderers. Where you live is a nice, quiet place that is, if you'll forgive me saying so, just a little boring. But outside....' His face became animated with the possibilities that awaited her.

'I think I could handle it,' she said softly.

'I'm sure you could. Would you have to ask your father?'

'I'm not a child. I make those decisions myself.'

'Good. Then the answer is yes?'

'I'll think about it.'

'You'll let me know soon? I need an assistant and if it's not to be you, I'll have to make other arrangements.'

579

'I'll give you an answer in a few days.'

Rotondo slumped back in his seat. He closed his eyes and tried to think of the things he would have to do on the lake. He found it simpler than listening to Klemansky going through another of his routines with young women.

The northern bore had been drilled on a plain of unremitting flatness. The surface was largely clay with wide bands of yellow where rainwater had evaporated and left its stain as a reminder of rare times. There were low islands of sand, and colonies of rocks in which once great slabs were cracking and crumbling into small stones.

The bore site consisted of a pipe, a pool, a windmill, a cooling tank and a drinking trough. It had the look of a place abandoned by living things. Water spurted from the pipe and steam drifted up, to mingle with the heat haze. Otherwise, nothing moved. Past storms had piled sand against the sides of the tank and trough, giving the impression of buildings all but engulfed by encroaching dunes. The rocks that dotted the area lay like tumbled headstones. With its blades unmoving on this windless day, the windmill was a gaunt skeleton presiding over a deserted graveyard.

Adam had half expected to find Jimmy there, grinning and complaining of some minor catastrophe like dirt in the buggy's petrol tank. But there was no Jimmy, no cattle, and not even the comforting clank of the windmill.

The faint, broad imprint of the buggy's tyres were on every sandy patch. He had seen them yesterday. Jimmy had been here and, evidently, had driven around the bore several times. Finding no obvious track away from the bore, Adam headed north. He travelled towards a place where he knew feed grew and saw some cattle in the distance. They were along the bed of a small watercourse, standing in the shade cast by low trees.

Tails flicking, bodies swaying, they watched him approach. He stopped well short of the watercourse, not wanting to stampede them away from their shelter. He climbed on to the roof of the Land Rover and looked around. There was no sign of anything or anyone else. Getting back in the vehicle, he drove in a wide circle around the cattle. He found no trace of vehicle tracks.

Hc drove on, towards the Neales.

Jimmy could see the heifers edging closer. They wanted to drink but were frightened by his presence beside the trough. He could not rise. He tried, but his legs would not move and where his shoulders used to be was now a fiery cross.

With a great effort, he managed to lift his arm and gripped the edge of the trough. Summoning all his strength, he tried to lift himself. His arm shook with the effort but he was weak and could not move his body. He let his arm fall to the ground.

His fingers were wet. He sucked them and pressed the damp palm against his lips.

Behind him, the gate that he had pushed shut now sprung open under the weight of a bull thirsting for water. It shouldered its way into the compound. A dozen larger but lesser animals followed.

The bull, red eyes flicking from one side of the yard to the other, advanced on the trough. It saw Jimmy and stopped. It began pawing the ground.

S·E·V·E·N

Klemansky had commissioned a tailor to make special flameproof overalls for the record attempt. They were all white and had a shark motif on the left breast pocket. His boots and elbow-length gloves, also made from fire-resistant fabric, were powder blue. The helmet was white with a central band of stars and stripes to match the design on the tail fin of the car.

He dressed in the tent where the car had been garaged. He emerged wearing sun-glasses and carrying his gloves and helmet in one hand. His walking-stick swung from the other elbow. He limped past Gronwald and Rotondo and stopped where Cassie was standing, trying to be inconspicuous.

'Can you take photographs?'

She was surprised, and even embarrassed to be noticed. Since they had arrived, and the men had immersed themselves in technical matters, Cassie had felt like an intruder; not unwelcome but out of place.

'I suppose so. Yes.' Nina had shown her how to use the Leicas.

'Well then, you're the official photographer.' He began to put on his helmet.'

'Just like that? Don't I need a camera?'

'I have one. It's in my bag.' He nodded towards the large marquee. 'It's one of those new Japanese cameras. Ever shot in thirty-five millimetre?'

'I've used a Leica.'

He paused and squinted at her. 'Leica? The German camera?'

'Nina has a couple.'

He laughed. 'I can see you're used to nothing but the best. If you can use a Leica, you're definitely the team photographer.'

She got the camera. He showed her how the inbuilt light meter worked, standing beside her so she had to lean against his shoulder.

'It's got colour film in. Thirty-six exposures. Shoot as much as you like. We've got plenty more film.'

'What do you want me to take?' She was excited by the challenge but awed by the responsibility.

'Me.' He smiled from within the white helmet. The banded crown of stars and stripes sparkled in the sun. 'Before I get in, getting in, sitting in the Shark, having the belts tightened. Things like that. And then some of the others around the car, particularly the doctor and Oscar. Do you know how to change lenses?'

'Not on this.' She offered him the camera. He took off the lens and replaced it.

'When the car's running, put a long lens on. Fire off a couple of shots, just for the archives.'

'Where should I stand?'

'With Paolo or Oscar. Don't wander off on your own. I might run over you.' He pulled on one powder-blue glove. 'And then I'd lose all that precious film.'

She photographed him putting on his second glove. She had the car in the background and took care with the composition. Nina had spent a lot of time discussing the framing of subjects.

'Hey, you're good.'

She laughed. 'Don't pass judgement until you see the results. For all you know, I might be cutting your head off.'

'No, you're a pro. I can tell.'

She felt good. Useful, in this camp of specialists.

Cassie took many photographs. Not as many as she had seen Nina take on an assignment but enough, she felt, to cover the subject of Michel Klemansky preparing to drive the Great White Shark at Lake Eyre for the first time. She tried to think as Nina would, and take photographs that an international magazine would publish.

Oscar Gronwald took her by the elbow and led her away from the tail of the car, where she had been standing to get a dramatic shot that emphasized its great length.

'You'll get burnt there,' he said cheerily. 'We're about to fire the engine up.'

She stood clear, chastened by his words. Oscar had been friendly enough, but she had been the only person at the tail while everyone else, who knew what was about to happen, had been near the front.

She had expected that Klemansky would press a button and drive the Shark away. Instead, starting the jet proved to be a complex and exciting process. It had, Cassie reflected, the elements of some primitive ritual, which seemed appropriate considering the desolate location.

One of the Land Rovers was brought in and stationed beside the car. The unit carried a large auxiliary engine on the back, with rows of batteries and several thick cables, coiled on pegs like garden hose. The cables were plugged into connections on the side of the Shark. A shaft was then extended from the auxiliary motor and locked into a pick-up point just behind the cockpit.

Oscar stood near the nose of the car but to one side, to be well clear of the air intake. He raised one arm and waved it in a curious, circular motion. In the cockpit, Klemansky lifted a hand in response. From where she stood, Cassie could see only the top of his helmet and his arm. The perspex canopy was raised, hinged at the rear and rising vertically so that it resembled a transparent egg balancing on its end.

A mechanic on the back of the Land Rover also raised his hand and then bent to press a button which activated a starter motor that whirled the big auxiliary engine into life. When it began to throb, the Land Rover shook.

Cassie wondered what would happen next. She could see Gronwald continuing to swing his arm around, and began to imagine nothing was working until she became aware of a new and almost primeval sound. It was a deep, whirring noise, like some great animal aroused in anger.

The back of the Shark spat a sheet of flame. The whirring grew louder and, for an instant, oily black smoke gushed from the rear orifice. The car began to tremble. The noise became a shriek and the Shark's great white body shook on its wheels. A huge lick of fire burst from the rear and, like a flame on a gas stove, changed to blue and then dissolved to a withering vapour.

The noise became unbearable and she covered her ears.

Gronwald stopped waving, Klemansky lowered his arm, and the mechanic on the Land Rover stopped the auxiliary engine and began disconnecting the shaft and the thick cables. Cassie realized she had forgotten to take a photograph. Hurriedly, she raised the camera, grimacing with the pain caused by the noise, and took a shot. The Land Rover drove away and Gronwald and another man ran to the front of the car to close the cockpit. Cassie put a longer lens on the camera and took a photograph of the canopy being fastened in place.

Then the noise rose to an even shriller level and the car moved. Klemansky turned and headed for the start of the blue line. A blast of hot air hit Cassie and spun her around, almost knocking her from her feet. She crouched, back to the blast, until the car had moved away.

The car faded to a burning red dot chased by a fine mist of

584

powdered salt. Gronwald got in a vehicle and set off on the twenty-mile drive to the other end of the strip, where the refuelling team was waiting.

Rotondo watched him go, his face bearing the expression of a husband whose wife is in labour.

'How fast will he go?' Cassie asked.

He turned suddenly, unaware anyone had been near. 'Who?'

'Michel.' Cassie wished she had not spoken for her words seemed to have derailed his train of thought.

'Maybe three hundred.' His eyes were on the blue line, which led to a tiny puff of white.

'But Michel said he would only be doing two hundred miles an hour.'

He glanced at her, his bushy eyebrows knotted in some other problem. 'Forgive me. I think in kilometres. Three hundred kilometres is about one hundred and eighty-six miles an hour. That is what I would like him to do. But knowing Michel, anything is possible.'

'You think this is dangerous, don't you?'

'Certainly.' He was again squinting towards the horizon. 'This is the most dangerous activity known to man. Much better for Michel if he had wanted to be a lion tamer or an alligator wrestler.'

'Alligator wrestler?'

'In Florida in the south-eastern corner of the United States there are men who make their living by wrestling alligators. You know?' He snapped his arms together. 'They make a good living. They live to be wealthy old men. But no man has ever driven a car powered by a jet engine and tried to travel at eight hundred and forty-six kilometres an hour.' He glanced at her. 'That's five hundred in your measurement which is Michel's avowed goal. Now that we're here, and I realize that we are on a location which is straight out of the stone age, I'm beginning to think we are all mad, me especially.'

'Then why are you involved?'

'Because, young lady, I am an engineer. I cannot resist a challenge, and I am a fool.' He excused himself and walked towards the marquee where there was a two-way radio, connected to the refuellers at the other end of the track.

'How long before the car comes back?' Cassie called out.

He stopped at the entrance to the tent and looked at his watch. 'In about half an hour.'

It was twenty minutes before Rotondo reappeared.

'The car did two hundred and sixteen. That's miles, not kilometres. Much too fast at this stage.' He displayed a mandatory frown, but had trouble maintaining it. 'All systems seem to be working. Michel reports that the car is stable. It shows no apparent inclination to weave or wander off course. Mind you, we are only talking about two-fifths of the speed the car was designed to do.'

He walked towards the track, and she fell into step beside him. With the first run over, the Italian seemed anxious to talk. He talked of wind resistance and how it increased at the cube of the speed. Cassie didn't follow that but Rotondo pressed on. He explained how they had used a revolutionary new paint to reduce surface friction and thus gain a few precious miles per hour. He told her how important were the suspension settings. They determined what clearance the car's body had – the closer it travelled to the surface, the better – and the angle at which it travelled. The nose could be raised or lowered, he explained. Half a degree could be critical at the vehicle's theoretical top speed. Too low at the front, and the nose would apply too great a pressure on the front wheels. Too high, and the car would take off ... literally.

'We are developing enough power to fly.' His face was sombre. 'The trick is to keep it on the ground at a speed four times greater than a jet fighter needs to become airborne.'

Their conversation was interrupted by a noise like thunder rolling through distant mountains.

'Here he comes,' he said quietly, and gripped Cassie's hand.

The Shark emerged from the distant vapours as a grey spot chased by a billowing umbrella of white. For some seconds, the image became an illusion that wobbled and stretched and then broke into three. The lower objects dissolved in haze and only one dark spot could be seen, high above the lake. Rotondo made a noise as though he were choking. He had heard the reports of Campbell's crash at Utah. The British team had seen such a thing and thought it an aberration caused by the rising layers of hot air, but it had been the Bluebird somersaulting.

The image returned to earth and solidified. He sighed and Cassie felt his grip on her hand slacken.

The car raced towards them, nose stuck to the blue line, its shape becoming more distinct as it passed each tall mile post. And behind it came the blur of exhaust gases and salt, and the awful thunderous scream.

At least two miles from them, the noise subsided as Klemansky took his foot from the throttle. At the mile post, the braking parachute popped from the tail. The Shark glided to a halt.

Klemansky was ecstatic. 'Two hundred and seventy-five, Paolo,' he shouted as Rotondo ran to the car. The driver had opened the canopy and lifted himself to the side of the cockpit.

586

'That is too fast.' Rotondo was breathless from worry, rather than from running.

'I could have taken it over three hundred easily.'

'You were supposed to test it at two hundred.'

'Why? It wanted to go faster. We'll have the record within a week.'

Rotondo was smiling despite his efforts to appear stern. 'We will not. We need at least two weeks of tests. But how did it feel?'

'Sensational.'

Rotondo turned to Cassie, who was clicking pictures. 'You see what I have to endure? I ask the driver to give me a report and he says "sensational". I ask you, what does that mean?'

Klemansky slid to the ground. 'It means we're going to get this record.'

'I need to know details.'

'We'll talk tonight, Paolo. Why don't you go and look at those instruments you planted all over this fabulous machine, and see what they say and then do your sums. And when you've done that and thought about what the figures mean, you and I can talk.' He squeezed Rotondo's shoulder and walked to Cassie. 'Get some good pictures?'

She was still excited from the sight of the car at speed. 'I think so.'

'Good. You and I are going back to the homestead. I have an idea.'

'We're not doing more runs?' Rotondo looked up in surprise.

'No. You do your sums and let the boys get on with their re-fuelling practice. We've learned all we need to learn in one day.' He led Cassie towards the marquee. 'I'm going to get changed and then you and I are leaving. Do you know my idea?'

'No.'

'You're going to take me flying over the lake.'

'I am?'

'You'd like to, wouldn't you?'

'Of course. But why?'

'To take some photographs. The track from the air. The base camp. The Shark at rest. Me in the plane, looking down. All those things. Do I have a pilot?'

'Sure.'

He stopped walking and held her elbow tightly. 'I hadn't thought of that. As well as my personal assistant, you could be my personal pilot.'

'You have an aircraft?'

'I'll buy one.'

'What sort?' She laughed.

His eyes were dazzling. 'What sort would you like?'

At mid-afternoon, Adam returned to the northern bore. He had seen no sign of Jimmy and found no fresh tracks. He was now deeply worried. His friend had been gone for almost two days. Adam had checked all the places where he anticipated finding him. There had been tracks at a couple. But he had seen remarkably few cattle, which caused Adam to wonder if Jimmy had driven off into some remote part of the property in pursuit of straying cattle. If that were true, and Jimmy had broken down, then a large area would have to be searched, and the best way to do that was from the air.

He headed back towards the homestead, intending to take the Cessna out immediately.

Nina received two telegrams in the morning. The first was from the editor of the *Sunday Mail.* He praised her story and photographs, and said the article was being used as the main feature in the next issue of the newspaper. Fortunately, he did not mention the subject matter. Mrs Wilson, who had come into the radio room at the time the message was broadcast, had learnt not to ask questions about Nina's work and had retreated, curious but uninformed. She had seen the contented smile on Nina's face and had beamed her most understanding smile in response, but that was as close as they came to an exchange.

The second telegram was from Josef Hoffman. He wanted to see the record breaker in action, he said, and intended flying to Kalinda tomorrow, if they had room. Nina prepared the spare bedroom. She wished Adam had had the foresight to have added a couple more bedrooms for guests when the homestead was being constructed. They were often short of space these days.

When Adam returned, he drove in at a much faster pace than normal. He went to Stella, before coming on to the main homestead.

Nina knew from the empty Land Rover that the search had been unsuccessful and from her husband's long face that he was now extremely worried. He explained what he had done and what he had found.

She made tea. 'What do you think's happened?'

Adam splashed his face with water from the sink tap. This was normally a wrist-slapping offence but she said nothing. He looked hot and almost distraught. He spoke through a veil of dripping water. 'He's probably gone off after some strays. There are a lot of cattle missing. He could have broken down. Maybe got stuck.'

'Could he have had an accident?'

He nodded and wiped water from his jaw. 'But that's the least likely thing. He's probably just stranded somewhere. He would have had a bit of water with him but no food. There's a lot of country out there. Places I've never been to. It's the newest block on the property.' He grinned feebly. 'It's about time I had a good look at it.'

'What are you going to do?'

'Fly out. I mightn't be able to land to pick him up but at least I could spot him and maybe drop some tucker.'

'Fly?'

'I'l take the Cessna and go straight out, while there's still some light.'

She shook her head. 'You can't. Cassie's taken it.'

'When?'

'Half an hour ago.'

'Where?' His voice was growing louder.

'To the lake. Klemansky wanted to go. He needed to take some photographs.'

'She's taken Klemansky to the lake?'

Nina raised her hands, palms towards Adam in an attempt to mollify him. 'She's not going to land on the salt. She knows that's not allowed.'

'But where the hell's the plane when we need it?'

She chewed her lip. She had little practice in handling Adam when he was angry.

'You said she was taking pictures?'

She nodded. 'Apparently Klemansky has asked her to take shots of the record attempt. She photographed the first trial run this morning. She was very excited.'

'Excited. The man's conning her.'

'Maybe, but she didn't think that.'

'And they've taken the Cessna to take pictures of the lake? For heaven's sake, it's been there a million years. They could have waited another day.'

'She wasn't to know,' Nina said in a thin voice and Adam said what she was thinking.

'She knew Jimmy was missing.'

The kettle began to boil. Grateful for the diversion, Nina turned. 'What will you do?'

He sighed, the anger dissipating in despair. 'Take the helicopter, I suppose.'

'But it's so far.'

589

'I can't leave Jimmy out there another night. He could be hurt.... God knows. He's certain to be hungry. And Stella's sick with worry.'

'Please take Danny.'

'I'll have him follow me in the four-wheel-drive.'

'Don't do anything silly.'

'Do I ever do anything silly?'

She put her arms around his neck. 'Constantly.' She pulled his head towards her and kissed loose drops of water from his cheeks. 'And please don't be angry with Cassie. She's so excited about this record business, and being asked to take photographs.'

'Who's providing the film?'

She held him at arm's length. 'They are. And I hope you're joking.'

'I don't like this Klemansky. I wish he would camp on the lake, break the record and go home.'

'He's paying us a lot of money. Money we could do with.'

'It won't be enough if something's happened to Jimmy and we can't find him because Klemansky wants pretty pictures of the lake.'

After he had left, Nina remembered the telegram from Josef. She ran to the verandah but Adam was already in the Land Rover and driving towards the shed where he kept the helicopter.

The plan worried Daniel. 'The motor needs service,' he said, resting against the frame of the helicopter. 'We were going to take the heads off and do the valves, remember?'

'We've got to find Jimmy and I'd like to do it before the sun goes down.'

'Will she do the trip?'

'There's only one way to find out.' When Daniel continued to mumble his concern, Adam said, 'I think Jimmy's worth taking a risk for, don't you?'

'Not in that thing. Not with a sick motor.'

'It's not sick. Just a little off-colour.'

'Why don't we take the truck and your Land Rover? Then there'd be the two of us. We could spread out.'

'Because we can see ten times as much from the air. Come on. We're wasting time.'

Adam refuelled the machine, while Daniel went to get more food and sleeping bags, in case they had to spend the night camped out. The sun was already in the final quarter of the sky when they left. Adam flew directly to the bore. Daniel followed, winding his way through the sand ridges, until the strange little flying machine, looking like some spindly insect, became a mere dot in the sky and then disappeared from sight.

The Reverend Roger Montgomery was making his last visit to Marree. The mission at Beltana was being closed and he would soon be travelling to Adelaide for reassignment. His face bore a look of such intense cheerfulness that Nellie knew Saleem Benn had told the minister the news about her health.

He lied about how well she looked and they talked about trivial things. He was on his way north to William Creek and Oodnadatta and across to Coober Pedy and the smaller opal fields at Mintabi, to say goodbye to friends. The outback was changing. The mission hospital at Innamincka had been abandoned, the days were numbered for the mission at Oodnadatta, and now even the Smith of Dunesk Mission at Beltana, the very core of the Australian Inland Mission's operations in the north, was being closed. They had known days that would never return. They looked at each other sadly.

'You know I'm dying?'

Roger Montgomery's vocation had required him to talk to and comfort many dying people, but he found it difficult to face Nellie. 'Saleem said you were sick.'

'I wanted to thank you for everything you've done for me over the years.'

'Oh, Nellie.' He looked up with agonzied eyes. 'I feel that so much I've done for you, to you, has brought you nothing but misery.'

Saleem Benn had retreated to a corner of the room. He had the ability to fade and become as passive as a painting when not involved in a conversation.

Nellie was smiling. 'You've been a good friend.' The smile became a laugh. 'At least I've got the satisfaction of knowing that most of the bad things that happened to me in my life were my own fault. Not many people can say that.'

He tried to match her good humour. 'Or be honest enough to.'

'Maybe.' She searched for Saleem Benn and found him in the shadows. She smiled and he nodded.

'I've had some terrific times. Done some outrageous things. Done a few good things. I liked it at Innamincka.'

He sat with his hands locked between his knees. 'You did good work there.'

There was a silence. The room was dark, even though it was still light outside. 'It was good to do something useful,' she said.

'It's the best sort of work, when you feel you're doing something that's helping other people.'

591

'The trouble is,' she said, drumming her fingers on the armrests of the chair, 'that now it seems like it was all for nothing, because there's no one left up there. The place has become a ghost town.'

'It might spring back to life one day.'

'It'll never be like it was.'

'Things never are.' The room was filled with dark sighs.

'I was really sad when they closed the hospital.' Nellie leaned back and gazed up at the ceiling. Spider webs hung from the corners. She had intended to sweep them away. They could stay now. 'When Innamincka ended, it felt like a big part of me had died. It was a strange feeling. I was real depressed.'

'We all were.' He coughed. 'How's Daniel?'

'I haven't seen him for a while.'

Saleem Benn moved. 'He is developing into a good man. He is still working with Adam Ross, who treasures him.'

'Adam still doesn't know?'

The Afghan shook his head. 'I sent a note to Daniel the other day. I told him his mother was not well and suggested it would be wise for him to come to Marree soon to see her.'

Nellie smiled weakly. 'It better be real soon.'

Roger looked from one to the other. 'I'll be going to William Creek tomorrow. I'll let him know if you like ... that he should come as soon as he can.'

'That'd be good,' she said. 'I'd like to see Daniel again.'

Adam had never flown the helicopter so high. He was, he guessed, about eight hundred feet above the plain, having spent the last half hour coaxing the machine to that altitude. He could see all the way to the lake and the southern arm of the Neales.

Delicately, and conscious of being so far above the ground in such a flimsy device, he let the nose swing towards the sun. He was searching for shadows: the tell-tale cross of an erect man or the fat blob that the buggy would cast, with its wide chassis and four squat tyres. The plain lay beneath him like a faded abstract painting. It was a bleached pink and blotched with yellowed water stains and flat islands of white sand. Lines of rock, as uneven as cracks in a pavement, erupted at various places. Near the horizon, he could see low stands of scrub but they cast the soft and even shadows that belonged in this stark landscape. Of Jimmy and the buggy there was no sign.

The engine misfired. The aircraft slewed to one side and Adam felt a sharp fear jolt his throat. He had the sudden, clear sensation of being on his own. No engine, no blades, no frame, no seat. Just him and that huge fall to the coloured plain.

The engine caught. The tubular frame that had taken him so many hours to weld shuddered and then the whole machine stabilized. He could feel the blades whirring evenly above his head. Behind him, the old VW engine resumed its comforting, puttering beat. He took a deep breath and began to descend.

Adam flew to the bore and fluttered down near the windmill. He switched off, got out and walked around. A few times, he looked up, trying to imagine where he had been in the sky. Tasting bile in his throat, he walked to the trough and rinsed his mouth. He washed his face, then sat on the edge of the metal structure to await the arrival of Daniel in the four-wheel-drive.

After a few minutes he stood up. What was the point in waiting? Daniel could be another hour and there would be no light left to continue the search. He decided to fly to the west for half an hour; that area was one he hadn't searched in the Land Rover, and besides, he'd had such a fright that he wanted to get out and do something.

He gathered stones and made an arrow that pointed to the west. Daniel would certainly see that and know in which direction he had flown.

The motor was reluctant to start but with a splutter and one crackling backfire it began to run and then settled down to its normal idle. He listened to it for several seconds and then increased the revolutions. It seemed to be running perfectly. He tightened the seat belt, and took off.

Rising no more than ten feet, Adam flew towards the sun. The engine ran evenly and after ten minutes he climbed to thirty feet. A line of low trees appeared. They marked the course of a sandy creek. He slowed, but maintained height so that the aircraft was hovering by the time he reached the creek. He turned and slowly followed the sandy bed, searching for tracks.

A mile further on he saw hoof marks. Nearby was an area where the creek banks had crumbled into powdery sand and here he found tracks. He landed and walked over to investigate. The marks were broad and had the imprint of the buggy's tyres. Jimmy had crossed here. At least he was on his track.

Bending low to avoid the swinging blade, he stepped back into the helicopter and, taking off, flew along the line of the wheel-tracks. They led to a gibber desert. He sought more elevation, hoping the greater height would give him some indication of the path Jimmy had followed but the tracks vanished in the glossy mass of stones.

The gibbers stretched all the way to the west. To the north, Adam could just make out a line of sand-hills. Hoping to find tracks there, he banked to the right and flew towards the hills. He had never been over this part of his property and looked around with interest, noting the places where bushes grew or where there were signs of grass.

He came to the sand-hills, and realized he had now been gone almost half an hour. He would have to return, or risk flying back to the bore in the dark. He crossed one ridge, seeing plenty of feed for his cattle growing on its side but discovering no tracks. Other ridges, as even as waves pounding in towards a beach, ran to the horizon. He crossed more ridges and was about to turn for the bore when he glanced to his left. At the far end of the sand-hill was an object that seemed out of place. It was in shadow because of the low angle of the sun, but it seemed to be rectangular. He pulled back the stick, to climb and give himself a better view.

The engine stuttered, then cut. The helicopter turned sharply and dipped. Adam tried to pull the nose up but the machine was sliding sideways, angling towards the crest of the nearest ridge. Frantically, he tried to straighten it. The engine made a popping noise. The big blade spun, but sluggishly and uselessly.

The helicopter began to rotate, spiralling down like a leaf caught in a strong breeze. Giddied and disoriented, Adam could only lift one arm to protect his face. The sand and the bushes that grew along the ridge rushed towards him in a series of blurred images.

The tail hit first, then a blade which dug deep into the sand. With a hideous tearing of metal, the helicopter flipped upside down.

Adam felt the scratch of a bush, smelled petrol. The violent somersaulting continued. Then he hit something hard, and all movement ceased.

E·I·G·H·T

The sun was setting when Cassie landed the Cessna at the homestead air strip. Nina was waiting beside the car, her arms folded tightly across her chest. For Nina to be there was so unusual that Cassie went through the process of switching off with her stomach churning in anticipation of some catastrophe. She scrambled from the plane, leaving Klemansky standing beneath the wing with the camera bag over his shoulder. Her welcome was a barrage of questions.

'Where have you been? Did you have trouble? Did you land somewhere? I've been so worried. It's been five hours since you took off. What have you been doing?'

Cassie stopped. Nina was never like this. 'I'm all right,' she said, her face puzzled.

'But it's been five hours. Oh God, Cassie, how could you?'

'How could I what? Nina, you're starting to talk like a mother, and a pretty neurotic one at that.'

'Don't you speak to me like that.'

'Well, what's going on?'

'You've been out for five hours and the plane can't stay up for that long. I've been worried sick that you must have run out of gas.'

'We landed.'

'Cassie, how could you? You know your father said never to land on the lake.'

'We didn't land on the lake.' Arms folded, Cassie matched Nina's stance.

'Oh my God. Where then?'

'On a clay pan. It was perfectly safe. Michel wanted some pictures of him standing at the edge of the lake.'

Klemansky walked towards them and deposited the camera bag at Cassie's feet. 'I'll see you later. Thanks for the great pictures.' He smiled cheekily at Nina and limped towards his distant caravan. 'Don't worry, Mrs Ross,' he called out without turning. 'I feel like the exercise. It's a nice evening for walking.'

'I do not like that man,' Nina said when he was out of range. 'And while you were out all afternoon taking photographs of him –'

'They weren't all of Michel.'

'While you were out, your father had a desperate need to use the Cessna.' She told Cassie about the search for Jimmy. 'And now he's gone out in that wretched little whirly-thing of his and I have been worried sick about him. And you.'

'There's been no sign of Jimmy?' Cassie's face was gaunt.

'None. Your father's very worried. And, I must say, very angry.'

Cassie turned her head defiantly, preparing for fresh accusations.

'I know you took the plane in good faith but how could you just fly away taking pictures for that creep, and stay away for so long, when you knew Jimmy was missing.'

'I just thought he was late coming home.'

Nina sighed. 'I suspect you never even thought about Jimmy. You were so dazzled by that flashy racing driver that you jumped in the plane and did what he wanted without any other consideration. Cassie, you knew your father was out and looking for Jimmy.'

'But I didn't know he wouldn't find him. No one was really worried. Were you?'

Nina was taken aback. 'Well no. I guess I thought Adam would find him.'

'I seem to recall that when you and I were talking at breakfast, you were concerned with what school Patrick should go to. I don't remember you even mentioned Jimmy so don't try and make it sound like I've done something terrible.'

'Your father is angry,' Nina said softly.

'I'll straighten him out.'

Nina had to smile at that. Cassie had spoken with such certainty. 'I'm sure you will,' she said but looked away, not wanting to surrender the mood. Adam always gave in to Cassie; she felt it important to provide the balance. So she said, 'Because he's had to go out without the Cessna, he probably won't be home tonight.'

'He's on his own?'

Cassie had a way of turning simple questions into accusations, as a means of deflecting criticism from herself.

'No, he is not,' Nina growled. 'I wouldn't let him go off on his own in that little mechanical grasshopper of his. Daniel went with him. Thank God for Daniel.'

'Good old Danny boy.'

'Yes, he is good. And reliable. He went out after him in the Land Rover. They took food and camping gear.' The sun had set and Nina shivered with the first touch of a cool breeze.

'I'll take the plane out at first light.'

596

'And get him out of that fragile little thing?'

Cassie raised her right hand. 'Promise.'

Nina's head bobbed up and down. 'That would be good. I have the most terrible feeling about all this.'

'Dad'll find Jimmy.'

'It's not Jimmy. I have this terrible premonition that something's going to happen to your father.'

The breeze turned the blades of the windmill, cranking the pump into life. Metal rubbed on metal and, with a wheeze of washers in dry pipes, water was sucked from the steaming pool and propelled to the cooling tank. Daniel ignored the rhythmical clanking and splashing. Standing beside the stone arrow, he peered towards the western sky. The sun had gone. Soon there would be no light. Anxiously, he searched for a sign of Adam and the little helicopter.

Had Adam meant him to follow? He thought not. Adam would have flown only a short way out, searching for Jimmy while some daylight remained. The arrow was merely to let him know the direction he had taken. Daniel made one circuit of the windmill, examining the sky around him. Towards the lake, he saw a distant formation of birds, possibly pelicans or swans. They were drawn across the horizon like stitches on the hem of a blue cloth; but there was no sign of the helicopter.

Supposing Adam had found Jimmy? He would have landed. And if Jimmy were hurt or sick, Adam would wait with him.

He searched the sky once more. Night was close now and the evening star was already bright. He searched around it, seeking a dark spot moving across the deepening blue or the faint flash of a spinning blade. He turned on the lights of his four-wheel-drive, to act as a beacon, and then made one final sweep of the western horizon.

To the right of the evening star was a smudge that he had not noticed before. It seemed to be growing from the sharp line that defined the edge of the earth and, as he watched, it rose higher. Smoke? Daniel ran to the windmill and climbed until his head was just below the turning blades. From his elevated position, he looked again. It was a long way away, but it was smoke.

If Adam found Jimmy and wanted to attract his attention, he would light a fire.

Rapidly, Daniel descended the tower and ran back to the vehicle. He started the engine, took a bearing from the evening star, and drove across the dark plain towards the place where he had seen the smoke.

* * *

597

Jimmy greeted the night with dread. The coming of darkness was like a curtain ending a show. He could almost hear Cedric Carter calling out the familiar words. 'That's it, ladies and gentlemen, the end of another great performance but don't forget we open again tomorrow. Same time, same location. And if you can't come, tell your friends and tell them they'll see what you've just seen: the greatest show on earth.'

Where was the band that used to strike up on cue to rouse the audience to cheers and get them out of the tent quickly so the circus people could go to bed or get on with their drinking?

One steer, braver than the rest, came forward and nuzzled him.

Another night meant at least another twelve hours lying beside the trough. No one would come looking for him in the dark. Another night of shivering and lying in cow dung. Another night of starving and feeling thirsty. The only water he could get was by wetting his fingers in the trough and sucking them and that was not enough, and the effort of lifting his arm caused so much pain that it was almost not worth it.

His head still ached as though a fire burned at the base of his skull. He had no feeling from the shoulders down. They must have hit him hard, with something solid like a rifle butt or the back of an axe. His skull could be cracked. Maybe they'd broken his back.

The cattle were restless. They were still nervous about approaching the trough with him lying beside it, but this was the time when they drank.

The daring one nudged him again and he shouted at it. Or tried to. The noise came out like a squeak but it was effective and he heard the animal swing away.

Where was Adam? He'd been listening all day for the sound of an aircraft but all he'd heard had been the crunching of dust beneath the hooves of cattle and their soft murmurings of protest.

Another night, then possibly another day. How long could he last? His face was lying half in dust and half on a large pat of dung. Once more, he tried to move away. Just a couple of inches would do, but the effort sent an excruciating pain through his neck.

He lay still for several seconds, breathing heavily. I'm not going to die, he told himself. If it kills me I'm going to stay alive. With one eye open, he saw the vague outline of the bull, head lowered and staring at him.

'I just said something stupid,' he said and tried to laugh but produced a dry, crackling sound.

'If you're going to put your horns in me, old feller, go for the left arm.'

The animal stared back, unmoving.

'Just my luck,' Jimmy said. 'I come up with a good line and all I got for an audience is a real boofhead.'

He heard the sound of other cattle drinking from the side of the trough.

'Hey boof, go and drink with the boys.'

The bull's head swayed to one side. It advanced a step. Jimmy closed his eyes. He was tired and hungry and frightened. 'Don't forget,' he mumbled, 'go for the left arm. You'll have a lot of fun trying to find it.'

And then he thought: Adam, get here quickly mate. I can't stand much more of this.

First Adam felt the heat. It played on his back and around his neck. Then he smelled pungent aromas that were so strong they made his nose twitch in revulsion. There were danger signals in the smells too, automatic warnings that scratched at his semi-consciousness. He opened his eyes and coughed. Sand sprayed across his face. He tried to wipe his eyes but his hand was somewhere underneath him and he could not move it. The heat became fiercer, the smells more intense. He heard a sound he recognized. It was the crackle of flames.

He was covered in sand. It was in his ears, through his hair, caked to his face in sticky slabs. He sat up. Only then did he realize that he was not standing and that he was in a strange place.

A scorching heat touched him and, with a sudden burst of energy, he scrambled to his feet. Something was tied around his hips and became entangled in his legs. He fell, rolling downhill over soft sand and through bushes that scratched. He came to rest in a bush whose limbs danced with a yellow glow, and turned.

The helicopter was on top of a sand-hill and in the final stages of being consumed by fire. The frame was a pretzel of white-hot tubes, the motor a deep red glow at the heart of the blaze. All around it, bushes were burning. Petrol must have poured from the ruptured tank because long canals of fire ran from the wreckage.

He tried to stand, to get away from a nearby bush which was flaming like a gas lantern, but again fell. His seat belt was still around him. Part of the seat was attached to the belt and it was the twisted metal frame that had caught his legs. He fumbled with the clasp and, as it came loose, realized that his left hand hurt.

After taking a few unsteady steps and reaching cooler air, he stopped to examine the blaze. The front of his machine had been torn off. The tail rotor and one half of the big main blade were gone. He could see pieces of wreckage scattered near the burning bushes.

599

He looked up at the sky but the stars above were overwhelmed by the reddish glow that spread from the ridge. He was alive and it was a miracle. He thought of Nina. 'Well, my love,' he said, compelled to talk aloud to emphasize the reality of his survival, 'you won't have to worry about me flying that thing again.'

He sat on the sand and began to shake. He was sore in a few places. His hand throbbed and his hip ached and he could feel a leg stiffening. He had cut his head above the ear. What a mess, he thought. He, the rescuer, was now in need of rescue.

He recalled where he had flown and tried to estimate how far he might be from the bore, where Daniel would be waiting. He needed to climb to the top of the ridge, to survey the scene and get some idea of the nature of the countryside in which he had crashed. He began to trudge up the slope, skirting the fires. Bushes were either erupting in flames or disintegrating in showers of ash and sparks. The sand was soft and he slid backwards with every step. His hip hurt. Finally, he found it easier to crawl.

Near the top, a second wave of shock hit him and his hands shook so badly he had to stop and sit with his arms folded around his knees. He'd been lucky. Had the front of the tubular frame, the body he had so lovingly crafted, not broken and thrown him clear he would have burned like one of the bushes flaring on the side of the hill.

The main fire was easing. The tubes were melting in places and the twisted and glowing skeleton was folding on itself. In another hour or two, nothing would be left but a heap of molten metal. He had no food or water. He could be here for days. And what would happen to Jimmy?

Unsteadily, he got to his feet and climbed the last few steps to the crest. For a few moments he stood there, enjoying the breeze and staring, mesmerized, into the fire. Then he turned to look beyond the sand-hill.

Far in the distance but travelling directly towards him was a single, bright light.

Distances in the outback are deceptive by day, but duplicitous at night. A moving light becomes a will-o'-the-wisp that leads the imagination along fanciful paths. At first, Adam was certain the light came from Daniel's Land Rover. But as the minutes passed and the beam remained a single light that did not seem to be moving, he began to wonder. He stared intently. Could the light be much closer than he thought? The distance was impossible to estimate but the light now looked duller, possibly a hurricane lantern being carried by someone. He even shouted out, feeling foolish and receiving no answer. Suddenly, the light was moving again, sharply focused and a long way away. It flickered, as though bouncing over rough terrain.

It disappeared, and Adam felt a crush of disappointment. Seconds later, it was back, yellowed and fainter and heading in another direction. Then the light swung back towards the beacon made by the funeral pyre of his home-made flying machine. Now it looked like a motor bike.

This is ridiculous, he told himself, and sat in the sand and waited.

It took half an hour for the vehicle to draw close enough for the single light to divide into two. It was another twenty minutes before the Land Rover swung around the end of the sand-hill and drove along the valley towards the place where Adam waited.

'What the hell happened?' Daniel's face was dusty and anxious. The fire had diminished to a necklace of glowing embers, strung down the bosom of the hill. The young man stared at the scene in bewilderment.

'I saved you a job.' Adam had practised the greeting. 'There'll be no need to pull the heads off and do the valves.'

Daniel's eyes went from the ring of smouldering sticks to the blob of metal. 'That's the helicopter?'

'Was,' Adam corrected and told him what had happened. He got water from the back of the vehicle and had a long drink.

'No sign of Jimmy?'

'I saw his tracks.' He drank more water. 'Lost them again, though.'

Around the two men, the night breeze sighed. The motor of the Land Rover, hot from its long grind in low gear, cracked and groaned as the cool air embraced warm metal.

'You were a bit lucky.'

'Just a bit.'

'You've cut your head.'

'It's only small.' Adam felt the wound. He used some water to wash blood from his ear. 'You saw the fire from the bore?'

'Saw some smoke. It was right on last light. Lucky to see it.'

'Thank God for a man with good eyes. It's a long way from the bore.'

'Took me a few hours to get here. Want some tucker?'

'No. Not yet.' Adam stepped closer and squeezed Daniel's shoulder. 'You've no idea how good it is to see you,' he said and shook his head.

'Why don't you hop in and I'll take you back home?'

Adam climbed in the vehicle but asked Daniel to drive along the valley between the sand-hills. He had seen something just before the crash.

601

The area was sandy and covered by thick clumps of growth. As a result, Daniel had to follow a weaving course and it was five minutes before his lights shone on the object Adam had glimpsed from the air.

It was the buggy.

They got out and circled the little vehicle. It was upside down, with its front tyres and seat backs touching the ground and with its tail in the air. Adam examined the buggy while Daniel walked around it, in a circle illuminated by the lights of the Land Rover.

'Reckon he rolled it?' Daniel called out, his head down as he searched for tracks.

'Doesn't make sense. He wouldn't tip it over on flat country like this. Give us a hand will you?' Adam was trying to turn the vehicle back on its wheels but his left hand was too sore to use. Together, they rolled it upright.

Adam examined it. 'Nothing broken.'

'There are some tracks over there.'

'Jimmy's?'

'Don't think so. There are a lot of foot marks and a couple of a big wheeltracks, like a truck would make.'

Together, they walked to the spot. They examined the area in silence, taking care not to trample on the faint marks.

'What do you reckon?' Daniel asked.

'Looks like someone's come along. Maybe they gave Jimmy a lift.'

Daniel followed the tracks to the limit of the light cast by the headlamps. 'They went this way. Turned around there.' He pointed to where Adam stood. 'Then came back in this direction.'

'How clear are the tracks?'

'Pretty faint. Probably a couple of days old.'

'Reckon you could follow them?'

'In the dark?'

'You're the one with the good eyes.' Adam walked to where Daniel stood scratching his head in uncertainty. 'It's worth a go. They might lead to Jimmy.'

With the buggy in tow, they drove slowly along the valley until the tracks swung to the right. The marks were more difficult to distinguish in this area, because they had driven clear of sand ridges and were travelling over harder ground. Just when they thought they had lost the trail, Daniel glimpsed a tread-mark in a patch of sand to their right. They turned, and drove into another valley formed by sand-hills. These ran parallel with the ridge on which Adam had crashed, so they were now travelling opposite to their original bearing but a mile away.

602

Halfway along the valley, Daniel stopped. 'Something happened here,' he said and both men got out. They examined an area where the sand had been much disturbed. Footprints, vague and softened by wind, formed a circle that was bisected by wheeltracks. At the far end of the circle ran a long groove.

'Something was dragged along the ground,' Adam said, and followed the furrow until it petered out. Mystified, they got back in the Land Rover and continued to follow the wheeltracks. They turned around the end of the sand-hill and ran through the next valley. Once clear of the hills, the tracks ran straight across a plain. Gradually, the marks disappeared.

Daniel stopped the vehicle. 'What do we do now?'

'Either camp here and try to pick up the trail in the morning or keep on going.' A hand spotlight lay on the floor. He connected it, got out of the vehicle and swung the beam around them. 'Nothing. What do you reckon, Danny?'

'Up to you.' Daniel joined him in peering along the bright path of the beam. It revealed a monotony of small stones and sand. 'Don't like the idea of Jimmy being stuck out here somewhere.'

'He could have been picked up by some bloke from one of the neighbouring properties and be having a good night's sleep.'

'They'd have radioed.'

'Probably.' Adam nursed his aching hand. 'There's something wrong about all this.'

Daniel agreed, and they drove on. They saw no more tyre marks but maintained the same course, guiding themselves by the stars. Occasionally, Adam swung the spotlight in an arc but the beam revealed nothing but the uninterrupted plain.

After half an hour, Adam rapped the dashboard. 'Might as well stop. We could sail right past him like this.' He stepped out, taking the light with him. He flashed it around them. Off to their left, faint in the feeble light at the limit of the bead, was a hill. 'We'll camp over there.'

Daniel turned the Land Rover towards the hill. As he drove, Adam leaned out the window, playing the spotlight on the horizon. 'That's a big hill,' he said, fanning the light to left and right, and noting with surprise that there was thick timber at the base of the hill, and that grass grew on the flats and up the slopes.

'Ever been here before?'

'Never.' Adam swung the spotlight and let out a roar of triumph. Angling in towards their path and clearly defined in the bright light were wheeltracks.

'What a fluke,' Daniel chortled, and turned the Land Rover to follow the tracks.

They led around the tip of the hill, curled to the left, and came to a fence.

'What the hell!' Adam got out. The tyre marks continued under the wire. He walked back to Daniel who was still behind the wheel. 'There are a lot of tyre marks here. It looks like there've been trucks driving in and out, but there's no gate.'

'This is still Kalinda?'

'I think we've stumbled on something interesting.' Adam went to the tool-box and found a pair of pliers. He cut the fence and waved the Land Rover through.

On board again, he shone the spotlight ahead of them. The track curled past tapering ridges of rock and turned towards a collection of large boulders. Beyond was a stockyard. Cattle milled around the fence.

'What the hell's going on here?' Daniel said but as Adam didn't know, he didn't answer.

They drove to the stockyard gate. Adam shone the torch around them.

'Nothing but cattle,' Daniel said. 'And all with our brand.'

'We haven't branded the cattle up here,' Adam said softly. He shone the light into the stockyard. There was a trough and next to it, a big bull.

'That's a good-looking animal,' Daniel said.

'It's not ours.'

'It's got our brand. What's going on here?'

Some steers near the gate ran away as Adam got out of the vehicle. In the yard the bull stared blindly into the vehicle's lights. Its head was down and its tail swished from side to side.

'Be careful,' Daniel called. 'He looks a cranky one.'

Adam advanced. There was something on the ground near the bull. He clapped his good hand against his thigh and shouted. The bull faced him, its head low, its horns swaying, so that first one tip, then the other, pointed towards him as though measuring the distance for a charge. It pawed the dirt.

Adam shouted again and waved his arms. The shape near the animal looked like a man, and a terrible fear was welling within him. He took a step forward. The bull's nostrils quivered and almost touched the ground.

Behind him, Adam heard Daniel shouting. Then the engine note rose to a scream, and, with horn blaring, the Land Rover charged through the gate.

The bull turned and loped away, snorting and shaking its head in anger.

Adam dashed forward. The figure now revealed was of a black

604

man plastered in dust and manure and curled into a ball. He was lying on his left side, with his right arm protecting his face. His shirt was in shreds. The man's back was sliced and bleeding where the bull had been goring him. He did not move.

Adam paused, shocked by the sight, then advanced timidly, fearful of what he might discover. He rolled the bloodied figure on to its back.

Jimmy Kettle, one eye half open, stared up at him.

'Jimmy?'

The eye fluttered. 'G'day,' he croaked. 'Where ya been?'

Daniel ran to join them. 'You all right Jimmy?' he shouted.

'Not too good,' Jimmy said and fainted.

N·I·N·E

Cassie took off before dawn. She flew directly to the northern bore and then circled high above the windmill, searching for any sign of her father or the Land Rover. Finding neither, she banked to the east. She checked along the shore of the lake and the southern part of the river delta. Then she turned the Cessna to the west.

Ten minutes later, a faint line of dust rising from the plain attracted her attention. She banked towards it, then put the aircraft into a shallow dive when she recognized the Land Rover. She circled once around the vehicle, answered the waves of her father and Daniel, noticed the buggy hitched to the back and landed nearby on a broad stretch of clay.

The Land Rover stopped beside the Cessna. Adam got out and helped her from the cabin.

'Where's your little grasshopper?' she said.

'We had a bonfire.'

'It's burnt?' Then she noticed the cut on his head and his swollen hand. 'Oh my God, you're hurt.'

He waved the injured hand. 'I might have broken something. It's not a worry. We've got Jimmy.' She tried to talk but he stopped her. 'He's hurt. We need to get him home and get the doctor. We'll put him in the plane.'

She followed him to the Land Rover, returning Daniel's waved greeting.

Jimmy was unconscious. The men lifted him from the back seat.

'What happened?'

'We don't know. We found him like this. He'd been gored by a bull.'

She ran ahead to prepare the cabin. They put Jimmy across the back seats.

'I'll go with Cassie,' Adam said, 'and keep an eye on Jimmy. Will you be all right?'

Daniel nodded. Adam shook his hand and climbed into the Cessna.

When they were high above the plain, Cassie turned to her father. 'Are you angry with me?'

Adam leaned towards her. She met him halfway and kissed the tip of his nose.

'You don't taste angry,' she said.

He kissed her proffered nose. 'I was pretty steamed up yesterday but you make it hard to stay angry.'

'Good. I don't like the man I care about most in the whole world being angry with me. Now tell me what happened.'

Cassie called the Flying Doctor on the aircraft radio. As a result, his twin-engined aerial ambulance landed at Kalinda only an hour and a quarter after the Cessna. Stella had bathed Jimmy and fed him a little thin soup. He muttered a few incoherent words and then slept.

The doctor examined him and dressed the wounds on his back. While he was being carried to the aircraft, he strapped Adam's hand.

'Your friend may have a fractured skull,' he said, winding the bandage carefully across the palm. 'A few ribs could be broken and I'm not sure whether there's an injury to the neck or not. We'll take a few X-rays. You two must have had some accident.'

'We had separate accidents. I don't know what happened to Jimmy.'

'Car crash?'

'We found his car upside down but he was twenty miles away.'

The doctor looked up. 'He couldn't have walked that far.'

'I'd like to ask him what happened.'

'He won't be talking for a day or two. How did you hurt your hand?'

'I just fell down a sand-hill.' Adam wasn't going to mention the helicopter. The aircraft had not been registered and he had no licence to build, let alone fly it.

'Take a bit more care. You're not as young as you used to be.' The doctor, who was in his late twenties, flashed the affable smile strong young men reserve for once-strong old men.

Adam recognized a young buck's instinctive challenge to an old champion. 'I'll remember that.'

His hand bound, he and Nina walked with Stella to the aircraft. Stella was flying to the hospital with Jimmy. 'Look after him,' Adam said, 'and make sure you let me know what he says when he can talk. I'm very curious to know what happened.'

'What he's said so far doesn't make any sense,' she said. 'He was rambling about the old days. He said something about Gooly.'

'The storekeeper? He's been gone for years.'

'Nothing made sense.' She reached the aircraft and took Adam's hand. 'Thank you for finding him and bringing him back to me.'

'Just make sure he gets well.'

They stood back while the plane taxied to the end of the strip. Nina took his hand.

'I want to hear you tell me you'll never fly that little mechanized broomstick of yours again.'

'I can guarantee that.'

'You're not going to try and fix it?'

'What's left wouldn't fit into a bucket.'

She smiled then, as the implication of his words sunk in, looked aghast. 'Was it as bad as that?'

'Worse. You're very lucky to have me.'

Still holding his hand, she took one step back and studied his face. 'After all these years, I still can't tell when you're being serious and when you're joking.'

'I'm serious.' His eyes were ablaze with deception. 'In fact, I'm so shaken up by everything I feel like going to bed.'

She stayed her ground, recognizing the sparkle in his eyes.

'On your own, of course.'

'No.' The Flying Doctor's aircraft had begun its take-off run. As it lifted, Adam led Nina towards their car. 'As I'm lucky to be alive, I feel like celebrating.'

'Have I ever told you that you're hornier than one of your rams?'

'Not for a long time.' They got in the car. She drove him to the house.

Josef arrived that afternoon. He now owned a twin-engined Beechcraft which he flew low over the house to announce his arrival. He had the undercarriage lowered and one wheel cut a wire running from the radio mast. He was full of apologies once he learned of the damage he had caused but, within an hour, was in one of the four-wheel-drives and being driven to the lake by Cassie. Klemansky was due to make another test run that afternoon and Josef wanted to be there to see it.

The Hoffman family's wine business had expanded dramatically. His father had died in 1958 and Josef was now in control. He had made some radical changes. Instead of making wine only from what was grown on their own vines, Josef now bought grapes from other growers, and not only in the Barossa Valley. He had travelled to every vineyard along the Murray and in Coonawarra, Padthaway and McLaren Vale, seeking the product he desired. He was developing a reputation as a master blender. Josef was beginning to extol the virtues of cabernet sauvignon grapes when Cassie took a sandy creek crossing a little too quickly. His head hit the roof. 'Hey! Just because I cut a wire on your radio doesn't mean you have to punish me like this.'

'Sorry. I don't want to be late for the test run.'

'Just get me there in one piece.' He pushed himself back into the seat, and gazed critically at the driver. If she were a wine, Cassie would be red, full bodied and approaching the best time for tasting. And then he thought: here I go again, regarding her as some sort of consumable item rather than the daughter of my oldest friend.

Josef had realized, after the episode of eight years ago, that he had a problem with Cassie. It wasn't, he convinced himself, love or infatuation or any of those things – which he had experienced with other women and could handle – but a kind of magnetic and irresistible attraction. He was drawn to her, compelled to stare at her and subject to the greatest temptations when in her presence. He knew that if she walked in a certain fashion, sat in a particular pose or smiled in a special way, his muscles would turn to warm jelly. Which was one reason why he had been to Kalinda only six times in the last eight years. He didn't trust himself with her.

So he looked at her and tried to find flaws. She was not as classically good looking as her mother had been. She had more of Adam's earthiness, although she did have a sparkle that neither of them possessed, and she could say and do the most outrageous things. You would never mistake her for a city girl. Her hands were roughened from hard work and her arms, while slender, were muscular. When she shook hands it was a test of strength as much as a greeting: her saying, 'let's see how good you are, buster,' and if a man didn't measure up, he was likely to get his fingers cracked. He didn't know any woman in Adelaide who did that. And her skin was not just brown but tanned and her face, which had never known a softening cream, already had creases around the eyes. He liked her that way, and melted whenever the lines crinkled into a smile.

She turned and smiled. He shifted uncomfortably in the seat.

'Do you always fly that new twin of yours so low?'

'Only over your house.'

She concentrated on driving over a patch of rocks that made the springs stutter.

'It's good to have you back. We don't see much of you these days.'

'No. The wine business keeps me occupied.'

'Dad misses you.'

Josef was surprised and then flattered. He had never imagined Adam missing anyone.

'You two practically grew up together.'

'That's true.' He braced himself for another rough passage over rocks. 'They were good days.'

'Pretty wild days from the stories Dad used to tell me.'

Josef laughed. 'It'd be good to spend more time in the bush, I suppose.'

'You don't sound too sure about it.'

'Well, I don't have much time for that sort of thing. Not with the way the wine business is developing.' He wriggled into a new position, so that he faced her. 'I'm off to Europe next year.'

'For good?' There was alarm in her voice, and that pleased him.

'No. Just to visit a few of the famous wine producers. I'm off to Germany.' On an impulse, he added, 'You ought to come.'

'To Germany?'

'Why not?' She laughed and he recoiled, offended. 'What's so funny about coming to Germany with me?'

'Nothing.' She reached across and brushed his arm with her fingers. 'It's just that this seems to be a time when everyone wants to take me somewhere.'

'Everyone?' He was jealous. He recognized the feeling immediately and was ashamed but he was still jealous.

'Well, Peppino wants to take me to Adelaide.' She giggled.

'Who the hell's Peppino?'

'Giuseppe Portelli.' She rolled each syllable extravagantly. 'You know. You've met him.'

'The truck driver?'

'Trucking millionaire might be more accurate these days.'

'The young Italian bloke?'

'That's Peppino. He's got a big business now. He brought the jet car and all Michel's equipment up from Adelaide.'

Josef's eyes had narrowed at the mention of Klemansky but his focus quickly returned to the Italian. 'And this Peppino wants to take you to Adelaide?'

'In his truck.' They both laughed.

'And who else wants to take you somewhere?' Josef was more relaxed, Peppino's challenge having been vanquished.

'Michel,' she said brightly and Josef squirmed. 'He wants to take me around the world.'

'The American?'

'He's part-Russian, part-French. He's really a man of the world.'

'And why does this Russian-French-American want to take you around the world?'

'To work for him.'

'Doing what?' Josef drummed his fingers on the lid of the glove-box.

'Acting as his assistant. Writing letters, making bookings, handling the money.'

'You're joking.'

The crinkles around her eyes disappeared. 'Why should I?'

'Well, what do you know about these things?'

'I do it for Dad.'

'Your father is not Michel Klemansky.'

'I don't see the point.' She changed to a lower gear to plough through soft sand. 'As a matter of fact, he wants me to fly his private aircraft.'

'Where?'

'In Europe and America.'

'You?'

She stretched her back to achieve maximum height. 'At least when I fly I don't run into people's radio masts.'

Josef was silent for a long time. Then he smiled and said, 'Well, I guess you won't be going to Germany.'

'I'm not sure that I'll be going anywhere. There's so much to be done around here. And now Jimmy's hurt and Dad's got a broken hand ...'

'What have you told Klemansky?'

'Nothing yet. I haven't made up my mind. By the way, don't mention this to Dad, please.'

'About Klemansky's offer?'

'No.'

'Haven't you discussed it with him?'

'I'll make up my mind first, then I'll discuss it with him.'

He chuckled to himself. At least she's as tough on Adam as she is on me, he thought, and felt better. 'And what do you think you might do?'

'I might end up taking a truck ride to Adelaide.' She smiled and Josef felt his muscles turn to warm jelly.

Klemansky made several runs in the late afternoon. They were not as fast as in the Shark's first outing. Rotondo had installed instruments to record the downward pressure on each wheel at set speeds, and the American stuck to the recommended pace. The timekeepers used the runs as a rehearsal, and produced rolls of figures as well as photographs which showed the car passing the marker at the end of the timed strip. The speed was recorded at the bottom of the print.

Klemansky presented one print to Cassie. It showed

611

187.340 mph. 'Keep that as an historical memento,' he said, ignoring Josef who was beside her. 'It will probably be the slowest run the car ever does on Lake Eyre.'

When the American had gone, Josef said, 'I don't like him.'

Cassie raised one quizzical eyebrow. 'Why is it none of the Australian men like him?' She walked away to take a photograph and Josef was left standing on the salt, feeling foolish and angry.

Why was I crazy enough to mention Germany? he wondered. She'd never go; anyway, not with me. And Adam would go off his rocker if he knew I'd suggested such a thing. In any case, I'm nearly twice her age and people would stare at us and think she was my daughter, and instead of creating a good impression with the winemakers I'm trying to court, they'd all think I was just a dirty old man.

I should spend tomorrow with Adam, commiserate with him, talk about old times, and then go home.

Cassie had her back to him. She was trying to photograph the mechanics working on the Shark and bending forward to get the best angle.

Josef watched and sighed.

In bed that night, Nina leaned across and felt Adam's brow. 'Just want to see if you've got a fever.'

'I'm not sick. Just bruised.'

'And you've got a broken hand.'

'But not a fever.'

She lay back, but was restless. Adam asked her why.

'I can't hold your hand. I like to go to sleep holding your hand.' So she scrambled across him and he moved, and they lay beside each other holding hands.

They talked about Josef and how well he was doing in the wine business. 'He's so enthusiastic about what he's doing at the moment.'

She squeezed his hand and sniggered.

'What's wrong?' he asked.

'I think Joe's a little keen on Cassie.' She felt Adam stiffen. 'Oh, it's nothing serious. He just looks at her in a certain way. A kind of sad way, like someone on a diet who looks at cream cakes and knows he's not supposed to eat them, but can't help thinking about it.'

'Joe does that?'

'Haven't you ever noticed?'

'No,' Adam said, but there was uncertainty in his voice. He remembered the conversation he'd had with Josef years ago, when

612

Cassie was about seventeen and Adam had behaved like a suspicious father. 'Do you think it's serious?'

'Goodness me, no. But it's funny, every male around the place seems to have his eye on your daughter. Klemansky, Josef, Peppino –'

'Is he still keen on her?'

'Oh Adam, you're so blind sometimes.'

'I knew he used to like her, when she was just a kid, but I thought that had all passed. He's such a wealthy young man of the world these days.'

'He still likes her. He's just too much of a gentleman to be obvious about it.'

'He's a nice bloke.'

'He is.'

A car over in Klemansky's camp was turning and its lights splashed across the window. 'And then of course there's Daniel.'

'What do you mean?'

'I mean Daniel likes Cassie.'

Adam raised himself on one elbow. 'We all like Cassie.'

'Don't try to sound naïve. Daniel adores Cassie like a puppy loves its mistress.'

'Daniel? But he's younger than she is by a few years.'

'Unfortunately, my love, a man who adores a woman does not always stop to consider such things. But the poor thing. I feel sorry for Danny. Cassie treats him like he was her little brother.'

'He's a real gem, that one,' Adam said after a long pause. 'Good eyes. I was lucky that he spotted the smoke from such a distance. Sizes up a situation quickly, too.' He told how Daniel had driven into the stockyard to frighten away the bull.

'I hope Jimmy gets better soon.' She shook his arm. 'That reminds me. When you were talking to the doctor and giving him Jimmy's details, you said his name was Black. Why'd you say that?'

Adam made a wheezing sound. 'Whenever he goes to town, he calls himself Black.'

She waited, presuming he would say more but he stayed silent.

'I think Kettle's a nice name,' she said. 'It suits him. Jimmy Kettle's much more colourful, more appropriate, than Jimmy Black.'

He grunted.

'Does that mean that you agree?'

'I like Jimmy Kettle.'

'But Jimmy doesn't?'

He couldn't tell her the reason Jimmy had changed his name to Black so he said, 'I think he gets a little embarrassed by it.'

'People make jokes about a name like Kettle?'

'Probably did when he was a boy. Other kids can be pretty cruel when you're young.' Adam was pleased with that explanation. It sounded logical.

'*I* like it,' she said firmly, glad she had used the name Kettle, not Black, in the story that was due to be published in tomorrow's *Sunday Mail.*

T·E·N

It was a morning when the breeze was cool and the light so pure that the edges of the earth were drawn closer, to lie almost within grasp. It was a morning when hawks soared high to sprinkle the sky with faint black stars. It was the morning Roger Montgomery reached Kalinda. He arrived soon after breakfast. He apologized for his early arrival, commiserated with Adam, was concerned about Jimmy, and told the family of the closing of the mission. Then he went to find Daniel.

An hour later, Giuseppe Portelli arrived. Since delivering the Shark and its accoutrements, he had been out to an oil drilling site north-east of Oodnadatta. He sat with Nina, Cassie and Adam on the verandah. Adam had a sling around his wrist.

'I came because I've been hearing some funny things,' Portelli said, delicately balancing the cup of coffee Nina had made for him. At Kalinda these days, Mrs Wilson usually made the tea but Nina allowed no one but herself to make coffee for guests.

Adam sat back, his eyes owlish in anticipation of worrying news. Only a serious matter would have brought his friend so far.

'Like what?' Cassie prompted.

'They were saying up at Oodnadatta that someone found stolen cattle at your place.'

'Kalinda?' It was Cassie again. Adam was silent.

'Apparently some bloke reckoned he stumbled across a yard you'd built in some secret place to hold all those stolen cattle.'

'That's preposterous,' Nina said.

Portelli shrugged. 'I know, but it's what they're saying.'

Adam stood and walked to the edge of the verandah. Without looking back, he told Portelli the story of the stockyard he and Daniel had found. 'I was going to let the police know but I wanted to hear what Jimmy had to say. He was there. He might have seen someone.'

Cassie spoke. 'Who was this man who was supposed to have stumbled on the stolen cattle?'

'And what was he doing on Kalinda property in the first place?' Nina added.

'I don't know the answers to either of those questions. No one seems to know who the bloke was. He was just someone passing through.'

'Passing through!' Nina exploded. 'And he goes a hundred miles off course to enter our property and find stolen cattle in a place Adam had never been to?'

Portelli raised his shoulders defensively. 'I'm just telling you what people are saying.'

Nina slumped in her chair. 'I'm sorry, Peppino. It's just that I'm beginning to smell something very bad here.'

'It's starting to make sense.' Adam was still gazing out. 'All the cattle we looked at, even that big bull that's probably worth a lot of money, had been branded with our brand. On some, you could still see other brands underneath.' He turned to face the others. 'Now who the hell would go to all that trouble? Why would someone steal cattle and then put our brand on them.'

'It doesn't make sense,' Cassie said.

'Unless they were trying to frame you,' Nina said.

'Exactly,' Adam said. 'Make it look as though I've been stealing cattle. But why?'

No one spoke.

'Peppino, did anyone up at Oodnadatta say they've been losing a lot of stock lately?'

He shook his head. 'Not that I heard.'

'What did the men up there say they were going to do?' Nina asked.

'One bloke who apparently has a big property up that way reckoned he was going to drive out and have a look for himself.'

'Like hell he is.' Adam said. 'If some man thinks he can just drive on to my property and snoop around because he thinks I've been stealing cattle –'

'Dad'll flatten him.' Cassie threw a perfect left. 'And when he gets up, I'll knock him down again.'

'I think we should have another look,' Adam said. He angled his head towards Cassie. 'Feel like flying me out there this afternoon?'

'Love to.'

'Mind if I come?' Portelli asked.

'You trust-a me to fly-a you, Peppino, hch?'

'Sure. Why-a not.' He grinned and held out his cup to Nina, who was offering to pour more coffee.

Daniel came to see Adam. Roger Montgomery had brought a

message from his mother. She was now very sick and he should go to Marree as soon as possible.

'She's got worse. I know this is a bad time, what with your crook hand and Jimmy being in hospital –'

'You should go straight away?'

Roger, who was in the background, nodded silently.

'It's a rotten time,' Daniel said apologetically.

'Can't be helped. Do you want to go this afternoon?'

Daniel turned to the minister.

'That would be good. Mrs Khan would like that.'

'You go after lunch, Danny. Take my Land Rover. And I know I've never met your mother but give her my best wishes.'

Daniel nodded his thanks and left. Roger remained.

'She's a fine woman, his mother.' He shuffled his feet, as though he meant to say more.

'I'm sure she is,' Adam said. 'How bad is she?'

'She's not going to get better.'

'What a terrible shame. She can't be too old.'

Roger waved a hand. 'It would be good if you could meet her. She adores Daniel and is so proud of how well he's doing here.'

'I was thinking he'd be a good man to manage the place one day.'

Hesitantly but hopefully, Roger asked, 'Would you perhaps have some reason to go to Marree?' He shuffled his feet again. 'It would be a marvellous thing if you could actually tell her, in person, about your plans for Daniel. That sort of news would make her very happy.'

'Well, I don't know.' Adam examined his friend with curiosity. Roger must know how hard it would be for him to get away now and he must also know that Adam rarely had reason to travel to Marree. He couldn't remember the last time he'd been to the town. He removed his hat and scratched his head. 'There's no one else to look after the place. It would be extremely difficult ... to go all that way just to pass on a message like that.'

Roger waited.

'Maybe I could write her a letter?'

A gentle shake of the head. 'Not the same as you being there; you, the man who has charge of her son's future ...'

'Oh cut it out Roger ...'

'No, it's true Adam. She has enormous respect for you.'

'I've never met the woman.'

Roger's lips puffed, as though he were choking on a sentence that wouldn't come out. He coughed to clear the way for the words he intended. 'But you seeing her, face to face, and talking about her son, telling her all those good things about Daniel, would be such a good thing to do. I'm sure you'd find it worthwhile.' Roger's thick brows hovered above expectant eyes.

Adam frowned. 'I don't know why you're pressing me like this Roger. It must be very important to you.'

I should tell him, Roger thought. The man deserves to know that we're talking about Nellie and his son. Despite the promises he'd made all those years ago, he should tell. 'Adam,' he began and sighed, trying to find the way.

'Look Roger,' Adam cut in quickly, anxious to end this conversation, 'maybe I could go down to Marree in a week or two.'

It was a suggestion made without conviction, but Roger seized it with gratitude. He could remain true to Nellie and yet still bring the couple together. 'That would be marvellous.'

'I will if I can.'

'Thank you, Adam.' He watched, smiling, as Adam hurried away.

Saleem Goolamadail sat beneath the tree, with dust coating his face and flies crawling in his ears and up his nostrils, and was pleased. Opposite him, Ginger Thompson squatted in front of the small campfire and checked the blackened billy can to see if the water was boiling.

'So they are already talking about Mr Adam Ross, the cattle thief?' Goolamadail said and could not stop smiling.

'I would've told half a dozen blokes,' Thompson put another stick on the fire. 'By the end of the day, I even had a cove come up to me in the bar and tell me the story.'

'Excellent.'

'I think I stirred one bloke up enough to go out for 'imself. He was real riled up.'

Goolamadail brushed away some flies. 'With any luck, he'll be absent, searching for stolen cattle, at the very time we are stealing his.'

'That'd be nice, wouldn't it?'

'That would be a delightful irony.' Goolamadail stood. 'Well, we'll have some tea, and then we start.'

'Where will I see you again, boss?'

'At Coward Springs.'

'You'll be ready? I don't want to be 'angin' around.'

'Ginger, the trucks will all be going down the old track to the south. They will be miles away from us. There is no danger. We will be merely two travellers on our way to Adelaide.'

'With all the cops that'll be around, the quicker we're outa this area, the better.'

'Relax, my friend. You're about to become a wealthy man.'

Thompson breathed deeply and swiped at some flies. 'I'll relax when the money's in the bank.'

Alex Rafter had been in Sydney on business and in Melbourne on pleasure, and when he reached Adelaide Airport he was weary and a little confused. What made him confused was that he wasn't sure where he should live, whom he should work for, or if he should get married.

He was twenty-seven and a lawyer. There were many lawyers in Adelaide but he was one of the good young ones. Rafter had reached that exciting, bewildering stage in life where every opportunity is golden and every decision complex.

In Sydney, he had been offered a good position with one of the major oil companies whose legal manager wanted him to move there and join the head office in a senior position. And he had been to Melbourne where his girl-friend lived, and she wanted him to move to that city. Her father was a solicitor who had a business in Collins Street and he was prepared to give Rafter a job. But Rafter liked Adelaide, worked for a small firm of solicitors and had dreams of one day becoming a partner.

He had never had so many big decisions thrust at him at once. Corporate life, with an oak-panelled office, company car, expense account and, before too long, a yacht on Sydney Harbour? Or move to Collins Street, where some of the best legal minds in the country operated, but where he would be working for a silver-haired fox who would require marriage to his daughter as the first step in the climb to partnership? Or stay where he was? He liked Adelaide, and didn't particularly like the pace of Sydney or the conservatism of Melbourne.

He bought a newspaper and waited for a taxi. By the time the queue had shuffled him to the front of the line, he had glanced through the news pages and had folded the paper at the first feature. The large photograph of the one-armed aboriginal meant nothing to him, although the story looked interesting. 'Jimmy Kettle: The Demon of the Ring Becomes a Phantom of the Bush.'

He glanced at the story again when he had settled in the back seat of the cab. There was another smaller photograph. It was of a tall, powerful-looking man, who was either in his late forties or early fifties. Looking at that man's face, Rafter felt a prickling sensation creep over him. He was drifting back many years, to a time when the face was younger but still hard, and the man wore a beard. He read the lines beneath the picture. Adam Ross, master of Kalinda. Ross meant nothing. But Adam!

619

As the taxi headed towards his house in North Adelaide, the young lawyer thought of the days when he had been a boy of nine and had helped two Australian soldiers escape from Greece.

In another part of Adelaide, another man was reading the same article and looking at the same pictures, only he was more interested in the one-armed aboriginal. The reader was a big man, as most policemen are, and wide across the neck and fat in the belly, as policemen who have achieved high rank sometimes are. He read the story with great interest, and went to get a file he kept at home.

He spent the next hour sitting on his back porch, ignoring the sounds of children playing with a football on the lawn of the house next door. He read the file carefully and then lit his pipe and sat, staring across the small garden with the carefully tended rose bushes, and thinking. Then he got up and walked to the telephone. After he had made a long phone call, he went to the bedroom and started to pack a bag.

Daniel left for Marree immediately after lunch. Half an hour later, Cassie took off in the Cessna to fly to the place Adam now called Horseshoe Hills. Her passengers were three men: her father, Portelli and Josef, who was anxious to see the new land which had been acquired since his last visit.

'How much have you got now?' he said, his voice jocular, speaking as an adult would ask a boy how many marbles he had in a bag.

'Two and a half thousand square miles.'

Cassie corrected her father. 'Two thousand, five hundred and ten.'

'And you've never seen these hills before?'

'We put the bore in. We haven't had much of a chance to explore the rest of it. It's around five hundred extra square miles. That's a lot of land.'

'Our vineyard covers about sixty acres.' Josef said. 'That's about a quarter of a square mile.' He almost added 'and it's probably worth just as much as all of Kalinda' but didn't because it might have sounded boastful, which wasn't his intention. It was just that property became more valuable the closer you got to the city. And they had water at Tanunda. 'You'll end up owning half of Australia.'

'Only the half people don't want.'

Josef gazed through the window. 'Not a lot of water down there.'

Portelli laughed.

'If you're about to start one of your lectures about moving south to where there are rivers,' Adam said, turning in the front seat, 'we'll slow down and let you out.'

'You don't like it?' Portelli asked Josef. 'This is God's own country.'

Josef made a great show of examining the view. 'I would have thought God could have done better. After all, he had first choice.'

Portelli laughed nervously. In his family, no one would ever make jokes about the creator, let alone contemplate such sacrilege at fifteen hundred feet above the ground.

They reached the hills and made a wide sweep above the area. A small truck was parked near the stockyard.

Cassie landed on the flat plain near the entrance to the enclosed valley. They were walking towards the fence when the truck was driven out to meet them. Two men were in the front. Both got out. They were wearing bushman's gear of wide-brimmed hats, light-brown shirts, moleskin trousers and elastic-sided riding boots. The older man walked forward. Adam had met him a few times. He had a cattle station north of Oodnadatta.

'Hello Ross,' he said, stopping and thrusting his thumbs in his belt.

Adam nodded. 'G'day.' The man's name was Albert Kelly but after his surly greeting, Adam was not going to use the old man's first name. Neither did he feel comfortable about plain Kelly – in these parts, to address a man by his surname was close to an insult and he had no desire for a slanging match with old Albert Kelly.

'Come to see how this little operation of yours was getting on, have you?'

'I've come to see what's going on.'

The old man jabbed a finger towards the valley. 'What's going on is that you've got at least a hundred head of stolen prime cattle in there, all bearing your brand.'

The other man joined Kelly. 'And they've all bloody well got other bloody brands under your bloody brand.'

Kelly nodded his support. 'You've even got the bull that was stolen from Anna Creek. It's worth a couple of thousand quid.'

'You're a bloody thief,' the younger man shouted.

'You just calm down and listen for a minute.' Adam moved closer.

'I don't want to listen to you. The only time I want to hear you say something is when the judge asks you if you've got anything to say before he puts you away for ten years.'

'We've been losing cattle on and off for years,' the other man said. 'Never thought it was you, you thieving bastard.'

'Will you two shut up for a minute?' Adam was conscious of his

621

broken hand. The younger man had stepped closer and was opening and clenching his fists. Cassie stood beside Adam, who said: 'We have not stolen anyone's cattle.'

'We seen them for ourselves,' Kelly said.

'We did not take them. We did not put them there. We didn't build the yards.'

'We didn't even know this place was here,' Cassie added.

'And who are you?'

'I'm Cassandra Ross, his daughter, and if you don't shut up and listen to him, I'll come over there and flatten you.'

Kelly gasped, then started to laugh. 'Never had a sheila talk to me like that.'

Cassie took a step forward. 'You call me a sheila and I *will* flatten you. You call me Miss Ross.'

'Jesus bloody Christ,' the younger man said, looking across at Kelly. 'I think she bloody well means it.'

Cassie wagged a fist at him. 'And if you don't stop swearing, I'll knock your teeth so far down your throat that every time you go to sit down, you'll bite yourself.'

Kelly looked at Adam. 'Is she for real?'

Adam held up his bandaged hand, as if this explained a great deal. 'She certainly is. Now, are you going to listen to what I have to say?'

The men were silent, but had their eyes on Cassie. Quietly, Josef and Portelli took positions next to Adam.

Kelly pointed at the Italian. 'I know you, don't I?'

'The name's Portelli and I run a trucking business.'

'So you're the bloke who's been shifting the cattle for him.'

The hairs on Portelli's neck began to bristle. 'If you are suggesting that I haul stolen cattle –'

Josef shuffled forward, hands casually stuffed in his pockets. 'My name is Josef Hoffman, gentlemen. I come from Tanunda and I was invited by Mr Ross to accompany him here today to see what we might discover. Only two days ago, an associate of Mr Ross was found here, badly injured and possibly attacked by a person or persons unknown. That was Mr Ross's first visit to this site, a fact which can be readily confirmed by the testimony of other persons.'

'Who the hell are you?' Kelly said, his voice rising.

'I told you. Hoffman. Hard of hearing are you sir? I'll speak up. I've heard what you said to both Mr Ross and Mr Portelli. Your remarks are clearly slanderous. To prove a case of slander, you need someone else to hear what you said. I heard what you said. I'm the witness.' Josef raced on, without giving the men a chance to interrupt. 'From my experience, I would say Mr Ross could reasonably expect a settlement in his favour of at least twenty thousand pounds. In Mr Portelli's case, the slander was not so vicious but you have certainly traduced him –'

'I've what?'

'Traduced. Impugned his character. Bearing in mind the importance of good reputation in his sort of business, I would say his claim could well be the same as Mr Ross's. Twenty thousand pounds – each.'

'What are you saying?'

'I've been saying, gentlemen, that the pair of you have been talking bullshit.'

Kelly scratched an eyebrow. 'That's the first thing you've said that I've understood.'

'Well, why don't you just calm down and let Mr Ross talk.'

'I just want to know who's been stealing these cattle,' Kelly said, glancing from Josef to Cassie who still had her fists clenched menacingly.

'So do I,' said Adam. Gently, he pushed Josef back in case he started talking again. 'I haven't had a good look round but I suspect most of these cattle are mine.'

'They've got other brands,' the younger man said. 'And then yours over the top.'

'I know. Someone's been playing a very funny game out here and I want to find out who it is, and what game he's playing.'

'So do we.'

'Good. We're on the same side. Now, as Mr Hoffman was saying, a friend of mine was found out here the other day. Me and one of my men discovered him. He was badly hurt. We don't know how or by who. He's in hospital and as soon as he can talk, we should know more. He'd come up this way looking for missing cattle.'

Kelly pulled the brim of his hat lower over his face. 'You reporting this to the police?'

'Yes. Now, I've got a question for you. What made you come here?'

'How do you mean?'

Cassie joined in again. 'That's a simple enough question. What are you doing on our property? Who told you there were stolen cattle here?'

Kelly scratched his chest and looked at the other man. 'I think it was you, wasn't it, Harry?'

'No. It was a bloke in the pub.'

'Do you know the man?' Adam spoke quietly.

Kelly shook his head.

'Well, Mr Kelly, next time you want to come on my property for any reason, you write to me or get on the radio and wait for an invitation. I don't like what you've done.'

'You're trespassing,' Josef said from behind Adam.

'I was steamed up.'

'Next time talk to me. Don't come blundering on my place like this.'

'But we thought you were pinching our cattle,' the younger man said.

'Well, you were wrong.'

'What about the bull?' Kelly said. 'They've been looking for that.'

'Nothing leaves here till the police are notified,' Adam said.

Kelly nodded. 'I'll go along with that.'

'You certainly will. Now, you two have got a long drive back to your place.'

Kelly and the other man left. As they passed the group, Kelly tipped his hat. 'Goodbye Miss Ross,' he said and smiled.

In the aircraft on the way back, Portelli sat in the front, next to Cassie. 'You were pretty good back there. But what were you going to do if they called your bluff?'

Her smile developed sharp edges. 'I wasn't bluffing.'

'You were going to hit them?'

'Sure.'

'You know how to fight?'

'When I was a kid, Dad showed me how to defend myself. We used to spend hours boxing. Only make-believe, of course.'

'That wouldn't have been make-believe back there.'

'Well then I would have thrown my left hook. Jimmy showed me how to do that.'

Portelli laughed, disbelievingly. 'Jimmy hasn't got a left arm.'

'I have, and that's the one we're talking about.' She shook it at Portelli, then surveyed him, as a buyer assesses an animal before purchase. 'One day, when you're feeling game, we'll put on the gloves.'

Adam leaned across and touched Portelli's shoulder. 'Don't fall for that one, Peppino. Cassie reckons any gentlemen would hold back and let her get in two good punches. And if she hit you with two of her specials, you'd be sitting on the ground with a surprised expression on your face.'

'Talking of surprises,' Josef said, anxious to end a conversation in which Portelli and Cassie were the principals, 'what do you reckon those characters we surprised are going to do?'

'Talk to each other all the way to Oodnadatta,' Adam said, 'and end up convincing themselves that I was lying.'

'So what will you do? They'll talk to others.'

'I'm going to radio the police first thing in the morning. I tried the other day, but the sergeant was out.'

'What we need,' Cassie said, 'is to hear from Stella. She's going to get a message through when Jimmy's able to talk and tell us what happened.'

'What you need,' Josef said with a patient sigh, 'is to join the twentieth century and get the telephone connected.'

'It'll get up here one day.'

'Jesus Adam, we've had it for a hundred years.'

'Things just take a little longer up here.' Adam settled into the seat and closed his eyes. He was thinking about how he could use the land and water he had seen at Horseshoe Hills.

E·L·E·V·E·N

The Shark made six test runs on Monday. The first two, undertaken early in the morning when conditions were at their best, were fast. On the second run, Klemansky touched 320 miles per hour. This generated much excitement in the camp because it was the first time the car had exceeded 300, and it had done so with ease. The driver, however, reported a tendency for the nose to weave. As a result, Rotondo made some adjustments to the front. He had microscopic changes made to the suspension settings and altered the angle of the trim tabs which were set on either side of the frontal air intake. These tabs were in the shape of tiny swept-back wings and could be adjusted to provide more or less downthrust at the nose. Rotondo eased the angle and then installed instruments within the chassis to measure the effect during the afternoon's runs. He specified two tests at 250 miles per hour, and two at 275.

The engine specialist in the team also made adjustments to the big jet motor. He noticed the presence of salt on the turbine blades and told Rotondo he would have to strip the engine after another dozen runs.

Rotondo was depressed but the news seemed to make Klemansky even more cheerful than he had been all day.

'The car feels great,' he announced. 'This news just means we go for the record sooner, rather than later.'

He sought out Cassie. She was photographing a mechanic making an adjustment at the front of the car. The man was inside the air intake, with only his hips and legs showing, so that he seemed to have been partly swallowed by the monstrous machine. Klemansky put his hand over the lens. He smiled good-humouredly.

'What's your answer?'

His action had not only ruined the shot but gave her a shock. She swallowed deeply. 'About what?'

'The job. We said a few days. It's a few days.'

She straightened. 'So much has happened. Dad's hurt. Jimmy's in hospital. There's an awful lot to do around here.'

'You can't devote yourself to helping your father all your life. There's more to the world than a big salt lake and a few sand-hills.'

'Oh, I know.'

He kissed her cheek. He had never done that. 'Just tell me you're still considering the offer.'

She brushed hair behind her ear. 'I am.'

'Good. And tell me you'd like to do it.'

'I would.'

'Even better. Have you thought any more about what sort of aircraft you'd like to fly?'

'Were you serious about that?'

'I certainly was. Do you know they're now making small jets for private use? They fly at 600 miles per hour. Do you think you could handle a plane like that?'

'You'd buy one? And let me fly it?'

'Why not? I think it's appropriate that the man who drives a jet car should be flown in a jet plane, don't you?'

She looked down. 'I don't know.'

He put his finger under her chin and raised her face. 'It was a genuine offer.'

'I'll think about it.'

'Just tell me again you'd like to do it.'

'It sounds great.'

'Fine. That will do me.' He used the finger to blow a kiss and limped to the car.

She found Rotondo sitting at a card-table and doing calculations. Framing a picture so that he appeared to be sitting alone on the lake, she took his photograph. He looked up at the snap of the shutter.

'Busy?' she said.

He put down his pencil. 'Just sums. I'm always doing sums.'

'Michel seems happy.'

'It does not take much to make him feel that way. Despite the fact that he is the one at risk in this project, he does not appreciate the magnitude of the risk.'

She was silent.

'Salt is getting in the engine,' he said, leaning so far back in his canvas chair that she thought he must tip over. 'We have only twelve more runs to make before we must dismantle, clean and check all the parts. And do it out here.' He waved at the salt around him.

'What does that mean?'

'If we pull the engine apart and find nothing corroded by salt, it means a delay of at least one week. If we find corrosion and have to replace parts ...' His hands became moths that fluttered to the table.

'Michel seems anxious to go for the record.'

'Of course. He is an impatient man. He is also rich and brave and that is a very dangerous combination.'

'But could you try for the record? I mean, is everything ready?'

He looked towards the strip, with its blue line drawing his imagination towards possibilities as vague as the horizon. 'The stewards have arrived and are anxious that we get cracking, as they put it. The timekeepers are in position and all this equipment works. The track is prepared. The driver is ready and eager. The only thing not ready is the car.'

'Is something wrong?'

'I do not know. It is not thoroughly tested.'

'Michel did over 300 today and seemed so pleased,' she said, hoping to ease his concern.

'He wants to do 500. That is a different world. And unfortunately, it is a world we know very little about.' He stood and stretched and put his pencil on the table. 'Every day, Michel tells me how much this venture is costing. He tells me how much each additional day costs him. He tells me of the other things he wants to do, and of his business appointments in America and Europe. The trouble is, you see, he is a man of action, of deeds, and I am a man of theory, of thoughts. And I fear, Miss Ross, that I am going to be pushed into letting him make the attempt – to enter that world of speed we do not understand – before I am convinced the car is ready.'

The room within the Marree police station was dark and filled with the smell of old dust. It was a bright, clear day outside but it was dark in the room because it was the sergeant's office and he never allowed the blinds to be raised, and it was dusty because the aboriginal who did the dusting couldn't see what he was doing and wasn't allowed to move any of the papers stacked on the filing cabinets or on the sergeant's desk.

Wes Butler had been sergeant of police at Marree for two years. He didn't like the heat and his eyes reacted badly to glare, so he spent as much time as he could in his office with the blinds down.

The big man on the other side of the desk peered at him. 'You spoke to Ross this morning?'

'Yes, and it must have been about the same man, Inspector, although he called him Jimmy Black.' Butler examined the picture in the newspaper the inspector had brought with him. 'The Flying Doctor took him to hospital down south. He's pretty bad I hear.'

'And they think there's some cattle-stealing going on?'

'Ross isn't sure. He thinks one bull belongs to Anna Creek. The rest of them could be his own stock.'

The inspector tapped his fingers lightly on the desk. 'Well, that's your business. Mine is this man Kettle. I've come up here to see him and you tell me he's down in Adelaide. You'll find out which hospital?'

The sergeant made a note. He was an exceptionally tall man with a body that ran without any indentation from armpits to hips. He was round-shouldered and slumped in the chair like a creased pillow.

'And you know nothing about this business?'

'I've been here two years.' Butler's chin grazed his chest. 'There's nothing on the files. I've never heard anyone in town talking about it.'

'It was a long time ago.'

Butler straightened to take a deep breath. 'Still, I can understand your special interest. What would you like me to do?'

'I'd like to talk to this man Ross. There were several men involved at the time. He might know who they were.' The inspector looked at a file in his hands. 'The man who brought the body in was called Saleem Benn.'

'Oh, he still lives here.'

Slowly, the inspector put his papers on the desk. 'Is he an old man?'

'Very.'

'How's his memory?'

'Oh, he's not senile if that's what you mean. He's still very astute. He'd be the smartest man in town. And the wealthiest.'

'What is he? An Indian?'

'Afghan. A fine old gentleman. He runs some stores in the district.'

'An honest man?'

'Absolutely.'

'I might have a word with him in the morning.' He prepared to light his pipe. 'And then I might see Ross.'

'He lives west of Lake Eyre. It's about a day's drive from here.'

The inspector lit a match but left it hovering above the tobacco. 'I might go up there. I'd like to see this place where Jimmy Kettle has been hiding all these years.'

The telephone was a relatively recent fitting in Saleem Benn's store. He didn't like it. It seemed to be used principally by people who either tried to sell him things he didn't need or wanted to borrow money.

629

However, when his nephew's son hurried to the house to tell him there was a call from Stella in Adelaide, he moved quickly. He had learned about Jimmy's misfortune from Daniel, and was anxious to hear any news.

What he heard caused him to sit down, until his nephew's son came to enquire if he were feeling unwell. Nodding him away, he rose and walked to the house where Nellie was staying. Daniel opened the door. 'I have news from Jimmy.'

Daniel led the Afghan into the lounge-room, where Nellie reclined on a couch. On seeing him, she sat up.

He beamed. 'You look much better.'

'I'm happy because my son is here.'

'Uncle has news about Jimmy,' Daniel said and offered the old man a chair.

Saleem Benn was reluctant to rush into the subject that had brought him here. It was impolite to come straight to the point, but the information was so extraordinary that he felt an aberration was excusable. He compromised by making a rambling introduction, explaining how he had come to receive the phone call from Stella.

'And how is Jimmy?' Nellie asked.

The old man stroked his nose, to aid his recall. 'He has a fractured skull. He has a small break in his spine, here.' He touched the base of his neck. 'He has many cuts on his back.'

'From the bull?' Daniel asked.

'The cuts on his back were caused by the horns of the bull, yes. And he has many other minor injuries, like abrasions and cuts and bruises.'

'That bull would've killed him if we hadn't got there when we did.'

'Possibly. But his worst injuries were not caused by the bull. And this is where the story becomes a tale of dastardly deeds and, from my family's point of view, a matter of shame.'

The others waited in silence. Outside, the sun had almost set and the simple muslin drapes on the window glowed like burnished copper.

'You remember Goolamadail?'

Both nodded. Nellie's face seemed to have whitened and stretched.

Saleem Benn gave the sigh of a person settling back into a painful position. 'According to our friend Jimmy, he found that wretch of a nephew of mine and two other men in the stockyard in the hills.' He glanced at Daniel. 'The place you told me about. Apparently one of the men attacked him from behind and caused those terrible injuries to his head and neck. I did not understand the

630

rest of Stella's story very well but apparently Jimmy, through some miracle, was able to escape from them, and then hide and overhear what they had to say.'

He paused for so long Nellie said: 'And?'

'Jimmy believes Goolamadail and his associates are planning to steal many cattle and have Adam Ross blamed.'

Nellie lay back on the couch. 'So it was Gooly. I might have known. I wish I'd killed him when I had the chance.'

Daniel looked at her in astonishment.

'I broke his nose. He attacked me in the store and I hit him with an iron pot or something.'

The young man frowned. 'I didn't know you'd ever been up that way.'

She glanced at Saleem Benn.

'It was a long time ago. I wish I'd hit him harder now.'

'He is an evil man, the black sheep of our flock,' Saleem Benn said, drawing Daniel's eyes away from his mother. 'Adam Ross threw him out of the store at William Creek – acting on my behalf of course. Goolamadail had been stealing from me.'

'And now he's stealing cattle and trying to get ...' She hesitated. 'Trying to get Mr Ross blamed.'

'Have the police been told?' Daniel said.

'I will go to the sergeant tomorrow.' The old man raised a long, thin finger. 'We must also let Adam Ross know. That was why Stella telephoned me, to see if we could pass the message on. Unhappily it is not the sort of message one can transmit by radio. It is too complex and too personal. If we send such information by the wireless, Goolamadail or one of his henchmen could be listening and be warned.'

'I'll drive up tonight.' Daniel saw the look of alarm on Nellie's face. 'It's urgent, Mum. I have to go.'

'It's a long way in the dark.'

'Don't worry. I've got good eyes.' He saw her blink. 'Hey, don't start howling or doing anything like that. After I give Adam the news, I'll come back.'

It was dark. Daniel drove to the pumps at the front of the store to fill the Land Rover's tank. He parked behind a truck, whose driver had gone inside to buy food. He, too, went into the store. The other man was at the counter. The man took off his hat and ran grimy fingers through his hair.

'Which way are you heading?' Daniel asked pleasantly.

A cigarette was stuck to the man's lower lip. 'South.'

'I'm going north.'

'Road's crook.'

'I know. I come from up that way.'

The man ordered tobacco and chocolates.

'How long are you going to be?' Daniel asked.

'What's it to you?'

'I want to get petrol and you're blocking the pumps.'

'Yeah?' The man didn't bother looking at him. 'Be through in a minute. Then I'm gonna fill the truck. Just 'ave to wait, won't ya?'

Daniel shrugged and walked outside. The truck was a battered old International. The paint had faded from exposure to the sun and the tyres were well chewed. This truck, he reckoned, had done a lot of hard work and not much of it on made roads. The front number-plate was so stone-chipped as to be almost illegible but he could just make out the numbers. He walked around the back. The rear plate was badly chipped, too. That was unusual. The rear number plate shouldn't be marked by stones. He strolled to the front of the truck. The numbers were different.

Daniel walked past the driver's door. He heard a shuffling noise. Someone was inside. He stopped and looked through the window. A man was lying across the front seat, with a blanket over his head and upper body. It was difficult to see him clearly, because the only light came from the store but it was certainly a man; not a child or a woman. The legs moved.

'You all right, mate?' Daniel asked.

At that moment, the driver came out of the store. 'What ya doin' there?'

'Nothing.' Daniel moved away from the truck. 'Is your friend sick?'

The man took the cigarette out of his mouth and blew smoke towards Daniel. 'Why don't ya get back in yer car and mind yer own business?' The young Afghan attendant walked out of the store. The man thrust a ten-pound note in his hands. 'Give us a tenner's worth.' He glared at Daniel, who drifted into the shadows.

Daniel walked back to the middle of the street. Marree at night was a dark town and the street – broad, dusty and unlit – was the darkest part of town. There were few patches of light. The brightest was off to his right at the railway marshalling yards, where a forest of stanchions sprouted dazzling beams, each illuminating its own string of empty rail tracks and empty carriages. The railway station and its cluster of sheds and cottages were all dark angles and squat shadows. On the far side of the line the hotel formed a rectangle of black against a charcoal sky. A solitary light shone through its bar door. Down the road on his side of the rail tracks, a globe shone from a wall. It wore a halo of frenzied insects. With his back to the

632

store and the Afghan quarter where he had been raised, Daniel examined the town. Three bright spots in all of Marree. It was as dark and lifeless as a cemetery.

The smell of cooking fires was in the air.

Daniel shivered. Marree was the only town he'd ever known. He didn't like it much, especially at night when it reminded him of a kerosene lantern with the wick turned down: all dull and smoky and about to go out.

He turned around to see how the refuelling was progressing. Rashid, the young Afghan attendant, was still filling the tank. The driver whose outline was etched by the faint light escaping through the store's open doorway stood near the front of the truck. His hat twisted, the head turning in several directions as though the man were looking for someone.

Me, thought Daniel, and not wanting trouble, walked down the street. He went as far as the place where the solitary electric light bulb shone on a wall, but he stood on the other side of the road, out of sight. He went over the message he had to deliver to Adam, to make sure he had it right.

The driver got in the truck. The motor stuttered into life, the lights came on and the truck swung on to the road. Daniel waited for it to pass.

Instead of passing, the driver headed for the light. There he stopped, motor thumping in an uneven idle, while he took out a broad sheet of paper and studied it. Daniel could see him clearly. Then he saw the second man rise. He came up like a ghost, with his head shrouded in a blanket, but then slipped that off, shook his head and used his fingers to push his long black hair in place.

It was Goolamadail. Daniel peered, striving to be certain because it was many years since he had seen Saleem Benn's disgraced nephew. But there was no doubt. Even the ugly broken nose. It was Gooly, the man who had attacked Jimmy.

The driver folded the paper, Goolamadail leaned back in his seat and the truck drove away.

At first, Daniel didn't know what to do. He stood on the road and watched the tail light of the truck be swallowed by its own dust. Then he turned and ran back to the Land Rover.

Rashid was waiting, the long pump hose in his hand. 'In a hurry, Danny?'

Daniel jumped into the Land Rover. 'Go to your father's uncle. Tell him I've seen Gooly.'

'Who?' The youth still held the hose.

'Gooly. He'll understand. He's in that truck.'

* * *

Daniel caught the truck at a place where the road climbed a low ridge. The International was not going quickly. Daniel passed it in a shower of small stones and, just beyond the ridge, braked and turned to block the path of the other vehicle.

The truck slewed to a halt.

'What the hell ya doin'?' the driver roared but then broke into a fit of coughing caused by the pall of dust which enveloped both vehicles.

Daniel got out and walked to the passenger's side of the cabin. Goolamadail's frightened eyes stared at him.

'What do you want?'

Daniel pulled the door open. 'You forgot your change back at the shop. The young feller sent me after you.' He extended his hand.

'I never left nothin' in the shop,' the driver said, and coughed again.

'A fiver's a fiver.'

Tentatively, Goolamadail reached out. Daniel grabbed his wrist and pulled him from the truck. He was a light man, and the strength of Daniel's action sent him sprawling into bushes at the other side of the road.

'The police want you too,' Daniel said and began to climb into the cabin. The driver reversed. He planted his left leg on Daniel's chest and kicked.

Daniel fell back on to the road. The truck then moved forward, clearing the tail of the Land Rover, and accelerated away.

Daniel got up and ran to Goolamadail. The Afghan had risen to his hands and knees but the young man jumped on his back and drove him face first into the ground.

Knees on Goolamadail's back, Daniel took off his belt and looped it around the man's neck. He drew the buckle tight against the throat.

'Who are you?' Goolamadail wheezed.

Daniel needed to get his breath. 'I work for Adam Ross,' he said eventually, 'and I'm a friend of Jimmy's.'

'Who?' Goolamadail tried to turn.

'That one-armed bloke you clobbered.' He stood and, like a man with a dog on a leash, pulled Goolamadail to his feet. He led him to the Land Rover.

Goolamadail walked with his hands to his throat. When he reached the vehicle, he leaned against the bull bar. 'Where's Ginger?'

'Your mate? Down the road. He didn't want to stay.' Daniel started knotting the loose end of his belt to the bar.

'What are you doing?'

'Tying you on. I'm driving you back to the police station.'

'I cannot run like this!'

'Then climb on the bonnet.' Daniel picked him up bodily and threw him across the front of the Land Rover. Goolamadail lay, head over the front, legs spread wide on either side of the bonnet. 'Now you can stay up there by hanging on' – he took Goolamadail's hands and placed them, one at a time, on the top rung of the bull bar – 'or you can try to get off, and if you do that, I'll run over you. So hang on.'

He got in the Land Rover and drove back to Marree.

Peppino Portelli was with Cassie on the back verandah. It was the prospect of talking to her privately that had kept him at Kalinda. Always, it seemed to him, either the middle-aged Mr Hoffman or the flashy American Klemansky had dominated her time.

He began by telling her how well he had done in business.

'I know that, Peppino. You can spare me your life story. What are you getting at?'

'Well, I'm building a house in the Adelaide hills.'

'What for?'

'To live in, of course.' She could be exasperating, but he ploughed on. 'It will have five bedrooms, three bathrooms all made from the finest imported marble –'

'What are you going to do? Run a guest house or open a museum?'

'Cassandra, this is serious.'

'I'm sorry.' She ran her hand down her face, pulling an appropriate expression into place. 'Go on. What's the kitchen like?'

He smiled, encouraged by the question. 'Huge. The biggest refrigerator you've ever seen. A deep-freeze that's even bigger and a pantry that you have to walk into. The living room is forty-five feet by thirty and it will lead out on to a balcony with a view across all of Adelaide to the sea.'

'And you're going to just live in it?'

'What do you mean "just"?'

'Well, it sounds too good for an ordinary house.'

'It will be the finest house in Adelaide. Finest new house, that is. Some of the old ones are very nice.'

'Why do you want such a big house?'

'So my wife will know how much I love her,' he said simply, and sat with his hands on his knees.

'Peppino!' She stood up and clapped her hands. 'You didn't tell me you were getting married.'

His eyes journeyed from hope to dismay and return. She could be joking. 'I haven't asked yet,' he said softly.

'You haven't asked and you're building a house with five bedrooms and three bathrooms with Italian marble and a balcony that has views across Adelaide to the sea?'

One hand made a brief foray from the knees but quickly went back, to clasp the other. 'I was going to ask your father.'

'My father?' She slumped in the chair, then sprang upright. 'You want to marry Dad?'

He jumped to his feet. 'You are insulting.'

'You can't mean you want to marry me.'

'Why not?'

'Because we've never ... Well, we haven't said anything or done anything.'

'Why do you think I've kept on coming out here all these years?'

'To make money?'

He pointed a fist at her, his temper about to erupt, but she laughed.

'Look, Peppino, I like you and I know you like me but we've never talked about getting married.'

'It is proper that I speak to your father first, to get his permission.'

'To do what?'

'To raise the subject with you.'

'Peppino, that is the strangest way ...' She could not finish because Adam strode on to the verandah.

'I'm going to Marree,' he said.

'Now?'

'Straight away. Nina and I are driving down.'

'What on earth's happened?'

'We just got an urgent message from Saleem Benn. It was radioed through the police channel in Marree. It seems they've caught the man responsible for the attack on Jimmy and they want me there immediately.'

'Dad, I could fly you down first thing in the morning.'

He shook his head. 'I want to be there tonight.' He moved forward and took Portelli's hand. 'I'm sorry I've got to dash. Thanks for all your help. I'll see you soon, I hope.'

'Yes,' Portelli said softly. 'I hope so too.'

The aboriginal constable slept in the room next to the lock-up at the Marree police station. About one o'clock in the morning, he was roused by a steady tapping on the front door. Rubbing his eyes he went to the door.

636

'What do you want?' he mumbled.

'Wanna talk to ya,' the man's voice said.

'Come back in the morning.'

'Someone's lost, and I can't find the Birdsville Track.'

'Who's lost?' The constable scratched his head and opened the door. 'I don't understand you mister.'

A rifle barrel bumped his chest. Ginger Thompson forced his way into the room. 'Where's the man yer got 'ere?'

The constable said nothing. Thompson prodded him, harder than before and the man stumbled and fell. He got up to find the rifle at his throat.

'Where is 'e?' The Afghan with a nose all over his face?'

The man gestured with his thumb. 'Out the back. In the cell.'

'Get ya keys, unlock the cell, let 'im out.'

He followed the constable to the lock-up. The man switched on a light. Within the cell, Goolamadail sat up, blinking in surprise.

'Don't say nothing'. You,' Thompson pushed the constable in the back, 'opener door.'

The constable unlocked the door. Goolamadail arose and, holding his back, left the cell. He had to pass the constable, who spun suddenly, grabbed him and pushed him towards Thompson.

Thompson bounced off the wall. The black man leaped at him and grabbed the rifle. For several seconds they wrestled, each man with two hands on the gun and each striving to gain an advantage. The constable was strong and he was angry, which made him stronger. He was taller than Thompson and he forced the other man against the wall.

Goolamadail grasped the heavy ring of keys and hit the constable on the back of the head. The man let go the rifle and then tried to seize it again but he was too late. Thompson swung the butt into the man's belly. When he doubled forward, Thompson clubbed him across the back of the skull.

The constable collapsed on the floor.

'You all right?' Thompson gasped.

Goolamadail nodded. He still held the keys.

'Well, don't just stand there. Drag 'im inter the cell and lock 'im in.' Thompson looked anxiously around them. ''Urry up. All er noise mighter woke up some un.'

Goolamadail dragged the unconscious constable into the cell and closed the door. He turned off the light. The two men went into the police station.

'The truck's outside,' Thompson whispered, leading the way. 'We can be inner Flinders before dawn an' they'll never find us.'

In front of them, the door swung open wide. The frame was filled by the tall silhouette of Sergeant Butler. He was holding his service revolver.

'What the hell's going on?' He waved the gun from one man to the other.

Thompson shot him.

The impact spun the sergeant through the doorway. He landed at the side of the path. He struggled to sit up. Thompson ran past him.

'Hey!' The sergeant made a gurgling sound and, with a supreme effort, raised his pistol.

Goolamadail, still in the room and too frightened to move, called out. Thompson stopped, turned and began to lift the rifle. The bullet from the sergeant's revolver hit him in the middle of the forehead.

Goolamadail saw his friend fall and land, with part of his head blown away, beneath the sign that said POLICE.

One arm braced on the footpath, the sergeant struggled to turn towards Goolamadail.

'Now,' he said, but that was all he said. Very slowly, like a tall tree falling in a forest, he toppled to the ground.

He did not move. Goolamadail stayed in the doorway, not knowing what to do. He heard a dog bark. Someone was shouting.

The noises made him move. He darted forward and picked up the sergeant's revolver. He hurried towards the truck but then saw a man running along the street, pulling on a shirt as he ran, so Goolamadail turned and went the other way. He came to a corner and heard more voices behind him.

He ran down another street, crossed the complex of railway lines, and entered the Afghan part of town.

Behind him someone called out. He ran harder.

T·W·E·L·V·E

Near the store, Goolamadail stopped running. He was out of breath and the sounds of pursuit had diminished. Revolver dangling from one hand, he looked back. A man was standing at the place where Goolamadail had crossed the last set of railway tracks. The man peered down the road where the Afghan was bent, panting and distressed, and then looked the other way, in the direction of the Birdsville Track. Goolamadail could see him clearly because the man was outlined by the lights of the railway marshalling yards but it was obvious the man could not see him.

In the distance, lights flashed. A car was coming from the north, along the track from Oodnadatta and William Creek. It had extremely bright lights and he knew that as soon as the car swung around the bend near the marshalling yards, the long beams would illuminate all the road, and he would be revealed.

He hurried past the store and turned down a side street. There he stopped, and watched as the first wash of light from the approaching car brightened the dusty surface of the main road. He held the gun ready. He could walk out, stop the car, get rid of the driver and commandeer the vehicle. With such good lights it had to be a modern car and he could probably drive a long way before dawn. He might even reach Hawker.

He waited, emboldened by the thought of easy escape, but the lights suddenly disappeared. He risked walking back to the road. The car had turned across the railway lines, and driven into the main part of town.

Now he did not know what to do. He looked back, along the side street. Fifty yards away was a house with a big, square vehicle parked in its front yard. He walked to it. It was a Land Rover. Perfect. He would steal it. The north was full of Land Rovers so it was not the sort of vehicle to arouse special interest. He was now sufficiently calm to consider that he might get a good price for it down south.

He tried the driver's door. It was locked. He slapped his knee in frustration. Who on earth would bother to lock a vehicle in this town? He looked up and down the street but there were no other cars. Then he examined the house. It was probably one of the homes his accursed uncle owned, although it was so long since he had been in Marree that he had no idea who lived here now. There was no light.

He walked to the door and tried the handle. It was unlocked. He wished Ginger were here because Ginger was good at this sort of thing. Then he recalled his last vision of Ginger and felt sick and frightened, and wondered how close the searchers were. They would have found the policeman. Soon they would be scouring the town.

He opened the door.

Nellie was sitting on the edge of her bed. The sound of the gunshots had woken her but Daniel, who was in the back room, still slept. She thought of rousing him but he was a heavy sleeper – she always said he would sleep through an earthquake – and he had not gone to bed until midnight.

There were no more shots, if they were shots; it could have been a car backfiring, although she thought she had heard people shouting. Maybe some rowdy drunks.

She was about to lie down again when the front-door latch clicked. She wasn't frightened. She assumed Daniel had been awake after all and had slipped out to see what was happening. Now he must be returning to the house.

She got up, went to the front door and switched on the light.

Goolamadail, bent forward in a crouch, let out a hiss.

'You're in gaol,' she said, and sat heavily in the nearest chair. 'Daniel,' she screamed, and regretted it, for only then did she notice the gun.

Goolamadail's hand shook. 'Be quiet.' He walked closer. 'What are you doing here?'

She gripped the chair, unable to speak.

'It's you?' His eyes had grown extraordinarily wide. 'It is really you?'

The question helped calm her. 'No. It's someone else. I'll say this for you, Gooly. You never change. You're still as stupid as ever.'

He raised the gun as though to strike her but at that moment Daniel walked into the room. Not fully awake, he was bare chested and buttoning up his trousers.

'What's up?'

'We got a visitor.'

He faced Goolamadail. 'What are you doing here?'

640

The question was asked in a mild voice. He paused on the final button.

'Just go back to bed,' Nellie said, hoping to get her son out of the room.

'Do not move.' The sharp voice made Daniel blink and stand up straight. 'It is you! What are you doing here?'

Wearily, Nellie stood. 'I've got to say this, Gooly. Your conversation's become even more boring than I remember. They're the same questions you asked me.'

'Who is he?' Goolamadail waggled the gun.

'He's my son.'

The barrel went from mother to son, the motion as regular as a metronome. Nellie thought he was going to shoot and feeling exhausted, let herself fall back in the chair. "Just me, Gooly. Only shoot me. I'm the one you hate.'

'I did not come here to shoot you. I need the keys to your car.'

Nellie looked up at Daniel. There was something in her eyes that made him say: 'I haven't got them.'

Nearby a dog barked. At the sound Goolamadail grew even more agitated. 'Don't be foolish and don't waste my time. I have to get going at once.'

'How did you get out of gaol?' Daniel asked.

'That is none of your business.'

'I heard guns,' Nellie said.

'Be quiet.' He aimed the revolver at Daniel. 'Where are the keys?'

'I don't have them.' Daniel raised his open hands as proof.

'Let me see. Keep your hands in the air. Turn around.' The Afghan shuffled forward and felt in the pockets of the young man's pants. When he found nothing but a crumpled handkerchief, he shoved Daniel forward. 'Where are they?' His voice was so throttled by stress that he produced almost no sound.

'Rashid has them.' It was all Daniel could think of. The keys were on the floor beside his bed.

'Who is Rashid?' Goolamadail's face reddened.

'The young bloke at the store. He filled the tank for me.'

Daniel lowered his hands and turned. When he saw Goolamadail's face he stepped back; he had seen that look on wild cattle when they sensed they were cornered. It preceded some crazed, panicky charge.

'And he has the keys? Why?'

'He wanted to drive the Land Rover.' Daniel tried to sound reasonable, soothing.

'Can you start the car without keys?'

641

'No.'

'It can be done. I know people who do it very simply.'

'I don't know how.'

'You can try.'

'I might set fire to the car.'

Goolamadail used the butt of the pistol to scratch his cheek. 'Where is Rashid?'

'Next door.'

'Get the keys.'

'It'll take me five minutes.' His mother's eyes were urgent, trying to transmit another message.

'I have her.' Goolamadail pointed the revolver at Nellie. 'If you're not back in ten minutes, I will shoot her.'

'And what good will that do you?' Nellie said.

He leaned towards her. 'It might give me a sense of very real satisfaction.'

'And Daniel won't have to come back in the house. Where will that leave you, Gooly? In the usual place. Up to your ears in shit.' She glanced across at her son. 'Sorry Daniel.'

'That's all right,' he said. 'I thought you put it pretty well.'

'Stop talking!' Gooly shouted. 'Go and get the keys. If you are not back soon –'

'You'll do what, you little slime?' Nellie said.

'I will start to hurt you. One blow with this –' he held up the gun '– every ten minutes.'

'If you touch my mother,' Daniel said, 'I will tie you under the Land Rover and head for the bush.'

Goolamadail smiled, pleased to have rattled the young man. 'Go and get the keys. Say nothing to anyone. Be back here in ten minutes. Believe me, it would give me much pleasure to shoot this woman.'

Daniel left the house and ran. He thought of going to Saleem Benn's house but his uncle was an old man and not much help against an armed man as desperate as Goolamadail. Better to get the police. He could be at the station in two minutes. Still wearing only his long pants, he sprinted across the railway tracks, crossed the road near the hotel, and ran along the street that led to the Marree police station. As he drew closer, he saw lights in the nearest houses and people standing in groups on the footpath.

In the middle of the road was Adam's Mercedes-Benz. Its lights were still blazing. In their glare he saw Adam and Nina talking to two men.

He ran up and grabbed the astonished Adam by the arm.

'Gooly's got out,' he gasped.

'I know. There's been a shooting. Where on earth did you come from, looking like that?'

Daniel was shaking his head, needing air and wanting Adam to listen.

'He's got Mum. He's in our house.'

A large man in pyjamas was bending down, examining something in the gateway of the police station.

He looked up, glanced from Adam to Daniel, and then resumed examining the object on the ground.

'Gooly's got a gun. He wants a car to get away in.' Daniel blurted out the words. 'Quick. If I'm not back soon, he's going to start shooting.'

'Where?'

'At Mum's house. It's on the other side of the line.'

Adam pushed him towards the Mercedes. 'Hop in. Show me where it is.'

Daniel looked around him. 'Shouldn't we get the police?'

'There are no police. The sergeant's been shot. The constable's unconscious inside.'

Nina moved forward. 'We came down to see the sergeant. I think he's dead. There's another body there too.'

'You say Gooly's got a gun?' Adam asked, his voice sharp.

Daniel nodded. He could see the soles of a pair of boots, toes-up, beside the big man in the gateway.

'What sort? Rifle? Hand-gun?'

'Hand-gun. Revolver. Adam, he's going to start shooting soon. He's off his head.'

Adam pushed him into a back seat, then sat behind the wheel. Nina slid into the other front seat.

'Where do you think you're going?' he said.

'With you. We've no time to argue.'

The big man in pyjamas appeared at Nina's door. 'Do you folks know something I don't?'

Adam leaned towards him. 'Who are you?'

'A police officer. Visiting from Adelaide.'

'We think the man who escaped from here is in a house on the other side of town,' Nina said. 'He has this young man's mother as hostage.'

'Do you want a lift?' Adam said, anxiously dabbing at the accelerator pedal.

'No. I've got to get someone to make contact with a doctor. Then I'll get a weapon and follow you. Where is this house?'

Daniel shouted: 'First street past the store on the other side of town.' He rapped the back of the driver's seat. 'Adam, please hurry.'

'Just park near the house,' the man said, adjusting his pyjamas. 'Wait for me.'

Adam waved and drove off.

Adam turned off the lights, switched off the engine and let the car coast towards the house.

'So he expects you to return with the keys?' Adam whispered.

'Yes. From Rashid.'

Adam took a key from the Mercedes' ring. 'Here's the key to our front door. You go in and give it to Gooly.'

Nina touched Adam's shoulder. 'That policeman said to wait.'

'We can't wait,' Daniel said. 'He's got a gun and he's got Mum and he's nuts.'

'You feel game?' Adam asked.

'I've got to go in.'

'OK. Try and get him out of the house quickly. I'll be outside the door. When he comes out I'll clobber him.'

Nina shook Adam's shoulder. 'You've only got one good hand.'

He offered her his best imitation of a confident smile. 'I only need one with Gooly.' Back to Daniel: 'You reckon you can handle it?'

'Yes.'

'For God's sake be careful,' Nina said.

Daniel got out of the car and moved stealthily towards the house.

'Good luck,' Adam whispered, and hid behind the Land Rover in the front yard. Daniel walked to the door, tapped lightly, and entered. Adam waited for the door to close, then crept to the verandah. A rocking-chair was near the door. He knelt beside it.

The front room was empty and the house was in darkness. Daniel stood inside the door, letting his eyes grow accustomed to the gloom.

'We are here.' Goolamadail's voice came from the kitchen. He moved out, pushing Nellie ahead of him.

'You all right?' Daniel said.

'Silence. Do you have the key?'

Daniel held up the key but the Afghan could not see it and switched on a lamp.

'Give it to me. What did the boy say?'

'Nothing. He went back to sleep.'

'You took a long time.'

'He couldn't find it. He wasn't properly awake.'

'And there is no one outside?'

644

'No.'

Goolamadail went to the window and parted the curtains. 'I have been thinking,' he said, peering at the road. ' I will take the woman with me as hostage.'

'You're not taking anyone.' Daniel moved to shield his mother.

Goolamadail sneered. 'If that silly gesture means I am supposed to shoot you in order to reach the woman, that is quite all right by me. You are the cause of the trouble tonight.' He stopped. A light had flashed across the window. 'You brought someone!'

'No.' Daniel held Nellie behind him.

'There is a car.'

Daniel remembered the fat man in pyjamas. 'If you hurry you can still get away.'

Another beam touched the glass. 'There is a second car. You have led them here.' The Afghan's voice was a trickle of despair. 'You have deceived me.'

'I don't know who they are.'

'Devil!' Goolamadail aimed the gun.

Daniel threw himself against Nellie, and the pair of them fell to the floor. A bullet whistled over his head. It plucked a cheap framed picture from the wall and spun it along the ceiling.

Daniel grabbed a chair. Goolamadail aimed again. The door swung open and Adam, yelling like a crazy man, burst in.

Goolamadail pivoted and stared at the intruder in disbelief.

'Hello, Gooly.' Adam lifted his bandaged hand. 'Been a long time. I hear you've gone into the cattle-stealing business.'

'You?' Goolamadail croaked. 'What is happening? Are all my devils visiting me at once?'

Behind him, Daniel got to his feet and lunged at the Afghan. Hearing the noise, Goolamadail turned and swung the heavy revolver. It struck Daniel on the side of the head, stunning him, but he held on and dragged the man to the floor.

Goolamadail freed an arm, and pointed the gun at Adam. 'You will die,' he screamed.

What happened then seemed to take place in slow motion. Adam was conscious of moving along the wall, trying to avoid the bullet. He was aware that Daniel, aching and only partly conscious, was somehow grappling with the Afghan. And he saw a dark woman, Daniel's mother, rise and throw herself over the hand that held the gun.

The sound was a muffled roar that stunned the ears. The woman's back rose like a sheet billowing in a single puff of wind.

Adam pulled her clear. He kicked the gun from Goolamadail's hand and saw that Daniel, shaking his head and lifting himself from the floor, had hooked one large arm around the Afghan's throat.

Gently, Adam lifted Daniel's mother in his arms. At first, he saw only the wound and felt sick. An awful stain was spreading across her middle. Then he looked into her face.

Her lips formed the word: 'Adam.'

On the floor, Daniel had locked both arms around Goolamadail's neck. It was a murderous hold, fierce enough to snap a steer's neck and applied by a man who had lost all control.

'For God's sake don't!' Adam shouted and saw Daniel look at him, and gulp, and release his grip. Goolamadail sank to the floor.

There was a thunder of feet and the police inspector led a charge into the room.

Daniel stood, holding the limp Afghan by his shirt collar. 'Here's your man,' he said and threw Goolamadail at the feet of the man in the doorway.

'The woman?' The inspector was dressed and holding a shotgun.

'Shot,' Adam said and he heard Daniel make a strange wheezing sound.

'We're getting a doctor.' the inspector said.

'There isn't one in town.'

'There's one on the way from Leigh Creek. We need him for the sergeant.' He went to the door and called out, 'He's OK, lady.'

Nina pushed past him. 'Adam?'

'I'm all right.' He sat in a chair and pulled Nellie to his chest.

'Oh my God. Is that Danny's mother?'

Adam looked up at his wife and his face was stretched into a mask of disbelief. 'Nina, this is Nellie.'

T·H·I·R·T·E·E·N

Three stood around the bed, each with a face that had been whitened by shock then further bleached by the light from a single unshielded bulb. Nellie lay on the bed. Her eyes were closed. She was breathing, but every breath was sharp and short and the bloodstain on the towel pressed against her middle rose and fell and spread with each breath.

Nina adjusted the towel. Another towel, bloodstained and crumpled, lay in a corner. Nina held out her other hand and Adam, who had been near the wall, stepped forward and took it.

'Still bleeding,' she whispered. 'I don't know what else we can do.'

'Nothing,' he said in a voice hollow with despair. 'We can't move her. We just have to wait for the doctor to get here.' He let his head sag to one side until it touched Nina's hair. 'She's a fighter. She'll hang on as long as she can.'

Daniel had put on a shirt. Now he sat at the end of the bed and, with the new pressure on the mattress, Nellie stirred. No one spoke. Nellie's laboured breathing sawed at the silence.

There was a padding of footsteps and the inspector appeared at the doorway, his head projecting into the room but his body deferentially not intruding on their space.

'The doctor from Leigh Creek is on his way,' he said. 'He'll be coming straight here.'

'The sergeant?' Nina asked.

'Sergeant Butler died a few minutes ago, ma'am. How is she?' Nina gulped but nodded. The head withdrew.

Daniel turned and stared at Adam. 'What did he say?'

Adam shook his head, finding it hard to produce the words. 'The sergeant's dead.' He gripped Nina's hand tightly.

Outside, a dog barked. Another answered. They had been barking at each other for the last twenty minutes.

'I wish someone would shut them up,' Adam muttered. He looked at his watch, trying to think ahead. 'It'll take the doctor at least an hour and a half to get here. It's not a good road at night.'

'I think she's breathing easier,' Daniel said, willing it to be so. He let his head sink forward. He stayed like that for a few moments, then straightened. Through narrowed eyes, he looked at Adam. 'I didn't know you knew her.'

Adam nodded and mouthed 'yes' but no sound emerged.

'Your mother and Adam were very good friends,' Nina said.

Daniel's face crinkled in surprise. 'She never said anything about that.'

'She used to live at Kalinda.'

'Mum did?'

'Many years ago. When Adam first went there.'

Adam smiled, pleased to find refuge in the past. 'She raised Cassie when she was only a toddler.'

Daniel shook his head in bewilderment. 'But she always spoke as though she didn't know anyone up there.'

Adam raised one shoulder. 'It was a long time ago. We were together at Coober Pedy, too.'

'With Jimmy?' Daniel had heard Jimmy's stories of the opal mining days.

'And Josef.' Adam was silent and the dogs barked again. 'We lost track of her many years ago. Before the war.'

'And your mother's been on her own all these years?' Nina said, determined to steer the conversation along easier lines.

'Yes.' Daniel blinked, still trying to absorb what he had just been told. 'She used to help run the hospital at Innamincka. She stayed up there and sent me to school here.'

'And never remarried?'

'No. I think she really loved my father. I don't remember him. He was killed in an accident. I don't think she ever got over his death.'

In a shuffle of slippered feet, Saleem Benn appeared. 'I have just been told.' He was breathless but his words suggested that some nephew's son would suffer for the omission. He saw Nellie and a whimper of concern escaped the trap of his clenched teeth.

'She's lost a lot of blood,' Adam said.

The old man's eyes went to the towel. 'And the wound.... how bad is it?'

'Pretty bad,' Adam said. He touched his right side. 'The bullet hit here. Gooly was trying to shoot me. She threw herself on the gun.'

'She saved Adam's life,' Nina said.

Saleem Benn's head tipped forward. 'Yes. She would do such a thing. I have come to know her well in recent years. She is a fine woman.'

648

Adam faced him. 'Why didn't you tell me Nellie was Daniel's mother?'

'Her name's Ellen,' Daniel said.

The old man touched Daniel's shoulder. 'Your mother chose to call herself Ellen only in recent years.' He looked around him. 'Do none of you know?'

The group was silent. Nina spoke first. 'Know what?'

Saleem Benn sighed. 'I think it is time for the truth to be told. There has been silence and needless suffering for too long.' He moved wearily to the edge of the bed. Respectfully, Daniel stood and the Afghan sat in his place. He patted the young man's hand. 'It is a story that few people know. Myself. The minister of religion who has been a friend of yours for many years.'

'Roger?' Adam said. He felt Nina push closer to him.

'The Reverend Montgomery, yes. And the woman who is Jimmy Kettle's wife. Nellie who now calls herself Ellen, swore each of us to secrecy. Believe me, it has been a great burden to bear. One that has caused me a great distress and, at times, forced me to speak untruths.' He smiled ruefully at Daniel.

'What are you talking about?' Adam said.

Saleem Benn's eyes were sad and rheumy. 'The pledge was made many years ago, when she left Kalinda. Do you recall? There was a woman who wanted to take your daughter from you.'

'Mrs Maguire.' Adam turned to Nina: 'Heather's mother.'

'That was the time. Have you never guessed why Nellie left?'

The others were all looking at Adam. He shook his head vigorously, feeling he was being accused of something. 'I often wondered. I worried about it for years. It didn't make sense.'

'I don't understand any of this,' Daniel said.

'I searched for her for so long,' Adam said to Nina. 'You know the story.'

'No, none of you know the story,' Saleem Benn corrected. He gestured towards Daniel. 'This boy, treasured as though he were my own grandson, has been loved as one of my own because he is the son of my dearest friend.' He had come without his glasses and spent a few moments wiping his eyes. 'His father is not dead. Nor is he named Khalid. The father is alive, but unaware that he has this fine boy as a son.'

Nina tightened her hold on Adam's hand.

'Dear lady,' Saleem Benn said, smiling at her, 'you who have been a delight and comfort to my dearest and most respected friend, you know, don't you? You have guessed.'

'Daniel is Adam's son?' she said weakly.

'Of course.'

649

A beetle slapped the naked globe. Far away, another dog barked. Saleem Benn clasped his hands.

'She was with child,' he continued, speaking almost in a whisper. 'Your child, Adam Ross. But you were not married ...' he paused and grasped Daniel's hand. 'She thought there would be such disgrace that they would take your daughter from you.' His free hand fluttered through the air as delicately as a butterfly. 'Since then, other things, terrible things, have happened to keep her from you.' Saleem Benn changed his position on the bed. The movement caused Nellie to groan. Her head moved from side to side. She opened her eyes.

Adam stepped towards her.

'Nellie,' he said and she lifted the fingers of one hand. Tenderly, he took the hand. 'I'm here with Daniel.'

Her eyes were glazed. They roamed past Adam, across the ceiling and focused on Daniel. Then she turned back towards Adam.

'Yes, it's me,' he said, weeping warm tears. 'With Daniel.' He squeezed her fingers gently. 'Daniel our son.'

Nellie smiled and closed her eyes.

'There's a doctor coming. You hang on,' he said. But Nellie was gone.

They moved to the other room and sat in chairs far apart, Adam and Daniel facing each other but insulated by separate memories. Saleem Benn nodded, as though asleep, but his face was contented.

Nina was concerned about Adam. The only light was a wedge that came through the partly opened kitchen door, and in the gloom his face seemed even more worn and his hair grey. 'We should think about going to bed,' she suggested. The men agreed in whispered monosyllables, but no one moved.

After a while, Daniel rocked forward and leaned his elbows on his knees. He tilted his head towards Adam. The effort appeared to exhaust him.

'You're my father.' It was not a question but his acceptance of the fact.

Saleem Benn answered. 'Indeed he is. It is a fact that will bring you much pride when time has given you the opportunity to absorb all that you have learned tonight.'

'Adam sighed. 'I wish I'd known a long time ago.'

'Yes, it would have been better.' The Afghan's long and elegant fingers met in front of his face. 'But she was a proud woman, and stubborn. A thing you must remember is that she acted from the most unselfish motives. She left Kalinda to protect you, not because

650

she was angry, as she made it appear.'

'What should I call you?' Daniel said, still gazing mournfully at Adam.

At first Adam did not understand. Then he smiled and the relief of having to consider something so trivial after the events of the last few hours started him laughing. 'For heaven's sake, Danny, I don't know. I'm still going to call you Danny.'

'Do I have to call you Dad?'

Laughing and wiping his eyes at the same time, Adam stood, walked towards Daniel and opened his arms. The younger man stood, head lowered, eyes wide.

'Mum always said my father was a good man,' Daniel said and they embraced.

Saleem Benn tipped his fingers towards Nina. 'The mother knows her son is with his father at last. Do you not think so?'

'I hope so.'

His body followed the inclination of his hands. 'Will this be difficult for you?'

'Having a new son in the family?' Her eyes went to the two men. 'I don't think so. Daniel was already like one of the family. Now he truly is.'

He slid his chair closer to hers. 'The fact that there was another woman; that does not bother you?'

He was near enough for her to reach out and touch his hand. 'I knew of Nellie. Adam often spoke of her. I only wish I'd had the opportunity to meet her.'

'She was a woman capable of the most noble deeds.' He placed one hand over hers and leaned closer. 'Although impulsive and sometimes erratic. Not always wise, but unfailingly honest. I must confess I have had little time for women in my life but in the last few years, I grew to love that one as my daughter.' His watery eyes blinked savagely. 'And now I have lost her.'

At the other side of the room, Adam released his hold on Daniel and stepped back. He looked towards Nina and she thought he blushed. 'I don't normally hug men,' he said. 'He's a strong son of a gun.'

'You pair are going to have a great deal of talking to do,' Nina said.

'Cassie and Patrick will be surprised.'

She rolled her eyes. 'We'll all have a lot to talk about.'

Adam moved to her and took her hand. 'I didn't know. Truly. I didn't even suspect such a thing.'

She kissed the palm of his hand. 'I'm glad we know now. And there's a lot of time to make up for. You've found a son who's....'

651

She paused. 'How old are you Daniel?'

'Twenty-one.' He was standing with one hand lightly on Adam's shoulder, the physical connection a subconscious one, the action of a blind man touching an object to verify its existence.

'A grown man. Old enough to vote.' She examined them critically. 'Possibly even better looking than his father.'

'Well thank you,' Adam said and Daniel grinned, and then no one spoke. A lethargy settled on the room.

'I think it's time for some sleep,' Nina said. 'We can talk in the morning.'

'There is a room prepared in my house,' Saleem Benn began, but then halted, interrupted by the sound of a car approaching. It stopped outside the house. Adam went to the door. The imposing form of the police inspector appeared on the verandah.

'Mr Ross,' he said softly. 'I haven't disturbed you?'

'No. We're all still up.'

'Good.' He lowered himself into the rocking-chair. 'Lord what a night.'

'Yes.' The man seemed intent on staying, so Adam offered him tea.

'No, thank you. Just a few things I wanted to say. First, the doctor. He should be here soon. I'll have him look at the constable and then put him to bed for a few hours in the hotel.'

'How is the constable?'

'He has a severe headache.' The inspector noticed Adam's bandaged hand and pointed to it. 'Is that new?'

'No. I did it a few days ago.'

The man clasped his forehead. 'I'm not sure what I've seen and what I haven't. And it's late and I'm getting old. Anyone here need a doctor?'

'No.'

The man's eyes darkened into rings of concern. 'The doctor will need to examine the body. For the report.'

'I understand.'

'Good.' He moved and the chair squeaked. 'I've been talking to that man Goolamadail. Extraordinary.'

'What is?' Adam was beginning to feel uneasy.

'The story he's been telling me. By the way, did you see the Sunday paper?'

He shook his head. 'We don't get the papers where I live.'

'I suppose not.' He made the chair rock. 'This fellow we have over in the gaol has been talking non-stop. He's been saying the strangest things.'

'Goolamadail's a strange man.'

The inspector was eyeing Adam with great intensity. 'Mr Ross, I was wondering if you would call into the police station in the morning. Around nine. Would that be possible?'

'I think so.'

'Good. There are a number of things I want to discuss with you. They're mainly to do with the things this Goolamadail fellow has been saying. It may take a little while.'

'That's OK.'

'Mr. Ross, I need your assurance that you will call in to see me, and that you won't just drive on home.'

Adam straightened. 'What on earth are you suggesting?'

'Nothing at this stage. It's just that this man has been making rather vivid claims; you know, accusations.'

'Against me?'

The inspector pushed himself from the chair. 'I think in all the excitement and confusion, I forgot to introduce myself. I apologize.'

'That's all right. I'm Adam Ross.'

'Oh, I know.' He smiled and shook Adam's extended hand. 'My name's Russell Mailey. I think you might have known my father.'

'Mailey?' Adam's legs felt weak.

'Yes. He was a policeman too. Died up this way many years ago.'

F·O·U·R·T·E·E·N

Next morning, an aircraft arrived at Kalinda with supplies that Klemansky had ordered. Cassie went to the strip, talked to the pilot and watched the items being unloaded. The operation was almost completed when Klemansky drove up.

'Some things the eminent Italian doctor felt he needed urgently,' he said to Cassie, standing beside her and leaning heavily on his stick.

'Is your leg aching?'

'It does some mornings.' His smile exuded stoicism. He hurried to change the subject. 'Paolo felt he simply had to have more equipment to carry out more tests and more things to make more changes. I'm afraid the man is a born fiddler. Can't leave things alone. And so we have to have a plane at God knows how much an hour to fly in items we'll probably never use.' The grumpy tone vanished immediately and he winked at her. 'Still, it *has* given me this chance to bring in a few things I needed. Some good wine and gourmet items. I feel like cooking again.'

'You had food flown up?' Cassie had never contemplated such an extravagance. Food came on the hoof or by truck.

'I wanted something for the special dinner I will cook when I break the record in a few days' time.'

'A few days?'

'Oh sure. The car's fantastic. I'll give Paolo a day or two to play around, to make him feel he's justified his role in this project, and then I'll take the Shark out and knock over Cobb's record.'

'Won't that be dangerous? I mean, doing it so soon?'

He rested both hands on the cane. 'No, but don't tell anyone. The more that people think there's an element of danger, the more interest we arouse. The more interest, the more publicity and the more publicity, the more money we make.' He grinned like a schoolboy revealing his plans for a practical joke.

'You can make money from all this?' She had only heard talk of how much everything cost.

'Sure.' He seemed surprised and she felt she had disappointed him by asking such a question. 'In fact, it'll be part of your job to see we make money. I'm sure you understand how it works. Personal appearances, endorsements for products. That sort of thing.'

'You want me to do that?'

'Well, you can watch how I go about it at first. Then you take over. You know the sort of thing: "The fastest man on earth relies on Rolex watches to keep him on time," or "Michel Klemansky can't waste time over breakfast so he eats Kellogg's Corn Flakes."'

'Oh.' She'd never seen 'that sort of thing' but vowed to learn. 'They pay for that?'

'Big money.'

'How much?'

'As much as we can squeeze out of them.' All this time he had not faced her but had been watching his man checking the boxes from the aircraft. The man brought two to Klemansky.

'Just put them in my car,' he said and turned to Cassie. 'I bought a little extra. Something for a special meal tonight. Do you like fish?'

'We rarely eat fish up here.'

'Excellent. You will eat trout tonight. I will devise a special way to prepare it and name it in your honour.'

'Tonight?'

'At seven. My caravan?'

She smiled nervously. 'I suppose so. Isn't it about time I had you over for dinner?'

'There's plenty of time for that later. Tonight will be my pleasure. At seven.' He nodded, almost a military dismissal, and limped towards his car. At the door he stopped. 'When's your father coming back?'

'I don't know,' she called. 'Maybe not for a day or two.'

'And your friend's all right? The black man with the missing arm?' He grinned.

'I guess so. We haven't heard too much.'

Cassie went back to the house. Peppino was on the verandah, playing with Patrick. The boy was engaged in an arm wrestle; his two against one of Peppino's.

'You're just in time to save me,' Peppino said.

Cassie picked up Patrick who kicked vigorously. 'You little devil. Why aren't you doing your lessons?'

'Because I don't want to.'

'Daddy will be angry.'

'Daddy's not here.'

'You're a spoiled brat.'

'And you're an ugly old maid.'

She dropped him on the floor. 'Where did you hear that?'

'What?' He straightened his clothes.

'That I'm an ugly old maid.'

'I heard Mummy and Mrs Wilson talking.'

'And?' She had a threatening look, which he recognized. He backed away, to give himself a start in any chase that might ensue.

'They were saying if you didn't get married soon you'd end up being an old maid.'

'Who said that?'

'They both did.'

'Patrick, you're lying again.'

'Am not.'

'You are.' She took one step forward and his feet dithered, preparing for flight. 'And who said I was ugly?'

'Everyone says that.'

'It's true.' Peppino chimed in and grinned.

She waved a finger at him. 'You can stay out of this.' He raised a hand in surrender.

'Mummy said you were ugly.'

'She did not.'

'She did.'

'Nina would not say that. When she comes home, I'm going to tell her you said that.'

'She won't believe you.'

'Yes she will.'

'She believes me, not you.'

'Peppino will tell her.'

Patrick looked doubtfully at the man who had been his wrestling adversary. 'He won't be here. He's going.'

'He'll be back and then he'll tell her.'

'She won't believe him either.'

'Patrick, you're a little turd.'

'What's that?'

'A shit.'

'I'm going to tell Mummy you swore.'

'And I'm going to wallop you.' She advanced and he fled. When he was gone, she smiled apologetically at Peppino. 'He's spoiled rotten.'

'He's just a kid,' Peppino said.

'But a rotten one.'

'He's got a lot of fire in him.'

'It bursts out in the wrong places.'

'He'll be OK. Boys are boys.'

'Nina wants to send him to boarding-school.'

'And your father?'

'I think he likes to have him around.'

'And you?'

'I hope he goes.' She flopped into the chair beside Peppino. 'It'd be good for him. A bit of discipline would soon straighten him out.'

He sat quietly, enjoying her presence.

'When are you going back?'

'This morning,' he said. 'I've got a million things to do. I should have been back two days ago.'

'When will you return?'

His head turned towards her. 'Does that mean you're going to miss me?'

She waved a hand as though brushing a fly. 'I can hardly wait until I see you again.'

'One day you're going to mean that.' He shifted to the farthest corner of the chair.

'Is that a promise?'

'It is.'

She grinned impishly. 'I hope you're a patient man.'

He squirmed uncomfortably. 'I am. But this is very difficult for me. I'd like to take you out but there's nowhere to go. I can't take you to a dance, or the theatre or to see a film. We can't go to parties. We can't do any of those normal things.'

'Poor Peppino.'

'And poor Cassandra. I'd give you a terrific time.'

'And then marry me and carry me off to your big house with five bedrooms in the Adelaide hills.'

'Don't make fun of me.'

'I'm not.'

'You are. You always have. But that's the way you are. I think it's just the way you have of showing your affection.'

She covered her eyes.

'The problem is we can never be alone. You don't know me, Cassandra.'

'I've known you for years.'

'I mean really know me. As I truly am.'

She scratched her head. 'You could always cook me a meal.'

'What?'

'Well, that's what Michel's doing.'

'Klemansky's coming here to cook a meal?'

'I didn't say he was coming here. I said he was cooking a meal. And for me.'

He bristled. 'Where?'

'In his place.'

'His place? Where's that? What are you talking about?'

'What-a you-a talk about, eh?' She flung her hands in extravagant gestures. 'In his caravan, of course. He cooks there. I've had a meal there before.'

'With him?'

'Well, I certainly wouldn't eat in there on my own. Of course with him, and he was the cook, or the chef as he calls it. He's a very good cook.'

'What did Adam say? Did he know?'

'He knew and why should he say anything? He does let me eat, you know.'

'Just the two of you?'

'Well, I invited the Australian Army but they couldn't make it.'

He shrank in the chair. 'So there were only the two of you?'

'Just Michel and me. Or Michel and I. I'll have to ask Mrs Wilson.' She giggled.

'I think it is most improper.'

'And I don't. Peppino, if you could cook, I'd let you make dinner for me. But you can't cook.'

He pushed himself to his feet. 'There is almost no greater insult, or stupidity, than to accuse an Italian male, especially one from the south of Italy, of not being able to cook.' He walked a few paces along the verandah with his hands clasped behind his back. 'It is a very big insult.'

'You can cook?'

He spun around. 'My father owns a ristorante. He is very famous.' She was still grinning and that tossed a few more coals on the fire within him. He held up his hand, displaying three fingers. 'I will be back in three days. I will prepare a meal that you will never forget.'

'Why? Are you going to poison me?'

'Will you stop laughing?' His anger was beginning to crack and the first signs of a smile were breaking through. 'Do you like pasta?'

'What's that?'

He rolled his eyes towards the ceiling. 'Spaghetti. Macaroni. Vermicelli.'

'I don't like spaghetti.'

'When have you ever eaten it?'

'Often. Mrs Wilson gets it by the carton.'

'You mean spaghetti in cans?'

'Yes.' She was unsettled by his expression of disbelief. 'That's the way it comes.'

'Cassandra,' he said, advancing like an army about to start a seige, 'spaghetti in cans is as much like the real thing as ... as ...' He stopped, both his words and his advance. 'Well, I can't think of anything because it is nothing like the real thing.'

'And you make the real thing?'

He kissed his finger tips. 'I will get the real thing, the genuine pasta. I will bring tomatoes and olives and garlic.'

'I don't like garlic.'

'You will like mine.' He sat beside her but ignored her, talking to the ceiling. 'We will dine out here, just you and me on the verandah. You like wine?'

'Some.'

'I will select an excellent wine.'

'Where will you cook?'

'In a corner of Mrs Wilson's kitchen. She will help. She likes me.'

'Because you always eat her cooking.'

His eyes slid from the ceiling to her. 'When are you dining with Klemansky?'

'Tonight. He's had fish flown from Adelaide.'

'The man wastes his money.'

'And you don't?'

'Never.'

Lightly, she slapped the armrest of her chair. 'Then how come you're travelling all the way back here when you should be doing work somewhere else?'

'That is not a waste. That is an investment in the future.' He rose and kissed her hand. He had never done that. 'I'll be back in three days' time.'

'I won't have lunch that day.' Her eyes twinkled.

'Just you and me, here?' He pointed to the floor at her feet.

'It's a bargain.'

'Goodbye.'

'*Arrivederci*,' she said with a bow and he left smiling.

Peppino felt good, even though he knew he had been lying a little. He had to return in a few days, irrespective of whether he cooked for Cassie or not. Klemansky had told him in confidence that he intended making his record bid by the end of the week, and wanted to start moving his equipment out of Kalinda by the weekend.

Soon after Peppino left, the Flying Doctor radio telegram service transmitted a message that puzzled Cassie. It was for her father, and it was from someone in Adelaide named Alex Rafter. The message said Rafter had seen Adam's picture in the newspaper and he wanted Adam to telephone him. He gave his telephone number and address.

659

She sent a reply that Adam was in Marree, and gave Saleem Benn's telephone number.

Adam awoke late, feeling wretched. Mailey's son. What was it he had said? 'You might have known my father.' He thought of telling Nina, who knew nothing of Sergeant Mailey, but said nothing. When he arose, Adam felt weak, as though his body had been drained of some vital substance; he had trouble walking and his mind was numbed.

Three dogs were sniffing around the fence outside the Marree police station. A group of people stood on the other side of the road. They talked quietly, looking but not daring to approach the place where two men had died. It was a hot morning and swarms of insects had been attracted by the meaty aromas. Far above, the hawks soared, remote, detached, almost pure.

Adam arrived with Nina. He parked the Mercedes, a manoeuvre that sent two of the dogs curling nervously along the fence. The third remained, its body twitching in readiness to wag a tail or spur four legs into instant flight. Adam was in no mood to pat a strange dog and the animal dipped out of his way.

Inspector Mailey was inside. The desk was already littered with unwashed cups.

'Thank you for coming.' He waved them into chairs. 'I haven't been to bed so please forgive my appearance.'

They mumbled a chorus of forgiveness, and refused his offer of coffee.

'I'll come straight to the point. First, cattle stealing.' He put on his glasses and examined the first sheet on a sheaf of papers. 'Saleem Goolamadail is being held pending several charges, obviously, but the initial one, for which he was originally incarcerated by Sergeant Butler, was to do with an alleged assault on a Mr James or Jimmy Black. Is that right?'

Adam looked at Nina and shrugged. 'That's what we understand. Jimmy was badly hurt the other day. I found him. He couldn't talk at the time and he was taken down to Adelaide.'

Nina leaned forward. 'He's now regained consciousness and said that he was attacked by Goolamadail and two other men. He also said they were planning some sort of cattle-stealing operation.'

'So I understand.' He had a ball-point pen, which he used to tap his lip. 'You're Mrs Ross?'

'Yes.'

'Is that an American accent I detect, Mrs Ross?' He smiled pleasantly.

'Yes. I've lived in Australia for almost eight years now but they

660

say you never lose an accent.'

'It's delightful.' He began drilling with the pen. 'May I ask your first name?'

'Nina.'

He began to write.

'Actually, it's Melina.' She spelled it.

His eyes were tired but flashed interest. 'Melina Ross?'

'Yes.'

'Not Melina O'Sullivan.'

She smiled and blinked in surprise at the same time. 'Well yes. I write under that name.'

'I find your stories most interesting.' She nodded her thanks. 'But let me return to the subject of cattle stealing. This fellow Goolamadail said some extraordinary things last night, both before and after he busted out of here. He didn't deny that he knew something about a cattle-stealing operation. But he said you, Mr Ross, were running that operation, and had for some years, and he further said that he had been approached by you to help dispose of the stolen cattle. In other words, he was to act as some kind of agent for the sale. He claims that he was waiting to meet you before deciding whether to go ahead with any action or not.' Mailey put the pen on the desk.

'That's not true.'

'You deny the allegation?'

'Absolutely.'

'That's fine.' He made some notes. Adam and Nina glanced nervously at each other.

'Maybe,' Adam said, 'you should have someone talk to Jimmy in hospital. He could tell your man all he knows. We're a bit in the dark about what he saw or heard, or what happened.'

'I've already taken steps to see that Jimmy' – he glanced at a note – 'Black is interviewed.'

'Good.'

'Mr Ross, I had a long and most interesting talk to Saleem Goolamadail –'

'We call him Gooly.'

He smiled. 'Saves time, doesn't it? Well, I talked to Gooly before the escape and the fatal shootings and I spoke to him again after those incidents, at some length. We discussed several subjects.'

Adam shifted uneasily in his seat.

'Cattle stealing was one. Because of all that happened, I am disinclined to take his word too seriously, or was. However, this morning we had a report from Oodnadatta that several people up there have reported the loss of stock and at least two of them are blaming you. In fact one grazier' – again he referred to notes – 'a Mr Albert Kelly, has reported to the police that he personally saw stolen cattle, rebranded with your brand, in a compound on your property. Mr Ross, that is a most serious accusation.'

'I have not stolen any cattle.'

Adam's eyes met Mailey's until the inspector looked down. 'Well, there may have to be some investigation.' He looked up briefly. 'I will not be carrying it out. A relieving officer will be sent up here and he will be charged with the responsibility of conducting further investigations.' He smiled at Nina. 'We police talk a lot of gobbledegook, don't we?'

She returned his smile, intrigued by this juggler of other people's accusations.

'In other words, the new man can sort out the mess. Is that better?'

'Much,' she said. 'But tell me, inspector, do you really believe what this man says?'

'I don't have to believe him, ma'am. But I do have to take notice of what he says.' He turned from her to Adam and his smile disappeared on the journey. 'However, it was another matter that brought me to this part of the world. In fact, it was an article in the weekend newspaper that aroused my interest. An article by your wife, Mr Ross. You might not have seen the paper but I'm sure you're familiar with the article.'

He saw Adam's dumbfounded look, and glanced at Nina, then back to Adam. He produced a copy of the *Sunday Mail.* 'It's on page nineteen.'

Adam turned to the page and his face became ashen.

'You haven't read the story, Mr Ross?'

Nina reached for Adam's hand. 'I wanted to surprise Jimmy. It was a great story ...' Her voice sank to a whisper for Adam was staring at her, his eyes awash with soft accusations.

'Is the man in that photograph Jimmy Black?' Mailey could have been addressing the floor.

Adam studied the page again. Mailey's eyes darted up for the answer.

'Mr Ross?'

'Why do you want to know, sergeant?'

'Inspector,' he said, so softly the correction could scarcely be heard. 'My father was the sergeant.'

Nina saw the expression on Adam's face and knew something was terribly wrong. She took the newspaper and, with dismay growing within her, looked at the bold display.

'Mr Ross, it was the name Jimmy Kettle that brought me here. If

Jimmy Kettle is Jimmy Black, that is something I need to know.'
He paused. 'So please, answer the question.'

Adam nodded. 'Yes.'

'Thank you.'

'Now please answer mine.'

'Why do I want to know? What's Jimmy Kettle to me?' He had been playing with the pen and put it on the desk, neatly parallel with the edge of his sheaf of notes. 'My father had a number of qualities that made him a bad parent but a good policeman. You see, he lived for his work. He wasn't home much.' He reached for the pen. 'He died when I was at school. I really didn't know him all that well, but a lot of people, especially other policemen, did know him and they've told me a great deal about him.

'He was a hard man. Very hard. Tough. You know the sort of person? What used to be called a man's man. Certainly not a woman's man.' He stopped, lost in some private recollection. 'He died more than thirty years ago, under strange circumstances. There was an investigation and it was all explained, or at least it was to the satisfaction of the officials of the time. But there were still several perplexing aspects to the affair.'

The aboriginal constable entered the room. His head was bandaged.

'Are you sure you wouldn't like some coffee or tea?' Mailey asked, and Nina was reminded of the rhyme about the spider and the fly. Adam had already refused. She offered the constable a sympathetic smile. He withdrew.

'In case you're not familiar with the story,' Mailey said, in a way that suggested such a possibility was unlikely, 'my father travelled to Coober Pedy to investigate an alleged robbery. While there, he apparently became involved in another investigation. It seems that he found in Coober Pedy a person who was, or whom he considered to be, a fugitive. Now it all gets rather clouded at this point because we have to rely largely on verbal information, rather than written reports. My father put very little of this secondary investigation down on paper. He probably intended to write a full report on his return but, of course, he never returned.

'Apparently, he left Coober Pedy in pursuit of this man, who was in the company of several other persons. We do however, have descriptions. A boy, a young aboriginal woman and a white youth of powerful build with blonde hair.' He took a deep breath and marched the butt of the pen across the desk. 'My father reached William Creek without having apprehended these four persons. He was in a motor car. The next thing we know is that his body was found somewhere to the south-west of Lake Eyre – not too far from where you have your property Mr Ross – in a situation which suggested that he had died of thirst. The body was so decomposed that a proper and satisfactory post-mortem examination was not possible. Nor, apparently, was it considered to be needed.

'The affair always puzzled friends and associates of my father. They told my mother he was not the sort of man to die in that way. Another man would abandon a broken-down motor car and walk across the sand-hills until he died of thirst. Not my father. Or so they said.' He laid the pen to rest again and folded his arms. 'Now, Mr Ross, I have always wondered how my father died; whether he perished in the way the report suggested, or whether something else happened to him. There were many puzzles and vague areas in the report but the one certain fact was the name of the man, the alleged fugitive, that my father discovered at Coober Pedy, and then attempted to follow on that final, fatal mission of his.' He turned to Nina, as though she alone needed to hear the name. 'That man was an aboriginal circus boxer by the name of Jimmy Kettle.'

Nina clutched at Adam's hand.

'I never forgot the name, but I hadn't seen any reference to it until this story of yours appeared on Sunday.' He smiled. 'It was a good story, but a very strange experience for me to read about someone who seemed so elusive as not to have existed. Do you understand the feeling?'

Neither spoke. Mailey scratched an ear. 'So I came north, intending to drive to this property of yours, to have a chat to this Jimmy Kettle, now older and going grey and unfortunate enough to have lost an arm somewhere along the pathway of life. I should point out I'm here in my own time. Taking a few days off, as they say. And, of course, on the way north I stumble into this sorry business.

'Now, Mr Ross, while I'm having a fairly heavy conversation with this Gooly character, he tells me a number of truly extraordinary things. He says you're a cattle thief, the master mind of a major operation. You're now aware of that accusation. But do you know what else he said about you?' He leaned back in the chair and, although he was not smoking, pursed his lips and blew a steam of air towards the ceiling. 'Before he knew my name or my special interest, this man told me that Mr Adam Ross, when only a young man, had killed a policeman by the name of Mailey.'

F·I·F·T·E·E·N

Without speaking, Adam drove from the police station. Nina sat quietly beside him, worried about the conversation with Inspector Mailey, worried about the way her husband looked and worried about him driving the car with a broken hand but she, too, said nothing. She understood his silences these days, and waited for him to choose the moment to talk. Nina had become expert at interpreting the signs, and the expression on his face told her that confused thoughts were whirling through his mind. Once he had them sorted out, divided into their separate categories and ready to be discussed, he would talk.

He crossed the railway line but instead of turning towards Saleem Benn's house, he drove the Mercedes on towards the sign-post that leaned drunkenly away from the town and had 'Birdsville 325' inscribed on its board. He turned on to that road, passed a wired-in yard that contained three goats and a heap of old ice chests, rusting drums and truck tyres, and let the car roll to a halt.

'I thought you were going to take me up the Birdsville Track,' she said, still looking ahead and trying to make it easier for him to begin.

'No.' His fingers tapped the rim of the steering wheel.

'You will one day?'

He nodded.

'How's your hand?'

He lifted it and moved it, to demonstrate that it still worked, and then turned in the seat to face her. 'There's so much to tell you.'

She took his good hand. 'I'm sorry about the story. I don't know exactly what I've done wrong but I know I've caused you a lot of trouble.'

'It's not your fault. You couldn't have known.' He was not looking at her, which was unusual. For their most intimate conversations, his eyes normally melted into her but now they were somewhere else, moving constantly as a counter-balance to his roving thoughts.

'He said you'd killed a policeman.'

'Yes.'

'You did?'

'Yes. A long time ago. His father, apparently.'

'Oh, Adam.' Now their eyes were in contact. 'And Jimmy? He was involved too?'

'Me, Jimmy, Josef and Saleem Benn.'

She swayed back in astonishment. 'All four of you?'

'Nellie knew too, although she wasn't there. We've kept it a secret all these years.' Nervously, his fingers played on her hand. 'It's a long story and I'll tell you everything soon, but not now, please.'

She waited, then said: 'Why did you kill him?'

'He was trying to kill the others. We had a fight.'

'He was after Jimmy?'

'Yes.' He saw the question in her eyes. 'No. Jimmy hadn't done anything wrong. Mailey was a –' Adam stopped. 'Please, I'll tell you everything later. At the moment, I just can't –' His head sagged. She ruffled his hair.

'And I had to go and write a story about Jimmy Kettle. I was so sure everyone would be pleased. I did it to give Jimmy some recognition.' She let her head touch his shoulder. 'I'm so sorry.'

'It's my fault.' Adam straightened and she moved away. They faced each other again. 'I should have told you all about it years ago. The whole story. It wasn't fair of me not to let you know. We were fools to think no one would find out.'

They sat in silence for a while, with Adam drawing nourishment from Nina's presence. In front of the car, a willy-willy spun across the road, the swirling column of dust drawing dried leaves and twigs into its spirals and slapping the car with its gritty outer winds.

'Just like a little tornado,' she said but Adam was thinking of other things.

'I wish you had told me,' she said when the air was calm once more and the only sound was a fly, trapped in the car and attacking the windscreen in a series of frenzied bursts. 'And not just to stop me writing that stupid article, either. If I'd known, I could have shared this thing with you. We could have talked about it. You could have got it out of your system.'

'And now the inspector knows.'

'It could be bad?'

'Of course. I killed the man.'

'What can Inspector Mailey do?'

'Whatever he likes.'

She thought for a while. 'You could deny everything. The others aren't going to say anything.'

666

'No. I've had enough of running away.'

'Is it possible you could go to gaol?'

'When it happened, we thought they might hang us.'

'Oh, Adam, don't say that.' She pressed his hand. 'As soon as you're feeling better, we're going to sit down somewhere on our own and you're going to tell me the whole story. And then, we're going to work out what we should do. You and I. This is a problem we can share, and together we'll find a solution.'

'Together.' He smiled.

'You look as though you could do with a long sleep.'

'About one week, I'd say.' He leaned across and kissed her. 'I do love you. You know that, don't you?'

'Yes. It's nice to hear you say it, though.'

'And all this business. It hasn't changed how you feel?'

'You mean what the inspector was saying?'

'And Nellie and Daniel.'

'Well, I don't think I've ever known a day like the last twenty-four hours and I'm shocked. Maybe stunned is a better word. So much has happened. I know you've killed people but that was in the war. Now you're being accused of murder.'

'It wasn't that.'

'I know, or I think I do. I'm sure you'll tell me in your own good time. But I'm still confused and distressed. I mean about Nellie and Daniel. It was just awful what happened to her. And so terrible that she kept the secret about Daniel all these years.' She laughed but it was a nervous trill. 'I guess I'll just have to get used to having three children.'

'I'm sorry you're being dragged through all this.'

'Adam, I love you more than I have loved anyone, more than I could ever love anyone, and right now I love you more than ever.'

He spent some time considering what she had said. 'That sounds pretty good to me.'

'I'm glad you approve.' They kissed. 'Now Mr Ross, where are you taking me? Up to Birdsville, or back to where there are people waiting anxiously to see us?'

At Saleem Benn's house, Adam took Daniel to one side and told him what happened at the police station.

'What he said was true,' Adam said, liking the way Daniel returned his gaze and listened without interrupting. 'I did kill that man. I broke his neck. It happened more than thirty years ago and I'll tell you the whole story one day soon, but right now, the thing that Nina and I have to work out is what to do next.'

667

Daniel sat quietly, nodding to himself. 'All this explains something.'

'What's that?' Adam felt exhausted and his voice was hoarse.

'Why you shouted at me when I was wrestling with Gooly. I was going to break *his* neck. No doubt about it. I was out to kill him. And then you screamed out at me, and you gave me such a shock I stopped. It wasn't just the noise but something in your voice.' He looked at Adam. 'It was fear.'

Adam sighed. 'Probably was. I didn't want you doing what I'd done all those years ago.' He took Daniel by the arm. 'Come on. I have to tell your uncle what happened.'

'He's not really my uncle, is he?'

'I think he'd still like you to call him that. Come on.'

At first with disbelief and then in mounting despair, Saleem Benn listened to Adam's account of what had happened at the police station. The lines on his weathered face deepened into ridges of anguish. The appearance of the son of that devil Mailey was like the return of a long-forgotten nightmare. Having said that, he cursed the mother of Saleem Goolamadail for having been delivered of such carrion and then cursed himself for not having strangled the child at birth. Then the old man beat his brow, demanding to know what foul or sacrilegious deeds of his in the past were now being punished, and lamenting that retribution was being visited on his friends and not solely on himself.

'It's not your fault,' Adam said, upset at the old man's distress. 'Things just happen.'

'No. That is too crude a philosophy, if you will forgive me saying so. There is a purpose to all this. I do not understand, but I know there is a reason. I will spend tonight in contemplation.' He had been pacing the room. Now he sat down, his face grey with fatigue. 'So what is the situation now? What does this son of the devil Mailey want?'

Nina answered. 'He asked Adam not to go away. He said he wasn't under arrest but he should stay in town for a day or two. He said we would be staying for Nellie's funeral, anyhow.' She saw the enquiring look on the Afghan's face. 'We understand the funeral will be in two days' time.'

'In the meantime, there's no man at Kalinda to run things,' Adam said ruefully. 'Cassie's on her own. Klemansky's got his team there which is one hell of a confusing sideshow.'

'Josef's there,' Nina added, to calm him.

'He can't run the property.'

'But he can keep an eye on things. At least for a day or two.'

Daniel had been sitting quietly in the corner. 'I'll go back.'

'You can't miss the funeral.'

'I'll drive up to Kalinda this afternoon, and come back. I'll be here in time.'

Saleem Benn raised both hands. 'Please, get back to Mailey. What is happening? Does the son know the story of the father's death?'

'Only what Gooly told him,' Adam said. 'He was very decent really. When he realized I wasn't going to say anything, he said it'd be a good idea if I had a talk to a solicitor.'

'In my limited experience, the men of law walk hand in hand with the forces of darkness. They are an evil, forced on us by the system that they perpetuate.' The old man withdrew into a silence punctuated by much muttering. 'Do you think it is essential for you to hire the services of such a man?'

'Yes,' Nina said forcefully. 'And I will find the right man. It's my fault all this has developed in the way it has, so it's up to me to help.'

'You didn't know.' Eyes closed, Adam shook his head. He was about to say more when Rashid, the young man from the store, appeared. There was a telephone call for Mr Ross.

'I'll take it,' Nina said, rising. She was more used to telephones. 'You stay and talk. If it's really urgent, I'll come and get you.'

Nina returned ten minutes later. 'You will never guess who that was,' she said and then saved Adam the bother of guessing by continuing immediately, 'it was Alex.'

Adam showed no recognition. 'Who's Alex?'

'Alex Raftopoulos. The boy from Greece.'

'You have had a telephone call from Greece?' the Afghan asked, his voice a squeak of respect for an instrument he had previously denigrated.

She laughed. 'No. He now lives in Adelaide. He migrated here years ago. He's changed his name. It's a long story and he's going to tell me more when I see him.'

'He's coming here?' Adam asked, suddenly aroused from his despondency.

'No. I'm going to see him.' She clapped her hands. 'I think the call must mean a change in our luck.'

Saleem Benn raised one eyebrow, tilting wrinkles so that his forehead resembled the ravaged slope of a mountainside.

'Alex is a solicitor. He tells me he is a good one. And he is going to help us.'

Adam pressed his forehead, trying to comprehend. 'How will you get to Adelaide?'

669

'By train, I suppose.' Clearly, she had not thought of that.

'You've got a five-day wait.'

'I've got an idea,' Daniel said. 'I'll get Cassie to bring the plane down. She can fly you.'

'I don't like Cassie flying to Adelaide.' Adam's objection was quiet but final.

Nina grabbed his hands. 'I have a better idea. I'll go with Josef. His twin's much faster, anyhow.'

'If I go now, Joe could be here this evening,' Daniel said, sharing Nina's enthusiasm.

'And I could be in Adelaide tonight.'

'It'll be dark.'

'He can fly that new plane of his at night. Adam,' she said, squeezing his hands. 'I have to see Jimmy, to see how he is and to find out precisely what happened. That's vital. Then I have to talk to Alex, to see what he can do. We can't waste a day.'

Daniel was already heading for the door. 'I'll go now. If Josef's at the house, he could be here by four o'clock.'

'And I could be in Adelaide in time to be having dinner with Alex.'

'Alex Raftopoulos?' Adam was recalling the serious boy of nine.

'Now Alex Rafter, twenty-seven, and sounds very much like a switched-on young lawyer. He saw the story too, so thank God it's done some good.'

'And he wants to help?'

'Eagerly.'

Adam sat back. He gazed at Nina with his mouth open. 'Alex. So he's a lawyer after all.'

'Yes. Wouldn't Dimitri be proud?'

Adam took half an hour to tell Nina and Daniel the story of Sergeant Mailey. Then Daniel drove rapidly up the Oodnadatta Track to William Creek.

He reached Kalinda in the middle of the afternoon. Josef was at the homestead. He had planned going out to the lake to watch Dr Rotondo and the mechanics make some changes to the jet car but immediately agreed to fly to Marree, collect Nina, and continue on to Adelaide.

He was gone before Cassie returned. She had been checking sheep near one of the bores.

Daniel followed her into the kitchen. While Mrs Wilson made tea, he told the two women of the events in Marree. He had been speaking for a few minutes when Patrick entered the room, the boy having been attracted by the tinkling of cups, a noise which announced food. Patrick sat quietly and listened to the rest of the story. He said: 'Did your mother get shot?' Mrs Wilson tried to stifle any further words but Daniel said 'yes', smiling tolerantly, and explained how his mother had died in preventing Goolamadail from shooting Patrick's father.

'If your mother hadn't been shot would my father have been shot?'

'Possibly,' Mrs Wilson interjected and gave the boy a biscuit.

'Who was your mother?' Patrick asked the question with the biscuit poised.

'Shut up, Patrick,' Cassie said and rammed the biscuit into his mouth.

'No one you know, darling,' Mrs Wilson said. Daniel was silent and left the room.

'Is Daniel crying?'

'Oh Patrick, don't be such a drongo,' Cassie said, glowering at him. 'His mother is dead. Of course he's sad.'

'But men don't cry.'

'Sometimes they do,' Mrs Wilson said.

'I've never seen Daniel cry before.'

'His mother never died before,' Cassie said. 'She only died last night. He's very upset. And he came all the way up here to let us know.'

'Why didn't Mummy and Daddy come back?'

'They had things to do,' Cassie said and looked at Mrs Wilson to see if she knew what those things were. The older woman shook her head. 'Danny has to go back to Marree in a couple of days for the funeral.'

'What's a funeral?'

'It's what they have when they bury people.'

'Why do they bury people?'

Cassie withdrew before the few questions became an inquisition. 'You tell him, Mrs Wilson. You're more patient than me.'

'Than I,' Mrs Wilson chided, her voice gentle.

'Than I, who am off to see if Daniel is all right.'

'Who is off.'

'This very instant.' She left with a back-handed wave. Daniel was on the verandah.

She stopped at a discreet distance. 'Are you all right?'

'Yes.' He turned. His eyes were dry.

'Oh. I thought –' she sat in a chair and he sat beside her. 'The little brat can be rough.'

'Kids are kids.'

'Not the ones who are monsters.'

671

'Your brother's not a monster.'

'He's my half-brother. I'm very proud of that fact. If ever he makes me feel ashamed to be related I think of that and only feel half-ashamed.'

A flock of cockatoos wheeled past the verandah. Spreading wings of flashing white and fanning their sulphurous crests, they settled near the horseyards and began pecking at the ground.

'Some other things happened at Marree,' Daniel said, still watching the birds.

Cassie had heard about Jimmy's message, the apprehension of Goolamadail and the shootings. 'Something else?'

'Two things you should know about. Really your father should tell you.' He still found it simple and reasonable to say 'your' and not 'our' father. 'But he isn't here and there are things happening that you'll hear about, and they won't make sense unless you know the truth.'

'Two things?'

'Yes.'

'You make it all sound very mysterious, Danny.'

He had the look of a person who longs to be somewhere else. 'There was a policeman in town. An inspector from Adelaide.' And he told her the story of Mailey. It was a long story; what had happened in the 1920s, and what had transpired in Marree that morning. The cockatoos had flown away long before the tale was ended.

She glanced at her watch. 'I'd almost forgotten. I'm having dinner with Michel and I have to rush. I don't feel like going over there now.'

Daniel sat quietly, not yet finished but waiting for the right moment before resuming.

Cassie found one more question. 'Do you think this lawyer in Adelaide, the Greek man that Dad used to know during the war, will be able to help?'

'Nina seems to think so. She's seeing him tonight.'

Cassie hunched over her knees. 'I think I'll call off dinner. I couldn't stand small-talk tonight.'

'It might do you good. Take your mind off things.'

'I wish I could help.'

'There's nothing much that you can do. Not up here.'

She got up, as though to leave.

'Before you go.'

'Is it important Danny?' She put one levelled hand against her chin. 'I'm just about up to here in disasters and worries.'

'Well, it's not really a disaster –'

672

'Maybe tomorrow then.' She started to walk away, then stopped when she saw the intense expression on his face. 'Is it about Inspector Mailey?'

'Nothing to do with him. It's about my mother.'

She returned quickly and sat beside him. 'I'm sorry. I was so caught up in my own thoughts ... Forgive me Danny. What is it?'

'I don't know how to start this.'

'Dad always says the beginning is a good place.' She crossed her knees, locked her fingers and gave Daniel her total attention. He looked away.

'The trouble is, I don't know where the beginning is. Did you know –' He broke off and let his head sag backwards. 'Did you know my mother used to live here?'

'At Kalinda?' Cassie untangled her legs. 'Danny, she couldn't. Dad built this place. There was no one here before then.'

'She lived here when your Dad was here. She used to look after you.'

'Your mother did?'

'I always thought her name was Ellen, but I found out last night that her first name was really Nellie.'

Cassie leaned back so far her head touched the wall. 'Your mother was Nellie?'

He nodded, still dreading what he had to say.

'She was lovely,' Cassie said, here eyes focused on the ceiling. 'She came here eight or nine years ago. We had a talk.'

'Mum did?' It was his turn to be surprised.

'Nellie, yes. I remembered her vaguely as a kid. Dad says I loved her.' She reached out, almost touching him. 'And she was your mother. Oh Danny, oh my God, it was *Nellie* who was shot.' Her fingers played nervous games. Another flock of cockatoos, fewer birds this time, descended on the horseyards, but her eyes and mind were elsewhere. Eventually she said, 'Thank you for telling me.'

'There's more. My uncle told me last night.'

'Saleem Benn?'

'Yes. You see, Cassie, I never knew my father. I'd always thought he was dead because that was what Mum had said.'

'And?'

'Last night I found out he's alive and I found out who he is.'

Each stared frankly into the other's eyes, hers curious, his hurting.

'My father is your father.'

She blinked, then almost smiled, certain he must be joking, but no trace of levity showed on the face of the young man staring so

673

intensely, sorrowfully at her. There was a great distance behind those eyes.

She sank into the chair, risked one more glance at him and covered her face.

'You're telling me that ...'

He waited but she had run out of words.

'I'm saying my mother was the woman you knew as Nellie, and my father is your father, Adam Ross.'

She lifted one hand to reveal an eye. 'And you believe that?'

'Saleem Benn says it's true. Your father didn't know.'

'Dad didn't know?'

'No.' They sat in silence.

She let her hand fall so far back it banged the wall. 'My God, another half-brother.'

'Yes.' There appeared the first hint of a smile. 'I was a bit worried to hear what you were saying about Patrick.'

She hit the wall again. 'This is incredible.'

'I still can't believe it myself.'

'And Nellie, I mean your mother, left here in 1939?'

'I was born at Oodnadatta six months later. She left here so that woman in Sydney wouldn't take you away from your father. She was frightened there would be a scandal.'

Cassie stood and walked to the edge of the verandah. 'And your mother never told you anything about this?'

'All she ever told me was that my father had left when I was a baby, and then had an accident and got killed. She always said that she loved him and couldn't marry anyone else.'

'She said that?'

'And she always told me my father was a fine man.' There was another long pause.

'And she was sick? I mean, just recently?'

'She was dying.'

'She knew that?'

'Yes.'

'And she threw herself on the gun when Gooly tried to shoot Dad?'

'Yes. I heard Gooly shout "I'll kill you" or something like that.'

'She knew what she was doing?'

'Yes, I think so.'

Cassie leaned on the verandah rail and watched the late afternoon sun draw sharp shadows on the red soil. 'I'm going to my room.' She walked to Daniel, bent, and kissed him. 'I'm sorry about your mother. Not just last night. Everything.'

He stood up. She offered her hand and grinned. 'I guess I should say welcome to the family. A bit late, I suppose.'

She went to her room. There her thoughts raced along new paths. Her father had slept with Nellie, had sex with a coloured woman. How long had they slept together? Probably all the time she was at Kalinda. Had they loved each other or had it been a sordid affair, the kind of liaison Mrs Wilson sometimes gossiped about?

She was shocked. Not that a white man had slept with a coloured woman. That was all right. But her father! And they weren't married. That was the thing. She didn't care who slept together and had babies, as long as they were married. But her father and Nellie, the woman who looked after his baby daughter after his wife had died?

Cassie lay on the bed and gazed up at the ceiling, lost in new thoughts.

Cassie had never eaten trout. The fish was delicious but she had difficulty separating the flesh from the fine bones. Her dexterity was hampered by the consumption of too much wine. It seemed to her that Klemansky had provided more wine than on the last occasion and he kept filling her glass. And whereas he had given her a choice of drinks at their first dinner, on this occasion she had had no say. He insisted she was drinking wine and because she arrived late and was flustered by Daniel's news, and because she was in a mood to capitulate to simple demands, she drank wine. It was good, obviously expensive and, somehow, delivered very cold from the tiny refrigerator in the American's caravan. By the end of the meal, she was dizzy, inclined to giggle and talking more than she meant to.

'Do you think people who aren't married should have babies?' she asked and was shocked to detect a slur in her voice.

Klemansky refilled her glass and put the bottle on the table. He had been looking at her in the strangest way, she thought; part amusement, part something else.

'Definitely not.'

'Neither do I.'

'But they should certainly sleep together.'

She had been about to sip some wine but returned the glass to the table. 'They should?'

'Certainly. If they like each other.'

'Ah.'

'Or if they feel like it.'

'If they like it or if they feel each other.' She reflected on her answer. 'Did I say it right?'

'You did.'

'That doesn't leave much, does it?' She giggled. 'Who shouldn't sleep together then?'

'Those who don't want to.'

'I don't understand that.' Nor did she understand why he seemed to be drinking so little of his own wine when it was so good and when he had gone to so much trouble to have it brought up here.

'It's very simple. People who do not like each other should not have to go to bed together. By the way, I hate that term "sleeping together" when it usually means anything but sleeping, don't you?'

She sipped more wine. 'And people who do like each other; they have to?'

She meant it to be funny. She was feeling really good now. Much better than this afternoon. But he didn't seem to think she was being humorous. He concentrated on the label on the current bottle of wine, and frowned.

'*Have* is a difficult word. They are not forced to, by any law, written or unwritten. But they may have a feeling of inevitability, a sense of irresistible attraction, which compels them to experience the other person. In other words, through this deep seated, instinctive impulse, they go to bed with the other person because they have to. Not to do so would be wrong.'

'Oh.'

His eyes switched from the label to her. 'It's funny, but years ago people thought differently. For unmarried couples to go to bed was scandalous. Of course, things have changed so much in recent times. Especially for women.' Without even looking at the bottle, he took it and filled her glass. 'Attitudes towards women have gone through a revolution. What was once considered shocking is now thought to be normal. Women were once not allowed out of the house. Now they talk politics, smoke, drink, go to bed with whom they like, even with other women. I think it's a healthy trend, don't you?'

She raised one eyebrow.

'I'm told Australian country women are particularly strong.' For the first time in the last half hour, he sipped some of his own wine.

'I can crack a stockwhip.'

The glass obscured most of his face. 'What are you suggesting?'

'Nothing.' She giggled without meaning to. 'But I haven't met the man who can handle a whip like I can.'

His eyes darted across her; he seemed greatly amused. 'We could have a very interesting time when we go overseas. You could use the whip to your heart's content. I know people who would be interested.'

'You want me to take the stockwhip?'

'If you wish. You can take your spurs, if you like. Maybe a branding iron or two.'

She balanced her glass near her nose. 'Do you have cattle?'

'A few old bulls and cows.' He laughed. 'I'd like to see some of them running with a red hot iron in pursuit.'

'You get them on the ground first. You have to hold them down.'

Delicately, he touched his nose. 'I can see I must take you to New York. You'd be a sensation.'

'I'm pretty good right here.' Both laughed.

'Ah, Cassie, Cassie,' he said, sliding down from one pinnacle but preparing for the assault on another. 'How do you think of me?'

She peeped over the rim of her glass. He reached across, took it from her hand and put it on the table.

'I want an answer.'

'The answer is yes. What was the question?'

'How do you think of me. As a racing driver, some sort of crazy nut, a rich American?'

'I don't know.'

'Or as a friend?'

'Ah.' She reached for the glass. 'And if I say as a friend, we have to go to bed together, right?'

'Right.' The eyes had narrowed. 'Friends like us should go to bed together.'

'I don't feel tired.'

'Good.'

She giggled.

He stood, and limped to the light switch. He turned it off. A lamp glowed in the far end of the caravan. 'It was too bright,' he said and limped back.

'Is your leg still sore?'

'Yes.' He undid his belt.

'What are you doing?'

'My leg aches. It needs massaging. I have to massage it every night, ever since the crash at Monaco.' He shook off his shoes. 'Would you massage it for me?'

'I don't think I'd be very good.'

'I'll show you how.'

'I have massaged Patrick,' she added, suddenly remembering nights when she had tried to ease the stiffness from her little brother's legs, usually after too many hours on his horse.

'Patrick?'

'My brother. Correction, my half-brother. I have a lot of half-

677

brothers. They seem to pop out of the woodwork.' She raised a hand to stifle a laugh. 'Where does it hurt?'

'Where does what hurt?'

'Your leg. You wanted me to massage it and make it better, remember?'

'Here.' He wiggled his ankle and moved nearer her, his injured leg raised, hands poised like a tightrope walker getting his balance.

'You look funny.'

He sat down, frowning.

She sat opposite him. 'Have I offended you?'

He shook his head. 'Why do you ask?'

'You look offended.'

'Merely puzzled.' He reached out and put his hand on her shoulder. 'You're a very unusual young woman.'

'Is that bad?' She searched for the wine glass and sipped from it. 'I don't try to be unusual. In fact, I think I'm very usual.' She giggled. 'Is there such a word? I mean, in that sense?'

'Who knows?' He raised a hand in a helpless gesture. 'Are we going to sit here all night and exchange silly sentences?'

She put down the glass, folded her hands demurely on her lap and faced him. 'I'm sorry.'

'For what?'

'Being silly.'

He held out his hand. It was a graceful gesture, much like the poses Cassie had seen on classical paintings in some of Mrs Wilson's books. The Greek god offering contact to a mere mortal. 'Come here,' he said softly.

'I am here.'

But he continued to extend the hand. His smile was tolerant, benign, and she moved closer.

'What now?'

'You're an extraordinarily attractive woman.'

'You just said I was silly.' She began to twist away, but gently, he turned her face towards him. He kissed her.

It was a long kiss. She could hear insects chirping and the hiss of a gas flame. When it was over, she touched her lips. 'Why did you do that?'

'Why not?' He smiled. 'You're beautiful and beautiful women deserve to be kissed.'

'Michel, I don't think we should ...' Her protest trailed into a long silence. He kissed her again. Then he slid behind her, put both arms around her and kissed the back of her neck. It was a delicious sensation and she shivered. His tongue played with her ear. She squirmed away. He followed her, kissing her cheek, then her ear, then the neck. His breath played on the fine hairs that ran down to her spine.

'Oh Michel.' It could have been a protest or a gasp of ecstasy.

His hands cupped her breasts. 'You're magnificent,' he said and his teeth nibbled the top of one shoulder.

I shouldn't let him do this, she thought, but the sensation was incredible, as though someone had opened the door to a hidden chamber and now emotions that had been pent up, hidden for years, began to pour through in a great gushing torrent. Her body shook. She tried to stop it, to control herself, but the shaking grew worse. Or better. It was a wonderful feeling. His hand was inside her blouse. She felt her nipples rise. The fingers were stroking, circling, delicately fondling her.

A voice told her she must protest. 'This is not right,' she whispered. 'We shouldn't be doing this.'

He moved to one side and kissed her ear. 'Everyone does it.'

'But we're not in love.'

Now he faced her and placed a finger against her lips. 'Shh,' he whispered and unbuttoned her blouse.

'Why are you doing that, Michel?'

He pushed the blouse clear of her shoulders and leant down, running his tongue along the exposed swell of her breasts. 'You're superb,' he said and she felt his fingers fumbling with the catch to her bra.

'I must be getting better,' she said and felt light headed again. She shook her head. She'd had far too much to drink.

'Better?' the voice came from her cleavage.

'First I was unusual, then extraordinary, then beautiful, then ... what was it? Magnificent. Now I'm superb.'

He raised his head. 'You've got a good memory. As well as magnificent breasts.' He removed the bra and kissed her on each nipple. He pulled her close, squeezing her around his face. Then he swayed back and stared expectantly at her. She stood up. He stayed on the seat and smiled at her. He expected her to continue undressing but she began to put on the bra again.

'What are you doing?'

She didn't know what to say that wouldn't sound childish or immature, so she said, 'I'm cold.'

'I'm cold too. There's a very simple solution.' Klemansky took a deep breath, as though having made a resolution, and reached for her hand. Again, it was the classical gesture, the move of a man who had never known failure. 'Come here.'

'Where?'

'To bed.'

'Why?' It was a little girl's voice and she wondered where it had come from.

'To get warm.'

She had the bra back in place. He was smiling at her, planning a second removal.

'How about your ankle?'

'Well, you can begin by massaging my leg. Why not? You can start here.' He tapped his thigh.

'It hurts up there?'

'It aches all over.'

'All over?' She placed a hand on the table to steady herself. 'What sort of accident was it?'

'A big one. Why don't you come and lie down? You can massage my leg and get warm at the same time.'

'Where?'

He took her arm and began to guide her to the other end of the caravan.

She stopped and tried to remove his hand. 'Did you put something in the wine?'

'No. Why?'

'I feel funny.'

'Then lie down.'

'I should go home.'

'Lie down first.' He held on to her arm. She was surprised at the strength of his grip.

'No.' She spread both hands against his shoulders.

'You're a very attractive girl. I could show you so much, teach you a great deal.'

'I should go home. I don't feel well.'

'If you don't feel well, come here.' He opened a curtain, to reveal a bed that was spread across the width of the caravan. She pulled back. 'You want to come to Europe with me, don't you?'

'I'm going home.' He pulled her forward, off-balance. 'Please, Michel.'

'My leg's aching.'

'Please.'

He shook her arm and it hurt. 'What are you? Queer or something?'

'What do you mean?'

He had her in a distorted dancing pose: one hand held her arm high, the other was locked around the small of her back. Grunting with exertion, he pulled her close to him. She turned her head away.

'I'll say this for you,' he said. 'You're strong. Let's see how you make love!'

'No.' She stamped on his foot. With a howl, he stepped back, releasing her. He clenched his right fist and raised it.

The scuffling had helped clear her head. She thought of Jimmy and his boxing lessons, swayed to the right and threw a left hook.

Her timing was faulty and her fist struck him a glancing blow on the tip of the nose. He stumbled back and fell on the bed. 'You goddam bitch,' he shouted, feeling his nose. A smear of blood coloured his finger. 'You won't get the fucking job now.'

'I don't want a fucking job.' She backed away.

He stood, wiping more blood from his nose. 'I ought to smear you over these walls.'

'You touch me and I'll take the stockwhip to you.'

'Like hell you will. No woman does that to me.' He picked up a heavy torch.

'You come one step closer and I'll get the whip.'

'And do what, you ugly bitch?'

'Solve all your problems.' Her right arm swung an imaginary whip. 'I reckon I can take the balls off a bull at fifteen feet. Yours shouldn't be any problem.'

He stepped forward, threatening her with the torch. 'You and who else?'

'Just me.' Clumsily, she fastened the buttons on her blouse. 'And after I finish with you, my brother could have what was left of you. He'd tear you apart.'

'Your kid brother Patrick?' He laughed.

'My big brother Daniel.'

'He's not your brother.' Even so, Klemansky paused. Daniel had the build of a weight lifter. And he was always hanging around Cassie. He didn't want to tangle with him.

'Didn't you know? Daniel's my new brother.' She swayed and tried to steady herself but knocked over the wine. 'He'd take your arms off,' she said, trying to wipe spilled wine from her legs. 'He's as strong as a bullock.'

"And you're as clumsy as one.' Klemansky frowned and threw the torch on the bed. 'Get out. You're drunk.'

'And you're a louse. And a liar.' She couldn't think of other words. Those weren't strong enough, but her mind wasn't working properly.

She backed out of the caravan. It was black outside. She tried to run to the homestead but, being giddy, stumbled and fell. She felt sick and now she felt frightened.

A strong arm grabbed her elbow and she quaked with fright.

'It's only me,' Daniel said.

'Oh God, you gave me such a scare.' Gratefully she took his

681

other hand. He pulled her to her feet. 'What on earth are you doing here?' she gasped.

'I didn't feel like staying indoors. I just wanted to think about things. And then I thought it'd be a good idea if I was around to walk you home. You know, just in case. I don't like that bloke.'

'You're a good judge.' She leaned on him.

'Are you all right? What happened?'

'Nothing.'

'You sure? Why were you running?'

'I wanted to get home. I was feeling sick.'

'Come on. I'll help you.'

Arm in arm, they walked to the homestead.

S·I·X·T·E·E·N

The morning of Nellie's funeral dawned still and hot and grew hotter as the sun climbed and scraped colour from the sky. Marree was never a busy town but fewer people than usual moved on this day, because of the heat and the flies and the awareness of death that funerals bring to small communities. Those who ventured into the sun made short, ambling journeys. Even the town dogs, habitual street dwellers with dusty flanks raked deep by the scars of hungry days, crawled out of sight beneath the trees near the hotel. The railway station was deserted, a concrete ship in a sea of rails. The train from the south had been cancelled because of a strike and the only movement came from a fluttering of hawks, gathered around a strip of line where feed had spilled from stock trucks. As the morning progressed, an occasional willy-willy raised chimneys of dust far away in the country beyond the wide, dry bed of the Frome River.

It was a good day for a burial; a day to put the dead to rest and not to contemplate the miseries of those who were left.

The funeral was set for eleven o'clock. At ten, Inspector Mailey called at Saleem Benn's house to see Adam. He had more information to pass on about the cattle-stealing allegations. Could they meet after the service? And would Adam be in a position to make a statement regarding his knowledge of events connected with the death of Mailey's father?

Adam told the inspector that his wife Nina had been in Adelaide, consulting a lawyer. She had telephoned him yesterday to say that they were gathering information. Possibly she would reach Marree today.

At ten-twenty, a single-engined aircraft flew low over town, the signal that it was about to land and that the crew required transportation back to Marree. Adam heard the plane, ran outside and recognized his Cessna. He drove to the airstrip to collect Cassie and Daniel. No sooner had he taken them to the house than a second aircraft buzzed the buildings. It came in low, almost touching a radio mast.

'That must be Joe,' Cassie drawled, even before they recognized the aircraft. He drove back to the airstrip. The twin had already landed by the time he arrived.

Nina was first out. She was tired and gaunt but smiled, and there was more than an expression of pleasure at being reunited: her eyes had the sparkle of triumph.

Josef got out, waved, but stayed with the aircraft. The other passengers emerged but stayed dutifully behind Nina.

'We've had a very busy time,' Nina said in a voice aching with fatigue.

The first man was young, short and thick-set. His black hair was thinning prematurely. His face was unnaturally broad, due mainly to a huge smile.

'Adam, this is Alex.'

They shook hands, then wrestled each other into a hug.

'He's been marvellous,' she said, pushing them apart, 'but we'll talk later. There are more people you have to meet.'

A slim aborigine with an excessively creased face stood shyly behind Nina.

'This is Nelson Cannaroola. He is Jimmy's cousin. He was in the creek at Port Augusta the night you first saw Sergeant Mailey.' They shook hands.

A stooped and bearded man, somewhere in his eighties, shuffled up to Adam. 'You introduced me to this gentleman when we drove south through Coober Pedy,' Nina said and she could not keep pride from her voice. 'I remembered the meeting and I remembered the name and Alex tracked him down yesterday.'

Adam, jaw agape, shook the man's hand. 'Dexter Paradine.'

'Good to see you,' the old man said.

'It was Mr Paradine's first flight.'

He ignored Nina's comment. 'I saw Mailey shoot old Horrie Smith,' Paradine said, nodding with satisfaction, for he was at the age when others assume an old man's memory is gone. 'He assaulted me and he stole a car which was never returned to its rightful owner.' He could have been giving evidence.

Alex interrupted him. 'Mr Paradine was kind enough to agree to this long flight, to help his old friend, Mr Ross. Now, Adam, is the Afghan gentleman Saleem Benn in town?'

Still stunned by the arrival of so many, Adam could only nod.

'Good. I presume he'll testify on our behalf?'

'Certainly.'

'Excellent. Let's get in the car. I want to tell you what I have in mind and I understand you have a funeral to attend?'

'Yes.'

'My condolences. Nina explained.' He shook Adam's hand again, and went to the car.

Josef joined them. 'What do you think of little Alex?'

'I can't get over it.'

'He's a cross between Perry Mason and a bulldozer. And has he been working hard! Hasn't stopped. He's always either on the telephone or on the way to see someone.' Josef looped an arm across Adam's shoulder. 'Nina's been going just as hard. She hasn't had more than two hours' sleep since she left. That's not a bad wife you've got there.'

'I know. You've been busy too.'

'Getting a few flying hours up. I saw Jimmy and he's going to be all right. We know the full story and Alex has got it all written out.' He looked around them, squinting in the cruel light. 'Sad day, old mate, isn't it?'

'Yes.' Adam felt old this morning. His shoulders were a little stooped. 'It could be an important day, too. I've got to see Inspector Mailey after the funeral.'

'Don't worry. We'll turn Alex loose on him.' Josef attempted a confident smile but he was filled with a gnawing dread. Nellie was gone, and Mailey had returned.

At Lake Eyre, Dr Paolo Rotondo received the message from the timekeepers and strode angrily to the end of the record strip. The Shark was slowing, its striped parachute whirling and filling in the jet stream behind the car.

When Klemansky stopped, Rotondo went to the nose and unlatched the cockpit cover. 'What did you think you were doing? *Madonna mia*, do you know how fast that was?'

Klemansky removed his helmet which had baffled his ears from the verbal onslaught. He grinned happily. 'How fast, Paolo?'

'*Cretino!* What are you trying to do? I ask for a run at two hundred and fifty and you do three hundred and seventy!'

'Are we talking kilometres or miles?'

'*Miles!*' He screamed the word.

Klemansky wriggled deeper into the seat and smiled in satisfaction. 'I though it was a quick one.'

'I wanted two fifty!'

Klemansky shouted back. 'And I almost got to Cobb's speed.'

'This was a test run. I needed data.'

'Jesus Christ, Paolo, you're always after data. You should go and lock yourself in a laboratory somewhere and play with mice. We're after a record. We want speed. And I just gave it to you.'

'You could have crashed.'

'I didn't.'

The Italian walked in a circle of fury. 'I am sick of all this. I am dealing with a madman. Worse, I am dealing with a child, an imbecile who does not realize what we are trying to do.'

'We are trying to go fast, you stupid bastard.'

'Stupid! That's the word for you. I am tired of all this. I have had enough.'

Klemansky climbed from the cockpit and slid to the ground. 'Good. So have I.'

Gronwald was standing back, trying to stay out of range. Klemansky signalled to him.

'Oscar, come here.'

Gronwald hesitated.

'Goddam it, come here.' He jabbed a finger at Rotondo. 'And you get off the lake.'

'With pleasure.' Rotondo strode angrily towards a Land Rover.

'Michel, please calm down,' Gronwald said.

'I'm calm, and I want you to have the Shark ready for an attempt on the record. The proper goddam thing. No more of this pissing around. That's our next run. We go for five hundred.'

Gronwald's face became contorted in doubt. 'Michel, we need Paolo. There are still things that he wanted to do.'

'Oscar, he'll keep on testing things until he wears the goddam car out.' When the Swede still seemed unsure, Klemansky said, 'You have two days Oscar. Get it ready. Have everything organized.'

'But there are things –'

'Two days. If you don't want to do it, you can leave too and I'll take the Shark out like it is.' He stalked to the tent.

The church was small and stifling in the heat of the late morning. An arrangement of paper flowers filled one corner of the wooden building. It had been there for so long the red roses had turned an insipid pink and the stalks were strips of unevenly faded green. A stained-glass window was behind the altar. Plain glass filled the windows on either side of the building and the insects that hovered above the pews turned blue or red or golden brown, depending on which shaft of light was penetrated.

There were few mourners: those who had known Nellie, those who were curious, and an old woman who had been to every funeral in Marree since her husband died. A grey-haired, grey-faced woman, as starched and crisp as a well-loved old shirt, played an organ which produced notes of asthmatic quality. At her side was a small boy who pumped air for the organ and coughed persistently.

686

The Reverend Roger Montgomery drove to town to conduct the service. On the way, he had detoured to a homestead where the manager's wife kept a small flower garden. She had made a wreath of daisies, geraniums and green leaves with a centre-piece of Sturt's Desert Pea. Roger was particularly pleased with that. The exotic desert flower, with its waxy tongue of brilliant red and glossy black and which brought a wild beauty to the most desolate places, seemed a perfect choice; a bloom to match the spirit of the woman on whose coffin the wreath reposed.

The service was brief. Hymns were sung in a stumbling, follow-the-leader fashion, for, although the words were provided, the only ones who knew the melodies were Roger, who sang in a strong if flat voice, and the woman at the back of the church, who knew every hymn sung at every funeral. The woman at the organ kept silent, all her concentration needed to read the music. The boy pumped and coughed.

Four men bore the slim coffin to the hearse. Adam and Daniel were at the front, Josef and one of Saleem Benn's nephews, who was representing the old man, at the back.

At the cemetery, Saleem Benn joined them. He wore the flowing robes of his camel-riding days.

'I think I was wearing this on the first occasion I met Nellie,' he told Adam and squeezed his hand in greeting. 'I recall not being impressed. It is fitting, I think, that I should be so dressed as a token of my repentance.' He pressed Adam's hand again, and stood beside Daniel. Adam was flanked by Nina and Cassie.

'I know you loved her,' Nina said softly, as they walked towards the grave which a man had spent all of one day digging. 'And I know Daniel was born out of that love. So I think it would be good if you were to stand with your son.'

Adam turned to her and she was frightened to see how tired and worn he looked. 'No,' he said. 'He probably wants to be with Saleem Benn. The old fellow raised him. He's like a father.'

'He would rather be with you.'

'But I don't want to leave you on your own.'

'I'll be with Cassie.' As if to express her agreement, Cassie linked arms with Nina. 'And we'll be close. Please, Adam. It's what Nellie would want.'

Adam moved towards his son. Saleem Benn saw him coming, smiled contentedly, and whispered to Daniel: 'Stand with your father. It is proper on a day like today.'

Adam and Daniel stood side by side while the others shuffled into place. Adam held out his hand for Nina and pulled her close to him and his newly-found son. Thus they stood, while Nellie was

buried in a graveyard of rock and raw earth and leaning tomb-
stones.

A dog sauntered in from the street and sat behind the thin line of
humans. There were more willy-willies rising from the mirages
beyond the Frome and, high above them, a solitary hawk made a
lonely circle in the sky.

'I knew this woman well,' Roger said, addressing the small
group. Bible in hand he stood beside the open grave and faced the
mourners but his eyes were far away, seeing sights on the other side
of the vapours that danced on the plains. He stood motionless for
so long that Nina, who had covered more than one major funeral in
her journalistic career, thought he had forgotten what he meant to
say. Eventually his eyes came back to the group and he smiled and
shut the Bible. 'In fact, I was with her many years ago when she
made a decision that required an immense amount of courage. It
was a decision which took her away from a home where she had
lived happily for some years, a home in which there dwelled people
who loved her and whom she, in turn, loved deeply.'

A fly settled on Roger's face. He brushed it away.

'People often talk of soldiers in war giving their lives. It's what
we call the supreme sacrifice. All those years ago, our dear sister,
whom we are now committing to God's mercy, made a sacrifice of
supreme dimensions, but instead of forfeiting her life, she sacrificed
other things – her chance to remain with those she loved, her future
happiness – and I think that took a great deal more courage.

'Now, why did she do this?' Again he paused and gazed beyond
them. 'The answer is simple. She did it to help those she loved. She
sacrificed herself, she forfeited her future, she abandoned the
possibility of her own happiness, so that others might be spared
anguish and loneliness. It was a decision which required more
bravery and determination than most of us possess. It may not have
been a wise decision. It may have caused her unnecessary hardship
and even imposed grief on those who did not, who could not
understand.' He raised the Bible to his chest. 'Wise or not, it was
the action of a remarkably caring and selfless woman.'

At that point, Roger appeared to remember the speech he had
prepared and spoke about Nellie's work for the Australian Inland
Mission at Innamincka, and how she would be remembered with
affection by the people who lived along the Cooper. He offered his
condolences to Daniel and to all her friends, and closed with a
prayer.

The coffin was lowered into the grave. The few who were there
stood in silence, faces dripping perspiration, hands flicking at flies.

In the desert beyond the Frome, the swirling columns of dust had spun themselves into oblivion and the solitary hawk that once circled high above the graveyard had vanished.

Inspector Mailey stood near the gateway to the cemetery. Roger stopped and spoke to him for several minutes. When the minister had gone, Mailey waited for Adam.

'I know this is a bad day to be talking of the things we have to discuss, Mr Ross, but the matter is very important.' He had small eyes, as intense and nervous as an eagle's. 'And I have very little time.'

'After lunch, inspector?'

'That would be fine. Give me a chance to cool off. You'll come to the police station?'

'Yes, but there will be several of us.'

'Good. Each can make a contribution?'

'Indeed.'

'In that case, they'll be very welcome. Shall we say two o'clock?'

S·E·V·E·N·T·E·E·N

Mailey shared the late Sergeant Butler's aversion to bright light and heat, and left the shades down in the main office of the police station. He sat at the sergeant's desk.

'I hadn't expected so many.' The inspector ran a querulous eye around the ring of people assembled in the room. Adam had introduced them but it was Alex who took the floor.

'Three are here because they are family.' Alex indicated Cassie, Daniel and Nina. 'Mr Ross feels it is important that they hear all that is said in this matter.'

Adam nodded agreement.

'The others all have important statements to make.' Saleem Benn looked at Nelson Cannaroola, who stared intently at his own knees. Josef sat beside Dexter Paradine. The old man was eager to talk, and kept licking his lips to ensure words would flow easily. 'But perhaps I should clarify something before we begin,' Alex continued. 'Am I correct, inspector, in understanding that you are not here in an official capacity but have travelled here as a matter of personal interest?'

'Correct, Mr Rafter.'

'So this is not an official enquiry?'

'This was to be Mr Ross and myself having a talk,' Mailey said with heavy irony. 'I had not expected to odds to be nine to one.'

'You will soon understand the reason.'

'Good.' Mailey lit his pipe.

'Therefore,' Alex said, returning to his theme, 'as this is an informal gathering, nothing that will be said will have any relevance in any possible future inquiry and –'

'Mr Rafter.' The inspector drew on his pipe and fixed his bright little eyes on Alex. 'You know the law as well as I do. Possibly better. You know you can say what you like now and deny what you like later. But you should be aware that I will remember all that you tell me and therefore, you give me information at your peril, or rather, that of your clients.'

Alex began to speak, but Mailey help up a hand. 'I came here because of something I read in a newspaper article. The name that interested me in that article was the name of Jimmy Kettle. Are you aware of *why* I was interested?'

'I am.'

'And are you aware that my interest in Mr Ross has been aroused by information given to me by a Mr Saleem Goolamadail – who shall afterwards, mercifully, be referred to as Gooly?'

Alex suppressed a smile. 'Yes inspector. I'm aware of that. Mr Ross, however, feels that now is the time for the truth, and all of it, in the matter of your father's death, to be told.'

Mailey sat back and sucked on his pipe. 'Go ahead then, Mr Rafter.'

Alex took a deep breath and rubbed his hands together. 'Mr Ross and Mr Kettle have been friends for more than thirty years. They first met in a boxing match at Port Augusta. At that time, Mr Kettle was employed in a circus run by a Mr Cedric Carter. He was the star performer in the circus boxing troupe. In those days, of course, Mr Kettle had not lost his left arm.'

Mailey's pipe tilted in acknowledgement. 'Are you saying they fought in a boxing match?'

'Yes.'

'Who won?' The inspector regarded Adam with interest.

'Mr Ross.'

Now it was Cassie who looked at Adam and her eyes were wide with surprise, but she said nothing.

'Mr Ross befriended Mr Kettle and went with him that night to a camp where there were several members of Mr Kettle's family, plus other members of the aboriginal community. Now inspector, at this time your father was a sergeant of police based at Port Augusta.'

Mailey nodded, not necessarily agreeing but registering the statement.

'During the night, there was a raid. A group of white men arrived at the camp armed with various weapons. They were searching for Jimmy Kettle.'

'Why?'

'Inspector, the instigator of this raid was a notorious businessman from Port Pirie who, it seems, had been beaten up by Jimmy Kettle some weeks before. He was out for revenge. He brought with him as a prisoner the woman we buried today. She was then only a girl of course, and was known as Nellie Arlton.' Alex looked to Adam for confirmation. He was working without notes. Alex had thought of adding that the businessman, in fact, ran a brothel and that Nellie had worked for him; but Daniel was listening intently and

691

Alex saw no reason to add injury to an already traumatic day.

Mailey shifted in his chair. 'Why did this character bring Nellie Arlton or, as she later called herself, Mrs Khan with him?'

'Because she was at the time friendly with Jimmy Kettle. She was, in fact, a hostage – there to make sure Kettle surrendered. Well, the raid failed. Kettle and Mr Ross were sleeping some distance away in a cave. They heard a noise and went down to see what was happening. They found that the Port Pirie businessman I mentioned, a Mr Harris, had engaged someone to lead the raid. That someone was Sergeant Mailey.'

'Now, hang on –'

Alex leaned across the table. 'I have a sworn statement from Mr Kettle, dictated in hospital and signed by him.' He took an envelope from his pocket and gave it to Mailey. 'Read it later. It is a horrifying story. Mr Kettle was a witness to what happened that night. So are two people in this room, Mr Ross and Mr Cannaroola. Mr Cannaroola is Mr Kettle's cousin.' He turned to the aboriginal. 'Nelson, what did you see?'

In that shadowed room, the creases on Cannaroola's dark face glistened like fine stripes of war paint. His teeth flashed. 'I saw a big feller with an axe chop up two little boys. I saw plenty of killing.'

'How many of your people were killed?'

'Five.'

'Some of your family?'

'My two little brothers.'

'Did your people kill any of the white men?'

'No. They had guns and axes. We were trying to run away.'

'And you saw a policeman?'

'Yes.'

'Who?'

'Sergeant Mailey. He was a big fat feller.'

'You knew him?'

'Yes.'

'How?'

'He'd bashed me up a few times before.'

'Sergeant Mailey had beaten you?'

'Yes. He was plenty tough, that feller.'

'And what did he do that night?'

'He bashed my father.'

'And?'

'He shot the white man.'

'What white man?'

'The little feller with the funny voice. Harris – the one who wanted to catch Jimmy.'

'Sergeant Mailey shot him?'

'Yes.'

'How?'

'With a gun.'

Alex touched his forehead. 'No, I mean how was it that Sergeant Mailey shot the white man?'

'The white feller was wrestling with Jimmy.'

'Jimmy had come back?'

'Yes.' He nodded towards Adam. 'Him and this feller came back to help us. Anyhow, Sergeant Mailey, he said he was going to shoot Jimmy but he shot the white feller instead. Jimmy had the bloke by the throat.'

'And Mailey shot him?'

'Yes.'

'Dead?'

'Yes.'

Alex turned to Adam. 'You saw all this?'

'Clearly. Jimmy had hold of Harris and was threatening to break his neck unless Mailey dropped the gun. Mailey just laughed and kept coming. Then he fired but he hit the other man because Jimmy was hiding behind him.'

Alex swung back towards Nelson Cannaroola. 'Was there a police investigation of these killings?'

'No.'

'Did the police ever come?'

'Yes. A few of them came out to clean up.'

'How do you know?'

'I saw them. I was hiding.'

'But there was no investigation, no trial, no arrest?'

'No.'

'What did your people do after the raid?'

'We kept out of the way. We knew Sergeant Mailey would kill us if he found us or if we talked.'

'So you didn't talk?'

'No. It wasn't the first time,' Cannaroola said addressing the inspector. 'Sergeant Mailey, he was a plenty bad feller. He'd bashed up plenty of black fellers, killed a few.'

'Do you have any questions, inspector?' Alex asked.

Mailey leaned forward. 'Mr Cannaroola, how did you see all these things you described? It was the middle of the night.'

Cannaroola pointed towards the ceiling. 'Full moon.'

'There was some cloud,' Adam said, 'but when the moon was out, it was bright.'

Mailey leaned back and cradled his pipe bowl. 'Go on,

693

Mr Rafter. What else have you got to say?'

'After the raid, Adam Ross, Jimmy Kettle and Nellie Arlton – they'd managed to rescue her – fled in fear of their lives. They dared not go back to Port Augusta, so they headed north.'

'They met us,' Josef said, and Mailey strained to see him clearly, for Josef was in the darkest part of the room. 'I was a kid at the time. I was travelling with my parents and my sister up to Coober Pedy. We gave them a lift. I can remember the first time we saw them. They'd been walking through the bush and they were as thirsty as hell. All scratched and dusty too.'

'And you took them to the opal fields at Coober Pedy?' Alex said.

'Yes. Adam dug a house next to our bus. We lived above ground. For the next few months, we all dug for opals. We had one lease. Adam had another. Jimmy helped on Adam's lease.'

The inspector moved so vigorously that his chair scratched on the floor. 'All this is very interesting, Mr Rafter, but is it relevant to the purpose of this gathering, which is to explain how my father died, and whether or not Mr Ross was involved?'

'It is most relevant, inspector. Your father, Sergeant Mailey, began a systematic search of the State for the people who had been witness to the shooting of and the murder of the aborigines. This search was a private quest. It was not authorized. It was not to bring Mr Ross or Mr Kettle to face charges for any misdemeanours, but to get rid of them. To kill them. To dispose of the witnesses to his crime.'

'That is your surmise, Mr Rafter.'

'Perhaps if I could continue, inspector?'

'We're here to talk.'

'Thank you.' Alex dug his hands in his trouser pockets and once more addressed Josef.

'When did Sergeant Mailey arrive at Coober Pedy?'

'Maybe six months later. He came up because someone reported the theft of opal but it turned out that he'd been travelling all over the State looking for any sign of Jimmy Kettle and the fair-headed young bloke who'd also seen the massacre at the camp. That was Adam, of course.'

'And what did he do?'

'He arrested Adam and Jimmy.'

Alex moved, to stand beside Adam. 'How did he arrest you, Mr Ross?'

'I went into the post office one day. Mailey was hiding in the shadows and hit me over the back of the head with a big piece of timber.'

'He didn't say "what's your name" or "you're under arrest" or any such words?'

'He just hit me from behind. When I woke up, Jimmy and I were in the town's old lock-up.'

'How had he arrested Jimmy?'

'In the same way.'

'With a blow from behind?'

'Yes.'

'Did he talk to you while you were in that lock-up?'

'Yes. He told us he was going to take us south and then shoot us on the way. He would pretend that we had tried to escape.'

'He was quite specific in that threat?'

'Oh yes. He boasted about it. It was very hot in the cell and he wouldn't give us any water. I remember that too. He seemed to be enjoying himself that day.'

Alex moved to where Dexter Paradine sat. The old man looked up eagerly.

'Mr Paradine has been at Coober Pedy for more than forty years. He was there at the time Sergeant Mailey came to the town and arrested the two men.'

'I remember it very clearly,' Paradine said, blinking through his thick glasses and not needing to be prompted further. 'I remonstrated with the sergeant – he was a great big man, with a red face – because of the rough way he treated those two young fellows but he just pushed me around. He was a violent man.'

'He pushed you? You mean knocked you down?'

'Yes.' Paradine shoved with both hands. 'Like this.'

'Had you pushed him?'

'No. I was trying to talk to him.'

'What happened next?'

'Well, as I recall, he threw those two young fellows in the lock-up. They were both out like a light. The lock-up hadn't been used for years. You wouldn't put a dog in there, and he didn't feed them or give them water. I remember, he told us that if any of us went near the gaol, he'd treat us as accomplices and shoot us.'

'Did he say why he had arrested them?'

'He said they were murderers. He said they'd killed some men down south.'

'They'd killed some men?'

'Yes. That's what he said.'

'Did you believe him?'

Before Paradine could answer, Mailey rapped the desk. 'Mr Rafter, this might be an informal session but you know there's absolutely no point to a question like that. What this gentleman did

695

or did not think is as important to this discussion as what he had for breakfast.'

Alex delivered a vestigial bow. Paradine seemed confused. 'Does the inspector want to know what I had for breakfast?'

'No.' Alex smiled at everyone but Paradine. 'It was merely an expression. Please continue.'

'Well, we didn't know what to think. After all, Mailey was a policeman, but we did form a delegation to lodge a complaint against the way he was behaving.'

'And what was the response?'

'He threatened us.'

'In what way?'

'A violent way.'

'Physically violent?'

Paradine laughed. It was a dry wheezing sound. 'He shot Horrie Smith.'

'He shot someone?'

'I didn't tell you that, did I?'

'No, you didn't.' Alex's eyes darted towards the inspector and back to Paradine. 'What happened?'

'Horrie was trying to stop him shooting the two young fellows and the sergeant knocked him to the ground and when Horrie was still trying to stop him, Mailey shot him.'

'What with?'

Paradine's face curled into a look of astonishment. 'A gun, of course.'

'A rifle?'

'No. His revolver. His police revolver.'

'At close range?'

'He couldn't have got any closer. Horrie was at his feet.'

'So he shot a man lying on the ground?'

'Yes. The sergeant went berserk.'

'Did he kill this Horrie Smith?'

'No. He was a tough old buzzard, Horrie. He got shot through the lung.'

Inspector Mailey cleared his throat so loudly that both Alex and Paradine turned towards him. 'Mr Paradine, you said the sergeant was trying to shoot the two men. I presume you meant Mr Ross and Mr Kettle.' Paradine nodded vigorously. 'Why? Why was he trying to shoot them?'

'They were running away,' Paradine said, as though explaining the obvious.

'They had broken out of gaol?'

Josef stood. 'We broke them out. Nellie and me.' He sat down again.

Mailey's eagle eyes switched to Josef. 'Why?'

'Because we knew Sergeant Mailey meant to kill them.'

'How did you know that?'

'Adam and Jimmy told us. I sneaked up to the gaol and dropped a flask of water through the window. They were dying of thirst.'

Mailey seemed unimpressed. 'Did you actually hear the sergeant threaten to kill them?'

'Not personally.'

'The whole town knew,' Paradine interjected. 'There was no doubt the man meant to get rid of them. He was mad.'

'Thank you, Mr Paradine,' Mailey said, his eyes closed. 'I take it you're a qualified psychiatrist?'

'I know a crazy man when I see one,' Paradine said, his voice thin with strain. 'After he shot Horrie, he just took the postmaster's car and drove off. Never brought it back.'

'He asked the postmaster if he could borrow his car?' Alex said reasonably.

'He waved his gun at the man and threatened to blow his head off if he didn't give it to him.' He sat back, his face smouldering. 'He was crazy all right. Mean and crazy.'

Alex went to his briefcase and glanced at some notes. 'Do you have any more questions you want to ask Mr Paradine?'

'Not at the moment, thank you.' Mailey draped one arm over the back of the chair. 'We do seem to be travelling a long road, Mr Rafter. I hope the journey is nearing its end.'

'It is. But every stop along the way is important.' Alex patted Paradine's shoulder. 'Thank you very much for your contribution.'

Watching Paradine, Adam saw disappointment on the old man's face. He wanted to keep going and for a moment, Adam was back at Coober Pedy in 1929 at the weekly sing-song around a bonfire. Paradine had been the best singer in town but a merciless monopolizer of the night's entertainment. Adam closed his eyes and pictured a younger Dexter Paradine, one arm outstretched and oblivious to the jeers of his comrades, bursting into another song.

'There might be some more questions later,' Alex said. 'In the meantime, we go back to Coober Pedy, where two young men are fleeing for their lives –'

'Let's just say fleeing, Mr Rafter.'

'As you wish, inspector. And Sergeant Mailey has commandeered a motor car to follow them.'

'Commandeer's a funny term,' Paradine said, leaning forward so he could be seen by all the others. 'The sergeant was going to blow the postmaster's head off if he didn't give it to him.'

'Thank you, Mr Paradine.'

'The man never got his car back. That was worth a lot of money in those days.'

'Quite true. Thank you.' Alex returned a sheet of paper to his briefcase. 'Now let me go back a little. Mr Hoffman said that he and the girl Nellie, or Miss Arlton as she was then, had helped Mr Ross and Mr Kettle to get out of the old lock-up. The four of them were then pursued by Sergeant Mailey. This was at night. They headed out into the desert.'

'I'd plotted a course during the day,' Josef said and smiled at Cassie who was looking at him, her face alive with interest. She thought she knew all the stories concerning her father's younger days, but this was new. 'We had to avoid any roads or tracks – Mailey had been shooting at us.'

'You were breaking prisoners out of gaol,' the inspector said in a dogmatic tone.

'Correct. To save them being murdered on the way south to Port Augusta.'

'So you allege.'

'I certainly do.'

Alex crossed the room to sever the visual line between Josef and the inspector. 'Miss Arlton –'

'Why don't you just use first names?' Josef said. 'I don't know who you're talking about when you say Miss Arlton or Mr Kettle. After all, this isn't a bloody court of law.'

'It certainly isn't,' Mailey said drily.

'Very well. Nellie became separated from the others in the dark. She was subsequently caught by the sergeant, who beat her.'

'What do you mean by that?' Mailey had relit his pipe and was having trouble keeping the tobacco burning.

Adam spoke. 'The sergeant took off his belt and whipped her with the buckle. He hit her until she was semi-conscious.' Adam glanced at Daniel who was sitting with his chin buried in his hands. 'He then assaulted her.'

The inspector's eyes roved from Adam to Alex. 'Does Mr Ross mean there was another alleged beating?'

Alex leaned across the desk and whispered, 'She was raped.'

Mailey angled his head to see past Alex. 'You were there, Mr Ross?'

'No. Nellie told me later. She was scarred by the belt.'

'She always had scars on her back,' Daniel said, sitting up, having heard the latter part of the conversation.

'They were from the buckle of the belt.'

'That is hearsay, Mr Ross.'

Adam looked to Alex for explanation. 'It means it is not some-

698

thing you saw, but something another person told you. It would not be admissible evidence in a court.'

'Exactly,' the inspector said, and then spent several seconds rekindling his pipe. 'A court would not allow such a statement.'

'But if Nellie were still alive, and told you what happened ...'

'The word "if" doesn't mean much in court either, Mr Ross,' Mailey removed his pipe and aimed the stem at Alex. 'How close are we to Lake Eyre? I seem to be getting a whole bucketful of allegations about my father tipped over me. He allegedly shot people, bashed men, raped women but let's not forget that he was the one who died. Now what happened?'

'There were four witnesses to the death of your father,' Alex said. 'One is in hospital.'

'Jimmy Kettle?'

'Correct. The other three are here. Mr Ross – sorry, Adam, Josef and Saleem Benn.' He looked at the Afghan. 'Do I call you Saleem?'

The Afghan bowed his head.

'In those days, Saleem operated a business hauling supplies by camel to remote settlements. He was camped along the route taken that night by Adam, Josef and Jimmy. They joined his caravan, which was heading towards William Creek.'

Saleem Benn leaned forward. 'Adam Ross was badly burned, especially on the legs and on the hands.'

'How come?'

'There had been a fire.'

'At the lock-up,' Josef added hastily. 'Adam and Jimmy were trapped inside. Adam carried Jimmy out and got burnt.'

The inspector leaned forward and put both elbows on the desk. 'Now just a minute. I'm losing track of this conversation.' He looked at a sheet of paper to check Josef's name. 'Mr Hoffman, you say there was a fire at the lock-up. What was the building made of?'

Josef thought for a moment. 'Stone.'

Mailey rocked back in his chair and it squeaked, as though about to break. 'Then how did it catch fire?'

Josef grinned ruefully. 'Nellie and I were trying to pull the door off with a tow rope.'

'And a car I presume?'

'Yes. Nellie got confused and drove backwards into the door. The petrol tank split and it caught fire.'

'The gaol?'

'Yes. And the car.'

Mailey busied himself with his pipe, so that his hands covered his face. 'I'm pleased that my father is not the only person accused of destroying things. You burnt down the gaol, Mr Hoffman?'

'I don't know. We didn't stay. The sergeant was shooting at us.'

'I must say I can understand why.' The words were delivered with a fine slice of sarcasm.

'May I return to Saleem's evidence, inspector?'

'It's hardly evidence, Mr Rafter.'

'Well, may we hear what he has to say? In other words, what he would say if he were called to give evidence in court, should there be any need.'

Mailey sighed. 'Your point is taken and fully understood Mr Rafter.'

Alex gestured towards Saleem Benn. It was a magician's flourish, exposing the palm to prove he had nothing in his hand. The Afghan looked about him uncertainly. 'You took the three men to William Creek?' Alex prompted.

'Yes. On my camels. We camped outside the town and I went in alone.'

'Why?'

'To see if the devil Mailey was there.'

'Please call him Sergeant Mailey.'

Saleem Benn nodded gravely towards the inspector. 'My apologies for an unthinking remark. There was no intention on my part of giving offence to you.'

Mailey removed the pipe and gave an elaborate nod of acknowledgement. 'Tell me sir, had you met Sergeant Mailey before this?'

'No.'

'So he was a stranger to you?'

'Yes. All I knew of him was what had been told to me by the three young men who were now travelling with me.'

'So your impression of the sergeant was coloured by their highly unusual and provocative story?'

Saleem Benn rested the tip of an index finger on each side of his nose. 'I did not believe them.'

'Well, why on earth did you take them with you to William Creek?'

'Because they were in need.' There was a silence before the Afghan spoke again. 'I went into the hotel. The sergeant was there, but in hiding outside the building. The publican, who was a friend of mine, although unhappily long since deceased, told me about this strange man, who had arrived there by car and was now waiting for someone else to arrive; a hunter in hiding beside the trap, and a person he regarded as being most sinister.'

Mailey snorted.

'When the sergeant finally entered the building and began asking me questions, I took an instant dislike to the man.' Saleem Benn inclined his head towards the inspector. 'Please do not regard this as offensive to you. I am only explaining my feeling then, with all the frankness I can muster.'

'Understood.'

'Thank you.' Again the Afghan touched his nose, as if the action closed a circuit that intensified recollection of that night. 'I decided then that to deliver the three young men to the policeman would be to lead innocent lambs to the slaughter.'

'All as a result of your intuitive feelings?'

The Afghan's pale eyes focused on the inspector as though recognizing his presence for the first time. 'Having seen and spoken to the sergeant, I now believed the things that had been told to me. I now felt the young men were in grave danger. And I resolved to take them elsewhere.'

'Where to?' Alex rejoined the conversation.

'I knew of a mound spring in country where only I had ever travelled. It was west of the great lake. It is now on the property owned by Mr Adam Ross.'

Cassie looked at Nina who turned to Adam. Cassie leaned forward. 'Which one's that?' she whispered, but her father put a finger to his lips.

Alex smiled indulgently. 'You can talk to each other later. Saleem, you headed for that spring intending to camp overnight?'

'Yes. Unhappily, I had underestimated the diligence and cunning of Sergeant Mailey, and he followed us there.'

'Were you aware of that – that he was tracking you?'

'No.'

'And he followed your caravan to the mound spring?'

'I had chosen a roundabout route and taken care to leave the least possible trail, but he was a clever man and followed us.'

'In the car he had commandeered?'

'Yes, but at a great distance, so we would not be aware of his presence. He came upon us very late at night, while we slept. We were his prisoners before we were truly aware of what was happening. He tied us up with a strong rope. He had me trussed most cruelly, so that I thought I would choke.'

The inspector narrowed already slatted eyes. 'He tied you, Mr Benn?'

The Afghan sniffed. 'Yes. My legs were bent back, a rope was around my throat, and my arms were behind me and most tightly bound.'

'Why you? He wasn't after you.'

701

'He wanted no one alive who could testify against him.'

There was a long silence. Finally, Adam stood.

'I think it's time for me to join in.' He was aware of the two women staring up at him; Cassie eager to learn more, Nina dreading what she might hear.

'Your turn, Mr Ross?' The inspector said. 'The last in line. Why's that?'

'Because I'm the man who killed your father.' He raised his arms. 'I killed him with my bare hands and I ran away. This is where I stop running.'

E·I·G·H·T·E·E·N

Alex walked across the room. 'I'm hot and dry. Do you think it would be possible to have a cup of tea before we continue?'

Mailey coughed and called for the constable. Cassie went with the man to help make the tea. Nina reached for Adam's hand but said nothing. Alex checked his notes.

Mailey spent the time studying each person in turn, but said nothing.

When the tea was served and the early rattles had subsided, Alex moved to the centre of the room. 'Adam,' he began, 'Saleem has described how he was surprised in his sleep by Sergeant Mailey, and was subsequently bound, hand and foot.'

'And neck,' the Afghan interjected.

'But *you* were not caught. Please tell us why.'

'Before the sergeant arrived, I'd been unable to sleep. Saleem Benn told you that I had burns. They were hurting, and I went to the spring, to get water. I stayed there, out of sight of the others.'

'And you were there,' Alex said, his voice slow and deliberate, 'when Sergeant Mailey arrived?'

'Yes. That's the only thing that saved our lives.'

'Please explain that.'

'Well, the sergeant had a gun.' He paused. 'He tied up Saleem Benn and Jimmy. He left Josef free, and made him dig a hole.'

'A hole?'

'Yes. A grave.'

Josef shifted uncomfortably. 'He told me it was a joke. I was just a kid and thought he was telling me the truth. But in fact, he had me dig a grave big enough for three bodies.'

The inspector put his pipe on the desk and sat with his hands forming a bridge to cover the lower part of his face. His eyes never left Adam.

'When Josef had finished the grave, Sergeant Mailey picked up the shovel and tried to smash in the back of Josef's head. I managed to get close, and I called out to Josef and he sort of turned and fell, and I threw myself at Mailey.'

'I saw all this happening,' the old Afghan said. 'I thought we were about to die and had been praying. The devil – I beg your pardon – Sergeant Mailey had previously whispered to me that he meant to shoot me and bury me as a Christian. He was a warped man.'

'Whispered?' the inspector said in a sharp voice.

'He did not want the boy – that is, Mr Hoffman – to hear what he said to me. The boy was still occupied digging the grave. It took him a very long time.'

Alex moved to a far wall and leaned against a filing cabinet. 'Adam, you said you leaped towards the sergeant, to stop him hitting Josef with the shovel. It was a shovel?'

'Yes. A big one.'

'What happened?'

'My legs and hands were bad and I couldn't move very well, and I sort of bounced off him. He tried to hit me with the shovel but I managed to duck and then Josef threw himself at the sergeant.'

'I was a diversion.' Josef grinned. 'The sergeant knocked me over as though I were a ten-pin, but at least he took his eye off Adam for a few seconds.'

'Which saved my life. Anyhow, we started to wrestle.'

Saleem Benn moved the fingers of one extended hand to attract Alex's attention. 'It was a titanic struggle. A powerful youth against a monster of a man. Adam Ross was fighting for all our lives, but truly I thought he must lose. The sergeant was a huge man, very wide and very angry, and Adam Ross you must remember, was burned on his hands. I recall hearing him scream with pain and yet not relent. It was truly horrifying but in some ways a magnificent spectacle. A battle to the death, with the lives of four people at stake. I was bound, Jimmy Kettle was trussed just as effectively, the boy Josef was in a state of paralysis from the vicious blow he had received. Only Adam Ross stood between us and death.'

There was a long silence. Outside, a car passed the building. In another room, another man coughed.

'This is all very dramatic,' the inspector said softly.

Alex moved from the cabinet. 'The sworn statement by Jimmy Kettle says essentially the same thing.'

'So you and the sergeant were fighting,' Inspector Mailey said, his attention concentrated on Adam. 'This big powerful man and a youth with bad burns. What happened? Did you find a gun, or get hold of the shovel? Did you bash his skull in?'

Adam turned towards his family. 'I broke his neck.'

Outside the man coughed again.

704

Very slowly, the inspector settled back in his chair. The movement released a chorus of protesting squeaks. 'And you broke his neck?' He raised his hands. 'With your arms?'

'I thought he was about to break mine,' Adam said and lapsed into silence.

'I had prayed that Allah would give my friend great strength,' Saleem Benn said and stopped, satisfied that the explanation was complete.

'The sergeant died instantly,' Josef said. 'There was this terrible snapping sound, like a dry branch breaking . . .'

No one spoke, and Josef felt compelled to continue. 'Adam couldn't get free. They were tangled together. I wasn't strong enough to break the sergeant's death grip. I had to untie Jimmy and get him to help.'

'I think that will be enough,' Alex said, his voice quiet and his face wreathed in concern for the inspector who was sitting still, eyes wide open but looking at no one.

Adam took a deep breath. 'I had no intention of killing him. I was trying to stop him killing my friends.'

'Which would certainly have happened,' Saleem Benn added quickly. 'There is no doubt that the sergeant, however dear he may have been to you, was in a murderous mood when we encountered him and was filled with a passionate desire to end our lives and leave our bodies in a place where they would never be discovered. He may have been a good man when you knew him, dear sir, but in those last days of his life, he was truly possessed by the devil. I am sorry to be the one to say such a distressing thing, but it is the truth.' He sheltered behind an archway of slender fingers.

The inspector got out of the chair and walked to a window. He toyed with the blind but left it down. 'In the report I read, Mr Benn, you were the person who supposedly found the body. When you brought it in, it was virtually a skeleton and, ah, dismembered. How was that accomplished?'

'I went back later.'

'And you brought back the body as you found it?'

'Yes. I merely reported I had found the body in that condition, which was the truth.'

'It was said my father had died of thirst.'

'That was the assumption of other people.'

Mailey turned slowly. 'Mr Ross, if you had no intention of killing the sergeant but were truly fighting for your life and the lives of others, as you all assert, why didn't you report the matter to the police?'

'Would you?' Adam waited, as if expecting the inspector to reply but Mailey remained silent and each man looked deep into the other's eyes, searching for uncertainty. Eventually, Mailey turned back to the window and stood there, shoulders square and hands locked behind his back.

'I was nineteen,' Adam said. 'I knew very little about policemen. I presumed that some of the men I'd seen killing aborigines in the camp at Port Augusta were policemen.'

'You didn't know that for a fact,' the inspector said.

'No, but I knew Sergeant Mailey was a policeman and he was giving orders.'

'What sort of orders?'

'Orders to kill.'

Alex, who had taken a seat, glanced obliquely at the inspector, but Mailey remained, erect and unmoving, in front of the opaque screen.

'He was shouting out to his men to kill them all, not to let any get away.' As Adam said this, he saw Mailey's shoulders rise and fall, and the man seemed to diminish a little in height. 'He spoke as though he was used to giving them orders and they acted like men used to taking orders from him.'

'So you assumed they were policemen?' Alex offered.

'Yes.'

'I must say,' Saleem Benn said, 'that after the death of Sergeant Mailey, Adam Ross indicated that he wanted to go to the authorities, to tell the truth about the whole affair.'

The inspector turned his head. 'And what changed his mind, Mr Benn?'

'Concern for Jimmy Kettle.'

'What do you mean?' The inspector growled the question.

'Jimmy Kettle is black. He had seen some of his family slaughtered. Others had been beaten on previous occasions.'

Nelson Cannaroola, who had been sitting quietly with his hands on his knees, said: 'I had me older brother bashed to death just a few weeks before Sergeant Mailey came to the camp.'

The inspector walked quickly to the desk and leaned on it, his arms outstretched, his neck thrust towards the aborigine. 'Are you saying police bashed him?'

'Yes. With an iron bar.'

'I presume you have names?'

'Yes.'

'Who did it –' He checked his list of names. 'Mr Cannaroola. Who killed your brother?'

'Your father.' The eyes were unflinching, but without malice. 'He was a bad feller, that man.'

706

Mailey slumped into the chair.

Saleem Benn resumed, his voice softer than before. 'Jimmy Kettle said that if Adam Ross went to the police, we would all be put in cells. He believed that if he were put in a cell, he would be murdered. Either beaten to death or hanged by his own trouser belt. It had happened to friends.'

'So you said nothing.'

'No,' Adam said. 'Until now.'

'And somehow this Gooly character found out the story?'

'Somehow.'

Saleem Benn waved a hand. 'Some years ago I was ill. A fever. Apparently I talked while in a delirium and my nephew heard me say certain things. Later, he attempted to blackmail me.'

'Gooly tried to blackmail you?'

'Yes. He is to our family as slime is to a wall of stone.'

Mailey began to refill his pipe. 'I wonder if I could ask everyone to leave the room, just for a while.' They began to rise, pleased to get up. 'Except for Mr Ross. I need to have a word with him in private. Do you mind, Mr Ross?'

Adam had been first to his feet. He sat down again.

When the others had left the room, Mailey said, 'Before we talk any more about this business of my father's death, there are a few things you should be aware of, regarding the allegations against you of cattle stealing. First, a temporary replacement for the late Sergeant Butler will be here as soon as the trains start running again. This cattle-stealing business is really a matter for him, rather than me. However, I will leave him a report with a number of recommendations, which he may or may not feel inclined to act upon. The essence of my recommendations is that I feel the allegations made by this Gooly-bird have about as much substance as a jug full of steam. In other words, I think he's talking a lot of crap.'

Adam was surprised. 'Thank you.'

Mailey waved the thanks aside. 'The new man may form a different conclusion. Now, the second thing. I'm afraid we've been keeping that sick friend of yours, Jimmy Kettle, rather busy. I've had one of my officers go along and see him about this conversation he says he overheard between Gooly-dooly and his offsiders. You know the one I mean? Where he thought they were planning some big cattle-stealing operation?' He waited for Adam's slow nod. Mailey scratched his scalp. 'My officer said Kettle was most helpful. As a result of what he told us, we sent information out to certain police stations. We had a message this morning. It seems that a number of large convoys of road trains have been intercepted. All were laden with cattle. The drivers, I am reasonably sure, are honest men, just going about their normal business and thinking they were engaged in a legitimate job of moving cattle south. The cattle, incidentally, were all due to be shipped out of the country.

'We checked with the shipping company and a man there has given us a good description of the person he's been dealing with; in other words, the man we would presume has been organizing all this. The description fits our friend Gooly. I thought you might like to know that too, Mr Ross.'

'Thank you.'

'A third thing. I didn't intrude at the funeral this morning but I was there.'

'I saw you.'

'A strange thing happened this morning. After the funeral, the minister ...' He paused for Adam to supply the name.

'Roger Montgomery.'

'He came up to me and spoke for a few minutes. I understand you and Mrs Khan – Nellie Arlton – were once very close?'

'Yes. We lived together many years ago. Daniel, who was here a few minutes ago, is our son.'

'You were only made aware of that fact recently, I understand.' Mailey concerned himself with his pipe.

'Yes.'

'I'm not trying to pry into personal matters but what Mr Montgomery said might interest you. And he gave me this information to indicate what sort of a person this Gooly was, as a means, I'm sure, of helping to get you off the hook – the cattle-stealing allegations. Do you follow me?'

'I think I follow you but I don't understand you.'

'Did you know Mrs Khan had been subjected to a kind of blackmail?'

Adam shook his head.

'Did Gooly have some reason to hate her?'

'He tried to force himself on her many years ago.' Adam leaned forward. 'Was Gooly blackmailing her?'

'Mr Montgomery told me Gooly somehow found out about your son, Daniel. This was when Daniel was only a kid. Apparently, Mrs Khan was on her way to your property with the intention of re-establishing contact with you. I don't fully understand and nor do I need to, but it would seem she left you in confusing circumstances?'

'Yes. Just before the war.'

'Gooly threatened her. More accurately, he threatened you, through her. He told her if she ever came back to the area he would

708

do his best to disgrace you. You know, as the father of an illegitimate son by a black woman.' He looked up at the ceiling. 'Which is why she disappeared from your life in the first place – according to Mr Montgomery.'

Adam covered his face. 'I didn't know that.'

'I think Mr Montgomery was the only person she ever told. Please don't think I have any intention of meddling or any wish to cause embarrassment. I just thought you'd like to know.'

Adam looked up. 'Thank you.'

'She sounds like she was an unusual woman.'

'Very.'

Mailey swung his feet on to the desk. 'What was interesting to me, of course, was that Gooly had attempted blackmail. The information merely adds to the picture I'm forming of this character. He's a nicely rounded, thoroughly despicable rogue. I wouldn't believe a word he said which means, Mr Ross, that as far as the cattle-stealing allegations are concerned, I'd say you're off the hook.'

Adam stood. 'Thank heavens for that.'

'The new man will have to confirm it, of course.'

'Of course.'

'But I wouldn't lose any sleep over it.'

Adam nodded thanks.

'Now about this other matter.' Adam sat down again. 'Mr Ross, I came up here looking for Jimmy Kettle and I found you. I came hoping to discover what had really happened to my father, and I discovered things I didn't want to hear. They are only allegations, of course.'

'We told you the truth.'

Mailey blew smoke and watched it curl towards the ceiling. 'Does this room bother you, being so dark?' he asked suddenly.

'No.'

'Good. At least the room's bearable like this. It's a furnace outside. How do you put up with the heat?'

'You get used to it.'

'I suppose so.' He took out his handkerchief and wiped his forehead, as though the conversation required to be ended with such a gesture. Then he looked at Adam in a way that was almost furtive. 'Do you know what I couldn't get used to when I was a kid?'

Adam waited.

'I couldn't get used to my father beating my mother.' Mailey's eyes went to the ceiling again. 'Did your father ever beat your mother Mr Ross?'

'My mother died when I was young.'

709

'I wish my father had.' His little eyes darted to Adam. 'Does that shock you?'

Adam shrugged. This was a conversation that properly required only one participant.

'My earliest recollections are of a man who hit people. I thought my mother was dark around the eyes naturally. It was years before I realized they were bruises.'

He didn't want to continue for a while and Adam shared his silence.

'You don't talk a lot, Mr Ross.'

'I've learned that there are times when it pays to keep quiet.'

'It's a shame other people haven't learned the same lesson. By the way, I like your friends.'

'Despite the fact that they were saying things you didn't want to hear?'

'Mr Ross, I didn't say I liked what they said, I said I liked them. In my business, you hear some nice people say terrible things and some terrible people say nice things.' The pipe had gone out and he put it on the desk. 'What did you think when you found out who I was?'

Adam shrugged, trying to recall. 'So much that was bad had happened already that day. I felt like I was in some sort of nightmare that I couldn't wake up from.'

'Were you frightened?'

Adam considered the question. 'Yes, I think so. It was like being dragged backwards into your past – the very worst part of it.'

Mailey leaned forward. 'What you told me was true? You people hadn't got together and decided to embellish the facts a little? After all, you had thirty-two years to work out a good story.' He smiled as one failed thief might console another.

'It was true, inspector.'

Mailey nodded to himself. After a while, he said, 'I'm a better policeman than my father was. Do you know that?'

'I'll have to take your word for it.'

'Please do. It's true. Those men who knew my father said he was a good cop but they meant tough cop. Tough, that was the word for him. And persistent. Doggedly persistent. If he got on to a job, he'd never give up. Doesn't make for a good policeman, though. He didn't have compassion or judgement, and a policeman without those qualities is flawed. Fatally flawed. What do you think of me, Mr Ross?'

'I think you're probably a decent man.'

'Decent.' Mailey extended his lips, as though the word was too awkward to digest. 'I thank you for that and I hope you're right.

710

But do you know that I hated my father? And now that you know it, you'll certainly be wondering why I came up here. Why not let the old bastard lie in peace, eh?'

'Why did you come?'

'Because I'm concerned with the truth. For all these years, I've wondered what really happened to him. I knew him well enough to know he wasn't the sort of man to wander away from a motor car and die of thirst. He was a good bushman, Mr Ross. Are you a good bushman?'

'I think so.'

'I'm sure you are. I'd like to think you could respect another man for being a good bushman, even if you could not respect him in other ways.' He took a deep breath which seemed, temporarily, to transport him to another scene. 'Anyhow, I always doubted the conclusions of the report and when I saw the name Jimmy Kettle, all the old feelings were stirred up again.'

'So you came up here?'

'Yes. Your wife wrote that story. Stirred up quite a hornets' nest, didn't she?' He seemed amused. 'Wives do the funniest things. Are you happily married, Mr Ross?'

'Very.'

'You're a lucky man.' He moved his left hand on the desk as though playing chords on a piano. 'I'm sure you're aware that the events you told me about today justify the opening of an inquiry and possibly the laying of charges. I'm not quite sure what they would be, although I have an officer in my area who specializes in thinking up great charges.' His lips moved, as if they were about to part in a smile, but he brought them under control. 'So if we wanted to, we could make life very unpleasant for you.'

'I'm sure you could.'

'Oh we could. There's no doubt about that. However, none of that would do much good for the reputation of a police officer who was buried with honours more than thirty years ago. It wouldn't do much good for the force as a whole. In fact, it could open such a can of worms that it might do a great deal of harm.' He blew a stream of smokeless air towards the ceiling. 'I came searching for the truth and I believe I've found it. I think you and your friends were telling the truth, Mr Ross. I must confess to being appalled and ashamed to have heard the things I have heard today, but he who searches for the truth is rarely going to like what he finds.'

Adam waited until the inspector's eyes resumed contact with his.

'So what will you do?'

'What would you like me to do?'

'Have some afternoon tea with us then drive back down south.'

711

Mailey laughed. 'Do you think I'm a simple man?'

'No. But I think you're honest and I think you're a realist.'

The inspector let his head sag almost to the top of the desk. 'I like you, Mr Ross. Not just for inviting me to tea either.' With a great effort, he raised his head. 'By heavens I'm tired. I have hardly slept these last three days. So one thing I am not going to do is start driving back to Adelaide. I would go no more than one mile before I fell asleep at the wheel.' He smiled a defeated smile. 'So as soon as we finish here, I'm going back to the hotel to have a beer, go to my room, and attempt to sleep for fifteen hours.'

Adam sat up, back straight and hands on his knees. 'And what should I do? You asked me the other day not to leave town.'

Mailey stood. 'I think you should join your friends waiting so anxiously outside and go and have afternoon tea.' The inspector held out his right hand. 'Maybe we'll meet again some day under more favourable circumstances.'

'I'd like that.'

'So would I, Mr Ross, so would I.'

They shook hands.

N·I·N·E·T·E·E·N

Patrick had a difficult time accepting Daniel's new status in the Ross family. After the news had been broken that the tall, dark young man who worked on the property and did what everyone else told him to do was, in fact, his half-brother, Patrick mounted his horse and went for a long ride among the sand-hills. He liked it out there. Whenever he had some problem to consider or merely to worry about, he rode out to where the brooding dunes offered the twin consolations of privacy and silence. There was no one to interfere; no bossy half-sister to tell him what he should be doing; no father who was so busy working that he had no time to spare for games or to show him how to do things and yet who seemed to expect him to know how to perform the feats that Daniel and Cassie did with ease.

Patrick found the whip too long and heavy and Cassie always laughed at the way it got tangled in his legs; and whenever he tried to hammer nails, which Daniel did so rapidly and expertly, he either bent the nail or hit his thumb. He could ride a horse well. His father had shown him how, but that was years ago. They told him he could ride before he could walk. So he liked to ride because he did it well and no one ever laughed at him when he was in the saddle.

His horse was a chestnut which he called Silver. The colour was wrong but he had named it after the horse the Lone Ranger rode. He had seen that Silver in a comic book but it was the rider, rather than the horse, that had fired his imagination. On Silver he thought of himself as the Lone Ranger, galloping from some mysterious place to overcome evil and then riding off, with men admiring him and women loving him but no one knowing who he was. He longed to have a Tonto who would follow him, blindly and faithfully, but there were no Indians at Kalinda. There were some Afghans at Marree and he'd always thought Daniel was an Afghan. Some of the young men had sharp faces a little like Tonto; but none of them wore feathers or rode horses.

He did have a mask which he had made and kept hidden from everyone else, and wore only when he was out here, among the dunes. Today, he didn't feel like wearing a mask. How could a grown man suddenly be your brother? He found it hard to grasp the concept of a half-brother even though the only sister he had was a half-sister. No one had ever really explained what the 'half' meant, unless it meant they were older, because Cassie was a grown-up and so was Daniel who maybe wasn't as old as Cassie but was certainly bigger. The only other person he knew who had sisters was Elizabeth, Jimmy and Stella's youngest girl. She had two sisters. Lizzie was sixteen and Marie and Yvonne were older but at least they were all around the same age. But they were sisters and maybe sisters were different to brothers. He didn't know anyone who had a brother.

What Patrick could not understand was why it had taken Daniel so long to become his brother or even his half-brother. Was it that a half-brother only became your brother halfway through his life? And if that was so, what had he been before? Daniel had always been at Kalinda, and Daniel had always been able to do everything so that his father relied on him more and more. A sudden thought gripped the boy. Supposing someone else came to work at Kalinda, and was good, and his father liked him too. Would he become a half-brother?

The idea filled him with despair. It was so difficult trying to do the things that Daniel did, without facing the prospect of some other man coming along, and being good with the sheep and the cattle and able to build things and know when to clean the water troughs and how to drive the cars and trucks and to repair the machinery. If that happened, he would never get close to his father because his father liked people who could do things. His father was always saying what a good man Daniel was and now he had made him a half-brother.

Patrick, still only in his seventh year, used to like Daniel. Now, he wasn't so sure.

Adam, Nina and Josef were near the site of the original mound spring. Nina had started a vegetable garden at its edge.

'Now you know why the ground was so soft,' Josef said. 'I did all the original digging.'

'Your humour is macabre.' Nina led them back towards the house. She clapped her hands. 'Let's forget all that. It's in the past. Let's concentrate on the future.'

Adam, walking beside his wife, knew what to expect. Nina was not about to lapse into idle chatter. She had something in mind.

714

This was her way of sliding into the chosen subject.

'All right,' said Josef, taking the bait. He was weary, having just flown from Coober Pedy, where he had taken Dexter Paradine. 'What are we going to discuss? Something fascinating, like the future of red wines in Australia or something dull, like raising beef cattle in areas of marginal rainfall?'

'I thought we'd talk about Cassie.'

'You're worried about Cassie?' Josef asked. As far as he knew Cassie was well and had absorbed the events and implications of the last days with remarkable aplomb.

'Concerned is probably a better word.' Nina turned towards him. 'Because of all that's happened, we've been thinking about the children. All three of them.'

'Naturally.'

'And on the way back from Marree, Adam and I decided that Patrick should go to boarding-school as soon as he's old enough. We've been talking about it for a long time and we've finally agreed it would be best for him.'

'Where? In Adelaide?'

'I think so. We'll have to find a good school.'

'And you'd want him to have an uncle who'd take him home for the weekends.'

'That would be fantastic of you Joe.' She touched his wrist. Nina was an intuitive exponent of body contact. She worked on a scale of smiles, touches and kisses which were her automatic responses to favours. She was a great toucher; Josef melted and looked quickly at Adam, as though so warm a contact deserved a flash of jealousy.

Adam was thinking about a small boy at a strange school in a big city. 'We don't like the idea for a lot of reasons, but Nina's convinced me that it would be best for him in the long run.' He and Nina traded uneasy smiles. 'But if you were around, just in case he needed somewhere to go or someone to talk to ...'

'Of course.'

'We wouldn't expect you to take him every weekend but occasionally would be a real help. We don't like the idea of the little bloke down there on his own for a few months at a time.'

'Be pleased to.'

'Which brings us back to the number one child,' Nina said. 'Cassie is sensationally efficient and capable around the property.'

'Agreed.'

'But she's never been anywhere. Josef, do you know she has never travelled out of South Australia?'

'She was born in New South Wales,' Adam said.

'And came here as a baby.' It seemed to Josef that these were

715

fragments from previous conversations. 'So we've been thinking –'

'*You've* been thinking,' Adam said.

Nina signalled a look that was part affection, part reproach. 'You've known Cassie since she was born. You like her. You understand her.'

Josef felt the hairs rise at the back of his neck.

'And you were telling me you're planning to go to Europe to visit some of the vineyards and great wine-makers.'

'Yes I am.' His voice seemed to belong to someone else.

'Would it be possible, would it be too great an imposition, for her to travel with you?'

Adam turned to Josef. 'I said to Nina she should go with her if she wants Cassie to see Europe. We shouldn't impose on someone else.'

'I can't go,' Nina said. 'Not for some time. I have commissions for two stories and I just can't get away to Europe. And when I do go, I want Adam to go too.'

'I can't get away. Not while Jimmy's crook.'

She touched Josef's arm. 'There's also the question of Michel Klemansky.'

'Oh?' He tried to keep his voice level and flat, as if he'd never thought of the man in association with Cassie. 'What's that?'

'I think Cassie's rather under his spell. He's had her working for him, as official photographer which of course is all nonsense, but which she takes very seriously. I think there's even more to it than that. Daniel's got the impression that she's considering going away with him – that he's offered her some sort of position.'

'Oh my God.'

'Exactly.' She was now holding his arm. 'So we were thinking ... you're such a good friend. We know she'd be safe with you.' She blushed. 'I don't mean it that way. I mean you'd make sure she was packed and caught the aircraft and didn't lose her passport, and saw a doctor if she got sick. Things like that.'

'Act like her uncle.'

'Would it be possible?'

'It's a lot to ask,' Adam said, clearing the path towards refusal.

'Well, I don't know.' Josef's heart was racing. He frowned, hoping the strength of his expression would overwhelm any others that might betray him. 'It's mainly business visits that I'd planned.'

'It'd be too hard,' Adam said.

'No.' Josef seemed to be wrestling with difficulties and surmounting them. 'I had thought of doing a bit of sightseeing too.'

'To what places?' Nina was eager.

'Well, the wine-makers I planned visiting were in Germany and

France. Then I thought I might go to Switzerland and down into Italy.'

'Oh, Josef. Would it be possible? We'd pay for all of Cassie's costs, of course. Even give her enough to buy you the occasional meal.'

He returned her smile. 'Let me think about it.'

'We need to get her away. For so many reasons.'

'I understand. I'll check through the schedule tonight.' His mind was a cauldron of mixed thoughts.

Adam seemed to be staring at him with a peculiar intensity and he looked away.

When Peppino returned to Kalinda, the first person he met was Dr Rotondo. The designer of the Great White Shark was still at the base, out of the team yet unable to leave. It was not a matter of waiting for transport to the south; he was unable to abandon a project which he had inspired and to which he was still devoted.

The concept of running a pure jet car had been his. The Shark was his loving creation, devised by him, drawn by him and fashioned by craftsmen who followed his every instruction. In the last months, his passionate wish had been that this revolutionary machine be tested and developed in gradual stages, based on soundly acquired engineering data, so that it had the best possible chance of success. His clash with Klemansky had destroyed that hope.

Rotondo had believed that the car was more important than the driver, but he now realized that, as far as most people were concerned, he was wrong. The world's press had been congregating at Kalinda and few journalists bothered to write about the car. They had once, when the design was first revealed, but now it was old news; just a 'jet car'. If they discussed it at all, it was only in the most basic and often inaccurate terms. The focus of interest was now entirely on Klemansky.

No one had interviewed Rotondo. Even his dismissal had passed without notice because he was not a person to be noticed. And being the sort of man who could be engrossed in a project and not be aware of other people's perceptions had led him into another, even more fundamental error. That had been to assume others would automatically recognize his premier role in this venture. To him it seemed so obvious that he was the project's most important person that he devoted none of his energy to advocating his own cause.

He came from a country where creative people were accorded honour. Klemansky came from a world where the powerful seized

717

fame, and where honours were accorded not to the talented, but to the wealthy.

Rotondo had been caught in a conflict between systems. Without realizing a battle was in progress, he had lost.

'I had no idea,' Peppino said. 'I thought everything was going according to schedule. He said he intended breaking the record on Friday and asked me to be ready to start moving things out at the weekend.'

'Just like that,' Rotondo said, restraining his arms but allowing his hands to flap. 'The man talks as though he merely has to press a button to break the record.'

'Is he crazy?'

'Worse. He's a fool.' Rotondo said he had attempted a reconciliation, because he knew his services were vital to success but Klemansky had not budged and had used the crudest terms to confirm his unchanged attitude. 'I realize now that he always meant to get rid of me.'

'For heaven's sake, why?'

'He sees me as a rival. He wants all the glory. A shared triumph isn't enough for him. He wants everything.' This time Rotondo's arms got away from him and they rose in the manner of a large bird struggling to fly. 'The man believes the car is now good enough to give him the world record. He is convinced he no longer needs me.'

'But you did say you quit.' Peppino offered the words cautiously.

Rotondo raised his shoulders. Now he could have been a vulture hunching over a corpse. 'I did not mean it. You are Italian. You understand.' He gave a melancholy smile. 'I played into his hands.'

'So what will you do?'

'Stay here. Witness the triumph if, in fact, Klemansky does break the record as he is very likely to do and feel like an alien, someone who has had absolutely no part in the achievement. If he succeeds, Klemansky will claim all the laurels and the world will present them to him. It is the way things happen.' He sighed. 'If on the other hand he fails, I will feel . . .' He groped for the word. 'Devastated. I will know it should not have happened this way. I will feel the blame is mine. And you may be sure Klemansky will agree.' He laughed, but the sound was sad.

Peppino had been anticipating a romantic dinner with Cassie but surprised himself by inviting Rotondo to join them. It was a spur-of-the-moment decision, made because he felt sorry for a fellow Italian who seemed so thoroughly miserable. The invitation made and accepted, Peppino then regretted his impetuosity. Cassie would be either annoyed that he had ruined the concept of a dinner for two by inviting an outsider, or pleased because she wouldn't have to undergo the ordeal of dining with him alone. Whichever her response, it would be bad for him.

Cassie liked the idea. She, too, was sorry for Rotondo. She knew some sort of schism had developed between the two principals of the record project although it was not until Peppino explained that she became aware of the extent of the breach. Like Peppino, she admired the man for his dignified manner and obvious ability. And she sent Peppino's spirits into high orbit by declaring that he had shown remarkable understanding and generosity by making the offer. She loved him for it. Those were her words and he felt so elated as to become giddy.

The preparation of dinner was chaotic, in a joyful way. Mrs Wilson abandoned the kitchen to the three of them. Peppino attempted to do everything, which had always been his intention but he was frustrated by his guests. Cassie was in a mischievous mood and insisted in meddling and sampling ingredients, while Rotondo, bursting from the dark mood which had engulfed him, revealed a flair for culinary matters and promoted himself to assistant chef and chief adviser.

Peppino had gone to great lengths to assemble the necessary items for the meal. For the pasta course, he had brought small, juicy, sweet tomatoes – he knew an Italian who grew exactly the correct type in the back yard of his Adelaide home – plus fresh basil, which Cassie had never seen; virgin olive oil (and he explained how much healthier and tastier the virgin oil was compared to the varieties with which she was familiar); cloves of garlic which caused her to turn up her nose in anticipation of offensive aromas only to have Rotonto launch into a learned exposition on its remarkable qualities and how to avoid the anti-social after-effects; black olives, which she was at first reluctant to taste and then disinclined to leave alone; and fresh Parmesan cheese which he had her grate to keep her occupied and away from the olives. The pasta itself was a spaghetti which he had purchased from an Italian food shop in one of the suburbs. Rotondo attended to its boiling while Peppino prepared the tomato sauce.

The main course was scaloppine and salad, which at first caused Cassie some amusement. The idea of anyone bringing meat to Kalinda she found hilarious, for the freezer was stocked with three months supply of beef. But, as with everything else, Peppino had bought the veal from a special supplier and ensured it and the other commodities survived the journey in good condition by transporting them in large ice boxes. The salad was a simple mix of lettuce and radicchio, a red and white veined, slightly bitter leaf, but the secret was in the dressing which he mixed on the spot with

719

much theatrical flourishing of oil and vinegar.

For dessert, he had brought fresh eggs and aged Marsala and whisked up a zabaglione.

For wine, he produced several bottles of vino bianco. These he had transported in one ice box and water from the melting ice had caused the labels to float away. He put them back in place, apologised for the wrinkles and soppy edges, and then helped consume the contents with gusto.

Rotondo, after several months of tension and a couple of days of misery, became highly animated as the evening progressed. He began to speak in Italian. He and Peppino conversed and then sang some songs.

'Is that Italian?' Cassie asked, after one particularly lively exchange.

'Yes,' Peppino said and apologized. 'We are extremely rude to do that in front of you.'

'No.' Her eyes were wide with the joy of discovery. 'It sounds lovely. I've never heard you talk Italian.'

'Honly-a broken Hinglish eh?'

'Oh, Peppino. I wish you'd taught me Italian when you first came here. It sounds like music.'

'It's never too late –'

Peppino couldn't say any more because Rotondo began singing again and dragged the others into his melody.

It was the best meal Cassie could remember. It was also the most entertaining and with the songs sung and zabaglione consumed, they were on the verandah drinking coffee. The coffee, too, had been carefully chosen for the occasion. Peppino had selected the blend and brought a large quantity together with an expresso machine, as a gift for Nina.

As often happens at the end of a boisterous evening, there was a time when no one spoke and the silence honed itself into a fine edge.

Eventually, Peppino spoke to the doctor. 'What are you thinking of, my friend?'

'The car. The record. Tomorrow. What else?' He rolled sad eyes from Peppino to Cassie.

'Will you go to watch?' she asked.

He shook his head. 'No. There would be a scene. He would go crazy. It would be bad.'

'But what if they need you?'

'Oh, they need me. There is no doubt about that.'

'It's a terrible situation.'

'Yes.'

'Very unfair.'

He was silent.

'Shouldn't someone speak to Michel?' Both men looked at her. 'I mean if he's doing something wrong, if there are things that should be done to the car, and aren't being done ...' She let the sentence fade away. Rotondo was not listening. His eyes had glazed and he was slipping back into his former morose state.

'Hey Paolo,' Peppino called. 'Cheer up. I'll get Cassandra to see him.'

'No, Peppino,' she said softly but he charged ahead.

'She's a lady and you were telling me he's a lady's man. He'd listen to her.' He swung towards Cassie and winked. 'Wouldn't he? You could talk sense into his head.'

'Well, I don't know.'

'She's a very sensible person.' Peppino was determined to cheer his compatriot and ignored Cassie's signals of caution. 'And she's really onside with Klemansky. She's his official photographer.' Again he swung back to her. 'Aren't you?'

'I was,' she said but he missed the point.

'He shouldn't go out tomorrow and give the car full power,' Rotondo whispered. 'Not yet. There are things we should have done, tests that have to be carried out.'

'But you designed it to go at five hundred,' Peppino said cheerfully.

'You are assuming my design is perfect. No design of any complex mechanical device is ever perfect. Not without refinement. Not without tuning. Not without testing.'

'But it might work fine.'

He gave Peppino a pitying look. 'That is the remark of a gambler. That is the sort of thing Klemansky would say, only he would be more bombastic. He would say, "it will work fine" and convince himself.' He rapped the table and made the coffee cups jump in their saucers. 'The man is an idiot and a gambler and this is a deadly business for a person like that to be in.'

'Why's he doing it?' Cassie said.

'I do not know. I gave up trying to understand him a long time ago.'

Peppino stood and poured more coffee. 'You should try and see Klemansky,' he announced. 'And you should do it tonight. He is still awake. I can see the light in his caravan.'

'But what could I say?'

Rotondo cast sheep-dog eyes at Cassie. 'He likes flattery. He is used to being surrounded by acolytes.'

'But what should she say?' Peppino said, sensing Cassie was on the verge of agreeing.

721

'That he should wait. There is a much greater chance of success if a few more trial runs are conducted.' He leaned forward earnestly. 'It is principally a matter of the vehicle's behaviour, not of its performance. I need to know if it is likely to veer or lift or become unstable. Do you know we are using a jet engine that was developed for use in an American fighter plane?'

Both nodded.

'Do you know that the Sabre, laden with fuel and armaments – bombs, rockets, cannons, all those terrible things – weighs more than the Great White Shark? *More.* Think about that. What it means is that we have a car with enough power to lift off and climb vertically, like a rocket. I deliberately went for the lightest possible weight in the design of this machine, to give it the best possible performance, and that puts even greater stress on the shape and the balance. It is those factors, not weight, that keep it on its wheels. The challenge is to go as fast as an aircraft, but the problem is to keep it on the ground.'

After a long pause, Cassie said: 'Does Michel understand this?'

'Of course, but he chooses not to recognize such facts.'

'Why?'

'To remain sane. Not to lose his nerve. After all, he is the one who has to ride in such a machine.'

T·W·E·N·T·Y

Klemansky wrote two letters and then carefully re-read them.

Dear Paolo,
   Well, my dear friend, you were correct. We should not have gone so early. You were right, I was wrong, you are still here on earth, I am not. Hopefully, that gives you very little satisfaction.
   Paolo, I want you to know that despite the friction between us in recent times I have always had and still have (this is written the night before, so have is correct) the greatest respect for your ability and judgement. I think you're the best in your field. If I hadn't always felt that, I would never have engaged you or bought your crazy concept in the first place. I hope you know me well enough to realize that what I say is true. I may be an unreasonable bastard much of the time, but I do have a certain knack in surrounding myself with good people, and you were the best.
   What you may not understand is why I've acted the way I have in the last few days.
   I'm running out of money. I don't mean I'm flat broke or anything like that but the squeeze is sure being applied. Each of the recent aircraft that has flown in supples has also brought mail that contains sad, bad, tidings. The business in the States is going from one disaster to another. As you know, we lost money last year, but the way things are going these twelve months, last year might seem to be pretty good!
   So what all this means is I have to watch the dollars and get the hell out of here as quickly as I can. Or rather, that was my objective. There is no way I could afford an engine rebuild. Even another week's rental to the Rosses would be a severe embarrassment. And I don't have enough to pay that talkative countryman of yours for the use of all his trucks.
   So it's do or die. Literally.
   I needed the record to get the money that will pour in. If

you're reading this letter, it means I didn't get the record, and it means that in a week or two, there are going to be a whole lot of people coming around looking for money for all sorts of goods and services.

My advice to you is to get the hell out of the country. In case you can't beat the creditors, tell them you didn't work for me and we parted company some time ago. Just to help you with that line, I've attached a letter accepting your resignation (for personal reasons) and post-dated it so there should be no argument.

Needless to say, I hope you don't get to read this letter, although, should we be successful tomorrow I might keep it and show it to you one day just to prove what a humble guy I really am. Or was. If I get the record, I might turn into a real bastard, unbearable all the time.

Michel

PS I enjoyed having you with me in the racing team. I mightn't have been the world's best driver but we had some good times. MK

Klemansky folded the letter and its attachment and put the two sheets in an envelope, which he sealed. Carefully and neatly, he wrote Rotondo's name on the envelope. Then he picked up the second letter.

Dear Father,

If we have not been as close as we should have been, that has not been your fault but mine. My one regret is that the situation now can never be rectified.

I know I have done many things that have brought you dismay and even shame. But please understand that having a father like you has not been easy. You are so successful, so respected and so respectable that to emulate you has been almost impossible. Not being able to follow, I have gone in a different direction. The decision was caused, not by lack of love or respect, but out of a strong, almost consuming need to be independent, to be seen and recognized as a separate individual.

I guess most people will have looked upon me as being successful, although you and I know differently. The one thing I can honestly say I did well was to drive fast cars quicker than most people. This last venture was to try and prove no one ever was quicker. Please respect me for that.

Your loving son,
Michel

PS Try and explain all this to Mother.

* * *

Someone knocked on the door. It was done so discreetly as to be almost inaudible.

'Oscar?' Klemansky called. He knew Gronwald had been working on the car. 'I thought you'd still be out at the lake.' He put his hand across the letter to his father, and then grew impatient because the door was still closed. 'Well come in, for Christ's sake.'

There was another knock.

He walked to the door and opened it. A swath of light, yellowed by its journey to the great blackness outside, shone on Cassie. She retreated one step.

'Oh.' He scratched the back of his head. 'Brought the bull whip?'

'No.' Her lip curled in brief acknowledgement of his humour but then the mouth straightened and uncertainty returned, for he was a shadowy outline in a bright doorway and she had no way of guessing the expression on his face.

'Forget something?'

'I wanted to talk to you. Just a few minutes.'

'Uh huh.' His body filled the doorway.

'About tomorrow.'

Slowly, just a little too casually, he leaned forward and looked in either direction. 'On your own?'

'Yes.' Already she regretted having come. Venturing to his caravan, with her hands clasped meekly in front of her, had put her in the role of suppliant. For an instant, seeing the light on his face and assuming the strained expression was arrogance, she wished she had indeed brought the whip. Calming herself, she said, 'I've been talking to Dr Rotondo.'

'Dear old Paolo,' he said with heavy irony, and emitted a weary sigh. 'And you have a message, a last-minute plea?'

'I want to talk to you.'

'In your own right, as the former official photographer? You haven't given the camera back by the way.' Without waiting for her response, he withdrew from the doorway. 'Oh well, come on in. You know where everything is. Take a seat.'

Any thought of flattering him as a means of achieving the objective had vanished by the time she entered the caravan. But she was conscious of the promise she had made to Rotondo, so she began: 'I've had dinner with Giuseppe Portelli . . .'

'Ah yes,' he said, flashing a smile at the name. 'The little Italian with the big trucks.'

'He's not exactly little.' Peppino was at least as tall as Klemansky and considerably broader.

He laughed. 'You know what I mean.'

725

She did not, but continued. 'Dr Rotondo was there as well.'

'Nice of you to feed him.'

His flippancy seemed strained and she wondered how much he'd had to drink. 'What Dr Rotondo said worried me. He seemed so concerned.'

'I'm sure.'

'No, really Michel.'

'You've heard he's been dismissed?'

'He told me.'

'Should've got rid of him a long time ago. He ceased to be really productive months ago. He's what we call a back-room boy. Someone who's great in theory but should never be allowed out of the laboratory or workshop. Hopeless in the field. He's so full of theories and he's got his head so jammed up with sums that he doesn't want to do anything.'

Her disbelief seeped through.

'No, it's true. Rotondo was good in the design phase. I'll give him that. Jet propulsion was a neat idea and he had some good men build my car. But that's it. Period. I should never have brought him here.'

He was sitting at the table, brushing his fingers across the letter to his father. He seemed unaware of it for a moment, and then picked up the sheet of paper and folded it in several places.

'Dr Rotondo told me he doesn't think the Shark is ready,' Cassie said.

'As far as he is concerned, it never will be ready. He just wants to keep on fiddling with it.'

'I don't think so.'

'That's touching, my dear, but what you think is hardly relevant, let alone likely to be accurate.' He opened one hand, as though it were holding a glass. 'The car is as good as it's ever likely to be. The track is right. The timekeepers are ready. The stewards are in place with their little pens and rubberstamps all poised. So why wait?'

She had the feeling she was not only losing the argument but had made no headway. 'They could wait another week, surely?' The question sounded lame, even to her.

'Why?' He pushed the imaginary glass away. 'And why should I keep paying large sums of money to keep all these people here? Who do you think pays for all their transportation, their food, their accommodation? Who do you think pays your father to rent space in the goddam shearers' quarters and pays for the cook and pays for a waitress who's not even here but has dashed off down to Adelaide?'

She rushed to Stella's defence. 'Jimmy's in hospital. She had to go.'

726

'I'm still paying just as much.' He leaned forward, his eyes full of pity for someone who could not understand a simple problem. 'I'm sorry your friend is in hospital. I'm sorry you had to feed Rotondo tonight. I'm sorry you had to listen to all his bleating about how necessary he is to the team. But the truth is, every extra day we stay here costs me a fortune – me, not the eminent doctor – and the truth is there is absolutely no reason for us to sit around doing fancy sums when we should be doing what we came here to do. Which is to go out and break the record.'

He stared at her, but missed contact with her eyes.

'Michel, have you been drinking?'

He slammed the table and the caravan rocked. 'Of course not.'

'You seem ... strange.'

'Great.' He gave a shrill laugh. 'I'm glad you didn't say queer.' His eyes wandered around the caravan, seeking some object that might share the joke; and suddenly she understood.

'Are you frightened?' She posed the question quietly and with sympathy.

He swung his bad leg over the other knee. 'What sort of question's that?'

'It just seems to me that you might be. I think I would be.'

'You're not me and thank heavens for that. All the world is grateful for that.'

Her eyes were keen. 'You must have so many things going through your mind. This is not a good night for you to be on your own, is it?'

'Are you volunteering?'

'No. But it seems to me it would be better if you had someone to talk to.'

'My God. The girl's a psychiatrist. Who do you think I am? The prisoner in the condemned cell, and you're the priest, come to hear my confession?'

'No.'

'Well, leave me alone.' His hands played with the folded sheet of paper.

She stood to leave. She was getting nowhere and only embarrassing him. The envelope, which he had covered with his arm, was now revealed. She read the name: Paolo Rotondo. 'You've written to Dr Rotondo?'

Hastily he covered the letter. 'Just a formal confirmation of his dismissal. The chance for me to tell him a few truths. Put the little wop in his place.'

'Michel that's horrible.'

'I'm a horrible guy. Why don't you get out of here?'

727

She paused near the door. 'I'm sure if you wanted to do more testing, say for another week, Dad wouldn't charge you anything. I mean for the accommodation or meals.'

He stood and his face was flushed. 'Will you leave me alone?'

She left and didn't look back, and heard the sound of something heavy being thrown against a wall.

Long before dawn, there came the growl of motors and, like beasts aroused from a winter's sleep, a convoy of vehicles rolled out of Kalinda. Dark shapes linked by strands of light, they headed towards the lake.

The first to leave were the mechanics and refuellers, then Oscar Gronwald and some of the specialist members of the team. Close behind were the timekeepers, who needed to make one final check of their equipment, then the stewards who would supervise the whole attempt and were following the others because they didn't know the way. Bringing up the rear were the journalists and photographers and the television crews. They followed because it was the news reporter's role to follow. They had no part to play other than to be there, and to watch, and to record the deeds of others. So they breathed dust and followed dim tail lights and endured the long, dark drive to the record strip on Lake Eyre with one purpose: to be in place at the appropriate time, and to tell the story of the day when the world's first jet-propelled land speed record contender carried Michel Klemansky to glory or failure in his bid to become the fastest man on earth.

The best conditions for the attempt were likely to be at dawn. Therefore Klemansky timed his departure to have him arrive at the lake site half an hour before sun-up. Gronwald had left one of his men to drive the American, and to ensure he departed on time.

Adam had been watching Klemansky's caravan, and left only when he did. He had no desire to reach the lake too early and get in the way of those who had work to do, and he thought it wise to have someone follow the American's car in case he had trouble on the way to the lake.

'It'd be a great record attempt if a hundred people were waiting out on the salt and the driver was forty miles back up the track with a broken fan-belt,' he said, but he need not have worried. Klemansky's car made the journey without incident. Adam travelled with Nina, Patrick and Alex Rafter. The young solicitor had accepted their invitation to spend some days at Kalinda. He was flying south with Josef tomorrow. Patrick was in the back, sleeping with his head on the basket of food Mrs Wilson had prepared; she had been up, cooking, since three-thirty. Cassie was in the second Land Rover with Josef, Peppino and Dr Rotondo. The designer had been reluctant to join them, yet found it impossible to stay away. It was cold. Rotondo wore heavy clothing and a scarf around his face. Cassie suspected it was more for disguise than warmth.

Daniel had stayed at the homestead. It was his choice. There were things to do and he knew that someone other than Mrs Wilson and Jimmy's girls should be at the property.

First light came to the lake by stealth. No one saw it arrive. It was just there, a split in the night that defined where the land ended and the sky began. Out of it spread a thin greyness that washed across the heavens like water slowly flooding a pavement. It erased the stars and bleached the moon, and turned cold shadows into tents and trucks and flagpoles with dead banners. The salt glowed a silvery blue and people stamped their feet and blew warm breath on cold fingers.

Within the largest tent, a generator hummed and bright lights shone. Several men pushed the Great White Shark and it rolled out, cold and quiet and sinister, its tyres crunching the damp salt, its gaudy mouth poised to devour whatever lay before it.

The timekeepers were in place at the ten and eleven-mile marks. The refuelling crew was at the far end of the strip. Some journalists had elected to watch from beside the measured mile, because that was where the first news of a new record would be given, and their cars were speeding down the service road, well to one side of the main strip. Radios were being tested and the air crackled with metallic voices counting to ten and demanding acknowledgements to half-understood messages.

The sky had turned the colour of mother-of-pearl.

'The weather's good,' Oscar Gronwald said in greeting Klemansky.

'How's the car?'

'Ready.' The Swede was concerned by the expression on Klemansky's face. 'Michel, what's wrong?'

'I haven't got my stick.'

'Where is it?'

'In the caravan.'

'Oh well –' Gronwald was anxious to get moving but there was something so morbid about the other man's expression that he stayed where he was. 'Well Michel, what's the problem?'

'I broke it last night.' Klemansky attempted a smile and failed. 'Hit the wall with it.'

'Well,' Gronwald said, filling an awkward gap while he thought

729

of something to say. 'Let's face it, you're not going to be doing a lot of walking today.' When that brought no response he added: 'I'll fix it when we get back. Put it together with glue and some of my silver tape. Give it character.'

'Oscar, I wanted it today.'

'Michel, you don't need it,' he said gently and wondered what was wrong with the man.

'I was counting on taking it in the car.'

He forced a laugh. 'You certainly don't need it in the Shark.'

'I had a space for it.'

'A good luck charm? C'mon Michel, you don't believe in those things.'

'It used to belong to my grandfather. My father gave it to me.'

'I'll fix it.' He moved close to Klemansky and caught the stale stench of liquor. 'Are you sure you're OK?'

'I didn't want to break it.'

'No. Well, you get ready.' He patted Klemansky on the shoulder to start him on the journey to the tent where he would don his driving gear. 'Better get ready. We should go while there's no wind.'

Klemansky cleared his throat. 'The car's ready?'

'Yes,' Gronwald reiterated. 'Everything's done.'

'Good for five hundred?' He smiled and the confident look that Gronwald knew had returned, and the Swede felt better.

'Good for whatever speed you want, Michel.'

Klemansky walked towards the tent. 'Keep people away from me, won't you Oscar?' he said, without looking back. He was not limping. ''Specially the stewards. I don't want any of them within fifty feet of me.'

Because you've been drinking, Gronwald thought and felt a pang of deep concern. But he said, 'OK,' and walked to where the Great White Shark waited, all glistening highlights and rounded shadows, with its nose pointing towards the bright stain that marked the place where the rim of the sun would soon appear.

Cassie still had Klemansky's camera. She took a photograph of the car against the soft, pearly sky and then stood back, watching Oscar Gronwald and his men standing beside the car, occasionally polishing an already bright spot and not knowing what else to do as they waited for the driver to reappear.

Adam was near the main tent. Nina was pouring coffee and most of their group were clustered around her. Peppino took Adam to one side.

'There's something I've been wanting to ask you,' he said. 'This is probably a strange time but ...' The words trailed off nervously.

730

'What's up?' Adam was curious. Peppino was normally direct. Adam admired him for that.

'Well, I'm building a new house in Adelaide.' He hesitated. 'So I can live there.'

Adam smiled, his curiosity stretching. 'Right. Just like I built a new house for me to live in a few years ago.'

'That's correct.' They smiled at each other.

Adam lowered his head, inviting Peppino to say more but the man's mind had become stranded on some obstacle.

'Do you want me to come down and give you a hand painting it?'

'No.' Peppino erupted into laughter. 'I want Cassandra to live there. I want to marry her.'

Adam held out a hand, to steady himself. 'Cassie?'

'Yes. Hadn't you suspected?'

Adam's eyes shifted towards Nina, who was pouring coffee, and back to Peppino. 'I hadn't really thought about it.'

'Well, I love her and I want to marry her and that's why I'm building this house. It's for her. I'm doing well in business, Adam.'

'I know that. You've done very well.'

'And I could afford a wife and provide for her.'

Adam wiped his mouth to suppress a grin. 'What does Cassie say about all this?'

'I wanted to speak to you first, to get your permission.'

'My permission for you to marry my daughter?'

'Well, not quite that.' Peppino looked down shyly, and Adam thought that if the young man had been carrying a hat, he would now be playing nervously with the brim. His hands moved like that. 'That's a bit old-fashioned. I only wanted to let you know what my intentions were and get your permission to talk to Cassandra.'

'And what will you say to her?'

'I'll ask her to marry me.'

They faced each other, neither certain whether to smile or not.

'Well, go ahead,' Adam said. 'Talk to her by all means, and ask her for yourself.'

'I should tell you I have already raised the subject in a kind of a way.'

'Oh. And what was her reaction?'

'She laughed.' Peppino delivered a warm Neapolitan smile.

'But you'll try again?'

'Oh, that wasn't a formal proposal or anything like that. I had to speak to you first.'

'I appreciate that, Peppino.'

'Thank you.' They shook hands.

Adam went to Nina and accepted a cup of coffee and a scone that Mrs Wilson had baked. He took Nina's arm and walked her away from the others.

'Guess what?' he said and told her of the conversation with Peppino.

'You look pleased,' she said.

'Well, he's a nice young fellow.'

'He's a lovely man, and maybe she'll want to marry him one day.'

He sipped coffee without taking his eyes from her. 'I can sense a "but".'

'But not yet.'

'She's twenty-five.'

Nina shook her head. 'She should, she *must* see something of the world before she ties herself down to married life.'

'I can't imagine Cassie tying herself down to anything.'

'More than ever, I'm convinced she should go to Europe. Two months there, with Josef as chaperon, would do wonders for her.'

'And Peppino?'

'He'll wait.'

T·W·E·N·T·Y-O·N·E

Klemansky emerged from his tent and saw Cassie. He signalled to her.

'I see you're still on the job,' he said, indicating the camera.

'I was going to give it back to you.'

'Keep it. A memento of Michel Klemansky and the Great White Shark and the two weeks when the world's greatest circus came to Lake Eyre. Have you taken any good photographs this morning?'

'A few.' Self-consciously, she fingered the camera. 'At least I think so. It's still pretty dark.'

'The sun is about to make an appearance.' He waved a hand. 'And I shall ride off into the rising sun, like a medieval knight astride a thunderbolt. I thought of calling the car Thunderbolt. Did you know that?'

'No.'

'Someone else thought of it first.' He looked around them. 'Not one cameraman in sight. The Press are boring. They've all gone to the same place, to see the car at maximum speed.' He delivered the last words with a cynical flourish. 'And there they will see a blur, a smear of white on a lake of white.' He paused, knotting his brow. 'I chose the wrong colour. I wasn't thinking. Should have made it bright red or blue. The camera won't distinguish the car on this background. Anyhow, they've all rushed off to the measured mile, playing follow the leader as the Press always do, and no one is here to record an historic moment, to take the real picture, which is me preparing to go out on this great, dead lake, and become the fastest man on wheels.'

She lifted the camera, offering it as she might have tempted him with a chocolate. 'Do you want me to take a picture?'

He swung the helmet by its strap. 'Why not? We'll start at the tent. Michel Klemansky walks out to face the dawn. That sort of shot. How much film have you got?'

'Plenty.'

'Good.' He walked quickly back to the tent. 'Inside or out?'

'Out. There's more light.'

'Spoken like a real pro.' He let his eyes roam across her body. 'I can't work you out.'

She faced him, cordially defiant. 'There's nothing to work out.'

'What you see is what you get, eh?' He posed with the helmet in the crook of one arm. 'Whereas with me –'

She pressed the button.

'Take another one.' He let the helmet dangle casually from one hand. 'That was a strange conversation we had last night. Do you want me to smile?'

'No. Look serious.' She took the photograph. 'It was a short conversation.'

'I broke my cane last night. You know, my walking-stick?'

She nodded, 'How?'

'I hit the wall with it after you left.'

She busied herself adjusting the camera. 'I heard something.'

'I was angry.'

'With me?'

He turned and swung the helmet in a circle. 'Not really. More with myself, I guess. Do you want me to put these gloves on?'

'OK.' She took a picture of him pulling on the long gloves, and then with his arms folded.

'The walking-stick was something my grandfather had given to my father and he handed it down to me.'

'Can you fix it?'

He seemed not to have heard her. 'My father gave it to me a long time before the accident at Monaco. He must have known something.' He smiled to himself. 'I can't recall anything else he gave me since I was a kid. Except advice. He was always giving me advice. But the stick was special. It was beautifully carved. Did you ever look at it closely?'

'No.'

'It was beautiful. And I smashed it against the wall.' His breath escaped in a sorrowful gush. 'And do you know why?'

She retreated behind eyes of child-like innocence.

'Because I felt exposed. You asked me if I was frightened. Of course I was frightened, but I certainly wasn't about to admit it and yet you knew.'

'I just thought ... Well, it seemed to me that you should be. I mean, this is a very –' She stopped, not wanting to use such a provocative word as dangerous. 'This is a very difficult thing you're doing.'

'I was scared stiff last night.'

'You were?' She was genuinely surprised. 'You struck me as

being the sort of man who's afraid of nothing.'

'Oh sure. I'm the kind of guy who cracks a few bones, then comes out of the anaesthetic and cracks a few jokes. Afraid of nothing. You build up an image of yourself that becomes so complete you even start to believe it yourself. Occasionally the façade crumbles.' He grinned a sick man's smile. 'As you saw last night.'

'Michel, why go now? You're the only one who's been insisting that the record attempt takes place today.'

'There are reasons.'

'You could call it off.'

'No. There are situations that become unstoppable. This is one. It's gone too far.'

'Dr Rotondo came out with us.'

'I thought he would.'

'He couldn't stay away.'

His face became strong again. 'Keep him away from me. He's the last person I want to speak to today. If I saw him I'd hit him.'

'For God's sake why?'

'Because he's a reasonable man, and I'm beyond reason.'

She fiddled with the camera, not wanting to look at him. 'He's saying you don't have to try for five hundred. He was saying four hundred will give you the record.'

'You see? I told you he was that sort of man.' He let the swinging helmet bump against his leg. 'The car has the power to do five hundred. I know that. I've said my objective is five hundred. Anything less will be regarded as failure.'

'Dr Rotondo said you could do four hundred today, get the record, do some more tests, and then go for higher speeds.'

'What are you, his PR girl?'

'I just want you to do the right thing, and not hurt yourself.'

'You care?'

'Of course I care.'

He held out his hand. She took it and he pulled her roughly to him. He kissed her, then pushed her away. Off-balance, she clutched the camera, which swung wildly from her neck.

'Thank you,' he said softly. 'I have had many women love me but I don't think any of them have ever cared for me.'

'Why not just try for four hundred?'

'Because there are people to whom I have promised a speed of five hundred. It is a magic number. There are advertising campaigns based on that figure. Do you understand? There are very large sums of money involved.'

'Michel, money's not that important.'

735

He laughed softly. 'Oh, my sweet, innocent girl. How little you know about the way the world works. Money is all-important.'

They faced each other, not speaking in the soft light. He shook his head, as though not believing what he saw. 'You really are concerned about me, aren't you?'

'Yes.'

'Despite the things I've done?'

'Last night I saw a different man.'

'Hah!' He slapped his thigh. 'Last night was the night before the big event. Nerves. Tension. You understand? I always get that way before a race or something really important. Morbid. Depressed. It's all gone. Today I'm confident because I'm the person who's about to become the fastest man in the world.' He moved closer and took her hand. 'Still like what you see?'

'Yes.'

He kissed her. It was a long and tender kiss and she felt herself becoming limp. When she opened her eyes, he was smiling.

'Have you ever been kissed before?'

'Yes,' she said, knowing he didn't believe her.

'You must promise not to wish me good luck. That is very bad luck.'

'What do I say?'

'Break a leg.'

'I can't say that.'

'Then say nothing.' He kissed her again. 'I'm sorry I behaved so badly. I thought you were like the others.'

She nodded, with her eyes closed and moist.

'Shall we say seven tonight, in my caravan?'

'Let me cook.'

He laughed. 'I can't wait. Now, we mustn't miss the sunrise. It will give you your best photographs. Michel Klemansky climbing into the Great White Shark at the dawn of a new speed era. I should have been a caption writer, don't you think?' He walked towards the car. 'Come, the Press photographers have deserted us. You have a world exclusive.'

As he neared the car, the first dazzling sliver of raw sunlight burst over the horizon, like molten metal spilling from a dark cauldron. Following Klemansky, Cassie felt a faint breeze touch her face.

Cassie took photographs of Klemansky climbing into the car, being strapped in the seat, having his air supply connected. With the canopy raised and the driver exposed to the cool morning air, she was accepted as a necessary addition to the small team entrusted with the responsibility of getting the car under way. That attitude changed, however, immediately the canopy was lowered. With Klemansky sealed in place, his link with Cassie was severed. He was reduced to a bright helmet and darkened sun visor, glimpsed only vaguely through the glinting perspex panels; she was an intruder with a camera, one who got in the way. The men, she thought, behaved like servants who resented an outsider's intimate contact with their master. She moved away, beyond the range of their bitter expressions and well clear of their harried paths around the vehicle.

The Land Rover with the starting unit rolled into position and the main cable was plugged into the long white body, an umbilical cord from diminutive parent to massive infant. The starter motor throbbed, whirring the jet engine into life. The tail disgorged flames and the placid air beyond the flames suddenly boiled into streams of writhing images.

Having put a long lens on the camera, Cassie took several pictures, and then walked to the place where the others were standing. Their hands covered their ears.

'He will of course go as fast as he can,' Rotondo shouted, to be heard above the engine's scream.

'I think so. I told him what you said.'

'And he took no notice.' His face was agitated, and he moved his nose like a hound searching for a scent. 'There is a breeze. I've lost the feel of it because of all the disturbed air from the jet, but he cannot run if there is too much wind.'

Alarmed by his expression, Cassie joined in the search for the errant breeze.

He waved his hands in a gesture of futility. 'I must speak to Oscar,' he said and hurried towards the Shark but before he had taken more than a few steps, Gronwald got in a vehicle and drove off at high speed. Rotondo walked back, waving his hands and still searching for signs of a natural wind in the ruffled and heated air pulsating from the jet.

He walked to the side of the tent. Cassie joined him. 'What do you think?' she asked and then volunteered her opinion. 'I can't feel any breeze now.'

'No.' He sounded uncertain. 'Could you take me to the time-keepers?'

'Now?'

'We will see him start, then be in position for the second run. I want to hear the time for the first run and ascertain if there is any wind and see how the track behaved.'

'The track?'

737

'Oh yes. We are testing the salt, too. It may break up. We do not know.' He was interrupted by the rising howl of the jet engine. With the concentrated, hurtful sound of a dozen destructive storms, the Great White Shark began to roll along the blue line.

They ran to one of the Land Rovers. 'We're going to the measured mile,' Cassie shouted to her father. Both groups jumped in their vehicles and raced down the service track, while on the record strip, the jet car accelerated slowly away until it disappeared behind the shimmering screen of its own exhaust.

It was like the start of a Grand Prix. No matter how he tried to slow his racing heart and calm the jangling nerves that made his wrists flutter, Klemansky could not stop the nervous spasms that shook his body. It would pass, he knew, because he was always like this at the start of an important event. A minute or two was all he needed. In a race that meant the opening lap. Here it meant the record, because he had to be up to full speed in less than a minute. To do five hundred, he must pass through the measured mile in a fraction over seven seconds. Three breaths. Seven seconds. No time to relax or ease himself into the routine.

The Shark was still accelerating gradually and travelling slowly. He glanced at the air speed indicator. Only one hundred and thirty five. It was quiet. He could hear a whistling behind him and was conscious of a slight quivering around the front wheels, which were just behind his shoulders. He was right in the nose of the car. If he hit something he would be the first to know. It was a macabre joke which he repeated to himself each run. This time, he did not smile.

The trembling continued. His hands were all right because they had the tiny steering-wheel to grip, but his lower arms shook nervously and irregularly, vibrating like tuning forks. He must concentrate. Remember what he had to do. Just keep it straight, apply the power evenly and in the precise amounts required, watch the gauges, count the mile posts. It was simple. Much easier than driving in a race. No other traffic. No drivers nibbling at his tail or cutting across his line in a corner. All he had to do was go fast and stay straight.

It was a deceptive car to drive. Unlike a Formula One machine or a big sports racer, which delivered the power in one whamming hammer blow and spun the back wheels and required delicate co-ordination between the right foot on the accelerator pedal and the hands on the wheel and great deftness in changing gears and judging engine revolutions, this was a simple, if monstrously powerful, device. There was no clutch to depress, no gear lever to shift, no violent burst of power to spin the wheels. He was riding a

738

jet engine. All he had to do was press a pedal to feed the engine more kerosene. The power arrived smoothly and almost instantly but the speed came later. It was a weird sensation because the car ran faster and faster, at an accelerating pace, long after he had issued the command. It was like being on elastic, and catapulting up to speed.

But finesse was required. Too little power early on and he would not be travelling fast enough at the first timing marker. Too much and the Shark could yaw or patter out of control.

A quick glance at the instruments. Two eighty-five. A marker flashed past. He hadn't recognized it and cursed himself. The fourth or fifth mile? Time to gamble. He depressed the pedal. The whistle, errily distant now, became shrill and almost painful and another sound, the rush of air over and under and around him, became a roar and for an instant he was a boy travelling with his father on an express train which thundered into a tunnel. He used to like that, and would press his face to the window and feel the glass vibrate.

The Shark was vibrating. No time to look at the instruments now. All his attention was on the rectangular frame of perspex in front of his eyes, with its view of pale sky and grey salt. The blue line was rushing beneath his legs, only the line was no longer straight. It had become a writhing snake, and it was moving to one side. The perspex was shaking and the steering-wheel was buzzing in his hands and the salt and the sky joined in a fuzzy union of greys. The blue snake had moved further to one side. He was off the line. The first temptation was to turn back, pick up the line, but Klemansky was too good for that.

He was shouting in silence, telling himself what to do. 'Doesn't matter. Stay parallel. The salt's good. Don't budge or you'll flip the goddam thing.'

He lapsed into groans. The vibration was awful. His hands ached, his wrists felt as if they were on a jackhammer. Oh, Jesus, he couldn't see. His eyes weren't working. A terrible shaking had moved up his spine and even though he pressed the back of his helmet hard against the head rest, he couldn't stop his eyes and his jaw and his skull from moving and buzzing and hurting.

The blue line, as blurred and nonsensical as a stripe moving across a television screen, passed beneath him. It took nearly a second, or another two hundred and fifty yards, for the message to register: he was running, across the track.

He began to scream; not through fear, but to do something violent because what he had to do with his hands required the utmost delicacy and every instinct demanded a wild, impulsive move. He turned the wheel one degree. No more. Still screaming, he saw a blur of banners and a dark patch of people and shapes. To the right was the line, out of focus, but there, and constant.

Another banner. The kilometre. Then another. The end of the measured mile. His brain worked, even if the senses were bombarding it with scrambled messages.

He was through. Gradually he eased back on the pedal. The vibrations slowed, then died away. He realized he hadn't taken a breath for some time and let deep draughts of air hiss through his teeth. He could see now. The horizon settled to a sharp distinction between sky and lake. The blue line was well to his right. How had he strayed so far?

Another mile post passed and he closed the throttle. At the next marker, he applied the brakes for the first time then released them, just as Paolo had said he should. For the first time, he thought of other people. The radio crackled and a voice, sharp as a splinter, gave an incomprehensible message.

'Three miles out,' he said, not caring what had been said but pleased to have heard a voice. He braked again.

At the nineteen-mile marker, he pressed the button that fired the parachute and felt the tail quiver and then the sensation of a giant hand gripping the car and trying to pull it back.

The mechanics and the refuellers were waiting. They were dancing and waving their arms. Following the great loop in the blue line, he turned the Shark and pointed it back down the strip. The refuelling vehicles scurried into place. One man tried to open the canopy before he had shut off the fuel supply. Klemansky waved him away.

The howl of the engine faded. The perspex lifted. The man was at the point where laughter gives way to tears. 'Five hundred and nineteen miles per hour,' he managed to say.

'Is Oscar here yet?' Klemansky said, and was proud that he could be so matter-of-fact.

The steward near the timekeepers' box was surprised to find Dr Paolo Rotondo there. He had thought, he explained in a bemused yet infinitely polite tone, that the designer of the car would be with the car. Rotondo said the reasons were complex and repeated his question: how had the car looked as it passed through the measured mile.

The man grinned. 'Bloody quick.'

'Was it stable?'

The steward shrugged. 'It went past so fast it was hard to tell. Made a hell of a racket.'

'Did the nose appear to be lifting? Did the car waver off course?'

'Not as far as I could see.'

'Was there a wind blowing?'

'You mean from the car?'

'No. Was there a wind blowing across the track?'

A faint breeze was stirring the air. The man moistened a finger and used it to check the direction of the wind. 'You mean like this?'

'Yes. But was it stronger? Were there gusts?'

'When the car passed?'

'Yes.'

'I don't remember. I was concentrating on the car.'

Rotondo scratched his chin. 'What do you do for a living? Are you a professional steward?'

The man laughed nervously. 'No. I'm an undertaker.'

Rotondo walked to Adam and Cassie, who were standing nearby. 'The man is an undertaker. What does that mean?'

Adam looked at Cassie who looked away. 'It means he buries people.' He coughed.

Rotondo's eyes widened and he put his hand to his chest. For a moment, Adam thought he was going to bless himself. 'I think it's just a coincidence,' he murmured, and returned to the steward who was standing with his hands clasped in front of him.

'I need to go on the track,' Rotondo said. 'I have your permission?'

The man was confused by such a request. He checked his watch. 'The car has to make its second run within an hour of the first.'

'I'm aware of that. I need to see the track.'

'How long will you be?'

'Possibly ten minutes.'

'Just wait a moment.' The man went to a radio on a small table, and called the base at the far end of the track. A voice that rang like echoes from within an iron boiler answered him. The steward returned, his face wearing the classic mask of petty authority. 'You have ten minutes, no more,' he intoned.

Rotondo got in the Land Rover with Adam and Cassie, who turned at ninety degrees to the service road and drove to the record strip. They stopped at the edge and walked towards the central blue line.

A gust of wind cooled their cheeks.

Rotondo stopped. 'There are gusts,' he said gravely. 'That one was two or three miles an hour in strength.'

'And that's a problem?' Adam asked.

'From the side, yes. It can be tolerated from the front or the rear. Not the side.' The wind disappeared.

741

'It's gone,' Cassie said.

'Better that it blew constantly. In puffs it is most deadly.' He resumed walking. They intercepted the tracks of the car and stood between them. They looked in either direction.

'He's gone in a big sweep,' Adam said, squinting along the tracks.

Over a distance of a mile or more, they could see where the indentations left by the tyres had swung from one side of the blue line to the other. Where they stood, the marks were at least forty yards from the centre line. Further in the distance, they swung even wider and then, near the horizon, curved back again.

The Italian swallowed and the exercise seemed to cause him pain for his face became contorted. 'He had either a problem of stability,' he said in a strained voice, 'or there was a side wind, a gust that blew him off course.' They followed his gaze towards the horizon. 'He did well to bring it back. I would say that at this point, he was almost out of control.'

Adam and Cassie were silent as Rotondo bent to examine the surface. 'Some pulverization of the salt has occurred, but not a great deal.' He pressed a thumb into the slight but wide groove left by one set of wheels. 'A little moisture has been brought to the surface. Not enough to cause concern.' He squatted to study the wheel marks from a lower angle.

'What are you looking for?' Adam asked.

'Unevenness. Any sign that the suspension is pounding. I cannot tell. I should be with the car.' He stood up and brushed salt from his hands.

Another ruffle of wind crossed the track. He turned to Adam. 'What does that mean, wind like that? Does it get stronger or go away?'

Adam frowned. 'I rarely get out to the lake so I wouldn't know. Back home, however, if the wind starts after sun-up at this time of the year, it usually gets stronger. For an hour or so anyhow.' He glanced at Cassie who nodded confirmation.

Rotondo's feet began to jiggle in agitation. 'They will have completed refuelling. They will almost have fitted the new tyres. I must speak to Michel.'

'The man has a radio,' Adam said, and Rotondo ran towards the car.

Only one front wheel had to be bolted in place. A fitter stood patiently beside the rig that carried the streamlined wheel cover, ready to fit it back on to the body. A mechanic ran towards Oscar Gronwald, who had arrived in time to supervise the final work on the car.

742

'Dr Rotondo's on the radio. He wants to speak to the boss.'

'Not possible,' Gronwald said, not bothering to look up. He checked the tightness of the wheel. 'He's strapped in, plugged in, locked in. What the hell does Paolo want anyhow?'

'He just says it's urgent.'

'Where is he?' Job finished, Gronwald stood up and signalled the man with the wheel cover to put it in position.

'At the measured mile.'

Gronwald pondered. Michel had said the doctor had become unbalanced but the Swede respected Rotondo who knew more about the car than anyone. 'OK,' he said, moving towards the radio. 'I'll be back in a minute.'

Rotondo's voice erupted from the radio in a scratching burst of noise. 'Oscar, did Michel report any problem with handling or keeping it on line?'

'He said it vibrated. Over.'

'I'm at the time trap. The car moved at least sixty yards to the left.'

'He didn't say anything about that. Over.'

'There's been some wind, Oscar. He should wait or abort.' Rotondo spoke with such urgency that his voice was distorted.

'Say again.'

He screamed into the radio. 'I said there is wind and he shouldn't go.'

Oscar was silent for a few seconds. 'How bad's the wind? Over.'

'It comes in gusts.'

'Is it blowing now?'

'Oscar, it is gusting. Do you understand?'

'Just a minute.' Gronwald ran back to the car. He unclipped the canopy.

'What are you doing?' Klemanskey disconnected the air supply mouthpiece so he could speak clearly.

'I have Paolo on the radio. He's at the measured mile. He said there's a wind blowing.'

Klemansky thumped the steering-wheel. 'Can you feel a wind?'

Gronwald shook his head. 'There's none here but he says it's blowing in gusts down at the ten-mile mark.'

Klemansky felt the twitching resume in his belly. He had to do it this time. He was one half of the way through the ordeal, the worst half, the first run, and there was no way he could do it all again. He lifted the tinted visor and squinted up into the anxious face of the Swede. 'What's he want me to do?'

'Wait.'

'Like hell. We've got five nineteen up, Oscar. We're halfway there.'

743

'He seems worried, Michel.'

'Of course he's worried. He's worried we're going to get the record without him.' That was it. Envy. Spitefulness. A small voice within him was trying to say Paolo Rotondo was not like that and if the doctor was worried, there was a good reason for it; but a stronger voice told him that if he didn't drive back down the track, if he didn't go for that second run, he would never get back in the car again.

The Swede bit his lip. His eyes roved, searching for a wind.

'Jesus Christ, Oscar, will you close the canopy? We've only got another fifteen minutes and I'm not going to sit here and let the record go.'

'Do you want me to check again?'

'I want you to close the goddam lid. Shut me in. I want to go.'

'He sounded genuine, Michel.'

'Can you feel any wind?'

'No.'

'Well, I'm not going to wait around for it to start blowing.' He reached up with a gloved hand and pulled the canopy down. Gronwald secured the outside catch. The starting crew moved into place to wind the jet engine into life. Gronwald went back to the radio.

'He's coming, Paolo,' he said and switched off.

Rotondo put down the radio and turned to Adam. There was a look of disbelief on his face. 'He took no notice. He's on the way.'

A stronger gust of wind ruffled papers on the table where the radio stood. The steward, who had been with the timekeepers, waved to Rotondo. 'He's just about to leave,' the man shouted and his face was bright with excitement.

Klemansky felt better. This was like the halfway mark in a race, a time when he was always more relaxed, more in control of the car, even enjoying himself. The turnaround had been performed rapidly and without a hitch.

He rolled past the first marker and its banner was still. There was no wind. In any case, he had raced in thunderstorms and he wasn't going to call the attempt off with the record almost in his pocket because someone thought he noticed a puff of wind. Paolo always had been neurotic about wind on this lake.

The air was still. The track felt good. The car was perfect. New tyres had probably fixed the vibration. To hell with Rotondo. Michel Klemansky had become the first man to travel faster than five hundred miles an hour on land. One more run and it would be the world record. Segrave, Campbell, Cobb, Klemansky. He felt good.

He gave the engine a little more power. The next marker passed. He scanned the instruments and saw the needle pass the one-fifty mark. My God, five fifty might be possible this time.

Three. Four. Five. The posts whipped by, each one appearing and flashing past more rapidly than the last. Six. The needle swung over three hundred and he was conscious of two things: a greater surge of acceleration, and a fluttering of the last banner.

The vibration returned. He was over four hundred now and the instruments were dancing and the terrible buzzing sensation was climbing up his spine. His teeth hurt. The clarity of vision was going to be replaced by a grey blur. Never mind. Twenty seconds would see him through. Just follow the blue line. But the line, a vague blue blur, was moving. It flickered to one side. He was screaming, no roaring, fighting to bring the car back to the line but something was pushing him away.

Another banner went by and it was flapping and it was close.

The car came out of the horizon in a sudden, bewildering burst of speed, a monster darting from its lair. It began as a flat, misshapen thing, weaving and growing larger each second and being chased by an evil cloud of gas and atomized salt. And then it changed direction. The painted mouth turned as if to snap at the post that marked the start of the measured mile, slewed momentarily back towards the centre of the strip and then, with horrifying abruptness, jerked to the right.

At undiminished speed, the Great White Shark ran off the course.

Its wheels hit the rough salt and the noise changed from a banshee howl to a hideous screech. The car lifted, banged down hard again and shot across the service road. It was no more than fifty yards from where people were grouped near the timekeepers' table.

A white storm of salt erupted in its wake. The car disappeared.

Adam had not moved. He was aware of Cassie's fingernails cutting into his arm but he could not see her because of the noxious fog that engulfed them. Together, they coughed and bent and shook while the noise of the car continued as a rolling, rumbling thunder.

When the sound grew less, they straightened and saw in the distance, a white spot with a bright red centre racing towards the middle of the lake. And then it became an illusion: the red glow supported a white tower which grew higher and higher on a base of

745

billowing cloud, and then everything fell slowly back into the haze which cloaked the horizon.

Pieces of wreckage formed remote islands of black and white and steaming grey. From some twisted fragments rose columns of smoke. The smoke climbed, thin and unbending, because there was no wind. It had gone and the lake was quiet.

Dr Paolo Rotondo sifted through some pieces of the wreckage. Behind him stood Cassie, hands to her face. Peppino was beside her, with one arm across her shoulder.

Josef stood with Adam and Nina.

Five hundred yards away, Oscar Gronwald was directing one of his men to a small object that sparkled near a salt island. His commands, harsh and shrill, drifted to them. Far behind them, another vehicle was making the long journey from the graded strip to the place where the Great White Shark had disintegrated.

'I'd like to go soon,' Nina said softly. 'We should get Cassie away from here.'

Adam mumbled agreement and moved towards his daughter. 'I think it's time we were moving,' he said.

She turned, allowing Peppino's arm to fall uselessly by his side. 'Oh Dad, I just can't believe this has happened.'

He put his hat back on; he'd had it off, holding it deferentially in one hand, as though he were attending a funeral. He made soothing noises. 'Let me take you home. We can't do anything here.'

She put both arms around him and gripped him so hard he had difficulty in breathing. 'Michel was frightened,' she said, her voice a whimper. 'Don't you understand what that means?'

'Hush,' he loosened her grip and held her hands.

'Those last moments, the whole of that final run must have been horrible for him. He knew what was likely to happen.' Her eyes were wide and unnaturally bright. 'He could foresee it. He must have thought about it all last night, all this morning. And yet he still got in the car and then it happened.' Her voice slid into silence.

Adam stroked Cassie's hair. Behind them, he could see Dr Rotondo bending to pick up something. What on earth was he looking for? Klemansky was dead, scattered across the salt in small lumps of incinerated flesh and yet the Italian was concerned with recovering fragments of machinery. Adam burned with a sudden, illogical flare of anger. Was Rotondo trying to put the pieces of his precious car back together again so that someone else could have a go at the record?

'It must have been just horrible,' Cassie repeated and cried again and, with the release of those fresh tears, Adam felt his anger towards Rotondo dissipate as suddenly as it had come. The poor bloke would be even more distressed than he was. He'd built the car that had carried Klemansky to his death. Adam pressed Cassie against his chest.

'Dad, Michel only pretended to be brave.'

'No, he was brave.'

She shook her head savagely. 'Maybe he was brave, but he was frightened. He pretended that he was reckless and bold and afraid of nothing, but he was really frightened by this whole business. Oh Dad, I know, because he told me. And yet he went ahead and got in the car. And now, look.' She pulled one hand free and waved it towards the islands of smouldering debris. 'There's nothing left of the car or of him but little bits and pieces.' The last words burst from her, carried on a torrent of sobbing.

He tried to walk her back to the Land Rover but she spread her feet, refusing to move. He held her until the crying stopped. Nina came over and put a hand on her shoulder. She smiled sadly at Adam.

'He was a nice man.' Cassie looked from one to the other. 'I know you didn't like him but he was nice. I got to know him. I really did. And now he's gone.' Her words ended in a squeak of despair.

Adam nodded. 'Of course,' he said and suddenly felt tears welling up within him. He pressed his face into her hair so that Nina wouldn't see. Cassie was crying again, sobbing noisily, and he rocked with her, unable to halt his own tears. Cassie's distress had torn him open, exposing all the grief that was stored and hidden within him. He was crying because she was crying and he had never known her to be so upset; it frightened him and, worse, it made him feel helpless and vulnerable. And he was crying because of Nellie and all the anguish of the last few days and because he felt so worn and useless.

Roughly, he wiped his face.

Cassie was speaking, face pressed against his chest, her voice muffled by his shirt. 'I was the last person to talk to him before he got in the car.'

'Don't talk any more. We'll go home.'

'He wanted me to go away with him. To Europe and America. He wanted me to be his manager.' Cassie drew back, to face them both. 'I was going to say no, but after this morning I think I might have said yes. He was so nice. So honest. He told me that he was frightened last night.'

Nina looked at Adam, pleading with him to take Cassie to the car. He tried to move but she stayed obstinately in place.

747

'I saw him last night. I tried to get him to wait, to postpone the run until the car was ready. I wasn't much good.' Her eyes swung to Nina and back to Adam. 'If I'd been any good, if I'd just tried a little harder, I might have stopped him. And then he might ...'

Adam thrust her away from him. 'Now listen to me Cassie. Michel drove that car not because anyone made him but because he felt he had to. It was his decision. No one else's. He knew the risks better than anyone.' Her eyes were closed and he shook her. 'Are you listening to what I'm saying?'

'Yes.' A brief flicker of the eyelids.

'Don't ever blame yourself, or anyone else for that matter. Michel knew what he was doing. He knew that people sometimes died trying to break land speed records. For heaven's sake, he often talked about it, about how dangerous it was. He even seemed to boast about it.'

Her voice was a murmur. 'Dr Rotondo said the car wasn't ready.'

'And Michel said it was?'

'Yes.'

'Well there you are. It was his decision. He knew the risks. He knew what Rotondo was saying. He was determined to go for the record today. There was nothing you could have done about it.' He put a finger under her chin and lifted her face. 'Do you understand what I'm saying?'

She kept her eyes down. 'I think he liked me, Dad.' And to Nina: 'He really did. I could sense it.'

Nina shook her head.

'Come on,' Adam said and, this time, persuaded her to move away.

'I liked him. After this morning, I know that I liked him and I'm sure he liked me. I mean really and sincerely.'

Flanked by her father and Nina, she walked unsteadily towards the Land Rover. Behind them, Paolo Rotondo had put his hands in his pockets and was staring up at the sky.

That night, long after everyone had gone to bed, Cassie got up and walked to the verandah. She found Adam standing at the rail, staring at the brilliant display of stars.

They talked for a long time. First, about Klemansky. She spoke and Adam listened while she poured out all her feelings about the man. They were silent for a while and then they talked about Nellie. She asked questions. Adam answered, at first in monosyllables and then in long, rambling recollections of earlier years. He told her everything. As he talked, Cassie leaned against him and

748

he was reminded of the nights he and his daughter had shared under the stars, long before he built this house, when the two of them used to tend the sheep and trap marauding dingoes. That was after Nellie had gone ...

Finally, they talked about Daniel.

'I'm glad we found out,' she said. 'Even though it's funny suddenly having another brother.'

'And another son. That is a strange sensation.' She let her head touch his shoulder. 'Although it shouldn't be too hard for you,' he added. 'You've always treated him like a brother. You've bullied him since the day he arrived at Kalinda.'

She laughed and felt better.

They were silent for a long time. When she was little and they were out among the dunes tracking a dingo, they would go for hours without talking. She liked that. Silence was good when shared.

The sky was growing lighter. Was it nearly dawn? She took his hand. 'Have I ever told you, Adam Ross, how much I love you?'

He gave a grunt of surprise. 'There are some things you don't have to say.'

'But I want you to know I love you and I'm very proud of you.'

'Even after all the things you've learned about me in the last couple of days?'

'More than ever.'

He put an arm around her and kissed her forehead.

'You're supposed to say that you love me too,' she scolded.

'But you know that.'

'A daughter still likes to be reminded.'

'I love you too, Cassie Ross.'

'And you're proud of me.'

'And I'm proud of you. Very proud.' He laughed softly. 'Come on, it's time we got to bed.'

'Do you think you could sleep now?'

'Yes. Until lunchtime. How about you?'

She nodded. 'I feel better. I needed to talk.'

With his arm around her shoulder, he led her from the verandah. 'I do love you, Cassie.'

'Gosh, twice in one night.'

'One morning,' he corrected and opened the door into the house.

The next afternoon, Nina was alone with Josef. 'The other day,' she began, with the weary emphasis of someone talking about a time long ago, 'we were discussing the possibility of Cassie travelling to Europe.'

Josef nodded sombrely.

'These have been terrible, confusing days for her.'

'For everyone.'

'But for Cassie especially. I think she had grown very fond of Klemansky.'

Josef hesitated while he considered her words. 'Fond?' he asked, his face wrinkled by doubt. 'Do you mean she was in love with that man?'

'I don't know whether it was as serious as that, but something happened between them, just before that last run, which has deeply affected her.' She took his hand in hers. 'Dear Josef, please promise that you'll take Cassie with you. There are so many reasons why she should get away from here for a while.' She squeezed his fingers. 'That's if you're still planning to go.'

'Well yes, I am.' He avoided her eyes. His mind was in a turmoil. Cassie in love with Klemansky? He felt jealous. That was madness. The man was dead and she was the daughter of his best friend.

'Please, Josef.'

He should say no. Cassie could go to Sydney. Maybe holiday up on the Great Barrier Reef. Meet a nice young man.

'Will you be too busy?' Suddenly embarrassed, Nina pressed his hand. 'I'm sorry. You'll have too much to do. It is a business trip. I shouldn't have asked.'

'No.' He shook his head earnestly. He wanted Cassie to go. Heavens, how he wanted her with him.

'So it's possible?'

A long pause. 'Yes.'

'Please. I'd be eternally grateful. And she wouldn't be a bother. We'd meet all her costs, of course ...'

He smiled and raised a hand in protest. 'It would be my pleasure.'

'You'll take her?'

'Of course.'

'Josef, you're a darling.' She kissed him and he felt rotten.

BOOK
S·E·V·E·N
Cassie

O · N · E

April, 1962: Alsace, France

It was a small town in the mountains and it was surrounded by vineyards and pine forests. Some farms were scattered across the valley. Their land ran to the edge of the peak, which hid all but the highest tower of an old castle on the peak. The farmhouses were jumbles of stone and moss. Cold, ancient and everlasting, they sat in fields of grapevines whose ranks were raked in rows of leafy green. The farms had been there since feudal times. The town was newer. It was built along a ridge, which gave travellers a tantalizing view of the old tower projecting above the pines, and it was on the main tourist road of the region, the *Route du Vin d'Alsace.* The Rhine was to the east, less than half an hour's drive away but out of sight. Beyond the river and lying under the silvery haze created by its own affluence, was West Germany.

There were only a dozen houses in the town. All had shingle roofs that sloped at sharp angles to let snow slide free in the cold months, and white-painted stone and brick walls with large window-boxes to let blooms splash bright colours in the warm months. The town did not spread from the road but followed it, clinging to its turns as faithfully as leaves on a vine.

Apart from the houses, the town had a small store, a primitive garage and a hotel. The hotel was like a larger version of one of the houses; a rectangular three-storeyed building whose longer sides ran parallel with the road.

Josef climbed wearily from the rented Citroën. This was the fourth town he had tried. All the hotels had been full. Already, the setting sun was flirting with the tips of the pine forest and, anticipating another rebuff, he walked to the arched entrance way. The door was locked. He pressed the button. No one answered, and he had visions of Cassie and himself either sleeping in the car or having to drive all the way to Strasbourg.

The Citroën's horn beeped a distant signal and he looked back to see Cassie, who was still in the car, pointing towards the end of the building. He walked around the corner, descended some stone steps, and found a small door beneath a sign that said 'Restaurant'. He waved to Cassie, and grinned. He was not good with doors; he either went to the wrong one or pushed when he should have pulled.

He knocked. A woman called out in French for him to enter. He went inside and found himself in a long room with a polished tile floor, walls of roughly hewn stone and a ceiling dominated by massive timber beams. Wooden tables and chairs were arranged in neat rows. The tables were covered by red and white chequered cloths. Lights – electric but in the shape of old gas lamps – hung from the ceiling. A woman, wiping her hands on an apron which matched the tablecloths, was at the far end of the room. She had grey hair and a formidable shape. She studied Josef, and spoke in German.

'How did you know I spoke German?' he said, in German.

'You are not German?' She advanced, still rubbing her hands.

'I'm Australian.'

She cocked her head to one side. 'English?' she said and fashioned a few grotesque words in the language.

'Yes,' he said but he reverted to German. 'My parents were born in Germany.'

'Ah, where?'

'Not far from here. Near Wiesbaden.'

'Not far?' She shook one hand as though she had burnt the fingers. 'You want a meal?'

'Yes. And two rooms, if you have them available.'

'Two?' Her expression suggested he had asked the impossible. She pushed past him. 'You have a car?'

'Yes.' She was already through the door. He followed her to the Citroën. She nodded to Cassie, who had raised hopeful eyes, and turned with her hands on her hips.

'I have one room available, not two. Do you and your daughter mind sharing a room?'

Josef was beyond wincing at such a remark. In the five weeks that he and Cassie had been in Europe, many people had assumed that she was his daughter. 'I'll have to ask,' he said, pleased that the woman spoke little English. Cassie's eyes switched from the woman to Josef. 'Madame has a room, which is the good news. The other news, which is not necessarily bad, is that she only has one. So you can sleep in the hotel and I'll curl in the car.'

'Is that what she suggested?'

'No. She wants to know if we mind sharing.' He winked. 'She

754

called you my daughter, but I think she knows better.'

Cassie smiled sweetly. 'I don't mind sharing a room with you, Father.'

Without following the words, the woman understood the meaning and went to the back of the car. 'Open,' she commanded. Josef unlocked the boot and the woman lifted out their two suitcases. He attempted to take the load from her but she shouldered him aside and carrying the bags with ease, led them to a room on the first floor. It smelled of floor polish and freshly laundered linen. It had a small window above a large flower-box, and two beds.

'Two beds?' she asked. She had thick eyebrows and they lined up at a cynical angle.

'Yes, that's good.' Josef enjoyed giving her his blandest, most innocent smile of thanks.

'One night?'

'Unfortunately, yes. We have to go tomorrow.'

'To Wiesbaden?' The eyebrows were still inclined just in case, Josef imagined, he wanted to recant and ask for a double bed.

'We've been there. We met an uncle.'

'That was good.'

'Yes. He was thrilled to meet my daughter after all these years.'

She narrowed her eyes, then smiled. 'You can register when you come down for dinner. Just your passport will do.'

She offered him her hand and almost crushed his.

'Have a pleasant evening. Dinner is in half an hour. You will eat here. We have very good food.'

'I wouldn't think of going anywhere else.' He massaged his fingers.

She smiled contentedly and nodded to Cassie. 'Eat good,' she said in English.

'Thank you.'

When she had left the room Cassie said. 'What was she saying?'

'Usual things. Dinner's in half an hour. By the way, I don't think she believes you're my daughter.'

'Oh.'

'She thinks I'm a dirty old man.'

'How clever of her.' She opened her case. 'If I need help, I'll whistle for her.'

'Fine,' Josef said, checking all the joints on the fingers of his right hand, 'but once you two make a deal, whatever you do, don't let her shake on it.'

The business part of the trip was almost at an end. In thirty-five days of travel, they had visited many of Europe's best-known vineyards and most famous wine-makers. Josef had learned a lot, talked a lot, made friends in many establishments and discussed the possibility of importing wines with several companies. It had not been all work, however, for Josef had made considerable changes to his original itinerary once Cassie's participation was confirmed. The journey was no longer merely 'an old wino's wog pub crawl' as Jimmy – out of hospital and back at Kalinda – had described it before Cassie's departure. Mindful of Nina's desire that his young charge see more of Europe than the aromatic interiors of noble cellars, Josef had amended the schedule to include a few cities, many good restaurants, an occasional museum or cathedral, a couple of night clubs and even a cruise on the Rhine.

They had flown from Sydney to Paris where they spent three days, allegedly to recover from the rigours of a thirty-hour flight. In reality, they spent most of their time seeing the city. Not resting in their hotel was no great hardship, because it was a seedy place, much favoured by strange women with dogs. It had an antiquated elevator that resembled a bird cage, moved slowly and broke down regularly.

The hotel was near the Place de la République. They walked to Notre-Dame, strolled along the Avenue des Champs Elysées, climbed the Arc de Triomphe and saw the city from the observation deck on the Eiffel Tower. They went shopping. Cassie bought shoes and long boots and a coat with a fur collar, for it was still cold when they arrived and she was fresh from the tail-end of a scorching Australian summer.

Near the shop was a bookstall with a magazine poster proclaiming in French: AT LAST. THE TRUE STORY. WHAT WENT WRONG AT LAKE EYRE. There had been so many stories, so many screaming, outrageous posters. Josef whisked Cassie in the other direction. She had been good; much better than in those first months after the crash, but there was no need to remind her of the man.

The idea was to keep her occupied, to show her dazzling new things, so on the first night, having not slept for almost two days, they went to the Folies Bergère. Josef had long nursed a desire to visit the most famous night-club in the world. At first, he was wildly stimulated by the spectacle of so much glittering nudity but then, suffering from jet lag and an oversupply of bared torsos, drifted into a state of semi-comatose euphoria.

Cassie was shocked, not for reasons of morality but because she considered it unthinkable that women would bare their breasts and dance and parade in public. Once she got used to the idea and overcame the feeling that all the men in the audience were looking at her out of the corners of their eyes, she began to enjoy the show. The fact that the costumes were so elaborate and covered so little puzzled her but after some time she began to admire the routine and compare the girls and even to wonder how she might look in similar outfits. She felt daring and light headed enough to ask Josef, but by this time he was almost asleep, and leaning on her shoulder.

On the second night, they contemplated dining at Maxims until they saw the prices on the menu outside, and instead ate at a crowded but cheap restaurant. On the third night, they went to the Crazy Horse night club and discussed the nudity in most sophisticated terms. The next morning, hovering between a dream-like unreality and very real exhaustion they took delivery of a Citroën rent-a-car and headed towards the wine-growing regions where Josef had appointments.

Josef spoke a little French and taught Cassie how to count and how to say 'yes' and 'no', 'please' and 'thankyou'. She learned one stock saying: 'Je ne parle pas français. Parlez-vous anglais?' but became so proficient that people refused to believe she could not speak French. Therefore, she kept quiet and let Josef do the talking. Josef would attempt introductions whereupon the person being visited would either display massive indifference to anything other than a quick over-the-counter sale, or reveal exquisite manners and a matching command of English. The latter visits were delights.

For a week they visited vineyards, talking business and sampling products, dining in modern restaurants and ancient châteaux, trudging up manicured slopes and exploring musty cellars.

At the end of the week and by now acclimatized if still not rested, they left France for Luxembourg and then travelled northeast along the valley of the Mosel, to visit the first of the German vineyards.

For Cassie, the Mosel was a picture book of fantasies brought to life. Here was a river that never ran dry, and was so wide and deep and free of snags that big boats – cheery, colourful ferries or long, flat barges – plied up and down and even had room to pass each other. There were hills, always hills, climbing up from the river and combed in neat rows of lustrous green and rich, earthy brown. Everything was so precise, so tidy, so verdant, so abundant – and so well watered.

She thought of Kalinda; dusty, sandy, flat, windswept, raw Kalinda. She gazed again at the painted scenery and the constantly flowing river and, for the first time, felt a pang of homesickness.

They stayed at Cochem, a town all scrubbed and shiny bright in a fold of the rumpled hills, and then followed the Mosel to the Rhine.

Along that great river, they spent ten days visiting wine-makers, became tourists in Bonn and Cologne and then went back to the Rhine for a three-day cruise that Josef had arranged as a surprise for Cassie. It rained for all those three days but at least, and at last, they got some rest. Despite mists that sheathed the hills and sudden squalls that stippled the surface of the river, Cassie found the cruise romantic and, because of the poor visibility, mysterious. Great barges churned past unseen, their mournful horns sighing laments, their powerful engines fading in the fog. Occasionally, the rain eased and the mist would part to reveal a castle, perched like a nest on a crag. Then the mist would drift back and the castle would slip from sight, as elusive as an image in a half-remembered dream.

They visited more wine-makers, saw Josef's uncle in Wiesbaden, travelled flat-out up the autobahn to Hamburg to see the city where Josef's maternal grandfather had been a clockmaker, and then headed south again. They collected mail in Frankfurt, spent one day in Heidelberg and another on the fringe of the Black Forest at Baden-Baden, and then crossed the Rhine back into France, to see some of the vineyards in Alsace.

Once those visits were completed, Josef intended driving south to Switzerland and then into Italy. There would be no more business calls. After Alsace, the journey was to be purely a holiday; he would be completing Cassie's European education, showing her Switzerland and the lakes of northern Italy, then Verona, Venice, Florence and Rome. The fact that he had been to none of these places didn't bother him. He had read about them and would continue to act the role of guide and world-wise traveller.

The woman with the iron grip had been modest. The meal served in the restaurant at her small hotel was not merely very good, as she had promised. It was excellent. Josef and Cassie ate well and drank a little too much of the local wine because, as he said, work was almost over and they should celebrate, 'to mark the end of the days of hardship'. They drank to that.

They even talked about Klemansky. That was something of a milestone; a sign, he felt, that the man was, at last, dead and buried.

'He knew a lot about wine,' Cassie said, as if discussing some absent friend and even speculated that the white they were drinking was the same wine the American had produced for their second, disastrous dinner. She told Josef about that night, and laughed.

'I'm not a good drunk,' she said, and had some more.

Towards the end of the evening the woman joined them, bringing another bottle of wine from the hotel's own vineyard. It was late when they went upstairs to their room.

758

'This is going to be fun,' Cassie said, pirouetting towards her bed. She bounced on her mattress.

Josef, who had the look of someone who is about to do something he knows he shouldn't, was surprised. 'It is?'

'Well, we can talk. Most nights, we have to go to our own rooms and I usually feel like talking about all the things we've done and seen, but there's no one to talk to. You're always somewhere else.'

'Well, that's the way it has to be.'

She bounced on the mattress once more. 'Why?'

'Because it is.'

'Josef Hoffman,' she said, rollicking into her German voice, 'das ist nein gut. In fact, as an answer, das ist a load of grosse rubbish.'

He sat on his bed. 'Your German is awful.'

'I thought it sounded pretty good.'

'About as good as the Italian you used to speak to that Peppino character.'

'I think my German's better.' She fell back on the bed. 'Peppino's coming to Italy.'

'You told me. You got a letter from him.'

'I'd like to see him again.'

'You won't. Not unless we go out of our way.'

'I'd still like to see him.' She bounced into an upright position. 'Oh, I feel like going out. To a night club or somewhere bright, where they've got a floorshow.'

He laughed. 'We're a long way from Paris.'

She stood and performed a showgirl's walk to the door and back. She hummed some music and with a flourish removed the jacket she had been wearing. 'Do you remember the first night in Paris?'

'Sure.'

'You do not. You fell asleep.'

'I did not. Not until the end, anyhow. We went to the Folies Bergère.'

'You didn't see a thing.' Hips swaying excessively, she did another lap of the room.

'Who are you supposed to be? One of the Folies girls?'

'I think I'd make a good showgirl.'

'You do?' The voice hovered between mocking and challenging. Josef felt warm around the neck and loosened his collar.

'I looked at myself in the mirror. I reckon I'm as good as they are.'

'But you can crack a stock-whip. I'll bet none of them can.'

'No one wants to see a naked girl with a whip.'

'Don't you be too sure of that.'

'Das ist noddle-talk, mein Josef.' Her voice deepened to a

Marlene Dietrich growl. 'The men want girls with long legs. Beautiful faces. Gorgeous bodies.' She imitated the strut of the black dancer who had been the Folies star.

Josef giggled.

'You don't think I look beautiful?'

'I think you look great.'

'Then why did you laugh?'

'Because I hadn't imagined you like that. It's a surprise.'

'I told you, I did it in front of the mirror. I got curious so I took my clothes off and practised in the hotel room.'

'In Paris?'

'And a few other places since.' She leaned forward, gave a slow and lecherous wink and then turned her back to him. 'I've got one of the routines down pat.' She busied herself for a few moments.

Josef became uneasy. 'Now Cassie ... you're a little tipsy.'

'No, it's OK.' She turned and her blouse was undone. 'Now this is how it goes.'

'Cassie, please.'

'No, watch.' She removed her blouse and put it on her head, arranging it to form a rough turban. 'That's my fancy head-dress, all full of diamonds and glittering threads. How's it look?'

'Great,' he said in a quiet voice.

She stepped out of her skirt, pulled the flimsy cover off her bed, and tied it over her shoulders like a cloak. 'And then I make my entrance like this.' She backed to the door and then, one arm raised above her head with the wrist bent at a fetching angle and the other hand on her hip, advanced towards him. Her hips swayed, her legs swung in slow, sensuous arcs. She stopped in front of him. 'Of course, I need music. What do you think?'

His eyes were slightly above the level of her navel. He coughed. 'You need higher heels and a string of diamonds around your neck.'

'Oh, I've got something.' She turned hurriedly and fossicked in her suitcase. When she faced him, she was wearing a gold chain. 'Not diamonds, but they give you the idea.'

'They do indeed.'

She laughed and folded her arms across her chest. 'I feel silly with the bra on. I couldn't believe it when I first saw those girls with nothing covering them, but you get used to it after a while, don't you? In fact, if someone came out of the stage wearing a bra, you'd look at her, wouldn't you?'

'Yes, you would.'

She put her hands behind her back. 'Should I?'

His clenched fist touched his lips. 'No.'

'All the girls here seem to do it.'

'Only the ones at places like the Folies Bergère, Cassie.'

'But they're the most beautiful girls. I was really embarrassed at first but after a while I realized they looked really lovely. Very natural.'

'Well, I don't know if that's the word.'

'I look good like that.'

'I'm sure you do.'

'You don't believe me.' Once again she put her hands behind her back, fingers feeling for the catch of her brassière. 'I'm tempted ...'

He looked down, not knowing what to do.

'What does a man feel when he sees a woman like that? You know, with her tits showing. Is that the right word?'

'I know what you mean.'

'How do you feel? What does it make you think?'

'Jesus, Cassie, that's an impossible question to ask your old uncle.'

'You're not my uncle and you're not old. You're a dynamic man of the world. How do you react?'

'I get hot flushes.'

She laughed. 'No, seriously.'

'I am serious.'

'Hot flushes.' Again it was the Dietrich voice. She stood in front of him, her face glowing from the wine, her hands poised behind her back, and he didn't know whether he wanted her to remove the bra or not. The male in him said yes, but the friend of Adam Ross said no.

'I'm like most men. I admire beauty in a woman. I'm affected by seeing ... seeing things that are normally hidden.'

'I wonder why we cover ourselves up?'

'To keep warm.' His voice was husky.

'To make ourselves more enticing. More intriguing, more irresistible to males who suffer from hot flushes.' She launched into another swaying, posturing parade. When she was once more in front of him, she spun slowly and squeezed her arms against her chest so that her breasts swelled and strained to burst free. 'I remember how that stripper did it at the Crazy Horse,' she said and raised one arm to cover all but her eyes. The other hand went to the catch.

'No, Cassie.' He heard himself telling her to stop and he was surprised because he longed to reach out and pull the damned thing off her.

'I'm bigger than some of them.'

'I can see that. There's no need to take it off.' Another voice was shouting silent contradictions.

761

'They wobble a bit when I dance around, but I think I still look good.'

'I'm sure you do. Why don't you sit down?' He admired the voice that said that. It sounded firm but reasonable and there was no hint of the lust that was burning within him. He had no idea how he had managed to speak so calmly; it was as though he had been temporarily inhabited by a different, better person.

She sat on her bed. 'I've never shown myself to any man. I was going to take it off, just like they did in Paris.' Blouse draped across her head, bed cover over her shoulders, gold chain around her neck, she sat in her underwear and looked at him with eyes that were partly glazed. 'I feel a bit giddy.'

'We had a lot of wine.'

'We've had a lot of wine ever since we arrived.' She put the blouse on the bed and shook her hair. 'Do you think I'd be a good showgirl?'

'I don't know if you'd like the life, wearing feathers and baring your breasts twice a night, six nights a week.'

She sat up straight. 'That's what I needed. Feathers.'

'You don't need anything Cassie. You're beautiful as you are.'

'No, I'm not. I'm not beautiful. I'm just drunk.'

'*I* think you're beautiful.'

She undid the bed cover and let it fall around her hips. 'Do you know I've never had a man make love to me?'

He searched for an answer. 'Well, that's good.'

'Why?'

He took longer to reply. 'Men like to marry a virgin.'

'I think that's ridiculous.'

'No, it's good.'

'You've never been married.'

'No. I've thought about it.'

'I bet you've made love to a woman.'

Josef let his head hang. 'Why do you say that?'

'Because you're so experienced. You seem to know everything about women.'

He kept his head low but looked up. 'I know so much no woman has ever wanted to marry me.'

'Have you?'

'What?'

'Made love.'

'Yes.'

'I knew. Did you make love to Sarah?'

'Sarah Mandleton?' They had spent much time on their drives talking about Josef's old girl-friends. Because Sarah had once

762

travelled to Kalinda, she had assumed a special status. Josef had been kind to her, and enhanced his own reputation, by converting Sarah into a woman of incredible beauty and saintly manner. He preferred to preserve the lie and said: 'No. Not Sarah.'

'Who then?'

'A girl I knew a long time ago.'

'Was she beautiful?'

'Of course.'

'What was her name?'

He shook his head and smiled. 'That wouldn't be fair.' Ah, he thought, the old hypocrite is back in residence, preserving the honour and reputation of the fictional innocent.

'You're very noble.'

He said nothing.

'What was it like?'

'Making love?'

'Yes.' She leaned forward eagerly. 'No one's ever told me.'

'Well,' he said, groping for words, 'it was a long time ago.'

'But it was good?'

'Yes,' he said and was astonished to see that his reply seemed to satisfy her.

'I thought it would be.' She yawned. 'Suddenly, I feel so tired.'

There was no bathroom in the room, so he offered to leave while she changed.

She laughed. 'I haven't got much more to do. Just turn your back. That's if you want to. I don't mind.'

It would be so easy, he thought, to walk to the other bed, bend down and kiss her, remove those two flimsy garments, and do what she craved for him to do. Instead, he lay on the bed and faced the wall.

'You're such a saint,' she said, and there was no trace of irony in her voice.

T·W·O

With his commercial obligations fulfilled and his desires held in check only by an untrusted conscience, Josef became an impatient traveller. He whizzed Cassie through Switzerland in three days. She was left reeling, with calendar images of snowy peaks and picturesque lakes, while he was so exhausted at the end of each day's drive that there was little likelihood of his succumbing to temptation by filling Cassie with wine and then suggesting she do her Folies impersonation.

Before the trip began, there were times when he had dreamed of two months of constant debauchery, and he had felt positively evil in accepting the implicit trust of Adam and Nina, when his own fantasies had been so vivid. But after their arrival in Europe, something strange had happened. He'd looked at himself honestly, and not liked what he saw. Maybe it was the fact that he was in a foreign country and viewing so many things in a new way that made him conduct such a critical examination. He was no longer young – something he knew but had not really recognized – and the sight of a tired, wrinkled and balding man staring at him from the convex surface of a well-lit bathroom mirror had shocked him. Nor was he particularly good looking; certainly not in the way he remembered and, therefore, imagined himself. His picture of Josef Hoffman was of a young man projecting an air of wholesome virility, and who could topple any criticism by turning on a smile of beguiling innocence. That was a difficult image to sustain when the face staring back at him was of an older, worn and slightly dissolute stranger.

The night in the small hotel in Alsace had shaken him, and the vibrations persisted. Certainly Cassie was drunk, or sufficiently dazed by alcohol to have lost her inhibitions but even so, she had offered herself to him. That was what shocked him. The wine had skimmed away the barriers and what he'd seen was the real Cassie. 'Here,' she had said, 'you can have me if you want me.' The prey was lying down for the hunter who had followed her stealthily, erratically and shamefully, for years.

All through Switzerland he tried to clear his thoughts. At first, he was so shaken by the fact that he could have slept with Cassie and turned all his wild dreams into reality, that he was filled with self-loathing. He saw himself as a lecher, posing as her friend and confidant, graciously assuring her family that he would be her guardian and mentor, while planning to take her on a stage-by-stage tour of the Kama Sutra.

That image had lasted as long as Lugarno, where the Citroën punctured a tyre. While he waited for a garageman to repair the tyre, and while Cassie walked among the shops, Josef went through a further exercise in self-denigration. He had done nothing, that night in Alsace, because that was the sort of man he had become: a person who fantasized but shrank from opportunity.

What the hell was he? To start with he was forty-eight and Cassie was twenty-two years younger. Whereas she was vibrant and still refreshingly innocent, he was jaded and devious. He felt rotten. And old.

And then Cassie returned, bearing a gift and smiling in anticipation of the pleasure it would bring him. He unwrapped a box that contained a Swiss Army knife with his name engraved on the side.

Did he really like it? Of course. And did he think Dad and Daniel would like one each? He was certain they would, he said, as his fingernails explored the crevices and pulled up blades and scissors and a small magnifying glass. She hurried back down the street and a realization came to him. She liked him. She trusted him, confided in him and had, in the past weeks, become increasingly fond of him, even if the person she found attractive was different to the character whose portrait Josef painted so clearly in his mind.

The garageman had repaired the tyre and replaced the wheel long before Cassie returned. Josef sat in the car wondering. Who had the correct image of Josef Hoffman? The subject himself or the young woman travelling with him? The tarnished and weary man with the cynical inner view, or the perceptive young innocent?

They drove away from Lugarno, crossed the lakes and entered Italy.

'What do you think of me, Cassie?' He had taken a ticket from the toll-booth and was steering the car south on the autostrada to Milan.

'I think you're nice.'

'No, I'm serious.'

'So am I. You *are* nice.' She broke off some chocolate from a large block and offered it to him. 'Do you mean more than that, more than nice?'

'Yes.'

'Are you fishing for compliments?' She smiled past the piece of chocolate that protruded from her mouth like a rectangular cigar.

'No. I'd just like the truth. I've been feeling pretty bad these last couple of days.'

'Sick?'

'Guilty.'

'About what?'

'Lots of things. The other night, for instance. Our last night in France.'

One of her cheeks bulged from the press of chocolate. 'I was drunk.'

'Do you remember what you did?'

'Of course.'

'Were you really going to parade naked for me?'

She swallowed some chocolate, which stifled a laugh. 'I wouldn't have been naked. I had on my knickers and the bed cover.'

'And your blouse.'

'On my head.' She giggled and covered her mouth. 'I must have looked a scream.'

'It was a bit unusual.' A red sport car, lights flashing aggressively, swept past. Josef flashed back and muttered a profanity.

'Gosh, he's going fast,' she said and another car overtook them, its lights flashing and snatching at the sports car in front. She watched both cars race out of sight. 'Would I have taken my top off?' She paused. 'Yes.'

'Why?'

'Why not? It's the way the girls were in those night clubs. I think it looks ... daring.'

'And you want to be daring?'

She swallowed again. 'Sometimes.'

'When?'

'There are times. Not now. It'd be silly in the car. But I wanted to in the room. We'd had a nice dinner, some good wine.'

'A bit too much.'

'But it was nice. No, I just felt good. I felt daring and very European.' She bent forward and turned to see his face more clearly. 'Is that why you feel bad? Because I didn't take my bra off?'

He glanced at her, then moved his eyes quickly back to the road. 'I felt bad because I wanted you to.'

She pressed herself against the seat. 'I thought you would. That's why I did it. All the men in the night clubs seemed to like that sort

766

of thing. I mean they paid a lot of money to look, didn't they?'

'Men do like it,' he said, and pulled out to pass a line of trucks.

'But you asked me to stop. I would have kept going. I thought you would have wanted me to ... what's the word? ... bare myself.' She smiled sadly. 'I thought I must have been a bit of a flop.'

'No,' he said quickly.

'I thought you either didn't like what I was doing or you were being very noble.'

'I liked it and I was not being noble.'

'Then why did you tell me to stop?'

'I guess it was my conscience. After all, I'm the baby-sitter.' She hit his arm. 'Don't you dare say that.'

'Let's just say that I remembered my obligations.'

'Rats to your obligations.' She offered him more chocolate and then grabbed their road map as a row of destination signs loomed ahead. 'We follow the A9,' she said, and put the map down.

They were silent as he passed a series of turn-offs. They followed the overhead arrows indicating *Milano.*

'I've been thinking a lot since Michel died. He wanted to make love to me. Did you know that?'

He swallowed awkwardly. 'No.'

'He did.' She paused. 'I wish he had. I think it would have been good. Don't you?'

'Cassie, how would I know?'

'You know what I mean.' She shook her head emphatically. 'I was stupid. I should have let him make love to me. Just to see what it was like. Having sex is the most normal thing to do.' She said that with the earnest enthusiasm that only an innocent can muster. 'Haven't you seen the way the animals behave at Kalinda?'

'Cassie!'

'Well, it's true. My heavens, the camels ...'

Josef laughed and slapped his forehead. He did it like an Italian, even though they had just entered the country.

'Don't be such an old fuddy duddy. Tell me, Josef, have you ever wanted to sleep with me?' she said, munching steadily. They flashed under the last sign.

'Yes.' He looked at her but she was staring to one side, absorbing her first views of Italy. An old stone town spread down the side of the mountain.

'I've thought of it too. Not always. Just some nights.'

'You never said anything.'

She turned slowly. 'Neither did you.'

Josef felt good. Not justified, but less isolated. 'I thought about it a lot.'

'Really?' She seemed amused, as though they were discussing the foibles of other people.

'Do you know, even before we left Australia I wondered whether we ... well, if we might go to bed.' He could scarcely tell her how constant were his fantasies, but admitting this much made him feel as though a great load had suddenly been removed.

She laughed. 'I didn't think about it then, but I did after Paris.'

'Way back then?'

'Yes.' She scratched at his shoulder. 'Is that why you felt bad? Because you secretly wanted to make love to me, and felt guilty?'

'I guess so.'

'Well, I felt the same way and I didn't feel bad, or guilty.'

'How did you feel?'

'Kind of frustrated. Disappointed. I've never had sex with anyone. You have.' She lowered her eyebrows defensively. 'You told me. Remember that girl long ago?'

He nodded and was tempted to tell her the truth, but resisted. 'So you were curious?'

'Yes.' She laughed but any sound was swallowed in the noise of the car. 'It wasn't love or anything like that.'

Josef felt as thought he'd swallowed ice. He'd never thought of himself as a sex object, there to satisfy curiosity. Anyone who'd ever made love to him had been in love with him, or so he imagined. Except the girls in Cairo, although they'd all said they loved him, and it was fun to believe them and let them get on with their tricks. He said, 'No. Of course not.'

'Why did you want to sleep with me? Was it because men just have to have women? I've been told that.'

'That's true, I suppose.' The fine, revealing spirit of honesty was slipping away.

'And you really were attracted to me? I mean, the other night, when I did that ridiculous dance.'

'Sure. You looked beautiful.'

'But not irresistible?' It was a serious question although the lips were smiling.

'You'll never know how close it was.'

'That's good.' She pulled a face. 'And now I still don't know what it's like. Sex I mean.'

'You'll find out soon enough.' He heard himself say it, and knew the words had closed the episode.

'We won't do it, will we?'

'No.'

She seemed satisfied with that. 'But you think I'm attractive?'

'Yes Cassie, very, very attractive.'

'I think you're very strong. And very noble.'

'Really?'

'Yes. And that answers your question. I think you're strong and noble.' She scratched his shoulder again, as a kitten would. 'And very sexy. We've got to find you a suitable woman.'

He drove on to Milan, feeling old.

T·H·R·E·E

They got lost trying to find their hotel in Milan but ate well at a small restaurant, whose owner put them on the right road. They saw the outside of La Scala and walked around the Duomo trying to count the statues. They spent an hour in the piazza and watched a sword swallower and a man selling mechanical birds that he wound up and flew. They looked in shop windows and had an ice cream and coffee at one o'clock in the morning. They had trouble finding their way back to the hotel and went to bed happy.

Their hotel had a tiny garden at the side. It was enclosed by a wall that was hidden beneath a flowering vine. There were several shrubs in large ceramic tubs and half a dozen tables beneath umbrellas. They ate breakfast there.

Cassie had been raised on the principle of eating a substantial breakfast, which could vary from porridge, bacon and eggs, toast and jam and tea, to something simpler like grilled steak and tomatoes. She had found the Continental practice of eating rolls and drinking coffee almost barbaric in the degree of punishment it inflicted on the hungry traveller. At least at this hotel they provided a basket of rolls of excellent quality. They were all crust and empty inside; she liked that.

'You'll get fat,' Josef said, envying her for the fact that she never seemed to put on weight.

'No one could ever get fat on a Continental breakfast.' She buttered another roll.

'No one else in Europe eats four rolls for breakfast.'

'I haven't finished.' The waiter brought another basket of rolls, put them on the table and winked. 'I like Italians,' she said, when the waiter had gone. 'They're good sports.'

'He thinks you're trying for a new world record.'

'Talking of Italians, Peppino is due to fly into Rome today.'

Josef took a roll for himself. 'He is?' he said with little interest.

She reached for her handbag and withdrew the letter she had received in Frankfurt. 'He's going to see some of his family.'

'How long's he staying?'

'A month.'

'Where's the family?'

She checked the letter. 'Near Naples. Where's that?'

'Down the other end of Italy. In the south.'

'Far from here?'

'Too far. We're going east to Venice.'

'He's staying in a hotel in Rome for one day and then going to Naples.'

'Uh-huh.' Josef was busy spreading strawberry jam.

'I'd like to see Peppino.'

He looked at her, his doubtful eyes hovering above the roll. 'Do you really like him?'

'I miss him.'

'Like you miss your father?'

'No. Differently. Peppino's a lot of fun really. Did I tell you he wanted to marry me?'

'You didn't. Nina mentioned something about it.' It was one of the reasons she had thought it wise for Cassie to go away. 'It's not a serious thing, is it?'

'I think it is with him. He's built a house.'

'For you?'

She smiled, pleased to see such consternation on Josef's face. 'For his bride,' she said coyly.

'Pick a bride, any bride. Is that the way he works?'

'I think that's being a bit uncharitable. He just seems to think it was time he got married.'

'Probably his family. Italian parents like their sons to get married, although they usually want to have a say in who the unlucky girl's going to be.'

'I thought I might ring him.'

'On the telephone?'

'Unless there's some other way.'

'Italian telephones don't work.'

'You haven't used one.'

'It's a well-known fact.' He dabbed his lips with the napkin. 'Where will you call him?'

'He gave me the name of the hotel where he's staying in Rome.'

He looked at his watch. 'We haven't got too long. I'd like to be on the road to Verona soon.'

'I won't be long.'

'What are you going to say to him?'

'I'm going to tell him the Italians make good bread rolls.' She stood up, clutching the letter and her bag. 'Don't let them take the

771

rolls away. I might want more when I come back.'

'I'll guard them with my life. Give Peppino my best.' He smiled knowingly. 'If you get through.'

She was back within ten minutes. 'Couldn't get through?' he said.

She smiled but there was no happiness on her face. 'They put me straight through. It was a good line.'

'And what happened?'

'The man who answered said "pronto" or something like that, but couldn't speak English.'

He assumed the knowing look of a veteran traveller. 'So it was all a waste of time?'

'No. He got someone who spoke English.'

Josef drank some coffee. 'Cassie, we've got to leave soon. You'd better tell me what happened or we'll still be here when they serve lunch.'

'Peppino's not there. He hasn't booked in yet.'

He looked genuinely sorry. 'Well, that's bad luck. Still, you'll see him when you get back to Australia.'

She nodded. 'I left my name and gave the man the name of the hotel we're staying at in Venice. He might ring me there from Naples.'

'Yes, he might.' Josef pushed the basket towards her. 'Time for one more.'

They got lost leaving Milan and then drove one full lap of the ring road encircling the country's second-biggest city, because Cassie became confused with the way Italians spelt their place-names. It was only when they approaching the *Venezia* signs for the second time that she guessed it might be a funny way to spell Venice.

They had a late lunch at a town on the southern shores of Lake Garda. By now, Cassie was well aware that the names on the destination boards rarely matched the printing on her map and guided Josef unerringly to *Sermione* on *Largo di Garda*. Verona was their destination that night. Finding it was simple because the Italians used Shakespeare's spelling.

They were entranced by the city. And it was while they were having coffee at a footpath café near the Roman arena that that Josef met Ursula von Dannenberg.

She was at the table next to theirs. They met because the waiter, stressed by a sudden influx of customers, gave their change to her. She studied Josef for several seconds, trying to decide what language to use and, while the decision was being made, Josef looked across. Each blushed to be caught staring at the other.

In Italian, she said, 'This must be yours,' and handed him the stack of one-thousand-lire notes. 'He's given you plenty so you can leave him a tip.'

Not understanding, Josef said. 'Thank you.'

She tilted her head and replied in the same language. 'Ah, so you speak English. I was wondering. One never knows how to address strangers in a city like this.'

Josef nodded his agreement. Cassie was examining the woman with interest. She was, Cassie guessed, in her early forties. She was slim and wearing a grey suit that fitted so perfectly it must have been tailored. She wore glasses that focused attention on eyes of sky blue. Her hair had been blonde and was turning grey; not a strand out of place.

'You are American?' By the phrasing, she expected him to say no.

'Australian.'

'Oh.' She smiled. 'There are so many Americans over here these days.' Her own English had an American accent, but it was obviously not her native language.

'You're not Italian?' Josef said, leaving himself a comfortable exit from the conversation if he were wrong.

'No, German.'

'On holidays?' he enquired in German. 'Or some other reason?'

One carefully maintained eyebrow rose a millimetre. She answered in the same language. 'I'm here on holidays, yes. Or I was.'

'Was?'

'I fear I have been stranded.' She glanced across at the floodlit walls of the ancient arena. 'I was travelling with a friend. There was an argument over the most stupid thing. I fear she has gone, driven off home, and left me here.' She smiled, more embarrassed than upset.

'She?' Josef prompted, and Cassie, who had no idea of what they were talking about, drank some coffee and busied herself by studying their faces.

'A friend. Maybe an ex-friend.' The woman lit a cigarette. 'It is not wise for two women to travel together. Better the way you two are doing it.' She waved the cigarette towards Cassie. 'I hope she is not your daughter or something ridiculous like that?'

'No.' Josef smiled at Cassie but stayed in German. 'It's something even worse. She is the daughter of a friend of mine. I am showing her Europe.'

'That is very good of you.'

'I also had some business to do.'

'Oh. What sort of business are you in?' She leaned back and directed a fine stream of smoke towards Josef. 'Let me guess.'

He matched her pose. Cassie was intrigued.

'You are in textiles. Either a manufacturer or possibly a grower of fine wool. I understand Australians are the world's largest producers of wool.'

Josef was delighted. 'I am flattered, but you're wrong.'

'Ah. But you have the appearance. You dress well but in a nice casual way, like someone who is used to fine living but also perhaps the outdoors – which is why I thought maybe you grew wool.'

'I'm a wine producer.'

'You're not.' She looked across at Cassie, as though seeking confirmation and received a bemused smile.

'I've known you only two minutes and already you're doubting me.' Josef was enjoying the exchange. 'I assure you it's true. I have a vineyard in South Australia. We make our own wines. Reds and whites. Good wines.'

'Forgive me. I have never met an Australian wine-maker.' She stubbed out the partly smoked cigarette. 'Then your business is my business.'

'You make wine?'

'My family does. We have for many generations.'

'She's a wine-maker,' he said to Cassie, and Cassie smiled and said, 'Oh.'

'You do not speak German?' the woman said in English.

'No.'

'Forgive me. I have been very rude. My name is Ursula von Dannenberg.'

'I'm Cassie Ross.' They smiled across adjoining tables.

'She and her father have a big sheep station out in the middle of nowhere,' Josef said.

'Sheep. You grow wool?'

'Yes.'

Ursula turned to Josef. 'You see? I was almost correct but with the wrong person.' She laughed. It was a stronger, more peasant-like laugh than the well-groomed exterior would have suggested. 'And you, Mr Wine-maker?'

'Hoffman. Josef Hoffman.'

'That is a good German name.'

'My parents were born in Germany.'

'Which explains your proficiency in German. I was most impressed.'

'Thank you.' More people were arriving. When one couple looked longingly at the spare seats at her table, Josef suggested Ursula join them. They drank more coffee. Ursula told them about the argument with her friend. It had been over their next destination. Ursula had wanted to go to Venice, the other woman to Florence.

'My friend had been there, I had not,' she said. 'She said it was dirty and boring. I said I wanted to see for myself. It was stupid really. You certainly get to know people on a long journey, is that not true?'

'Indeed,' Josef said. 'What will you do now?'

She shrugged and laughed. 'I have not really thought about that. I'm still in a state of shock about her departure. It was her car. She just got in and drove off.'

'We're going to Venice tomorrow,' Cassie said, and Josef looked pleased that someone else had said that.

Ursula seemed not to have heard. 'I will stay in Italy. I am not going home, which is just what she would hope I would do. I have two more weeks yet. I will see what I can.'

Josef glanced at Cassie who nodded. 'Why don't you come to Venice with us?'

She smiled wistfuly. 'That is kind of you, but no, I could not. It would be too much of an imposition.'

'Absolutely no trouble. We have a large car, and there's no one in the back seat.'

Cassie sat in the back seat all the way to the car park in Venice. Normally, she sat beside Josef or did the driving, but she was happy to surrender her front seat because Ursula and Josef seemed to get on so well. They chatted non-stop, sometimes in English but often in German until, aware that Cassie was behind them, they would revert to English. They did not give the impression, Cassie noted, of always being aware of her presence, and this excited her. She had been worrying about Josef; a possible cure for his woman-less life seemed to be at hand.

By the time they had locked the car among hundreds of other vehicles on the sprawling Venetian car park and were transferring to a launch for their journey to the hotel, Josef had eyes for no one but the slim German woman. He had learned considerably more about her. She was a widow, she had an eighteen-year-old daughter, and she lived near Endingen, not far from the Rhine in the south-western corner of West Germany. Her family had owned the vineyard for two hundred and twenty years.

She was a woman of wealth and good taste, Cassie decided. Ursula dressed with a simple elegance and wore discreet but expensive jewellery. She was polite in a refined but natural way, had a good, earthy humour, spoke German, English, French and Italian, was passable at Spanish, knew a little Dutch and was learning

Japanese. Josef thought that quaint but she considered Japanese to be an important language of the future. She had a good ear, she explained, which she had possibly inherited from her mother who spoke seven languages and had been a concert violinist.

Cassie, who was looking at the woman to fill a specific role, thought she had two more important qualifications. She was about the right age for Josef. (A younger woman would be hopeless and inspire Josef to play superman; he needed an older woman who was worldly and tolerant and would let him be himself.) Ursula also let Josef talk, liked to hear his stories, and seemed to respect what he had to say.

By the time the launch reached the landing near the hotel, Cassie was wondering how she could get away and leave them on their own. The answer came when they reached the lobby of the hotel.

There was a message for her. Someone had come to see her, and had recently gone to the coffee lounge across the street. Curious she walked there while Josef completed the booking-in formalities and in the shop, sitting beside a window and beaming with delight, was Peppino.

They kissed; only in greeting but it was exciting all the same. He had received her message in Rome and caught a morning flight to Venice.

'What about Naples and your family?'

'I'm going tomorrow,' he said. 'I wanted to see you first.'

He was still holding her, although at a respectful distance. She leaned forward, her head shaking in disbelief. 'I thought you might ring me. That was all.'

'When I discovered you were in Italy, I had to come and see you.'

'But it must have cost you so much.'

'Do you think I worked so hard all those years just to keep my money in the bank?' He was pleased she made no effort to move away. 'And now that you are here and we are together, there is something most important I must say to you.'

'Oh?'

'I want you to come with me to Naples.'

She turned releasing his grip, and sat at the table. 'I can't. I'm with Josef. You know. Mr Hoffman, Dad's friend.'

'I know Joe.' He couldn't stop smiling. He looked more Italian, she thought, with his fine leather jacket and boots, and a stance that one could mistake for being haughty. He was a handsome man and had grown a thick moustache since she had last seen him. She leaned across the table and touched it. 'It suits you.'

He nodded. 'Couldn't you leave Joe for a few days? It's very important.'

She thought of Ursula. 'I don't know,' she said, reluctant to blurt out what was forming in her mind. 'How long can you stay here?'

'I have to go tomorrow.'

'Why's it so important for me to go to Naples?'

His eyes roamed across her face. 'It's my family. Specifically my mother. She wants me to get married.'

She leaned back. 'Peppino!'

'She has selected a girl for me.' He waved his hands, grappling for an explanation she would comprehend. 'It's the way. She's worried that I'm not married. She writes to me that if I'm not going to take a woman why didn't I become a priest like her brother Giorgio did. I tell her I'm interested in an Australian girl, a lovely, good, very Australian girl, and she says what's wrong with Italian girls? For hundreds of years, our family men have been marrying Italian girls; why do I want to break the tradition? I tell her, if you saw the girl, you'd know.'

Cassie's eyes had never been so wide.'You want to show me to them?'

'I don't want to have to marry someone else.'

'You don't have to marry anyone, Peppino.'

He smiled demurely. 'You don't know my family.'

'They can't make you?'

His shoulders rose in slow motion. 'There are things a son is expected to do. The one good part of all this,' he added, unable to resist the barb, 'is that the girl they have selected is beautiful. Very talented and highly intelligent.'

'How can she be intelligent if she's considering marrying you?'

He shook his head. 'You haven't changed.'

'Would you want me to?'

'No.' He took both her hands. 'I've missed you. How's it been? Have you had a good time?'

'Wonderful. I love Italy.'

He bent forward to bring his eyes to her level. 'Will you come to Naples? I could show you Capri, Amalfi, Positano, Sorrento. And if we have time, Vesuvius and Pompeii. There would not just be my family.'

'I don't want to end up as some sort of exhibit in a competition.'

Eyes pressed tightly to shut out such a possibility, he shook his head. 'I want to be with you. I'd like you to meet my family. And I'd like to be able to say to my mother: "You see. That is the woman I love. Now, I may not be able to marry her because she might reject me as being unworthy but I have to try. I have to make this woman love me too." And then I would say to my mother: "Now that you have seen her, you can understand why I can marry no one else."'

777

A waiter approached and asked if an extra coffee was required. Peppino waved him away.

'That's what you want to do?' Cassie said, touched by the way Peppino had spoken.

'Yes.'

She thought. 'What's Naples like?'

'Magnificent. Decadent. Inspiring. Filthy. I love it. There is no city like it on earth.'

She hesitated. 'Do you really think I should go?'

He fondled his new moustache, as though needing time to contemplate the question.

'Considering all the points for and against, I think the answer is "yes".'

Josef professed to be annoyed and thought of a dozen reasons why she should stay in Venice. But it was a lame argument, advanced because he thought he should object, not because he wanted her to stay.

'You will have a much better time without me,' she said pointedly. 'You and Ursula don't want to be dragging a third body around with you.'

'That's ridiculous.' He cleared his throat. 'How long will you be?'

'Three days.'

'You'll be all right? You'll look after yourself? You won't do anything silly with that young fellow?'

'I'll probably be safer with him than I was with you,' she said, and winked. He blushed, and she added. 'Take care of Ursula, Josef. I think you might have found a really nice woman.'

'Cassie, you're being absurd and presumptuous.'

'I know.'

None of them had been to Venice, so for the rest of the day they behaved as tourists. The four of them walked through St Mark's Square, explored a few narrow streets, posed for photographs on arched bridges and visited a glass works. However, the arrival of Peppino had automatically divided the group into two pairs and as the day progressed, the division became greater. Late in the afternoon Cassie and Peppino took one gondola and Josef and Ursula another. They anticipated following a set course but the boatmen went along different canals. They did not meet again until midnight when the couples, content to be in each other's company, met on a bridge near the hotel. Josef, Cassie noted, was smiling serenely.

The next morning, Cassie and Peppino flew to Naples.

778

F·O·U·R

Having been raised in the parched but pure desolation of Kalinda, Cassie had arrived in Europe as an alien might land on Planet Earth. She, who was used to the whisper of the wind, was greeted by the tumult of crowds. She, who knew well only one town – William Creek, population eighteen – had to contend with cities of millions. She, who came from a place where time was measured by the seasons, was brushed aside by people desperate to save minutes. Instead of the eerie quiet of a bush track, she was confronted by paved roads filled with chaotic traffic. Streams of cars, buses, bicycles, and anything with wheels and a horn to blare or a bell to ring were all propelled, it seemed, by neurotics disputing a strip of territory or striving to win a fraction of time at someone else's expense.

In her weeks in Europe, she had come to anticipate the grandeur of historic cities, to be awed by the remnants of past civilizations and to note the emphasis of human achievement rather than the simple glory of nature. She had become used to the jostle of crowds, the menace of pickpockets, the threat of speeding cars and scooters (which came at you from the wrong side of the road), the co-existence of magnificence and decadence, the crowded buildings, the narrow streets, the noise. But nothing had prepared her for Naples.

They landed within sight of Vesuvius. At least, Peppino said it was close. Smog lacquered the sky, rendering opaque all scenery beyond a few buildings that skirted the airport, but he pointed to a broad smear that ran below the thickest of the silvery sheen and announced that that was the base of the great volcano.

They caught a bus to the city. The vehicle, laden with businessmen immersed in newspapers, first drove past farms, then blocks of tall apartments patched with lines of washing, and finally descended towards the bay. The streets narrowed and curved through rows of buildings stained with the neglect of ages. Walls reverberated to the stuttering bark of motor scooters and the dull boom of diesel engines. Exhaust fumes blued the air.

They passed garbage heaped against the sides of buildings and stacked in neat piles in the middle of the road. Many times they halted, locked in a smoking, rumbling jam of endless proportions. Drivers leaned on their horns, cursed those ahead and grinned at each other. Scooters with two, three or four on board – never one – curled through impossible gaps, bees among a swarm of stalled locusts.

The businessmen on board spared Naples an occasional glance but, knowing what to expect, stayed with their newspapers. It was already warm. Some fanned themselves.

Their journey lurched from one unwelcomed halt to the next. Through one dark and narrow street, the tyres of the bus shuddered on rough paving. Cassie looked up. She saw flowers in a window and equally colourful washing hanging from the level above that. Children played on the footpath. Suddenly the road widened and they were surrounded by majestic buildings, fronted by vast columns and surmounted by statues.

Two small motor cycles raced past, each with a girl on the back, each billowing smoke, each performing a continuous sequence of spectacular avoidances, each inspiring a ripple of protesting horns.

The bus came to the bay and turned along a broad promenade. On one side, Cassie saw stately buildings, palm trees, gardens; on the other, barrowmen selling food, wharves, flags, yachts and ferries bearing signs that read Capri and Sorrento. There were little boats with people fishing and on a distant hill, mansions and tall trees and gardens bursting with exotic colour.

Peppino had been silent. 'It is a city of contrasts.' He turned to Cassie with his face a mixture of sadness and pride. 'It takes time to appreciate, much longer to understand.'

They had been stopped at street lights. Now the signals changed, and the movement of traffic resumed with the ferocity of a Grand Prix start.

'It's so noisy.' Cassie had to shout to be heard. 'And crazy.'

'Yes. I've missed it.'

They caught a taxi from the city. Only in the taxi did Peppino confess he was unsure of the welcome they would receive from his father. When Cassie became apprehensive, he held her hand and assured her that Alfonso Portelli could be the warmest and most loving parent in the world. However – and he fluttered his eyelids to make her believe it was a minor qualification – he was very traditional, a trifle autocratic, believed that no one else's opinion deserved to share the same room as his, and had a military bearing which could intimidate strangers.

'He sounds delightful,' Cassie said nervously. 'If you'd told me this yesterday, I wouldn't have got on the plane.'

'I know.' His smile said he had been extraordinarily clever. 'One thing you must not do is discuss the war.'

'Why?'

Alfonso Portelli, he explained, had been a officer in the Italian Army. He had fought in North Africa, been captured by the British and spent three years in a prisoner-of-war camp in Canada. According to Peppino, there were two consequences of his father's incarceration. He was good at digging potatoes (he laughed when he said this) and he spoke a little English.

'But why shouldn't I mention the war?'

'Because he is a proud man. He was a good officer – he was decorated for bravery early in the war – and he is ashamed that battles were being fought and won while he was forced to grow vegetables in Canada.'

The Portelli family lived in an apartment in the hills to the north-east of Naples. It was a big apartment, occupying one floor of a four-storey building, and it had a long balcony with views from Vesuvius to the Sorrento Peninsula. That was on clear days, which were becoming increasingly rare. On the day that Peppino returned home, the clear view was of the rooftops of buildings down the lower slopes of the hill. The city was seen as through a veil. The bay dissolved into a glowing haze of factory smoke and exhaust gases. There was no trace of the world's most famous volcano or of the peninsula that pointed its tapering mountains towards the fabled Isle of Capri.

Peppino's father was a tall, lean man who still maintained the bearing of a military officer despite having run a restaurant for sixteen years. Alfonso Portelli greeted his son formally, almost resentfully, Cassie thought, and she wondered how much of that sentiment was due to her presence. The family had received little warning of her visit and she was now experiencing a prickling sensation of being unwelcome. Not that they were discourteous. They were polite, strangers with impeccable manners compelled by breeding and tradition to perform in a certain way, but they were obviously ruffled by her presence.

Having shaken his son's hand, the father guided Peppino towards his mother and turned his attention to Cassie. 'How do you do?' he said, in an English flawed by lack of practice. And that was all; no smile, no more stumbling words of greeting, no gushing torrent of warm Italian. He waited in silence for his wife to finish weeping against her son's cheek before introducing Cassie. Marisella Portelli was short; stout but not fat, and greyer than her husband. She had been a good-looking woman, Cassie decided, although her face was now a ruin of worry lines. Cassie accepted her proffered hand and smiled, but the woman looked away, embarrassed by tears which still ran down her face. She had been much more interested in examining Cassie when they entered the apartment; at that time, Signora Portelli, stationed at a respectable distance behind her husband, had not taken her eyes off the girl her son had brought from Vehice.

The reason for such intense interest and the reason for the cold greeting was revealed when Peppino and Cassie reached the balcony. More than thirty people were assembled there. A party had been organized, to surprise the returning son. It was then that Cassie discovered there were, in fact, two guests of honour – Peppino and a dark-haired girl of stunningly good looks. Her name was Anna. She was the girl chosen by the parents as a suitable wife for their eldest son.

A glass of wine in his hand, Peppino took Cassie to a vacant space at the edge of the balcony. 'I am sorry,' he said. 'I did not know that there would be a party.'

A man walked past and slapped Peppino on the back. He said something. Peppino responded and they both laughed.

'I thought only my family would be here,' he continued, when the man had gone. 'I had no idea there would be so many people.'

'They seem happy to see you.'

'I hardly remember most of them. It's been so long since I was in Naples.'

At the far end of the balcony stood Anna. She was encircled by older people, but a gap in the throng allowed her to see Peppino. She smiled shyly.

'She's very beautiful,' Cassie said.

His lips pouted in a noncommittal way. 'I find it very embarrassing. It's like someone bringing a horse out of a stable and saying: "Here, what do you think of this one? It has a nice appearance and a very good pedigree. If it is not fast enough for racing, you can always use it for breeding."'

'Peppino, that's awful.'

'Not as awful as you think. My mother has already told me that boys are dominant in her family. She is the only daughter in a brood of six, so she is likely to have sons, not daughters.'

'That's good?'

'Oh, that's very good.' He sipped wine to extinguish some of the fire within him.

She drank some wine too, and admired the view.

782

'The air over Naples has become very dirty,' he said.

'It wasn't like this before?'

'During the war, I used to stand out here and look at the ships in the harbour. There were air raids. They were colourful and exciting. The view was very clear from here. And you could always see Vesuvius. Its peak is about there.' He pointed into the smog. 'It's very wide and for much of the year, there's snow on top. It erupted once just before the war ended. That was most spectacular. At night, all the clouds were bright orange from the reflected light and I remember watching from here with my mother. Her face was glowing from so much light in the sky. There was a great tower of flame shooting in the air and molten lava on the rim of the mountain. I can still remember the way my mother held me. She was frightened. To me, it was just a big display of fireworks but she knew what could happen. She imagined we were to become a second Pompeii.'

The air was warm and dense with the fragrance of flowers and the pungent smell of diesel smoke. The aromas drifted past in confusing waves.

'Have you had a chance to talk to your father?'

'Yes. He said I should not have brought you here.'

She looked down. He leaned on the balcony and squinted into the haze.

'And what did you say?'

'That he should not have invited Anna. I said I wanted only to see my family, not a selection committee. He was not amused.'

'I don't think I should stay.'

He turned, leaving one elbow on the wide marble edge. 'If you leave, it will mean we are surrendering to them and their old-fashioned ways.'

'But Peppino, I feel so out of place. I don't know anyone, I don't speak the same language, and I feel as though everyone resents me being here.'

'No. Only my parents feel resentment and they do not resent you. They are annoyed at me. They feel I am trying to thwart their well laid-out plans. And they are quite right. I am not going to let them tell me whom I should marry. No, we will meet people and smile. We will have lunch. And then we will say goodbye to everyone and you and I will go to Naples and I will show you the city.'

'You can't leave all these people.'

'They are only here for lunch.'

'Well then, you can't leave your family.'

'I will see them tonight.'

'Where will I stay tonight?'

'Here of course.'

'There's no room.'

'We have plenty of room.' He waved his arm at the crowd. 'Things are not always this busy.'

'But what about Anna?'

He brought his face close to hers. 'She can go home like the other guests. Now stop complaining and have a good time. This is a party and I can promise you one thing. You will enjoy the food. My mother is an excellent cook. We are having pasta with clams. Do you like clams?'

Cassie was reeling from the pace of Peppino's conversation. 'I've never had them.'

His face became elongated in distress for someone so deprived. 'They are shellfish. The clams from around Naples are the best in the world. You will love them. My mother's spaghetti con vongole is something you will not forget.' With a flourish, he kissed the tips of his fingers. 'Now come, and meet some people.'

Peppino stayed gallantly by her side, introducing her and interpreting when possible, until they came to a couple who spoke English. He was a doctor, his wife a journalist. They shook hands. Cassie was conscious of the woman's smooth, cool hands; hers seemed so rough and hot by comparison. The couple had spent a year in America. He was now a heart specialist; she wrote about fashion for a Neapolitan newspaper. At that stage in the conversation, Peppino was dragged to one side by a brother. Waving helplessly, he left Cassie in their care.

'So you live in the Australian outlands,' the doctor said.

'Outlands?' Cassie was puzzled.

'You have the wrong word,' his wife suggested. 'It is not outlands but it is out-something.'

'Outback?'

'Yes,' he said. 'I have been mystified by the expression. What does it mean?'

Cassie tried to explain. She ended by saying: 'It means out the back of beyond.'

'You live out the back of beyond?'

'Yes. Near Lake Eyre in South Australia.'

His face settled into an expression that suggested either the explanation made sense or he was too polite to query it.

His wife was more frank. 'I do not understand. You live at the back of beyond. Beyond?' She repeated the word in Italian and her husband nodded. Yes, that was the word. 'Is there such a place?'

784

Cassie was enjoying the exchange, but wishing she could speak Italian. It seemed wrong that, in Italy, Italians had to speak English so that someone visiting their country could have a pleasant conversation.

'No,' she said. 'There is no town called Beyond. It is an expression.' She waited for them to confirm their understanding. 'We say something is back of beyond when we mean it is way beyond where most people live.'

'Ah, I understand,' he said, and retreated into confusion.

His wife said, 'And you live out the back of that?'

'Yes.'

'How far?'

'Way out.'

'So the outback is further out than the back of beyond?'

'No,' Cassie said, 'the outback is the back of beyond. Once you travel beyond beyond, you're in the outback.'

The doctor turned to the journalist. 'Well, you're the one who is good with words. Explain that to me.' His wife lifted her hands in defeat.

'I wish I could speak Italian,' Cassie said. 'Then I could explain.'

'No,' the woman said laughing. 'There is absolutely no way of explaining what you have said in Italian.'

Peppino returned briefly. 'How are you all getting on?'

'Famously,' the doctor said. 'Your visitor had given us a fascinating lesson on colloquial Australian terms.'

'Oh,' said Peppino. 'And confused you?'

'Thoroughly.'

'Good. She always confused me.' He moved closer to Cassie. 'Are you all right?'

'Fine. We're having a nice talk.'

'I'll be back.' He waved and left. Cassie saw Alfonso Portelli take Peppino by the elbow and guide him towards Anna.

The couple beamed the universal expressions of persons prepared to resume a conversation. 'We won't go into where you live again,' the doctor said, 'but I believe you are the daughter of a good friend of Giuseppe's.'

'Yes. My father's known him for many years. Since ...' She almost said Peppino. '... since Giuseppe first came to Australia.'

'His parents did not want him to go.'

'Really?'

'Oh, they were most upset.'

'He's done very well. Giuseppe operates a large transport company.'

'And what does your father do?'

'He raises sheep and cattle.'

'A farmer.'

The wife corrected him. 'More like a rancher, probably.'

'Yes. We have lots of land.'

'And you have been travelling through Europe?' the woman asked.

'Yes.'

'On your own?'

'No, with a friend.'

'Ah. The friend has gone home.'

'No. I'll be going back to Venice in a few days.'

'I see. You'll rejoin her there.' Cassie let that pass without correction. 'So this is merely a brief diversion to see the poor underdeveloped south of Italy?' The woman smiled with an intense sweetness.

'Well, to see Naples.'

'And what do you think?'

'I've just arrived.'

They laughed. All new arrivals were stunned by first impressions.

Peppino's younger sister came with bottles of wine and refilled their glasses. The doctor lowered his head to intercept his overfilled glass. 'And you and Giuseppe met at the airport? By chance perhaps?'

Alarm bells began to ring within Cassie but the game had become too confusing for anything but the truth. 'No, we met up in Venice.'

'Oh.' They glanced at each other and he continued. 'He flew from Australia to Venice?'

'He landed at Rome.'

'And came to see you?' she said.

'Yes.' Cassie was aware that they were both looking towards Anna.

'Giuseppe and your father must be very close friends,' the doctor said.

'Yes.' From the other side of the balcony, the sound of Peppino's laughter came to her.

'I see the two principals are together,' the woman said.

'I beg your pardon?'

'Giuseppe and Anna.' She made sure Cassie was looking. 'Anna Bertaggia. The one talking to Giuseppe. The party is partly for her, to celebrate her performance last week.'

'What did she do?'

'Played the piano. It was her first public performance.'

786

'As a featured soloist,' her husband added. 'She is a player of exceptional promise.'

'And very pretty. How old is she?' Cassie hoped her question sounded like the curiosity of a music lover, not of a rival.

The woman referred to her husband. 'About twenty?'

'Possibly twenty-one. I'm not sure. I'm not good at judging women's ages.' Cassie knew he was making comparisons and, for the first time in her life, she felt a twinge of inferiority. She was the only person on the balcony who could not speak Italian, her manners lacked the polish of these worldly people, her hands were roughened by years of hard work, she was not as pretty as the doll-like Anna and now there was a new factor, one she had never before considered: she was too old.

F·I·V·E

In the afternoon, Peppino took Cassie to the city, but after an hour spent admiring statues and dodging swarms of smoking Lambrettas and tiny Fiats, they walked to a wharf and caught a ferry to Sorrento. Peppino seemed to rejoice in the sights, sounds and smells of his native city. The reason for the ferry ride he said, as Cassie recovered from a coughing bout caused by inhaling a burst of diesel fumes, was to see Naples from its famous bay. That was the best way to appreciate the port, the city and the majestic setting.

It was true. As they sat on the rear deck of the ferry, the clamour faded and the palm trees and tall buildings shrank in size and the claw of hills that grasped Naples grew wider and more prominent. They talked, and Peppino pointed out landmarks before they disappeared behind the shroud spun by the city itself.

They got off the ferry at Sorrento. They walked for a while. It was warm, so they found an outdoor café with tables sheltered by trees. Cassie wanted ice cream. She ordered, Peppino having coached her in what to say.

'*Due gelati, per favore,*' she said and Peppino smiled proudly.

The waiter bombarded Cassie with a torrent of words. Peppino answered.

'What did I say wrong?' she asked, when the waiter had gone.

'Nothing. Your Italian was perfect. He asked what flavours we wanted.'

Two small boys on bicycles rode along the footpath. They weaved between the tables.

'Just practising for when they're old enough to own motor bikes,' Peppino said, and she watched them ride away, racing each other.

'Was my Italian really good?'

'First class.'

'Just like an Italian?'

He wobbled one hand, seeking the correct level of compliment. 'Maybe with a slight English accent.'

'An English accent?'

'Well, the sort of accent you expect in people who speak English.'

'We have accents?'

'Very definitely.'

She brushed her chin. 'I'd never thought of that.'

He smiled, enjoying being with her in his country.

'Peppino, why don't you make fun of the way I speak Italian ... or try to?'

He seemed genuinely perplexed. 'But why? What you said then was very good.'

'But you told me what to say.'

'Why not?'

'I can remember when you first used to come out to Kalinda. I gave you a terrible time. You-a know-a what-a I mean-a, eh?'

He grinned. 'That was fun.'

'I still made it hard for you.'

'No. I had to learn. You were a big help.'

'I did nothing but tease you.'

'That helped. It made me aware of what I was doing wrong.'

The waiter brought two glass bowls piled high with multi-coloured ice-cream. She sat back, astonished by the size of the helping. He raised his spoon, posed but waiting for her to start.

'Why don't you get your own back now?' she said.

He lowered the spoon. 'All I want to do is eat this. This is the one thing I've missed.' She still waited. 'Because I don't want to,' he said. 'There is no point. That was a long time ago, and you did not mean to hurt.'

'I must have seemed very cruel to you.'

'No.'

'Just a silly little girl?'

'Not even that. You did not know ... It was meant kindly. I knew that.'

'It's only since I've been over here that I'm beginning to realize what it must have been like for you. Joe does most of our talking, and he's good. He speaks German, of course.'

'Of course. He still remembers it?'

'Oh he's marvellous. But when we were in Germany, I couldn't follow what was going on. It was like being deaf.'

He nodded sympathetically.

'You must have been very brave, to have come out on your own, not speaking any English, and then heading off into the bush like you did. And you're such a cultured person. I don't think I really appreciated that till I came here.'

'We do tend to judge people by the way they talk, don't we? We humans have a nasty habit of judging others by their inadequacies, rather than by their achievements.'

She agreed. 'Anyhow, I'm sorry.'

'What for?'

'Giving you such a hard time, even if it was only in fun. I was pretty stupid.'

'We will both be stupid if we don't eat our ice cream.' Once more he lifted the spoon. 'May we start? It is not good when it melts.'

Halfway through her plate, she paused. 'Will you teach me to speak Italian?'

'Certainly.'

'Is it difficult?'

'To speak properly, yes. To speak badly, no.'

'I would probably speak it badly.'

'That's all right. Most of us speak it badly. They say only the people of Florence speak Italian properly.'

'Who says that?'

'The people of Florence.'

She laughed and sprayed him with slivers of chocolate *gelato*. She reached across to wipe his shirt. He took her hand. 'Cassandra, I would like to teach you to speak my language. Then we could come back together, many times, and we could share in so much more.'

She allowed her hand to stay against his chest. 'I think I'd like that.'

His face grew serious. 'I have a question I must ask.'

She waited, intrigued by his sudden change of mood.

'It is about the American, Michel Klemansky.' He coughed discreetly. 'Do you still think about him?'

'Yes.' She reached across the table. 'But it's different now.'

He nodded a little too vigorously, determined to show that the answer satisfied him. He forced a smile.

'Peppino, there was nothing between us.'

'Of course not.' He played with his spoon. 'But you were very upset. I thought, maybe . . .'

She followed his lead and picked up her spoon. 'I was upset because it was a horrible accident and because, well, he'd said some things to me just before he was killed that made me think . . . well, made me feel close to him. He was a strange man – I know that now – but there was a good side, a very human side to him. I felt a bond with him on that morning.' Her spoon did a lap of the empty dish.

'Did you like him?' Peppino dared not look up.

'Yes. And I think he liked me.'

'He was the sort of man who would like many women.'

'Of course. I know that. He tried to make love to me.'

Peppino breathed deeply.

'I didn't let him.' She laughed. 'Come on, you've probably tried to make love to other women.' She gripped his arm and shook it gently, teasing him. 'You must have, being a red-blooded Neapolitan.'

He said nothing and seemed to slide within himself.

'Peppino, I did not let him make love to me.' She shook his arm again and he nodded but did not look up. 'All right, let me tell you. On that last morning he showed me another side of his character. He was very human, even vulnerable, and I was touched. He told me he was frightened. He told me he hadn't slept all night. I felt sorry for him and close to him that morning because he told me things he didn't tell other people.'

'Like a priest,' he said, still not looking at her, 'hearing confession.'

'Maybe. I don't know. What he told me was that of all the women he had known, none really cared for him. They liked his money and the glamorous life he led, but they didn't show any concern for him.'

'And he thought you did?'

'He said so. Yes.'

'And did you?'

'Yes.' She lowered her face to meet his eyes. 'Peppino, I didn't love him. I was concerned for him. I was shocked by his death and for a while I felt guilty because I thought I could have stopped him; you know, influenced him to wait until Dr Rotondo considered the car was ready.'

He shook his head sadly. 'You could not. No one could have stopped him'

'I know that now. Peppino, I might have been a bit dazzled by him, and I certainly felt a bond between us on that last day, but that was all. I wasn't in love with the man.'

Peppino was staring out across the bay. 'In many ways he was a very brave man. To be frightened of something and still go ahead and do it requires a special kind of courage.'

'Yes.' She smiled, pleased they agreed.

'And his ghost is not around to haunt us?'

'No.' She leaned closer. 'Believe me Peppino.'

He shuffled his seat until he was alongside her. He put his arm around her shoulders. 'Why am I talking about these things when it is such a beautiful day, heh?'

They returned to the Portelli apartment at dusk. A few guests were still there. They included Anna and her parents.

'They have been invited to dinner,' Peppino told Cassie, waggling his eyebrows dramatically. 'My parents do not give up easily.'

She took him to one side. 'Peppino, this is all very difficult but please remember I haven't said I'm going to marry you.'

'I know.'

'Well, there are times I feel I'm being pushed.'

He raised both hands. 'No pushing. but there are three decisions to be made in this affair. Yours is one, and that has still to be made. You are undecided, is that correct?'

'Yes.'

'That's OK. But the other two decisions are mine, and they have been made.'

'Two?'

'Yes. The first was that I wanted to marry you. I decided that a long time ago.'

Her smiled softened. 'And the second?'

'The second is that I do not want to marry Anna Bertaggia, even if you will not have me.'

'She's very pretty.'

'Not as pretty as you.'

'Don't be silly and don't try to butter me up. She's much better looking. I know that.'

'I prefer your looks.'

'She's very talented. She plays the piano. She gives concerts.'
'So?'

'Well, I can't play the piano.'

'You can ride a camel and crack a whip. She can't do that.'
'Be serious.'

'I am. If I want music in the house, I can put on a record. Maybe one of hers, if she ever makes a record.'

'Peppino, she's beautiful, she's probably very clever and she's Italian.'

'If you like her so much, we can adopt her.'

She let her hands dangle by her sides. 'What am I going to do with you?'

'Marry me.'

'So we can go camel riding and whip cracking?'

'Why not? With you, it would be fun.'

'I don't know what to say.'

'The word in Italian is "*si*".' He took her hand. 'Why don't we go and talk to Anna?'

'What about?'

'Just small talk. I promise I won't mention adoption.' He led her to the couch where Anna was sitting. 'Hi,' he said, 'do you speak English?'

She shook her head, then smiled at Cassie, with the helpless expression common between people who cannot communicate. Peppino spoke to her briefly in Italian, then turned to Cassie. 'Do you mind if we talk for just a few minutes?'

'No, of course not.'

He spoke for ten minutes. Gradually, Anna's smile faded and she listened with a growing intensity. Occasionally, she glanced at Casssie. When he had finished, she reached across and shook Cassie's hand.

'*Grazie,*' Cassie said, using one of her few Italian words. 'And what was that for?' The three of them sat on the couch. Anna listened with apparent interest.

'I told her about my work, what the country is like where I work and where my trucks operate, and I told her about Kalinda. I mentioned your father, and I told her what you did on the property.'

'Did you say I could ride a camel and crack a whip?'

'No. Would you like me to tell her?' He smiled and Cassie smiled and, warmed by the exchange, Anna smiled too.

'Was that all?' Cassie asked.

'Well, it was a very long story which I made as brief as possible.'

'Did you say anything about us?'

Anna had fixed her huge eyes on him. 'Yes. I said we were very good friends and that if I ever did marry, it would probably be to an Australian girl. Someone like you.'

'Someone like me?'

'That's roughly what I said. It's a phrase that's extremely difficult to translate.'

'Why did she shake my hand?'

'She may have misunderstood me.'

'And thought you said you were definitely going to marry me?'

His smile almost divided his face. 'Like I said, Italian is a very difficult language to be precise in.'

'Unless you come from Florence?'

'Precisely.'

She returned Anna's sweet look of sympathy and then gave Peppino a much sharper look. 'When I learn Italian, you won't be able to lie to me.'

He leaned back on the couch. 'I like what you're implying.'

* * *

During the evening, Peppino had a long conversation with his parents. It ended with his mother retiring temporarily to her bedroom. Peppino then talked to his father for some time before rejoining Cassie. He seemed distressed.

'What's wrong?' she asked.

'Ridiculous, emotional Italian families.' He sat with her, his mouth working as though chewing something. 'Would you believe that my mother thought I was coming back to live here permanently? She said, "Well, you've been in Australia and made some money. Now come home where you belong." And I said I belong in Australia. "I'm a naturalized citizen of Australia." And she said "Once an Italian always an Italian." Would you believe that? My mother and father too, although he didn't say as much, always thought I was coming back. I told them I'll come back to see them as often as I can. I told them that while I may be an Italian in spirit, I'm an Australian in fact, I said they can come and see me and I can come and see them but that they'd better accept the fact that I live in Australia, I intend to stay there, and I'm not coming back home. Not to live, anyhow.'

'The poor things,' she said. 'They could always come and stay with us.'

'Sure. I told them that.' It was some time before he realized what she had said.

'I meant to say "with you".'

He lifted his hands. 'Of course.' But the dismal expression had gone.

Another guest who stayed for dinner was Peppino's cousin, Gino Scarlatti. He was a dentist who was wealthy enough to own two cars. Peppino borrowed the smaller and older model, and next day took Cassie out in the car.

They drove through the city, blowing the squeaky horn constantly, darting with the sudden rushes of cars and scooters, making impossible passing manoeuvres, judging clearances to the nearest centimetre, filling whatever space was free and disputing what was not and generally behaving so irresponsibly that they blended in perfectly with the normal traffic. It was, Cassie said, like being in the middle of a cattle rush, only more fun.

Once clear of the city, they took the road to Pompeii. For two hours they walked the pavements of the excavated Roman city. It was an eerie experience for Cassie. To her, an old building was the original homestead her father had built, and here was a city which had been hidden under the ashes of a volcanic eruption for almost seventeen hundred years. She asked Peppino to tell her what had happened. He bought her a booklet.

'This is my first time here too,' he said, so they read the book and explored Pompeii together.

For lunch they ate rolls filled with prosciutto and drank mineral water. They walked some more, ate ice cream and then drove on to Salerno. There, Peppino turned west on the road to Amalfi. It was a narrow strip that curved through every fold in the hills forming the northern coast of the Gulf of Salerno. The scenery was breathtaking. Whitewashed buildings clung to clifftops or peppered the slopes. The lower hillsides were terraced into orchards and vineyards. Where there was space at the foot of a valley or a shore where boats could be beached, there was a village. The sea was a ceramic blue ruffled only by the passage of fishing boats.

Because the road was so narrow and twisting, and because every bend required a warning toot on the horn and produced a squeal of tyres, the journey to Amalfi was protracted and noisy but exciting. Several times they had to slow, to squeeze past oncoming vehicles. When they reached Amalfi they were glad to park the car near the harbour and walk through the town. They inspected the statue to the man who invented the compass, climbed the steps to the chequered cathedral where the remains of Saint Andrew were buried and strolled through shops glittering with colourful plates and jugs. They walked along the breakwater to look at the moored yachts and then returned to the car.

They drove to Positano and walked down to the sea because the town's roads were too narrow for cars. They had dinner at a restaurant on the beach and then drove across the peninsula to Sorrento and back around the bay to Naples.

It was after eleven when they reached the Portelli's apartment.

'I had no idea Italy was so beautiful,' Cassie said.

'Or that we built our roads like serpents.' He let his hand wiggle towards her. She caught it and held it.

'Thank you for a lovely day.'

'Tomorrow we go to Capri.'

'And then I have to go back.'

'I have the phone number of your hotel in Venice. I could call Joe and tell him you're staying.'

'No. I have to go.' She drew a long, deep breath. 'Peppino. I've been thinking. When everything's so beautiful here, when your family's here, when your food's so good, why do you live in Australia?'

'Because I like it.'

'But do you prefer it?'

'Yes.' He shrugged. 'I love Italy. I love Naples. I love the area around Naples. But I want to live in Australia.'

'Why?'

'Many things.' His head moved like a hound searching for scent. 'Opportunity. That's the big thing. There is more opportunity, more chance for a person like myself to make his fortune, to lead a good life. Italy is a beautiful country but it is old, tired and crowded. It is a land of the past. Where I have chosen to live is a land of the future.'

'But will you stay? After what I've seen today, I can understand much better what your parents were saying. I think if I'd been born here, I'd want to come back.'

'That's because it's all new to you.'

'It's so full of history. And it's such a beautiful place. The sea today was just gorgeous.'

He laughed. 'You are from the outback. The sea is a revelation to you, no matter where you find it. And remember, Cassandra, I have been taking you to the best places. There are many parts of this country and certainly of Naples you would not want to see.'

She was quiet for a few moments. 'I suppose what I'm saying Peppino is this: are you likely to change your mind?'

'Ah,' he said, understanding causing his eyes to sparkle. 'You are saying: "Will he persuade me to marry him, take me to his big new house in Adelaide, and then sell the lot and move back to Naples, where we will be living in the spare bedroom of his parents' apartment." Is that it?'

'Something like that.'

'My dear Cassandra.' He took both her hands. 'I solemnly swear...'

She giggled. 'Next thing you'll be on your knees.'

He knelt. 'I swear as an Australian citizen that I will not vamoose, nick off, or otherwise leave the country except on holidays.'

'So help you God.'

'Yes. Exactly.' He stood up. 'We will come back regularly. Maybe once a year, if business is good.'

'And if it's not?'

'Twice a year. I don't want to be around if things are going badly.' He grew serious again. 'I made my decision a long time ago. Nothing has happened to change my mind. Now let me ask you a question. Would you want to live in Italy?'

'I hadn't thought about it.'

'Think about it.' He looked at his watch. 'You've got a minute.'

'Peppino, I've only been in the country a few days.'

'That's enough to form an opinion.'

796

'Well, I don't know. I like it. I'm stunned by it. The people seem nice.'

He lowered his watch. 'Before you give your answer, I should warn you that if you want to live here you'll have to marry someone else. I'm staying in Australia.'

'You're a nut.' Playfully, she raised her left fist.

'That's the dreaded Jimmy Kettle left hook you're about to throw, is it?'

'That's it.' She laughed and lowered her arm. 'I've had such a wonderful time, Peppino.'

He held out his hands and she took them. 'So have I. Tell me Cassandra, and this is very serious, have you learned to like me a little more in the last few days?'

Her reply was so delayed he had time to smile nervously, change to a serious expression and then smile again. 'Yes,' she said softly. 'I have. Maybe more than a little. I've also discovered that there's another Giuseppe Portelli and I like him too. Very much.'

Despite the late hour Cassie wrote a letter to Adam before going to bed that night.

Dear Dad,

I think I'm in love. Before you start getting all upset and thinking that I've met up with some ritzy Contentinal playboy out to marry into the Ross millions, let me calm you down by saying it is someone you know and, I think, respect. It's Peppino. Hey now, how that's for a surprise?

As you probably know, Peppino is over here to visit his family in Naples. He came up to Venice to see Josef and myself, which was a real surprise. Well, I have to confess he came to see me, but Josef was there too. By the way, Josef, who is very well thank you, seems to have found himself a lady friend!!! She is a very glamorous German lady whose family has been in the wine business for simply hundreds of years. But back to Peppino.

He persuaded me to come down to Naples and see the south of Italy, which wasn't on our original schedule. He also wanted me to meet his family and some of his friends. I didn't want to leave Josef on his own but he's with Ursula (that's her name) and I think being alone and having me out of the way was just what he wanted.

Anyhow, Josef is in Venice with Ursula and I'm in Naples, staying with Peppino's family. They are nice, I think, but it's hard to tell because they don't speak English. It's really funny. They wanted him to marry this Italian girl – a pretty young thing who

797

plays the piano and seems nice although I can't tell because I can't talk to her. They had a surprise party for Peppino the day we arrived. Talk about embarrassing. They had invited this girl along, so Peppino could give her the once-over. Just like the stud bull sales only the other way around, if you know what I mean. Peppino got stuck into his parents and told them he would marry the girl he wanted, not the one they wanted and it all got pretty tense but now things seem to have calmed down. He can't be pushed around, I'll say that for our boy.

We've had a couple of days together. We've driven through Naples (more exciting than driving through William Creek, believe me) and been to see some lovely places on the sea, like Sorrento and Amalfi. Today we walked through Pompeii, which was like stepping back two thousand years. I'll tell you about it when I get home.

Being with Peppino has been really good because it's given me the chance to see him in his original environment and to understand why he's like he is. He speaks beautiful Italian (I think) and must be witty because he makes people laugh a lot. He's also very kind and helpful to me. He's taught me a few words in Italian and never laughs at me (remember me? I feel so ashamed now of the way I used to poke fun at his English).

What I'm saying, Dad, is I've seen Peppino in a different light. He makes more sense to me now – if that makes sense to you! – because I can see that he's a man from two cultures. He's part sophisticated Italian, part Australian bushie. He's clever, resourceful, determined and considerate. Having come to Italy and seen Naples, I feel I'm now much closer to understanding and appreciating him than I could ever have done just by staying home.

As I said, I think I'm in love but I haven't said anything to him yet. He still says he wants to marry me, which, I must confess, I now find a very interesting thought. However, I haven't quite decided but I wanted to write and warn you so that if I come home all starry-eyed and dreamy, you'll know what's happened.

Could you bear the thought of me living in Adelaide?

Don't you dare show this letter to anyone, but please give my love to Nina and Danny and everyone at Kalinda. Tell Nina she was right. I should have come to Europe a hundred years ago.

I've got gifts for everyone except Patrick and I'll get something for him in Rome before we catch the plane home. How is the little twerp? Enjoying school? I hope they knock some sense into him. If you happen to see him, give him my love and pull his ear

for me. Hey, do you miss me telling you how to run the place? I miss you too.
    Love and *arrivederci,*
    Cassie

The next morning they caught the ferry to Capri. They took a boat ride to the Blue Grotto but spent most of their time browsing around the town or following paths along the clifftops. In the late afternoon, they caught the ferry back to Naples. The air was clearer and, for the first time, they saw Vesuvius. Taking the sighting as an omen, Peppino reached into his pocket and produced a small box. He pressed it into Cassie's hand.
    'What is it?'
    'Something I've had for a little while,' he said.
    She saw the flash of diamonds. 'Is it what I think it is?'
    He made a feeble attempt at humour. 'It's not a cabbage.' His hands shook.
    'It's a ring?'
    'Yes.' They touched heads.
    In a hushed voice, she said, 'If I put it on, does it mean we're engaged?'
    'It means you have accepted my proposal and made me the happiest man on earth.'
    'You're on a boat,' she pointed out.
    'Well then, the happiest man on land or sea.'
    She sat with her head against him, staring at the ring. 'It is beautiful, Peppino. I'm overwhelmed.'
    'Too overwhelmed to take it out of the box?'
    She kissed his cheek. 'Yes. Why don't you put it on my finger for me?'

Even the parents mellowed that night, if not into a state of joy, then certainly into a warm contentment that their eldest son was so happy. Peppino had a long talk to his father and mother. Both kissed Cassie. The mother wept.
    'Now my mother can stop worrying that I'd let the chance go by to become a priest,' Peppino said. 'Do you know why she started to cry?'
    'I thought she must have been sad at losing you.'
    'She cried when I said we'd be married in Australia. She had visions of a big wedding in Naples.' He looked at her with sudden concern. 'That's all right by you, isn't it?'
    She laughed. 'I hadn't thought about it.'
    'It would be a disaster here. An expensive disaster. There would

799

be a thousand guests. You would know half a dozen people and I would have forgotten the rest. No, it will be in Australia.'

'I'm glad we decided.'

He looked at her uncertainly, trying to lift the remark by its fine edge and put it in its place. Then his face became sad. 'Do you have to go to Venice tomorrow?'

'Joe's expecting me. We have bookings. I'd love to stay Peppino, really, but I can't. He's gone to so much trouble organizing things.'

The telephone rang. Peppino's younger sister answered, then called to Peppino, saying there was a man speaking English on the line. A few moments later, Peppino returned for Cassie.

'It's Josef,' he said. 'Your guardian.'

'He is not my guardian,' she muttered and Peppino ducked out of the way.

'Hi,' Josef shouted, his voice tinny over the long distance. 'How's Naples?'

'Fine. How's Venice?'

'Fine.'

'How have you been?'

'Good. And you?'

'Oh fine. How's Ursula? Still there?'

'Oh sure. She's well.'

Peppino stood beside Cassie trying to follow the conversation.

Both spoke at once and then there was a pause. 'I've had a lot of trouble getting through,' Josef said. 'I booked the call over an hour ago.'

'Oh. How did you find the number?'

'Peppino gave it to me.'

'Oh.' She looked at Peppino and smiled. 'Is there anything wrong?'

'No. Everything's fine. Great. Couldn't be better.'

'Are you and Ursula hitting it off?'

'You could say that.'

'Oh, that sounds interesting.'

'Cassie.' He stretched out the name in a way that meant he was about to ask her a great favour. 'How much do you want to see Venice? What I mean is, you've seen some of it. Do you want to see more?'

'Well, I don't know.' Peppino kissed her ear and raised his eyebrows, wondering what it was she didn't know.

'And Florence. I was wondering how important that was to you.'

'Josef, what are you trying to ask me?'

'Well, I was wondering if we could meet up in Rome in about two weeks' time.' There was a long hesitation. 'We have to catch the plane then.'

'I know.'

'Is it a problem? Could you go somewhere, or do something for the next fortnight?'

'Well ...' she began.

'You see, Ursula wants to see a few places up here in the north and then she suggested I should go and see her family winery.'

'In Germany?'

'It's not that far really. There could be some business we could do.'

'I'm sure.' She was smiling so broadly Peppino shook her arm, demanding to be let in on the conversation. 'Just a minute Josef.'

'What is it?' Peppino said when she had covered the mouthpiece.

'Joe's wanting to know if I would mind not going back to Venice. He suggests we meet in Rome in two weeks. That's if I can find something to do, or some place to stay –'

'You're joking?'

'No. Can I stay?'

'You want to?' His face was still disbelieving.

She lifted the phone. 'If it's important to you Joe, you go ahead. I'm sure I can make other arrangements.'

'You don't mind?' His voice surged with hope.

'No. Of course not. I'm sure it must be important.'

'It is. Believe me.'

'We'll meet at the hotel in Rome in two weeks then?'

'To the day. You'll be able to get there?'

'Of course.' Peppino put his arms around her waist. 'Good luck in Germany, Joe.'

'Thank you. This could be a big break for me.'

'Do a lot of business.'

'I will.' Another pause. 'You're sure you don't mind?'

'Not at all. Give my love to Ursula.'

'I will. How's Peppino? Been giving you a hard time?'

'No. Just the opposite.'

'OK. Got to run. Thanks again.'

Having put the telephone down, Cassie danced on her toes and clapped her hands. 'Joe's in love.'

'With the German lady?'

'Yes. They're going back to Germany. He says to do business.' She burst into laughter.

'Did he say he was in love?'

'No, but he is. I can tell.'

'And you can stay?'

'We can have another two weeks together, if you'd like that.'

'Cassandra, I know I'm in Naples but I feel as though I'm in heaven.'

801

BOOK
E·I·G·H·T
Patrick

O · N · E

December, 1965: Adelaide

Patrick Ross was regarded by those charged with his education as a bright but difficult student. He passed exams easily, if not with distinction and, in the four years he had been a boarder at school, had shown a flair for avoiding study and doing the minimal amount of homework. He was also good at sport.

Now ten, Patrick was enjoying the end-of-year atmosphere at school. The final examinations were over, there was no study to avoid, the teachers were relaxed and the students were eagerly anticipating their holidays. In ten days' time, Patrick was due to catch the train to William Creek, to spend the six-week summer vacation at Kalinda.

Normally he spent the weekends with Cassie and Peppino in their big house in the Adelaide Hills although occasionally he went to stay with his Uncle Joe at Tanunda. For the last weekend of the year, however, he had been given permission to do something special. His best friend at school was Damon Gallagher, whose parents owned a yacht. They were sailing to Kangaroo Island and Patrick had been invited to join them.

Mr Gallagher was a stockbroker. He wanted to leave at four o'clock on the Friday, so he had a car collect the boys from school and take them to the Outer Harbour where his yacht, *Quo Vadis*, was moored. Patrick liked the water and was an excellent swimmer – he was the under-eleven champion at school – but he had never been sailing and his imagination had conjured pictures of them putting to sea in something the size of a rowing-boat. The one subject he liked at school was Australian history and he had been intrigued by drawings of the explorer Charles Sturt sailing down the Murray in a longboat with a small mast and oars projecting from the sides. That was the kind of boat he expected. He was staggered by the appearance of the Gallagher's yacht. *Quo Vadis* was a 48-foot schooner. The hull was painted deep blue and had a white stripe running from bow to stern. It could sleep eight in comfort, sparkled with polished brass and had wooden fittings that were as glossy as a grand piano. Patrick was consumed by two emotions: love for such a glorious-looking tool of adventure, and envy for Damon Gallagher.

There were five on board: Mr and Mrs Gallagher, Damon and Patrick and Simon Bannister, who worked for Damon's father and helped sail the boat. They left at four – Mr Gallagher liked to do things on time – and set a south-westerly course across the Gulf of St Vincent for Edithburg, on the heel of the Yorke Peninsula. It was warm and a light breeze was blowing. They arrived after dark and anchored near a place where Mr Gallagher and Simon often went fishing.

On the way across the gulf, Patrick was allowed to steer the boat until the wind grew so strong that Simon took the wheel again. He and Damon had helped set the sails, something Damon professed to know a great deal about and, for part of the journey, the two boys sat at the bow and watched the graceful hull divide the sea into hissing streams of foam. But for most of the time, Patrick stood at the back rail and watched the dinghy dancing in their wake.

'Dad won't let anyone ride in there,' Damon said, with the voice of a seasoned sailor. 'He says if anyone fell out, it would take too long to turn the *Quo Vadis* around and they'd either drown or be taken by a shark before we got back.'

Patrick rarely took any of Damon's more melodramatic pronouncements too seriously because he knew his friend was given to romantic exaggerations and so he looked at the little boat, scudding and twisting on the end of its line, and longed to be on board. There, he could be master of his own ship and drift off into the wonderful world of his imagination.

They fished that night. Simon showed Patrick how to bait his hook and helped him untangle his line when it became knotted, but the boy caught nothing. Damon hooked one fish but his father said it was too small and made him throw it back in the sea.

Both men caught big fish and that was exciting but then the boys were put to bed because they were the youngest. Patrick hated being the youngest and longed to grow up, so he alone could decide what to do and when to do it. On this night, however, being sent to bed wasn't so bad because the two of them were in bunks in the bow of the boat, and the bunks were high and curved in towards each other. Water slapped against the outside of the hull and they could talk without being heard by the others.

At first, Damon talked about the islands and ports he had been to in the boat and Patrick listened but found it boring because he didn't know any of the places his friend seemed to find so interesting. Then Patrick told stories about Kalinda and Lake Eyre but Damon couldn't imagine a place so big or so dry and so he changed the subject. Each recounted tales of the worst things he had done. This was more interesting. Tales of daring and disobedience, even if postscripted by a beating, were lively fare at eleven o'clock at night in a yacht anchored off a lonely shore.

Damon had sunk a speedboat his father owned.

'How?'

'I pulled the plugs out.'

'What plugs?' Patrick, who knew animals and machinery but not boats, also knew that Damon used his considerable inventive talents to embellish his best stories. 'Boats don't have plugs.;'

'They do. You pull them out when the boat's running to drain water out of it and then you them back in again when you stop.'

'Where are they? In the bottom?'   .

'No, of course not. They're at the back. Anyhow, we'd stopped and Dad was on the land and I was playing in the boat and I pulled the plugs out and the boat sank.'

'Right down?'

'It was in ten feet of water.' Both muffled laughs of delight. 'It had a big V8 engine and the water got in and ruined it.'

'Ruined it?' Patrick struggled to hold his mouth in place.

'It cost five hundred pounds to fix.'

Patrick almost dared not ask the next question. 'What happened to you?'

'Oh I got off before it sank.'

'No, I mean what did your father do to you?'

'Nothing.'

'Nothing?' Patrick's eyes swelled to bursting point.

'The worse the things you do, the less your parents do. Do something little and they wallop you. You know, break a vase or crack a window or something like that. But do something really big and they don't know what to do.'

Patrick considered that logic for several seconds. 'I didn't get beaten over what happened at my sister's wedding either.'

'What happened?' Damon was wide awake, his body aglow with the joy of recollecting his great escapade.

'She married an Italian ...'

'Your sister married a wog?'

'She's a lot older than me,' he said, as though that were sufficient explanation. 'And he's not really a wog. Peppino's been here a long time.'

'What's his name?' Damon had raised himself on one elbow.

'Peppino.'

The other boy dissolved into guffaws of disbelief. Patrick swung his pillow at him.

'They'll hear you and come in and make us go to sleep if you don't shut up.'

Damon controlled himself. 'Is that really his name?'

'It's short for Giuseppe, I think. That's what Cassie said. She's my sister. He's nice, so don't laugh at him.'

Damon covered his mouth. 'All right. Go on. What did you do?'

'Well, we had the wedding at the homestead and people came from all over the place. Peppino's parents came out from Italy.' He raised the pillow when Damon seemed about to laugh. 'Now don't you start that again.'

'I won't. What were they like? Did they speak English?'

'No.'

'Does Peppino?' He managed to resist a giggle.

'Of course he does.'

'A lot of Italians don't,' Damon said, in a learned way. 'Wouldn't you think the parents would have taught themselves English, seeing they were coming out for the wedding?'

'Well they didn't, and that was the problem. We had this big tent out in front of the house where we had all the drinks and there was a band playing inside and people went in there to have a drink and to get out of the sun and to listen to music.'

'Must have been a big tent.'

'It was huge. It was all striped and had flags on it.' For a moment, Patrick was lost among the recollections of the day.

'So what happened? Come on. Don't go to sleep yet.'

'Well, my mother was busy and my dad was helping serve drinks and Cassie was trying to talk to everyone and so there was no one to talk to Mr and Mrs Portelli.'

'Who are they?'

'Peppino's parents, you twit.' They exchanged blows with their pillows, then settled back into the story. 'I got them more drinks and they bowed and smiled – they were really funny – and they patted my hair, and I hate people doing that, don't you?'

'Makes my skin creep.'

'So I was talking to them and I asked them if they'd like to see the camels.'

'I thought you said they couldn't speak English?'

'They couldn't, well not properly, but I kept talking and they kept smiling and when I started to walk over to the yards where the camels were, they followed me. They were talking to each other and smiling as though I was really cute, you know?'

'Yeah. I've got an aunt like that. She makes me puke.'

'When we got to the camels, Mrs Portelli got a bit frightened because one of them was making a lot of noise. You know what camels are like.'

'Yeah.' Damon had seen some camels in a circus.

'So I said, "Do you want me to ride one for you?" You know, to show them that the camels weren't dangerous. And they didn't know what I said, I suppose, but Mr Portelli smiled and nodded and she just stayed behind him where it was safe, and so I undid the gates and brought one of the camels out.'

'Can you really ride a camel?'

'Sure. Even without a saddle. Anyhow, I got it to get down and I climbed on and then it made a lot of noise and Mrs Portelli started to squeal.'

Damon put both hands to his face.

'It got up with me on its back and I had only a halter on it because all I meant to do was ride it back into the yard but she made so much noise that it took fright.'

'It probably wasn't used to Italian.'

'I hadn't thought of that. Anyhow, it bolted.'

'And?' His hands were ready for the explosion.

'I tried to turn it but it got more frightened because people were yelling and it ran straight into the big tent and got tangled in the ropes and pulled it down.'

'It never!' Damon's grammar tended to collapse when he was excited.

'There were at least twenty people inside, including my father and the band.'

Damon's hands couldn't hold in the noise so he rolled face down on the pillow.

'I went another half a mile before I could slow the camel down. Then I got off and led it back.'

One eye appeared above the pillow. 'What happened?'

'Everyone was laughing.'

'Even your father?'

'He said later it was the best thing that happened all day. My sister would have skinned me but there were too many people around. Peppino thought it was a big joke.'

'And your mother?'

'She said I could have killed myself.'

Damon wiped his face. 'Aren't mothers like that? You do something that's real fun and all they think about is that you might catch a cold or cut your finger. They're really sickening.'

Both boys were silent for a while. The boat was rocking gently.

'What's your father like?' Damon asked.

'Good.'

'Mine's very strict. He expects me to be perfect.'

'So does mine.'

'All fathers are like that. Why does yours make you go to school when he didn't have to go?' Damon had heard the story of Adam's lack of formal education.

'To get rid of me, I suppose. I don't know why I have to learn all the things we get at school if I'm going to go back to Kalinda. I'd learn more from Danny.'

'He's your brother?'

Patrick nodded. 'He can do everything. He can mend the cars, he can fix machinery, he can ride, he flies Dad's plane, he knows all about sheep and cattle, and I'll bet he didn't learn any of those things at school.'

'Which school did he go to?'

'Marree.'

'I haven't heard of that one.'

'It's only small.'

Damon sat up in the bunk and rearranged the blankets. 'How come your father never learned to read or write?'

Patrick had told his friend that story more than a year ago. He was sorry he had. It was a fact he was ashamed of; all the other boys had fathers who had either been to the same school or to one of similarly exalted status. All, he was sure, were extremely literate men. Only he had a father who had never been educated. 'He can read and write,' he said grudgingly.

'You told me he couldn't.'

'He can. He taught himself.'

'How could you teach yourself something like that?'

'Well he did. Or someone helped him.' He rolled to one side. 'What are we going to do tomorrow?'

'Go down to Kangaroo Island. Do some more fishing. Maybe go swimming.'

'I mean you and me. What are we going to do that's special?'

'Like what?'

'Well, like ride in the dinghy.'

'Dad won't let us.'

'It'd be great though, wouldn't it?'

'He wouldn't let us.'

'What if we just got in and hid there?'

'Talk sense. He'd see us.'

'Could we take it for a row then?'

'When?'

'When we get wherever we're going. While the others fish, maybe you and me could go for a row.'

'I don't think Dad would let us.'

'Gee, doesn't your father let you do anything?'

''Course he does.'

'Have you ever taken the dinghy out? On your own, without one of the grown-ups?'

Damon lay back and closed his eyes. 'No.'

'Why?'

'He says it's dangerous.'

Patrick rolled on his side. 'I'll bet it's not as dangerous as riding a camel. 'Specially a camel without a saddle.'

They were up at dawn and under way almost immediately. The wind had turned and Mr Gallagher suggested a change of destination. Instead of tacking towards Kangaroo Island, he proposed following the southern coast of the Yorke Peninsula and then crossing to the Gambier Islands, at the lower end of Spencer Gulf. There was good fishing there. Did anyone object? He was the sort of man to whom few ever raised an objection, particularly his family, an employee or a ten-year-old guest like Patrick, so *Quo Vadis* followed a course towards Cape Spencer at the tip of the peninsula, and then swung into the blue-grey waters of the gulf. By lunch-time, they were anchored in the lee of Wedge Island, the largest of the Gambier group.

In the afternoon, Mr Gallagher tried fishing from the yacht but caught nothing. He decided to go ashore and fish from the rocks. Damon asked to go with him.

'Rock fishing's too dangerous for kids,' Mr Gallagher said, and he and Simon put their angling gear in the dinghy and headed for the shore.

Mrs Gallagher went below to sleep. She was a woman who spent a great deal of her energy in socializing and regarded weekends on the yacht as an opportunity for her to catch up on lost rest.

The wind had dropped. It was hot on deck. A few gulls circled the boat.

'What are we going to do?' Patrick said, sitting by the rail and letting his legs dangle over the side. Like Damon, he was wearing only his swimming costume.

'Do you want to try fishing again?'

'There are no fish and the lines always get in a tangle,' Patrick said.

'Do you want to play Chinese Checkers?'

'I can play that at school.'

The gulls drifted towards the island and Patrick wished he were a bird. Birds could go anywhere. 'Why don't we have a swim?'

'We're not allowed.'

'Who said?'

'No one, but I know we're not allowed.' Damon thought of adding that it was too dangerous to swim out here but he was concerned that his friend might accuse him of being scared.

'We could swim to the beach.'

'It's too far.'

'It's only a hundred yards.' Patrick kicked his legs. 'Can't you swim that far?'

'It's not that.'

'What is it then?' Damon sat beside him, saying nothing. 'I'll give you a race. First one to the dinghy wins.'

'You can always beat me,' Damon said, his voice beginning to change into a whine of defeat.

'You do over-arm and I'll swim breast-stroke.'

'We're not supposed to leave the yacht, though.'

'No one said so.'

'But I know we're not.'

'If no one said so, it's all right.' Patrick walked to the ladder at the stern. 'Come on, you can go first.'

'I don't want to go first. I don't want to race.'

'Well, I'll see you on the beach.' Patrick lowered himself into the water. 'Come on, you can say I made you do it.' He struck out for the island and a few seconds later, heard splashing as his friend entered the water behind him.

He reached the beach and stood at the water's edge, waiting for Damon to join him. Mr Gallagher and Simon had walked around a rocky headland and were out of sight. Patrick went to the dinghy and pushed it towards the water, until its bottom was moving with each wave, and lightly scraping the sand. He climbed in.

'What are you doing?' Damon gasped. He was so tired from the swim that he had difficulty standing.

'Just sitting.'

'You'll get washed out.'

'That's all right, I'll paddle it in.'

'Don't you lose any of the oars.'

Patrick took out the oars and put them on the beach. 'Now we won't lose them.' He climbed back into the dinghy. 'Come on. Get in.'

Damon hesitated.

'Gee, you're a chicken,' Patrick said and Damon got in.

The boat moved on a small wave. 'We'll be floating next,'

Damon said, his rising tone blending fear with excitement.

'Well, so what?' Deliberately, Patrick put one foot over the side and pushed. The dinghy glided from the beach.

'You're nuts,' Damon said but giggled. 'Now you're better get us back in.'

Patrick leaned over the side, and paddled. The boat turned in a slow half-circle until it was pointing out towards the yacht. Damon paddled on the other side and the dinghy spun faster. 'We're going around in circles,' he said and looked anxiously at the growing distance between themselves and the beach. 'We're going out to sea. We must be caught in a current.'

A small wave rolled under the boat and Damon, who had been attempting to stand, fell over. Fearfully, he clutched at the side of the dinghy. 'We're going to get into trouble.'

'Stop whingeing. We'll be all right.' Patrick paddled harder but the boat slewed off course and drifted even further away from land. Eventually, Patrick grew tired of paddling and sat back. 'If you hadn't made me take out the oars, we'd be all right.'

'I didn't make you. You're the one that did it. I didn't even want to leave the yacht.'

Patrick looked around them. The current was taking them towards rocks that projected from a headland at the end of the beach. 'If we both paddle at once and in the same direction we might get back.'

'I don't want to paddle.'

'Well, I can't do it on my own.'

'It's your fault we're out here.'

'Well, help me.'

'I can't. I'm too tired.'

'You haven't done anything.'

'I have so. I swam all the way to the beach.'

'So did I.'

'But *I* didn't want to swim to the beach.'

Defeated by such reasoning, Patrick sat in the dinghy, slumped forward and wondering if he could swim and somehow tow the dinghy back to shore.

The two fishermen came into sight. They were standing on the rocks at the tip of the headland. Damon stood up and began to shout.

'What are you doing?' Patrick said, tugging at the boy's costume.

'Waving to Dad.'

'But he'll kill you.'

Damon sat down but his shouts had been effective. The men waved, showing signs of agitation rather than greeting. Simon immediately put down his rod and began hurrying over the rocks towards them. Mr Gallagher was slower but followed, scrambling over the slippery terrain with less agility than his employee.

'You're heading for the rocks,' Mr Gallagher shouted, gesticulating with both arms. 'Row the other way.'

Damon was shivering with fright.

'Damon!' his father roared.

'We haven't got the oars,' the boy called out.

'Where are they?'

'On the beach.'

The father threw his cap on the ground. 'What are you doing in the boat, anyhow?' He stood where he was, leaving any rescue to Simon.

'He's going to kill me,' Damon muttered.

'I thought you said he only punished you for little things?' Patrick said.

By now, Simon had reached the nearest rocks. He was fifty yards away. Wearing a shirt and rolled-up pants, he called out: 'Have you lost the oars, Damon?'

'Yes,' the boy answered, happier to be dealing with the younger man. Simon was about thirty and good with boats. He always treated Damon well. 'They're safe. They're back on the beach.'

Simon grinned. 'A fat lot of use they are there. Have you tried paddling with your hands?'

'Yes. It doesn't work.'

He stroked his chin. 'Well, if you keep on coming as you are, you'll end up on the rocks and we don't want a hole in the boat, do we?'

Patrick waved his hand. 'I could swim and try to tow it away.'

Simon looked at the sweeping current. 'I don't think you'd be strong enough, son. Looks like I better come out and give you a hand.' He dived in.

Damon's father hadn't moved. As Simon swam towards the dinghy, Mr Gallagher called out: 'What are you doing in the boat anyway Damon? I left you on the schooner.'

'We were playing.'

'I'll give you playing when I get to you.'

'He's going to kill me,' the boy whispered, rolling his eyes at Patrick.

Simon was a powerful swimmer but the current was difficult and, burdened by the drag from his clothes, he took more than a minute to reach the boat. He grabbed the bow. 'Whew! That was hard.'

'Do you want to get in?' Damon asked. Both boys were at the front.

'No. I'll turn it around first.' He spat out water. 'Whose idea was this?'

'Mine,' Patrick said.

'Wasn't a good one, was it?'

'No.'

'OK, here we go.' He kicked and, with one arm holding the bow and the other stroking the water, began to swing the boat around.

'Should we paddle?' Patrick said.

'Why not?' Simon blew out a stream of water and kept swimming.

He turned the nose of the boat and, with both boys leaning over the side to paddle, gradually moved the dinghy away from the rocks. When he had covered twenty yards, Simon draped both his arms over the side.

'I need a rest,' he said.

'Can you stand?' Damon said.

Simon's face twisted into a grin. 'There's thirty feet of water under me.'

'Do you want to come into the boat?' Patrick asked.

'Might as well. Then we can all paddle it back to the beach.' He held out one hand.

Patrick went to help him but a strange thing happened. Simon suddenly rose in the air and in a flurry of broken water, was catapulted away from the boat. As he moved away, his mouth opened but he made no sound. His hands clawed at the air and then, just as suddenly, he was pulled under the surface. With a frightful plopping sound, water rushed to fill the space where Simon had been.

In astonishment, the boys looked at each other, then back out to sea. About thirty yards away, Simon reappeared. His face was a ghastly white. He cried out, not in pain but surprise. One arm flapped the water.

Patrick was still struggling to comprehend what had happened, but he had done a basic lifesaving course at school and he knew that Simon, quite obviously, was drowning. Damon was screaming out, but making no sense. Patrick dived from the boat.

He swam as hard as he could towards the man. He could hear Damon shrieking hysterically. Then he had a sensation of a great presence and something travelling at an impossible speed brushed against him. It was big and its touch burned, and he was pushed off course. He stopped swimming. He could see Simon clearly. One hand was above the water and he was uttering little gasping noises, like a child might make. And then, with a terrifying jerk, Simon accelerated away from him, his head cutting a thick wake as it raced in a wide curve. Then he disappeared.

T·W·O

Shark attacks are horrible things, the manifestation of everyone's deepest and least rational fears. A monster from another age and another, hidden world snatches a man and devours him, but is never seen.

That was a terrible part of the story of Simon Bannister's death: the great fish that killed him was not sighted. It rubbed against Patrick and took most of the skin from his thigh, but no one saw it. There was only the ghastly sight of a man with one hand raised being propelled through the water, before being dragged under, to be torn apart and eaten.

Not a trace of the body was found, which added to the story the newspapers had to tell. There was much speculation about what sort of shark had taken Simon. Most people thought it was a Great White. They were found in those waters, and the sheer ferocity of the attack suggested the predator had been this, the most deadly of the species. Those who knew sharks speculated that the mankiller must have been at least twenty feet long.

Newspapers published accounts of previous shark attacks and a spate of statistics about huge sharks, both sighted and caught. There was even one commentary about the stupidity of people who swam in such waters. Simon Bannister achieved notoriety in death as a foolhardy adventurer who chose the wrong place for his final swim.

What the story did have was a hero and a ten-year-old one at that.

Patrick Ross, a boy from the outback who was a student at one of Adelaide's best schools, had dived in to attempt rescue. The monster had even grazed him with its sandpaper-tough skin as it rushed past to finish off its victim. The story was a major one for journalists, but they had to wait two days before they were able to interview the young hero.

The *Quo Vadis* had stayed at Wedge Island for several hours, while Gallagher radioed for help from vessels in the vicinity and continued a vain search for the missing man. Then he sailed for Port Lincoln, to report the happening to the police and to get medical attention for Patrick, whose skinned thigh was extremely painful. The boy was also in shock and had been dazed and sick since the attack. A Port Lincoln doctor put him in hospital for twenty-four hours. Patrick flew to Adelaide on the Monday, accompanied by Damon and his mother.

Automatically, Damon's father had accused his son of suggesting the swim and of taking the boat. Damon had been numbed into silence. But because they thought their son was at fault, the parents had taken care to exonerate both boys from any blame. They told no one that the oars had been left on the beach or that the dinghy was drifting. Their story was that, for some inexplicable reason, Simon had decided to swim out to the boat.

By now, Patrick feared the truth would come out and he would be blamed for Simon's death. He dreaded meeting people, going back to school, even facing his own parents. He was sick on the aircraft.

To his astonishment, he found Adelaide airport crowded by people who cheered him as he limped through the terminal. There were bright lights and cameras and reporters with a barrage of questions. No one asked what he and Damon were doing in the boat. Mr Gallagher, in his report to the police, said simply that the boys were in the dinghy and Simon had decided to swim out to them.

After several minutes of trying to answer questions about the shark and what he saw and why he dived in the water, Patrick realized that no one was going to blame him for anything. They thought he was marvellous. He soon learned what answers they liked best and avoided the fact that he had no idea there was a shark in the water. With masterly understatement, he said he dived in because Simon needed help. The journalists loved that answer. They talked to each other a lot. Someone mentioned something about a medal. He did interviews for television and had his photograph taken by men who grovelled in front of him with cameras that whirred and snapped. They asked him to put his sore leg up on a chair and not smile but look serious. One photographer even borrowed a walking-stick from an old man and gave it to Patrick and asked him to lean on it. The photographer wrote a caption in his notebook and showed it to the boy. He had written: 'After brush with death, young hero returns to Adelaide.' After checking that he had spelled Patrick's name correctly, the man patted the boy on the head and left, looking pleased with himself. Patrick shared the feeling. He no longer felt sick.

Cassie was at the airport, looking strange with her swollen belly.

'Are you really all right, Patrick?' she asked, once he was free of the journalists.

'Sure.' He had learned, almost instantly, the value of understatement.

'How's your leg?'

'It's sore but it's all right.'

'And you. You're really OK?' She put an arm around him, and he knew she was not going to ask him difficult questions.

He nodded. 'I was sick on the plane.'

'Oh.' She smiled. 'I hope you feel up to another flight. Mum and Dad will be here this afternoon. They're flying down.'

'Oh.' He wasn't sure whether that was good news. His mother would be easy but his father seemed to know when he was hiding things.

'They're going to take you home.'

'But school doesn't finish for another week.'

'That's all right. I've spoken to the headmaster. You're excused. I told them you'd been in hospital.'

He felt a sudden and unexpected surge of disappointment. Normally, time away from school was to be treasured but, after the adulation of the past half hour, he had begun to relish the thought of returning to school. Still pale, his thigh strapped and in genuine pain, it would have been good to have paraded for his schoolmates, and shown them that the whole incident hadn't frightened him, not the way it had affected Damon.

'Couldn't I go back to school for one day?' he pleaded.

'Good heavens,' she said, tightening her hold on him, 'you *must* be sick.' And, proud of her little brother, she walked with him to the car park.

Adam landed the Cessna at Adelaide that afternoon. Few people were at the airport and he and Nina had to wait for a taxi to take them on the forty-minute journey to Cassie's house. Nina had time to telephone Cassie and be assured that Patrick was well, his leg was mending and he was happily watching television in the big games room of the Portelli house.

It was Nina's second visit to Adelaide within three weeks. The first visit had been for the launching of her book, *A New Look at an Old Country*. Nina's first book, it was a collection of her favourite photographs and stories about Australia. She didn't like the title and had wanted to call it *Nina's Collection* but the publisher had overruled her. In frustration, she had suggested *Kangaroo Tales* as an alternative and had been appalled to discover someone in the organization liked the name.

The launch had been a disaster. She was thrust into radio and television interviews on programmes few people listened to or watched, and was guest of honour at a press conference attended by one embarrassed journalist. Several signing sessions at city book stores resulted in the sale of sixteen books, many for staff members.

The book flopped.

Halted by traffic signals, the taxi stopped outside one of Adelaide's biggest booksellers. 'It's not in the window,' she said mournfully.

'What's not?' Adam had been thinking of Patrick.

'The book that was going to be the world's number one bestseller.'

He peered across her, towards the window. Adam was now fifty-five and should have been wearing his glasses. 'It'll become a bestseller. It just takes time for the word to get around.'

'I think the word might have gotten around.' She opened the door and said to the driver, 'Could you park up ahead? I'll only be a minute.'

'Where are you off to?' Adam called but she was gone.

Nina darted into the store. Display stands of books, all new since she was last in town, were near the door. She searched for *A New Look* under the banner 'latest releases' but it was not there. She bought a book on aeroplanes for Patrick and hurried out. The cab driver could have been carved from stone but Adam was fidgeting.

'I thought I'd get this for Patrick.' She produced the book.

'See yours?'

'At the back. Buried and almost out of sight. I can understand now why Hemingway shot himself.'

'I found something to read while you were inside. Got it from a paper boy.' He gave her a copy of *The News*. Across the front page was the headline: 'Shark Hero: First Picture.' Beneath it was a picture of Patrick with his bandaged leg draped over a chair.

Cassie, six months pregnant and radiant, led them to the huge room where Patrick sprawled across a couch. He had been watching TV.

'I wanted to go to school but Cassie wouldn't let me,' he complained.

Nina rushed to him and hugged him. Over her shoulder, Patrick smiled a greeting to his father. 'She wouldn't take me back to school. Not even for one hour,' he said, when Nina had withdrawn to examine him more closely.

'You wanted to go to school?' Adam said, pleased that his son raised such a trifling subject. He had been apprehensive, fearing the boy might still be in shock. He had expected a tearful outburst but this was normal: Patrick was complaining about something Cassie had done.

'It's true,' Cassie confessed cheerfully. 'The little brat wanted to go to school.'

'Have you seen the afternoon paper?' Nina said. 'Patrick's picture is on page one. They're calling him a hero. Which he is.' She kissed his forehead.

'You should have seen the crowd at the airport,' Cassie said. 'There were reporters and photographers and people from television.'

Adam felt a great urge to take his son and hug him and kiss him and tell him how thankful he was that he had escaped the shark and how proud he was that he had thought only of saving the man, but he thought: He knows all that. I'm his father and he knows I love him. So instead of doing any of those things he sat beside Patrick and ruffled his hair and asked about his leg.

'It's all right.' Patrick smiled shyly. 'They said it was the skin of the shark that hurt me. It's rough like a file.'

Nina shuddered. 'Let's not talk about that. Look what I bought you.' She gave him the book. Immediately he began looking at the pictures. 'They say it's got all the latest jets in it.'

He nodded. Was that all they were going to say about the shark attack? No more questions?

Cassie was reading the story in the newspaper. 'They say here you dived in and almost landed on the shark. What's wrong? Didn't you see it?' But she was grinning and he knew that she was joking, so he grinned back.

'Cassie, please.'

'Oh it's all right, Nina. He can handle it, can't you, Patrick?' She passed him the paper. 'Here, read about yourself.'

'I thought I'd find him in bed, under sedation or asleep.'

'He's been watching *Skippy*.' Cassie laughed and Patrick felt good, relieved. Cassie was proud of him. As far as he could remember, she had never been proud of him before. She was always teasing him and making him feel bad.

He liked the picture. It filled up almost the whole front page. Then he turned to page two, as the footnote instructed him to do and read the rest of the story. As he read, a strange realization developed within him. What he was reading was what everyone would believe. The story in the newspaper, although wrong in some facts and certainly wrong because of the notable omissions, would become accepted as fact. It didn't matter what he said from now on. This was the truth, because it was in print and because people wanted to believe it.

'What's it like reading about yourself?' Cassie asked.

'Funny.'

'There's one thing I can't understand,' Adam said and Patrick knew what was coming and felt a chill rise up through his middle. Adam had been reading the paper over his son's shoulder. 'And that is, why this poor Bannister fellow would decide to swim out to the boat.'

'The man had grown careless,' Nina said quickly, and Patrick knew that this was a critical moment. He could speak now, and tell them exactly what happened and they would hate him forever because he had persuaded Damon to swim ashore with him, and he had got in the dinghy, and he had taken the oars out, and he had kicked the boat clear of the beach, and he had made Simon swim out to save the dinghy being washed on to the rocks; or he could say nothing. The truth was in the newspaper.

'I suppose so,' Adam said, in the way he did when he was talking to himself rather than to others.

'Let's talk about other things,' Nina said and she turned to Cassie. 'You're still feeling well?'

'I'm fine. I feel great.'

'You look well fed,' Adam said and grinned as Cassie shook her left fist at him. 'When's Peppino due back?'

'He's leaving Broken Hill tomorrow. Be here about five.'

'He's well?'

'Putting on weight and happy as Larry.'

Still holding the newspaper, Patrick closed his eyes. He saw Simon grasping the side of the dinghy and saying 'Whose idea was this?' and smiling in a way that meant he understood. Patrick had been able to tell the truth then, but it was too late now. He shuddered.

Nina looked at him anxiously. 'You're going straight to bed.'

'No.' It was a mild protest, done for show.

'Yes you are, young man. You were in hospital yesterday. You're still not well.' As he was trundled off to bed Patrick heard his father ask Cassie if she would telephone her doctor and ask him to call around.

Josef visited them later that evening. The doctor had just departed, having given Patrick a sedative and administered to the parents a warning that reaction to the incident was likely to continue and possibly grow worse in the next few days.

'So what are you going to do?' Josef asked Adam.

'Take him home tomorrow. Let him ride his horse and do a few things around the property, to take his mind off this other business.'

'How's his leg? Didn't the shark hit him?'

'I think it must be hurting but he's not saying much.'

'Must be a brave little bugger.'

Adam nodded.

'I heard on the radio that they might give him a medal.'

'I think the sooner people forget about it, the better for him.'

'Maybe. I'll bet it changes him though, and for the good. You know, it often needs something terrible to happen to bring out the best in a person.'

'Not at ten, Joe, not that young.'

'No.' Josef spent a few moments in contemplation. He knew Adam had been worried about Patrick. The school reports hadn't been good. 'I'll bet he's a different boy from now on. You'll see.'

They went out on the terrace. It was a view that Adam found miraculous and for a full minute, he and his friend stood in silence, looking at the tall eucalypti and the tapering shadows of the hills and, in the distance, the lights of the city, laid out neatly like a sparkling diamond on the velvet tray of evening.

Adam had not seen Josef for a year. The previous occasion had been at Tanunda, at a party to celebrate Josef's fiftieth birthday. Ursula von Dannenburg had flown out to surprise the guest-of-honour; which was not the novelty it might have been because Josef was expecting her at Tanunda one week later on one of their regular 'business' meetings.

Josef broke the silence. 'I'm off to Germany again next month.'

'Why don't you marry the woman and save yourself all this travelling?'

This would be the fourth time Josef had flown to Germany to see Ursula. She had been in Australia twice.

'It's a business arrangement,' Josef said, his voice tart.

'But you told me a year ago that you were sleeping with her.'

Josef blushed and looked behind to ensure no one had joined them on the terrace. 'I mean we have to do all this travelling back and forth for business reasons. Ursula cannot leave her business. I can't leave mine.'

'Why don't you put a manager in?'

'It wouldn't work.'

'Why doesn't she?'

'She says the same thing.'

'So you're just going to fly backwards and forwards, seeing each other every six months or so?;'

Josef shrugged and concentrated on the view of Adelaide.

'Do you like her enough to want to marry her?'

'Yes, I think so.'

'You should be certain.'

'I am.' Josef turned from the view, his chin set resolutely.

'And how about Ursula? Would she want to marry you?'

'She says so. But hers is a family business that's been running for a couple of hundred years and she can't just walk out on it and come to live in Australia.'

Adam moved closer. 'What would you like to do? Get married?'

He nodded. 'I've left it a bit late, I suppose.'

'Never too late, Joe. Look, I know I'm the world's worst person to talk about romantic affairs after some of the things I've been involved with, but if you just keep shuttling backwards and forwards like this and do nothing about it, she's going to find herself a nice, convenient German bloke and you're going to end up a lonely old man.'

'I'm old now.'

'Who isn't?' They shared a quiet laugh. 'Look Joe, you've got a few choices. If the only problems are to do with business, you can decide to do one of the following things. First, she can sell up and come to live in Australia.'

Josef shook his head. 'She wouldn't do that.'

'Sell or live here?'

'Sell.'

'OK. Scrub that. Second, you could sell and go and live in Germany.'

'I don't want to sell. And I don't want to live in Germany. Not all the time, anyhow.'

'So we come down to the third choice. Merge.'

'What?'

'Merge. Join the businesses. Make one wine-producing company out of two.'

Josef scratched his cheek. 'How?'

'You're the businessman. You work it out. She buys part of your company, and you purchase part of hers.'

'Hers is worth more than mine.'

'Well, you might end up owning just a little bit of hers. In other words, you could each buy into the other's company. You could import some of her wines –'

'We do already.'

'Import more. Do something.'

'It's not that easy.'

'Neither is having to fly halfway around the world to see someone you love. Do you want to keep doing that forever?'

'No.'

'Well, do something and do it soon.' Adam was quiet for a while. 'Your problem is finding someone to manage the business, right?'

823

'Well, it won't run itself if I'm not here. But people who know the wine business aren't that easy to find.'

'Not in this country?'

'No. There are a lot in Germany, of course.'

Adam turned slowly towards him. 'Well there's your answer. Get Ursula to find a good, reliable young bloke who's looking for an opportunity and who'd like to live out here.'

'And?'

'And if you've got someone running the place and if she can find someone to run hers –'

'Oh she has already has. She doesn't run it on a day-to-day basis. She just has to keep an eye on things.'

'Josef, you've got no problem. Arrange some sort of business tie-up. Get her to find you a really good manager –'

'Wine-maker.'

'Whatever you need. And then you could spend some of the year in Germany seeing how that side of the operation is going, and some of the year out here.'

'I'd be travelling just as much,' he protested.

'It's not the travel that's the problem,' Adam said patiently. 'It's being alone. And this way, you two could travel together and live together.'

Josef pressed his chin into his upraised hand. 'I'm sure there'd be a lot of problems.'

'I'm sure there would and I'm sure you could overcome them.'

'Do you think so?'

'If you wanted to.'

Josef grinned. 'You make life sound so simple. "Do this, do that, and things'll be right."

'They won't get right unless you do something,' Adam said, and went inside to see Patrick.

The boy was almost asleep. Adam sat on his bed.

'How's the leg?'

'Good.'

'It can't be good. It must be hurting.'

Patrick was surprised. Always in the past, he had been expected to understate any injury. Now, when he was understating his father was being sympathetic. 'A bit,' he suggested and was pleased to see the smile of approval.

'The doctor was saying you might be feeling a little bit bad for a while.'

'How do you mean?' Patrick asked.

'It's a thing called shock. It's nothing to do with being brave or

824

anything like that. It's just a natural reaction by the body to a really bad experience.'

'What's it do?'

'Well, it's hard to explain. You see, if a man has a really shocking experience –' Adam was careful to say 'man' – something like you've been through, where another person's been killed, and you've been in great danger; well, the body can take a while to wake up to what's happened.'

'What happens then?'

'Funny things. I know in the war, when I got frightened –'

'Did you get frightened?' Patrick had never considered such a possibility.

'Often. You go through an experience, and you do what you have to do – just like you jumped in the water and tried to help that man – and at first, you don't think about what could have happened, but it can catch up with you later. I know, I used to feel cold and clammy, and I'd sweat and I'd start shaking.'

'I was sick in Port Lincoln and on the plane.'

'Well, there you are.' Adam brushed Patrick's hair from his eyes. 'What I'm trying to say is that you should take it easy for a few days. Don't rush around. Just get better.'

'I'm not sick, Dad.'

'I know. But if you start shaking or feeling frightened, don't feel bad. It happens to everyone.'

'Even you?'

'It happened to me more times than I could tell you Patrick.'

Adam kissed him on the top of the head. It was a strange sensation. Patrick couldn't remember the last time his father had kissed him. Certainly not when he'd first left home to go to school. They had shaken hands, like men.

Patrick wished his father would stay at his bedside for a long time. If it were long enough, he might even find the strength to tell him what had really happened at Wedge Island.

But Adam said, 'You'd better go to sleep. We've got a long way to go tomorrow. If your leg's good enough, you might even be able to go for a ride on Silver when we get home. He's been missing you.'

Patrick nodded and watched his father leave the room. But when he closed his eyes, he saw Simon, and Simon was holding on to the side of the dinghy with his legs deep and inviting in the water and saying 'Whose idea was this?' and smiling at him. And then the shark came, but this time he saw it and it was huge with great bloodstained jaws.

Nina ran in when she heard the screams. Adam followed and the two of them sat with their son until, finally, he fell asleep.

825

T·H·R·E·E

March, 1970: Adelaide

Patrick was not looking forward to the weekend. Cassie and the kids were still in Italy with Peppino, visiting his family in Naples, so there was no point going to an empty house. Uncle Josef was in Sydney on business. Alex Rafter was in town and had said he could stay with him any time, but Patrick didn't like staying with the lawyer. He was always asking him what he was going to do when he left school and hassling him about the need to have a career and that made him feel guilty, because Patrick had no idea what he wanted to do. Most people at school expected him to go back to Kalinda and run the place some day, but Daniel did that so well that there was no point even contemplating life as a grazier. He didn't know enough about running the property whereas Daniel knew everything, and there was no way that he'd go back to the bush and work for his half-brother.

His sister, Uncle Josef and Alex Rafter were the only people he was authorized to visit at weekends. So that was that. He'd stay at school.

Damon Gallagher's father had bought a Jaguar and the family was driving to Mount Gambier for the weekend. Damon said it was to run in the new car and talked as though he were an expert on running-in procedures, but Patrick knew that Damon was a nincompoop with machinery and didn't even know how to drive. Patrick did. He had been driving the old 'flying ladder' for years and last Christmas his father had let him drive the Land Rover almost all the way to William Creek.

Damon left on the Friday afternoon, talking constantly about the Jaguar and how fast it would go when it was run in, and that left Patrick with just a few boarders who had nowhere to go for the weekend. The only boy around his age was Arnold Reckitt, whose parents lived in New Guinea and who stayed in school every Saturday and Sunday. At sixteen, he was little more than a year older than Patrick, although slightly smaller in size. He had a face like a weasel and a reputation for getting into trouble. He was known by all, even the staff, as Reckless Reckitt. No one ever called him Arnold. He was good at science, if adventurous, and eighteen months earlier had carried out an impromptu experiment which had burned down part of the science laboratory. He had been saved from expulsion only by the fact that his father had an important post in the diplomatic service, had used all his skills of diplomacy on the headmaster, and had paid for the repairs.

'Whiskers has gone for the weekend,' Reckitt told Patrick. Whiskers was a bearded maths teacher, dreaded by all for his sudden bursts of temper. 'He's left his Morris Minor.'

'Why?' The teacher and his faded red Minor convertible were regarded as inseparable.

'Needs two new tyres and he can't afford to buy them yet.' Reckitt was the conduit for school gossip. One advantage of never leaving the place was that everyone, including the gardener, caretaker and cook, talked to him.

Patrick wondered what Reckitt was getting at. His eyes had shifted into the narrow focus of a hatcher of plots.

'You reckon you can drive a car.' It was not a question but a challenge and Patrick was unable to resist challenges that questioned his abilities.

'Sure. I've been driving for years.'

'Reckon you could drive a Minor?'

Patrick blanched. 'You're not thinking of taking Whiskers' car?'

With a sly smile of triumph, Reckitt produced the keys. They swung from a large enamelled badge that showed an ox crossing a ford. It was a distinctive and familiar keyring. The teacher jangled and played with it constantly during lessons.

'Where did you get that?' Patrick was aghast.

'I know where he hides them.' Only the clicking of the swinging keys broke the silence. 'Well?'

'Well, what?'

'Do you want to drive?'

'We can't take his car.'

'Why not? It's there.'

'What if he comes back?'

'He won't. Whiskers has gone off to Kingston for a dirty weekend with Lois-the-lungs.' Lois was the headmaster's secretary.

'Oh cut it out,' Patrick scoffed, not knowing whether to smile or not. 'How do you know that?'

'Reggie the caretaker heard him making the reservations on the phone and he told the cook and I heard him tell her. I was in the pantry, nicking some biscuits.'

827

Patrick frowned, full of admiration for Reckitt's ability to learn all the most interesting news but disappointed that the well-upholstered Lois had undertaken so sordid a venture. He liked Lois.

'So he won't be back till Sunday night.' Reckitt swung the keys again. 'Come on. Just once around the block.'

Patrick stalled the engine twice before he managed to get the car moving but, once he had the feel of the clutch, he found the Minor easy to drive. Reckitt discovered the light switch and they turned on to the road that ran at the back of the school. The first circuit was accomplished and they did another. Patrick was preparing to drive back into the school grounds when Reckitt grabbed the steering-wheel. Patrick slowed the car to a jerky halt.

'Why don't we go into town?' the older boy suggested.

'You're nuts, Reckless.'

'Aw, c'mon, you're a good driver.' Reckitt, the master psychologist, paused to let the compliment do its work. 'We could be in town in fifteen minutes, do one run up King William Street, have a milk shake, and then come back.'

'What if someone sees us?'

'Like who? Everyone's away and it's dark, anyhow.'

'I don't know the way.'

'I'll show you.'

'I haven't got any money for a milk shake.'

'I have. I'll shout you.'

Traffic was light as they approached the northern end of King William Street which was just as well because Patrick had never driven in a town before, let alone venture down the State capital's main and busiest thoroughfare.

He made the turn neatly, just missing a couple who were crossing the street and had the wit and agility to jump backwards out of his way. Reckitt looked back and chortled. 'You should see the looks on their faces.'

Patrick joined his laughter. He was feeling confident now and drove across the next series of intersections without problems. At the next junction, a car approached from their left.

'He's got to give way to you,' Reckitt said and Patrick, realizing this meant he should not slow, kept his foot off the brake pedal. He watched the other car with the intensity of a hawk selecting its prey. As a result, he did not see the truck travelling across the intersection from the other direction until the blare of its horn drew his startled eyes to the right. He saw bright lights, the tall, square shape of a furniture van and braked as hard as he could.

The faulty tyres that the owner intended to replace slid on the road and the Minor slewed across the intersection. The van driver tried to avoid the little convertible but his bumper bar caught the mudguard and tore it off. Deflected off-course, the van mounted the footpath and crashed into a shop window.

Unhurt but stunned by the enormity of the accident, Patrick sat in the ruins of the Minor until the police arrived. The last view he had of his passenger was of Reckless Reckitt bolting down a side-street.

At school on Monday morning, Patrick implicated no one else. In the morning he was caned. In the afternoon he was expelled.

Alex Rafter saw Inspector Russell Mailey to ascertain if any prosecution was likely. Mailey had become a friend of the Rosses and had spent his previous holiday at Kalinda. Despite his bulk, he proved to be an accomplished horse rider. He had gone riding with Patrick several times.

'There are a couple of factors in the kid's favour, Alex,' the inspector said. 'The first is that Patrick doesn't have a driver's licence so we can't take it away from him. The second is, the school's headmaster thinks someone else put him up to it, because while he's inclined to be wild, he's no thief. He got a medal for bravery four or five years ago, didn't he?'

'Yes. He tried to save a man who was taken by a shark.'

'Well, that helps. In other words, he's not the sort of boy you'd sling into reform school. There's also the question of the teacher's car.'

'Adam has said he's prepared to pay for the cost of its repair or replacement.'

Mailey growled into his pipe. 'Luckily, the thing was worth about one fourteenth part of Sweet Fanny Adams. If it was a dog, you'd have taken it to the vet and had it put down.'

'But there was a lot of other damage. The truck, the shop.'

'Insurance, Alex, insurance.' He sucked noisily. 'We'll just let them pay and hope no one notices the rise in premiums next year.'

'So there'll be no charges against the boy?'

Mailey shook his head. 'It would be a good thing if Adam could keep him out of cars for a while, though. Maybe just restrict his driving to the back blocks of William Creek until he's old enough to be unleashed on an unsuspecting public.'

Adam flew down the next day. He came alone because Nina was in Alice Springs, getting material for her second book. The first had failed in Australia but sold reasonably well in America and she was now contracted to a New York publisher.

Josef returned from Sydney the same day. He and Adam met that night in the hotel where Adam was staying.

'Patrick hasn't been the same since the shark attack,' Adam confided. 'He was always pretty unruly but he didn't do the stupid things he's done in the last four and a half years. It's almost as though he's trying to get himself punished.'

'All kids go through a period of being naughty.'

'It's more than that. He's being naughty, as you call it, in a senseless way. Two years ago, they were showing pictures in the school theatre and he crawled up in the dark and tied the housemaster's shoelaces together so that the fellow fell flat on his face when the pictures were over.'

Josef sniggered. 'I rather like that.'

'The master didn't. Last year, Patrick climbed the school clock tower. That's almost a hanging offence and the silly little blighter did it when there was a function on, and all the staff were around. Everyone saw him. When he was twelve, he and a mate were given the job one weekend of mowing the lawn in the headmaster's house. They cut the grass all right but they mowed the gardens too.'

'That's a bit off.'

'He's had so many canings but it doesn't make any difference.' He made a noise that was part laugh, part lament. 'He's as game as Ned Kelly. Some of the things he's done have been risky. I guess other boys dare him. I don't know. For instance, he climbed to the very top of the highest tree in the park and was apparently swinging from side to side like a goanna up a gum tree. They were going to get the fire brigade to bring him down by ladder but he managed to climb down by himself.'

'He's got a nerve then.'

'Maybe too much. I've warned him. Seems to do no good either.' Adam shook his head sadly. 'He does silly things at home, too. Leaves the gate of the horseyard open. Things he never used to do.'

'He was always good with horses.'

'I know. His school work's gone off, as well. He used to like history. Now he fails in it. He used to be so good at swimming and now he never goes in the water.'

'That's understandable,' Josef said, looking sombre.

'I know, but he's given up football, too. He was good at that.'

'And now this.' They stood quietly together. 'What are you going to do?'

'Find another school, if another school will have him.'

Josef offered to help. He knew influential people.

'The problem is,' Adam said, 'I don't fully understand my own

830

son. He's my flesh and blood but we're so different. I don't know why he does the things he does. I don't really know what he likes doing. I don't know what he wants to do, what he wants to be.'

Josef looked up in surprise. 'Won't he work on Kalinda?'

'Not necessarily. Nina doesn't want him to. She says he doesn't seem to have any aptitude for station work and I think she's right. He doesn't know how to do some of the simplest things around the property and he doesn't seem at all interested in finding out. He never asks me to show him how to do something.'

Josef hesitated. 'Maybe he finds it hard to ask.'

'How do you mean?'

'Well, some people are like that. They won't ask because they expect people to offer. And the trouble is, you're so good at doing most things, he probably feels a bit intimidated. And, of course, there's Daniel, who's also good at everything.'

'Danny didn't know much when he started. He used to ask me a lot of questions.'

'He's different to Patrick.'

'He certainly is.'

Josef ran his fingers across his scalp. He had thinned on top in the last few years and he arranged what hair was left with care. 'Do you think the problem could be one of communication?'

Adam's brow knotted into ridges of uncertainty.

'You're having trouble getting through to him,' Josef continued, 'and he's not passing any information on to you. The result: an impasse. Neither understands the other.'

'What are you saying?'

'The problem could be yours as much as his.'

The ridges on Adam's forehead rose in protest. 'I didn't take a teacher's car and run it into the side of a truck in the main street of Adelaide.'

'I'm not talking about that, although that little incident could be connected in some way.' Before Adam could protest again, he went on: 'What I'm saying is that he might be just like you and not able to express himself clearly.'

'I can express myself clearly.'

'Well, easily or comfortably might have been better words. Let's face it Adam, there have been times when I could have got more conversation out of a drain pipe than out of you.'

The ruffled expression softened to a grin. 'That's a weird analogy.'

Josef regarded Adam with astonishment. 'I never thought I'd hear you say something like that. Analogy! Whatever happened to the simple bush bloke who couldn't read or write?'

The grin broadened. 'He married an American writer, who makes him read all her work.' He nodded contentedly, then glanced sharply at his friend. 'You're saying because I mightn't talk much, Patrick thinks I'm not interested in him, and because he doesn't talk much, I think he's not interested in what I'm doing. Is that it?'

'Something like that.'

Adam considered all that Josef had said and then let his head sag forward, as though in defeat. 'I think the trouble is that we've spoilt him. He's had it too easy.'

'All parents tend to spoil their kids.'

'No. We've given him anything he's wanted and a lot of things he didn't want but got anyhow.' Adam's eyes reflected the deep regret within him. 'I've got a feeling it might have been lot better to have kept him up at the property instead of sending him down here. I could have spent more time with him, with us doing things together, like I did with Cassie. He mightn't have got the same education but what he's got doesn't seem to have done him all that much good. He's mixing with a strange lot, too. Some of the kids at the school can't do anything. Not in a practical sense. They wouldn't know how to hammer a nail, put a fence post in, mend a roof. None of those things. They've never known what it was like to want for anything. The parents have got big houses, yachts, fancy cars –'

Josef smiled mischievously. 'You've got a big house and fancy cars and I'll bet none of them own as much land as you.'

'*Touché.*'

'*Touché,*' Josef said, recalling a conversation of long ago.

'The trouble is,' Adam said, 'that I've changed. I've got money. Life's too easy. If Patrick had had to walk around at nights with me, trapping dingoes like Cassie had to, he'd have turned out differently.'

'You can't blame him for that.'

'No.' He sighed. 'The world's changed, Joe. That's the trouble. It's no one's fault but it's different, and I'm finding it harder to understand.'

'It moves faster.'

He need not have spoken, for Adam was still going. 'And you know something else? By sending Patrick down here, to mix with city boys and snobs, I've turned my own son into both those things, and I can't stand snobs, and I don't understand city boys.'

'Well,' Josef said, ending the conversation by standing, 'if I'm to find another school for young Patrick, I'd better look for one full of poor kids from the country.'

832

'Might be cheaper than this one.'

'I'll also look for one where the schoolmasters have bicycles.'

Both laughed. 'How's Ursula?' Adam felt a pang of conscience for not having enquired sooner.'

'Didn't I tell you? I'm about to become a grandfather.'

Adam's day had been long and difficult and Josef's meaning eluded him.

'You know Ursula has a daughter, Lisa?'

'I didn't know her name but I knew she had a daughter.'

'Well, Lisa's married and last year she had a baby.'

'And?'

'So Ursula's a grandmother.' He waited. 'And I'm about to become a grandfather.'

The fog lifted slowly. 'You two have finally decided?'

'I'm going over in June. We're getting married in Germany.'

'Before I say congratulations, may I say it's about time?'

They shook hands and Josef smiled a lot. 'I'm really happy, now it's all been decided.'

'And you finally sorted out the business of the two businesses?' Adam knew Ursula's fellow shareholders had been reluctant to sell any part of their enterprise to Josef, or to buy any share in his operation.

He nodded. 'I'm selling out.'

'To Ursula?'

'No. To a tobacco company. They want to diversify into wine. They've offered me an amount too large to refuse.'

'So what will you do?'

'Become a rich, married man of leisure.' He preened himself. 'I think it was what I was really cut out to be.'

Through his contacts, Josef found a school prepared to take Patrick. It was a good school – without the social standing of the one from which the boy had been expelled – but it had an impressive reputation for dealing with difficult students. Patrick would start at the beginning of the next term. Therefore, with a few weeks to fill in, Adam took him back to Kalinda.

On the long flight to the homestead, Adam tried to discuss the motive for the prank but the attempt soon degenerated into accusations by the father and sullen silences from the son. Not knowing how to deal with someone who had inherited his own ability to resist conversation, Adam dropped the subject, intending to try again in a few days. Patrick seemed greatly distressed by the affair. To be punished was something he could accept and, in fact, had accepted so many times for such a variety of misdemeanours that

833

he was quite proficient at it. While he seemed to court canings, some of his ventures had such an element of boldness about them that he had earned the respect of his fellow students and a grudging admiration from some of the staff. The puzzling thing to Adam was that the escapades which involved most risk and daring were always illicit. It was as though he were saying: 'No one else but I can do that. Now punish me.'

The expulsion, however, had brought him disgrace and that was something he had never experienced. There was no glory in this incident. Not only had he taken a car illegally, wrecked it and caused damage to other property, but he had shown himself to be a poor driver. That was what hurt. He had boasted to other boys about his ability to drive a car and yet, in his first public outing, he had made a fool of himself.

Having no luck with his attempt at trying to understand the incident, Adam was silent for some time and concentrated on flying the Cessna. He continually referred to the map, something he never did when flying around Kalinda, and noticed that Patrick seemed intrigued by what he was doing. He explained how he had lodged a flight plan and now had to stick to it and then, despite Patrick asking no question, explained what a flight plan was. He had to follow a set route, fly at a specified altitude, and reach nominated points at certain times. It was difficult on his own, he added, and passed his son the map and gave him his watch.

To his surprise, Patrick showed skill at navigation. He appeared to have an instinctive ability to relate what he saw on the map to the terrain over which they were flying, had a good idea of direction and an understanding of scale which impressed him.

'Where did you learn to read a map?' Adam said, in a voice which he hoped suggested admiration.

'At school.' Patrick was gazing to the right at the blue folds of the Flinders Ranges and did not turn. 'We used to go bush walking.'

'I didn't know that.'

'One of the teachers liked it.' That was all. The engine droned a dirge for the death of a promising exchange.

A little later, Adam tried again. 'Ever thought of flying? You used to be keen on aeroplanes when you were younger.'

'You mean flying, like you're flying?'

'Yes. In your own plane.'

Patrick had often dreamed of it. He would like to fly a jet fighter like the Mirage that the Australian air force used, or one of the big new Boeing 747 jumbos. 'No,' he said, still looking out to the right.

'You'd probably be a good pilot.'

'Why?'

'Well, you're good at sports. You've got a good eye, good co-ordination.'

'It's supposed to be difficult.'

'I think it's easier than driving a car.' Patrick shot a quick, accusing glance at his father and Adam wished he hadn't said that. 'You could get a licence in a couple of years' time,' Adam said quickly, trying to plough under his inadvertent reminder of the weekend. 'I'd be prepared to pay for your instruction. Would you like to do that?'

'Maybe.'

'You could practise in this. That would give you a flying start.' He nudged his son. 'That was a joke.'

'It wasn't very good.'

'Have you ever heard me tell a good joke?'

Patrick looked at his father and smiled. 'No.'

A barrier had just collapsed and Adam sensed it. 'You've never flown the Cessna, have you?'

Patrick's eyes widened. 'No.'

'Do you want to have a go?'

'I'm not allowed to, am I?'

'Well, not on your own but I'm here and I don't think anyone's going to object if you just fly it for a little while.' He turned and carefully searched the rear seats. 'I can't see anyone back there, can you?'

'No.' The boy's fingers were already circling in anticipation of touching the wheel. 'But who's going to navigate?'

The question was posed with such solemnity that Adam felt compelled to reply in the same vein. 'Good point. I will.' He took back the map.

For the next twenty minutes, Patrick flew the plane. He soon learned to keep the nose pointing at the horizon and cured a tendency to dip one wing. To Adam's great joy, Patrick began asking questions and Adam explained how the engine was started, how the throttle controlled their speed, how the propeller drew them through the air and how the shape of the wing provided lift. He offered to explain more when they were on the ground and able to walk around the aircraft. Patrick practised a few gentle turns but when the Cessna began to climb and yaw drunkenly, Adam took over. They both laughed, each from an excitement of a different kind.

F·O·U·R

The next few days were important to Patrick, because in that time he made a profound discovery. It concerned the way people varied according to where they lived. There were two main groups, he reckoned, and they were separated by a line that ran somewhere across the top of the State. South of the line were the superior ones. They were the sophisticates, people like the parents and teachers he had met at school who seemed to know most things, knew what to wear for every occasion and performed the rituals of society with a well-oiled grace. These were the people he admired.

North of the line, the folk were rougher, they tolerated uncouth types and they spoke a slower and less complex language. These people were all right, Patrick felt, in their own environment and some were even admired by their own kind, but they were hopelessly out of place south of the line. They always seemed incongruous in the city. They looked different with their lined and sunburned faces, they wore hats and they got lost.

His father was like that. Patrick came to realize, to his great distress, that everyone at Kalinda – with the notable exception of his mother who was American and therefore not really a normal person – fitted into the latter category.

He suspected the line occurred somewhere around Leigh Creek because it was at the big coal-mining settlement that the thought began to develop. His father landed there to refuel. The two of them went into the small airport terminal, to go to the men's room and to have a drink. At this stage, Patrick had never felt so close to his father. He was in a euphoric state from having flown the Cessna and he had experienced the rare enjoyment of having his father explain interesting things to him. But then something happened that changed that, and emphasized the gap between father and son; for Patrick longed to be from the south, and his father was a northerner.

Another, larger aircraft landed, on its way to Adelaide. The name of a mining company was on the side. Several men, some wearing ties, disembarked. Patrick recognized one of them as Damon Gallagher's father. The boy moved behind Adam, to be hidden from Mr Gallagher's sight.

Noticing the manoeuvre, Adam studied the approaching group with renewed interest, to see what had prompted Patrick's strange reaction.

'Isn't that Mr Gallagher?' he said. The two men had met at the inquest into Simon Bannister's death.

'Yes,' the boy whispered.

'Do you want to say hello?'

'No.'

Gallagher was involved in an animated discussion with his companions and spared Adam no more than a cursory nod. The boy moved around Adam to stay out of sight. Adam said nothing to Patrick. He assumed his son was fearful of being drawn into a discussion about his expulsion. He was wrong. Patrick was ashamed to be seen with him and hoped neither would be recognized. He had literally died from embarrassment when the two fathers had met at the Coroner's court because Mr Gallagher knew that his father had never been to school and believed he couldn't read or write.

Patrick had cursed himself many times for the foolish moment when he had revealed that information to a blabber-mouth like Damon Gallagher. Damon had told his father. Mr Gallagher, according to the son, had initially expressed disbelief, then laughed and thought it a great joke but then delivered the first of several stern lectures about the need to study and do well at school to avoid ending up an illiterate moron like Patrick Ross's father.

Patrick held his breath until the group entered the men's room. He then hurried his father out to the refuelled Cessna. From deep within him, an instinctive feeling was emerging that said his father and Damon's father belonged to different worlds. Mr Gallagher, with his white shirt and tie and carefully brushed hair was educated, urbane and could move comfortably in any circle of men. He was a product of the city and of schools like the one Patrick had been thrown out of, which, somehow, created superior people. His father, with his open-necked shirt and moleskins and tousled hair, belonged in one place only: the bush. He was, in Patrick's critical eye, an alien in every territory but his own. Mr Gallagher was polished; his father was rough.

He loved his father, with a kind of instinctive, animal desperation but he did not admire him. And when they walked to the plane, he thought how much he resented the fact that of all the boys at his former school, he'd been the only one with a father who had never been educated and had the rough hands of a worker.

The second incident that influenced Patrick happened soon after he reached Kalinda. It involved Daniel. His half-brother was now thirty and therefore aged. He managed the property. Daniel seemed confident in everything he did, which had always made Patrick uncomfortable in his presence because, in the last eight or nine years, the boy felt he was always being compared with the man. Daniel never got into trouble, which made Patrick's surprise all the greater when he entered the kitchen and found his half-brother kissing Elizabeth Kettle.

Jimmy's and Stella's youngest daughter was now twenty-five and working in the big house as cook and housekeeper. Mrs Wilson had retired two years ago. She was in her late seventies and suffering from arthritis. She still lived in her little house on the property, but Lizzie did all the work.

Daniel grinned. 'What's up, young feller?'

Patrick blushed and was so embarrassed he wasn't able to reverse out of the kitchen. Mouth open, he stared at the couple.

'It's all right, Pat.' Daniel was the only one who ever called him that. 'Me and Lizzie are engaged.'

Lizzie smiled. She was the prettiest of the Kettle girls. The others had left the property. Marie was working in Peppino's office in Adelaide and Yvonne was a nurse at Port Augusta.

'I didn't know you were engaged.'

'Well, you wouldn't, would you? We've been up here and you've been down in the big smoke.'

'Driving through Adelaide,' Lizzie said, unable to resist the addition. She had only just heard the story and thought it hilarious.

Patrick scowled at her. He had once liked Lizzie. She was the only one at Kalinda who ever played with him in the days before he was sent off to school. He mumbled something and left the kitchen. He saddled Silver and rode out to the sand-hills. Out there, where he used to play his Lone Ranger games, he dismounted and let the horse search for grass while he sat on the soft slope and thought.

Daniel was going to marry a black woman?

He had never thought of people as having different colours until he had gone south and learned the distinctions mainly in gossip sessions in the school yard. He liked Lizzie – or he used to until she had made fun of him – and had never thought of her as anything but a rather skinny girl with big teeth. But now he knew she was black and different and somehow not as good. She couldn't help that, of course, but all his friends at school told jokes about aborigines and while blacks might have been nice people and not to blame for being inferior, they were certainly not the sort of people

838

that someone in your family married.

If Damon Gallagher had an older brother, he would never in a million years contemplate marring an aboriginal woman. Not a Gallagher. They knew exactly what was right and what was wrong, what was acceptable and what was not.

If Daniel and Lizzie got married, how would he ever introduce them to his friends? He couldn't. It would be just too embarrassing.

Kalinda had experienced a string of good seasons. Adam now had thirty-eight thousand sheep and nearly five hundred head of prime beef cattle. Most of the cattle were up near the Horseshoe Hills, where an outstation had been built. It was not the house that Jimmy had imagined, being tiny, with only one room and a verandah but it was built in a spectacular location on the side of a hill near the great pillars of rock. It had water pumped to it from the spring. Since Cassie had married, Adam had employed another three men (much to Cassie's delight because it proved, she said, that she had done the work of three men) and one was always stationed at Horseshoe Hills. Jimmy liked to spend as much time as he could there. He was driving back to the homestead when he saw Patrick on his horse, emerging from the region of dunes. He stopped and waited for the boy to ride to him. Jimmy was in a Japanese four-wheel drive that Adam had bought, to see if it matched up to the Land Rovers he had used for so long. The Toyota was cheaper and not in such short supply as the British vehicle.

Jimmy had not seen Patrick since the Christmas holidays. He was pleased to see the boy but he was a specialist in laconic greetings. 'G'day,' he said.

'Hello, Jimmy.' Meeting his friends and explaining what had happened was an ordeal Patrick detested.

'Thought you were supposed to be at school?' He managed to put one foot on the steering-wheel and make it seem like a natural movement.

Patrick leaned forward to stroke Silver's neck. 'I was.'

'Get thrown out or something?'

Jimmy always had a way of guessing. He was grinning, suggesting that, no matter how bad the news, it would be a bit of a giggle. Patrick nodded and scratched an eyelid.

'Fair Dinkum? You're not pulling my leg?'

'No. I got expelled.'

'What's that mean?'

'Thrown out.'

'It's a fancy school term, is it? Oh well, that's what you get for going to a fancy school. When they kick you out, they call it some-

839

thing else. When I went to school, they threw me out by the scruff of the neck and just said "piss off and don't come back" but it wasn't a very fancy school.'

Patrick was not smiling.

'What did you do? Something interesting?'

While he told him, Patrick studied Jimmy. The aborigine had always been an old man but now he looked older than ever. He had never really recovered from the beating he'd got from the cattle thieves. His hair was still thick but mostly grey and he was skinny with the loose flesh that athletic men get when they grow old and thin. Patrick liked Jimmy, even though he always teased him.

'Was there just you in the car?'

Slowly, Patrick shook his head.

'Who was the other bloke?'

'Just someone.'

'Not going to say, eh? One of your school mates?'

'Yes.'

'What happened to him?'

'He ran away.'

'Why didn't you?'

'It didn't seem right.'

'And you didn't think of it in time, eh?' Jimmy always smiled like a boy which was strange for someone so old.

He returned the smile. 'I didn't think of it.'

'And this bloke never came forward and owned up?'

'No.'

'Sounds like a bit of a prick. Tell me Patrick, me boy, whose idea was it to take the car? Yours or this other kid's?'

Patrick had always said it was his because he had never implicated anyone else. He had seen Reckless Reckitt once, briefly, before the session with the headmaster and Reckless had said he would be expelled if he were involved, so Patrick said nothing.

'Don't want to say?' Jimmy coaxed.

'I've always said it was mine. I haven't told anyone else that another boy was involved.'

'But it was the other kid's idea.' Jimmy lifted his foot from the wheel. 'You needn't say nothing. Old Jimmy can read the truth in your baby blue eyes.'

'I haven't got baby blue eyes.'

'Just kidding. And you haven't told your dad about the other kid?'

'No. I told the headmaster that there was no one else and if I tell Dad he might tell the head and then there'd be more trouble.'

'I don't think your dad would do that.' He shifted in the seat.

'Have you heard about Lizzie and Danny?'

'Daniel told me.'

'What do you think?' Jimmy's broad grin left no doubt about his feelings.

'It's good.'

'Lizzie's a good cook.'

'I know.'

'Sort of makes us family, doesn't it?'

'What does?' He could feel the hairs tingling on the back of his neck.

'My daughter marrying your brother. It means we're going to be related. I'll probably be your half-step father or your half father-in-law or something. I never could keep up with who was who in your family.' He put his legs back in place on the floor. 'Anyhow, I got to get back. See you later, kid. And don't worry. I got chucked out of school too, and it didn't do me no harm.'

He drove away.

Patrick sat on the horse, not moving and trying to gather together all the bits Jimmy had scattered in his direction. He could end up like Jimmy, a man who talked badly and had no skills and was always talking about the old days when he was a fighter. And he and Jimmy would be related? That was true. If Daniel married Lizzie, Jimmy Kettle would be part of the family.

Slowly, with his head in a turmoil of terrible possibilities, Patrick rode back to the homestead.

A day later, Kalinda had an unexpected visitor. The Reverend Roger Montgomery called in, on his way to attend a convention in Alice Springs.

'Everyone thinks I'm crazy for driving up,' he explained to Adam, 'but you know how I like driving, and this gives me a chance to see a few old friends.'

Adam gave him Nina's address in Alice Springs. She would be in the Centre for another week.

'I enjoyed her first book,' Roger said.

'Some people didn't like the title.'

'Oh, I thought it was most appropriate.' He was a loyal friend who presumed the choice of the title had been Nina's.

'She didn't like it.'

'Oh.' He reconsidered. 'It was possibly just a little long.'

'The book sold well in America.'

'So I heard. That's excellent.' Roger polished his glasses. 'Apparently they didn't consider the title too long, but you know how the Americans are with language.'

841

'They changed the name of it.'

'Oh.'

'They called it *Down Under.*'

'*Down Under?*' Roger seemed about to remove his glasses but restrained himself. 'Just that? What strange people.'

'It sold well.'

'Well, that's the test I suppose. Is she doing a story about The Ghan in this new book of hers?'

'I think she might be.'

'She should, while it's still around.' Roger explained that there was talk of the railway being re-routed, to avoid areas south and west of Lake Eyre where frequent washouts had damaged the line and disrupted services.

'It's about time,' Adam said, doubting that any work would be done. He'd heard these rumours before. 'If they'd built the line properly in the first place it wouldn't get undermined or washed away every time there was rain.'

'I don't think it's just a question of rebuilding it.' Roger paused, not sure how to break the news. 'What they're talking about is taking it somewhere else, way over to the west, where there aren't any creeks and there's not so much sand.'

Adam was alarmed. 'And what sort of service would we get?'

Roger coughed. 'None.'

'What do you mean? Only one train a week?'

'No. None. They'd pull the line up.'

'That'd be crazy, Roger. They went to so much trouble to build the thing in the first place and they only modernized it twelve or thirteen years ago. They wouldn't just rip it up.'

The minister nodded sadly. 'Governments have been known to do things that defy logic.'

'And what about people like us, who live along the line and depend on it?'

'There aren't enough of you. The changes are only mooted, but they're being suggested in the interests of the twin gods that all politicians worship, progress and economics. All too often, progress is just another name for needless change, although something certainly should be done to fix the line.'

'Well why don't they fix it, instead of cutting us off?'

'Because of the second god, economics. They can say it will save money eventually and they can point to all the jobs that will be created for the people who have to build the new line.'

'What about the hardships for those who live along the existing line?'

'Ah.' Roger raised a hand, as though about to begin a sermon.

'Politics is a game of numbers. On the one hand, there are a few thousand people who will gain temporary employment during the construction of such a line. On the other are a few like yourself who live here, and will be permanently disadvantaged. Politicians rarely look beyond the next election, I'm afraid, so who do you think will win?'

Adam was silent.

'It's only talk,' Roger said, to comfort him.

'But you think it has substance?'

'Yes.'

'It would make things difficult for us.'

Roger laughed. 'You've never had it easy!'

Wryly, Adam joined in. 'So what's new, eh?'

'Precisely. Whatever happens you'll cope. By the way, how's the young one, Patrick? Doing well at school?'

Adam told him of his son's expulsion.

'Would you like me to talk to him?' Roger offered, when Adam had finished.

'He doesn't like to speak about it.'

'Maybe he should. It could help. Often, we bottle up things that are better brought out into the open.' When Adam still looked doubtful, he said: 'It's what I do best; a little bit of talking and a lot of listening. A bit of wise counselling and a lot of letting him say what's on his mind might help the lad.'

Roger's opportunity came that afternoon. He saw Patrick ride back to the yards and unsaddle Silver. He wandered across. As Patrick was leaving, with the saddle held in front of him, Roger said, 'Do you remember me, Patrick? I'm Roger Montgomery.'

Patrick slung the saddle across the top rail of the yard and shook hands. 'You're an old friend of Dad's?'

'That's right. I used to be the minister up in this area years ago. Funny thing, my next posting was at Port Lincoln.' He smiled as though that should have meant something.

'Oh?'

'Yes. I was there at the time of that terrible business.'

'Oh.' Now Patrick understood. 'The shark.'

'You were quite a hero.'

Patrick took the saddle off the fence and started walking towards the shed. Roger fell into step beside him, with his hands behind his back and his head bent forward.

'Everyone was talking about it. They thought it was quite an exceptional thing that you had done.'

Without turning or stopping, Patrick said, 'Did Dad tell you I'd been expelled from school?'

'He did, actually.'

'Did he ask you to talk to me?'

'No.' They were matching step, each with his head down. 'I just thought I'd say hello. Why, would you like to talk?'

'No thank you.'

'I'm a good listener.'

Without answering, Patrick entered the shed and put the saddle away. Roger waited for him. 'It can sometimes help to talk about things.'

'I don't want to talk about it.'

'That's fair enough.'

Patrick walked towards the hangar and the minister followed. 'I flew the plane the other day,' the boy said.

'Did you now?' It sounded perilously like a statement of disbelief.

'You can ask Dad. He let me fly for a while, south of Leigh Creek.'

Roger swallowed, censuring himself. 'And how did you go?'

'All right.'

'Enjoy it?'

The boy shrugged, obviously unwilling to carry on with the subject.

'It seems to me that you're a lad with a lot of ability and a lot of good points.'

Patrick spared him a brief, quizzical glance. It demanded an explanation.

'You ride a horse very well.'

'Everyone can do that.'

'No, they can't.' He adopted his most humble expression. 'I can't.'

'But you're a reverend.'

'I don't see what that has to do with it. Ministers of religion can play cricket or football, climb mountains, do all sorts of things. It's just that I can't ride and neither can many people. Very few boys in the city can ride horses.'

'They don't need a horse in the city. A horse would look silly.'

'Possibly.' He locked hands firmly behind his back. 'You do many things very well, Patrick, and I'm sure you could do even more if you tried. Your father can do a lot of things well. You take after him.'

'No, I don't.'

'Oh, you're just like him, in so many ways.'

'No, I'm not.'

Roger tried to laugh. 'Well, at least you're modest. I think that's

844

one thing people liked about you all those years ago, when you won that medal for bravery. You were just a nice, ordinary, modest kid. A very brave boy. Braver than most grown men.'

'I don't want to talk about it, please.'

'Why not? That's something you can be proud of.'

'Because I don't want to.'

They were near the entrance to the hangar. Roger stopped and turned the boy to face him. 'Patrick, it's often better to talk about things than to keep them bottled up inside. If there's something about the incident that still worries you, and you think it might help to talk about it, to get it off your chest, to brush it out of your system for all time, then try talking about it to me.'

Patrick had gone pale. 'I'm not worried about anything.'

'I talk to a lot of people who go through traumatic experiences. A few weeks ago I had to talk to a man whose son had been killed in a car accident. The father had been driving the car. Can you imagine how he must have felt?' Roger paused for some sign of understanding but Patrick was looking down at the ground.

'That poor man blamed himself. I got him to talk about the accident. It was a very difficult thing for him to do but by going through the whole episode, even the most painful parts, I was able to learn what was troubling him and convince him that it wasn't really his fault. Certainly his son is dead, and that can never be changed, but at least the man doesn't feel as guilty as he did. Patrick, he was destroying himself with guilt, over something that wasn't really his fault.'

Patrick looked up. 'What's that got to do with the price of fish?'

Roger frowned. 'I wasn't trying to be flippant.'

'Well, I don't want to talk about the shark. I didn't kill anyone.' He strode into the hangar. Roger followed.

'Of course not. You tried to save someone from being killed. Someone who, through his own stupidity, put both your lives at risk.'

Patrick spun around. 'Simon was not stupid.'

'Well,' Roger continued, feeling he was on the verge of having the boy reveal what troubled him, 'he certainly did a reckless, even an insane thing. No one just goes for a swim in waters like those.'

'He didn't.'

'He did, Patrick, he did. Now, I'm sorry if that man was a friend of yours but the fact is that he died, and even worse, he risked your life, because of an act of stupidity on his part.'

'Will you shut up?'

Roger raised a finger. 'Don't be rude to me. I'm trying to help.'

'I don't want you to help.'

845

'Patrick, please.'

The boy ran to the wall and lifted a heavy piece of timber. He held it like a club. 'Will you go away?'

'Patrick!'

Patrick advanced and the minister retreated. 'Go away,' the boy shouted. Wiping his lips, Roger backed out of the hangar.

'I think I should talk to your father.'

'Yes, why don't you? Everyone talks to my father.'

Roger left. Patrick threw the piece of timber to one side and, heart pounding, walked to the Cessna. He stood at the nose of the plane, one hand on a propeller blade and watched Roger Montgomery hurry back towards the homestead. There would be trouble. As soon as his father heard what the minister had to say, he'd come running over and then he'd get belted. And that would mean there was nowhere he could go. He wasn't wanted at school. He wouldn't be wanted here any more.

He'd heard of boys running away from home but didn't know how to go about it. He could try. He didn't know where he'd go or how he could get anywhere in this country. Kalinda was so isolated. He could always take Silver and hide out in the sand-hills. They'd find him, though.

There was no time to re-saddle Silver and get away before his father came. He should hide. He walked to the side of the aircraft, opened the door and climbed abroad. He slid into the pilot's seat.

There was another way. He could kill himself. He'd read about people doing that. It would make everyone really sorry, too, and that would be good. He wondered what was the best way to do it, and if it hurt.

In the distance, he heard a door slam.

He wished he could fly this plane as high as it would go and then dive it down on the house. That would show them. Then he'd never know the shame of having his brother marry a black girl and he'd never be related to Jimmy Kettle or end up like him, and no one would ever find out why Simon Bannister had to get in the water that day.

He saw his father leave the house. Behind him and waving his hands, was Roger Montgomery. One of the old Land Rovers drove past the hangar. Great. That was Daniel. Now they were all here, except his mother, but she'd find out and cry a lot and that would be just as good.

He knew how to start the motor. His father had told him and he had watched him at Leigh Creek. He went through each process, just as his father had done, and pressed the starter. The propeller spun in a series of jerks and then the exhaust pipes spat smoke and

846

the engine started. The propeller became a blur and a terrible noise filled the hangar. The Cessna crept forward. How did he stop it? His father hadn't told him that. He became frightened. Looking out, he saw his father running towards the building.

Rocking from side to side, the plane rolled through the open doors. It was gathering speed. He hadn't touched the throttle. Why was it going faster?

Adam dived to one side to avoid the propeller. He grabbed at the passing wing strut and managed to hold on for a few moments but lost his grip and rolled along the ground in the wake of the Cessna.

The Land Rover skidded to a halt beside him. Daniel jumped out.

'You all right?' He pulled his father to his feet.

'I'm OK. Quick. After him.'

'Who's in the plane?'

'Patrick.'

They saw the aircraft fishtailing as Patrick discovered how to turn it. It performed a quarter-turn to the left and headed towards the house, then swung violently to the right.

'You drive,' Daniel shouted and vaulted into the back of the vehicle. 'Get me alongside if you can, on the right-hand side.'

Adam set off in pursuit of the plane which was now heading towards the horseyards. Near the fence, Patrick swung to the left and the aircraft, wobbling from the violence of the turn, lost some speed. It began to accelerate again but the delay enabled Adam to catch it. He drove behind the tail and accelerated towards the high wing.

'For heaven's sake be careful,' he shouted, as he brought the nose of the Land Rover beneath the wing. In the outside mirror, he could see Daniel poised to jump. It was like hunting down wild cattle; he would drive, Daniel would leap off, take a few rapid steps and grab the galloping bull.

Daniel leaped from the vehicle and ran, arms flailing, legs striding in huge, unbalanced steps that somehow got him to the wing strut. Just as he finally lost his balance, he gripped the strut and let his boots drag in the dirt for a few moments while he gathered strength for the next manoeuvre.

Adam pulled away from the Cessna, to be well clear in case the aircraft turned or Daniel fell.

The plane ran over a rough patch of ground and Daniel, balancing like a gymnast with one leg groping for a place on the footplate, almost lost his hold. He slipped and the other leg dragged across some stones. The Cessna was now aimed at the little house where Mrs Wilson lived. Hearing the noise, she came to the front door. Her eyesight was not good, but she could see an aeroplane, with a man out the side and a young face peering through the screen, bearing down on her.

Daniel got a foot on the plate, swung forward and managed to open the door. He sprawled across the seat and, with his legs projecting through the open door, reached across and pulled back the throttle.

The plane slowed to a waddle.

'Left, Patrick,' he gasped. 'Turn it to the left.'

The boy complied. Daniel crawled inside, and switched off.

'The first rule of flying,' he said, still sucking in great quantities of air, 'is not to start 'em if you can't stop 'em.'

It was a peace offering, a way out, but it went unrecognized.

'I can fly.' Sullenly Patrick sat with his hands on the wheel.

'Don't be a dill, Pat.' He rubbed sore ribs. 'What were you trying to do? Kill yourself?'

Mrs Wilson was calling out, demanding to know what was happening.

'Yes,' Patrick said.

'Don't talk like a smart alec. You nearly ran your dad down and you've just about given Mrs Wilson a heart attack.' The boy was not looking at him, and Daniel shook him. 'Face me, will you. I want to help you.'

'I don't want your help. I hate you.'

'Hate me. Why?'

'Because you're going to marry a nigger.'

F·I·V·E

Patrick returned to Adelaide in disgrace. The incident with the Cessna seemed to cure him of his passion for misbehaviour because his passage through the new school was relatively calm, but it also ended his blossoming relationship with his father. When Daniel had dragged him by the ear from the pilot's seat, Patrick had poured out his hatred for Kalinda and the people who lived there, and his contempt for their way of life. After that, Adam rarely spoke to him and when he did, Patrick seldom answered.

Patrick left school at seventeen, having just – to Nina's great relief – missed the possibility of being conscripted into the army for service in Vietnam. He was tall, fair like his father but not as broad across the shoulders, and good looking in a slightly vulnerable way. Nina thought he was developing talent as a writer and tried to get him accepted as a cadet journalist on one of the Adelaide papers. When that was unsuccessful, she found him a job with a small advertising agency. He liked that. He was working with young people who epitomized the spirit of the age. Australia was on a boom inspired by its massive mineral resources and the office, like much of the country, was buoyant with optimism and complacency. The two principals were in their early thirties and drove Porsches. There was a free-and-easy atmosphere in the office. Ties were allowed only when the account executives called on certain clients. Everyone wore jeans and smoked either the most fashionable brand of cigarette or rolled their own from plants that grew in the little garden out the back of their converted terrace house. They were people who were certain they knew what was wrong with the world, were almost as sure about the cure, and praised or damned wines with a vehemence others reserved for politicians. Those were their great passions: discussing what was wrong with a world ruined by their elders, and drinking wines produced by the same benighted generation.

It was at the agency that Patrick discovered sex need not be practised in the dark or after office hours. It was also there that

Patrick discovered he looked good in front of the camera. He was at a shoot one day when a male model failed to arrive. Patrick stood in for him. The campaign was successful and he was offered other modelling jobs, which his boss allowed him to take. They worked erratic shifts at the agency and didn't seem to mind when people started or finished as long as the work was done.

They knew his mother was an American, which made him different, and a writer of some note, which gave him distinction. He rarely spoke about his father although his fellow workers knew Mr Ross lived in the outback and owned a huge tract of land. They assumed Patrick was rich and could probably afford a Porsche too, but chose not to flaunt his wealth. The girls liked him for that.

No one knew he had been expelled from one of the State's most prestigious schools. No one associated him with the small boy who, in the previous decade, had been the hero of a shark attack.

In 1976, the agency opened an office in Sydney and Patrick, now nearly twenty-one, was transferred there. He didn't like the new boss. The man expected punctuality and seemed to be intent on stifling the creativity of young people, so after six months, Patrick quit. He concentrated on modelling, made good money – vast amounts some weeks – and found a flat in Paddington.

He drifted into acting. On the advice of a friend he applied for a bit-part in a film. He was hired for a crowd scene but the director wanted someone with fair hair to climb a clock tower, and as he had neither a suitable stunt man nor a blond wig for a dark volunteer, he sent the eager Patrick up the building.

The tower was easier to climb than the one at his old school. At the top, the young man had time to reflect that a stunt that had once earned him a caning was now worth five hundred dollars.

He graduated to a supporting role in a cops-and-robbers TV show. That lasted a year.

In 1978 he went to England.

That was the year Adam knew they were in for a bad drought.

For a time, Kalinda had enjoyed a string of good seasons. Rain had fallen in successive years and they had witnessed the remarkable sight of the lake being filled to the highest erosion marks cut into its jutting headlands. Feed had grown in previously desolate places, the cattle had become fat and sleek, the sheep had multiplied and grown fine fleece and Adam had prospered. He used his profit, plus borrowed money, to purchase even better quality breeding stock, to sink more bores and to fence large paddocks. He also built houses for his new workers and their families and replaced his old Land Rovers with new Toyotas.

His sheep and cattle could now reach every corner of his two thousand, five hundred and ten square miles, the paddocks were well fenced, he had constructed roads on his property and had put down fifteen landing strips.

His underground bores and springs gave him a never-ending supply of water. None of his stock should ever die of thirst. All he lacked was a guarantee of the grass and top-feed to keep them alive. Without rain for a few years, the pastures would wither and his animals would perish.

There had been no worthwhile rain for eighteen months. The grass which had flourished in previous years had died or was reduced to straw. Mulga trees which had bloomed a brilliant yellow in the good times became wizened skeletons. Even the top-feed which had sustained stock in the driest seasons began to shrivel and lose its leaves. Some bushes died. Some were uprooted in the dust storms, which became more frequent.

Two years earlier, the shearers had handled forty thousand merinos but by 1978, Adam had sold half of his flock at poor prices to conserve feed for his breeding stock and strongest animals. Whereas he had sent three hundred head of cattle to market in 1976, he now had only three hundred on the property and none was sent to the sales.

One dry day followed the other with a searing monotony. Skies were no longer blue but the colour of long-dead ash, and the wind, when it blew, brought the lick of a blast furnace.

Saleem Benn, now feeling his great age and disinclined to leave Marree, was pessimistic. He had known a time like this, when the pelicans flew south and the hawks flapped lazily on the ground and each breath of scorched air brought a foreboding of worse to come. That time had been back in the 1920s, when he had taken a caravan of thirty camels to Cordillo Downs. Ten camels had perished and he had suffered so badly from thirst and the dreadful heat that he had barely survived the fourteen-month journey.

His old friend's gloomy reminiscence depressed Adam. It underscored a thought that had been worrying him for some time. More and more, he was thinking he'd made a mistake by settling at Kalinda. True, he had built the property from nothing and in those early days, that was seen as an admirable thing. He had erected houses and sheds, sunk bores, graded roads, made fences, raised sheep, bred cattle. By most standards, he was a success. Even an outstanding success, given the quality of the arid country he had settled in. But the one adversary he couldn't overcome, and the one that could beat him, at any time, was nature.

If it rained, he would be all right. If it didn't and the drought

851

lasted as long as the one that Saleem Benn recalled with such distaste, then he would go broke. He would lose everything.

What he had considered to be a good fight – man indulging in a righteous battle to tame a wilderness and turn it into productive land – was, he was beginning to think, more of an exercise in futility. He was battling against the way things were and had always been; maybe even the way things were meant to be. He was up against the natural order, which was the most stupid and unnatural of all battles to undertake.

Despite the houses, the sheds, the bores, the fences and all the stock, whether he succeeded or failed at Kalinda would be decided by one thing. Rain.

Maybe he should have done something else, or gone somewhere else, like Josef was always advocating. He went to bed that night wondering if he had wasted forty years of his life.

Cassie arrived in the company plane. Peppino used the aircraft to service units in the field. The pilot was on his way to a drilling site on the western side of the Simpson Desert. He let Cassie get out, waved goodbye, and took off again.

'Just like a bus,' she told Adam. 'He'll pick me up tomorrow afternoon.'

Cassie was now in her forty-second year. She could have been mistaken for a woman in her mid-thirties until a closer examination revealed the fine wrinkles around her eyes, a legacy of her early years in the bush. She dressed like a city woman but walked like a country girl, with large springy strides. The three men she had left behind in Adelaide, she said, were quite capable of caring for themselves. Peppino had the makings of a paunch which would suit a man of his substance. The boys were fine and doing well at school. Giovanni, or Johnny as he was always known, was now twelve and by far the tallest boy in his class. Enrico, or Rick, was ten, still nuggety, and the sensation of the junior football team.

'Peppino's diversifying – again,' she announced when they were assembled for lunch. They all smiled – Nina and Adam, Lizzie and Daniel, Stella and Jimmy – but there was no suggestion that they hadn't taken the remark seriously. All of Peppino's diversifications had been successful. He still supplied equipment and services to mineral and geological survey companies but now had contracts for delivering city newspapers to country centres, owned three tuna-fishing boats that operated around the Eyre Peninsula and into the waters of the Great Australian Bight and operated car and truck dealerships in Adelaide, Port Pirie, Whyalla, Port Lincoln and Broken Hill. He was a millionaire several times over.

852

'He's going into tourism,' Cassie said.

'Holidays?' Adam asked.

'Taking people on holidays, yes. He's done some research, as always. He reckons tourism is the fastest growing industry in the world.'

'Holidays?' Adam's voice echoed with doubt. 'But there's a drought and it's getting worse. People won't have the money to get away.'

'Dad, fewer and fewer people live in the outback. Old fossils like you are becoming extinct.' She was sitting next to him and touched his shoulder, as though delicately fingering a museum exhibit. 'Most people in this country live in the cities and the only time they're aware of a drought is when meat and vegetables get dearer.'

'What sort of holidays?' Adam asked, reluctant to yield.

'By coach. He's proposing tours of the outback, 'specially to some of the out-of-the-way-places.'

'Not Ayers Rock?' Nina said.

'Every tourist company goes to Ayers Rock.'

'So you'll go somewhere else?' Lizzie asked.

'Peppino knows a lot of fascinating places from all his travels. You know the story: wherever a mining company has dug or drilled, my man has driven. He's got drivers who know their way across deserts and into the most remote and beautiful places. Peppino knows the people who live there and he even owns the company that can sell him the coaches.'

'How does he handle so many different businesses?' Adam shook his head in puzzled admiration.

'He has a lot of good men in his organization, and one fabulously gifted woman.'

'You talking about Marie?' Jimmy said and they all laughed. 'How is she?'

'Fine. She's doing very well in her new job.' Jimmy's eldest daughter was secretary to the man who ran the fishing and news-paper delivery operations.

'Does she really get free newspapers?'

Cassie laughed. 'Probably.'

Jimmy shook his head but failed to dislodge the look of wonderment. In his eyes, working at a steady job and getting something for nothing was the pinnacle of achievement. 'Fish too?' he asked.

'We all get fish.'

'For nix?'

'They're our fish.'

Cassie asked about the property and Adam and Daniel outlined the depressing story of the drought.

'No one's aware of it down south yet,' she said.

'That figures. At times I feel as though we're living in a different

853

country. We're losing our railway, we're getting rid of stock, the feed's drying up ...' He stared gloomily across the room.

'You should do like Peppino does and diversify.'

'Into what? You can't grow wheat or crops up here. It's getting marginal even for grazing.' He jabbed the air with his left fist. 'Do you know what happened the other day? A group of government officials came in by plane. They were doing a survey of the State's water resources and one young cove who must have been all of twenty-five gave me a lecture about what I was doing wrong.'

'I don't think he was long out of university,' Nina added, with a tolerant smile.

'Yes,' Adam said. 'This young feller reckoned I shouldn't raise sheep in this country. According to him, I should pack up and walk off and leave it all to the blackfellers.'

'That'd be all right,' Jimmy said and ducked as Adam pretended to throw his serviette at him.

'The trouble is, the young fellow was probably right.' Adam sighed. 'For a hundred years, they've been urging us to move into the backblocks and settle. We were opening up the country, or at least, that's what I thought we were supposed to be doing. And now a whole new generation who wouldn't know which end of an axe to use are telling us we were wrong. What they'd like would be for us to head down south and camp on the beach and go on social security.'

'You should be in politics, Pop.' Cassie pulled his ear. 'What you need to do, my fiery old fossil of a father, is to go into tourism.'

'And run buses?'

'No. Have people stay here. We could bring up coach loads of people. You could show them the lake, the sand-hills, a mound spring, Horseshoe Hills, a bore.'

He laughed. 'Bore would be right. They'd be bored stiff.'

She held out her right hand. 'Want to bet that it wouldn't work?'

He took her hand. 'Ten dollars. Who'd run it? Where would people stay?'

'You've got shearers' quarters.' She looked around the table. 'And any amount of talent. Nina, Lizzie, Stella.'

Adam laughed. 'Woman's work, eh?'

'No. We'd just need the best brains available.' She gripped his hand before he could lift it. 'Tell me, have you heard from Patrick?'

Adam's face lost its animation. 'He's in London.'

Nina leaned forward with her hands clasped. 'I think he's finding things pretty tough.'

S·I·X

Patrick liked London but, at first, found it hard to make money. One hurdle in the way of earning his keep was that he was not supposed to work. He was an alien in a land where tens of thousands of young men couldn't get jobs and he had entered Britain on the stipulation that he did not seek employment. Another hurdle was that, even if he lied about his birthplace, work for a person with his talents was extremely difficult to find for London was bursting with unemployed actors and models.

For seven weeks he approached television studios, film production houses and advertising agencies, showing them his portfolio of stills from unfamiliar campaigns and discussing his role in a TV series none of them had seen. On the Tuesday of the eighth week, he put on a phoney accent and got a part-time job in a travel company that conducted overland bus tours to India and Nepal. On the same day, he had another stroke of luck. He ran into Damon Gallagher, who had been living in London for a year.

Damon had a Range Rover and a two-bedroom flat in Hampstead. Patrick, who had been staying in cramped quarters at Earl's Court, moved in with him.

Damon allegedly worked for his father. 'Represented' was the word he used. As far as Patrick could determine, Damon did nothing but read the newspapers every day, have an occasional business lunch and make telephone calls to Adelaide. The expenses he incurred were handy for Australian tax purposes.

Damon's voice had always tended more towards British pronunciation than Australian and, while his accent had not changed, he now used British terms like 'dear boy', 'super' and 'do you know what I mean'. He felt at home.

He offered Patrick a job which wouldn't interfere with his part-time labours for the travel company. 'The old man said we should spend a bit more money and I said I could do with a driver. You do have a licence?' He gave a nervous laugh, remembering the King William Street exploit.

Patrick produced an International Driver's Licence. 'Super,' Damon said, and Patrick became the chauffeur for the London representative of Mazell, Gallagher and Tomkins. He now had two jobs, neither of which required a great deal of effort.

He worked Thursdays and Fridays at the travel agency. He sat in an office plastered with maps of Greece, Turkey, Iran, Afghanistan, Pakistan and India and spent hours offering meaningful advice to impecunious young women who were seeking the adventure of a lifetime. If the girl were particularly attractive, Patrick would suggest dinner, borrow the Range Rover and offer her the bonus of the experience of a lifetime.

'If the bus trip's not good, at least you can say you got something worthwhile for the money,' he would say in parting, to those who seemed to have a sense of humour.

When the woman who ran the agency (and whose husband drove one of the buses) discovered Patrick knew a few words of Pushtu, taught to him by Daniel many years ago, he became the company's resident expert on Afghanistan. He studied the map with interest and even read a few books about the country.

The job with Damon usually involved going to lunch. They got a map of London and began to tick off all the restaurants they had visited. Occasionally, Damon took some guest to lunch and then Patrick would dutifully deliver them to the restaurant and collect them after the meal but, mostly, they ate together.

Having a good address, money, a Range Rover and almost unlimited time, Damon had gathered around him friends who prized such things. The young man's status had been boosted by the acquisition of his own, full-time driver but those who met Patrick soon realized the appointment was a bit of a joke: merely a way for two old school chums to get together and have fun, and let the willing father in far-off Australia pay for the sowing of the young men's wild oats.

Patrick discovered that Damon had developed a preference for male friends. That suited him. Patrick could make as vigorous a play as he liked for any girl they met, even if she were a friend of Damon, without there being a risk of jealousy. It became a convenient arrangement. Damon encouraged Patrick in his efforts to bed girls and even went with him on what he termed 'wench patrols', if ever his friend appeared to be negotiating a lean period in his love life. For Patrick, blessed by a hard body and gentle features – twin attributes that girls found attractive – such periods were rare. As his part of an unexpressed bargain, Patrick knew what functions to attend and which to avoid and what nights to spend away from the Hampstead flat.

It was a pleasant, if wasteful, period in Patrick's life. He was achieving little in a professional sense and was living off a young man he found amusing but considered to be inferior. However, he had picked up the rudiments of the travel business, had more than fifty female entries in his little book of telephone numbers, spent little of his own money, was learning his way round the streets of London and knew where to find most of the interesting restaurants.

Towards the end of summer, Damon met someone new and spent much of his time travelling on his own to Kensington. Patrick presumed it was a new male friend and was surprised when he was presented to a young woman whom Damon introduced only as Farah. She was an Iranian student. At first, Patrick thought his friend's preferences had undergone a change of polarity and was envious, because Farah looked like a Persian version of Sophia Loren, but then he discovered that she had an older brother with whom Damon had become infatuated. Damon was hoping Patrick would be a sport and show some interest in the girl.

The sister, Damon explained, had led a sheltered life before coming to London. She knew men could be friends but had no idea the relationship could become deeper. Farah would be scandalized if she discovered her brother was having an affair with another man. It was up to Patrick, he said with a wink, to keep her occupied and her mind on other things.

Farah's brother was called Rezi. After he finished university, he was to follow his father into the Iranian diplomatic service. He was tall and thin, with large eyes and a face of feline angularity.

'Isn't he the most beautiful thing you've ever seen?' Damon gushed in a rare moment. Normally, he didn't discuss his friends.

'He's super.'

Damon missed the irony. 'Farah's nice too, but, you know ...'

'Yes.'

'I do appreciate what you're doing for me. If she ever suspected ...'

Patrick couldn't see how the girl didn't suspect her brother and Damon were more than just casual friends. They spent every weekend together. Damon had eyes only for the exquisite Rezi. Patrick had even seen them holding hands. But Farah, apparently, believed chess was their consuming interest and would let them go away to play undisturbed while Patrick took her to the theatre, to some new restaurant or for a drive in the Range Rover.

She was an extraordinarily pretty girl, but boring. Sex was forbidden. Patrick made a few attempts to have her sample its delights but soon gave up. He complained to Damon, who promptly offered to pay him to spend time with the girl. This

857

Patrick did, comforting himself with the knowledge that, in his third concurrent job in London, he must be the only man in the city being paid not to have sex with a woman.

Towards the end of 1978, both Damon and Rezi had cause to be agitated but for different reasons, neither of which was to do with any deterioration in their relationship. Damon's upset came from the decision by Mazell, Gallagher and Tomkins to close the London office. 'We're out of a job, dear boy,' he told Patrick. 'There's either a new man in the head office or there's been a change in the taxation laws. Whatever it is, we're out on our ears.'

Rezi's concern was for the deteriorating political situation in his own country and for a corresponding decline in his father's health. He had received a letter from Tehran. His father was sick and wanted Rezi to return immediately to Iran, to take charge of the family's affairs and to help counter certain accusations being made against him. Rumours were spreading that the old man was illicitly sending large sums of money out of the country. Naturally, the presence of his son and daughter in London, where they lived in luxury and entertained lavishly, added substance to those stories. He wanted them to return home at once.

By coincidence, an official from the Iranian embassy had called on Rezi only an hour after the letter arrived. The man had wandered through the apartment, examining furniture and paintings and questioning Rezi about what money his father sent him. He had even had the effrontery to ask how much he paid for his suits. More disturbing was that he had questioned Rezi about some of his sister's friends. It was rumoured, the man said, that Farah was frequently seen in the company of known dissidents.

This worried Rezi for Iran was in a state of turmoil. There was talk of revolution. Accusations of disloyalty were rife. His father was in great danger and so unwell that he would have difficulty in defending himself against any charges. The family could lose everything. And the son and daughter of an accused man mightn't be safe in London. The dreaded SAVAK had tentacles that reached everywhere, even to England.

That night, in the flat he shared with Patrick, Damon said, 'Rezi feels he should go back. It would devastate me if he left and I stayed. Not that I can afford to stay on in London now.'

Patrick found the conversation embarrassing but sat quietly.

'So I'm thinking of going as far as Tehran with him.'

Patrick studied Damon's face to see if this was a serious proposal. It was. 'Wouldn't that be dangerous?'

'Why, for heaven's sake?'

'Well, there's been trouble over there. Riots, shooting, that sort

858

of thing. Didn't they pot a few hundred people in some square in Tehran the other day?'

'A media beat-up, dear boy. In any case, the Persians have been shooting people ever since the invention of gunpowder. It's like football: a national sport. No, it's perfectly safe. I was reading that the jolly old Queen is even planning a state visit in the royal yacht. If it's safe enough for the royal family, it'll be safe enough for a colonial as common as me.'

Patrick rubbed his chin in doubt. 'But you'll be going with Rezi and this is a Muslim country.'

'I do remember my geography, or social studies or whatever it was.'

'And if they found an Australian man in bed with an Iranian man, they'd probably do something very unpleasant to you.'

Damon looked grim. 'I still want to go.'

'Just for a few more hours together on a jet?'

'I wasn't thinking of flying.' He enjoyed the look of consternation on Patrick's face. 'Don't look so surprised. You send people off by bus every few weeks. Why shouldn't we do it in style?'

'We?'

'You, me, Rezi and his sister. Plenty of room in the old wagon.'

'We drive them all the way to Tehran?'

'Why not? We can take out time through Europe, see a bit of France, have a week or two in Saint Tropez and Cannes. You know what I mean?'

'And take as long as possible getting to Iran.'

'Of course.' He grinned triumphantly.

'Damon, what do we do after we drop them off in Tehran?'

'To be perfectly frank, I hadn't really thought that far ahead. Keep on going I suppose.'

'All the way to Australia?'

'Well, until the road peters out. Then we put the old Rover on a ship, send it back home and sell it for a fortune.' He saw the doubtful look in Patrick's eyes. 'What's wrong? Don't want to go home yet?'

'I hadn't thought about it.'

'It'd be a bit of fun. Especially Europe. I've hardly seen anything of the continent.' Patrick still seemed uncertain.

'The journey is feasible, isn't it? I mean, there *is* a road?'

'Yes. It's supposed to be good all the way to Tehran.'

'Well, there we are. We'll go for a drive. And you never know,' he winked, 'a week on the French Riviera might persuade Rezi to stay in Europe and forget about going home.'

* * *

859

They left England just before Christmas. One aspect of the journey that Patrick had not considered concerned his relationship with Farah.

She had grown fond of him during their weeks together in London and presumed he felt the same about her. For Farah, who was excessively romantic, the journey was to be a bittersweet episode in her life; each day would be more exciting and yet sadder than the last, each night a rehearsal for their final farewell. He might even contemplate suicide. She was twenty, coated in western sophistication yet immature, vulnerable and essentially Iranian at the core.

Patrick, whose interest in women was confined to sexual adventures, regarded Farah as a lost cause. As he was no longer being paid to show interest in her, or to divert her attention from the other two (which was an impossibility, anyhow, in such a crowded vehicle), he attempted neither. At first she was hurt, then she became resentful. There was one period, just beyond the English Channel, when she thought his long silences might be caused by distress due to their imminent separation, but a hard laugh and some forthright language soon dispelled that illusion. They headed south across France with Farah feeling greatly confused. Her confusion worsened when, having been inexplicably spurned by Patrick, she sought comfort from her brother and found she was in competition with Damon. Rezi and the shorter, less attractive Australian, had eyes only for each other. They talked, touched and looked at each other in ways that suggested, even to her innocent eyes, pastimes other than chess. By Cannes, she was outraged. There was no question of Damon having time to persuade Rezi to change his mind. After only two days on the French Riviera, an angry and insistent Farah had them all back in the Range Rover and speeding to the east.

Thirteen days later, having disposed of Italy, Yugoslavia, Greece and Turkey, they were at the Iranian border. Snow was piled high at the side of the road and it was freezing cold. They joined a queue of trucks whose drivers slept or gossiped, like men accustomed to lengthy delays. A much larger number of vehicles was leaving Iran and many were packed in a way that suggested hasty exits, but Farah was as oblivious to that as she was to the majestic cap of nearby Mount Ararat. Her sole concern was to re-enter Iran. She, whose Islamic sense of propriety had swollen as the distance to her homeland diminished, yearned to reach Tehran and rid her brother of the influence of these vile westerners.

Crossing the border took six hours. The Turks were slow but polite whereas the Iranians were irascible and flustered by the clamour of individuals attempting to leave the country. Patrick and the others might have been there longer had not Rezi discovered an official who found his appearance fetching, and allowed them to move many places up the line.

Once inside Iran, they followed the highway towards the city of Tabriz. A constant trickle of traffic came towards them, among them many new Mercedes-Benz saloons and locally-made Peycans bearing roof-racks crammed with snow-flecked luggage.

'I think the situation here might be a little worse than we were led to believe,' Patrick said softly. He was driving and meant his words for Damon, who was sharing the back seat with Rezi.

'No,' Farah answered. She was much more animated since leaving Turkey. 'Some people have been fleeing the country but they are the greedy ones who have amassed fortunes overseas and would rather be with their money than with their kinsfolk. We can do without them.'

'Who told you that?' Rezi snapped. He intended making life difficult for his sister once they reached Tehran. London was full of Iranian dissidents and Muslim fundamentalists and she had fallen under their influence. What she didn't realize was that those ratbag students and religious revolutionaries were the enemies of the Shah and, therefore, of their family. Their father was a senior government official, a loyal servant of the King from the time of his coronation, and if the Shahanshah, King of Kings, Light of the Aryans, Muhammad Rezi Pahlavi fell, so would their family. All of them. They'd have all their money and property confiscated and probably end up in gaol. Their father would be tortured. Farah was too stupid to understand that. She had always been easily swayed by someone with a silken tongue and a holy glint in his eyes.

And now she was ruining this journey for him. If she persisted with her obnoxious behaviour, he would take the most exquisite revenge on her once they were home. If she levelled accusations against him, he would brand her a whore who had slept with men in London. He had photographs of her sitting with Patrick, which he could display in case such a situation arose. There were other photographs too, of her standing beside western men – Englishmen, Germans, Americans – at parties he had given in the past year. Those pictures were all the proof he would need to discredit her in a society where the merest hint of a woman's immorality – provided it was made by a male – carried the weight of truth.

'What nonsense are you talking now?' he said.

'It's not nonsense. Yusef told me.' Yusef was a fellow student, much given to praising some obscure religious leader exiled in Paris.

861

'Yusef is a goat who deserves to have his throat slit to silence his bleatings.'

They continued to argue for some minutes, Farah repeating the things her fellow student had been saying, and Rezi constantly winking at Damon as though the discussion were a farce being staged for the two visitors.

The country was dry, but fertile. They passed many farms, with fields ploughed in broad, lumpy rows. At a place where mountains squeezed the farms into a narrow valley, the road followed a series of sharp turns around great outcroppings of rock. They came to a road block. It was formed simply of two trucks, parked in such a way that vehicles had to slow to thread their way past. A number of young men stood in the gap between the trucks. They were armed with rifles but wore ordinary clothes, not uniforms.

'Bandits?' Patrick asked with trepidation, having travelled so fast that there was no chance of him stopping and turning back. He had heard tales of dacoits causing trouble for foreigners, but that was much further to the east, around the Khyber Pass.

'No,' Farah said and wound down her window, as she was on the side where people would expect to find the driver.

Her brother reached forward and tapped her shoulder. 'You be quiet,' he commanded and opened his own window. 'What do you want?' he called out in his own language.

A young man walked to his door. He was no more than eighteen and had a moustache as fine as a camel-hair brush. A bandolier stretched from his shoulder to his hip. He examined all four persons within the vehicle and seemed particularly interested in Patrick. His companions surrounded the vehicle, peering through the windows. One opened the back, and began rifling through the luggage.

'Are you carrying weapons?' the leader said.

'No,' Rezi answered.

'Are you Iranian?'

'Yes.'

'Why are you in a car with the steering on that side?' He was chewing something and seemed about to spit.

'It is a British car.'

'And you?' He had a pistol and waved it as casually as a cigarette towards Patrick. 'Are you Iranian too?'

'He does not understand you,' Rezi said, his expression suggesting Patrick was to be pitied. 'He speaks only English.'

The young man cleared something caught between his front teeth. 'He is American?'

'He is Australian. So is the man beside me.'

'Oh.' The young man seemed puzzled. 'Not American?'

862

'No.'

'Are you carrying American cigarettes?'

Rezi let his abnormally large eyes flash signals of understanding. 'We have English cigarettes. Would some of those interest you?'

'You have a packet?'

'Certainly.' Rezi delved into a bag and passed the young man the cigarettes. As though signalled, the man searching the back of the vehicle withdrew and slammed the tailgate.

'Where have you driven from?' the leader asked.

'England.'

'In this car?'

'Yes. My friends are driving on to Australia.'

The man put the packet in the pocket of his jacket. 'You have a cigarette for my friend?'

Rezi looked doubtful. 'How many do you need?'

'Just one cigarette. Make it two. One for me to smoke now. One for him.' The second man, holding a rifle in both hands, pressed against his companion.

'Certainly.' Rezi searched for an open packet. 'Why are you stopping cars?'

'We are looking for guns.'

Rezi smiled. He passed over two cigarettes and a box of matches. 'Have you found any?'

The young man lit his cigarette and pointed casually towards a van parked off the road. Only then did Rezi notice the bodies of two men lying near the front wheels.

'OK. You can go.' He waved them on, and walked back to a truck which had ground to a stop behind the Range Rover.

There were many soldiers in Tabriz, all armed and strolling in groups. A tank was stationed at one intersection. At the next were the blackened shells of two burnt cars. Many shops were closed.

They found a service station, joined a queue of waiting vehicles and refilled the car's tank, plus two drums they carried in the back. They bought some food and left the city.

An hour out of Tabriz, they passed a convoy of military vehicles heading towards the city. Motor-cycle riders escorting the convoy waved them to the side of the road until the trucks had passed.

'I'm beginning to think this was not one of your better ideas,' Patrick confided to the image of Damon, whose eyes smouldered in the rearview mirror. His friend had hardly spoken since the border.

Again, Farah answered for someone else. 'No, it will be better when we get closer to the capital. It has always been bad up in this corner of the country. There are many trouble-makers who want an independent nation.'

Rezi growled from the back seat. 'That is nonsense.'

'It is not. They get support from the Soviet Union.'

'I am not disputing that. I am saying it is nonsense to say that things will be better in Tehran.'

Damon said, 'You think it will be dangerous there?'

'Who knows?' Rezi patted Damon's hand. 'But there will certainly be trouble in Tehran.'

'Should we go back?'

Hearing Damon's question, Patrick began to slow.

'Keep going,' Farah shouted. 'Tabriz is an outpost, full of dissidents. It will be perfectly all right in the capital.' She turned to her brother. 'And there is no question of us leaving Iran again, just so that you can be with your' – she pointed an accusing finger at Damon – 'friend. Chess, indeed. I know what's been going on.'

Rezi leaned forward and slapped her face. 'From now on, you will not talk unless I give you permission.'

She held her hand to her jaw. Her eyes were shocked but not unconquered. 'I will, I know –'

He slapped her on the other cheek; not viciously but firmly, as a person might discipline a dog. 'I think I will tell Father that you should marry that old carpet merchant who used to be interested in you before you went to London.'

'You wouldn't dare.'

'Oh, I would.' He moved closer with a reptilian grace. 'You have not been away so long that you have forgotten how things are, surely?'

'I will tell Father what you have been up to.'

'And I have photographs.' He laughed.

'What do you mean?'

'Nothing.' He sat back and looked out the window, no longer interested in her. 'But once they are shown to people, no one will want to marry you, even the old carpet merchant.'

'What photographs?'

He bent forward and raised his hand. 'Silence.'

Patrick, being signalled back on to the highway by one of the military policemen, turned to Rezi. 'Take it easy, sport,' he said.

Rezi waved a hand in warning. 'This is our affair and this is our country. Do not interfere.'

Feeling he should say something as the owner of the vehicle, Damon said, 'Stay out of it, Patrick,' but his voice shook. He inclined his head towards the Iranian. 'You really think we should go on?'

Rezi had been watching the last of the convoy. 'I think it is too late to do anything else.'

That night they slept in the car. Damon had driven the final shift and pulled off the road at a place where the Range Rover could be hidden behind trees. He suggested that Patrick sleep in the driver's seat. 'You're the better driver,' he said, 'and if anything happens we might want to make a quick getaway.' He then climbed in the back with Rezi. Farah said nothing.

They slept badly. Many trucks passed during the night and because the area was bounded by hills, the booming echoes of the big diesel motors sounded long before lights could be seen through the trees and continued long after they had passed. It was cold and Patrick, feeling chilled and stiff, started up the V8 an hour before dawn and resumed their journey to Tehran.

Near Qazvin, they encountered another road block.

This time, the men were older. One, wearing a filthy turban, approached the car. He was by far the oldest of the group. He carried no arms but those behind him all had rifles or pistols. The old man ordered everyone out of the car.

He was intrigued by the vehicle and inspected it minutely, even bending to read the words moulded on the tyres. He stopped in front of Rezi. 'You are American?'

'I am one of you,' Rezi replied indignantly, but was required to produce his papers as proof.

The man's tanned face was pockmarked so that his skin had the colour and texture of rotting timber. He singled out Patrick, whose height and fair colouring distinguished him in the company of so many shorter and darker people. 'He is American?'

Rezi shook his head. 'Australian.'

That meant nothing to the old man.

'Australia,' Patrick repeated and when there was still no response, he said 'Kangaroo' and hopped down the road. The men with the guns laughed. 'Kangaroo,' Patrick said again, and held his hands paw-like, under his chin.

The old man nodded several times and permitted his ravaged face to soften into a smile. He pointed to Damon. 'He is American?' This was less of a question; there had to be at least one American, the man was saying, in a foreign car with four persons on board.

Sadly, Rezi shook his head. One of the men bearing a rifle, which he held across his shoulders like a bullock's yoke, smiled broadly. He was enjoying the exchange but had the dull eyes of a man who would shoot if things became boring.

865

'He too is Australian,' Rezi said.

Damon attempted to smile. The old man felt the foreigner's coat, touched his collar, examined Damon's hands and ran one roughened finger along his cheek, playing with the fresh stubble. He turned and said something to his companions. They laughed and Rezi's face became flushed.

The man wiped his hand along the side of his turban and spoke to Damon.

'He wants you to hop like a kangaroo,' Rezi explained.

'The old bastard,' Damon muttered.

'Do as he says,' Patrick said, 'and smile.'

Damon hopped once and the old man opened his mouth in pleasure, revealing a few yellowed teeth. He pointed to Farah but did not waste words on a woman.

'My sister,' Rezi said. 'She understands what you say.'

All the men examined her as though assessing her value on the market.

'You have been away?' the old man said, giving Rezi back his passport.

'Yes. For several years. How are things in Tehran?'

The man's cheeks bunched like boils. 'Who knows? They say there has been fighting.'

'In the capital?' Farah blurted out the words.

The old man ignored her. 'Where were you?'

'In London,' Rezi said.

'What were you doing there?'

'Studying. So was my sister.'

'And why are you returning?'

Rezi hesitated. 'This is the right time for a man to be in his own country.'

The man nodded. 'Let us pray that it is the right time for you, eh?'

'Yes, indeed. Thank you.'

'You have family in Tehran?'

'Yes. My mother and father and some brothers. And two sisters,' he added as an afterthought.

'Let us hope that you find them. You may go.' He turned and walked away. The man with the rifle across his shoulders stayed, hands draped over the gun, his eyes wandering across the vehicle with a look that could have been envy.

'Let us go quickly,' Rezi said. Greatly disturbed, he got in the car.

'Who were those people?' Damon asked.

'I don't know.'

866

'Don't you think you should have asked them, dear boy?'

'Do you wish to deliver me to my family beneath a blanket?' He let one hand touch Damon. 'They are the people who would rule our country and take us back to the dark ages. Don't worry. Order will soon be restored. The Shah and his forces are all-powerful.'

Josef Hoffman had argued with Ursula. Their relationship had become stormy in recent months and he returned on his own to Adelaide. He visited Peppino and Cassie.

'I don't know who looks the worst, you or Peppino,' Cassie said when her husband left the room to make a phone call. She examined Josef's lined face with concern. 'You both look as though the world is about to come crashing around your shoulders.'

Josef hadn't been thinking about other people's worries. 'What's wrong with Peppino?' he asked.

'Nothing that a rest wouldn't fix. It's just that he's been working flat out and never takes a day off. Quite simply, he's worn to a frazzle. He needs a break.'

'Why don't you two go away?'

She shook her head. 'The boys are at school and there are so many businesses to run ...'

'Do you want me to take him off your hands for a few days?' He smiled and immediately looked younger, even allowing for the thinning hair and the network of worry lines.

She said nothing, waiting for him to elaborate.

My God, you're a good looking woman, Josef thought. Better now than you were twenty years ago. More mature, more interesting. 'I'd been thinking that a few days in the bush might help calm me down,' he said. 'So I'd been contemplating flying up north.'

'Kalinda?'

'Where else? Peppino could come with me. He could pretend he was examining something to do with your latest tourist operation.'

She laughed. 'He could, actually. Dad's been turning the old shearers' quarters into a motel. Peppino wants to check on what's being done.'

'So you're going ahead with all that?'

'Absolutely. Dad's not all that keen but we've bulldozed his objections to one side.' She clapped her hands lightly. 'When are you going?'

'I was thinking of flying up in a day or two.'

'Good. I'll tell him he's going.'

'There'll be no argument, no reasons why he can't possibly spare the time?'

'Of course.' She grinned. 'But he'll go. You won't let him work,

867

will you? He does desperately need a few days of doing nothing.'

'I'll talk to Adam and, between us, we'll work out something to make sure Peppino puts his mind into neutral. Maybe we'll slip him on a horse and take him out in the sandhills.'

She wrinkled her nose. 'Have you ever seen Peppino on a horse?'

He shrugged. 'Maybe a Land Cruiser would be better.'

'Much. How long can you spare?'

'I thought of going up for a week.'

'Great.' She took Josef's hand in hers. The skin was softer, these days. He remembered the roughness when she was just a youngster and they'd spent the night together huddled near a fire.

'Three days is all I can spare, really Joe.' Peppino was still objecting when the shoreline of Lake Eyre South came into sight. 'We've got some problems with the dealership at Broken Hill and I should get over there as soon as possible.'

The engine coughed momentarily.

'Dirt in one of the injectors,' Peppino said, automatically analysing the problem.

The engine note became smooth again and Josef shook his head. 'Just a hiccup. It's had a few late nights.' He grinned, determined to make this man relax. Peppino had problems with the tuna-fishing boats, too. He'd heard all about it on the way up from Adelaide. 'I'll fly you over to Broken Hill on the way back if you like. How about that?'

Peppino nodded. He had his head turned, listening to the motor.

They were near the lake when the propeller fluttered to a stop and a raucous whistle replaced the drone of the engine. Neither man spoke, but Peppino grasped the sides of his seat.

Josef tried to restart the motor but failed. 'Just a slight problem,' he said, determined to sound calm but shouting the words. 'Luckily, we're almost over the salt, so I'll put her down there and see what's wrong.'

Josef aimed for the edge of the lake. It looked muddy and soft but he had no choice. It was the only flat area he could reach.

They were almost down when Peppino saw the fence. It was a dilapidated old wire fence, broken in places but running across the salt. Peppino called a warning, but the plane was sinking rapidly and there was nothing Josef could do. The wheels caught in the wire.

The plane somersaulted on to the salt and, shedding wings and great slices of aluminium, skidded upside down across a muddy inlet of Lake Eyre South. Before it stopped, there was a gush of fuel and what was left of the aircraft caught fire.

868

S·E·V·E·N

They saw the smoke long before they saw the city. There must have been a number of truly big fires because columns of dark grey stained the sky in many places and then blended with the broad layer of smoke that was spread above Tehran. From a distance, the smoke looked like a gigantic but shadowy table with many legs.

As they entered the outskirts of the city a flight of jets passed low above them and the glass in the Range Rover shook.

The city was filthy. Garbage and broken glass were strewn across the footpaths and smoke curled from rubbish tins. Damaged and burnt cars were abandoned and the gutters were flooded with oily water. Many buildings had been singed by fire. Banners that had once hung from street lamps had been torn down and lay shredded on the roads. They passed one footpath blocked by fallen masonry. Nearby, a shop burned fiercely although no one was attempting to put out the blaze. A jeep laden with soldiers cut in front of them and turned down an alley. They glimpsed an overturned van and a mob of young men who threw stones, then ran.

'Keep going,' Rezi said. He was leaning forward, his head and shoulders thrust between the front seats. 'Whatever you do, don't stop unless it is absolutely imperative.'

'Like up ahead?' Patrick said. A tank was rumbling towards them, its long cannon wagging like an accusing finger. He slowed.

'Go to the other side of the road,' Rezi commanded and Patrick swung the vehicle between a central row of light standards and drove down the left side.

'Just like home,' he said and waved to the officer sitting in the turret. Not sure who he was, the man gave a half salute. Patrick darted back to the other side of the road. They passed the smoking ruins of a tall building whose walls had been painted with signs and bore a crude representation of Uncle Sam.

'May I ask a pertinent question?' Damon said, gripping Rezi's arm. 'If this is an eruption by people who want the Shah to leave, in other words, if this is people who are for the Shah versus people who are against the Shah, whose jolly side are you on?'

Rezi did not turn. 'My father is a high-ranking government official.'

'Which means he's pro-Shah?' Patrick said.

'It is the government of the Shah, yes.'

Farah, who was pressed into the corner, said, 'Yusef says the Shah is in league with Satan.'

Rezi raised his hand and she cowered against the glass. 'If you speak once more, I will throw you out of this car.'

'Hey, steady on,' Patrick said.

'He's only joking, dear boy.'

'I am not, my dear Damon,' Rezi said in an icy voice. 'Words like that could have us all killed. My family, too.'

Her film-star eyes poured out defiance.

'You see,' Rezi said, more to himself than the others, 'educating women is not only a waste of money, it is dangerous.'

The jet fighters flew back and the whole car shook.

Far ahead, the road appeared to be blocked. People were running, or fighting – it was hard to tell which – and, in a great mass, surged from one side of the road to the other, like water sloshing across a basin. Above them arched trails of pale smoke.

'Tear-gas.' Rezi dug his fingers into Patrick's left arm. 'We must not get involved in that. Take the next turn to the right.'

'Where will that take us?' Patrick asked but turned all the same. They heard gunfire.

'Trust him,' Damon said. He was frightened, and beyond constructive thought.

'Now left,' Rezi said, after they had covered several blocks. With a shattering burst of noise, a helicopter flew above them then disappeared behind a tall building. Patrick, looking up briefly, saw men with rifles on the roof.

'I hope you know where you're taking us,' he muttered.

'To our family apartment. We will be safe there. It is a quiet part of town.'

For twenty minutes, he guided them along a succession of back streets, avoiding main roads and crowds. There were no fires here. Far to their left rose the silhouettes of tall buildings made vague by smoke and behind them, hazy but majestic, the Elburz mountains. Damavand was the highest peak in that range, Patrick remembered from the map on the wall in London, and Damavand was higher than any mountain in Europe. What a beautiful city this must have been, he thought, and concentrated on following Rezi's directions.

They turned left again, and entered a hilly district where the streets were lined with trees. They passed one house that had been gutted by fire. The front wall was intact but its two windows were sad eyes stained by mascara runs of sooty water. Ominously, another house in the same street had its door smashed and all its windows broken. The rendered walls were chipped and there were signs of a small fire having burned near one corner. Rezi and Farah exchanged worried glances, but said nothing.

'Far to go?' Patrick was anxious for reassurance.

'Not far,' Rezi said in a hushed voice. They turned right into a street where the branches of trees met to form a tunnel. An old bus was parked in a way that almost blocked the road. Several men stood behind it. Most carried sticks or weapons of some sort. They turned to look at the Range Rover.

'What do I do?' Patrick braked.

'Go around them.'

'I can't.'

'Go over them then.'

Patrick had almost stopped. He looked in the outside mirror and, to his horror, saw men behind him. He hadn't noticed them. They were moving on to the roadway and began running towards the vehicle.

One hand on the horn, Patrick drove towards the bus. Two men, one brandishing a stick, the other carrying a rifle, stood in his way.

'Don't stop!' Rezi screamed. Farah had covered her face. Patrick heard the crack of a stick striking the back of the vehicle. He turned to the right, and jolted over the gutter, intending to drive along the footpath. More men were in his way. One lifted a rifle so Patrick swerved the vehicle away from them and charged through a hedge. They bounced on to the front lawn of a large house. He glimpsed a woman's face in an upstairs window, saw in the mirror men pursuing them through the gap in the hedge and swung to the left, churning across a garden of low shrubs.

A wooden fence divided this house from the next. He drove through it. Farah screamed. With a post cart-wheeling over the bonnet, the car ran through a ditch that made their heads crack the roof, and then charged across another lawn. There was a driveway at the far side of the grass. Patrick turned left, showering red gravel from each of the four tyres as he accelerated towards the road.

The driveway was sealed by tall metal gates. Farah was still screaming. The Range Rover hit the gates in the middle and they flew apart. One enterprising pursuer, keeping track of their progress through the gardens, had run along the footpath to intercept them but arrived just as the vehicle burst out. A gate hit him with tremendous force, catapulting the man on to the roadway.

Patrick wrenched the wheel to the right, steadied the vehicle as it swayed across the road, and glimpsed a dozen men in howling pursuit.

'Where to?' Patrick's heart raced but the excitement had cleansed his mind. He felt like shouting in elation.

'To the left. Here.' Rezi grabbed his shoulder.

There were more men in this street and they turned at the scream of the tyres. Behind the group was a car surrounded by another mob. Several houses in the street were ablaze.

'Stop,' Rezi said, his voice choked by disbelief.

'That is our apartment.' Farah began wailing.

'Which one?'

Farah pointed to a burning building. It was the one nearest the mob who surrounded the car. As they approached, the men started to rock the encircled car from side to side. Gaining momentum, they tipped it on its side and then, with much shouting, rolled it on its roof. They stood back and a fire bomb splashed across the exposed belly of the car. There was a roar of approval.

A window opened and a man crawled out. Immediately, he was seized by the mob.

'That is my father,' Rezi whimpered and Patrick drove forward. It was not a question of wanting to help or of being heroic; he could not stay, for in his mirrors he could see that his recent pursuers had turned the corner.

Some of the men near the burning car swung around to face them but most were concerned with the man they had caught. Patrick drove straight for them. A tall man in a white turban and with robes stained by grease stood in front of the others. His intentions were clear because he waved an old sword above his head. He did not leap to one side, as his companions did, and Patrick hit him. Robes flying, the man somersaulted on to the front of the Range Rover. He hit the windscreen and Patrick had a brief but vivid impression of a bearded and astonished face sliding across the glass. With a clatter, the sword landed on the roof. The man fell off.

The other men were turning. Rezi's father was on his feet. He was wearing a dark business suit and, being stunned, seemed greatly concerned about the state of his clothing. The lapels and shoulders of his coat had been ripped, exposing the padding, and he was trying to push one pad back into place. His nose bled.

Sticks beat against the sides of the vehicle but Patrick drove on, until he was level with the burning car.

'Grab him,' he shouted and jumped from the Range Rover, expecting the others to follow. He had run over a man who was squirming on the ground, holding his ankle. He stepped over him, punched another man and grabbed Rezi's father by the arm. Not

872

recognizing him, the man fought back.

'Rezi, your son, he's in the car,' Patrick shouted and pulled him towards the car. Several men grabbed him. A tug-of-war ensued with the father in the middle, weeping, bleeding and losing more of his coat as Patrick pulled on one arm and a group of Iranians held the other.

'For God's sake, give me a hand,' Patrick shouted and glanced back. Until that point, he had not been frightened – there had been no time – but what he saw now filled him with horror. The car was full of people. Farah had been dragged out on the road. Damon and Rezi were still in the back but were submerged beneath a whirl of robes and flailing arms.

Someone jumped on Patrick's back and he felt a sharp blow across the legs. He fell, losing his grip on the father's arm. Another man jumped on his back but he shook both his assailants clear and got to his feet, to fight his way to the door of the car.

Rezi's father had fallen to his hands and knees. A thick-set man with a lustrous black beard stood astride him, like a rider standing in the stirrups, pulled out a knife, and cut the father's throat. The other men shouted their approval.

The bearded man dragged the limp body to its feet and thrust it at Patrick. 'Here, American,' the man said in English, 'take your servant to the devil with you.'

Patrick, hands in the air to avoid touching what had once been Rezi's father, let the body slip to the road. The mob advanced.

He turned and jerked open the door. A young man was behind the wheel and had switched off the engine. Patrick grabbed his leg and pulled him out. He got in and tried to shut the door but one of the mob, holding a large spanner as a weapon, thrust his head and shoulders into the gap. Patrick kicked him in the face and managed to grab the spanner as the man disappeared. He felt a sharp pain in his side and spun around to see a boy in the passenger's seat, grinning and wielding a pen knife. He lunged again but Patrick moved to one side and hit him across the face with the spanner. He kicked him out, locked the door and turned to the back where Damon and Rezi were struggling with three men. Rezi was on the floor, wedged between the seats.

An Iranian saw him and bared his teeth an instant before Patrick removed them with a lusty swipe of the spanner. He saw two more heads, delivered two more hard blows – he didn't care if he killed, and then, feeling the vehicle shake as the mob got hold of it, started up the motor.

He searched for Farah and saw her near the front of the car. Two men had her. One held a pistol to her head and, as Patrick

873

watched, pulled the trigger. They threw the girl away. The man with the gun aimed at Patrick's head. He ducked and heard the windscreen shatter. Head down, he pushed the lever into first gear and tried to accelerate away. There was a loud communal howling and the car trembled but did not move. A side window exploded in a shower of glass. He tried again and still the weight of the mob held the vehicle in place. Now Patrick tried reverse. The mob was not expecting that, and he rolled back several feet. A great roar went up. He sat up, projecting his face just above the base of the windscreen and saw men racing from the front of the car to the rear.

He pushed the second, smaller lever into low range, re-engaged first gear and floored the accelerator pedal. The Range Rover lurched forward, dragging a dozen people with it. Rapidly, he changed gears to gain momentum. He ran over something and there was a hideous screaming. Speed gained, he shuffled the smaller lever back into high range and sped down the road, trailing bruised bodies as the car gathered pace.

He heard sounds of a renewed struggle in the back and, when well clear of the mob, twisted in his seat to see what was happening. He stopped the car.

Damon was sitting up and wrestling with the Iranian with broken teeth. The man had a knife. This time Patrick hit him on the top of the head. The man slumped across Damon in a grotesque embrace.

The mob, seeing them stopped, had begun to run after them.

'For God's sake get rid of him,' Patrick said.

'How?' Damon seemed unable to move.

Patrick leaned back and opened the door. 'Throw him out.' He grabbed the man by the collar and tipped him head-first on to the road.

The crowd was too close, so Patrick drove away, with the open door flapping in the wind.

'The door's open,' Damon gasped.

'Well, either close it or throw the other blokes out.'

He heard Damon grunting. 'They're too heavy. They're both on top of Rezi.'

Patrick turned around the first corner, drove another block and, in a deserted street, stopped. He jumped out and helped Damon drag out the unconscious Iranians.

Rezi was groaning.

'He's covered in blood,' Damon said.

'So are you.'

Damon wiped his face which was scored by scratch marks. 'You've got a big patch of blood on your side.'

'I think a young kid stuck a knife in me,' Patrick said, and climbed back in the car. He drove off.

Damon hit the back of the driver's seat. 'We've left Farah behind.'

'She's dead. I saw them shoot her. Rezi's old man got killed too.'

Damon was silent for a long time. He pulled Rezi on to the seat and felt for his pulse. 'His heart's still beating.'

'Good. We're going to need him.'

'They almost killed him. How can you be so callous?'

'Because this is his country and I haven't got a clue where to go.'

Daniel made a bumpy landing on the track that skirted the edge of the lake. He and Adam got out of the Cessna and ran to where the old Land Rover was parked. One of the men from Muloorina was waiting there. Long before they reached him, it was obvious that there was no reason to hurry. The man was rolling a cigarette. He shook his head and they slowed to a walk.

'Found it this morning,' he said, avoiding the anguish in their eyes. 'Didn't know what it was at first.' He led them out on to the salt, towards the great streaks of ash and blackened metal that were scattered across the inlet.

'There were two on board. Men, I'd say. You can't really tell.'

'So no one ...' Adam began, but then didn't know how to finish the question.

'No hope.' The man shook his head. 'I figured they tried to land for some reason and got tangled up in the old fence. They dragged a length of wire right across the lake with them.'

They passed a piece of wing. It was bent and jagged at one end, but it had been spared the fames and was identifiable.

'It would have been quick,' the man said, as though that made things better, and stopped to let the two men walk on by themselves, to the place where Josef and Peppino had died.

E·I·G·H·T

What Patrick did know was that he had to get out of Tehran. He remembered that, in their final approach to the place where Rezi's family lived, the mountains had formed a stunning backdrop to the city, so now he drove away from the mountains. They were his only guide. He kept them behind him, constantly checking as he drove through a labyrinth of small streets until, finally, he came to a wide but deserted road. He turned left, away from the mountains. He checked the sun, burning dull yellow through the pall of smoke. Patrick was confused by the skies of the northern hemisphere because by night the constellations were upside-down and by day the sun rose and set in the wrong places, but, by forcing himself to think logically and remember where he was, he deduced that they were travelling south. There was a map in the car but he had no idea where it had got to in the shambles of the last few minutes and he was certainly not going to stop and search for it. He tried to remember the map of Iran that was pinned to the wall of the travel agency in London. Afghanistan, Pakistan and India were to the east so if that were to be their direction, he would have to bear left somewhere. But where? He had no idea. South of Tehran was the Persian Gulf. That was all he could remember. That and the fact that Iran was a large country, the biggest traversed by the bus on its overland journey to India.

He drove quickly, knowing that even if he were heading away from their ultimate destination, it was imperative that they get away from the mad crowds that were rampaging through the city. At one intersection, he halted to let a number of army jeeps race across. They were laden with soldiers in battledress. The leading jeep had gone no more than a hundred metres when an explosion ripped it into three large pieces which continued, flaming and twisting, down the road. The bodies of the soldiers became rag dolls that were tossed, limp and burning, high in the air.

Damon, who was sitting dazed in the back, said, 'What was that? What happened?' like a little boy at the cinema.

The second and third jeeps slewed violently across the road and soldiers jumped out. There was the rattle of gunfire.

'Either a bomb or a rocket,' Patrick guessed and accelerated across the intersection. He had no intention of waiting to find out.

'The place has gone mad,' Damon said, making a personal complaint to those who had spoiled his first visit to Tehran. He was cradling Rezi's head in his lap. 'You seem to be driving very quickly, dear boy. Don't forget we want to get this thing back to Adelaide in one piece so we can make a killing on the used-car market.'

'You won't get a zac for it if we get a rocket up the tail pipe,' Patrick said and kept his foot hard on the throttle.

'Do you have any idea where we're going?'

'None.'

'Do you think this is wise then?'

'What, Damon? Do I think what's wise?' Patrick was looking in the mirrors. A long way back, a vehicle with a flashing blue light was racing down the middle of the street. Patrick turned at the next corner.

'Where are we going now?'

'There's a police car behind us.'

'I told you you were going too fast.'

Patrick sought Damon's eyes in the mirror. 'If you'd like to be a big help, you could do three things.'

'What are they?' The voice was suspicious.

'Pick the map up, get Rezi to wake up, and shut up.'

'There's no need to use that tone. I've had a bad experience.'

'Well, I'm sorry for you, Damon, particularly as I've had such a terrific time,' Patrick said, his voice weary, 'but if you could find the map, we might be able to work out where we should be going.'

A helicopter clattered overhead, racing towards the spirals of smoke that marked the site where the jeep had exploded.

'I don't like this place.'

'Damon, look for the map.'

'Where is it?'

'You had it.'

'I did?'

'You and Rezi were using it.'

'We were?'

'Look, I know you're feeling crook but try and find it.'

Damon put Rezi to one side and spent several minutes searching for the map. He found it under a seat. 'I have it. Now what do you want?'

'I think we're going south. Try and find the name of a city to the south.'

'I'm not much good with maps.'

'Well, give it to me.' Patrick stretched an arm behind the seat. 'And you try to wake Rezi.'

Damon handed Patrick the map. 'Did they really kill Farah?'

'Yes.'

'You saw it?'

'Yes. A man shot her. Then he tried to shoot me.' Patrick put his finger against the hold in the laminated windscreen.

'And they killed Rezi's father? How?'

'I don't think you want to know.'

'You saw it happen?'

'They threw the body at me.'

'Oh God.' There was a long silence, then: 'What have we got involved in, Patrick?'

'Something we don't understand. Just try and wake Rezi.'

Their road joined a wider highway. Patrick saw a sign to Qom and Esfahan. He slowed, studied the map, and followed the sign. 'This will do us,' he said.

'You know where we are?'

'More or less.'

'Then we're all right?'

'Except we're going in the wrong direction. But at least we'll get out of Tehran.'

Rezi recovered consciousness before they reached Qom. Damon gave him water and explained what had happened while Patrick took advantage of a deserted stretch of road to pour the contents of a drum into the petrol tank.

'You saw my father die?' Rezi asked when Patrick climbed back into the vehicle. Patrick nodded. 'There was no doubt? You are sure he was dead?'

'No doubt.'

Damon dabbed water on Rezi's face. The Iranian brushed him away. He did not enquire about Farah.

'Where are you driving to now?'

Patrick smiled foolishly. 'I don't know. Oh, I know this road goes to Qom and Esfahan and then eventually down to the Persian Gulf but I don't have any destination in mind. I just wanted to get out of the city.'

Rezi clicked his fingers and Damon passed him the map.

'I was thinking,' Patrick said, 'that we should try to get out of Iran. I thought we should head for Afghanistan.' He let the idea sink in. 'Do you want to leave Iran?'

'Yes, yes.' Rezi touched a cut above his eye. 'I don't know. I mean, I don't really know what I should do.'

'You can't go back to Tehran.'

'No.'

'We were lucky to get out. We mightn't be so lucky next time.'

Rezi was studying the map.

'Is it far to Afghanistan?' Damon asked.

'We have to cross two-thirds of the country. It will take at least two days.'

'The buses used to go up near the Caspian Sea,' Patrick said. He had been studying the map.

'We've come the other way,' Rezi said. 'We are down south.'

'Well, where can we go?' Damon leaned forward anxiously. 'And are you going with us?'

Rezi waved a hand, demanding silence.

Patrick restarted the engine.

'Where are you going?' Damon asked anxiously.

'There are trucks coming. I don't want to be sitting here, waiting to be shot at.'

Rezi waved a hand imperiously. 'Go. I have an idea.'

Patrick drove on, accelerating swiftly to keep his distance from the trucks, waiting patiently for the Iranian to expound his thought. He drove two kilometres before Rezi spoke.

'We will need more fuel.'

'I just put some in,' Patrick said, to reassure him.

Again the hand waved, silencing foolish words. He was a different, more abrasive person in his own country. 'We will need more for the journey I have in mind. Stop at the next gas station you see, if it seems safe.'

'Where are we going, Rezi?' Patrick was willing to be led, but not blindly.

'Across the Dasht-e-Kavir. The Salt Desert.'

'How big is that?' Damon asked.

'Vast.' He took pity on his friend and patted his hand. 'The main trouble will be in the cities. Therefore, we will avoid the cities. There should be no wild mobs in the Dasht-e-Kavir, so that is the best way for us to go.'

'Where will that take us?'

'To the east. Towards Afghanistan.'

'So you're coming with us?' Damon said anxiously.

'I have no choice.'

It was a less than gracious answer, Patrick thought, but he asked, 'Are there roads?'

'According to the map, yes. I have not been there.'

'Who normally goes there?'

'No one.' Rezi touched the cut on his head and examined his

879

finger for blood. 'The last person I know of who crossed the desert was Alexander the Great.'

Damon leaned forward and squeezed Patrick's shoulder. 'He's only joking. Rezi has a great sense of humour.'

Unsmiling, Patrick drove on, searching for a place to buy fuel.

They came to a town with low buildings of stone and mud, and on the fringe of the town they found a garage. There were no vehicles in sight. Some children playing near the petrol pumps ran to the back of the garage when the Range Rover approached. Patrick and Rezi followed the children and found the garage owner and his family hiding in the workshop. The man was in fear of his life and refused to come out. Revolutionaries had been through the town seeking and killing the Shah's supporters or those who were purported to favour the existing regime; soldiers and police had been through searching for revolutionaries. The man had nine children. He had the smallest ones and his wife hidden under a tarpaulin.

Rezi explained that they were neither revolutionaries nor soldiers but merely tourists seeking petrol. He pushed forward the blond Patrick as proof. After much talk and an offer to pay twice the legal price, the man came out and filled their tank and empty drum. By now convinced that they were no threat, he studied the map and showed Rezi a track that would take them to Jandag, a town on the southern side of the desert. From there, they could follow a better road to Tabas. From Tabas, it would be relatively simple to travel the four or five hundred kilometres to the Afghan border.

'How are things at Tabas?' Rezi asked.

The man shrugged. 'Who knows? Maybe all right. It is remote. But things are bad at Esfahan. There has been much slaughter.'

'It is insanity.'

The man shrugged, not wanting to be drawn into expressing an opinion. 'They say the Shah is leaving.'

'That's impossible.'

'It might have seemed so once. Not now.' The man went back in the garage and returned with a gift of fruit. 'Keep away from the towns,' he advised, 'and do not enter into a discussion with anyone. Our country has suddenly become a nest of spies.'

At a junction twenty kilometres down the road, they turned off the bitumen and headed east along a primitive track that took them into the Dasht-e-Kavir.

Patrick drove for the rest of the afternoon and a curious thing happened. The further he drove, the more relaxed he became. He felt at home. This was like the Australian outback. A strong feeling

880

of being back in familiar, comfortable, even loved country was seeping through him and that was strange, because in recent years he had worked hard at cleansing his spirit of any bush influence. He now regarded himself as a city person, a sophisticate who had no links, other than the chance of birth, with the outback. He was amused when people discovered he came from near Lake Eyre and flattered when they regarded his story as one of advancement: the boy from the bush who made it in the city and was even on TV. Kalinda, he had convinced himself, was in a remote and wretched part of Australia where only people of inferior intellect (like Jimmy and Daniel) or masochistic tendencies (like his bull-headed father) or who had no choice (like his mother) could live.

And yet, as he drove through a desert crossed by the armies of antiquity, he recalled pleasant times in a land where the pioneering had been done by his father. He was taken back to his earliest years and realized, with surprise, that the memories were good. He thought of the days when he used to ride Silver across country like this, with his Lone Ranger mask in place and the soft walls of the Kalinda dunes shielding him from reality. He remembered fiery sunsets and violent dawns and felt again the sting of a dust storm or the cool splatter of a thunderstorm. He thought of the silence and the pure air, the bellow of cattle and the swirl of dust. He imagined kangaroos bounding over the plains and hawks drawing tight circles in the sky.

He thought of his mother and father. He had written to his mother – not as many times as she wrote to him, but mothers were expected to fulfil obligations while sons, he knew, would always be excused. He never wrote to his father. But out here in the salt desert of Iran, he thought of his father, wondered what he was doing and wondered, with a deep concern, whether his father ever thought of him.

It was late at night in Adelaide. Adam was on the terrace at Cassie's house, gazing at the lights of the city but thinking of other places. Nina came looking for him. 'I was wondering where you were,' she said, standing beside him at the rail. 'Everyone thought you must have slipped off to bed.'

'No, I was just thinking.

She brushed a lock of hair from his forehead.

'How are the boys?'

'Cassie's with them, trying to get them to go to sleep,' she said softly. 'I don't think they fully understand yet.'

'And you got on to Ursula?'

She had already told him, but she said, 'Yes. She's flying out.'

'Why?' He growled the word because if Ursula and Josef hadn't argued, Joe would still be in Europe and Peppino would be here with him on the terrace. And Cassie wouldn't be inside, not crying and trying to be brave and facing thirty or forty years of life without her husband. 'She can't do anything.'

'Don't blame her, Adam. It's not her fault. It's not anyone's fault.'

He looked into her eyes and then shook his head and turned away, to stare at the lights of Adelaide once more. 'Cassie's amazing,' he said after a long silence.

'Yes,' she said, and then: 'Why?'

'She hasn't cried yet. After all that's happened, I haven't seen her cry.'

'She will. One day it will just happen. I think you should be around, to provide a broad shoulder.' She let her head touch him. 'She keeps saying she was the one who talked Josef into taking Peppino up north.'

He shook his head again. He was never good with words and they were useless now.

'We could stay here for a while,' Nina suggested. 'Just until Cassie gets used ... just to keep Cassie and the boys company.'

'Things are pretty bad back home, what with the drought and all. I was thinking I should sell those sheep.' He sighed and she said nothing, knowing that he hadn't finished. 'But you're right. We should be here. I guess Danny and Jimmy can look after the place for a while.'

'I guess so.'

He kept his eyes on the lights, watching distant cars trace ghostly patterns through the night.

After a while he said, 'Just before you came out, I was thinking about Patrick. I had such a strange feeling.'

She leaned against his shoulder. 'Like what?'

'Can't explain. It was just a strange feeling.'

'As though something was wrong?'

'I don't know. It was a bit like a dream. I had the feeling Patrick was calling out to me.'

'You might have dozed off.' she suggested. 'It's very late and you have been known to fall asleep on your feet.'

He rapped the railing. 'No, I was definitely awake. When was the last time you heard from him?'

'Oh, a few weeks ago.'

'More like a few months. He doesn't write often.'

'He's inherited his father's gift for sparse communication.'

She meant it kindly, but he frowned and said, 'You're right. I've been bad at that.'

'Adam, I was joking.'

'No, it's true. And not just with my children. I've been thinking of a million things I should have said to Joe.'

'Adam, you were Josef's best and truest friend. He knew that. In any case, it's not what people say to each other, it's what they do that counts.'

He made a whimpering sound. 'And Peppino. God ...'

'Please don't do this to yourself, Adam. We can't step back into the past and make things happen differently.'

'I hardly saw him in recent times.'

'Peppino was very busy.'

'He was a good man, Nina. One of the best.'

'Yes.'

'Cassie was lucky. He loved her. He was a good husband. That man could work. And so clever. Always thinking up ideas and they all made money,' He rubbed a cheek. 'It's hard to realize that he's gone. That they've both gone.' He searched for the stars, but they were hidden by cloud.

She took his arm and put it around her. 'At least Cassie won't have to worry about money,' she said softly.

'No.' He breathed deeply and shivered. It was cold on the terrace. 'We'll stay with Cassie awhile.'

'Yes. It'd be good for her. And for us.'

'I'm going to spend more time with my kids.'

She nodded, so that her hair ruffled his chin.

'Is London a good place for Patrick to be?'

She was surprised by the question. Adam had always regarded London as being remote; not good or bad. She was careful with her answer. 'It's an exciting place. And we know he's staying with Damon Gallagher and that's comforting. At least we know he's with a friend.' Adam looked doubtful, so she added, 'And the Gallaghers are a good family. Damon would be a good influence.'

He was quiet for a long time. Insects were chirping in the trees and the night throbbed with their clockwork sounds.

'I was thinking,' Adam said, 'that I haven't given him enough time. Maybe I expected too much from him. I don't know.'

She nuzzled closer. 'I think he's the sort of young man who has to do things for himself, make his own mistakes, discover what he wants to be.'

'I wish he'd wanted to live in the bush. I could have helped him more.'

'I think he's inherited my love of cities.'

He was surprised. 'Would you still rather live in the city?'

'Not now. I was a city girl once, though, and Patrick probably

883

has got that from the O'Sullivan side of the family.'

Adam turned, so that his back was to the view. 'Do you think we should go to London?'

She was astonished. Adam had never made such a suggestion. 'To see Patrick?'

'Yes. Not now, of course, but maybe when things have settled down. We could take Cassie and the boys.'

'Would you leave Kalinda for a few months?'

He thought for a while. 'I'd have to, wouldn't I? I can't spend time with a son who lives in London and stay on the property. And you were saying you reckon Danny and Jimmy could look after the place for a while.'

'I'm sure they could. In fact, Danny would love to prove that he can run things without you being around.'

Adam pulled Nina close. 'In the past, I've always put Kalinda in front of everything else. There was always so much to do.' The sound of a car horn, blaring impatience at some unseen obstruction, drifted up to them. 'I don't know whether I was right or wrong. I'm not too sure about a lot of things these days. I do know that I don't want to lose our son.'

She kissed his cheek. 'I'd love to see Patrick.'

Adam looked around them, suddenly stirred by a thought. 'I wonder where the young blighter is?' They had not been able to make contact with Patrick since the crash. They had cabled and tried to telephone his apartment. Nina presumed that he and Damon had left London on business for a few days.

She checked her watch. 'It's a good time to ring London now.'

They went inside. Alex Rafter was on his own, finishing a whisky. 'You found him, I see,' he said to Nina and stood. 'I must be going. Cassie's just gone back in to check on the boys.' He searched for his coat. 'They're forecasting rain for tomorrow. I just heard the news. By the way, the Shah's left Iran. The whole country's erupting.'

'Really?' Nina tried to show interest.

'That's the end of the rug business I suppose.' Alex grimaced. He had been importing Persian carpets as a sideline to his legal practice. 'There's a real bloodbath going on. All the pro-Shah people are being lined up and shot. Nasty place to be at the moment.' He headed for the door.

'I'm just about to make coffee,' Nina said and steered him back to a couch. 'You sit down and talk to Adam for a moment. I'll put the water on and make a phone call.'

'To London,' Adam said. He still regarded the telephone as a miraculous device.

Cassie was back in the room when Nina returned. 'The boys are sound asleep at last,' she said, but Nina was not listening. White-faced, she slumped in a chair.

'What is it?' Adam asked.

'I got through to London straight away,' Nina said in a voice that seemed to come from some distant, hollow place. 'There was a woman in the apartment. She's the new tenant.' Her eyes were glazed. Slowly, they moved towards Adam. 'She said that Patrick and Damon and two friends left London a few weeks ago to drive to Iran.'

The sun was high on the third day of the journey when the Range Rover drove out of the Salt Desert and into the hills. The road improved. For the first time since leaving Tehran, Damon was at the wheel. Rezi was beside him, studying the map and trying to determine the name of the small town they could see in the distance. Patrick was asleep on the back seat. He had driven for most of the night.

'I think we are beyond Tabas but I don't know.' Rezi said. The track had been extremely rough and progress slow. They had followed one wrong road for more than fifty kilometres. All he was sure of was that they were now travelling in an easterly direction. 'We should get fuel. If we can fill up once more, we will be able to reach Afghanistan.'

Damon's eyelids hung heavily, giving his fleshy face a spaniel look, but there was no question of his falling asleep. Fear and exhaustion mixed a powerful potion that kept him in a state of stunned wakefulness. Not alert but incapable of rest, he drove slowly, mechanically, an automaton on a treadmill.

He shook his head. 'I'm sorry, Rezi. What did you say?'

'That we should get fuel.'

'Will it be safe?'

'We must have it. It will not be safe to run out of fuel.'

'No. Of course not. Where will we get it?'

'At this next town.'

'Next town. Right.' It was difficult to see through the shattered windscreen and Damon's weary eyes scanned the view several times before registering that they were on the point of entering a town. The buildings were the colour of the stone and earth, but sharper in outline. 'Oh, we're here.'

Nervously, Rezi looked at him. 'Do you want Patrick to drive? I could wake him.'

Damon was slow to answer. 'No. I'm perfectly all right.'

They drove into the town. The road was paved with stone.

885

Narrow and rough, it ran between low, ochre walls but then opened on to a square. The area was dusty, with trees around its perimeter and a monument in its middle. The monument had been broken. Pieces of a statue lay on the ground. In front of them, their neatness a contrast to the casual scattering of broken marble, was a row of six posts. The bodies of six men, blindfolded and bound by the wrists and ankles, were tied to the posts. Their heads lolled in the careless pose of death.

On the other side of the square was a garage.

'Keep going.' Rezi saw a group of men emerge from beneath the trees, but Damon, eyes blinking in a laboured fashion, had slowed.

'Why are you stopping?' Rezi screamed.

'There's a service station.'

'By all that's weird and wonderful, have you gone crazy? Drive off. They're shooting people here.'

Some of the men were running towards them.

'But we want petrol,' Damon said, his voice dull.

A man reached the Range Rover and tried to open Rezi's door. It was locked. The man had an axe in his hands and used it to smash the window.

Patrick was awake. 'For God's sake get going!'

'But there are people in front,' Damon said.

'Drive over them.'

The mob had surrounded the car and, almost in unison, all the remaining windows caved in. The doors were wrenched open and the three men hauled out on to the street. The mob howled in triumph.

A man of enormous size wrapped his arms around Patrick and lifted him bodily.

'We have an American devil!' he shouted.

Someone splashed petrol across the Range Rover, then threw a match. Flames leaped around the car. Still shouting, the mob drew away from the blaze, back into the square, back towards the six posts.

N·I·N·E

For more than six months, no news of Patrick or his companions reached the world outside Iran. It was known that two Australians named Ross and Gallagher and two Iranians had driven into the country from Turkey. They had been in a Range Rover with British registration and they had entered Iran a few days before the Shah fled Tehran. From that point onwards, there was absolutely no information. No one had seen them, there were no records of them staying at any hotel, and no sighting had been reported of the missing vehicle. Not that there was much interest. This was a time when the staff of the American Embassy had been taken hostage and public executions were daily happenings. With thousands being slaughtered, the disappearance of two young Iranians was nothing; the affair of the Australians was a puzzle that intrigued few people. In a country consuming itself in a frenzy of destruction and death, the answer seemed all too obvious.

Ross, Gallagher and the others had had the miserable luck to drive into Iran at precisely the wrong time. That was the official view. Obviously, they had fallen foul of one of the mobs or of the army or of one of the killing agencies. They had been shot and buried with the thousands of other nameless victims of a righteous revolution. Their car was one of hundreds burned beyond recognition.

One night, just before Christmas 1979, Adam sat up in bed and reached for Nina's hand.

'He's alive,' he said.

'You were dreaming?' She turned on the light.

'I don't think so. I heard Patrick talking to me.'

She moved closer to him. 'I often dream of him. I see him as a little boy, riding his horse or playing games ...'

'No, no,' Adam said impatiently. 'It wasn't like that. It was Patrick like he is now. A man. He was trying to tell me something.'

There was fresh pain in her eyes. 'Was he all right?'

'I don't know.'

'What did he say?'

He shook his head. 'Something has happened. That's all I know. And he's alive.'

She turned off the light and held his hand even more tightly.

There was another rumble. This time, the walls shook and the bars on the window buzzed like tuning forks. Grit cascaded from the ceiling. Outside, some people were shouting and some were screaming. From the distance came the boom and rattle of collapsing bricks.

Patrick rubbed his filthy hands on his threadbare jeans and moved into the corner where the walls seemed strongest. Another shower of grit fell from the ceiling. The bars began to quiver and a third tremor rolled in. It started as a low, benign sound, like thunder in a far-away valley, but then there was the sharp crack of splitting wood and the deeper gasp of the earth dividing, and the wall with the barred window fell over. Part of the roof collapsed.

The corner where Patrick stood trembled and the ceiling above him sagged. He dashed out, stumbling over the fallen wall in his haste to get clear of the cell before the whole building came down. The ground shook, moving left, right, left, and he was tossed on to his hands and knees. He looked back. His cell, the place where he had spent half a year of his life, was folding like cards in a stack. Left wall, back wall, roof, right wall. It was the same all along the building. Walls tumbled, dust rose.

Once there had been a high brick wall around the prison but parts of it had fallen and he could see the town, or what used to be the town. Now it was rubble and strange broken walls. Dust and smoke were rising and in the distance a great spout of water shot into the air. Just outside the wall a power pole had snapped. Broken wires writhed and spat sparks.

Strange noises filled the air: the gush of water, the hiss of escaping gas, the sizzle of electricity, the crackle of flames, the cries of people.

When the ground ceased shaking and the deep rumbling faded, Patrick got to his feet and examined the ruins of the prison. At that moment, he thought of Damon. He had not seen his friend for five weeks. He had no idea where he was kept. If they had still been questioning Damon and taking him on daily visits to the ghastly 'persuasion' chamber, then he would probably have been in the central part of the complex and if he had been there when the earthquake struck, then he was dead because the middle of the building had collapsed and it had been three storeys high.

He could smell the pungent aroma of gas.

A man dressed in military uniform came running towards him. The man was shouting. Patrick stiffened but the man run by, still shouting.

He tried to think but it was difficult. He had been in the dark so long the light hurt. His head ached and he felt a large lump on the back of his skull. He had no idea what had caused that. He had to get out. Not just from the prison. That would be easy. Merely step through a gap in the wall, avoid the wires that flicked and spluttered across the road like electrified snakes, and he was free. No, he had to get out of this town and out of Iran. He had to get away from the people who had beaten him with truncheons and put a clamp on his scrotum and pressed burning cigarettes under his armpits. The men who one week insisted he worked for the CIA and the next demanded his confession as a Soviet spy. Patrick began to shake. He gripped one hand with the other and forced himself to think. The first thing was to find Damon. He had a desperate need to find someone he could talk to in English.

He stared at the heap of blackened bricks that had been his cell. The next two cells were destroyed. No hint of a wall, no suggestion of life. Where there had been two cubes of brick housing two men, there was now a flattened pyramid of rubble. He walked further and, as he walked, the damage was less severe. One cell had lost only part of the outer wall and a corner of its roof. The next had tilted at an angle but seemed intact.

Tentatively he called out Damon's name. There was no reply. He crawled to the cell with the gap in its wall and saw a figure in the corner. It was a man, coated in dust and sitting with his arms around his knees.

'Damon?'

The man looked up and shook dust from his head. It was Rezi. Patrick shuffled across to him. 'Where's Damon?'

Rezi's eyes were glazed. 'The building fell down.'

'I know. Where's Damon?'

'What happened?'

He shook Rezi. 'Where's Damon?'

Rezi tapped the wall beside him.

'In there?'

Rezi nodded. 'What happened?'

'Earthquake.'

The door to the cell still stood but the wall had crumbled around it. On hands and knees, Patrick crawled into the corridor. A guard lay face down on the floor with a heavy wooden beam angled across his shoulders. Patrick got up and stepped over the man's body. The next cell appeared to have broken away from the rest of the building. A shower of masonry fell as Patrick moved into the room and he stood still for a few moments, fearful of another tremor. When the dust cleared, he saw a heap of bricks across the bench where the prisoner would sleep. An arm projected from the pile.

'Damon?' Patrick called out, unable to move any closer.

A thin voice answered, but it came through a hole in the dividing wall. It was a small hole, no more than two bricks wide. Patrick pressed his face to the opening. 'Are you in there, Damon?'

'Patrick?' The voice was a squeak of hope.

'Can you get out?'

'I think the roof's about to fall in on me.'

'Hang on.' Patrick returned to the dead warder and prised keys from his clenched right hand. He went to the door of Damon's cell but the wall had settled and the door would not move. Patrick went back into the adjoining cell.

'You'll have to get out through here,' he said and, using a brick as a hammer, began chipping at the edges of the hole.

'It's too small.'

'Just stand clear. Are you all right?'

'I think so. Was it an earthquake?'

Patrick knocked two bricks out of the way. 'A big one. The town's destroyed.'

'You've been outside?'

'Just for a while.' He hammered another brick out of its mortar. 'OK. Try and squeeze through.'

He grabbed Damon's extended hands and pulled him through. Part of the wall came with him and, as they scurried out of the cell, the whole wall and ceiling collapsed behind them.

Leading the way, Patrick crawled back into Rezi's cell and out through the broken wall. Both men followed. Near the breached outer wall, Patrick stopped. 'There are live wires outside so take care.' Both his companions were thin and covered in dust. Damon was still wearing shirt and jeans but Rezi had been dressed in a filthy robe. The Iranian leaned forward, both hands on his knees.

'Are you two all right?

'Bloodied but unbowed,' Damon gasped and put Rezi's arm across his shoulder.

Two men appeared from the ruins of the building. One walked in a circle and fell down.

'Let's get out of here,' Patrick said and led the way through the gap in the wall.

A car raced past them, then slid to a stop as the driver braked to avoid a wide split that yawned across the road. On the other side of the gap was a truck laden with bags of cement. Its engine idled but the cabin was abandoned.

From the far side of the town came a loud explosion. The air reeked of gas.

Patrick walked past the cement truck, then stopped. There was no sign of the driver. He climbed aboard. 'Come on.' He beckoned his companions.

Rezi scrambled up but Damon hesitated. 'The road's got a big hole in it.'

'I'll go the other way,' Patrick said. 'Get in. We're not going to walk to Afghanistan.'

At nightfall, they reached a village near the border. They had bathed in a stream and drank their fill, but they had no food and were almost out of diesel fuel.

'We must eat.' Rezi said. Near-starvation had drawn skin tight over his cheekbones and his eyes bulged unnaturally.

'We have no money,' said Damon, ever the pessimist.

'We have a load of cement,' Patrick suggested. Both men looked at him, neither understanding. 'Trade,' he added, focusing on Rezi. 'You could exchange a few bags for some food and a bit of diesel, perhaps?'

Using his fingers as a comb, Rezi brushed back his hair and went to the first house. He returned five minutes later. 'Drive to the third house on the left,' he said.

'How did you get on?' Patrick asked.

Rezi waved a hand in the direction of the house. 'Later. Time for talk later.' His voice was gravelly and he seemed close to exhaustion. He had been tortured; that much he had told them but otherwise he had remained silent since their escape.

Patrick stopped outside the house. 'Do you want me to come with you?'

He shook head head slowly. 'Several men will frighten them. Let me go alone.'

This time he was gone for half an hour. It was cold in the truck and Patrick and Damon were shivering when Rezi returned with a man carrying a torch. 'Get out,' Rezi said, as the other man inspected their load. Patrick hesitated. Rezi wiped his lips. He had been eating. 'It's perfectly safe. There is food in the house. While you eat, my friend will take the truck and fill the tank.'

Patrick got down. Reluctantly and stiffly, Damon followed. They followed Rezi into the house. They sat at a wooden table in a room illuminated only by a small log fire. A woman, all shawls and shadows, brought food.

'He knew of my father,' Rezi said and tore off a piece of un-leavened bread. 'This is a village where people are neither pro-revolution nor pro-Shah. They just get on with life. However, they are peaceful people and dislike what has been happening.'

'What tale did you tell them about us?' Damon said.

'I told the truth. I said we were political prisoners who were awaiting execution.'

'We were?'

Rezi's large eyes swept across Damon. 'Surely you were under no illusions?' He ate more bread. 'I told him we were set free by an earthquake. He is a religious man and agrees it was an act of God.'

'And he knew your father?'

'He knew of my father. Happily, he was regarded as a good man in the former government. Honest and fair.'

Patrick had been eating wolfishly. 'What's he going to do for us?'

'In exchange for all the cement,' Rezi said, his eyes darting from one to the other to make sure they understood the extent of the bargain, 'he has agreed to give us some old but warm clothes, both as a disguise and to keep us from freezing because there is snow where we are heading. In addition, he will fill the tank of the truck and put two drums on the back.'

'How far will that take us?' Damon said, with a show of petu-lance.

'Deep into Afghanistan. Who knows where?'

'We won't get across the border. We have no papers.'

Wearily, Rezi tapped the table. 'That is the rest of the bargain. Once he has unloaded the cement, he will lead us across the border, at a place where there are no controls.'

'He knows the way?'

'Very well,' Rezi said and, for the first time since their release, smiled. 'He travels the route regularly. He is a smuggler.'

For four hours they drove, following tracks that grew progressively rougher and climbed higher into mountains. The man led in a small van. At a place where snow lay on either side of the rocky track, he stopped and spoke to Rezi.

'He says we should travel without lights from now on. You must also disconnect the brake lights, in case someone sees the red light flashing when you slow down.'

'How are we going to do that?' Damon said but Patrick was already out of the cabin. He returned a few minutes later, blowing on his fingers to stimulate warmth.

'I took the bulbs out,' he said and drove off slowly, trying to follow the van as it climbed a precipitous track across a dark mountain. For fifteen minutes they travelled at little more than walking pace, bumping across rocks and trying to keep the wide truck on a gradually narrowing track. At one point, the guide stopped and Patrick almost ran into the back of his van. The man got out and, taking Patrick by the hand, led him to a section of the track where the edge had broken away. He indicated where Patrick should drive: partly up the embankment, then down, in a slither of snow, to the track on the other side.

They began to descend. Now Patrick had the truck in first gear and a foot hard on the brake. At times, with all wheels locked, they slid down steep inclines but eventually came to a flat area where the outline of tall trees rose high above them. Here the guide stopped. He spoke to Rezi.

'This is as far as he goes. There is a track to the left. We take it. He says we should not put our lights on until we come to another intersection, in about half an hour's time. We turn left again' – he turned to the man and checked, and the man nodded – 'and follow the road all the way up to Herat.'

'How close are we to the border?' Patrick said.

'We have crossed it.'

'Thank God for that,' Damon said and they all shook hands.

Their guide moved forward and, like a traffic policeman, directed them to the track. With a wave to the man, Patrick drove slowly down through the trees, into Afghanistan.

A few hours later and at a border crossing more than one thousand kilometres to the north-east, the first Russian tanks in a massive army of invasion rolled out of the Soviet Union and headed south towards Kabul.

T·E·N

August, 1980

In the weeks after his seventieth birthday, Adam Ross did a great deal of thinking. He had plenty of time, as he was not as active on the property as he had been in past years. The numbers of stock had been so drastically reduced that there wasn't as much to do at mustering or shearing time, although just keeping the stock alive was a battle. There wasn't much money coming in and a painfully large amount going out, largely to pay the interest on his loans, but all he was trying to do was hold on; just see out the drought and have something left, to start rebuilding when the rains came.

On many days, after he had seen sheep die from hunger and watched bony cattle wobble across the plains, Adam would think about his years at Kalinda and wonder again if all the effort had been worthwhile. He was not normally a pessimistic person but the drought and the disappearance of Patrick had affected him profoundly. And now that he was an old man who had journeyed far beyond youth to reach the daunting peaks of age, he had an acute awareness of failure and a realization that little time was left to correct past mistakes.

Increasingly, he was feeling that he should have left the place as it was. Maybe it was an area where no one should have tried to raise sheep and cattle. Maybe it should have been left to the wind and the sun and the occasional mob of foraging kangaroos, the way it had been for thousands of years.

The drought had brought home to him the irony of the situation. If no rain fell for five years – more than enough to kill all the stock and ruin him – the kangaroos would merely hop away and return when there was water. The trees would wither and some might die, but the survivors would flourish when rain fell and propagate in profusion. Grass would sprout again. The only things that would not survive the dry years were the foreigners: the sheep, the cattle and the people who were dedicated to raising strange beasts in a hostile land.

But there were other occasions when his stubborn streak widened and he swore that he would not give in, and he planned tactics to outlast the drought and prepare for the return of the good times. In those moods, he blessed the fate that had delivered him a son like Daniel.

Daniel ran Kalinda now. He was a good man. Nellie would be proud. He thought of Nellie a lot these days. He was finding that age presents the past in confusing ways and the times when Nellie had been such a strong force in his life either seemed long, long ago or only yesterday. He remembered her as a young woman, which was good. Nellie was always so young in spirit. They'd had such a pitifully short time together.

Sometimes, purely out of curiosity and never because of unhappiness with his present situation, Adam wondered what his life would have been like if Nellie hadn't run away. They would have married. He would still have gone to the war. He would probably have met Nina. They would not have made love like they did in Greece – or maybe they would have; he wasn't too sure about that – but they would certainly not be married and that would have meant Patrick would not have been born. Patrick. Most of his thinking these days was about his younger son. He had not known Daniel until he was practically grown up and he had not truly known Patrick after that age. He had been busy with work and content to leave most of Patrick's upbringing to the super-efficient Nina, but somewhere along the way he'd let the boy down. Now it was too late.

In all the time since Patrick had disappeared Adam had never told anyone he believed his son was dead. Just the opposite: he would say he was sure the young fellow was alive, and people would agree and smile sadly and think he was a foolish old man. After all, it was more than a year. They now knew the names of the two young Iranians with whom Patrick and Damon Gallagher were travelling, they knew the father of the Iranians had been a government official of high rank, and they knew that that man and all his family were dead. They had been slaughtered by a mob around the time Patrick and the others should have reached Tehran. It was a simple deduction to imagine the two young Australians being at the house at the time of the slayings and dying in the frenzy of killing.

The practical side of Adam said the boy was dead. In fact, there were times – private times when he couldn't sleep and lay staring into the dark and imagining all the dreadful things that could have happened – when he wished that a telegram would come saying 'we regret to advise ...' At least it would be definite. The uncertainty was almost unbearable.

The radio telephone rang. It was a difficult thing to operate and Adam often spoke when the button wasn't down or disconnected people unintentionally.

The caller was Cassie. 'Are you sitting down?'

He was silent for a while, all the dreadful possibilities of accidents to his grandsons whirling through his head. 'What's happened?' he said slowly but forgot to press the button and had to repeat the question.

'The boys are fine. It's nothing like that. It's good news – I think.'

'Oh.' Adam sat back and breathed heavily. 'Well, what's up?'

'I've just had a phone call from the Gallaghers. You know, Damon's parents?'

'Yes, of course.' Suddenly Adam's heart was pumping. Nina had come into the room. 'Cassie,' he whispered to her, and gripped her hand.

'Are you ready for this?' Cassie said. 'Damon has been found, and he's alive.'

'Damon!' Adam pulled Nina on to his knee.

'He's in Pakistan. Very sick, but alive and safe.'

'And Patrick?'

There was a pause. 'We don't know yet. The message was confused. But it seems that Patrick might be alive and in Afghanistan.'

Much happened in the next four days. Adam and Nina flew to Adelaide, saw the Gallaghers and spent hours telephoning the Department of Foreign Affairs in Canberra and the Australian Embassy in Islamabad. Nina also contacted a few of the senior newspaper executives she knew in Australia and even a couple of editors in America, to ask them to pass on whatever information they could gather from their correspondents in Pakistan.

The story they heard had many gaps, but essentially, it was this: Damon Gallagher was in a hospital in Peshawar, not far from the Khyber Pass. He had been wounded in fighting between Soviet troops and Afghan rebels. The rebels had managed to bring him across the border into Pakistan. An Australian diplomat had seen him in hospital but Damon had been too sick to pass on any but the sketchiest of details. However, it seemed that he and Patrick had been imprisoned in Iran, had somehow managed to escape and – by means which were still unclear – had entered Afghanistan and come into contact with one of the resistance groups. It was believed that Patrick was still with this Mujahedin band. They were understood to be operating in the area between Kandahar and Ghazni, in the south-eastern sector of the country. Ominously, heavy fighting had been reported from that region.

Damon was expected to be in hospital for several weeks. He had been wounded in an ambush and had lost a great deal of blood, a condition exacerbated by the long and arduous journey to Peshawar. It was thought he would be able to give a more lucid account of events in about a week's time.

It was this latter piece of information which made Adam decide: he was going to Peshawar.

He thought Nina might object, point out that he was an old man, and could do no good in a strange country like Pakistan. Instead, she thought it was a good idea.

'We'll both go mad if we have to wait here for news,' she said.

'Both of us?'

She folded her arms. 'Why not?' The eyes challenged but twinkled.

'Because it might be dangerous.'

She ignored that. 'You need someone to look after you.'

He snorted. 'I do not.'

'I'd be worried if I weren't there.'

'I'd be worried if you were.'

'Adam, I have to be close to where Patrick is. I thought I'd lost him.' She turned her head for a few moments. 'I have to be there. To find out what happened. To be near. Can you understand?'

'I'll still be worried.'

'Well, I'll be there to comfort you.'

'And to tell me not to worry?'

'Of course.'

'I was thinking,' he said slowly, as he always did when broaching an idea, 'that it might be a good idea to take Daniel along.'

'Daniel?'

'If Patrick really is in Afghanistan, and can't get out, we might have to go in there and try to bring him out.'

Alarmed, she pulled away from him.

'I'm just saying "if",' he continued, but his face had the look which told her his mind was set. 'Nina, if Patrick needs help, we're going to get it for him.'

'What sort of help?'

'I have no idea.'

'But you'd consider going into Afghanistan?'

'If necessary.'

'Adam, there's a war going on there.'

'And our son is there. Or so we think.'

She drew a deep breath. 'Adam, you're seventy.'

'And my son is dear to me and I haven't done enough for him in the past.'

897

She took his hand. 'Let's just see what the situation is when we get to Pakistan.'

'Certainly.'

She nodded, knowing she could expect no more concessions. 'Why Daniel?'

'Lots of reasons. He's strong. He's sensible. He's good in an emergency. And he was raised as an Afghan. He speaks the language.'

She seemed to be looking beyond him, into some frightening part of the future. 'You want Daniel there in case you go into Afghanistan.'

He held her hands so tightly she winced. 'If Patrick's alive and can be got out, I'm going to get him out.'

'Oh God.' She turned her face from him. 'I don't want to lose all my men.'

He waited until their eyes met again. 'I want you to do some things for me.'

'What?' She didn't look up.

'Daniel will need a passport. Could you start doing what's got to be done?'

'I suppose so.'

'And we'll need plane tickets, accommodation, visas, those things.'

She nodded. 'What are you going to do?'

'See Cassie. Then fly to Marree. I want to talk to Saleem Benn.'

'No I'm fine, really Dad,' Cassie looked well. A little tired, perhaps, but that was understandable. Since Peppino's death, she had immersed herself in the affairs of Portelli Enterprises. She had disposed of the car and truck dealerships and was about to finalize a deal to lease the fishing boats to an operator at Port Lincoln. She now had fewer worries and a substantial amount of cash. She planned investing some of it in the burgeoning tourist side of the business.

Cassie guided Adam towards a kitchen chair. 'And though you haven't got around to asking me yet, I'd be delighted to go up to Kalinda and run things while you're away.'

'How did you know I was going to ask you?'

'Through that miraculous invention, the telephone. Nina rang me.'

'You're sure you can do it?'

'Absolutely. It'll be a nice break.'

'We shouldn't be too long.'

'Just don't worry. I can handle it.'

'Danny won't be up there.' Adam looked anxiously at her. 'I'm taking him with me to Pakistan.'

'Good. You need someone to look after you.'

He shook his head in mock despair. 'Why do you torment me so in my old age?'

'Because you love it.' She poured him a cup of tea. 'Nina says you're thinking of going into Afghanistan.'

'Only if we have to. It'd be a last resort.'

'Dad, Afghanistan is not Lake Eyre. A war is being fought there. The Russians have got bombers and tanks and all sorts of things. I've seen it on television. There are horrifying stories in the paper.' He was avoiding her eyes. She touched his hand. 'Dad, you won't, will you?'

He had an exploratory sip of his tea. 'If you were stuck in some out-of-the-way place, wouldn't you expect me to come and get you?'

'Patrick is not just stuck in some out-of-the-way place. He might be – and might's the word because we don't know – somewhere in a country we know very little about. We don't know where he is, but we do know that there's a major war going on. I wouldn't expect you to go into Afghanistan for anyone. There are some things that are just not possible, even for you.' She passed him a tin of biscuits. 'Now you promise me.'

He took a biscuit but didn't answer her. She had a way of extracting pledges he didn't wish to make.

'We have to face the possibility that he may not be alive,' she said softly.

'He's alive.' He waved the cup to change the subject. 'What about the boys and their schooling? Will you leave them here?'

'I'll take them with me. I'll teach them a few things they won't learn in that fancy school of theirs, like how to crack a stockwhip and ride a camel.'

He laughed. 'Not too many camels on the place these days.'

'I'm going to do a lot of things while you're away,' she said and winked mischievously. 'I'll transform the place.'

'There's a drought. You won't be able to put more stock on the land. There's no feed.'

'I'm not talking about stock. I'm talking about tourists. That's where you're going to make your money in the future.' She leaned back. 'I'm going to jazz up that half-baked motel you've got up there and make it into something really good and I'm going to establish a desert garden that will be the talk of the outback.'

He smiled tolerantly. It was good to see her enthusiastic about something, even if it didn't make sense. 'What's a desert garden?

899

Are you going to stick in some date palms?'

'You're such an old fossil. Nothing like that.' She thrust another biscuit at him. 'I've been reading about native vegetation – Australian desert flora – and there are some beautiful plants we could grow there. We'll put plantations of native trees and shrubs near the homestead and out at some of the bores, where there's plenty of water. It'll transform the place.'

He looked down and smiled. 'I never thought I'd end up growing flowers instead of wool.'

'Not exactly flowers, Dad.'

'Well what?'

'We'll make Kalinda a desert showpiece. Just leave it to me.'

For all the fifty-one years that Adam had known Saleem Benn, the Afghan's face had been deeply lined, so that any expression was shaded and scored by ridges of emphasis. Now that he had attained an age few men reach, the abundant creases had deepened into crevices and a frown was a bewildering complex of folded skin. He was frowning now.

'It was so long ago,' the old man said. 'Those I knew would be long since dead.'

'Maybe some names,' Adam suggested. 'Family names. People we could track down.'

One finger, long and tapered, like a bird's claw, tapped the arm of the Afghan's chair. He sat, as always these days, in his favourite corner of his favourite room. Sometimes the present confused him but he had clear recollections of the past, and his mind was reeling through memories of a land he had left in the closing years of the nineteenth century.

'We came from Kabul.' The voice was croaky.

Adam nodded, waiting patiently for Saleem Benn to continue.

'But we spent much time in Peshawar. It was in Peshawar that we met that scoundrel who engaged my uncle and my brothers and myself to bring camels to Australia.'

Again Adam nodded. He knew the story.

'For a circus.' The old man smiled. 'I was only a young man but I remember Peshawar very well. That is where the boy is in hospital?'

'Damon Gallagher, yes.'

'We were in Peshawar almost a year. That was long before they talked of such a country as Pakistan.' The wrinkles formed a mask of regret, not for the change of name but for the passing of an age he remembered so vividly. 'The British who were there knew the area as the North-West Frontier. It was an extremely colourful place. A veritable crossroads of the world, with men of all races strolling the streets. We always carried weapons. My uncle had a rifle that was old, even then. It was ornately decorated and very long.' One hand rose, as delicately as tissue paper wafting on a current, and indicated great height. 'It was as tall as he was, and he was a tall man, much taller than I. We all carried knives.' He grinned impishly. 'The British thought we were very fierce. If they could see me now!'

'They would consider you a wise man,' Adam said in Pushtu.

The wrinkles on one side of the old man's face congregated in a wince.

'I got it wrong?'

'I know what you meant, dear friend. One of my regrets, which I will surely take with me to the grave, is that I did not teach you to be proficient in the language of my ancestors. You showed great potential.' He sighed. 'It could have been a most useful asset on your forthcoming journey.'

'I'm taking Daniel.'

'Good. He is fluent.'

'Perhaps you could spare time to teach me on my return?'

Saleem Benn cackled with mirth. 'Perhaps that is the reason Allah has spared me for so long. I can think of no other.' Wiping his eyes, he looked at Adam. 'But I have forgotten. What was it you wanted?'

'Names. If I had some family to see, some contact who might be able to help us get into Afghanistan, it would be very useful.'

'I will need paper and a pen.'

Adam got them for him. Saleem Benn's rheumy eyes followed him as he moved.

'There is risk in what you are contemplating?'

'Possibly.'

'I was thinking, my friend, that while you are a mere colt compared to this old and tired horse, you are still not as sprightly as you once were.'

'And I should take care?'

'As I well know, age is an insidious trap and has a way of allowing us to step in its snares.' He stopped to clear his throat. 'Therefore, may I suggest that you let Daniel do that which should properly be performed by a young man.' He leaned forward and extended a hand. He waited until Adam gripped it. 'My grandfather lived to be one hundred and eighteen years of age. I have set my own personal target one hundred and ten. I would like to hold a small celebration on that day, and I would like you to be present, as an old friend and as the person for whom I have the deepest respect. Therefore, may I make this request? Please take care of

901

yourself, to ensure you return safe and well, so that the celebration in a few years hence will not be spoiled by your absence.'

Adam laughed. 'You're asking me not to do anything silly.'

'I have never grown accustomed to the direct manner of speech you people use in this country.' He shook his head, then examined the pen and paper. 'Now you brought me these for some purpose. Do you recall what it was?'

'Names,' Adam said gently. 'In Peshawar and within Afghanistan.'

'Ah yes. Peshawar. It was a most colourful place. People from all races seemed to gather there. A veritable crossroads of the world.' He glanced up at Adam and smiled, happy to be transported back to his youth. 'The road from the Khyber Pass enters the town by way of a slight rise and then turns like this.' His hand glided through a bend. 'On the left-hand side of the road there is a merchant, an honourable man, who was known to my uncle.'

He began writing down names.

E·L·E·V·E·N

The sun had been up for two hours when the big helicopters appeared on the horizon. There were three of them. Two flew together, scudding across the plain. The other was a long way back and flying at a much higher altitude.

Fareed had been waiting for them. He put down his binoculars. 'Right on time. It is a good thing for us that the Russians are so stupid. It helps us to plan our day.' He passed the glasses to Patrick who was lying beside him on the shelf of broken rock. Both were aware of the enemy's liking for routine. The helicopters only flew in good weather and, on clear days, took off from the big base at Kandahar at the same time. It did make life a little easier, but neither man was smiling. The aircraft were heading straight for the village, and they knew what gunships could do to a community.

Anxiously, Patrick turned to his Afghan companion. 'Do you think there was an informer?'

'There is always an informer when the Russians come so unerringly towards a target.' Fareed examined the village below them with the dispassionate calm of a person observing an ant that is about to be trodden on. 'We will find him.'

Patrick raised the glasses. 'How?'

'If the Russians have come here to work, our informer may be the only man to survive.' He glanced across at Patrick, who was lying on his stomach, focusing on the approaching helicopters. 'He will have left the village sometime during the night. Few traitors have a taste for suicide.' He put out his hand to cover the lenses. 'Put them down now. They are getting close and the glass might reflect.' Fareed was a brave man but all the Mujahedin feared the power of the gunships.

They had been in that village the previous night. Fareed's small band had entered after sunset, met the head men to discuss the progress of the war, shared a meal, rested and left at three in the morning. They had reached their mountain retreat before dawn.

The other seven men had taken the jeeps and the weapons

deeper into the hills. Fareed and Patrick had stayed to observe the daily display of air power.

The helicopters always patrolled the highway linking Kandahar to Ghazni and Kabul and they always searched the country on either side of the road in their relentless quest for rebel targets. This morning, however, they were not making random sweeps of the countryside. Like vultures coming to a feast, they were flying directly towards the village.

Now Patrick could hear the rapid whoot-whoot-whoot of the big aircraft. The leading two machines had fanned out, to approach the village from either side. The other stayed back, still high but hovering. Patrick felt a terrible chill within him because he knew what was going to happen. Someone had reported that a band of Mujahedin had stayed in the village, so the people were to be punished. He had seen other villages which had received similar treatment.

A small truck drove clear of the houses. Several people were running for the shelter of a rocky watercourse which meandered past the settlement.

In perfect unison, the two helicopters landed. Troops spilled from each, running in the crouch peculiar to helicopter people, and entered the village. From his vantage point Patrick heard the crackle of rifle fire. A continuous wailing sound, punctured by shouts and screams, drifted up into the mountains. After a few minutes, the soldiers returned to the helicopters which waited, blades scything the air, for the next stage of the punitive raid to begin.

The third gunship descended and followed the earthen track that ran through the centre of the village. It carried napalm and rapid-fire cannons and for ten chaotic seconds, it unleashed its weapons on a miserable collection of mud and stone buildings which sheltered those who had survived the first onslaught. Houses were pulverized, then engulfed in flames.

His single, annihilating, run completed, the helicopter pilot started to climb but then saw the dust trail of the fleeing truck. He swooped on the vehicle and, with a burst of cannon fire that lasted less than two seconds, blew it from the road. He then circled back towards the village, taking care to avoid the great columns of smoke that poured from the ruins.

The other helicopters took off.

Fareed put his hand on Patrick's arm. 'Do not move. They will look this way.'

'They did that because we were there.'

'It is a cruel war. Keep your face down.'

904

The three gunships were coming towards the mountains. Patrick, lying still, fondled his Kalashnikov.

'Do not even contemplate it,' Fareed said. 'I too am angry, possibly more than you, but you might as well throw stones as fire a rifle at one of these. They are only vulnerable from the top and then only to something much heavier than the little toys we carry.'

'Why the hell don't they give us rockets?'

'It is your people who do not send us the weapons we need.' As he spoke, the first helicopter rattled over a ridge near them and the mountainside erupted in dust and swirling winds.

'I'm not an American,' Patrick shouted, his voice shaking because the gunship was close and he was frightened. Fareed was scared too, he knew, but the Afghan was better at disguising his emotions.

'You could make the Americans send us what we need. We are fighting your war for you!'

Patrick, head down, flashed his teeth at the Afghan. 'Excuse me, but I thought I was fighting your war for you.'

Fareed had not taken his hand from Patrick's arm. The other gunships were standing clear of the mountain and their noise beat down on them. 'Let us just say,' he shouted, to be heard above the racket, 'that we are fighting each other's war.'

The first helicopter climbed and swung back to join the others.

'They're going.' Patrick couldn't hide the thrill in his voice. This was like a deadly game of hide-and-seek. The other players – the villages down on the plain – had been caught but Fareed and himself were the lucky ones who had got away. Patrick had seen plenty of killing since he had been in Afghanistan and his reaction was always the same. He was ashamed, but he couldn't help it: there was a primeval sense of elation that where others had lost, he had won. They had died, he had survived.

'They do not like the mountains,' Fareed said. 'The mountains are our territory. The Russians know we are short of rockets but they know we have some. Over our mountains, they are likely to get one of our rockets up their boom!'

'Bum,' Patrick corrected.

Fareed laughed. 'I don't know how they could ever have thought you were Russian.'

'Well, your mates did. The trouble was, no one in that group spoke English.'

'And they almost shot you. What a waste that would have been.' He looked at the departing aircraft and sat up. 'Come. They're out of range.'

They stood, and ignoring the smoke from the devastated village, followed the path down to the camp.

Fareed's group was one of three rebel units involved in a planned attack on a government fort. The fort was small and to the southeast of Ghazni. It had no great strategic significance but it was there, which was the prime irritant, and it was reported to contain a cache of arms and ammunition and those were items the Mujahedin needed desperately. The plan was simple, as most rebel schemes were. They would storm the fort, overwhelm the garrison, take what booty they could carry and get away before Soviet gunships or tanks arrived. How the attack was to be carried out had yet to be resolved. All three rebel groups were to meet in the mountains and work out the details. The assault on the fort was scheduled to take place in three nights' time, when there would be no moon.

The meeting place was a narrow gorge which gave the rebels almost total protection from air strikes. It had been used several times as a base for planning other attacks or hiding after a strike against government or Russian troops.

On this occasion, Fareed's tiny band was the first of the groups to enter the mountains. When Fareed and Patrick finally reached the site, the jeeps were already hidden beneath broken branches near the entrance to the gorge. One man stood guard. Inside the gorge, ammunition and supplies had been stacked beneath a ledge that jutted from the cliff face. The other six men were seated in a grove of myrtle. Two of them, an old man with hawk's eyes, and a tall, intense Pathan whose curly black hair and thick beard suggested he was wearing an Astrakhan balaclava, were loading shells for the heavy machine-gun.

The others were talking animatedly when Fareed and Patrick walked through the narrow pass. Some of them stood, not because their leader approached but because they were stiff from the long wait and anxious for news. They had heard the sound of the gunships. Fareed sat on a rock and told his men what he had seen.

Patrick stayed well back. He was accepted as part of the band, having been with them for four months, but he wanted to be alone. The attack had sickened him. The brief surge of elation he had felt at having escaped the questing eyes of the gunship crews was gone. Now there was only horror. He had seen some terrible sights in this war but nothing like this morning's. He could accept seeing men die in battle, could tolerate the thought of prisoners being tortured, and knew that tens of thousands of ordinary citizens had already died in a war that was not about winning territory but was being fought to destroy the spirit of a proud people. What made today different

906

was that a whole village had died because he had been there. That was all the reason that the airborne extermination squad needed. He and the others had been there. So, zap! The village is annihilated. Women who had hidden out of sight, children who had slept and not seen him enter or leave, had all perished. And he, who was safely hidden in the rocks, had watched them die.

For one terrifying instant, Patrick was taken back fifteen years, to Wedge Island.

He turned and walked away. He was wiping his face when Fareed joined him.

'Are you not feeling well?' With concern, Fareed examined the man the Mujahedin had once considered a Soviet spy and was now one of his most trusted men. Patrick stared back. These days, Fareed reflected, the tall Australian looked like an Afghan freedom fighter. His turban and his loose clothes were the same as those worn by others in the band, his hair and beard were dyed black and even his blue eyes were not out of place in a country where thousands traced their ancestry back to the invading mercenaries of Alexander the Great.

'I'm OK. I was just thinking about this morning.'

'It does not pay to dwell on some of the things we see.'

'But, Fareed,' Patrick said, his eyes roving the sheer walls of the gorge, 'doesn't it make you think? Doesn't it make you doubt what you're doing? Because we've come here to prepare for an attack on some piddling little fort to try and win ourselves enough ammo to go and attack some other piddling little fort, all those people died. Every last one of them, even the bloke in the little truck.'

Fareed's eyes narrowed. 'What is ammo?'

Patrick's eyes descended from the heights and scanned Fareed's face. The question was a serious one. 'Ammunition. Bullets for the damned Kalashnikovs and more shells for the bloody useless Dashaka.'

'It's not useless,' the Afghan snapped.

'You know what I mean. It weighs a ton and last time it jammed.'

'The shells had not been properly loaded on the belt.' He made a clucking sound with his mouth. 'What you're saying is just what those godless Russians want us to say. You realize that, don't you?'

Once again, Patrick looked up at the towering walls.

'Patrick, the people who help us know they are taking risks. They take those risks willingly because they believe it is worthwhile. If we lie down and surrender, those monsters will never leave our country and their lackeys in Kabul will make life worse and worse for us. We have to keep fighting and while we fight many innocent people will die, because the Russians think we are weak and will be influenced by their atrocities. Well, we will fight until we are victorious or we are all martyred but we will never stop.'

'Or until you run out of ammo,' Patrick said, attempting a grin.

'We will still fight.' Fareed took his hand, his little finger looping through Patrick's.

It was a habit that still embarrassed the young man. Despite the months in Afghanistan, he found it strange to see men whom he knew as deadly killers and who would slit the throat of a person who hinted at homosexuality, walking hand in hand.

Fareed jiggled his finger to get his attention. 'We should rest. The others may not get here until late tonight, or possibly the night after, in view of what has happened this morning.'

'We just wait?' Patrick still marvelled at the patience of Afghan men.

'Yes.' He tweaked Patrick's finger. 'After this next attack, we should think about getting you across the border into Pakistan.'

'Reckon you could do without me after all these months?'

'I believe it may be time for you to go. You have had extraordinary luck but luck, like time, eventually runs out.'

Damon Gallagher had been wounded in an ambush near Qalat, north of Kandahar. The journey from southern Afghanistan to the hospital in Peshawar had taken eight days. He had been unconscious for the first part, which had been by jeep over rough tracks. He had been semi-conscious and screaming with pain for the second and longest part, which had seen him strapped to the back of a mule and crossing mountains near the Pakistan border. On the third part, he had been in a truck, trying to remain silent to match the stoicism of the wounded Afghans packed in with him, but praying for death.

He was clean and freshly shaven, but haggard and thin. His eyes had the strained hopelessness of a person who has given up trying to combat pain. Nina remembered Damon as a chubby boy. As the three of them sat beside his bed and listened to his story, she found herself looking at a young man whose face was emaciated and lined and who could be mistaken for a badly worn forty-year-old and she wondered what her son, who was the same age, looked like at this moment. And if, in fact, he were still alive.

Damon spoke slowly and in a raspy voice. He and Patrick had been with a small band of Mujahedin rebels. They had been travelling at night in three jeeps. Two nights before the ambush, they had fired the last of their rockets in an attack on an army convoy and were fleeing towards the shelter of some mountains, having hidden in villages during the day and driven only at night.

There was a river that had to be crossed. Rivers were always dangerous places because the approaches could be mined. Patrick had walked ahead, testing the path and checking the depth of the water.

'And it could have been mined?' Adam was aghast. 'Why don't those people use mine detectors?'

'They don't have any, Mr Ross.'

'And Patrick went ahead?' Nina said weakly.

'The Afghans do it. It's their way. The will of Allah and all that. They're crazy people. And they're fighting a lop-sided war. It's broomsticks and 303s against jets and tanks.' He didn't resume for some time and the faint, lazy buzz of the traffic and the shouts of people from the streets of Peshawar swirled through the room. 'What we didn't know was that there was this bloody big Russian tank dug in on the other side. It was just waiting for us.'

Outside, there was a banging, as though two trucks had collided. Damon seemed not to notice. 'They let Patrick get across and waited for the jeeps to come down. I was in the first jeep. They blasted us out of the water. I didn't hear the noise. I just felt the thump and then we were spinning and that's all I remember. I got this' – he touched his broken leg – 'and a load of scrap metal in the belly.'

'And Patrick?' Nina asked the question for them all.

He lifted his shoulders. 'I don't know. Obviously someone got away because they brought me out. But I didn't see him again.' He regarded them with pity and then made a whimpering sound. 'The next thing I saw was the back of that mule.'

They visited Damon several times in the next few days and gradually pieced together an account of what had happened to Patrick since he had left London. Damon told of their tribulations in Iran and of their escape across the border. In Afghanistan, Patrick, Damon and Rezi had driven to Herat and joined the Asian Highway, the only sealed road across the country.

They had started the 1,093-kilometre journey to Kabul in high spirits. Unaware that there had been a political crisis in the country or that Soviet forces were pouring across the border to prop up a tottering pro-Communist regime, they followed the highway on its long loop to the south.

About two hundred kilometres down the highway, they had come to a road block. Soldiers were searching for insurgents and, because they had no papers, they were arrested. Their truck was confiscated. They were put in an army truck and driven down the highway towards a military base. However, they were waylaid by rebels, who killed the soldiers on board and then commandeered their weapons and the truck.

The presence of three foreigners confused the rebels, who split up immediately after the attack. One lot took the truck and Rezi. Damon never saw his Iranian friend again.

The other men, who were in a Russian-made jeep, took Patrick and Damon to their village, where they were questioned at length. That had been a tedious and frustrating affair as none of the inquisitors spoke English. Patrick's few words of Pushtu caused great suspicion. He was regarded as being a Russian infiltrator, sent behind the lines before the invasion. He had the fair skin and hair of a Russian, which was sufficient evidence for some of the hotheads to demand his execution.

One of the rebels, who spoke Russian and tried for several days to trap Patrick into revealing a fluency in the language, had become so incensed by the prisoner's stubbornness that he had led Patrick out to a tree, bound him, blindfolded him and gone through the motions of shooting him by firing squad. The other Afghans had thought this a great joke.

Curiously, Damon had not been pressed so hard but that, he thought, was because of his dark colouring, his scrawny physique (he had lost a great deal of weight in the Iranian prison) and the fact that he spoke not one word of the language. Patrick, however, had continued to be regarded with great suspicion, even when a rebel who spoke some English arrived to take over the questioning. He established that Patrick and his friend came from a country no one there had heard of, and were trying to drive home in a car they did not possess. Again, most of the Afghans thought this a great joke and it was, Damon reflected, their entertainment value that probably kept them alive. They stayed with the group for some weeks. It was at a time when the war was in its earliest phase but there was considerable fighting in the region. The men who had captured them were forced to leave their village but took their two puzzling prisoners with them. They were fortunate, Damon said, because although the rebels captured several men in a number of those early skirmishes, they never took any other prisoners.

The turning point in their relationship with the rebels came when the men were the victims of a surprise attack by Soviet commandos. The soldiers, with the slanted eyes of men from the Muslim provinces along Afghanistan's northern frontier, were landed by helicopter and stormed the camp where the rebels had gathered after a raid. Patrick had helped fight them off. Although unarmed, he had gone to the aid of the leader and pulled a man off his back.

From that time on they were trusted, if not understood.

Eventually, they had been passed into the care of another group of Mujahedin who were operating more to the east. The leader of

910

this group spoke English. He had been studying medicine at a university in Pakistan when the war broke out and had returned to fight the Russians. He and Patrick had become good friends. Damon had been with this man's group when injured in the ambush.

'What is the man's name?' Adam asked.

'Fareed.'

Peshawar was perched on a rim of Pakistan's western frontier. It guarded a place where the mountains of the Hindu Kush were breached by the ravines of the Khyber Pass and by wild streams that ravelled together to form the mighty Indus River. Midway between the Mediterranean and ancient Cathay, it was a place where centuries of travellers had passed, rested, traded or fought. It was a dusty, untidy jumble of a city, as haphazard as a bird's nest scattered by the wind.

In a street that was a cauldron of exotic smells, strident noises, bright colours and biblical faces, Adam and Daniel found a man whose grandfather's name had been on Saleem Benn's list. He was a tailor. Legs crossed, he sat at the front of his shop, stitching the lapel of a jacket. He had the remarkable knack, Adam observed, of ignoring the solid stream of passers-by – boys on bicycles, refugees in solid groups of confused misery, the poor, men who passed in earnest conversation and silent women cloaked in tent-like chadoris – and yet of spotting instantly a potential customer. That was why he was so eager to talk. He thought Adam and Daniel might order a suit or one of his fine, handmade shirts.

He led them to the back of the shop. It was so narrow Adam could have touched both side walls at once. At the rear of the building and flanked by bolts of the finest woven cloth, Adam explained how he had been given the name of the tailor's grandfather. Naturally, the man had never met Saleem Benn but knew of the family. He showed polite interest in the fact that many Afghan or Pathan families now dwelt in the same part of Australia as his visitors. Yes, of course he knew about Australia. He was a keen follower of cricket and rattled off the names of Dennis Lillee and Allan Border, to prove his knowledge was current. How could he help them?

Adam explained that his younger son was thought to be with a Mujahedin band operating somewhere between Kandahar and Ghazni. He was last seen near the town of Qalat, when the group had been ambushed by a Soviet tank. Another Australian had been wounded and brought to the hospital in Peshawar.

The tailor, dressed in white skull-cap and kameez partouk, the

911

pyjamas-like outfit of the region, listened attentively, fingering a sample of fine English tweed while Adam spoke.

'There has been some heavy fighting in recent weeks,' the man said, his eyes dark with gloom. 'Many thousands of refugees have come here. Peshawar is literally bursting at the seams with Afghans who have been driven from their homes.'

Adam explained that they wanted to find someone who came from the area where Patrick was last seen. They needed to talk to a person who knew of Fareed and who might know if Patrick had survived the ambush.

'You want to know if your son is alive,' the man said simply.

'Yes.'

The tailor nodded. He had sons. He understood. 'It may be difficult, but I can ask. Someone may know.'

'If he is alive, we want to get him out.'

The man's eyes rolled in surprise. 'You wish to engage men to rescue him?'

'We'll go in ourselves, if we have to,' Daniel said. The man's eyes measured him for the task.

'My elder son speaks the language,' Adam said.

'So what you need is this.' The tailor raised one hand, preparing to tick off the fingers. 'Information about whether your other son is still alive and if so, where he might be.'

'Yes,' Adam said and the tailor tucked one finger out of the way.

'You require information on a man called Fareed, who is a Mujahedin leader.'

'Correct.'

'There are several Mujahedin groups. What you might call factions. Not all are friendly with each other. Some are represented here. Inquiries could be made.' He touched another finger. 'And then you need to know the name of someone who might be willing to enter Afghanistan to attempt rescue or, alternatively, show you the way in. In effect, act as your guide.'

'That's right.'

'These enquiries could take several days. I am not without other things to do.' His face bore the look of a man whose dearest wish was being thwarted by cruel circumstance. When he was certain they expected to be rebuffed, he smiled; a man who could sell quality suits in a city like Peshawar had to possess theatrical flair. 'However, it is not every day I am visited by two Australians who have a friend who was a friend of my grandfather.'

Adam bowed slightly, just as Saleem Benn would have done.

'So I shall enquire among my friends.'

'If you could find the time to help us, perhaps you could also spare the time to make each of us a suit.'

'Perhaps,' the man said, affecting nonchalance. He lifted the sample of English tweed. 'Is it hot in your country or cold?'

T·W·E·L·V·E

Fareed's men waited in the gorge for six days before the second group of Mujahedin arrived. There had been much Soviet activity in the area and it had been too dangerous to travel to the mountains. Twenty men were in the band but they were pitifully short of arms.

'It will have to be a very brief attack,' Fareed said to Patrick. 'There are not enough weapons to go around and only sufficient ammunition for about two hours of firing. If we do not succeed in that time, we will have to fall back.'

'Or get shot,' Patrick added cynically.

'If that is the will of Allah.'

'What if we have the front gate on the verge of falling down when we run out of bullets?'

'Ask me that question if the situation arises.'

Despite his erudition and knowledge of other people's ways, Fareed's attitude to life and death varied little from that of the humblest tribesman who believed his destiny was predetermined. It made such a man a difficult companion in war. 'Inshallah and all that,' as Patrick used to growl whenever a rebel performed a feat that combined stunning bravery with monumental foolhardiness. A man with an old rifle would charge a tank and thereby draw fire on the whole band. The solitary operator of an anti-aircraft gun would fire on a jet far beyond the range of his weapon, reveal his location and die when other planes came to riddle him at their leisure. A sneak attack on an armed fort, that needed stealth because the defenders outnumbered the attackers by ten to one, would suddenly erupt into a screaming charge, because that was the Afghan way.

They were brave men and deadly killers, but not given to subtlety in the way they waged war on a hated enemy. Little wonder that the life expectancy of these so-called Freedom Fighters was beginning to be measured in months.

Fareed was different in some ways, which explained why he had survived a year of bitter guerrilla warfare. He respected the gunships and tried to keep clear of tanks, unless his party was armed with appropriate weapons. But in normal fighting, he was inclined to plan so far and then put his trust in the will of Allah.

The third lot of rebels arrived and the leaders spent hours discussing the latest information gleaned from sympathizers in the area. Then they evolved a battle plan. Patrick could imagine its simplicity. The main topics would be where to put the heavy machine-gun, where to station the rocket launchers that the last band had brought with them, when the attacking party should leave the nearest cover, and at what time the firing should start. And then? Just storm the walls and kill the enemy.

He had a bad feeling about this venture but, risky though it felt, he would not contemplate staying out of the action. He had to be involved because he now believed in the Afghans' cause. Their methods might be crude, their tactics primitive and their chances poor but they were right. They were the good guys, fighting for their country, their beliefs, their way of life. And he? Well, he was no Lone Ranger riding out of the hills on a white horse, but he was on the side of good in a struggle against evil, he had come to the aid of a desperate people, and he had proved himself to be a courageous and resourceful fighter. For the first time in his life, Patrick felt he was doing something that was truly worthwhile.

While Adam and Daniel checked through Saleem Benn's list, Nina had been following other avenues. She went to the Australian and American embassies in Islamabad and presented herself as both the mother of a young man missing in Afghanistan and a journalist of international renown. She was given sympathy and an extensive briefing and cautioned to do nothing provocative. Journalists, both embassies advised, were regarded with suspicion on either side of the Khyber Pass.

Nina also sought out press contacts whose names had been given by her newspaper friends. Some were journalists working in the capital. Others were correspondents who were using Peshawar as the most convenient base for filing stories on the Afghan conflict and on the ever-increasing flow of refugees crossing the border.

The latter journalists were the most useful. The nature of their work required them to establish contact with various Mujahedin groups and they were able to tell her which ones were most likely to have the information she sought. One British journalist confided that the leader of one faction was 'PR-conscious'. This Afghan man had spent some years in America and knew the value of publicity. A good story could influence governments to send aid or prompt a flood of donations which would allow him to spend money on his own shopping list of necessities. For the promise of a story written by Melina O'Sullivan, he could be most co-operative.

'There's only one problem, dear lady,' the journalist added. 'I don't know where Dadmir Mohammad is these days. There was an attempt on his life recently. A few of his men got blown up by a car bomb, but he got away.'

'And you don't know where he went to?'

'Oh, he's still around Peshawar. You can be sure of that. But he's been forced into hiding. I haven't seen sight nor sound of him for ten days.'

The tailor had discovered that Dadmir Mohammad's forces were fighting in the area where Patrick had last been seen. He knew nothing of the man's reputation for seeking publicity but was aware of one vital piece of information that was denied the British journalist. He knew how to find him.

Through the brother of his nephew's wife, he arranged a meeting. 'He will see only two people,' the tailor said, when they met that night.

'You and Daniel go,' Nina said.

'No.' The tailor waved a hand furiously. 'He specifically wants to meet the person who will write the story. Whatever he can do, he will do only on the strict understanding that there will be a story published that is favourable to his cause.'

'Well, I hope I can do that,' Nina said. 'I will write the truth.'

'Tell him that.'

The meeting was at midnight. A car met them at the rear of a restaurant two blocks away from their hotel. They were driven to a house on the outskirts of the city. The house was surrounded by a high wall and set behind a long garden. As they drove in, Adam saw sentries at several points. Two men checked the car again near the house.

Dadmir Mohammad was more like a businessman than the popular image of a freedom fighter. He was a large, grey-haired man who smoked a cigar and seemed in need of sleep. Fareed was one of his commanders. He knew of Patrick. He was a good man.

'Is he alive?' Nina leaned forward anxiously. Adam stayed back. Something in the man's attitude worried him.

Dadmir removed his cigar and examined his visitors. 'As far as I know, yes.'

'There was an ambush,' Adam said. 'A Russian tank was involved. Patrick's friend, another young Australian, was badly hurt.'

'Not too badly, I think.' He blew smoke between them. 'He is in hospital here, am I right?'

'Yes.'

'Then he's a lucky man. Go to the refugee camps. See how many children you can count without legs or arms, eh?'

Nina slumped forward. 'Our son has been missing for two years.'

He stopped her with a wave of his cigar. For the first time, Adam noticed a man standing in the corner. Silent and unmoving, he blended with the curtains.

'You are a journalist, Mrs Ross?'

'I write under my maiden name, Melina O'Sullivan.'

'Yes, I understand the system.' The cigar fanned the air. 'Tell me, who do you write for?'

She listed the magazines and newspapers which had published her articles in recent years.

'You will write for all of them?'

'No. Only one magazine but possibly several newspapers.'

'An American magazine?'

'Possibly.'

'Make it certainly.'

She glanced at Adam. 'Well, I think I could manage that.'

'We need American weapons. To get them, we need Congressional approval. To get that, we need publicity. And the publicity must be in America.'

Her head tilted into the merest hint of a bow. 'I understand.'

'Good. What sort of story will you write?'

Nina had anticipated this question. Her sole desire was to get Patrick safely out of the country and so, to exert the leverage she required, there could be only one answer. 'I will write the story of Patrick Ross, who fought alongside the freedom fighters of Afghanistan.'

There was the suggestion of a smile. 'So he will have to come out?'

'Yes.'

'He is a valuable man where he is.'

'He's more valuable to you here, out of Afghanistan, where I can talk to him and then write the story.'

He leaned towards Adam, one husband addressing another. 'Is your wife a good writer, Mr Ross?'

'Yes she is. She writes books, too.'

He swung back towards Nina. 'Would you write a book about this?'

'Possibly. I'd need some photographs.'

The cigar described an arc that sliced through all obstacles. 'They can be supplied.' He pressed a buzzer and a man entered with coffee. He waited until the coffee was poured. 'Now, about your son. Patrick Ross was not injured in that ambush. We lost three men, however, plus the other Australian who had to be evacuated. Four men in all. It was a very small group to start with.'

'But Patrick's all right?' she asked.

'He leads a charmed life, apparently.'

Adam leaned back and exchanged glances with Nina. Then he said, 'What does he do with the group?'

Dadmir Mohammad spread his hands and spoke around the cigar. 'He fights.'

Nina covered her mouth.

'We have a small party leaving tomorrow night to carry in some necessary supplies for my forces. Two vehicles only. If we are to search for your son and bring him back, we will need a third vehicle.'

'But some of your men can bring him out?' Nina asked.

He shook his head. 'We have no men to spare.'

There was an awkward silence, which Adam broke. 'If there are any costs involved, I'd be willing to pay.'

He shrugged. 'Regrettably, there are costs. War is not only cruel, it is expensive. I understand Mr Ross that you are prepared to enter Afghanistan?'

'If necessary.'

'It may be. I can spare a driver, a guide who knows the way, but he cannot travel alone.' He looked at Nina. 'So either your husband goes, or your son stays where he is. I'm sorry.'

Adam leaned forward. 'We're prepared to go.'

Dadmir Mohammad scratched an eyebrow. 'Ah yes, you have another son.' He glanced at a sheet of paper on his desk. 'Is it true he speaks our language?'

'It is true,' Adam answered in Pushtu.

'You too?'

'Only a little. My son is fluent.'

'May I ask, how is such a thing possible?'

'He was raised by an Afghan friend of mine.'

'In Australia?'

'Yes. At Marree.'

'Ah.' The name meant nothing. 'How fortuitous. This other son ... he is resourceful, able to use a gun?'

'All those things.'

'The country you will enter is very hard.'

'We live in hard country.'

'Ah. Which is why you have Afghans for neighbours.'

'I had never thought of that.'

He smiled smugly. 'Your son is the same size as you?'

918

'Yes. A little taller but as broad.'

'I will have a man come to your hotel in the morning. He will bring clothes. Do not take anything other than what he gives you. No sunglasses; they are the sign of a westerner. No papers to identify you. Nothing.'

'You mentioned guns. Should we take something?'

The Afghan spoke to the guard in the corner and held out his hand. The man passed him a pistol. 'A hand-gun for each of you might be a good idea. You can purchase ones like this at a gun-smith's.' He passed it to Adam. 'Can you use such a weapon?'

Adam turned it in his hand. 'I think so.'

'And your son?'

'He's a very good shot.'

Nina had both hands to her face. 'Will they be necessary?'

'Almost certainly not, Mrs Ross.' He winked, a strangely incon-gruous gesture from a man who showed so little emotion. 'It is just a ploy on my part to get more weapons into Afghanistan.' He took the pistol and passed it back to the guard, who wiped it lovingly. 'You see, after this little venture, I am hoping your husband will donate the pistols to the cause. My men will certainly make good use of them.' Again his eyes went to the sheet of paper and he coughed apologetically. 'Mr Ross, this will be a gruelling trip. You are in good health?'

Adam smiled without seeming to be amused. 'You mean, am I too old?'

The other man waggled his head.

'I don't think so, Mr Dadmir. And I am used to roughing it.'

'We live in the desert,' Nina said softly.

Dadmir Mohammad ground his cigar into an ashtray blackened by use. 'You should be prepared to leave tomorrow night, Mr Ross. You and your son, who speaks our language.'

'Very well. What time?'

'When you are called for.' He pointed a finger at Nina. 'Your stories will be very important for us. What will you say in them?'

'Whatever is the truth.'

He nodded, then noticed Adam curling a finger as though anxious to gain his attention. 'Yes Mr Ross?'

'You said something about us having to search for Patrick. Don't you know where he is?'

Dadmir Mohammad examined his watch. 'I know where he is tonight. He is preparing to attack a fort.'

'Oh my God,' Nina said.

'Dear lady, it is a small fort. They do this sort of thing all the time.'

919

Adam was white. 'And where will he be when we reach the area?'

'You should arrive there in two or three days' time. There are several places where your son and Fareed could be. These raids they carry out are hit-and-run affairs, you see, and it all depends on where they run to.'

T·H·I·R·T·E·E·N

The fort was small, little more than a tower surmounting a stone building that covered an area the size of two tennis courts. It stood on a large outcropping of rock. Because the stone walls were the colour of the natural rock, it was difficult to determine where the outcrop ended and the fort began. The effect was compounded by the age of the building. The base structure, with walls two metres thick, was at least three hundred years old and was covered by the scars of countless battles and the dross of age. The tower was a more recent addition, being only one hundred and forty years old. It had been raised by the British during the time of the first Anglo-Afghan war.

The fort was near a pass, which was the reason for its existence. The road to the pass curved out of a wide valley, ran below the fort at a place where any traveller was exposed to its cannon, and then climbed into the mountains.

The Mujahedin arrived before dawn. They had walked all night through the mountains, lugging the equipment they would need for the attack. They now spread across the nearest hill. Some rested, some ate, some slept; all waited for the day to pass. The sites for the rocket launchers and the big Dashaka had been chosen. Most had only to keep out of sight until it was time to move against the fort.

Early in the morning, Patrick accompanied Fareed to a vantage-point on the hill. Lying in the shadows cast by a low and scraggy bush, they surveyed their target and assessed how long it might take men to cross the open land to the rock on which the fort squatted like an upended mushroom. In the afternoon, Patrick returned on his own to lie beneath the bush, allow a cool breeze to blow across his body and study the fort once more. Occasionally, he saw men moving on the walls. Few soldiers seemed to be stationed there. While he watched, two trucks drove up and were parked near the main entrance. Some men walked into the fort. The trucks had followed a strange, wandering path, which meant the area outside was mined. He waited for the trucks to leave. They followed the same route. Patrick sketched it on a pad.

The three Mujahedin bands totalled forty men. Four of them had already been sent to the nearest fort, about fifty kilometres away, to create a diversion. They had taken a few of the precious rocket-propelled grenades and, at a set time, were to fire them into the other fort. The four men were then to get away. Hopefully, when the first garrison radioed for help, the troops at the second fort would believe they had a fight on their own hands and would stay where they were.

The remaining thirty-six rebels were to be divided into two sections. One lot would launch the rockets and fire the heavy machine-gun. The others would advance on the fort. Patrick was in the second group. There were not sufficient weapons for all the men, so six would have to go with nothing but knives. They were to pick up the rifle of any man who fell – on either side – and help carry back captured guns and ammunition.

When the sun went down the men, having prayed, moved slowly out of the hills and began advancing on the fort. According to the plan, they had an hour to reach a position near the front of the building. They would follow Patrick's sketched route through the minefield to the main gate. When the first salvo of rockets was fired, they would attack. They carried ropes and hooks to scale the walls.

That was the plan. In fact, a man walking wide of the main group stepped on a mine after thirty minutes and a rebel in the hills immediately launched his rocket. Other rockets followed. There was a loud explosion within the fort.

Fareed cursed in Pushtu, Farsi and English but broke into a run because all the men had begun to charge. Patrick ran behind Fareed who, in turn, was following another man. All the attackers were now shouting and ignoring the carefully plotted but tortuous path to the main gate.

The man in front of Fareed trod on a mine and somersaulted above an eruption of yellow. Fareed dodged to one side. Patrick followed. He was carrying a rifle and had a rope coiled around one shoulder and had trouble keeping his balance as he sprinted across the rough terrain.

Behind them, the big Dashaka began pumping out its lethal hail but, as yet, no one in the fort had responded. Heart pounding, cold air searing his lungs, Patrick ran hard because he knew the silence from the fort wouldn't last. Once the confusion and panic had settled, the defenders would show interest in the men charging through the minefield and put machine-guns and sharpshooters on the walls to pick them off.

922

Fareed was drawing away from him. Gripping the rope, which was slipping from his shoulder, Patrick kept running until he reached the base of the rock and began the climb. One rocket landed near them and howls of protest came from the throats of the rebels. Then another rocket hit the centre of the fort and a loud explosion was followed by a vivid sheet of flame, which cast light across the rocky outcrop. The rebels, brightly lit and vulnerable, cheered wildly.

A man near Patrick fell, but he had only slipped and got up again.

From the fort came the harsh, staccato bark of a light cannon. Another joined in. The soldiers had started to fight back but they were firing at the hills.

Fareed reached the wall and pressed himself against the worn stone. A few seconds later, the heavily burdened Patrick joined him.

'Give me your rope.'

Patrick passed it to the Afghan and stood, bent over his rifle and sucking in breath, while Fareed swung the hook towards the top of the wall. He missed the first time but the hook caught on the next throw. Other men reached the wall. Other ropes snaked to the top.

'You and I will open the gate.' Fareed waited for Patrick's acknowledgement before starting to scale the wall, his woollen shawl billowing as he climbed. Above them, Patrick heard the first sharp snap of a rifle being fired. Another Mujahedin reached the top first and it was he who had the attention of the defenders when Fareed clambered over the parapet. This saved his life. There were three soldiers defending this section. All were jumpy and all converged on the first man over the wall. He died, happily martyred at the throat of his enemy, while Fareed had time to get to his feet and calmly shoot the first soldier to notice his arrival. Then he shot the second man, who was slower. The third soldier, no older than seventeen, dropped his gun.

'You would like to join the Mujahedin?' Fareed asked and the young man gave a sickly smile. Eyes on the soldier, Fareed helped Patrick over the wall. 'That boy is going to take us down to the gate and open it for us,' he said, and prodded the soldier in the ribs.

Two more rebels joined them. Both were breathless but bared their teeth in the joy of achievement and the wondrous shock of still being alive.

The government soldier, shivering with fear, led them down a winding stone stairway. Fareed turned to Patrick. 'It goes well, eh?' He looked pleased. Fareed enjoyed few things these days but he liked fighting.

One of the rockets had exploded near the gate, setting fire to a store-room and killing several soldiers, whose bodies sprawled across the cobbled road that led to the central courtyard. Three surviving soldiers guarded the massive gate. All were looking outwards. Two manned a machine-gun in a turret on top of the entrance. The third was preparing to operate a searchlight and sweep the area at the front of the fort. None was given the choice of fighting or surrendering. A rapid burst of fire from behind delivered the gate into the hands of the attackers.

Patrick opened the gate and a dozen Mujahedin poured through. The battle was over in minutes. There were no Soviet troops in the fort. A few of the government soldiers who survived elected to join the Mujahedin and, as an initial test of their enthusiasm for the cause, led Fareed to the armoury. While he and some men were examining what bounty the fort had to offer, other rebels gathered guns and ammunition from fallen soldiers. They waited at the gate, carrying an assortment of deadly weapons and smiling triumphantly at Patrick, who was maintaining an increasingly nervous watch down the valley. He knew the attack had been bungled. The firing had started half an hour too early, which meant a radio message would have gone out before the second fort was bombarded. The other fort was bigger and manned by Russians. It had tanks, including some of the new, light, high-speed variety. They could cover the distance between forts in less than an hour.

Fareed returned, demanding more men to carry some of the munitions he had discovered. An argument began. The leader of the second band, which had provided the force with most men, wanted to seize more weapons. Fareed's need was to carry a greater proportion of ammunition. After ten minutes of shouting and hand waving, in which most members of all parties joined in, it was decided that the cache should be carried to the gate where each group could select what it wanted.

By now, Patrick was extremely agitated. The Mujahedin were haggling like women at the meat market while a squadron of fleet Russian tanks could be on its way. He pulled Fareed to one side.

'We must leave. They will have sent a message to the other fort. If we delay any longer or have too much to carry, we'll never make it to the mountains.'

Fareed was in no mood for negative thoughts. His face still flushed with the euphoria of victory, he beamed at his friend. He slapped Patrick's shoulder. 'We have won a great battle.'

'And now we have to get out, and quickly.'

The Afghan's eyes fluttered until the words had passed. 'First we take what we need. It is why we came.'

'The tanks will be here.'

Fareed's smile faded and Patrick realized the other man doubted his courage. 'You watch for the tanks,' Fareed sneered. 'We will gather the arms we need.'

Patrick waited another ten minutes. Each shadow in the wide valley seemed to move. He heard noises but fear was playing tricks with his imagination. Every distant rumble that he heard as the purr of an engine swelled into the laughter of rebels staggering under the burden of a dismantled cannon. Every faint clip-clopping that echoed through the archway and had him scanning the sky for the silhouette of a gunship became the footsteps of a man running over stone stairs.

Eventually, Fareed was at his side. One shoulder sagged under the weight of a bandoleer glistening with cartridges. He wore a new gunbelt, with grenades dangling from its side. 'No tanks?' The question was meant as an insult.

'No. Not yet.'

'You will help us carry our treasure, I trust?' He pointed to a metal case, which Patrick lifted on to his shoulder. It felt as heavy as a bag of cement. They had at least a kilometre to walk before they reached the hills and then a night trekking over rough mountain paths.

They left the fort. All bore heavy loads, some shared by several men. They had taken five prisoners. Each was a soldier conscripted into the government army and each now was professing an earnest desire to fight the Soviet invaders. They were made to go ahead. Almost immediately, one of them stepped on a mine and was left howling and clutching at the stump of a leg.

A great rush of flames surged up the fort's tower. There was a cheer. The last men out had splashed petrol over the structure and ignited it as they left.

'Great,' Patrick said, although Fareed was not near and no one else understood English. 'Now we have a nice bright beacon to guide the Russians.' He heard the sound of a single rifle shot. The wounded man stopped screaming.

They were near the hills when he heard the harsh rumble of tanks. Some men dropped their loads and started to run. Patrick saw Fareed turn and try to lift a metal case dropped by bolting rebels. He moved towards the Afghan.

'Let me give you a hand,' he said and Fareed looked up, his expression struggling between regret and fear.

'We need these,' he gasped. 'They're rockets.'

925

'Not much good to us if we're not around to fire them,' Patrick said, but he helped Fareed lift the case. Weighed down and unbalanced by their loads, they jogged towards the hills.

The leading tank entered the minefield ringing the fort. A muffled explosion sounded and the tank jiggled to one side but the mines were designed to maim men, not cripple armoured tanks, and it kept coming. There was the dull thud of a signal pistol being fired and a starshell burst above the fleeing rebels. The first guns jabbered into life.

No answering fire would come from the Dashaka, Patrick knew, because the big gun would have been dismantled immediately the fort was taken. Already, it was being carried back to the meeting-place in the mountains.

Two men running ahead of them were cut down by raking fire from a tank that had circled to one side and was now racing in from their left. It was close, its sinister outline pinpricked by flashes of white fire. Fareed stumbled, pulling the rocket case with him. Unbalanced, Patrick fell heavily. The case on his shoulders landed on his back, winding him. He lay on his face, unable to move. He heard more shooting, then the grind of tanks passing him. It was too late to run away so he feigned death, hoping for a chance to escape when the tanks had gone.

He was conscious of men running, screams, rifle fire, the pounding of heavy guns, the thrash of metal treads. Then boots scraped a rock close to him and someone pulled the metal case from his back. Cold steel touched his neck. The toe of a boot thrust its way under his ribs and rolled him on his back. Now the steel touched his forehead. He opened one eye. The shadows loomed above him. One bent forward. Rough hands pulled him to his feet.

Adam felt ridiculous, dressed in what he regarded as pyjamas and with eighteen feet of cloth wrapped around the top of his head. By comparison, Daniel looked good, as though born to wear such clothes which, Adam reflected, was almost the truth considering his son had been raised as an Afghan. Only the absence of a beard or moustache distinguished him from the other men in the convoy.

All the personal gear they were carrying into Afghanistan – some nuts and dried fruit, warmer clothing for the nights and two nine-millimetre automatic hand-guns – was in a haversack stashed under the seat of their Mahindra jeep. It was a small vehicle, about the size of the original wartime jeep, and Adam, who was travelling in the back, had little room for his head or legs. He was sharing the rear compartment with sacks of vegetables and jerrycans of fuel which were stacked on wooden boxes, and every bump brought him the rough caress of a bulging sack or a rap from the hard edge of a metal container.

They had travelled for two days, following the two trucks carrying arms to Dadmir Mohammad's forces in Afghanistan. Daniel rode in the front seat because he spoke the language. On the way from Peshawar to the border, in a region where fierce-looking farmers raised crops of hashish and opium, there were frequent check-points. These were primarily to save an innocent traveller from the embarrassment of discovering a heroin manufacturing operation and thus meeting the traditional fate of inquisitive strangers. The region was off limits to any but locals or nomadic Pathans.

Officials at a check-point interrogated either or both of the front-seat occupants. Adam, surrounded by sacks and cans and awkwardly out of reach, mumbled a few words and played the role of a doddery old man travelling in the back.

Early in the journey, the driver had been greatly amused by Daniel's command of Pushtu.

'Do I not speak it well?' Daniel asked.

'Too well.' The man laughed. 'You remind me of my grandfather. He uses the same words.'

Adam thought this hilarious and looked forward to telling Saleem Benn that his version of the language, which he had so often threatened to teach to Adam, was regarded as being archaic. It was one of the few amusing aspects of the journey. The dust was blinding, the tracks rough, the heat intense by day and the cold chilling by night, and the succession of check-points within Pakistan had racked his nerves because the officials shouted and gesticulated and seemed inclined to send them back. How the trucks got through amazed him. They were heavily laden with the distinctive devices of war and those items were covered by the flimsiest shield of vegetables. He presumed, after a dozen checks had failed to unearth so much as a single round of ammunition, that an appropriate official had been bribed or that the Pakistanis were fully aware of what was in the truck and were entirely sympathetic. He hoped it was the latter. He was disappointed with some of the things he had discovered in this part of the world. Everything and everyone seemed to have a price. Corruption was endemic. You could get into a forbidden place, buy prohibited goods, find a way around any hurdle, if you had sufficient money and access to the right man. Dadmir Mohammad had blithely added a thousand American dollars to the agreed price for the use of the jeep and driver. He said it was for an additional 'connection' involved in the transaction. Even the tailor, who had been a helpful and, indeed, vital ally, had made sure he would not be out of pocket by demanding an exorbitant deposit for the two suits he would start to make only when (and if) Adam and Daniel returned to Peshawar.

Later on the second day, the trucks stopped among low hills. 'We are to wait here,' the driver said. They waited. The driver dozed. Two men from the trucks, each bearing a rifle, climbed to the top of a prominent hill. They crouched there, as unmoving and still as the rocks that dotted the crest. After a hour, two other men appeared. The newcomers wore thick jackets but carried no guns. They talked briefly but with great animation and then all four walked down to the road. The jeep driver awoke and joined them.

He returned after five minutes. 'We are to wait for sunset, then go to their village. They will show us the way.'

Th village was twelve kilometres away but the journey took almost an hour. They travelled without lights and the track was rough and cut by many dry watercourses.

Adam was surprised by the size of the village. Many times larger than William Creek, it sprawled across undulating land near the base of what seemed, in the dark, to be a large mountain. The houses were shadowy boxes, low and flat-roofed and made of mud and stone. There were, Adam guessed, at least a hundred buildings which would have made this insignificant village in Afghanistan a big town in the Australian outback.

They drove to the back of one house and entered an enclosed yard. Another building, dilapidated with age, stood in a corner of the yard. Several men were waiting there. Rapidly they began unloading the trucks. They carried Russian rifles, Chinese rockets, Czech pistols, American anti-tank missiles and a variety of armaments and explosives through the door of the old building and down into a cavernous cellar.

The guide took Daniel by the elbow and led him towards the house. Adam followed. 'There is a man here who has information about your brother,' he said and Daniel translated. They were taken to a room where several men sat at a table. One, thickset and wearing clothes that were ragged and stained, looked up.

'This is the man,' the guide said. 'He has travelled a long way.'

'You know of my brother?' Daniel blundered into the question without bothering to go through the ritual of introduction and polite inquiries. 'The one called Patrick Ross?'

The man's eyes were burdened by an immense weariness. 'Ah, Part-reek.' He nodded sagely.

'Do you know where he is?'

'No.'

Angrily, Daniel spun towards the guide. 'You said he knew.'

928

The guide abandoned Pushtu and unleashed a stampede of Farsi. The man snapped back. The exchange continued for more than a minute, rising in ferocity and then gradually subsiding. The other men at the table, who had examined Adam and Daniel with great interest when the argument began, drifted back into their chatter.

The guide moved close to Daniel. 'The man is very tired. There was a big battle. Not a good one.'

'And Patrick?' asked Adam, who had followed most of the guide's words.

'He does not know.'

'But Patrick was involved?' Daniel said.

The guide asked the man. 'Yes, he was.'

'Is Patrick safe?'

'He does not know.'

'He hasn't seen him?'

'He knows nothing.'

'But you said he did.' A week in Peshawar and the long, rough ride had reduced Daniel's tolerance of devious people and misleading conversations.

'No.' The guide smiled innocently. 'This man knows where there is a man who knows.'

'About Patrick?'

'Apparently.'

'And where is this man?'

'At a camp in the hills.'

'Do you know where the camp is?'

The guide was reluctant to answer, but eventually said, 'Yes. It is a long way from here.'

'How far?'

'At least three hours by jeep.'

Daniel explained the conversation to his father. 'Let's go, then,' Adam said.

The guide shook his head. 'I am too tired.'

'I will drive,' Daniel said. 'You show me where to go.'

The man licked his lips. 'It is a very rough road.'

'I am used to very rough roads.'

'It is dangerous.'

'Because of the Russians?'

'Yes. There is a fort in the area. Often, they patrol in the night.'

'Is it more dangerous in daylight?'

'Of course.'

'Then we should go tonight.'

The guide frowned.

'We cannot wait,' Adam said, when he had caught up. Still the

929

man was reluctant. 'Does he want more money?'

Now the guide was offended. Daniel spoke to him for some time. 'He says it's a question of going over dangerous terrain and he is tired. He's worried that he might make a mistake.'

'Please tell him it's most urgent. Maybe he could rest for a while, and then travel.'

Daniel put this proposition.

'Yes,' the guide said. 'I will eat, then sleep for one hour.'

The guide slept for nearly two hours and it was after eleven when they left the village. A fine slice of moon lit the sky but progress was slow. The guide drove, stopping frequently to search the night and listen for sounds. Once, they heard a helicopter but it was in the distance. When the noise of its engines faded they drove on.

Just as their driver had underestimated the amount of time he needed for sleep, so had he miscalculated the duration of the journey. They took nearly seven hours to reach the camp. The sky was already bright when they were taken to a bend in a gorge and told to wait while someone went to fetch the man who knew about 'Part-reek'.

The man who returned was Fareed. His forehead was bandaged and his hair, thrust up by the wrapping, was tousled from sleep.

'It began well,' he said in English when they were sitting together to eat unleavened bread, raw onion and dried apricot. 'We took the fort. Patrick was at my side. Together, we secured the gate and that was the turning point. With the gate in our hands, victory was guaranteed. He's a good fighter, your son. Many times I have seen him do brave acts.'

'Thank you,' Adam said, without emotion. Fareed insisted on telling a chronological story and Adam wanted to know the ending.

'We gained much in the way of arms. They are essential to us. We are so poorly equipped, we have to capture weapons in order to fight on.'

'So I believe.'

'We found so much. It was a veritable treasure trove of the items we sorely needed.' He ran through an inventory of rifles, cannons, machine-guns and missiles. He was staring at Adam but seeming to look beyond him. 'I was overjoyed at our good fortune but conscious of the need to make a hasty exit. There is another fort nearby, you see, and there are Russians there, with tanks.'

Adam remained silent as did Daniel, who sat patiently listening to the Afghan. Father and son shared the growing feeling that this long exposition was the prelude to a tale of tragedy.

'We poor Afghans have been so long denied modern weapons or

930

even bullets to fire from ancient rifles that some of my people were like starving men turned loose at a banquet. Even Patrick succumbed to the excitement.'

'What did he do?' Adam asked the question gently.

'Stayed there too long. I was conscious of the threat from the tanks and of the need for haste, but unfortunately Patrick and the more excitable of my men remained at the fort too long.'

'What happened?'

'The tanks came.' He looked away. 'We were almost in the hills. Each man carried a heavy load – far too much, but you must understand how they were – and the whole group was moving slowly. We were perfect targets.'

Adam drew breath in a hiss.

Fareed raised a hand. 'No. He is alive. Forgive me for not telling you earlier.' He touched the bandage in explanation of his forgetfulness and then went on. 'We were together. I was helping him carry some of his load when the tanks started firing on us. They are a new type of Soviet tank. Quite small and very fast.'

Adam nodded impatiently. 'What happened?'

'We fell. In addition to the box we shared, Patrick was carrying another metal box on his shoulders. When he fell, the box crushed him.'

'Oh my God.'

'No, I have used the wrong expression. Not crushed, but landed on top of him. It seemed to knock him senseless. I got up and ran to avoid a tank that was bearing down on us. I diverted their attention from Patrick. They almost got me.' He touched the bandage. 'It was very confusing. Many men were lost. Thirty-six stormed the fort. Only nine got back here.'

'And Patrick? You said he was alive.'

'Yes.' He leaned back. 'Not all our people fight in bands like ours, Mr Ross. Many are behind enemy lines, in the cities, within the forts.' He paused to make sure Adam understood. 'We have had information passed on to us concerning Patrick. He was captured and taken to a fort where they are convinced they have got themselves an American soldier. These fools imagine they have won themselves a very great prize because the communist puppets in Kabul and their masters in the Kremlin are telling the world they are fighting American, Chinese and Pakistani troops, who have invaded Afghanistan. Seeing there are no American soldiers in my country, Mr Ross, an American captive is a very great rarity, especially one who is not an American but an Australian.' He chortled at the absurdity of the situation but quickly grew serious again. 'Such a prisoner is beyond the interviewing capabilities of anyone at the fort where Patrick is being held, so he is being moved.'

'And he's all right?'

'Our informant made no reference to any injuries.'

Adam's head sagged forward. 'So he's a prisoner of the Russians?'

'There are Russians in the fort, although many of the soldiers there are Afghan government troops.'

'You said he was being moved.'

'To Kabul. That's where all important prisoners are taken.' He sighed. 'It will not be a pleasant experience. They will want a confession.'

Adam was silent, his mind racing ahead to the horrors awaiting Patrick.

Daniel said, 'When is he being taken there?'

Fareed raised his eyebrows. 'That I do not know. Wait here.' He left the tent but returned a few minutes later. 'In the morning. The information we have is that he will be transferred tomorrow, to reach Kabul before midday.' He smiled wickedly. 'In our country at the moment, the days belong to the enemy but the nights belong to us. Therefore, they do important things in daylight.'

Adam glanced at Daniel. 'Are you thinking what I'm thinking?'

'Yes. I think I am and I think we should.'

'And what are you thinking?' Fareed said, his eyes darting from one to the other.

'That we should not let him be taken to Kabul.'

F·O·U·R·T·E·E·N

'You cannot even contemplate rescue,' Fareed said, his face set. 'I feel for him as though he were my brother but we cannot risk many lives merely to save one man.'

Adam took some time to answer. He disliked this man but Fareed had the power to decide his son's fate. 'Patrick is more than one man,' he said. 'He represents your cause.'

The Afghan's brow wrinkled. 'He is not even one of my people. What are you talking about?'

'The Russians will say he is an American, or whatever suits them.'

'The Russians are liars.'

'But not everyone knows that. Many will believe what they are told. And you know what the result of that will be.'

'What?'

'The world will begin to believe what the communists are saying. They will think there are foreign troops here and you are not true freedom fighters but just mercenaries who are working for the CIA.' Adam had heard those accusations in Peshawar. He saw Fareed wince. 'In other words, he will be used to convince the world that the Russian lies are, in fact, the truth – that foreign troops are fighting in Afghanistan.'

The tilt of Fareed's head acknowledged the point.

'There's another reason why we should rescue him,' Adam said. 'Your boss, Dadmir Mohammad, wants Patrick safely out of the country so that a famous writer can tell his story to the world. That means your story too, and the story of the Mujahedin.'

'The famous writer is your wife. I know what Dadmir wants. We have a radio. We are in touch.'

'She is a very good writer,' Adam said hastily, dismayed by the cynicism in Fareed's voice.

'She wants him saved because she is his mother.'

'She is also a great writer. Millions of people will read her story. What she writes will tell people the truth about what's going on in your country. It may make the American government increase aid.'

'More weapons?'

'And better weapons.'

'Rescuing one man will do all this?'

'It could.'

Fareed selected a dried apricot. 'How do you propose we carry out this rescue?'

'I don't know. It depends on where he is.'

Fareed chewed until the fruit was soft. 'We could not reach him while he's in the fort. There's no time, anyhow. If we do make an attempt, it would have to be once he was taken from the fort.'

'And how would they move him?'

'Possibly by air, if they think he's important enough. Otherwise by road. There would be a convoy with soldiers. They guard against attacks, even though they know we prefer to strike at night.'

Daniel said, 'Can we find out when's he leaving and how?'

Fareed's expression suggested the apricot had suddenly turned bitter. 'We have excellent informants, my friend, but as yet the enemy do not provide us with timetables or running schedules.'

Daniel persisted. 'And there's no way of finding out?'

'There is no telephone line from our man in the enemy stronghold to here. We would like it, but we don't have it.' Seeing Daniel smart under the sarcasm, he relented. 'It is extraordinarily difficult to get information out from a place like that. It has to be brought out on foot. We may not hear from our man there for another week. Or ever again, if he has pressed his luck too far. Our enemies are ruthless and not averse to shooting a few innocent men to get the one they want.'

'So what do we do?' Adam said.

'I might suggest you get some sleep. I will talk to what remains of my band and see what they think. This afternoon, we will talk again.'

'We don't have to sleep,' Adam said, not daring to waste time.

'You can do nothing for several hours. Let me see what can be done. We will meet this afternoon.' Not waiting for an answer, he left.

'I don't like him,' Daniel said.

'Me neither.' Adam scratched his chin. 'One good thing is that he seems to think a lot of Patrick.'

'But maybe not enough.'

Needing to think, Fareed walked deep into the gorge. There were two parts to the Ross argument. The first impressed him. Patrick in Russian hands could damage their cause in a profound way and slow down aid to the Mujahedin. The second part, about a story to be written by a woman who was Patrick's mother, he found ludicrous. It was the sort of thing that the fat slug Dadmir Mohammad would think of: a scheme to build his own reputation and, in some way, to fatten his purse.

But something had to be done. He reached the end of the gorge convinced that the Russians must not take Patrick to the capital. First, they would loosen his tongue and have him spill out names and then they would put him on display as proof of a foreign invasion of the country. It wouldn't be good for his own reputation, either. Patrick had served with his band. And Patrick, he could not forget, knew the disaster at the fort could be blamed on him because he had dallied too long and allowed his men to be caught in a defenceless position.

He sought out one of his men and put forward a plan to ensure that Patrick was taken by road.

'And we would then ambush the convoy?' the man said.

'It might be interesting.'

'You are crazy, Fareed. We've never attacked a convoy in daylight.' But the man smiled, as though the thought appealed.

'Therefore, they won't be expecting it.'

The man nodded, his great hooked nose bobbing like a parrot's beak. 'It would be good.'

'The idea begins to appeal, eh?' Fareed knew this man. He was brave and courted martyrdom. He accepted the fact that sooner or later he would die in battle. What did it matter when, as long as the end was a glorious one?

'Fareed, how can we kill the godless Russians and not kill the young Part-reek?'

'We can't.'

The man pondered that statement. 'Therefore, we are to kill everyone?'

'Yes. The father himself convinced me. It is vital to our cause that Patrick does not reach Kabul. We destroy the convoy. We kill all on board.'

Patrick had been allowed to sleep for the first time in almost three days but, after a few hours, he was roused by someone shaking his shoulder. It was done gently. He sat up.

It was the Russian, the man with the kind eyes who had flown to the fort yesterday. 'I'm sorry to disturb you,' he said, in his curiously accented English. 'I have good news and I thought you would wish to know.'

Patrick rubbed his cheeks.

'We are going to Kabul.' The man's eyes shone. 'You and I.

935

They are sending a helicopter. Imagine that. Have you ever flown in a helicopter?'

'No.' No point talking about the one his father had built.

'Well, it will be an invigorating experience. I flew down here in one. The scenery is very interesting. Stark, possibly like parts of Arizona or Utah, but you will be able to see for yourself and be able to make comparisons.'

Patrick shuffled across the cot until his back touched the cold stone wall.

'Kabul is interesting but I fear you will not see any likeness to any city you know.' The man laughed pleasantly. 'It is not New York.'

'I'm not American.'

'Oh dear. Let us not start that again.'

'I'm not.'

'If you say so.'

'I'm an Australian. I was on my way home and I got caught up in this business by accident.'

The Russian sat on the cot beside Patrick. He joined him in staring at the wall opposite them. 'Where we are going,' he said softly, 'there will be many people who will want to ask you many questions. Many people. Some of them are terrible bores. Others are –' He glanced quickly at Patrick. 'Well, others are not what you would call nice people. Some are Afghans. A barbaric race, given to enjoying the sight of human suffering. Others you will meet are from my country but you must understand that we are a most diverse nation with many different ethnic groups. Some are not people I would choose as friends.' He stared at the wall again. 'Do you understand what I am saying?'

'No.'

He whistled softly. 'You are tired. I should have been more thoughtful. Please forgive me.' He said nothing for a long time. Patrick closed his eyes.

'You've heard of Ghengis Khan?'

Patrick opened his eyes.

'There are people in my country who can trace their bloodlines back to him or his lieutenants. They have wild eyes.' He turned and pulled his eyes into a slant. 'They can be most unsettling when one first confronts them. You will meet a few in Kabul.'

Patrick let his head rest against the wall.

'Please do not tell them that story.'

'What story?'

'That most imaginative tale about you trying to drive to ... where was it you said?'

936

'Australia.'

'Yes, to Australia. They have extremely short tempers and do not like having their time wasted with foolish stories.'

'It's not a foolish story. It's the truth.'

'My friend, a word of advice. When we get to Kabul, do not ever give one of these men an answer like that.' He took Patrick's hand and examined the fingers. Patrick pulled his hand away. 'It's all right,' the Russian said. 'I was merely trying to imagine those fingers without nails.'

Patrick laughed.

'It's good that you have a sense of humour.' The man lapsed into another silence. The whistle of passing jets sounded through the barred window.

'MIGs, I would say. We have total control of the sky.' He was hunched across the edge of the cot. 'You've sold quite a few of your F16s to Pakistan, I understand. Are they a good aircraft?'

Patrick pressed the side of his face to the wall. 'I'm an Australian.'

'Were you in Vietnam?'

'No.'

'Of course not. You were too young. The imperialist forces were defeated when you were only ... let me guess. Sixteen?'

Patrick did not answer.

'You may well be an Australian but Australia sent forces to Vietnam. When Uncle Sam snaps his fingers, the kangaroo jumps.'

Patrick laughed.

'You have a fine sense of humour.'

'So do you.'

'A man needs a sense of humour.' The Russian nodded to himself. 'Yours will be a great asset which may help you through the first day or so.'

'Good.'

He turned to face Patrick. 'Please, do not make the error I have seen so many brave but misguided men make. They think they can hold out, maintain their stories, outlast the inquisitors. Believe me, my dear young friend, it is just not possible.'

'No?'

'Absolutely not.' He shifted his position on the cot to bring his whole body towards Patrick. 'No matter what you were told before you were sent in here, no matter what cover story you were given to memorize in case of capture, no matter how bravely you endure the experience that awaits you at the hands of those monsters in Kabul, you will be broken and you will tell the truth.' He stood. 'And it could all be avoided.'

937

'What could?'

An expression of great sadness spread across the Russian's face. 'What they propose doing to you. And do you know how it could be avoided?'

'How?'

'By telling me the truth.'

'I have.'

The man sat on the cot once more and leaned forward with a smile on his face. 'There are more than two hundred million Americans. What harm would there be in claiming that there was one more?'

'You mean pretend to be an American?'

'If that's how you want to put it. Say "yes, I am an American" and "yes, I was sent into Afghanistan" and that's all there will be to it. From that moment on, you will receive nothing but the best of treatment.'

'That's a promise?'

'Indeed.' The man stood. 'Rest again. I'll be back in the morning, just before the helicopter arrives. Change your story, and we could have a very pleasant trip.'

The Russian went to the door and waited for a guard to turn the lock.

'Do you know what I like about you?' Patrick said.

'No. What?' The man stood in the open doorway.

'You've got a great sense of humour.'

The door closed. Patrick lay back on the cot. A helicopter. Prisoners were thrown out of helicopters. He had seen that. Men tossed to their deaths. Women, stripped of their clothes, flung out at a thousand feet. It would be quick. Better than being tortured in some Kabul dungeon. And if prisoners could be thrown out, why couldn't a prisoner jump out?

He rolled on his side. When was the last time he had contemplated suicide? Back in Kalinda, when he'd climbed into the Cessna. He smiled to himself. He'd been a crazy kid. He wondered if his father still had the Cessna or if he still flew. He was an old man now but probably still pretending he was young and thinking there was nothing he couldn't do. He would have liked to have told his father what really happened in the shark attack, and at least die with that out in the open.

Thinking of Kalinda, and of his father whom he loved but had never understood, Patrick drifted off to sleep.

There was little food in the camp but Fareed saw that some was brought for Adam and Daniel. A decision had been made, he announced as they ate their nan bread. His group would ambush the convoy in the morning. A site had been chosen for the attack.

'You're certain Patrick will be taken by road?' Adam asked.

'We are taking steps to ensure that no helicopter will be available for such a menial task as transporting a prisoner.'

'What'll you be doing?'

'What is necessary to keep them occupied.' He smiled enigmatically. 'Take my word for it. Patrick will be moved by road.'

Adam asked what role they would play in the ambush.

'You wish to be involved?'

'Of course.'

'You can use a rifle?'

'We both can.'

'Are you familiar with the Kalashnikov?'

'No. It's Russian?'

'Yes. It's good. Simple to use. I will have two brought to you. Familiarize yourselves with them.'

Adam's wrinkles deepened. 'You can spare two?'

'For this one exercise. We are in the most unusual situation at the moment of having more weapons than men.'

'How many of us will be involved?'

'All of my men, plus you two.'

'How many's that?'

'Six.'

'There are only four of you?'

'Myself and three men.'

'That'll be enough?'

'That is all we have.' He flicked the loose tail of his turban away from his shoulder. 'It will be a small convoy. Possibly no more than two vehicles.'

'And we're going to stop them with rifles?'

'We have some new weapons. You yourself helped deliver them last night, I understand. They will be more than adequate for the job.'

'And we'll be able to get Patrick out?'

'If it is God's will.'

Adam stirred uneasily. 'What is the plan?'

'We leave tonight, in one vehicle driven by the man who brought you here. We will stop the vehicle in a safe place and then walk to the site we have chosen for the ambush.'

'And then?'

'I will explain more when we get there.' He rose and lifted a hand in farewell. 'I will send a man with the rifles.'

F·I·F·T·E·E·N

It was a small truck of great age. The battery was flat and they had to push it to start the engine. Adam was dismayed.

'This is what we have to use as a getaway vehicle?'

'It runs,' Fareed said, in the voice of one who accepts miracles. 'And it is all we have.'

The driver, Fareed and one of his men were to travel in the cabin. Adam, Daniel and the other two rebels were to sit in the back, sharing the space with a wooden crate.

'What's in the box?' Adam asked Fareed, as they were about to climb in the back.

'You will find out.'

Adam took Fareed by the arm and the Afghan was surprised by the strength of the grip. 'Tell me now.'

Fareed tried to shake his arm free. 'They are to stop the trucks.'

'What are they? Rockets, bombs, missiles?'

'Anti-tank missiles. The very latest.'

Adam let him go. 'You'll blow a hole right through a truck with one of those.'

'No. We can take out the front of a truck and leave the back intact.'

'You'd better.'

'We can. It is simple. And don't threaten me, old man.'

'Don't call me old man.' Adam lifted a finger and waved it beneath Fareed's nose. 'Or I'll call you boy.'

Fareed bared his teeth in an imitation of a smile. 'I see now where Patrick gets his spirit. But do not try to give me orders and never, never put your hand on me again.'

'Let's get a few things straight.' Adam took the rifle from his shoulder and held it at his side. 'You're running this show and I'm told you're a good man, so I expect you'll run it well. But Daniel and I have got our necks on the block too, so don't keep us in the dark. When we get to wherever we're going, I expect to be told exactly what you intend doing, and precisely what we have to do. I don't want to foul-up because no one knows what's going on.'

'You will be told all you need to know.'

'I said tell me everything.'

Fareed dismissed him with a haughty wave. 'You are old and an amateur.'

Adam lifted a finger and pointed it, like a pistol, between Fareed's eyes. 'I was killing people before you were born, sonny.'

'You were a criminal or a soldier?'

'I was in the last war. In Greece and New Guinea.'

'That was a long time ago.'

'I've got a good memory.'

Fareed made a derisive snort. 'That was a different war. This is a guerrilla operation. It's very different.'

Adam smiled. 'There's no nothing so foolish as a young man who thinks he knows everything. In Greece, I fought behind the lines for a year and a half. We lived in caves. I carried wounded men up mountains. We fought the Germans and I'll bet they're every bit as tough as the Russians. We were short of food, clothes, bullets and we were outnumbered a hundred to one but we kept on fighting them.'

'We do not have proper weapons.'

'I've looked a man in the eyes and killed him with a spear. He was armed with a rifle and I used a wooden spear because I had nothing else. Have you had to use a spear, Fareed? You've got missiles in there to stop tanks but have you ever had to stand over a man who was about to shoot you and then stuck a spear through his chest?' He jabbed Fareed in the chest. 'I have, so don't call me an amateur.'

The other men were looking on with interest. Fareed glanced nervously at them.

'I don't want my son killed because some galoot puts a rocket into the back of a truck,' Adam continued, his voice lower. 'This is going to be risky. I've got no illusions. I also know that you're putting your life on the line to help Patrick and I admire you for that. But if we don't know what's going on, if we're not thoroughly briefed, if your men don't know precisely what they should be doing, then we're all going to end up dead.'

'If that is God's will.'

'My philosophy,' Adam said, 'is to give God all the help he needs to see that we stay alive.'

'I see you are a philosopher, as well as an ancient warrior?'

'I'm a man who has a feeling you're keeping something back from us.'

For a moment, the Afghan's eyes were fierce. Then his face

941

relaxed. 'Let us save our venom for the enemy.'

Adam agreed. 'And there will be no secrets?'

'I will tell you everything when we get to the site of the ambush. You will like the place. It is very good for killing Russians.'

'I just want to save my son.'

'Of course. We have a common purpose.'

Adam and Daniel climbed in the back of the truck. The last man in was one of the rebels. Fareed spoke to him briefly, then got in the cabin.

As the old truck bounced and banged over the rough track out of the gorge, Daniel leaned close to Adam's ear. 'I think we've got a problem.' He had to shout to be heard above the noise.

'Why?'

'Do you see the last feller to get in?'

Adam was facing the man. He was young and thin and had a thick moustache. He avoided Adam's eyes. 'What about him?'

'I heard what Fareed said to him before he climbed in. He told him to stay with us. Fareed said that if they killed Patrick, he was to shoot us.'

Fareed had chosen the site with care. The place where they were to carry out the ambush was good, without being so good that it was obvious and would therefore draw suspicion. What made it outstanding was that the spot was close to another feature which would be certain to gain the attention of any soldiers in the convoy. This other feature was a perfect – and, therefore, perfectly obvious – place from which to launch an attack on any vehicles travelling the highway.

Three hundred metres from the chosen location was a bend, where the road had to thread its way through a split in a range of low hills. A jumble of boulders lay at each side of the gap. They provided enough shelter to hide a hundred men.

'The guards will be extremely nervous and alert as they drive through there,' Fareed said. 'But once through, they will relax and have a big let-down in concentration. We are here, waiting. Just as they reach for a cigarette, we will attack.'

The area Fareed had selected was covered with smaller rocks and honeycombed with holes. Along with the missiles and rifles, they had brought a spade, which was used to enlarge some of the holes sufficiently to hide a man. The idea was that the six men would loosely bury themselves to avoid detection from the air and only emerge when the convoy approached.

'How will you know which is the correct convoy?' Adam asked.

'There is little traffic. Occasionally, there is a large procession of

military vehicles. Sometimes hundreds pass with tanks and helicopters escorting them. This convoy will be small. Just a couple of
vehicles. I will know.'

The plan was to split the group into two. Fareed and two of his
men were to be at the far end of the trap. They would have the
anti-tank missiles. Adam, Daniel and one rebel – the young man
with the thick moustache – were at the other end, with Kalashnikovs. Fareed would launch the attack by firing the first missile.
Adam, Daniel and the other man were at the back to prevent
anyone reversing out of the trap.

'How do we know the Russians won't shoot Patrick once we
start firing?' Adam said.

'We don't. We must rely on surprise. I will be one hundred
metres down the road from you and I will fire at the *second* vehicle.
That is the one most likely to be carrying the prisoner. Omar, who
will be another fifty metres further on, will then fire at the *first*
vehicle. Rahim, who is an excellent shot, will be with Omar.
Immediately, he will fire to kill the two drivers. All that should take
four seconds, maybe five. If there are other vehicles in the convoy,
you will fire at them. As far as the leading two vehicles are
concerned, it is very likely that any soldiers on board will leap out,
because the front of the vehicles will probably be ablaze. You will
shoot them.'

'And you?'

'Once I have fired my missile, I will use the rifle and join in.'

'You all know Patrick?'

'Like a brother, Mr Ross. We will not mistake him for a Russian,
have no fear.'

'And once we have Patrick, we dash for our truck.' It was hidden
in a gully, about a kilometre from the highway. The driver was
guarding it.

'Precisely.'

'And hope the truck starts.'

'It is a very fine truck. Just old.'

'And with a flat battery.'

'But it is a good truck.'

They had several hours to wait for dawn. Once, they heard a helicopter approaching and a large, noisy shadow, with a spotlight
blazing down on the road, swept above them. Ten minutes later, a
dozen army trucks and a group of armoured cars drove past.

'Well, at least they don't go fast along here,' Daniel whispered.
He and Adam were in adjoining holes. It was cold and they had too
much on their minds to sleep. The third man was to one side and

943

slightly behind them. He was dozing.

'I've been thinking,' Adam said. 'If this other bloke's been told to put bullets in us, we're going to spend just as much time watching him as we are the Russians. So I think we'd better get him out of the way. What do you reckon?'

Daniel thought. 'Do you mean shoot him?'

'Nothing as drastic as that. Just put him out of action. Tie him up.' Adam stretched, to make himself more comfortable. 'Then we could concentrate on the job we've got to do.'

'Like me to look after him?'

'Reckon you can? You'd have to be quiet.'

'I reckon.' Daniel crawled from the hole. He left his rifle, taking only the pistol. Adam waited, listening for noises. He heard nothing until a faint rustling heralded Daniel's return. He brought the Afghan with him. The man was gagged and crawled on hands and knees. Daniel carried the Afghan's rifle.

'I thought it might be better to have him here, where we could keep an eye on him.' Daniel pushed the man into a vacant hole and used the Afghan's turban to bind his wrists and ankles.

Daniel bent over the man. 'I know you were told to shoot us,' he whispered in Pushtu. Even in the dark, he saw the man's eyes widen. No one in Fareed's band was aware that he spoke their language. 'Let me now tell you that if you move or make a noise, I will cut your throat and leave your body for the vultures.'

He returned to his own hiding place.

'I've been thinking,' Adam said and Daniel, who had carefully placed the second Kalashnikov alongside his own, leaned closer to hear. 'If Fareed told this young fellow to shoot us if Patrick gets shot, they must think there's a fair chance of him getting shot.'

'Probably.'

'They might even want him dead.'

'Why? He's one of their band.'

'These blokes have a funny attitude towards death. They don't seem to mind the idea of dying. And killing one of their own is acceptable if the result justifies it.'

'But why would they kill Patrick?'

'Because it's simpler. It would be much easier to put one of those anti-tank things straight through the middle of whatever's carrying Patrick than fiddle around trying to knock a front wheel off and then having a bit of a gun-fight.'

'They'd kill everyone?'

'Sure. That way there's no messy rifle fire, no one to shoot back.'

'But if they don't want Patrick alive, why bother with the

ambush? Why not let the Russians take him to Kabul and save themselves all this trouble?'

'Because of something stupid I said. I forgot I was talking to a fanatic.'

'What did you say?'

'I reminded Fareed how valuable a propaganda weapon Patrick would be in Russian hands.'

'So he'd rather have him dead?'

'Possibly.'

Daniel was silent for a while and they heard the distant beat of a helicopter engine. It was flying high, a long way from the road. When it had gone, Daniel said, 'So Fareed's likely to fire his rockets into the middle of the vehicles and wipe everyone out in one nice little burst and then go home for breakfast. What can we do? He's up there with all those fancy gadgets and we're down the other end of the road.'

'I thought I might go and give him a hand,' Adam said. 'Do you reckon you could handle things down this end on your own?'

'Probably. What are you going to do?'

'Pay Fareed a visit.'

'Take it easy.' There was concern in Daniel's voice. 'You're not as young as you used to be.'

'If I was as young as that,' Adam said, tapping Daniel's shoulder, 'I wouldn't need you here.' He crawled away, moving a little stiffly, Daniel thought, but making not a sound.

The Russian entered the cell, scowling. 'Hurry,' he told Patrick. 'We are leaving early. They have a car waiting for us.'

Patrick swung his legs over the side of the cot. 'It's still dark.'

'I can see that. The sun will be up soon. Be quick.'

'I thought we were going by helicopter?'

'There has been a change of plan. About two hours ago, bandits raided some airfields.'

'Do much damage?' Patrick asked cheerfully.

'None at all. But all helicopters are needed to hunt down the bandits and teach them a lesson. Now hurry. We have a long journey ahead of us.'

'Do I get something to eat?'

'You can eat in Kabul.' They moved out of the cell. The Russian fell into step beside Patrick. 'I suppose you miss the traditional style of breakfast. What was your favourite? Flapjacks and bacon rashers?'

'What are flapjacks?'

The Russian scratched an eyebrow. 'I'll say this for you, my

945

friend. You have been very well trained. It may allow you to endure another hour in the skilled hands of my associates in Kabul.'

In the courtyard, a Russian jeep waited, engine idling, steam billowing from a chilled exhaust. One soldier was at the wheel. Another, holding a rifle across his chest, sat beside him.

'Put out your hands.' Patrick did as he was bid and the Russian clamped handcuffs to his wrists. He pocketed the key. A truck drove into the courtyard. Six soldiers, all in battledress, climbed into the open back.

'You should feel flattered. We are providing you with an escort. Now get in.' He pushed Patrick into the back of the jeep and climbed in after him. They drove out of the courtyard and headed for the highway to Kabul.

Early in the morning, two jets flew past at great speed, chased by collapsing tunnels of sound. There were no helicopters, even at the time when they normally patrolled the highway, and Fareed was pleased. The diversions had worked. He had asked for quick attacks on airfields in the south, to suggest the start of a major campaign down there. The Russians would not waste a helicopter on taxi duty today. Patrick would be sent by road.

Just when it was growing uncomfortably hot in the dirt and sweaty dust rings were forming across his neck, Fareed heard the sound of the vehicles approaching. He wriggled out of the earth, lifted the missile launcher, and once more focused on the spot on the road which he had selected as the target zone.

The vehicles appeared through the gap. Fareed's heart beat faster. It was certainly the convoy and there were only two vehicles: a large truck with an open back and with soldiers sitting on either side, and a jeep following close behind. They were not moving quickly. The soldiers, who had travelled through the gap facing outwards and with rifles at the ready, turned and settled back in place.

Fareed put his eye to the sight.

The barrel of a pistol touched the back of his head. 'Destroy the jeep and I'll blow your brains out,' Adam whispered.

Fareed's head jerked back, hitting the pistol.

'Just take it easy. Show me how good you are. Take the front wheel off.'

'What are you doing here?' the Afghan hissed.

'Making sure Patrick stays alive.' Adam tapped him with the gun. 'Here they come.'

They kept their faces low as the truck roared past. The jeep entered the target zone. Fareed hesitated. The shot he had intended

946

was almost front-on and would have skewered the jeep down the middle. No one could survive a strike like that. With the pistol rubbing his ear, he swung the device, following the jeep and waiting until it was almost side-on. It filled the sight. He fired.

The missile struck the front, tearing away metal but corkscrewing beyond the road and exploding over rocks. The jeep, with its front gaping like an opened sardine can, slithered off the road, hit some holes, and rolled on its side.

Farther up the road, the leading truck suddenly erupted in flames. A missile had struck it from the rear. Adam saw pieces of metal and men and blazing canvas cart-wheeling through the air and was on his feet, scrambling to reach the up-ended jeep.

At the other end of the trap, Daniel burst from hiding and dashed towards the others.

Another explosion shook the truck and burning fragments cascaded on the road. Several rifle shots rang out.

The jeep had come to rest on a ridge between holes. It see-sawed on its side, with flames dancing around its broken engine. The driver hung lifeless through his window. A soldier crawled through the space where the windscreen had been and fell into a hole. His chest was bleeding. He tried to keep moving but rolled on his back and lay there, making gurgling noises.

The jeep's canvas top was ripped. Adam grabbed an end and pulled it clear of the roof frame. Two men were huddled in the back. He gripped the jacket of the top man and hauled him out. A stranger stared at him. The man got to his feet, swaying unsteadily, and slowly raised his hands.

Adam heard the shot, saw the man spin and fall, and saw Fareed standing near him with the rifle at his hip.

'Oh for Christ's sake,' Adam screamed, pushing Fareed away, 'the man had surrendered.' Anxiously, he bent to help the second man, who was upside down and struggling to get out. 'There was no need to –'

There was another shot and Adam's legs were knocked from under him. He fell against the jeep, the impact causing it to rock wildly.

Fareed walked closer, rifle at the ready.

'I told you never to touch me.' He lifted the Kalashnikov.

Daniel had pounded along the road. 'Hey!' he shouted, still at full speed and, as Fareed turned, he threw himself at the Afghan with the lunge he used to fell wild bulls. He hit Fareed so hard the man toppled in a sliding tangle of arms and billowing robes. Daniel followed him, lifted him and hit him again. He threw him in front of the jeep and ran to Adam.

Adam's eyes were glazed. 'What did he do?'

'Shot you. Let me have a look.'

They were both on the ground when the man in the jeep crawled out. He looked at Daniel and then at Adam.

'Am I dreaming?' Patrick said.

Adam gripped his younger son's manacled hands, closed his eyes as though trying not to cry and fainted.

Omar and Rahim ran back, anxious to get away before others reached the scene. They saw the unconscious Fareed lying crumpled in the hole at the nose of the jeep, tested his body with a toe and assumed he had been shot in the skirmish. They were not surprised. He was always a daring fighter and likely to be martyred. They greeted Patrick with joy.

'Where is Azim?' they asked.

Daniel had forgotten the other man. Leaving Omar and Rahim to pick up his father, he ran back to Azim. He untied him. 'I believe I should shoot you,' he said. 'If I tell the others of the treachery you planned, they will shoot you.'

'It was not my plan.'

'That is the only reason I have not cut your throat.' He pulled Azim to his feet. 'Now go and help the others. You will be judged on what you do for the rest of this day.'

When Daniel rejoined the group, Patrick held out a set of keys. 'The Russian had them,' he said, jogging to keep up the pace of the two men carrying Adam. 'For heaven's sake, undo these handcuffs, will you?'

'And how are you, Pat?' Daniel said and they both laughed at the absurdity of a normal greeting at a time like this.

The first aircraft arrived just before they reached the gully where the truck was hidden. It was a spotter plane, a slow, noisy aircraft that turned in tight circles above the column of smoke rising from the highway. It climbed and made a series of exploratory sweeps across country on either side of the road. By the time it flew their way, the men were among rocks and the pilot flew on without seeing them.

By now, Adam had regained consciousness. The bullet had gouged a hole in his thigh. They attempted to bind the wound, then Daniel carried him to the truck.

'What now, Pat?' Daniel said. 'You're the soldier. What do we do next?'

'Move. The next thing *they'll* do is send other planes. First jets, then helicopters. We can't stay here.'

'Would they attack an old truck?'

948

'Probably.'

Daniel checked Adam's wound. The leg was sticky with bright red blood. 'Is there a doctor nearby, or a village?'

'I don't know where we are.'

Daniel asked the same question of Omar.

'There is no doctor,' he replied, surprised to hear the *feranghi* speak his language. 'But there is a village.'

'How far?'

The man shrugged. 'Half an hour. Perhaps less.'

'My father needs attention. If he could be given shelter in some house ...'

'It will be bad for everyone if we are found in the village. Bad for us. Bad for the villagers. The Russians will come and destroy everything.'

'He may die if we don't get someone to attend to that leg.'

The man shrugged, a gesture of compassion from a practical person. 'He is one. In the village there are hundreds.'

Adam waved his hand to attract their attention. Daniel and Patrick squatted beside him. He gripped Patrick's hand but spoke to Daniel. 'No village. Be the first place they'd look.'

'You need help.'

Adam's teeth were clenched in pain. He shook his head. 'No village. But get out of here. Too close.'

Patrick agreed. 'They'll have helicopters here soon.'

Daniel turned to his brother. 'Well, what do we do, Pat? This is your part of the world.'

Patrick took a deep breath. This was the first day on which Daniel had ever asked his advice. 'We get the hell out of here,' he said. 'And we go east, towards Pakistan.'

They had to push the truck. The ground was so rough that little speed could be gained and the engine spluttered and backfired but refused to start. Only when several exhausting minutes of pushing brought them to a downhill slope did the truck roll fast enough to spark the engine into stammering, belching life. It pumped out vast clouds of blue smoke. In dismay, Patrick watched the smoke rise above the gully. Had they sent up a signal, they could not have defined more clearly their location.

The realization that he was in charge came slowly to Patrick. It was a good sensation. It gave him a feeling of strength; not through having power over others but through being able to act quickly and decisively and do what he knew should be done. The three Mujahedin were now waiting for his orders. They knew him as Fareed's deputy. Instinctively, they looked to him for guidance.

949

And they were getting nervous.

'Quick,' he shouted. His Pushtu was basic but usually sufficient. He had Adam lifted gently and put into the back of the truck and then hustled the others to get in with him.

He sat with the driver. 'Slow,' he said. 'No dust.'

The man understood the words but not the reason. He presumed Patrick was concerned solely for the comfort of his father but there was an additional and more important motive. To travel rapidly would suggest flight and stir up excessive dust. Either factor was sufficient to lure an inquisitive pilot, whereas a slow-moving truck might not be seen and, if it were, might not arouse suspicion.

The driver followed a track that led towards the mountains. It was more of a donkey trail than a road for wheeled vehicles but it was wide enough to allow the truck to make slow progress.

They had entered low hills when a sudden blast of noise shook the truck and whisked the land around them into whirlpools of dust. The belly of a jet fighter flashed overhead. It came from the rear and was so low Patrick could clearly see the racks of rockets beneath the wings. The truck wobbled in the turbulence.

The plane climbed and turned and the mountains groaned with rumbling echoes.

The driver went faster.

'Slow,' Patrick shouted and bent to see where the jet had gone. It was still turning and had lowered its wing flaps to make another, slower pass. The pilot wanted to have a good look at them. Patrick rapped on the back window of the cabin and saw Daniel's face pressed to the small glass panel. 'Get everyone down,' he shouted. 'Out of sight.'

The jet was approaching them again. Patrick remembered a story Alex Rafter had told him about Greece. It was about Alex, the boy, waving to a German pilot who had waved back and flown away. So Patrick leaned out the window and smiled and waved a cordial greeting. He saw the pilot staring.

He heard the crack of a rifle shot. One of the Afghans had found the target too tempting.

'You bloody fool,' he shouted but no one could hear a puny human's voice above the rush of power from the jet as the pilot, having seen the rifleman, swung the fighter into another climbing turn. The Russian's intentions were obvious. He would take his time, approach from the rear and blast them out of the hills.

'Stop.' Patrick knew they had a chance if they got clear of the road but to stay in the truck was death. Confused, the driver kept going and was searching for the plane. 'Stop!' Patrick screamed again, and the Afghan stamped on the brake pedal so savagely that

950

the old truck skidded sideways.

Patrick jumped out and ran to the back. One of the Afghans was already out but kneeling, and taking aim at the distant jet. Daniel dragged Adam to the tail-gate and passed him down to Patrick. Adam clutched a rifle.

'What do you think you're going to do with that?' Patrick grunted as he hoisted Adam on to his shoulder.

'Take it home as a souvenir.' Adam gasped as Patrick stumbled under the load and headed towards an eroded gutter. It was shallow but it was close and it cut a jagged path away from the track. He fell into it, meaning to put his father down gently but spilling him on his back. Adam yelled with pain, but clung to the rifle.

Face down where he had fallen in the ditch, Patrick heard the pitiful bark of rifles, felt the ground shake and, as he turned, saw the truck rise and jolt forward. Then the fighter hurtled past and the air was thick with whirling pieces of metal and hideous noises.

Daniel fell on top of him, his arms splayed out, the rifle he had been carrying clattering to the ground. The jet was climbing, fouling the pure sky with its thunder.

The last three members of Fareed's rebel band had chosen to confront the Soviet jet with their Soviet rifles and were splattered across the chopped wreckage of the truck. The driver had run to the other side of the trail. Now, he hobbled towards them, holding one knee.

Daniel had not moved. Patrick pushed him clear, and got to his knees.

'You all right?' Adam said.

Patrick spat dirt.

'And Daniel?'

'He's out of it.' He felt Daniel's pulse. 'Still alive. He got hit by something. His turban's been knocked off.'

With difficulty, Adam pulled himself into a sitting position. 'Any blood?'

Patrick had been checking for bleeding. 'Bit on the back of the head. In the ears. Why? Are you thinking of giving him some?'

Adam made a harsh, throaty sound. 'Great time to crack jokes.'

'Best time.' He looked around them. 'Things couldn't be worse. No truck. No men. You've got a hole in your leg you could ride a bike through and Daniel's out like a light. And the Russians will have troops here in half an hour to mop up whatever's left.'

Adam gripped the Kalashnikov. 'Well, you'd better get moving.'

Patrick stood and picked up Daniel's fallen rifle. 'How? And where to?'

'You're in charge, son.' Adam groaned and felt his leg. 'But anywhere would be better than here.'

The driver was standing nearby, trying to pull a sliver of metal from his knee. Patrick walked across and spoke to him.

'I'm still not too sure of their lingo,' he said when he returned, 'but I think he's saying there's a settlement of some sort on the other side of the mountain.'

'Tell you what. You take Daniel. Go with the guide. Find a good hiding place. Then come back for me.'

'I don't like leaving you.'

'No choice.' Adam waved a hand. 'Go.'

Patrick nodded. 'I'll be back soon.'

'Quick as you can. Here.' Adam lifted his hand and Patrick took it. 'Good on you. See you soon, eh?'

S·I·X·T·E·E·N

Adam either slept or fainted. He wasn't sure which. When he awoke, it was hot and he was lying in the gutter and he could hear the flat drone of an aircraft engine. He stayed low. It was probably another spotter plane, checking how successful the jet's attack had been.

The aircraft circled several times. Lying back, not moving but with his eyes open, Adam watched the high-winged plane sweep overhead. The pilot stayed well out of rifle range, then turned to the west.

Adam sat up. The leg had stopped bleeding. He lifted the sodden bandage and found the hole in his thigh was sealed with a jelly-like wad of ugly red. The wound was the shape of a large bird's claw. He examined it dispassionately, clinically, as though it were someone else's leg and the crippling wound someone else's misfortune.

He picked up the rifle and put it on the edge of the gutter. From here, he could see what remained of the three Afghans. Brave men. Foolhardy, stupid to the point of being suicidal, but fearless. Was that the same thing as being brave? He wasn't sure, but it took guts for the three of them to blast away at the fighter with its armour and cannon and rockets. It was as futile as the past challenging the future, yet magnificent in a wretchedly sad way. Not a bad way to go, he thought, and wondered about his own chances of survival; and if he ever did get out of here, whether he'd lose his leg. Then he looked at the empty and lifeless landscape and felt lonely and, at that moment, accepted as fact that he would not leave this place. This was where he would die.

For a brief moment, he was frightened. Then the fear left him. It oozed away. It wasn't replaced by anything. He didn't feel brave, not like the Afghans were brave. He just felt nothing. Numb. As if he'd already ceased living and what happened next didn't count.

He wondered what he would do if soldiers came. He didn't want to kill anyone but he wasn't going to lie down and be shot. He knew they wouldn't be looking for prisoners so he'd die fighting. Die. It was strange thinking about that. Death, the act of dying, was the certain fate of all persons but few thought about it. At least, he hadn't. He'd always been too busy. Now he thought about it. He wondered which way he would go. A tank, perhaps, could come up the road and blow him to smithereens, or one of those big helicopters might drop napalm on him. He wouldn't like that. Possibly soldiers would come and one would put a single shot through his head.

He could always scrape away that vile-looking clot on his leg and let his blood drain out.

The thought of that made him sick, and then he heard the sound of a helicopter. It was far away but he saw it, a slim little grasshopper above the horizon and heading straight for him.

'Are you OK, Dad?' He hadn't heard Patrick approach. Great sentry I'd make, he thought, and almost fainted again.

'Come on. Put your arms around my neck.'

Adam did as he was told. 'You're bigger than I remember you, Patrick.'

'You haven't seen me for a long time. Now shut up and let me get you out of here.' Patrick strained to lift him. 'There's a chopper coming and if he spots us, we'll be in trouble. Can you hang on to your gun?'

'Sure.' Adam gritted his teeth and thought what a strange death it would be to die on the back of your son. Patrick was strong. He was running. The jarring sent terrible spasms of pain through his leg. He swore he would not cry out but despite the resolve every step dislodged a groan.

Patrick followed a narrow path up the hill. It was rough and zig-zagged between rocks so large that Adam's elbows brushed against them. The track became steeper. Patrick slowed, unable to maintain the pace and wheezing for breath.

At a bend in the track where a small bush sprouted between boulders, he stopped, unable to go any further. He lowered Adam to the ground and helped him shuffle behind a boulder. He sank down beside his father, gulping in air.

'That was a good run,' Adam said and didn't recognize the old, thin voice that uttered such nonsensical words.

Patrick let his head loll to one side. He was grey with fatigue.

'Where's Daniel?'

Patrick gestured with his thumb. 'Good spot.' He sucked in air. 'Further up. They won't see him.' He got to his hands and knees and peeped around the rock. The helicopter was close now and rising. 'He'll have a bit of a look-see before he lands.' Patrick sucked in more air. 'So keep down.'

Adam curled against the base of the rock. Gently, Patrick moved his father's legs until they were close to the rock and then covered him with branches from the bush.

The helicopter was hovering above the wreckage. It was not one of the big gunships but a smaller machine. That's good, Patrick thought, because it won't have the firepower of the larger aircraft, or be carrying a dozen commandos. He closed his eyes for a few seconds and breathed deeply, recharging his reserves of energy. He felt his father's hand touch his outstretched leg.

'You OK?'

'Sure.' He crawled closer and rearranged the branches to give better cover. 'At least you're not as heavy as Danny.'

'How is he?'

'Sleeping. He might have concussion.' He looked around the rock. The helicopter was still above the truck. 'I'll get you up to him in a minute. We'll just wait and see what these fellows are up to.'

At that moment, the noise emitted by the helicopter changed to a higher pitch and it began to move, following the main trail up into the hills.

'Don't look up,' Patrick said softly. 'They'll see a face. It stands out.'

Keeping his head down, Adam smiled to himself. He was back in Greece, keeping low so the Germans wouldn't see the distinctive outline of a pale human face. Nothing changed in war except the enemy, and the fact that the Germans used to climb mountains and the Russians flew over them.

The helicopter crossed a ridge and flew out of sight. In silence they waited. 'What do we do now?' Adam said.

Patrick raised a finger to his lips. 'Stay where we are.' He was crouched forward, as though kneeling in prayer. He had one rifle beside him. 'They'll be looking for movement.' He listened intently for several seconds, gathering the scraps of sound floating in the hills. 'Sometimes they put a few men down and let them lie low for a while and then the chopper goes off and tries to flush –'

His voice was drowned by the sudden roar of the helicopter, which burst over a crest near them.

'Head down,' Patrick shouted and, bent in a foetal crouch, he pressed himself against a boulder. The machine passed directly above them and the branches covering Adam danced and whipped in the vortex of disturbed air. The noise eased. Patrick lifted his head and crawled to the edge of the boulder. The helicopter was turning above the remains of the truck. As slowly and as cautiously as a wild dog settling down for the night, it circled once over its chosen spot and landed.

Two soldiers, helmeted and carrying guns, jumped out. The helicopter took off immediately.

Crouched low, the men on the ground advanced to the truck and prodded the bodies of the three Afghans. One soldier searched the truck while the other stood guard. The helicopter stayed above them. The grey barrel of a machine-gun drooped from its side.

One man waved and the helicopter flew away, following its original route along the trail and over the crest. It returned a few minutes later and landed. Three more soldiers got out. Once more the helicopter took off but this time it flew to the west.

'He's going,' Patrick whispered. 'But he's left five men down by the truck.'

'A good time for us to go?' Adam said, pushing the branches off him.

'Very good. As soon as they find this track, they'll come up for a look.'

'I'll walk,' Adam said. 'You just give me a hand.'

Patrick shook his head. 'You wouldn't make a dozen steps. Anyhow, the track's too narrow. It's single-file.'

'I'm too heavy.'

'Dad, I'm a big boy. I can carry you. Now just shut up.' Gently, he hoisted his father on to his shoulders and used the branch to erase the marks they had made on the earth. Then slowly he began to climb through the boulders.

Daniel was lying under a shallow ledge near the crest of the hill. He was conscious, and on his own.

'Where's the driver?' Patrick hissed.

Daniel, mouth open and eyes glazed, could not answer. Painfully, he shook his head.

Patrick helped Adam to the ground. 'The Afghan's gone.'

'Where?'

'Who knows? Can't blame him for saving his own hide.'

Adam dragged himself under the ledge. 'How are you, Danny?'

Daniel managed to nod. He licked his lips.

'Have we got any water?' Adam asked Patrick, who was on his knees and looking back down the narrow track.

'We've got rifles and about a hundred rounds. But no water and no food.'

Adam touched the back of Daniel's head. 'He's got a lump the size of an emu egg.'

'Must have been hit by a bit of metal.' He turned and grinned. 'Lucky it was his head.'

Adam crawled alongside Patrick. 'As soon as you've had enough rest, you should get him out of here.'

'Danny?'

'Yes. Try and find that village.' Adam inched forward until he had a better view of the track. 'They may have a jeep or a truck that could get you into Pakistan.'

'What about you?'

'Well, I thought it might be handy if you had someone here to keep an eye on the track. You know, make things awkward for any Russians who tried to follow you.'

'You mean you're going to stay here?'

'Why not?'

Patrick rubbed his face. 'Dad, you know why not. I'm not going to leave you here.'

'Yes you are. Look, I'm worn out from all this moving around. I need to rest.'

'Dad, we're not talking about you having a rest. We're talking about me abandoning you.'

Adam shook his head stubbornly.

'Dad, if the Russians come up the hill, you won't hold them off for long.'

'Maybe for long enough.' Adam slid the rifle forward and aimed it down the track. 'I mightn't be able to walk but I still reckon I could fire one of these.'

'Dad, I can't.'

He seized Patrick's wrist. 'You've got to, son. No point in the three of us waiting around. You can't carry me and Danny.' Patrick looked away. Adam shook his wrist. 'If you go now and take Danny with you, you might be all right.'

Patrick swung around. 'I don't want to leave you.'

'I don't particularly want you to go.' Adam tried to smile. 'But you've got to.'

'Let me take you and come back for Danny.'

'No. He can walk. He'll need your help but you've got a chance with him.'

'Dad!'

'For once in your life will you do what I ask you?' When he saw the flush of hurt on Patrick's face, he added, 'I'm an old man. I've lived my life. You two are young. Do you understand what I'm saying?'

Patrick nodded.

'This is best. But you've got to go now.'

Patrick looked down the track, and then back to Adam. 'I'll come back for you.'

Adam smiled. 'I don't know if that's such a good idea.'

'I will.'

'I know you want to, but I'd feel a lot happier if you two got out safely. I want you alive and back with your mother, not getting yourself killed trying to save an old bloke like me. Now get going.'

Patrick wormed his way under the ledge and pulled Daniel into the open. 'Can you stand?' he asked and Daniel, eyes blinking slowly, nodded.

Patrick shuffled back to Adam. 'How many rounds have you got left?'

'Enough.'

'If they come, stay under the ledge. They mightn't see you.'

'Sure.'

'Jesus, Dad, there's so much I want to talk to you about.'

'Me too.' Adam held up his hand and took Patrick's. 'You turned out really well. I'm proud of you.'

'I wish we –'

'I wish you'd get out of here. Just tell your mother I love her, OK?'

'I love you too, Dad.'

'Me too.'

He watched them leave. Daniel, still dazed, leaning heavily on Patrick's shoulder. They followed the track down the other side of the ridge and were soon out of sight.

Adam put the rifle against a rock and counted his ammunition. He had forty-five rounds. Sufficient to keep any intruders busy for ten minutes or so, he thought. He pushed himself into a seated position and studied the area.

The ledge under which Daniel had been hidden was wide and gave good protection from the air but any man climbing up the path would look straight into it, making it useless as a long-term defensive position. Be all right for a few shots. No more. Across the track, the ground rose into an area covered with large rocks and a few big, rounded boulders. They gave good protection from the side but were exposed from the air. If the Russians brought back another helicopter, he'd be as exposed as a lizard basking in the sun. The ledge was best, if he could just cover the opening in some way.

Near him were several rocks that were large enough to block the opening beneath the ledge. He tried to dislodge some of them but they were too heavy. He squirmed his way to a smaller rock and, using his back and his one good leg, was able to lever it out of its resting place and push it across until it was touching the lip of the ledge.

He crawled back to where he had left his rifle and surveyed his handiwork. That would do. As a last resort, he could get under the ledge and lie behind the rock. It was a little wider than his shoulders. He could fire from there, and be difficult to hit.

He heard a noise and looked down the track. Two soldiers were climbing up.

There was no question of hiding and letting them pass. If they followed the track, they would catch Patrick and Daniel. He had to stop them.

He took careful aim at the second man who was crouched low, moving slowly and taking care not to dislodge stones. He fired. The soldier seemed to spring backwards, like a clumsy gymnast attempting a back flip, and disappeared among rocks. When the leading soldier spun around, confused by the cry of his companion and the rifle's ringing echoes, Adam fired again. The soldier fell on his knees and slid sideways off the track.

Adam pulled back out of sight. Bile rose in his throat. He was back in Greece and he was sick of killing people. He closed his eyes and saw the soldier with the stubble on his chin and a spear through his chest and he felt like throwing the rifle down the hill and rolling on his back and letting life drain out of him. But if he didn't stop these men, they would kill his sons.

He gripped the rifle again and peeped around the rock. He saw no movement, heard no sound. There were three more down there, somewhere. He wished they would yell out in surprise, call to their companions or make some noise, but there was nothing. He shivered. These were professionals. Young, hard, trained to kill. And he was seventy and had a hole in his leg. He pulled back out of sight again and felt sick with fear. Biting hard on his bottom lip, he made himself think. What would they do?

They won't come charging up the track, he told himself. They'll probably send one man to have a look and the others, if they come, will climb another way.

Adam waited another minute. Still he could hear nothing. He was certain they would be climbing to see what had happened to their companions. They might even have reached them. If that was so, they would be fanning out. He looked around him. Off to his left but separated by a deep fissure was a rocky knob. It was higher than his position and if a soldier scaled that, he would have a clear shot at him.

Adam squirmed away from his sniping position and, dragging his injured leg, crossed the path and moved up into the rocks on the other side.

The pain was awful but he persuaded himself that the more it hurt, the less likely he was to faint. He dragged himself up until he was ringed by boulders. He looked across at the high knob. He was protected here. He also had a clear view of the track below.

He waited.

The first sign was the rattle of a small stone. It came from down the hill. After another minute, Adam noticed a movement, the sort that is so faint the viewer begins to doubt what he has seen. It looked like a small rock moving. Adam watched and saw it again. It was a camouflaged helmet. After a while the man moved again and now Adam could see him clearly. He was moving slowly, patiently, and constantly searching the ground above him. He was near the place where Adam had shot the first two soldiers.

The man stopped and again searched the ridges above him. Then he glanced to his right and, very slowly, raised his hand as if signalling someone. Adam followed the line of the signal and saw a movement on top of the high rocks. Up there on the knob, where a sniper would have an easy shot at someone lying in Adam's original position, was another soldier. He was prone and, but for the acknowledgement of the signal, did not move.

Adam raised the Kalashnikov.

He squeezed the trigger. He pumped out three rounds, saw the man's jacket lift around the shoulders, and swung the rifle down towards the other man. The soldier on the track was scrambling for cover. Adam held his finger on the trigger. The man ran in a pool of spurting dust and flying rock chips, then fell and rolled out of sight. Quickly, Adam turned back to the man on the high rocks. He had not moved. One arm swung limply over the edge.

One man left, maybe two. He could have missed the man on the track. He waited for the last echoes of gunfire to crackle into the distance and then listened. A soft moaning, as faint as the rustle of trees in a dawn breeze, drifted up the hill. Adam heard a man's voice uttering a few urgent words; scraping sounds; the rattle of stones.

He reloaded, pulled his leg into a more comfortable position and waited.

The next move caught him by surprise. From down the track, someone began firing an automatic weapon that sent bullets singing around the boulders. One spray followed another in short, lethal bursts. Adam kept his head down, more in fear of being struck by a ricochet than a direct hit.

A minute of intermittent firing was followed by an eerie silence. Adam pulled himself to another position and put one eye beyond the rock. He fired once. A withering response splattered across the boulders, showering him with fragments of stone. He closed his eyes and pressed his face to the ground and, when the firing ended, lifted his gun and sent a single shot down the track, not bothering to select a target.

Another burst hammered the rocks.

He saw where these shots came from and fired again. There was a short, stuttering response. A stone chip cut his cheek. He was wiping his face when another, longer burst swept the area. A bush at the end of the rocks dissolved into twigs and blew away.

Adam waited, expecting more fire or the man to advance. Nothing happened.

He was finding it difficult to estimate time but he guessed half an hour passed. There was no movement, no more firing, no sign of a soldier. Now he began to suffer from alternate spells of either intense pain or giddiness. He didn't want to pass out. It would be ridiculous to faint and have a squad of Russian soldiers go charging past him after the boys. He moved, knowing the effort and the pain would keep him awake. Sliding on his belly, he went back to his original position and stayed there for several minutes, thinking about Patrick and Daniel and wondering how far they had progressed down the track.

For a while the pain eased and, with a clearer head, he tried to anticipate what the Russians would do. They would have a radio and whoever was left would be signalling for help. They probably believed several rebels were hiding in the hills. So what would they do?

He had another wave of giddiness and it took several minutes for him to answer his own question. They would send more troops. How? In a helicopter.

As though keyed to his thoughts, the first woofling beat of a big helicopter's rotors drummed through the hills. Without bothering to search for it, Adam slithered towards the ledge and dragged himself under the shelf. The noise was loud. He squirmed into place behind the rock, protected from above and out of sight of anyone climbing up the track.

The helicopter came sweeping around the curve of the hill. Roaring and hissing and beating the air, it rocked to a halt just beyond the shelf where Adam hid. He could see the lower half of the great machine as it hung in the air, like a hawk hovering over its prey. Then its tail lifted and the cannon began their deadly pounding, firing so rapidly that one blast merged with the next in the insane chatter of destruction.

The rocky hiding place where Adam had made his recent stand shattered under the onslaught.

When the firing stopped, the gunship moved out from the hill in a slow quarter-circle and, once more, blasted away at the rocks. Great lumps of stone bombarded the ledge. Tucked out of sight behind the protecting rock, Adam covered his ears and pressed his face into the ground and waited for the storm of steel and stone to pass.

The cannons stopped. The helicopter lifted its nose and swung out of sight.

A thick layer of grit covered Adam. He wiped his face and readied the Kalashnikov.

Within a minute, a soldier appeared. He moved cautiously, crouching low with his eyes intent on the devastation among the boulders. Adam let him climb to the top and poke among the chipped ruins. No other soldier appeared. The Russian turned. His face was puzzled and just a little fearful. He was only young, fair and about Patrick's build. He is probably a nice boy, Adam thought, who is loved by his parents and has a girl-friend, and who doesn't want to be here and doesn't know what this war is all about.

The Russian looked towards the ledge.

Adam shot him. It was a simple shot but he felt as if he had killed his own son and he vomited.

The helicopter had flown to a higher position. Now it turned, raised its tail and started the long aerial slide back to the hilltop. It came straight for Adam.

They carry napalm, he thought. The pilot won't worry about cannons this time. He'll come in and drop the stuff all over the top of the hill and that will be that. My little hole in the ground will be full of flaming jelly.

For an instant, Adam considered turning the gun on himself but the thought vanished in a rush of anger. He didn't want to die and he wasn't going to let some shadowy figure in an ugly-looking flying machine spray him with liquid fire. Not without a fight. He steadied the rifle and waited for the target to draw within range.

Before he could press the trigger, there was a loud whooshing noise and something rushed past the ledge, laying a dense trail of smoke. Spiralling and weaving, it raced towards the helicopter. The pilot saw it coming and tried to lift, but the smoke trail rose too, and when the source of the smoke met the gunship, both disappeared in a fearful flash. The sky filled with whirling flames.

The smoke cleared from the gap beneath the ledge. Adam saw shoes, then knees, then Patrick's face.

'Thank God,' Patrick said and reached in to pull his father clear.

S·E·V·E·N·T·E·E·N

The men in the little band of Mujahedin were ecstatic. Never before had they shot down one of the feared Soviet gunships. What was more, they had performed the feat with one of the new weapons brought to them by the *feranghi*, who were the very men they had now saved. Because other helicopters had been heard during the night, they could not light a fire to celebrate their great victory but they sat together in the camp in the mountains and talked for many hours.

Just before midnight, the leader came to see Patrick. 'I have sent a man to the village. In the village is an old but excellent truck which is owned by a very good friend of mine. My man should return with the truck in two hours. Be ready to leave immediately. You must be out of the country by dawn.'

Daniel translated for his brother. Head swathed in a bandage, he was seated beside Patrick.

'How is your head?' the leader asked.

'There is a battle going on inside.' Gingerly, Daniel put both hands to his forehead. 'But it will pass.'

'Indeed. So will the red eyes.'

Daniel nodded his thanks but left one hand holding his brow.

Adam lay between his sons. He had been conscious for only brief periods since they had begun the long walk through the mountains. He stirred.

Daniel leaned closer. 'Are you awake?' he asked softly.

Adam opened one eye. 'Daniel?'

'It's me.'

He reached out with his other hand. 'And Patrick?'

Patrick touched the extended fingers. 'I'm OK.'

'He carried you here,' Daniel said.

'I'm alive? I mean, this isn't heaven and we are all together?'

'We're all alive, this is Afghanistan, not heaven, and tomorrow we'll be in Pakistan.'

'With Nina?' The voice creaked with suffering.

'Soon.'

He lay back, nodding to himself. 'I remember that big helicopter coming in. What happened?'

'Do you remember our driver?'

Adam nodded again.

'He didn't run out on us. He went for help. He ran into this band of rebels who were on their way to see what all the noise was about. They've got some of the new ground-to-air missiles. Apparently it was among the stuff that you and Daniel helped to smuggle into the country.'

'Good on us,' Adam said weakly.

'That's what they reckon. Anyhow, they blew the gunship out of the sky and we brought you here. We're close to the border.' He adjusted the blanket that was around his father. 'Feel up to a nice long drive?'

'Sure. When do we leave?'

'In about two hours.'

Adam reached out for Daniel. 'I can't see you, so hang on to my hand.' He enjoyed the comforting grip for a few moments. 'You feel strong enough. Is your head OK?'

'Better than your leg.' Daniel pressed his father's fingers. 'They tell me you made quite a stand up there on the pass. Held off half the Russian army. You must have been busy.'

'Yes.' Adam was smiling. He closed his eyes.

'Thanks for that.'

But Adam was already asleep.

Peshawar

The doctor waited for Nina to leave the ward. The man had a small face with a large, beaked nose. His hair was glossy and brushed back. It shone like feathers. Nina thought he resembled a crow.

'Your husband is in remarkable condition for a person of his age.' He walked with his hands behind his back and with his neck jutting out. 'We had contemplated amputation, you know.'

'I know.' She remembered that night, when Adam had been brought to the hospital.

'However, all that is passed. He seems to have great recuperative powers and should mend completely.'

'I'm most grateful for all you've done.'

'He will need crutches for some time. He may always require a walking-stick.'

'I bought him one in the market the other day.'

'Not a sword-stick, I trust.' The doctor smiled broadly and Nina felt a mad urge to feed him birdseed. 'The market is filled with scoundrels who would like to sell you all sorts of deadly weapons. Sword-sticks are very popular.'

'This one is just a plain old walking-stick. We've had quite enough of deadly weapons, thank you.'

They shook hands. His eyes were extraordinarily intense. 'It is a long flight home. I hope you will be comfortable.'

'Thank you.'

A car was waiting outside the hospital. Dadmir Mohammad sat in the back. 'I thought it wiser to see you here rather than at the hotel or my house,' he said when she reached the car window. 'You are leaving tomorrow?'

'Yes. We'll be in Australia in two days' time.'

'Ah, home. No place like it, is there?'

'No.'

'Which is why we continue to fight this uneven battle. It is our homes that are being destroyed, our families who are being killed and maimed, our homeland which has been invaded.'

'I understand that very clearly.'

'And you will say that in your stories?'

'Certainly.'

'Will there be a book?'

'I think so.'

'That is excellent.' He did not smile. 'We are sorry to be losing a warrior like your son.'

'I'm not.'

He lit a cigar. 'Please remember, write only the truth.'

'I will.'

'And please remember us, when you are safely at home.'

'We will. Thank you for everything.'

He dismissed her thanks with a wave and tapped the driver on the shoulder. The car pulled out from the kerb, to join the chaotic traffic of Peshawar.

Patrick went to the hospital early that night. 'I wanted to see you before the others arrived,' he said, and started to fidget with the hem of the sheet.

'What's up?' Adam had put on weight in the last week but was still so thin that when he smiled, waves of deep wrinkles washed across his cheeks.

Patrick cleared his throat. 'It's something I've been wanting to tell you for a long time.'

Adam settled against the pillows, saying nothing.

'Do you know you're a difficult man to talk to?'

The waves spread to Adam's forehead. 'Is that what you wanted to tell me?'

'No, of course not.'

Again Adam was silent.

'You don't say anything.'

'If I was talking, you wouldn't be able to say anything and then I wouldn't hear what it was you wanted to tell me.'

Patrick pulled at the sheet. 'I got a letter from Cassie today.'

Eagerly Adam bent forward. 'How is she?'

'Fine. The boys are well. They're all up at Kalinda.'

Adam shook his head wistfully. 'You've no idea how much I'm looking forward to being back there.'

'Cassie says the drought's worse. Jimmy's trying to sell the last of the sheep.' He had his head bent low and glanced across at his father. 'You gave up a lot by coming out here, looking for me, didn't you?'

Adam gazed up at the ceiling. 'I reckon it was worth it.'

'Could you lose everything?'

'Possibly. I owe the banks a lot.'

Patrick's head sagged even lower. 'I'll make it up somehow.'

'You haven't got any making up to do.' He patted the sheets near Patrick's hand. 'Is that what you wanted to tell me about?'

'No.'

'Do you want me to keep quiet, or do you want me to keep on talking while you get up the nerve to say whatever it is that's on your mind?'

'No.'

'No, what?'

Patrick released his grip on the hem. 'Do you remember the shark attack?'

'Of course.'

'It's about Simon Bannister.'

Adam was listening but seemed not to be breathing. Their eyes met and Patrick looked away again.

'You once said you couldn't understand why he went in the water. I've never forgotten you saying that.'

'That's true. It used to puzzle me.'

Patrick straightened his back. 'He dived in to stop us being washed on to the rocks.' His eyes flicked towards Adam, whose face carried a strange half-smile. 'Damon and I were playing around in the dinghy. It was my idea. I'd put the oars on the beach and pushed us out into the water. Then we got caught in a current and were drifting towards some rocks. Simon swam out to push the boat clear.'

966

'And the shark attacked him?'

'Yes. I was about to help him get in the dinghy.'

Adam bent towards Patrick. 'This has worried you all these years?'

He nodded.

'Why did you jump in the water?'

'To try and help him. I thought he was drowning.'

'Did you see the shark?'

'Not at first.'

Adam reached out to touch the top of Patrick's head. 'What's worried you most all this time?'

'The fact that it was my fault. He got in the water because I'd done something stupid.'

'Patrick, there's one thing you should remember. You might have been skylarking in the boat but you didn't make him go in the water.'

'Yes I did. He had to try and save the boat.'

'But you didn't make him. Mr Gallagher did.'

Blinking in bewilderment, Patrick stared up at his father.

'I saw Mr Gallagher at the inquest, remember?' Adam said and, slowly, Patrick inclined his head. 'We were talking afterwards. Mr Gallagher got very upset and I tried to comfort him and then he told me that when he saw the dinghy drifting, he ordered Simon Bannister to swim out so the boat wouldn't be damaged.'

'Mr Gallagher did?'

'He blamed himself for that poor man's death. He probably still does. He told him to go in the water. The other man worked for him and did what he was told.'

Patrick leaned forward until his face touched the sheet. Adam stroked the back of his head. 'Did I ever tell you about the time I killed a policeman?'

He used the sheet to wipe his eyes. 'Don't turn it into a joke, Dad.'

'It's not a joke. It's true, unhappily. Would you like me to tell you the story? It happened a long time ago.'

They talked for a long time and about many things. Adam closed his eyes. Patrick thought he had fallen asleep until his father's hand groped for his.

'Does it embarrass you if I hold your hand?' His father's half-opened eyes searched for his.

'No. The Afghans do it all the time.'

'Do they now?' He closed his eyes again. 'I must tell Saleem Benn.'

967

'How is your old friend?'

Adam raised his eyebrows without opening his eyes. 'Good. A bit weary these days.' The face crinkled. 'We'd be a good pair.'

'You'll be fine as soon as we get you back to Kalinda.'

'That's what I need. To get home.' He pushed himself into an upright position and opened his eyes. 'I don't know what's wrong with me. I can't stop sleeping.'

'You've had a pretty rough time. You could do with a bit of a rest.'

Adam nodded contentedly. 'Thank heavens you didn't say I'm not as young as I used to be. The next person who says that will get thrown out of the room.'

'I'll give you a hand if you like.'

Adam's closed lips muffled a tiny explosion of mirth. 'You're probably right. I could do with a bit of help.'

The sounds of the city seeped into the ward. The grind of motors, the strident demands of horns and bells, the burble of voices were as constant as the rumble of surf on a distant shore.

'Noisy place,' Adam said.

'Yes. Would you like me to leave you alone for a while?'

Adam tightened his grip on his son's hand. 'No. We've been apart too much.' He let his head roll towards Patrick. 'You're not going away again, are you?'

Patrick swayed back in the flimsy hospital chair. 'I thought I might find something useful to do around the place.'

'At Kalinda?'

He spoke earnestly. 'You could probably do with a bit of help, so long as you show me what to do.'

'That'd be easy. You were always good on a horse.'

'What I was thinking of, though, was doing something on the tourism side.'

Adam let his eyes wander across the ceiling. 'Cassie's always saying there's good money in that.'

'Well, there is. I know a bit about the business. I might have a talk to her.'

Adam glanced down at Patrick. 'We'll have to get rid of this drought first.'

'How bad is it?'

'Worst ever. Families that have been on the land for a hundred years are walking off and leaving their properties.'

'How about us?'

'It'll rain.'

'When?'

'Eventually.'

968

'Can we wait that long?'

'I can. How about you?'

Patrick grinned. 'Well if you can, I can.'

'That's what I like to hear.' Adam let his eyes close. 'I might sleep for a little while. I'll try and dream about Kalinda after a big storm and see how good it looks.'

'You do that.'

'You won't leave?'

'No.'

'Nina and Daniel should be here soon. You'll wake me when they come?'

'As soon as they walk through the door.'

He sat with his father and held his hand. After a while, the deep lines drawn across Adam's face softened and Patrick knew he was dreaming of rain and his beloved Kalinda.

E·I·G·H·T·E·E·N

On the way to Kalinda, they stopped at Marree. Saleem Benn was in the corner of the darkest room, sitting in his favourite chair. He rose with some difficulty to greet them. His face was thinner than they remembered, his white beard more wispy. With great dignity, he shook Patrick's outstretched hand and said 'well done' and 'welcome home' several times and remarked on what a fine young man he had grown into. Then, with a flourish he embraced Daniel.

He moved to Nina and held both her hands in his. His eyes filled with tears and he blinked rapidly.

'I am not weeping, dear lady,' he said, refusing to wipe his face. 'What you see is merely joy overflowing. You have brought them all back. Truly, it is a miracle.'

At last he turned to Adam, who stood on crutches near the doorway. 'Ah, Adam Ross,' he said, walking towards his friend with both hands clasped. Now the tears coursed down his cheeks. 'There was a time when I doubted that I would see you again. I heard from your worthy daughter that you and Daniel had ventured into that troubled land. In truth, I thought it was a valiant but hopeless quest ...' He gripped Adam's hand in a sawing motion. 'Now you are back and I will die a contented man.'

'Not yet,' Adam said, struggling to stay balanced on the crutches. 'There's that birthday party you promised.'

'Oh yes.' The old man was nodding. 'You have a year or two to wait. Did you return just for that?'

'Of course,' Adam said and they embraced.

'Well done,' Saleem Benn said.

'They all did well,' Nina said.

'We brought you some gifts,' Daniel said and produced several parcels. One contained a long coat, trimmed with fur and elaborately stitched in the Afghan style.

'Now when would I wear such a magnificent-looking garment?'

'At the party,' Adam said. 'It was made by a tailor whose grandfather was a tailor in Peshawar in your time. You sent me to him.

He was at the same address.'

'Ah. So you found him,' Saleem Benn said as Patrick helped him put on the coat, and then to Adam: 'Peshawar was a colourful place. A veritable crossroads of the world, with men of all races strolling the streets. They all carried weapons.'

'Many still do,' Adam said and Saleem Benn nodded contentedly.

Adam had never seen the land so dry. On the drive from William Creek to the homestead, dust lay thick in the wheeltracks and spun in violent, choking eddies behind the car. Everywhere, drift sand spread its deadly embrace, piling against bushes and rocks and filling the hollow ribs of long-dead animals. There was no sign of life. He peered into the distance but saw no slinking dingo, no bounding kangaroo, no circling hawk. Creeks that floods had carved into sharp, raw channels were now rounded into powdery troughs. The dunes, once softened by a fuzz of grey bush and green vine, had become red blisters on a scorched plain and their sides were covered by scabs of withered vegetation.

All around, the desert sizzled with mirages.

'And you're going to bring tourists, city folk, up here to see this?' Adam said much later, when he and Cassie were walking near the stockyard.

'What do you mean "going to"? We are already.' She turned to face him, her eyes still bright with the joy of having everyone back at Kalinda. 'We had a group of Japanese up here last week and they loved it.'

'Japanese?'

'Sure. They've got money. They don't just buy our wool ... when we've got some to sell. They want to see where it comes from. And they love to visit strange places.'

He shook his head in disbelief and settled himself more comfortably on the crutches. 'They must have thought this was a strange place. What happened?'

'Well, first we flew them over Lake Eyre, and that was great. That lake's your biggest asset, Dad.'

'It is?' He looked at her bright, eager face and thought: you're an astonishing woman, Cassie. That lake claimed the life of your mother, your husband and that American adventurer you were keen on, and yet you can divorce yourself from those memories and see that great stretch of salt as an asset. He said, 'And how's that?'

'Because it's unique. There's nothing like it in the world, at least not that tourists can get to. The Japanese all looked down at it and

971

went 'wow' and then started firing off cameras until the cabin was clicking and chattering like a nest of crickets.'

'Is that so?'

'Yes,' she said, knowing he was mocking her. She nudged him in the ribs. 'They couldn't believe it was so big. Anyhow, we landed on the new strip near the lake ...' She paused, smiling.

'What new strip?'

'We built one. Jimmy's amazing on the grader.'

'You built a new airstrip?'

'Right next to the lake. It's not exactly mountainous country and we only had a few anthills to knock over and a bit of sand to smooth out. We've got a picnic area there, too. A bough shelter, seats, a barbecue.'

'You've been busy.'

'We did the strip in three days. It took another few days to build the other things, but yes, we have been busy.' She started to walk and he followed her. 'Anyhow, we landed at the new strip and Jimmy was waiting with the camels. We're giving tourists rides on our camels.'

'Oh are we?'

'They'll be very popular.'

He laughed. 'You've got it all worked out. What happened to the Japanese?'

'Well, they started to mount the camels for their ride out on to the salt, but one of the men was running around with a movie camera and he spooked Rajah and the rotten old beast bolted.'

'With someone on board?'   .

'A very proper Japanese gentleman with a baseball cap and a T-shirt with "Sexy Boy" written across the front. So Rajah set off at a gallop with Jimmy after him, and then all the other camels bolted, but they went in different directions. A couple went north into the sand-hills, one went south and almost ended up in a swamp and the rest headed for home.'

Adam paled. 'All with a Japanese tourist on board?'

'Almost all. What's more, they stayed on board. No one fell off which was a miracle. It took us two hours to round them all up.'

Adam rubbed his chin, suddenly contemplating such things as insurance premiums and lawsuits. 'How terrible.'

'Terrible? The Japanese loved it. They all thought it was the greatest adventure of their lives. Particularly Sexy Boy. He was a real sport.'

'You're still going to have camel rides?'

'Certainly. It's a great attraction and tourists will pay good money to be bounced around.'

'What are you going to do to make sure no more camels bolt off?'

'We're building a yard out there. And we'll have them all tethered together. We've got it worked out.'

'We don't want anyone getting hurt.'

'No, Dad.' They walked to the motel buildings. Several hectares of ground beyond the buildings had been dug up. A forest of small plants showed above beds mulched with chopped spinifex.

'What the devil have you done here?' Adam scratched his head.

'This is the first of our desert gardens,' she said and took him on a tour of inspection. She and the boys, plus Stella and Lizzie, had done the planting. They had put in trees like desert oak, desert poplar and colony wattle, ground cover such as parakeelya and Sturt's desert pea and a host of shrubs – mainly the honey and rattlepod grevilleas.

'We want to attract a lot of birds,' she said.

Adam looked around at the hundreds of mulched mounds, each sprouting a small tree, bush or vine. 'What for?' he said. 'We've got birds. There are always birds around.'

'We want to attract pretty, colourful birds. Cockatoos, galahs and rosellas. Tourists love them. Do you know you can get a thousand dollars for one of our parrots overseas? And we've got hundreds of them flying around, wild and free. We just need the feed to attract them to the homestead and these plants will do it.' She bent down and lifted a handful of chopped spinifex. 'How do you like this? We finally found a use for all this rotten stuff.'

'You've been mowing the spinifex?'

'Jimmy did. He slashed it and we filled about ten truck loads.' She displayed scratch marks on her hands and wrists. 'It's terrible stuff, but it makes good mulch. It'll keep the moisture in and the weeds out.'

Adam waved the toe of his injured leg towards a black plastic pipe showing through the mulch. 'What's this?'

'Irrigation. We bring water from the bore and drip it on to the roots. We let it go deep down so that the plants grow properly.'

'Bore water'll kill them.'

'Not this water. I had it analysed. It's not too salty and we chose plants that can tolerate it.'

He shuffled around, examining the spread of plants. 'You put in a lot.'

'Eight hundred.' She breathed deeply, proud of what had been done. 'It's just the start. We're going to put in more, and then other plantations out at some of the bores.'

'The rabbits will eat them.'

'Not the ones we'll put in. We'll select the best natives.' She shook his arm. 'You're just an old cynic.'

He grinned. 'I suppose that's better than being an old fossil.'

'Only marginally,' she said and turned to the motel buildings. 'We haven't done much to these yet, but I've got it all planned out. We're going to change the rooms, make them more comfortable, improve the bathrooms, things like that. People don't mind roughing it during the day, but they like to be comfortable at night.' She grinned. 'We're going to put in electric blankets for the winter nights.'

The motel had once been the shearers' quarters. Adam had regarded the original buildings as providing an extreme standard of comfort for the outback because they had only two beds to a room and the floors were concrete and the doors and windows were sealed to keep the dust out.

His head shook slowly in a lament for the passing of things he understood. 'You're going to spoil them,' he said softly.

'You can't spoil people who are going to pay top money to stay at our place.'

'Talking of money,' he said, 'where are we getting the money for all this?'

'Portelli Enterprises. This is our contribution. We'll provide the facilities needed, you turn on the rough inland charm.' She stood in front of him, smiling. 'You've no idea how pleased I am to see you here.'

'You've no idea how glad I am to be back.'

She was silent for a few moments. 'No one else but you could have got Patrick out.'

He smiled and it was perilously close to a blush. 'We were lucky. And don't forget, it was Daniel and me. My God, Cassie, he's a good man.'

'I know that.' She reached out impishly, to touch the tip of his nose. 'But then you're blessed with outstanding children who can do anything.'

He laughed. 'Patrick's changed. Looks good, doesn't he?'

'Very. I hardly recognized him. He's a man.'

'He carried me out.'

'I know. I'm proud of him.' She sighed. 'I've got a lot of catching up to do with Patrick. We haven't been that close.'

Adam nodded contentedly.

'And I'm proud of you too, Adam Ross, cynical old fossil that you are.'

He used his toe to paw at the ground. 'So here we are, in the middle of the biggest drought we've ever known, and we're going

974

into the gardening and tourist business.'

'We are, and we're doing it so we can keep Kalinda.'

'It might be difficult,' he said, squinting towards the sun. 'The bank still expects us to pay off their loan and unless we put some more stock in this property soon, we're not going to get that sort of money.'

'We'll get tourists, Dad.'

'That'll help.' Breathing deeply, searching the air for a hint of rain, he looked around him. 'But it won't be enough. I suppose you want people to come here to see a working outback property.'

She nodded vigorously. 'I thought people might even like to help with some of the work. You know, ride the horses at mustering time, go out with us when we check the bores. Things like that. I think that would be popular.'

'With the Japanese?'

'With everyone.'

He continued to examine the sky. 'You could be right. But if they want to see a working property, it's got to be doing some work and that means we need more stock. And before we can buy stock, we need feed on the ground and that means we need rain.'

She nodded with him. Suddenly she was miserable.

'Hey, don't look like that,' he said, shuffling his crutches so that he could put one arm around her shoulder. 'You've done wonders, and when it rains and the feed comes back, we'll be right. Then we'll run a place that combines two things: a working sheep station and a tourist centre.'

'Will you be able to borrow more money to buy sheep?'

'If it rains and we get the feed, certainly.'

'All right,' she said. 'We'll combine the two. Sheep and tourists.'

'Right.'

'You really like what we've done?'

'I think this garden will look great when everything grows.'

'It'll take a couple of years. I want to take you out to the new airstrip too, and show you what we've done.'

'I'd love to see it.'

They headed towards the house. 'Dad, how long can you last without rain?'

He shrugged noncommittally. 'A few months. There's a lot owing.'

'Tell the bank about what we're doing up here and how we're diversifying into tourism. That should bring us in a steady cashflow. They'd like that.'

'I will. The trouble is, they need a big sum and that means at least the promise of the money from a wool clip.'

975

She joined him in studying the sky. 'There hasn't been a drop of rain since you left.'

'And when it does rain, it'll probably flood.' They reached the verandah and she helped him up the steps. 'And by the time that happens, we'll probably have walked off this place and left it to the bank and we'll all be living on your back terrace.'

'At least there's a nice view from there,' she said, and went inside to make a cup of tea.

It took Nina another week to finish her story on Patrick's life with the Mujahedin. Her agent in America had presold the rights to the *New York Times*, which intended running the ten thousand-word story over three issues. The agent also had several publishers vying for the rights to her book.

Nina had to complete the book within three months. She had drafted an outline and had a selection of photographs supplied by Dadmir Mohammad. 'It'll be a rush,' she told Adam, 'but it can be done. And whoever buys it will pay an advance of around fifty thousand dollars, so that should bring a smile to the bank manager's face.'

'A fifth of a smile,' Adam said, doing some rapid calculation. He frowned. 'But we can't touch that. It's your writing money.'

She threw up her hands. 'I thought we'd been through all that years ago. Kalinda is where I live too, Adam Ross. I share in the good times and when there are debts to be paid, I share in the responsibility of paying them.'

He shook his head stubbornly.

'Adam, it'll help. Surely it would take pressure off the loan if the bank knew that fifty thousand US dollars were on their way.'

'You shouldn't have to pay, Nina. It's not right.'

'It's not right that we should lose Kalinda. Look, I know you're a proud man, but you've got to be practical.' When he said nothing, she added, 'I could always lend it to you.'

He looked up.

'Would that satisfy your strange sense of honour?'

'I don't like borrowing money from a woman,' he said and started to smile. 'Especially a good-looking one.'

'You're quaint.'

He scratched an ear. 'Cassie's always calling me an old fossil.'

'More of a relic.' She kissed his forehead. 'A relic of a different and better age. You're a nice, old-fashioned man. I thought that even when we were alone in that cellar in Greece.'

He seized her wrist and laughed. 'You thought what?'

'That you were old-fashioned.'

'In Greece?' He kissed her full on the lips.

'My, that didn't taste like a fossil.'

'Do you know what I thought in that cellar?'

'What?' She remained within kissing range.

'I thought what a good-looking woman you were.'

She straightened momentarily. 'What do you mean "were"?'

He held her wrist. 'Your eyes are sparkling just like they were in that cellar.'

'You couldn't see.'

'I could. There was a candle.'

'So there was.'

'Don't tell me you'd forgotten.'

'I only remember you.'

He pulled her on to his knee.

'Careful of your leg,' she said before he kissed her again.

Patrick spent a few days camped at the new airstrip near the lake, helping Jimmy and Daniel build the camel yards. It was dry and hot at the site and the work was hard, but they were good days. Daniel treated him as an equal and yet showed him what to do, while Jimmy kept up a commentary of constant and witty derogation. The old man hadn't changed. His hair was now the colour of gunmetal and his skin was more leathery than ever, but he still enjoyed nothing more than deflating egos.

He had a few prepared lines. On one occasion, he was resting within the bough shelter and said, 'Sing out when you need a hand.'

It was his standard one-armed-man joke. Normally, he added, 'If you want two, get someone else', but Patrick called his bluff. 'I could do with a hand now, Jimmy,' he cried out while lifting a particularly heavy piece of timber. Jimmy took a stuffed glove from his pocket and casually tossed it to him.

The morning after they returned to the homestead, Patrick decided to ride out to the dunes where he had spent so much time as a boy. Silver was no longer there, of course, but he saddled another horse that was about the same size and colour. He was ready to mount when Jimmy ambled up and asked where he was going.

'Just for a ride.'

'Wouldn't be going out to the sand-hills?'

Patrick was taken aback. The dunes were his private place. No one knew about them. Or at least, that had been the childhood pretence. All he could think to say was, 'Why?'

'Thought you might need this.' Jimmy produced the Lone Ranger mask. He held it out, the only suggestion of a smile being a glint buried deep behind his eyes.

Patrick felt as though he were shrinking in size. He was ten again. A little kid who had a special hiding place. And now it was discovered.

'Well, do you want it or not?' The smile was close and it was not going to be one of Jimmy's sharp smiles that sliced the pretence from you but a warm, understanding one.

Patrick took the rag mask, and turned it over in his hand. 'Where did you find this?'

'Oh, I've had it for a few years. From about the time you almost put the old Cessna through Mrs Wilson's bedroom.'

Patrick held it up. 'You know what this is?'

'Sure. Your cowboy mask. I thought you might want to keep it. You know, as a memento.' He grinned. 'You used to wear it a lot.'

'When did you see me?'

'When you'd put it on and then go and ride up and down the sand-hills. You used to play around for hours.'

'And you were there?'

Jimmy nodded.

'I never saw you.'

'I can be hard to see, when I want to.' He lifted a foot and bent his one arm so that his pose resembled a stunted tree. 'I've got the colouring and the shape,' he said, then relaxed so suddenly that he seemed in danger of falling apart. 'I used to follow you out.'

'To the dunes?'

'They're not far. Just a short run for a feller like me who used to be good on his feet and didn't mind a bit of exercise as long as it was in a good cause.'

'But why?'

'To keep an eye on you.'

'What for?' The question was bent around an accusation.

Jimmy straightened in indignation. 'To make sure you didn't get into any trouble.'

'You went all the way out there just to ...' Patrick groped for the correct words '... baby-sit me?'

The question delighted Jimmy. 'Something like that.'

'Dad asked you?'

'No. I just wanted to make sure you were okay. You were only a little bloke and that was a big horse. And that's rough country out there.'

'And you followed me out all those times just to make sure I didn't get hurt?'

'Yep.'

'Why didn't you ever let me know you were out there?'

'Didn't want to spoil your game. You always seemed to be

978

having a good time. What were you playing?'

'I was pretending I was the Lone Ranger.' He saw Jimmy's puzzled look. 'He was an American comic book hero. A masked cowboy who fought against evil.'

Jimmy nodded contentedly. 'It looked like a lot of fun. You sure killed a lot of baddies.'

Both laughed.

Patrick put the mask in his pocket and mounted the horse. 'I'm just going back to see what it's like. Want a lift out there?'

'Sure, why not?' Jimmy said and let Patrick haul him up on to the rump of the horse.

They had been at Kalinda for two weeks. Adam's leg was growing stronger and he now walked with the stick which Nina had bought in Peshawar. He was at the Number Two bore with Daniel.

'It's worse now than when we first came here,' Adam said, scuffing the dry ground with the tip of his walking-stick. 'There was no water then but at least there was feed. Look at the place now. There's tons of underground water but nothing for stock to eat. It really is a desert.'

Daniel had his father's gift of using silence to signify agreement.

'I had hoped to leave all this to you one day. I don't mean for you to own it entirely,' Adam added hastily, stirring at the earth with his stick. 'To have a share of it, along with Cassie and Patrick, but to run it. It would have been yours. You know what I mean?'

Daniel knew.

'I didn't have much luck with the bank.'

'What happened?'

'Just a phone conversation, which isn't a very satisfactory way of doing business, but I thought I should let them know I was back in the country.' Adam cleared his throat. 'And let them know about Nina's book and the money that's coming.'

'And?'

'There's a new man there. I don't know him, which is a problem. He was polite, but he reminded me that we're a mile behind in the payments. It seems we're not the only ones. Everyone up this way's suffering from the drought.'

'So they want their money?'

'Yes. I've got a month.' He limped towards the bore, which began to clank as the blades turned in a breeze. 'It's funny, isn't it? You think you're doing the right thing. You make improvements, buy better quality stock, borrow money to put in new equipment to make the place more productive so you can earn more money.' He reached a fence and raised his weak leg to rest it on the lower rail.

'And then we have the worst drought in living memory. It'll end one day, of course, and the country will come back to life and things'll probably be good for another fifty or hundred years.' He sighed. 'Josef was right.'

Daniel leaned against a post. They merged as one: the lifeless post, the languid human. 'How do you mean?'

'He said I should have gone south, to a place where there's regular rainfall. Trouble was I couldn't afford it.'

'I don't like it down south. I like it up here.'

Adam laughed.

'What's up?'

'You reminded me of someone.'

'Who?'

'Me.'

Daniel smiled slowly. 'What do you think of Cassie's ideas?'

'Good.'

'So do I.' He turned as the windmill spun more rapidly. The wind had strengthened. He saw Adam breathe deeply, testing the air.

'Rain?'

'Could be,' Adam said, examining the sky. 'Let's get back to the house.'

Cassie planned returning to Adelaide in a few days' time. She had been washing clothes and was on the verandah, sniffing the wind and eyeing a faint row of clouds gathering on the western horizon, when Adam and Daniel returned.

Adam took her by the elbow and led her inside. 'You'll frighten them away if you keep looking at them,' he said and went into the kitchen. She recognized the signal and put a kettle on the stove.

Nina came from her room. Flexing her fingers after a morning's typing, she sat at the table beside Adam.

'How's it going?' he asked.

'Very harrowing. Writing about your son fighting with a bunch of rebel tribesmen is just the most extraordinary experience.' She stretched both arms high above her shoulders. 'But speaking as a writer, not as a mother, I think it's going well.'

'The Americans should like this book,' Adam said, but he was not looking at her. His eyes were on the window.

'I hope so.' She leaned against his shoulder. 'What's so interesting?'

'There are rain clouds on the horizon,' Cassie said.

Nina got up and hurried to the verandah. Adam followed her. The clouds were no more than a smear of dark grey, a band of sediment lying at the bottom of a drained sky. Nina started laughing.

980

'What's so funny?'

'I was thinking that this must be one of the few places on earth where someone would go rushing out of the house to look at a cloud. And not a very impressive cloud at that. I mean, if I were an artist, I wouldn't dash inside again to grab my easel and paints.'

'You wouldn't need much paint.'

She agreed and they went back inside. 'They are rain clouds,' he mused. 'But they might never come over here. They could stay where they are, blow somewhere else, or just pass overhead and not give us more than a few drops.'

'So you don't think it'll rain?' Nina asked.

'I don't dare hope.'

The storm came that afternoon. There was much wind and dust and great, swirling columns of dead leaves and grass, but little rain. A few drops pattered on the homestead's iron roof. Lightning flashed and thunder rumbled across the plains and echoed from the sand-hills, but the clouds passed.

'It'll probably pour over the lake,' Adam said, gazing wistfully to the east.

'That'd be right,' Jimmy said breezily. 'It always rains where you don't want it. Who ever heard of a lake with water in it? How could you ride camels on a lake like that.'

After dinner, Adam went outside to peer at the sky. He came in after nine o'clock. 'There's still a lot of cloud about,' he said without sounding hopeful and, after talking again to Cassie about how long she would spend in Adelaide and when she might return to Kalinda, went to bed.

The sound of distant thunder woke him. It was almost one in the morning. He tried to get up without disturbing Nina, but tripped while searching in the dark for his walking-stick.

'What is it?' she whispered.

'Thunder.' Another roll sounded.

'Isn't that a long way away?'

'Yes,' he said, pulling on his pants. 'But I thought I'd have a look. Just to see where the lightning is.'

'You shouldn't be walking around in the dark.'

'No. Do you want to come with me?'

She got up, put on her dressing gown and slippers and followed him to the front steps. He was already sitting there. A cool wind was blowing, touching them in uneven gusts. He used the stick to point to the west.

'There's a big storm over there.' He breathed deeply. 'There's rain, too. You can smell it.'

She sat beside him and pulled his arm around her. 'Hold on to me. I'm cold.'

He held her tightly. 'If it rained, I mean if it really rained, would you mind if I used that fifty thousand of yours to buy good quality merinos? They'd still be cheap if I got in early, and if we had good breeding stock on the place, the bank would see us out for a bit longer. And then with the wool clip, we could pay off most of the loan.'

'Of course,' she said, then jumped when lightning flashed nearby. 'That was close.'

He stood up and walked away from the house.

'Where are you going?' she whispered.

'Just having a look.'

'Adam, there's nothing to see. It's pitch black.'

Another flash, which was followed almost immediately by a clap of thunder that rattled the homestead windows, illuminated the area. She saw Adam staring up at the sky, as though in prayer.

'You should come inside. You'll catch cold out there.'

He walked further from the house and disappeared into the night. She turned on the verandah light. His was a ghostly figure, plodding into the darkness, leaning towards the stick, but with the face still upturned.

The first drop touched his cheek. 'It's raining,' he called out, touching his face and holding the palm towards Nina as proof of a miracle.

'It rained this morning.' She stood near the verandah railing, with her arms folded across her body, shivering with cold.

'No, Nina, this is the real thing.' A sudden burst of rain came thudding across the plain towards him. He heard it and turned to face it.

She could see it in the vague light, a grey cloud sweeping towards him. 'Adam, come back to the house. You'll get saturated.'

But he stood there, with his arms outstretched in welcome. When the rain hit him, he let out a whoop of joy. She could see him, a pillar of reflected light surrounded by transparent rods of water. The ground around him erupted into splashing, sprouting puddles. He yelled out once more.

'You'll wake everyone,' she wailed. 'And you'll catch your death of cold.'

'Let's wake everyone.' He swung a hand above his head in triumph. 'This is the real thing, Nina. We're in for a real soaking.'

She let her head sag forward and began to laugh. 'You're the one who's in for a soaking. And you're crazy.'

Cassie appeared at the other end of the verandah 'What's happening?'

982

'Your father is doing a rain dance.'

'Cassie,' Adam shouted, lifting his stick high in the air and almost toppling over. 'Rain! Rain! Beautiful rain!'

Cassie darted inside and returned with an umbrella. It was stiff from lack of use and, frustrated, she thew it down and ran out to join her father.

The rain grew heavier.

'You'll both drown,' Nina called out, but neither Adam nor Cassie moved. Their hair was plastered to their faces, but they were laughing; wiping their eyes, spluttering from the flow of water and laughing like children playing under a hose on a hot summer's day.

She heard the splash of heavy footsteps and Daniel ran into the light. He was covered by a riding coat and wore his hat, but he took it off and stood with Adam and Cassie, face upwards, drinking in the rain. He threw an arm around his father's shoulder and tugged so hard that Adam almost fell.

Then Jimmy dashed from his house. He had formed a hood from a sheet of canvas. He by-passed the others and went straight to the verandah.

'I thought you were having a party and had forgotten to invite me.' He shed the canvas and shook himself. 'White people are nuts,' he confided to Nina.

She hugged him, then ran inside to fetch Patrick.

He emerged, rubbing his eyes and staring in amazement at the three figures in the rain.

'They've all gone troppo,' Jimmy said.

The three were dancing a jig. Cassie and Daniel flanked Adam. Each had a supporting arm around him.

'In the morning,' Adam said, wiping away water that streamed down his nose, 'I'm going to ring up the stock agent and get him to buy those sheep.'

'Is it going to keep on raining?' Cassie asked. As though in answer, a dazzling chain of lightning forked across the western horizon.

'There's a lot more coming,' Adam shouted. 'All the creeks will be flooded, the roads will be washed out, the airstrips will be unusable, the sheds will leak and it'll be wonderful,' he kissed Cassie, 'because there'll be growth everywhere.'

On the verandah, Patrick took off his pyjama top.

'You're not going out?' Nina said.

'I sure am.'

'You'll catch your death of cold.'

With a swift lunge, he grabbed his mother and lifted her into his arms. 'You're coming out too. This looks like too great a party to miss.'

983

Jimmy stood back to avoid being splashed by the rain and watched Patrick carry Nina, kicking and protesting and laughing, to join the others. When Patrick reached them and put Nina down, they all joined hands.

Jimmy leaned against the verandah post. 'Well,' he said to himself, 'it looks like we won't have to pack up and leave this dry old place after all.' And then to the others, who were standing in a circle, presenting their faces to the downpour: 'Don't drink too much of that water. We want some of it left to grow grass.'

The oldest of Cassie's sons came out on to the verandah. He was rubbing his eyes. 'What's happening, Uncle Jimmy? Is something wrong? Why was Grandpa calling out?'

Jimmy picked up the boy and sat with him in one of the chairs. The lad had the bright eyes of Peppino but the build of a Ross. 'No, Johnny, everything's good. Your old grandpa's calling out because he's very happy.'